The Desire Series
The Financier &
The Titan

Theodore Dreiser

TABLE OF CONTENTS

THE FINANCIER

THE TITAN

THE FINANCIER

CHAPTER I

The Philadelphia into which Frank Algernon Cowperwood was born was a city of two hundred and fifty thousand and more. It was set with handsome parks, notable buildings, and crowded with historic memories. Many of the things that we and he knew later were not then in existence—the telegraph, telephone, express company, ocean steamer, city delivery of mails. There were no postage-stamps or registered letters. The street car had not arrived. In its place were hosts of omnibuses, and for longer travel the slowly developing railroad system still largely connected by canals.

Cowperwood's father was a bank clerk at the time of Frank's birth, but ten years later, when the boy was already beginning to turn a very sensible, vigorous eye on the world, Mr. Henry Worthington Cowperwood, because of the death of the bank's president and the consequent moving ahead of the other officers, fell heir to the place vacated by the promoted teller, at the, to him, munificent salary of thirty-five hundred dollars a year. At once he decided, as he told his wife joyously, to remove his family from 21 Buttonwood Street to 124 New Market Street, a much better neighborhood, where there was a nice brick house of three stories in height as opposed to their present two-storied domicile. There was the probability that some day they would come into something even better, but for the present this was sufficient. He was exceedingly grateful.

Henry Worthington Cowperwood was a man who believed only what he saw and was content to be what he was—a banker, or a prospective one. He was at this time a significant figure—tall, lean, inquisitorial, clerkly—with nice, smooth, closely-cropped side whiskers coming to almost the lower lobes of his ears. His upper lip was smooth and curiously long, and he had a long, straight nose and a chin that tended to be pointed. His eyebrows were bushy, emphasizing vague, grayish-green eyes, and his hair was short and smooth and nicely parted. He wore a frock-coat always—it was quite the thing in financial circles in those days—and a high hat. And he kept his hands and nails immaculately clean. His manner might have been called severe, though really it was more cultivated than austere.

Being ambitious to get ahead socially and financially, he was very careful of whom or with whom he talked. He was as much afraid of expressing a rabid or unpopular political or social opinion as he was of being seen with an evil character, though he had really no opinion of great political significance to express. He was neither anti- nor pro-slavery, though the air was stormy with abolition sentiment and its opposition. He believed sincerely that vast fortunes were to be made out of railroads if one only had the capital and that curious thing, a magnetic personality—the ability to win the confidence of others. He was sure that Andrew Jackson was all wrong in his opposition to Nicholas Biddle and the United States Bank, one of the great issues of the day; and he was worried, as he might well be, by the perfect storm of wildcat money which was floating about and which was constantly coming to his bank—discounted, of course, and handed out again to anxious borrowers at a profit. His bank was the Third National of Philadelphia, located in that center of all Philadelphia and indeed, at that time, of practically all national finance—Third Street—and its owners conducted a brokerage business as a side line. There was a perfect plague of State banks, great and small, in those days, issuing notes practically without regulation upon insecure and unknown assets and failing and suspending with astonishing rapidity; and a knowledge of all these was an important requirement of Mr. Cowperwood's position. As a result, he had become the soul of caution. Unfortunately, for him, he lacked in a great measure the two things that are necessary for distinction in any field—magnetism and vision. He was not destined to be a great financier, though he was marked out to be a moderately successful one.

Mrs. Cowperwood was of a religious temperament—a small woman, with light-brown hair and clear, brown eyes, who had been very attractive in her day, but had become rather prim and matter-of-fact and inclined to take very seriously the maternal care of her three sons and one daughter. The former, captained by Frank, the eldest, were a source of considerable annoyance to her, for they were forever making expeditions to different parts of the city, getting in with bad boys, probably, and seeing and hearing things they should neither see nor hear.

Frank Cowperwood, even at ten, was a natural-born leader. At the day school he attended, and later at the Central High School, he was looked upon as one whose common sense could unquestionably be trusted in all cases. He was a sturdy youth, courageous and defiant. From the very start of his life, he wanted to know about economics and politics. He cared nothing for books. He was a clean, stalky, shapely boy, with a bright, clean-cut, incisive face; large, clear, gray eyes; a wide forehead; short, bristly, dark-brown hair. He had an incisive, quick-motioned, self-sufficient manner, and was forever asking questions with a keen desire for an intelligent reply. He never had an ache or pain, ate his food with gusto, and ruled his brothers with a rod of iron. "Come on, Joe!" "Hurry, Ed!" These commands were issued in no rough but always a sure way, and Joe and Ed came. They looked up to Frank from the first as a master, and what he had to say was listened to eagerly.

He was forever pondering, pondering—one fact astonishing him quite as much as another—for he could not figure out how this thing he had come into—this life—was organized. How did all these people get into the world? What were they doing here? Who started things, anyhow? His mother told him the story of Adam and Eve, but he didn't believe it. There was a fish-market not so very far from his home, and there, on his way to see his father at the bank, or conducting his brothers on after-school expeditions, he liked to look at a certain tank in front of one store where were kept odd specimens of sea-life brought in by the Delaware Bay fishermen. He saw once there a sea-horse—just a queer little sea-animal that looked somewhat like a horse—and another time he saw an electric eel which Benjamin Franklin's discovery had explained. One day he saw a squid and a lobster put in the tank, and in connection with them was witness to a tragedy which stayed with him all his life and cleared things up considerably intellectually. The lobster, it appeared from the talk of the idle bystanders, was offered no food, as the squid was considered his rightful prey. He lay at the bottom of the clear glass tank on the yellow sand, apparently seeing nothing—you could not tell in which way his beady, black buttons of eyes were looking—but apparently they were never off the body of the squid. The latter, pale and waxy in texture, looking very much like pork fat or jade, moved about in torpedo fashion; but his movements were apparently never out of the eyes of his enemy, for by degrees small portions of his body began to disappear, snapped off by the relentless claws of his pursuer. The lobster would leap like a catapult to where the squid was apparently idly dreaming, and the squid, very alert, would dart away, shooting out at the same time a cloud of ink, behind which it would disappear. It was not always completely successful, however. Small portions of its body or its tail were frequently left in the claws of the monster below. Fascinated by the drama, young Cowperwood came daily to watch.

One morning he stood in front of the tank, his nose almost pressed to the glass. Only a portion of the squid remained, and his ink-bag was emptier than ever. In the corner of the tank sat the lobster, poised apparently for action.

The boy stayed as long as he could, the bitter struggle fascinating him. Now, maybe, or in an hour or a day, the squid might die, slain by the lobster, and the lobster would eat him. He looked again at the greenish-copperish engine of destruction in the corner and wondered when this would be. To-night, maybe. He would come back to-night.

He returned that night, and lo! the expected had happened. There was a little crowd around the tank. The lobster was in the corner. Before him was the squid cut in two and partially devoured.

2

"He got him at last," observed one bystander. "I was standing right here an hour ago, and up he leaped and grabbed him. The squid was too tired. He wasn't quick enough. He did back up, but that lobster he calculated on his doing that. He's been figuring on his movements for a long time now. He got him to-day."

Frank only stared. Too bad he had missed this. The least touch of sorrow for the squid came to him as he stared at it slain. Then he gazed at the victor.

"That's the way it has to be, I guess," he commented to himself. "That squid wasn't quick enough." He figured it out.

"The squid couldn't kill the lobster—he had no weapon. The lobster could kill the squid—he was heavily armed. There was nothing for the squid to feed on; the lobster had the squid as prey. What was the result to be? What else could it be? He didn't have a chance," he concluded finally, as he trotted on homeward.

The incident made a great impression on him. It answered in a rough way that riddle which had been annoying him so much in the past: "How is life organized?" Things lived on each other—that was it. Lobsters lived on squids and other things. What lived on lobsters? Men, of course! Sure, that was it! And what lived on men? he asked himself. Was it other men? Wild animals lived on men. And there were Indians and cannibals. And some men were killed by storms and accidents. He wasn't so sure about men living on men; but men did kill each other. How about wars and street fights and mobs? He had seen a mob once. It attacked the Public Ledger building as he was coming home from school. His father had explained why. It was about the slaves. That was it! Sure, men lived on men. Look at the slaves. They were men. That's what all this excitement was about these days. Men killing other men—negroes.

He went on home quite pleased with himself at his solution.

"Mother!" he exclaimed, as he entered the house, "he finally got him!"

"Got who? What got what?" she inquired in amazement. "Go wash your hands."

"Why, that lobster got that squid I was telling you and pa about the other day."

"Well, that's too bad. What makes you take any interest in such things? Run, wash your hands."

"Well, you don't often see anything like that. I never did." He went out in the back yard, where there was a hydrant and a post with a little table on it, and on that a shining tin-pan and a bucket of water. Here he washed his face and hands.

"Say, papa," he said to his father, later, "you know that squid?"

"Yes."

"Well, he's dead. The lobster got him."

His father continued reading. "Well, that's too bad," he said, indifferently.

But for days and weeks Frank thought of this and of the life he was tossed into, for he was already pondering on what he should be in this world, and how he should get along. From seeing his father count money, he was sure that he would like banking; and Third Street, where his father's office was, seemed to him the cleanest, most fascinating street in the world.

CHAPTER II

The growth of young Frank Algernon Cowperwood was through years of what might be called a comfortable and happy family existence. Buttonwood Street, where he spent the first ten years of his life, was a lovely place for a boy to live. It contained mostly small two and three-story red brick houses, with small white marble steps leading up to the front door, and thin, white marble trimmings outlining the front door and windows. There were trees in the street—plenty of them. The road pavement was of big, round cobblestones, made bright and clean by the rains; and the sidewalks were of red brick, and always damp and cool. In the rear was a yard, with trees and grass and sometimes flowers, for the lots were almost always one hundred feet deep, and the house-fronts, crowding close to the pavement in front, left a comfortable space in the rear.

The Cowperwoods, father and mother, were not so lean and narrow that they could not enter into the natural tendency to be happy and joyous with their children; and so this family, which increased at the rate of a child every two or three years after Frank's birth until there were four children, was quite an interesting affair when he was ten and they were ready to move into the New Market Street home. Henry Worthington Cowperwood's connections were increased as his position grew more responsible, and gradually he was becoming quite a personage. He already knew a number of the more prosperous merchants who dealt with his bank, and because as a clerk his duties necessitated his calling at other banking-houses, he had come to be familiar with and favorably known in the Bank of the United States, the Drexels, the Edwards, and others. The brokers knew him as representing a very sound organization, and while he was not considered brilliant mentally, he was known as a most reliable and trustworthy individual.

In this progress of his father young Cowperwood definitely shared. He was quite often allowed to come to the bank on Saturdays, when he would watch with great interest the deft exchange of bills at the brokerage end of the business. He wanted to know where all the types of money came from, why discounts were demanded and received, what the men did with all the money they received. His father, pleased at his interest, was glad to explain so that even at this early age—from ten to fifteen—the boy gained a wide knowledge of the condition of the country financially—what a State bank was and what a national one; what brokers did; what stocks were, and why they fluctuated in value. He began to see clearly what was meant by money as a medium of exchange, and how all values were calculated according to one primary value, that of gold. He was a financier by instinct, and all the knowledge that pertained to that great art was as natural to him as the emotions and subtleties of life are to a poet. This medium of exchange, gold, interested him intensely. When his father explained to him how it was mined, he dreamed that he owned a gold mine and waked to wish that he did. He was likewise curious about stocks and bonds and he learned that some stocks and bonds were not worth the paper they were written on, and that others were worth much more than their face value indicated.

"There, my son," said his father to him one day, "you won't often see a bundle of those around this neighborhood." He referred to a series of shares in the British East India Company, deposited as collateral at two-thirds of their face value for a loan of one hundred thousand dollars. A Philadelphia magnate had hypothecated them for the use of the ready cash. Young Cowperwood looked at them curiously. "They don't look like much, do they?" he commented.

"They are worth just four times their face value," said his father, archly.

Frank reexamined them. "The British East India Company," he read. "Ten pounds—that's pretty near fifty dollars."

"Forty-eight, thirty-five," commented his father, dryly. "Well, if we had a bundle of those we wouldn't need to work very hard. You'll notice there are scarcely any pin-marks on them. They aren't sent around very much. I don't suppose these have ever been used as collateral before."

Young Cowperwood gave them back after a time, but not without a keen sense of the vast ramifications of finance. What was the East India Company? What did it do? His father told him.

At home also he listened to considerable talk of financial investment and adventure. He heard, for one thing, of a curious character by the name of Steemberger, a great beef speculator from Virginia, who was attracted to Philadelphia in those days by the hope of

4

large and easy credits. Steemberger, so his father said, was close to Nicholas Biddle, Lardner, and others of the United States Bank, or at least friendly with them, and seemed to be able to obtain from that organization nearly all that he asked for. His operations in the purchase of cattle in Virginia, Ohio, and other States were vast, amounting, in fact, to an entire monopoly of the business of supplying beef to Eastern cities. He was a big man, enormous, with a face, his father said, something like that of a pig; and he wore a high beaver hat and a long frock-coat which hung loosely about his big chest and stomach. He had managed to force the price of beef up to thirty cents a pound, causing all the retailers and consumers to rebel, and this was what made him so conspicuous. He used to come to the brokerage end of the elder Cowperwood's bank, with as much as one hundred thousand or two hundred thousand dollars, in twelve months—post-notes of the United States Bank in denominations of one thousand, five thousand, and ten thousand dollars. These he would cash at from ten to twelve per cent. under their face value, having previously given the United States Bank his own note at four months for the entire amount. He would take his pay from the Third National brokerage counter in packages of Virginia, Ohio, and western Pennsylvania bank-notes at par, because he made his disbursements principally in those States. The Third National would in the first place realize a profit of from four to five per cent. on the original transaction; and as it took the Western bank-notes at a discount, it also made a profit on those.

There was another man his father talked about—one Francis J. Grund, a famous newspaper correspondent and lobbyist at Washington, who possessed the faculty of unearthing secrets of every kind, especially those relating to financial legislation. The secrets of the President and the Cabinet, as well as of the Senate and the House of Representatives, seemed to be open to him. Grund had been about, years before, purchasing through one or two brokers large amounts of the various kinds of Texas debt certificates and bonds. The Republic of Texas, in its struggle for independence from Mexico, had issued bonds and certificates in great variety, amounting in value to ten or fifteen million dollars. Later, in connection with the scheme to make Texas a State of the Union, a bill was passed providing a contribution on the part of the United States of five million dollars, to be applied to the extinguishment of this old debt. Grund knew of this, and also of the fact that some of this debt, owing to the peculiar conditions of issue, was to be paid in full, while other portions were to be scaled down, and there was to be a false or pre-arranged failure to pass the bill at one session in order to frighten off the outsiders who might have heard and begun to buy the old certificates for profit. He acquainted the Third National Bank with this fact, and of course the information came to Cowperwood as teller. He told his wife about it, and so his son, in this roundabout way, heard it, and his clear, big eyes glistened. He wondered why his father did not take advantage of the situation and buy some Texas certificates for himself. Grund, so his father said, and possibly three or four others, had made over a hundred thousand dollars apiece. It wasn't exactly legitimate, he seemed to think, and yet it was, too. Why shouldn't such inside information be rewarded? Somehow, Frank realized that his father was too honest, too cautious, but when he grew up, he told himself, he was going to be a broker, or a financier, or a banker, and do some of these things.

Just at this time there came to the Cowperwoods an uncle who had not previously appeared in the life of the family. He was a brother of Mrs. Cowperwood's—Seneca Davis by name—solid, unctuous, five feet ten in height, with a big, round body, a round, smooth head rather bald, a clear, ruddy complexion, blue eyes, and what little hair he had of a sandy hue. He was exceedingly well dressed according to standards prevailing in those days, indulging in flowered waistcoats, long, light-colored frock-coats, and the invariable (for a fairly prosperous man) high hat. Frank was fascinated by him at once. He had been a planter in Cuba and still owned a big ranch there and could tell him tales of Cuban life— rebellions, ambuscades, hand-to-hand fighting with machetes on his own plantation, and things of that sort. He brought with him a collection of Indian curies, to say nothing of an independent fortune and several slaves—one, named Manuel, a tall, raw-boned black, was his constant attendant, a bodyservant, as it were. He shipped raw sugar from his plantation in boat-loads to the Southwark wharves in Philadelphia. Frank liked him because he took life in a hearty, jovial way, rather rough and offhand for this somewhat quiet and reserved household.

"Why, Nancy Arabella," he said to Mrs Cowperwood on arriving one Sunday afternoon, and throwing the household into joyous astonishment at his unexpected and unheralded appearance, "you haven't grown an inch! I thought when you married old brother Hy here that you were going to fatten up like your brother. But look at you! I swear to Heaven you don't weigh five pounds." And he jounced her up and down by the waist, much to the perturbation of the children, who had never before seen their mother so familiarly handled.

Henry Cowperwood was exceedingly interested in and pleased at the arrival of this rather prosperous relative; for twelve years before, when he was married, Seneca Davis had not taken much notice of him.

"Look at these little putty-faced Philadelphians," he continued, "They ought to come down to my ranch in Cuba and get tanned up. That would take away this waxy look." And he pinched the cheek of Anna Adelaide, now five years old. "I tell you, Henry, you have a rather nice place here." And he looked at the main room of the rather conventional three-story house with a critical eye.

Measuring twenty by twenty-four and finished in imitation cherry, with a set of new Sheraton parlor furniture it presented a quaintly harmonious aspect. Since Henry had become teller the family had acquired a piano—a decided luxury in those days—brought from Europe; and it was intended that Anna Adelaide, when she was old enough, should learn to play. There were a few uncommon ornaments in the room—a gas chandelier for one thing, a glass bowl with goldfish in it, some rare and highly polished shells, and a marble Cupid bearing a basket of flowers. It was summer time, the windows were open, and the trees outside, with their widely extended green branches, were pleasantly visible shading the brick sidewalk. Uncle Seneca strolled out into the back yard.

"Well, this is pleasant enough," he observed, noting a large elm and seeing that the yard was partially paved with brick and enclosed within brick walls, up the sides of which vines were climbing. "Where's your hammock? Don't you string a hammock here in summer? Down on my veranda at San Pedro I have six or seven."

"We hadn't thought of putting one up because of the neighbors, but it would be nice," agreed Mrs. Cowperwood. "Henry will have to get one."

"I have two or three in my trunks over at the hotel. My niggers make 'em down there. I'll send Manuel over with them in the morning."

He plucked at the vines, tweaked Edward's ear, told Joseph, the second boy, he would bring him an Indian tomahawk, and went back into the house.

"This is the lad that interests me," he said, after a time, laying a hand on the shoulder of Frank. "What did you name him in full, Henry?"

"Frank Algernon."

"Well, you might have named him after me. There's something to this boy. How would you like to come down to Cuba and be a planter, my boy?"

"I'm not so sure that I'd like to," replied the eldest.

"Well, that's straight-spoken. What have you against it?"

"Nothing, except that I don't know anything about it."

"What do you know?"

The boy smiled wisely. "Not very much, I guess."

"Well, what are you interested in?"

"Money!"

"Aha! What's bred in the bone, eh? Get something of that from your father, eh? Well, that's a good trait. And spoken like a man, too! We'll hear more about that later. Nancy, you're breeding a financier here, I think. He talks like one."

He looked at Frank carefully now. There was real force in that sturdy young body—no doubt of it. Those large, clear gray eyes were full of intelligence. They indicated much and revealed nothing.

"A smart boy!" he said to Henry, his brother-in-law. "I like his get-up. You have a bright family."

Henry Cowperwood smiled dryly. This man, if he liked Frank, might do much for the boy. He might eventually leave him some of his fortune. He was wealthy and single.

Uncle Seneca became a frequent visitor to the house—he and his negro body-guard, Manuel, who spoke both English and Spanish, much to the astonishment of the children; and he took an increasing interest in Frank.

"When that boy gets old enough to find out what he wants to do, I think I'll help him to do it," he observed to his sister one day; and she told him she was very grateful. He talked to Frank about his studies, and found that he cared little for books or most of the study he was compelled to pursue. Grammar was an abomination. Literature silly. Latin was of no use. History—well, it was fairly interesting.

"I like bookkeeping and arithmetic," he observed. "I want to get out and get to work, though. That's what I want to do."

"You're pretty young, my son," observed his uncle. "You're only how old now? Fourteen?"

"Thirteen."

"Well, you can't leave school much before sixteen. You'll do better if you stay until seventeen or eighteen. It can't do you any harm. You won't be a boy again."

"I don't want to be a boy. I want to get to work."

"Don't go too fast, son. You'll be a man soon enough. You want to be a banker, do you?"

"Yes, sir!"

"Well, when the time comes, if everything is all right and you've behaved yourself and you still want to, I'll help you get a start in business. If I were you and were going to be a banker, I'd first spend a year or so in some good grain and commission house. There's good training to be had there. You'll learn a lot that you ought to know. And, meantime, keep your health and learn all you can. Wherever I am, you let me know, and I'll write and find out how you've been conducting yourself."

He gave the boy a ten-dollar gold piece with which to start a bank-account. And, not strange to say, he liked the whole Cowperwood household much better for this dynamic, self-sufficient, sterling youth who was an integral part of it.

CHAPTER III

It was in his thirteenth year that young Cowperwood entered into his first business venture. Walking along Front Street one day, a street of importing and wholesale establishments, he saw an auctioneer's flag hanging out before a wholesale grocery and from the interior came the auctioneer's voice: "What am I bid for this exceptional lot of Java coffee, twenty-two bags all told, which is now selling in the market for seven dollars and thirty-two cents a bag wholesale? What am I bid? What am I bid? The whole lot must go as one. What am I bid?"

"Eighteen dollars," suggested a trader standing near the door, more to start the bidding than anything else. Frank paused.

"Twenty-two!" called another.

"Thirty!" a third. "Thirty-five!" a fourth, and so up to seventy-five, less than half of what it was worth.

"I'm bid seventy-five! I'm bid seventy-five!" called the auctioneer, loudly. "Any other offers? Going once at seventy-five; am I offered eighty? Going twice at seventy-five, and"—he paused, one hand raised dramatically. Then he brought it down with a slap in the palm of the other—"sold to Mr. Silas Gregory for seventy-five. Make a note of that, Jerry," he called to his red-haired, freckle-faced clerk beside him. Then he turned to another lot of grocery staples—this time starch, eleven barrels of it.

Young Cowperwood was making a rapid calculation. If, as the auctioneer said, coffee was worth seven dollars and thirty-two cents a bag in the open market, and this buyer was getting this coffee for seventy-five dollars, he was making then and there eighty-six dollars and four cents, to say nothing of what his profit would be if he sold it at retail. As he recalled, his mother was paying twenty-eight cents a pound. He drew nearer, his books tucked under his arm, and watched these operations closely. The starch, as he soon heard, was valued at ten dollars a barrel, and it only brought six. Some kegs of vinegar were knocked down at one-third their value, and so on. He began to wish he could bid; but he had no money, just a little pocket change. The auctioneer noticed him standing almost directly under his nose, and was impressed with the stolidity—solidity—of the boy's expression.

"I am going to offer you now a fine lot of Castile soap—seven cases, no less—which, as you know, if you know anything about soap, is now selling at fourteen cents a bar. This soap is worth anywhere at this moment eleven dollars and seventy-five cents a case. What am I bid? What am I bid? What am I bid?" He was talking fast in the usual style of auctioneers, with much unnecessary emphasis; but Cowperwood was not unduly impressed. He was already rapidly calculating for himself. Seven cases at eleven dollars and seventy-five cents would be worth just eighty-two dollars and twenty-five cents; and if it went at half—if it went at half—

"Twelve dollars," commented one bidder.

"Fifteen," bid another.

"Twenty," called a third.

"Twenty-five," a fourth.

Then it came to dollar raises, for Castile soap was not such a vital commodity. "Twenty-six." "Twenty-seven." "Twenty-eight." "Twenty-nine." There was a pause. "Thirty," observed young Cowperwood, decisively.

The auctioneer, a short lean faced, spare man with bushy hair and an incisive eye, looked at him curiously and almost incredulously but without pausing. He had, somehow, in spite of himself, been impressed by the boy's peculiar eye; and now he felt, without knowing why, that the offer was probably legitimate enough, and that the boy had the money. He might be the son of a grocer.

"I'm bid thirty! I'm bid thirty! I'm bid thirty for this fine lot of Castile soap. It's a fine lot. It's worth fourteen cents a bar. Will any one bid thirty-one? Will any one bid thirty-one? Will any one bid thirty-one?"

"Thirty-one," said a voice.

"Thirty-two," replied Cowperwood. The same process was repeated.

"I'm bid thirty-two! I'm bid thirty-two! I'm bid thirty-two! Will anybody bid thirty-three? It's fine soap. Seven cases of fine Castile soap. Will anybody bid thirty-three?"

Young Cowperwood's mind was working. He had no money with him; but his father was teller of the Third National Bank, and he could quote him as reference. He could sell all of his soap to the family grocer, surely; or, if not, to other grocers. Other people were anxious to get this soap at this price. Why not he?

The auctioneer paused.

8

"Thirty-two once! Am I bid thirty-three? Thirty-two twice! Am I bid thirty-three? Thirty-two three times! Seven fine cases of soap. Am I bid anything more? Once, twice! Three times! Am I bid anything more?"—his hand was up again—"and sold to Mr.—?" He leaned over and looked curiously into the face of his young bidder.

"Frank Cowperwood, son of the teller of the Third National Bank," replied the boy, decisively.

"Oh, yes," said the man, fixed by his glance.

"Will you wait while I run up to the bank and get the money?"

"Yes. Don't be gone long. If you're not here in an hour I'll sell it again."

Young Cowperwood made no reply. He hurried out and ran fast; first, to his mother's grocer, whose store was within a block of his home.

Thirty feet from the door he slowed up, put on a nonchalant air, and strolling in, looked about for Castile soap. There it was, the same kind, displayed in a box and looking just as his soap looked.

"How much is this a bar, Mr. Dalrymple?" he inquired.

"Sixteen cents," replied that worthy.

"If I could sell you seven boxes for sixty-two dollars just like this, would you take them?"

"The same soap?"

"Yes, sir."

Mr. Dalrymple calculated a moment.

"Yes, I think I would," he replied, cautiously.

"Would you pay me to-day?"

"I'd give you my note for it. Where is the soap?"

He was perplexed and somewhat astonished by this unexpected proposition on the part of his neighbor's son. He knew Mr. Cowperwood well—and Frank also.

"Will you take it if I bring it to you to-day?"

"Yes, I will," he replied. "Are you going into the soap business?"

"No. But I know where I can get some of that soap cheap."

He hurried out again and ran to his father's bank. It was after banking hours; but he knew how to get in, and he knew that his father would be glad to see him make thirty dollars. He only wanted to borrow the money for a day.

"What's the trouble, Frank?" asked his father, looking up from his desk when he appeared, breathless and red faced.

"I want you to loan me thirty-two dollars! Will you?"

"Why, yes, I might. What do you want to do with it?"

"I want to buy some soap—seven boxes of Castile soap. I know where I can get it and sell it. Mr. Dalrymple will take it. He's already offered me sixty-two for it. I can get it for thirty-two. Will you let me have the money? I've got to run back and pay the auctioneer."

His father smiled. This was the most business-like attitude he had seen his son manifest. He was so keen, so alert for a boy of thirteen.

"Why, Frank," he said, going over to a drawer where some bills were, "are you going to become a financier already? You're sure you're not going to lose on this? You know what you're doing, do you?"

"You let me have the money, father, will you?" he pleaded. "I'll show you in a little bit. Just let me have it. You can trust me."

He was like a young hound on the scent of game. His father could not resist his appeal.

"Why, certainly, Frank," he replied. "I'll trust you." And he counted out six five-dollar certificates of the Third National's own issue and two ones. "There you are."

Frank ran out of the building with a briefly spoken thanks and returned to the auction room as fast as his legs would carry him. When he came in, sugar was being auctioned. He made his way to the auctioneer's clerk.

"I want to pay for that soap," he suggested.

9

"Now?"

"Yes. Will you give me a receipt?"

"Yep."

"Do you deliver this?"

"No. No delivery. You have to take it away in twenty-four hours."

That difficulty did not trouble him.

"All right," he said, and pocketed his paper testimony of purchase.

The auctioneer watched him as he went out. In half an hour he was back with a drayman—an idle levee-wharf hanger-on who was waiting for a job.

Frank had bargained with him to deliver the soap for sixty cents. In still another half-hour he was before the door of the astonished Mr. Dalrymple whom he had come out and look at the boxes before attempting to remove them. His plan was to have them carried on to his own home if the operation for any reason failed to go through. Though it was his first great venture, he was cool as glass.

"Yes," said Mr. Dalrymple, scratching his gray head reflectively. "Yes, that's the same soap. I'll take it. I'll be as good as my word. Where'd you get it, Frank?"

"At Bixom's auction up here," he replied, frankly and blandly.

Mr. Dalrymple had the drayman bring in the soap; and after some formality—because the agent in this case was a boy—made out his note at thirty days and gave it to him.

Frank thanked him and pocketed the note. He decided to go back to his father's bank and discount it, as he had seen others doing, thereby paying his father back and getting his own profit in ready money. It couldn't be done ordinarily on any day after business hours; but his father would make an exception in his case.

He hurried back, whistling; and his father glanced up smiling when he came in.

"Well, Frank, how'd you make out?" he asked.

"Here's a note at thirty days," he said, producing the paper Dalrymple had given him. "Do you want to discount that for me? You can take your thirty-two out of that."

His father examined it closely. "Sixty-two dollars!" he observed. "Mr. Dalrymple! That's good paper! Yes, I can. It will cost you ten per cent.," he added, jestingly. "Why don't you just hold it, though? I'll let you have the thirty-two dollars until the end of the month."

"Oh, no," said his son, "you discount it and take your money. I may want mine."

His father smiled at his business-like air. "All right," he said. "I'll fix it to-morrow. Tell me just how you did this." And his son told him.

At seven o'clock that evening Frank's mother heard about it, and in due time Uncle Seneca. "What'd I tell you, Cowperwood?" he asked. "He has stuff in him, that youngster. Look out for him."

Mrs. Cowperwood looked at her boy curiously at dinner. Was this the son she had nursed at her bosom not so very long before? Surely he was developing rapidly.

"Well, Frank, I hope you can do that often," she said.

"I hope so, too, ma," was his rather noncommittal reply.

Auction sales were not to be discovered every day, however, and his home grocer was only open to one such transaction in a reasonable period of time, but from the very first young Cowperwood knew how to make money. He took subscriptions for a boys' paper; handled the agency for the sale of a new kind of ice-skate, and once organized a band of neighborhood youths into a union for the purpose of purchasing their summer straw hats at wholesale. It was not his idea that he could get rich by saving. From the first he had the notion that liberal spending was better, and that somehow he would get along.

It was in this year, or a little earlier, that he began to take an interest in girls. He had from the first a keen eye for the beautiful among them; and, being good-looking and magnetic himself, it was not difficult for him to attract the sympathetic interest of those in whom he was interested. A twelve-year old girl, Patience Barlow, who lived further up the street, was the first to attract his attention or be attracted by him. Black hair and snapping black eyes were her portion, with pretty pigtails down her back, and dainty feet and ankles to match a dainty figure. She was a Quakeress, the daughter of Quaker parents, wearing a demure little bonnet. Her disposition, however, was vivacious, and she liked this self-reliant, self-sufficient, straight-spoken boy. One day, after an exchange of glances from time to time, he said, with a smile and the courage that was innate in him: "You live up my way, don't you?" "Yes," she replied, a little flustered—this last manifested in a nervous swinging of her school-bag—"I live at number one-forty-one."

"I know the house," he said. "I've seen you go in there. You go to the same school my sister does, don't you? Aren't you Patience Barlow?" He had heard some of the boys speak her name. "Yes. How do you know?"

"Oh, I've heard," he smiled. "I've seen you. Do you like licorice?"

He fished in his coat and pulled out some fresh sticks that were sold at the time.

"Thank you," she said, sweetly, taking one.

"It isn't very good. I've been carrying it a long time. I had some taffy the other day."

"Oh, it's all right," she replied, chewing the end of hers.

"Don't you know my sister, Anna Cowperwood?" he recurred, by way of self-introduction. "She's in a lower grade than you are, but I thought maybe you might have seen her."

"I think I know who she is. I've seen her coming home from school."

"I live right over there," he confided, pointing to his own home as he drew near to it, as if she didn't know. "I'll see you around here now, I guess."

"Do you know Ruth Merriam?" she asked, when he was about ready to turn off into the cobblestone road to reach his own door.

"No, why?"

"She's giving a party next Tuesday," she volunteered, seemingly pointlessly, but only seemingly.

"Where does she live?"

"There in twenty-eight."

"I'd like to go," he affirmed, warmly, as he swung away from her.

"Maybe she'll ask you," she called back, growing more courageous as the distance between them widened. "I'll ask her."

"Thanks," he smiled.

And she began to run gayly onward.

He looked after her with a smiling face. She was very pretty. He felt a keen desire to kiss her, and what might transpire at Ruth Merriam's party rose vividly before his eyes.

This was just one of the early love affairs, or puppy loves, that held his mind from time to time in the mixture of after events. Patience Barlow was kissed by him in secret ways many times before he found another girl. She and others of the street ran out to play in the snow of a winter's night, or lingered after dusk before her own door when the days grew dark early. It was so easy to catch and kiss her then, and to talk to her foolishly at parties. Then came Dora Fitler, when he was sixteen years old and she was fourteen; and Marjorie Stafford, when he was seventeen and she was fifteen. Dora Fitter was a brunette, and Marjorie Stafford was as fair as the morning, with bright-red cheeks, bluish-gray eyes, and flaxen hair, and as plump as a partridge.

It was at seventeen that he decided to leave school. He had not graduated. He had only finished the third year in high school; but he had had enough. Ever since his thirteenth year his mind had been on finance; that is, in the form in which he saw it manifested in Third Street. There had been odd things which he had been able to do to earn a little money now and then. His Uncle Seneca had allowed him to act as assistant weigher at the sugar-docks in Southwark, where three-hundred-pound bags were weighed into the government bonded warehouses under the eyes of United States inspectors. In certain emergencies he was called to assist his father, and was paid for it. He even made an arrangement with Mr. Dalrymple to assist him on Saturdays; but when his father became cashier of his bank, receiving an

11

income of four thousand dollars a year, shortly after Frank had reached his fifteenth year, it was self-evident that Frank could no longer continue in such lowly employment.

Just at this time his Uncle Seneca, again back in Philadelphia and stouter and more domineering than ever, said to him one day:

"Now, Frank, if you're ready for it, I think I know where there's a good opening for you. There won't be any salary in it for the first year, but if you mind your p's and q's, they'll probably give you something as a gift at the end of that time. Do you know of Henry Waterman & Company down in Second Street?"

"I've seen their place."

"Well, they tell me they might make a place for you as a bookkeeper. They're brokers in a way—grain and commission men. You say you want to get in that line. When school's out, you go down and see Mr. Waterman—tell him I sent you, and he'll make a place for you, I think. Let me know how you come out."

Uncle Seneca was married now, having, because of his wealth, attracted the attention of a poor but ambitious Philadelphia society matron; and because of this the general connections of the Cowperwoods were considered vastly improved. Henry Cowperwood was planning to move with his family rather far out on North Front Street, which commanded at that time a beautiful view of the river and was witnessing the construction of some charming dwellings. His four thousand dollars a year in these pre-Civil-War times was considerable. He was making what he considered judicious and conservative investments and because of his cautious, conservative, clock-like conduct it was thought he might reasonably expect some day to be vice-president and possibly president, of his bank.

This offer of Uncle Seneca to get him in with Waterman & Company seemed to Frank just the thing to start him off right. So he reported to that organization at 74 South Second Street one day in June, and was cordially received by Mr. Henry Waterman, Sr. There was, he soon learned, a Henry Waterman, Jr., a young man of twenty-five, and a George Waterman, a brother, aged fifty, who was the confidential inside man. Henry Waterman, Sr., a man of fifty-five years of age, was the general head of the organization, inside and out— traveling about the nearby territory to see customers when that was necessary, coming into final counsel in cases where his brother could not adjust matters, suggesting and advising new ventures which his associates and hirelings carried out. He was, to look at, a phlegmatic type of man—short, stout, wrinkled about the eyes, rather protuberant as to stomach, red-necked, red-faced, the least bit popeyed, but shrewd, kindly, good-natured, and witty. He had, because of his naturally common-sense ideas and rather pleasing disposition built up a sound and successful business here. He was getting strong in years and would gladly have welcomed the hearty cooperation of his son, if the latter had been entirely suited to the business.

He was not, however. Not as democratic, as quick-witted, or as pleased with the work in hand as was his father, the business actually offended him. And if the trade had been left to his care, it would have rapidly disappeared. His father foresaw this, was grieved, and was hoping some young man would eventually appear who would be interested in the business, handle it in the same spirit in which it had been handled, and who would not crowd his son out.

Then came young Cowperwood, spoken of to him by Seneca Davis. He looked him over critically. Yes, this boy might do, he thought. There was something easy and sufficient about him. He did not appear to be in the least flustered or disturbed. He knew how to keep books, he said, though he knew nothing of the details of the grain and commission business. It was interesting to him. He would like to try it.

"I like that fellow," Henry Waterman confided to his brother the moment Frank had gone with instructions to report the following morning. "There's something to him. He's the cleanest, briskest, most alive thing that's walked in here in many a day."

12

"Yes," said George, a much leaner and slightly taller man, with dark, blurry, reflective eyes and a thin, largely vanished growth of brownish-black hair which contrasted strangely with the egg-shaped whiteness of his bald head. "Yes, he's a nice young man. It's a wonder his father don't take him in his bank."

"Well, he may not be able to," said his brother. "He's only the cashier there."

"That's right."

"Well, we'll give him a trial. I bet anything he makes good. He's a likely-looking youth."

Henry got up and walked out into the main entrance looking into Second Street. The cool cobble pavements, shaded from the eastern sun by the wall of buildings on the east—of which his was a part—the noisy trucks and drays, the busy crowds hurrying to and fro, pleased him. He looked at the buildings over the way—all three and four stories, and largely of gray stone and crowded with life—and thanked his stars that he had originally located in so prosperous a neighborhood. If he had only brought more property at the time he bought this!

"I wish that Cowperwood boy would turn out to be the kind of man I want," he observed to himself, meditatively. "He could save me a lot of running these days."

Curiously, after only three or four minutes of conversation with the boy, he sensed this marked quality of efficiency. Something told him he would do well.

CHAPTER IV

The appearance of Frank Cowperwood at this time was, to say the least, prepossessing and satisfactory. Nature had destined him to be about five feet ten inches tall. His head was large, shapely, notably commercial in aspect, thickly covered with crisp, dark-brown hair and fixed on a pair of square shoulders and a stocky body. Already his eyes had the look that subtle years of thought bring. They were inscrutable. You could tell nothing by his eyes. He walked with a light, confident, springy step. Life had given him no severe shocks nor rude awakenings. He had not been compelled to suffer illness or pain or deprivation of any kind. He saw people richer than himself, but he hoped to be rich. His family was respected, his father well placed. He owed no man anything. Once he had let a small note of his become overdue at the bank, but his father raised such a row that he never forgot it. "I would rather crawl on my hands and knees than let my paper go to protest," the old gentleman observed; and this fixed in his mind what scarcely needed to be so sharply emphasized—the significance of credit. No paper of his ever went to protest or became overdue after that through any negligence of his.

He turned out to be the most efficient clerk that the house of Waterman & Co. had ever known. They put him on the books at first as assistant bookkeeper, vice Mr. Thomas Trixler, dismissed, and in two weeks George said: "Why don't we make Cowperwood head bookkeeper? He knows more in a minute than that fellow Sampson will ever know."

"All right, make the transfer, George, but don't fuss so. He won't be a bookkeeper long, though. I want to see if he can't handle some of these transfers for me after a bit."

The books of Messrs. Waterman & Co., though fairly complicated, were child's play to Frank. He went through them with an ease and rapidity which surprised his erstwhile superior, Mr. Sampson.

"Why, that fellow," Sampson told another clerk on the first day he had seen Cowperwood work, "he's too brisk. He's going to make a bad break. I know that kind. Wait a little bit until we get one of those rush credit and transfer days." But the bad break Mr. Sampson anticipated did not materialize. In less than a week Cowperwood knew the financial condition of the Messrs. Waterman as well as they did—better—to a dollar. He knew how

13

their accounts were distributed; from what section they drew the most business; who sent poor produce and good—the varying prices for a year told that. To satisfy himself he ran back over certain accounts in the ledger, verifying his suspicions. Bookkeeping did not interest him except as a record, a demonstration of a firm's life. He knew he would not do this long. Something else would happen; but he saw instantly what the grain and commission business was—every detail of it. He saw where, for want of greater activity in offering the goods consigned—quicker communication with shippers and buyers, a better working agreement with surrounding commission men—this house, or, rather, its customers, for it had nothing, endured severe losses. A man would ship a tow-boat or a car-load of fruit or vegetables against a supposedly rising or stable market; but if ten other men did the same thing at the same time, or other commission men were flooded with fruit or vegetables, and there was no way of disposing of them within a reasonable time, the price had to fall. Every day was bringing its special consignments. It instantly occurred to him that he would be of much more use to the house as an outside man disposing of heavy shipments, but he hesitated to say anything so soon. More than likely, things would adjust themselves shortly.

The Watermans, Henry and George, were greatly pleased with the way he handled their accounts. There was a sense of security in his very presence. He soon began to call Brother George's attention to the condition of certain accounts, making suggestions as to their possible liquidation or discontinuance, which pleased that individual greatly. He saw a way of lightening his own labors through the intelligence of this youth; while at the same time developing a sense of pleasant companionship with him.

Brother Henry was for trying him on the outside. It was not always possible to fill the orders with the stock on hand, and somebody had to go into the street or the Exchange to buy and usually he did this. One morning, when way-bills indicated a probable glut of flour and a shortage of grain—Frank saw it first—the elder Waterman called him into his office and said:

"Frank, I wish you would see what you can do with this condition that confronts us on the street. By to-morrow we're going to be overcrowded with flour. We can't be paying storage charges, and our orders won't eat it up. We're short on grain. Maybe you could trade out the flour to some of those brokers and get me enough grain to fill these orders."

"I'd like to try," said his employee.

He knew from his books where the various commission-houses were. He knew what the local merchants' exchange, and the various commission-merchants who dealt in these things, had to offer. This was the thing he liked to do—adjust a trade difficulty of this nature. It was pleasant to be out in the air again, to be going from door to door. He objected to desk work and pen work and poring over books. As he said in later years, his brain was his office. He hurried to the principal commission-merchants, learning what the state of the flour market was, and offering his surplus at the very rate he would have expected to get for it if there had been no prospective glut. Did they want to buy for immediate delivery (forty-eight hours being immediate) six hundred barrels of prime flour? He would offer it at nine dollars straight, in the barrel. They did not. He offered it in fractions, and some agreed to take one portion, and some another. In about an hour he was all secure on this save one lot of two hundred barrels, which he decided to offer in one lump to a famous operator named Genderman with whom his firm did no business. The latter, a big man with curly gray hair, a gnarled and yet pudgy face, and little eyes that peeked out shrewdly through fat eyelids, looked at Cowperwood curiously when he came in.

"What's your name, young man?" he asked, leaning back in his wooden chair.

"Cowperwood."

"So you work for Waterman & Company? You want to make a record, no doubt. That's why you came to me?"

Cowperwood merely smiled.

"Well, I'll take your flour. I need it. Bill it to me."

Cowperwood hurried out. He went direct to a firm of brokers in Walnut Street, with whom his firm dealt, and had them bid in the grain he needed at prevailing rates. Then he returned to the office.

"Well," said Henry Waterman, when he reported, "you did that quick. Sold old Genderman two hundred barrels direct, did you? That's doing pretty well. He isn't on our books, is he?"

"No, sir."

"I thought not. Well, if you can do that sort of work on the street you won't be on the books long."

Thereafter, in the course of time, Frank became a familiar figure in the commission district and on 'change (the Produce Exchange), striking balances for his employer, picking up odd lots of things they needed, soliciting new customers, breaking gluts by disposing of odd lots in unexpected quarters. Indeed the Watermans were astonished at his facility in this respect. He had an uncanny faculty for getting appreciative hearings, making friends, being introduced into new realms. New life began to flow through the old channels of the Waterman company. Their customers were better satisfied. George was for sending him out into the rural districts to drum up trade, and this was eventually done.

Near Christmas-time Henry said to George: "We'll have to make Cowperwood a liberal present. He hasn't any salary. How would five hundred dollars do?"

"That's pretty much, seeing the way times are, but I guess he's worth it. He's certainly done everything we've expected, and more. He's cut out for this business."

"What does he say about it? Do you ever hear him say whether he's satisfied?"

"Oh, he likes it pretty much, I guess. You see him as much as I do."

"Well, we'll make it five hundred. That fellow wouldn't make a bad partner in this business some day. He has the real knack for it. You see that he gets the five hundred dollars with a word from both of us."

So the night before Christmas, as Cowperwood was looking over some way-bills and certificates of consignment preparatory to leaving all in order for the intervening holiday, George Waterman came to his desk.

"Hard at it," he said, standing under the flaring gaslight and looking at his brisk employee with great satisfaction.

It was early evening, and the snow was making a speckled pattern through the windows in front.

"Just a few points before I wind up," smiled Cowperwood.

"My brother and I have been especially pleased with the way you have handled the work here during the past six months. We wanted to make some acknowledgment, and we thought about five hundred dollars would be right. Beginning January first we'll give you a regular salary of thirty dollars a week."

"I'm certainly much obliged to you," said Frank. "I didn't expect that much. It's a good deal. I've learned considerable here that I'm glad to know."

"Oh, don't mention it. We know you've earned it. You can stay with us as long as you like. We're glad to have you with us."

Cowperwood smiled his hearty, genial smile. He was feeling very comfortable under this evidence of approval. He looked bright and cheery in his well-made clothes of English tweed.

On the way home that evening he speculated as to the nature of this business. He knew he wasn't going to stay there long, even in spite of this gift and promise of salary. They were grateful, of course; but why shouldn't they be? He was efficient, he knew that; under him things moved smoothly. It never occurred to him that he belonged in the realm of clerkdom. Those people were the kind of beings who ought to work for him, and who would. There was nothing savage in his attitude, no rage against fate, no dark fear of failure.

15

These two men he worked for were already nothing more than characters in his eyes—their business significated itself. He could see their weaknesses and their shortcomings as a much older man might have viewed a boy's.

After dinner that evening, before leaving to call on his girl, Marjorie Stafford, he told his father of the gift of five hundred dollars and the promised salary.

"That's splendid," said the older man. "You're doing better than I thought. I suppose you'll stay there."

"No, I won't. I think I'll quit sometime next year."

"Why?"

"Well, it isn't exactly what I want to do. It's all right, but I'd rather try my hand at brokerage, I think. That appeals to me."

"Don't you think you are doing them an injustice not to tell them?"

"Not at all. They need me." All the while surveying himself in a mirror, straightening his tie and adjusting his coat.

"Have you told your mother?"

"No. I'm going to do it now."

He went out into the dining-room, where his mother was, and slipping his arms around her little body, said: "What do you think, Mammy?"

"Well, what?" she asked, looking affectionately into his eyes.

"I got five hundred dollars to-night, and I get thirty a week next year. What do you want for Christmas?"

"You don't say! Isn't that nice! Isn't that fine! They must like you. You're getting to be quite a man, aren't you?"

"What do you want for Christmas?"

"Nothing. I don't want anything. I have my children."

He smiled. "All right. Then nothing it is."

But she knew he would buy her something.

He went out, pausing at the door to grab playfully at his sister's waist, and saying that he'd be back about midnight, hurried to Marjorie's house, because he had promised to take her to a show.

"Anything you want for Christmas this year, Margy?" he asked, after kissing her in the dimly-lighted hall. "I got five hundred to-night."

She was an innocent little thing, only fifteen, no guile, no shrewdness.

"Oh, you needn't get me anything."

"Needn't I?" he asked, squeezing her waist and kissing her mouth again.

It was fine to be getting on this way in the world and having such a good time.

CHAPTER V

The following October, having passed his eighteenth year by nearly six months, and feeling sure that he would never want anything to do with the grain and commission business as conducted by the Waterman Company, Cowperwood decided to sever his relations with them and enter the employ of Tighe & Company, bankers and brokers.

Cowperwood's meeting with Tighe & Company had come about in the ordinary pursuance of his duties as outside man for Waterman & Company. From the first Mr. Tighe took a keen interest in this subtle young emissary.

"How's business with you people?" he would ask, genially; or, "Find that you're getting many I.O.U.'s these days?"

Because of the unsettled condition of the country, the over-inflation of securities, the slavery agitation, and so forth, there were prospects of hard times. And Tighe—he could not have told you why—was convinced that this young man was worth talking to in regard to all this. He was not really old enough to know, and yet he did know.

"Oh, things are going pretty well with us, thank you, Mr. Tighe," Cowperwood would answer.

"I tell you," he said to Cowperwood one morning, "this slavery agitation, if it doesn't stop, is going to cause trouble."

A negro slave belonging to a visitor from Cuba had just been abducted and set free, because the laws of Pennsylvania made freedom the right of any negro brought into the state, even though in transit only to another portion of the country, and there was great excitement because of it. Several persons had been arrested, and the newspapers were discussing it roundly.

"I don't think the South is going to stand for this thing. It's making trouble in our business, and it must be doing the same thing for others. We'll have secession here, sure as fate, one of these days." He talked with the vaguest suggestion of a brogue.

"It's coming, I think," said Cowperwood, quietly. "It can't be healed, in my judgment. The negro isn't worth all this excitement, but they'll go on agitating for him—emotional people always do this. They haven't anything else to do. It's hurting our Southern trade."

"I thought so. That's what people tell me."

He turned to a new customer as young Cowperwood went out, but again the boy struck him as being inexpressibly sound and deep-thinking on financial matters. "If that young fellow wanted a place, I'd give it to him," he thought.

Finally, one day he said to him: "How would you like to try your hand at being a floor man for me in 'change? I need a young man here. One of my clerks is leaving."

"I'd like it," replied Cowperwood, smiling and looking intensely gratified. "I had thought of speaking to you myself some time."

"Well, if you're ready and can make the change, the place is open. Come any time you like."

"I'll have to give a reasonable notice at the other place," Cowperwood said, quietly. "Would you mind waiting a week or two?"

"Not at all. It isn't as important as that. Come as soon as you can straighten things out. I don't want to inconvenience your employers."

It was only two weeks later that Frank took his departure from Waterman & Company, interested and yet in no way flustered by his new prospects. And great was the grief of Mr. George Waterman. As for Mr. Henry Waterman, he was actually irritated by this defection.

"Why, I thought," he exclaimed, vigorously, when informed by Cowperwood of his decision, "that you liked the business. Is it a matter of salary?"

"No, not at all, Mr. Waterman. It's just that I want to get into the straight-out brokerage business."

"Well, that certainly is too bad. I'm sorry. I don't want to urge you against your own best interests. You know what you are doing. But George and I had about agreed to offer you an interest in this thing after a bit. Now you're picking up and leaving. Why, damn it, man, there's good money in this business."

"I know it," smiled Cowperwood, "but I don't like it. I have other plans in view. I'll never be a grain and commission man." Mr. Henry Waterman could scarcely understand why obvious success in this field did not interest him. He feared the effect of his departure on the business.

And once the change was made Cowperwood was convinced that this new work was more suited to him in every way—as easy and more profitable, of course. In the first place, the firm of Tighe & Co., unlike that of Waterman & Co., was located in a handsome green-gray stone building at 66 South Third Street, in what was then, and for a number of years afterward, the heart of the financial district. Great institutions of national and international import and repute were near at hand—Drexel & Co., Edward Clark & Co., the Third National Bank, the First National Bank, the Stock Exchange, and similar institutions. Almost a score of smaller banks and brokerage firms were also in the vicinity. Edward Tighe, the head and brains of this concern, was a Boston Irishman, the son of an immigrant who had flourished and done well in that conservative city. He had come to Philadelphia to interest himself in the speculative life there. "Sure, it's a right good place for those of us who are awake," he told his friends, with a slight Irish accent, and he considered himself very much awake. He was a medium-tall man, not very stout, slightly and prematurely gray, and with a manner which was as lively and good-natured as it was combative and self-reliant. His upper lip was ornamented by a short, gray mustache.

"May heaven preserve me," he said, not long after he came there, "these Pennsylvanians never pay for anything they can issue bonds for." It was the period when Pennsylvania's credit, and for that matter Philadelphia's, was very bad in spite of its great wealth. "If there's ever a war there'll be battalions of Pennsylvanians marching around offering notes for their meals. If I could just live long enough I could get rich buyin' up Pennsylvania notes and bonds. I think they'll pay some time; but, my God, they're mortal slow! I'll be dead before the State government will ever catch up on the interest they owe me now."

It was true. The condition of the finances of the state and city was most reprehensible. Both State and city were rich enough; but there were so many schemes for looting the treasury in both instances that when any new work had to be undertaken bonds were necessarily issued to raise the money. These bonds, or warrants, as they were called, pledged interest at six per cent.; but when the interest fell due, instead of paying it, the city or State treasurer, as the case might be, stamped the same with the date of presentation, and the warrant then bore interest for not only its original face value, but the amount then due in interest. In other words, it was being slowly compounded. But this did not help the man who wanted to raise money, for as security they could not be hypothecated for more than seventy per cent. of their market value, and they were not selling at par, but at ninety. A man might buy or accept them in foreclosure, but he had a long wait. Also, in the final payment of most of them favoritism ruled, for it was only when the treasurer knew that certain warrants were in the hands of "a friend" that he would advertise that such and such warrants—those particular ones that he knew about—would be paid.

What was more, the money system of the United States was only then beginning slowly to emerge from something approximating chaos to something more nearly approaching order. The United States Bank, of which Nicholas Biddle was the progenitor, had gone completely in 1841, and the United States Treasury with its subtreasury system had come in 1846; but still there were many, many wildcat banks, sufficient in number to make the average exchange-counter broker a walking encyclopedia of solvent and insolvent institutions. Still, things were slowly improving, for the telegraph had facilitated stock-market quotations, not only between New York, Boston, and Philadelphia, but between a local broker's office in Philadelphia and his stock exchange. In other words, the short private wire had been introduced. Communication was quicker and freer, and daily grew better.

Railroads had been built to the South, East, North, and West. There was as yet no stock-ticker and no telephone, and the clearing-house had only recently been thought of in New York, and had not yet been introduced in Philadelphia. Instead of a clearing-house service, messengers ran daily between banks and brokerage firms, balancing accounts on pass-books, exchanging bills, and, once a week, transferring the gold coin, which was the only thing that could be accepted for balances due, since there was no stable national currency. "On 'change," when the gong struck announcing the close of the day's business, a company of young men, known as "settlement clerks," after a system borrowed from London, gathered in the center of the room and compared or gathered the various trades of the day in a ring, thus eliminating all those sales and resales between certain firms which naturally canceled each other. They carried long account books, and called out the transactions—

18

"Delaware and Maryland sold to Beaumont and Company," "Delware and Maryland sold to Tighe and Company," and so on. This simplified the bookkeeping of the various firms, and made for quicker and more stirring commercial transactions.

Seats "on 'change" sold for two thousand dollars each. The members of the exchange had just passed rules limiting the trading to the hours between ten and three (before this they had been any time between morning and midnight), and had fixed the rates at which brokers could do business, in the face of cut-throat schemes which had previously held. Severe penalties were fixed for those who failed to obey. In other words, things were shaping up for a great 'change business, and Edward Tighe felt, with other brokers, that there was a great future ahead.

CHAPTER VI

The Cowperwood family was by this time established in its new and larger and more tastefully furnished house on North Front Street, facing the river. The house was four stories tall and stood twenty-five feet on the street front, without a yard.

Here the family began to entertain in a small way, and there came to see them, now and then, representatives of the various interests that Henry Cowperwood had encountered in his upward climb to the position of cashier. It was not a very distinguished company, but it included a number of people who were about as successful as himself—heads of small businesses who traded at his bank, dealers in dry-goods, leather, groceries (wholesale), and grain. The children had come to have intimacies of their own. Now and then, because of church connections, Mrs. Cowperwood ventured to have an afternoon tea or reception, at which even Cowperwood attempted the gallant in so far as to stand about in a genially foolish way and greet those whom his wife had invited. And so long as he could maintain his gravity very solemnly and greet people without being required to say much, it was not too painful for him. Singing was indulged in at times, a little dancing on occasion, and there was considerably more "company to dinner," informally, than there had been previously.

And here it was, during the first year of the new life in this house, that Frank met a certain Mrs. Semple, who interested him greatly. Her husband had a pretentious shoe store on Chestnut Street, near Third, and was planning to open a second one farther out on the same street.

The occasion of the meeting was an evening call on the part of the Semples, Mr. Semple being desirous of talking with Henry Cowperwood concerning a new transportation feature which was then entering the world—namely, street-cars. A tentative line, incorporated by the North Pennsylvania Railway Company, had been put into operation on a mile and a half of tracks extending from Willow Street along Front to Germantown Road, and thence by various streets to what was then known as the Cohocksink Depot; and it was thought that in time this mode of locomotion might drive out the hundreds of omnibuses which now crowded and made impassable the downtown streets. Young Cowperwood had been greatly interested from the start. Railway transportation, as a whole, interested him, anyway, but this particular phase was most fascinating. It was already creating widespread discussion, and he, with others, had gone to see it. A strange but interesting new type of car, fourteen feet long, seven feet wide, and nearly the same height, running on small iron car-wheels, was giving great satisfaction as being quieter and easier-riding than omnibuses; and Alfred Semple was privately considering investing in another proposed line which, if it could secure a franchise from the legislature, was to run on Fifth and Sixth streets.

Cowperwood, Senior, saw a great future for this thing; but he did not see as yet how the capital was to be raised for it. Frank believed that Tighe & Co. should attempt to become the selling agents of this new stock of the Fifth and Sixth Street Company in the event it succeeded in getting a franchise. He understood that a company was already formed, that a large amount of stock was to be issued against the prospective franchise, and that these shares were to be sold at five dollars, as against an ultimate par value of one hundred. He wished he had sufficient money to take a large block of them.

Meanwhile, Lillian Semple caught and held his interest. Just what it was about her that attracted him at this age it would be hard to say, for she was really not suited to him emotionally, intellectually, or otherwise. He was not without experience with women or girls, and still held a tentative relationship with Marjorie Stafford; but Lillian Semple, in spite of the fact that she was married and that he could have legitimate interest in her, seemed not wiser and saner, but more worth while. She was twenty-four as opposed to Frank's nineteen, but still young enough in her thoughts and looks to appear of his own age. She was slightly taller than he—though he was now his full height (five feet ten and one-half inches)—and, despite her height, shapely, artistic in form and feature, and with a certain unconscious placidity of soul, which came more from lack of understanding than from force of character. Her hair was the color of a dried English walnut, rich and plentiful, and her complexion waxen—cream wax—with lips of faint pink, and eyes that varied from gray to blue and from gray to brown, according to the light in which you saw them. Her hands were thin and shapely, her nose straight, her face artistically narrow. She was not brilliant, not active, but rather peaceful and statuesque without knowing it. Cowperwood was carried away by her appearance. Her beauty measured up to his present sense of the artistic. She was lovely, he thought—gracious, dignified. If he could have his choice of a wife, this was the kind of a girl he would like to have.

As yet, Cowperwood's judgment of women was temperamental rather than intellectual. Engrossed as he was by his desire for wealth, prestige, dominance, he was confused, if not chastened by considerations relating to position, presentability and the like. None the less, the homely woman meant nothing to him. And the passionate woman meant much. He heard family discussions of this and that sacrificial soul among women, as well as among men—women who toiled and slaved for their husbands or children, or both, who gave way to relatives or friends in crises or crucial moments, because it was right and kind to do so— but somehow these stories did not appeal to him. He preferred to think of people—even women—as honestly, frankly self-interested. He could not have told you why. People seemed foolish, or at the best very unfortunate not to know what to do in all circumstances and how to protect themselves. There was great talk concerning morality, much praise of virtue and decency, and much lifting of hands in righteous horror at people who broke or were even rumored to have broken the Seventh Commandment. He did not take this talk seriously. Already he had broken it secretly many times. Other young men did. Yet again, he was a little sick of the women of the streets and the bagnio. There were too many coarse, evil features in connection with such contacts. For a little while, the false tinsel-glitter of the house of ill repute appealed to him, for there was a certain force to its luxury—rich, as a rule, with red-plush furniture, showy red hangings, some coarse but showily-framed pictures, and, above all, the strong-bodied or sensuously lymphatic women who dwelt there, to (as his mother phrased it) prey on men. The strength of their bodies, the lust of their souls, the fact that they could, with a show of affection or good-nature, receive man after man, astonished and later disgusted him. After all, they were not smart. There was no vivacity of thought there. All that they could do, in the main, he fancied, was this one thing. He pictured to himself the dreariness of the mornings after, the stale dregs of things when only sleep and thought of gain could aid in the least; and more than once, even at his age, he shook his head. He wanted contact which was more intimate, subtle, individual, personal.

So came Lillian Semple, who was nothing more to him than the shadow of an ideal. Yet she cleared up certain of his ideas in regard to women. She was not physically as vigorous or brutal as those other women whom he had encountered in the lupanars, thus far—raw, unashamed contraveners of accepted theories and notions—and for that very reason he liked her. And his thoughts continued to dwell on her, notwithstanding the hectic days which now passed like flashes of light in his new business venture. For this stock exchange world in which he now found himself, primitive as it would seem to-day, was most fascinating to Cowperwood. The room that he went to in Third Street, at Dock, where the brokers or their agents and clerks gathered one hundred and fifty strong, was nothing to speak of artistically—a square chamber sixty by sixty, reaching from the second floor to the roof of a four-story building; but it was striking to him. The windows were high and narrow; a large-faced clock faced the west entrance of the room where you came in from the stairs; a collection of telegraph instruments, with their accompanying desks and chairs, occupied the northeast corner. On the floor, in the early days of the exchange, were rows of chairs where the brokers sat while various lots of stocks were offered to them. Later in the history of the exchange the chairs were removed and at different points posts or floor-signs indicating where certain stocks were traded in were introduced. Around these the men who were interested gathered to do their trading. From a hall on the third floor a door gave entrance to a visitor's gallery, small and poorly furnished; and on the west wall a large blackboard carried current quotations in stocks as telegraphed from New York and Boston. A wicket-like fence in the center of the room surrounded the desk and chair of the official recorder; and a very small gallery opening from the third floor on the west gave place for the secretary of the board, when he had any special announcement to make. There was a room off the southwest corner, where reports and annual compendiums of chairs were removed and at different signs indicating where certain stocks of various kinds were kept and were available for the use of members.

Young Cowperwood would not have been admitted at all, as either a broker or broker's agent or assistant, except that Tighe, feeling that he needed him and believing that he would be very useful, bought him a seat on 'change—charging the two thousand dollars it cost as a debt and then ostensibly taking him into partnership. It was against the rules of the exchange to sham a partnership in this way in order to put a man on the floor, but brokers did it. These men who were known to be minor partners and floor assistants were derisively called "eighth chasers" and "two-dollar brokers," because they were always seeking small orders and were willing to buy or sell for anybody on their commission, accounting, of course, to their firms for their work. Cowperwood, regardless of his intrinsic merits, was originally counted one of their number, and he was put under the direction of Mr. Arthur Rivers, the regular floor man of Tighe & Company.

Rivers was an exceedingly forceful man of thirty-five, well-dressed, well-formed, with a hard, smooth, evenly chiseled face, which was ornamented by a short, black mustache and fine, black, clearly penciled eyebrows. His hair came to an odd point at the middle of his forehead, where he divided it, and his chin was faintly and attractively cleft. He had a soft voice, a quiet, conservative manner, and both in and out of this brokerage and trading world was controlled by good form. Cowperwood wondered at first why Rivers should work for Tighe—he appeared almost as able—but afterward learned that he was in the company. Tighe was the organizer and general hand-shaker, Rivers the floor and outside man.

It was useless, as Frank soon found, to try to figure out exactly why stocks rose and fell. Some general reasons there were, of course, as he was told by Tighe, but they could not always be depended on.

"Sure, anything can make or break a market"—Tighe explained in his delicate brogue—"from the failure of a bank to the rumor that your second cousin's grandmother has a cold. It's a most unusual world, Cowperwood. No man can explain it. I've seen breaks in stocks that you could never explain at all—no one could. It wouldn't be possible to find out why they broke. I've seen rises the same way. My God, the rumors of the stock exchange! They beat the devil. If they're going down in ordinary times some one is unloading, or they're rigging the market. If they're going up—God knows times must be good or somebody must be buying—that's sure. Beyond that—well, ask Rivers to show you the ropes. Don't you ever lose for me, though. That's the cardinal sin in this office." He grinned maliciously, even if kindly, at that.

Cowperwood understood—none better. This subtle world appealed to him. It answered to his temperament.

There were rumors, rumors, rumors—of great railway and street-car undertakings, land developments, government revision of the tariff, war between France and Turkey, famine in Russia or Ireland, and so on. The first Atlantic cable had not been laid as yet, and news of any kind from abroad was slow and meager. Still there were great financial figures in the held, men who, like Cyrus Field, or William H. Vanderbilt, or F. X. Drexel, were doing marvelous things, and their activities and the rumors concerning them counted for much.

Frank soon picked up all of the technicalities of the situation. A "bull," he learned, was one who bought in anticipation of a higher price to come; and if he was "loaded up" with a "line" of stocks he was said to be "long." He sold to "realize" his profit, or if his margins were exhausted he was "wiped out." A "bear" was one who sold stocks which most frequently he did not have, in anticipation of a lower price, at which he could buy and satisfy his previous sales. He was "short" when he had sold what he did not own, and he "covered" when he bought to satisfy his sales and to realize his profits or to protect himself against further loss in case prices advanced instead of declining. He was in a "corner" when he found that he could not buy in order to make good the stock he had borrowed for delivery and the return of which had been demanded. He was then obliged to settle practically at a price fixed by those to whom he and other "shorts" had sold.

He smiled at first at the air of great secrecy and wisdom on the part of the younger men. They were so heartily and foolishly suspicious. The older men, as a rule, were inscrutable. They pretended indifference, uncertainty. They were like certain fish after a certain kind of bait, however. Snap! and the opportunity was gone. Somebody else had picked up what you wanted. All had their little note-books. All had their peculiar squint of eye or position or motion which meant "Done! I take you!" Sometimes they seemed scarcely to confirm their sales or purchases—they knew each other so well—but they did. If the market was for any reason active, the brokers and their agents were apt to be more numerous than if it were dull and the trading indifferent. A gong sounded the call to trading at ten o'clock, and if there was a noticeable rise or decline in a stock or a group of stocks, you were apt to witness quite a spirited scene. Fifty to a hundred men would shout, gesticulate, shove here and there in an apparently aimless manner; endeavoring to take advantage of the stock offered or called for.

"Five-eighths for five hundred P. and W.," some one would call—Rivers or Cowperwood, or any other broker.

"Five hundred at three-fourths," would come the reply from some one else, who either had an order to sell the stock at that price or who was willing to sell it short, hoping to pick up enough of the stock at a lower figure later to fill his order and make a little something besides. If the supply of stock at that figure was large Rivers would probably continue to bid five-eighths. If, on the other hand, he noticed an increasing demand, he would probably pay three-fourths for it. If the professional traders believed Rivers had a large buying order, they would probably try to buy the stock before he could at three-fourths, believing they could sell it out to him at a slightly higher price. The professional traders were, of course, keen students of psychology; and their success depended on their ability to guess whether or not a broker representing a big manipulator, like Tighe, had an order large enough to affect the market sufficiently to give them an opportunity to "get in and out," as they termed it, at a profit before he had completed the execution of his order. They were like hawks watching for an opportunity to snatch their prey from under the very claws of their opponents.

Four, five, ten, fifteen, twenty, thirty, forty, fifty, and sometimes the whole company would attempt to take advantage of the given rise of a given stock by either selling or offering to buy, in which case the activity and the noise would become deafening. Given groups might be trading in different things; but the large majority of them would abandon what they were doing in order to take advantage of a speciality. The eagerness of certain young brokers or clerks to discover all that was going on, and to take advantage of any given rise or fall, made for quick physical action, darting to and fro, the excited elevation of explanatory fingers. Distorted faces were shoved over shoulders or under arms. The most ridiculous grimaces were purposely or unconsciously indulged in. At times there were situations in which some individual was fairly smothered with arms, faces, shoulders, crowded toward him when he manifested any intention of either buying or selling at a profitable rate. At first it seemed quite a wonderful thing to young Cowperwood—the very physical face of it—for he liked human presence and activity; but a little later the sense of the thing as a picture or a dramatic situation, of which he was a part faded, and he came down to a clearer sense of the intricacies of the problem before him. Buying and selling stocks, as he soon learned, was an art, a subtlety, almost a psychic emotion. Suspicion, intuition, feeling—these were the things to be "long" on.

Yet in time he also asked himself, who was it who made the real money—the stock-brokers? Not at all. Some of them were making money, but they were, as he quickly saw, like a lot of gulls or stormy petrels, hanging on the lee of the wind, hungry and anxious to snap up any unwary fish. Back of them were other men, men with shrewd ideas, subtle resources. Men of immense means whose enterprise and holdings these stocks represented, the men who schemed out and built the railroads, opened the mines, organized trading enterprises, and built up immense manufactories. They might use brokers or other agents to buy and sell on 'change; but this buying and selling must be, and always was, incidental to the actual fact—the mine, the railroad, the wheat crop, the flour mill, and so on. Anything less than straight-out sales to realize quickly on assets, or buying to hold as an investment, was gambling pure and simple, and these men were gamblers. He was nothing more than a gambler's agent. It was not troubling him any just at this moment, but it was not at all a mystery now, what he was. As in the case of Waterman & Company, he sized up these men shrewdly, judging some to be weak, some foolish, some clever, some slow, but in the main all small-minded or deficient because they were agents, tools, or gamblers. A man, a real man, must never be an agent, a tool, or a gambler—acting for himself or for others—he must employ such. A real man—a financier—was never a tool. He used tools. He created. He led.

Clearly, very clearly, at nineteen, twenty, and twenty-one years of age, he saw all this, but he was not quite ready yet to do anything about it. He was certain, however, that his day would come.

CHAPTER VII

In the meantime, his interest in Mrs. Semple had been secretly and strangely growing. When he received an invitation to call at the Semple home, he accepted with a great deal of pleasure. Their house was located not so very far from his own, on North Front Street, in the neighborhood of what is now known as No. 956. It had, in summer, quite a wealth of green leaves and vines. The little side porch which ornamented its south wall commanded a charming view of the river, and all the windows and doors were topped with lunettes of small-paned glass. The interior of the house was not as pleasing as he would have had it. Artistic impressiveness, as to the furniture at least, was wanting, although it was new and good. The pictures were—well, simply pictures. There were no books to speak of—the Bible, a few current novels, some of the more significant histories, and a collection of antiquated odds and ends in the shape of books inherited from relatives. The china was good—of a delicate pattern. The carpets and wall-paper were too high in key. So it went. Still, the personality of Lillian Semple was worth something, for she was really pleasing to look upon, making a picture wherever she stood or sat.

There were no children—a dispensation of sex conditions which had nothing to do with her, for she longed to have them. She was without any notable experience in social life, except such as had come to the Wiggin family, of which she was a member—relatives and a few neighborhood friends visiting. Lillian Wiggin, that was her maiden name—had two brothers and one sister, all living in Philadelphia and all married at this time. They thought she had done very well in her marriage.

It could not be said that she had wildly loved Mr. Semple at any time. Although she had cheerfully married him, he was not the kind of man who could arouse a notable passion in any woman. He was practical, methodic, orderly. His shoe store was a good one—well-stocked with styles reflecting the current tastes and a model of cleanliness and what one might term pleasing brightness. He loved to talk, when he talked at all, of shoe manufacturing, the development of lasts and styles. The ready-made shoe—machine-made to a certain extent—was just coming into its own slowly, and outside of these, supplies of which he kept, he employed bench-making shoemakers, satisfying his customers with personal measurements and making the shoes to order.

Mrs. Semple read a little—not much. She had a habit of sitting and apparently brooding reflectively at times, but it was not based on any deep thought. She had that curious beauty of body, though, that made her somewhat like a figure on an antique vase, or out of a Greek chorus. It was in this light, unquestionably, that Cowperwood saw her, for from the beginning he could not keep his eyes off her. In a way, she was aware of this but she did not attach any significance to it. Thoroughly conventional, satisfied now that her life was bound permanently with that of her husband, she had settled down to a staid and quiet existence.

At first, when Frank called, she did not have much to say. She was gracious, but the burden of conversation fell on her husband. Cowperwood watched the varying expression of her face from time to time, and if she had been at all psychic she must have felt something. Fortunately she was not. Semple talked to him pleasantly, because in the first place Frank was becoming financially significant, was suave and ingratiating, and in the next place he was anxious to get richer and somehow Frank represented progress to him in that line. One spring evening they sat on the porch and talked—nothing very important—slavery, street-cars, the panic—it was on then, that of 1857—the development of the West. Mr. Semple wanted to know all about the stock exchange. In return Frank asked about the shoe business, though he really did not care. All the while, inoffensively, he watched Mrs. Semple. Her manner, he thought, was soothing, attractive, delightful. She served tea and cake for them. They went inside after a time to avoid the mosquitoes. She played the piano. At ten o'clock he left.

Thereafter, for a year or so, Cowperwood bought his shoes of Mr. Semple. Occasionally also he stopped in the Chestnut Street store to exchange the time of the day. Semple asked his opinion as to the advisability of buying some shares in the Fifth and Sixth Street line, which, having secured a franchise, was creating great excitement. Cowperwood gave him his best judgment. It was sure to be profitable. He himself had purchased one hundred shares at five dollars a share, and urged Semple to do so. But he was not interested in him personally. He liked Mrs. Semple, though he did not see her very often.

24

About a year later, Mr. Semple died. It was an untimely death, one of those fortuitous and in a way insignificant episodes which are, nevertheless, dramatic in a dull way to those most concerned. He was seized with a cold in the chest late in the fall—one of those seizures ordinarily attributed to wet feet or to going out on a damp day without an overcoat—and had insisted on going to business when Mrs. Semple urged him to stay at home and recuperate. He was in his way a very determined person, not obstreperously so, but quietly and under the surface. Business was a great urge. He saw himself soon to be worth about fifty thousand dollars. Then this cold—nine more days of pneumonia—and he was dead. The shoe store was closed for a few days; the house was full of sympathetic friends and church people. There was a funeral, with burial service in the Callowhill Presbyterian Church, to which they belonged, and then he was buried. Mrs. Semple cried bitterly. The shock of death affected her greatly and left her for a time in a depressed state. A brother of hers, David Wiggin, undertook for the time being to run the shoe business for her. There was no will, but in the final adjustment, which included the sale of the shoe business, there being no desire on anybody's part to contest her right to all the property, she received over eighteen thousand dollars. She continued to reside in the Front Street house, and was considered a charming and interesting widow.

Throughout this procedure young Cowperwood, only twenty years of age, was quietly manifest. He called during the illness. He attended the funeral. He helped her brother, David Wiggin, dispose of the shoe business. He called once or twice after the funeral, then stayed away for a considerable time. In five months he reappeared, and thereafter he was a caller at stated intervals—periods of a week or ten days.

Again, it would be hard to say what he saw in Semple. Her prettiness, wax-like in its quality, fascinated him; her indifference aroused perhaps his combative soul. He could not have explained why, but he wanted her in an urgent, passionate way. He could not think of her reasonably, and he did not talk of her much to any one. His family knew that he went to see her, but there had grown up in the Cowperwood family a deep respect for the mental force of Frank. He was genial, cheerful, gay at most times, without being talkative, and he was decidedly successful. Everybody knew he was making money now. His salary was fifty dollars a week, and he was certain soon to get more. Some lots of his in West Philadelphia, bought three years before, had increased notably in value. His street-car holdings, augmented by still additional lots of fifty and one hundred and one hundred and fifty shares in new lines incorporated, were slowly rising, in spite of hard times, from the initiative five dollars in each case to ten, fifteen, and twenty-five dollars a share—all destined to go to par. He was liked in the financial district and he was sure that he had a successful future. Because of his analysis of the brokerage situation he had come to the conclusion that he did not want to be a stock gambler. Instead, he was considering the matter of engaging in bill-brokering, a business which he had observed to be very profitable and which involved no risk as long as one had capital. Through his work and his father's connections he had met many people—merchants, bankers, traders. He could get their business, or a part of it, he knew. People in Drexel & Co. and Clark & Co. were friendly to him. Jay Cooke, a rising banking personality, was a personal friend of his.

Meanwhile he called on Mrs. Semple, and the more he called the better he liked her. There was no exchange of brilliant ideas between them; but he had a way of being comforting and social when he wished. He advised her about her business affairs in so intelligent a way that even her relatives approved of it. She came to like him, because he was so considerate, quiet, reassuring, and so ready to explain over and over until everything was quite plain to her. She could see that he was looking on her affairs quite as if they were his own, trying to make them safe and secure.

"You're so very kind, Frank," she said to him, one night. "I'm awfully grateful. I don't know what I would have done if it hadn't been for you."

She looked at his handsome face, which was turned to hers, with child-like simplicity.

"Not at all. Not at all. I want to do it. I wouldn't have been happy if I couldn't."

His eyes had a peculiar, subtle ray in them—not a gleam. She felt warm toward him, sympathetic, quite satisfied that she could lean on him.

"Well, I am very grateful just the same. You've been so good. Come out Sunday again, if you want to, or any evening. I'll be home."

It was while he was calling on her in this way that his Uncle Seneca died in Cuba and left him fifteen thousand dollars. This money made him worth nearly twenty-five thousand dollars in his own right, and he knew exactly what to do with it. A panic had come since Mr. Semple had died, which had illustrated to him very clearly what an uncertain thing the brokerage business was. There was really a severe business depression. Money was so scarce that it could fairly be said not to exist at all. Capital, frightened by uncertain trade and money conditions, everywhere, retired to its hiding-places in banks, vaults, tea-kettles, and stockings. The country seemed to be going to the dogs. War with the South or secession was vaguely looming up in the distance. The temper of the whole nation was nervous. People dumped their holdings on the market in order to get money. Tighe discharged three of his clerks. He cut down his expenses in every possible way, and used up all his private savings to protect his private holdings. He mortgaged his house, his land holdings—everything; and in many instances young Cowperwood was his intermediary, carrying blocks of shares to different banks to get what he could on them.

"See if your father's bank won't loan me fifteen thousand on these," he said to Frank, one day, producing a bundle of Philadelphia & Wilmington shares. Frank had heard his father speak of them in times past as excellent.

"They ought to be good," the elder Cowperwood said, dubiously, when shown the package of securities. "At any other time they would be. But money is so tight. We find it awfully hard these days to meet our own obligations. I'll talk to Mr. Kugel." Mr. Kugel was the president.

There was a long conversation—a long wait. His father came back to say it was doubtful whether they could make the loan. Eight per cent., then being secured for money, was a small rate of interest, considering its need. For ten per cent. Mr. Kugel might make a call-loan. Frank went back to his employer, whose commercial choler rose at the report.

"For Heaven's sake, is there no money at all in the town?" he demanded, contentiously. "Why, the interest they want is ruinous! I can't stand that. Well, take 'em back and bring me the money. Good God, this'll never do at all, at all!"

Frank went back. "He'll pay ten per cent.," he said, quietly.

Tighe was credited with a deposit of fifteen thousand dollars, with privilege to draw against it at once. He made out a check for the total fifteen thousand at once to the Girard National Bank to cover a shrinkage there. So it went.

During all these days young Cowperwood was following these financial complications with interest. He was not disturbed by the cause of slavery, or the talk of secession, or the general progress or decline of the country, except in so far as it affected his immediate interests. He longed to become a stable financier; but, now that he saw the inside of the brokerage business, he was not so sure that he wanted to stay in it. Gambling in stocks, according to conditions produced by this panic, seemed very hazardous. A number of brokers failed. He saw them rush in to Tighe with anguished faces and ask that certain trades be canceled. Their very homes were in danger, they said. They would be wiped out, their wives and children put out on the street.

This panic, incidentally, only made Frank more certain as to what he really wanted to do—now that he had this free money, he would go into business for himself. Even Tighe's offer of a minor partnership failed to tempt him.

"I think you have a nice business," he explained, in refusing, "but I want to get in the note-brokerage business for myself. I don't trust this stock game. I'd rather have a little business of my own than all the floor work in this world."

26

"But you're pretty young, Frank," argued his employer. "You have lots of time to work for yourself." In the end he parted friends with both Tighe and Rivers. "That's a smart young fellow," observed Tighe, ruefully.

"He'll make his mark," rejoined Rivers. "He's the shrewdest boy of his age I ever saw."

CHAPTER VIII

Cowperwood's world at this time was of roseate hue. He was in love and had money of his own to start his new business venture. He could take his street-car stocks, which were steadily increasing in value, and raise seventy per cent. of their market value. He could put a mortgage on his lots and get money there, if necessary. He had established financial relations with the Girard National Bank—President Davison there having taken a fancy to him—and he proposed to borrow from that institution some day. All he wanted was suitable investments—things in which he could realize surely, quickly. He saw fine prospective profits in the street-car lines, which were rapidly developing into local ramifications.

He purchased a horse and buggy about this time—the most attractive-looking animal and vehicle he could find—the combination cost him five hundred dollars—and invited Mrs. Semple to drive with him. She refused at first, but later consented. He had told her of his success, his prospects, his windfall of fifteen thousand dollars, his intention of going into the note-brokerage business. She knew his father was likely to succeed to the position of vice-president in the Third National Bank, and she liked the Cowperwoods. Now she began to realize that there was something more than mere friendship here. This erstwhile boy was a man, and he was calling on her. It was almost ridiculous in the face of things—her seniority, her widowhood, her placid, retiring disposition—but the sheer, quiet, determined force of this young man made it plain that he was not to be balked by her sense of convention.

Cowperwood did not delude himself with any noble theories of conduct in regard to her. She was beautiful, with a mental and physical lure for him that was irresistible, and that was all he desired to know. No other woman was holding him like that. It never occurred to him that he could not or should not like other women at the same time. There was a great deal of palaver about the sanctity of the home. It rolled off his mental sphere like water off the feathers of a duck. He was not eager for her money, though he was well aware of it. He felt that he could use it to her advantage. He wanted her physically. He felt a keen, primitive interest in the children they would have. He wanted to find out if he could make her love him vigorously and could rout out the memory of her former life. Strange ambition. Strange perversion, one might almost say.

In spite of her fears and her uncertainty, Lillian Semple accepted his attentions and interest because, equally in spite of herself, she was drawn to him. One night, when she was going to bed, she stopped in front of her dressing table and looked at her face and her bare neck and arms. They were very pretty. A subtle something came over her as she surveyed her long, peculiarly shaded hair. She thought of young Cowperwood, and then was chilled and shamed by the vision of the late Mr. Semple and the force and quality of public opinion.

"Why do you come to see me so often?" she asked him when he called the following evening.

"Oh, don't you know?" he replied, looking at her in an interpretive way.

"No."

"Sure you don't?"

"Well, I know you liked Mr. Semple, and I always thought you liked me as his wife. He's gone, though, now."

"And you're here," he replied.

"And I'm here?"

"Yes. I like you. I like to be with you. Don't you like me that way?"

"Why, I've never thought of it. You're so much younger. I'm five years older than you are."

"In years," he said, "certainly. That's nothing. I'm fifteen years older than you are in other ways. I know more about life in some ways than you can ever hope to learn—don't you think so?" he added, softly, persuasively.

"Well, that's true. But I know a lot of things you don't know." She laughed softly, showing her pretty teeth.

It was evening. They were on the side porch. The river was before them.

"Yes, but that's only because you're a woman. A man can't hope to get a woman's point of view exactly. But I'm talking about practical affairs of this world. You're not as old that way as I am."

"Well, what of it?"

"Nothing. You asked why I came to see you. That's why. Partly."

He relapsed into silence and stared at the water.

She looked at him. His handsome body, slowly broadening, was nearly full grown. His face, because of its full, clear, big, inscrutable eyes, had an expression which was almost babyish. She could not have guessed the depths it veiled. His cheeks were pink, his hands not large, but sinewy and strong. Her pale, uncertain, lymphatic body extracted a form of dynamic energy from him even at this range.

"I don't think you ought to come to see me so often. People won't think well of it." She ventured to take a distant, matronly air—the air she had originally held toward him.

"People," he said, "don't worry about people. People think what you want them to think. I wish you wouldn't take that distant air toward me."

"Why?"

"Because I like you."

"But you mustn't like me. It's wrong. I can't ever marry you. You're too young. I'm too old."

"Don't say that!" he said, imperiously. "There's nothing to it. I want you to marry me. You know I do. Now, when will it be?"

"Why, how silly! I never heard of such a thing!" she exclaimed. "It will never be, Frank. It can't be!"

"Why can't it?" he asked.

"Because—well, because I'm older. People would think it strange. I'm not long enough free."

"Oh, long enough nothing!" he exclaimed, irritably. "That's the one thing I have against you—you are so worried about what people think. They don't make your life. They certainly don't make mine. Think of yourself first. You have your own life to make. Are you going to let what other people think stand in the way of what you want to do?"

"But I don't want to," she smiled.

He arose and came over to her, looking into her eyes.

"Well?" she asked, nervously, quizzically.

He merely looked at her.

"Well?" she queried, more flustered.

He stooped down to take her arms, but she got up.

"Now you must not come near me," she pleaded, determinedly. "I'll go in the house, and I'll not let you come any more. It's terrible! You're silly! You mustn't interest yourself in me."

28

She did show a good deal of determination, and he desisted. But for the time being only. He called again and again. Then one night, when they had gone inside because of the mosquitoes, and when she had insisted that he must stop coming to see her, that his attentions were noticeable to others, and that she would be disgraced, he caught her, under desperate protest, in his arms.

"Now, see here!" she exclaimed. "I told you! It's silly! You mustn't kiss me! How dare you! Oh! oh! oh!—"

She broke away and ran up the near-by stairway to her room. Cowperwood followed her swiftly. As she pushed the door to he forced it open and recaptured her. He lifted her bodily from her feet and held her crosswise, lying in his arms.

"Oh, how could you!" she exclaimed. "I will never speak to you any more. I will never let you come here any more if you don't put me down this minute. Put me down!"

"I'll put you down, sweet," he said. "I'll take you down," at the same time pulling her face to him and kissing her. He was very much aroused, excited.

While she was twisting and protesting, he carried her down the stairs again into the living-room, and seated himself in the great armchair, still holding her tight in his arms.

"Oh!" she sighed, falling limp on his shoulder when he refused to let her go. Then, because of the set determination of his face, some intense pull in him, she smiled. "How would I ever explain if I did marry you?" she asked, weakly. "Your father! Your mother!"

"You don't need to explain. I'll do that. And you needn't worry about my family. They won't care."

"But mine," she recoiled.

"Don't worry about yours. I'm not marrying your family. I'm marrying you. We have independent means."

She relapsed into additional protests; but he kissed her the more. There was a deadly persuasion to his caresses. Mr. Semple had never displayed any such fire. He aroused a force of feeling in her which had not previously been there. She was afraid of it and ashamed.

"Will you marry me in a month?" he asked, cheerfully, when she paused.

"You know I won't!" she exclaimed, nervously. "The idea! Why do you ask?"

"What difference does it make? We're going to get married eventually." He was thinking how attractive he could make her look in other surroundings. Neither she nor his family knew how to live.

"Well, not in a month. Wait a little while. I will marry you after a while—after you see whether you want me."

He caught her tight. "I'll show you," he said.

"Please stop. You hurt me."

"How about it? Two months?"

"Certainly not."

"Three?"

"Well, maybe."

"No maybe in that case. We marry."

"But you're only a boy."

"Don't worry about me. You'll find out how much of a boy I am."

He seemed of a sudden to open up a new world to her, and she realized that she had never really lived before. This man represented something bigger and stronger than ever her husband had dreamed of. In his young way he was terrible, irresistible.

"Well, in three months then," she whispered, while he rocked her cozily in his arms.

CHAPTER IX

Cowperwood started in the note brokerage business with a small office at No. 64 South Third Street, where he very soon had the pleasure of discovering that his former excellent business connections remembered him. He would go to one house, where he suspected ready money might be desirable, and offer to negotiate their notes or any paper they might issue bearing six per cent. interest for a commission and then he would sell the paper for a small commission to some one who would welcome a secure investment. Sometimes his father, sometimes other people, helped him with suggestions as to when and how. Between the two ends he might make four and five per cent. on the total transaction. In the first year he cleared six thousand dollars over and above all expenses. That wasn't much, but he was augmenting it in another way which he believed would bring great profit in the future.

Before the first street-car line, which was a shambling affair, had been laid on Front Street, the streets of Philadelphia had been crowded with hundreds of springless omnibuses rattling over rough, hard, cobblestones. Now, thanks to the idea of John Stephenson, in New York, the double rail track idea had come, and besides the line on Fifth and Sixth Streets (the cars running out one street and back on another) which had paid splendidly from the start, there were many other lines proposed or under way. The city was as eager to see street-cars replace omnibuses as it was to see railroads replace canals. There was opposition, of course. There always is in such cases. The cry of probable monopoly was raised. Disgruntled and defeated omnibus owners and drivers groaned aloud.

Cowperwood had implicit faith in the future of the street railway. In support of this belief he risked all he could spare on new issues of stock shares in new companies. He wanted to be on the inside wherever possible, always, though this was a little difficult in the matter of the street-railways, he having been so young when they started and not having yet arranged his financial connections to make them count for much. The Fifth and Sixth Street line, which had been but recently started, was paying six hundred dollars a day. A project for a West Philadelphia line (Walnut and Chestnut) was on foot, as were lines to occupy Second and Third Streets, Race and Vine, Spruce and Pine, Green and Coates, Tenth and Eleventh, and so forth. They were engineered and backed by some powerful capitalists who had influence with the State legislature and could, in spite of great public protest, obtain franchises. Charges of corruption were in the air. It was argued that the streets were valuable, and that the companies should pay a road tax of a thousand dollars a mile. Somehow, however, these splendid grants were gotten through, and the public, hearing of the Fifth and Sixth Street line profits, was eager to invest. Cowperwood was one of these, and when the Second and Third Street line was engineered, he invested in that and in the Walnut and Chestnut Street line also. He began to have vague dreams of controlling a line himself some day, but as yet he did not see exactly how it was to be done, since his business was far from being a bonanza.

In the midst of this early work he married Mrs. Semple. There was no vast to-do about it, as he did not want any and his bride-to-be was nervous, fearsome of public opinion. His family did not entirely approve. She was too old, his mother and father thought, and then Frank, with his prospects, could have done much better. His sister Anna fancied that Mrs. Semple was designing, which was, of course, not true. His brothers, Joseph and Edward, were interested, but not certain as to what they actually thought, since Mrs. Semple was good-looking and had some money.

It was a warm October day when he and Lillian went to the altar, in the First Presbyterian Church of Callowhill Street. His bride, Frank was satisfied, looked exquisite in a trailing gown of cream lace—a creation that had cost months of labor. His parents, Mrs. Seneca Davis, the Wiggin family, brothers and sisters, and some friends were present. He was a little opposed to this idea, but Lillian wanted it. He stood up straight and correct in black broadcloth for the wedding ceremony—because she wished it, but later changed to a smart business suit for traveling. He had arranged his affairs for a two weeks' trip to New York and Boston. They took an afternoon train for New York, which required five hours to reach. When they were finally alone in the Astor House, New York, after hours of make-believe and public pretense of indifference, he gathered her in his arms.

"Oh, it's delicious," he exclaimed, "to have you all to myself."

She met his eagerness with that smiling, tantalizing passivity which he had so much admired but which this time was tinged strongly with a communicated desire. He thought he should never have enough of her, her beautiful face, her lovely arms, her smooth, lymphatic body. They were like two children, billing and cooing, driving, dining, seeing the sights. He was curious to visit the financial sections of both cities. New York and Boston appealed to him as commercially solid. He wondered, as he observed the former, whether he should ever leave Philadelphia. He was going to be very happy there now, he thought, with Lillian and possibly a brood of young Cowperwoods. He was going to work hard and make money. With his means and hers now at his command, he might become, very readily, notably wealthy.

CHAPTER X

The home atmosphere which they established when they returned from their honeymoon was a great improvement in taste over that which had characterized the earlier life of Mrs. Cowperwood as Mrs. Semple. They had decided to occupy her house, on North Front Street, for a while at least. Cowperwood, aggressive in his current artistic mood, had objected at once after they were engaged to the spirit of the furniture and decorations, or lack of them, and had suggested that he be allowed to have it brought more in keeping with his idea of what was appropriate. During the years in which he had been growing into manhood he had come instinctively into sound notions of what was artistic and refined. He had seen so many homes that were more distinguished and harmonious than his own. One could not walk or drive about Philadelphia without seeing and being impressed with the general tendency toward a more cultivated and selective social life. Many excellent and expensive houses were being erected. The front lawn, with some attempt at floral gardening, was achieving local popularity. In the homes of the Tighes, the Leighs, Arthur Rivers, and others, he had noticed art objects of some distinction—bronzes, marbles, hangings, pictures, clocks, rugs.

It seemed to him now that his comparatively commonplace house could be made into something charming and for comparatively little money. The dining-room for instance which, through two plain windows set in a hat side wall back of the veranda, looked south over a stretch of grass and several trees and bushes to a dividing fence where the Semple property ended and a neighbor's began, could be made so much more attractive. That fence—sharp-pointed, gray palings—could be torn away and a hedge put in its place. The wall which divided the dining-room from the parlor could be knocked through and a hanging of some pleasing character put in its place. A bay-window could be built to replace the two present oblong windows—a bay which would come down to the floor and open out on the lawn via swiveled, diamond-shaped, lead-paned frames. All this shabby, nondescript furniture, collected from heaven knows where—partly inherited from the Semples and the Wiggins and partly bought—could be thrown out or sold and something better and more harmonious introduced. He knew a young man by the name of Ellsworth, an architect newly graduated from a local school, with whom he had struck up an interesting friendship—one of those inexplicable inclinations of temperament. Wilton Ellsworth was an artist in spirit, quiet, meditative, refined. From discussing the quality of a certain building on Chestnut Street which was then being erected, and which Ellsworth pronounced atrocious, they had fallen to discussing art in general, or the lack of it, in America. And it occurred to him that Ellsworth was the man to carry out his decorative views to a nicety. When he suggested the young man to Lillian, she placidly agreed with him and also with his own ideas of how the house could be revised.

So while they were gone on their honeymoon Ellsworth began the revision on an estimated cost of three thousand dollars, including the furniture. It was not completed for nearly three weeks after their return; but when finished made a comparatively new house. The dining-room bay hung low over the grass, as Frank wished, and the windows were diamond-paned and leaded, swiveled on brass rods. The parlor and dining-room were separated by sliding doors; but the intention was to hang in this opening a silk hanging depicting a wedding scene in Normandy. Old English oak was used in the dining-room, an American imitation of Chippendale and Sheraton for the sitting-room and the bedrooms. There were a few simple water-colors hung here and there, some bronzes of Hosmer and Powers, a marble venus by Potter, a now forgotten sculptor, and other objects of art—nothing of any distinction. Pleasing, appropriately colored rugs covered the floor. Mrs. Cowperwood was shocked by the nudity of the Venus which conveyed an atmosphere of European freedom not common to America; but she said nothing. It was all harmonious and soothing, and she did not feel herself capable to judge. Frank knew about these things so much better than she did. Then with a maid and a man of all work installed, a program of entertaining was begun on a small scale.

Those who recall the early years of their married life can best realize the subtle changes which this new condition brought to Frank, for, like all who accept the hymeneal yoke, he was influenced to a certain extent by the things with which he surrounded himself. Primarily, from certain traits of his character, one would have imagined him called to be a citizen of eminent respectability and worth. He appeared to be an ideal home man. He delighted to return to his wife in the evenings, leaving the crowded downtown section where traffic clamored and men hurried. Here he could feel that he was well-stationed and physically happy in life. The thought of the dinner-table with candles upon it (his idea); the thought of Lillian in a trailing gown of pale-blue or green silk—he liked her in those colors; the thought of a large fireplace flaming with solid lengths of cord-wood, and Lillian snuggling in his arms, gripped his immature imagination. As has been said before, he cared nothing for books, but life, pictures, trees, physical contact—these, in spite of his shrewd and already gripping financial calculations, held him. To live richly, joyously, fully—his whole nature craved that.

And Mrs. Cowperwood, in spite of the difference in their years, appeared to be a fit mate for him at this time. She was once awakened, and for the time being, clinging, responsive, dreamy. His mood and hers was for a baby, and in a little while that happy expectation was whispered to him by her. She had half fancied that her previous barrenness was due to herself, and was rather surprised and delighted at the proof that it was not so. It opened new possibilities—a seemingly glorious future of which she was not afraid. He liked it, the idea of self-duplication. It was almost acquisitive, this thought. For days and weeks and months and years, at least the first four or five, he took a keen satisfaction in coming home evenings, strolling about the yard, driving with his wife, having friends in to dinner, talking over with her in an explanatory way the things he intended to do. She did not understand his financial abstrusities, and he did not trouble to make them clear.

But love, her pretty body, her lips, her quiet manner—the lure of all these combined, and his two children, when they came—two in four years—held him. He would dandle Frank, Jr., who was the first to arrive, on his knee, looking at his chubby feet, his kindling eyes, his almost formless yet bud-like mouth, and wonder at the process by which children came into the world. There was so much to think of in this connection—the spermatozoic beginning, the strange period of gestation in women, the danger of disease and delivery. He had gone

32

through a real period of strain when Frank, Jr., was born, for Mrs. Cowperwood was frightened. He feared for the beauty of her body—troubled over the danger of losing her; and he actually endured his first worry when he stood outside the door the day the child came. Not much—he was too self-sufficient, too resourceful; and yet he worried, conjuring up thoughts of death and the end of their present state. Then word came, after certain piercing, harrowing cries, that all was well, and he was permitted to look at the new arrival. The experience broadened his conception of things, made him more solid in his judgment of life. That old conviction of tragedy underlying the surface of things, like wood under its veneer, was emphasized. Little Frank, and later Lillian, blue-eyed and golden-haired, touched his imagination for a while. There was a good deal to this home idea, after all. That was the way life was organized, and properly so—its cornerstone was the home.

It would be impossible to indicate fully how subtle were the material changes which these years involved—changes so gradual that they were, like the lap of soft waters, unnoticeable. Considerable—a great deal, considering how little he had to begin with—wealth was added in the next five years. He came, in his financial world, to know fairly intimately, as commercial relationships go, some of the subtlest characters of the steadily enlarging financial world. In his days at Tighe's and on the exchange, many curious figures had been pointed out to him—State and city officials of one grade and another who were "making something out of politics," and some national figures who came from Washington to Philadelphia at times to see Drexel & Co., Clark & Co., and even Tighe & Co. These men, as he learned, had tips or advance news of legislative or economic changes which were sure to affect certain stocks or trade opportunities. A young clerk had once pulled his sleeve at Tighe's.

"See that man going in to see Tighe?"

"Yes."

"That's Murtagh, the city treasurer. Say, he don't do anything but play a fine game. All that money to invest, and he don't have to account for anything except the principal. The interest goes to him."

Cowperwood understood. All these city and State officials speculated. They had a habit of depositing city and State funds with certain bankers and brokers as authorized agents or designated State depositories. The banks paid no interest—save to the officials personally. They loaned it to certain brokers on the officials' secret order, and the latter invested it in "sure winners." The bankers got the free use of the money a part of the time, the brokers another part: the officials made money, and the brokers received a fat commission. There was a political ring in Philadelphia in which the mayor, certain members of the council, the treasurer, the chief of police, the commissioner of public works, and others shared. It was a case generally of "You scratch my back and I'll scratch yours." Cowperwood thought it rather shabby work at first, but many men were rapidly getting rich and no one seemed to care. The newspapers were always talking about civic patriotism and pride but never a word about these things. And the men who did them were powerful and respected.

There were many houses, a constantly widening circle, that found him a very trustworthy agent in disposing of note issues or note payment. He seemed to know so quickly where to go to get the money. From the first he made it a principle to keep twenty thousand dollars in cash on hand in order to be able to take up a proposition instantly and without discussion. So, often he was able to say, "Why, certainly, I can do that," when otherwise, on the face of things, he would not have been able to do so. He was asked if he would not handle certain stock transactions on 'change. He had no seat, and he intended not to take any at first; but now he changed his mind, and bought one, not only in Philadelphia, but in New York also. A certain Joseph Zimmerman, a dry-goods man for whom he had handled various note issues, suggested that he undertake operating in street-railway shares for him, and this was the beginning of his return to the floor.

In the meanwhile his family life was changing—growing, one might have said, finer and more secure. Mrs. Cowperwood had, for instance, been compelled from time to time to make a subtle readjustment of her personal relationship with people, as he had with his. When Mr. Semple was alive she had been socially connected with tradesmen principally—retailers and small wholesalers—a very few. Some of the women of her own church, the First Presbyterian, were friendly with her. There had been church teas and sociables which she and Mr. Semple attended, and dull visits to his relatives and hers. The Cowperwoods, the Watermans, and a few families of that caliber, had been the notable exceptions. Now all this was changed. Young Cowperwood did not care very much for her relatives, and the Semples had been alienated by her second, and to them outrageous, marriage. His own family was closely interested by ties of affection and mutual prosperity, but, better than this, he was drawing to himself some really significant personalities. He brought home with him, socially—not to talk business, for he disliked that idea—bankers, investors, customers and prospective customers. Out on the Schuylkill, the Wissahickon, and elsewhere, were popular dining places where one could drive on Sunday. He and Mrs. Cowperwood frequently drove out to Mrs. Seneca Davis's, to Judge Kitchen's, to the home of Andrew Sharpless, a lawyer whom he knew, to the home of Harper Steger, his own lawyer, and others. Cowperwood had the gift of geniality. None of these men or women suspected the depth of his nature—he was thinking, thinking, thinking, but enjoyed life as he went.

One of his earliest and most genuine leanings was toward paintings. He admired nature, but somehow, without knowing why, he fancied one could best grasp it through the personality of some interpreter, just as we gain our ideas of law and politics through individuals. Mrs. Cowperwood cared not a whit one way or another, but she accompanied him to exhibitions, thinking all the while that Frank was a little peculiar. He tried, because he loved her, to interest her in these things intelligently, but while she pretended slightly, she could not really see or care, and it was very plain that she could not.

The children took up a great deal of her time. However, Cowperwood was not troubled about this. It struck him as delightful and exceedingly worth while that she should be so devoted. At the same time, her lethargic manner, vague smile and her sometimes seeming indifference, which sprang largely from a sense of absolute security, attracted him also. She was so different from him! She took her second marriage quite as she had taken her first—a solemn fact which contained no possibility of mental alteration. As for himself, however, he was bustling about in a world which, financially at least, seemed all alteration—there were so many sudden and almost unheard-of changes. He began to look at her at times, with a speculative eye—not very critically, for he liked her—but with an attempt to weigh her personality. He had known her five years and more now. What did he know about her? The vigor of youth—those first years—had made up for so many things, but now that he had her safely...

There came in this period the slow approach, and finally the declaration, of war between the North and the South, attended with so much excitement that almost all current minds were notably colored by it. It was terrific. Then came meetings, public and stirring, and riots; the incident of John Brown's body; the arrival of Lincoln, the great commoner, on his way from Springfield, Illinois, to Washington via Philadelphia, to take the oath of office; the battle of Bull Run; the battle of Vicksburg; the battle of Gettysburg, and so on. Cowperwood was only twenty-five at the time, a cool, determined youth, who thought the slave agitation might be well founded in human rights—no doubt was—but exceedingly dangerous to trade. He hoped the North would win; but it might go hard with him personally and other financiers. He did not care to fight. That seemed silly for the individual man to do. Others might—there were many poor, thin-minded, half-baked creatures who would put themselves up to be shot; but they were only fit to be commanded or shot down. As for him, his life was sacred to himself and his family and his personal interests. He recalled seeing, one day, in one of the quiet side streets, as the working-men were coming

34

home from their work, a small enlisting squad of soldiers in blue marching enthusiastically along, the Union flag flying, the drummers drumming, the fifes blowing, the idea being, of course, to so impress the hitherto indifferent or wavering citizen, to exalt him to such a pitch, that he would lose his sense of proportion, of self-interest, and, forgetting all—wife, parents, home, and children—and seeing only the great need of the country, fall in behind and enlist. He saw one workingman swinging his pail, and evidently not contemplating any such denouement to his day's work, pause, listen as the squad approached, hesitate as it drew close, and as it passed, with a peculiar look of uncertainty or wonder in his eyes, fall in behind and march solemnly away to the enlisting quarters. What was it that had caught this man, Frank asked himself. How was he overcome so easily? He had not intended to go. His face was streaked with the grease and dirt of his work—he looked like a foundry man or machinist, say twenty-five years of age. Frank watched the little squad disappear at the end of the street round the corner under the trees.

This current war-spirit was strange. The people seemed to him to want to hear nothing but the sound of the drum and fife, to see nothing but troops, of which there were thousands now passing through on their way to the front, carrying cold steel in the shape of guns at their shoulders, to hear of war and the rumors of war. It was a thrilling sentiment, no doubt, great but unprofitable. It meant self-sacrifice, and he could not see that. If he went he might be shot, and what would his noble emotion amount to then? He would rather make money, regulate current political, social and financial affairs. The poor fool who fell in behind the enlisting squad—no, not fool, he would not call him that—the poor overwrought working-man—well, Heaven pity him! Heaven pity all of them! They really did not know what they were doing.

One day he saw Lincoln—a tall, shambling man, long, bony, gawky, but tremendously impressive. It was a raw, slushy morning of a late February day, and the great war President was just through with his solemn pronunciamento in regard to the bonds that might have been strained but must not be broken. As he issued from the doorway of Independence Hall, that famous birthplace of liberty, his face was set in a sad, meditative calm. Cowperwood looked at him fixedly as he issued from the doorway surrounded by chiefs of staff, local dignitaries, detectives, and the curious, sympathetic faces of the public. As he studied the strangely rough-hewn countenance a sense of the great worth and dignity of the man came over him.

"A real man, that," he thought; "a wonderful temperament." His every gesture came upon him with great force. He watched him enter his carriage, thinking "So that is the railsplitter, the country lawyer. Well, fate has picked a great man for this crisis."

For days the face of Lincoln haunted him, and very often during the war his mind reverted to that singular figure. It seemed to him unquestionable that fortuitously he had been permitted to look upon one of the world's really great men. War and statesmanship were not for him; but he knew how important those things were—at times.

CHAPTER XI

It was while the war was on, and after it was perfectly plain that it was not to be of a few days' duration, that Cowperwood's first great financial opportunity came to him. There was a strong demand for money at the time on the part of the nation, the State, and the city. In July, 1861, Congress had authorized a loan of fifty million dollars, to be secured by twenty-year bonds with interest not to exceed seven per cent., and the State authorized a loan of three millions on much the same security, the first being handled by financiers of Boston, New York, and Philadelphia, the second by Philadelphia financiers alone. Cowperwood had no hand in this. He was not big enough. He read in the papers of gatherings of men whom he knew personally or by reputation, "to consider the best way to aid the nation or the State"; but he was not included. And yet his soul yearned to be of them. He noticed how often a rich man's word sufficed—no money, no certificates, no collateral, no anything—just his word. If Drexel & Co., or Jay Cooke & Co., or Gould & Fiske were rumored to be behind anything, how secure it was! Jay Cooke, a young man in Philadelphia, had made a great strike taking this State loan in company with Drexel & Co., and selling it at par. The general opinion was that it ought to be and could only be sold at ninety. Cooke did not believe this. He believed that State pride and State patriotism would warrant offering the loan to small banks and private citizens, and that they would subscribe it fully and more. Events justified Cooke magnificently, and his public reputation was assured. Cowperwood wished he could make some such strike; but he was too practical to worry over anything save the facts and conditions that were before him.

His chance came about six months later, when it was found that the State would have to have much more money. Its quota of troops would have to be equipped and paid. There were measures of defense to be taken, the treasury to be replenished. A call for a loan of twenty-three million dollars was finally authorized by the legislature and issued. There was great talk in the street as to who was to handle it—Drexel & Co. and Jay Cooke & Co., of course.

Cowperwood pondered over this. If he could handle a fraction of this great loan now—he could not possibly handle the whole of it, for he had not the necessary connections—he could add considerably to his reputation as a broker while making a tidy sum. How much could he handle? That was the question. Who would take portions of it? His father's bank? Probably. Waterman & Co.? A little. Judge Kitchen? A small fraction. The Mills-David Company? Yes. He thought of different individuals and concerns who, for one reason and another—personal friendship, good-nature, gratitude for past favors, and so on—would take a percentage of the seven-percent. bonds through him. He totaled up his possibilities, and discovered that in all likelihood, with a little preliminary missionary work, he could dispose of one million dollars if personal influence, through local political figures, could bring this much of the loan his way.

One man in particular had grown strong in his estimation as having some subtle political connection not visible on the surface, and this was Edward Malia Butler. Butler was a contractor, undertaking the construction of sewers, water-mains, foundations for buildings, street-paving, and the like. In the early days, long before Cowperwood had known him, he had been a garbage-contractor on his own account. The city at that time had no extended street-cleaning service, particularly in its outlying sections and some of the older, poorer regions. Edward Butler, then a poor young Irishman, had begun by collecting and hauling away the garbage free of charge, and feeding it to his pigs and cattle. Later he discovered that some people were willing to pay a small charge for this service. Then a local political character, a councilman friend of his—they were both Catholics—saw a new point in the whole thing. Butler could be made official garbage-collector. The council could vote an annual appropriation for this service. Butler could employ more wagons than he did now—dozens of them, scores. Not only that, but no other garbage-collector would be allowed. There were others, but the official contract awarded him would also, officially, be the end of the life of any and every disturbing rival. A certain amount of the profitable proceeds would have to be set aside to assuage the feelings of those who were not contractors. Funds would have to be loaned at election time to certain individuals and organizations—but no matter. The amount would be small. So Butler and Patrick Gavin Comiskey, the councilman (the latter silently) entered into business relations. Butler gave up driving a wagon himself. He hired a young man, a smart Irish boy of his neighborhood, Jimmy Sheehan, to be his assistant, superintendent, stableman, bookkeeper, and what not. Since he soon began to make between four and five thousand a year, where before he made two thousand, he moved into a brick house in an outlying section of the south side, and sent his children to school. Mrs. Butler gave up making soap and feeding pigs. And since then times had been exceedingly good with Edward Butler.

He could neither read nor write at first; but now he knew how, of course. He had learned from association with Mr. Comiskey that there were other forms of contracting—sewers, water-mains, gas-mains, street-paving, and the like. Who better than Edward Butler to do it? He knew the councilmen, many of them. Het met them in the back rooms of saloons, on Sundays and Saturdays at political picnics, at election councils and conferences, for as a beneficiary of the city's largess he was expected to contribute not only money, but advice. Curiously he had developed a strange political wisdom. He knew a successful man or a coming man when he saw one. So many of his bookkeepers, superintendents, time-keepers had graduated into councilmen and state legislators. His nominees—suggested to political conferences—were so often known to make good. First he came to have influence in his councilman's ward, then in his legislative district, then in the city councils of his party—Whig, of course—and then he was supposed to have an organization.

Mysterious forces worked for him in council. He was awarded significant contracts, and he always bid. The garbage business was now a thing of the past. His eldest boy, Owen, was a member of the State legislature and a partner in his business affairs. His second son, Callum, was a clerk in the city water department and an assistant to his father also. Aileen, his eldest daughter, fifteen years of age, was still in St. Agatha's, a convent school in Germantown. Norah, his second daughter and youngest child, thirteen years old, was in attendance at a local private school conducted by a Catholic sisterhood. The Butler family had moved away from South Philadelphia into Girard Avenue, near the twelve hundreds, where a new and rather interesting social life was beginning. They were not of it, but Edward Butler, contractor, now fifty-five years of age, worth, say, five hundred thousand dollars, had many political and financial friends. No longer a "rough neck," but a solid, reddish-faced man, slightly tanned, with broad shoulders and a solid chest, gray eyes, gray hair, a typically Irish face made wise and calm and undecipherable by much experience. His big hands and feet indicated a day when he had not worn the best English cloth suits and tanned leather, but his presence was not in any way offensive—rather the other way about. Though still possessed of a brogue, he was soft-spoken, winning, and persuasive.

He had been one of the first to become interested in the development of the street-car system and had come to the conclusion, as had Cowperwood and many others, that it was going to be a great thing. The money returns on the stocks or shares he had been induced to buy had been ample evidence of that, He had dealt through one broker and another, having failed to get in on the original corporate organizations. He wanted to pick up such stock as he could in one organization and another, for he believed they all had a future, and most of all he wanted to get control of a line or two. In connection with this idea he was looking for some reliable young man, honest and capable, who would work under his direction and do what he said. Then he learned of Cowperwood, and one day sent for him and asked him to call at his house.

Cowperwood responded quickly, for he knew of Butler, his rise, his connections, his force. He called at the house as directed, one cold, crisp February morning. He remembered the appearance of the street afterward—broad, brick-paved sidewalks, macadamized roadway, powdered over with a light snow and set with young, leafless, scrubby trees and lamp-posts. Butler's house was not new—he had bought and repaired it—but it was not an unsatisfactory specimen of the architecture of the time. It was fifty feet wide, four stories tall, of graystone and with four wide, white stone steps leading up to the door. The window arches, framed in white, had U-shaped keystones. There were curtains of lace and a glimpse of red plush through the windows, which gleamed warm against the cold and snow outside. A trim Irish maid came to the door and he gave her his card and was invited into the house.

"Is Mr. Butler home?"

37

"I'm not sure, sir. I'll find out. He may have gone out."

In a little while he was asked to come upstairs, where he found Butler in a somewhat commercial-looking room. It had a desk, an office chair, some leather furnishings, and a bookcase, but no completeness or symmetry as either an office or a living room. There were several pictures on the wall—an impossible oil painting, for one thing, dark and gloomy; a canal and barge scene in pink and nile green for another; some daguerreotypes of relatives and friends which were not half bad. Cowperwood noticed one of two girls, one with reddish-gold hair, another with what appeared to be silky brown. The beautiful silver effect of the daguerreotype had been tinted. They were pretty girls, healthy, smiling, Celtic, their heads close together, their eyes looking straight out at you. He admired them casually, and fancied they must be Butler's daughters.

"Mr. Cowperwood?" inquired Butler, uttering the name fully with a peculiar accent on the vowels. (He was a slow-moving man, solemn and deliberate.) Cowperwood noticed that his body was hale and strong like seasoned hickory, tanned by wind and rain. The flesh of his cheeks was pulled taut and there was nothing soft or flabby about him.

"I'm that man."

"I have a little matter of stocks to talk over with you" ("matter" almost sounded like "mather"), "and I thought you'd better come here rather than that I should come down to your office. We can be more private-like, and, besides, I'm not as young as I used to be."

He allowed a semi-twinkle to rest in his eye as he looked his visitor over.

Cowperwood smiled.

"Well, I hope I can be of service to you," he said, genially.

"I happen to be interested just at present in pickin' up certain street-railway stocks on 'change. I'll tell you about them later. Won't you have somethin' to drink? It's a cold morning."

"No, thanks; I never drink."

"Never? That's a hard word when it comes to whisky. Well, no matter. It's a good rule. My boys don't touch anything, and I'm glad of it. As I say, I'm interested in pickin' up a few stocks on 'change; but, to tell you the truth, I'm more interested in findin' some clever young felly like yourself through whom I can work. One thing leads to another, you know, in this world." And he looked at his visitor non-committally, and yet with a genial show of interest.

"Quite so," replied Cowperwood, with a friendly gleam in return.

"Well," Butler meditated, half to himself, half to Cowperwood, "there are a number of things that a bright young man could do for me in the street if he were so minded. I have two bright boys of my own, but I don't want them to become stock-gamblers, and I don't know that they would or could if I wanted them to. But this isn't a matter of stock-gambling. I'm pretty busy as it is, and, as I said awhile ago, I'm getting along. I'm not as light on my toes as I once was. But if I had the right sort of a young man—I've been looking into your record, by the way, never fear—he might handle a number of little things—investments and loans—which might bring us each a little somethin'. Sometimes the young men around town ask advice of me in one way and another—they have a little somethin' to invest, and so—"

He paused and looked tantalizingly out of the window, knowing full well Cowperwood was greatly interested, and that this talk of political influence and connections could only whet his appetite. Butler wanted him to see clearly that fidelity was the point in this case—fidelity, tact, subtlety, and concealment.

"Well, if you have been looking into my record," observed Cowperwood, with his own elusive smile, leaving the thought suspended.

Butler felt the force of the temperament and the argument. He liked the young man's poise and balance. A number of people had spoken of Cowperwood to him. (It was now Cowperwood & Co. The company was fiction purely.) He asked him something about the

38

street; how the market was running; what he knew about street-railways. Finally he outlined his plan of buying all he could of the stock of two given lines—the Ninth and Tenth and the Fifteenth and Sixteenth—without attracting any attention, if possible. It was to be done slowly, part on 'change, part from individual holders. He did not tell him that there was a certain amount of legislative pressure he hoped to bring to bear to get him franchises for extensions in the regions beyond where the lines now ended, in order that when the time came for them to extend their facilities they would have to see him or his sons, who might be large minority stockholders in these very concerns. It was a far-sighted plan, and meant that the lines would eventually drop into his or his sons' basket.

"I'll be delighted to work with you, Mr. Butler, in any way that you may suggest," observed Cowperwood. "I can't say that I have so much of a business as yet—merely prospects. But my connections are good. I am now a member of the New York and Philadelphia exchanges. Those who have dealt with me seem to like the results I get."

"I know a little something about your work already," reiterated Butler, wisely.

"Very well, then; whenever you have a commission you can call at my office, or write, or I will call here. I will give you my secret operating code, so that anything you say will be strictly confidential."

"Well, we'll not say anything more now. In a few days I'll have somethin' for you. When I do, you can draw on my bank for what you need, up to a certain amount." He got up and looked out into the street, and Cowperwood also arose.

"It's a fine day now, isn't it?"

"It surely is."

"Well, we'll get to know each other better, I'm sure."

He held out his hand.

"I hope so."

Cowperwood went out, Butler accompanying him to the door. As he did so a young girl bounded in from the street, red-cheeked, blue-eyed, wearing a scarlet cape with the peaked hood thrown over her red-gold hair.

"Oh, daddy, I almost knocked you down."

She gave her father, and incidentally Cowperwood, a gleaming, radiant, inclusive smile. Her teeth were bright and small, and her lips bud-red.

"You're home early. I thought you were going to stay all day?"

"I was, but I changed my mind."

She passed on in, swinging her arms.

"Yes, well—" Butler continued, when she had gone. "Then we'll leave it for a day or two. Good day."

"Good day."

Cowperwood, warm with this enhancing of his financial prospects, went down the steps; but incidentally he spared a passing thought for the gay spirit of youth that had manifested itself in this red-cheeked maiden. What a bright, healthy, bounding girl! Her voice had the subtle, vigorous ring of fifteen or sixteen. She was all vitality. What a fine catch for some young fellow some day, and her father would make him rich, no doubt, or help to.

CHAPTER XII

It was to Edward Malia Butler that Cowperwood turned now, some nineteen months later when he was thinking of the influence that might bring him an award of a portion of the State issue of bonds. Butler could probably be interested to take some of them himself, or could help him place some. He had come to like Cowperwood very much and was now being carried on the latter's books as a prospective purchaser of large blocks of stocks. And Cowperwood liked this great solid Irishman. He liked his history. He had met Mrs. Butler, a rather fat and phlegmatic Irish woman with a world of hard sense who cared nothing at all for show and who still liked to go into the kitchen and superintend the cooking. He had met Owen and Callum Butler, the boys, and Aileen and Norah, the girls. Aileen was the one who had bounded up the steps the first day he had called at the Butler house several seasons before.

There was a cozy grate-fire burning in Butler's improvised private office when Cowperwood called. Spring was coming on, but the evenings were cool. The older man invited Cowperwood to make himself comfortable in one of the large leather chairs before the fire and then proceeded to listen to his recital of what he hoped to accomplish.

"Well, now, that isn't so easy," he commented at the end. "You ought to know more about that than I do. I'm not a financier, as you well know." And he grinned apologetically.

"It's a matter of influence," went on Cowperwood. "And favoritism. That I know. Drexel & Company and Cooke & Company have connections at Harrisburg. They have men of their own looking after their interests. The attorney-general and the State treasurer are hand in glove with them. Even if I put in a bid, and can demonstrate that I can handle the loan, it won't help me to get it. Other people have done that. I have to have friends—influence. You know how it is."

"Them things," Butler said, "is easy enough if you know the right parties to approach. Now there's Jimmy Oliver—he ought to know something about that." Jimmy Oliver was the whilom district attorney serving at this time, and incidentally free adviser to Mr. Butler in many ways. He was also, accidentally, a warm personal friend of the State treasurer.

"How much of the loan do you want?"

"Five million."

"Five million!" Butler sat up. "Man, what are you talking about? That's a good deal of money. Where are you going to sell all that?"

"I want to bid for five million," assuaged Cowperwood, softly. "I only want one million but I want the prestige of putting in a bona fide bid for five million. It will do me good on the street."

Butler sank back somewhat relieved.

"Five million! Prestige! You want one million. Well, now, that's different. That's not such a bad idea. We ought to be able to get that."

He rubbed his chin some more and stared into the fire.

And Cowperwood felt confident when he left the house that evening that Butler would not fail him but would set the wheels working. Therefore, he was not surprised, and knew exactly what it meant, when a few days later he was introduced to City Treasurer Julian Bode, who promised to introduce him to State Treasurer Van Nostrand and to see that his claims to consideration were put before the people. "Of course, you know," he said to Cowperwood, in the presence of Butler, for it was at the latter's home that the conference took place, "this banking crowd is very powerful. You know who they are. They don't want any interference in this bond issue business. I was talking to Terrence Relihan, who represents them up there"—meaning Harrisburg, the State capital—"and he says they won't stand for it at all. You may have trouble right here in Philadelphia after you get it—they're pretty powerful, you know. Are you sure just where you can place it?"

"Yes, I'm sure," replied Cowperwood.

"Well, the best thing in my judgment is not to say anything at all. Just put in your bid. Van Nostrand, with the governor's approval, will make the award. We can fix the governor, I think. After you get it they may talk to you personally, but that's your business."

Cowperwood smiled his inscrutable smile. There were so many ins and outs to this financial life. It was an endless network of underground holes, along which all sorts of influences were moving. A little wit, a little nimbleness, a little luck-time and opportunity—these sometimes availed. Here he was, through his ambition to get on, and nothing else, coming into contact with the State treasurer and the governor. They were going to consider his case personally, because he demanded that it be considered—nothing more. Others more influential than himself had quite as much right to a share, but they didn't take it. Nerve, ideas, aggressiveness, how these counted when one had luck!

He went away thinking how surprised Drexel & Co. and Cooke & Co. would be to see him appearing in the field as a competitor. In his home, in a little room on the second floor next his bedroom, which he had fixed up as an office with a desk, a safe, and a leather chair, he consulted his resources. There were so many things to think of. He went over again the list of people whom he had seen and whom he could count on to subscribe, and in so far as that was concerned—the award of one million dollars—he was safe. He figured to make two per cent. on the total transaction, or twenty thousand dollars. If he did he was going to buy a house out on Girard Avenue beyond the Butlers', or, better yet, buy a piece of ground and erect one; mortgaging house and property so to do. His father was prospering nicely. He might want to build a house next to him, and they could live side by side. His own business, aside from this deal, would yield him ten thousand dollars this year. His street-car investments, aggregating fifty thousand, were paying six per cent. His wife's property, represented by this house, some government bonds, and some real estate in West Philadelphia amounted to forty thousand more. Between them they were rich; but he expected to be much richer. All he needed now was to keep cool. If he succeeded in this bond-issue matter, he could do it again and on a larger scale. There would be more issues. He turned out the light after a while and went into his wife's boudoir, where she was sleeping. The nurse and the children were in a room beyond.

"Well, Lillian," he observed, when she awoke and turned over toward him, "I think I have that bond matter that I was telling you about arranged at last. I think I'll get a million of it, anyhow. That'll mean twenty thousand. If I do we'll build out on Girard Avenue. That's going to be the street. The college is making that neighborhood."

"That'll be fine, won't it, Frank!" she observed, and rubbed his arm as he sat on the side of the bed.

Her remark was vaguely speculative.

"We'll have to show the Butlers some attention from now on. He's been very nice to me and he's going to be useful—I can see that. He asked me to bring you over some time. We must go. Be nice to his wife. He can do a lot for me if he wants to. He has two daughters, too. We'll have to have them over here."

"I'll have them to dinner sometime," she agreed cheerfully and helpfully, "and I'll stop and take Mrs. Butler driving if she'll go, or she can take me."

She had already learned that the Butlers were rather showy—the younger generation—that they were sensitive as to their lineage, and that money in their estimation was supposed to make up for any deficiency in any other respect. "Butler himself is a very presentable man," Cowperwood had once remarked to her, "but Mrs. Butler—well, she's all right, but she's a little commonplace. She's a fine woman, though, I think, good-natured and good-hearted." He cautioned her not to overlook Aileen and Norah, because the Butlers, mother and father, were very proud of them.

Mrs. Cowperwood at this time was thirty-two years old; Cowperwood twenty-seven. The birth and care of two children had made some difference in her looks. She was no longer as softly pleasing, more angular. Her face was hollow-cheeked, like so many of Rossetti's and Burne-Jones's women. Her health was really not as good as it had been—the care of two children and a late undiagnosed tendency toward gastritis having reduced her. In short she was a little run down nervously and suffered from fits of depression. Cowperwood had noticed this. He tried to be gentle and considerate, but he was too much of a utilitarian and practical-minded observer not to realize that he was likely to have a sickly wife on his hands later. Sympathy and affection were great things, but desire and charm must endure or one

41

was compelled to be sadly conscious of their loss. So often now he saw young girls who were quite in his mood, and who were exceedingly robust and joyous. It was fine, advisable, practical, to adhere to the virtues as laid down in the current social lexicon, but if you had a sickly wife—And anyhow, was a man entitled to only one wife? Must he never look at another woman? Supposing he found some one? He pondered those things between hours of labor, and concluded that it did not make so much difference. If a man could, and not be exposed, it was all right. He had to be careful, though. Tonight, as he sat on the side of his wife's bed, he was thinking somewhat of this, for he had seen Aileen Butler again, playing and singing at her piano as he passed the parlor door. She was like a bright bird radiating health and enthusiasm—a reminder of youth in general.

"It's a strange world," he thought; but his thoughts were his own, and he didn't propose to tell any one about them.

The bond issue, when it came, was a curious compromise; for, although it netted him his twenty thousand dollars and more and served to introduce him to the financial notice of Philadelphia and the State of Pennsylvania, it did not permit him to manipulate the subscriptions as he had planned. The State treasurer was seen by him at the office of a local lawyer of great repute, where he worked when in the city. He was gracious to Cowperwood, because he had to be. He explained to him just how things were regulated at Harrisburg. The big financiers were looked to for campaign funds. They were represented by henchmen in the State assembly and senate. The governor and the treasurer were foot-free; but there were other influences—prestige, friendship, social power, political ambitions, etc. The big men might constitute a close corporation, which in itself was unfair; but, after all, they were the legitimate sponsors for big money loans of this kind. The State had to keep on good terms with them, especially in times like these. Seeing that Mr. Cowperwood was so well able to dispose of the million he expected to get, it would be perfectly all right to award it to him; but Van Nostrand had a counter-proposition to make. Would Cowperwood, if the financial crowd now handling the matter so desired, turn over his award to them for a consideration—a sum equal to what he expected to make—in the event the award was made to him? Certain financiers desired this. It was dangerous to oppose them. They were perfectly willing he should put in a bid for five million and get the prestige of that; to have him awarded one million and get the prestige of that was well enough also, but they desired to handle the twenty-three million dollars in an unbroken lot. It looked better. He need not be advertised as having withdrawn. They would be content to have him achieve the glory of having done what he started out to do. Just the same the example was bad. Others might wish to imitate him. If it were known in the street privately that he had been coerced, for a consideration, into giving up, others would be deterred from imitating him in the future. Besides, if he refused, they could cause him trouble. His loans might be called. Various banks might not be so friendly in the future. His constituents might be warned against him in one way or another.

Cowperwood saw the point. He acquiesced. It was something to have brought so many high and mighties to their knees. So they knew of him! They were quite well aware of him! Well and good. He would take the award and twenty thousand or thereabouts and withdraw. The State treasurer was delighted. It solved a ticklish proposition for him.

"I'm glad to have seen you," he said. "I'm glad we've met. I'll drop in and talk with you some time when I'm down this way. We'll have lunch together."

The State treasurer, for some odd reason, felt that Mr. Cowperwood was a man who could make him some money. His eye was so keen; his expression was so alert, and yet so subtle. He told the governor and some other of his associates about him.

So the award was finally made; Cowperwood, after some private negotiations in which he met the officers of Drexel & Co., was paid his twenty thousand dollars and turned his share of the award over to them. New faces showed up in his office now from time to time— among them that of Van Nostrand and one Terrence Relihan, a representative of some

42

other political forces at Harrisburg. He was introduced to the governor one day at lunch. His name was mentioned in the papers, and his prestige grew rapidly.

Immediately he began working on plans with young Ellsworth for his new house. He was going to build something exceptional this time, he told Lillian. They were going to have to do some entertaining—entertaining on a larger scale than ever. North Front Street was becoming too tame. He put the house up for sale, consulted with his father and found that he also was willing to move. The son's prosperity had redounded to the credit of the father. The directors of the bank were becoming much more friendly to the old man. Next year President Kugel was going to retire. Because of his son's noted coup, as well as his long service, he was going to be made president. Frank was a large borrower from his father's bank. By the same token he was a large depositor. His connection with Edward Butler was significant. He sent his father's bank certain accounts which it otherwise could not have secured. The city treasurer became interested in it, and the State treasurer. Cowperwood, Sr., stood to earn twenty thousand a year as president, and he owed much of it to his son. The two families were now on the best of terms. Anna, now twenty-one, and Edward and Joseph frequently spent the night at Frank's house. Lillian called almost daily at his mother's. There was much interchange of family gossip, and it was thought well to build side by side. So Cowperwood, Sr., bought fifty feet of ground next to his son's thirty-five, and together they commenced the erection of two charming, commodious homes, which were to be connected by a covered passageway, or pergola, which could be inclosed with glass in winter.

The most popular local stone, a green granite was chosen; but Mr. Ellsworth promised to present it in such a way that it would be especially pleasing. Cowperwood, Sr., decided that he could afford to spent seventy-five thousand dollars—he was now worth two hundred and fifty thousand; and Frank decided that he could risk fifty, seeing that he could raise money on a mortgage. He planned at the same time to remove his office farther south on Third Street and occupy a building of his own. He knew where an option was to be had on a twenty-five-foot building, which, though old, could be given a new brownstone front and made very significant. He saw in his mind's eye a handsome building, fitted with an immense plate-glass window; inside his hardwood fixtures visible; and over the door, or to one side of it, set in bronze letters, Cowperwood & Co. Vaguely but surely he began to see looming before him, like a fleecy tinted cloud on the horizon, his future fortune. He was to be rich, very, very rich.

CHAPTER XIII

During all the time that Cowperwood had been building himself up thus steadily the great war of the rebellion had been fought almost to its close. It was now October, 1864. The capture of Mobile and the Battle of the Wilderness were fresh memories. Grant was now before Petersburg, and the great general of the South, Lee, was making that last brilliant and hopeless display of his ability as a strategist and a soldier. There had been times—as, for instance, during the long, dreary period in which the country was waiting for Vicksburg to fall, for the Army of the Potomac to prove victorious, when Pennsylvania was invaded by Lee—when stocks fell and commercial conditions were very bad generally. In times like these Cowperwood's own manipulative ability was taxed to the utmost, and he had to watch every hour to see that his fortune was not destroyed by some unexpected and destructive piece of news.

His personal attitude toward the war, however, and aside from his patriotic feeling that the Union ought to be maintained, was that it was destructive and wasteful. He was by no means so wanting in patriotic emotion and sentiment but that he could feel that the Union, as it had now come to be, spreading its great length from the Atlantic to the Pacific and from the snows of Canada to the Gulf, was worth while. Since his birth in 1837 he had seen the nation reach that physical growth—barring Alaska—which it now possesses. Not so much earlier than his youth Florida had been added to the Union by purchase from Spain; Mexico, after the unjust war of 1848, had ceded Texas and the territory to the West. The boundary disputes between England and the United States in the far Northwest had been finally adjusted. To a man with great social and financial imagination, these facts could not help but be significant; and if they did nothing more, they gave him a sense of the boundless commercial possibilities which existed potentially in so vast a realm. His was not the order of speculative financial enthusiasm which, in the type known as the "promoter," sees endless possibilities for gain in every unexplored rivulet and prairie reach; but the very vastness of the country suggested possibilities which he hoped might remain undisturbed. A territory covering the length of a whole zone and between two seas, seemed to him to possess potentialities which it could not retain if the States of the South were lost.

At the same time, the freedom of the negro was not a significant point with him. He had observed that race from his boyhood with considerable interest, and had been struck with virtues and defects which seemed inherent and which plainly, to him, conditioned their experiences.

He was not at all sure, for instance, that the negroes could be made into anything much more significant than they were. At any rate, it was a long uphill struggle for them, of which many future generations would not witness the conclusion. He had no particular quarrel with the theory that they should be free; he saw no particular reason why the South should not protest vigorously against the destruction of their property and their system. It was too bad that the negroes as slaves should be abused in some instances. He felt sure that that ought to be adjusted in some way; but beyond that he could not see that there was any great ethical basis for the contentions of their sponsors. The vast majority of men and women, as he could see, were not essentially above slavery, even when they had all the guarantees of a constitution formulated to prevent it. There was mental slavery, the slavery of the weak mind and the weak body. He followed the contentions of such men as Sumner, Garrison, Phillips, and Beecher, with considerable interest; but at no time could he see that the problem was a vital one for him. He did not care to be a soldier or an officer of soldiers; he had no gift for polemics; his mind was not of the disputatious order—not even in the realm of finance. He was concerned only to see what was of vast advantage to him, and to devote all his attention to that. This fratricidal war in the nation could not help him. It really delayed, he thought, the true commercial and financial adjustment of the country, and he hoped that it would soon end. He was not of those who complained bitterly of the excessive war taxes, though he knew them to be trying to many. Some of the stories of death and disaster moved him greatly; but, alas, they were among the unaccountable fortunes of life, and could not be remedied by him. So he had gone his way day by day, watching the coming in and the departing of troops, seeing the bands of dirty, disheveled, gaunt, sickly men returning from the fields and hospitals; and all he could do was to feel sorry. This war was not for him. He had taken no part in it, and he felt sure that he could only rejoice in its conclusion—not as a patriot, but as a financier. It was wasteful, pathetic, unfortunate.

The months proceeded apace. A local election intervened and there was a new city treasurer, a new assessor of taxes, and a new mayor; but Edward Malia Butler continued to have apparently the same influence as before. The Butlers and the Cowperwoods had become quite friendly. Mrs. Butler rather liked Lillian, though they were of different religious beliefs; and they went driving or shopping together, the younger woman a little critical and ashamed of the elder because of her poor grammar, her Irish accent, her plebeian tastes—as though the Wiggins had not been as plebeian as any. On the other hand the old lady, as she was compelled to admit, was good-natured and good-hearted. She loved to give, since she had plenty, and sent presents here and there to Lillian, the children, and others. "Now youse must come over and take dinner with us"—the Butlers had arrived at the evening-dinner period—or "Youse must come drive with me to-morrow."

"Aileen, God bless her, is such a foine girl," or "Norah, the darlin', is sick the day."

But Aileen, her airs, her aggressive disposition, her love of attention, her vanity, irritated and at times disgusted Mrs. Cowperwood. She was eighteen now, with a figure which was subtly provocative. Her manner was boyish, hoydenish at times, and although convent-trained, she was inclined to balk at restraint in any form. But there was a softness lurking in her blue eyes that was most sympathetic and human.

St. Timothy's and the convent school in Germantown had been the choice of her parents for her education—what they called a good Catholic education. She had learned a great deal about the theory and forms of the Catholic ritual, but she could not understand them. The church, with its tall, dimly radiant windows, its high, white altar, its figure of St. Joseph on one side and the Virgin Mary on the other, clothed in golden-starred robes of blue, wearing haloes and carrying scepters, had impressed her greatly. The church as a whole—any Catholic church—was beautiful to look at—soothing. The altar, during high mass, lit with a half-hundred or more candles, and dignified and made impressive by the rich, lacy vestments of the priests and the acolytes, the impressive needlework and gorgeous colorings of the amice, chasuble, cope, stole, and maniple, took her fancy and held her eye. Let us say there was always lurking in her a sense of grandeur coupled with a love of color and a love of love. From the first she was somewhat sex-conscious. She had no desire for accuracy, no desire for precise information. Innate sensuousness rarely has. It basks in sunshine, bathes in color, dwells in a sense of the impressive and the gorgeous, and rests there. Accuracy is not necessary except in the case of aggressive, acquisitive natures, when it manifests itself in a desire to seize. True controlling sensuousness cannot be manifested in the most active dispositions, nor again in the most accurate.

There is need of defining these statements in so far as they apply to Aileen. It would scarcely be fair to describe her nature as being definitely sensual at this time. It was too rudimentary. Any harvest is of long growth. The confessional, dim on Friday and Saturday evenings, when the church was lighted by but a few lamps, and the priest's warnings, penances, and ecclesiastical forgiveness whispered through the narrow lattice, moved her as something subtly pleasing. She was not afraid of her sins. Hell, so definitely set forth, did not frighten her. Really, it had not laid hold on her conscience. The old women and old men hobbling into church, bowed in prayer, murmuring over their beads, were objects of curious interest like the wood-carvings in the peculiar array of wood-reliefs emphasizing the Stations of the Cross. She herself had liked to confess, particularly when she was fourteen and fifteen, and to listen to the priest's voice as he admonished her with, "Now, my dear child." A particularly old priest, a French father, who came to hear their confessions at school, interested her as being kind and sweet. His forgiveness and blessing seemed sincere—better than her prayers, which she went through perfunctorily. And then there was a young priest at St. Timothy's, Father David, hale and rosy, with a curl of black hair over his forehead, and an almost jaunty way of wearing his priestly hat, who came down the aisle Sundays sprinkling holy water with a definite, distinguished sweep of the hand, who took her fancy. He heard confessions and now and then she liked to whisper her strange thoughts to him while she actually speculated on what he might privately be thinking. She could not, if she tried, associate him with any divine authority. He was too young, too human. There was something a little malicious, teasing, in the way she delighted to tell him about herself, and then walk demurely, repentantly out. At St. Agatha's she had been rather a difficult person to deal with. She was, as the good sisters of the school had readily perceived, too full of life, too active, to be easily controlled. "That Miss Butler," once observed Sister Constantia, the Mother Superior, to Sister Sempronia, Aileen's immediate mentor, "is a very spirited girl, you may have a great deal of trouble with her unless you use a good deal of tact. You may have to coax her with little gifts. You will get on better." So Sister Sempronia had sought to find what Aileen was most interested in, and bribe her therewith. Being intensely conscious of her father's competence, and vain of her personal superiority, it was not so easy to do. She had wanted to go home occasionally, though; she had wanted to be allowed to wear the sister's rosary of large beads with its pendent cross of ebony and its silver Christ, and this was held up as a great privilege. For keeping quiet in class, walking softly, and speaking softly—as much as it was in her to do—for not stealing into other girl's rooms after lights were out, and for abandoning crushes on this and that sympathetic sister, these awards and others, such as walking out in the grounds on Saturday afternoons, being allowed to have all the flowers she wanted, some extra dresses, jewels, etc., were offered. She liked music and the idea of painting, though she had no talent in that direction; and books, novels, interested her, but she could not get them. The rest— grammar, spelling, sewing, church and general history—she loathed. Deportment—well, there was something in that. She had liked the rather exaggerated curtsies they taught her, and she had often reflected on how she would use them when she reached home.

When she came out into life the little social distinctions which have been indicated began to impress themselves on her, and she wished sincerely that her father would build a better home—a mansion—such as those she saw elsewhere, and launch her properly in society. Failing in that, she could think of nothing save clothes, jewels, riding-horses, carriages, and the appropriate changes of costume which were allowed her for these. Her family could not entertain in any distinguished way where they were, and so already, at eighteen, she was beginning to feel the sting of a blighted ambition. She was eager for life. How was she to get it?

Her room was a study in the foibles of an eager and ambitious mind. It was full of clothes, beautiful things for all occasions—jewelry—which she had small opportunity to wear— shoes, stockings, lingerie, laces. In a crude way she had made a study of perfumes and cosmetics, though she needed the latter not at all, and these were present in abundance. She was not very orderly, and she loved lavishness of display; and her curtains, hangings, table ornaments, and pictures inclined to gorgeousness, which did not go well with the rest of the house.

Aileen always reminded Cowperwood of a high-stepping horse without a check-rein. He met her at various times, shopping with her mother, out driving with her father, and he was always interested and amused at the affected, bored tone she assumed before him—the "Oh, dear! Oh, dear! Life is so tiresome, don't you know," when, as a matter of fact, every moment of it was of thrilling interest to her. Cowperwood took her mental measurement exactly. A girl with a high sense of life in her, romantic, full of the thought of love and its possibilities. As he looked at her he had the sense of seeing the best that nature can do when she attempts to produce physical perfection. The thought came to him that some lucky young dog would marry her pretty soon and carry her away; but whoever secured her would have to hold her by affection and subtle flattery and attention if he held her at all.

"The little snip"—she was not at all—"she thinks the sun rises and sets in her father's pocket," Lillian observed one day to her husband. "To hear her talk, you'd think they were descended from Irish kings. Her pretended interest in art and music amuses me."

"Oh, don't be too hard on her," coaxed Cowperwood diplomatically. He already liked Aileen very much. "She plays very well, and she has a good voice."

"Yes, I know; but she has no real refinement. How could she have? Look at her father and mother."

"I don't see anything so very much the matter with her," insisted Cowperwood. "She's bright and good-looking. Of course, she's only a girl, and a little vain, but she'll come out of that. She isn't without sense and force, at that."

Aileen, as he knew, was most friendly to him. She liked him. She made a point of playing the piano and singing for him in his home, and she sang only when he was there. There was something about his steady, even gait, his stocky body and handsome head, which attracted her. In spite of her vanity and egotism, she felt a little overawed before him at times—keyed up. She seemed to grow gayer and more brilliant in his presence.

The most futile thing in this world is any attempt, perhaps, at exact definition of character. All individuals are a bundle of contradictions—none more so than the most capable.

In the case of Aileen Butler it would be quite impossible to give an exact definition. Intelligence, of a raw, crude order she had certainly—also a native force, tamed somewhat by the doctrines and conventions of current society, still showed clear at times in an elemental and not entirely unattractive way. At this time she was only eighteen years of age—decidedly attractive from the point of view of a man of Frank Cowperwood's temperament. She supplied something he had not previously known or consciously craved. Vitality and vivacity. No other woman or girl whom he had ever known had possessed so much innate force as she. Her red-gold hair—not so red as decidedly golden with a suggestion of red in it—looped itself in heavy folds about her forehead and sagged at the base of her neck. She had a beautiful nose, not sensitive, but straight-cut with small nostril openings, and eyes that were big and yet noticeably sensuous. They were, to him, a pleasing shade of blue-gray-blue, and her toilet, due to her temperament, of course, suggested almost undue luxury, the bangles, anklets, ear-rings, and breast-plates of the odalisque, and yet, of course, they were not there. She confessed to him years afterward that she would have loved to have stained her nails and painted the palms of her hands with madder-red. Healthy and vigorous, she was chronically interested in men—what they would think of her—and how she compared with other women.

The fact that she could ride in a carriage, live in a fine home on Girard Avenue, visit such homes as those of the Cowperwoods and others, was of great weight; and yet, even at this age, she realized that life was more than these things. Many did not have them and lived.

But these facts of wealth and advantage gripped her; and when she sat at the piano and played or rode in her carriage or walked or stood before her mirror, she was conscious of her figure, her charms, what they meant to men, how women envied her. Sometimes she looked at poor, hollow-chested or homely-faced girls and felt sorry for them; at other times she flared into inexplicable opposition to some handsome girl or woman who dared to brazen her socially or physically. There were such girls of the better families who, in Chestnut Street, in the expensive shops, or on the drive, on horseback or in carriages, tossed their heads and indicated as well as human motions can that they were better-bred and knew it. When this happened each stared defiantly at the other. She wanted ever so much to get up in the world, and yet namby-pamby men of better social station than herself did not attract her at all. She wanted a man. Now and then there was one "something like," but not entirely, who appealed to her, but most of them were politicians or legislators, acquaintances of her father, and socially nothing at all—and so they wearied and disappointed her. Her father did not know the truly elite. But Mr. Cowperwood—he seemed so refined, so forceful, and so reserved. She often looked at Mrs. Cowperwood and thought how fortunate she was.

CHAPTER XIV

The development of Cowperwood as Cowperwood & Co. following his arresting bond venture, finally brought him into relationship with one man who was to play an important part in his life, morally, financially, and in other ways. This was George W. Stener, the new

47

city treasurer-elect, who, to begin with, was a puppet in the hands of other men, but who, also in spite of this fact, became a personage of considerable importance, for the simple reason that he was weak. Stener had been engaged in the real estate and insurance business in a small way before he was made city treasurer. He was one of those men, of whom there are so many thousands in every large community, with no breadth of vision, no real subtlety, no craft, no great skill in anything. You would never hear a new idea emanating from Stener. He never had one in his life. On the other hand, he was not a bad fellow. He had a stodgy, dusty, commonplace look to him which was more a matter of mind than of body. His eye was of vague gray-blue; his hair a dusty light-brown and thin. His mouth—there was nothing impressive there. He was quite tall, nearly six feet, with moderately broad shoulders, but his figure was anything but shapely. He seemed to stoop a little, his stomach was the least bit protuberant, and he talked commonplaces—the small change of newspaper and street and business gossip. People liked him in his own neighborhood. He was thought to be honest and kindly; and he was, as far as he knew. His wife and four children were as average and insignificant as the wives and children of such men usually are.

Just the same, and in spite of, or perhaps, politically speaking, because of all this, George W. Stener was brought into temporary public notice by certain political methods which had existed in Philadelphia practically unmodified for the previous half hundred years. First, because he was of the same political faith as the dominant local political party, he had become known to the local councilman and ward-leader of his ward as a faithful soul—one useful in the matter of drumming up votes. And next—although absolutely without value as a speaker, for he had no ideas—you could send him from door to door, asking the grocer and the blacksmith and the butcher how he felt about things and he would make friends, and in the long run predict fairly accurately the probable vote. Furthermore, you could dole him out a few platitudes and he would repeat them. The Republican party, which was the new-born party then, but dominant in Philadelphia, needed your vote; it was necessary to keep the rascally Democrats out—he could scarcely have said why. They had been for slavery. They were for free trade. It never once occurred to him that these things had nothing to do with the local executive and financial administration of Philadelphia. Supposing they didn't? What of it?

In Philadelphia at this time a certain United States Senator, one Mark Simpson, together with Edward Malia Butler and Henry A. Mollenhauer, a rich coal dealer and investor, were supposed to, and did, control jointly the political destiny of the city. They had representatives, benchmen, spies, tools—a great company. Among them was this same Stener—a minute cog in the silent machinery of their affairs.

In scarcely any other city save this, where the inhabitants were of a deadly average in so far as being commonplace was concerned, could such a man as Stener have been elected city treasurer. The rank and file did not, except in rare instances, make up their political program. An inside ring had this matter in charge. Certain positions were allotted to such and such men or to such and such factions of the party for such and such services rendered—but who does not know politics?

In due course of time, therefore, George W. Stener had become persona grata to Edward Strobik, a quondam councilman who afterward became ward leader and still later president of council, and who, in private life was a stone-dealer and owner of a brickyard. Strobik was a benchman of Henry A. Mollenhauer, the hardest and coldest of all three of the political leaders. The latter had things to get from council, and Strobik was his tool. He had Stener elected; and because he was faithful in voting as he was told the latter was later made an assistant superintendent of the highways department.

Here he came under the eyes of Edward Malia Butler, and was slightly useful to him. Then the central political committee, with Butler in charge, decided that some nice, docile man who would at the same time be absolutely faithful was needed for city treasurer, and Stener was put on the ticket. He knew little of finance, but was an excellent bookkeeper; and, anyhow, was not corporation counsel Regan, another political tool of this great triumvirate, there to advise him at all times? He was. It was a very simple matter. Being put on the ticket was equivalent to being elected, and so, after a few weeks of exceedingly trying platform experiences, in which he had stammered through platitudinous declarations that the city needed to be honestly administered, he was inducted into office; and there you were.

Now it wouldn't have made so much difference what George W. Stener's executive and financial qualifications for the position were, but at this time the city of Philadelphia was still hobbling along under perhaps as evil a financial system, or lack of it, as any city ever endured—the assessor and the treasurer being allowed to collect and hold moneys belonging to the city, outside of the city's private vaults, and that without any demand on the part of anybody that the same be invested by them at interest for the city's benefit. Rather, all they were expected to do, apparently, was to restore the principal and that which was with them when they entered or left office. It was not understood or publicly demanded that the moneys so collected, or drawn from any source, be maintained intact in the vaults of the city treasury. They could be loaned out, deposited in banks or used to further private interests of any one, so long as the principal was returned, and no one was the wiser. Of course, this theory of finance was not publicly sanctioned, but it was known politically and journalistically, and in high finance. How were you to stop it?

Cowperwood, in approaching Edward Malia Butler, had been unconsciously let in on this atmosphere of erratic and unsatisfactory speculation without really knowing it. When he had left the office of Tighe & Co., seven years before, it was with the idea that henceforth and forever he would have nothing to do with the stock-brokerage proposition; but now behold him back in it again, with more vim than he had ever displayed, for now he was working for himself, the firm of Cowperwood & Co., and he was eager to satisfy the world of new and powerful individuals who by degrees were drifting to him. All had a little money. All had tips, and they wanted him to carry certain lines of stock on margin for them, because he was known to other political men, and because he was safe. And this was true. He was not, or at least up to this time had not been, a speculator or a gambler on his own account. In fact he often soothed himself with the thought that in all these years he had never gambled for himself, but had always acted strictly for others instead. But now here was George W. Stener with a proposition which was not quite the same thing as stock-gambling, and yet it was.

During a long period of years preceding the Civil War, and through it, let it here be explained and remembered, the city of Philadelphia had been in the habit, as a corporation, when there were no available funds in the treasury, of issuing what were known as city warrants, which were nothing more than notes or I.O.U.'s bearing six per cent. interest, and payable sometimes in thirty days, sometimes in three, sometimes in six months—all depending on the amount and how soon the city treasurer thought there would be sufficient money in the treasury to take them up and cancel them. Small tradesmen and large contractors were frequently paid in this way; the small tradesman who sold supplies to the city institutions, for instance, being compelled to discount his notes at the bank, if he needed ready money, usually for ninety cents on the dollar, while the large contractor could afford to hold his and wait. It can readily be seen that this might well work to the disadvantage of the small dealer and merchant, and yet prove quite a fine thing for a large contractor or note-broker, for the city was sure to pay the warrants at some time, and six per cent. interest was a fat rate, considering the absolute security. A banker or broker who gathered up these things from small tradesmen at ninety cents on the dollar made a fine thing of it all around if he could wait.

Originally, in all probability, there was no intention on the part of the city treasurer to do any one an injustice, and it is likely that there really were no funds to pay with at the time. However that may have been, there was later no excuse for issuing the warrants, seeing that the city might easily have been managed much more economically. But these warrants, as can readily be imagined, had come to be a fine source of profit for note-brokers, bankers, political financiers, and inside political manipulators generally and so they remained a part of the city's fiscal policy.

There was just one drawback to all this. In order to get the full advantage of this condition the large banker holding them must be an "inside banker," one close to the political forces of the city, for if he was not and needed money and he carried his warrants to the city treasurer, he would find that he could not get cash for them. But if he transferred them to some banker or note-broker who was close to the political force of the city, it was quite another matter. The treasury would find means to pay. Or, if so desired by the note-broker or banker—the right one—notes which were intended to be met in three months, and should have been settled at that time, were extended to run on years and years, drawing interest at six per cent. even when the city had ample funds to meet them. Yet this meant, of course, an illegal interest drain on the city, but that was all right also. "No funds" could cover that. The general public did not know. It could not find out. The newspapers were not at all vigilant, being pro-political. There were no persistent, enthusiastic reformers who obtained any political credence. During the war, warrants outstanding in this manner arose in amount to much over two million dollars, all drawing six per cent. interest, but then, of course, it began to get a little scandalous. Besides, at least some of the investors began to want their money back.

In order, therefore, to clear up this outstanding indebtedness and make everything shipshape again, it was decided that the city must issue a loan, say for two million dollars— no need to be exact about the amount. And this loan must take the shape of interest-bearing certificates of a par value of one hundred dollars, redeemable in six, twelve, or eighteen months, as the case may be. These certificates of loan were then ostensibly to be sold in the open market, a sinking-fund set aside for their redemption, and the money so obtained used to take up the long-outstanding warrants which were now such a subject of public comment.

It is obvious that this was merely a case of robbing Peter to pay Paul. There was no real clearing up of the outstanding debt. It was the intention of the schemers to make it possible for the financial politicians on the inside to reap the same old harvest by allowing the certificates to be sold to the right parties for ninety or less, setting up the claim that there was no market for them, the credit of the city being bad. To a certain extent this was true. The war was just over. Money was high. Investors could get more than six per cent. elsewhere unless the loan was sold at ninety. But there were a few watchful politicians not in the administration, and some newspapers and non-political financiers who, because of the high strain of patriotism existing at the time, insisted that the loan should be sold at par. Therefore a clause to that effect had to be inserted in the enabling ordinance.

This, as one might readily see, destroyed the politicians' little scheme to get this loan at ninety. Nevertheless since they desired that the money tied up in the old warrants and now not redeemable because of lack of funds should be paid them, the only way this could be done would be to have some broker who knew the subtleties of the stock market handle this new city loan on 'change in such a way that it would be made to seem worth one hundred and to be sold to outsiders at that figure. Afterward, if, as it was certain to do, it fell below that, the politicians could buy as much of it as they pleased, and eventually have the city redeem it at par.

George W. Stener, entering as city treasurer at this time, and bringing no special financial intelligence to the proposition, was really troubled. Henry A. Mollenhauer, one of the men who had gathered up a large amount of the old city warrants, and who now wanted his money, in order to invest it in bonanza offers in the West, called on Stener, and also on the mayor. He with Simpson and Butler made up the Big Three.

"I think something ought to be done about these warrants that are outstanding," he explained. "I am carrying a large amount of them, and there are others. We have helped the city a long time by saying nothing; but now I think that something ought to be done. Mr. Butler and Mr. Simpson feel the same way. Couldn't these new loan certificates be listed on the stock exchange and the money raised that way? Some clever broker could bring them to par."

Stener was greatly flattered by the visit from Mollenhauer. Rarely did he trouble to put in a personal appearance, and then only for the weight and effect his presence would have. He called on the mayor and the president of council, much as he called on Stener, with a lofty, distant, inscrutable air. They were as office-boys to him.

In order to understand exactly the motive for Mollenhauer's interest in Stener, and the significance of this visit and Stener's subsequent action in regard to it, it will be necessary to scan the political horizon for some little distance back. Although George W. Stener was in a way a political henchman and appointee of Mollenhauer's, the latter was only vaguely acquainted with him. He had seen him before; knew of him; had agreed that his name should be put on the local slate largely because he had been assured by those who were closest to him and who did his bidding that Stener was "all right," that he would do as he was told, that he would cause no one any trouble, etc. In fact, during several previous administrations, Mollenhauer had maintained a subsurface connection with the treasury, but never so close a one as could easily be traced. He was too conspicuous a man politically and financially for that. But he was not above a plan, in which Simpson if not Butler shared, of using political and commercial stool-pigeons to bleed the city treasury as much as possible without creating a scandal. In fact, for some years previous to this, various agents had already been employed—Edward Strobik, president of council, Asa Conklin, the then incumbent of the mayor's chair, Thomas Wycroft, alderman, Jacob Harmon, alderman, and others—to organize dummy companies under various names, whose business it was to deal in those things which the city needed—lumber, stone, steel, iron, cement—a long list—and of course, always at a fat profit to those ultimately behind the dummy companies, so organized. It saved the city the trouble of looking far and wide for honest and reasonable dealers.

Since the action of at least three of these dummies will have something to do with the development of Cowperwood's story, they may be briefly described. Edward Strobik, the chief of them, and the one most useful to Mollenhauer, in a minor way, was a very spry person of about thirty-five at this time—lean and somewhat forceful, with black hair, black eyes, and an inordinately large black mustache. He was dapper, inclined to noticeable clothing—a pair of striped trousers, a white vest, a black cutaway coat and a high silk hat. His markedly ornamental shoes were always polished to perfection, and his immaculate appearance gave him the nickname of "The Dude" among some. Nevertheless he was quite able on a small scale, and was well liked by many.

His two closest associates, Messrs. Thomas Wycroft and Jacob Harmon, were rather less attractive and less brilliant. Jacob Harmon was a thick wit socially, but no fool financially. He was big and rather doleful to look upon, with sandy brown hair and brown eyes, but fairly intelligent, and absolutely willing to approve anything which was not too broad in its crookedness and which would afford him sufficient protection to keep him out of the clutches of the law. He was really not so cunning as dull and anxious to get along.

Thomas Wycroft, the last of this useful but minor triumvirate, was a tall, lean man, candle-waxy, hollow-eyed, gaunt of face, pathetic to look at physically, but shrewd. He was an iron-molder by trade and had gotten into politics much as Stener had—because he was useful; and he had managed to make some money—via this triumvirate of which Strobik was the ringleader, and which was engaged in various peculiar businesses which will now be indicated.

The companies which these several henchmen had organized under previous administrations, and for Mollenhauer, dealt in meat, building material, lamp-posts, highway supplies, anything you will, which the city departments or its institutions needed. A city contract once awarded was irrevocable, but certain councilmen had to be fixed in advance and it took money to do that. The company so organized need not actually slaughter any cattle or mold lamp-posts. All it had to do was to organize to do that, obtain a charter, secure a contract for supplying such material to the city from the city council (which Strobik, Harmon, and Wycroft would attend to), and then sublet this to some actual beef-slaughterer or iron-founder, who would supply the material and allow them to pocket their profit which in turn was divided or paid for to Mollenhauer and Simpson in the form of political donations to clubs or organizations. It was so easy and in a way so legitimate. The particular beef-slaughterer or iron-founder thus favored could not hope of his own ability thus to obtain a contract. Stener, or whoever was in charge of the city treasury at the time, for his services in loaning money at a low rate of interest to be used as surety for the proper performance of contract, and to aid in some instances the beef-killer or iron-founder to carry out his end, was to be allowed not only the one or two per cent. which he might pocket (other treasurers had), but a fair proportion of the profits. A complacent, confidential chief clerk who was all right would be recommended to him. It did not concern Stener that Strobik, Harmon, and Wycroft, acting for Mollenhauer, were incidentally planning to use a little of the money loaned for purposes quite outside those indicated. It was his business to loan it.

However, to be going on. Some time before he was even nominated, Stener had learned from Strobik, who, by the way, was one of his sureties as treasurer (which suretyship was against the law, as were those of Councilmen Wycroft and Harmon, the law of Pennsylvania stipulating that one political servant might not become surety for another), that those who had brought about this nomination and election would by no means ask him to do anything which was not perfectly legal, but that he must be complacent and not stand in the way of big municipal perquisites nor bite the hands that fed him. It was also made perfectly plain to him, that once he was well in office a little money for himself was to be made. As has been indicated, he had always been a poor man. He had seen all those who had dabbled in politics to any extent about him heretofore do very well financially indeed, while he pegged along as an insurance and real-estate agent. He had worked hard as a small political henchman. Other politicians were building themselves nice homes in newer portions of the city. They were going off to New York or Harrisburg or Washington on jaunting parties. They were seen in happy converse at road-houses or country hotels in season with their wives or their women favorites, and he was not, as yet, of this happy throng. Naturally now that he was promised something, he was interested and compliant. What might he not get?

When it came to this visit from Mollenhauer, with its suggestion in regard to bringing city loan to par, although it bore no obvious relation to Mollenhauer's subsurface connection with Stener, through Strobik and the others, Stener did definitely recognize his own political subservience—his master's stentorian voice—and immediately thereafter hurried to Strobik for information.

"Just what would you do about this?" he asked of Strobik, who knew of Mollenhauer's visit before Stener told him, and was waiting for Stener to speak to him. "Mr. Mollenhauer talks about having this new loan listed on 'change and brought to par so that it will sell for one hundred."

Neither Strobik, Harmon, nor Wycroft knew how the certificates of city loan, which were worth only ninety on the open market, were to be made to sell for one hundred on 'change, but Mollenhauer's secretary, one Abner Sengstack, had suggested to Strobik that, since Butler was dealing with young Cowperwood and Mollenhauer did not care particularly for his private broker in this instance, it might be as well to try Cowperwood.

So it was that Cowperwood was called to Stener's office. And once there, and not as yet recognizing either the hand of Mollenhauer or Simpson in this, merely looked at the peculiarly shambling, heavy-cheeked, middle-class man before him without either interest or

52

sympathy, realizing at once that he had a financial baby to deal with. If he could act as adviser to this man—be his sole counsel for four years!

"How do you do, Mr. Stener?" he said in his soft, ingratiating voice, as the latter held out his hand. "I am glad to meet you. I have heard of you before, of course."

Stener was long in explaining to Cowperwood just what his difficulty was. He went at it in a clumsy fashion, stumbling through the difficulties of the situation he was suffered to meet.

"The main thing, as I see it, is to make these certificates sell at par. I can issue them in any sized lots you like, and as often as you like. I want to get enough now to clear away two hundred thousand dollars' worth of the outstanding warrants, and as much more as I can get later."

Cowperwood felt like a physician feeling a patient's pulse—a patient who is really not sick at all but the reassurance of whom means a fat fee. The abstrusities of the stock exchange were as his A B C's to him. He knew if he could have this loan put in his hands—all of it, if he could have the fact kept dark that he was acting for the city, and that if Stener would allow him to buy as a "bull" for the sinking-fund while selling judiciously for a rise, he could do wonders even with a big issue. He had to have all of it, though, in order that he might have agents under him. Looming up in his mind was a scheme whereby he could make a lot of the unwary speculators about 'change go short of this stock or loan under the impression, of course, that it was scattered freely in various persons' hands, and that they could buy as much of it as they wanted. Then they would wake to find that they could not get it; that he had it all. Only he would not risk his secret that far. Not he, oh, no. But he would drive the city loan to par and then sell. And what a fat thing for himself among others in so doing. Wisely enough he sensed that there was politics in all this—shrewder and bigger men above and behind Stener. But what of that? And how slyly and shrewdly they were sending Stener to him. It might be that his name was becoming very potent in their political world here. And what might that not mean!

"I tell you what I'd like to do, Mr. Stener," he said, after he had listened to his explanation and asked how much of the city loan he would like to sell during the coming year. "I'll be glad to undertake it. But I'd like to have a day or two in which to think it over."

"Why, certainly, certainly, Mr. Cowperwood," replied Stener, genially. "That's all right. Take your time. If you know how it can be done, just show me when you're ready. By the way, what do you charge?"

"Well, the stock exchange has a regular scale of charges which we brokers are compelled to observe. It's one-fourth of one per cent. on the par value of bonds and loans. Of course, I may hav to add a lot of fictitious selling—I'll explain that to you later—but I won't charge you anything for that so long as it is a secret between us. I'll give you the best service I can, Mr. Stener. You can depend on that. Let me have a day or two to think it over, though."

He shook hands with Stener, and they parted. Cowperwood was satisfied that he was on the verge of a significant combination, and Stener that he had found someone on whom he could lean.

CHAPTER XV

The plan Cowperwood developed after a few days' meditation will be plain enough to any one who knows anything of commercial and financial manipulation, but a dark secret to those who do not. In the first place, the city treasurer was to use his (Cowperwood's) office as a bank of deposit. He was to turn over to him, actually, or set over to his credit on the city's books, subject to his order, certain amounts of city loans—two hundred thousand dollars at first, since that was the amount it was desired to raise quickly—and he would then go into the market and see what could be done to have it brought to par. The city treasurer was to ask leave of the stock exchange at once to have it listed as a security. Cowperwood would then use his influence to have this application acted upon quickly. Stener was then to dispose of all city loan certificates through him, and him only. He was to allow him to buy for the sinking-fund, supposedly, such amounts as he might have to buy in order to keep the price up to par. To do this, once a considerable number of the loan certificates had been unloaded on the public, it might be necessary to buy back a great deal. However, these would be sold again. The law concerning selling only at par would have to be abrogated to this extent—i.e., that the wash sales and preliminary sales would have to be considered no sales until par was reached.

There was a subtle advantage here, as Cowperwood pointed out to Stener. In the first place, since the certificates were going ultimately to reach par anyway, there was no objection to Stener or any one else buying low at the opening price and holding for a rise. Cowperwood would be glad to carry him on his books for any amount, and he would settle at the end of each month. He would not be asked to buy the certificates outright. He could be carried on the books for a certain reasonable margin, say ten points. The money was as good as made for Stener now. In the next place, in buying for the sinking-fund it would be possible to buy these certificates very cheap, for, having the new and reserve issue entirely in his hands, Cowperwood could throw such amounts as he wished into the market at such times as he wished to buy, and consequently depress the market. Then he could buy, and, later, up would go the price. Having the issues totally in his hands to boost or depress the market as he wished, there was no reason why the city should not ultimately get par for all its issues, and at the same time considerable money be made out of the manufactured fluctuations. He, Cowperwood, would be glad to make most of his profit that way. The city should allow him his normal percentage on all his actual sales of certificates for the city at par (he would have to have that in order to keep straight with the stock exchange); but beyond that, and for all the other necessary manipulative sales, of which there would be many, he would depend on his knowledge of the stock market to reimburse him. And if Stener wanted to speculate with him—well.

Dark as this transaction may seem to the uninitiated, it will appear quite clear to those who know. Manipulative tricks have always been worked in connection with stocks of which one man or one set of men has had complete control. It was no different from what subsequently was done with Erie, Standard Oil, Copper, Sugar, Wheat, and what not. Cowperwood was one of the first and one of the youngest to see how it could be done. When he first talked to Stener he was twenty-eight years of age. When he last did business with him he was thirty-four.

The houses and the bank-front of Cowperwood & Co. had been proceeding apace. The latter was early Florentine in its decorations with windows which grew narrower as they approached the roof, and a door of wrought iron set between delicately carved posts, and a straight lintel of brownstone. It was low in height and distinguished in appearance. In the center panel had been hammered a hand, delicately wrought, thin and artistic, holding aloft a flaming brand. Ellsworth informed him that this had formerly been a money-changer's sign used in old Venice, the significance of which had long been forgotten.

The interior was finished in highly-polished hardwood, stained in imitation of the gray lichens which infest trees. Large sheets of clear, beveled glass were used, some oval, some oblong, some square, and some circular, following a given theory of eye movement. The fixtures for the gas-jets were modeled after the early Roman flame-brackets, and the office safe was made an ornament, raised on a marble platform at the back of the office and lacquered a silver-gray, with Cowperwood & Co. lettered on it in gold. One had a sense of reserve and taste pervading the place, and yet it was also inestimably prosperous, solid and assuring. Cowperwood, when he viewed it at its completion, complimented Ellsworth cheerily. "I like this. It is really beautiful. It will be a pleasure to work here. If those houses are going to be anything like this, they will be perfect."

"Wait till you see them. I think you will be pleased, Mr. Cowperwood. I am taking especial pains with yours because it is smaller. It is really easier to treat your father's. But yours—"

He went off into a description of the entrance-hall, reception-room and parlor, which he was arranging and decorating in such a way as to give an effect of size and dignity not really conformable to the actual space.

And when the houses were finished, they were effective and arresting—quite different from the conventional residences of the street. They were separated by a space of twenty feet, laid out as greensward. The architect had borrowed somewhat from the Tudor school, yet not so elaborated as later became the style in many of the residences in Philadelphia and elsewhere. The most striking features were rather deep-recessed doorways under wide, low, slightly floriated arches, and three projecting windows of rich form, one on the second floor of Frank's house, two on the facade of his father's. There were six gables showing on the front of the two houses, two on Frank's and four on his father's. In the front of each house on the ground floor was a recessed window unconnected with the recessed doorways, formed by setting the inner external wall back from the outer face of the building. This window looked out through an arched opening to the street, and was protected by a dwarf parapet or balustrade. It was possible to set potted vines and flowers there, which was later done, giving a pleasant sense of greenery from the street, and to place a few chairs there, which were reached via heavily barred French casements.

On the ground floor of each house was placed a conservatory of flowers, facing each other, and in the yard, which was jointly used, a pool of white marble eight feet in diameter, with a marble Cupid upon which jets of water played. The yard which was enclosed by a high but pierced wall of green-gray brick, especially burnt for the purpose the same color as the granite of the house, and surmounted by a white marble coping which was sown to grass and had a lovely, smooth, velvety appearance. The two houses, as originally planned, were connected by a low, green-columned pergola which could be enclosed in glass in winter.

The rooms, which were now slowly being decorated and furnished in period styles were very significant in that they enlarged and strengthened Frank Cowperwood's idea of the world of art in general. It was an enlightening and agreeable experience—one which made for artistic and intellectual growth—to hear Ellsworth explain at length the styles and types of architecture and furniture, the nature of woods and ornaments employed, the qualities and peculiarities of hangings, draperies, furniture panels, and door coverings. Ellsworth was a student of decoration as well as of architecture, and interested in the artistic taste of the American people, which he fancied would some day have a splendid outcome. He was wearied to death of the prevalent Romanesque composite combinations of country and suburban villa. The time was ripe for something new. He scarcely knew what it would be; but this that he had designed for Cowperwood and his father was at least different, as he said, while at the same time being reserved, simple, and pleasing. It was in marked contrast to the rest of the architecture of the street. Cowperwood's dining-room, reception-room, conservatory, and butler's pantry he had put on the first floor, together with the general entry-hall, staircase, and coat-room under the stairs. For the second floor he had reserved the library, general living-room, parlor, and a small office for Cowperwood, together with a boudoir for Lillian, connected with a dressing-room and bath.

On the third floor, neatly divided and accommodated with baths and dressing-rooms, were the nursery, the servants' quarters, and several guest-chambers.

Ellsworth showed Cowperwood books of designs containing furniture, hangings, etageres, cabinets, pedestals, and some exquisite piano forms. He discussed woods with him— rosewood, mahogany, walnut, English oak, bird's-eye maple, and the manufactured effects such as ormolu, marquetry, and Boule, or buhl. He explained the latter—how difficult it was to produce, how unsuitable it was in some respects for this climate, the brass and tortoise-shell inlay coming to swell with the heat or damp, and so bulging or breaking. He told of the difficulties and disadvantages of certain finishes, but finally recommended ormolu furniture for the reception room, medallion tapestry for the parlor, French renaissance for the dining-room and library, and bird's-eye maple (dyed blue in one instance, and left its natural color in another) and a rather lightly constructed and daintily carved walnut for the other rooms. The hangings, wall-paper, and floor coverings were to harmonize—not match—and the piano and music-cabinet for the parlor, as well as the etagere, cabinets, and pedestals for the reception-rooms, were to be of buhl or marquetry, if Frank cared to stand the expense.

Ellsworth advised a triangular piano—the square shapes were so inexpressibly wearisome to the initiated. Cowperwood listened fascinated. He foresaw a home which would be chaste, soothing, and delightful to look upon. If he hung pictures, gilt frames were to be the setting, large and deep; and if he wished a picture-gallery, the library could be converted into that, and the general living-room, which lay between the library and the parlor on the second-floor, could be turned into a combination library and living-room. This was eventually done; but not until his taste for pictures had considerably advanced.

It was now that he began to take a keen interest in objects of art, pictures, bronzes, little carvings and figurines, for his cabinets, pedestals, tables, and etageres. Philadelphia did not offer much that was distinguished in this realm—certainly not in the open market. There were many private houses which were enriched by travel; but his connection with the best families was as yet small. There were then two famous American sculptors, Powers and Hosmer, of whose work he had examples; but Ellsworth told him that they were not the last word in sculpture and that he should look into the merits of the ancients. He finally secured a head of David, by Thorwaldsen, which delighted him, and some landscapes by Hunt, Sully, and Hart, which seemed somewhat in the spirit of his new world.

The effect of a house of this character on its owner is unmistakable. We think we are individual, separate, above houses and material objects generally; but there is a subtle connection which makes them reflect us quite as much as we reflect them. They lend dignity, subtlety, force, each to the other, and what beauty, or lack of it, there is, is shot back and forth from one to the other as a shuttle in a loom, weaving, weaving. Cut the thread, separate a man from that which is rightfully his own, characteristic of him, and you have a peculiar figure, half success, half failure, much as a spider without its web, which will never be its whole self again until all its dignities and emoluments are restored.

The sight of his new house going up made Cowperwood feel of more weight in the world, and the possession of his suddenly achieved connection with the city treasurer was as though a wide door had been thrown open to the Elysian fields of opportunity. He rode about the city those days behind a team of spirited bays, whose glossy hides and metaled harness bespoke the watchful care of hostler and coachman. Ellsworth was building an attractive stable in the little side street back of the houses, for the joint use of both families. He told Mrs. Cowperwood that he intended to buy her a victoria—as the low, open, four-wheeled coach was then known—as soon as they were well settled in their new home, and that they were to go out more. There was some talk about the value of entertaining—that he would have to reach out socially for certain individuals who were not now known to him. Together with Anna, his sister, and his two brothers, Joseph and Edward, they could use the two houses jointly. There was no reason why Anna should not make a splendid match. Joe and Ed might marry well, since they were not destined to set the world on fire in commerce. At least it would not hurt them to try.

"Don't you think you will like that?" he asked his wife, referring to his plans for entertaining.

She smiled wanly. "I suppose so," she said.

56

CHAPTER XVI

It was not long after the arrangement between Treasurer Stener and Cowperwood had been made that the machinery for the carrying out of that political-financial relationship was put in motion. The sum of two hundred and ten thousand dollars in six per cent. interest-bearing certificates, payable in ten years, was set over to the credit of Cowperwood & Co. on the books of the city, subject to his order. Then, with proper listing, he began to offer it in small amounts at more than ninety, at the same time creating the impression that it was going to be a prosperous investment. The certificates gradually rose and were unloaded in rising amounts until one hundred was reached, when all the two hundred thousand dollars' worth—two thousand certificates in all—was fed out in small lots. Stener was satisfied. Two hundred shares had been carried for him and sold at one hundred, which netted him two thousand dollars. It was illegitimate gain, unethical; but his conscience was not very much troubled by that. He had none, truly. He saw visions of a halcyon future.

It is difficult to make perfectly clear what a subtle and significant power this suddenly placed in the hands of Cowperwood. Consider that he was only twenty-eight—nearing twenty-nine. Imagine yourself by nature versed in the arts of finance, capable of playing with sums of money in the forms of stocks, certificates, bonds, and cash, as the ordinary man plays with checkers or chess. Or, better yet, imagine yourself one of those subtle masters of the mysteries of the higher forms of chess—the type of mind so well illustrated by the famous and historic chess-players, who could sit with their backs to a group of rivals playing fourteen men at once, calling out all the moves in turn, remembering all the positions of all the men on all the boards, and winning. This, of course, would be an overstatement of the subtlety of Cowperwood at this time, and yet it would not be wholly out of bounds. He knew instinctively what could be done with a given sum of money— how as cash it could be deposited in one place, and yet as credit and the basis of moving checks, used in not one but many other places at the same time. When properly watched and followed this manipulation gave him the constructive and purchasing power of ten and a dozen times as much as his original sum might have represented. He knew instinctively the principles of "pyramiding" and "kiting." He could see exactly not only how he could raise and lower the value of these certificates of loan, day after day and year after year—if he were so fortunate as to retain his hold on the city treasurer—but also how this would give him a credit with the banks hitherto beyond his wildest dreams. His father's bank was one of the first to profit by this and to extend him loans. The various local politicians and bosses—Mollenhauer, Butler, Simpson, and others—seeing the success of his efforts in this direction, speculated in city loan. He became known to Mollenhauer and Simpson, by reputation, if not personally, as the man who was carrying this city loan proposition to a successful issue. Stener was supposed to have done a clever thing in finding him. The stock exchange stipulated that all trades were to be compared the same day and settled before the close of the next; but this working arrangement with the new city treasurer gave Cowperwood much more latitude, and now he had always until the first of the month, or practically thirty days at times, in which to render an accounting for all deals connected with the loan issue.

And, moreover, this was really not an accounting in the sense of removing anything from his hands. Since the issue was to be so large, the sum at his disposal would always be large, and so-called transfers and balancing at the end of the month would be a mere matter of bookkeeping. He could use these city loan certificates deposited with him for manipulative purposes, deposit them at any bank as collateral for a loan, quite as if they were his own, thus raising seventy per cent. of their actual value in cash, and he did not hesitate to do so. He could take this cash, which need not be accounted for until the end of the month, and cover other stock transactions, on which he could borrow again. There was no limit to the resources of which he now found himself possessed, except the resources of his own energy, ingenuity, and the limits of time in which he had to work. The politicians did not realize what a bonanza he was making of it all for himself, because they were as yet unaware of the subtlety of his mind. When Stener told him, after talking the matter over with the mayor, Strobik, and others that he would formally, during the course of the year, set over on the city's books all of the two millions in city loan, Cowperwood was silent—but with delight. Two millions! His to play with! He had been called in as a financial adviser, and he had given his advice and it had been taken! Well. He was not a man who inherently was troubled with conscientious scruples. At the same time he still believed himself financially honest. He was no sharper or shrewder than any other financier—certainly no sharper than any other would be if he could.

It should be noted here that this proposition of Stener's in regard to city money had no connection with the attitude of the principal leaders in local politics in regard to street-railway control, which was a new and intriguing phase of the city's financial life. Many of the leading financiers and financier-politicians were interested in that. For instance, Messrs. Mollenhauer, Butler, and Simpson were interested in street-railways separately on their own account. There was no understanding between them on this score. If they had thought at all on the matter they would have decided that they did not want any outsider to interfere. As a matter of fact the street-railway business in Philadelphia was not sufficiently developed at this time to suggest to any one the grand scheme of union which came later. Yet in connection with this new arrangement between Stener and Cowperwood, it was Strobik who now came forward to Stener with an idea of his own. All were certain to make money through Cowperwood—he and Stener, especially. What was amiss, therefore, with himself and Stener and with Cowperwood as their—or rather Stener's secret representative, since Strobik did not dare to appear in the matter—buying now sufficient street-railway shares in some one line to control it, and then, if he, Strobik, could, by efforts of his own, get the city council to set aside certain streets for its extension, why, there you were—they would own it. Only, later, he proposed to shake Stener out if he could. But this preliminary work had to be done by some one, and it might as well be Stener. At the same time, as he saw, this work had to be done very carefully, because naturally his superiors were watchful, and if they found him dabbling in affairs of this kind to his own advantage, they might make it impossible for him to continue politically in a position where he could help himself just the same. Any outside organization such as a street-railway company already in existence had a right to appeal to the city council for privileges which would naturally further its and the city's growth, and, other things being equal, these could not be refused. It would not do for him to appear, however, both as a shareholder and president of the council. But with Cowperwood acting privately for Stener it would be another thing.

The interesting thing about this proposition as finally presented by Stener for Strobik to Cowperwood, was that it raised, without appearing to do so, the whole question of Cowperwood's attitude toward the city administration. Although he was dealing privately for Edward Butler as an agent, and with this same plan in mind, and although he had never met either Mollenhauer or Simpson, he nevertheless felt that in so far as the manipulation of the city loan was concerned he was acting for them. On the other hand, in this matter of the private street-railway purchase which Stener now brought to him, he realized from the very beginning, by Stener's attitude, that there was something untoward in it, that Stener felt he was doing something which he ought not to do.

"Cowperwood," he said to him the first morning he ever broached this matter—it was in Stener's office, at the old city hall at Sixth and Chestnut, and Stener, in view of his oncoming prosperity, was feeling very good indeed—"isn't there some street-railway property around town here that a man could buy in on and get control of if he had sufficient money?"

Cowperwood knew that there were such properties. His very alert mind had long since sensed the general opportunities here. The omnibuses were slowly disappearing. The best routes were already preempted. Still, there were other streets, and the city was growing. The incoming population would make great business in the future. One could afford to pay almost any price for the short lines already built if one could wait and extend the lines into larger and better areas later. And already he had conceived in his own mind the theory of the "endless chain," or "argeeable formula," as it was later termed, of buying a certain property on a long-time payment and issuing stocks or bonds sufficient not only to pay your seller, but to reimburse you for your trouble, to say nothing of giving you a margin wherewith to invest in other things—allied properties, for instance, against which more bonds could be issued, and so on, ad infinitum. It became an old story later, but it was new at that time, and he kept the thought closely to himself. None the less he was glad to have Stener speak of this, since street-railways were his hobby, and he was convinced that he would be a great master of them if he ever had an opportunity to control them.

"Why, yes, George," he said, noncommittally, "there are two or three that offer a good chance if a man had money enough. I notice blocks of stock being offered on 'change now and then by one person and another. It would be good policy to pick these things up as they're offered, and then to see later if some of the other stockholders won't want to sell out. Green and Coates, now, looks like a good proposition to me. If I had three or four hundred thousand dollars that I thought I could put into that by degrees I would follow it up. It only takes about thirty per cent. of the stock of any railroad to control it. Most of the shares are scattered around so far and wide that they never vote, and I think two or three hundred thousand dollars would control that road." He mentioned one other line that might be secured in the same way in the course of time.

Stener meditated. "That's a good deal of money," he said, thoughtfully. "I'll talk to you about that some more later." And he was off to see Strobik none the less.

Cowperwood knew that Stener did not have any two or three hundred thousand dollars to invest in anything. There was only one way that he could get it—and that was to borrow it out of the city treasury and forego the interest. But he would not do that on his own initiative. Some one else must be behind him and who else other than Mollenhauer, or Simpson, or possibly even Butler, though he doubted that, unless the triumvirate were secretly working together. But what of it? The larger politicians were always using the treasury, and he was thinking now, only, of his own attitude in regard to the use of this money. No harm could come to him, if Stener's ventures were successful; and there was no reason why they should not be. Even if they were not he would be merely acting as an agent. In addition, he saw how in the manipulation of this money for Stener he could probably eventually control certain lines for himself.

There was one line being laid out to within a few blocks of his new home—the Seventeenth and Nineteenth Street line it was called—which interested him greatly. He rode on it occasionally when he was delayed or did not wish to trouble about a vehicle. It ran through two thriving streets of red-brick houses, and was destined to have a great future once the city grew large enough. As yet it was really not long enough. If he could get that, for instance, and combine it with Butler's lines, once they were secured—or Mollenhauer's, or Simpson's, the legislature could be induced to give them additional franchises. He even dreamed of a combination between Butler, Mollenhauer, Simpson, and himself. Between them, politically, they could get anything. But Butler was not a philanthropist. He would have to be approached with a very sizable bird in hand. The combination must be obviously advisable. Besides, he was dealing for Butler in street-railway stocks, and if this particular line were such a good thing Butler might wonder why it had not been brought to him in the first place. It would be better, Frank thought, to wait until he actually had it as his own, in which case it would be a different matter. Then he could talk as a capitalist. He began to dream of a city-wide street-railway system controlled by a few men, or preferably himself alone.

CHAPTER XVII

The days that had been passing brought Frank Cowperwood and Aileen Butler somewhat closer together in spirit. Because of the pressure of his growing affairs he had not paid so much attention to her as he might have, but he had seen her often this past year. She was now nineteen and had grown into some subtle thoughts of her own. For one thing, she was beginning to see the difference between good taste and bad taste in houses and furnishings.

"Papa, why do we stay in this old barn?" she asked her father one evening at dinner, when the usual family group was seated at the table.

"What's the matter with this house, I'd like to know?" demanded Butler, who was drawn up close to the table, his napkin tucked comfortably under his chin, for he insisted on this when company was not present. "I don't see anything the matter with this house. Your mother and I manage to live in it well enough."

"Oh, it's terrible, papa. You know it," supplemented Norah, who was seventeen and quite as bright as her sister, though a little less experienced. "Everybody says so. Look at all the nice houses that are being built everywhere about here."

"Everybody! Everybody! Who is 'everybody,' I'd like to know?" demanded Butler, with the faintest touch of choler and much humor. "I'm somebody, and I like it. Those that don't like it don't have to live in it. Who are they? What's the matter with it, I'd like to know?"

The question in just this form had been up a number of times before, and had been handled in just this manner, or passed over entirely with a healthy Irish grin. To-night, however, it was destined for a little more extended thought.

"You know it's bad, papa," corrected Aileen, firmly. "Now what's the use getting mad about it? It's old and cheap and dingy. The furniture is all worn out. That old piano in there ought to be given away. I won't play on it any more. The Cowperwoods—"

"Old is it!" exclaimed Butler, his accent sharpening somewhat with his self-induced rage. He almost pronounced it "owled." "Dingy, hi! Where do you get that? At your convent, I suppose. And where is it worn? Show me where it's worn."

He was coming to her reference to Cowperwood, but he hadn't reached that when Mrs. Butler interfered. She was a stout, broad-faced woman, smiling-mouthed most of the time, with blurry, gray Irish eyes, and a touch of red in her hair, now modified by grayness. Her cheek, below the mouth, on the left side, was sharply accented by a large wen.

"Children! children!" (Mr. Butler, for all his commercial and political responsibility, was as much a child to her as any.) "Youse mustn't quarrel now. Come now. Give your father the tomatoes."

There was an Irish maid serving at table; but plates were passed from one to the other just the same. A heavily ornamented chandelier, holding sixteen imitation candles in white porcelain, hung low over the table and was brightly lighted, another offense to Aileen.

"Mama, how often have I told you not to say 'youse'?" pleaded Norah, very much disheartened by her mother's grammatical errors. "You know you said you wouldn't."

"And who's to tell your mother what she should say?" called Butler, more incensed than ever at this sudden and unwarranted rebellion and assault. "Your mother talked before ever you was born, I'd have you know. If it weren't for her workin' and slavin' you wouldn't have any fine manners to paradin' before her. I'd have you know that. She's a better woman nor any you'll be runnin' with this day, you little baggage, you!"

"Mama, do you hear what he's calling me?" complained Norah, hugging close to her mother's arm and pretending fear and dissatisfaction.

"Eddie! Eddie!" cautioned Mrs. Butler, pleading with her husband. "You know he don't mean that, Norah, dear. Don't you know he don't?"

She was stroking her baby's head. The reference to her grammar had not touched her at all.

Butler was sorry that he had called his youngest a baggage; but these children—God bless his soul—were a great annoyance. Why, in the name of all the saints, wasn't this house good enough for them?

"Why don't you people quit fussing at the table?" observed Callum, a likely youth, with black hair laid smoothly over his forehead in a long, distinguished layer reaching from his left to close to his right ear, and his upper lip carrying a short, crisp mustache. His nose was short and retrousse, and his ears were rather prominent; but he was bright and attractive. He and Owen both realized that the house was old and poorly arranged; but their father and mother liked it, and business sense and family peace dictated silence on this score.

"Well, I think it's mean to have to live in this old place when people not one-fourth as good as we are are living in better ones. The Cowperwoods—why, even the Cowperwoods—"

"Yes, the Cowperwoods! What about the Cowperwoods?" demanded Butler, turning squarely to Aileen—she was sitting beside him—his big, red face glowing.

"Why, even they have a better house than we have, and he's merely an agent of yours."

"The Cowperwoods! The Cowperwoods! I'll not have any talk about the Cowperwoods. I'm not takin' my rules from the Cowperwoods. Suppose they have a fine house, what of it? My house is my house. I want to live here. I've lived here too long to be pickin' up and movin' away. If you don't like it you know what else you can do. Move if you want to. I'll not move."

It was Butler's habit when he became involved in these family quarrels, which were as shallow as puddles, to wave his hands rather antagonistically under his wife's or his children's noses.

"Oh, well, I will get out one of these days," Aileen replied. "Thank heaven I won't have to live here forever."

There flashed across her mind the beautiful reception-room, library, parlor, and boudoirs of the Cowperwoods, which were now being arranged and about which Anna Cowperwood talked to her so much—their dainty, lovely triangular grand piano in gold and painted pink and blue. Why couldn't they have things like that? Her father was unquestionably a dozen times as wealthy. But no, her father, whom she loved dearly, was of the old school. He was just what people charged him with being, a rough Irish contractor. He might be rich. She flared up at the injustice of things—why couldn't he have been rich and refined, too? Then they could have—but, oh, what was the use of complaining? They would never get anywhere with her father and mother in charge. She would just have to wait. Marriage was the answer—the right marriage. But whom was she to marry?

"You surely are not going to go on fighting about that now," pleaded Mrs. Butler, as strong and patient as fate itself. She knew where Aileen's trouble lay.

"But we might have a decent house," insisted Aileen. "Or this one done over," whispered Norah to her mother.

"Hush now! In good time," replied Mrs. Butler to Norah. "Wait. We'll fix it all up some day, sure. You run to your lessons now. You've had enough."

Norah arose and left. Aileen subsided. Her father was simply stubborn and impossible. And yet he was sweet, too. She pouted in order to compel him to apologize.

"Come now," he said, after they had left the table, and conscious of the fact that his daughter was dissatisfied with him. He must do something to placate her. "Play me somethin' on the piano, somethin' nice." He preferred showy, clattery things which exhibited her skill and muscular ability and left him wondering how she did it. That was what education was for—to enable her to play these very difficult things quickly and forcefully. "And you can have a new piano any time you like. Go and see about it. This looks pretty good to me, but if you don't want it, all right." Aileen squeezed his arm. What was the use of arguing with her father? What good would a lone piano do, when the whole house and the whole family atmosphere were at fault? But she played Schumann, Schubert, Offenbach, Chopin, and the old gentleman strolled to and fro and mused, smiling. There was real feeling and a thoughtful interpretation given to some of these things, for Aileen was not without sentiment, though she was so strong, vigorous, and withal so defiant; but it was all lost on him. He looked on her, his bright, healthy, enticingly beautiful daughter, and wondered what was going to become of her. Some rich man was going to marry her—some fine, rich young man with good business instincts—and he, her father, would leave her a lot of money.

There was a reception and a dance to be given to celebrate the opening of the two Cowperwood homes—the reception to be held in Frank Cowperwood's residence, and the dance later at his father's. The Henry Cowperwood domicile was much more pretentious, the reception-room, parlor, music-room, and conservatory being in this case all on the ground floor and much larger. Ellsworth had arranged it so that those rooms, on occasion, could be thrown into one, leaving excellent space for promenade, auditorium, dancing—anything, in fact, that a large company might require. It had been the intention all along of the two men to use these houses jointly. There was, to begin with, a combination use of the various servants, the butler, gardener, laundress, and maids. Frank Cowperwood employed a governess for his children. The butler was really not a butler in the best sense. He was Henry Cowperwood's private servitor. But he could carve and preside, and he could be used in either house as occasion warranted. There was also a hostler and a coachman for the joint stable. When two carriages were required at once, both drove. It made a very agreeable and satisfactory working arrangement.

The preparation of this reception had been quite a matter of importance, for it was necessary for financial reasons to make it as extensive as possible, and for social reasons as exclusive. It was therefore decided that the afternoon reception at Frank's house, with its natural overflow into Henry W.'s, was to be for all—the Tighes, Steners, Butlers, Mollenhauers, as well as the more select groups to which, for instance, belonged Arthur Rivers, Mrs. Seneca Davis, Mr. and Mrs. Trenor Drake, and some of the younger Drexels and Clarks, whom Frank had met. It was not likely that the latter would condescend, but cards had to be sent. Later in the evening a less democratic group if possible was to be entertained, albeit it would have to be extended to include the friends of Anna, Mrs. Cowperwood, Edward, and Joseph, and any list which Frank might personally have in mind. This was to be the list. The best that could be persuaded, commanded, or influenced of the young and socially elect were to be invited here.

It was not possible, however, not to invite the Butlers, parents and children, particularly the children, for both afternoon and evening, since Cowperwood was personally attracted to Aileen and despite the fact that the presence of the parents would be most unsatisfactory. Even Aileen as he knew was a little unsatisfactory to Anna and Mrs. Frank Cowperwood; and these two, when they were together supervising the list of invitations, often talked about it.

"She's so hoidenish," observed Anna, to her sister-in-law, when they came to the name of Aileen. "She thinks she knows so much, and she isn't a bit refined. Her father! Well, if I had her father I wouldn't talk so smart."

Mrs. Cowperwood, who was before her secretaire in her new boudoir, lifted her eyebrows.

"You know, Anna, I sometimes wish that Frank's business did not compel me to have anything to do with them. Mrs. Butler is such a bore. She means well enough, but she doesn't know anything. And Aileen is too rough. She's too forward, I think. She comes over here and plays upon the piano, particularly when Frank's here. I wouldn't mind so much for myself, but I know it must annoy him. All her pieces are so noisy. She never plays anything really delicate and refined."

"I don't like the way she dresses," observed Anna, sympathetically. "She gets herself up too conspicuously. Now, the other day I saw her out driving, and oh, dear! you should have seen her! She had on a crimson Zouave jacket heavily braided with black about the edges, and a turban with a huge crimson feather, and crimson ribbons reaching nearly to her waist.

Imagine that kind of a hat to drive in. And her hands! You should have seen the way she held her hands—oh—just so—self-consciously. They were curved just so"—and she showed how. "She had on yellow gauntlets, and she held the reins in one hand and the whip in the other. She drives just like mad when she drives, anyhow, and William, the footman, was up behind her. You should just have seen her. Oh, dear! oh, dear! she does think she is so much!" And Anna giggled, half in reproach, half in amusement.

"I suppose we'll have to invite her; I don't see how we can get out of it. I know just how she'll do, though. She'll walk about and pose and hold her nose up."

"Really, I don't see how she can," commented Anna. "Now, I like Norah. She's much nicer. She doesn't think she's so much."

"I like Norah, too," added Mrs. Cowperwood. "She's really very sweet, and to me she's prettier."

"Oh, indeed, I think so, too."

It was curious, though, that it was Aileen who commanded nearly all their attention and fixed their minds on her so-called idiosyncrasies. All they said was in its peculiar way true; but in addition the girl was really beautiful and much above the average intelligence and force. She was running deep with ambition, and she was all the more conspicuous, and in a way irritating to some, because she reflected in her own consciousness her social defects, against which she was inwardly fighting. She resented the fact that people could justly consider her parents ineligible, and for that reason her also. She was intrinsically as worth while as any one. Cowperwood, so able, and rapidly becoming so distinguished, seemed to realize it. The days that had been passing had brought them somewhat closer together in spirit. He was nice to her and liked to talk to her. Whenever he was at her home now, or she was at his and he was present, he managed somehow to say a word. He would come over quite near and look at her in a warm friendly fashion.

"Well, Aileen"—she could see his genial eyes—"how is it with you? How are your father and mother? Been out driving? That's fine. I saw you to-day. You looked beautiful."

"Oh, Mr. Cowperwood!"

"You did. You looked stunning. A black riding-habit becomes you. I can tell your gold hair a long way off."

"Oh, now, you mustn't say that to me. You'll make me vain. My mother and father tell me I'm too vain as it is."

"Never mind your mother and father. I say you looked stunning, and you did. You always do."

"Oh!"

She gave a little gasp of delight. The color mounted to her cheeks and temples. Mr. Cowperwood knew of course. He was so informed and intensely forceful. And already he was so much admired by so many, her own father and mother included, and by Mr. Mollenhauer and Mr. Simpson, so she heard. And his own home and office were so beautiful. Besides, his quiet intensity matched her restless force.

Aileen and her sister were accordingly invited to the reception but the Butlers mere and pere were given to understand, in as tactful a manner as possible, that the dance afterward was principally for young people.

The reception brought a throng of people. There were many, very many, introductions. There were tactful descriptions of little effects Mr. Ellsworth had achieved under rather trying circumstances; walks under the pergola; viewings of both homes in detail. Many of the guests were old friends. They gathered in the libraries and dining-rooms and talked. There was much jesting, some slappings of shoulders, some good story-telling, and so the afternoon waned into evening, and they went away.

Aileen had created an impression in a street costume of dark blue silk with velvet pelisse to match, and trimmed with elaborate pleatings and shirrings of the same materials. A toque of blue velvet, with high crown and one large dark-red imitation orchid, had given her a jaunty, dashing air. Beneath the toque her red-gold hair was arranged in an enormous chignon, with one long curl escaping over her collar. She was not exactly as daring as she seemed, but she loved to give that impression.

"You look wonderful," Cowperwood said as she passed him.

"I'll look different to-night," was her answer.

She had swung herself with a slight, swaggering stride into the dining-room and disappeared. Norah and her mother stayed to chat with Mrs. Cowperwood.

"Well, it's lovely now, isn't it?" breathed Mrs. Butler. "Sure you'll be happy here. Sure you will. When Eddie fixed the house we're in now, says I: 'Eddie, it's almost too fine for us altogether—surely it is,' and he says, says 'e, 'Norah, nothin' this side o' heavin or beyond is too good for ye'—and he kissed me. Now what d'ye think of that fer a big, hulkin' gossoon?"

"It's perfectly lovely, I think, Mrs. Butler," commented Mrs. Cowperwood, a little bit nervous because of others.

"Mama does love to talk so. Come on, mama. Let's look at the dining-room." It was Norah talking.

"Well, may ye always be happy in it. I wish ye that. I've always been happy in mine. May ye always be happy." And she waddled good-naturedly along.

The Cowperwood family dined hastily alone between seven and eight. At nine the evening guests began to arrive, and now the throng was of a different complexion—girls in mauve and cream-white and salmon-pink and silver-gray, laying aside lace shawls and loose dolmans, and the men in smooth black helping them. Outside in the cold, the carriage doors were slamming, and new guests were arriving constantly. Mrs. Cowperwood stood with her husband and Anna in the main entrance to the reception room, while Joseph and Edward Cowperwood and Mr. and Mrs. Henry W. Cowperwood lingered in the background. Lillian looked charming in a train gown of old rose, with a low, square neck showing a delicate chemisette of fine lace. Her face and figure were still notable, though her face was not as smoothly sweet as it had been years before when Cowperwood had first met her. Anna Cowperwood was not pretty, though she could not be said to be homely. She was small and dark, with a turned-up nose, snapping black eyes, a pert, inquisitive, intelligent, and alas, somewhat critical, air. She had considerable tact in the matter of dressing. Black, in spite of her darkness, with shining beads of sequins on it, helped her complexion greatly, as did a red rose in her hair. She had smooth, white well-rounded arms and shoulders. Bright eyes, a pert manner, clever remarks—these assisted to create an illusion of charm, though, as she often said, it was of little use. "Men want the dolly things."

In the evening inpour of young men and women came Aileen and Norah, the former throwing off a thin net veil of black lace and a dolman of black silk, which her brother Owen took from her. Norah was with Callum, a straight, erect, smiling young Irishman, who looked as though he might carve a notable career for himself. She wore a short, girlish dress that came to a little below her shoe-tops, a pale-figured lavender and white silk, with a fluffy hoop-skirt of dainty laced-edged ruffles, against which tiny bows of lavender stood out in odd places. There was a great sash of lavender about her waist, and in her hair a rosette of the same color. She looked exceedingly winsome—eager and bright-eyed.

But behind her was her sister in ravishing black satin, scaled as a fish with glistening crimsoned-silver sequins, her round, smooth arms bare to the shoulders, her corsage cut as low in the front and back as her daring, in relation to her sense of the proprieties, permitted. She was naturally of exquisite figure, erect, full-breasted, with somewhat more than gently swelling hips, which, nevertheless, melted into lovely, harmonious lines; and this low-cut corsage, receding back and front into a deep V, above a short, gracefully draped overskirt of black tulle and silver tissue, set her off to perfection. Her full, smooth, roundly modeled neck was enhanced in its cream-pink whiteness by an inch-wide necklet of black jet cut in many faceted black squares. Her complexion, naturally high in tone because of the pink of health, was enhanced by the tiniest speck of black court-plaster laid upon her cheekbone; and her hair, heightened in its reddish-gold by her dress, was fluffed loosely and adroitly about her eyes. The main mass of this treasure was done in two loose braids caught up in a black spangled net at the back of her neck; and her eyebrows had been emphasized by a pencil into something almost as significant as her hair. She was, for the occasion, a little too emphatic, perhaps, and yet more because of her burning vitality than of her costume. Art for her should have meant subduing her physical and spiritual significance. Life for her meant emphasizing them.

"Lillian!" Anna nudged her sister-in-law. She was grieved to think that Aileen was wearing black and looked so much better than either of them.

"I see," Lillian replied, in a subdued tone.

"So you're back again." She was addressing Aileen. "It's chilly out, isn't it?"

"I don't mind. Don't the rooms look lovely?"

She was gazing at the softly lighted chambers and the throng before her.

Norah began to babble to Anna. "You know, I just thought I never would get this old thing on." She was speaking of her dress. "Aileen wouldn't help me—the mean thing!"

Aileen had swept on to Cowperwood and his mother, who was near him. She had removed from her arm the black satin ribbon which held her train and kicked the skirts loose and free. Her eyes gleamed almost pleadingly for all her hauteur, like a spirited collie's, and her even teeth showed beautifully.

Cowperwood understood her precisely, as he did any fine, spirited animal.

"I can't tell you how nice you look," he whispered to her, familiarly, as though there was an old understanding between them. "You're like fire and song."

He did not know why he said this. He was not especially poetic. He had not formulated the phrase beforehand. Since his first glimpse of her in the hall, his feelings and ideas had been leaping and plunging like spirited horses. This girl made him set his teeth and narrow his eyes. Involuntarily he squared his jaw, looking more defiant, forceful, efficient, as she drew near.

But Aileen and her sister were almost instantly surrounded by young men seeking to be introduced and to write their names on dance-cards, and for the time being she was lost to view.

CHAPTER XVIII

The seeds of change—subtle, metaphysical—are rooted deeply. From the first mention of the dance by Mrs. Cowperwood and Anna, Aileen had been conscious of a desire toward a more effective presentation of herself than as yet, for all her father's money, she had been able to achieve. The company which she was to encounter, as she well knew, was to be so much more impressive, distinguished than anything she had heretofore known socially. Then, too, Cowperwood appeared as something more definite in her mind than he had been before, and to save herself she could not get him out of her consciousness.

A vision of him had come to her but an hour before as she was dressing. In a way she had dressed for him. She was never forgetful of the times he had looked at her in an interested way. He had commented on her hands once. To-day he had said that she looked "stunning," and she had thought how easy it would be to impress him to-night—to show him how truly beautiful she was.

She had stood before her mirror between eight and nine—it was nine-fifteen before she was really ready—and pondered over what she should wear. There were two tall pier-glasses in her wardrobe—an unduly large piece of furniture—and one in her closet door. She stood before the latter, looking at her bare arms and shoulders, her shapely figure, thinking of the fact that her left shoulder had a dimple, and that she had selected garnet garters decorated with heart-shaped silver buckles. The corset could not be made quite tight enough at first, and she chided her maid, Kathleen Kelly. She studied how to arrange her hair, and there was much ado about that before it was finally adjusted. She penciled her eyebrows and plucked at the hair about her forehead to make it loose and shadowy. She cut black court-plaster with her nail-shears and tried different-sized pieces in different places. Finally, she found one size and one place that suited her. She turned her head from side to side, looking at the combined effect of her hair, her penciled brows, her dimpled shoulder, and the black beauty-spot. If some one man could see her as she was now, some time! Which man? That thought scurried back like a frightened rat into its hole. She was, for all her strength, afraid of the thought of the one—the very deadly—the man.

And then she came to the matter of a train-gown. Kathleen laid out five, for Aileen had come into the joy and honor of these things recently, and she had, with the permission of her mother and father, indulged herself to the full. She studied a golden-yellow silk, with cream-lace shoulder-straps, and some gussets of garnet beads in the train that shimmered delightfully, but set it aside. She considered favorably a black-and-white striped silk of odd gray effect, and, though she was sorely tempted to wear it, finally let it go. There was a maroon dress, with basque and overskirt over white silk; a rich cream-colored satin; and then this black sequined gown, which she finally chose. She tried on the cream-colored satin first, however, being in much doubt about it; but her penciled eyes and beauty-spot did not seem to harmonize with it. Then she put on the black silk with its glistening crimsoned-silver sequins, and, lo, it touched her. She liked its coquettish drapery of tulle and silver about the hips. The "overskirt," which was at that time just coming into fashion, though avoided by the more conservative, had been adopted by Aileen with enthusiasm. She thrilled a little at the rustle of this black dress, and thrust her chin and nose forward to make it set right. Then after having Kathleen tighten her corsets a little more, she gathered the train over her arm by its train-band and looked again. Something was wanting. Oh, yes, her neck! What to wear—red coral? It did not look right. A string of pearls? That would not do either. There was a necklace made of small cameos set in silver which her mother had purchased, and another of diamonds which belonged to her mother, but they were not right. Finally, her jet necklet, which she did not value very highly, came into her mind, and, oh, how lovely it looked! How soft and smooth and glistening her chin looked above it. She caressed her neck affectionately, called for her black lace mantilla, her long, black silk dolman lined with red, and she was ready.

The ball-room, as she entered, was lovely enough. The young men and young women she saw there were interesting, and she was not wanting for admirers. The most aggressive of these youths—the most forceful—recognized in this maiden a fillip to life, a sting to existence. She was as a honey-jar surrounded by too hungry flies.

But it occurred to her, as her dance-list was filling up, that there was not much left for Mr. Cowperwood, if he should care to dance with her.

Cowperwood was meditating, as he received the last of the guests, on the subtlety of this matter of the sex arrangement of life. Two sexes. He was not at all sure that there was any law governing them. By comparison now with Aileen Butler, his wife looked rather dull, quite too old, and when he was ten years older she would look very much older.

"Oh, yes, Ellsworth had made quite an attractive arrangement out of these two houses—better than we ever thought he could do." He was talking to Henry Hale Sanderson, a young banker. "He had the advantage of combining two into one, and I think he's done more with my little one, considering the limitations of space, than he has with this big one. Father's has the advantage of size. I tell the old gentleman he's simply built a lean-to for me."

His father and a number of his cronies were over in the dining-room of his grand home, glad to get away from the crowd. He would have to stay, and, besides, he wanted to. Had he better dance with Aileen? His wife cared little for dancing, but he would have to dance with her at least once. There was Mrs. Seneca Davis smiling at him, and Aileen. By George, how wonderful! What a girl!

"I suppose your dance-list is full to overflowing. Let me see." He was standing before her and she was holding out the little blue-bordered, gold-monogrammed booklet. An orchestra was playing in the music room. The dance would begin shortly. There were delicately constructed, gold-tinted chairs about the walls and behind palms.

He looked down into her eyes—those excited, life-loving, eager eyes.

"You're quite full up. Let me see. Nine, ten, eleven. Well, that will be enough. I don't suppose I shall want to dance very much. It's nice to be popular."

"I'm not sure about number three. I think that's a mistake. You might have that if you wish."

She was falsifying.

"It doesn't matter so much about him, does it?"

His cheeks flushed a little as he said this.

"No."

Her own flamed.

"Well, I'll see where you are when it's called. You're darling. I'm afraid of you." He shot a level, interpretive glance into her eyes, then left. Aileen's bosom heaved. It was hard to breathe sometimes in this warm air.

While he was dancing first with Mrs. Cowperwood and later with Mrs. Seneca Davis, and still later with Mrs. Martyn Walker, Cowperwood had occasion to look at Aileen often, and each time that he did so there swept over him a sense of great vigor there, of beautiful if raw, dynamic energy that to him was irresistible and especially so to-night. She was so young. She was beautiful, this girl, and in spite of his wife's repeated derogatory comments he felt that she was nearer to his clear, aggressive, unblinking attitude than any one whom he had yet seen in the form of woman. She was unsophisticated, in a way, that was plain, and yet in another way it would take so little to make her understand so much. Largeness was the sense he had of her—not physically, though she was nearly as tall as himself—but emotionally. She seemed so intensely alive. She passed close to him a number of times, her eyes wide and smiling, her lips parted, her teeth agleam, and he felt a stirring of sympathy and companionship for her which he had not previously experienced. She was lovely, all of her—delightful.

"I'm wondering if that dance is open now," he said to her as he drew near toward the beginning of the third set. She was seated with her latest admirer in a far corner of the general living-room, a clear floor now waxed to perfection. A few palms here and there made embrasured parapets of green. "I hope you'll excuse me," he added, deferentially, to her companion.

"Surely," the latter replied, rising.

"Yes, indeed," she replied. "And you'd better stay here with me. It's going to begin soon. You won't mind?" she added, giving her companion a radiant smile.

"Not at all. I've had a lovely waltz." He strolled off.

Cowperwood sat down. "That's young Ledoux, isn't it? I thought so. I saw you dancing. You like it, don't you?"

"I'm crazy about it."

"Well, I can't say that myself. It's fascinating, though. Your partner makes such a difference. Mrs. Cowperwood doesn't like it as much as I do."

His mention of Lillian made Aileen think of her in a faintly derogative way for a moment.

"I think you dance very well. I watched you, too." She questioned afterwards whether she should have said this. It sounded most forward now—almost brazen.

"Oh, did you?"

"Yes."

He was a little keyed up because of her—slightly cloudy in his thoughts—because she was generating a problem in his life, or would if he let her, and so his talk was a little tame. He was thinking of something to say—some words which would bring them a little nearer together. But for the moment he could not. Truth to tell, he wanted to say a great deal.

"Well, that was nice of you," he added, after a moment. "What made you do it?"

He turned with a mock air of inquiry. The music was beginning again. The dancers were rising. He arose.

He had not intended to give this particular remark a serious turn; but, now that she was so near him, he looked into her eyes steadily but with a soft appeal and said, "Yes, why?"

They had come out from behind the palms. He had put his hand to her waist. His right arm held her left extended arm to arm, palm to palm. Her right hand was on his shoulder, and she was close to him, looking into his eyes. As they began the gay undulations of the waltz she looked away and then down without answering. Her movements were as light and airy as those of a butterfly. He felt a sudden lightness himself, communicated as by an invisible current. He wanted to match the suppleness of her body with his own, and did. Her arms, the flash and glint of the crimson sequins against the smooth, black silk of her closely fitting dress, her neck, her glowing, radiant hair, all combined to provoke a slight intellectual intoxication. She was so vigorously young, so, to him, truly beautiful.

"But you didn't answer," he continued.

"Isn't this lovely music?"

He pressed her fingers.

She lifted shy eyes to him now, for, in spite of her gay, aggressive force, she was afraid of him. His personality was obviously so dominating. Now that he was so close to her, dancing, she conceived of him as something quite wonderful, and yet she experienced a nervous reaction—a momentary desire to run away.

"Very well, if you won't tell me," he smiled, mockingly.

He thought she wanted him to talk to her so, to tease her with suggestions of this concealed feeling of his—this strong liking. He wondered what could come of any such understanding as this, anyhow?

"Oh, I just wanted to see how you danced," she said, tamely, the force of her original feeling having been weakened by a thought of what she was doing. He noted the change and smiled. It was lovely to be dancing with her. He had not thought mere dancing could hold such charm.

"You like me?" he said, suddenly, as the music drew to its close.

She thrilled from head to toe at the question. A piece of ice dropped down her back could not have startled her more. It was apparently tactless, and yet it was anything but tactless. She looked up quickly, directly, but his strong eyes were too much for her.

"Why, yes," she answered, as the music stopped, trying to keep an even tone to her voice. She was glad they were walking toward a chair.

"I like you so much," he said, "that I have been wondering if you really like me." There was an appeal in his voice, soft and gentle. His manner was almost sad.

"Why, yes," she replied, instantly, returning to her earlier mood toward him. "You know I do."

"I need some one like you to like me," he continued, in the same vein. "I need some one like you to talk to. I didn't think so before—but now I do. You are beautiful—wonderful."

"We mustn't," she said. "I mustn't. I don't know what I'm doing." She looked at a young man strolling toward her, and asked: "I have to explain to him. He's the one I had this dance with."

Cowperwood understood. He walked away. He was quite warm and tense now—almost nervous. It was quite clear to him that he had done or was contemplating perhaps a very treacherous thing. Under the current code of society he had no right to do it. It was against the rules, as they were understood by everybody. Her father, for instance—his father—every one in this particular walk of life. However, much breaking of the rules under the surface of things there might be, the rules were still there. As he had heard one young man remark once at school, when some story had been told of a boy leading a girl astray and to a disastrous end, "That isn't the way at all."

Still, now that he had said this, strong thoughts of her were in his mind. And despite his involved social and financial position, which he now recalled, it was interesting to him to see how deliberately and even calculatingly—and worse, enthusiastically—he was pumping the bellows that tended only to heighten the flames of his desire for this girl; to feed a fire that might ultimately consume him—and how deliberately and resourcefully!

Aileen toyed aimlessly with her fan as a black-haired, thin-faced young law student talked to her, and seeing Norah in the distance she asked to be allowed to run over to her.

"Oh, Aileen," called Norah, "I've been looking for you everywhere. Where have you been?"

"Dancing, of course. Where do you suppose I've been? Didn't you see me on the floor?"

"No, I didn't," complained Norah, as though it were most essential that she should. "How late are you going to stay?"

"Until it's over, I suppose. I don't know."

"Owen says he's going at twelve."

"Well, that doesn't matter. Some one will take me home. Are you having a good time?"

"Fine. Oh, let me tell you. I stepped on a lady's dress over there, last dance. She was terribly angry. She gave me such a look."

"Well, never mind, honey. She won't hurt you. Where are you going now?"

Aileen always maintained a most guardian-like attitude toward her sister.

"I want to find Callum. He has to dance with me next time. I know what he's trying to do. He's trying to get away from me. But he won't."

Aileen smiled. Norah looked very sweet. And she was so bright. What would she think of her if she knew? She turned back, and her fourth partner sought her. She began talking gayly, for she felt that she had to make a show of composure; but all the while there was ringing in her ears that definite question of his, "You like me, don't you?" and her later uncertain but not less truthful answer, "Yes, of course I do."

CHAPTER XIX

The growth of a passion is a very peculiar thing. In highly organized intellectual and artistic types it is so often apt to begin with keen appreciation of certain qualities, modified by many, many mental reservations. The egoist, the intellectual, gives but little of himself and asks much. Nevertheless, the lover of life, male or female, finding himself or herself in sympathetic accord with such a nature, is apt to gain much.

Cowperwood was innately and primarily an egoist and intellectual, though blended strongly therewith, was a humane and democratic spirit. We think of egoism and intellectualism as closely confined to the arts. Finance is an art. And it presents the operations of the subtlest of the intellectuals and of the egoists. Cowperwood was a financier. Instead of dwelling on the works of nature, its beauty and subtlety, to his material disadvantage, he found a happy mean, owing to the swiftness of his intellectual operations, whereby he could, intellectually and emotionally, rejoice in the beauty of life without interfering with his perpetual material and financial calculations. And when it came to women and morals, which involved so much relating to beauty, happiness, a sense of distinction and variety in living, he was but now beginning to suspect for himself at least that apart from maintaining organized society in its present form there was no basis for this one-life, one-love idea. How had it come about that so many people agreed on this single point, that it was good and necessary to marry one woman and cleave to her until death? He did not know. It was not for him to bother about the subtleties of evolution, which even then was being noised abroad, or to ferret out the curiosities of history in connection with this matter. He had no time. Suffice it that the vagaries of temperament and conditions with which he came into immediate contact proved to him that there was great dissatisfaction with that idea. People did not cleave to each other until death; and in thousands of cases where they did, they did not want to. Quickness of mind, subtlety of idea, fortuitousness of opportunity, made it possible for some people to right their matrimonial and social infelicities; whereas for others, because of dullness of wit, thickness of comprehension, poverty, and lack of charm, there was no escape from the slough of their despond. They were compelled by some devilish accident of birth or lack of force or resourcefulness to stew in their own juice of wretchedness, or to shuffle off this mortal coil—which under other circumstances had such glittering possibilities—via the rope, the knife, the bullet, or the cup of poison.

"I would die, too," he thought to himself, one day, reading of a man who, confined by disease and poverty, had lived for twelve years alone in a back bedroom attended by an old and probably decrepit housekeeper. A darning-needle forced into his heart had ended his earthly woes. "To the devil with such a life! Why twelve years? Why not at the end of the second or third?"

Again, it was so very evident, in so many ways, that force was the answer—great mental and physical force. Why, these giants of commerce and money could do as they pleased in this life, and did. He had already had ample local evidence of it in more than one direction. Worse—the little guardians of so-called law and morality, the newspapers, the preachers, the police, and the public moralists generally, so loud in their denunciation of evil in humble places, were cowards all when it came to corruption in high ones. They did not dare to utter a feeble squeak until some giant had accidentally fallen and they could do so without danger to themselves. Then, O Heavens, the palaver! What beatings of tom-toms! What mouthings of pharisaical moralities—platitudes! Run now, good people, for you may see clearly how evil is dealt with in high places! It made him smile. Such hypocrisy! Such cant! Still, so the world was organized, and it was not for him to set it right. Let it wag as it would. The thing for him to do was to get rich and hold his own—to build up a seeming of virtue and dignity which would pass muster for the genuine thing. Force would do that. Quickness of wit. And he had these. "I satisfy myself," was his motto; and it might well have been emblazoned upon any coat of arms which he could have contrived to set forth his claim to intellectual and social nobility.

But this matter of Aileen was up for consideration and solution at this present moment, and because of his forceful, determined character he was presently not at all disturbed by the problem it presented. It was a problem, like some of those knotty financial complications which presented themselves daily; but it was not insoluble. What did he want to do? He couldn't leave his wife and fly with Aileen, that was certain. He had too many connections. He had too many social, and thinking of his children and parents, emotional as well as financial ties to bind him. Besides, he was not at all sure that he wanted to. He did not intend to leave his growing interests, and at the same time he did not intend to give up Aileen immediately. The unheralded manifestation of interest on her part was too attractive. Mrs. Cowperwood was no longer what she should be physically and mentally, and that in itself to him was sufficient to justify his present interest in this girl. Why fear anything, if only he could figure out a way to achieve it without harm to himself? At the same time he thought it might never be possible for him to figure out any practical or protective program for either himself or Aileen, and that made him silent and reflective. For by now he was intensely drawn to her, as he could feel—something chemic and hence dynamic was uppermost in him now and clamoring for expression.

At the same time, in contemplating his wife in connection with all this, he had many qualms, some emotional, some financial. While she had yielded to his youthful enthusiasm for her after her husband's death, he had only since learned that she was a natural conservator of public morals—the cold purity of the snowdrift in so far as the world might see, combined at times with the murky mood of the wanton. And yet, as he had also learned, she was ashamed of the passion that at times swept and dominated her. This irritated Cowperwood, as it would always irritate any strong, acquisitive, direct-seeing temperament. While he had no desire to acquaint the whole world with his feelings, why should there be concealment between them, or at least mental evasion of a fact which physically she subscribed to? Why do one thing and think another? To be sure, she was devoted to him in her quiet way, not passionately (as he looked back he could not say that she had ever been that), but intellectually. Duty, as she understood it, played a great part in this. She was dutiful. And then what people thought, what the time-spirit demanded—these were the great things. Aileen, on the contrary, was probably not dutiful, and it was obvious that she had no temperamental connection with current convention. No doubt she had been as well instructed as many another girl, but look at her. She was not obeying her instructions.

In the next three months this relationship took on a more flagrant form. Aileen, knowing full well what her parents would think, how unspeakable in the mind of the current world were the thoughts she was thinking, persisted, nevertheless, in so thinking and longing. Cowperwood, now that she had gone thus far and compromised herself in intention, if not in deed, took on a peculiar charm for her. It was not his body—great passion is never that, exactly. The flavor of his spirit was what attracted and compelled, like the glow of a flame to a moth. There was a light of romance in his eyes, which, however governed and controlled—was directive and almost all-powerful to her.

When he touched her hand at parting, it was as though she had received an electric shock, and she recalled that it was very difficult for her to look directly into his eyes. Something akin to a destructive force seemed to issue from them at times. Other people, men particularly, found it difficult to face Cowperwood's glazed stare. It was as though there were another pair of eyes behind those they saw, watching through thin, obscuring curtains. You could not tell what he was thinking.

And during the next few months she found herself coming closer and closer to Cowperwood. At his home one evening, seated at the piano, no one else being present at the moment, he leaned over and kissed her. There was a cold, snowy street visible through the interstices of the hangings of the windows, and gas-lamps flickering outside. He had come in early, and hearing Aileen, he came to where she was seated at the piano. She was wearing a rough, gray wool cloth dress, ornately banded with fringed Oriental embroidery in blue and burnt-orange, and her beauty was further enhanced by a gray hat planned to match her dress, with a plume of shaded orange and blue. On her fingers were four or five rings, far too many—an opal, an emerald, a ruby, and a diamond—flashing visibly as she played.

She knew it was he, without turning. He came beside her, and she looked up smiling, the reverie evoked by Schubert partly vanishing—or melting into another mood. Suddenly he bent over and pressed his lips firmly to hers. His mustache thrilled her with its silky touch. She stopped playing and tried to catch her breath, for, strong as she was, it affected her breathing. Her heart was beating like a triphammer. She did not say, "Oh," or, "You mustn't," but rose and walked over to a window, where she lifted a curtain, pretending to look out. She felt as though she might faint, so intensely happy was she.

Cowperwood followed her quickly. Slipping his arms about her waist, he looked at her flushed cheeks, her clear, moist eyes and red mouth.

"You love me?" he whispered, stern and compelling because of his desire.

"Yes! Yes! You know I do."

He crushed her face to his, and she put up her hands and stroked his hair.

A thrilling sense of possession, mastery, happiness and understanding, love of her and of her body, suddenly overwhelmed him.

"I love you," he said, as though he were surprised to hear himself say it. "I didn't think I did, but I do. You're beautiful. I'm wild about you."

"And I love you" she answered. "I can't help it. I know I shouldn't, but—oh—" Her hands closed tight over his ears and temples. She put her lips to his and dreamed into his eyes. Then she stepped away quickly, looking out into the street, and he walked back into the living-room. They were quite alone. He was debating whether he should risk anything further when Norah, having been in to see Anna next door, appeared and not long afterward Mrs. Cowperwood. Then Aileen and Norah left.

CHAPTER XX

This definite and final understanding having been reached, it was but natural that this liaison should proceed to a closer and closer relationship. Despite her religious upbringing, Aileen was decidedly a victim of her temperament. Current religious feeling and belief could not control her. For the past nine or ten years there had been slowly forming in her mind a notion of what her lover should be like. He should be strong, handsome, direct, successful, with clear eyes, a ruddy glow of health, and a certain native understanding and sympathy—a love of life which matched her own. Many young men had approached her. Perhaps the nearest realization of her ideal was Father David, of St. Timothy's, and he was, of course, a priest and sworn to celibacy. No word had ever passed between them but he had been as conscious of her as she of him. Then came Frank Cowperwood, and by degrees, because of his presence and contact, he had been slowly built up in her mind as the ideal person. She was drawn as planets are drawn to their sun.

It is a question as to what would have happened if antagonistic forces could have been introduced just at this time. Emotions and liaisons of this character can, of course, occasionally be broken up and destroyed. The characters of the individuals can be modified or changed to a certain extent, but the force must be quite sufficient. Fear is a great deterrent—fear of material loss where there is no spiritual dread—but wealth and position so often tend to destroy this dread. It is so easy to scheme with means. Aileen had no spiritual dread whatever. Cowperwood was without spiritual or religious feeling. He looked at this girl, and his one thought was how could he so deceive the world that he could enjoy her love and leave his present state undisturbed. Love her he did surely.

Business necessitated his calling at the Butlers' quite frequently, and on each occasion he saw Aileen. She managed to slip forward and squeeze his hand the first time he came—to steal a quick, vivid kiss; and another time, as he was going out, she suddenly appeared from behind the curtains hanging at the parlor door.

"Honey!"

The voice was soft and coaxing. He turned, giving her a warning nod in the direction of her father's room upstairs.

She stood there, holding out one hand, and he stepped forward for a second. Instantly her arms were about his neck, as he slipped his about her waist.

"I long to see you so."

"I, too. I'll fix some way. I'm thinking."

He released her arms, and went out, and she ran to the window and looked out after him. He was walking west on the street, for his house was only a few blocks away, and she looked at the breadth of his shoulders, the balance of his form. He stepped so briskly, so incisively. Ah, this was a man! He was her Frank. She thought of him in that light already. Then she sat down at the piano and played pensively until dinner.

And it was so easy for the resourceful mind of Frank Cowperwood, wealthy as he was, to suggest ways and means. In his younger gallivantings about places of ill repute, and his subsequent occasional variations from the straight and narrow path, he had learned much of the curious resources of immorality. Being a city of five hundred thousand and more at this time, Philadelphia had its nondescript hotels, where one might go, cautiously and fairly protected from observation; and there were houses of a conservative, residential character, where appointments might be made, for a consideration. And as for safeguards against the production of new life—they were not mysteries to him any longer. He knew all about them. Care was the point of caution. He had to be cautious, for he was so rapidly coming to be an influential and a distinguished man. Aileen, of course, was not conscious, except in a vague way, of the drift of her passion; the ultimate destiny to which this affection might lead was not clear to her. Her craving was for love—to be fondled and caressed—and she really did not think so much further. Further thoughts along this line were like rats that showed their heads out of dark holes in shadowy corners and scuttled back at the least sound. And, anyhow, all that was to be connected with Cowperwood would be beautiful. She really did not think that he loved her yet as he should; but he would. She did not know that she wanted to interfere with the claims of his wife. She did not think she did. But it would not hurt Mrs. Cowperwood if Frank loved her—Aileen—also.

How shall we explain these subtleties of temperament and desire? Life has to deal with them at every turn. They will not down, and the large, placid movements of nature outside of man's little organisms would indicate that she is not greatly concerned. We see much punishment in the form of jails, diseases, failures, and wrecks; but we also see that the old tendency is not visibly lessened. Is there no law outside of the subtle will and power of the individual to achieve? If not, it is surely high time that we knew it—one and all. We might then agree to do as we do; but there would be no silly illusion as to divine regulation. Vox populi, vox Dei.

So there were other meetings, lovely hours which they soon began to spend the moment her passion waxed warm enough to assure compliance, without great fear and without thought of the deadly risk involved. From odd moments in his own home, stolen when there was no one about to see, they advanced to clandestine meetings beyond the confines of the city. Cowperwood was not one who was temperamentally inclined to lose his head and neglect his business. As a matter of fact, the more he thought of this rather unexpected affectional development, the more certain he was that he must not let it interfere with his business time and judgment. His office required his full attention from nine until three, anyhow. He could give it until five-thirty with profit; but he could take several afternoons off, from three-thirty until five-thirty or six, and no one would be the wiser. It was customary for Aileen to drive alone almost every afternoon a spirited pair of bays, or to ride a mount, bought by her father for her from a noted horse-dealer in Baltimore. Since Cowperwood also drove and rode, it was not difficult to arrange meeting-places far out on the Wissahickon or the Schuylkill road. There were many spots in the newly laid-out park, which were as free from interruption as the depths of a forest. It was always possible that they might encounter some one; but it was also always possible to make a rather plausible explanation, or none at all, since even in case of such an encounter nothing, ordinarily, would be suspected.

So, for the time being there was love-making, the usual billing and cooing of lovers in a simple and much less than final fashion; and the lovely horseback rides together under the green trees of the approaching spring were idyllic. Cowperwood awakened to a sense of joy in life such as he fancied, in the blush of this new desire, he had never experienced before. Lillian had been lovely in those early days in which he had first called on her in North Front Street, and he had fancied himself unspeakably happy at that time; but that was nearly ten years since, and he had forgotten. Since then he had had no great passion, no notable liaison; and then, all at once, in the midst of his new, great business prosperity, Aileen. Her young body and soul, her passionate illusions. He could see always, for all her daring, that she knew so little of the calculating, brutal world with which he was connected. Her father had given her all the toys she wanted without stint; her mother and brothers had coddled her, particularly her mother. Her young sister thought she was adorable. No one imagined for one moment that Aileen would ever do anything wrong. She was too sensible, after all, too eager to get up in the world. Why should she, when her life lay open and happy before her—a delightful love-match, some day soon, with some very eligible and satisfactory lover? "When you marry, Aileen," her mother used to say to her, "we'll have a grand time here. Sure we'll do the house over then, if we don't do it before. Eddie will have to fix it up, or I'll do it meself. Never fear."

"Yes—well, I'd rather you'd fix it now," was her reply.

Butler himself used to strike her jovially on the shoulder in a rough, loving way, and ask, "Well, have you found him yet?" or "Is he hanging around the outside watchin' for ye?"

If she said, "No," he would reply: "Well, he will be, never fear—worse luck. I'll hate to see ye go, girlie! You can stay here as long as ye want to, and ye want to remember that you can always come back."

Aileen paid very little attention to this bantering. She loved her father, but it was all such a matter of course. It was the commonplace of her existence, and not so very significant, though delightful enough.

But how eagerly she yielded herself to Cowperwood under the spring trees these days! She had no sense of that ultimate yielding that was coming, for now he merely caressed and talked to her. He was a little doubtful about himself. His growing liberties for himself seemed natural enough, but in a sense of fairness to her he began to talk to her about what their love might involve. Would she? Did she understand? This phase of it puzzled and frightened Aileen a little at first. She stood before him one afternoon in her black riding-habit and high silk riding-hat perched jauntily on her red-gold hair; and striking her riding-skirt with her short whip, pondering doubtfully as she listened. He had asked her whether she knew what she was doing? Whither they were drifting? If she loved him truly enough? The two horses were tethered in a thicket a score of yards away from the main road and from the bank of a tumbling stream, which they had approached. She was trying to discover if she could see them. It was pretense. There was no interest in her glance. She was thinking of him and the smartness of his habit, and the exquisiteness of this moment. He had such a charming calico pony. The leaves were just enough developed to make a diaphanous lacework of green. It was like looking through a green-spangled arras to peer into the woods beyond or behind. The gray stones were already faintly messy where the water rippled and sparkled, and early birds were calling—robins and blackbirds and wrens.

"Baby mine," he said, "do you understand all about this? Do you know exactly what you're doing when you come with me this way?"

"I think I do."

She struck her boot and looked at the ground, and then up through the trees at the blue sky.

"Look at me, honey."

"I don't want to."

"But look at me, sweet. I want to ask you something."

"Don't make me, Frank, please. I can't."

"Oh yes, you can look at me."

"No."

She backed away as he took her hands, but came forward again, easily enough.

"Now look in my eyes."

"I can't."

"See here."

"I can't. Don't ask me. I'll answer you, but don't make me look at you."

His hand stole to her cheek and fondled it. He petted her shoulder, and she leaned her head against him.

"Sweet, you're so beautiful," he said finally, "I can't give you up. I know what I ought to do. You know, too, I suppose; but I can't. I must have you. If this should end in exposure, it would be quite bad for you and me. Do you understand?"

"Yes."

"I don't know your brothers very well; but from looking at them I judge they're pretty determined people. They think a great deal of you."

"Indeed, they do." Her vanity prinked slightly at this.

"They would probably want to kill me, and very promptly, for just this much. What do you think they would want to do if—well, if anything should happen, some time?"

He waited, watching her pretty face.

"But nothing need happen. We needn't go any further."

"Aileen!"

"I won't look at you. You needn't ask. I can't."

"Aileen! Do you mean that?"

"I don't know. Don't ask me, Frank."

"You know it can't stop this way, don't you? You know it. This isn't the end. Now, if—"

He explained the whole theory of illicit meetings, calmly, dispassionately. "You are perfectly safe, except for one thing, chance exposure. It might just so happen; and then, of course, there would be a great deal to settle for. Mrs. Cowperwood would never give me a divorce; she has no reason to. If I should clean up in the way I hope to—if I should make a million—I wouldn't mind knocking off now. I don't expect to work all my days. I have always planned to knock off at thirty-five. I'll have enough by that time. Then I want to travel. It will only be a few more years now. If you were free—if your father and mother were dead"—curiously she did not wince at this practical reference—"it would be a different matter."

He paused. She still gazed thoughtfully at the water below, her mind running out to a yacht on the sea with him, a palace somewhere—just they two. Her eyes, half closed, saw this happy world; and, listening to him, she was fascinated.

"Hanged if I see the way out of this, exactly. But I love you!" He caught her to him. "I love you—love you!"

"Oh, yes," she replied intensely, "I want you to. I'm not afraid."

"I've taken a house in North Tenth Street," he said finally, as they walked over to the horses and mounted them. "It isn't furnished yet; but it will be soon. I know a woman who will take charge."

"Who is she?"

"An interesting widow of nearly fifty. Very intelligent—she is attractive, and knows a good deal of life. I found her through an advertisement. You might call on her some afternoon when things are arranged, and look the place over. You needn't meet her except in a casual way. Will you?"

She rode on, thinking, making no reply. He was so direct and practical in his calculations.

"Will you? It will be all right. You might know her. She isn't objectionable in any way. Will you?"

"Let me know when it is ready," was all she said finally.

CHAPTER XXI

The vagaries of passion! Subtleties! Risks! What sacrifices are not laid willfully upon its altar! In a little while this more than average residence to which Cowperwood had referred was prepared solely to effect a satisfactory method of concealment. The house was governed by a seemingly recently-bereaved widow, and it was possible for Aileen to call without seeming strangely out of place. In such surroundings, and under such circumstances, it was not difficult to persuade her to give herself wholly to her lover, governed as she was by her wild and unreasoning affection and passion. In a way, there was a saving element of love, for truly, above all others, she wanted this man. She had no thought or feeling toward any other. All her mind ran toward visions of the future, when, somehow, she and he might be together for all time. Mrs. Cowperwood might die, or he might run away with her at thirty-five when he had a million. Some adjustment would be made, somehow. Nature had given her this man. She relied on him implicitly. When he told her that he would take care of her so that nothing evil should befall, she believed him fully. Such sins are the commonplaces of the confessional.

It is a curious fact that by some subtlety of logic in the Christian world, it has come to be believed that there can be no love outside the conventional process of courtship and marriage. One life, one love, is the Christian idea, and into this sluice or mold it has been endeavoring to compress the whole world. Pagan thought held no such belief. A writing of divorce for trivial causes was the theory of the elders; and in the primeval world nature apparently holds no scheme for the unity of two beyond the temporary care of the young. That the modern home is the most beautiful of schemes, when based upon mutual sympathy and understanding between two, need not be questioned. And yet this fact should not necessarily carry with it a condemnation of all love not so fortunate as to find so happy a denouement. Life cannot be put into any mold, and the attempt might as well be abandoned at once. Those so fortunate as to find harmonious companionship for life should congratulate themselves and strive to be worthy of it. Those not so blessed, though they be written down as pariahs, have yet some justification. And, besides, whether we will or not, theory or no theory, the basic facts of chemistry and physics remain. Like is drawn to like. Changes in temperament bring changes in relationship. Dogma may bind some minds; fear, others. But there are always those in whom the chemistry and physics of life are large, and in whom neither dogma nor fear is operative. Society lifts its hands in horror; but from age to age the Helens, the Messalinas, the Du Barrys, the Pompadours, the Maintenons, and the Nell Gwyns flourish and point a freer basis of relationship than we have yet been able to square with our lives.

These two felt unutterably bound to each other. Cowperwood, once he came to understand her, fancied that he had found the one person with whom he could live happily the rest of his life. She was so young, so confident, so hopeful, so undismayed. All these months since they had first begun to reach out to each other he had been hourly contrasting her with his wife. As a matter of fact, his dissatisfaction, though it may be said to have been faint up to this time, was now surely tending to become real enough. Still, his children were pleasing to him; his home beautiful. Lillian, phlegmatic and now thin, was still not homely. All these years he had found her satisfactory enough; but now his dissatisfaction with her began to increase. She was not like Aileen—not young, not vivid, not as unschooled in the commonplaces of life. And while ordinarily, he was not one who was inclined to be querulous, still now on occasion, he could be. He began by asking questions concerning his wife's appearance—irritating little whys which are so trivial and yet so exasperating and discouraging to a woman. Why didn't she get a mauve hat nearer the shade of her dress? Why didn't she go out more? Exercise would do her good. Why didn't she do this, and why didn't she do that? He scarcely noticed that he was doing this; but she did, and she felt the undertone—the real significance—and took umbrage.

"Oh, why—why?" she retorted, one day, curtly. "Why do you ask so many questions? You don't care so much for me any more; that's why. I can tell."

He leaned back startled by the thrust. It had not been based on any evidence of anything save his recent remarks; but he was not absolutely sure. He was just the least bit sorry that he had irritated her, and he said so.

"Oh, it's all right," she replied. "I don't care. But I notice that you don't pay as much attention to me as you used to. It's your business now, first, last, and all the time. You can't get your mind off of that."

He breathed a sigh of relief. She didn't suspect, then.

But after a little time, as he grew more and more in sympathy with Aileen, he was not so disturbed as to whether his wife might suspect or not. He began to think on occasion, as his mind followed the various ramifications of the situation, that it would be better if she did. She was really not of the contentious fighting sort. He now decided because of various calculations in regard to her character that she might not offer as much resistance to some ultimate rearrangement, as he had originally imagined. She might even divorce him. Desire, dreams, even in him were evoking calculations not as sound as those which ordinarily generated in his brain.

No, as he now said to himself, the rub was not nearly so much in his own home, as it was in the Butler family. His relations with Edward Malia Butler had become very intimate. He was now advising with him constantly in regard to the handling of his securities, which were numerous. Butler held stocks in such things as the Pennsylvania Coal Company, the Delaware and Hudson Canal, the Morris and Essex Canal, the Reading Railroad. As the old gentleman's mind had broadened to the significance of the local street-railway problem in Philadelphia, he had decided to close out his other securities at such advantageous terms as he could, and reinvest the money in local lines. He knew that Mollenhauer and Simpson were doing this, and they were excellent judges of the significance of local affairs. Like Cowperwood, he had the idea that if he controlled sufficient of the local situation in this field, he could at last effect a joint relationship with Mollenhauer and Simpson. Political legislation, advantageous to the combined lines, could then be so easily secured. Franchises and necessary extensions to existing franchises could be added. This conversion of his outstanding stock in other fields, and the picking up of odd lots in the local street-railway, was the business of Cowperwood. Butler, through his sons, Owen and Callum, was also busy planning a new line and obtaining a franchise, sacrificing, of course, great blocks of stock and actual cash to others, in order to obtain sufficient influence to have the necessary legislation passed. Yet it was no easy matter, seeing that others knew what the general advantages of the situation were, and because of this Cowperwood, who saw the great source of profit here, was able, betimes, to serve himself—buying blocks, a part of which only went to Butler, Mollenhauer or others. In short he was not as eager to serve Butler, or any one else, as he was to serve himself if he could.

In this connection, the scheme which George W. Stener had brought forward, representing actually in the background Strobik, Wycroft, and Harmon, was an opening wedge for himself. Stener's plan was to loan him money out of the city treasury at two per cent., or, if he would waive all commissions, for nothing (an agent for self-protective purposes was absolutely necessary), and with it take over the North Pennsylvania Company's line on Front Street, which, because of the shortness of its length, one mile and a half, and the brevity of the duration of its franchise, was neither doing very well nor being rated very high. Cowperwood in return for his manipulative skill was to have a fair proportion of the stock—twenty per cent. Strobik and Wycroft knew the parties from whom the bulk of the stock could be secured if engineered properly. Their plan was then, with this borrowed treasury money, to extend its franchise and then the line itself, and then later again, by issuing a great block of stock and hypothecating it with a favored bank, be able to return the principal to the city treasury and pocket their profits from the line as earned. There was no trouble in this, in so far as Cowperwood was concerned, except that it divided the stock very badly among these various individuals, and left him but a comparatively small share— for his thought and pains.

But Cowperwood was an opportunist. And by this time his financial morality had become special and local in its character. He did not think it was wise for any one to steal anything from anybody where the act of taking or profiting was directly and plainly considered stealing. That was unwise—dangerous—hence wrong. There were so many situations wherein what one might do in the way of taking or profiting was open to discussion and doubt. Morality varied, in his mind at least, with conditions, if not climates. Here, in Philadelphia, the tradition (politically, mind you—not generally) was that the city treasurer might use the money of the city without interest so long as he returned the principal intact. The city treasury and the city treasurer were like a honey-laden hive and a queen bee around which the drones—the politicians—swarmed in the hope of profit. The one disagreeable thing in connection with this transaction with Stener was that neither Butler, Mollenhauer nor Simpson, who were the actual superiors of Stener and Strobik, knew anything about it. Stener and those behind him were, through him, acting for themselves. If the larger powers heard of this, it might alienate them. He had to think of this. Still, if he refused to make advantageous deals with Stener or any other man influential in local affairs, he was cutting off his nose to spite his face, for other bankers and brokers would, and gladly. And besides it was not at all certain that Butler, Mollenhauer, and Simpson would ever hear.

In this connection, there was another line, which he rode on occasionally, the Seventeenth and Nineteenth Street line, which he felt was a much more interesting thing for him to think about, if he could raise the money. It had been originally capitalized for five hundred thousand dollars; but there had been a series of bonds to the value of two hundred and fifty thousand dollars added for improvements, and the company was finding great difficulty in meeting the interest. The bulk of the stock was scattered about among small investors, and it would require all of two hundred and fifty thousand dollars to collect it and have himself elected president or chairman of the board of directors. Once in, however, he could vote this stock as he pleased, hypothecating it meanwhile at his father's bank for as much as he could get, and issuing more stocks with which to bribe legislators in the matter of extending the line, and in taking up other opportunities to either add to it by purchase or supplement it by working agreements. The word "bribe" is used here in this matter-of-fact American way, because bribery was what was in every one's mind in connection with the State legislature. Terrence Relihan—the small, dark-faced Irishman, a dandy in dress and manners—who represented the financial interests at Harrisburg, and who had come to Cowperwood after the five million bond deal had been printed, had told him that nothing could be done at the capital without money, or its equivalent, negotiable securities. Each significant legislator, if he yielded his vote or his influence, must be looked after. If he, Cowperwood, had any scheme which he wanted handled at any time, Relihan had intimated to him that he would be glad to talk with him. Cowperwood had figured on this Seventeenth and Nineteenth Street line scheme more than once, but he had never felt quite sure that he was willing to undertake it. His obligations in other directions were so large. But the lure was there, and he pondered and pondered.

Stener's scheme of loaning him money wherewith to manipulate the North Pennsylvania line deal put this Seventeenth and Nineteenth Street dream in a more favorable light. As it was he was constantly watching the certificates of loan issue, for the city treasury,—buying large quantities when the market was falling to protect it and selling heavily, though cautiously, when he saw it rising and to do this he had to have a great deal of free money to permit him to do it. He was constantly fearful of some break in the market which would affect the value of all his securities and result in the calling of his loans. There was no storm in sight. He did not see that anything could happen in reason; but he did not want to spread himself out too thin. As he saw it now, therefore if he took one hundred and fifty thousand dollars of this city money and went after this Seventeenth and Nineteenth Street matter it would not mean that he was spreading himself out too thin, for because of this new proposition could he not call on Stener for more as a loan in connection with these other ventures? But if anything should happen—well—

"Frank," said Stener, strolling into his office one afternoon after four o'clock when the main rush of the day's work was over—the relationship between Cowperwood and Stener had long since reached the "Frank" and "George" period—"Strobik thinks he has that North Pennsylvania deal arranged so that we can take it up if we want to. The principal stockholder, we find, is a man by the name of Coltan—not Ike Colton, but Ferdinand. How's that for a name?" Stener beamed fatly and genially.

Things had changed considerably for him since the days when he had been fortuitously and almost indifferently made city treasurer. His method of dressing had so much improved since he had been inducted into office, and his manner expressed so much more good feeling, confidence, aplomb, that he would not have recognized himself if he had been permitted to see himself as had those who had known him before. An old, nervous shifting of the eyes had almost ceased, and a feeling of restfulness, which had previously been restlessness, and had sprung from a sense of necessity, had taken its place. His large feet were incased in good, square-toed, soft-leather shoes; his stocky chest and fat legs were made somewhat agreeable to the eye by a well-cut suit of brownish-gray cloth; and his neck was now surrounded by a low, wing-point white collar and brown-silk tie. His ample chest, which spread out a little lower in around and constantly enlarging stomach, was ornamented by a heavy-link gold chain, and his white cuffs had large gold cuff-buttons set with rubies of a very notable size. He was rosy and decidedly well fed. In fact, he was doing very well indeed.

He had moved his family from a shabby two-story frame house in South Ninth Street to a very comfortable brick one three stories in height, and three times as large, on Spring Garden Street. His wife had a few acquaintances—the wives of other politicians. His children were attending the high school, a thing he had hardly hoped for in earlier days. He was now the owner of fourteen or fifteen pieces of cheap real estate in different portions of the city, which might eventually become very valuable, and he was a silent partner in the South Philadelphia Foundry Company and the American Beef and Pork Company, two corporations on paper whose principal business was subletting contracts secured from the city to the humble butchers and foundrymen who would carry out orders as given and not talk too much or ask questions.

"Well, that is an odd name," said Cowperwood, blandly. "So he has it? I never thought that road would pay, as it was laid out. It's too short. It ought to run about three miles farther out into the Kensington section."

"You're right," said Stener, dully.

"Did Strobik say what Colton wants for his shares?"

"Sixty-eight, I think."

"The current market rate. He doesn't want much, does he? Well, George, at that rate it will take about"—he calculated quickly on the basis of the number of shares Cotton was holding—"one hundred and twenty thousand to get him out alone. That isn't all. There's Judge Kitchen and Joseph Zimmerman and Senator Donovan"—he was referring to the State senator of that name. "You'll be paying a pretty fair price for that stud when you get it. It will cost considerable more to extend the line. It's too much, I think."

Cowperwood was thinking how easy it would be to combine this line with his dreamed-of Seventeenth and Nineteenth Street line, and after a time and with this in view he added:

"Say, George, why do you work all your schemes through Strobik and Harmon and Wycroft? Couldn't you and I manage some of these things for ourselves alone instead of for three or four? It seems to me that plan would be much more profitable to you."

80

"It would, it would!" exclaimed Stener, his round eyes fixed on Cowperwood in a rather helpless, appealing way. He liked Cowperwood and had always been hoping that mentally as well as financially he could get close to him. "I've thought of that. But these fellows have had more experience in these matters than I have had, Frank. They've been longer at the game. I don't know as much about these things as they do."

Cowperwood smiled in his soul, though his face remained passive.

"Don't worry about them, George," he continued genially and confidentially. "You and I together can know and do as much as they ever could and more. I'm telling you. Take this railroad deal you're in on now, George; you and I could manipulate that just as well and better than it can be done with Wycroft, Strobik, and Harmon in on it. They're not adding anything to the wisdom of the situation. They're not putting up any money. You're doing that. All they're doing is agreeing to see it through the legislature and the council, and as far as the legislature is concerned, they can't do any more with that than any one else could—than I could, for instance. It's all a question of arranging things with Relihan, anyhow, putting up a certain amount of money for him to work with. Here in town there are other people who can reach the council just as well as Strobik." He was thinking (once he controlled a road of his own) of conferring with Butler and getting him to use his influence. It would serve to quiet Strobik and his friends. "I'm not asking you to change your plans on this North Pennsylvania deal. You couldn't do that very well. But there are other things. In the future why not let's see if you and I can't work some one thing together? You'll be much better off, and so will I. We've done pretty well on the city-loan proposition so far, haven't we?"

The truth was, they had done exceedingly well. Aside from what the higher powers had made, Stener's new house, his lots, his bank-account, his good clothes, and his changed and comfortable sense of life were largely due to Cowperwood's successful manipulation of these city-loan certificates. Already there had been four issues of two hundred thousand dollars each. Cowperwood had bought and sold nearly three million dollars' worth of these certificates, acting one time as a "bull" and another as a "bear." Stener was now worth all of one hundred and fifty thousand dollars.

"There's a line that I know of here in the city which could be made into a splendidly paying property," continued Cowperwood, meditatively, "if the right things could be done with it. Just like this North Pennsylvania line, it isn't long enough. The territory it serves isn't big enough. It ought to be extended; but if you and I could get it, it might eventually be worked with this North Pennsylvania Company or some other as one company. That would save officers and offices and a lot of things. There is always money to be made out of a larger purchasing power."

He paused and looked out the window of his handsome little hardwood office, speculating upon the future. The window gave nowhere save into a back yard behind another office building which had formerly been a residence. Some grass grew feebly there. The red wall and old-fashioned brick fence which divided it from the next lot reminded him somehow of his old home in New Market Street, to which his Uncle Seneca used to come as a Cuban trader followed by his black Portuguese servitor. He could see him now as he sat here looking at the yard.

"Well," asked Stener, ambitiously, taking the bait, "why don't we get hold of that—you and me? I suppose I could fix it so far as the money is concerned. How much would it take?"

Cowperwood smiled inwardly again.

"I don't know exactly," he said, after a time. "I want to look into it more carefully. The one trouble is that I'm carrying a good deal of the city's money as it is. You see, I have that two hundred thousand dollars against your city-loan deals. And this new scheme will take two or three hundred thousand more. If that were out of the way—"

He was thinking of one of the inexplicable stock panics—those strange American depressions which had so much to do with the temperament of the people, and so little to do with the basic conditions of the country. "If this North Pennsylvania deal were through and done with—"

He rubbed his chin and pulled at his handsome silky mustache.

"Don't ask me any more about it, George," he said, finally, as he saw that the latter was beginning to think as to which line it might be. "Don't say anything at all about it. I want to get my facts exactly right, and then I'll talk to you. I think you and I can do this thing a little later, when we get the North Pennsylvania scheme under way. I'm so rushed just now I'm not sure that I want to undertake it at once; but you keep quiet and we'll see." He turned toward his desk, and Stener got up.

"I'll make any sized deposit with you that you wish, the moment you think you're ready to act, Frank," exclaimed Stener, and with the thought that Cowperwood was not nearly as anxious to do this as he should be, since he could always rely on him (Stener) when there was anything really profitable in the offing. Why should not the able and wonderful Cowperwood be allowed to make the two of them rich? "Just notify Stires, and he'll send you a check. Strobik thought we ought to act pretty soon."

"I'll tend to it, George," replied Cowperwood, confidently. "It will come out all right. Leave it to me."

Stener kicked his stout legs to straighten his trousers, and extended his hand. He strolled out in the street thinking of this new scheme. Certainly, if he could get in with Cowperwood right he would be a rich man, for Cowperwood was so successful and so cautious. His new house, this beautiful banking office, his growing fame, and his subtle connections with Butler and others put Stener in considerable awe of him. Another line! They would control it and the North Pennsylvania! Why, if this went on, he might become a magnate—he really might—he, George W. Stener, once a cheap real-estate and insurance agent. He strolled up the street thinking, but with no more idea of the importance of his civic duties and the nature of the social ethics against which he was offending than if they had never existed.

CHAPTER XXII

The services which Cowperwood performed during the ensuing year and a half for Stener, Strobik, Butler, State Treasurer Van Nostrand, State Senator Relihan, representative of "the interests," so-called, at Harrisburg, and various banks which were friendly to these gentlemen, were numerous and confidential. For Stener, Strobik, Wycroft, Harmon and himself he executed the North Pennsylvania deal, by which he became a holder of a fifth of the controlling stock. Together he and Stener joined to purchase the Seventeenth and Nineteenth Street line and in the concurrent gambling in stocks.

By the summer of 1871, when Cowperwood was nearly thirty-four years of age, he had a banking business estimated at nearly two million dollars, personal holdings aggregating nearly half a million, and prospects which other things being equal looked to wealth which might rival that of any American. The city, through its treasurer—still Mr. Stener—was a depositor with him to the extent of nearly five hundred thousand dollars. The State, through its State treasurer, Van Nostrand, carried two hundred thousand dollars on his books. Bode was speculating in street-railway stocks to the extent of fifty thousand dollars. Relihan to the same amount. A small army of politicians and political hangers-on were on his books for various sums. And for Edward Malia Butler he occasionally carried as high as one hundred thousand dollars in margins. His own loans at the banks, varying from day to day on variously hypothecated securities, were as high as seven and eight hundred thousand dollars. Like a spider in a spangled net, every thread of which he knew, had laid, had tested, he had surrounded and entangled himself in a splendid, glittering network of connections, and he was watching all the details.

His one pet idea, the thing he put more faith in than anything else, was his street-railway manipulations, and particularly his actual control of the Seventeenth and Nineteenth Street line. Through an advance to him, on deposit, made in his bank by Stener at a time when the stock of the Seventeenth and Nineteenth Street line was at a low ebb, he had managed to pick up fifty-one per cent. of the stock for himself and Stener, by virtue of which he was able to do as he pleased with the road. To accomplish this, however, he had resorted to some very "peculiar" methods, as they afterward came to be termed in financial circles, to get this stock at his own valuation. Through agents he caused suits for damages to be brought against the company for non-payment of interest due. A little stock in the hands of a hireling, a request made to a court of record to examine the books of the company in order to determine whether a receivership were not advisable, a simultaneous attack in the stock market, selling at three, five, seven, and ten points off, brought the frightened stockholders into the market with their holdings. The banks considered the line a poor risk, and called their loans in connection with it. His father's bank had made one loan to one of the principal stockholders, and that was promptly called, of course. Then, through an agent, the several heaviest shareholders were approached and an offer was made to help them out. The stocks would be taken off their hands at forty. They had not really been able to discover the source of all their woes; and they imagined that the road was in bad condition, which it was not. Better let it go. The money was immediately forthcoming, and Cowperwood and Stener jointly controlled fifty-one per cent. But, as in the case of the North Pennsylvania line, Cowperwood had been quietly buying all of the small minority holdings, so that he had in reality fifty-one per cent. of the stock, and Stener twenty-five per cent. more.

This intoxicated him, for immediately he saw the opportunity of fulfilling his long-contemplated dream—that of reorganizing the company in conjunction with the North Pennsylvania line, issuing three shares where one had been before and after unloading all but a control on the general public, using the money secured to buy into other lines which were to be boomed and sold in the same way. In short, he was one of those early, daring manipulators who later were to seize upon other and ever larger phases of American natural development for their own aggrandizement.

In connection with this first consolidation, his plan was to spread rumors of the coming consolidation of the two lines, to appeal to the legislature for privileges of extension, to get up an arresting prospectus and later annual reports, and to boom the stock on the stock exchange as much as his swelling resources would permit. The trouble is that when you are trying to make a market for a stock—to unload a large issue such as his was (over five hundred thousand dollars' worth)—while retaining five hundred thousand for yourself, it requires large capital to handle it. The owner in these cases is compelled not only to go on the market and do much fictitious buying, thus creating a fictitious demand, but once this fictitious demand has deceived the public and he has been able to unload a considerable quantity of his wares, he is, unless he rids himself of all his stock, compelled to stand behind it. If, for instance, he sold five thousand shares, as was done in this instance, and retained five thousand, he must see that the public price of the outstanding five thousand shares did not fall below a certain point, because the value of his private shares would fall with it. And if, as is almost always the case, the private shares had been hypothecated with banks and trust companies for money wherewith to conduct other enterprises, the falling of their value in the open market merely meant that the banks would call for large margins to protect their loans or call their loans entirely. This meant that his work was a failure, and he might readily fail. He was already conducting one such difficult campaign in connection with this city-loan deal, the price of which varied from day to day, and which he was only too anxious to have vary, for in the main he profited by these changes.

But this second burden, interesting enough as it was, meant that he had to be doubly watchful. Once the stock was sold at a high price, the money borrowed from the city treasurer could be returned; his own holdings created out of foresight, by capitalizing the future, by writing the shrewd prospectuses and reports, would be worth their face value, or little less. He would have money to invest in other lines. He might obtain the financial direction of the whole, in which case he would be worth millions. One shrewd thing he did, which indicated the foresight and subtlety of the man, was to make a separate organization or company of any extension or addition which he made to his line. Thus, if he had two or three miles of track on a street, and he wanted to extend it two or three miles farther on the same street, instead of including this extension in the existing corporation, he would make a second corporation to control the additional two or three miles of right of way. This corporation he would capitalize at so much, and issue stocks and bonds for its construction, equipment, and manipulation. Having done this he would then take the sub-corporation over into the parent concern, issuing more stocks and bonds of the parent company wherewith to do it, and, of course, selling these bonds to the public. Even his brothers who worked for him did not know the various ramifications of his numerous deals, and executed his orders blindly. Sometimes Joseph said to Edward, in a puzzled way, "Well, Frank knows what he is about, I guess."

On the other hand, he was most careful to see that every current obligation was instantly met, and even anticipated, for he wanted to make a great show of regularity. Nothing was so precious as reputation and standing. His forethought, caution, and promptness pleased the bankers. They thought he was one of the sanest, shrewdest men they had ever met.

However, by the spring and summer of 1871, Cowperwood had actually, without being in any conceivable danger from any source, spread himself out very thin. Because of his great success he had grown more liberal—easier—in his financial ventures. By degrees, and largely because of his own confidence in himself, he had induced his father to enter upon his street-car speculations, to use the resources of the Third National to carry a part of his loans and to furnish capital at such times as quick resources were necessary. In the beginning the old gentleman had been a little nervous and skeptical, but as time had worn on and nothing but profit eventuated, he grew bolder and more confident.

"Frank," he would say, looking up over his spectacles, "aren't you afraid you're going a little too fast in these matters? You're carrying a lot of loans these days."

"No more than I ever did, father, considering my resources. You can't turn large deals without large loans. You know that as well as I do."

"Yes, I know, but—now that Green and Coates—aren't you going pretty strong there?"

"Not at all. I know the inside conditions there. The stock is bound to go up eventually. I'll bull it up. I'll combine it with my other lines, if necessary."

Cowperwood stared at his boy. Never was there such a defiant, daring manipulator.

"You needn't worry about me, father. If you are going to do that, call my loans. Other banks will loan on my stocks. I'd like to see your bank have the interest."

So Cowperwood, Sr., was convinced. There was no gainsaying this argument. His bank was loaning Frank heavily, but not more so than any other. And as for the great blocks of stocks he was carrying in his son's companies, he was to be told when to get out should that prove necessary. Frank's brothers were being aided in the same way to make money on the side, and their interests were also now bound up indissolubly with his own.

With his growing financial opportunities, however, Cowperwood had also grown very liberal in what might be termed his standard of living. Certain young art dealers in Philadelphia, learning of his artistic inclinations and his growing wealth, had followed him up with suggestions as to furniture, tapestries, rugs, objects of art, and paintings—at first the American and later the foreign masters exclusively. His own and his father's house had not been furnished fully in these matters, and there was that other house in North Tenth Street, which he desired to make beautiful. Aileen had always objected to the condition of

84

her own home. Love of distinguished surroundings was a basic longing with her, though she had not the gift of interpreting her longings. But this place where they were secretly meeting must be beautiful. She was as keen for that as he was. So it became a veritable treasure-trove, more distinguished in furnishings than some of the rooms of his own home. He began to gather here some rare examples of altar cloths, rugs, and tapestries of the Middle Ages. He bought furniture after the Georgian theory—a combination of Chippendale, Sheraton, and Heppelwhite modified by the Italian Renaissance and the French Louis. He learned of handsome examples of porcelain, statuary, Greek vase forms, lovely collections of Japanese ivories and netsukes. Fletcher Gray, a partner in Cable & Gray, a local firm of importers of art objects, called on him in connection with a tapestry of the fourteenth century weaving. Gray was an enthusiast and almost instantly he conveyed some of his suppressed and yet fiery love of the beautiful to Cowperwood.

"There are fifty periods of one shade of blue porcelain alone, Mr. Cowperwood," Gray informed him. "There are at least seven distinct schools or periods of rugs—Persian, Armenian, Arabian, Flemish, Modern Polish, Hungarian, and so on. If you ever went into that, it would be a distinguished thing to get a complete—I mean a representative—collection of some one period, or of all these periods. They are beautiful. I have seen some of them, others I've read about."

"You'll make a convert of me yet, Fletcher," replied Cowperwood. "You or art will be the ruin of me. I'm inclined that way temperamentally as it is, I think, and between you and Ellsworth and Gordon Strake"—another young man intensely interested in painting—"you'll complete my downfall. Strake has a splendid idea. He wants me to begin right now—I'm using that word 'right' in the sense of 'properly,'" he commented—"and get what examples I can of just the few rare things in each school or period of art which would properly illustrate each. He tells me the great pictures are going to increase in value, and what I could get for a few hundred thousand now will be worth millions later. He doesn't want me to bother with American art."

"He's right," exclaimed Gray, "although it isn't good business for me to praise another art man. It would take a great deal of money, though."

"Not so very much. At least, not all at once. It would be a matter of years, of course. Strake thinks that some excellent examples of different periods could be picked up now and later replaced if anything better in the same held showed up."

His mind, in spite of his outward placidity, was tinged with a great seeking. Wealth, in the beginning, had seemed the only goal, to which had been added the beauty of women. And now art, for art's sake—the first faint radiance of a rosy dawn—had begun to shine in upon him, and to the beauty of womanhood he was beginning to see how necessary it was to add the beauty of life—the beauty of material background—how, in fact, the only background for great beauty was great art. This girl, this Aileen Butler, her raw youth and radiance, was nevertheless creating in him a sense of the distinguished and a need for it which had never existed in him before to the same degree. It is impossible to define these subtleties of reaction, temperament on temperament, for no one knows to what degree we are marked by the things which attract us. A love affair such as this had proved to be was little less or more than a drop of coloring added to a glass of clear water, or a foreign chemical agent introduced into a delicate chemical formula.

In short, for all her crudeness, Aileen Butler was a definite force personally. Her nature, in a way, a protest against the clumsy conditions by which she found herself surrounded, was almost irrationally ambitious. To think that for so long, having been born into the Butler family, she had been the subject, as well as the victim of such commonplace and inartistic illusions and conditions, whereas now, owing to her contact with, and mental subordination to Cowperwood, she was learning so many wonderful phases of social, as well as financial, refinement of which previously she had guessed nothing. The wonder, for instance, of a future social career as the wife of such a man as Frank Cowperwood. The beauty and resourcefulness of his mind, which, after hours of intimate contact with her, he was pleased to reveal, and which, so definite were his comments and instructions, she could not fail to sense. The wonder of his financial and artistic and future social dreams. And, oh, oh, she was his, and he was hers. She was actually beside herself at times with the glory, as well as the delight of all this.

At the same time, her father's local reputation as a quondam garbage contractor ("slop-collector" was the unfeeling comment of the vulgarian cognoscenti); her own unavailing efforts to right a condition of material vulgarity or artistic anarchy in her own home; the hopelessness of ever being admitted to those distinguished portals which she recognized afar off as the last sanctum sanctorum of established respectability and social distinction, had bred in her, even at this early age, a feeling of deadly opposition to her home conditions as they stood. Such a house compared to Cowperwood's! Her dear, but ignorant, father! And this great man, her lover, had now condescended to love her—see in her his future wife. Oh, God, that it might not fail! Through the Cowperwoods at first she had hoped to meet a few people, young men and women—and particularly men—who were above the station in which she found herself, and to whom her beauty and prospective fortune would commend her; but this had not been the case. The Cowperwoods themselves, in spite of Frank Cowperwood's artistic proclivities and growing wealth, had not penetrated the inner circle as yet. In fact, aside from the subtle, preliminary consideration which they were receiving, they were a long way off.

None the less, and instinctively in Cowperwood Aileen recognized a way out—a door—and by the same token a subtle, impending artistic future of great magnificence. This man would rise beyond anything he now dreamed of—she felt it. There was in him, in some nebulous, unrecognizable form, a great artistic reality which was finer than anything she could plan for herself. She wanted luxury, magnificence, social station. Well, if she could get this man they would come to her. There were, apparently, insuperable barriers in the way; but hers was no weakling nature, and neither was his. They ran together temperamentally from the first like two leopards. Her own thoughts—crude, half formulated, half spoken—nevertheless matched his to a degree in the equality of their force and their raw directness.

"I don't think papa knows how to do," she said to him, one day. "It isn't his fault. He can't help it. He knows that he can't. And he knows that I know it. For years I wanted him to move out of that old house there. He knows that he ought to. But even that wouldn't do much good."

She paused, looking at him with a straight, clear, vigorous glance. He liked the medallion sharpness of her features—their smooth, Greek modeling.

"Never mind, pet," he replied. "We will arrange all these things later. I don't see my way out of this just now; but I think the best thing to do is to confess to Lillian some day, and see if some other plan can't be arranged. I want to fix it so the children won't suffer. I can provide for them amply, and I wouldn't be at all surprised if Lillian would be willing to let me go. She certainly wouldn't want any publicity."

He was counting practically, and man-fashion, on her love for her children.

Aileen looked at him with clear, questioning, uncertain eyes. She was not wholly without sympathy, but in a way this situation did not appeal to her as needing much. Mrs. Cowperwood was not friendly in her mood toward her. It was not based on anything save a difference in their point of view. Mrs. Cowperwood could never understand how a girl could carry her head so high and "put on such airs," and Aileen could not understand how any one could be so lymphatic and lackadaisical as Lillian Cowperwood. Life was made for riding, driving, dancing, going. It was made for airs and banter and persiflage and coquetry. To see this woman, the wife of a young, forceful man like Cowperwood, acting, even though she were five years older and the mother of two children, as though life on its romantic and enthusiastic pleasurable side were all over was too much for her. Of course

Lillian was unsuited to Frank; of course he needed a young woman like herself, and fate would surely give him to her. Then what a delicious life they would lead!

"Oh, Frank," she exclaimed to him, over and over, "if we could only manage it. Do you think we can?"

"Do I think we can? Certainly I do. It's only a matter of time. I think if I were to put the matter to her clearly, she wouldn't expect me to stay. You look out how you conduct your affairs. If your father or your brother should ever suspect me, there'd be an explosion in this town, if nothing worse. They'd fight me in all my money deals, if they didn't kill me. Are you thinking carefully of what you are doing?"

"All the time. If anything happens I'll deny everything. They can't prove it, if I deny it. I'll come to you in the long run, just the same."

They were in the Tenth Street house at the time. She stroked his cheeks with the loving fingers of the wildly enamored woman.

"I'll do anything for you, sweetheart," she declared. "I'd die for you if I had to. I love you so."

"Well, pet, no danger. You won't have to do anything like that. But be careful."

CHAPTER XXIII

Then, after several years of this secret relationship, in which the ties of sympathy and understanding grew stronger instead of weaker, came the storm. It burst unexpectedly and out of a clear sky, and bore no relation to the intention or volition of any individual. It was nothing more than a fire, a distant one—the great Chicago fire, October 7th, 1871, which burned that city—its vast commercial section—to the ground, and instantly and incidentally produced a financial panic, vicious though of short duration in various other cities in America. The fire began on Saturday and continued apparently unabated until the following Wednesday. It destroyed the banks, the commercial houses, the shipping conveniences, and vast stretches of property. The heaviest loss fell naturally upon the insurance companies, which instantly, in many cases—the majority—closed their doors. This threw the loss back on the manufacturers and wholesalers in other cities who had had dealings with Chicago as well as the merchants of that city. Again, very grievous losses were borne by the host of eastern capitalists which had for years past partly owned, or held heavy mortgages on, the magnificent buildings for business purposes and residences in which Chicago was already rivaling every city on the continent. Transportation was disturbed, and the keen scent of Wall Street, and Third Street in Philadelphia, and State Street in Boston, instantly perceived in the early reports the gravity of the situation. Nothing could be done on Saturday or Sunday after the exchange closed, for the opening reports came too late. On Monday, however, the facts were pouring in thick and fast; and the owners of railroad securities, government securities, street-car securities, and, indeed, all other forms of stocks and bonds, began to throw them on the market in order to raise cash. The banks naturally were calling their loans, and the result was a stock stampede which equaled the Black Friday of Wall Street of two years before.

Cowperwood and his father were out of town at the time the fire began. They had gone with several friends—bankers—to look at a proposed route of extension of a local steam-railroad, on which a loan was desired. In buggies they had driven over a good portion of the route, and were returning to Philadelphia late Sunday evening when the cries of newsboys hawking an "extra" reached their ears.

"Ho! Extra! Extra! All about the big Chicago fire!"

"Ho! Extra! Extra! Chicago burning down! Extra! Extra!"

The cries were long-drawn-out, ominous, pathetic. In the dusk of the dreary Sunday afternoon, when the city had apparently retired to Sabbath meditation and prayer, with that tinge of the dying year in the foliage and in the air, one caught a sense of something grim and gloomy.

"Hey, boy," called Cowperwood, listening, seeing a shabbily clothed misfit of a boy with a bundle of papers under his arm turning a corner. "What's that? Chicago burning!"

He looked at his father and the other men in a significant way as he reached for the paper, and then, glancing at the headlines, realized the worst.

ALL CHICAGO BURNING

FIRE RAGES UNCHECKED IN COMMERCIAL SECTION SINCE YESTERDAY EVENING. BANKS, COMMERCIAL HOUSES, PUBLIC BUILDINGS IN RUINS. DIRECT TELEGRAPHIC COMMUNICATION SUSPENDED SINCE THREE O'CLOCK TO-DAY. NO END TO PROGRESS OF DISASTER IN SIGHT.

"That looks rather serious," he said, calmly, to his companions, a cold, commanding force coming into his eyes and voice. To his father he said a little later, "It's panic, unless the majority of the banks and brokerage firms stand together."

He was thinking quickly, brilliantly, resourcefully of his own outstanding obligations. His father's bank was carrying one hundred thousand dollars' worth of his street-railway securities at sixty, and fifty thousand dollars' worth of city loan at seventy. His father had "up with him" over forty thousand dollars in cash covering market manipulations in these stocks. The banking house of Drexel & Co. was on his books as a creditor for one hundred thousand, and that loan would be called unless they were especially merciful, which was not likely. Jay Cooke & Co. were his creditors for another one hundred and fifty thousand. They would want their money. At four smaller banks and three brokerage companies he was debtor for sums ranging from fifty thousand dollars down. The city treasurer was involved with him to the extent of nearly five hundred thousand dollars, and exposure of that would create a scandal; the State treasurer for two hundred thousand. There were small accounts, hundreds of them, ranging from one hundred dollars up to five and ten thousand. A panic would mean not only a withdrawal of deposits and a calling of loans, but a heavy depression of securities. How could he realize on his securities?—that was the question—how without selling so many points off that his fortune would be swept away and he would be ruined?

He figured briskly the while he waved adieu to his friends, who hurried away, struck with their own predicament.

"You had better go on out to the house, father, and I'll send some telegrams." (The telephone had not yet been invented.) "I'll be right out and we'll go into this thing together. It looks like black weather to me. Don't say anything to any one until after we have had our talk; then we can decide what to do."

Cowperwood, Sr., was already plucking at his side-whiskers in a confused and troubled way. He was cogitating as to what might happen to him in case his son failed, for he was deeply involved with him. He was a little gray in his complexion now, frightened, for he had already strained many points in his affairs to accommodate his son. If Frank should not be able promptly on the morrow to meet the call which the bank might have to make for one hundred and fifty thousand dollars, the onus and scandal of the situation would be on him.

On the other hand, his son was meditating on the tangled relation in which he now found himself in connection with the city treasurer and the fact that it was not possible for him to support the market alone. Those who should have been in a position to help him were now as bad off as himself. There were many unfavorable points in the whole situation. Drexel & Co. had been booming railway stocks—loaning heavily on them. Jay Cooke & Co. had been backing Northern Pacific—were practically doing their best to build that immense transcontinental system alone. Naturally, they were long on that and hence in a ticklish position. At the first word they would throw over their surest securities—government bonds, and the like—in order to protect their more speculative holdings. The bears would see the point. They would hammer and hammer, selling short all along the line. But he did not dare to do that. He would be breaking his own back quickly, and what he needed was time. If he could only get time—three days, a week, ten days—this storm would surely blow over.

The thing that was troubling him most was the matter of the half-million invested with him by Stener. A fall election was drawing near. Stener, although he had served two terms, was slated for reelection. A scandal in connection with the city treasury would be a very bad thing. It would end Stener's career as an official—would very likely send him to the penitentiary. It might wreck the Republican party's chances to win. It would certainly involve himself as having much to do with it. If that happened, he would have the politicians to reckon with. For, if he were hard pressed, as he would be, and failed, the fact that he had been trying to invade the city street-railway preserves which they held sacred to themselves, with borrowed city money, and that this borrowing was liable to cost them the city election, would all come out. They would not view all that with a kindly eye. It would be useless to say, as he could, that he had borrowed the money at two per cent. (most of it, to save himself, had been covered by a protective clause of that kind), or that he had merely acted as an agent for Stener. That might go down with the unsophisticated of the outer world, but it would never be swallowed by the politicians. They knew better than that.

There was another phase to this situation, however, that encouraged him, and that was his knowledge of how city politics were going in general. It was useless for any politician, however loftly, to take a high and mighty tone in a crisis like this. All of them, great and small, were profiting in one way and another through city privileges. Butler, Mollenhauer, and Simpson, he knew, made money out of contracts—legal enough, though they might be looked upon as rank favoritism—and also out of vast sums of money collected in the shape of taxes—land taxes, water taxes, etc.—which were deposited in the various banks designated by these men and others as legal depositories for city money. The banks supposedly carried the city's money in their vaults as a favor, without paying interest of any kind, and then reinvested it—for whom? Cowperwood had no complaint to make, for he was being well treated, but these men could scarcely expect to monopolize all the city's benefits. He did not know either Mollenhauer or Simpson personally—but he knew they as well as Butler had made money out of his own manipulation of city loan. Also, Butler was most friendly to him. It was not unreasonable for him to think, in a crisis like this, that if worst came to worst, he could make a clean breast of it to Butler and receive aid. In case he could not get through secretly with Stener's help, Cowperwood made up his mind that he would do this.

His first move, he decided, would be to go at once to Stener's house and demand the loan of an additional three or four hundred thousand dollars. Stener had always been very tractable, and in this instance would see how important it was that his shortage of half a million should not be made public. Then he must get as much more as possible. But where to get it? Presidents of banks and trust companies, large stock jobbers, and the like, would have to be seen. Then there was a loan of one hundred thousand dollars he was carrying for Butler. The old contractor might be induced to leave that. He hurried to his home, secured his runabout, and drove rapidly to Stener's.

As it turned out, however, much to his distress and confusion, Stener was out of town—down on the Chesapeake with several friends shooting ducks and fishing, and was not expected back for several days. He was in the marshes back of some small town. Cowperwood sent an urgent wire to the nearest point and then, to make assurance doubly sure, to several other points in the same neighborhood, asking him to return immediately. He was not at all sure, however, that Stener would return in time and was greatly nonplussed and uncertain for the moment as to what his next step would be. Aid must be forthcoming from somewhere and at once.

Suddenly a helpful thought occurred to him. Butler and Mollenhauer and Simpson were long on local street-railways. They must combine to support the situation and protect their interests. They could see the big bankers, Drexel & Co. and Cooke & Co., and others and urge them to sustain the market. They could strengthen things generally by organizing a buying ring, and under cover of their support, if they would, he might sell enough to let him out, and even permit him to go short and make something—a whole lot. It was a brilliant thought, worthy of a greater situation, and its only weakness was that it was not absolutely certain of fulfillment.

He decided to go to Butler at once, the only disturbing thought being that he would now be compelled to reveal his own and Stener's affairs. So reentering his runabout he drove swiftly to the Butler home.

When he arrived there the famous contractor was at dinner. He had not heard the calling of the extras, and of course, did not understand as yet the significance of the fire. The servant's announcement of Cowperwood brought him smiling to the door.

"Won't you come in and join us? We're just havin' a light supper. Have a cup of coffee or tea, now—do."

"I can't," replied Cowperwood. "Not to-night, I'm in too much of a hurry. I want to see you for just a few moments, and then I'll be off again. I won't keep you very long."

"Why, if that's the case, I'll come right out." And Butler returned to the dining-room to put down his napkin. Aileen, who was also dining, had heard Cowperwood's voice, and was on the qui vive to see him. She wondered what it was that brought him at this time of night to see her father. She could not leave the table at once, but hoped to before he went. Cowperwood was thinking of her, even in the face of this impending storm, as he was of his wife, and many other things. If his affairs came down in a heap it would go hard with those attached to him. In this first clouding of disaster, he could not tell how things would eventuate. He meditated on this desperately, but he was not panic-stricken. His naturally even-molded face was set in fine, classic lines; his eyes were as hard as chilled steel.

"Well, now," exclaimed Butler, returning, his countenance manifesting a decidedly comfortable relationship with the world as at present constituted. "What's up with you to-night? Nawthin' wrong, I hope. It's been too fine a day."

"Nothing very serious, I hope myself," replied Cowperwood, "But I want to talk with you a few minutes, anyhow. Don't you think we had better go up to your room?"

"I was just going to say that," replied Butler—"the cigars are up there."

They started from the reception-room to the stairs, Butler preceding and as the contractor mounted, Aileen came out from the dining-room in a frou-frou of silk. Her splendid hair was drawn up from the base of the neck and the line of the forehead into some quaint convolutions which constituted a reddish-gold crown. Her complexion was glowing, and her bare arms and shoulders shone white against the dark red of her evening gown. She realized there was something wrong.

"Oh, Mr. Cowperwood, how do you do?" she exclaimed, coming forward and holding out her hand as her father went on upstairs. She was delaying him deliberately in order to have a word with him and this bold acting was for the benefit of the others.

"What's the trouble, honey?" she whispered, as soon as her father was out of hearing. "You look worried."

"Nothing much, I hope, sweet," he said. "Chicago is burning up and there's going to be trouble to-morrow. I have to talk to your father."

She had time only for a sympathetic, distressed "Oh," before he withdrew his hand and followed Butler upstairs. She squeezed his arm, and went through the reception-room to the parlor. She sat down, thinking, for never before had she seen Cowperwood's face wearing such an expression of stern, disturbed calculation. It was placid, like fine, white wax, and quite as cold; and those deep, vague, inscrutable eyes! So Chicago was burning. What would happen to him? Was he very much involved? He had never told her in detail of his affairs. She would not have understood fully any more than would have Mrs. Cowperwood. But she was worried, nevertheless, because it was her Frank, and because she was bound to him by what to her seemed indissoluble ties.

Literature, outside of the masters, has given us but one idea of the mistress, the subtle, calculating siren who delights to prey on the souls of men. The journalism and the moral pamphleteering of the time seem to foster it with almost partisan zeal. It would seem that a censorship of life had been established by divinity, and the care of its execution given into the hands of the utterly conservative. Yet there is that other form of liaison which has nothing to do with conscious calculation. In the vast majority of cases it is without design or guile. The average woman, controlled by her affections and deeply in love, is no more capable than a child of anything save sacrificial thought—the desire to give; and so long as this state endures, she can only do this. She may change—Hell hath no fury, etc.—but the sacrificial, yielding, solicitous attitude is more often the outstanding characteristic of the mistress; and it is this very attitude in contradistinction to the grasping legality of established matrimony that has caused so many wounds in the defenses of the latter. The temperament of man, either male or female, cannot help falling down before and worshiping this nonseeking, sacrificial note. It approaches vast distinction in life. It appears to be related to that last word in art, that largeness of spirit which is the first characteristic of the great picture, the great building, the great sculpture, the great decoration—namely, a giving, freely and without stint, of itself, of beauty. Hence the significance of this particular mood in Aileen.

All the subtleties of the present combination were troubling Cowperwood as he followed Butler into the room upstairs.

"Sit down, sit down. You won't take a little somethin'? You never do. I remember now. Well, have a cigar, anyhow. Now, what's this that's troublin' you to-night?"

Voices could be heard faintly in the distance, far off toward the thicker residential sections.

"Extra! Extra! All about the big Chicago fire! Chicago burning down!"

"Just that," replied Cowperwood, hearkening to them. "Have you heard the news?"

"No. What's that they're calling?"

"It's a big fire out in Chicago."

"Oh," replied Butler, still not gathering the significance of it.

"It's burning down the business section there, Mr. Butler," went on Cowperwood ominously, "and I fancy it's going to disturb financial conditions here to-morrow. That is what I have come to see you about. How are your investments? Pretty well drawn in?"

Butler suddenly gathered from Cowperwood's expression that there was something very wrong. He put up his large hand as he leaned back in his big leather chair, and covered his mouth and chin with it. Over those big knuckles, and bigger nose, thick and cartilaginous, his large, shaggy-eyebrowed eyes gleamed. His gray, bristly hair stood up stiffly in a short, even growth all over his head.

"So that's it," he said. "You're expectin' trouble to-morrow. How are your own affairs?"

"I'm in pretty good shape, I think, all told, if the money element of this town doesn't lose its head and go wild. There has to be a lot of common sense exercised to-morrow, or to-night, even. You know we are facing a real panic. Mr. Butler, you may as well know that. It may not last long, but while it does it will be bad. Stocks are going to drop to-morrow ten or fifteen points on the opening. The banks are going to call their loans unless some arrangement can be made to prevent them. No one man can do that. It will have to be a combination of men. You and Mr. Simpson and Mr. Mollenhauer might do it—that is, you could if you could persuade the big banking people to combine to back the market. There is going to be a raid on local street-railways—all of them. Unless they are sustained the bottom is going to drop out. I have always known that you were long on those. I thought you and Mr. Mollenhauer and some of the others might want to act. If you don't I might as well confess that it is going to go rather hard with me. I am not strong enough to face this thing alone."

He was meditating on how he should tell the whole truth in regard to Stener.

"Well, now, that's pretty bad," said Butler, calmly and meditatively. He was thinking of his own affairs. A panic was not good for him either, but he was not in a desperate state. He could not fail. He might lose some money, but not a vast amount—before he could adjust things. Still he did not care to lose any money.

"How is it you're so bad off?" he asked, curiously. He was wondering how the fact that the bottom was going to drop out of local street-railways would affect Cowperwood so seriously. "You're not carryin' any of them things, are you?" he added.

It was now a question of lying or telling the truth, and Cowperwood was literally afraid to risk lying in this dilemma. If he did not gain Butler's comprehending support he might fail, and if he failed the truth would come out, anyhow.

"I might as well make a clean breast of this, Mr. Butler," he said, throwing himself on the old man's sympathies and looking at him with that brisk assurance which Butler so greatly admired. He felt as proud of Cowperwood at times as he did of his own sons. He felt that he had helped to put him where he was.

"The fact is that I have been buying street-railway stocks, but not for myself exactly. I am going to do something now which I think I ought not to do, but I cannot help myself. If I don't do it, it will injure you and a lot of people whom I do not wish to injure. I know you are naturally interested in the outcome of the fall election. The truth is I have been carrying a lot of stocks for Mr. Stener and some of his friends. I do not know that all the money has come from the city treasury, but I think that most of it has. I know what that means to Mr. Stener and the Republican party and your interests in case I fail. I don't think Mr. Stener started this of his own accord in the first place—I think I am as much to blame as anybody—but it grew out of other things. As you know, I handled that matter of city loan for him and then some of his friends wanted me to invest in street-railways for them. I have been doing that ever since. Personally I have borrowed considerable money from Mr. Stener at two per cent. In fact, originally the transactions were covered in that way. Now I don't want to shift the blame on any one. It comes back to me and I am willing to let it stay there, except that if I fail Mr. Stener will be blamed and that will reflect on the administration. Naturally, I don't want to fail. There is no excuse for my doing so. Aside from this panic I have never been in a better position in my life. But I cannot weather this storm without assistance, and I want to know if you won't help me. If I pull through I will give you my word that I will see that the money which has been taken from the treasury is put back there. Mr. Stener is out of town or I would have brought him here with me."

Cowperwood was lying out of the whole cloth in regard to bringing Stener with him, and he had no intention of putting the money back in the city treasury except by degrees and in such manner as suited his convenience; but what he had said sounded well and created a great seeming of fairness.

"How much money is it Stener has invested with you?" asked Butler. He was a little confused by this curious development. It put Cowperwood and Stener in an odd light.

"About five hundred thousand dollars," replied Cowperwood.

The old man straightened up. "Is it as much as that?" he said.

"Just about—a little more or a little less; I'm not sure which."

The old contractor listened solemnly to all Cowperwood had to say on this score, thinking of the effect on the Republican party and his own contracting interests. He liked Cowperwood, but this was a rough thing the latter was telling him—rough, and a great deal to ask. He was a slow-thinking and a slow-moving man, but he did well enough when he did think. He had considerable money invested in Philadelphia street-railway stocks— perhaps as much as eight hundred thousand dollars. Mollenhauer had perhaps as much more. Whether Senator Simpson had much or little he could not tell. Cowperwood had told him in the past that he thought the Senator had a good deal. Most of their holdings, as in the case of Cowperwood's, were hypothecated at the various banks for loans and these loans invested in other ways. It was not advisable or comfortable to have these loans called, though the condition of no one of the triumvirate was anything like as bad as that of Cowperwood. They could see themselves through without much trouble, though not without probable loss unless they took hurried action to protect themselves.

He would not have thought so much of it if Cowperwood had told him that Stener was involved, say, to the extent of seventy-five or a hundred thousand dollars. That might be adjusted. But five hundred thousand dollars!

"That's a lot of money," said Butler, thinking of the amazing audacity of Stener, but failing at the moment to identify it with the astute machinations of Cowperwood. "That's something to think about. There's no time to lose if there's going to be a panic in the morning. How much good will it do ye if we do support the market?"

"A great deal," returned Cowperwood, "although of course I have to raise money in other ways. I have that one hundred thousand dollars of yours on deposit. Is it likely that you'll want that right away?"

"It may be," said Butler.

"It's just as likely that I'll need it so badly that I can't give it up without seriously injuring myself," added Cowperwood. "That's just one of a lot of things. If you and Senator Simpson and Mr. Mollenhauer were to get together—you're the largest holders of street-railway stocks—and were to see Mr. Drexel and Mr. Cooke, you could fix things so that matters would be considerably easier. I will be all right if my loans are not called, and my loans will not be called if the market does not slump too heavily. If it does, all my securities are depreciated, and I can't hold out."

Old Butler got up. "This is serious business," he said. "I wish you'd never gone in with Stener in that way. It don't look quite right and it can't be made to. It's bad, bad business," he added dourly. "Still, I'll do what I can. I can't promise much, but I've always liked ye and I'll not be turning on ye now unless I have to. But I'm sorry—very. And I'm not the only one that has a hand in things in this town." At the same time he was thinking it was right decent of Cowperwood to forewarn him this way in regard to his own affairs and the city election, even though he was saving his own neck by so doing. He meant to do what he could.

"I don't suppose you could keep this matter of Stener and the city treasury quiet for a day or two until I see how I come out?" suggested Cowperwood warily.

"I can't promise that," replied Butler. "I'll have to do the best I can. I won't lave it go any further than I can help—you can depend on that." He was thinking how the effect of Stener's crime could be overcome if Cowperwood failed.

"Owen!"

He stepped to the door, and, opening it, called down over the banister.

"Yes, father."

"Have Dan hitch up the light buggy and bring it around to the door. And you get your hat and coat. I want you to go along with me."

"Yes, father."

He came back.

"Sure that's a nice little storm in a teapot, now, isn't it? Chicago begins to burn, and I have to worry here in Philadelphia. Well, well—" Cowperwood was up now and moving to the door. "And where are you going?"

"Back to the house. I have several people coming there to see me. But I'll come back here later, if I may."

"Yes, yes," replied Butler. "To be sure I'll be here by midnight, anyhow. Well, good night. I'll see you later, then, I suppose. I'll tell you what I find out."

He went back in his room for something, and Cowperwood descended the stair alone. From the hangings of the reception-room entryway Aileen signaled him to draw near.

"I hope it's nothing serious, honey?" she sympathized, looking into his solemn eyes.

It was not time for love, and he felt it.

"No," he said, almost coldly, "I think not."

"Frank, don't let this thing make you forget me for long, please. You won't, will you? I love you so."

"No, no, I won't!" he replied earnestly, quickly and yet absently.

"I can't! Don't you know I won't?" He had started to kiss her, but a noise disturbed him. "Sh!"

He walked to the door, and she followed him with eager, sympathetic eyes.

What if anything should happen to her Frank? What if anything could? What would she do? That was what was troubling her. What would, what could she do to help him? He looked so pale—strained.

CHAPTER XXIV

The condition of the Republican party at this time in Philadelphia, its relationship to George W. Stener, Edward Malia Butler, Henry A. Mollenhauer, Senator Mark Simpson, and others, will have to be briefly indicated here, in order to foreshadow Cowperwood's actual situation. Butler, as we have seen, was normally interested in and friendly to Cowperwood. Stener was Cowperwood's tool. Mollenhauer and Senator Simpson were strong rivals of Butler for the control of city affairs. Simpson represented the Republican control of the State legislature, which could dictate to the city if necessary, making new election laws, revising the city charter, starting political investigations, and the like. He had many influential newspapers, corporations, banks, at his beck and call. Mollenhauer represented the Germans, some Americans, and some large stable corporations—a very solid and respectable man. All three were strong, able, and dangerous politically. The two latter counted on Butler's influence, particularly with the Irish, and a certain number of ward leaders and Catholic politicians and laymen, who were as loyal to him as though he were a part of the church itself. Butler's return to these followers was protection, influence, aid, and good-will generally. The city's return to him, via Mollenhauer and Simpson, was in the shape of contracts—fat ones—street-paving, bridges, viaducts, sewers. And in order for him to get these contracts the affairs of the Republican party, of which he was a beneficiary as well as a leader, must be kept reasonably straight. At the same time it was no more a part of his need to keep the affairs of the party straight than it was of either Mollenhauer's or Simpson's, and Stener was not his appointee. The latter was more directly responsible to Mollenhauer than to any one else.

As Butler stepped into the buggy with his son he was thinking about this, and it was puzzling him greatly.

"Cowperwood's just been here," he said to Owen, who had been rapidly coming into a sound financial understanding of late, and was already a shrewder man politically and socially than his father, though he had not the latter's magnetism. "He's been tellin' me that he's in a rather tight place. You hear that?" he continued, as some voice in the distance was calling "Extra! Extra!" "That's Chicago burnin', and there's goin' to be trouble on the stock exchange to-morrow. We have a lot of our street-railway stocks around at the different banks. If we don't look sharp they'll be callin' our loans. We have to 'tend to that the first thing in the mornin'. Cowperwood has a hundred thousand of mine with him that he wants me to let stay there, and he has some money that belongs to Stener, he tells me."

94

"Stener?" asked Owen, curiously. "Has he been dabbling in stocks?" Owen had heard some rumors concerning Stener and others only very recently, which he had not credited nor yet communicated to his father. "How much money of his has Cowperwood?" he asked.

Butler meditated. "Quite a bit, I'm afraid," he finally said. "As a matter of fact, it's a great deal—about five hundred thousand dollars. If that should become known, it would be makin' a good deal of noise, I'm thinkin'."

"Whew!" exclaimed Owen in astonishment. "Five hundred thousand dollars! Good Lord, father! Do you mean to say Stener has got away with five hundred thousand dollars? Why, I wouldn't think he was clever enough to do that. Five hundred thousand dollars! It will make a nice row if that comes out."

"Aisy, now! Aisy, now!" replied Butler, doing his best to keep all phases of the situation in mind. "We can't tell exactly what the circumstances were yet. He mayn't have meant to take so much. It may all come out all right yet. The money's invested. Cowperwood hasn't failed yet. It may be put back. The thing to be settled on now is whether anything can be done to save him. If he's tellin' me the truth—and I never knew him to lie—he can get out of this if street-railway stocks don't break too heavy in the mornin'. I'm going over to see Henry Mollenhauer and Mark Simpson. They're in on this. Cowperwood wanted me to see if I couldn't get them to get the bankers together and have them stand by the market. He thought we might protect our loans by comin' on and buyin' and holdin' up the price."

Owen was running swiftly in his mind over Cowperwood's affairs—as much as he knew of them. He felt keenly that the banker ought to be shaken out. This dilemma was his fault, not Stener's—he felt. It was strange to him that his father did not see it and resent it.

"You see what it is, father," he said, dramatically, after a time. "Cowperwood's been using this money of Stener's to pick up stocks, and he's in a hole. If it hadn't been for this fire he'd have got away with it; but now he wants you and Simpson and Mollenhauer and the others to pull him out. He's a nice fellow, and I like him fairly well; but you're a fool if you do as he wants you to. He has more than belongs to him already. I heard the other day that he has the Front Street line, and almost all of Green and Coates; and that he and Stener own the Seventeenth and Nineteenth; but I didn't believe it. I've been intending to ask you about it. I think Cowperwood has a majority for himself stowed away somewhere in every instance. Stener is just a pawn. He moves him around where he pleases."

Owen's eyes gleamed avariciously, opposingly. Cowperwood ought to be punished, sold out, driven out of the street-railway business in which Owen was anxious to rise.

"Now you know," observed Butler, thickly and solemnly, "I always thought that young felly was clever, but I hardly thought he was as clever as all that. So that's his game. You're pretty shrewd yourself, aren't you? Well, we can fix that, if we think well of it. But there's more than that to all this. You don't want to forget the Republican party. Our success goes with the success of that, you know"—and he paused and looked at his son. "If Cowperwood should fail and that money couldn't be put back—" He broke off abstractedly. "The thing that's troublin' me is this matter of Stener and the city treasury. If somethin' ain't done about that, it may go hard with the party this fall, and with some of our contracts. You don't want to forget that an election is comin' along in November. I'm wonderin' if I ought to call in that one hundred thousand dollars. It's goin' to take considerable money to meet my loans in the mornin'."

It is a curious matter of psychology, but it was only now that the real difficulties of the situation were beginning to dawn on Butler. In the presence of Cowperwood he was so influenced by that young man's personality and his magnetic presentation of his need and his own liking for him that he had not stopped to consider all the phases of his own relationship to the situation. Out here in the cool night air, talking to Owen, who was ambitious on his own account and anything but sentimentally considerate of Cowperwood, he was beginning to sober down and see things in their true light. He had to admit that Cowperwood had seriously compromised the city treasury and the Republican party, and incidentally Butler's own private interests. Nevertheless, he liked Cowperwood. He was in no way prepared to desert him. He was now going to see Mollenhauer and Simpson as much to save Cowperwood really as the party and his own affairs. And yet a scandal. He did not like that—resented it. This young scalawag! To think he should be so sly. None the less he still liked him, even here and now, and was feeling that he ought to do something to help the young man, if anything could help him. He might even leave his hundred-thousand-dollar loan with him until the last hour, as Cowperwood had requested, if the others were friendly.

"Well, father," said Owen, after a time, "I don't see why you need to worry any more than Mollenhauer or Simpson. If you three want to help him out, you can; but for the life of me I don't see why you should. I know this thing will have a bad effect on the election, if it comes out before then; but it could be hushed up until then, couldn't it? Anyhow, your street-railway holdings are more important than this election, and if you can see your way clear to getting the street-railway lines in your hands you won't need to worry about any elections. My advice to you is to call that one-hundred-thousand-dollar loan of yours in the morning, and meet the drop in your stocks that way. It may make Cowperwood fail, but that won't hurt you any. You can go into the market and buy his stocks. I wouldn't be surprised if he would run to you and ask you to take them. You ought to get Mollenhauer and Simpson to scare Stener so that he won't loan Cowperwood any more money. If you don't, Cowperwood will run there and get more. Stener's in too far now. If Cowperwood won't sell out, well and good; the chances are he will bust, anyhow, and then you can pick up as much on the market as any one else. I think he'll sell. You can't afford to worry about Stener's five hundred thousand dollars. No one told him to loan it. Let him look out for himself. It may hurt the party, but you can look after that later. You and Mollenhauer can fix the newspapers so they won't talk about it till after election."

"Aisy! Aisy!" was all the old contractor would say. He was thinking hard.

CHAPTER XXV

The residence of Henry A. Mollenhauer was, at that time, in a section of the city which was almost as new as that in which Butler was living. It was on South Broad Street, near a handsome library building which had been recently erected. It was a spacious house of the type usually affected by men of new wealth in those days—a structure four stories in height of yellow brick and white stone built after no school which one could readily identify, but not unattractive in its architectural composition. A broad flight of steps leading to a wide veranda gave into a decidedly ornate door, which was set on either side by narrow windows and ornamented to the right and left with pale-blue jardinieres of considerable charm of outline. The interior, divided into twenty rooms, was paneled and parqueted in the most expensive manner for homes of that day. There was a great reception-hall, a large parlor or drawing-room, a dining-room at least thirty feet square paneled in oak; and on the second floor were a music-room devoted to the talents of Mollenhauer's three ambitious daughters, a library and private office for himself, a boudoir and bath for his wife, and a conservatory. Mollenhauer was, and felt himself to be, a very important man. His financial and political judgment was exceedingly keen. Although he was a German, or rather an American of German parentage, he was a man of a rather impressive American presence. He was tall and heavy and shrewd and cold. His large chest and wide shoulders supported a head of distinguished proportions, both round and long when seen from different angles. The frontal bone descended in a protruding curve over the nose, and projected solemnly over the eyes, which burned with a shrewd, inquiring gaze. And the nose and mouth and chin below, as well as his smooth, hard cheeks, confirmed the impression that he knew very well what he wished in this world, and was very able without regard to let or hindrance to get it. It was a big face, impressive, well modeled. He was an excellent friend of Edward Malia Butler's, as such friendships go, and his regard for Mark Simpson was as sincere as that of one tiger for another. He respected ability; he was willing to play fair when fair was the game. When it was not, the reach of his cunning was not easily measured.

When Edward Butler and his son arrived on this Sunday evening, this distinguished representative of one-third of the city's interests was not expecting them. He was in his library reading and listening to one of his daughters playing the piano. His wife and his other two daughters had gone to church. He was of a domestic turn of mind. Still, Sunday evening being an excellent one for conference purposes generally in the world of politics, he was not without the thought that some one or other of his distinguished confreres might call, and when the combination footman and butler announced the presence of Butler and his son, he was well pleased.

"So there you are," he remarked to Butler, genially, extending his hand. "I'm certainly glad to see you. And Owen! How are you, Owen? What will you gentlemen have to drink, and what will you smoke? I know you'll have something. John"—to the servitor—"see if you can find something for these gentlemen. I have just been listening to Caroline play; but I think you've frightened her off for the time being."

He moved a chair into position for Butler, and indicated to Owen another on the other side of the table. In a moment his servant had returned with a silver tray of elaborate design, carrying whiskies and wines of various dates and cigars in profusion. Owen was the new type of young financier who neither smoked nor drank. His father temperately did both.

"It's a comfortable place you have here," said Butler, without any indication of the important mission that had brought him. "I don't wonder you stay at home Sunday evenings. What's new in the city?"

"Nothing much, so far as I can see," replied Mollenhauer, pacifically. "Things seem to be running smooth enough. You don't know anything that we ought to worry about, do you?"

"Well, yes," said Butler, draining off the remainder of a brandy and soda that had been prepared for him. "One thing. You haven't seen an avenin' paper, have you?"

"No, I haven't," said Mollenhauer, straightening up. "Is there one out? What's the trouble anyhow?"

"Nothing—except Chicago's burning, and it looks as though we'd have a little money-storm here in the morning."

"You don't say! I didn't hear that. There's a paper out, is there? Well, well—is it much of a fire?"

"The city is burning down, so they say," put in Owen, who was watching the face of the distinguished politician with considerable interest.

"Well, that is news. I must send out and get a paper. John!" he called. His man-servant appeared. "See if you can get me a paper somewhere." The servant disappeared. "What makes you think that would have anything to do with us?" observed Mollenhauer, returning to Butler.

"Well, there's one thing that goes with that that I didn't know till a little while ago and that is that our man Stener is apt to be short in his accounts, unless things come out better than some people seem to think," suggested Butler, calmly. "That might not look so well before election, would it?" His shrewd gray Irish eyes looked into Mollenhauer's, who returned his gaze.

"Where did you get that?" queried Mr. Mollenhauer icily. "He hasn't deliberately taken much money, has he? How much has he taken—do you know?"

"Quite a bit," replied Butler, quietly. "Nearly five hundred thousand, so I understand. Only I wouldn't say that it has been taken as yet. It's in danger of being lost."

"Five hundred thousand!" exclaimed Mollenhauer in amazement, and yet preserving his usual calm. "You don't tell me! How long has this been going on? What has he been doing with the money?"

"He's loaned a good deal—about five hundred thousand dollars to this young Cowperwood in Third Street, that's been handlin' city loan. They've been investin' it for themselves in one thing and another—mostly in buyin' up street-railways." (At the mention of street-railways Mollenhauer's impassive countenance underwent a barely perceptible change.) "This fire, accordin' to Cowperwood, is certain to produce a panic in the mornin', and unless he gets considerable help he doesn't see how he's to hold out. If he doesn't hold out, there'll be five hundred thousand dollars missin' from the city treasury which can't be put back. Stener's out of town and Cowperwood's come to me to see what can be done about it. As a matter of fact, he's done a little business for me in times past, and he thought maybe I could help him now—that is, that I might get you and the Senator to see the big bankers with me and help support the market in the mornin'. If we don't he's goin' to fail, and he thought the scandal would hurt us in the election. He doesn't appear to me to be workin' any game—just anxious to save himself and do the square thing by me—by us, if he can." Butler paused.

Mollenhauer, sly and secretive himself, was apparently not at all moved by this unexpected development. At the same time, never having thought of Stener as having any particular executive or financial ability, he was a little stirred and curious. So his treasurer was using money without his knowing it, and now stood in danger of being prosecuted! Cowperwood he knew of only indirectly, as one who had been engaged to handle city loan. He had profited by his manipulation of city loan. Evidently the banker had made a fool of Stener, and had used the money for street-railway shares! He and Stener must have quite some private holdings then. That did interest Mollenhauer greatly.

"Five hundred thousand dollars!" he repeated, when Butler had finished. "That is quite a little money. If merely supporting the market would save Cowperwood we might do that, although if it's a severe panic I do not see how anything we can do will be of very much assistance to him. If he's in a very tight place and a severe slump is coming, it will take a great deal more than our merely supporting the market to save him. I've been through that before. You don't know what his liabilities are?"

"I do not," said Butler.

"He didn't ask for money, you say?"

"He wants me to l'ave a hundred thousand he has of mine until he sees whether he can get through or not."

"Stener is really out of town, I suppose?" Mollenhauer was innately suspicious.

"So Cowperwood says. We can send and find out."

Mollenhauer was thinking of the various aspects of the case. Supporting the market would be all very well if that would save Cowperwood, and the Republican party and his treasurer. At the same time Stener could then be compelled to restore the five hundred thousand dollars to the city treasury, and release his holdings to some one—preferably to him—Mollenhauer. But here was Butler also to be considered in this matter. What might he not want? He consulted with Butler and learned that Cowperwood had agreed to return the five hundred thousand in case he could get it together. The various street-car holdings were not asked after. But what assurance had any one that Cowperwood could be so saved? And could, or would get the money together? And if he were saved would he give the money back to Stener? If he required actual money, who would loan it to him in a time like this—in case a sharp panic was imminent? What security could he give? On the other hand, under pressure from the right parties he might be made to surrender all his street-railway holdings for a song—his and Stener's. If he (Mollenhauer) could get them he would not particularly care whether the election was lost this fall or not, although he felt satisfied, as had Owen, that it would not be lost. It could be bought, as usual. The defalcation—if Cowperwood's

98

failure made Stener's loan into one—could be concealed long enough, Mollenhauer thought, to win. Personally as it came to him now he would prefer to frighten Stener into refusing Cowperwood additional aid, and then raid the latter's street-railway stock in combination with everybody else's, for that matter—Simpson's and Butler's included. One of the big sources of future wealth in Philadelphia lay in these lines. For the present, however, he had to pretend an interest in saving the party at the polls.

"I can't speak for the Senator, that's sure," pursued Mollenhauer, reflectively. "I don't know what he may think. As for myself, I am perfectly willing to do what I can to keep up the price of stocks, if that will do any good. I would do so naturally in order to protect my loans. The thing that we ought to be thinking about, in my judgment, is how to prevent exposure, in case Mr. Cowperwood does fail, until after election. We have no assurance, of course, that however much we support the market we will be able to sustain it."

"We have not," replied Butler, solemnly.

Owen thought he could see Cowperwood's approaching doom quite plainly. At that moment the door-bell rang. A maid, in the absence of the footman, brought in the name of Senator Simpson.

"Just the man," said Mollenhauer. "Show him up. You can see what he thinks."

"Perhaps I had better leave you alone now," suggested Owen to his father. "Perhaps I can find Miss Caroline, and she will sing for me. I'll wait for you, father," he added.

Mollenhauer cast him an ingratiating smile, and as he stepped out Senator Simpson walked in.

A more interesting type of his kind than Senator Mark Simpson never flourished in the State of Pennsylvania, which has been productive of interesting types. Contrasted with either of the two men who now greeted him warmly and shook his hand, he was physically unimpressive. He was small—five feet nine inches, to Mollenhauer's six feet and Butler's five feet eleven inches and a half, and then his face was smooth, with a receding jaw. In the other two this feature was prominent. Nor were his eyes as frank as those of Butler, nor as defiant as those of Mollenhauer; but for subtlety they were unmatched by either—deep, strange, receding, cavernous eyes which contemplated you as might those of a cat looking out of a dark hole, and suggesting all the artfulness that has ever distinguished the feline family. He had a strange mop of black hair sweeping down over a fine, low, white forehead, and a skin as pale and bluish as poor health might make it; but there was, nevertheless, resident here a strange, resistant, capable force that ruled men—the subtlety with which he knew how to feed cupidity with hope and gain and the ruthlessness with which he repaid those who said him nay. He was a still man, as such a man might well have been—feeble and fish-like in his handshake, wan and slightly lackadaisical in his smile, but speaking always with eyes that answered for every defect.

"Av'nin', Mark, I'm glad to see you," was Butler's greeting.

"How are you, Edward?" came the quiet reply.

"Well, Senator, you're not looking any the worse for wear. Can I pour you something?"

"Nothing to-night, Henry," replied Simpson. "I haven't long to stay. I just stopped by on my way home. My wife's over here at the Cavanaghs', and I have to stop by to fetch her."

"Well, it's a good thing you dropped in, Senator, just when you did," began Mollenhauer, seating himself after his guest. "Butler here has been telling me of a little political problem that has arisen since I saw you. I suppose you've heard that Chicago is burning?"

"Yes; Cavanagh was just telling me. It looks to be quite serious. I think the market will drop heavily in the morning."

"I wouldn't be surprised myself," put in Mollenhauer, laconically.

"Here's the paper now," said Butler, as John, the servant, came in from the street bearing the paper in his hand. Mollenhauer took it and spread it out before them. It was among the earliest of the "extras" that were issued in this country, and contained a rather impressive spread of type announcing that the conflagration in the lake city was growing hourly worse since its inception the day before.

"Well, that is certainly dreadful," said Simpson. "I'm very sorry for Chicago. I have many friends there. I shall hope to hear that it is not so bad as it seems."

The man had a rather grandiloquent manner which he never abandoned under any circumstances.

"The matter that Butler was telling me about," continued Mollenhauer, "has something to do with this in a way. You know the habit our city treasurers have of loaning out their money at two per cent.?"

"Yes?" said Simpson, inquiringly.

"Well, Mr. Stener, it seems, has been loaning out a good deal of the city's money to this young Cowperwood, in Third Street, who has been handling city loans."

"You don't say!" said Simpson, putting on an air of surprise. "Not much, I hope?" The Senator, like Butler and Mollenhauer, was profiting greatly by cheap loans from the same source to various designated city depositories.

"Well, it seems that Stener has loaned him as much as five hundred thousand dollars, and if by any chance Cowperwood shouldn't be able to weather this storm, Stener is apt to be short that amount, and that wouldn't look so good as a voting proposition to the people in November, do you think? Cowperwood owes Mr. Butler here one hundred thousand dollars, and because of that he came to see him to-night. He wanted Butler to see if something couldn't be done through us to tide him over. If not"—he waved one hand suggestively—"well, he might fail."

Simpson fingered his strange, wide mouth with his delicate hand. "What have they been doing with the five hundred thousand dollars?" he asked.

"Oh, the boys must make a little somethin' on the side," said Butler, cheerfully. "I think they've been buyin' up street-railways, for one thing." He stuck his thumbs in the armholes of his vest. Both Mollenhauer and Simpson smiled wan smiles.

"Quite so," said Mollenhauer. Senator Simpson merely looked the deep things that he thought.

He, too, was thinking how useless it was for any one to approach a group of politicians with a proposition like this, particularly in a crisis such as bid fair to occur. He reflected that if he and Butler and Mollenhauer could get together and promise Cowperwood protection in return for the surrender of his street-railway holdings it would be a very different matter. It would be very easy in this case to carry the city treasury loan along in silence and even issue more money to support it; but it was not sure, in the first place, that Cowperwood could be made to surrender his stocks, and in the second place that either Butler or Mollenhauer would enter into any such deal with him, Simpson. Butler had evidently come here to say a good word for Cowperwood. Mollenhauer and himself were silent rivals. Although they worked together politically it was toward essentially different financial ends. They were allied in no one particular financial proposition, any more than Mollenhauer and Butler were. And besides, in all probability Cowperwood was no fool. He was not equally guilty with Stener; the latter had loaned him money. The Senator reflected on whether he should broach some such subtle solution of the situation as had occurred to him to his colleagues, but he decided not. Really Mollenhauer was too treacherous a man to work with on a thing of this kind. It was a splendid chance but dangerous. He had better go it alone. For the present they should demand of Stener that he get Cowperwood to return the five hundred thousand dollars if he could. If not, Stener could be sacrificed for the benefit of the party, if need be. Cowperwood's stocks, with this tip as to his condition, would, Simpson reflected, offer a good opportunity for a little stock-exchange work on the part of his own brokers. They could spread rumors as to Cowperwood's condition and then offer to take his shares off his hands—for a song, of course. It was an evil moment that led Cowperwood to Butler.

"Well, now," said the Senator, after a prolonged silence, "I might sympathize with Mr. Cowperwood in his situation, and I certainly don't blame him for buying up street-railways if he can; but I really don't see what can be done for him very well in this crisis. I don't know about you, gentlemen, but I am rather certain that I am not in a position to pick other people's chestnuts out of the fire if I wanted to, just now. It all depends on whether we feel that the danger to the party is sufficient to warrant our going down into our pockets and assisting him."

At the mention of real money to be loaned Mollenhauer pulled a long face. "I can't see that I will be able to do very much for Mr. Cowperwood," he sighed.

"Begad," said Buler, with a keen sense of humor, "it looks to me as if I'd better be gettin' in my one hundred thousand dollars. That's the first business of the early mornin'." Neither Simpson nor Mollenhauer condescended on this occasion to smile even the wan smile they had smiled before. They merely looked wise and solemn.

"But this matter of the city treasury, now," said Senator Simpson, after the atmosphere had been allowed to settle a little, "is something to which we shall have to devote a little thought. If Mr. Cowperwood should fail, and the treasury lose that much money, it would embarrass us no little. What lines are they," he added, as an afterthought, "that this man has been particularly interested in?"

"I really don't know," replied Butler, who did not care to say what Owen had told him on the drive over.

"I don't see," said Mollenhauer, "unless we can make Stener get the money back before this man Cowperwood fails, how we can save ourselves from considerable annoyance later; but if we did anything which would look as though we were going to compel restitution, he would probably shut up shop anyhow. So there's no remedy in that direction. And it wouldn't be very kind to our friend Edward here to do it until we hear how he comes out on his affair." He was referring to Butler's loan.

"Certainly not," said Senator Simpson, with true political sagacity and feeling.

"I'll have that one hundred thousand dollars in the mornin'," said Butler, "and never fear."

"I think," said Simpson, "if anything comes of this matter that we will have to do our best to hush it up until after the election. The newspapers can just as well keep silent on that score as not. There's one thing I would suggest"—and he was now thinking of the street-railway properties which Cowperwood had so judiciously collected—"and that is that the city treasurer be cautioned against advancing any more money in a situation of this kind. He might readily be compromised into advancing much more. I suppose a word from you, Henry, would prevent that."

"Yes; I can do that," said Mollenhauer, solemnly.

"My judgement would be," said Butler, in a rather obscure manner, thinking of Cowperwood's mistake in appealing to these noble protectors of the public, "that it's best to let sleepin' dogs run be themselves."

Thus ended Frank Cowperwood's dreams of what Butler and his political associates might do for him in his hour of distress.

The energies of Cowperwood after leaving Butler were devoted to the task of seeing others who might be of some assistance to him. He had left word with Mrs. Stener that if any message came from her husband he was to be notified at once. He hunted up Walter Leigh, of Drexel & Co., Avery Stone of Jay Cooke & Co., and President Davison of the Girard National Bank. He wanted to see what they thought of the situation and to negotiate a loan with President Davison covering all his real and personal property.

"I can't tell you, Frank," Walter Leigh insisted, "I don't know how things will be running by to-morrow noon. I'm glad to know how you stand. I'm glad you're doing what you're doing—getting all your affairs in shape. It will help a lot. I'll favor you all I possibly can. But if the chief decides on a certain group of loans to be called, they'll have to be called, that's all. I'll do my best to make things look better. If the whole of Chicago is wiped out, the insurance companies—some of them, anyhow—are sure to go, and then look out. I suppose you'll call in all your loans?"

"Not any more than I have to."

"Well, that's just the way it is here—or will be."

The two men shook hands. They liked each other. Leigh was of the city's fashionable coterie, a society man to the manner born, but with a wealth of common sense and a great deal of worldly experience.

"I'll tell you, Frank," he observed at parting, "I've always thought you were carrying too much street-railway. It's great stuff if you can get away with it, but it's just in a pinch like this that you're apt to get hurt. You've been making money pretty fast out of that and city loans."

He looked directly into his long-time friend's eyes, and they smiled.

It was the same with Avery Stone, President Davison, and others. They had all already heard rumors of disaster when he arrived. They were not sure what the morrow would bring forth. It looked very unpromising.

Cowperwood decided to stop and see Butler again for he felt certain his interview with Mollenhauer and Simpson was now over. Butler, who had been meditating what he should say to Cowperwood, was not unfriendly in his manner. "So you're back," he said, when Cowperwood appeared.

"Yes, Mr. Butler."

"Well, I'm not sure that I've been able to do anything for you. I'm afraid not," Butler said, cautiously. "It's a hard job you set me. Mollenhauer seems to think that he'll support the market, on his own account. I think he will. Simpson has interests which he has to protect. I'm going to buy for myself, of course."

He paused to reflect.

"I couldn't get them to call a conference with any of the big moneyed men as yet," he added, warily. "They'd rather wait and see what happens in the mornin'. Still, I wouldn't be down-hearted if I were you. If things turn out very bad they may change their minds. I had to tell them about Stener. It's pretty bad, but they're hopin' you'll come through and straighten that out. I hope so. About my own loan—well, I'll see how things are in the mornin'. If I raisonably can I'll lave it with you. You'd better see me again about it. I wouldn't try to get any more money out of Stener if I were you. It's pretty bad as it is."

Cowperwood saw at once that he was to get no aid from the politicians. The one thing that disturbed him was this reference to Stener. Had they already communicated with him—warned him? If so, his own coming to Butler had been a bad move; and yet from the point of view of his possible failure on the morrow it had been advisable. At least now the politicians knew where he stood. If he got in a very tight corner he would come to Butler again—the politicians could assist him or not, as they chose. If they did not help him and he failed, and the election were lost, it was their own fault. Anyhow, if he could see Stener first the latter would not be such a fool as to stand in his own light in a crisis like this.

"Things look rather dark to-night, Mr. Butler," he said, smartly, "but I still think I'll come through. I hope so, anyhow. I'm sorry to have put you to so much trouble. I wish, of course, that you gentlemen could see your way clear to assist me, but if you can't, you can't. I have a number of things that I can do. I hope that you will leave your loan as long as you can."

He went briskly out, and Butler meditated. "A clever young chap that," he said. "It's too bad. But he may come out all right at that."

Cowperwood hurried to his own home only to find his father awake and brooding. To him he talked with that strong vein of sympathy and understanding which is usually characteristic of those drawn by ties of flesh and blood. He liked his father. He sympathized with his painstaking effort to get up in the world. He could not forget that as a boy he had had the loving sympathy and interest of his father. The loan which he had from the Third

National, on somewhat weak Union Street Railway shares he could probably replace if stocks did not drop too tremendously. He must replace this at all costs. But his father's investments in street-railways, which had risen with his own ventures, and which now involved an additional two hundred thousand—how could he protect those? The shares were hypothecated and the money was used for other things. Additional collateral would have to be furnished the several banks carrying them. It was nothing except loans, loans, loans, and the need of protecting them. If he could only get an additional deposit of two or three hundred thousand dollars from Stener. But that, in the face of possible financial difficulties, was rank criminality. All depended on the morrow.

Monday, the ninth, dawned gray and cheerless. He was up with the first ray of light, shaved and dressed, and went over, under the gray-green pergola, to his father's house. He was up, also, and stirring about, for he had not been able to sleep. His gray eyebrows and gray hair looked rather shaggy and disheveled, and his side-whiskers anything but decorative. The old gentleman's eyes were tired, and his face was gray. Cowperwood could see that he was worrying. He looked up from a small, ornate escritoire of buhl, which Ellsworth had found somewhere, and where he was quietly tabulating a list of his resources and liabilities. Cowperwood winced. He hated to see his father worried, but he could not help it. He had hoped sincerely, when they built their houses together, that the days of worry for his father had gone forever.

"Counting up?" he asked, familiarly, with a smile. He wanted to hearten the old gentleman as much as possible.

"I was just running over my affairs again to see where I stood in case—" He looked quizzically at his son, and Frank smiled again.

"I wouldn't worry, father. I told you how I fixed it so that Butler and that crowd will support the market. I have Rivers and Targool and Harry Eltinge on 'change helping me sell out, and they are the best men there. They'll handle the situation carefully. I couldn't trust Ed or Joe in this case, for the moment they began to sell everybody would know what was going on with me. This way my men will seem like bears hammering the market, but not hammering too hard. I ought to be able to unload enough at ten points off to raise five hundred thousand. The market may not go lower than that. You can't tell. It isn't going to sink indefinitely. If I just knew what the big insurance companies were going to do! The morning paper hasn't come yet, has it?"

He was going to pull a bell, but remembered that the servants would scarcely be up as yet. He went to the front door himself. There were the Press and the Public Ledger lying damp from the presses. He picked them up and glanced at the front pages. His countenance fell. On one, the Press, was spread a great black map of Chicago, a most funereal-looking thing, the black portion indicating the burned section. He had never seen a map of Chicago before in just this clear, definite way. That white portion was Lake Michigan, and there was the Chicago River dividing the city into three almost equal portions—the north side, the west side, the south side. He saw at once that the city was curiously arranged, somewhat like Philadelphia, and that the business section was probably an area of two or three miles square, set at the juncture of the three sides, and lying south of the main stem of the river, where it flowed into the lake after the southwest and northwest branches had united to form it. This was a significant central area; but, according to this map, it was all burned out. "Chicago in Ashes" ran a great side-heading set in heavily leaded black type. It went on to detail the sufferings of the homeless, the number of the dead, the number of those whose fortunes had been destroyed. Then it descanted upon the probable effect in the East. Insurance companies and manufacturers might not be able to meet the great strain of all this.

"Damn!" said Cowperwood gloomily. "I wish I were out of this stock-jobbing business. I wish I had never gotten into it." He returned to his drawing-room and scanned both accounts most carefully.

Then, though it was still early, he and his father drove to his office. There were already messages awaiting him, a dozen or more, to cancel or sell. While he was standing there a messenger-boy brought him three more. One was from Stener and said that he would be back by twelve o'clock, the very earliest he could make it. Cowperwood was relieved and yet distressed. He would need large sums of money to meet various loans before three. Every hour was precious. He must arrange to meet Stener at the station and talk to him before any one else should see him. Clearly this was going to be a hard, dreary, strenuous day.

Third Street, by the time he reached there, was stirring with other bankers and brokers called forth by the exigencies of the occasion. There was a suspicious hurrying of feet—that intensity which makes all the difference in the world between a hundred people placid and a hundred people disturbed. At the exchange, the atmosphere was feverish. At the sound of the gong, the staccato uproar began. Its metallic vibrations were still in the air when the two hundred men who composed this local organization at its utmost stress of calculation, threw themselves upon each other in a gibbering struggle to dispose of or seize bargains of the hour. The interests were so varied that it was impossible to say at which pole it was best to sell or buy.

Targool and Rivers had been delegated to stay at the center of things, Joseph and Edward to hover around on the outside and to pick up such opportunities of selling as might offer a reasonable return on the stock. The "bears" were determined to jam things down, and it all depended on how well the agents of Mollenhauer, Simpson, Butler, and others supported things in the street-railway world whether those stocks retained any strength or not. The last thing Butler had said the night before was that they would do the best they could. They would buy up to a certain point. Whether they would support the market indefinitely he would not say. He could not vouch for Mollenhauer and Simpson. Nor did he know the condition of their affairs.

While the excitement was at its highest Cowperwood came in. As he stood in the door looking to catch the eye of Rivers, the 'change gong sounded, and trading stopped. All the brokers and traders faced about to the little balcony, where the secretary of the 'change made his announcements; and there he stood, the door open behind him, a small, dark, clerkly man of thirty-eight or forty, whose spare figure and pale face bespoke the methodic mind that knows no venturous thought. In his right hand he held a slip of white paper. "The American Fire Insurance Company of Boston announces its inability to meet its obligations." The gong sounded again.

Immediately the storm broke anew, more voluble than before, because, if after one hour of investigation on this Monday morning one insurance company had gone down, what would four or five hours or a day or two bring forth? It meant that men who had been burned out in Chicago would not be able to resume business. It meant that all loans connected with this concern had been, or would be called now. And the cries of frightened "bulls" offering thousand and five thousand lot holdings in Northern Pacific, Illinois Central, Reading, Lake Shore, Wabash; in all the local streetcar lines; and in Cowperwood's city loans at constantly falling prices was sufficient to take the heart out of all concerned. He hurried to Arthur Rivers's side in the lull; but there was little he could say.

"It looks as though the Mollenhauer and Simpson crowds aren't doing much for the market," he observed, gravely.

"They've had advices from New York," explained Rivers solemnly. "It can't be supported very well. There are three insurance companies over there on the verge of quitting, I understand. I expect to see them posted any minute."

They stepped apart from the pandemonium, to discuss ways and means. Under his agreement with Stener, Cowperwood could buy up to one hundred thousand dollars of city loan, above the customary wash sales, or market manipulation, by which they were making money. This was in case the market had to be genuinely supported. He decided to buy sixty thousand dollars worth now, and use this to sustain his loans elsewhere. Stener would pay him for this instantly, giving him more ready cash. It might help him in one way and another; and, anyhow, it might tend to strengthen the other securities long enough at least to allow him to realize a little something now at better than ruinous rates. If only he had the means "to go short" on this market! If only doing so did not really mean ruin to his present position. It was characteristic of the man that even in this crisis he should be seeing how the very thing that of necessity, because of his present obligations, might ruin him, might also, under slightly different conditions, yield him a great harvest. He could not take advantage of it, however. He could not be on both sides of this market. It was either "bear" or "bull," and of necessity he was "bull." It was strange but true. His subtlety could not avail him here. He was about to turn and hurry to see a certain banker who might loan him something on his house, when the gong struck again. Once more trading ceased. Arthur Rivers, from his position at the State securities post, where city loan was sold, and where he had started to buy for Cowperwood, looked significantly at him. Newton Targool hurried to Cowperwood's side.

"You're up against it," he exclaimed. "I wouldn't try to sell against this market. It's no use. They're cutting the ground from under you. The bottom's out. Things are bound to turn in a few days. Can't you hold out? Here's more trouble."

He raised his eyes to the announcer's balcony.

"The Eastern and Western Fire Insurance Company of New York announces that it cannot meet its obligations."

A low sound something like "Haw!" broke forth. The announcer's gavel struck for order.

"The Erie Fire Insurance Company of Rochester announces that it cannot meet its obligations."

Again that "H-a-a-a-w!"

Once more the gavel.

"The American Trust Company of New York has suspended payment."

"H-a-a-a-w!"

The storm was on.

"What do you think?" asked Targool. "You can't brave this storm. Can't you quit selling and hold out for a few days? Why not sell short?"

"They ought to close this thing up," Cowperwood said, shortly. "It would be a splendid way out. Then nothing could be done."

He hurried to consult with those who, finding themselves in a similar predicament with himself, might use their influence to bring it about. It was a sharp trick to play on those who, now finding the market favorable to their designs in its falling condition, were harvesting a fortune. But what was that to him? Business was business. There was no use selling at ruinous figures, and he gave his lieutenants orders to stop. Unless the bankers favored him heavily, or the stock exchange was closed, or Stener could be induced to deposit an additional three hundred thousand with him at once, he was ruined. He hurried down the street to various bankers and brokers suggesting that they do this—close the exchange. At a few minutes before twelve o'clock he drove rapidly to the station to meet Stener; but to his great disappointment the latter did not arrive. It looked as though he had missed his train. Cowperwood sensed something, some trick; and decided to go to the city hall and also to Stener's house. Perhaps he had returned and was trying to avoid him.

Not finding him at his office, he drove direct to his house. Here he was not surprised to meet Stener just coming out, looking very pale and distraught. At the sight of Cowperwood he actually blanched.

"Why, hello, Frank," he exclaimed, sheepishly, "where do you come from?"

"What's up, George?" asked Cowperwood. "I thought you were coming into Broad Street."

"So I was," returned Stener, foolishly, "but I thought I would get off at West Philadelphia and change my clothes. I've a lot of things to 'tend to yet this afternoon. I was coming in to see you." After Cowperwood's urgent telegram this was silly, but the young banker let it pass.

"Jump in, George," he said. "I have something very important to talk to you about. I told you in my telegram about the likelihood of a panic. It's on. There isn't a moment to lose. Stocks are 'way down, and most of my loans are being called. I want to know if you won't let me have three hundred and fifty thousand dollars for a few days at four or five per cent. I'll pay it all back to you. I need it very badly. If I don't get it I'm likely to fail. You know what that means, George. It will tie up every dollar I have. Those street-car holdings of yours will be tied up with me. I won't be able to let you realize on them, and that will put those loans of mine from the treasury in bad shape. You won't be able to put the money back, and you know what that means. We're in this thing together. I want to see you through safely, but I can't do it without your help. I had to go to Butler last night to see about a loan of his, and I'm doing my best to get money from other sources. But I can't see my way through on this, I'm afraid, unless you're willing to help me." Cowperwood paused. He wanted to put the whole case clearly and succinctly to him before he had a chance to refuse—to make him realize it as his own predicament.

As a matter of fact, what Cowperwood had keenly suspected was literally true. Stener had been reached. The moment Butler and Simpson had left him the night before, Mollenhauer had sent for his very able secretary, Abner Sengstack, and despatched him to learn the truth about Stener's whereabouts. Sengstack had then sent a long wire to Strobik, who was with Stener, urging him to caution the latter against Cowperwood. The state of the treasury was known. Stener and Strobik were to be met by Sengstack at Wilmington (this to forefend against the possibility of Cowperwood's reaching Stener first)—and the whole state of affairs made perfectly plain. No more money was to be used under penalty of prosecution. If Stener wanted to see any one he must see Mollenhauer. Sengstack, having received a telegram from Strobik informing him of their proposed arrival at noon the next day, had proceeded to Wilmington to meet them. The result was that Stener did not come direct into the business heart of the city, but instead got off at West Philadelphia, proposing to go first to his house to change his clothes and then to see Mollenhauer before meeting Cowperwood. He was very badly frightened and wanted time to think.

"I can't do it, Frank," he pleaded, piteously. "I'm in pretty bad in this matter. Mollenhauer's secretary met the train out at Wilmington just now to warn me against this situation, and Strobik is against it. They know how much money I've got outstanding. You or somebody has told them. I can't go against Mollenhauer. I owe everything I've got to him, in a way. He got me this place."

"Listen, George. Whatever you do at this time, don't let this political loyalty stuff cloud your judgment. You're in a very serious position and so am I. If you don't act for yourself with me now no one is going to act for you—now or later—no one. And later will be too late. I proved that last night when I went to Butler to get help for the two of us. They all know about this business of our street-railway holdings and they want to shake us out and that's the big and little of it—nothing more and nothing less. It's a case of dog eat dog in this game and this particular situation and it's up to us to save ourselves against everybody or go down together, and that's just what I'm here to tell you. Mollenhauer doesn't care any more for you to-day than he does for that lamp-post. It isn't that money you've paid out to me that's worrying him, but who's getting something for it and what. Well they know that you and I are getting street-railways, don't you see, and they don't want us to have them. Once they get those out of our hands they won't waste another day on you or me. Can't you see that? Once we've lost all we've invested, you're down and so am I—and no one is going to turn a hand for you or me politically or in any other way. I want you to understand that, George, because it's true. And before you say you won't or you will do anything because Mollenhauer says so, you want to think over what I have to tell you."

106

He was in front of Stener now, looking him directly in the eye and by the kinetic force of his mental way attempting to make Stener take the one step that might save him—Cowperwood—however little in the long run it might do for Stener. And, more interesting still, he did not care. Stener, as he saw him now, was a pawn in whosoever's hands he happened to be at the time, and despite Mr. Mollenhauer and Mr. Simpson and Mr. Butler he proposed to attempt to keep him in his own hands if possible. And so he stood there looking at him as might a snake at a bird determined to galvanize him into selfish self-interest if possible. But Stener was so frightened that at the moment it looked as though there was little to be done with him. His face was a grayish-blue: his eyelids and eye rings puffy and his hands and lips moist. God, what a hole he was in now!

"Say that's all right, Frank," he exclaimed desperately. "I know what you say is true. But look at me and my position, if I do give you this money. What can't they do to me, and won't. If you only look at it from my point of view. If only you hadn't gone to Butler before you saw me."

"As though I could see you, George, when you were off duck shooting and when I was wiring everywhere I knew to try to get in touch with you. How could I? The situation had to be met. Besides, I thought Butler was more friendly to me than he proved. But there's no use being angry with me now, George, for going to Butler as I did, and anyhow you can't afford to be now. We're in this thing together. It's a case of sink or swim for just us two—not any one else—just us—don't you get that? Butler couldn't or wouldn't do what I wanted him to do—get Mollenhauer and Simpson to support the market. Instead of that they are hammering it. They have a game of their own. It's to shake us out—can't you see that? Take everything that you and I have gathered. It is up to you and me, George, to save ourselves, and that's what I'm here for now. If you don't let me have three hundred and fifty thousand dollars—three hundred thousand, anyhow—you and I are ruined. It will be worse for you, George, than for me, for I'm not involved in this thing in any way—not legally, anyhow. But that's not what I'm thinking of. What I want to do is to save us both—put us on easy street for the rest of our lives, whatever they say or do, and it's in your power, with my help, to do that for both of us. Can't you see that? I want to save my business so then I can help you to save your name and money." He paused, hoping this had convinced Stener, but the latter was still shaking.

"But what can I do, Frank?" he pleaded, weakly. "I can't go against Mollenhauer. They can prosecute me if I do that. They can do it, anyhow. I can't do that. I'm not strong enough. If they didn't know, if you hadn't told them, it might be different, but this way—" He shook his head sadly, his gray eyes filled with a pale distress.

"George," replied Cowperwood, who realized now that only the sternest arguments would have any effect here, "don't talk about what I did. What I did I had to do. You're in danger of losing your head and your nerve and making a serious mistake here, and I don't want to see you make it. I have five hundred thousand of the city's money invested for you—partly for me, and partly for you, but more for you than for me"—which, by the way, was not true—"and here you are hesitating in an hour like this as to whether you will protect your interest or not. I can't understand it. This is a crisis, George. Stocks are tumbling on every side—everybody's stocks. You're not alone in this—neither am I. This is a panic, brought on by a fire, and you can't expect to come out of a panic alive unless you do something to protect yourself. You say you owe your place to Mollenhauer and that you're afraid of what he'll do. If you look at your own situation and mine, you'll see that it doesn't make much difference what he does, so long as I don't fail. If I fail, where are you? Who's going to save you from prosecution? Will Mollenhauer or any one else come forward and put five hundred thousand dollars in the treasury for you? He will not. If Mollenhauer and the others have your interests at heart, why aren't they helping me on 'change today? I'll tell you why. They want your street-railway holdings and mine, and they don't care whether you go to jail afterward or not. Now if you're wise you will listen to me. I've been loyal to you, haven't I? You've made money through me—lots of it. If you're wise, George, you'll go to your office and write me your check for three hundred thousand dollars, anyhow, before you do a single other thing. Don't see anybody and don't do anything till you've done that. You can't be hung any more for a sheep than you can for a lamb. No one can prevent you from giving me that check. You're the city treasurer. Once I have that I can see my way out of this, and I'll pay it all back to you next week or the week after—this panic is sure to end in that time. With that put back in the treasury we can see them about the five hundred thousand a little later. In three months, or less, I can fix it so that you can put that back. As a matter of fact, I can do it in fifteen days once I am on my feet again. Time is all I want. You won't have lost your holdings and nobody will cause you any trouble if you put the money back. They don't care to risk a scandal any more than you do. Now what'll you do, George? Mollenhauer can't stop you from doing this any more than I can make you. Your life is in your own hands. What will you do?"

Stener stood there ridiculously meditating when, as a matter of fact, his very financial blood was oozing away. Yet he was afraid to act. He was afraid of Mollenhauer, afraid of Cowperwood, afraid of life and of himself. The thought of panic, loss, was not so much a definite thing connected with his own property, his money, as it was with his social and political standing in the community. Few people have the sense of financial individuality strongly developed. They do not know what it means to be a controller of wealth, to have that which releases the sources of social action—its medium of exchange. They want money, but not for money's sake. They want it for what it will buy in the way of simple comforts, whereas the financier wants it for what it will control—for what it will represent in the way of dignity, force, power. Cowperwood wanted money in that way; Stener not. That was why he had been so ready to let Cowperwood act for him; and now, when he should have seen more clearly than ever the significance of what Cowperwood was proposing, he was frightened and his reason obscured by such things as Mollenhauer's probable opposition and rage, Cowperwood's possible failure, his own inability to face a real crisis. Cowperwood's innate financial ability did not reassure Stener in this hour. The banker was too young, too new. Mollenhauer was older, richer. So was Simpson; so was Butler. These men, with their wealth, represented the big forces, the big standards in his world. And besides, did not Cowperwood himself confess that he was in great danger—that he was in a corner. That was the worst possible confession to make to Stener—although under the circumstances it was the only one that could be made—for he had no courage to face danger.

So it was that now, Stener stood by Cowperwood meditating—pale, flaccid; unable to see the main line of his interests quickly, unable to follow it definitely, surely, vigorously—while they drove to his office. Cowperwood entered it with him for the sake of continuing his plea.

"Well, George," he said earnestly, "I wish you'd tell me. Time's short. We haven't a moment to lose. Give me the money, won't you, and I'll get out of this quick. We haven't a moment, I tell you. Don't let those people frighten you off. They're playing their own little game; you play yours."

"I can't, Frank," said Stener, finally, very weakly, his sense of his own financial future, overcome for the time being by the thought of Mollenhauer's hard, controlling face. "I'll have to think. I can't do it right now. Strobik just left me before I saw you, and—"

"Good God, George," exclaimed Cowperwood, scornfully, "don't talk about Strobik! What's he got to do with it? Think of yourself. Think of where you will be. It's your future—not Strobik's—that you have to think of."

"I know, Frank," persisted Stener, weakly; "but, really, I don't see how I can. Honestly I don't. You say yourself you're not sure whether you can come out of things all right, and three hundred thousand more is three hundred thousand more. I can't, Frank. I really can't. It wouldn't be right. Besides, I want to talk to Mollenhauer first, anyhow."

"Good God, how you talk!" exploded Cowperwood, angrily, looking at him with ill-concealed contempt. "Go ahead! See Mollenhauer! Let him tell you how to cut your own throat for his benefit. It won't be right to loan me three hundred thousand dollars more, but it will be right to let the five hundred thousand dollars you have loaned stand unprotected and lose it. That's right, isn't it? That's just what you propose to do—lose it, and everything else besides. I want to tell you what it is, George—you've lost your mind. You've let a single message from Mollenhauer frighten you to death, and because of that you're going to risk your fortune, your reputation, your standing—everything. Do you really realize what this means if I fail? You will be a convict, I tell you, George. You will go to prison. This fellow Mollenhauer, who is so quick to tell you what not to do now, will be the last man to turn a hand for you once you're down. Why, look at me—I've helped you, haven't I? Haven't I handled your affairs satisfactorily for you up to now? What in Heaven's name has got into you? What have you to be afraid of?"

Stener was just about to make another weak rejoinder when the door from the outer office opened, and Albert Stires, Stener's chief clerk, entered. Stener was too flustered to really pay any attention to Stires for the moment; but Cowperwood took matters in his own hands.

"What is it, Albert?" he asked, familiarly.

"Mr. Sengstack from Mr. Mollenhauer to see Mr. Stener."

At the sound of this dreadful name Stener wilted like a leaf. Cowperwood saw it. He realized that his last hope of getting the three hundred thousand dollars was now probably gone. Still he did not propose to give up as yet.

"Well, George," he said, after Albert had gone out with instructions that Stener would see Sengstack in a moment. "I see how it is. This man has got you mesmerized. You can't act for yourself now—you're too frightened. I'll let it rest for the present; I'll come back. But for Heaven's sake pull yourself together. Think what it means. I'm telling you exactly what's going to happen if you don't. You'll be independently rich if you do. You'll be a convict if you don't."

And deciding he would make one more effort in the street before seeing Butler again, he walked out briskly, jumped into his light spring runabout waiting outside—a handsome little yellow-glazed vehicle, with a yellow leather cushion seat, drawn by a young, high-stepping bay mare—and sent her scudding from door to door, throwing down the lines indifferently and bounding up the steps of banks and into office doors.

But all without avail. All were interested, considerate; but things were very uncertain. The Girard National Bank refused an hour's grace, and he had to send a large bundle of his most valuable securities to cover his stock shrinkage there. Word came from his father at two that as president of the Third National he would have to call for his one hundred and fifty thousand dollars due there. The directors were suspicious of his stocks. He at once wrote a check against fifty thousand dollars of his deposits in that bank, took twenty-five thousand of his available office funds, called a loan of fifty thousand against Tighe & Co., and sold sixty thousand Green & Coates, a line he had been tentatively dabbling in, for one-third their value—and, combining the general results, sent them all to the Third National. His father was immensely relieved from one point of view, but sadly depressed from another. He hurried out at the noon-hour to see what his own holdings would bring. He was compromising himself in a way by doing it, but his parental heart, as well as is own financial interests, were involved. By mortgaging his house and securing loans on his furniture, carriages, lots, and stocks, he managed to raise one hundred thousand in cash, and deposited it in his own bank to Frank's credit; but it was a very light anchor to windward in this swirling storm, at that. Frank had been counting on getting all of his loans extended three or four days at least. Reviewing his situation at two o'clock of this Monday afternoon, he said to himself thoughtfully but grimly: "Well, Stener has to loan me three hundred thousand—that's all there is to it. And I'll have to see Butler now, or he'll be calling his loan before three."

He hurried out, and was off to Butler's house, driving like mad.

CHAPTER XXVI

Things had changed greatly since last Cowperwood had talked with Butler. Although most friendly at the time the proposition was made that he should combine with Mollenhauer and Simpson to sustain the market, alas, now on this Monday morning at nine o'clock, an additional complication had been added to the already tangled situation which had changed Butler's attitude completely. As he was leaving his home to enter his runabout, at nine o'clock in the morning of this same day in which Cowperwood was seeking Stener's aid, the postman, coming up, had handed Butler four letters, all of which he paused for a moment to glance at. One was from a sub-contractor by the name of O'Higgins, the second was from Father Michel, his confessor, of St. Timothy's, thanking him for a contribution to the parish poor fund; a third was from Drexel & Co. relating to a deposit, and the fourth was an anonymous communication, on cheap stationery from some one who was apparently not very literate—a woman most likely—written in a scrawling hand, which read:

DEAR SIR—This is to warn you that your daughter
Aileen is running around with a man that she shouldn't,
Frank A. Cowperwood, the banker. If you don't believe
it, watch the house at 931 North Tenth Street. Then you
can see for yourself.

There was neither signature nor mark of any kind to indicate from whence it might have come. Butler got the impression strongly that it might have been written by some one living in the vicinity of the number indicated. His intuitions were keen at times. As a matter of fact, it was written by a girl, a member of St. Timothy's Church, who did live in the vicinity of the house indicated, and who knew Aileen by sight and was jealous of her airs and her position. She was a thin, anemic, dissatisfied creature who had the type of brain which can reconcile the gratification of personal spite with a comforting sense of having fulfilled a moral duty. Her home was some five doors north of the unregistered Cowperwood domicile on the opposite side of the street, and by degrees, in the course of time, she made out, or imagined that she had, the significance of this institution, piecing fact to fancy and fusing all with that keen intuition which is so closely related to fact. The result was eventually this letter which now spread clear and grim before Butler's eyes.

The Irish are a philosophic as well as a practical race. Their first and strongest impulse is to make the best of a bad situation—to put a better face on evil than it normally wears. On first reading these lines the intelligence they conveyed sent a peculiar chill over Butler's sturdy frame. His jaw instinctively closed, and his gray eyes narrowed. Could this be true? If it were not, would the author of the letter say so practically, "If you don't believe it, watch the house at 931 North Tenth Street"? Wasn't that in itself proof positive—the hard, matter-of-fact realism of it? And this was the man who had come to him the night before seeking aid—whom he had done so much to assist. There forced itself into his naturally slow-moving but rather accurate mind a sense of the distinction and charm of his daughter—a considerably sharper picture than he had ever had before, and at the same time a keener understanding of the personality of Frank Algernon Cowperwood. How was it he had failed to detect the real subtlety of this man? How was it he had never seen any sign of it, if there had been anything between Cowperwood and Aileen?

Parents are frequently inclined, because of a time-flattered sense of security, to take their children for granted. Nothing ever has happened, so nothing ever will happen. They see their children every day, and through the eyes of affection; and despite their natural charm and their own strong parental love, the children are apt to become not only commonplaces, but ineffably secure against evil. Mary is naturally a good girl—a little wild, but what harm can befall her? John is a straight-forward, steady-going boy—how could he get into trouble? The astonishment of most parents at the sudden accidental revelation of evil in connection with any of their children is almost invariably pathetic. "My John! My Mary! Impossible!" But it is possible. Very possible. Decidedly likely. Some, through lack of experience or understanding, or both, grow hard and bitter on the instant. They feel themselves astonishingly abased in the face of notable tenderness and sacrifice. Others collapse before the grave manifestation of the insecurity and uncertainty of life—the mystic chemistry of our being. Still others, taught roughly by life, or endowed with understanding or intuition, or both, see in this the latest manifestation of that incomprehensible chemistry which we call life and personality, and, knowing that it is quite vain to hope to gainsay it, save by greater subtlety, put the best face they can upon the matter and call a truce until they can think. We all know that life is unsolvable—we who think. The remainder imagine a vain thing, and are full of sound and fury signifying nothing.

So Edward Butler, being a man of much wit and hard, grim experience, stood there on his doorstep holding in his big, rough hand his thin slip of cheap paper which contained such a terrific indictment of his daughter. There came to him now a picture of her as she was when she was a very little girl—she was his first baby girl—and how keenly he had felt about her all these years. She had been a beautiful child—her red-gold hair had been pillowed on his breast many a time, and his hard, rough fingers had stroked her soft cheeks, lo, these thousands of times. Aileen, his lovely, dashing daughter of twenty-three! He was lost in dark, strange, unhappy speculations, without any present ability to think or say or do the right thing. He did not know what the right thing was, he finally confessed to himself. Aileen! Aileen! His Aileen! If her mother knew this it would break her heart. She mustn't! She mustn't! And yet mustn't she?

The heart of a father! The world wanders into many strange by-paths of affection. The love of a mother for her children is dominant, leonine, selfish, and unselfish. It is concentric. The love of a husband for his wife, or of a lover for his sweetheart, is a sweet bond of agreement and exchange trade in a lovely contest. The love of a father for his son or daughter, where it is love at all, is a broad, generous, sad, contemplative giving without thought of return, a hail and farewell to a troubled traveler whom he would do much to guard, a balanced judgment of weakness and strength, with pity for failure and pride in achievement. It is a lovely, generous, philosophic blossom which rarely asks too much, and seeks only to give wisely and plentifully. "That my boy may succeed! That my daughter may be happy!" Who has not heard and dwelt upon these twin fervors of fatherly wisdom and tenderness?

As Butler drove downtown his huge, slow-moving, in some respects chaotic mind turned over as rapidly as he could all of the possibilities in connection with this unexpected, sad, and disturbing revelation. Why had Cowperwood not been satisfied with his wife? Why should he enter into his (Butler's) home, of all places, to establish a clandestine relationship of this character? Was Aileen in any way to blame? She was not without mental resources of her own. She must have known what she was doing. She was a good Catholic, or, at least, had been raised so. All these years she had been going regularly to confession and communion. True, of late Butler had noticed that she did not care so much about going to church, would sometimes make excuses and stay at home on Sundays; but she had gone, as a rule. And now, now—his thoughts would come to the end of a blind alley, and then he would start back, as it were, mentally, to the center of things, and begin all over again.

He went up the stairs to his own office slowly. He went in and sat down, and thought and thought. Ten o'clock came, and eleven. His son bothered him with an occasional matter of interest, but, finding him moody, finally abandoned him to his own speculations. It was

111

twelve, and then one, and he was still sitting there thinking, when the presence of Cowperwood was announced.

Cowperwood, on finding Butler not at home, and not encountering Aileen, had hurried up to the office of the Edward Butler Contracting Company, which was also the center of some of Butler's street-railway interests. The floor space controlled by the company was divided into the usual official compartments, with sections for the bookkeepers, the road-managers, the treasurer, and so on. Owen Butler, and his father had small but attractively furnished offices in the rear, where they transacted all the important business of the company.

During this drive, curiously, by reason of one of those strange psychologic intuitions which so often precede a human difficulty of one sort or another, he had been thinking of Aileen. He was thinking of the peculiarity of his relationship with her, and of the fact that now he was running to her father for assistance. As he mounted the stairs he had a peculiar sense of the untoward; but he could not, in his view of life, give it countenance. One glance at Butler showed him that something had gone amiss. He was not so friendly; his glance was dark, and there was a certain sternness to his countenance which had never previously been manifested there in Cowperwood's memory. He perceived at once that here was something different from a mere intention to refuse him aid and call his loan. What was it? Aileen? It must be that. Somebody had suggested something. They had been seen together. Well, even so, nothing could be proved. Butler would obtain no sign from him. But his loan—that was to be called, surely. And as for an additional loan, he could see now, before a word had been said, that that thought was useless.

"I came to see you about that loan of yours, Mr. Butler," he observed, briskly, with an old-time, jaunty air. You could not have told from his manner or his face that he had observed anything out of the ordinary.

Butler, who was alone in the room—Owen having gone into an adjoining room—merely stared at him from under his shaggy brows.

"I'll have to have that money," he said, brusquely, darkly.

An old-time Irish rage suddenly welled up in his bosom as he contemplated this jaunty, sophisticated undoer of his daughter's virtue. He fairly glared at him as he thought of him and her.

"I judged from the way things were going this morning that you might want it," Cowperwood replied, quietly, without sign of tremor. "The bottom's out, I see."

"The bottom's out, and it'll not be put back soon, I'm thinkin'. I'll have to have what's belongin' to me to-day. I haven't any time to spare."

"Very well," replied Cowperwood, who saw clearly how treacherous the situation was. The old man was in a dour mood. His presence was an irritation to him, for some reason—a deadly provocation. Cowperwood felt clearly that it must be Aileen, that he must know or suspect something.

He must pretend business hurry and end this. "I'm sorry. I thought I might get an extension; but that's all right. I can get the money, though. I'll send it right over."

He turned and walked quickly to the door.

Butler got up. He had thought to manage this differently.

He had thought to denounce or even assault this man. He was about to make some insinuating remark which would compel an answer, some direct charge; but Cowperwood was out and away as jaunty as ever.

The old man was flustered, enraged, disappointed. He opened the small office door which led into the adjoining room, and called, "Owen!"

"Yes, father."

"Send over to Cowperwood's office and get that money."

"You decided to call it, eh?"

"I have."

Owen was puzzled by the old man's angry mood. He wondered what it all meant, but thought he and Cowperwood might have had a few words. He went out to his desk to write a note and call a clerk. Butler went to the window and stared out. He was angry, bitter, brutal in his vein.

"The dirty dog!" he suddenly exclaimed to himself, in a low voice. "I'll take every dollar he's got before I'm through with him. I'll send him to jail, I will. I'll break him, I will. Wait!"

He clinched his big fists and his teeth.

"I'll fix him. I'll show him. The dog! The damned scoundrel!"

Never in his life before had he been so bitter, so cruel, so relentless in his mood.

He walked his office floor thinking what he could do. Question Aileen—that was what he would do. If her face, or her lips, told him that his suspicion was true, he would deal with Cowperwood later. This city treasurer business, now. It was not a crime in so far as Cowperwood was concerned; but it might be made to be.

So now, telling the clerk to say to Owen that he had gone down the street for a few moments, he boarded a street-car and rode out to his home, where he found his elder daughter just getting ready to go out. She wore a purple-velvet street dress edged with narrow, flat gilt braid, and a striking gold-and-purple turban. She had on dainty new boots of bronze kid and long gloves of lavender suede. In her ears was one of her latest affectations, a pair of long jet earrings. The old Irishman realized on this occasion, when he saw her, perhaps more clearly than he ever had in his life, that he had grown a bird of rare plumage.

"Where are you going, daughter?" he asked, with a rather unsuccessful attempt to conceal his fear, distress, and smoldering anger.

"To the library," she said easily, and yet with a sudden realization that all was not right with her father. His face was too heavy and gray. He looked tired and gloomy.

"Come up to my office a minute," he said. "I want to see you before you go."

Aileen heard this with a strange feeling of curiosity and wonder. It was not customary for her father to want to see her in his office just when she was going out; and his manner indicated, in this instance, that the exceptional procedure portended a strange revelation of some kind. Aileen, like every other person who offends against a rigid convention of the time, was conscious of and sensitive to the possible disastrous results which would follow exposure. She had often thought about what her family would think if they knew what she was doing; she had never been able to satisfy herself in her mind as to what they would do. Her father was a very vigorous man. But she had never known him to be cruel or cold in his attitude toward her or any other member of the family, and especially not toward her. Always he seemed too fond of her to be completely alienated by anything that might happen; yet she could not be sure.

Butler led the way, planting his big feet solemnly on the steps as he went up. Aileen followed with a single glance at herself in the tall pier-mirror which stood in the hall, realizing at once how charming she looked and how uncertain she was feeling about what was to follow. What could her father want? It made the color leave her cheeks for the moment, as she thought what he might want.

Butler strolled into his stuffy room and sat down in the big leather chair, disproportioned to everything else in the chamber, but which, nevertheless, accompanied his desk. Before him, against the light, was the visitor's chair, in which he liked to have those sit whose faces he was anxious to study. When Aileen entered he motioned her to it, which was also ominous to her, and said, "Sit down there."

She took the seat, not knowing what to make of his procedure. On the instant her promise to Cowperwood to deny everything, whatever happened, came back to her. If her father was about to attack her on that score, he would get no satisfaction, she thought. She owed it to Frank. Her pretty face strengthened and hardened on the instant. Her small, white teeth set themselves in two even rows; and her father saw quite plainly that she was consciously bracing herself for an attack of some kind. He feared by this that she was guilty, and he was all the more distressed, ashamed, outraged, made wholly unhappy. He fumbled in the left-hand pocket of his coat and drew forth from among the various papers the fatal communication so cheap in its physical texture. His big fingers fumbled almost tremulously as he fished the letter-sheet out of the small envelope and unfolded it without saying a word. Aileen watched his face and his hands, wondering what it could be that he had here. He handed the paper over, small in his big fist, and said, "Read that."

Aileen took it, and for a second was relieved to be able to lower her eyes to the paper. Her relief vanished in a second, when she realized how in a moment she would have to raise them again and look him in the face.

DEAR SIR—This is to warn you that your daughter
Aileen is running around with a man that she shouldn't,
Frank A. Cowperwood, the banker. If you don't believe
it, watch the house at 931 North Tenth Street. Then you
can see for yourself.

In spite of herself the color fled from her cheeks instantly, only to come back in a hot, defiant wave.

"Why, what a lie!" she said, lifting her eyes to her father's. "To think that any one should write such a thing of me! How dare they! I think it's a shame!"

Old Butler looked at her narrowly, solemnly. He was not deceived to any extent by her bravado. If she were really innocent, he knew she would have jumped to her feet in her defiant way. Protest would have been written all over her. As it was, she only stared haughtily. He read through her eager defiance to the guilty truth.

"How do ye know, daughter, that I haven't had the house watched?" he said, quizzically. "How do ye know that ye haven't been seen goin' in there?"

Only Aileen's solemn promise to her lover could have saved her from this subtle thrust. As it was, she paled nervously; but she saw Frank Cowperwood, solemn and distinguished, asking her what she would say if she were caught.

"It's a lie!" she said, catching her breath. "I wasn't at any house at that number, and no one saw me going in there. How can you ask me that, father?"

In spite of his mixed feelings of uncertainty and yet unshakable belief that his daughter was guilty, he could not help admiring her courage—she was so defiant, as she sat there, so set in her determination to lie and thus defend herself. Her beauty helped her in his mood, raised her in his esteem. After all, what could you do with a woman of this kind? She was not a ten-year-old girl any more, as in a way he sometimes continued to fancy her.

"Ye oughtn't to say that if it isn't true, Aileen," he said. "Ye oughtn't to lie. It's against your faith. Why would anybody write a letter like that if it wasn't so?"

"But it's not so," insisted Aileen, pretending anger and outraged feeling, "and I don't think you have any right to sit there and say that to me. I haven't been there, and I'm not running around with Mr. Cowperwood. Why, I hardly know the man except in a social way."

Butler shook his head solemnly.

"It's a great blow to me, daughter. It's a great blow to me," he said. "I'm willing to take your word if ye say so; but I can't help thinkin' what a sad thing it would be if ye were lyin' to me. I haven't had the house watched. I only got this this mornin'. And what's written here may not be so. I hope it isn't. But we'll not say any more about that now. If there is anythin' in it, and ye haven't gone too far yet to save yourself, I want ye to think of your mother and your sister and your brothers, and be a good girl. Think of the church ye was raised in, and the name we've got to stand up for in the world. Why, if ye were doin' anything wrong, and the people of Philadelphy got a hold of it, the city, big as it is, wouldn't be big enough to hold us. Your brothers have got a reputation to make, their work to do here. You and your sister want to get married sometime. How could ye expect to look the world in the face and do anythin' at all if ye are doin' what this letter says ye are, and it was told about ye?"

The old man's voice was thick with a strange, sad, alien emotion. He did not want to believe that his daughter was guilty, even though he knew she was. He did not want to face what he considered in his vigorous, religious way to be his duty, that of reproaching her sternly. There were some fathers who would have turned her out, he fancied. There were others who might possibly kill Cowperwood after a subtle investigation. That course was not for him. If vengeance he was to have, it must be through politics and finance—he must drive him out. But as for doing anything desperate in connection with Aileen, he could not think of it.

"Oh, father," returned Aileen, with considerable histrionic ability in her assumption of pettishness, "how can you talk like this when you know I'm not guilty? When I tell you so?" The old Irishman saw through her make-believe with profound sadness—the feeling that one of his dearest hopes had been shattered. He had expected so much of her socially and matrimonially. Why, any one of a dozen remarkable young men might have married her, and she would have had lovely children to comfort him in his old age.

"Well, we'll not talk any more about it now, daughter," he said, wearily. "Ye've been so much to me during all these years that I can scarcely belave anythin' wrong of ye. I don't want to, God knows. Ye're a grown woman, though, now; and if ye are doin' anythin' wrong I don't suppose I could do so much to stop ye. I might turn ye out, of course, as many a father would; but I wouldn't like to do anythin' like that. But if ye are doin' anythin' wrong"—and he put up his hand to stop a proposed protest on the part of Aileen—"remember, I'm certain to find it out in the long run, and Philadelphy won't be big enough to hold me and the man that's done this thing to me. I'll get him," he said, getting up dramatically. "I'll get him, and when I do—" He turned a livid face to the wall, and Aileen saw clearly that Cowperwood, in addition to any other troubles which might beset him, had her father to deal with. Was this why Frank had looked so sternly at her the night before?

"Why, your mother would die of a broken heart if she thought there was anybody could say the least word against ye," pursued Butler, in a shaken voice. "This man has a family—a wife and children, Ye oughtn't to want to do anythin' to hurt them. They'll have trouble enough, if I'm not mistaken—facin' what's comin' to them in the future," and Butler's jaw hardened just a little. "Ye're a beautiful girl. Ye're young. Ye have money. There's dozens of young men'd be proud to make ye their wife. Whatever ye may be thinkin' or doin', don't throw away your life. Don't destroy your immortal soul. Don't break my heart entirely."

Aileen, not ungenerous—fool of mingled affection and passion—could now have cried. She pitied her father from her heart; but her allegiance was to Cowperwood, her loyalty unshaken. She wanted to say something, to protest much more; but she knew that it was useless. Her father knew that she was lying.

"Well, there's no use of my saying anything more, father," she said, getting up. The light of day was fading in the windows. The downstairs door closed with a light slam, indicating that one of the boys had come in. Her proposed trip to the library was now without interest to her. "You won't believe me, anyhow. I tell you, though, that I'm innocent just the same."

Butler lifted his big, brown hand to command silence. She saw that this shameful relationship, as far as her father was concerned, had been made quite clear, and that this trying conference was now at an end. She turned and walked shamefacedly out. He waited until he heard her steps fading into faint nothings down the hall toward her room. Then he arose. Once more he clinched his big fists.

"The scoundrel!" he said. "The scoundrel! I'll drive him out of Philadelphy, if it takes the last dollar I have in the world."

CHAPTER XXVII

For the first time in his life Cowperwood felt conscious of having been in the presence of that interesting social phenomenon—the outraged sentiment of a parent. While he had no absolute knowledge as to why Butler had been so enraged, he felt that Aileen was the contributing cause. He himself was a father. His boy, Frank, Jr., was to him not so remarkable. But little Lillian, with her dainty little slip of a body and bright-aureoled head, had always appealed to him. She was going to be a charming woman one day, he thought, and he was going to do much to establish her safely. He used to tell her that she had "eyes like buttons," "feet like a pussy-cat," and hands that were "just five cents' worth," they were so little. The child admired her father and would often stand by his chair in the library or the sitting-room, or his desk in his private office, or by his seat at the table, asking him questions.

This attitude toward his own daughter made him see clearly how Butler might feel toward Aileen. He wondered how he would feel if it were his own little Lillian, and still he did not believe he would make much fuss over the matter, either with himself or with her, if she were as old as Aileen. Children and their lives were more or less above the willing of parents, anyhow, and it would be a difficult thing for any parent to control any child, unless the child were naturally docile-minded and willing to be controlled.

It also made him smile, in a grim way, to see how fate was raining difficulties on him. The Chicago fire, Stener's early absence, Butler, Mollenhauer, and Simpson's indifference to Stener's fate and his. And now this probable revelation in connection with Aileen. He could not be sure as yet, but his intuitive instincts told him that it must be something like this.

Now he was distressed as to what Aileen would do, say if suddenly she were confronted by her father. If he could only get to her! But if he was to meet Butler's call for his loan, and the others which would come yet to-day or on the morrow, there was not a moment to lose. If he did not pay he must assign at once. Butler's rage, Aileen, his own danger, were brushed aside for the moment. His mind concentrated wholly on how to save himself financially.

He hurried to visit George Waterman; David Wiggin, his wife's brother, who was now fairly well to do; Joseph Zimmerman, the wealthy dry-goods dealer who had dealt with him in the past; Judge Kitchen, a private manipulator of considerable wealth; Frederick Van Nostrand, the State treasurer, who was interested in local street-railway stocks, and others. Of all those to whom he appealed one was actually not in a position to do anything for him; another was afraid; a third was calculating eagerly to drive a hard bargain; a fourth was too deliberate, anxious to have much time. All scented the true value of his situation, all wanted time to consider, and he had no time to consider. Judge Kitchen did agree to lend him thirty thousand dollars—a paltry sum. Joseph Zimmerman would only risk twenty-five thousand dollars. He could see where, all told, he might raise seventy-five thousand dollars by hypothecating double the amount in shares; but this was ridiculously insufficient. He had figured again, to a dollar, and he must have at least two hundred and fifty thousand dollars above all his present holdings, or he must close his doors. To-morrow at two o'clock he would know. If he didn't he would be written down as "failed" on a score of ledgers in Philadelphia.

What a pretty pass for one to come to whose hopes had so recently run so high! There was a loan of one hundred thousand dollars from the Girard National Bank which he was particularly anxious to clear off. This bank was the most important in the city, and if he retained its good will by meeting this loan promptly he might hope for favors in the future whatever happened. Yet, at the moment, he did not see how he could do it. He decided, however, after some reflection, that he would deliver the stocks which Judge Kitchen, Zimmerman, and others had agreed to take and get their checks or cash yet this night. Then

116

he would persuade Stener to let him have a check for the sixty thousand dollars' worth of city loan he had purchased this morning on 'change. Out of it he could take twenty-five thousand dollars to make up the balance due the bank, and still have thirty-five thousand for himself.

The one unfortunate thing about such an arrangement was that by doing it he was building up a rather complicated situation in regard to these same certificates. Since their purchase in the morning, he had not deposited them in the sinking-fund, where they belonged (they had been delivered to his office by half past one in the afternoon), but, on the contrary, had immediately hypothecated them to cover another loan. It was a risky thing to have done, considering that he was in danger of failing and that he was not absolutely sure of being able to take them up in time.

But, he reasoned, he had a working agreement with the city treasurer (illegal of course), which would make such a transaction rather plausible, and almost all right, even if he failed, and that was that none of his accounts were supposed necessarily to be put straight until the end of the month. If he failed, and the certificates were not in the sinking-fund, he could say, as was the truth, that he was in the habit of taking his time, and had forgotten. This collecting of a check, therefore, for these as yet undeposited certificates would be technically, if not legally and morally, plausible. The city would be out only an additional sixty thousand dollars—making five hundred and sixty thousand dollars all told, which in view of its probable loss of five hundred thousand did not make so much difference. But his caution clashed with his need on this occasion, and he decided that he would not call for the check unless Stener finally refused to aid him with three hundred thousand more, in which case he would claim it as his right. In all likelihood Stener would not think to ask whether the certificates were in the sinking-fund or not. If he did, he would have to lie— that was all.

He drove rapidly back to his office, and, finding Butler's note, as he expected, wrote a check on his father's bank for the one hundred thousand dollars which had been placed to his credit by his loving parent, and sent it around to Butler's office. There was another note, from Albert Stires, Stener's secretary, advising him not to buy or sell any more city loan— that until further notice such transactions would not be honored. Cowperwood immediately sensed the source of this warning. Stener had been in conference with Butler or Mollenhauer, and had been warned and frightened. Nevertheless, he got in his buggy again and drove directly to the city treasurer's office.

Since Cowperwood's visit Stener had talked still more with Sengstack, Strobik, and others, all sent to see that a proper fear of things financial had been put in his heart. The result was decidedly one which spelled opposition to Cowperwood.

Strobik was considerably disturbed himself. He and Wycroft and Harmon had also been using money out of the treasury—much smaller sums, of course, for they had not Cowperwood's financial imagination—and were disturbed as to how they would return what they owed before the storm broke. If Cowperwood failed, and Stener was short in his accounts, the whole budget might be investigated, and then their loans would be brought to light. The thing to do was to return what they owed, and then, at least, no charge of malfeasance would lie against them.

"Go to Mollenhauer," Strobik had advised Stener, shortly after Cowperwood had left the latter's office, "and tell him the whole story. He put you here. He was strong for your nomination. Tell him just where you stand and ask him what to do. He'll probably be able to tell you. Offer him your holdings to help you out. You have to. You can't help yourself. Don't loan Cowperwood another damned dollar, whatever you do. He's got you in so deep now you can hardly hope to get out. Ask Mollenhauer if he won't help you to get Cowperwood to put that money back. He may be able to influence him."

There was more in this conversation to the same effect, and then Stener hurried as fast as his legs could carry him to Mollenhauer's office. He was so frightened that he could scarcely breathe, and he was quite ready to throw himself on his knees before the big German-American financier and leader. Oh, if Mr. Mollenhauer would only help him! If he could just get out of this without going to jail!

"Oh, Lord! Oh, Lord! Oh, Lord!" he repeated, over and over to himself, as he walked. "What shall I do?"

The attitude of Henry A. Mollenhauer, grim, political boss that he was—trained in a hard school—was precisely the attitude of every such man in all such trying circumstances.

He was wondering, in view of what Butler had told him, just how much he could advantage himself in this situation. If he could, he wanted to get control of whatever street-railway stock Stener now had, without in any way compromising himself. Stener's shares could easily be transferred on 'change through Mollenhauer's brokers to a dummy, who would eventually transfer them to himself (Mollenhauer). Stener must be squeezed thoroughly, though, this afternoon, and as for his five hundred thousand dollars' indebtedness to the treasury, Mollenhauer did not see what could be done about that. If Cowperwood could not pay it, the city would have to lose it; but the scandal must be hushed up until after election. Stener, unless the various party leaders had more generosity than Mollenhauer imagined, would have to suffer exposure, arrest, trial, confiscation of his property, and possibly sentence to the penitentiary, though this might easily be commuted by the governor, once public excitement died down. He did not trouble to think whether Cowperwood was criminally involved or not. A hundred to one he was not. Trust a shrewd man like that to take care of himself. But if there was any way to shoulder the blame on to Cowperwood, and so clear the treasurer and the skirts of the party, he would not object to that. He wanted to hear the full story of Stener's relations with the broker first. Meanwhile, the thing to do was to seize what Stener had to yield.

The troubled city treasurer, on being shown in Mr. Mollenhauer's presence, at once sank feebly in a chair and collapsed. He was entirely done for mentally. His nerve was gone, his courage exhausted like a breath.

"Well, Mr. Stener?" queried Mr. Mollenhauer, impressively, pretending not to know what brought him.

"I came about this matter of my loans to Mr. Cowperwood."

"Well, what about them?"

"Well, he owes me, or the city treasury rather, five hundred thousand dollars, and I understand that he is going to fail and that he can't pay it back."

"Who told you that?"

"Mr. Sengstack, and since then Mr. Cowperwood has been to see me. He tells me he must have more money or he will fail and he wants to borrow three hundred thousand dollars more. He says he must have it."

"So!" said Mr. Mollenhauer, impressively, and with an air of astonishment which he did not feel. "You would not think of doing that, of course. You're too badly involved as it is. If he wants to know why, refer him to me. Don't advance him another dollar. If you do, and this case comes to trial, no court would have any mercy on you. It's going to be difficult enough to do anything for you as it is. However, if you don't advance him any more—we will see. It may be possible, I can't say, but at any rate, no more money must leave the treasury to bolster up this bad business. It's much too difficult as it now is." He stared at Stener warningly. And he, shaken and sick, yet because of the faint suggestion of mercy involved somewhere in Mollenhauer's remarks, now slipped from his chair to his knees and folded his hands in the uplifted attitude of a devotee before a sacred image.

"Oh, Mr. Mollenhauer," he choked, beginning to cry, "I didn't mean to do anything wrong. Strobik and Wycroft told me it was all right. You sent me to Cowperwood in the first place. I only did what I thought the others had been doing. Mr. Bode did it, just like I have been doing. He dealt with Tighe and Company. I have a wife and four children, Mr. Mollenhauer. My youngest boy is only seven years old. Think of them, Mr. Mollenhauer! Think of what my arrest will mean to them! I don't want to go to jail. I didn't think I was doing anything very wrong—honestly I didn't. I'll give up all I've got. You can have all my stocks and houses and lots—anything—if you'll only get me out of this. You won't let 'em send me to jail, will you?"

His fat, white lips were trembling—wabbling nervously—and big hot tears were coursing down his previously pale but now flushed cheeks. He presented one of those almost unbelievable pictures which are yet so intensely human and so true. If only the great financial and political giants would for once accurately reveal the details of their lives!

Mollenhauer looked at him calmly, meditatively. How often had he seen weaklings no more dishonest than himself, but without his courage and subtlety, pleading to him in this fashion, not on their knees exactly, but intellectually so! Life to him, as to every other man of large practical knowledge and insight, was an inexplicable tangle. What were you going to do about the so-called morals and precepts of the world? This man Stener fancied that he was dishonest, and that he, Mollenhauer, was honest. He was here, self-convicted of sin, pleading to him, Mollenhauer, as he would to a righteous, unstained saint. As a matter of fact, Mollenhauer knew that he was simply shrewder, more far-seeing, more calculating, not less dishonest. Stener was lacking in force and brains—not morals. This lack was his principal crime. There were people who believed in some esoteric standard of right—some ideal of conduct absolutely and very far removed from practical life; but he had never seen them practice it save to their own financial (not moral—he would not say that) destruction. They were never significant, practical men who clung to these fatuous ideals. They were always poor, nondescript, negligible dreamers. He could not have made Stener understand all this if he had wanted to, and he certainly did not want to. It was too bad about Mrs. Stener and the little Steners. No doubt she had worked hard, as had Stener, to get up in the world and be something—just a little more than miserably poor; and now this unfortunate complication had to arise to undo them—this Chicago fire. What a curious thing that was! If any one thing more than another made him doubt the existence of a kindly, overruling Providence, it was the unheralded storms out of clear skies—financial, social, anything you choose—that so often brought ruin and disaster to so many.

"Get Up, Stener," he said, calmly, after a few moments. "You mustn't give way to your feelings like this. You must not cry. These troubles are never unraveled by tears. You must do a little thinking for yourself. Perhaps your situation isn't so bad."

As he was saying this Stener was putting himself back in his chair, getting out his handkerchief, and sobbing hopelessly in it.

"I'll do what I can, Stener. I won't promise anything. I can't tell you what the result will be. There are many peculiar political forces in this city. I may not be able to save you, but I am perfectly willing to try. You must put yourself absolutely under my direction. You must not say or do anything without first consulting with me. I will send my secretary to you from time to time. He will tell you what to do. You must not come to me unless I send for you. Do you understand that thoroughly?"

"Yes, Mr. Mollenhauer."

"Well, now, dry your eyes. I don't want you to go out of this office crying. Go back to your office, and I will send Sengstack to see you. He will tell you what to do. Follow him exactly. And whenever I send for you come at once."

He got up, large, self-confident, reserved. Stener, buoyed up by the subtle reassurance of his remarks, recovered to a degree his equanimity. Mr. Mollenhauer, the great, powerful Mr. Mollenhauer was going to help him out of his scrape. He might not have to go to jail after all. He left after a few moments, his face a little red from weeping, but otherwise free of telltale marks, and returned to his office.

Three-quarters of an hour later, Sengstack called on him for the second time that day— Abner Sengstack, small, dark-faced, club-footed, a great sole of leather three inches thick under his short, withered right leg, his slightly Slavic, highly intelligent countenance burning with a pair of keen, piercing, inscrutable black eyes. Sengstack was a fit secretary for Mollenhauer. You could see at one glance that he would make Stener do exactly what Mollenhauer suggested. His business was to induce Stener to part with his street-railway holdings at once through Tighe & Co., Butler's brokers, to the political sub-agent who would eventually transfer them to Mollenhauer. What little Stener received for them might well go into the treasury. Tighe & Co. would manage the "'change" subtleties of this without giving any one else a chance to bid, while at the same time making it appear an open-market transaction. At the same time Sengstack went carefully into the state of the treasurer's office for his master's benefit—finding out what it was that Strobik, Wycroft, and Harmon had been doing with their loans. Via another source they were ordered to disgorge at once or face prosecution. They were a part of Mollenhauer's political machine. Then, having cautioned Stener not to set over the remainder of his property to any one, and not to listen to any one, most of all to the Machiavellian counsel of Cowperwood, Sengstack left.

Needless to say, Mollenhauer was greatly gratified by this turn of affairs. Cowperwood was now most likely in a position where he would have to come and see him, or if not, a good share of the properties he controlled were already in Mollenhauer's possession. If by some hook or crook he could secure the remainder, Simpson and Butler might well talk to him about this street-railway business. His holdings were now as large as any, if not quite the largest.

CHAPTER XXVIII

It was in the face of this very altered situation that Cowperwood arrived at Stener's office late this Monday afternoon.

Stener was quite alone, worried and distraught. He was anxious to see Cowperwood, and at the same time afraid.

"George," began Cowperwood, briskly, on seeing him, "I haven't much time to spare now, but I've come, finally, to tell you that you'll have to let me have three hundred thousand more if you don't want me to fail. Things are looking very bad today. They've caught me in a corner on my loans; but this storm isn't going to last. You can see by the very character of it that it can't."

He was looking at Stener's face, and seeing fear and a pained and yet very definite necessity for opposition written there. "Chicago is burning, but it will be built up again. Business will be all the better for it later on. Now, I want you to be reasonable and help me. Don't get frightened."

Stener stirred uneasily. "Don't let these politicians scare you to death. It will all blow over in a few days, and then we'll be better off than ever. Did you see Mollenhauer?"

"Yes."

"Well, what did he have to say?"

"He said just what I thought he'd say. He won't let me do this. I can't, Frank, I tell you!" exclaimed Stener, jumping up. He was so nervous that he had had a hard time keeping his seat during this short, direct conversation. "I can't! They've got me in a corner! They're after me! They all know what we've been doing. Oh, say, Frank"—he threw up his arms wildly—"you've got to get me out of this. You've got to let me have that five hundred thousand back and get me out of this. If you don't, and you should fail, they'll send me to the penitentiary. I've got a wife and four children, Frank. I can't go on in this. It's too big for me. I never should have gone in on it in the first place. I never would have if you hadn't persuaded me, in a way. I never thought when I began that I would ever get in as bad as all this. I can't go on, Frank. I can't! I'm willing you should have all my stock. Only give me back that five hundred thousand, and we'll call it even." His voice rose nervously as he talked, and he wiped his wet forehead with his hand and stared at Cowperwood pleadingly, foolishly.

Cowperwood stared at him in return for a few moments with a cold, fishy eye. He knew a great deal about human nature, and he was ready for and expectant of any queer shift in an individual's attitude, particularly in time of panic; but this shift of Stener's was quite too much. "Whom else have you been talking to, George, since I saw you? Whom have you seen? What did Sengstack have to say?"

"He says just what Mollenhauer does, that I mustn't loan any more money under any circumstances, and he says I ought to get that five hundred thousand back as quickly as possible."

"And you think Mollenhauer wants to help you, do you?" inquired Cowperwood, finding it hard to efface the contempt which kept forcing itself into his voice.

"I think he does, yes. I don't know who else will, Frank, if he don't. He's one of the big political forces in this town."

"Listen to me," began Cowperwood, eyeing him fixedly. Then he paused. "What did he say you should do about your holdings?"

"Sell them through Tighe & Company and put the money back in the treasury, if you won't take them."

"Sell them to whom?" asked Cowperwood, thinking of Stener's last words.

"To any one on 'change who'll take them, I suppose. I don't know."

"I thought so," said Cowperwood, comprehendingly. "I might have known as much. They're working you, George. They're simply trying to get your stocks away from you. Mollenhauer is leading you on. He knows I can't do what you want—give you back the five hundred thousand dollars. He wants you to throw your stocks on the market so that he can pick them up. Depend on it, that's all arranged for already. When you do, he's got me in his clutches, or he thinks he has—he and Butler and Simpson. They want to get together on this local street-railway situation, and I know it, I feel it. I've felt it coming all along. Mollenhauer hasn't any more intention of helping you than he has of flying. Once you've sold your stocks he's through with you—mark my word. Do you think he'll turn a hand to keep you out of the penitentiary once you're out of this street-railway situation? He will not. And if you think so, you're a bigger fool than I take you to be, George. Don't go crazy. Don't lose your head. Be sensible. Look the situation in the face. Let me explain it to you. If you don't help me now—if you don't let me have three hundred thousand dollars by to-morrow noon, at the very latest, I'm through, and so are you. There is not a thing the matter with our situation. Those stocks of ours are as good to-day as they ever were. Why, great heavens, man, the railways are there behind them. They're paying. The Seventeenth and Nineteenth Street line is earning one thousand dollars a day right now. What better evidence do you want than that? Green & Coates is earning five hundred dollars. You're frightened, George. These damned political schemers have scared you. Why, you've as good a right to loan that money as Bode and Murtagh had before you. They did it. You've been doing it for Mollenhauer and the others, only so long as you do it for them it's all right. What's a designated city depository but a loan?"

Cowperwood was referring to the system under which certain portions of city money, like the sinking-fund, were permitted to be kept in certain banks at a low rate of interest or no rate—banks in which Mollenhauer and Butler and Simpson were interested. This was their safe graft.

"Don't throw your chances away, George. Don't quit now. You'll be worth millions in a few years, and you won't have to turn a hand. All you will have to do will be to keep what you have. If you don't help me, mark my word, they'll throw you over the moment I'm out of this, and they'll let you go to the penitentiary. Who's going to put up five hundred thousand dollars for you, George? Where is Mollenhauer going to get it, or Butler, or anybody, in these times? They can't. They don't intend to. When I'm through, you're through, and you'll be exposed quicker than any one else. They can't hurt me, George. I'm an agent. I didn't ask you to come to me. You came to me in the first place of your own accord. If you don't help me, you're through, I tell you, and you're going to be sent to the penitentiary as sure as there are jails. Why don't you take a stand, George? Why don't you stand your ground? You have your wife and children to look after. You can't be any worse off loaning me three hundred thousand more than you are right now. What difference does it make—five hundred thousand or eight hundred thousand? It's all one and the same thing, if you're going to be tried for it. Besides, if you loan me this, there isn't going to be any trial. I'm not going to fail. This storm will blow over in a week or ten days, and we'll be rich again. For Heaven's sake, George, don't go to pieces this way! Be sensible! Be reasonable!"

He paused, for Stener's face had become a jelly-like mass of woe.

"I can't, Frank," he wailed. "I tell you I can't. They'll punish me worse than ever if I do that. They'll never let up on me. You don't know these people."

In Stener's crumpling weakness Cowperwood read his own fate. What could you do with a man like that? How brace him up? You couldn't! And with a gesture of infinite understanding, disgust, noble indifference, he threw up his hands and started to walk out. At the door he turned.

"George," he said, "I'm sorry. I'm sorry for you, not for myself. I'll come out of things all right, eventually. I'll be rich. But, George, you're making the one great mistake of your life. You'll be poor; you'll be a convict, and you'll have only yourself to blame. There isn't a thing the matter with this money situation except the fire. There isn't a thing wrong with my affairs except this slump in stocks—this panic. You sit there, a fortune in your hands, and you allow a lot of schemers, highbinders, who don't know any more of your affairs or mine than a rabbit, and who haven't any interest in you except to plan what they can get out of you, to frighten you and prevent you from doing the one thing that will save your life. Three hundred thousand paltry dollars that in three or four weeks from now I can pay back to you four and five times over, and for that you will see me go broke and yourself to the penitentiary. I can't understand it, George. You're out of your mind. You're going to rue this the longest day that you live."

He waited a few moments to see if this, by any twist of chance, would have any effect; then, noting that Stener still remained a wilted, helpless mass of nothing, he shook his head gloomily and walked out.

It was the first time in his life that Cowperwood had ever shown the least sign of weakening or despair. He had felt all along as though there were nothing to the Greek theory of being pursued by the furies. Now, however, there seemed an untoward fate which was pursuing him. It looked that way. Still, fate or no fate, he did not propose to be daunted. Even in this very beginning of a tendency to feel despondent he threw back his head, expanded his chest, and walked as briskly as ever.

In the large room outside Stener's private office he encountered Albert Stires, Stener's chief clerk and secretary. He and Albert had exchanged many friendly greetings in times past, and all the little minor transactions in regard to city loan had been discussed between them, for Albert knew more of the intricacies of finance and financial bookkeeping than Stener would ever know.

At the sight of Stires the thought in regard to the sixty thousand dollars' worth of city loan certificates, previously referred to, flashed suddenly through his mind. He had not deposited them in the sinking-fund, and did not intend to for the present—could not, unless considerable free money were to reach him shortly—for he had used them to satisfy other pressing demands, and had no free money to buy them back—or, in other words, release them. And he did not want to just at this moment. Under the law governing transactions of this kind with the city treasurer, he was supposed to deposit them at once to the credit of the city, and not to draw his pay therefor from the city treasurer until he had. To be very exact, the city treasurer, under the law, was not supposed to pay him for any transaction of this kind until he or his agents presented a voucher from the bank or other organization carrying the sinking-fund for the city showing that the certificates so purchased had actually been deposited there. As a matter of fact, under the custom which had grown up between him and Stener, the law had long been ignored in this respect. He could buy certificates of city loan for the sinking-fund up to any reasonable amount, hypothecate them where he pleased, and draw his pay from the city without presenting a voucher. At the end of the month sufficient certificates of city loan could usually be gathered from one source and another to make up the deficiency, or the deficiency could actually be ignored, as had been done on more than one occasion, for long periods of time, while he used money secured by hypothecating the shares for speculative purposes. This was actually illegal; but neither Cowperwood nor Stener saw it in that light or cared.

The trouble with this particular transaction was the note that he had received from Stener ordering him to stop both buying and selling, which put his relations with the city treasury on a very formal basis. He had bought these certificates before receiving this note, but had not deposited them. He was going now to collect his check; but perhaps the old, easy system of balancing matters at the end of the month might not be said to obtain any longer. Stires might ask him to present a voucher of deposit. If so, he could not now get this check for sixty thousand dollars, for he did not have the certificates to deposit. If not, he might get the money; but, also, it might constitute the basis of some subsequent legal action. If he did not eventually deposit the certificates before failure, some charge such as that of larceny might be brought against him. Still, he said to himself, he might not really fail even yet. If any of his banking associates should, for any reason, modify their decision in regard to calling his loans, he would not. Would Stener make a row about this if he so secured this check? Would the city officials pay any attention to him if he did? Could you get any district attorney to take cognizance of such a transaction, if Stener did complain? No, not in all likelihood; and, anyhow, nothing would come of it. No jury would punish him in the face of the understanding existing between him and Stener as agent or broker and principal. And, once he had the money, it was a hundred to one Stener would think no more about it. It would go in among the various unsatisfied liabilities, and nothing more would be thought about it. Like lightning the entire situation hashed through his mind. He would risk it. He stopped before the chief clerk's desk.

"Albert," he said, in a low voice, "I bought sixty thousand dollars' worth of city loan for the sinking-fund this morning. Will you give my boy a check for it in the morning, or, better yet, will you give it to me now? I got your note about no more purchases. I'm going back to the office. You can just credit the sinking-fund with eight hundred certificates at from seventy-five to eighty. I'll send you the itemized list later."

"Certainly, Mr. Cowperwood, certainly," replied Albert, with alacrity. "Stocks are getting an awful knock, aren't they? I hope you're not very much troubled by it?"

"Not very, Albert," replied Cowperwood, smiling, the while the chief clerk was making out his check. He was wondering if by any chance Stener would appear and attempt to interfere with this. It was a legal transaction. He had a right to the check provided he deposited the certificates, as was his custom, with the trustee of the fund. He waited tensely while Albert wrote, and finally, with the check actually in his hand, breathed a sigh of relief. Here, at least, was sixty thousand dollars, and to-night's work would enable him to cash the seventy-five thousand that had been promised him. To-morrow, once more he must see Leigh, Kitchen, Jay Cooke & Co., Edward Clark & Co.—all the long list of people to whom he owed loans and find out what could be done. If he could only get time! If he could get just a week!

CHAPTER XXIX

But time was not a thing to be had in this emergency. With the seventy-five thousand dollars his friends had extended to him, and sixty thousand dollars secured from Stires, Cowperwood met the Girard call and placed the balance, thirty-five thousand dollars, in a private safe in his own home. He then made a final appeal to the bankers and financiers, but they refused to help him. He did not, however, commiserate himself in this hour. He looked out of his office window into the little court, and sighed. What more could he do? He sent a note to his father, asking him to call for lunch. He sent a note to his lawyer, Harper Steger, a man of his own age whom he liked very much, and asked him to call also. He evolved in his own mind various plans of delay, addresses to creditors and the like, but alas! he was going to fail. And the worst of it was that this matter of the city treasurer's loans was bound to become a public, and more than a public, a political, scandal. And the charge of conniving, if not illegally, at least morally, at the misuse of the city's money was the one thing that would hurt him most.

How industriously his rivals would advertise this fact! He might get on his feet again if he failed; but it would be uphill work. And his father! His father would be pulled down with him. It was probable that he would be forced out of the presidency of his bank. With these thoughts Cowperwood sat there waiting. As he did so Aileen Butler was announced by his office-boy, and at the same time Albert Stires.

"Show in Miss Butler," he said, getting up. "Tell Mr. Stires to wait." Aileen came briskly, vigorously in, her beautiful body clothed as decoratively as ever. The street suit that she wore was of a light golden-brown broadcloth, faceted with small, dark-red buttons. Her head was decorated with a brownish-red shake of a type she had learned was becoming to her, brimless and with a trailing plume, and her throat was graced by a three-strand necklace of gold beads. Her hands were smoothly gloved as usual, and her little feet daintily shod. There was a look of girlish distress in her eyes, which, however, she was trying hard to conceal.

"Honey," she exclaimed, on seeing him, her arms extended—"what is the trouble? I wanted so much to ask you the other night. You're not going to fail, are you? I heard father and Owen talking about you last night."

"What did they say?" he inquired, putting his arm around her and looking quietly into her nervous eyes.

"Oh, you know, I think papa is very angry with you. He suspects. Some one sent him an anonymous letter. He tried to get it out of me last night, but he didn't succeed. I denied everything. I was in here twice this morning to see you, but you were out. I was so afraid that he might see you first, and that you might say something."

"Me, Aileen?"

"Well, no, not exactly. I didn't think that. I don't know what I thought. Oh, honey, I've been so worried. You know, I didn't sleep at all. I thought I was stronger than that; but I was so worried about you. You know, he put me in a strong light by his desk, where he could see my face, and then he showed me the letter. I was so astonished for a moment I hardly know what I said or how I looked."

"What did you say?"

"Why, I said: 'What a shame! It isn't so!' But I didn't say it right away. My heart was going like a trip-hammer. I'm afraid he must have been able to tell something from my face. I could hardly get my breath."

"He's a shrewd man, your father," he commented. "He knows something about life. Now you see how difficult these situations are. It's a blessing he decided to show you the letter instead of watching the house. I suppose he felt too bad to do that. He can't prove anything now. But he knows. You can't deceive him."

"How do you know he knows?"

124

"I saw him yesterday."

"Did he talk to you about it?"

"No; I saw his face. He simply looked at me."

"Honey! I'm so sorry for him!"

"I know you are. So am I. But it can't be helped now. We should have thought of that in the first place."

"But I love you so. Oh, honey, he will never forgive me. He loves me so. He mustn't know. I won't admit anything. But, oh, dear!"

She put her hands tightly together on his bosom, and he looked consolingly into her eyes. Her eyelids, were trembling, and her lips. She was sorry for her father, herself, Cowperwood. Through her he could sense the force of Butler's parental affection; the volume and danger of his rage. There were so many, many things as he saw it now converging to make a dramatic denouement.

"Never mind," he replied; "it can't be helped now. Where is my strong, determined Aileen? I thought you were going to be so brave? Aren't you going to be? I need to have you that way now."

"Do you?"

"Yes."

"Are you in trouble?"

"I think I am going to fail, dear."

"Oh, no!"

"Yes, honey. I'm at the end of my rope. I don't see any way out just at present. I've sent for my father and my lawyer. You mustn't stay here, sweet. Your father may come in here at any time. We must meet somewhere—to-morrow, say—to-morrow afternoon. You remember Indian Rock, out on the Wissahickon?"

"Yes."

"Could you be there at four?"

"Yes."

"Look out for who's following. If I'm not there by four-thirty, don't wait. You know why. It will be because I think some one is watching. There won't be, though, if we work it right. And now you must run, sweet. We can't use Nine-thirty-one any more. I'll have to rent another place somewhere else."

"Oh, honey, I'm so sorry."

"Aren't you going to be strong and brave? You see, I need you to be."

He was almost, for the first time, a little sad in his mood.

"Yes, dear, yes," she declared, slipping her arms under his and pulling him tight. "Oh, yes! You can depend on me. Oh, Frank, I love you so! I'm so sorry. Oh, I do hope you don't fail! But it doesn't make any difference, dear, between you and me, whatever happens, does it? We will love each other just the same. I'll do anything for you, honey! I'll do anything you say. You can trust me. They sha'n't know anything from me."

She looked at his still, pale face, and a sudden strong determination to fight for him welled up in her heart. Her love was unjust, illegal, outlawed; but it was love, just the same, and had much of the fiery daring of the outcast from justice.

"I love you! I love you! I love you, Frank!" she declared. He unloosed her hands.

"Run, sweet. To-morrow at four. Don't fail. And don't talk. And don't admit anything, whatever you do."

"I won't."

"And don't worry about me. I'll be all right."

He barely had time to straighten his tie, to assume a nonchalant attitude by the window, when in hurried Stener's chief clerk—pale, disturbed, obviously out of key with himself.

"Mr. Cowperwood! You know that check I gave you last night? Mr. Stener says it's illegal, that I shouldn't have given it to you, that he will hold me responsible. He says I can be arrested for compounding a felony, and that he will discharge me and have me sent to prison if I don't get it back. Oh, Mr. Cowperwood, I am only a young man! I'm just really starting out in life. I've got my wife and little boy to look after. You won't let him do that to me? You'll give me that check back, won't you? I can't go back to the office without it. He says you're going to fail, and that you knew it, and that you haven't any right to it."

Cowperwood looked at him curiously. He was surprised at the variety and character of these emissaries of disaster. Surely, when troubles chose to multiply they had great skill in presenting themselves in rapid order. Stener had no right to make any such statement. The transaction was not illegal. The man had gone wild. True, he, Cowperwood, had received an order after these securities were bought not to buy or sell any more city loan, but that did not invalidate previous purchases. Stener was browbeating and frightening his poor underling, a better man than himself, in order to get back this sixty-thousand-dollar check. What a petty creature he was! How true it was, as somebody had remarked, that you could not possibly measure the petty meannesses to which a fool could stoop!

"You go back to Mr. Stener, Albert, and tell him that it can't be done. The certificates of loan were purchased before his order arrived, and the records of the exchange will prove it. There is no illegality here. I am entitled to that check and could have collected it in any qualified court of law. The man has gone out of his head. I haven't failed yet. You are not in any danger of any legal proceedings; and if you are, I'll help defend you. I can't give you the check back because I haven't it to give; and if I had, I wouldn't. That would be allowing a fool to make a fool of me. I'm sorry, very, but I can't do anything for you."

"Oh, Mr. Cowperwood!" Tears were in Stires's eyes. "He'll discharge me! He'll forfeit my sureties. I'll be turned out into the street. I have only a little property of my own—outside of my salary!"

He wrung his hands, and Cowperwood shook his head sadly.

"This isn't as bad as you think, Albert. He won't do what he says. He can't. It's unfair and illegal. You can bring suit and recover your salary. I'll help you in that as much as I'm able. But I can't give you back this sixty-thousand-dollar check, because I haven't it to give. I couldn't if I wanted to. It isn't here any more. I've paid for the securities I bought with it. The securities are not here. They're in the sinking-fund, or will be."

He paused, wishing he had not mentioned that fact. It was a slip of the tongue, one of the few he ever made, due to the peculiar pressure of the situation. Stires pleaded longer. It was no use, Cowperwood told him. Finally he went away, crestfallen, fearsome, broken. There were tears of suffering in his eyes. Cowperwood was very sorry. And then his father was announced.

The elder Cowperwood brought a haggard face. He and Frank had had a long conversation the evening before, lasting until early morning, but it had not been productive of much save uncertainty.

"Hello, father!" exclaimed Cowperwood, cheerfully, noting his father's gloom. He was satisfied that there was scarcely a coal of hope to be raked out of these ashes of despair, but there was no use admitting it.

"Well?" said his father, lifting his sad eyes in a peculiar way.

"Well, it looks like stormy weather, doesn't it? I've decided to call a meeting of my creditors, father, and ask for time. There isn't anything else to do. I can't realize enough on anything to make it worth while talking about. I thought Stener might change his mind, but he's worse rather than better. His head bookkeeper just went out of here."

"What did he want?" asked Henry Cowperwood.

"He wanted me to give him back a check for sixty thousand that he paid me for some city loan I bought yesterday morning." Frank did not explain to his father, however, that he had hypothecated the certificates this check had paid for, and used the check itself to raise money enough to pay the Girard National Bank and to give himself thirty-five thousand in cash besides.

126

"Well, I declare!" replied the old man. "You'd think he'd have better sense than that. That's a perfectly legitimate transaction. When did you say he notified you not to buy city loan?"

"Yesterday noon."

"He's out of his mind," Cowperwood, Sr., commented, laconically.

"It's Mollenhauer and Simpson and Butler, I know. They want my street-railway lines. Well, they won't get them. They'll get them through a receivership, and after the panic's all over. Our creditors will have first chance at these. If they buy, they'll buy from them. If it weren't for that five-hundred-thousand-dollar loan I wouldn't think a thing of this. My creditors would sustain me nicely. But the moment that gets noised around!... And this election! I hypothecated those city loan certificates because I didn't want to get on the wrong side of Davison. I expected to take in enough by now to take them up. They ought to be in the sinking-fund, really."

The old gentleman saw the point at once, and winced.

"They might cause you trouble, there, Frank."

"It's a technical question," replied his son. "I might have been intending to take them up. As a matter of fact, I will if I can before three. I've been taking eight and ten days to deposit them in the past. In a storm like this I'm entitled to move my pawns as best I can."

Cowperwood, the father, put his hand over his mouth again. He felt very disturbed about this. He saw no way out, however. He was at the end of his own resources. He felt the side-whiskers on his left cheek. He looked out of the window into the little green court. Possibly it was a technical question, who should say. The financial relations of the city treasury with other brokers before Frank had been very lax. Every banker knew that. Perhaps precedent would or should govern in this case. He could not say. Still, it was dangerous—not straight. If Frank could get them out and deposit them it would be so much better.

"I'd take them up if I were you and I could," he added.

"I will if I can."

"How much money have you?"

"Oh, twenty thousand, all told. If I suspend, though, I'll have to have a little ready cash."

"I have eight or ten thousand, or will have by night, I hope."

He was thinking of some one who would give him a second mortgage on his house.

Cowperwood looked quietly at him. There was nothing more to be said to his father. "I'm going to make one more appeal to Stener after you leave here," he said. "I'm going over there with Harper Steger when he comes. If he won't change I'll send out notice to my creditors, and notify the secretary of the exchange. I want you to keep a stiff upper lip, whatever happens. I know you will, though. I'm going into the thing head down. If Stener had any sense—" He paused. "But what's the use talking about a damn fool?"

He turned to the window, thinking of how easy it would have been, if Aileen and he had not been exposed by this anonymous note, to have arranged all with Butler. Rather than injure the party, Butler, in extremis, would have assisted him. Now...!

His father got up to go. He was as stiff with despair as though he were suffering from cold.

"Well," he said, wearily.

Cowperwood suffered intensely for him. What a shame! His father! He felt a great surge of sorrow sweep over him but a moment later mastered it, and settled to his quick, defiant thinking. As the old man went out, Harper Steger was brought in. They shook hands, and at once started for Stener's office. But Stener had sunk in on himself like an empty gas-bag, and no efforts were sufficient to inflate him. They went out, finally, defeated.

"I tell you, Frank," said Steger, "I wouldn't worry. We can tie this thing up legally until election and after, and that will give all this row a chance to die down. Then you can get your people together and talk sense to them. They're not going to give up good properties like this, even if Stener does go to jail."

Steger did not know of the sixty thousand dollars' worth of hypothecated securities as yet. Neither did he know of Aileen Butler and her father's boundless rage.

CHAPTER XXX

There was one development in connection with all of this of which Cowperwood was as yet unaware. The same day that brought Edward Butler the anonymous communication in regard to his daughter, brought almost a duplicate of it to Mrs. Frank Algernon Cowperwood, only in this case the name of Aileen Butler had curiously been omitted.

Perhaps you don't know that your husband is running with another woman. If you don't believe it, watch the house at 931 North Tenth Street.

Mrs. Cowperwood was in the conservatory watering some plants when this letter was brought by her maid Monday morning. She was most placid in her thoughts, for she did not know what all the conferring of the night before meant. Frank was occasionally troubled by financial storms, but they did not see to harm him.

"Lay it on the table in the library, Annie. I'll get it."

She thought it was some social note.

In a little while (such was her deliberate way), she put down her sprinkling-pot and went into the library. There it was lying on the green leather sheepskin which constituted a part of the ornamentation of the large library table. She picked it up, glanced at it curiously because it was on cheap paper, and then opened it. Her face paled slightly as she read it; and then her hand trembled—not much. Hers was not a soul that ever loved passionately, hence she could not suffer passionately. She was hurt, disgusted, enraged for the moment, and frightened; but she was not broken in spirit entirely. Thirteen years of life with Frank Cowperwood had taught her a number of things. He was selfish, she knew now, self-centered, and not as much charmed by her as he had been. The fear she had originally felt as to the effect of her preponderance of years had been to some extent justified by the lapse of time. Frank did not love her as he had—he had not for some time; she had felt it. What was it?—she had asked herself at times—almost, who was it? Business was engrossing him so.

Finance was his master. Did this mean the end of her regime, she queried. Would he cast her off? Where would she go? What would she do? She was not helpless, of course, for she had money of her own which he was manipulating for her. Who was this other woman? Was she young, beautiful, of any social position? Was it—? Suddenly she stopped. Was it? Could it be, by any chance—her mouth opened—Aileen Butler?

She stood still, staring at this letter, for she could scarcely countenance her own thought. She had observed often, in spite of all their caution, how friendly Aileen had been to him and he to her. He liked her; he never lost a chance to defend her. Lillian had thought of them at times as being curiously suited to each other temperamentally. He liked young people. But, of course, he was married, and Aileen was infinitely beneath him socially, and he had two children and herself. And his social and financial position was so fixed and stable that he did not dare trifle with it. Still she paused; for forty years and two children, and some slight wrinkles, and the suspicion that we may be no longer loved as we once were, is apt to make any woman pause, even in the face of the most significant financial position. Where would she go if she left him? What would people think? What about the children? Could she prove this liaison? Could she entrap him in a compromising situation? Did she want to?

She saw now that she did not love him as some women love their husbands. She was not wild about him. In a way she had been taking him for granted all these years, had thought that he loved her enough not to be unfaithful to her; at least fancied that he was so engrossed with the more serious things of life that no petty liaison such as this letter indicated would trouble him or interrupt his great career. Apparently this was not true. What should she do? What say? How act? Her none too brilliant mind was not of much service in this crisis. She did not know very well how either to plan or to fight.

The conventional mind is at best a petty piece of machinery. It is oyster-like in its functioning, or, perhaps better, clam-like. It has its little siphon of thought-processes forced up or down into the mighty ocean of fact and circumstance; but it uses so little, pumps so faintly, that the immediate contiguity of the vast mass is not disturbed. Nothing of the subtlety of life is perceived. No least inkling of its storms or terrors is ever discovered except through accident. When some crude, suggestive fact, such as this letter proved to be, suddenly manifests itself in the placid flow of events, there is great agony or disturbance and clogging of the so-called normal processes. The siphon does not work right. It sucks in fear and distress. There is great grinding of maladjusted parts—not unlike sand in a machine—and life, as is so often the case, ceases or goes lamely ever after.

Mrs. Cowperwood was possessed of a conventional mind. She really knew nothing about life. And life could not teach her. Reaction in her from salty thought-processes was not possible. She was not alive in the sense that Aileen Butler was, and yet she thought that she was very much alive. All illusion. She wasn't. She was charming if you loved placidity. If you did not, she was not. She was not engaging, brilliant, or forceful. Frank Cowperwood might well have asked himself in the beginning why he married her. He did not do so now because he did not believe it was wise to question the past as to one's failures and errors. It was, according to him, most unwise to regret. He kept his face and thoughts to the future.

But Mrs. Cowperwood was truly distressed in her way, and she went about the house thinking, feeling wretchedly. She decided, since the letter asked her to see for herself, to wait. She must think how she would watch this house, if at all. Frank must not know. If it were Aileen Butler by any chance—but surely not—she thought she would expose her to her parents. Still, that meant exposing herself. She determined to conceal her mood as best she could at dinner-time—but Cowperwood was not able to be there. He was so rushed, so closeted with individuals, so closely in conference with his father and others, that she scarcely saw him this Monday night, nor the next day, nor for many days.

For on Tuesday afternoon at two-thirty he issued a call for a meeting of his creditors, and at five-thirty he decided to go into the hands of a receiver. And yet, as he stood before his principal creditors—a group of thirty men—in his office, he did not feel that his life was ruined. He was temporarily embarrassed. Certainly things looked very black. The city-treasurership deal would make a great fuss. Those hypothecated city loan certificates, to the extent of sixty thousand, would make another, if Stener chose. Still, he did not feel that he was utterly destroyed.

"Gentlemen," he said, in closing his address of explanation at the meeting, quite as erect, secure, defiant, convincing as he had ever been, "you see how things are. These securities are worth just as much as they ever were. There is nothing the matter with the properties behind them. If you will give me fifteen days or twenty, I am satisfied that I can straighten the whole matter out. I am almost the only one who can, for I know all about it. The market is bound to recover. Business is going to be better than ever. It's time I want. Time is the only significant factor in this situation. I want to know if you won't give me fifteen or twenty days—a month, if you can. That is all I want."

He stepped aside and out of the general room, where the blinds were drawn, into his private office, in order to give his creditors an opportunity to confer privately in regard to his situation. He had friends in the meeting who were for him. He waited one, two, nearly three hours while they talked. Finally Walter Leigh, Judge Kitchen, Avery Stone, of Jay Cooke & Co., and several others came in. They were a committee appointed to gather further information.

"Nothing more can be done to-day, Frank," Walter Leigh informed him, quietly. "The majority want the privilege of examining the books. There is some uncertainty about this entanglement with the city treasurer which you say exists. They feel that you'd better announce a temporary suspension, anyhow; and if they want to let you resume later they can do so."

"I'm sorry for that, gentlemen," replied Cowperwood, the least bit depressed. "I would rather do anything than suspend for one hour, if I could help it, for I know just what it means. You will find assets here far exceeding the liabilities if you will take the stocks at their normal market value; but that won't help any if I close my doors. The public won't believe in me. I ought to keep open."

"Sorry, Frank, old boy," observed Leigh, pressing his hand affectionately. "If it were left to me personally, you could have all the time you want. There's a crowd of old fogies out there that won't listen to reason. They're panic-struck. I guess they're pretty hard hit themselves. You can scarcely blame them. You'll come out all right, though I wish you didn't have to shut up shop. We can't do anything with them, however. Why, damn it, man, I don't see how you can fail, really. In ten days these stocks will be all right."

Judge Kitchen commiserated with him also; but what good did that do? He was being compelled to suspend. An expert accountant would have to come in and go over his books. Butler might spread the news of this city-treasury connection. Stener might complain of this last city-loan transaction. A half-dozen of his helpful friends stayed with him until four o'clock in the morning; but he had to suspend just the same. And when he did that, he knew he was seriously crippled if not ultimately defeated in his race for wealth and fame.

When he was really and finally quite alone in his private bedroom he stared at himself in the mirror. His face was pale and tired, he thought, but strong and effective. "Pshaw!" he said to himself, "I'm not whipped. I'm still young. I'll get out of this in some way yet. Certainly I will. I'll find some way out."

And so, cogitating heavily, wearily, he began to undress. Finally he sank upon his bed, and in a little while, strange as it may seem, with all the tangle of trouble around him, slept. He could do that—sleep and gurgle most peacefully, the while his father paced the floor in his room, refusing to be comforted. All was dark before the older man—the future hopeless. Before the younger man was still hope.

And in her room Lillian Cowperwood turned and tossed in the face of this new calamity. For it had suddenly appeared from news from her father and Frank and Anna and her mother-in-law that Frank was about to fail, or would, or had—it was almost impossible to say just how it was. Frank was too busy to explain. The Chicago fire was to blame. There was no mention as yet of the city treasurership. Frank was caught in a trap, and was fighting for his life.

In this crisis, for the moment, she forgot about the note as to his infidelity, or rather ignored it. She was astonished, frightened, dumbfounded, confused. Her little, placid, beautiful world was going around in a dizzy ring. The charming, ornate ship of their fortune was being blown most ruthlessly here and there. She felt it a sort of duty to stay in bed and try to sleep; but her eyes were quite wide, and her brain hurt her. Hours before Frank had insisted that she should not bother about him, that she could do nothing; and she had left him, wondering more than ever what and where was the line of her duty. To stick by her husband, convention told her; and so she decided. Yes, religion dictated that, also custom. There were the children. They must not be injured. Frank must be reclaimed, if possible. He would get over this. But what a blow!

CHAPTER XXXI

The suspension of the banking house of Frank A. Cowperwood & Co. created a great stir on 'change and in Philadelphia generally. It was so unexpected, and the amount involved was comparatively so large. Actually he failed for one million two hundred and fifty thousand dollars; and his assets, under the depressed condition of stock values, barely totaled seven hundred and fifty thousand dollars. There had been considerable work done on the matter of his balance-sheet before it was finally given to the public; but when it was, stocks dropped an additional three points generally, and the papers the next day devoted notable headlines to it. Cowperwood had no idea of failing permanently; he merely wished to suspend temporarily, and later, if possible, to persuade his creditors to allow him to resume. There were only two things which stood in the way of this: the matter of the five hundred thousand dollars borrowed from the city treasury at a ridiculously low rate of interest, which showed plainer than words what had been going on, and the other, the matter of the sixty-thousand-dollar check. His financial wit had told him there were ways to assign his holdings in favor of his largest creditors, which would tend to help him later to resume; and he had been swift to act. Indeed, Harper Steger had drawn up documents which named Jay Cooke & Co., Edward Clark & Co., Drexel & Co., and others as preferred. He knew that even though dissatisfied holders of smaller shares in his company brought suit and compelled readjustment or bankruptcy later, the intention shown to prefer some of his most influential aids was important. They would like it, and might help him later when all this was over. Besides, suits in plenty are an excellent way of tiding over a crisis of this kind until stocks and common sense are restored, and he was for many suits. Harper Steger smiled once rather grimly, even in the whirl of the financial chaos where smiles were few, as they were figuring it out.

"Frank," he said, "you're a wonder. You'll have a network of suits spread here shortly, which no one can break through. They'll all be suing each other."

Cowperwood smiled.

"I only want a little time, that's all," he replied. Nevertheless, for the first time in his life he was a little depressed; for now this business, to which he had devoted years of active work and thought, was ended.

The thing that was troubling him most in all of this was not the five hundred thousand dollars which was owing the city treasury, and which he knew would stir political and social life to the center once it was generally known—that was a legal or semi-legal transaction, at least—but rather the matter of the sixty thousand dollars' worth of unrestored city loan certificates which he had not been able to replace in the sinking-fund and could not now even though the necessary money should fall from heaven. The fact of their absence was a matter of source. He pondered over the situation a good deal. The thing to do, he thought, if he went to Mollenhauer or Simpson, or both (he had never met either of them, but in view of Butler's desertion they were his only recourse), was to say that, although he could not at present return the five hundred thousand dollars, if no action were taken against him now, which would prevent his resuming his business on a normal scale a little later, he would pledge his word that every dollar of the involved five hundred thousand dollars would eventually be returned to the treasury. If they refused, and injury was done him, he proposed to let them wait until he was "good and ready," which in all probability would be never. But, really, it was not quite clear how action against him was to be prevented—even by them. The money was down on his books as owing the city treasury, and it was down on the city treasury's books as owing from him. Besides, there was a local organization known as the Citizens' Municipal Reform Association which occasionally conducted investigations in connection with public affairs. His defalcation would be sure to come to the ears of this body and a public investigation might well follow. Various private individuals knew of it already. His creditors, for instance, who were now examining his books.

This matter of seeing Mollenhauer or Simpson, or both, was important, anyhow, he thought; but before doing so he decided to talk it all over with Harper Steger. So several days after he had closed his doors, he sent for Steger and told him all about the transaction, except that he did not make it clear that he had not intended to put the certificates in the sinking-fund unless he survived quite comfortably.

131

Harper Steger was a tall, thin, graceful, rather elegant man, of gentle voice and perfect manners, who walked always as though he were a cat, and a dog were prowling somewhere in the offing. He had a longish, thin face of a type that is rather attractive to women. His eyes were blue, his hair brown, with a suggestion of sandy red in it. He had a steady, inscrutable gaze which sometimes came to you over a thin, delicate hand, which he laid meditatively over his mouth. He was cruel to the limit of the word, not aggressively but indifferently; for he had no faith in anything. He was not poor. He had not even been born poor. He was just innately subtle, with the rather constructive thought, which was about the only thing that compelled him to work, that he ought to be richer than he was—more conspicuous. Cowperwood was an excellent avenue toward legal prosperity. Besides, he was a fascinating customer. Of all his clients, Steger admired Cowperwood most.

"Let them proceed against you," he said on this occasion, his brilliant legal mind taking in all the phases of the situation at once. "I don't see that there is anything more here than a technical charge. If it ever came to anything like that, which I don't think it will, the charge would be embezzlement or perhaps larceny as bailee. In this instance, you were the bailee. And the only way out of that would be to swear that you had received the check with Stener's knowledge and consent. Then it would only be a technical charge of irresponsibility on your part, as I see it, and I don't believe any jury would convict you on the evidence of how this relationship was conducted. Still, it might; you never can tell what a jury is going to do. All this would have to come out at a trial, however. The whole thing, it seems to me, would depend on which of you two—yourself or Stener—the jury would be inclined to believe, and on how anxious this city crowd is to find a scapegoat for Stener. This coming election is the rub. If this panic had come at any other time—"

Cowperwood waved for silence. He knew all about that. "It all depends on what the politicians decide to do. I'm doubtful. The situation is too complicated. It can't be hushed up." They were in his private office at his house. "What will be will be," he added.

"What would that mean, Harper, legally, if I were tried on a charge of larceny as bailee, as you put it, and convicted? How many years in the penitentiary at the outside?"

Steger thought a minute, rubbing his chin with his hand. "Let me see," he said, "that is a serious question, isn't it? The law says one to five years at the outside; but the sentences usually average from one to three years in embezzlement cases. Of course, in this case—"

"I know all about that," interrupted Cowperwood, irritably. "My case isn't any different from the others, and you know it. Embezzlement is embezzlement if the politicians want to have it so." He fell to thinking, and Steger got up and strolled about leisurely. He was thinking also.

"And would I have to go to jail at any time during the proceedings—before a final adjustment of the case by the higher courts?" Cowperwood added, directly, grimly, after a time.

"Yes, there is one point in all legal procedure of the kind," replied Steger, cautiously, now rubbing his ear and trying to put the matter as delicately as possible. "You can avoid jail sentences all through the earlier parts of a case like this; but if you are once tried and convicted it's pretty hard to do anything—as a matter of fact, it becomes absolutely necessary then to go to jail for a few days, five or so, pending the motion for a new trial and the obtaining of a certificate of reasonable doubt. It usually takes that long."

The young banker sat there staring out of the window, and Steger observed, "It is a bit complicated, isn't it?"

"Well, I should say so," returned Frank, and he added to himself: "Jail! Five days in prison!" That would be a terrific slap, all things considered. Five days in jail pending the obtaining of a certificate of reasonable doubt, if one could be obtained! He must avoid this! Jail! The penitentiary! His commercial reputation would never survive that.

The necessity of a final conference between Butler, Mollenhauer, and Simpson was speedily reached, for this situation was hourly growing more serious. Rumors were floating about in Third Street that in addition to having failed for so large an amount as to have further unsettled the already panicky financial situation induced by the Chicago fire, Cowperwood and Stener, or Stener working with Cowperwood, or the other way round, had involved the city treasury to the extent of five hundred thousand dollars. And the question was how was the matter to be kept quiet until after election, which was still three weeks away. Bankers and brokers were communicating odd rumors to each other about a check that had been taken from the city treasury after Cowperwood knew he was to fail, and without Stener's consent. Also that there was danger that it would come to the ears of that very uncomfortable political organization known as the Citizens' Municipal Reform Association, of which a well-known iron-manufacturer of great probity and moral rectitude, one Skelton C. Wheat, was president. Wheat had for years been following on the trail of the dominant Republican administration in a vain attempt to bring it to a sense of some of its political iniquities. He was a serious and austere man—one of those solemn, self-righteous souls who see life through a peculiar veil of duty, and who, undisturbed by notable animal passions of any kind, go their way of upholding the theory of the Ten Commandments over the order of things as they are.

The committee in question had originally been organized to protest against some abuses in the tax department; but since then, from election to election, it had been drifting from one subject to another, finding an occasional evidence of its worthwhileness in some newspaper comment and the frightened reformation of some minor political official who ended, usually, by taking refuge behind the skirts of some higher political power—in the last reaches, Messrs. Butler, Mollenhauer, and Simpson. Just now it was without important fuel or ammunition; and this assignment of Cowperwood, with its attendant crime, so far as the city treasury was concerned, threatened, as some politicians and bankers saw it, to give it just the club it was looking for.

However, the decisive conference took place between Cowperwood and the reigning political powers some five days after Cowperwood's failure, at the home of Senator Simpson, which was located in Rittenhouse Square—a region central for the older order of wealth in Philadelphia. Simpson was a man of no little refinement artistically, of Quaker extraction, and of great wealth-breeding judgment which he used largely to satisfy his craving for political predominance. He was most liberal where money would bring him a powerful or necessary political adherent. He fairly showered offices—commissionerships, trusteeships, judgeships, political nominations, and executive positions generally—on those who did his bidding faithfully and without question. Compared with Butler and Mollenhauer he was more powerful than either, for he represented the State and the nation. When the political authorities who were trying to swing a national election were anxious to discover what the State of Pennsylvania would do, so far as the Republican party was concerned, it was to Senator Simpson that they appealed. In the literal sense of the word, he knew. The Senator had long since graduated from State to national politics, and was an interesting figure in the United States Senate at Washington, where his voice in all the conservative and moneyed councils of the nation was of great weight.

The house that he occupied, of Venetian design, and four stories in height, bore many architectural marks of distinction, such as the floriated window, the door with the semipointed arch, and medallions of colored marble set in the walls. The Senator was a great admirer of Venice. He had been there often, as he had to Athens and Rome, and had brought back many artistic objects representative of the civilizations and refinements of older days. He was fond, for one thing, of the stern, sculptured heads of the Roman emperors, and the fragments of gods and goddesses which are the best testimony of the

artistic aspirations of Greece. In the entresol of this house was one of his finest treasures—
a carved and floriated base bearing a tapering monolith some four feet high, crowned by the
head of a peculiarly goatish Pan, by the side of which were the problematic remains of a
lovely nude nymph—just the little feet broken off at the ankles. The base on which the feet
of the nymph and the monolith stood was ornamented with carved ox-skulls intertwined
with roses. In his reception hall were replicas of Caligula, Nero, and other Roman
emperors; and on his stair-walls reliefs of dancing nymphs in procession, and priests
bearing offerings of sheep and swine to the sacrificial altars. There was a clock in some
corner of the house which chimed the quarter, the half, the three-quarters, and the hour in
strange, euphonious, and pathetic notes. On the walls of the rooms were tapestries of
Flemish origin, and in the reception-hall, the library, the living-room, and the drawing-
room, richly carved furniture after the standards of the Italian Renaissance. The Senator's
taste in the matter of paintings was inadequate, and he mistrusted it; but such as he had
were of distinguished origin and authentic. He cared more for his curio-cases filled with
smaller imported bronzes, Venetian glass, and Chinese jade. He was not a collector of these
in any notable sense—merely a lover of a few choice examples. Handsome tiger and
leopard skin rugs, the fur of a musk-ox for his divan, and tanned and brown-stained goat
and kid skins for his tables, gave a sense of elegance and reserved profusion. In addition the
Senator had a dining-room done after the Jacobean idea of artistic excellence, and a wine-
cellar which the best of the local vintners looked after with extreme care. He was a man
who loved to entertain lavishly; and when his residence was thrown open for a dinner, a
reception, or a ball, the best of local society was to be found there.

The conference was in the Senator's library, and he received his colleagues with the genial
air of one who has much to gain and little to lose. There were whiskies, wines, cigars on the
table, and while Mollenhauer and Simpson exchanged the commonplaces of the day
awaiting the arrival of Butler, they lighted cigars and kept their inmost thoughts to
themselves.

It so happened that upon the previous afternoon Butler had learned from Mr. David Pettie,
the district attorney, of the sixty-thousand-dollar-check transaction. At the same time the
matter had been brought to Mollenhauer's attention by Stener himself. It was Mollenhauer,
not Butler who saw that by taking advantage of Cowperwood's situation, he might save the
local party from blame, and at the same time most likely fleece Cowperwood out of his
street-railway shares without letting Butler or Simpson know anything about it. The thing to
do was to terrorize him with a private threat of prosecution.

Butler was not long in arriving, and apologized for the delay. Concealing his recent grief
behind as jaunty an air as possible, he began with:

"It's a lively life I'm leadin', what with every bank in the city wantin' to know how their
loans are goin' to be taken care of." He took a cigar and struck a match.

"It does look a little threatening," said Senator Simpson, smiling. "Sit down. I have just
been talking with Avery Stone, of Jay Cooke & Company, and he tells me that the talk in
Third Street about Stener's connection with this Cowperwood failure is growing very
strong, and that the newspapers are bound to take up the matter shortly, unless something
is done about it. I am sure that the news will also reach Mr. Wheat, of the Citizens' Reform
Association, very shortly. We ought to decide now, gentlemen, what we propose to do. One
thing, I am sure, is to eliminate Stener from the ticket as quietly as possible. This really
looks to me as if it might become a very serious issue, and we ought to be doing what we
can now to offset its effect later."

Mollenhauer pulled a long breath through his cigar, and blew it out in a rolling steel-blue
cloud. He studied the tapestry on the opposite wall but said nothing.

"There is one thing sure," continued Senator Simpson, after a time, seeing that no one else
spoke, "and that is, if we do not begin a prosecution on our own account within a
reasonable time, some one else is apt to; and that would put rather a bad face on the matter.

My own opinion would be that we wait until it is very plain that prosecution is going to be undertaken by some one else—possibly the Municipal Reform Association—but that we stand ready to step in and act in such a way as to make it look as though we had been planning to do it all the time. The thing to do is to gain time; and so I would suggest that it be made as difficult as possible to get at the treasurer's books. An investigation there, if it begins at all—as I think is very likely—should be very slow in producing the facts."

The Senator was not at all for mincing words with his important confreres, when it came to vital issues. He preferred, in his grandiloquent way, to call a spade a spade.

"Now that sounds like very good sense to me," said Butler, sinking a little lower in his chair for comfort's sake, and concealing his true mood in regard to all this. "The boys could easily make that investigation last three weeks, I should think. They're slow enough with everything else, if me memory doesn't fail me." At the same time he was cogitating as to how to inject the personality of Cowperwood and his speedy prosecution without appearing to be neglecting the general welfare of the local party too much.

"Yes, that isn't a bad idea," said Mollenhauer, solemnly, blowing a ring of smoke, and thinking how to keep Cowperwood's especial offense from coming up at this conference and until after he had seen him.

"We ought to map out our program very carefully," continued Senator Simpson, "so that if we are compelled to act we can do so very quickly. I believe myself that this thing is certain to come to an issue within a week, if not sooner, and we have no time to lose. If my advice were followed now, I should have the mayor write the treasurer a letter asking for information, and the treasurer write the mayor his answer, and also have the mayor, with the authority of the common council, suspend the treasurer for the time being—I think we have the authority to do that—or, at least, take over his principal duties but without for the time being, anyhow, making any of these transactions public—until we have to, of course. We ought to be ready with these letters to show to the newspapers at once, in case this action is forced upon us."

"I could have those letters prepared, if you gentlemen have no objection," put in Mollenhauer, quietly, but quickly.

"Well, that strikes me as sinsible," said Butler, easily. "It's about the only thing we can do under the circumstances, unless we could find some one else to blame it on, and I have a suggestion to make in that direction. Maybe we're not as helpless as we might be, all things considered."

There was a slight gleam of triumph in his eye as he said this, at the same time that there was a slight shadow of disappointment in Mollenhauer's. So Butler knew, and probably Simpson, too.

"Just what do you mean?" asked the Senator, looking at Butler interestedly. He knew nothing of the sixty-thousand-dollar check transaction. He had not followed the local treasury dealings very closely, nor had he talked to either of his confreres since the original conference between them. "There haven't been any outside parties mixed up with this, have there?" His own shrewd, political mind was working.

"No-o. I wouldn't call him an outside party, exactly, Senator," went on Butler suavely. "It's Cowperwood himself I'm thinkin' of. There's somethin' that has come up since I saw you gentlemen last that makes me think that perhaps that young man isn't as innocent as he might be. It looks to me as though he was the ringleader in this business, as though he had been leadin' Stener on against his will. I've been lookin' into the matter on me own account, and as far as I can make out this man Stener isn't as much to blame as I thought. From all I can learn, Cowperwood's been threatenin' Stener with one thing and another if he didn't give him more money, and only the other day he got a big sum on false pretenses, which might make him equally guilty with Stener. There's sixty-thousand dollars of city loan certificates that has been paid for that aren't in the sinking-fund. And since the reputation of the party's in danger this fall, I don't see that we need to have any particular

135

consideration for him." He paused, strong in the conviction that he had sent a most dangerous arrow flying in the direction of Cowperwood, as indeed he had. Yet at this moment, both the Senator and Mollenhauer were not a little surprised, seeing at their last meeting he had appeared rather friendly to the young banker, and this recent discovery seemed scarcely any occasion for a vicious attitude on his part. Mollenhauer in particular was surprised, for he had been looking on Butler's friendship for Cowperwood as a possible stumbling block.

"Um-m, you don't tell me," observed Senator Simpson, thoughtfully, stroking his mouth with his pale hand.

"Yes, I can confirm that," said Mollenhauer, quietly, seeing his own little private plan of browbeating Cowperwood out of his street-railway shares going glimmering. "I had a talk with Stener the other day about this very matter, and he told me that Cowperwood had been trying to force him to give him three hundred thousand dollars more, and that when he refused Cowperwood managed to get sixty thousand dollars further without his knowledge or consent."

"How could he do that?" asked Senator Simpson, incredulously. Mollenhauer explained the transaction.

"Oh," said the Senator, when Mollenhauer had finished, "that indicates a rather sharp person, doesn't it? And the certificates are not in the sinking-fund, eh?"

"They're not," chimed in Butler, with considerable enthusiasm.

"Well, I must say," said Simpson, rather relieved in his manner, "this looks like a rather good thing than not to me. A scapegoat possibly. We need something like this. I see no reason under the circumstances for trying to protect Mr. Cowperwood. We might as well try to make a point of that, if we have to. The newspapers might just as well talk loud about that as anything else. They are bound to talk; and if we give them the right angle, I think that the election might well come and go before the matter could be reasonably cleared up, even though Mr. Wheat does interfere. I will be glad to undertake to see what can be done with the papers."

"Well, that bein' the case," said Butler, "I don't see that there's so much more we can do now; but I do think it will be a mistake if Cowperwood isn't punished with the other one. He's equally guilty with Stener, if not more so, and I for one want to see him get what he deserves. He belongs in the penitentiary, and that's where he'll go if I have my say." Both Mollenhauer and Simpson turned a reserved and inquiring eye on their usually genial associate. What could be the reason for his sudden determination to have Cowperwood punished? Cowperwood, as Mollenhauer and Simpson saw it, and as Butler would ordinarily have seen it, was well within his human, if not his strictly legal rights. They did not blame him half as much for trying to do what he had done as they blamed Stener for letting him do it. But, since Butler felt as he did, and there was an actual technical crime here, they were perfectly willing that the party should have the advantage of it, even if Cowperwood went to the penitentiary.

"You may be right," said Senator Simpson, cautiously. "You might have those letters prepared, Henry; and if we have to bring any action at all against anybody before election, it would, perhaps, be advisable to bring it against Cowperwood. Include Stener if you have to but not unless you have to. I leave it to you two, as I am compelled to start for Pittsburg next Friday; but I know you will not overlook any point."

The Senator arose. His time was always valuable. Butler was highly gratified by what he had accomplished. He had succeeded in putting the triumvirate on record against Cowperwood as the first victim, in case of any public disturbance or demonstration against the party. All that was now necessary was for that disturbance to manifest itself; and, from what he could see of local conditions, it was not far off. There was now the matter of Cowperwood's disgruntled creditors to look into; and if by buying in these he should succeed in preventing the financier from resuming business, he would have him in a very precarious condition indeed. It was a sad day for Cowperwood, Butler thought—the day he had first tried to lead Aileen astray—and the time was not far off when he could prove it to him.

CHAPTER XXXIII

In the meantime Cowperwood, from what he could see and hear, was becoming more and more certain that the politicians would try to make a scapegoat of him, and that shortly. For one thing, Stires had called only a few days after he closed his doors and imparted a significant bit of information. Albert was still connected with the city treasury, as was Stener, and engaged with Sengstack and another personal appointee of Mollenhauer's in going over the treasurer's books and explaining their financial significance. Stires had come to Cowperwood primarily to get additional advice in regard to the sixty-thousand-dollar check and his personal connection with it. Stener, it seemed, was now threatening to have his chief clerk prosecuted, saying that he was responsible for the loss of the money and that his bondsmen could be held responsible. Cowperwood had merely laughed and assured Stires that there was nothing to this.

"Albert," he had said, smilingly, "I tell you positively, there's nothing in it. You're not responsible for delivering that check to me. I'll tell you what you do, now. Go and consult my lawyer—Steger. It won't cost you a cent, and he'll tell you exactly what to do. Now go on back and don't worry any more about it. I am sorry this move of mine has caused you so much trouble, but it's a hundred to one you couldn't have kept your place with a new city treasurer, anyhow, and if I see any place where you can possibly fit in later, I'll let you know."

Another thing that made Cowperwood pause and consider at this time was a letter from Aileen, detailing a conversation which had taken place at the Butler dinner table one evening when Butler, the elder, was not at home. She related how her brother Owen in effect had stated that they—the politicians—her father, Mollenhauer, and Simpson, were going to "get him yet" (meaning Cowperwood), for some criminal financial manipulation of something—she could not explain what—a check or something. Aileen was frantic with worry. Could they mean the penitentiary, she asked in her letter? Her dear lover! Her beloved Frank! Could anything like this really happen to him?

His brow clouded, and he set his teeth with rage when he read her letter. He would have to do something about this—see Mollenhauer or Simpson, or both, and make some offer to the city. He could not promise them money for the present—only notes—but they might take them. Surely they could not be intending to make a scapegoat of him over such a trivial and uncertain matter as this check transaction! When there was the five hundred thousand advanced by Stener, to say nothing of all the past shady transactions of former city treasurers! How rotten! How political, but how real and dangerous.

But Simpson was out of the city for a period of ten days, and Mollenhauer, having in mind the suggestion made by Butler in regard to utilizing Cowperwood's misdeed for the benefit of the party, had already moved as they had planned. The letters were ready and waiting. Indeed, since the conference, the smaller politicians, taking their cue from the overlords, had been industriously spreading the story of the sixty-thousand-dollar check, and insisting that the burden of guilt for the treasury defalcation, if any, lay on the banker. The moment Mollenhauer laid eyes on Cowperwood he realized, however, that he had a powerful personality to deal with. Cowperwood gave no evidence of fright. He merely stated, in his bland way, that he had been in the habit of borrowing money from the city treasury at a low rate of interest, and that this panic had involved him so that he could not possibly return it at present.

"I have heard rumors, Mr. Mollenhauer," he said, "to the effect that some charge is to be brought against me as a partner with Mr. Stener in this matter; but I am hoping that the city will not do that, and I thought I might enlist your influence to prevent it. My affairs are not in a bad way at all, if I had a little time to arrange matters. I am making all of my creditors an offer of fifty cents on the dollar now, and giving notes at one, two, and three years; but in this matter of the city treasury loans, if I could come to terms, I would be glad to make it a hundred cents—only I would want a little more time. Stocks are bound to recover, as you know, and, barring my losses at this time, I will be all right. I realize that the matter has gone pretty far already. The newspapers are likely to start talking at any time, unless they are stopped by those who can control them." (He looked at Mollenhauer in a complimentary way.) "But if I could be kept out of the general proceedings as much as possible, my standing would not be injured, and I would have a better chance of getting on my feet. It would be better for the city, for then I could certainly pay it what I owe it." He smiled his most winsome and engaging smile. And Mollenhauer seeing him for the first time, was not unimpressed. Indeed he looked at this young financial David with an interested eye. If he could have seen a way to accept this proposition of Cowperwood's, so that the money offered would have been eventually payable to him, and if Cowperwood had had any reasonable prospect of getting on his feet soon, he would have considered carefully what he had to say. For then Cowperwood could have assigned his recovered property to him. As it was, there was small likelihood of this situation ever being straightened out. The Citizens' Municipal Reform Association, from all he could hear, was already on the move—investigating, or about to, and once they had set their hands to this, would unquestionably follow it closely to the end.

"The trouble with this situation, Mr. Cowperwood," he said, affably, "is that it has gone so far that it is practically out of my hands. I really have very little to do with it. I don't suppose, though, really, it is this matter of the five-hundred-thousand-dollar loan that is worrying you so much, as it is this other matter of the sixty-thousand-dollar check you received the other day. Mr. Stener insists that you secured that illegally, and he is very much wrought up about it. The mayor and the other city officials know of it now, and they may force some action. I don't know."

Mollenhauer was obviously not frank in his attitude—a little bit evasive in his sly reference to his official tool, the mayor; and Cowperwood saw it. It irritated him greatly, but he was tactful enough to be quite suave and respectful.

"I did get a check for sixty thousand dollars, that's true," he replied, with apparent frankness, "the day before I assigned. It was for certificates I had purchased, however, on Mr. Stener's order, and was due me. I needed the money, and asked for it. I don't see that there is anything illegal in that."

"Not if the transaction was completed in all its details," replied Mollenhauer, blandly. "As I understand it, the certificates were bought for the sinking-fund, and they are not there. How do you explain that?"

"An oversight, merely," replied Cowperwood, innocently, and quite as blandly as Mollenhauer. "They would have been there if I had not been compelled to assign so unexpectedly. It was not possible for me to attend to everything in person. It has not been our custom to deposit them at once. Mr. Stener will tell you that, if you ask him."

"You don't say," replied Mollenhauer. "He did not give me that impression. However, they are not there, and I believe that that makes some difference legally. I have no interest in the matter one way or the other, more than that of any other good Republican. I don't see exactly what I can do for you. What did you think I could do?"

"I don't believe you can do anything for me, Mr. Mollenhauer," replied Cowperwood, a little tartly, "unless you are willing to deal quite frankly with me. I am not a beginner in politics in Philadelphia. I know something about the powers in command. I thought that you could stop any plan to prosecute me in this matter, and give me time to get on my feet again. I am not any more criminally responsible for that sixty thousand dollars than I am for the five hundred thousand dollars that I had as loan before it—not as much so. I did not create this panic. I did not set Chicago on fire. Mr. Stener and his friends have been reaping some profit out of dealing with me. I certainly was entitled to make some effort to save myself after all these years of service, and I can't understand why I should not receive some courtesy at the hands of the present city administration, after I have been so useful to it. I certainly have kept city loan at par; and as for Mr. Stener's money, he has never wanted for his interest on that, and more than his interest."

"Quite so," replied Mollenhauer, looking Cowperwood in the eye steadily and estimating the force and accuracy of the man at their real value. "I understand exactly how it has all come about, Mr. Cowperwood. No doubt Mr. Stener owes you a debt of gratitude, as does the remainder of the city administration. I'm not saying what the city administration ought or ought not do. All I know is that you find yourself wittingly or unwittingly in a dangerous situation, and that public sentiment in some quarters is already very strong against you. I personally have no feeling one way or the other, and if it were not for the situation itself, which looks to be out of hand, would not be opposed to assisting you in any reasonable way. But how? The Republican party is in a very bad position, so far as this election is concerned. In a way, however innocently, you have helped to put it there, Mr. Cowperwood. Mr. Butler, for some reason to which I am not a party, seems deeply and personally incensed. And Mr. Butler is a great power here—" (Cowperwood began to wonder whether by any chance Butler had indicated the nature of his social offense against himself, but he could not bring himself to believe that. It was not probable.) "I sympathize with you greatly, Mr. Cowperwood, but what I suggest is that you first See Mr. Butler and Mr. Simpson. If they agree to any program of aid, I will not be opposed to joining. But apart from that I do not know exactly what I can do. I am only one of those who have a slight say in the affairs of Philadelphia."

At this point, Mollenhauer rather expected Cowperwood to make an offer of his own holdings, but he did not. Instead he said, "I'm very much obliged to you, Mr. Mollenhauer, for the courtesy of this interview. I believe you would help me if you could. I shall just have to fight it out the best way I can. Good day."

And he bowed himself out. He saw clearly how hopeless was his quest.

In the meanwhile, finding that the rumors were growing in volume and that no one appeared to be willing to take steps to straighten the matter out, Mr. Skelton C. Wheat, President of the Citizens' Municipal Reform Association, was, at last and that by no means against his will, compelled to call together the committee of ten estimable Philadelphians of which he was chairman, in a local committee-hall on Market Street, and lay the matter of the Cowperwood failure before it.

"It strikes me, gentlemen," he announced, "that this is an occasion when this organization can render a signal service to the city and the people of Philadelphia, and prove the significance and the merit of the title originally selected for it, by making such a thoroughgoing investigation as will bring to light all the facts in this case, and then by standing vigorously behind them insist that such nefarious practices as we are informed were indulged in in this case shall cease. I know it may prove to be a difficult task. The Republican party and its local and State interests are certain to be against us. Its leaders are unquestionably most anxious to avoid comment and to have their ticket go through undisturbed, and they will not contemplate with any equanimity our opening activity in this matter; but if we persevere, great good will surely come of it. There is too much dishonesty in public life as it is. There is a standard of right in these matters which cannot permanently be ignored, and which must eventually be fulfilled. I leave this matter to your courteous consideration."

Mr. Wheat sat down, and the body before him immediately took the matter which he proposed under advisement. It was decided to appoint a subcommittee "to investigate" (to quote the statement eventually given to the public) "the peculiar rumors now affecting one of the most important and distinguished offices of our municipal government," and to report at the next meeting, which was set for the following evening at nine o'clock. The meeting adjourned, and the following night at nine reassembled, four individuals of very shrewd financial judgment having meantime been about the task assigned them. They drew up a very elaborate statement, not wholly in accordance with the facts, but as nearly so as could be ascertained in so short a space of time.

"It appears [read the report, after a preamble which explained why the committee had been appointed] that it has been the custom of city treasurers for years, when loans have been authorized by councils, to place them in the hands of some favorite broker for sale, the broker accounting to the treasurer for the moneys received by such sales at short periods, generally the first of each month. In the present case Frank A. Cowperwood has been acting as such broker for the city treasurer. But even this vicious and unbusiness-like system appears not to have been adhered to in the case of Mr. Cowperwood. The accident of the Chicago fire, the consequent depression of stock values, and the subsequent failure of Mr. Frank A. Cowperwood have so involved matters temporarily that the committee has not been able to ascertain with accuracy that regular accounts have been rendered; but from the manner in which Mr. Cowperwood has had possession of bonds (city loan) for hypothecation, etc., it would appear that he has been held to no responsibility in these matters, and that there have always been under his control several hundred thousand dollars of cash or securities belonging to the city, which he has manipulated for various purposes; but the details of the results of these transactions are not easily available.

"Some of the operations consisted of hypothecation of large amounts of these loans before the certificates were issued, the lender seeing that the order for the hypothecated securities was duly made to him on the books of the treasurer. Such methods appear to have been occurring for a long time, and it being incredible that the city treasurer could be unaware of the nature of the business, there is indication of a complicity between him and Mr. Cowperwood to benefit by the use of the city credit, in violation of the law.

"Furthermore, at the very time these hypothecations were being made, and the city paying interest upon such loans, the money representing them was in the hands of the treasurer's broker and bearing no interest to the city. The payment of municipal warrants was postponed, and they were being purchased at a discount in large amounts by Mr. Cowperwood with the very money that should have been in the city treasury. The bona fide holders of the orders for certificates of loans are now unable to obtain them, and thus the city's credit is injured to a greater extent than the present defalcation, which amounts to over five hundred thousand dollars. An accountant is now at work on the treasurer's books, and a few days should make clear the whole modus operandi. It is hoped that the publicity thus obtained will break up such vicious practices."

There was appended to this report a quotation from the law governing the abuse of a public trust; and the committee went on to say that, unless some taxpayer chose to initiate proceedings for the prosecution of those concerned, the committee itself would be called upon to do so, although such action hardly came within the object for which it was formed. This report was immediately given to the papers. Though some sort of a public announcement had been anticipated by Cowperwood and the politicians, this was, nevertheless, a severe blow. Stener was beside himself with fear. He broke into a cold sweat when he saw the announcement which was conservatively headed, "Meeting of the Municipal Reform Association." All of the papers were so closely identified with the political and financial powers of the city that they did not dare to come out openly and say what they thought. The chief facts had already been in the hands of the various editors and publishers for a week and more, but word had gone around from Mollenhauer, Simpson, and Butler to use the soft pedal for the present. It was not good for Philadelphia, for local

140

commerce, etc., to make a row. The fair name of the city would be smirched. It was the old story.

At once the question was raised as to who was really guilty, the city treasurer or the broker, or both. How much money had actually been lost? Where had it gone? Who was Frank Algernon Cowperwood, anyway? Why was he not arrested? How did he come to be identified so closely with the financial administration of the city? And though the day of what later was termed "yellow journalism" had not arrived, and the local papers were not given to such vital personal comment as followed later, it was not possible, even bound as they were, hand and foot, by the local political and social magnates, to avoid comment of some sort. Editorials had to be written. Some solemn, conservative references to the shame and disgrace which one single individual could bring to a great city and a noble political party had to be ventured upon.

That desperate scheme to cast the blame on Cowperwood temporarily, which had been concocted by Mollenhauer, Butler, and Simpson, to get the odium of the crime outside the party lines for the time being, was now lugged forth and put in operation. It was interesting and strange to note how quickly the newspapers, and even the Citizens' Municipal Reform Association, adopted the argument that Cowperwood was largely, if not solely, to blame. Stener had loaned him the money, it is true—had put bond issues in his hands for sale, it is true, but somehow every one seemed to gain the impression that Cowperwood had desperately misused the treasurer. The fact that he had taken a sixty-thousand-dollar check for certificates which were not in the sinking-fund was hinted at, though until they could actually confirm this for themselves both the newspapers and the committee were too fearful of the State libel laws to say so.

In due time there were brought forth several noble municipal letters, purporting to be a stern call on the part of the mayor, Mr. Jacob Borchardt, on Mr. George W. Stener for an immediate explanation of his conduct, and the latter's reply, which were at once given to the newspapers and the Citizens' Municipal Reform Association. These letters were enough to show, so the politicians figured, that the Republican party was anxious to purge itself of any miscreant within its ranks, and they also helped to pass the time until after election.

OFFICE OF THE MAYOR OF THE CITY OF PHILADELPHIA

GEORGE W. STENER, ESQ.,   October 18,
1871. City Treasurer.

DEAR SIR,—Information has been given
me that certificates of city loan to a large amount, issued
by you for sale on account of the city, and, I presume,
after the usual requisition from the mayor of the city, have
passed out of your custody, and that the proceeds of the
sale of said certificates have not been paid into the city
treasury.

I have also been informed that a large amount of the city's
money has been permitted to pass into the hands of some one
or more brokers or bankers doing business on Third Street,
and that said brokers or bankers have since met with
financial difficulties, whereby, and by reason of the above
generally, the interests of the city are likely to be very
seriously affected.

I have therefore to request that you will promptly advise me

of the truth or falsity of these statements, so that such
duties as devolve upon me as the chief magistrate of the
city, in view of such facts, if they exist, may be
intelligently discharged. Yours respectfully,

JACOB BORCHARDT, Mayor of Philadelphia.

OFFICE OF THE TREASURER OF THE CITY OF PHILADELPHIA

HON. JACOB BORCHARDT.   October 19, 1871.

DEAR SIR,—I have to acknowledge the receipt of your
communication of the 21st instant, and to express my regret
that I cannot at this time give you the information you ask.
There is undoubtedly an embarrassment in the city treasury,
owing to the delinquency of the broker who for several years
past has negotiated the city loans, and I have been, since
the discovery of this fact, and still am occupied in
endeavoring to avert or lessen the loss with which the city
is threatened. I am, very respectfully, GEORGE W. STENER.

OFFICE OF THE MAYOR OF THE CITY OF PHILADELPHIA

GEORGE W. STENER, ESQ.,   October 21, 1871.
City Treasurer.

DEAR SIR—Under the existing
circumstances you will consider this as a notice of
withdrawal and revocation of any requisition or authority by
me for the sale of loan, so far as the same has not been
fulfilled. Applications for loans may for the present be
made at this office. Very respectfully,

JACOB BORCHARDT, Mayor of Philadelphia.

And did Mr. Jacob Borchardt write the letters to which his name was attached? He did not.
Mr. Abner Sengstack wrote them in Mr. Mollenhauer's office, and Mr. Mollenhauer's
comment when he saw them was that he thought they would do—that they were very good,
in fact. And did Mr. George W. Stener, city treasurer of Philadelphia, write that very politic
reply? He did not. Mr. Stener was in a state of complete collapse, even crying at one time at
home in his bathtub. Mr. Abner Sengstack wrote that also, and had Mr. Stener sign it. And
Mr. Mollenhauer's comment on that, before it was sent, was that he thought it was "all
right." It was a time when all the little rats and mice were scurrying to cover because of the
presence of a great, fiery-eyed public cat somewhere in the dark, and only the older and
wiser rats were able to act.
Indeed, at this very time and for some days past now, Messrs. Mollenhauer, Butler, and
Simpson were, and had been, considering with Mr. Pettie, the district attorney, just what
could be done about Cowperwood, if anything, and in order to further emphasize the blame
in that direction, and just what defense, if any, could be made for Stener. Butler, of course,
was strong for Cowperwood's prosecution. Pettie did not see that any defense could be
made for Stener, since various records of street-car stocks purchased for him were spread
upon Cowperwood's books; but for Cowperwood—"Let me see," he said. They were

speculating, first of all, as to whether it might not be good policy to arrest Cowperwood, and if necessary try him, since his mere arrest would seem to the general public, at least, positive proof of his greater guilt, to say nothing of the virtuous indignation of the administration, and in consequence might tend to divert attention from the evil nature of the party until after election.

So finally, on the afternoon of October 26, 1871, Edward Strobik, president of the common council of Philadelphia, appeared before the mayor, as finally ordered by Mollenhauer, and charged by affidavit that Frank A. Cowperwood, as broker, employed by the treasurer to sell the bonds of the city, had committed embezzlement and larceny as bailee. It did not matter that he charged George W. Stener with embezzlement at the same time. Cowperwood was the scapegoat they were after.

CHAPTER XXXIV

The contrasting pictures presented by Cowperwood and Stener at this time are well worth a moment's consideration. Stener's face was grayish-white, his lips blue. Cowperwood, despite various solemn thoughts concerning a possible period of incarceration which this hue and cry now suggested, and what that meant to his parents, his wife and children, his business associates, and his friends, was as calm and collected as one might assume his great mental resources would permit him to be. During all this whirl of disaster he had never once lost his head or his courage. That thing conscience, which obsesses and rides some people to destruction, did not trouble him at all. He had no consciousness of what is currently known as sin. There were just two faces to the shield of life from the point of view of his peculiar mind-strength and weakness. Right and wrong? He did not know about those. They were bound up in metaphysical abstrusities about which he did not care to bother. Good and evil? Those were toys of clerics, by which they made money. And as for social favor or social ostracism which, on occasion, so quickly followed upon the heels of disaster of any kind, well, what was social ostracism? Had either he or his parents been of the best society as yet? And since not, and despite this present mix-up, might not the future hold social restoration and position for him? It might. Morality and immorality? He never considered them. But strength and weakness—oh, yes! If you had strength you could protect yourself always and be something. If you were weak—pass quickly to the rear and get out of the range of the guns. He was strong, and he knew it, and somehow he always believed in his star. Something—he could not say what—it was the only metaphysics he bothered about—was doing something for him. It had always helped him. It made things come out right at times. It put excellent opportunities in his way. Why had he been given so fine a mind? Why always favored financially, personally? He had not deserved it—earned it. Accident, perhaps, but somehow the thought that he would always be protected—these intuitions, the "hunches" to act which he frequently had—could not be so easily explained. Life was a dark, insoluble mystery, but whatever it was, strength and weakness were its two constituents. Strength would win—weakness lose. He must rely on swiftness of thought, accuracy, his judgment, and on nothing else. He was really a brilliant picture of courage and energy—moving about briskly in a jaunty, dapper way, his mustaches curled, his clothes pressed, his nails manicured, his face clean-shaven and tinted with health.

In the meantime, Cowperwood had gone personally to Skelton C. Wheat and tried to explain his side of the situation, alleging that he had done no differently from many others before him, but Wheat was dubious. He did not see how it was that the sixty thousand dollars' worth of certificates were not in the sinking-fund. Cowperwood's explanation of custom did not avail. Nevertheless, Mr. Wheat saw that others in politics had been profiting quite as much as Cowperwood in other ways and he advised Cowperwood to turn state's evidence. This, however, he promptly refused to do—he was no "squealer," and indicated as much to Mr. Wheat, who only smiled wryly.

Butler, Sr., was delighted (concerned though he was about party success at the polls), for now he had this villain in the toils and he would have a fine time getting out of this. The incoming district attorney to succeed David Pettie if the Republican party won would be, as was now planned, an appointee of Butler's—a young Irishman who had done considerable legal work for him—one Dennis Shannon. The other two party leaders had already promised Butler that. Shannon was a smart, athletic, good-looking fellow, all of five feet ten inches in height, sandy-haired, pink-cheeked, blue-eyed, considerable of an orator and a fine legal fighter. He was very proud to be in the old man's favor—to be promised a place on the ticket by him—and would, he said, if elected, do his bidding to the best of his knowledge and ability.

There was only one fly in the ointment, so far as some of the politicians were concerned, and that was that if Cowperwood were convicted, Stener must needs be also. There was no escape in so far as any one could see for the city treasurer. If Cowperwood was guilty of securing by trickery sixty thousand dollars' worth of the city money, Stener was guilty of securing five hundred thousand dollars. The prison term for this was five years. He might plead not guilty, and by submitting as evidence that what he did was due to custom save himself from the odious necessity of pleading guilty; but he would be convicted nevertheless. No jury could get by the fact in regard to him. In spite of public opinion, when it came to a trial there might be considerable doubt in Cowperwood's case. There was none in Stener's.

The practical manner in which the situation was furthered, after Cowperwood and Stener were formally charged may be quickly noted. Steger, Cowperwood's lawyer, learned privately beforehand that Cowperwood was to be prosecuted. He arranged at once to have his client appear before any warrant could be served, and to forestall the newspaper palaver which would follow it if he had to be searched for.

The mayor issued a warrant for Cowperwood's arrest, and, in accordance with Steger's plan, Cowperwood immediately appeared before Borchardt in company with his lawyer and gave bail in twenty thousand dollars (W. C. Davison, president of the Girard National Bank, being his surety), for his appearance at the central police station on the following Saturday for a hearing. Marcus Oldslaw, a lawyer, had been employed by Strobik as president of the common council, to represent him in prosecuting the case for the city. The mayor looked at Cowperwood curiously, for he, being comparatively new to the political world of Philadelphia, was not so familiar with him as others were; and Cowperwood returned the look pleasantly enough.

"This is a great dumb show, Mr. Mayor," he observed once to Borchardt, quietly, and the latter replied, with a smile and a kindly eye, that as far as he was concerned, it was a form of procedure which was absolutely unavoidable at this time.

"You know how it is, Mr. Cowperwood," he observed. The latter smiled. "I do, indeed," he said.

Later there followed several more or less perfunctory appearances in a local police court, known as the Central Court, where when arraigned he pleaded not guilty, and finally his appearance before the November grand jury, where, owing to the complicated nature of the charge drawn up against him by Pettie, he thought it wise to appear. He was properly indicted by the latter body (Shannon, the newly elected district attorney, making a demonstration in force), and his trial ordered for December 5th before a certain Judge Payderson in Part I of Quarter Sessions, which was the local branch of the State courts dealing with crimes of this character. His indictment did not occur, however, before the coming and going of the much-mooted fall election, which resulted, thanks to the clever political manipulations of Mollenhauer and Simpson (ballot-box stuffing and personal violence at the polls not barred), in another victory, by, however, a greatly reduced majority. The Citizens' Municipal Reform Association, in spite of a resounding defeat at the polls, which could not have happened except by fraud, continued to fire courageously away at those whom it considered to be the chief malefactors.

Aileen Butler, during all this time, was following the trend of Cowperwood's outward vicissitudes as heralded by the newspapers and the local gossip with as much interest and bias and enthusiasm for him as her powerful physical and affectional nature would permit. She was no great reasoner where affection entered in, but shrewd enough without it; and, although she saw him often and he told her much—as much as his natural caution would permit—she yet gathered from the newspapers and private conversation, at her own family's table and elsewhere, that, as bad as they said he was, he was not as bad as he might be. One item only, clipped from the Philadelphia Public Ledger soon after Cowperwood had been publicly accused of embezzlement, comforted and consoled her. She cut it out and carried it in her bosom; for, somehow, it seemed to show that her adored Frank was far more sinned against than sinning. It was a part of one of those very numerous pronunciamientos or reports issued by the Citizens' Municipal Reform Association, and it ran:

"The aspects of the case are graver than have yet been allowed to reach the public. Five hundred thousand dollars of the deficiency arises not from city bonds sold and not accounted for, but from loans made by the treasurer to his broker. The committee is also informed, on what it believes to be good authority, that the loans sold by the broker were accounted for in the monthly settlements at the lowest prices current during the month, and that the difference between this rate and that actually realized was divided between the treasurer and the broker, thus making it to the interest of both parties to 'bear' the market at some time during the month, so as to obtain a low quotation for settlement. Nevertheless, the committee can only regard the prosecution instituted against the broker, Mr. Cowperwood, as an effort to divert public attention from more guilty parties while those concerned may be able to 'fix' matters to suit themselves."

"There," thought Aileen, when she read it, "there you have it." These politicians—her father among them as she gathered after his conversation with her—were trying to put the blame of their own evil deeds on her Frank. He was not nearly as bad as he was painted. The report said so. She gloated over the words "an effort to divert public attention from more guilty parties." That was just what her Frank had been telling her in those happy, private hours when they had been together recently in one place and another, particularly the new rendezvous in South Sixth Street which he had established, since the old one had to be abandoned. He had stroked her rich hair, caressed her body, and told her it was all a prearranged political scheme to cast the blame as much as possible on him and make it as light as possible for Stener and the party generally. He would come out of it all right, he said, but he cautioned her not to talk. He did not deny his long and profitable relations with Stener. He told her exactly how it was. She understood, or thought she did. Anyhow, her Frank was telling her, and that was enough.

As for the two Cowperwood households, so recently and pretentiously joined in success, now so gloomily tied in failure, the life was going out of them. Frank Algernon was that life. He was the courage and force of his father: the spirit and opportunity of his brothers, the hope of his children, the estate of his wife, the dignity and significance of the Cowperwood name. All that meant opportunity, force, emolument, dignity, and happiness to those connected with him, he was. And his marvelous sun was waning apparently to a black eclipse.

Since the fatal morning, for instance, when Lillian Cowperwood had received that utterly destructive note, like a cannonball ripping through her domestic affairs, she had been walking like one in a trance. Each day now for weeks she had been going about her duties placidly enough to all outward seeming, but inwardly she was running with a troubled tide of thought. She was so utterly unhappy. Her fortieth year had come for her at a time when life ought naturally to stand fixed and firm on a solid base, and here she was about to be torn bodily from the domestic soil in which she was growing and blooming, and thrown out indifferently to wither in the blistering noonday sun of circumstance.

As for Cowperwood, Senior, his situation at his bank and elsewhere was rapidly nearing a climax. As has been said, he had had tremendous faith in his son; but he could not help seeing that an error had been committed, as he thought, and that Frank was suffering greatly for it now. He considered, of course, that Frank had been entitled to try to save himself as he had; but he so regretted that his son should have put his foot into the trap of any situation which could stir up discussion of the sort that was now being aroused. Frank was wonderfully brilliant. He need never have taken up with the city treasurer or the politicians to have succeeded marvelously. Local street-railways and speculative politicians were his undoing. The old man walked the floor all of the days, realizing that his sun was setting, that with Frank's failure he failed, and that this disgrace—these public charges—meant his own undoing. His hair had grown very gray in but a few weeks, his step slow, his face pallid, his eyes sunken. His rather showy side-whiskers seemed now like flags or ornaments of a better day that was gone. His only consolation through it all was that Frank had actually got out of his relationship with the Third National Bank without owing it a single dollar. Still as he knew the directors of that institution could not possibly tolerate the presence of a man whose son had helped loot the city treasury, and whose name was now in the public prints in this connection. Besides, Cowperwood, Sr., was too old. He ought to retire.

The crisis for him therefore came on the day when Frank was arrested on the embezzlement charge. The old man, through Frank, who had it from Steger, knew it was coming, still had the courage to go to the bank but it was like struggling under the weight of a heavy stone to do it. But before going, and after a sleepless night, he wrote his resignation to Frewen Kasson, the chairman of the board of directors, in order that he should be prepared to hand it to him, at once. Kasson, a stocky, well-built, magnetic man of fifty, breathed an inward sigh of relief at the sight of it.

"I know it's hard, Mr. Cowperwood," he said, sympathetically. "We—and I can speak for the other members of the board—we feel keenly the unfortunate nature of your position. We know exactly how it is that your son has become involved in this matter. He is not the only banker who has been involved in the city's affairs. By no means. It is an old system. We appreciate, all of us, keenly, the services you have rendered this institution during the past thirty-five years. If there were any possible way in which we could help to tide you over the difficulties at this time, we would be glad to do so, but as a banker yourself you must realize just how impossible that would be. Everything is in a turmoil. If things were settled—if we knew how soon this would blow over—" He paused, for he felt that he could not go on and say that he or the bank was sorry to be forced to lose Mr. Cowperwood in this way at present. Mr. Cowperwood himself would have to speak.

During all this Cowperwood, Sr., had been doing his best to pull himself together in order to be able to speak at all. He had gotten out a large white linen handkerchief and blown his nose, and had straightened himself in his chair, and laid his hands rather peacefully on his desk. Still he was intensely wrought up.

"I can't stand this!" he suddenly exclaimed. "I wish you would leave me alone now."

Kasson, very carefully dressed and manicured, arose and walked out of the room for a few moments. He appreciated keenly the intensity of the strain he had just witnessed. The moment the door was closed Cowperwood put his head in his hands and shook convulsively. "I never thought I'd come to this," he muttered. "I never thought it." Then he wiped away his salty hot tears, and went to the window to look out and to think of what else to do from now on.

146

As time went on Butler grew more and more puzzled and restive as to his duty in regard to his daughter. He was sure by her furtive manner and her apparent desire to avoid him, that she was still in touch with Cowperwood in some way, and that this would bring about a social disaster of some kind. He thought once of going to Mrs. Cowperwood and having her bring pressure to bear on her husband, but afterwards he decided that that would not do. He was not really positive as yet that Aileen was secretly meeting Cowperwood, and, besides, Mrs. Cowperwood might not know of her husband's duplicity. He thought also of going to Cowperwood personally and threatening him, but that would be a severe measure, and again, as in the other case, he lacked proof. He hesitated to appeal to a detective agency, and he did not care to take the other members of the family into his confidence. He did go out and scan the neighborhood of 931 North Tenth Street once, looking at the house; but that helped him little. The place was for rent, Cowperwood having already abandoned his connection with it.

Finally he hit upon the plan of having Aileen invited to go somewhere some distance off— Boston or New Orleans, where a sister of his wife lived. It was a delicate matter to engineer, and in such matters he was not exactly the soul of tact; but he undertook it. He wrote personally to his wife's sister at New Orleans, and asked her if she would, without indicating in any way that she had heard from him, write his wife and ask if she would not permit Aileen to come and visit her, writing Aileen an invitation at the same time; but he tore the letter up. A little later he learned accidentally that Mrs. Mollenhauer and her three daughters, Caroline, Felicia, and Alta, were going to Europe early in December to visit Paris, the Riviera, and Rome; and he decided to ask Mollenhauer to persuade his wife to invite Norah and Aileen, or Aileen only, to go along, giving as an excuse that his own wife would not leave him, and that the girls ought to go. It would be a fine way of disposing of Aileen for the present. The party was to be gone six months. Mollenhauer was glad to do so, of course. The two families were fairly intimate. Mrs. Mollenhauer was willing— delighted from a politic point of view—and the invitation was extended. Norah was overjoyed. She wanted to see something of Europe, and had always been hoping for some such opportunity. Aileen was pleased from the point of view that Mrs. Mollenhauer should invite her. Years before she would have accepted in a flash. But now she felt that it only came as a puzzling interruption, one more of the minor difficulties that were tending to interrupt her relations with Cowperwood. She immediately threw cold water on the proposition, which was made one evening at dinner by Mrs. Butler, who did not know of her husband's share in the matter, but had received a call that afternoon from Mrs. Mollenhauer, when the invitation had been extended.

"She's very anxious to have you two come along, if your father don't mind," volunteered the mother, "and I should think ye'd have a fine time. They're going to Paris and the Riveera."

"Oh, fine!" exclaimed Norah. "I've always wanted to go to Paris. Haven't you, Ai? Oh, wouldn't that be fine?"

"I don't know that I want to go," replied Aileen. She did not care to compromise herself by showing any interest at the start. "It's coming on winter, and I haven't any clothes. I'd rather wait and go some other time."

"Oh, Aileen Butler!" exclaimed Norah. "How you talk! I've heard you say a dozen times you'd like to go abroad some winter. Now when the chance comes—besides you can get your clothes made over there."

"Couldn't you get somethin' over there?" inquired Mrs. Butler. "Besides, you've got two or three weeks here yet."

"They wouldn't want a man around as a sort of guide and adviser, would they, mother?" put in Callum.

"I might offer my services in that capacity myself," observed Owen, reservedly.

"I'm sure I don't know," returned Mrs. Butler, smiling, and at the same time chewing a lusty mouthful. "You'll have to ast 'em, my sons."

Aileen still persisted. She did not want to go. It was too sudden. It was this. It was that. Just then old Butler came in and took his seat at the head of the table. Knowing all about it, he was most anxious to appear not to.

"You wouldn't object, Edward, would you?" queried his wife, explaining the proposition in general.

"Object!" he echoed, with a well simulated but rough attempt at gayety. "A fine thing I'd be doing for meself—objectin'. I'd be glad if I could get shut of the whole pack of ye for a time."

"What talk ye have!" said his wife. "A fine mess you'd make of it livin' alone."

"I'd not be alone, belave me," replied Butler. "There's many a place I'd be welcome in this town—no thanks to ye."

"And there's many a place ye wouldn't have been if it hadn't been for me. I'm tellin' ye that," retorted Mrs. Butler, genially.

"And that's not stretchin' the troot much, aither," he answered, fondly.

Aileen was adamant. No amount of argument both on the part of Norah and her mother had any effect whatever. Butler witnessed the failure of his plan with considerable dissatisfaction, but he was not through. When he was finally convinced that there was no hope of persuading her to accept the Mollenhauer proposition, he decided, after a while, to employ a detective.

At that time, the reputation of William A. Pinkerton, of detective fame, and of his agency was great. The man had come up from poverty through a series of vicissitudes to a high standing in his peculiar and, to many, distasteful profession; but to any one in need of such in themselves calamitous services, his very famous and decidedly patriotic connection with the Civil War and Abraham Lincoln was a recommendation. He, or rather his service, had guarded the latter all his stormy incumbency at the executive mansion. There were offices for the management of the company's business in Philadelphia, Washington, and New York, to say nothing of other places. Butler was familiar with the Philadelphia sign, but did not care to go to the office there. He decided, once his mind was made up on this score, that he would go over to New York, where he was told the principal offices were.

He made the simple excuse one day of business, which was common enough in his case, and journeyed to New York—nearly five hours away as the trains ran then—arriving at two o'clock. At the offices on lower Broadway, he asked to see the manager, whom he found to be a large, gross-featured, heavy-bodied man of fifty, gray-eyed, gray-haired, puffily outlined as to countenance, but keen and shrewd, and with short, fat-fingered hands, which drummed idly on his desk as he talked. He was dressed in a suit of dark-brown wool cloth, which struck Butler as peculiarly showy, and wore a large horseshoe diamond pin. The old man himself invariably wore conservative gray.

"How do you do?" said Butler, when a boy ushered him into the presence of this worthy, whose name was Martinson—Gilbert Martinson, of American and Irish extraction. The latter nodded and looked at Butler shrewdly, recognizing him at once as a man of force and probably of position. He therefore rose and offered him a chair.

"Sit down," he said, studying the old Irishman from under thick, bushy eyebrows. "What can I do for you?"

"You're the manager, are you?" asked Butler, solemnly, eyeing the man with a shrewd, inquiring eye.

"Yes, sir," replied Martinson, simply. "That's my position here."

"This Mr. Pinkerton that runs this agency—he wouldn't be about this place, now, would he?" asked Butler, carefully. "I'd like to talk to him personally, if I might, meaning no offense to you."

148

"Mr. Pinkerton is in Chicago at present," replied Mr. Martinson. "I don't expect him back for a week or ten days. You can talk to me, though, with the same confidence that you could to him. I'm the responsible head here. However, you're the best judge of that."

Butler debated with himself in silence for a few moments, estimating the man before him. "Are you a family man yourself?" he asked, oddly.

"Yes, sir, I'm married," replied Martinson, solemnly. "I have a wife and two children."

Martinson, from long experience conceived that this must be a matter of family misconduct—a son, daughter, wife. Such cases were not infrequent.

"I thought I would like to talk to Mr. Pinkerton himself, but if you're the responsible head—" Butler paused.

"I am," replied Martinson. "You can talk to me with the same freedom that you could to Mr. Pinkerton. Won't you come into my private office? We can talk more at ease in there."

He led the way into an adjoining room which had two windows looking down into Broadway; an oblong table, heavy, brown, smoothly polished; four leather-backed chairs; and some pictures of the Civil War battles in which the North had been victorious. Butler followed doubtfully. He hated very much to take any one into his confidence in regard to Aileen. He was not sure that he would, even now. He wanted to "look these fellys over," as he said in his mind. He would decide then what he wanted to do. He went to one of the windows and looked down into the street, where there was a perfect swirl of omnibuses and vehicles of all sorts. Mr. Martinson quietly closed the door.

"Now then, if there's anything I can do for you," Mr. Martinson paused. He thought by this little trick to elicit Butler's real name—it often "worked"—but in this instance the name was not forthcoming. Butler was too shrewd.

"I'm not so sure that I want to go into this," said the old man solemnly. "Certainly not if there's any risk of the thing not being handled in the right way. There's somethin' I want to find out about—somethin' that I ought to know; but it's a very private matter with me, and—" He paused to think and conjecture, looking at Mr. Martinson the while. The latter understood his peculiar state of mind. He had seen many such cases.

"Let me say right here, to begin with, Mr.—"

"Scanlon," interpolated Butler, easily; "that's as good a name as any if you want to use one. I'm keepin' me own to meself for the present."

"Scanlon," continued Martinson, easily. "I really don't care whether it's your right name or not. I was just going to say that it might not be necessary to have your right name under any circumstances—it all depends upon what you want to know. But, so far as your private affairs are concerned, they are as safe with us, as if you had never told them to any one. Our business is built upon confidence, and we never betray it. We wouldn't dare. We have men and women who have been in our employ for over thirty years, and we never retire any one except for cause, and we don't pick people who are likely to need to be retired for cause. Mr. Pinkerton is a good judge of men. There are others here who consider that they are. We handle over ten thousand separate cases in all parts of the United States every year. We work on a case only so long as we are wanted. We try to find out only such things as our customers want. We do not pry unnecessarily into anybody's affairs. If we decide that we cannot find out what you want to know, we are the first to say so. Many cases are rejected right here in this office before we ever begin. Yours might be such a one. We don't want cases merely for the sake of having them, and we are frank to say so. Some matters that involve public policy, or some form of small persecution, we don't touch at all—we won't be a party to them. You can see how that is. You look to me to be a man of the world. I hope I am one. Does it strike you that an organization like ours would be likely to betray any one's confidence?" He paused and looked at Butler for confirmation of what he had just said.

"It wouldn't seem likely," said the latter; "that's the truth. It's not aisy to bring your private affairs into the light of day, though," added the old man, sadly.

They both rested.

"Well," said Butler, finally, "you look to me to be all right, and I'd like some advice. Mind ye, I'm willing to pay for it well enough; and it isn't anything that'll be very hard to find out. I want to know whether a certain man where I live is goin' with a certain woman, and where. You could find that out aisy enough, I belave—couldn't you?"

"Nothing easier," replied Martinson. "We are doing it all the time. Let me see if I can help you just a moment, Mr. Scanlon, in order to make it easier for you. It is very plain to me that you don't care to tell any more than you can help, and we don't care to have you tell any more than we absolutely need. We will have to have the name of the city, of course, and the name of either the man or the woman; but not necessarily both of them, unless you want to help us in that way. Sometimes if you give us the name of one party—say the man, for illustration—and the description of the woman—an accurate one—or a photograph, we can tell you after a little while exactly what you want to know. Of course, it's always better if we have full information. You suit yourself about that. Tell me as much or as little as you please, and I'll guarantee that we will do our best to serve you, and that you will be satisfied afterward."

He smiled genially.

"Well, that bein' the case," said Butler, finally taking the leap, with many mental reservations, however, "I'll be plain with you. My name's not Scanlon. It's Butler. I live in Philadelphy. There's a man there, a banker by the name of Cowperwood—Frank A. Cowperwood—"

"Wait a moment," said Martinson, drawing an ample pad out of his pocket and producing a lead-pencil; "I want to get that. How do you spell it?"

Butler told him.

"Yes; now go on."

"He has a place in Third Street—Frank A. Cowperwood—any one can show you where it is. He's just failed there recently."

"Oh, that's the man," interpolated Martinson. "I've heard of him. He's mixed up in some city embezzlement case over there. I suppose the reason you didn't go to our Philadelphia office is because you didn't want our local men over there to know anything about it. Isn't that it?"

"That's the man, and that's the reason," said Butler. "I don't care to have anything of this known in Philadelphy. That's why I'm here. This man has a house on Girard Avenue—Nineteen-thirty-seven. You can find that out, too, when you get over there."

"Yes," agreed Mr. Martinson.

"Well, it's him that I want to know about—him—and a certain woman, or girl, rather." The old man paused and winced at this necessity of introducing Aileen into the case. He could scarcely think of it—he was so fond of her. He had been so proud of Aileen. A dark, smoldering rage burned in his heart against Cowperwood.

"A relative of yours—possibly, I suppose," remarked Martinson, tactfully. "You needn't tell me any more—just give me a description if you wish. We may be able to work from that." He saw quite clearly what a fine old citizen in his way he was dealing with here, and also that the man was greatly troubled. Butler's heavy, meditative face showed it. "You can be quite frank with me, Mr. Butler," he added; "I think I understand. We only want such information as we must have to help you, nothing more."

"Yes," said the old man, dourly. "She is a relative. She's me daughter, in fact. You look to me like a sensible, honest man. I'm her father, and I wouldn't do anything for the world to harm her. It's tryin' to save her I am. It's him I want." He suddenly closed one big fist forcefully.

Martinson, who had two daughters of his own, observed the suggestive movement.

"I understand how you feel, Mr. Butler," he observed. "I am a father myself. We'll do all we can for you. If you can give me an accurate description of her, or let one of my men see her at your house or office, accidentally, of course, I think we can tell you in no time at all if they are meeting with any regularity. That's all you want to know, is it—just that?"

"That's all," said Butler, solemnly.

"Well, that oughtn't to take any time at all, Mr. Butler—three or four days possibly, if we have any luck—a week, ten days, two weeks. It depends on how long you want us to shadow him in case there is no evidence the first few days."

"I want to know, however long it takes," replied Butler, bitterly. "I want to know, if it takes a month or two months or three to find out. I want to know." The old man got up as he said this, very positive, very rugged. "And don't send me men that haven't sinse—lots of it, plase. I want men that are fathers, if you've got 'em—and that have sinse enough to hold their tongues—not b'ys."

"I understand, Mr. Butler," Martinson replied. "Depend on it, you'll have the best we have, and you can trust them. They'll be discreet. You can depend on that. The way I'll do will be to assign just one man to the case at first, some one you can see for yourself whether you like or not. I'll not tell him anything. You can talk to him. If you like him, tell him, and he'll do the rest. Then, if he needs any more help, he can get it. What is your address?"

Butler gave it to him.

"And there'll be no talk about this?"

"None whatever—I assure you."

"And when'll he be comin' along?"

"To-morrow, if you wish. I have a man I could send to-night. He isn't here now or I'd have him talk with you. I'll talk to him, though, and make everything clear. You needn't worry about anything. Your daughter's reputation will be safe in his hands."

"Thank you kindly," commented Butler, softening the least bit in a gingerly way. "I'm much obliged to you. I'll take it as a great favor, and pay you well."

"Never mind about that, Mr. Butler," replied Martinson. "You're welcome to anything this concern can do for you at its ordinary rates."

He showed Butler to the door, and the old man went out. He was feeling very depressed over this—very shabby. To think he should have to put detectives on the track of his Aileen, his daughter!

CHAPTER XXXVI

The very next day there called at Butler's office a long, preternaturally solemn man of noticeable height and angularity, dark-haired, dark-eyed, sallow, with a face that was long and leathery, and particularly hawk-like, who talked with Butler for over an hour and then departed. That evening he came to the Butler house around dinner-time, and, being shown into Butler's room, was given a look at Aileen by a ruse. Butler sent for her, standing in the doorway just far enough to one side to yield a good view of her. The detective stood behind one of the heavy curtains which had already been put up for the winter, pretending to look out into the street.

"Did any one drive Sissy this mornin'?" asked Butler of Aileen, inquiring after a favorite family horse. Butler's plan, in case the detective was seen, was to give the impression that he was a horseman who had come either to buy or to sell. His name was Jonas Alderson, and be looked sufficiently like a horsetrader to be one.

"I don't think so, father," replied Aileen. "I didn't. I'll find out."

"Never mind. What I want to know is did you intend using her to-morrow?"

"No, not if you want her. Jerry suits me just as well."

"Very well, then. Leave her in the stable." Butler quietly closed the door. Aileen concluded at once that it was a horse conference. She knew he would not dispose of any horse in which she was interested without first consulting her, and so she thought no more about it. After she was gone Alderson stepped out and declared that he was satisfied. "That's all I need to know," he said. "I'll let you know in a few days if I find out anything."

He departed, and within thirty-six hours the house and office of Cowperwood, the house of Butler, the office of Harper Steger, Cowperwood's lawyer, and Cowperwood and Aileen separately and personally were under complete surveillance. It took six men to do it at first, and eventually a seventh, when the second meeting-place, which was located in South Sixth Street, was discovered. All the detectives were from New York. In a week all was known to Alderson. It had been agreed between him and Butler that if Aileen and Cowperwood were discovered to have any particular rendezvous Butler was to be notified some time when she was there, so that he might go immediately and confront her in person, if he wished. He did not intend to kill Cowperwood—and Alderson would have seen to it that he did not in his presence at least, but he would give him a good tongue-lashing, fell him to the floor, in all likelihood, and march Aileen away. There would be no more lying on her part as to whether she was or was not going with Cowperwood. She would not be able to say after that what she would or would not do. Butler would lay down the law to her. She would reform, or he would send her to a reformatory. Think of her influence on her sister, or on any good girl—knowing what she knew, or doing what she was doing! She would go to Europe after this, or any place he chose to send her.

In working out his plan of action it was necessary for Butler to take Alderson into his confidence and the detective made plain his determination to safeguard Cowperwood's person.

"We couldn't allow you to strike any blows or do any violence," Alderson told Butler, when they first talked about it. "It's against the rules. You can go in there on a search-warrant, if we have to have one. I can get that for you without anybody's knowing anything about your connection with the case. We can say it's for a girl from New York. But you'll have to go in in the presence of my men. They won't permit any trouble. You can get your daughter all right—we'll bring her away, and him, too, if you say so; but you'll have to make some charge against him, if we do. Then there's the danger of the neighbors seeing. You can't always guarantee you won't collect a crowd that way." Butler had many misgivings about the matter. It was fraught with great danger of publicity. Still he wanted to know. He wanted to terrify Aileen if he could—to reform her drastically.

Within a week Alderson learned that Aileen and Cowperwood were visiting an apparently private residence, which was anything but that. The house on South Sixth Street was one of assignation purely; but in its way it was superior to the average establishment of its kind—of red brick, white-stone trimmings, four stories high, and all the rooms, some eighteen in number, furnished in a showy but cleanly way. It's patronage was highly exclusive, only those being admitted who were known to the mistress, having been introduced by others. This guaranteed that privacy which the illicit affairs of this world so greatly required. The mere phrase, "I have an appointment," was sufficient, where either of the parties was known, to cause them to be shown to a private suite. Cowperwood had known of the place from previous experiences, and when it became necessary to abandon the North Tenth Street house, he had directed Aileen to meet him here.

The matter of entering a place of this kind and trying to find any one was, as Alderson informed Butler on hearing of its character, exceedingly difficult. It involved the right of search, which was difficult to get. To enter by sheer force was easy enough in most instances where the business conducted was in contradistinction to the moral sentiment of the community; but sometimes one encountered violent opposition from the tenants themselves. It might be so in this case. The only sure way of avoiding such opposition would be to take the woman who ran the place into one's confidence, and by paying her sufficiently insure silence. "But I do not advise that in this instance," Alderson had told Butler, "for I believe this woman is particularly friendly to your man. It might be better, in spite of the risk, to take it by surprise." To do that, he explained, it would be necessary to have at least three men in addition to the leader—perhaps four, who, once one man had been able to make his entrance into the hallway, on the door being opened in response to a ring, would appear quickly and enter with and sustain him. Quickness of search was the next thing—the prompt opening of all doors. The servants, if any, would have to be overpowered and silenced in some way. Money sometimes did this; force accomplished it at other times. Then one of the detectives simulating a servant could tap gently at the different doors—Butler and the others standing by—and in case a face appeared identify it or not, as the case might be. If the door was not opened and the room was not empty, it could eventually be forced. The house was one of a solid block, so that there was no chance of escape save by the front and rear doors, which were to be safe-guarded. It was a daringly conceived scheme. In spite of all this, secrecy in the matter of removing Aileen was to be preserved.

When Butler heard of this he was nervous about the whole terrible procedure. He thought once that without going to the house he would merely talk to his daughter declaring that he knew and that she could not possibly deny it. He would then give her her choice between going to Europe or going to a reformatory. But a sense of the raw brutality of Aileen's disposition, and something essentially coarse in himself, made him eventually adopt the other method. He ordered Alderson to perfect his plan, and once he found Aileen or Cowperwood entering the house to inform him quickly. He would then drive there, and with the assistance of these men confront her.

It was a foolish scheme, a brutalizing thing to do, both from the point of view of affection and any corrective theory he might have had. No good ever springs from violence. But Butler did not see that. He wanted to frighten Aileen, to bring her by shock to a realization of the enormity of the offense she was committing. He waited fully a week after his word had been given; and then, one afternoon, when his nerves were worn almost thin from fretting, the climax came. Cowperwood had already been indicted, and was now awaiting trial. Aileen had been bringing him news, from time to time, of just how she thought her father was feeling toward him. She did not get this evidence direct from Butler, of course— he was too secretive, in so far as she was concerned, to let her know how relentlessly he was engineering Cowperwood's final downfall—but from odd bits confided to Owen, who confided them to Callum, who in turn, innocently enough, confided them to Aileen. For one thing, she had learned in this way of the new district attorney elect—his probable attitude—for he was a constant caller at the Butler house or office. Owen had told Callum that he thought Shannon was going to do his best to send Cowperwood "up"—that the old man thought he deserved it.

In the next place she had learned that her father did not want Cowperwood to resume business—did not feel he deserved to be allowed to. "It would be a God's blessing if the community were shut of him," he had said to Owen one morning, apropos of a notice in the papers of Cowperwood's legal struggles; and Owen had asked Callum why he thought the old man was so bitter. The two sons could not understand it. Cowperwood heard all this from her, and more—bits about Judge Payderson, the judge who was to try him, who was a friend of Butler's—also about the fact that Stener might be sent up for the full term of his crime, but that he would be pardoned soon afterward.

Apparently Cowperwood was not very much frightened. He told her that he had powerful financial friends who would appeal to the governor to pardon him in case he was convicted; and, anyhow, that he did not think that the evidence was strong enough to convict him. He was merely a political scapegoat through public clamor and her father's influence; since the latter's receipt of the letter about them he had been the victim of Butler's enmity, and nothing more. "If it weren't for your father, honey," he declared, "I could have this

153

indictment quashed in no time. Neither Mollenhauer nor Simpson has anything against me personally, I am sure. They want me to get out of the street-railway business here in Philadelphia, and, of course, they wanted to make things look better for Stener at first; but depend upon it, if your father hadn't been against me they wouldn't have gone to any such length in making me the victim. Your father has this fellow Shannon and these minor politicians just where he wants them, too. That's where the trouble lies. They have to go on."

"Oh, I know," replied Aileen. "It's me, just me, that's all. If it weren't for me and what he suspects he'd help you in a minute. Sometimes, you know, I think I've been very bad for you. I don't know what I ought to do. If I thought it would help you any I'd not see you any more for a while, though I don't see what good that would do now. Oh, I love you, love you, Frank! I would do anything for you. I don't care what people think or say. I love you."

"Oh, you just think you do," he replied, jestingly. "You'll get over it. There are others."

"Others!" echoed Aileen, resentfully and contemptuously. "After you there aren't any others. I just want one man, my Frank. If you ever desert me, I'll go to hell. You'll see."

"Don't talk like that, Aileen," he replied, almost irritated. "I don't like to hear you. You wouldn't do anything of the sort. I love you. You know I'm not going to desert you. It would pay you to desert me just now."

"Oh, how you talk!" she exclaimed. "Desert you! It's likely, isn't it? But if ever you desert me, I'll do just what I say. I swear it."

"Don't talk like that. Don't talk nonsense."

"I swear it. I swear by my love. I swear by your success—my own happiness. I'll do just what I say. I'll go to hell."

Cowperwood got up. He was a little afraid now of this deep-seated passion he had aroused. It was dangerous. He could not tell where it would lead.

It was a cheerless afternoon in November, when Alderson, duly informed of the presence of Aileen and Cowperwood in the South Sixth Street house by the detective on guard drove rapidly up to Butler's office and invited him to come with him. Yet even now Butler could scarcely believe that he was to find his daughter there. The shame of it. The horror. What would he say to her? How reproach her? What would he do to Cowperwood? His large hands shook as he thought. They drove rapidly to within a few doors of the place, where a second detective on guard across the street approached. Butler and Alderson descended from the vehicle, and together they approached the door. It was now almost four-thirty in the afternoon. In a room within the house, Cowperwood, his coat and vest off, was listening to Aileen's account of her troubles.

The room in which they were sitting at the time was typical of the rather commonplace idea of luxury which then prevailed. Most of the "sets" of furniture put on the market for general sale by the furniture companies were, when they approached in any way the correct idea of luxury, imitations of one of the Louis periods. The curtains were always heavy, frequently brocaded, and not infrequently red. The carpets were richly flowered in high colors with a thick, velvet nap. The furniture, of whatever wood it might be made, was almost invariably heavy, floriated, and cumbersome. This room contained a heavily constructed bed of walnut, with washstand, bureau, and wardrobe to match. A large, square mirror in a gold frame was hung over the washstand. Some poor engravings of landscapes and several nude figures were hung in gold frames on the wall. The gilt-framed chairs were upholstered in pink-and-white-flowered brocade, with polished brass tacks. The carpet was of thick Brussels, pale cream and pink in hue, with large blue jardinieres containing flowers woven in as ornaments. The general effect was light, rich, and a little stuffy.

"You know I get desperately frightened, sometimes," said Aileen. "Father might be watching us, you know. I've often wondered what I'd do if he caught us. I couldn't lie out of this, could I?"

"You certainly couldn't," said Cowperwood, who never failed to respond to the incitement of her charms. She had such lovely smooth arms, a full, luxuriously tapering throat and neck; her golden-red hair floated like an aureole about her head, and her large eyes sparkled. The wondrous vigor of a full womanhood was hers—errant, ill-balanced, romantic, but exquisite, "but you might as well not cross that bridge until you come to it," he continued. "I myself have been thinking that we had better not go on with this for the present. That letter ought to have been enough to stop us for the time."

He came over to where she stood by the dressing-table, adjusting her hair.

"You're such a pretty minx," he said. He slipped his arm about her and kissed her pretty mouth. "Nothing sweeter than you this side of Paradise," he whispered in her ear.

While this was enacting, Butler and the extra detective had stepped out of sight, to one side of the front door of the house, while Alderson, taking the lead, rang the bell. A negro servant appeared.

"Is Mrs. Davis in?" he asked, genially, using the name of the woman in control. "I'd like to see her."

"Just come in," said the maid, unsuspectingly, and indicated a reception-room on the right. Alderson took off his soft, wide-brimmed hat and entered. When the maid went up-stairs he immediately returned to the door and let in Butler and two detectives. The four stepped into the reception-room unseen. In a few moments the "madam" as the current word characterized this type of woman, appeared. She was tall, fair, rugged, and not at all unpleasant to look upon. She had light-blue eyes and a genial smile. Long contact with the police and the brutalities of sex in her early life had made her wary, a little afraid of how the world would use her. This particular method of making a living being illicit, and she having no other practical knowledge at her command, she was as anxious to get along peacefully with the police and the public generally as any struggling tradesman in any walk of life might have been. She had on a loose, blue-flowered peignoir, or dressing-gown, open at the front, tied with blue ribbons and showing a little of her expensive underwear beneath. A large opal ring graced her left middle finger, and turquoises of vivid blue were pendent from her ears. She wore yellow silk slippers with bronze buckles; and altogether her appearance was not out of keeping with the character of the reception-room itself, which was a composite of gold-flowered wall-paper, blue and cream-colored Brussels carpet, heavily gold-framed engravings of reclining nudes, and a gilt-framed pier-glass, which rose from the floor to the ceiling. Needless to say, Butler was shocked to the soul of him by this suggestive atmosphere which was supposed to include his daughter in its destructive reaches.

Alderson motioned one of his detectives to get behind the woman—between her and the door—which he did.

"Sorry to trouble you, Mrs. Davis," he said, "but we are looking for a couple who are in your house here. We're after a runaway girl. We don't want to make any disturbance— merely to get her and take her away." Mrs. Davis paled and opened her mouth. "Now don't make any noise or try to scream, or we'll have to stop you. My men are all around the house. Nobody can get out. Do you know anybody by the name of Cowperwood?"

Mrs. Davis, fortunately from one point of view, was not of a particularly nervous nor yet contentious type. She was more or less philosophic. She was not in touch with the police here in Philadelphia, hence subject to exposure. What good would it do to cry out? she thought. The place was surrounded. There was no one in the house at the time to save Cowperwood and Aileen. She did not know Cowperwood by his name, nor Aileen by hers. They were a Mr. and Mrs. Montague to her.

"I don't know anybody by that name," she replied nervously.

"Isn't there a girl here with red hair?" asked one of Alderson's assistants. "And a man with a gray suit and a light-brown mustache? They came in here half an hour ago. You remember them, don't you?"

155

"There's just one couple in the house, but I'm not sure whether they're the ones you want. I'll ask them to come down if you wish. Oh, I wish you wouldn't make any disturbance. This is terrible."

"We'll not make any disturbance," replied Alderson, "if you don't. Just you be quiet. We merely want to see the girl and take her away. Now, you stay where you are. What room are they in?"

"In the second one in the rear up-stairs. Won't you let me go, though? It will be so much better. I'll just tap and ask them to come out."

"No. We'll tend to that. You stay where you are. You're not going to get into any trouble. You just stay where you are," insisted Alderson.

He motioned to Butler, who, however, now that he had embarked on his grim task, was thinking that he had made a mistake. What good would it do him to force his way in and make her come out, unless he intended to kill Cowperwood? If she were made to come down here, that would be enough. She would then know that he knew all. He did not care to quarrel with Cowperwood, in any public way, he now decided. He was afraid to. He was afraid of himself.

"Let her go," he said grimly, doggedly referring to Mrs. Davis, "But watch her. Tell the girl to come down-stairs to me."

Mrs. Davis, realizing on the moment that this was some family tragedy, and hoping in an agonized way that she could slip out of it peacefully, started upstairs at once with Alderson and his assistants who were close at his heels. Reaching the door of the room occupied by Cowperwood and Aileen, she tapped lightly. At the time Aileen and Cowperwood were sitting in a big arm-chair. At the first knock Aileen blanched and leaped to her feet. Usually not nervous, to-day, for some reason, she anticipated trouble. Cowperwood's eyes instantly hardened.

"Don't be nervous," he said, "no doubt it's only the servant. I'll go."

He started, but Aileen interfered. "Wait," she said. Somewhat reassured, she went to the closet, and taking down a dressing-gown, slipped it on. Meanwhile the tap came again. Then she went to the door and opened it the least bit.

"Mrs. Montague," exclaimed Mrs. Davis, in an obviously nervous, forced voice, "there's a gentleman downstairs who wishes to see you."

"A gentleman to see me!" exclaimed Aileen, astonished and paling. "Are you sure?"

"Yes; he says he wants to see you. There are several other men with him. I think it's some one who belongs to you, maybe."

Aileen realized on the instant, as did Cowperwood, what had in all likelihood happened. Butler or Mrs. Cowperwood had trailed them—in all probability her father. He wondered now what he should do to protect her, not himself. He was in no way deeply concerned for himself, even here. Where any woman was concerned he was too chivalrous to permit fear. It was not at all improbable that Butler might want to kill him; but that did not disturb him. He really did not pay any attention to that thought, and he was not armed.

"I'll dress and go down," he said, when he saw Aileen's pale face. "You stay here. And don't you worry in any way for I'll get you out of this—now, don't worry. This is my affair. I got you in it and I'll get you out of it." He went for his hat and coat and added, as he did so, "You go ahead and dress; but let me go first."

Aileen, the moment the door closed, had begun to put on her clothes swiftly and nervously. Her mind was working like a rapidly moving machine. She was wondering whether this really could be her father. Perhaps it was not. Might there be some other Mrs. Montague—a real one? Supposing it was her father—he had been so nice to her in not telling the family, in keeping her secret thus far. He loved her—she knew that. It makes all the difference in the world in a child's attitude on an occasion like this whether she has been loved and petted and spoiled, or the reverse. Aileen had been loved and petted and spoiled. She could not think of her father doing anything terrible physically to her or to any one else. But it was so hard to confront him—to look into his eyes. When she had attained a proper memory of him, her fluttering wits told her what to do.

"No, Frank," she whispered, excitedly; "if it's father, you'd better let me go. I know how to talk to him. He won't say anything to me. You stay here. I'm not afraid—really, I'm not. If I want you, I'll call you."

He had come over and taken her pretty chin in his hands, and was looking solemnly into her eyes.

"You mustn't be afraid," he said. "I'll go down. If it's your father, you can go away with him. I don't think he'll do anything either to you or to me. If it is he, write me something at the office. I'll be there. If I can help you in any way, I will. We can fix up something. There's no use trying to explain this. Say nothing at all."

He had on his coat and overcoat, and was standing with his hat in his hand. Aileen was nearly dressed, struggling with the row of red current-colored buttons which fastened her dress in the back. Cowperwood helped her. When she was ready—hat, gloves, and all—he said:

"Now let me go first. I want to see."

"No; please, Frank," she begged, courageously. "Let me, I know it's father. Who else could it be?" She wondered at the moment whether her father had brought her two brothers but would not now believe it. He would not do that, she knew. "You can come if I call." She went on. "Nothing's going to happen, though. I understand him. He won't do anything to me. If you go it will only make him angry. Let me go. You stand in the door here. If I don't call, it's all right. Will you?"

She put her two pretty hands on his shoulders, and he weighed the matter very carefully. "Very well," he said, "only I'll go to the foot of the stairs with you."

They went to the door and he opened it. Outside were Alderson with two other detectives and Mrs. Davis, standing perhaps five feet away.

"Well," said Cowperwood, commandingly, looking at Alderson.

"There's a gentleman down-stairs wishes to see the lady," said Alderson. "It's her father, I think," he added quietly.

Cowperwood made way for Aileen, who swept by, furious at the presence of men and this exposure. Her courage had entirely returned. She was angry now to think her father would make a public spectacle of her. Cowperwood started to follow.

"I'd advise you not to go down there right away," cautioned Alderson, sagely. "That's her father. Butler's her name, isn't it? He don't want you so much as he wants her."

Cowperwood nevertheless walked slowly toward the head of the stairs, listening.

"What made you come here, father?" he heard Aileen ask.

Butler's reply he could not hear, but he was now at ease for he knew how much Butler loved his daughter.

Confronted by her father, Aileen was now attempting to stare defiantly, to look reproachful, but Butler's deep gray eyes beneath their shaggy brows revealed such a weight of weariness and despair as even she, in her anger and defiance, could not openly flaunt. It was all too sad.

"I never expected to find you in a place like this, daughter," he said. "I should have thought you would have thought better of yourself." His voice choked and he stopped.

"I know who you're here with," he continued, shaking his head sadly. "The dog! I'll get him yet. I've had men watchin' you all the time. Oh, the shame of this day! The shame of this day! You'll be comin' home with me now."

"That's just it, father," began Aileen. "You've had men watching me. I should have thought—" She stopped, because he put up his hand in a strange, agonized, and yet dominating way.

"None of that! none of that!" he said, glowering under his strange, sad, gray brows. "I can't stand it! Don't tempt me! We're not out of this place yet. He's not! You'll come home with me now."

Aileen understood. It was Cowperwood he was referring to. That frightened her.

"I'm ready," she replied, nervously.

The old man led the way broken-heartedly. He felt he would never live to forget the agony of this hour.

CHAPTER XXXVII

In spite of Butler's rage and his determination to do many things to the financier, if he could, he was so wrought up and shocked by the attitude of Aileen that he could scarcely believe he was the same man he had been twenty-four hours before. She was so nonchalant, so defiant. He had expected to see her wilt completely when confronted with her guilt. Instead, he found, to his despair, after they were once safely out of the house, that he had aroused a fighting quality in the girl which was not incomparable to his own. She had some of his own and Owen's grit. She sat beside him in the little runabout—not his own—in which he was driving her home, her face coloring and blanching by turns, as different waves of thought swept over her, determined to stand her ground now that her father had so plainly trapped her, to declare for Cowperwood and her love and her position in general. What did she care, she asked herself, what her father thought now? She was in this thing. She loved Cowperwood; she was permanently disgraced in her father's eyes. What difference could it all make now? He had fallen so low in his parental feeling as to spy on her and expose her before other men—strangers, detectives, Cowperwood. What real affection could she have for him after this? He had made a mistake, according to her. He had done a foolish and a contemptible thing, which was not warranted however bad her actions might have been. What could he hope to accomplish by rushing in on her in this way and ripping the veil from her very soul before these other men—these crude detectives? Oh, the agony of that walk from the bedroom to the reception-room! She would never forgive her father for this—never, never, never! He had now killed her love for him—that was what she felt. It was to be a battle royal between them from now on. As they rode—in complete silence for a while—her hands clasped and unclasped defiantly, her nails cutting her palms, and her mouth hardened.

It is an open question whether raw opposition ever accomplishes anything of value in this world. It seems so inherent in this mortal scheme of things that it appears to have a vast validity. It is more than likely that we owe this spectacle called life to it, and that this can be demonstrated scientifically; but when that is said and done, what is the value? What is the value of the spectacle? And what the value of a scene such as this enacted between Aileen and her father?

The old man saw nothing for it, as they rode on, save a grim contest between them which could end in what? What could he do with her? They were riding away fresh from this awful catastrophe, and she was not saying a word! She had even asked him why he had come there! How was he to subdue her, when the very act of trapping her had failed to do so? His ruse, while so successful materially, had failed so utterly spiritually. They reached the house, and Aileen got out. The old man, too nonplussed to wish to go further at this time, drove back to his office. He then went out and walked—a peculiar thing for him to do; he had done nothing like that in years and years—walking to think. Coming to an open Catholic church, he went in and prayed for enlightenment, the growing dusk of the interior, the single everlasting lamp before the repository of the chalice, and the high, white altar set with candles soothing his troubled feelings.

He came out of the church after a time and returned home. Aileen did not appear at dinner, and he could not eat. He went into his private room and shut the door—thinking, thinking, thinking. The dreadful spectacle of Aileen in a house of ill repute burned in his brain. To think that Cowperwood should have taken her to such a place—his Aileen, his and his wife's pet. In spite of his prayers, his uncertainty, her opposition, the puzzling nature of the situation, she must be got out of this. She must go away for a while, give the man up, and then the law should run its course with him. In all likelihood Cowperwood would go to the penitentiary—if ever a man richly deserved to go, it was he. Butler would see that no stone was left unturned. He would make it a personal issue, if necessary. All he had to do was to let it be known in judicial circles that he wanted it so. He could not suborn a jury, that would be criminal; but he could see that the case was properly and forcefully presented; and if Cowperwood were convicted, Heaven help him. The appeal of his financial friends would not save him. The judges of the lower and superior courts knew on which side their bread was buttered. They would strain a point in favor of the highest political opinion of the day, and he certainly could influence that. Aileen meanwhile was contemplating the peculiar nature of her situation. In spite of their silence on the way home, she knew that a conversation was coming with her father. It had to be. He would want her to go somewhere. Most likely he would revive the European trip in some form—she now suspected the invitation of Mrs. Mollenhauer as a trick; and she had to decide whether she would go. Would she leave Cowperwood just when he was about to be tried? She was determined she would not. She wanted to see what was going to happen to him. She would leave home first—run to some relative, some friend, some stranger, if necessary, and ask to be taken in. She had some money—a little. Her father had always been very liberal with her. She could take a few clothes and disappear. They would be glad enough to send for her after she had been gone awhile. Her mother would be frantic; Norah and Callum and Owen would be beside themselves with wonder and worry; her father—she could see him. Maybe that would bring him to his senses. In spite of all her emotional vagaries, she was the pride and interest of this home, and she knew it.

It was in this direction that her mind was running when her father, a few days after the dreadful exposure in the Sixth Street house, sent for her to come to him in his room. He had come home from his office very early in the afternoon, hoping to find Aileen there, in order that he might have a private interview with her, and by good luck found her in. She had had no desire to go out into the world these last few days—she was too expectant of trouble to come. She had just written Cowperwood asking for a rendezvous out on the Wissahickon the following afternoon, in spite of the detectives. She must see him. Her father, she said, had done nothing; but she was sure he would attempt to do something. She wanted to talk to Cowperwood about that.

"I've been thinkin' about ye, Aileen, and what ought to be done in this case," began her father without preliminaries of any kind once they were in his "office room" in the house together. "You're on the road to ruin if any one ever was. I tremble when I think of your immortal soul. I want to do somethin' for ye, my child, before it's too late. I've been reproachin' myself for the last month and more, thinkin', perhaps, it was somethin' I had done, or maybe had failed to do, aither me or your mother, that has brought ye to the place where ye are to-day. Needless to say, it's on me conscience, me child. It's a heartbroken man you're lookin' at this day. I'll never be able to hold me head up again. Oh, the shame—the shame! That I should have lived to see it!"

"But father," protested Aileen, who was a little distraught at the thought of having to listen to a long preachment which would relate to her duty to God and the Church and her family and her mother and him. She realized that all these were important in their way; but Cowperwood and his point of view had given her another outlook on life. They had discussed this matter of families—parents, children, husbands, wives, brothers, sisters— from almost every point of view. Cowperwood's laissez-faire attitude had permeated and colored her mind completely. She saw things through his cold, direct "I satisfy myself" attitude. He was sorry for all the little differences of personality that sprang up between people, causing quarrels, bickerings, oppositions, and separation; but they could not be helped. People outgrew each other. Their points of view altered at varying ratios—hence changes. Morals—those who had them had them; those who hadn't, hadn't. There was no explaining. As for him, he saw nothing wrong in the sex relationship. Between those who were mutually compatible it was innocent and delicious. Aileen in his arms, unmarried, but loved by him, and he by her, was as good and pure as any living woman—a great deal purer than most. One found oneself in a given social order, theory, or scheme of things. For purposes of social success, in order not to offend, to smooth one's path, make things easy, avoid useless criticism, and the like, it was necessary to create an outward seeming— ostensibly conform. Beyond that it was not necessary to do anything. Never fail, never get caught. If you did, fight your way out silently and say nothing. That was what he was doing in connection with his present financial troubles; that was what he had been ready to do the other day when they were caught. It was something of all this that was coloring Aileen's mood as she listened at present.

"But father," she protested, "I love Mr. Cowperwood. It's almost the same as if I were married to him. He will marry me some day when he gets a divorce from Mrs. Cowperwood. You don't understand how it is. He's very fond of me, and I love him. He needs me."

Butler looked at her with strange, non-understanding eyes. "Divorce, did you say," he began, thinking of the Catholic Church and its dogma in regard to that. "He'll divorce his own wife and children—and for you, will he? He needs you, does he?" he added, sarcastically. "What about his wife and children? I don't suppose they need him, do they? What talk have ye?"

Aileen flung her head back defiantly. "It's true, nevertheless," she reiterated. "You just don't understand."

Butler could scarcely believe his ears. He had never heard such talk before in his life from any one. It amazed and shocked him. He was quite aware of all the subtleties of politics and business, but these of romance were too much for him. He knew nothing about them. To think a daughter of his should be talking like this, and she a Catholic! He could not understand where she got such notions unless it was from the Machiavellian, corrupting brain of Cowperwood himself.

"How long have ye had these notions, my child?" he suddenly asked, calmly and soberly. "Where did ye get them? Ye certainly never heard anything like that in this house, I warrant. Ye talk as though ye had gone out of yer mind."

"Oh, don't talk nonsense, father," flared Aileen, angrily, thinking how hopeless it was to talk to her father about such things anyhow. "I'm not a child any more. I'm twenty-four years of age. You just don't understand. Mr. Cowperwood doesn't like his wife. He's going to get a divorce when he can, and will marry me. I love him, and he loves me, and that's all there is to it."

"Is it, though?" asked Butler, grimly determined by hook or by crook, to bring this girl to her senses. "Ye'll be takin' no thought of his wife and children then? The fact that he's goin' to jail, besides, is nawthin' to ye, I suppose. Ye'd love him just as much in convict stripes, I suppose—more, maybe." (The old man was at his best, humanly speaking, when he was a little sarcastic.) "Ye'll have him that way, likely, if at all."

Aileen blazed at once to a furious heat. "Yes, I know," she sneered. "That's what you would like. I know what you've been doing. Frank does, too. You're trying to railroad him to prison for something he didn't do—and all on account of me. Oh, I know. But you won't hurt him. You can't! He's bigger and finer than you think he is and you won't hurt him in

160

the long run. He'll get out again. You want to punish him on my account; but he doesn't care. I'll marry him anyhow. I love him, and I'll wait for him and marry him, and you can do what you please. So there!"

"Ye'll marry him, will you?" asked Butler, nonplussed and further astounded. "So ye'll wait for him and marry him? Ye'll take him away from his wife and children, where, if he were half a man, he'd be stayin' this minute instead of gallivantin' around with you. And marry him? Ye'd disgrace your father and yer mother and yer family? Ye'll stand here and say this to me, I that have raised ye, cared for ye, and made somethin' of ye? Where would you be if it weren't for me and your poor, hard-workin' mother, schemin' and plannin' for you year in and year out? Ye're smarter than I am, I suppose. Ye know more about the world than I do, or any one else that might want to say anythin' to ye. I've raised ye to be a fine lady, and this is what I get. Talk about me not bein' able to understand, and ye lovin' a convict-to-be, a robber, an embezzler, a bankrupt, a lyin', thavin'—"

"Father!" exclaimed Aileen, determinedly. "I'll not listen to you talking that way. He's not any of the things that you say. I'll not stay here." She moved toward the door; but Butler jumped up now and stopped her. His face for the moment was flushed and swollen with anger.

"But I'm not through with him yet," he went on, ignoring her desire to leave, and addressing her direct—confident now that she was as capable as another of understanding him. "I'll get him as sure as I have a name. There's law in this land, and I'll have it on him. I'll show him whether he'll come sneakin' into dacent homes and robbin' parents of their children."

He paused after a time for want of breath and Aileen stared, her face tense and white. Her father could be so ridiculous. He was, contrasted with Cowperwood and his views, so old-fashioned. To think he could be talking of some one coming into their home and stealing her away from him, when she had been so willing to go. What silliness! And yet, why argue? What good could be accomplished, arguing with him here in this way? And so for the moment, she said nothing more—merely looked. But Butler was by no means done. His mood was too stormy even though he was doing his best now to subdue himself.

"It's too bad, daughter," he resumed quietly, once he was satisfied that she was going to have little, if anything, to say. "I'm lettin' my anger get the best of me. It wasn't that I intended talkin' to ye about when I ast ye to come in. It's somethin' else I have on me mind. I was thinkin', perhaps, ye'd like to go to Europe for the time bein' to study music. Ye're not quite yourself just at present. Ye're needin' a rest. It would be good for ye to go away for a while. Ye could have a nice time over there. Norah could go along with ye, if you would, and Sister Constantia that taught you. Ye wouldn't object to havin' her, I suppose?"

At the mention of this idea of a trip of Europe again, with Sister Constantia and music thrown in to give it a slightly new form, Aileen bridled, and yet half-smiled to herself now. It was so ridiculous—so tactless, really, for her father to bring up this now, and especially after denouncing Cowperwood and her, and threatening all the things he had. Had he no diplomacy at all where she was concerned? It was really too funny! But she restrained herself here again, because she felt as well as saw, that argument of this kind was all futile now.

"I wish you wouldn't talk about that, father," she began, having softened under his explanation. "I don't want to go to Europe now. I don't want to leave Philadelphia. I know you want me to go; but I don't want to think of going now. I can't."

Butler's brow darkened again. What was the use of all this opposition on her part? Did she really imagine that she was going to master him—her father, and in connection with such an issue as this? How impossible! But tempering his voice as much as possible, he went on, quite softly, in fact. "But it would be so fine for ye, Aileen. Ye surely can't expect to stay here after—" He paused, for he was going to say "what has happened." He knew she was very sensitive on that point. His own conduct in hunting her down had been such a breach of fatherly courtesy that he knew she felt resentful, and in a way properly so. Still, what could be greater than her own crime? "After," he concluded, "ye have made such a mistake ye surely wouldn't want to stay here. Ye won't be wantin' to keep up that—committin' a mortal sin. It's against the laws of God and man."

He did so hope the thought of sin would come to Aileen—the enormity of her crime from a spiritual point of view—but Aileen did not see it at all.

"You don't understand me, father," she exclaimed, hopelessly toward the end. "You can't. I have one idea, and you have another. But I don't seem to be able to make you understand now. The fact is, if you want to know it, I don't believe in the Catholic Church any more, so there."

The moment Aileen had said this she wished she had not. It was a slip of the tongue. Butler's face took on an inexpressibly sad, despairing look.

"Ye don't believe in the Church?" he asked.

"No, not exactly—not like you do."

He shook his head.

"The harm that has come to yer soul!" he replied. "It's plain to me, daughter, that somethin' terrible has happened to ye. This man has ruined ye, body and soul. Somethin' must be done. I don't want to be hard on ye, but ye must leave Philadelphy. Ye can't stay here. I can't permit ye. Ye can go to Europe, or ye can go to yer aunt's in New Orleans; but ye must go somewhere. I can't have ye stayin' here—it's too dangerous. It's sure to be comin' out. The papers'll be havin' it next. Ye're young yet. Yer life is before you. I tremble for yer soul; but so long as ye're young and alive ye may come to yer senses. It's me duty to be hard. It's my obligation to you and the Church. Ye must quit this life. Ye must lave this man. Ye must never see him any more. I can't permit ye. He's no good. He has no intintion of marryin' ye, and it would be a crime against God and man if he did. No, no! Never that! The man's a bankrupt, a scoundrel, a thafe. If ye had him, ye'd soon be the unhappiest woman in the world. He wouldn't be faithful to ye. No, he couldn't. He's not that kind." He paused, sick to the depths of his soul. "Ye must go away. I say it once and for all. I mane it kindly, but I want it. I have yer best interests at heart. I love ye; but ye must. I'm sorry to see ye go—I'd rather have ye here. No one will be sorrier; but ye must. Ye must make it all seem natcheral and ordinary to yer mother; but ye must go—d'ye hear? Ye must."

He paused, looking sadly but firmly at Aileen under his shaggy eyebrows. She knew he meant this. It was his most solemn, his most religious expression. But she did not answer. She could not. What was the use? Only she was not going. She knew that—and so she stood there white and tense.

"Now get all the clothes ye want," went on Butler, by no means grasping her true mood. "Fix yourself up in any way you plase. Say where ye want to go, but get ready."

"But I won't, father," finally replied Aileen, equally solemnly, equally determinedly. "I won't go! I won't leave Philadelphia."

"Ye don't mane to say ye will deliberately disobey me when I'm asking ye to do somethin' that's intended for yer own good, will ye daughter?"

"Yes, I will," replied Aileen, determinedly. "I won't go! I'm sorry, but I won't!"

"Ye really mane that, do ye?" asked Butler, sadly but grimly.

"Yes, I do," replied Aileen, grimly, in return.

"Then I'll have to see what I can do, daughter," replied the old man. "Ye're still my daughter, whatever ye are, and I'll not see ye come to wreck and ruin for want of doin' what I know to be my solemn duty. I'll give ye a few more days to think this over, but go ye must. There's an end of that. There are laws in this land still. There are things that can be done to those who won't obey the law. I found ye this time—much as it hurt me to do it. I'll find ye again if ye try to disobey me. Ye must change yer ways. I can't have ye goin' on as ye are. Ye understand now. It's the last word. Give this man up, and ye can have anything ye choose. Ye're my girl—I'll do everything I can in this world to make ye happy.

162

Why, why shouldn't I? What else have I to live for but me children? It's ye and the rest of them that I've been workin' and plannin' for all these years. Come now, be a good girl. Ye love your old father, don't ye? Why, I rocked ye in my arms as a baby, Aileen. I've watched over ye when ye were not bigger than what would rest in me two fists here. I've been a good father to ye—ye can't deny that. Look at the other girls you've seen. Have any of them had more nor what ye have had? Ye won't go against me in this. I'm sure ye won't. Ye can't. Ye love me too much—surely ye do—don't ye?" His voice weakened. His eyes almost filled.

He paused and put a big, brown, horny hand on Aileen's arm. She had listened to his plea not unmoved—really more or less softened—because of the hopelessness of it. She could not give up Cowperwood. Her father just did not understand. He did not know what love was. Unquestionably he had never loved as she had.

She stood quite silent while Butler appealed to her.

"I'd like to, father," she said at last and softly, tenderly. "Really I would. I do love you. Yes, I do. I want to please you; but I can't in this—I can't! I love Frank Cowperwood. You don't understand—really you don't!"

At the repetition of Cowperwood's name Butler's mouth hardened. He could see that she was infatuated—that his carefully calculated plea had failed. So he must think of some other way.

"Very well, then," he said at last and sadly, oh, so sadly, as Aileen turned away. "Have it yer own way, if ye will. Ye must go, though, willy-nilly. It can't be any other way. I wish to God it could."

Aileen went out, very solemn, and Butler went over to his desk and sat down. "Such a situation!" he said to himself. "Such a complication!"

CHAPTER XXXVIII

The situation which confronted Aileen was really a trying one. A girl of less innate courage and determination would have weakened and yielded. For in spite of her various social connections and acquaintances, the people to whom Aileen could run in an emergency of the present kind were not numerous. She could scarcely think of any one who would be likely to take her in for any lengthy period, without question. There were a number of young women of her own age, married and unmarried, who were very friendly to her, but there were few with whom she was really intimate. The only person who stood out in her mind, as having any real possibility of refuge for a period, was a certain Mary Calligan, better known as "Mamie" among her friends, who had attended school with Aileen in former years and was now a teacher in one of the local schools.

The Calligan family consisted of Mrs. Katharine Calligan, the mother, a dressmaker by profession and a widow—her husband, a house-mover by trade, having been killed by a falling wall some ten years before—and Mamie, her twenty-three-year-old daughter. They lived in a small two-story brick house in Cherry Street, near Fifteenth. Mrs. Calligan was not a very good dressmaker, not good enough, at least, for the Butler family to patronize in their present exalted state. Aileen went there occasionally for gingham house-dresses, underwear, pretty dressing-gowns, and alterations on some of her more important clothing which was made by a very superior modiste in Chestnut Street. She visited the house largely because she had gone to school with Mamie at St. Agatha's, when the outlook of the Calligan family was much more promising. Mamie was earning forty dollars a month as the teacher of a sixth-grade room in one of the nearby public schools, and Mrs. Calligan averaged on the whole about two dollars a day—sometimes not so much. The house they occupied was their own, free and clear, and the furniture which it contained suggested the size of their joint income, which was somewhere near eighty dollars a month.

Mamie Calligan was not good-looking, not nearly as good-looking as her mother had been before her. Mrs. Calligan was still plump, bright, and cheerful at fifty, with a fund of good humor. Mamie was somewhat duller mentally and emotionally. She was serious-minded—made so, perhaps, as much by circumstances as by anything else, for she was not at all vivid, and had little sex magnetism. Yet she was kindly, honest, earnest, a good Catholic, and possessed of that strangely excessive ingrowing virtue which shuts so many people off from the world—a sense of duty. To Mamie Calligan duty (a routine conformity to such theories and precepts as she had heard and worked by since her childhood) was the all-important thing, her principal source of comfort and relief; her props in a queer and uncertain world being her duty to her Church; her duty to her school; her duty to her mother; her duty to her friends, etc. Her mother often wished for Mamie's sake that she was less dutiful and more charming physically, so that the men would like her.

In spite of the fact that her mother was a dressmaker, Mamie's clothes never looked smart or attractive—she would have felt out of keeping with herself if they had. Her shoes were rather large, and ill-fitting; her skirt hung in lifeless lines from her hips to her feet, of good material but seemingly bad design. At that time the colored "jersey," so-called, was just coming into popular wear, and, being close-fitting, looked well on those of good form. Alas for Mamie Calligan! The mode of the time compelled her to wear one; but she had neither the arms nor the chest development which made this garment admirable. Her hat, by choice, was usually a pancake affair with a long, single feather, which somehow never seemed to be in exactly the right position, either to her hair or her face. At most times she looked a little weary; but she was not physically weary so much as she was bored. Her life held so little of real charm; and Aileen Butler was unquestionably the most significant element of romance in it.

Mamie's mother's very pleasant social disposition, the fact that they had a very cleanly, if poor little home, that she could entertain them by playing on their piano, and that Mrs. Calligan took an adoring interest in the work she did for her, made up the sum and substance of the attraction of the Calligan home for Aileen. She went there occasionally as a relief from other things, and because Mamie Calligan had a compatible and very understanding interest in literature. Curiously, the books Aileen liked she liked—Jane Eyre, Kenelm Chillingly, Tricotrin, and A Bow of Orange Ribbon. Mamie occasionally recommended to Aileen some latest effusion of this character; and Aileen, finding her judgment good, was constrained to admire her.

In this crisis it was to the home of the Calligans that Aileen turned in thought. If her father really was not nice to her, and she had to leave home for a time, she could go to the Calligans. They would receive her and say nothing. They were not sufficiently well known to the other members of the Butler family to have the latter suspect that she had gone there. She might readily disappear into the privacy of Cherry Street and not be seen or heard of for weeks. It is an interesting fact to contemplate that the Calligans, like the various members of the Butler family, never suspected Aileen of the least tendency toward a wayward existence. Hence her flight from her own family, if it ever came, would be laid more to the door of a temperamental pettishness than anything else.

On the other hand, in so far as the Butler family as a unit was concerned, it needed Aileen more than she needed it. It needed the light of her countenance to keep it appropriately cheerful, and if she went away there would be a distinct gulf that would not soon be overcome.

Butler, senior, for instance, had seen his little daughter grow into radiantly beautiful womanhood. He had seen her go to school and convent and learn to play the piano—to him a great accomplishment. Also he had seen her manner change and become very showy and her knowledge of life broaden, apparently, and become to him, at least, impressive. Her smart, dogmatic views about most things were, to him, at least, well worth listening to. She knew more about books and art than Owen or Callum, and her sense of social manners was perfect. When she came to the table—breakfast, luncheon, or dinner—she was to him always a charming object to see. He had produced Aileen—he congratulated himself. He had furnished her the money to be so fine. He would continue to do so. No second-rate upstart of a man should be allowed to ruin her life. He proposed to take care of her always—to leave her so much money in a legally involved way that a failure of a husband could not possibly affect her. "You're the charming lady this evenin', I'm thinkin'," was one of his pet remarks; and also, "My, but we're that fine!" At table almost invariably she sat beside him and looked out for him. That was what he wanted. He had put her there beside him at his meals years before when she was a child.

Her mother, too, was inordinately fond of her, and Callum and Owen appropriately brotherly. So Aileen had thus far at least paid back with beauty and interest quite as much as she received, and all the family felt it to be so. When she was away for a day or two the house seemed glum—the meals less appetizing. When she returned, all were happy and gay again.

Aileen understood this clearly enough in a way. Now, when it came to thinking of leaving and shifting for herself, in order to avoid a trip which she did not care to be forced into, her courage was based largely on this keen sense of her own significance to the family. She thought over what her father had said, and decided she must act at once. She dressed for the street the next morning, after her father had gone, and decided to step in at the Calligans' about noon, when Mamie would be at home for luncheon. Then she would take up the matter casually. If they had no objection, she would go there. She sometimes wondered why Cowperwood did not suggest, in his great stress, that they leave for some parts unknown; but she also felt that he must know best what he could do. His increasing troubles depressed her.

Mrs. Calligan was alone when she arrived and was delighted to see her. After exchanging the gossip of the day, and not knowing quite how to proceed in connection with the errand which had brought her, she went to the piano and played a melancholy air.

"Sure, it's lovely the way you play, Aileen," observed Mrs. Calligan who was unduly sentimental herself. "I love to hear you. I wish you'd come oftener to see us. You're so rarely here nowadays."

"Oh, I've been so busy, Mrs. Calligan," replied Aileen. "I've had so much to do this fall, I just couldn't. They wanted me to go to Europe; but I didn't care to. Oh, dear!" she sighed, and in her playing swept off with a movement of sad, romantic significance. The door opened and Mamie came in. Her commonplace face brightened at the sight of Aileen.

"Well, Aileen Butler!" she exclaimed. "Where did you come from? Where have you been keeping yourself so long?"

Aileen rose to exchange kisses. "Oh, I've been very busy, Mamie. I've just been telling your mother. How are you, anyway? How are you getting along in your work?"

Mamie recounted at once some school difficulties which were puzzling her—the growing size of classes and the amount of work expected. While Mrs. Calligan was setting the table Mamie went to her room and Aileen followed her.

As she stood before her mirror arranging her hair Aileen looked at her meditatively.

"What's the matter with you, Aileen, to-day?" Mamie asked. "You look so—" She stopped to give her a second glance.

"How do I look?" asked Aileen.

"Well, as if you were uncertain or troubled about something. I never saw you look that way before. What's the matter?"

"Oh, nothing," replied Aileen. "I was just thinking." She went to one of the windows which looked into the little yard, meditating on whether she could endure living here for any length of time. The house was so small, the furnishings so very simple.

"There is something the matter with you to-day, Aileen," observed Mamie, coming over to her and looking in her face. "You're not like yourself at all."

"I've got something on my mind," replied Aileen—"something that's worrying me. I don't know just what to do—that's what's the matter."

"Well, whatever can it be?" commented Mamie. "I never saw you act this way before. Can't you tell me? What is it?"

"No, I don't think I can—not now, anyhow." Aileen paused. "Do you suppose your mother would object," she asked, suddenly, "if I came here and stayed a little while? I want to get away from home for a time for a certain reason."

"Why, Aileen Butler, how you talk!" exclaimed her friend. "Object! You know she'd be delighted, and so would I. Oh, dear—can you come? But what makes you want to leave home?"

"That's just what I can't tell you—not now, anyhow. Not you, so much, but your mother. You know, I'm afraid of what she'd think," replied Aileen. "But, you mustn't ask me yet, anyhow. I want to think. Oh, dear! But I want to come, if you'll let me. Will you speak to your mother, or shall I?"

"Why, I will," said Mamie, struck with wonder at this remarkable development; "but it's silly to do it. I know what she'll say before I tell her, and so do you. You can just bring your things and come. That's all. She'd never say anything or ask anything, either, and you know that—if you didn't want her to." Mamie was all agog and aglow at the idea. She wanted the companionship of Aileen so much.

Aileen looked at her solemnly, and understood well enough why she was so enthusiastic— both she and her mother. Both wanted her presence to brighten their world. "But neither of you must tell anybody that I'm here, do you hear? I don't want any one to know— particularly no one of my family. I've a reason, and a good one, but I can't tell you what it is—not now, anyhow. You'll promise not to tell any one."

"Oh, of course," replied Mamie eagerly. "But you're not going to run away for good, are you, Aileen?" she concluded curiously and gravely.

"Oh, I don't know; I don't know what I'll do yet. I only know that I want to get away for a while, just now—that's all." She paused, while Mamie stood before her, agape.

"Well, of all things," replied her friend. "Wonders never cease, do they, Aileen? But it will be so lovely to have you here. Mama will be so pleased. Of course, we won't tell anybody if you don't want us to. Hardly any one ever comes here; and if they do, you needn't see them. You could have this big room next to me. Oh, wouldn't that be nice? I'm perfectly delighted." The young school-teacher's spirits rose to a decided height. "Come on, why not tell mama right now?"

Aileen hesitated because even now she was not positive whether she should do this, but finally they went down the stairs together, Aileen lingering behind a little as they neared the bottom. Mamie burst in upon her mother with: "Oh, mama, isn't it lovely? Aileen's coming to stay with us for a while. She doesn't want any one to know, and she's coming right away." Mrs. Calligan, who was holding a sugarbowl in her hand, turned to survey her with a surprised but smiling face. She was immediately curious as to why Aileen should want to come—why leave home. On the other hand, her feeling for Aileen was so deep that she was greatly and joyously intrigued by the idea. And why not? Was not the celebrated Edward Butler's daughter a woman grown, capable of regulating her own affairs, and welcome, of course, as the honored member of so important a family. It was very flattering to the Calligans to think that she would want to come under any circumstances.

"I don't see how your parents can let you go, Aileen; but you're certainly welcome here as long as you want to stay, and that's forever, if you want to." And Mrs. Calligan beamed on her welcomingly. The idea of Aileen Butler asking to be permitted to come here! And the hearty, comprehending manner in which she said this, and Mamie's enthusiasm, caused

Aileen to breathe a sigh of relief. The matter of the expense of her presence to the Calligans came into her mind.

"I want to pay you, of course," she said to Mrs. Calligan, "if I come."

"The very idea, Aileen Butler!" exclaimed Mamie. "You'll do nothing of the sort. You'll come here and live with me as my guest."

"No, I won't! If I can't pay I won't come," replied Aileen. "You'll have to let me do that." She knew that the Calligans could not afford to keep her.

"Well, we'll not talk about that now, anyhow," replied Mrs. Calligan. "You can come when you like and stay as long as you like. Reach me some clean napkins, Mamie." Aileen remained for luncheon, and left soon afterward to keep her suggested appointment with Cowperwood, feeling satisfied that her main problem had been solved. Now her way was clear. She could come here if she wanted to. It was simply a matter of collecting a few necessary things or coming without bringing anything. Perhaps Frank would have something to suggest.

In the meantime Cowperwood made no effort to communicate with Aileen since the unfortunate discovery of their meeting place, but had awaited a letter from her, which was not long in coming. And, as usual, it was a long, optimistic, affectionate, and defiant screed in which she related all that had occurred to her and her present plan of leaving home. This last puzzled and troubled him not a little.

Aileen in the bosom of her family, smart and well-cared for, was one thing. Aileen out in the world dependent on him was another. He had never imagined that she would be compelled to leave before he was prepared to take her; and if she did now, it might stir up complications which would be anything but pleasant to contemplate. Still he was fond of her, very, and would do anything to make her happy. He could support her in a very respectable way even now, if he did not eventually go to prison, and even there he might manage to make some shift for her. It would be so much better, though, if he could persuade her to remain at home until he knew exactly what his fate was to be. He never doubted but that some day, whatever happened, within a reasonable length of time, he would be rid of all these complications and well-to-do again, in which case, if he could get a divorce, he wanted to marry Aileen. If not, he would take her with him anyhow, and from this point of view it might be just as well as if she broke away from her family now. But from the point of view of present complications—the search Butler would make—it might be dangerous. He might even publicly charge him with abduction. He therefore decided to persuade Aileen to stay at home, drop meetings and communications for the time being, and even go abroad. He would be all right until she came back and so would she—common sense ought to rule in this case.

With all this in mind he set out to keep the appointment she suggested in her letter, nevertheless feeling it a little dangerous to do so.

"Are you sure," he asked, after he had listened to her description of the Calligan homestead, "that you would like it there? It sounds rather poor to me."

"Yes, but I like them so much," replied Aileen.

"And you're sure they won't tell on you?"

"Oh, no; never, never!"

"Very well," he concluded. "You know what you're doing. I don't want to advise you against your will. If I were you, though, I'd take your father's advice and go away for a while. He'll get over this then, and I'll still be here. I can write you occasionally, and you can write me."

The moment Cowperwood said this Aileen's brow clouded. Her love for him was so great that there was something like a knife thrust in the merest hint at an extended separation. Her Frank here and in trouble—on trial maybe and she away! Never! What could he mean by suggesting such a thing? Could it be that he didn't care for her as much as she did for him? Did he really love her? she asked herself. Was he going to desert her just when she was going to do the thing which would bring them nearer together? Her eyes clouded, for she was terribly hurt.

"Why, how you talk!" she exclaimed. "You know I won't leave Philadelphia now. You certainly don't expect me to leave you."

Cowperwood saw it all very clearly. He was too shrewd not to. He was immensely fond of her. Good heaven, he thought, he would not hurt her feelings for the world!

"Honey," he said, quickly, when he saw her eyes, "you don't understand. I want you to do what you want to do. You've planned this out in order to be with me; so now you do it. Don't think any more about me or anything I've said. I was merely thinking that it might make matters worse for both of us; but I don't believe it will. You think your father loves you so much that after you're gone he'll change his mind. Very good; go. But we must be very careful, sweet—you and I—really we must. This thing is getting serious. If you should go and your father should charge me with abduction—take the public into his confidence and tell all about this, it would be serious for both of us—as much for you as for me, for I'd be convicted sure then, just on that account, if nothing else. And then what? You'd better not try to see me often for the present—not any oftener than we can possibly help. If we had used common sense and stopped when your father got that letter, this wouldn't have happened. But now that it has happened, we must be as wise as we can, don't you see? So, think it over, and do what you think best and then write me and whatever you do will be all right with me—do you hear?" He drew her to him and kissed her. "You haven't any money, have you?" he concluded wisely.

Aileen, deeply moved by all he had just said, was none the less convinced once she had meditated on it a moment, that her course was best. Her father loved her too much. He would not do anything to hurt her publicly and so he would not attack Cowperwood through her openly. More than likely, as she now explained to Frank, he would plead with her to come back. And he, listening, was compelled to yield. Why argue? She would not leave him anyhow.

He went down in his pocket for the first time since he had known Aileen and produced a layer of bills. "Here's two hundred dollars, sweet," he said, "until I see or hear from you. I'll see that you have whatever you need; and now don't think that I don't love you. You know I do. I'm crazy about you."

Aileen protested that she did not need so much—that she did not really need any—she had some at home; but he put that aside. He knew that she must have money.

"Don't talk, honey," he said. "I know what you need." She had been so used to receiving money from her father and mother in comfortable amounts from time to time that she thought nothing of it. Frank loved her so much that it made everything right between them. She softened in her mood and they discussed the matter of letters, reaching the conclusion that a private messenger would be safest. When finally they parted, Aileen, from being sunk in the depths by his uncertain attitude, was now once more on the heights. She decided that he did love her, and went away smiling. She had her Frank to fall back on—she would teach her father. Cowperwood shook his head, following her with his eyes. She represented an additional burden, but give her up, he certainly could not. Tear the veil from this illusion of affection and make her feel so wretched when he cared for her so much? No. There was really nothing for him to do but what he had done. After all, he reflected, it might not work out so badly. Any detective work that Butler might choose to do would prove that she had not run to him. If at any moment it became necessary to bring common sense into play to save the situation from a deadly climax, he could have the Butlers secretly informed as to Aileen's whereabouts. That would show he had little to do with it, and they could try to persuade Aileen to come home again. Good might result—one could not tell. He would deal with the evils as they arose. He drove quickly back to his office, and Aileen returned to her home determined to put her plan into action. Her father had given her some little time in which to decide—possibly he would give her longer—but she would not wait. Having always had her wish granted in everything, she could not understand why she was not to have her way this time. It was about five o'clock now. She would wait until all the members of the family were comfortably seated at the dinner-table, which would be about seven o'clock, and then slip out.

On arriving home, however, she was greeted by an unexpected reason for suspending action. This was the presence of a certain Mr. and Mrs. Steinmetz—the former a well-known engineer who drew the plans for many of the works which Butler undertook. It was the day before Thanksgiving, and they were eager to have Aileen and Norah accompany them for a fortnight's stay at their new home in West Chester—a structure concerning the charm of which Aileen had heard much. They were exceedingly agreeable people—comparatively young and surrounded by a coterie of interesting friends. Aileen decided to delay her flight and go. Her father was most cordial. The presence and invitation of the Steinmetzes was as much a relief to him as it was to Aileen. West Chester being forty miles from Philadelphia, it was unlikely that Aileen would attempt to meet Cowperwood while there.

She wrote Cowperwood of the changed condition and departed, and he breathed a sigh of relief, fancying at the time that this storm had permanently blown over.

CHAPTER XXXIX

In the meanwhile the day of Cowperwood's trial was drawing near. He was under the impression that an attempt was going to be made to convict him whether the facts warranted it or not. He did not see any way out of his dilemma, however, unless it was to abandon everything and leave Philadelphia for good, which was impossible. The only way to guard his future and retain his financial friends was to stand trial as quickly as possible, and trust them to assist him to his feet in the future in case he failed. He discussed the possibilities of an unfair trial with Steger, who did not seem to think that there was so much to that. In the first place, a jury could not easily be suborned by any one. In the next place, most judges were honest, in spite of their political cleavage, and would go no further than party bias would lead them in their rulings and opinions, which was, in the main, not so far. The particular judge who was to sit in this case, one Wilbur Payderson, of the Court of Quarter Sessions, was a strict party nominee, and as such beholden to Mollenhauer, Simpson, and Butler; but, in so far as Steger had ever heard, he was an honest man.

"What I can't understand," said Steger, "is why these fellows should be so anxious to punish you, unless it is for the effect on the State at large. The election's over. I understand there's a movement on now to get Stener out in case he is convicted, which he will be. They have to try him. He won't go up for more than a year, or two or three, and if he does he'll be pardoned out in half the time or less. It would be the same in your case, if you were convicted. They couldn't keep you in and let him out. But it will never get that far—take my word for it. We'll win before a jury, or we'll reverse the judgment of conviction before the State Supreme Court, certain. Those five judges up there are not going to sustain any such poppycock idea as this."

Steger actually believed what he said, and Cowperwood was pleased. Thus far the young lawyer had done excellently well in all of his cases. Still, he did not like the idea of being hunted down by Butler. It was a serious matter, and one of which Steger was totally unaware. Cowperwood could never quite forget that in listening to his lawyer's optimistic assurances.

The actual beginning of the trial found almost all of the inhabitants of this city of six hundred thousand "keyed up." None of the women of Cowperwood's family were coming into court. He had insisted that there should be no family demonstration for the newspapers to comment upon. His father was coming, for he might be needed as a witness. Aileen had written him the afternoon before saying she had returned from West Chester and wishing him luck. She was so anxious to know what was to become of him that she could not stay away any longer and had returned—not to go to the courtroom, for he did not want her to do that, but to be as near as possible when his fate was decided, adversely or otherwise. She wanted to run and congratulate him if he won, or to console with him if he lost. She felt that her return would be likely to precipitate a collision with her father, but she could not help that.

The position of Mrs. Cowperwood was most anomalous. She had to go through the formality of seeming affectionate and tender, even when she knew that Frank did not want her to be. He felt instinctively now that she knew of Aileen. He was merely awaiting the proper hour in which to spread the whole matter before her. She put her arms around him at the door on the fateful morning, in the somewhat formal manner into which they had dropped these later years, and for a moment, even though she was keenly aware of his difficulties, she could not kiss him. He did not want to kiss her, but he did not show it. She did kiss him, though, and added: "Oh, I do hope things come out all right."

"You needn't worry about that, I think, Lillian," he replied, buoyantly. "I'll be all right."

He ran down the steps and walked out on Girard Avenue to his former car line, where he boarded a car. He was thinking of Aileen and how keenly she was feeling for him, and what a mockery his married life now was, and whether he would face a sensible jury, and so on and so forth. If he didn't—if he didn't—this day was crucial!

He stepped off the car at Third and Market and hurried to his office. Steger was already there. "Well, Harper," observed Cowperwood, courageously, "today's the day."

The Court of Quarter Sessions, Part I, where this trial was to take place, was held in famous Independence Hall, at Sixth and Chestnut Streets, which was at this time, as it had been for all of a century before, the center of local executive and judicial life. It was a low two-story building of red brick, with a white wooden central tower of old Dutch and English derivation, compounded of the square, the circle, and the octagon. The total structure consisted of a central portion and two T-shaped wings lying to the right and left, whose small, oval-topped old-fashioned windows and doors were set with those many-paned sashes so much admired by those who love what is known as Colonial architecture. Here, and in an addition known as State House Row (since torn down), which extended from the rear of the building toward Walnut Street, were located the offices of the mayor, the chief of police, the city treasurer, the chambers of council, and all the other important and executive offices of the city, together with the four branches of Quarter Sessions, which sat to hear the growing docket of criminal cases. The mammoth city hall which was subsequently completed at Broad and Market Streets was then building.

An attempt had been made to improve the reasonably large courtrooms by putting in them raised platforms of dark walnut surmounted by large, dark walnut desks, behind which the judges sat; but the attempt was not very successful. The desks, jury-boxes, and railings generally were made too large, and so the general effect was one of disproportion. A cream-colored wall had been thought the appropriate thing to go with black walnut furniture, but time and dust had made the combination dreary. There were no pictures or ornaments of any kind, save the stalky, over-elaborated gas-brackets which stood on his honor's desk, and the single swinging chandelier suspended from the center of the ceiling. Fat bailiffs and court officers, concerned only in holding their workless jobs, did not add anything to the spirit of the scene. Two of them in the particular court in which this trial was held contended hourly as to which should hand the judge a glass of water. One preceded his honor like a fat, stuffy, dusty majordomo to and from his dressing-room. His business was to call loudly, when the latter entered, "His honor the Court, hats off. Everybody please rise," while a second bailiff, standing at the left of his honor when he was seated, and between the jury-box and the witness-chair, recited in an absolutely unintelligible way that beautiful and dignified statement of collective society's obligation to the constituent units, which begins, "Hear ye! hear ye! hear ye!" and ends, "All those of you having just cause for complaint draw near and ye shall be heard." However, you would have thought it was of no import here. Custom and indifference had allowed it to sink to a mumble. A third bailiff guarded the door of the jury-room; and in addition to these there were present a court clerk—small, pale, candle-waxy, with colorless milk-and-water eyes, and thin, pork-fat-colored hair and beard, who looked for all the world like an Americanized and decidedly decrepit Chinese mandarin—and a court stenographer.

Judge Wilbur Payderson, a lean herring of a man, who had sat in this case originally as the examining judge when Cowperwood had been indicted by the grand jury, and who had bound him over for trial at this term, was a peculiarly interesting type of judge, as judges go. He was so meager and thin-blooded that he was arresting for those qualities alone. Technically, he was learned in the law; actually, so far as life was concerned, absolutely unconscious of that subtle chemistry of things that transcends all written law and makes for the spirit and, beyond that, the inutility of all law, as all wise judges know. You could have looked at his lean, pedantic body, his frizzled gray hair, his fishy, blue-gray eyes, without any depth of speculation in them, and his nicely modeled but unimportant face, and told him that he was without imagination; but he would not have believed you—would have fined you for contempt of court. By the careful garnering of all his little opportunities, the furbishing up of every meager advantage; by listening slavishly to the voice of party, and following as nearly as he could the behests of intrenched property, he had reached his present state. It was not very far along, at that. His salary was only six thousand dollars a year. His little fame did not extend beyond the meager realm of local lawyers and judges. But the sight of his name quoted daily as being about his duties, or rendering such and such a decision, was a great satisfaction to him. He thought it made him a significant figure in the world. "Behold I am not as other men," he often thought, and this comforted him. He was very much flattered when a prominent case came to his calendar; and as he sat enthroned before the various litigants and lawyers he felt, as a rule, very significant indeed. Now and then some subtlety of life would confuse his really limited intellect; but in all such cases there was the letter of the law. He could hunt in the reports to find out what really thinking men had decided. Besides, lawyers everywhere are so subtle. They put the rules of law, favorable or unfavorable, under the judge's thumb and nose. "Your honor, in the thirty-second volume of the Revised Reports of Massachusetts, page so and so, line so and so, in Arundel versus Bannerman, you will find, etc." How often have you heard that in a court of law? The reasoning that is left to do in most cases is not much. And the sanctity of the law is raised like a great banner by which the pride of the incumbent is strengthened.

Payderson, as Steger had indicated, could scarcely be pointed to as an unjust judge. He was a party judge—Republican in principle, or rather belief, beholden to the dominant party councils for his personal continuance in office, and as such willing and anxious to do whatever he considered that he reasonably could do to further the party welfare and the private interests of his masters. Most people never trouble to look into the mechanics of the thing they call their conscience too closely. Where they do, too often they lack the skill to disentangle the tangled threads of ethics and morals. Whatever the opinion of the time is, whatever the weight of great interests dictates, that they conscientiously believe. Some one has since invented the phrase "a corporation-minded judge." There are many such.

Payderson was one. He fairly revered property and power. To him Butler and Mollenhauer and Simpson were great men—reasonably sure to be right always because they were so powerful. This matter of Cowperwood's and Stener's defalcation he had long heard of. He knew by associating with one political light and another just what the situation was. The party, as the leaders saw it, had been put in a very bad position by Cowperwood's subtlety. He had led Stener astray—more than an ordinary city treasurer should have been led astray—and, although Stener was primarily guilty as the original mover in the scheme, Cowperwood was more so for having led him imaginatively to such disastrous lengths. Besides, the party needed a scapegoat—that was enough for Payderson, in the first place. Of course, after the election had been won, and it appeared that the party had not suffered so much, he did not understand quite why it was that Cowperwood was still so carefully included in the Proceedings; but he had faith to believe that the leaders had some just grounds for not letting him off. From one source and another he learned that Butler had some private grudge against Cowperwood. What it was no one seemed to know exactly. The general impression was that Cowperwood had led Butler into some unwholesome financial transactions. Anyhow, it was generally understood that for the good of the party, and in order to teach a wholesome lesson to dangerous subordinates—it had been decided to allow these several indictments to take their course. Cowperwood was to be punished quite as severely as Stener for the moral effect on the community. Stener was to be sentenced the maximum sentence for his crime in order that the party and the courts should appear properly righteous. Beyond that he was to be left to the mercy of the governor, who could ease things up for him if he chose, and if the leaders wished. In the silly mind of the general public the various judges of Quarter Sessions, like girls incarcerated in boarding-schools, were supposed in their serene aloofness from life not to know what was going on in the subterranean realm of politics; but they knew well enough, and, knowing particularly well from whence came their continued position and authority, they were duly grateful.

CHAPTER XL

When Cowperwood came into the crowded courtroom with his father and Steger, quite fresh and jaunty (looking the part of the shrewd financier, the man of affairs), every one stared. It was really too much to expect, most of them thought, that a man like this would be convicted. He was, no doubt, guilty; but, also, no doubt, he had ways and means of evading the law. His lawyer, Harper Steger, looked very shrewd and canny to them. It was very cold, and both men wore long, dark, bluish-gray overcoats, cut in the latest mode. Cowperwood was given to small boutonnieres in fair weather, but to-day he wore none. His tie, however, was of heavy, impressive silk, of lavender hue, set with a large, clear, green emerald. He wore only the thinnest of watch-chains, and no other ornament of any kind. He always looked jaunty and yet reserved, good-natured, and yet capable and self-sufficient. Never had he looked more so than he did to-day.

He at once took in the nature of the scene, which had a peculiar interest for him. Before him was the as yet empty judge's rostrum, and at its right the empty jury-box, between which, and to the judge's left, as he sat facing the audience, stood the witness-chair where he must presently sit and testify. Behind it, already awaiting the arrival of the court, stood a fat bailiff, one John Sparkheaver whose business it was to present the aged, greasy Bible to be touched by the witnesses in making oath, and to say, "Step this way," when the testimony was over. There were other bailiffs—one at the gate giving into the railed space before the judge's desk, where prisoners were arraigned, lawyers sat or pleaded, the defendant had a chair, and so on; another in the aisle leading to the jury-room, and still another guarding the door by which the public entered. Cowperwood surveyed Stener, who was one of the witnesses, and who now, in his helpless fright over his own fate, was without malice toward any one. He had really never borne any. He wished if anything now that he had followed Cowperwood's advice, seeing where he now was, though he still had faith that Mollenhauer and the political powers represented by him would do something for him with the governor, once he was sentenced. He was very pale and comparatively thin. Already he had lost that ruddy bulk which had been added during the days of his prosperity. He wore a new gray suit and a brown tie, and was clean-shaven. When his eye caught Cowperwood's steady beam, it faltered and drooped. He rubbed his ear foolishly. Cowperwood nodded.

"You know," he said to Steger, "I feel sorry for George. He's such a fool. Still I did all I could."

Cowperwood also watched Mrs. Stener out of the tail of his eye—an undersized, peaked, and sallow little woman, whose clothes fitted her abominably. It was just like Stener to marry a woman like that, he thought. The scrubby matches of the socially unelect or unfit always interested, though they did not always amuse, him. Mrs. Stener had no affection for Cowperwood, of course, looking on him, as she did, as the unscrupulous cause of her husband's downfall. They were now quite poor again, about to move from their big house into cheaper quarters; and this was not pleasing for her to contemplate.

Judge Payderson came in after a time, accompanied by his undersized but stout court attendant, who looked more like a pouter-pigeon than a human being; and as they came, Bailiff Sparkheaver rapped on the judge's desk, beside which he had been slumbering, and mumbled, "Please rise!" The audience arose, as is the rule of all courts. Judge Payderson stirred among a number of briefs that were lying on his desk, and asked, briskly, "What's the first case, Mr. Protus?" He was speaking to his clerk.

During the long and tedious arrangement of the day's docket and while the various minor motions of lawyers were being considered, this courtroom scene still retained interest for Cowperwood. He was so eager to win, so incensed at the outcome of untoward events which had brought him here. He was always intensely irritated, though he did not show it, by the whole process of footing delays and queries and quibbles, by which legally the affairs of men were too often hampered. Law, if you had asked him, and he had accurately expressed himself, was a mist formed out of the moods and the mistakes of men, which befogged the sea of life and prevented plain sailing for the little commercial and social barques of men; it was a miasma of misinterpretation where the ills of life festered, and also a place where the accidentally wounded were ground between the upper and the nether millstones of force or chance; it was a strange, weird, interesting, and yet futile battle of wits where the ignorant and the incompetent and the shrewd and the angry and the weak were made pawns and shuttlecocks for men—lawyers, who were playing upon their moods, their vanities, their desires, and their necessities. It was an unholy and unsatisfactory disrupting and delaying spectacle, a painful commentary on the frailties of life, and men, a trick, a snare, a pit and gin. In the hands of the strong, like himself when he was at his best, the law was a sword and a shield, a trap to place before the feet of the unwary; a pit to dig in the path of those who might pursue. It was anything you might choose to make of it—a door to illegal opportunity; a cloud of dust to be cast in the eyes of those who might choose, and rightfully, to see; a veil to be dropped arbitrarily between truth and its execution, justice and its judgment, crime and punishment. Lawyers in the main were intellectual mercenaries to be bought and sold in any cause. It amused him to hear the ethical and emotional platitudes of lawyers, to see how readily they would lie, steal, prevaricate, misrepresent in almost any cause and for any purpose. Great lawyers were merely great unscrupulous subtleties, like himself, sitting back in dark, close-woven lairs like spiders and awaiting the approach of unwary human flies. Life was at best a dark, inhuman, unkind, unsympathetic struggle built of cruelties and the law, and its lawyers were the most despicable representatives of the whole unsatisfactory mess. Still he used law as he would use any other trap or weapon to rid him of a human ill; and as for lawyers, he picked them up as he would any club or knife wherewith to defend himself. He had no particular respect for any of them—not even Harper Steger, though he liked him. They were tools to be used—knives, keys, clubs, anything you will; but nothing more. When they were through they were paid and dropped—put aside and forgotten. As for judges, they were merely incompetent lawyers, at a rule, who were shelved by some fortunate turn of chance, and who would not, in all likelihood, be as efficient as the lawyers who pleaded before them if they were put in the same position. He had no respect for judges—he knew too much about them. He knew how often they were sycophants, political climbers, political hacks, tools, time-servers, judicial door-mats lying before the financially and politically great and powerful who used them as such. Judges were fools, as were most other people in this dusty, shifty world. Pah! His inscrutable eyes took them all in and gave no sign. His only safety lay, he thought, in the magnificent subtlety of his own brain, and nowhere else. You could not convince Cowperwood of any great or inherent virtue in this mortal scheme of things. He knew too much; he knew himself.

When the judge finally cleared away the various minor motions pending, he ordered his clerk to call the case of the City of Philadelphia versus Frank A. Cowperwood, which was done in a clear voice. Both Dennis Shannon, the new district attorney, and Steger, were on their feet at once. Steger and Cowperwood, together with Shannon and Strobik, who had now come in and was standing as the representative of the State of Pennsylvania—the complainant—had seated themselves at the long table inside the railing which inclosed the space before the judge's desk. Steger proposed to Judge Payderson, for effect's sake more than anything else, that this indictment be quashed, but was overruled.

A jury to try the case was now quickly impaneled—twelve men out of the usual list called to serve for the month—and was then ready to be challenged by the opposing counsel. The business of impaneling a jury was a rather simple thing so far as this court was concerned. It consisted in the mandarin-like clerk taking the names of all the jurors called to serve in this court for the month—some fifty in all—and putting them, each written on a separate slip of paper, in a whirling drum, spinning it around a few times, and then lifting out the first slip which his hand encountered, thus glorifying chance and settling on who should be juror No. 1. His hand reaching in twelve times drew out the names of the twelve jurymen, who as their names were called, were ordered to take their places in the jury-box.

Cowperwood observed this proceeding with a great deal of interest. What could be more important than the men who were going to try him? The process was too swift for accurate judgment, but he received a faint impression of middle-class men. One man in particular, however, an old man of sixty-five, with iron-gray hair and beard, shaggy eyebrows, sallow complexion, and stooped shoulders, struck him as having that kindness of temperament and breadth of experience which might under certain circumstances be argumentatively swayed in his favor. Another, a small, sharp-nosed, sharp-chinned commercial man of some kind, he immediately disliked.

"I hope I don't have to have that man on my jury," he said to Steger, quietly.

"You don't," replied Steger. "I'll challenge him. We have the right to fifteen peremptory challenges on a case like this, and so has the prosecution."

When the jury-box was finally full, the two lawyers waited for the clerk to bring them the small board upon which slips of paper bearing the names of the twelve jurors were fastened in rows in order of their selection—jurors one, two, and three being in the first row; four, five, and six in the second, and so on. It being the prerogative of the attorney for the prosecution to examine and challenge the jurors first, Shannon arose, and, taking the board, began to question them as to their trades or professions, their knowledge of the case before the court, and their possible prejudice for or against the prisoner.

It was the business of both Steger and Shannon to find men who knew a little something of finance and could understand a peculiar situation of this kind without any of them (looking at it from Steger's point of view) having any prejudice against a man's trying to assist himself by reasonable means to weather a financial storm or (looking at it from Shannon's point of view) having any sympathy with such means, if they bore about them the least suspicion of chicanery, jugglery, or dishonest manipulation of any kind. As both Shannon and Steger in due course observed for themselves in connection with this jury, it was composed of that assorted social fry which the dragnets of the courts, cast into the ocean of the city, bring to the surface for purposes of this sort. It was made up in the main of managers, agents, tradesmen, editors, engineers, architects, furriers, grocers, traveling salesmen, authors, and every other kind of working citizen whose experience had fitted him for service in proceedings of this character. Rarely would you have found a man of great distinction; but very frequently a group of men who were possessed of no small modicum of that interesting quality known as hard common sense.

Throughout all this Cowperwood sat quietly examining the men. A young florist, with a pale face, a wide speculative forehead, and anemic hands, struck him as being sufficiently impressionable to his personal charm to be worth while. He whispered as much to Steger. There was a shrewd Jew, a furrier, who was challenged because he had read all of the news of the panic and had lost two thousand dollars in street-railway stocks. There was a stout wholesale grocer, with red cheeks, blue eyes, and flaxen hair, who Cowperwood said he thought was stubborn. He was eliminated. There was a thin, dapper manager of a small retail clothing store, very anxious to be excused, who declared, falsely, that he did not believe in swearing by the Bible. Judge Payderson, eyeing him severely, let him go. There were some ten more in all—men who knew of Cowperwood, men who admitted they were prejudiced, men who were hidebound Republicans and resentful of this crime, men who knew Stener—who were pleasantly eliminated.

By twelve o'clock, however, a jury reasonably satisfactory to both sides had been chosen.

CHAPTER XLI

At two o'clock sharp Dennis Shannon, as district attorney, began his opening address. He stated in a very simple, kindly way—for he had a most engaging manner—that the indictment as here presented charged Mr. Frank A. Cowperwood, who was sitting at the table inside the jury-rail, first with larceny, second with embezzlement, third with larceny as bailee, and fourth with embezzlement of a certain sum of money—a specific sum, to wit, sixty thousand dollars—on a check given him (drawn to his order) October 9, 1871, which was intended to reimburse him for a certain number of certificates of city loan, which he as agent or bailee of the check was supposed to have purchased for the city sinking-fund on the order of the city treasurer (under some form of agreement which had been in existence between them, and which had been in force for some time)—said fund being intended to take up such certificates as they might mature in the hands of holders and be presented for payment—for which purpose, however, the check in question had never been used.

"Now, gentlemen," said Mr. Shannon, very quietly, "before we go into this very simple question of whether Mr. Cowperwood did or did not on the date in question get from the city treasurer sixty thousand dollars, for which he made no honest return, let me explain to you just what the people mean when they charge him first with larceny, second with embezzlement, third with larceny as bailee, and fourth with embezzlement on a check. Now, as you see, there are four counts here, as we lawyers term them, and the reason there are four counts is as follows: A man may be guilty of larceny and embezzlement at the same time, or of larceny or embezzlement separately, and without being guilty of the other, and the district attorney representing the people might be uncertain, not that he was not guilty of both, but that it might not be possible to present the evidence under one count, so as to insure his adequate punishment for a crime which in a way involved both. In such cases, gentlemen, it is customary to indict a man under separate counts, as has been done in this case. Now, the four counts in this case, in a way, overlap and confirm each other, and it will be your duty, after we have explained their nature and character and presented the evidence, to say whether the defendant is guilty on one count or the other, or on two or three of the counts, or on all four, just as you see fit and proper—or, to put it in a better way, as the evidence warrants. Larceny, as you may or may not know, is the act of taking away the goods or chattels of another without his knowledge or consent, and embezzlement is the fraudulent appropriation to one's own use of what is intrusted to one's care and management, especially money. Larceny as bailee, on the other hand, is simply a more definite form of larceny wherein one fixes the act of carrying away the goods of another without his knowledge or consent on the person to whom the goods were delivered in trust that is, the agent or bailee. Embezzlement on a check, which constitutes the fourth charge, is simply a more definite form of fixing charge number two in an exact way and signifies appropriating the money on a check given for a certain definite purpose. All of these charges, as you can see, gentlemen, are in a way synonymous. They overlap and overlay each other. The people, through their representative, the district attorney, contend that Mr. Cowperwood, the defendant here, is guilty of all four charges. So now, gentlemen, we will proceed to the history of this crime, which proves to me as an individual that this defendant has one of the most subtle and dangerous minds of the criminal financier type, and we hope by witnesses to prove that to you, also."

Shannon, because the rules of evidence and court procedure here admitted of no interruption of the prosecution in presenting a case, then went on to describe from his own point of view how Cowperwood had first met Stener; how he had wormed himself into his confidence; how little financial knowledge Stener had, and so forth; coming down finally to the day the check for sixty thousand dollars was given Cowperwood; how Stener, as treasurer, claimed that he knew nothing of its delivery, which constituted the base of the charge of larceny; how Cowperwood, having it, misappropriated the certificates supposed to have been purchased for the sinking-fund, if they were purchased at all—all of which Shannon said constituted the crimes with which the defendant was charged, and of which he was unquestionably guilty.

"We have direct and positive evidence of all that we have thus far contended, gentlemen," Mr. Shannon concluded violently. "This is not a matter of hearsay or theory, but of fact. You will be shown by direct testimony which cannot be shaken just how it was done. If, after you have heard all this, you still think this man is innocent—that he did not commit the crimes with which he is charged—it is your business to acquit him. On the other hand, if you think the witnesses whom we shall put on the stand are telling the truth, then it is your business to convict him, to find a verdict for the people as against the defendant. I thank you for your attention."

The jurors stirred comfortably and took positions of ease, in which they thought they were to rest for the time; but their idle comfort was of short duration for Shannon now called out the name of George W. Stener, who came hurrying forward very pale, very flaccid, very tired-looking. His eyes, as he took his seat in the witness-chair, laying his hand on the Bible and swearing to tell the truth, roved in a restless, nervous manner.

His voice was a little weak as he started to give his testimony. He told first how he had met Cowperwood in the early months of 1866—he could not remember the exact day; it was during his first term as city treasurer—he had been elected to the office in the fall of 1864. He had been troubled about the condition of city loan, which was below par, and which could not be sold by the city legally at anything but par. Cowperwood had been recommended to him by some one—Mr. Strobik, he believed, though he couldn't be sure. It was the custom of city treasurers to employ brokers, or a broker, in a crisis of this kind, and he was merely following what had been the custom. He went on to describe, under steady promptings and questions from the incisive mind of Shannon, just what the nature of this first conversation was—he remembered it fairly well; how Mr. Cowperwood had said he thought he could do what was wanted; how he had gone away and drawn up a plan or thought one out; and how he had returned and laid it before Stener. Under Shannon's skillful guidance Stener elucidated just what this scheme was—which wasn't exactly so flattering to the honesty of men in general as it was a testimonial to their subtlety and skill.

After much discussion of Stener's and Cowperwood's relations the story finally got down to the preceding October, when by reason of companionship, long business understanding, mutually prosperous relationship, etc., the place had been reached where, it was explained, Cowperwood was not only handling several millions of city loan annually, buying and selling for the city and trading in it generally, but in the bargain had secured one five hundred thousand dollars' worth of city money at an exceedingly low rate of interest, which was being invested for himself and Stener in profitable street-car ventures of one kind and another. Stener was not anxious to be altogether clear on this point; but Shannon, seeing that he was later to prosecute Stener himself for this very crime of embezzlement, and that Steger would soon follow in cross-examination, was not willing to let him be hazy. Shannon wanted to fix Cowperwood in the minds of the jury as a clever, tricky person, and by degrees he certainly managed to indicate a very subtle-minded man. Occasionally, as one sharp point after another of Cowperwood's skill was brought out and made moderately clear, one juror or another turned to look at Cowperwood. And he noting this and in order to impress them all as favorably as possible merely gazed Stenerward with a steady air of intelligence and comprehension.

The examination now came down to the matter of the particular check for sixty thousand dollars which Albert Stires had handed Cowperwood on the afternoon—late—of October 9, 1871. Shannon showed Stener the check itself. Had he ever seen it? Yes. Where? In the office of District Attorney Pettie on October 20th, or thereabouts last. Was that the first time he had seen it? Yes. Had he ever heard about it before then? Yes. When? On October 10th last. Would he kindly tell the jury in his own way just how and under what circumstances he first heard of it then? Stener twisted uncomfortably in his chair. It was a hard thing to do. It was not a pleasant commentary on his own character and degree of moral stamina, to say the least. However, he cleared his throat again and began a description of that small but bitter section of his life's drama in which Cowperwood, finding himself in a tight place and about to fail, had come to him at his office and demanded that he loan him three hundred thousand dollars more in one lump sum.

There was considerable bickering just at this point between Steger and Shannon, for the former was very anxious to make it appear that Stener was lying out of the whole cloth about this. Steger got in his objection at this point, and created a considerable diversion from the main theme, because Stener kept saying he "thought" or he "believed."

"Object!" shouted Steger, repeatedly. "I move that that be stricken from the record as incompetent, irrelevant, and immaterial. The witness is not allowed to say what he thinks, and the prosecution knows it very well."

"Your honor," insisted Shannon, "I am doing the best I can to have the witness tell a plain, straightforward story, and I think that it is obvious that he is doing so."

"Object!" reiterated Steger, vociferously. "Your honor, I insist that the district attorney has no right to prejudice the minds of the jury by flattering estimates of the sincerity of the witness. What he thinks of the witness and his sincerity is of no importance in this case. I must ask that your honor caution him plainly in this matter."

"Objection sustained," declared Judge Payderson, "the prosecution will please be more explicit"; and Shannon went on with his case.

Stener's testimony, in one respect, was most important, for it made plain what Cowperwood did not want brought out—namely, that he and Stener had had a dispute before this; that Stener had distinctly told Cowperwood that he would not loan him any more money; that Cowperwood had told Stener, on the day before he secured this check, and again on that very day, that he was in a very desperate situation financially, and that if he were not assisted to the extent of three hundred thousand dollars he would fail, and that

177

then both he and Stener would be ruined. On the morning of this day, according to Stener, he had sent Cowperwood a letter ordering him to cease purchasing city loan certificates for the sinking-fund. It was after their conversation on the same afternoon that Cowperwood surreptitiously secured the check for sixty thousand dollars from Albert Stires without his (Stener's) knowledge; and it was subsequent to this latter again that Stener, sending Albert to demand the return of the check, was refused, though the next day at five o'clock in the afternoon Cowperwood made an assignment. And the certificates for which the check had been purloined were not in the sinking-fund as they should have been. This was dark testimony for Cowperwood.

If any one imagines that all this was done without many vehement objections and exceptions made and taken by Steger, and subsequently when he was cross-examining Stener, by Shannon, he errs greatly. At times the chamber was coruscating with these two gentlemen's bitter wrangles, and his honor was compelled to hammer his desk with his gavel, and to threaten both with contempt of court, in order to bring them to a sense of order. Indeed while Payderson was highly incensed, the jury was amused and interested.

"You gentlemen will have to stop this, or I tell you now that you will both be heavily fined. This is a court of law, not a bar-room. Mr. Steger, I expect you to apologize to me and your colleague at once. Mr. Shannon, I must ask that you use less aggressive methods. Your manner is offensive to me. It is not becoming to a court of law. I will not caution either of you again."

Both lawyers apologized as lawyers do on such occasions, but it really made but little difference. Their individual attitudes and moods continued about as before.

"What did he say to you," asked Shannon of Stener, after one of these troublesome interruptions, "on that occasion, October 9th last, when he came to you and demanded the loan of an additional three hundred thousand dollars? Give his words as near as you can remember—exactly, if possible."

"Object!" interposed Steger, vigorously. "His exact words are not recorded anywhere except in Mr. Stener's memory, and his memory of them cannot be admitted in this case. The witness has testified to the general facts."

Judge Payderson smiled grimly. "Objection overruled," he returned.

"Exception!" shouted Steger.

"He said, as near as I can remember," replied Stener, drumming on the arms of the witness-chair in a nervous way, "that if I didn't give him three hundred thousand dollars he was going to fail, and I would be poor and go to the penitentiary."

"Object!" shouted Stager, leaping to his feet. "Your honor, I object to the whole manner in which this examination is being conducted by the prosecution. The evidence which the district attorney is here trying to extract from the uncertain memory of the witness is in defiance of all law and precedent, and has no definite bearing on the facts of the case, and could not disprove or substantiate whether Mr. Cowperwood thought or did not think that he was going to fail. Mr. Stener might give one version of this conversation or any conversation that took place at this time, and Mr. Cowperwood another. As a matter of fact, their versions are different. I see no point in Mr. Shannon's line of inquiry, unless it is to prejudice the jury's minds towards accepting certain allegations which the prosecution is pleased to make and which it cannot possibly substantiate. I think you ought to caution the witness to testify only in regard to things that he recalls exactly, not to what he thinks he remembers; and for my part I think that all that has been testified to in the last five minutes might be well stricken out."

"Objection overruled," replied Judge Payderson, rather indifferently; and Steger who had been talking merely to overcome the weight of Stener's testimony in the minds of the jury, sat down.

Shannon once more approached Stener.

"Now, as near as you can remember, Mr. Stener, I wish you would tell the jury what else it was that Mr. Cowperwood said on that occasion. He certainly didn't stop with the remark that you would be ruined and go to the penitentiary. Wasn't there other language that was employed on that occasion?"

"He said, as far as I can remember," replied Stener, "that there were a lot of political schemers who were trying to frighten me, that if I didn't give him three hundred thousand dollars we would both be ruined, and that I might as well be tried for stealing a sheep as a lamb."

"Ha!" yelled Shannon. "He said that, did he?"

"Yes, sir; he did," said Stener.

"How did he say it, exactly? What were his exact words?" Shannon demanded, emphatically, pointing a forceful forefinger at Stener in order to key him up to a clear memory of what had transpired.

"Well, as near as I can remember, he said just that," replied Stener, vaguely. "You might as well be tried for stealing a sheep as a lamb."

"Exactly!" exclaimed Shannon, whirling around past the jury to look at Cowperwood. "I thought so."

"Pure pyrotechnics, your honor," said Steger, rising to his feet on the instant. "All intended to prejudice the minds of the jury. Acting. I wish you would caution the counsel for the prosecution to confine himself to the evidence in hand, and not act for the benefit of his case."

The spectators smiled; and Judge Payderson, noting it, frowned severely. "Do you make that as an objection, Mr. Steger?" he asked.

"I certainly do, your honor," insisted Steger, resourcefully.

"Objection overruled. Neither counsel for the prosecution nor for the defense is limited to a peculiar routine of expression."

Steger himself was ready to smile, but he did not dare to.

Cowperwood fearing the force of such testimony and regretting it, still looked at Stener, pityingly. The feebleness of the man; the weakness of the man; the pass to which his cowardice had brought them both!

When Shannon was through bringing out this unsatisfactory data, Steger took Stener in hand; but he could not make as much out of him as he hoped. In so far as this particular situation was concerned, Stener was telling the exact truth; and it is hard to weaken the effect of the exact truth by any subtlety of interpretation, though it can, sometimes, be done. With painstaking care Steger went over all the ground of Stener's long relationship with Cowperwood, and tried to make it appear that Cowperwood was invariably the disinterested agent—not the ringleader in a subtle, really criminal adventure. It was hard to do, but he made a fine impression. Still the jury listened with skeptical minds. It might not be fair to punish Cowperwood for seizing with avidity upon a splendid chance to get rich quick, they thought; but it certainly was not worth while to throw a veil of innocence over such palpable human cupidity. Finally, both lawyers were through with Stener for the time being, anyhow, and then Albert Stires was called to the stand.

He was the same thin, pleasant, alert, rather agreeable soul that he had been in the heyday of his clerkly prosperity—a little paler now, but not otherwise changed. His small property had been saved for him by Cowperwood, who had advised Steger to inform the Municipal Reform Association that Stires' bondsmen were attempting to sequestrate it for their own benefit, when actually it should go to the city if there were any real claim against him—which there was not. That watchful organization had issued one of its numerous reports covering this point, and Albert had had the pleasure of seeing Strobik and the others withdraw in haste. Naturally he was grateful to Cowperwood, even though once he had been compelled to cry in vain in his presence. He was anxious now to do anything he could to help the banker, but his naturally truthful disposition prevented him from telling anything except the plain facts, which were partly beneficial and partly not.

Stires testified that he recalled Cowperwood's saying that he had purchased the certificates, that he was entitled to the money, that Stener was unduly frightened, and that no harm would come to him, Albert. He identified certain memoranda in the city treasurer's books, which were produced, as being accurate, and others in Cowperwood's books, which were also produced, as being corroborative. His testimony as to Stener's astonishment on discovering that his chief clerk had given Cowperwood a check was against the latter; but Cowperwood hoped to overcome the effect of this by his own testimony later.

Up to now both Steger and Cowperwood felt that they were doing fairly well, and that they need not be surprised if they won their case.

CHAPTER XLII

The trial moved on. One witness for the prosecution after another followed until the State had built up an arraignment that satisfied Shannon that he had established Cowperwood's guilt, whereupon he announced that he rested. Steger at once arose and began a long argument for the dismissal of the case on the ground that there was no evidence to show this, that and the other, but Judge Payderson would have none of it. He knew how important the matter was in the local political world.

"I don't think you had better go into all that now, Mr. Steger," he said, wearily, after allowing him to proceed a reasonable distance. "I am familiar with the custom of the city, and the indictment as here made does not concern the custom of the city. Your argument is with the jury, not with me. I couldn't enter into that now. You may renew your motion at the close of the defendants' case. Motion denied."

District-Attorney Shannon, who had been listening attentively, sat down. Steger, seeing there was no chance to soften the judge's mind by any subtlety of argument, returned to Cowperwood, who smiled at the result.

"We'll just have to take our chances with the jury," he announced.

"I was sure of it," replied Cowperwood.

Steger then approached the jury, and, having outlined the case briefly from his angle of observation, continued by telling them what he was sure the evidence would show from his point of view.

"As a matter of fact, gentlemen, there is no essential difference in the evidence which the prosecution can present and that which we, the defense, can present. We are not going to dispute that Mr. Cowperwood received a check from Mr. Stener for sixty thousand dollars, or that he failed to put the certificate of city loan which that sum of money represented, and to which he was entitled in payment as agent, in the sinking-fund, as the prosecution now claims he should have done; but we are going to claim and prove also beyond the shadow of a reasonable doubt that he had a right, as the agent of the city, doing business with the city through its treasury department for four years, to withhold, under an agreement which he had with the city treasurer, all payments of money and all deposits of certificates in the sinking-fund until the first day of each succeeding month—the first month following any given transaction. As a matter of fact we can and will bring many traders and bankers who have had dealings with the city treasury in the past in just this way to prove this. The prosecution is going to ask you to believe that Mr. Cowperwood knew at the time he received this check that he was going to fail; that he did not buy the certificates, as he claimed, with the view of placing them in the sinking-fund; and that, knowing he was going to fail, and that he could not subsequently deposit them, he deliberately went to Mr. Albert

Stires, Mr. Stener's secretary, told him that he had purchased such certificates, and on the strength of a falsehood, implied if not actually spoken, secured the check, and walked away.

"Now, gentlemen, I am not going to enter into a long-winded discussion of these points at this time, since the testimony is going to show very rapidly what the facts are. We have a number of witnesses here, and we are all anxious to have them heard. What I am going to ask you to remember is that there is not one scintilla of testimony outside of that which may possibly be given by Mr. George W. Stener, which will show either that Mr. Cowperwood knew, at the time he called on the city treasurer, that he was going to fail, or that he had not purchased the certificates in question, or that he had not the right to withhold them from the sinking-fund as long as he pleased up to the first of the month, the time he invariably struck a balance with the city. Mr. Stener, the ex-city treasurer, may possibly testify one way. Mr. Cowperwood, on his own behalf, will testify another. It will then be for you gentlemen to decide between them, to decide which one you prefer to believe—Mr. George W. Stener, the ex-city treasurer, the former commercial associate of Mr. Cowperwood, who, after years and years of profit, solely because of conditions of financial stress, fire, and panic, preferred to turn on his one-time associate from whose labors he had reaped so much profit, or Mr. Frank A. Cowperwood, the well-known banker and financier, who did his best to weather the storm alone, who fulfilled to the letter every agreement he ever had with the city, who has even until this hour been busy trying to remedy the unfair financial difficulties forced upon him by fire and panic, and who only yesterday made an offer to the city that, if he were allowed to continue in uninterrupted control of his affairs he would gladly repay as quickly as possible every dollar of his indebtedness (which is really not all his), including the five hundred thousand dollars under discussion between him and Mr. Stener and the city, and so prove by his works, not talk, that there was no basis for this unfair suspicion of his motives. As you perhaps surmise, the city has not chosen to accept his offer, and I shall try and tell you why later, gentlemen. For the present we will proceed with the testimony, and for the defense all I ask is that you give very close attention to all that is testified to here to-day. Listen very carefully to Mr. W. C. Davison when he is put on the stand. Listen equally carefully to Mr. Cowperwood when we call him to testify. Follow the other testimony closely, and then you will be able to judge for yourselves. See if you can distinguish a just motive for this prosecution. I can't. I am very much obliged to you for listening to me, gentlemen, so attentively."

He then put on Arthur Rivers, who had acted for Cowperwood on 'change as special agent during the panic, to testify to the large quantities of city loan he had purchased to stay the market; and then after him, Cowperwood's brothers, Edward and Joseph, who testified to instructions received from Rivers as to buying and selling city loan on that occasion—principally buying.

The next witness was President W. C. Davison of the Girard National Bank. He was a large man physically, not so round of body as full and broad. His shoulders and chest were ample. He had a big blond head, with an ample breadth of forehead, which was high and sane-looking. He had a thick, squat nose, which, however, was forceful, and thin, firm, even lips. There was the faintest touch of cynical humor in his hard blue eyes at times; but mostly he was friendly, alert, placid-looking, without seeming in the least sentimental or even kindly. His business, as one could see plainly, was to insist on hard financial facts, and one could see also how he would naturally be drawn to Frank Algernon Cowperwood without being mentally dominated or upset by him. As he took the chair very quietly, and yet one might say significantly, it was obvious that he felt that this sort of legal-financial palaver was above the average man and beneath the dignity of a true financier—in other words, a bother. The drowsy Sparkheaver holding up a Bible beside him for him to swear by might as well have been a block of wood. His oath was a personal matter with him. It was good business to tell the truth at times. His testimony was very direct and very simple.

He had known Mr. Frank Algernon Cowperwood for nearly ten years. He had done business with or through him nearly all of that time. He knew nothing of his personal relations with Mr. Stener, and did not know Mr. Stener personally. As for the particular check of sixty thousand dollars—yes, he had seen it before. It had come into the bank on October 10th along with other collateral to offset an overdraft on the part of Cowperwood & Co. It was placed to the credit of Cowperwood & Co. on the books of the bank, and the bank secured the cash through the clearing-house. No money was drawn out of the bank by Cowperwood & Co. after that to create an overdraft. The bank's account with Cowperwood was squared.

Nevertheless, Mr. Cowperwood might have drawn heavily, and nothing would have been thought of it. Mr. Davison did not know that Mr. Cowperwood was going to fail—did not suppose that he could, so quickly. He had frequently overdrawn his account with the bank; as a matter of fact, it was the regular course of his business to overdraw it. It kept his assets actively in use, which was the height of good business. His overdrafts were protected by collateral, however, and it was his custom to send bundles of collateral or checks, or both, which were variously distributed to keep things straight. Mr. Cowperwood's account was the largest and most active in the bank, Mr. Davison kindly volunteered. When Mr. Cowperwood had failed there had been over ninety thousand dollars' worth of certificates of city loan in the bank's possession which Mr Cowperwood had sent there as collateral. Shannon, on cross-examination, tried to find out for the sake of the effect on the jury, whether Mr. Davison was not for some ulterior motive especially favorable to Cowperwood. It was not possible for him to do that. Steger followed, and did his best to render the favorable points made by Mr. Davison in Cowperwood's behalf perfectly clear to the jury by having him repeat them. Shannon objected, of course, but it was of no use. Steger managed to make his point.

He now decided to have Cowperwood take the stand, and at the mention of his name in this connection the whole courtroom bristled.

Cowperwood came forward briskly and quickly. He was so calm, so jaunty, so defiant of life, and yet so courteous to it. These lawyers, this jury, this straw-and-water judge, these machinations of fate, did not basically disturb or humble or weaken him. He saw through the mental equipment of the jury at once. He wanted to assist his counsel in disturbing and confusing Shannon, but his reason told him that only an indestructible fabric of fact or seeming would do it. He believed in the financial rightness of the thing he had done. He was entitled to do it. Life was war—particularly financial life; and strategy was its keynote, its duty, its necessity. Why should he bother about petty, picayune minds which could not understand this? He went over his history for Steger and the jury, and put the sanest, most comfortable light on it that he could. He had not gone to Mr. Stener in the first place, he said—he had been called. He had not urged Mr. Stener to anything. He had merely shown him and his friends financial possibilities which they were only too eager to seize upon. And they had seized upon them. (It was not possible for Shannon to discover at this period how subtly he had organized his street-car companies so that he could have "shaken out" Stener and his friends without their being able to voice a single protest, so he talked of these things as opportunities which he had made for Stener and others. Shannon was not a financier, neither was Steger. They had to believe in a way, though they doubted it, partly— particularly Shannon.) He was not responsible for the custom prevailing in the office of the city treasurer, he said. He was a banker and broker.

The jury looked at him, and believed all except this matter of the sixty-thousand-dollar check. When it came to that he explained it all plausibly enough. When he had gone to see Stener those several last days, he had not fancied that he was really going to fail. He had asked Stener for some money, it is true—not so very much, all things considered—one hundred and fifty thousand dollars; but, as Stener should have testified, he (Cowperwood) was not disturbed in his manner. Stener had merely been one resource of his. He was satisfied at that time that he had many others. He had not used the forceful language or made the urgent appeal which Stener said he had, although he had pointed out to Stener that it was a mistake to become panic-stricken, also to withhold further credit. It was true that Stener was his easiest, his quickest resource, but not his only one. He thought, as a matter of fact, that his credit would be greatly extended by his principal money friends if necessary, and that he would have ample time to patch up his affairs and keep things going until the storm should blow over. He had told Stener of his extended purchase of city loan to stay the market on the first day of the panic, and of the fact that sixty thousand dollars was due him. Stener had made no objection. It was just possible that he was too mentally disturbed at the time to pay close attention. After that, to his, Cowperwood's, surprise, unexpected pressure on great financial houses from unexpected directions had caused them to be not willingly but unfortunately severe with him. This pressure, coming collectively the next day, had compelled him to close his doors, though he had not really expected to up to the last moment. His call for the sixty-thousand-dollar check at the time had been purely fortuitous. He needed the money, of course, but it was due him, and his clerks were all very busy. He merely asked for and took it personally to save time. Stener knew if it had been refused him he would have brought suit. The matter of depositing city loan certificates in the sinking-fund, when purchased for the city, was something to which he never gave any personal attention whatsoever. His bookkeeper, Mr. Stapley, attended to all that. He did not know, as a matter of fact, that they had not been deposited. (This was a barefaced lie. He did know.) As for the check being turned over to the Girard National Bank, that was fortuitous. It might just as well have been turned over to some other bank if the conditions had been different.

Thus on and on he went, answering all of Steger's and Shannon's searching questions with the most engaging frankness, and you could have sworn from the solemnity with which he took it all—the serious business attention—that he was the soul of so-called commercial honor. And to say truly, he did believe in the justice as well as the necessity and the importance of all that he had done and now described. He wanted the jury to see it as he saw it—put itself in his place and sympathize with him.

He was through finally, and the effect on the jury of his testimony and his personality was peculiar. Philip Moultrie, juror No. 1, decided that Cowperwood was lying. He could not see how it was possible that he could not know the day before that he was going to fail. He must have known, he thought. Anyhow, the whole series of transactions between him and Stener seemed deserving of some punishment, and all during this testimony he was thinking how, when he got in the jury-room, he would vote guilty. He even thought of some of the arguments he would use to convince the others that Cowperwood was guilty. Juror No. 2, on the contrary, Simon Glassberg, a clothier, thought he understood how it all came about, and decided to vote for acquittal. He did not think Cowperwood was innocent, but he did not think he deserved to be punished. Juror No. 3, Fletcher Norton, an architect, thought Cowperwood was guilty, but at the same time that he was too talented to be sent to prison. Juror No. 4, Charles Hillegan, an Irishman, a contractor, and a somewhat religious-minded person, thought Cowperwood was guilty and ought to be punished. Juror No. 5, Philip Lukash, a coal merchant, thought he was guilty. Juror No. 6, Benjamin Fraser, a mining expert, thought he was probably guilty, but he could not be sure. Uncertain what he would do, juror No. 7, J. J. Bridges, a broker in Third Street, small, practical, narrow, thought Cowperwood was shrewd and guilty and deserved to be punished. He would vote for his punishment. Juror No. 8, Guy E. Tripp, general manager of a small steamboat company, was uncertain. Juror No. 9, Joseph Tisdale, a retired glue manufacturer, thought Cowperwood was probably guilty as charged, but to Tisdale it was no crime. Cowperwood was entitled to do as he had done under the circumstances. Tisdale would vote for his acquittal. Juror No. 10, Richard Marsh, a young florist, was for Cowperwood in a sentimental way. He had, as a matter of fact, no real convictions. Juror No. 11, Richard

Webber, a grocer, small financially, but heavy physically, was for Cowperwood's conviction. He thought him guilty. Juror No. 12, Washington B. Thomas, a wholesale flour merchant, thought Cowperwood was guilty, but believed in a recommendation to mercy after pronouncing him so. Men ought to be reformed, was his slogan.

So they stood, and so Cowperwood left them, wondering whether any of his testimony had had a favorable effect.

CHAPTER XLIII

Since it is the privilege of the lawyer for the defense to address the jury first, Steger bowed politely to his colleague and came forward. Putting his hands on the jury-box rail, he began in a very quiet, modest, but impressive way:

"Gentlemen of the jury, my client, Mr. Frank Algernon Cowperwood, a well-known banker and financier of this city, doing business in Third Street, is charged by the State of Pennsylvania, represented by the district attorney of this district, with fraudulently transferring from the treasury of the city of Philadelphia to his own purse the sum of sixty thousand dollars, in the form of a check made out to his order, dated October 9, 1871, and by him received from one Albert Stires, the private secretary and head bookkeeper of the treasurer of this city, at the time in question. Now, gentlemen, what are the facts in this connection? You have heard the various witnesses and know the general outlines of the story. Take the testimony of George W. Stener, to begin with. He tells you that sometime back in the year 1866 he was greatly in need of some one, some banker or broker, who would tell him how to bring city loan, which was selling very low at the time, to par—who would not only tell him this, but proceed to demonstrate that his knowledge was accurate by doing it. Mr. Stener was an inexperienced man at the time in the matter of finance. Mr. Cowperwood was an active young man with an enviable record as a broker and a trader on 'change. He proceeded to demonstrate to Mr. Stener not only in theory, but in fact, how this thing of bringing city loan to par could be done. He made an arrangement at that time with Mr. Stener, the details of which you have heard from Mr. Stener himself, the result of which was that a large amount of city loan was turned over to Mr. Cowperwood by Mr. Stener for sale, and by adroit manipulation—methods of buying and selling which need not be gone into here, but which are perfectly sane and legitimate in the world in which Mr. Cowperwood operated, did bring that loan to par, and kept it there year after year as you have all heard here testified to.

"Now what is the bone of contention here, gentlemen, the significant fact which brings Mr. Stener into this court at this time charging his old-time agent and broker with larceny and embezzlement, and alleging that he has transferred to his own use without a shadow of return sixty thousand dollars of the money which belongs to the city treasury? What is it? Is it that Mr. Cowperwood secretly, with great stealth, as it were, at some time or other, unknown to Mr. Stener or to his assistants, entered the office of the treasurer and forcibly, and with criminal intent, carried away sixty thousand dollars' worth of the city's money? Not at all. The charge is, as you have heard the district attorney explain, that Mr. Cowperwood came in broad daylight at between four and five o'clock of the afternoon preceeding the day of his assignment; was closeted with Mr. Stener for a half or three-quarters of an hour; came out; explained to Mr. Albert Stires that he had recently bought sixty thousand dollars' worth of city loan for the city sinking-fund, for which he had not been paid; asked that the amount be credited on the city's books to him, and that he be given a check, which was his due, and walked out. Anything very remarkable about that, gentlemen? Anything very strange? Has it been testified here to-day that Mr. Cowperwood was not the agent of the city for the transaction of just such business as he said on that occasion that he had transacted? Did any one say here on the witness-stand that he had not bought city loan as he said he had?

"Why is it then that Mr. Stener charges Mr. Cowperwood with larcenously securing and feloniously disposing of a check for sixty thousand dollars for certificates which he had a right to buy, and which it has not been contested here that he did buy? The reason lies just here—listen—just here. At the time my client asked for the check and took it away with him and deposited it in his own bank to his own account, he failed, so the prosecution insists, to put the sixty thousand dollars' worth of certificates for which he had received the check, in the sinking-fund; and having failed to do that, and being compelled by the pressure of financial events the same day to suspend payment generally, he thereby, according to the prosecution and the anxious leaders of the Republican party in the city, became an embezzler, a thief, a this or that—anything you please so long as you find a substitute for George W. Stener and the indifferent leaders of the Republican party in the eyes of the people."

And here Mr. Steger proceeded boldly and defiantly to outline the entire political situation as it had manifested itself in connection with the Chicago fire, the subsequent panic and its political consequences, and to picture Cowperwood as the unjustly maligned agent, who before the fire was valuable and honorable enough to suit any of the political leaders of Philadelphia, but afterward, and when political defeat threatened, was picked upon as the most available scapegoat anywhere within reach.

And it took him a half hour to do that. And afterward but only after he had pointed to Stener as the true henchman and stalking horse, who had, in turn, been used by political forces above him to accomplish certain financial results, which they were not willing to have ascribed to themselves, he continued with:

"But now, in the light of all this, only see how ridiculous all this is! How silly! Frank A. Cowperwood had always been the agent of the city in these matters for years and years. He worked under certain rules which he and Mr. Stener had agreed upon in the first place, and which obviously came from others, who were above Mr. Stener, since they were hold-over customs and rules from administrations, which had been long before Mr. Stener ever appeared on the scene as city treasurer. One of them was that he could carry all transactions over until the first of the month following before he struck a balance. That is, he need not pay any money over for anything to the city treasurer, need not send him any checks or deposit any money or certificates in the sinking-fund until the first of the month because— now listen to this carefully, gentlemen; it is important—because his transactions in connection with city loan and everything else that he dealt in for the city treasurer were so numerous, so swift, so uncalculated beforehand, that he had to have a loose, easy system of this kind in order to do his work properly—to do business at all. Otherwise he could not very well have worked to the best advantage for Mr. Stener, or for any one else. It would have meant too much bookkeeping for him—too much for the city treasurer. Mr. Stener has testified to that in the early part of his story. Albert Stires has indicated that that was his understanding of it. Well, then what? Why, just this. Would any jury suppose, would any sane business man believe that if such were the case Mr. Cowperwood would be running personally with all these items of deposit, to the different banks or the sinking-fund or the city treasurer's office, or would be saying to his head bookkeeper, 'Here, Stapley, here is a check for sixty thousand dollars. See that the certificates of loan which this represents are put in the sinking-fund to-day'? And why not? What a ridiculous supposition any other supposition is! As a matter of course and as had always been the case, Mr. Cowperwood had a system. When the time came, this check and these certificates would be automatically taken care of. He handed his bookkeeper the check and forgot all about it. Would you imagine a banker with a vast business of this kind doing anything else?"

Mr. Steger paused for breath and inquiry, and then, having satisfied himself that his point had been sufficiently made, he continued:

"Of course the answer is that he knew he was going to fail. Well, Mr. Cowperwood's reply is that he didn't know anything of the sort. He has personally testified here that it was only at the last moment before it actually happened that he either thought or knew of such an occurrence. Why, then, this alleged refusal to let him have the check to which he was legally entitled? I think I know. I think I can give a reason if you will hear me out."

Steger shifted his position and came at the jury from another intellectual angle:

"It was simply because Mr. George W. Stener at that time, owing to a recent notable fire and a panic, imagined for some reason—perhaps because Mr. Cowperwood cautioned him not to become frightened over local developments generally—that Mr. Cowperwood was going to close his doors; and having considerable money on deposit with him at a low rate of interest, Mr. Stener decided that Mr. Cowperwood must not have any more money—not even the money that was actually due him for services rendered, and that had nothing whatsoever to do with the money loaned him by Mr. Stener at two and one-half per cent. Now isn't that a ridiculous situation? But it was because Mr. George W. Stener was filled with his own fears, based on a fire and a panic which had absolutely nothing to do with Mr. Cowperwood's solvency in the beginning that he decided not to let Frank A. Cowperwood have the money that was actually due him, because he, Stener, was criminally using the city's money to further his own private interests (through Mr. Cowperwood as a broker), and in danger of being exposed and possibly punished. Now where, I ask you, does the good sense of that decision come in? Is it apparent to you, gentlemen? Was Mr. Cowperwood still an agent for the city at the time he bought the loan certificates as here testified? He certainly was. If so, was he entitled to that money? Who is going to stand up here and deny it? Where is the question then, as to his right or his honesty in this matter? How does it come in here at all? I can tell you. It sprang solely from one source and from nowhere else, and that is the desire of the politicians of this city to find a scapegoat for the Republican party.

"Now you may think I am going rather far afield for an explanation of this very peculiar decision to prosecute Mr. Cowperwood, an agent of the city, for demanding and receiving what actually belonged to him. But I'm not. Consider the position of the Republican party at that time. Consider the fact that an exposure of the truth in regard to the details of a large defalcation in the city treasury would have a very unsatisfactory effect on the election about to be held. The Republican party had a new city treasurer to elect, a new district attorney. It had been in the habit of allowing its city treasurers the privilege of investing the funds in their possession at a low rate of interest for the benefit of themselves and their friends. Their salaries were small. They had to have some way of eking out a reasonable existence. Was Mr. George Stener responsible for this custom of loaning out the city money? Not at all. Was Mr. Cowperwood? Not at all. The custom had been in vogue long before either Mr. Cowperwood or Mr. Stener came on the scene. Why, then, this great hue and cry about it now? The entire uproar sprang solely from the fear of Mr. Stener at this juncture, the fear of the politicians at this juncture, of public exposure. No city treasurer had ever been exposed before. It was a new thing to face exposure, to face the risk of having the public's attention called to a rather nefarious practice of which Mr. Stener was taking advantage, that was all. A great fire and a panic were endangering the security and well-being of many a financial organization in the city—Mr. Cowperwood's among others. It meant many possible failures, and many possible failures meant one possible failure. If Frank A. Cowperwood failed, he would fail owing the city of Philadelphia five hundred thousand dollars, borrowed from the city treasurer at the very low rate of interest of two and one-half per cent. Anything very detrimental to Mr. Cowperwood in that? Had he gone to the city treasurer and asked to be loaned money at two and one-half per cent.? If he had, was there anything criminal in it from a business point of view? Isn't a man entitled to borrow money from any source he can at the lowest possible rate of interest? Did Mr. Stener have to loan it to Mr. Cowperwood if he did not want to? As a matter of fact didn't he testify here to-day that he personally had sent for Mr. Cowperwood in the first place? Why, then, in Heaven's name, this excited charge of larceny, larceny as bailee, embezzlement, embezzlement on a check, etc., etc.?

"Once more, gentlemen, listen. I'll tell you why. The men who stood behind Stener, and whose bidding he was doing, wanted to make a political scapegoat of some one—of Frank Algernon Cowperwood, if they couldn't get any one else. That's why. No other reason under God's blue sky, not one. Why, if Mr. Cowperwood needed more money just at that time to tide him over, it would have been good policy for them to have given it to him and hushed this matter up. It would have been illegal—though not any more illegal than anything else that has ever been done in this connection—but it would have been safer. Fear, gentlemen, fear, lack of courage, inability to meet a great crisis when a great crisis appears, was all that really prevented them from doing this. They were afraid to place confidence in a man who had never heretofore betrayed their trust and from whose loyalty and great financial ability they and the city had been reaping large profits. The reigning city treasurer of the time didn't have the courage to go on in the face of fire and panic and the rumors of possible failure, and stick by his illegal guns; and so he decided to draw in his horns as testified here to-day—to ask Mr. Cowperwood to return all or at least a big part of the five hundred thousand dollars he had loaned him, and which Cowperwood had been actually using for his, Stener's benefit, and to refuse him in addition the money that was actually due him for an authorized purchase of city loan. Was Cowperwood guilty as an agent in any of these transactions? Not in the least. Was there any suit pending to make him return the five hundred thousand dollars of city money involved in his present failure? Not at all. It was simply a case of wild, silly panic on the part of George W. Stener, and a strong desire on the part of the Republican party leaders, once they discovered what the situation was, to find some one outside of Stener, the party treasurer, upon whom they could blame the shortage in the treasury. You heard what Mr. Cowperwood testified to here in this case to-day—that he went to Mr. Stener to forfend against any possible action of this kind in the first place. And it was because of this very warning that Mr. Stener became wildly excited, lost his head, and wanted Mr. Cowperwood to return him all his money, all the five hundred thousand dollars he had loaned him at two and one-half per cent. Isn't that silly financial business at the best? Wasn't that a fine time to try to call a perfectly legal loan?

"But now to return to this particular check of sixty thousand dollars. When Mr. Cowperwood called that last afternoon before he failed, Mr. Stener testified that he told him that he couldn't have any more money, that it was impossible, and that then Mr. Cowperwood went out into his general office and without his knowledge or consent persuaded his chief clerk and secretary, Mr. Albert Stires, to give him a check for sixty thousand dollars, to which he was not entitled and on which he, Stener, would have stopped payment if he had known.

"What nonsense! Why didn't he know? The books were there, open to him. Mr. Stires told him the first thing the next morning. Mr. Cowperwood thought nothing of it, for he was entitled to it, and could collect it in any court of law having jurisdiction in such cases, failure or no failure. It is silly for Mr. Stener to say he would have stopped payment. Such a claim was probably an after-thought of the next morning after he had talked with his friends, the politicians, and was all a part, a trick, a trap, to provide the Republican party with a scapegoat at this time. Nothing more and nothing less; and you may be sure no one knew it better than the people who were most anxious to see Mr. Cowperwood convicted."

Steger paused and looked significantly at Shannon.

"Gentlemen of the jury [he finally concluded, quietly and earnestly], you are going to find, when you think it over in the jury-room this evening, that this charge of larceny and larceny as bailee, and embezzlement of a check for sixty thousand dollars, which are contained in this indictment, and which represent nothing more than the eager effort of the district

187

attorney to word this one act in such a way that it will look like a crime, represents nothing more than the excited imagination of a lot of political refugees who are anxious to protect their own skirts at the expense of Mr. Cowperwood, and who care for nothing—honor, fair play, or anything else, so long as they are let off scot-free. They don't want the Republicans of Pennsylvania to think too ill of the Republican party management and control in this city. They want to protect George W. Stener as much as possible and to make a political scapegoat of my client. It can't be done, and it won't be done. As honorable, intelligent men you won't permit it to be done. And I think with that thought I can safely leave you."

Steger suddenly turned from the jury-box and walked to his seat beside Cowperwood, while Shannon arose, calm, forceful, vigorous, much younger.

As between man and man, Shannon was not particularly opposed to the case Steger had made out for Cowperwood, nor was he opposed to Cowperwood's having made money as he did. As a matter of fact, Shannon actually thought that if he had been in Cowperwood's position he would have done exactly the same thing. However, he was the newly elected district attorney. He had a record to make; and, besides, the political powers who were above him were satisfied that Cowperwood ought to be convicted for the looks of the thing. Therefore he laid his hands firmly on the rail at first, looked the jurors steadily in the eyes for a time, and, having framed a few thoughts in his mind began:

"Now, gentlemen of the jury, it seems to me that if we all pay strict attention to what has transpired here to-day, we will have no difficulty in reaching a conclusion; and it will be a very satisfactory one, if we all try to interpret the facts correctly. This defendant, Mr. Cowperwood, comes into this court to-day charged, as I have stated to you before, with larceny, with larceny as bailee, with embezzlement, and with embezzlement of a specific check—namely, one dated October 9, 1871, drawn to the order of Frank A. Cowperwood & Company for the sum of sixty thousand dollars by the secretary of the city treasurer for the city treasurer, and by him signed, as he had a perfect right to sign it, and delivered to the said Frank A. Cowperwood, who claims that he was not only properly solvent at the time, but had previously purchased certificates of city loan to the value of sixty thousand dollars, and had at that time or would shortly thereafter, as was his custom, deposit them to the credit of the city in the city sinking-fund, and thus close what would ordinarily be an ordinary transaction—namely, that of Frank A. Cowperwood & Company as bankers and brokers for the city buying city loan for the city, depositing it in the sinking-fund, and being promptly and properly reimbursed. Now, gentlemen, what are the actual facts in this case? Was the said Frank A. Cowperwood & Company—there is no company, as you well know, as you have heard testified here to-day, only Frank A. Cowperwood—was the said Frank A. Cowperwood a fit person to receive the check at this time in the manner he received it— that is, was he authorized agent of the city at the time, or was he not? Was he solvent? Did he actually himself think he was going to fail, and was this sixty-thousand-dollar check a last thin straw which he was grabbing at to save his financial life regardless of what it involved legally, morally, or otherwise; or had he actually purchased certificates of city loan to the amount he said he had in the way he said he had, at the time he said he had, and was he merely collecting his honest due? Did he intend to deposit these certificates of loans in the city sinking-fund, as he said he would—as it was understood naturally and normally that he would—or did he not? Were his relations with the city treasurer as broker and agent the same as they had always been on the day that he secured this particular check for sixty thousand dollars, or were they not? Had they been terminated by a conversation fifteen minutes before or two days before or two weeks before—it makes no difference when, so long as they had been properly terminated—or had they not? A business man has a right to abrogate an agreement at any time where there is no specific form of contract and no fixed period of operation entered into—as you all must know. You must not forget that in considering the evidence in this case. Did George W. Stener, knowing or suspecting that Frank A. Cowperwood was in a tight place financially, unable to fulfill any longer properly and honestly the duties supposedly devolving on him by this agreement, terminate it then and there on October 9, 1871, before this check for sixty thousand dollars was given, or did he not? Did Mr. Frank A. Cowperwood then and there, knowing that he was no longer an agent of the city treasurer and the city, and knowing also that he was insolvent (having, as Mr. Stener contends, admitted to him that he was so), and having no intention of placing the certificates which he subsequently declared he had purchased in the sinking-fund, go out into Mr. Stener's general office, meet his secretary, tell him he had purchased sixty thousand dollars' worth of city loan, ask for the check, get it, put it in his pocket, walk off, and never make any return of any kind in any manner, shape, or form to the city, and then, subsequently, twenty-four hours later, fail, owing this and five hundred thousand dollars more to the city treasury, or did he not? What are the facts in this case? What have the witnesses testified to? What has George W. Stener testified to, Albert Stires, President Davison, Mr. Cowperwood himself? What are the interesting, subtle facts in this case, anyhow? Gentlemen, you have a very curious problem to decide."

He paused and gazed at the jury, adjusting his sleeves as he did so, and looking as though he knew for certain that he was on the trail of a slippery, elusive criminal who was in a fair way to foist himself upon an honorable and decent community and an honorable and innocent jury as an honest man.

Then he continued:

"Now, gentlemen, what are the facts? You can see for yourselves exactly how this whole situation has come about. You are sensible men. I don't need to tell you. Here are two men, one elected treasurer of the city of Philadelphia, sworn to guard the interests of the city and to manipulate its finances to the best advantage, and the other called in at a time of uncertain financial cogitation to assist in unraveling a possibly difficult financial problem; and then you have a case of a quiet, private financial understanding being reached, and of subsequent illegal dealings in which one man who is shrewder, wiser, more versed in the subtle ways of Third Street leads the other along over seemingly charming paths of fortunate investment into an accidental but none the less criminal mire of failure and exposure and public calumny and what not. And then they get to the place where the more vulnerable individual of the two—the man in the most dangerous position, the city treasurer of Philadelphia, no less—can no longer reasonably or, let us say, courageously, follow the other fellow; and then you have such a spectacle as was described here this afternoon in the witness-chair by Mr. Stener—that is, you have a vicious, greedy, unmerciful financial wolf standing over a cowering, unsophisticated commercial lamb, and saying to him, his white, shiny teeth glittering all the while, 'If you don't advance me the money I ask for—the three hundred thousand dollars I now demand—you will be a convict, your children will be thrown in the street, you and your wife and your family will be in poverty again, and there will be no one to turn a hand for you.' That is what Mr. Stener says Mr. Cowperwood said to him. I, for my part, haven't a doubt in the world that he did. Mr. Steger, in his very guarded references to his client, describes him as a nice, kind, gentlemanly agent, a broker merely on whom was practically forced the use of five hundred thousand dollars at two and a half per cent. when money was bringing from ten to fifteen per cent. in Third Street on call loans, and even more. But I for one don't choose to believe it. The thing that strikes me as strange in all of this is that if he was so nice and kind and gentle and remote—a mere hired and therefore subservient agent—how is it that he could have gone to Mr. Stener's office two or three days before the matter of this sixty-thousand-dollar check came up and say to him, as Mr. Stener testifies under oath that he did say to him, 'If you don't give me three hundred thousand dollars' worth more of the city's money at once, to-day, I will fail, and you will be a convict. You will go to the penitentiary.'? That's what he said to him. 'I will fail and you will be a convict. They can't touch me, but they will arrest you. I am an agent merely.' Does that sound like a nice, mild, innocent, well-mannered agent, a hired broker, or doesn't it sound like a hard, defiant, contemptuous master—a man in control and ready to rule and win by fair means or foul?

"Gentlemen, I hold no brief for George W. Stener. In my judgment he is as guilty as his smug co-partner in crime—if not more so—this oily financier who came smiling and in sheep's clothing, pointing out subtle ways by which the city's money could be made profitable for both; but when I hear Mr. Cowperwood described as I have just heard him described, as a nice, mild, innocent agent, my gorge rises. Why, gentlemen, if you want to get a right point of view on this whole proposition you will have to go back about ten or twelve years and see Mr. George W. Stener as he was then, a rather poverty-stricken beginner in politics, and before this very subtle and capable broker and agent came along and pointed out ways and means by which the city's money could be made profitable; George W. Stener wasn't very much of a personage then, and neither was Frank A. Cowperwood when he found Stener newly elected to the office of city treasurer. Can't you see him arriving at that time nice and fresh and young and well dressed, as shrewd as a fox, and saying: 'Come to me. Let me handle city loan. Loan me the city's money at two per cent. or less.' Can't you hear him suggesting this? Can't you see him?

"George W. Stener was a poor man, comparatively a very poor man, when he first became city treasurer. All he had was a small real-estate and insurance business which brought him in, say, twenty-five hundred dollars a year. He had a wife and four children to support, and he had never had the slightest taste of what for him might be called luxury or comfort. Then comes Mr. Cowperwood—at his request, to be sure, but on an errand which held no theory of evil gains in Mr. Stener's mind at the time—and proposes his grand scheme of manipulating all the city loan to their mutual advantage. Do you yourselves think, gentlemen, from what you have seen of George W. Stener here on the witness-stand, that it was he who proposed this plan of ill-gotten wealth to that gentleman over there?"

He pointed to Cowperwood.

"Does he look to you like a man who would be able to tell that gentleman anything about finance or this wonderful manipulation that followed? I ask you, does he look clever enough to suggest all the subtleties by which these two subsequently made so much money? Why, the statement of this man Cowperwood made to his creditors at the time of his failure here a few weeks ago showed that he considered himself to be worth over one million two hundred and fifty thousand dollars, and he is only a little over thirty-four years old to-day. How much was he worth at the time he first entered business relations with the ex-city treasurer? Have you any idea? I can tell. I had the matter looked up almost a month ago on my accession to office. Just a little over two hundred thousand dollars, gentlemen—just a little over two hundred thousand dollars. Here is an abstract from the files of Dun & Company for that year. Now you can see how rapidly our Caesar has grown in wealth since then. You can see how profitable these few short years have been to him. Was George W. Stener worth any such sum up to the time he was removed from his office and indicted for embezzlement? Was he? I have here a schedule of his liabilities and assets made out at the time. You can see it for yourselves, gentlemen. Just two hundred and twenty thousand dollars measured the sum of all his property three weeks ago; and it is an accurate estimate, as I have reason to know. Why was it, do you suppose, that Mr. Cowperwood grew so fast in wealth and Mr. Stener so slowly? They were partners in crime. Mr. Stener was loaning Mr. Cowperwood vast sums of the city's money at two per cent. when call-rates for money in Third Street were sometimes as high as sixteen and seventeen per cent. Don't you suppose that Mr. Cowperwood sitting there knew how to use this very cheaply come-by money to the very best advantage? Does he look to you as though he didn't? You have seen him on the witness-stand. You have heard him testify. Very suave, very straightforward-seeming, very innocent, doing everything as a favor to Mr. Stener and his friends, of course, and yet making a million in a little over six years and allowing Mr. Stener to make one hundred and sixty thousand dollars or less, for Mr. Stener had some little money at the time this partnership was entered into—a few thousand dollars."

Shannon now came to the vital transaction of October 9th, when Cowperwood called on Stener and secured the check for sixty thousand dollars from Albert Stires. His scorn for this (as he appeared to think) subtle and criminal transaction was unbounded. It was plain larceny, stealing, and Cowperwood knew it when he asked Stires for the check.

"Think of it! [Shannon exclaimed, turning and looking squarely at Cowperwood, who faced him quite calmly, undisturbed and unashamed.] Think of it! Think of the colossal nerve of the man—the Machiavellian subtlety of his brain. He knew he was going to fail. He knew after two days of financial work—after two days of struggle to offset the providential disaster which upset his nefarious schemes—that he had exhausted every possible resource save one, the city treasury, and that unless he could compel aid there he was going to fail. He already owed the city treasury five hundred thousand dollars. He had already used the city treasurer as a cat's-paw so much, had involved him so deeply, that the latter, because of the staggering size of the debt, was becoming frightened. Did that deter Mr. Cowperwood? Not at all."

He shook his finger ominously in Cowperwood's face, and the latter turned irritably away. "He is showing off for the benefit of his future," he whispered to Steger. "I wish you could tell the jury that."

"I wish I could," replied Steger, smiling scornfully, "but my hour is over."

"Why [continued Mr. Shannon, turning once more to the jury], think of the colossal, wolfish nerve that would permit a man to say to Albert Stires that he had just purchased sixty thousand dollars' worth additional of city loan, and that he would then and there take the check for it! Had he actually purchased this city loan as he said he had? Who can tell? Could any human being wind through all the mazes of the complicated bookkeeping system which he ran, and actually tell? The best answer to that is that if he did purchase the certificates he intended that it should make no difference to the city, for he made no effort to put the certificates in the sinking-fund, where they belonged. His counsel says, and he says, that he didn't have to until the first of the month, although the law says that he must do it at once, and he knew well enough that legally he was bound to do it. His counsel says, and he says, that he didn't know he was going to fail. Hence there was no need of worrying about it. I wonder if any of you gentlemen really believed that? Had he ever asked for a check like that so quick before in his life? In all the history of these nefarious transactions was there another incident like that? You know there wasn't. He had never before, on any occasion, asked personally for a check for anything in this office, and yet on this occasion he did it. Why? Why should he ask for it this time? A few hours more, according to his own statement, wouldn't have made any difference one way or the other, would it? He could have sent a boy for it, as usual. That was the way it had always been done before. Why anything different now? I'll tell you why! [Shannon suddenly shouted, varying his voice tremendously.] I'll tell you why! He knew that he was a ruined man! He knew that his last semi-legitimate avenue of escape—the favor of George W. Stener—had been closed to him! He knew that honestly, by open agreement, he could not extract another single dollar from the treasury of the city of Philadelphia. He knew that if he left the office without this check and sent a boy for it, the aroused city treasurer would have time to inform his clerks, and that then no further money could be obtained. That's why! That's why, gentlemen, if you really want to know.

"Now, gentlemen of the jury, I am about done with my arraignment of this fine, honorable, virtuous citizen whom the counsel for the defense, Mr. Steger, tells you you cannot possibly convict without doing a great injustice. All I have to say is that you look to me like sane, intelligent men—just the sort of men that I meet everywhere in the ordinary walks of life, doing an honorable American business in an honorable American way. Now, gentlemen of the jury [he was very soft-spoken now], all I have to say is that if, after all you have heard and seen here to-day, you still think that Mr. Frank A. Cowperwood is an honest, honorable man—that he didn't steal, willfully and knowingly, sixty thousand dollars from the Philadelphia city treasury; that he had actually bought the certificates he said he had, and had intended to put them in the sinking-fund, as he said he did, then don't you dare to do anything except turn him loose, and that speedily, so that he can go on back to-day into Third Street, and start to straighten out his much-entangled financial affairs. It is the only thing for honest, conscientious men to do—to turn him instantly loose into the heart of this community, so that some of the rank injustice that my opponent, Mr. Steger, alleges has been done him will be a little made up to him. You owe him, if that is the way you feel, a prompt acknowledgment of his innocence. Don't worry about George W. Stener. His guilt is established by his own confession. He admits he is guilty. He will be sentenced without trial later on. But this man—he says he is an honest, honorable man. He says he didn't think he was going to fail. He says he used all that threatening, compelling, terrifying language, not because he was in danger of failing, but because he didn't want the bother of looking further for aid. What do you think? Do you really think that he had purchased sixty thousand dollars more of certificates for the sinking-fund, and that he was entitled to the money? If so, why didn't he put them in the sinking-fund? They're not there now, and the sixty thousand dollars is gone. Who got it? The Girard National Bank, where he was overdrawn to the extent of one hundred thousand dollars! Did it get it and forty thousand dollars more in other checks and certificates? Certainly. Why? Do you suppose the Girard National Bank might be in any way grateful for this last little favor before he closed his doors? Do you think that President Davison, whom you saw here testifying so kindly in this case feels at all friendly, and that that may possibly—I don't say that it does—explain his very kindly interpretation of Mr. Cowperwood's condition? It might be. You can think as well along that line as I can. Anyhow, gentlemen, President Davison says Mr. Cowperwood is an honorable, honest man, and so does his counsel, Mr. Steger. You have heard the testimony. Now you think it over. If you want to turn him loose—turn him loose. [He waved his hand wearily.] You're the judges. I wouldn't; but then I am merely a hard-working lawyer—one person, one opinion. You may think differently—that's your business. [He waved his hand suggestively, almost contemptuously.] However, I'm through, and I thank you for your courtesy. Gentlemen, the decision rests with you."

He turned away grandly, and the jury stirred—so did the idle spectators in the court. Judge Payderson sighed a sigh of relief. It was now quite dark, and the flaring gas forms in the court were all brightly lighted. Outside one could see that it was snowing. The judge stirred among his papers wearily, and turning to the jurors solemnly, began his customary explanation of the law, after which they filed out to the jury-room.

Cowperwood turned to his father who now came over across the fast-emptying court, and said:

"Well, we'll know now in a little while."

"Yes," replied Cowperwood, Sr., a little wearily. "I hope it comes out right. I saw Butler back there a little while ago."

"Did you?" queried Cowperwood, to whom this had a peculiar interest.

"Yes," replied his father. "He's just gone."

So, Cowperwood thought, Butler was curious enough as to his fate to want to come here and watch him tried. Shannon was his tool. Judge Payderson was his emissary, in a way. He, Cowperwood, might defeat him in the matter of his daughter, but it was not so easy to defeat him here unless the jury should happen to take a sympathetic attitude. They might convict him, and then Butler's Judge Payderson would have the privilege of sentencing him—giving him the maximum sentence. That would not be so nice—five years! He cooled a little as he thought of it, but there was no use worrying about what had not yet happened. Steger came forward and told him that his bail was now ended—had been the moment the jury left the room—and that he was at this moment actually in the care of the sheriff, of whom he knew—Sheriff Adlai Jaspers. Unless he were acquitted by the jury, Steger added, he would have to remain in the sheriff's care until an application for a certificate of reasonable doubt could be made and acted upon.

"It would take all of five days, Frank," Steger said, "but Jaspers isn't a bad sort. He'd be reasonable. Of course if we're lucky you won't have to visit him. You will have to go with this bailiff now, though. Then if things come out right we'll go home. Say, I'd like to win this case," he said. "I'd like to give them the laugh and see you do it. I consider you've been pretty badly treated, and I think I made that perfectly clear. I can reverse this verdict on a dozen grounds if they happen to decide against you."

He and Cowperwood and the latter's father now stalked off with the sheriff's subordinate—a small man by the name of "Eddie" Zanders, who had approached to take charge. They entered a small room called the pen at the back of the court, where all those on trial whose liberty had been forfeited by the jury's leaving the room had to wait pending its return. It was a dreary, high-ceiled, four-square place, with a window looking out into Chestnut Street, and a second door leading off into somewhere—one had no idea where. It was dingy, with a worn wooden floor, some heavy, plain, wooden benches lining the four sides, no pictures or ornaments of any kind. A single two-arm gas-pipe descended from the center of the ceiling. It was permeated by a peculiarly stale and pungent odor, obviously redolent of all the flotsam and jetsam of life—criminal and innocent—that had stood or sat in here from time to time, waiting patiently to learn what a deliberating fate held in store.

Cowperwood was, of course, disgusted; but he was too self-reliant and capable to show it. All his life he had been immaculate, almost fastidious in his care of himself. Here he was coming, perforce, in contact with a form of life which jarred upon him greatly. Steger, who was beside him, made some comforting, explanatory, apologetic remarks.

"Not as nice as it might be," he said, "but you won't mind waiting a little while. The jury won't be long, I fancy."

"That may not help me," he replied, walking to the window. Afterward he added: "What must be, must be."

His father winced. Suppose Frank was on the verge of a long prison term, which meant an atmosphere like this? Heavens! For a moment, he trembled, then for the first time in years he made a silent prayer.

CHAPTER XLIV

Meanwhile the great argument had been begun in the jury-room, and all the points that had been meditatively speculated upon in the jury-box were now being openly discussed.

It is amazingly interesting to see how a jury will waver and speculate in a case like this— how curious and uncertain is the process by which it makes up its so-called mind. So-called truth is a nebulous thing at best; facts are capable of such curious inversion and interpretation, honest and otherwise. The jury had a strongly complicated problem before it, and it went over it and over it.

Juries reach not so much definite conclusions as verdicts, in a curious fashion and for curious reasons. Very often a jury will have concluded little so far as its individual members are concerned and yet it will have reached a verdict. The matter of time, as all lawyers know, plays a part in this. Juries, speaking of the members collectively and frequently individually, object to the amount of time it takes to decide a case. They do not enjoy sitting and deliberating over a problem unless it is tremendously fascinating. The ramifications or the mystery of a syllogism can become a weariness and a bore. The jury-room itself may and frequently does become a dull agony.

On the other hand, no jury contemplates a disagreement with any degree of satisfaction. There is something so inherently constructive in the human mind that to leave a problem unsolved is plain misery. It haunts the average individual like any other important task left unfinished. Men in a jury-room, like those scientifically demonstrated atoms of a crystal which scientists and philosophers love to speculate upon, like finally to arrange themselves into an orderly and artistic whole, to present a compact, intellectual front, to be whatever they have set out to be, properly and rightly—a compact, sensible jury. One sees this same instinct magnificently displayed in every other phase of nature—in the drifting of sea-wood to the Sargasso Sea, in the geometric interrelation of air-bubbles on the surface of still water, in the marvelous unreasoned architecture of so many insects and atomic forms which make up the substance and the texture of this world. It would seem as though the physical substance of life—this apparition of form which the eye detects and calls real were shot through with some vast subtlety that loves order, that is order. The atoms of our so-called being, in spite of our so-called reason—the dreams of a mood—know where to go and what to do. They represent an order, a wisdom, a willing that is not of us. They build orderly in spite of us. So the subconscious spirit of a jury. At the same time, one does not forget the strange hypnotic effect of one personality on another, the varying effects of varying types on each other, until a solution—to use the word in its purely chemical sense—is reached. In a jury-room the thought or determination of one or two or three men, if it be definite enough, is likely to pervade the whole room and conquer the reason or the opposition of the majority. One man "standing out" for the definite thought that is in him is apt to become either the triumphant leader of a pliant mass or the brutally battered target of a flaming, concentrated intellectual fire. Men despise dull opposition that is without reason. In a jury-room, of all places, a man is expected to give a reason for the faith that is in him—if one is demanded. It will not do to say, "I cannot agree." Jurors have been known to fight. Bitter antagonisms lasting for years have been generated in these close quarters. Recalcitrant jurors have been hounded commercially in their local spheres for their unreasoned oppositions or conclusions.

After reaching the conclusion that Cowperwood unquestionably deserved some punishment, there was wrangling as to whether the verdict should be guilty on all four counts, as charged in the indictment. Since they did not understand how to differentiate between the various charges very well, they decided it should be on all four, and a recommendation to mercy added. Afterward this last was eliminated, however; either he was guilty or he was not. The judge could see as well as they could all the extenuating circumstances—perhaps better. Why tie his hands? As a rule no attention was paid to such recommendations, anyhow, and it only made the jury look wabbly.

So, finally, at ten minutes after twelve that night, they were ready to return a verdict; and Judge Payderson, who, because of his interest in the case and the fact that he lived not so far away, had decided to wait up this long, was recalled. Steger and Cowperwood were sent for. The court-room was fully lighted. The bailiff, the clerk, and the stenographer were there. The jury filed in, and Cowperwood, with Steger at his right, took his position at the gate which gave into the railed space where prisoners always stand to hear the verdict and listen to any commentary of the judge. He was accompanied by his father, who was very nervous.

For the first time in his life he felt as though he were walking in his sleep. Was this the real Frank Cowperwood of two months before—so wealthy, so progressive, so sure? Was this only December 5th or 6th now (it was after midnight)? Why was it the jury had deliberated so long? What did it mean? Here they were now, standing and gazing solemnly before them; and here now was Judge Payderson, mounting the steps of his rostrum, his frizzled hair standing out in a strange, attractive way, his familiar bailiff rapping for order. He did not look at Cowperwood—it would not be courteous—but at the jury, who gazed at him in return. At the words of the clerk, "Gentlemen of the jury, have you agreed upon a verdict?" the foreman spoke up, "We have."

"Do you find the defendant guilty or not guilty?"

"We find the defendant guilty as charged in the indictment."

How had they come to do this? Because he had taken a check for sixty thousand dollars which did not belong to him? But in reality it did. Good Lord, what was sixty thousand dollars in the sum total of all the money that had passed back and forth between him and George W. Stener? Nothing, nothing! A mere bagatelle in its way; and yet here it had risen up, this miserable, insignificant check, and become a mountain of opposition, a stone wall, a prison-wall barring his further progress. It was astonishing. He looked around him at the court-room. How large and bare and cold it was! Still he was Frank A. Cowperwood. Why should he let such queer thoughts disturb him? His fight for freedom and privilege and restitution was not over yet. Good heavens! It had only begun. In five days he would be out again on bail. Steger would take an appeal. He would be out, and he would have two long months in which to make an additional fight. He was not down yet. He would win his liberty. This jury was all wrong. A higher court would say so. It would reverse their verdict, and he knew it. He turned to Steger, where the latter was having the clerk poll the jury, in the hope that some one juror had been over-persuaded, made to vote against his will.

"Is that your verdict?" he heard the clerk ask of Philip Moultrie, juror No. 1.

"It is," replied that worthy, solemnly.

"Is that your verdict?" The clerk was pointing to Simon Glassberg.

"Yes, sir."

"Is that your verdict?" He pointed to Fletcher Norton.

"Yes."

So it went through the whole jury. All the men answered firmly and clearly, though Steger thought it might barely be possible that one would have changed his mind. The judge thanked them and told them that in view of their long services this night, they were dismissed for the term. The only thing remaining to be done now was for Steger to persuade Judge Payderson to grant a stay of sentence pending the hearing of a motion by the State Supreme Court for a new trial.

The Judge looked at Cowperwood very curiously as Steger made this request in proper form, and owing to the importance of the case and the feeling he had that the Supreme Court might very readily grant a certificate of reasonable doubt in this case, he agreed. There was nothing left, therefore, but for Cowperwood to return at this late hour with the deputy sheriff to the county jail, where he must now remain for five days at least—possibly longer.

The jail in question, which was known locally as Moyamensing Prison, was located at Tenth and Reed Streets, and from an architectural and artistic point of view was not actually displeasing to the eye. It consisted of a central portion—prison, residence for the sheriff or what you will—three stories high, with a battlemented cornice and a round battlemented tower about one-third as high as the central portion itself, and two wings, each two stories high, with battlemented turrets at either end, giving it a highly castellated and consequently, from the American point of view, a very prison-like appearance. The facade of the prison, which was not more than thirty-five feet high for the central portion, nor more than twenty-five feet for the wings, was set back at least a hundred feet from the street, and was continued at either end, from the wings to the end of the street block, by a stone wall all of twenty feet high. The structure was not severely prison-like, for the central portion was pierced by rather large, unbarred apertures hung on the two upper stories with curtains, and giving the whole front a rather pleasant and residential air. The wing to the right, as one stood looking in from the street, was the section known as the county jail proper, and was devoted to the care of prisoners serving short-term sentences on some judicial order. The wing to the left was devoted exclusively to the care and control of untried prisoners. The whole building was built of a smooth, light-colored stone, which on a snowy night like this, with the few lamps that were used in it glowing feebly in the dark, presented an eery, fantastic, almost supernatural appearance.

It was a rough and blowy night when Cowperwood started for this institution under duress. The wind was driving the snow before it in curious, interesting whirls. Eddie Zanders, the sheriff's deputy on guard at the court of Quarter Sessions, accompanied him and his father and Steger. Zanders was a little man, dark, with a short, stubby mustache, and a shrewd though not highly intelligent eye. He was anxious first to uphold his dignity as a deputy sheriff, which was a very important position in his estimation, and next to turn an honest penny if he could. He knew little save the details of his small world, which consisted of accompanying prisoners to and from the courts and the jails, and seeing that they did not get away. He was not unfriendly to a particular type of prisoner—the well-to-do or moderately prosperous—for he had long since learned that it paid to be so. To-night he offered a few sociable suggestions—viz., that it was rather rough, that the jail was not so far but that they could walk, and that Sheriff Jaspers would, in all likelihood, be around or could be aroused. Cowperwood scarcely heard. He was thinking of his mother and his wife and of Aileen.

When the jail was reached he was led to the central portion, as it was here that the sheriff, Adlai Jaspers, had his private office. Jaspers had recently been elected to office, and was inclined to conform to all outward appearances, in so far as the proper conduct of his office was concerned, without in reality inwardly conforming. Thus it was generally known among the politicians that one way he had of fattening his rather lean salary was to rent private rooms and grant special privileges to prisoners who had the money to pay for the same. Other sheriffs had done it before him. In fact, when Jaspers was inducted into office, several prisoners were already enjoying these privileges, and it was not a part of his scheme of things to disturb them. The rooms that he let to the "right parties," as he invariably put it, were in the central portion of the jail, where were his own private living quarters. They were unbarred, and not at all cell-like. There was no particular danger of escape, for a guard stood always at his private door instructed "to keep an eye" on the general movements of all the inmates. A prisoner so accommodated was in many respects quite a free person. His meals were served to him in his room, if he wished. He could read or play cards, or receive guests; and if he had any favorite musical instrument, that was not denied him. There was just one rule that had to be complied with. If he were a public character, and any newspaper men called, he had to be brought down-stairs into the private interviewing room in order that they might not know that he was not confined in a cell like any other prisoner.

Nearly all of these facts had been brought to Cowperwood's attention beforehand by Steger; but for all that, when he crossed the threshold of the jail a peculiar sensation of strangeness and defeat came over him. He and his party were conducted to a little office to the left of the entrance, where were only a desk and a chair, dimly lighted by a low-burning gas-jet. Sheriff Jaspers, rotund and ruddy, met them, greeting them in quite a friendly way. Zanders was dismissed, and went briskly about his affairs.

"A bad night, isn't it?" observed Jaspers, turning up the gas and preparing to go through the routine of registering his prisoner. Steger came over and held a short, private conversation with him in his corner, over his desk which resulted presently in the sheriff's face lighting up.

"Oh, certainly, certainly! That's all right, Mr. Steger, to be sure! Why, certainly!"

Cowperwood, eyeing the fat sheriff from his position, understood what it was all about. He had regained completely his critical attitude, his cool, intellectual poise. So this was the jail, and this was the fat mediocrity of a sheriff who was to take care of him. Very good. He would make the best of it. He wondered whether he was to be searched—prisoners usually were—but he soon discovered that he was not to be.

"That's all right, Mr. Cowperwood," said Jaspers, getting up. "I guess I can make you comfortable, after a fashion. We're not running a hotel here, as you know"—he chuckled to himself—"but I guess I can make you comfortable. John," he called to a sleepy factotum, who appeared from another room, rubbing his eyes, "is the key to Number Six down here?"

"Yes, sir."

"Let me have it."

John disappeared and returned, while Steger explained to Cowperwood that anything he wanted in the way of clothing, etc., could be brought in. Steger himself would stop round next morning and confer with him, as would any of the members of Cowperwood's family whom he wished to see. Cowperwood immediately explained to his father his desire for as little of this as possible. Joseph or Edward might come in the morning and bring a grip full of underwear, etc.; but as for the others, let them wait until he got out or had to remain permanently. He did think of writing Aileen, cautioning her to do nothing; but the sheriff now beckoned, and he quietly followed. Accompanied by his father and Steger, he ascended to his new room.

It was a simple, white-walled chamber fifteen by twenty feet in size, rather high-ceiled, supplied with a high-backed, yellow wooden bed, a yellow bureau, a small imitation-cherry table, three very ordinary cane-seated chairs with carved hickory-rod backs, cherry-stained also, and a wash-stand of yellow-stained wood to match the bed, containing a washbasin, a pitcher, a soap-dish, uncovered, and a small, cheap, pink-flowered tooth and shaving brush mug, which did not match the other ware and which probably cost ten cents. The value of this room to Sheriff Jaspers was what he could get for it in cases like this—twenty-five to thirty-five dollars a week. Cowperwood would pay thirty-five.

Cowperwood walked briskly to the window, which gave out on the lawn in front, now embedded in snow, and said he thought this was all right. Both his father and Steger were willing and anxious to confer with him for hours, if he wished; but there was nothing to say. He did not wish to talk.

"Let Ed bring in some fresh linen in the morning and a couple of suits of clothes, and I will be all right. George can get my things together." He was referring to a family servant who acted as valet and in other capacities. "Tell Lillian not to worry. I'm all right. I'd rather she would not come here so long as I'm going to be out in five days. If I'm not, it will be time enough then. Kiss the kids for me." And he smiled good-naturedly.

After his unfulfilled predictions in regard to the result of this preliminary trial Steger was almost afraid to suggest confidently what the State Supreme Court would or would not do; but he had to say something.

"I don't think you need worry about what the outcome of my appeal will be, Frank. I'll get a certificate of reasonable doubt, and that's as good as a stay of two months, perhaps longer. I don't suppose the bail will be more than thirty thousand dollars at the outside. You'll be out again in five or six days, whatever happens."

Cowperwood said that he hoped so, and suggested that they drop matters for the night. After a few fruitless parleys his father and Steger finally said good night, leaving him to his own private reflections. He was tired, however, and throwing off his clothes, tucked himself in his mediocre bed, and was soon fast asleep.

CHAPTER XLV

Say what one will about prison life in general, modify it ever so much by special chambers, obsequious turnkeys, a general tendency to make one as comfortable as possible, a jail is a jail, and there is no getting away from that. Cowperwood, in a room which was not in any way inferior to that of the ordinary boarding-house, was nevertheless conscious of the character of that section of this real prison which was not yet his portion. He knew that there were cells there, probably greasy and smelly and vermin-infested, and that they were enclosed by heavy iron bars, which would have as readily clanked on him as on those who were now therein incarcerated if he had not had the price to pay for something better. So much for the alleged equality of man, he thought, which gave to one man, even within the grim confines of the machinery of justice, such personal liberty as he himself was now enjoying, and to another, because he chanced to lack wit or presence or friends or wealth, denied the more comfortable things which money would buy.

The morning after the trial, on waking, he stirred curiously, and then it suddenly came to him that he was no longer in the free and comfortable atmosphere of his own bedroom, but in a jail-cell, or rather its very comfortable substitute, a sheriff's rented bedroom. He got up and looked out the window. The ground outside and Passayunk Avenue were white with snow. Some wagons were silently lumbering by. A few Philadelphians were visible here and there, going to and fro on morning errands. He began to think at once what he must do, how he must act to carry on his business, to rehabilitate himself; and as he did so he dressed and pulled the bell-cord, which had been indicated to him, and which would bring him an attendant who would build him a fire and later bring him something to eat. A shabby prison attendant in a blue uniform, conscious of Cowperwood's superiority because of the room he occupied, laid wood and coal in the grate and started a fire, and later brought him his breakfast, which was anything but prison fare, though poor enough at that.

After that he was compelled to wait in patience several hours, in spite of the sheriff's assumption of solicitous interest, before his brother Edward was admitted with his clothes. An attendant, for a consideration, brought him the morning papers, and these, except for the financial news, he read indifferently. Late in the afternoon Steger arrived, saying he had been busy having certain proceedings postponed, but that he had arranged with the sheriff for Cowperwood to be permitted to see such of those as had important business with him.

By this time, Cowperwood had written Aileen under no circumstances to try to see him, as he would be out by the tenth, and that either that day, or shortly after, they would meet. As he knew, she wanted greatly to see him, but he had reason to believe she was under surveillance by detectives employed by her father. This was not true, but it was preying on her fancy, and combined with some derogatory remarks dropped by Owen and Callum at the dinner table recently, had proved almost too much for her fiery disposition. But, because of Cowperwood's letter reaching her at the Calligans', she made no move until she read on the morning of the tenth that Cowperwood's plea for a certificate of reasonable doubt had been granted, and that he would once more, for the time being at least, be a free man. This gave her courage to do what she had long wanted to do, and that was to teach her father that she could get along without him and that he could not make her do anything she did not want to do. She still had the two hundred dollars Cowperwood had given her and some additional cash of her own—perhaps three hundred and fifty dollars in all. This she thought would be sufficient to see her to the end of her adventure, or at least until she could make some other arrangement for her personal well-being. From what she knew of the feeling of her family for her, she felt that the agony would all be on their side, not hers. Perhaps when her father saw how determined she was he would decide to let her alone and make peace with her. She was determined to try it, anyhow, and immediately sent word to Cowperwood that she was going to the Calligans and would welcome him to freedom.

In a way, Cowperwood was rather gratified by Aileen's message, for he felt that his present plight, bitter as it was, was largely due to Butler's opposition and he felt no compunction in striking him through his daughter. His former feeling as to the wisdom of not enraging Butler had proved rather futile, he thought, and since the old man could not be placated it might be just as well to have Aileen demonstrate to him that she was not without resources of her own and could live without him. She might force him to change his attitude toward her and possibly even to modify some of his political machinations against him, Cowperwood. Any port in a storm—and besides, he had now really nothing to lose, and instinct told him that her move was likely to prove more favorable than otherwise—so he did nothing to prevent it.

She took her jewels, some underwear, a couple of dresses which she thought would be serviceable, and a few other things, and packed them in the most capacious portmanteau she had. Shoes and stockings came into consideration, and, despite her efforts, she found that she could not get in all that she wished. Her nicest hat, which she was determined to take, had to be carried outside. She made a separate bundle of it, which was not pleasant to contemplate. Still she decided to take it. She rummaged in a little drawer where she kept her money and jewels, and found the three hundred and fifty dollars and put it in her purse. It wasn't much, as Aileen could herself see, but Cowperwood would help her. If he did not arrange to take care of her, and her father would not relent, she would have to get something to do. Little she knew of the steely face the world presents to those who have not been practically trained and are not economically efficient. She did not understand the bitter reaches of life at all. She waited, humming for effect, until she heard her father go downstairs to dinner on this tenth day of December, then leaned over the upper balustrade to make sure that Owen, Callum, Norah, and her mother were at the table, and that Katy, the housemaid, was not anywhere in sight. Then she slipped into her father's den, and, taking a note from inside her dress, laid it on his desk, and went out. It was addressed to "Father," and read:

Dear Father,—I just cannot do what you want me to. I have
made up my mind that I love Mr. Cowperwood too much, so I am
going away. Don't look for me with him. You won't find me
where you think. I am not going to him; I will not be
there. I am going to try to get along by myself for a
while, until he wants me and can marry me. I'm terribly
sorry; but I just can't do what you want. I can't ever
forgive you for the way you acted to me. Tell mama and Norah
and the boys good-by for me.

Aileen

To insure its discovery, she picked up Butler's heavy-rimmed spectacles which he employed always when reading, and laid them on it. For a moment she felt very strange, somewhat like a thief—a new sensation for her. She even felt a momentary sense of ingratitude coupled with pain. Perhaps she was doing wrong. Her father had been very good to her. Her mother would feel so very bad. Norah would be sorry, and Callum and Owen. Still, they did not understand her any more. She was resentful of her father's attitude. He might have seen what the point was; but no, he was too old, too hidebound in religion and conventional ideas—he never would. He might never let her come back. Very well, she would get along somehow. She would show him. She might get a place as a school-teacher, and live with the Calligans a long while, if necessary, or teach music.

She stole downstairs and out into the vestibule, opening the outer door and looking out into the street. The lamps were already flaring in the dark, and a cool wind was blowing. Her portmanteau was heavy, but she was quite strong. She walked briskly to the corner, which was some fifty feet away, and turned south, walking rather nervously and irritably, for this was a new experience for her, and it all seemed so undignified, so unlike anything she was accustomed to doing. She put her bag down on a street corner, finally, to rest. A boy whistling in the distance attracted her attention, and as he drew near she called to him: "Boy! Oh, boy!"

He came over, looking at her curiously.

"Do you want to earn some money?"

"Yes, ma'am," he replied politely, adjusting a frowsy cap over one ear.

"Carry this bag for me," said Aileen, and he picked it up and marched off.

In due time she arrived at the Calligans', and amid much excitement was installed in the bosom of her new home. She took her situation with much nonchalance, once she was properly placed, distributing her toilet articles and those of personal wear with quiet care. The fact that she was no longer to have the services of Kathleen, the maid who had served her and her mother and Norah jointly, was odd, though not trying. She scarcely felt that she had parted from these luxuries permanently, and so made herself comfortable.

Mamie Calligan and her mother were adoring slaveys, so she was not entirely out of the atmosphere which she craved and to which she was accustomed.

CHAPTER XLVI

Meanwhile, in the Butler home the family was assembling for dinner. Mrs. Butler was sitting in rotund complacency at the foot of the table, her gray hair combed straight back from her round, shiny forehead. She had on a dark-gray silk dress, trimmed with gray-and-white striped ribbon. It suited her florid temperament admirably. Aileen had dictated her mother's choice, and had seen that it had been properly made. Norah was refreshingly youthful in a pale-green dress, with red-velvet cuffs and collar. She looked young, slender, gay. Her eyes, complexion and hair were fresh and healthy. She was trifling with a string of coral beads which her mother had just given her.

"Oh, look, Callum," she said to her brother opposite her, who was drumming idly on the table with his knife and fork. "Aren't they lovely? Mama gave them to me."

"Mama does more for you than I would. You know what you'd get from me, don't you?"

"What?"

He looked at her teasingly. For answer Norah made a face at him. Just then Owen came in and took his place at the table. Mrs. Butler saw Norah's grimace.

"Well, that'll win no love from your brother, ye can depend on that," she commented.

"Lord, what a day!" observed Owen, wearily, unfolding his napkin. "I've had my fill of work for once."

"What's the trouble?" queried his mother, feelingly.

"No real trouble, mother," he replied. "Just everything—ducks and drakes, that's all."

"Well, ye must ate a good, hearty meal now, and that'll refresh ye," observed his mother, genially and feelingly. "Thompson"—she was referring to the family grocer—"brought us the last of his beans. You must have some of those."

"Sure, beans'll fix it, whatever it is, Owen," joked Callum. "Mother's got the answer."

"They're fine, I'd have ye know," replied Mrs. Butler, quite unconscious of the joke.

"No doubt of it, mother," replied Callum. "Real brain-food. Let's feed some to Norah."

"You'd better eat some yourself, smarty. My, but you're gay! I suppose you're going out to see somebody. That's why."

"Right you are, Norah. Smart girl, you. Five or six. Ten to fifteen minutes each. I'd call on you if you were nicer."

"You would if you got the chance," mocked Norah. "I'd have you know I wouldn't let you. I'd feel very bad if I couldn't get somebody better than you."

"As good as, you mean," corrected Callum.

"Children, children!" interpolated Mrs. Butler, calmly, looking about for old John, the servant. "You'll be losin' your tempers in a minute. Hush now. Here comes your father. Where's Aileen?"

Butler walked heavily in and took his seat.

John, the servant, appeared bearing a platter of beans among other things, and Mrs. Butler asked him to send some one to call Aileen.

"It's gettin' colder, I'm thinkin'," said Butler, by way of conversation, and eyeing Aileen's empty chair. She would come soon now—his heavy problem. He had been very tactful these last two months—avoiding any reference to Cowperwood in so far as he could help in her presence.

"It's colder," remarked Owen, "much colder. We'll soon see real winter now."

Old John began to offer the various dishes in order; but when all had been served Aileen had not yet come.

"See where Aileen is, John," observed Mrs. Butler, interestedly. "The meal will be gettin' cold."

Old John returned with the news that Aileen was not in her room.

"Sure she must be somewhere," commented Mrs. Butler, only slightly perplexed. "She'll be comin', though, never mind, if she wants to. She knows it's meal-time."

The conversation drifted from a new water-works that was being planned to the new city hall, then nearing completion; Cowperwood's financial and social troubles, and the state of the stock market generally; a new gold-mine in Arizona; the departure of Mrs. Mollenhauer the following Tuesday for Europe, with appropriate comments by Norah and Callum; and a Christmas ball that was going to be given for charity.

"Aileen'll be wantin' to go to that," commented Mrs. Butler.

"I'm going, you bet," put in Norah.

"Who's going to take you?" asked Callum.

"That's my affair, mister," she replied, smartly.

The meal was over, and Mrs. Butler strolled up to Aileen's room to see why she had not come down to dinner. Butler entered his den, wishing so much that he could take his wife into his confidence concerning all that was worrying him. On his desk, as he sat down and turned up the light, he saw the note. He recognized Aileen's handwriting at once. What could she mean by writing him? A sense of the untoward came to him, and he tore it open slowly, and, putting on his glasses, contemplated it solemnly.

So Aileen was gone. The old man stared at each word as if it had been written in fire. She said she had not gone with Cowperwood. It was possible, just the same, that he had run away from Philadelphia and taken her with him. This was the last straw. This ended it. Aileen lured away from home—to where—to what? Butler could scarcely believe, though, that Cowperwood had tempted her to do this. He had too much at stake; it would involve his own and Butler's families. The papers would be certain to get it quickly. He got up, crumpling the paper in his hand, and turned about at a noise. His wife was coming in. He pulled himself together and shoved the letter in his pocket.

"Aileen's not in her room," she said, curiously. "She didn't say anything to you about going out, did she?"

"No," he replied, truthfully, wondering how soon he should have to tell his wife.

"That's odd," observed Mrs. Butler, doubtfully. "She must have gone out after somethin'. It's a wonder she wouldn't tell somebody."

Butler gave no sign. He dared not. "She'll be back," he said, more in order to gain time than anything else. He was sorry to have to pretend. Mrs. Butler went out, and he closed the door. Then he took out the letter and read it again. The girl was crazy. She was doing an absolutely wild, inhuman, senseless thing. Where could she go, except to Cowperwood? She was on the verge of a public scandal, and this would produce it. There was just one thing to do as far as he could see. Cowperwood, if he were still in Philadelphia, would know. He would go to him—threaten, cajole, actually destroy him, if necessary. Aileen must come back. She need not go to Europe, perhaps, but she must come back and behave herself at least until Cowperwood could legitimately marry her. That was all he could expect now. She would have to wait, and some day perhaps he could bring himself to accept her wretched proposition. Horrible thought! It would kill her mother, disgrace her sister. He got up, took down his hat, put on his overcoat, and started out.

Arriving at the Cowperwood home he was shown into the reception-room. Cowperwood at the time was in his den looking over some private papers. When the name of Butler was announced he immediately went down-stairs. It was characteristic of the man that the announcement of Butler's presence created no stir in him whatsoever. So Butler had come. That meant, of course, that Aileen had gone. Now for a battle, not of words, but of weights of personalities. He felt himself to be intellectually, socially, and in every other way the more powerful man of the two. That spiritual content of him which we call life hardened to the texture of steel. He recalled that although he had told his wife and his father that the politicians, of whom Butler was one, were trying to make a scapegoat of him, Butler, nevertheless, was not considered to be wholly alienated as a friend, and civility must prevail. He would like very much to placate him if he could, to talk out the hard facts of life in a quiet and friendly way. But this matter of Aileen had to be adjusted now once and for all. And with that thought in his mind he walked quickly into Butler's presence.

The old man, when he learned that Cowperwood was in and would see him, determined to make his contact with the financier as short and effective as possible. He moved the least bit when he heard Cowperwood's step, as light and springy as ever.

"Good evening, Mr. Butler," said Cowperwood, cheerfully, when he saw him, extending his hand. "What can I do for you?"

"Ye can take that away from in front of me, for one thing," said Butler, grimly referring to his hand. "I have no need of it. It's my daughter I've come to talk to ye about, and I want plain answers. Where is she?"

"You mean Aileen?" said Cowperwood, looking at him with steady, curious, unrevealing eyes, and merely interpolating this to obtain a moment for reflection. "What can I tell you about her?"

"Ye can tell me where she is, that I know. And ye can make her come back to her home, where she belongs. It was bad fortune that ever brought ye across my doorstep; but I'll not bandy words with ye here. Ye'll tell me where my daughter is, and ye'll leave her alone from now, or I'll—" The old man's fists closed like a vise, and his chest heaved with suppressed rage. "Ye'll not be drivin' me too far, man, if ye're wise," he added, after a time, recovering his equanimity in part. "I want no truck with ye. I want my daughter."

"Listen, Mr. Butler," said Cowperwood, quite calmly, relishing the situation for the sheer sense of superiority it gave him. "I want to be perfectly frank with you, if you will let me. I may know where your daughter is, and I may not. I may wish to tell you, and I may not. She may not wish me to. But unless you wish to talk with me in a civil way there is no need of our going on any further. You are privileged to do what you like. Won't you come up-stairs to my room? We can talk more comfortably there."

Butler looked at his former protege in utter astonishment. He had never before in all his experience come up against a more ruthless type—suave, bland, forceful, unterrified. This man had certainly come to him as a sheep, and had turned out to be a ravening wolf. His incarceration had not put him in the least awe.

"I'll not come up to your room," Butler said, "and ye'll not get out of Philadelphy with her if that's what ye're plannin'. I can see to that. Ye think ye have the upper hand of me, I see, and ye're anxious to make something of it. Well, ye're not. It wasn't enough that ye come to me as a beggar, cravin' the help of me, and that I took ye in and helped ye all I could—ye had to steal my daughter from me in the bargain. If it wasn't for the girl's mother and her sister and her brothers—dacenter men than ever ye'll know how to be—I'd brain ye where ye stand. Takin' a young, innocent girl and makin' an evil woman out of her, and ye a married man! It's a God's blessin' for ye that it's me, and not one of me sons, that's here talkin' to ye, or ye wouldn't be alive to say what ye'd do."

The old man was grim but impotent in his rage.

"I'm sorry, Mr. Butler," replied Cowperwood, quietly. "I'm willing to explain, but you won't let me. I'm not planning to run away with your daughter, nor to leave Philadelphia. You ought to know me well enough to know that I'm not contemplating anything of that kind; my interests are too large. You and I are practical men. We ought to be able to talk this matter over together and reach an understanding. I thought once of coming to you and explaining this; but I was quite sure you wouldn't listen to me. Now that you are here I would like to talk to you. If you will come up to my room I will be glad to—otherwise not. Won't you come up?"

Butler saw that Cowperwood had the advantage. He might as well go up. Otherwise it was plain he would get no information.

"Very well," he said.

Cowperwood led the way quite amicably, and, having entered his private office, closed the door behind him.

"We ought to be able to talk this matter over and reach an understanding," he said again, when they were in the room and he had closed the door. "I am not as bad as you think, though I know I appear very bad." Butler stared at him in contempt. "I love your daughter, and she loves me. I know you are asking yourself how I can do this while I am still married; but I assure you I can, and that I do. I am not happily married. I had expected, if this panic hadn't come along, to arrange with my wife for a divorce and marry Aileen. My intentions are perfectly good. The situation which you can complain of, of course, is the one you encountered a few weeks ago. It was indiscreet, but it was entirely human. Your daughter does not complain—she understands." At the mention of his daughter in this connection Butler flushed with rage and shame, but he controlled himself.

"And ye think because she doesn't complain that it's all right, do ye?" he asked, sarcastically.

"From my point of view, yes; from yours no. You have one view of life, Mr. Butler, and I have another."

"Ye're right there," put in Butler, "for once, anyhow."

"That doesn't prove that either of us is right or wrong. In my judgment the present end justifies the means. The end I have in view is to marry Aileen. If I can possibly pull myself out of this financial scrape that I am in I will do so. Of course, I would like to have your consent for that—so would Aileen; but if we can't, we can't." (Cowperwood was thinking that while this might not have a very soothing effect on the old contractor's point of view, nevertheless it must make some appeal to his sense of the possible or necessary. Aileen's present situation was quite unsatisfactory without marriage in view. And even if he, Cowperwood, was a convicted embezzler in the eyes of the public, that did not make him so. He might get free and restore himself—would certainly—and Aileen ought to be glad to marry him if she could under the circumstances. He did not quite grasp the depth of Butler's religious and moral prejudices.) "Lately," he went on, "you have been doing all you can, as I understand it, to pull me down, on account of Aileen, I suppose; but that is simply delaying what I want to do."

"Ye'd like me to help ye do that, I suppose?" suggested Butler, with infinite disgust and patience.

"I want to marry Aileen," Cowperwood repeated, for emphasis' sake. "She wants to marry me. Under the circumstances, however you may feel, you can have no real objection to my doing that, I am sure; yet you go on fighting me—making it hard for me to do what you really know ought to be done."

"Ye're a scoundrel," said Butler, seeing through his motives quite clearly. "Ye're a sharper, to my way of thinkin', and it's no child of mine I want connected with ye. I'm not sayin', seein' that things are as they are, that if ye were a free man it wouldn't be better that she should marry ye. It's the one dacent thing ye could do—if ye would, which I doubt. But that's nayther here nor there now. What can ye want with her hid away somewhere? Ye can't marry her. Ye can't get a divorce. Ye've got your hands full fightin' your lawsuits and kapin' yourself out of jail. She'll only be an added expense to ye, and ye'll be wantin' all the money ye have for other things, I'm thinkin'. Why should ye want to be takin' her away from a dacent home and makin' something out of her that ye'd be ashamed to marry if you could? The laist ye could do, if ye were any kind of a man at all, and had any of that thing that ye're plased to call love, would be to lave her at home and keep her as respectable as possible. Mind ye, I'm not thinkin' she isn't ten thousand times too good for ye, whatever ye've made of her. But if ye had any sinse of dacency left, ye wouldn't let her shame her family and break her old mother's heart, and that for no purpose except to make her worse than she is already. What good can ye get out of it, now? What good can ye expect to come of it? Be hivins, if ye had any sinse at all I should think ye could see that for yerself. Ye're only addin' to your troubles, not takin' away from them—and she'll not thank ye for that later on."

He stopped, rather astonished that he should have been drawn into an argument. His contempt for this man was so great that he could scarcely look at him, but his duty and his need was to get Aileen back. Cowperwood looked at him as one who gives serious attention to another. He seemed to be thinking deeply over what Butler had said.

"To tell you the truth, Mr. Butler," he said, "I did not want Aileen to leave your home at all; and she will tell you so, if you ever talk to her about it. I did my best to persuade her not to, and when she insisted on going the only thing I could do was to be sure she would be comfortable wherever she went. She was greatly outraged to think you should have put detectives on her trail. That, and the fact that you wanted to send her away somewhere against her will, was the principal reasons for her leaving. I assure you I did not want her to go. I think you forget sometimes, Mr. Butler, that Aileen is a grown woman, and that she has a will of her own. You think I control her to her great disadvantage. As a matter of fact, I am very much in love with her, and have been for three or four years; and if you know anything about love you know that it doesn't always mean control. I'm not doing Aileen any injustice when I say that she has had as much influence on me as I have had on her. I love her, and that's the cause of all the trouble. You come and insist that I shall return your daughter to you. As a matter of fact, I don't know whether I can or not. I don't know that she would go if I wanted her to. She might turn on me and say that I didn't care for her any more. That is not true, and I would not want her to feel that way. She is greatly hurt, as I told you, by what you did to her, and the fact that you want her to leave Philadelphia. You can do as much to remedy that as I can. I could tell you where she is, but I do not know that I want to. Certainly not until I know what your attitude toward her and this whole proposition is to be."

He paused and looked calmly at the old contractor, who eyed him grimly in return.

"What proposition are ye talkin' about?" asked Butler, interested by the peculiar developments of this argument. In spite of himself he was getting a slightly different angle on the whole situation. The scene was shifting to a certain extent. Cowperwood appeared to be reasonably sincere in the matter. His promises might all be wrong, but perhaps he did love Aileen; and it was possible that he did intend to get a divorce from his wife some time and marry her. Divorce, as Butler knew, was against the rules of the Catholic Church, which he so much revered. The laws of God and any sense of decency commanded that Cowperwood should not desert his wife and children and take up with another woman— not even Aileen, in order to save her. It was a criminal thing to plan, sociologically speaking, and showed what a villain Cowperwood inherently was; but, nevertheless, Cowperwood was not a Catholic, his views of life were not the same as his own, Butler's, and besides and worst of all (no doubt due in part to Aileen's own temperament), he had compromised her situation very materially. She might not easily be restored to a sense of the normal and decent, and so the matter was worth taking into thought. Butler knew that ultimately he could not countenance any such thing—certainly not, and keep his faith with the Church—

but he was human enough none the less to consider it. Besides, he wanted Aileen to come back; and Aileen from now on, he knew, would have some say as to what her future should be.

"Well, it's simple enough," replied Cowperwood. "I should like to have you withdraw your opposition to Aileen's remaining in Philadelphia, for one thing; and for another, I should like you to stop your attacks on me." Cowperwood smiled in an ingratiating way. He hoped really to placate Butler in part by his generous attitude throughout this procedure. "I can't make you do that, of course, unless you want to. I merely bring it up, Mr. Butler, because I am sure that if it hadn't been for Aileen you would not have taken the course you have taken toward me. I understood you received an anonymous letter, and that afternoon you called your loan with me. Since then I have heard from one source and another that you were strongly against me, and I merely wish to say that I wish you wouldn't be. I am not guilty of embezzling any sixty thousand dollars, and you know it. My intentions were of the best. I did not think I was going to fail at the time I used those certificates, and if it hadn't been for several other loans that were called I would have gone on to the end of the month and put them back in time, as I always had. I have always valued your friendship very highly, and I am very sorry to lose it. Now I have said all I am going to say."

Butler looked at Cowperwood with shrewd, calculating eyes. The man had some merit, but much unconscionable evil in him. Butler knew very well how he had taken the check, and a good many other things in connection with it. The manner in which he had played his cards to-night was on a par with the way he had run to him on the night of the fire. He was just shrewd and calculating and heartless.

"I'll make ye no promise," he said. "Tell me where my daughter is, and I'll think the matter over. Ye have no claim on me now, and I owe ye no good turn. But I'll think it over, anyhow."

"That's quite all right," replied Cowperwood. "That's all I can expect. But what about Aileen? Do you expect her to leave Philadelphia?"

"Not if she settles down and behaves herself: but there must be an end of this between you and her. She's disgracin' her family and ruinin' her soul in the bargain. And that's what you are doin' with yours. It'll be time enough to talk about anything else when you're a free man. More than that I'll not promise."

Cowperwood, satisfied that this move on Aileen's part had done her a real service if it had not aided him especially, was convinced that it would be a good move for her to return to her home at once. He could not tell how his appeal to the State Supreme Court would eventuate. His motion for a new trial which was now to be made under the privilege of the certificate of reasonable doubt might not be granted, in which case he would have to serve a term in the penitentiary. If he were compelled to go to the penitentiary she would be safer—better off in the bosom of her family. His own hands were going to be exceedingly full for the next two months until he knew how his appeal was coming out. And after that—well, after that he would fight on, whatever happened.

During all the time that Cowperwood had been arguing his case in this fashion he had been thinking how he could adjust this compromise so as to retain the affection of Aileen and not offend her sensibilities by urging her to return. He knew that she would not agree to give up seeing him, and he was not willing that she should. Unless he had a good and sufficient reason, he would be playing a wretched part by telling Butler where she was. He did not intend to do so until he saw exactly how to do it—the way that would make it most acceptable to Aileen. He knew that she would not long be happy where she was. Her flight was due in part to Butler's intense opposition to himself and in part to his determination to make her leave Philadelphia and behave; but this last was now in part obviated. Butler, in spite of his words, was no longer a stern Nemesis. He was a melting man—very anxious to find his daughter, very willing to forgive her. He was whipped, literally beaten, at his own game, and Cowperwood could see it in the old man's eyes. If he himself could talk to Aileen personally and explain just how things were, he felt sure he could make her see that it would be to their mutual advantage, for the present at least, to have the matter amicably settled. The thing to do was to make Butler wait somewhere—here, possibly—while he went and talked to her. When she learned how things were she would probably acquiesce.

"The best thing that I can do under the circumstances," he said, after a time, "would be to see Aileen in two or three days, and ask her what she wishes to do. I can explain the matter to her, and if she wants to go back, she can. I will promise to tell her anything that you say."

"Two or three days!" exclaimed Butler, irritably. "Two or three fiddlesticks! She must come home to-night. Her mother doesn't know she's left the place yet. To-night is the time! I'll go and fetch her meself to-night."

"No, that won't do," said Cowperwood. "I shall have to go myself. If you wish to wait here I will see what can be done, and let you know."

"Very well," grunted Butler, who was now walking up and down with his hands behind his back. "But for Heaven's sake be quick about it. There's no time to lose." He was thinking of Mrs. Butler. Cowperwood called the servant, ordered his runabout, and told George to see that his private office was not disturbed. Then, as Butler strolled to and fro in this, to him, objectionable room, Cowperwood drove rapidly away.

CHAPTER XLVII

Although it was nearly eleven o'clock when he arrived at the Calligans', Aileen was not yet in bed. In her bedroom upstairs she was confiding to Mamie and Mrs. Calligan some of her social experiences when the bell rang, and Mrs. Calligan went down and opened the door to Cowperwood.

"Miss Butler is here, I believe," he said. "Will you tell her that there is some one here from her father?" Although Aileen had instructed that her presence here was not to be divulged even to the members of her family the force of Cowperwood's presence and the mention of Butler's name cost Mrs. Calligan her presence of mind. "Wait a moment," she said; "I'll see."

She stepped back, and Cowperwood promptly stepped in, taking off his hat with the air of one who was satisfied that Aileen was there. "Say to her that I only want to speak to her for a few moments," he called, as Mrs. Calligan went up-stairs, raising his voice in the hope that Aileen might hear. She did, and came down promptly. She was very much astonished to think that he should come so soon, and fancied, in her vanity, that there must be great excitement in her home. She would have greatly grieved if there had not been.

The Calligans would have been pleased to hear, but Cowperwood was cautious. As she came down the stairs he put his finger to his lips in sign for silence, and said, "This is Miss Butler, I believe."

"Yes," replied Aileen, with a secret smile. Her one desire was to kiss him. "What's the trouble darling?" she asked, softly.

"You'll have to go back, dear, I'm afraid," whispered Cowperwood. "You'll have everything in a turmoil if you don't. Your mother doesn't know yet, it seems, and your father is over at my place now, waiting for you. It may be a good deal of help to me if you do. Let me tell you—" He went off into a complete description of his conversation with Butler and his own views in the matter. Aileen's expression changed from time to time as the various phases of the matter were put before her; but, persuaded by the clearness with which he put the matter, and by his assurance that they could continue their relations as before uninterrupted, once this was settled, she decided to return. In a way, her father's surrender was a great triumph. She made her farewells to the Calligans, saying, with a smile, that they could not do without her at home, and that she would send for her belongings later, and returned with Cowperwood to his own door. There he asked her to wait in the runabout while he sent her father down.

"Well?" said Butler, turning on him when he opened the door, and not seeing Aileen.

"You'll find her outside in my runabout," observed Cowperwood. "You may use that if you choose. I will send my man for it."

"No, thank you; we'll walk," said Butler.

Cowperwood called his servant to take charge of the vehicle, and Butler stalked solemnly out.

He had to admit to himself that the influence of Cowperwood over his daughter was deadly, and probably permanent. The best he could do would be to keep her within the precincts of the home, where she might still, possibly, be brought to her senses. He held a very guarded conversation with her on his way home, for fear that she would take additional offense. Argument was out of the question.

"Ye might have talked with me once more, Aileen," he said, "before ye left. Yer mother would be in a terrible state if she knew ye were gone. She doesn't know yet. Ye'll have to say ye stayed somewhere to dinner."

"I was at the Calligans," replied Aileen. "That's easy enough. Mama won't think anything about it."

"It's a sore heart I have, Aileen. I hope ye'll think over your ways and do better. I'll not say anythin' more now."

Aileen returned to her room, decidedly triumphant in her mood for the moment, and things went on apparently in the Butler household as before. But those who imagine that this defeat permanently altered the attitude of Butler toward Cowperwood are mistaken.

In the meanwhile between the day of his temporary release and the hearing of his appeal which was two months off, Cowperwood was going on doing his best to repair his shattered forces. He took up his work where he left off; but the possibility of reorganizing his business was distinctly modified since his conviction. Because of his action in trying to protect his largest creditors at the time of his failure, he fancied that once he was free again, if ever he got free, his credit, other things being equal, would be good with those who could help him most—say, Cooke & Co., Clark & Co., Drexel & Co., and the Girard National Bank—providing his personal reputation had not been too badly injured by his sentence. Fortunately for his own hopefulness of mind, he failed fully to realize what a depressing effect a legal decision of this character, sound or otherwise, had on the minds of even his most enthusiastic supporters.

His best friends in the financial world were by now convinced that his was a sinking ship. A student of finance once observed that nothing is so sensitive as money, and the financial mind partakes largely of the quality of the thing in which it deals. There was no use trying to do much for a man who might be going to prison for a term of years. Something might be done for him possibly in connection with the governor, providing he lost his case before the Supreme Court and was actually sentenced to prison; but that was two months off, or more, and they could not tell what the outcome of that would be. So Cowperwood's repeated appeals for assistance, extension of credit, or the acceptance of some plan he had for his general rehabilitation, were met with the kindly evasions of those who were doubtful. They would think it over. They would see about it. Certain things were standing in the way. And so on, and so forth, through all the endless excuses of those who do not care to act. In these days he went about the money world in his customary jaunty way, greeting all those whom he had known there many years and pretending, when asked, to be very hopeful, to be doing very well; but they did not believe him, and he really did not care whether they did or not. His business was to persuade or over-persuade any one who could really be of assistance to him, and at this task he worked untiringly, ignoring all others.

"Why, hello, Frank," his friends would call, on seeing him. "How are you getting on?"

"Fine! Fine!" he would reply, cheerfully. "Never better," and he would explain in a general way how his affairs were being handled. He conveyed much of his own optimism to all those who knew him and were interested in his welfare, but of course there were many who were not.

In these days also, he and Steger were constantly to be met with in courts of law, for he was constantly being reexamined in some petition in bankruptcy. They were heartbreaking days, but he did not flinch. He wanted to stay in Philadelphia and fight the thing to a finish—putting himself where he had been before the fire; rehabilitating himself in the eyes of the public. He felt that he could do it, too, if he were not actually sent to prison for a long term; and even then, so naturally optimistic was his mood, when he got out again. But, in so far as Philadelphia was concerned, distinctly he was dreaming vain dreams.

One of the things militating against him was the continued opposition of Butler and the politicians. Somehow—no one could have said exactly why—the general political feeling was that the financier and the former city treasurer would lose their appeals and eventually be sentenced together. Stener, in spite of his original intention to plead guilty and take his punishment without comment, had been persuaded by some of his political friends that it would be better for his future's sake to plead not guilty and claim that his offense had been due to custom, rather than to admit his guilt outright and so seem not to have had any justification whatsoever. This he did, but he was convicted nevertheless. For the sake of appearances, a trumped-up appeal was made which was now before the State Supreme Court.

Then, too, due to one whisper and another, and these originating with the girl who had written Butler and Cowperwood's wife, there was at this time a growing volume of gossip relating to the alleged relations of Cowperwood with Butler's daughter, Aileen. There had been a house in Tenth Street. It had been maintained by Cowperwood for her. No wonder Butler was so vindictive. This, indeed, explained much. And even in the practical, financial world, criticism was now rather against Cowperwood than his enemies. For, was it not a fact, that at the inception of his career, he had been befriended by Butler? And what a way to reward that friendship! His oldest and firmest admirers wagged their heads. For they sensed clearly that this was another illustration of that innate "I satisfy myself" attitude which so regulated Cowperwood's conduct. He was a strong man, surely—and a brilliant one. Never had Third Street seen a more pyrotechnic, and yet fascinating and financially aggressive, and at the same time, conservative person. Yet might one not fairly tempt Nemesis by a too great daring and egotism? Like Death, it loves a shining mark. He should not, perhaps, have seduced Butler's daughter; unquestionably he should not have so boldly taken that check, especially after his quarrel and break with Stener. He was a little too aggressive. Was it not questionable whether—with such a record—he could be restored to his former place here? The bankers and business men who were closest to him were decidedly dubious.

But in so far as Cowperwood and his own attitude toward life was concerned, at this time—the feeling he had—"to satisfy myself"—when combined with his love of beauty and love and women, still made him ruthless and thoughtless. Even now, the beauty and delight of a girl like Aileen Butler were far more important to him than the good-will of fifty million people, if he could evade the necessity of having their good-will. Previous to the Chicago fire and the panic, his star had been so rapidly ascending that in the helter-skelter of great and favorable events he had scarcely taken thought of the social significance of the thing he was doing. Youth and the joy of life were in his blood. He felt so young, so vigorous, so like new grass looks and feels. The freshness of spring evenings was in him, and he did not care. After the crash, when one might have imagined he would have seen the wisdom of relinquishing Aileen for the time being, anyhow, he did not care to. She represented the best of the wonderful days that had gone before. She was a link between him and the past and a still-to-be triumphant future.

His worst anxiety was that if he were sent to the penitentiary, or adjudged a bankrupt, or both, he would probably lose the privilege of a seat on 'change, and that would close to him the most distinguished avenue of his prosperity here in Philadelphia for some time, if not forever. At present, because of his complications, his seat had been attached as an asset, and he could not act. Edward and Joseph, almost the only employees he could afford, were still acting for him in a small way; but the other members on 'change naturally suspected his brothers as his agents, and any talk that they might raise of going into business for themselves merely indicated to other brokers and bankers that Cowperwood was contemplating some concealed move which would not necessarily be advantageous to his creditors, and against the law anyhow. Yet he must remain on 'change, whatever happened, potentially if not actively; and so in his quick mental searchings he hit upon the idea that in order to forfend against the event of his being put into prison or thrown into bankruptcy, or both, he ought to form a subsidiary silent partnership with some man who was or would be well liked on 'change, and whom he could use as a cat's-paw and a dummy.

Finally he hit upon a man who he thought would do. He did not amount to much—had a small business; but he was honest, and he liked Cowperwood. His name was Wingate—Stephen Wingate—and he was eking out a not too robust existence in South Third Street as a broker. He was forty-five years of age, of medium height, fairly thick-set, not at all unprepossessing, and rather intelligent and active, but not too forceful and pushing in spirit. He really needed a man like Cowperwood to make him into something, if ever he was to be made. He had a seat on 'change, and was well thought of; respected, but not so very prosperous. In times past he had asked small favors of Cowperwood—the use of small loans at a moderate rate of interest, tips, and so forth; and Cowperwood, because he liked him and felt a little sorry for him, had granted them. Now Wingate was slowly drifting down toward a none too successful old age, and was as tractable as such a man would naturally be. No one for the time being would suspect him of being a hireling of Cowperwood's, and the latter could depend on him to execute his orders to the letter. He sent for him and had a long conversation with him. He told him just what the situation was, what he thought he could do for him as a partner, how much of his business he would want for himself, and so on, and found him agreeable.

"I'll be glad to do anything you say, Mr. Cowperwood," he assured the latter. "I know whatever happens that you'll protect me, and there's nobody in the world I would rather work with or have greater respect for. This storm will all blow over, and you'll be all right. We can try it, anyhow. If it don't work out you can see what you want to do about it later."

And so this relationship was tentatively entered into and Cowperwood began to act in a small way through Wingate.

CHAPTER XLVIII

By the time the State Supreme Court came to pass upon Cowperwood's plea for a reversal of the lower court and the granting of a new trial, the rumor of his connection with Aileen had spread far and wide. As has been seen, it had done and was still doing him much damage. It confirmed the impression, which the politicians had originally tried to create, that Cowperwood was the true criminal and Stener the victim. His semi-legitimate financial subtlety, backed indeed by his financial genius, but certainly on this account not worse than that being practiced in peace and quiet and with much applause in many other quarters—was now seen to be Machiavellian trickery of the most dangerous type. He had a wife and two children; and without knowing what his real thoughts had been the fruitfully imaginative public jumped to the conclusion that he had been on the verge of deserting them, divorcing Lillian, and marrying Aileen. This was criminal enough in itself, from the conservative point of view; but when taken in connection with his financial record, his trial, conviction, and general bankruptcy situation, the public was inclined to believe that he was all the politicians said he was. He ought to be convicted. The Supreme Court ought not to grant his prayer for a new trial. It is thus that our inmost thoughts and intentions burst at times via no known material agency into public thoughts. People know, when they cannot apparently possibly know why they know. There is such a thing as thought-transference and transcendentalism of ideas.

It reached, for one thing, the ears of the five judges of the State Supreme Court and of the Governor of the State.

During the four weeks Cowperwood had been free on a certificate of reasonable doubt both Harper Steger and Dennis Shannon appeared before the judges of the State Supreme Court, and argued pro and con as to the reasonableness of granting a new trial. Through his lawyer, Cowperwood made a learned appeal to the Supreme Court judges, showing how he had been unfairly indicted in the first place, how there was no real substantial evidence on which to base a charge of larceny or anything else. It took Steger two hours and ten minutes to make his argument, and District-Attorney Shannon longer to make his reply, during which the five judges on the bench, men of considerable legal experience but no great financial understanding, listened with rapt attention. Three of them, Judges Smithson, Rainey, and Beckwith, men most amenable to the political feeling of the time and the wishes of the bosses, were little interested in this story of Cowperwood's transaction, particularly since his relations with Butler's daughter and Butler's consequent opposition to him had come to them. They fancied that in a way they were considering the whole matter fairly and impartially; but the manner in which Cowperwood had treated Butler was never out of their minds. Two of them, Judges Marvin and Rafalsky, who were men of larger sympathies and understanding, but of no greater political freedom, did feel that Cowperwood had been badly used thus far, but they did not see what they could do about it. He had put himself in a most unsatisfactory position, politically and socially. They understood and took into consideration his great financial and social losses which Steger described accurately; and one of them, Judge Rafalsky, because of a similar event in his own life in so far as a girl was concerned, was inclined to argue strongly against the conviction of Cowperwood; but, owing to his political connections and obligations, he realized that it would not be wise politically to stand out against what was wanted. Still, when he and Marvin learned that Judges Smithson, Rainey, and Beckwith were inclined to convict Cowperwood without much argument, they decided to hand down a dissenting opinion. The point involved was a very knotty one. Cowperwood might carry it to the Supreme Court of the United States on some fundamental principle of liberty of action. Anyhow, other judges in other courts in Pennsylvania and elsewhere would be inclined to examine the decision in this case, it was so important. The minority decided that it would not do them any harm to hand down a dissenting opinion. The politicians would not mind as long as Cowperwood was convicted—would like it better, in fact. It looked fairer. Besides, Marvin and Rafalsky did not care to be included, if they could help it, with Smithson, Rainey, and Beckwith in a sweeping condemnation of Cowperwood. So all five judges fancied they were considering the whole matter rather fairly and impartially, as men will under such circumstances. Smithson, speaking for himself and Judges Rainey and Beckwith on the eleventh of February, 1872, said:

"The defendant, Frank A. Cowperwood, asks that the finding of the jury in the lower court (the State of Pennsylvania vs. Frank A. Cowperwood) be reversed and a new trial granted. This court cannot see that any substantial injustice has been done the defendant. [Here followed a rather lengthy resume of the history of the case, in which it was pointed out that the custom and precedent of the treasurer's office, to say nothing of Cowperwood's easy method of doing business with the city treasury, could have nothing to do with his responsibility for failure to observe both the spirit and the letter of the law.] The obtaining of goods under color of legal process [went on Judge Smithson, speaking for the majority] may amount to larceny. In the present case it was the province of the jury to ascertain the felonious intent. They have settled that against the defendant as a question of fact, and the court cannot say that there was not sufficient evidence to sustain the verdict. For what purpose did the defendant get the check? He was upon the eve of failure. He had already hypothecated for his own debts the loan of the city placed in his hands for sale—he had unlawfully obtained five hundred thousand dollars in cash as loans; and it is reasonable to suppose that he could obtain nothing more from the city treasury by any ordinary means. Then it is that he goes there, and, by means of a falsehood implied if not actual, obtains sixty thousand dollars more. The jury has found the intent with which this was done."

It was in these words that Cowperwood's appeal for a new trial was denied by the majority.

For himself and Judge Rafalsky, Judge Marvin, dissenting, wrote:

"It is plain from the evidence in the case that Mr. Cowperwood did not receive the check without authority as agent to do so, and it has not been clearly demonstrated that within his capacity as agent he did not perform or intend to perform the full measure of the obligation which the receipt of this check implied. It was shown in the trial that as a matter of policy it was understood that purchases for the sinking-fund should not be known or understood in the market or by the public in that light, and that Mr. Cowperwood as agent was to have an absolutely free hand in the disposal of his assets and liabilities so long as the ultimate result was satisfactory. There was no particular time when the loan was to be bought, nor was there any particular amount mentioned at any time to be purchased. Unless the defendant intended at the time he received the check fraudulently to appropriate it he could not be convicted even on the first count. The verdict of the jury does not establish this fact; the evidence does not show conclusively that it could be established; and the same jury, upon three other counts, found the defendant guilty without the semblance of shadow of evidence. How can we say that their conclusions upon the first count are unerring when they so palpably erred on the other counts? It is the opinion of the minority that the verdict of the jury in charging larceny on the first count is not valid, and that that verdict should be set aside and a new trial granted."

Judge Rafalsky, a meditative and yet practical man of Jewish extraction but peculiarly American appearance, felt called upon to write a third opinion which should especially reflect his own cogitation and be a criticism on the majority as well as a slight variation from and addition to the points on which he agreed with Judge Marvin. It was a knotty question, this, of Cowperwood's guilt, and, aside from the political necessity of convicting him, nowhere was it more clearly shown than in these varying opinions of the superior court. Judge Rafalsky held, for instance, that if a crime had been committed at all, it was not that known as larceny, and he went on to add:

"It is impossible, from the evidence, to come to the conclusion either that Cowperwood did not intend shortly to deliver the loan or that Albert Stires, the chief clerk, or the city treasurer did not intend to part not only with the possession, but also and absolutely with the property in the check and the money represented by it. It was testified by Mr. Stires that Mr. Cowperwood said he had bought certificates of city loan to this amount, and it has not been clearly demonstrated that he had not. His non-placement of the same in the sinking-fund must in all fairness, the letter of the law to the contrary notwithstanding, be looked upon and judged in the light of custom. Was it his custom so to do? In my judgment the doctrine now announced by the majority of the court extends the crime of constructive larceny to such limits that any business man who engages in extensive and perfectly legitimate stock transactions may, before he knows it, by a sudden panic in the market or a fire, as in this instance, become a felon. When a principle is asserted which establishes such a precedent, and may lead to such results, it is, to say the least, startling."

While he was notably comforted by the dissenting opinions of the judges in minority, and while he had been schooling himself to expect the worst in this connection and had been arranging his affairs as well as he could in anticipation of it, Cowperwood was still bitterly disappointed. It would be untrue to say that, strong and self-reliant as he normally was, he did not suffer. He was not without sensibilities of the highest order, only they were governed and controlled in him by that cold iron thing, his reason, which never forsook him. There was no further appeal possible save to the United States Supreme Court, as Steger pointed out, and there only on the constitutionality of some phase of the decision and his rights as a citizen, of which the Supreme Court of the United States must take cognizance. This was a tedious and expensive thing to do. It was not exactly obvious at the moment on what point he could make an appeal. It would involve a long delay—perhaps a year and a half, perhaps longer, at the end of which period he might have to serve his prison term anyhow, and pending which he would certainly have to undergo incarceration for a time.

Cowperwood mused speculatively for a few moments after hearing Steger's presentation of the case. Then he said: "Well, it looks as if I have to go to jail or leave the country, and I've decided on jail. I can fight this out right here in Philadelphia in the long run and win. I can get that decision reversed in the Supreme Court, or I can get the Governor to pardon me after a time, I think. I'm not going to run away, and everybody knows I'm not. These people who think they have me down haven't got one corner of me whipped. I'll get out of this thing after a while, and when I do I'll show some of these petty little politicians what it means to put up a real fight. They'll never get a damned dollar out of me now—not a dollar! I did intend to pay that five hundred thousand dollars some time if they had let me go. Now they can whistle!"

He set his teeth and his gray eyes fairly snapped their determination.

"Well, I've done all I can, Frank," pleaded Steger, sympathetically. "You'll do me the justice to say that I put up the best fight I knew how. I may not know how—you'll have to answer for that—but within my limits I've done the best I can. I can do a few things more to carry this thing on, if you want me to, but I'm going to leave it to you now. Whatever you say goes."

"Don't talk nonsense at this stage, Harper," replied Cowperwood almost testily. "I know whether I'm satisfied or not, and I'd soon tell you if I wasn't. I think you might as well go on and see if you can find some definite grounds for carrying it to the Supreme Court, but meanwhile I'll begin my sentence. I suppose Payderson will be naming a day to have me brought before him now shortly."

"It depends on how you'd like to have it, Frank. I could get a stay of sentence for a week maybe, or ten days, if it will do you any good. Shannon won't make any objection to that, I'm sure. There's only one hitch. Jaspers will be around here tomorrow looking for you. It's his duty to take you into custody again, once he's notified that your appeal has been denied. He'll be wanting to lock you up unless you pay him, but we can fix that. If you do want to wait, and want any time off, I suppose he'll arrange to let you out with a deputy; but I'm afraid you'll have to stay there nights. They're pretty strict about that since that Albertson case of a few years ago."

Steger referred to the case of a noted bank cashier who, being let out of the county jail at night in the alleged custody of a deputy, was permitted to escape. There had been emphatic and severe condemnation of the sheriff's office at the time, and since then, repute or no repute, money or no money, convicted criminals were supposed to stay in the county jail at night at least.

Cowperwood meditated this calmly, looking out of the lawyer's window into Second Street. He did not much fear anything that might happen to him in Jaspers's charge since his first taste of that gentleman's hospitality, although he did object to spending nights in the county jail when his general term of imprisonment was being reduced no whit thereby. All that he could do now in connection with his affairs, unless he could have months of freedom, could be as well adjusted from a prison cell as from his Third Street office—not quite, but nearly so. Anyhow, why parley? He was facing a prison term, and he might as well accept it without further ado. He might take a day or two finally to look after his affairs; but beyond that, why bother?

"When, in the ordinary course of events, if you did nothing at all, would I come up for sentence?"

"Oh, Friday or Monday, I fancy," replied Steger. "I don't know what move Shannon is planning to make in this matter. I thought I'd walk around and see him in a little while."

"I think you'd better do that," replied Cowperwood. "Friday or Monday will suit me, either way. I'm really not particular. Better make it Monday if you can. You don't suppose there is any way you can induce Jaspers to keep his hands off until then? He knows I'm perfectly responsible."

"I don't know, Frank, I'm sure; I'll see. I'll go around and talk to him to-night. Perhaps a hundred dollars will make him relax the rigor of his rules that much."

Cowperwood smiled grimly.

"I fancy a hundred dollars would make Jaspers relax a whole lot of rules," he replied, and he got up to go.

Steger arose also. "I'll see both these people, and then I'll call around at your house. You'll be in, will you, after dinner?"

"Yes."

They slipped on their overcoats and went out into the cold February day, Cowperwood back to his Third Street office, Steger to see Shannon and Jaspers.

CHAPTER XLIX

The business of arranging Cowperwood's sentence for Monday was soon disposed of through Shannon, who had no personal objection to any reasonable delay.

Steger next visited the county jail, close on to five o'clock, when it was already dark. Sheriff Jaspers came lolling out from his private library, where he had been engaged upon the work of cleaning his pipe.

"How are you, Mr. Steger?" he observed, smiling blandly. "How are you? Glad to see you. Won't you sit down? I suppose you're round here again on that Cowperwood matter. I just received word from the district attorney that he had lost his case."

"That's it, Sheriff," replied Steger, ingratiatingly. "He asked me to step around and see what you wanted him to do in the matter. Judge Payderson has just fixed the sentence time for Monday morning at ten o'clock. I don't suppose you'll be much put out if he doesn't show up here before Monday at eight o'clock, will you, or Sunday night, anyhow? He's perfectly reliable, as you know." Steger was sounding Jaspers out, politely trying to make the time of Cowperwood's arrival a trivial matter in order to avoid paying the hundred dollars, if possible. But Jaspers was not to be so easily disposed of. His fat face lengthened considerably. How could Steger ask him such a favor and not even suggest the slightest form of remuneration?

"It's ag'in' the law, Mr. Steger, as you know," he began, cautiously and complainingly. "I'd like to accommodate him, everything else being equal, but since that Albertson case three years ago we've had to run this office much more careful, and—"

"Oh, I know, Sheriff," interrupted Steger, blandly, "but this isn't an ordinary case in any way, as you can see for yourself. Mr. Cowperwood is a very important man, and he has a great many things to attend to. Now if it were only a mere matter of seventy-five or a hundred dollars to satisfy some court clerk with, or to pay a fine, it would be easy enough, but—" He paused and looked wisely away, and Mr. Jaspers's face began to relax at once. The law against which it was ordinarily so hard to offend was not now so important. Steger saw that it was needless to introduce any additional arguments.

"It's a very ticklish business, this, Mr. Steger," put in the sheriff, yieldingly, and yet with a slight whimper in his voice. "If anything were to happen, it would cost me my place all right. I don't like to do it under any circumstances, and I wouldn't, only I happen to know both Mr. Cowperwood and Mr. Stener, and I like 'em both. I don' think they got their rights in this matter, either. I don't mind making an exception in this case if Mr. Cowperwood don't go about too publicly. I wouldn't want any of the men in the district attorney's office to know this. I don't suppose he'll mind if I keep a deputy somewhere near all the time for looks' sake. I have to, you know, really, under the law. He won't bother him any. Just keep on guard like." Jaspers looked at Mr. Steger very flatly and wisely—almost placatingly under the circumstances—and Steger nodded.

"Quite right, Sheriff, quite right. You're quite right," and he drew out his purse while the sheriff led the way very cautiously back into his library.

"I'd like to show you the line of law-books I'm fixing up for myself in here, Mr. Steger," he observed, genially, but meanwhile closing his fingers gently on the small roll of ten-dollar bills Steger was handing him. "We have occasional use for books of that kind here, as you see. I thought it a good sort of thing to have them around." He waved one arm comprehensively at the line of State reports, revised statutes, prison regulations, etc., the while he put the money in his pocket and Steger pretended to look.

"A good idea, I think, Sheriff. Very good, indeed. So you think if Mr. Cowperwood gets around here very early Monday morning, say eight or eight-thirty, that it will be all right?"

"I think so," replied the sheriff, curiously nervous, but agreeable, anxious to please. "I don't think that anything will come up that will make me want him earlier. If it does I'll let you know, and you can produce him. I don't think so, though, Mr. Steger; I think everything will be all right." They were once more in the main hall now. "Glad to have seen you again, Mr. Steger—very glad," he added. "Call again some day."

Waving the sheriff a pleasant farewell, he hurried on his way to Cowperwood's house.

You would not have thought, seeing Cowperwood mount the front steps of his handsome residence in his neat gray suit and well-cut overcoat on his return from his office that evening, that he was thinking that this might be his last night here. His air and walk indicated no weakening of spirit. He entered the hall, where an early lamp was aglow, and encountered "Wash" Sims, an old negro factotum, who was just coming up from the basement, carrying a bucket of coal for one of the fireplaces.

"Mahty cold out, dis evenin', Mistah Coppahwood," said Wash, to whom anything less than sixty degrees was very cold. His one regret was that Philadelphia was not located in North Carolina, from whence he came.

"'Tis sharp, Wash," replied Cowperwood, absentmindedly. He was thinking for the moment of the house and how it had looked, as he came toward it west along Girard Avenue—what the neighbors were thinking of him, too, observing him from time to time out of their windows. It was clear and cold. The lamps in the reception-hall and sitting-room had been lit, for he had permitted no air of funereal gloom to settle down over this place since his troubles had begun. In the far west of the street a last tingling gleam of lavender and violet was showing over the cold white snow of the roadway. The house of gray-green stone, with its lighted windows, and cream-colored lace curtains, had looked especially attractive. He had thought for the moment of the pride he had taken in putting all this here, decorating and ornamenting it, and whether, ever, he could secure it for himself again. "Where is your mistress?" he added to Wash, when he bethought himself.

"In the sitting-room, Mr. Coppahwood, ah think."

Cowperwood ascended the stairs, thinking curiously that Wash would soon be out of a job now, unless Mrs. Cowperwood, out of all the wreck of other things, chose to retain him, which was not likely. He entered the sitting-room, and there sat his wife by the oblong center-table, sewing a hook and eye on one of Lillian, second's, petticoats. She looked up, at his step, with the peculiarly uncertain smile she used these days—indication of her pain, fear, suspicion—and inquired, "Well, what is new with you, Frank?" Her smile was something like a hat or belt or ornament which one puts on or off at will.

"Nothing in particular," he replied, in his offhand way, "except that I understand I have lost that appeal of mine. Steger is coming here in a little while to let me know. I had a note from him, and I fancy it's about that."

He did not care to say squarely that he had lost. He knew that she was sufficiently distressed as it was, and he did not care to be too abrupt just now.

"You don't say!" replied Lillian, with surprise and fright in her voice, and getting up.

She had been so used to a world where prisons were scarcely thought of, where things went on smoothly from day to day without any noticeable intrusion of such distressing things as courts, jails, and the like, that these last few months had driven her nearly mad. Cowperwood had so definitely insisted on her keeping in the background—he had told her so very little that she was all at sea anyhow in regard to the whole procedure. Nearly all that she had had in the way of intelligence had been from his father and mother and Anna, and from a close and almost secret scrutiny of the newspapers.

At the time he had gone to the county jail she did not even know anything about it until his father had come back from the court-room and the jail and had broken the news to her. It had been a terrific blow to her. Now to have this thing suddenly broken to her in this offhand way, even though she had been expecting and dreading it hourly, was too much.

She was still a decidedly charming-looking woman as she stood holding her daughter's garment in her hand, even if she was forty years old to Cowperwood's thirty-five. She was robed in one of the creations of their late prosperity, a cream-colored gown of rich silk, with dark brown trimmings—a fetching combination for her. Her eyes were a little hollow, and reddish about the rims, but otherwise she showed no sign of her keen mental distress. There was considerable evidence of the former tranquil sweetness that had so fascinated him ten years before.

"Isn't that terrible?" she said, weakly, her hands trembling in a nervous way. "Isn't it dreadful? Isn't there anything more you can do, truly? You won't really have to go to prison, will you?" He objected to her distress and her nervous fears. He preferred a stronger, more self-reliant type of woman, but still she was his wife, and in his day he had loved her much.

"It looks that way, Lillian," he said, with the first note of real sympathy he had used in a long while, for he felt sorry for her now. At the same time he was afraid to go any further along that line, for fear it might give her a false sense as to his present attitude toward her which was one essentially of indifference. But she was not so dull but what she could see that the consideration in his voice had been brought about by his defeat, which meant hers also. She choked a little—and even so was touched. The bare suggestion of sympathy brought back the old days so definitely gone forever. If only they could be brought back!

"I don't want you to feel distressed about me, though," he went on, before she could say anything to him. "I'm not through with my fighting. I'll get out of this. I have to go to prison, it seems, in order to get things straightened out properly. What I would like you to do is to keep up a cheerful appearance in front of the rest of the family—father and mother particularly. They need to be cheered up." He thought once of taking her hand, then decided not. She noted mentally his hesitation, the great difference between his attitude now and that of ten or twelve years before. It did not hurt her now as much as she once would have thought. She looked at him, scarcely knowing what to say. There was really not so much to say.

"Will you have to go soon, if you do have to go?" she ventured, wearily.

"I can't tell yet. Possibly to-night. Possibly Friday. Possibly not until Monday. I'm waiting to hear from Steger. I expect him here any minute."

To prison! To prison! Her Frank Cowperwood, her husband—the substance of their home here—and all their soul destruction going to prison. And even now she scarcely grasped why! She stood there wondering what she could do.

"Is there anything I can get for you?" she asked, starting forward as if out of a dream. "Do you want me to do anything? Don't you think perhaps you had better leave Philadelphia, Frank? You needn't go to prison unless you want to."

She was a little beside herself, for the first time in her life shocked out of a deadly calm.

He paused and looked at her for a moment in his direct, examining way, his hard commercial business judgment restored on the instant.

"That would be a confession of guilt, Lillian, and I'm not guilty," he replied, almost coldly. "I haven't done anything that warrants my running away or going to prison, either. I'm merely going there to save time at present. I can't be litigating this thing forever. I'll get out—be pardoned out or sued out in a reasonable length of time. Just now it's better to go, I think. I wouldn't think of running away from Philadelphia. Two of five judges found for me in the decision. That's pretty fair evidence that the State has no case against me."

His wife saw she had made a mistake. It clarified her judgment on the instant. "I didn't mean in that way, Frank," she replied, apologetically. "You know I didn't. Of course I know you're not guilty. Why should I think you were, of all people?"

She paused, expecting some retort, some further argument—a kind word maybe. A trace of the older, baffling love, but he had quietly turned to his desk and was thinking of other things.

At this point the anomaly of her own state came over her again. It was all so sad and so hopeless. And what was she to do in the future? And what was he likely to do? She paused half trembling and yet decided, because of her peculiarly nonresisting nature—why trespass on his time? Why bother? No good would really come of it. He really did not care for her any more—that was it. Nothing could make him, nothing could bring them together again, not even this tragedy. He was interested in another woman—Aileen—and so her foolish thoughts and explanations, her fear, sorrow, distress, were not important to him. He could take her agonized wish for his freedom as a comment on his probable guilt, a doubt of his innocence, a criticism of him! She turned away for a minute, and he started to leave the room.

"I'll be back again in a few moments," he volunteered. "Are the children here?"

"Yes, they're up in the play-room," she answered, sadly, utterly nonplussed and distraught.

"Oh, Frank!" she had it on her lips to cry, but before she could utter it he had bustled down the steps and was gone. She turned back to the table, her left hand to her mouth, her eyes in a queer, hazy, melancholy mist. Could it be, she thought, that life could really come to this—that love could so utterly, so thoroughly die? Ten years before—but, oh, why go back to that? Obviously it could, and thoughts concerning that would not help now. Twice now in her life her affairs had seemed to go to pieces—once when her first husband had died, and now when her second had failed her, had fallen in love with another and was going to be sent off to prison. What was it about her that caused such things? Was there anything wrong with her? What was she going to do? Where go? She had no idea, of course, for how long a term of years he would be sent away. It might be one year or it might be five years, as the papers had said. Good heavens! The children could almost come to forget him in five years. She put her other hand to her mouth, also, and then to her forehead, where there was a dull ache. She tried to think further than this, but somehow, just now, there was no further thought. Suddenly quite outside of her own volition, with no thought that she was going to do such a thing, her bosom began to heave, her throat contracted in four or five short, sharp, aching spasms, her eyes burned, and she shook in a vigorous, anguished, desperate, almost one might have said dry-eyed, cry, so hot and few were the tears. She could not stop for the moment, just stood there and shook, and then after a while a dull ache succeeded, and she was quite as she had been before.

"Why cry?" she suddenly asked herself, fiercely—for her. "Why break down in this stormy, useless way? Would it help?"

But, in spite of her speculative, philosophic observations to herself, she still felt the echo, the distant rumble, as it were, of the storm in her own soul. "Why cry? Why not cry?" She might have said—but wouldn't, and in spite of herself and all her logic, she knew that this tempest which had so recently raged over her was now merely circling around her soul's horizon and would return to break again.

CHAPTER L

The arrival of Steger with the information that no move of any kind would be made by the sheriff until Monday morning, when Cowperwood could present himself, eased matters. This gave him time to think—to adjust home details at his leisure. He broke the news to his father and mother in a consoling way and talked with his brothers and father about getting matters immediately adjusted in connection with the smaller houses to which they were now shortly to be compelled to move. There was much conferring among the different members of this collapsing organization in regard to the minor details; and what with his conferences with Steger, his seeing personally Davison, Leigh, Avery Stone, of Jay Cooke & Co., George Waterman (his old-time employer Henry was dead), ex-State Treasurer Van Nostrand, who had gone out with the last State administration, and others, he was very busy. Now that he was really going into prison, he wanted his financial friends to get together and see if they could get him out by appealing to the Governor. The division of opinion among the judges of the State Supreme Court was his excuse and strong point. He wanted Steger to follow this up, and he spared no pains in trying to see all and sundry who might be of use to him—Edward Tighe, of Tighe & Co., who was still in business in Third Street; Newton Targool; Arthur Rivers; Joseph Zimmerman, the dry-goods prince, now a millionaire; Judge Kitchen; Terrence Relihan, the former representative of the money element at Harrisburg; and many others.

Cowperwood wanted Relihan to approach the newspapers and see if he could not readjust their attitude so as to work to get him out, and he wanted Walter Leigh to head the movement of getting up a signed petition which should contain all the important names of moneyed people and others, asking the Governor to release him. Leigh agreed to this heartily, as did Relihan, and many others.

And, afterwards there was really nothing else to do, unless it was to see Aileen once more, and this, in the midst of his other complications and obligations, seemed all but impossible at times—and yet he did achieve that, too—so eager was he to be soothed and comforted by the ignorant and yet all embracing volume of her love. Her eyes these days! The eager, burning quest of him and his happiness that blazed in them. To think that he should be tortured so—her Frank! Oh, she knew—whatever he said, and however bravely and jauntily he talked. To think that her love for him should have been the principal cause of his being sent to jail, as she now believed. And the cruelty of her father! And the smallness of his enemies—that fool Stener, for instance, whose pictures she had seen in the papers. Actually, whenever in the presence of her Frank, she fairly seethed in a chemic agony for him—her strong, handsome lover—the strongest, bravest, wisest, kindest, handsomest man in the world. Oh, didn't she know! And Cowperwood, looking in her eyes and realizing this reasonless, if so comforting fever for him, smiled and was touched. Such love! That of a dog for a master; that of a mother for a child. And how had he come to evoke it? He could not say, but it was beautiful.

And so, now, in these last trying hours, he wished to see her much—and did—meeting her at least four times in the month in which he had been free, between his conviction and the final dismissal of his appeal. He had one last opportunity of seeing her—and she him—just before his entrance into prison this last time—on the Saturday before the Monday of his sentence. He had not come in contact with her since the decision of the Supreme Court had been rendered, but he had had a letter from her sent to a private mail-box, and had made an appointment for Saturday at a small hotel in Camden, which, being across the river, was safer, in his judgment, than anything in Philadelphia. He was a little uncertain as to how she would take the possibility of not seeing him soon again after Monday, and how she would act generally once he was where she could not confer with him as often as she chose. And in consequence, he was anxious to talk to her. But on this occasion, as he anticipated, and even feared, so sorry for her was he, she was not less emphatic in her protestations than she had ever been; in fact, much more so. When she saw him approaching in the distance, she went forward to meet him in that direct, forceful way which only she could attempt with him, a sort of mannish impetuosity which he both enjoyed and admired, and slipping her arms around his neck, said: "Honey, you needn't tell me. I saw it in the papers the other morning. Don't you mind, honey. I love you. I'll wait for you. I'll be with you yet, if it takes a dozen years of waiting. It doesn't make any difference to me if it takes a hundred, only I'm so sorry for you, sweetheart. I'll be with you every day through this, darling, loving you with all my might."

She caressed him while he looked at her in that quiet way which betokened at once his self-poise and yet his interest and satisfaction in her. He couldn't help loving Aileen, he thought who could? She was so passionate, vibrant, desireful. He couldn't help admiring her tremendously, now more than ever, because literally, in spite of all his intellectual strength, he really could not rule her. She went at him, even when he stood off in a calm, critical way, as if he were her special property, her toy. She would talk to him always, and particularly when she was excited, as if he were just a baby, her pet; and sometimes he felt as though she would really overcome him mentally, make him subservient to her, she was so individual, so sure of her importance as a woman.

Now on this occasion she went babbling on as if he were broken-hearted, in need of her greatest care and tenderness, although he really wasn't at all; and for the moment she actually made him feel as though he was.

"It isn't as bad as that, Aileen," he ventured to say, eventually; and with a softness and tenderness almost unusual for him, even where she was concerned, but she went on forcefully, paying no heed to him.

"Oh, yes, it is, too, honey. I know. Oh, my poor Frank! But I'll see you. I know how to manage, whatever happens. How often do they let visitors come out to see the prisoners there?"

"Only once in three months, pet, so they say, but I think we can fix that after I get there; only do you think you had better try to come right away, Aileen? You know what the feeling now is. Hadn't you better wait a while? Aren't you in danger of stirring up your father? He might cause a lot of trouble out there if he were so minded."

"Only once in three months!" she exclaimed, with rising emphasis, as he began this explanation. "Oh, Frank, no! Surely not! Once in three months! Oh, I can't stand that! I won't! I'll go and see the warden myself. He'll let me see you. I'm sure he will, if I talk to him."

She fairly gasped in her excitement, not willing to pause in her tirade, but Cowperwood interposed with her, "You're not thinking what you're saying, Aileen. You're not thinking. Remember your father! Remember your family! Your father may know the warden out there. You don't want it to get all over town that you're running out there to see me, do you? Your father might cause you trouble. Besides you don't know the small party politicians as I do. They gossip like a lot of old women. You'll have to be very careful what you do and how you do it. I don't want to lose you. I want to see you. But you'll have to mind what you're doing. Don't try to see me at once. I want you to, but I want to find out how the land lies, and I want you to find out too. You won't lose me. I'll be there, well enough."

He paused as he thought of the long tier of iron cells which must be there, one of which would be his—for how long?—and of Aileen seeing him through the door of it or in it. At the same time he was thinking, in spite of all his other calculations, how charming she was looking to-day. How young she kept, and how forceful! While he was nearing his full maturity she was a comparatively young girl, and as beautiful as ever. She was wearing a black-and-white-striped silk in the curious bustle style of the times, and a set of sealskin furs, including a little sealskin cap set jauntily on top her red-gold hair.

"I know, I know," replied Aileen, firmly. "But think of three months! Honey, I can't! I won't! It's nonsense. Three months! I know that my father wouldn't have to wait any three months if he wanted to see anybody out there, nor anybody else that he wanted to ask favors for. And I won't, either. I'll find some way."

Cowperwood had to smile. You could not defeat Aileen so easily.

"But you're not your father, honey; and you don't want him to know."

"I know I don't, but they don't need to know who I am. I can go heavily veiled. I don't think that the warden knows my father. He may. Anyhow, he doesn't know me; and he wouldn't tell on me if he did if I talked to him."

Her confidence in her charms, her personality, her earthly privileges was quite anarchistic. Cowperwood shook his head.

"Honey, you're about the best and the worst there is when it comes to a woman," he observed, affectionately, pulling her head down to kiss her, "but you'll have to listen to me just the same. I have a lawyer, Steger—you know him. He's going to take up this matter with the warden out there—is doing it today. He may be able to fix things, and he may not. I'll know to-morrow or Sunday, and I'll write you. But don't go and do anything rash until you hear. I'm sure I can cut that visiting limit in half, and perhaps down to once a month or once in two weeks even. They only allow me to write one letter in three months"—Aileen exploded again—"and I'm sure I can have that made different—some; but don't write me until you hear, or at least don't sign any name or put any address in. They open all mail and read it. If you see me or write me you'll have to be cautious, and you're not the most cautious person in the world. Now be good, will you?"

They talked much more—of his family, his court appearance Monday, whether he would get out soon to attend any of the suits still pending, or be pardoned. Aileen still believed in his future. She had read the opinions of the dissenting judges in his favor, and that of the three agreed judges against him. She was sure his day was not over in Philadelphia, and that he would some time reestablish himself and then take her with him somewhere else. She was sorry for Mrs. Cowperwood, but she was convinced that she was not suited to him— that Frank needed some one more like herself, some one with youth and beauty and force—her, no less. She clung to him now in ecstatic embraces until it was time to go. So far as a plan of procedure could have been adjusted in a situation so incapable of accurate adjustment, it had been done. She was desperately downcast at the last moment, as was he, over their parting; but she pulled herself together with her usual force and faced the dark future with a steady eye.

Monday came and with it his final departure. All that could be done had been done. Cowperwood said his farewells to his mother and father, his brothers and sister. He had a rather distant but sensible and matter-of-fact talk with his wife. He made no special point of saying good-by to his son or his daughter; when he came in on Thursday, Friday, Saturday, and Sunday evenings, after he had learned that he was to depart Monday, it was with the thought of talking to them a little in an especially affectionate way. He realized that his general moral or unmoral attitude was perhaps working them a temporary injustice. Still he was not sure. Most people did fairly well with their lives, whether coddled or deprived of opportunity. These children would probably do as well as most children, whatever happened—and then, anyhow, he had no intention of forsaking them financially, if he could help it. He did not want to separate his wife from her children, nor them from her. She should keep them. He wanted them to be comfortable with her. He would like to see them, wherever they were with her, occasionally. Only he wanted his own personal freedom, in so far as she and they were concerned, to go off and set up a new world and a new home with Aileen. So now on these last days, and particularly this last Sunday night, he was rather noticeably considerate of his boy and girl, without being too openly indicative of his approaching separation from them.

"Frank," he said to his notably lackadaisical son on this occasion, "aren't you going to straighten up and be a big, strong, healthy fellow? You don't play enough. You ought to get in with a gang of boys and be a leader. Why don't you fit yourself up a gymnasium somewhere and see how strong you can get?"

They were in the senior Cowperwood's sitting-room, where they had all rather consciously gathered on this occasion.

Lillian, second, who was on the other side of the big library table from her father, paused to survey him and her brother with interest. Both had been carefully guarded against any real knowledge of their father's affairs or his present predicament. He was going away on a journey for about a month or so they understood. Lillian was reading in a Chatterbox book which had been given her the previous Christmas.

"He won't do anything," she volunteered, looking up from her reading in a peculiarly critical way for her. "Why, he won't ever run races with me when I want him to."

"Aw, who wants to run races with you, anyhow?" returned Frank, junior, sourly. "You couldn't run if I did want to run with you."

"Couldn't I?" she replied. "I could beat you, all right."

"Lillian!" pleaded her mother, with a warning sound in her voice.

Cowperwood smiled, and laid his hand affectionately on his son's head. "You'll be all right, Frank," he volunteered, pinching his ear lightly. "Don't worry—just make an effort."

The boy did not respond as warmly as he hoped. Later in the evening Mrs. Cowperwood noticed that her husband squeezed his daughter's slim little waist and pulled her curly hair gently. For the moment she was jealous of her daughter.

"Going to be the best kind of a girl while I'm away?" he said to her, privately.

"Yes, papa," she replied, brightly.

"That's right," he returned, and leaned over and kissed her mouth tenderly. "Button Eyes," he said.

Mrs. Cowperwood sighed after he had gone. "Everything for the children, nothing for me," she thought, though the children had not got so vastly much either in the past.

Cowperwood's attitude toward his mother in this final hour was about as tender and sympathetic as any he could maintain in this world. He understood quite clearly the ramifications of her interests, and how she was suffering for him and all the others concerned. He had not forgotten her sympathetic care of him in his youth; and if he could have done anything to have spared her this unhappy breakdown of her fortunes in her old age, he would have done so. There was no use crying over spilled milk. It was impossible at times for him not to feel intensely in moments of success or failure; but the proper thing to do was to bear up, not to show it, to talk little and go your way with an air not so much of resignation as of self-sufficiency, to whatever was awaiting you. That was his attitude on this morning, and that was what he expected from those around him—almost compelled, in fact, by his own attitude.

"Well, mother," he said, genially, at the last moment—he would not let her nor his wife nor his sister come to court, maintaining that it would make not the least difference to him and would only harrow their own feelings uselessly—"I'm going now. Don't worry. Keep up your spirits."

He slipped his arm around his mother's waist, and she gave him a long, unrestrained, despairing embrace and kiss.

"Go on, Frank," she said, choking, when she let him go. "God bless you. I'll pray for you." He paid no further attention to her. He didn't dare.

"Good-by, Lillian," he said to his wife, pleasantly, kindly. "I'll be back in a few days, I think. I'll be coming out to attend some of these court proceedings."

To his sister he said: "Good-by, Anna. Don't let the others get too down-hearted."

"I'll see you three afterward," he said to his father and brothers; and so, dressed in the very best fashion of the time, he hurried down into the reception-hall, where Steger was waiting, and was off. His family, hearing the door close on him, suffered a poignant sense of desolation. They stood there for a moment, his mother crying, his father looking as though he had lost his last friend but making a great effort to seem self-contained and equal to his troubles, Anna telling Lillian not to mind, and the latter staring dumbly into the future, not knowing what to think. Surely a brilliant sun had set on their local scene, and in a very pathetic way.

CHAPTER LII

When Cowperwood reached the jail, Jaspers was there, glad to see him but principally relieved to feel that nothing had happened to mar his own reputation as a sheriff. Because of the urgency of court matters generally, it was decided to depart for the courtroom at nine o'clock. Eddie Zanders was once more delegated to see that Cowperwood was brought safely before Judge Payderson and afterward taken to the penitentiary. All of the papers in the case were put in his care to be delivered to the warden.

"I suppose you know," confided Sheriff Jaspers to Steger, "that Stener is here. He ain't got no money now, but I gave him a private room just the same. I didn't want to put a man like him in no cell." Sheriff Jaspers sympathized with Stener.

"That's right. I'm glad to hear that," replied Steger, smiling to himself.

"I didn't suppose from what I've heard that Mr. Cowperwood would want to meet Stener here, so I've kept 'em apart. George just left a minute ago with another deputy."

"That's good. That's the way it ought to be," replied Steger. He was glad for Cowperwood's sake that the sheriff had so much tact. Evidently George and the sheriff were getting along in a very friendly way, for all the former's bitter troubles and lack of means.

The Cowperwood party walked, the distance not being great, and as they did so they talked of rather simple things to avoid the more serious.

"Things aren't going to be so bad," Edward said to his father. "Steger says the Governor is sure to pardon Stener in a year or less, and if he does he's bound to let Frank out too."

Cowperwood, the elder, had heard this over and over, but he was never tired of hearing it. It was like some simple croon with which babies are hushed to sleep. The snow on the ground, which was enduring remarkably well for this time of year, the fineness of the day, which had started out to be clear and bright, the hope that the courtroom might not be full, all held the attention of the father and his two sons. Cowperwood, senior, even commented on some sparrows fighting over a piece of bread, marveling how well they did in winter, solely to ease his mind. Cowperwood, walking on ahead with Steger and Zanders, talked of approaching court proceedings in connection with his business and what ought to be done. When they reached the court the same little pen in which Cowperwood had awaited the verdict of his jury several months before was waiting to receive him.

Cowperwood, senior, and his other sons sought places in the courtroom proper. Eddie Zanders remained with his charge. Stener and a deputy by the name of Wilkerson were in the room; but he and Cowperwood pretended now not to see each other. Frank had no objection to talking to his former associate, but he could see that Stener was diffident and ashamed. So he let the situation pass without look or word of any kind. After some three-quarters of an hour of dreary waiting the door leading into the courtroom proper opened and a bailiff stepped in.

"All prisoners up for sentence," he called.

There were six, all told, including Cowperwood and Stener. Two· of them were confederate housebreakers who had been caught red-handed at their midnight task.

Another prisoner was no more and no less than a plain horse-thief, a young man of twenty-six, who had been convicted by a jury of stealing a grocer's horse and selling it. The last man was a negro, a tall, shambling, illiterate, nebulous-minded black, who had walked off with an apparently discarded section of lead pipe which he had found in a lumber-yard. His idea was to sell or trade it for a drink. He really did not belong in this court at all; but, having been caught by an undersized American watchman charged with the care of the property, and having at first refused to plead guilty, not quite understanding what was to be done with him, he had been perforce bound over to this court for trial. Afterward he had changed his mind and admitted his guilt, so he now had to come before Judge Payderson for sentence or dismissal. The lower court before which he had originally been brought had lost jurisdiction by binding him over to to higher court for trial. Eddie Zanders, in his self-appointed position as guide and mentor to Cowperwood, had confided nearly all of this data to him as he stood waiting.

The courtroom was crowded. It was very humiliating to Cowperwood to have to file in this way along the side aisle with these others, followed by Stener, well dressed but sickly looking and disconsolate.

The negro, Charles Ackerman, was the first on the list.

"How is it this man comes before me?" asked Payderson, peevishly, when he noted the value of the property Ackerman was supposed to have stolen.

"Your honor," the assistant district attorney explained, promptly, "this man was before a lower court and refused, because he was drunk, or something, to plead guilty. The lower court, because the complainant would not forego the charge, was compelled to bind him over to this court for trial. Since then he has changed his mind and has admitted his guilt to the district attorney. He would not be brought before you except we have no alternative. He has to be brought here now in order to clear the calendar."

Judge Payderson stared quizzically at the negro, who, obviously not very much disturbed by this examination, was leaning comfortably on the gate or bar before which the average criminal stood erect and terrified. He had been before police-court magistrates before on one charge and another—drunkenness, disorderly conduct, and the like—but his whole attitude was one of shambling, lackadaisical, amusing innocence.

"Well, Ackerman," inquired his honor, severely, "did you or did you not steal this piece of lead pipe as charged here—four dollars and eighty cents' worth?"

"Yassah, I did," he began. "I tell you how it was, jedge. I was a-comin' along past dat lumber-yard one Saturday afternoon, and I hadn't been wuckin', an' I saw dat piece o' pipe thoo de fence, lyin' inside, and I jes' reached thoo with a piece o' boad I found dey and pulled it over to me an' tuck it. An' aftahwahd dis Mistah Watchman man"—he waved his hand oratorically toward the witness-chair, where, in case the judge might wish to ask him some questions, the complainant had taken his stand—"come around tuh where I live an' accused me of done takin' it."

"But you did take it, didn't you?"

"Yassah, I done tuck it."

"What did you do with it?"

"I traded it foh twenty-five cents."

"You mean you sold it," corrected his honor.

"Yassah, I done sold it."

"Well, don't you know it's wrong to do anything like that? Didn't you know when you reached through that fence and pulled that pipe over to you that you were stealing? Didn't you?"

"Yassah, I knowed it was wrong," replied Ackerman, sheepishly. "I didn' think 'twuz stealin' like zackly, but I done knowed it was wrong. I done knowed I oughtn' take it, I guess."

"Of course you did. Of course you did. That's just it. You knew you were stealing, and still you took it. Has the man to whom this negro sold the lead pipe been apprehended yet?" the judge inquired sharply of the district attorney. "He should be, for he's more guilty than this negro, a receiver of stolen goods."

"Yes, sir," replied the assistant. "His case is before Judge Yawger."

"Quite right. It should be," replied Payderson, severely. "This matter of receiving stolen property is one of the worst offenses, in my judgment."

He then turned his attention to Ackerman again. "Now, look here, Ackerman," he exclaimed, irritated at having to bother with such a pretty case, "I want to say something to you, and I want you to pay strict attention to me. Straighten up, there! Don't lean on that gate! You are in the presence of the law now." Ackerman had sprawled himself comfortably down on his elbows as he would have if he had been leaning over a back-fence gate talking to some one, but he immediately drew himself straight, still grinning foolishly and apologetically, when he heard this. "You are not so dull but that you can understand what I am going to say to you. The offense you have committed—stealing a piece of lead pipe—is a crime. Do you hear me? A criminal offense—one that I could punish you very severely for. I could send you to the penitentiary for one year if I chose—the law says I may—one year at hard labor for stealing a piece of lead pipe. Now, if you have any sense you will pay strict attention to what I am going to tell you. I am not going to send you to the penitentiary right now. I'm going to wait a little while. I am going to sentence you to one year in the penitentiary—one year. Do you understand?" Ackerman blanched a little and licked his lips nervously. "And then I am going to suspend that sentence—hold it over your head, so that if you are ever caught taking anything else you will be punished for this offense and the next one also at one and the same time. Do you understand that? Do you know what I mean? Tell me. Do you?"

"Yessah! I does, sir," replied the negro. "You'se gwine to let me go now—tha's it."

The audience grinned, and his honor made a wry face to prevent his own grim grin.

"I'm going to let you go only so long as you don't steal anything else," he thundered. "The moment you steal anything else, back you come to this court, and then you go to the penitentiary for a year and whatever more time you deserve. Do you understand that? Now, I want you to walk straight out of this court and behave yourself. Don't ever steal anything. Get something to do! Don't steal, do you hear? Don't touch anything that doesn't belong to you! Don't come back here! If you do, I'll send you to the penitentiary, sure."

"Yassah! No, sah, I won't," replied Ackerman, nervously. "I won't take nothin' more that don't belong tuh me."

He shuffled away, after a moment, urged along by the guiding hand of a bailiff, and was put safely outside the court, amid a mixture of smiles and laughter over his simplicity and Payderson's undue severity of manner. But the next case was called and soon engrossed the interest of the audience.

It was that of the two housebreakers whom Cowperwood had been and was still studying with much curiosity. In all his life before he had never witnessed a sentencing scene of any kind. He had never been in police or criminal courts of any kind—rarely in any of the civil ones. He was glad to see the negro go, and gave Payderson credit for having some sense and sympathy—more than he had expected.

He wondered now whether by any chance Aileen was here. He had objected to her coming, but she might have done so. She was, as a matter of fact, in the extreme rear, pocketed in a crowd near the door, heavily veiled, but present. She had not been able to resist the desire to know quickly and surely her beloved's fate—to be near him in his hour of real suffering, as she thought. She was greatly angered at seeing him brought in with a line of ordinary criminals and made to wait in this, to her, shameful public manner, but she could not help admiring all the more the dignity and superiority of his presence even here. He was not even pale, as she saw, just the same firm, calm soul she had always known him to be. If he could only see her now; if he would only look so she could lift her veil and smile! He didn't, though; he wouldn't. He didn't want to see her here. But she would tell him all about it when she saw him again just the same.

The two burglars were quickly disposed of by the judge, with a sentence of one year each, and they were led away, uncertain, and apparently not knowing what to think of their crime or their future.

When it came to Cowperwood's turn to be called, his honor himself stiffened and straightened up, for this was a different type of man and could not be handled in the usual manner. He knew exactly what he was going to say. When one of Mollenhauer's agents, a close friend of Butler's, had suggested that five years for both Cowperwood and Stener would be about right, he knew exactly what to do. "Frank Algernon Cowperwood," called the clerk.

Cowperwood stepped briskly forward, sorry for himself, ashamed of his position in a way, but showing it neither in look nor manner. Payderson eyed him as he had the others.

"Name?" asked the bailiff, for the benefit of the court stenographer.

"Frank Algernon Cowperwood."

"Residence?"

"1937 Girard Avenue."

"Occupation?"

"Banker and broker."

Steger stood close beside him, very dignified, very forceful, ready to make a final statement for the benefit of the court and the public when the time should come. Aileen, from her position in the crowd near the door, was for the first time in her life biting her fingers nervously and there were great beads of perspiration on her brow. Cowperwood's father was tense with excitement and his two brothers looked quickly away, doing their best to hide their fear and sorrow.

"Ever convicted before?"

"Never," replied Steger for Cowperwood, quietly.

"Frank Algernon Cowperwood," called the clerk, in his nasal, singsong way, coming forward, "have you anything to say why judgment should not now be pronounced upon you? If so, speak."

Cowperwood started to say no, but Steger put up his hand.

"If the court pleases, my client, Mr. Cowperwood, the prisoner at the bar, is neither guilty in his own estimation, nor in that of two-fifths of the Pennsylvania State Supreme Court—the court of last resort in this State," he exclaimed, loudly and clearly, so that all might hear.

One of the interested listeners and spectators at this point was Edward Malia Butler, who had just stepped in from another courtroom where he had been talking to a judge. An obsequious court attendant had warned him that Cowperwood was about to be sentenced. He had really come here this morning in order not to miss this sentence, but he cloaked his motive under the guise of another errand. He did not know that Aileen was there, nor did he see her.

"As he himself testified at the time of his trial," went on Steger, "and as the evidence clearly showed, he was never more than an agent for the gentleman whose offense was subsequently adjudicated by this court; and as an agent he still maintains, and two-fifths of the State Supreme Court agree with him, that he was strictly within his rights and privileges in not having deposited the sixty thousand dollars' worth of city loan certificates at the time, and in the manner which the people, acting through the district attorney, complained that he should have. My client is a man of rare financial ability. By the various letters which have been submitted to your honor in his behalf, you will see that he commands the respect and the sympathy of a large majority of the most forceful and eminent men in his particular world. He is a man of distinguished social standing and of notable achievements. Only the most unheralded and the unkindest thrust of fortune has brought him here before you today—a fire and its consequent panic which involved a financial property of the most thorough and stable character. In spite of the verdict of the jury and the decision of three-fifths of the State Supreme Court, I maintain that my client is not an embezzler, that he has not committed larceny, that he should never have been convicted, and that he should not now be punished for something of which he is not guilty.

"I trust that your honor will not misunderstand me or my motives when I point out in this situation that what I have said is true. I do not wish to cast any reflection on the integrity of the court, nor of any court, nor of any of the processes of law. But I do condemn and deplore the untoward chain of events which has built up a seeming situation, not easily understood by the lay mind, and which has brought my distinguished client within the purview of the law. I think it is but fair that this should be finally and publicly stated here and now. I ask that your honor be lenient, and that if you cannot conscientiously dismiss this charge you will at least see that the facts, as I have indicated them, are given due weight in the measure of the punishment inflicted."

Steger stepped back and Judge Payderson nodded, as much as to say he had heard all the distinguished lawyer had to say, and would give it such consideration as it deserved—no more. Then he turned to Cowperwood, and, summoning all his judicial dignity to his aid, he began:

"Frank Algernon Cowperwood, you have been convicted by a jury of your own selection of the offense of larceny. The motion for a new trial, made in your behalf by your learned counsel, has been carefully considered and overruled, the majority of the court being entirely satisfied with the propriety of the conviction, both upon the law and the evidence. Your offense was one of more than usual gravity, the more so that the large amount of money which you obtained belonged to the city. And it was aggravated by the fact that you had in addition thereto unlawfully used and converted to your own use several hundred thousand dollars of the loan and money of the city. For such an offense the maximum punishment affixed by the law is singularly merciful. Nevertheless, the facts in connection with your hitherto distinguished position, the circumstances under which your failure was brought about, and the appeals of your numerous friends and financial associates, will be given due consideration by this court. It is not unmindful of any important fact in your career." Payderson paused as if in doubt, though he knew very well how he was about to proceed. He knew what his superiors expected of him.

"If your case points no other moral," he went on, after a moment, toying with the briefs, "it will at least teach the lesson much needed at the present time, that the treasury of the city is not to be invaded and plundered with impunity under the thin disguise of a business

225

transaction, and that there is still a power in the law to vindicate itself and to protect the public.

"The sentence of the court," he added, solemnly, the while Cowperwood gazed unmoved, "is, therefore, that you pay a fine of five thousand dollars to the commonwealth for the use of the county, that you pay the costs of prosecution, and that you undergo imprisonment in the State Penitentiary for the Eastern District by separate or solitary confinement at labor for a period of four years and three months, and that you stand committed until this sentence is complied with."

Cowperwood's father, on hearing this, bowed his head to hide his tears. Aileen bit her lower lip and clenched her hands to keep down her rage and disappointment and tears. Four years and three months! That would make a terrible gap in his life and hers. Still, she could wait. It was better than eight or ten years, as she had feared it might be. Perhaps now, once this was really over and he was in prison, the Governor would pardon him.

The judge now moved to pick up the papers in connection with Stener's case, satisfied that he had given the financiers no chance to say he had not given due heed to their plea in Cowperwood's behalf and yet certain that the politicians would be pleased that he had so nearly given Cowperwood the maximum while appearing to have heeded the pleas for mercy. Cowperwood saw through the trick at once, but it did not disturb him. It struck him as rather weak and contemptible. A bailiff came forward and started to hurry him away.

"Allow the prisoner to remain for a moment," called the judge.

The name, of George W. Stener had been called by the clerk and Cowperwood did not quite understand why he was being detained, but he soon learned. It was that he might hear the opinion of the court in connection with his copartner in crime. The latter's record was taken. Roger O'Mara, the Irish political lawyer who had been his counsel all through his troubles, stood near him, but had nothing to say beyond asking the judge to consider Stener's previously honorable career.

"George W. Stener," said his honor, while the audience, including Cowperwood, listened attentively. "The motion for a new trial as well as an arrest of judgment in your case having been overruled, it remains for the court to impose such sentence as the nature of your offense requires. I do not desire to add to the pain of your position by any extended remarks of my own; but I cannot let the occasion pass without expressing my emphatic condemnation of your offense. The misapplication of public money has become the great crime of the age. If not promptly and firmly checked, it will ultimately destroy our institutions. When a republic becomes honeycombed with corruption its vitality is gone. It must crumble upon the first pressure.

"In my opinion, the public is much to blame for your offense and others of a similar character. Heretofore, official fraud has been regarded with too much indifference. What we need is a higher and purer political morality—a state of public opinion which would make the improper use of public money a thing to be execrated. It was the lack of this which made your offense possible. Beyond that I see nothing of extenuation in your case."

Judge Payderson paused for emphasis. He was coming to his finest flight, and he wanted it to sink in.

"The people had confided to you the care of their money," he went on, solemnly. "It was a high, a sacred trust. You should have guarded the door of the treasury even as the cherubim protected the Garden of Eden, and should have turned the flaming sword of impeccable honesty against every one who approached it improperly. Your position as the representative of a great community warranted that.

"In view of all the facts in your case the court can do no less than impose a major penalty. The seventy-fourth section of the Criminal Procedure Act provides that no convict shall be sentenced by the court of this commonwealth to either of the penitentiaries thereof, for any term which shall expire between the fifteenth of November and the fifteenth day of February of any year, and this provision requires me to abate three months from the maximum of time which I would affix in your case—namely, five years. The sentence of the court is, therefore, that you pay a fine of five thousand dollars to the commonwealth for the use of the county"—Payderson knew well enough that Stener could never pay that sum— "and that you undergo imprisonment in the State Penitentiary for the Eastern District, by separate and solitary confinement at labor, for the period of four years and nine months, and that you stand committed until this sentence is complied with." He laid down the briefs and rubbed his chin reflectively while both Cowperwood and Stener were hurried out. Butler was the first to leave after the sentence—quite satisfied. Seeing that all was over so far as she was concerned, Aileen stole quickly out; and after her, in a few moments, Cowperwood's father and brothers. They were to await him outside and go with him to the penitentiary. The remaining members of the family were at home eagerly awaiting intelligence of the morning's work, and Joseph Cowperwood was at once despatched to tell them.

The day had now become cloudy, lowery, and it looked as if there might be snow. Eddie Zanders, who had been given all the papers in the case, announced that there was no need to return to the county jail. In consequence the five of them—Zanders, Steger, Cowperwood, his father, and Edward—got into a street-car which ran to within a few blocks of the prison. Within half an hour they were at the gates of the Eastern Penitentiary.

CHAPTER LIII

The Eastern District Penitentiary of Pennsylvania, standing at Fairmount Avenue and Twenty-first Street in Philadelphia, where Cowperwood was now to serve his sentence of four years and three months, was a large, gray-stone structure, solemn and momentous in its mien, not at all unlike the palace of Sforzas at Milan, although not so distinguished. It stretched its gray length for several blocks along four different streets, and looked as lonely and forbidding as a prison should. The wall which inclosed its great area extending over ten acres and gave it so much of its solemn dignity was thirty-five feet high and some seven feet thick. The prison proper, which was not visible from the outside, consisted of seven arms or corridors, ranged octopus-like around a central room or court, and occupying in their sprawling length about two-thirds of the yard inclosed within the walls, so that there was but little space for the charm of lawn or sward. The corridors, forty-two feet wide from outer wall to outer wall, were one hundred and eighty feet in length, and in four instances two stories high, and extended in their long reach in every direction. There were no windows in the corridors, only narrow slits of skylights, three and one-half feet long by perhaps eight inches wide, let in the roof; and the ground-floor cells were accompanied in some instances by a small yard ten by sixteen—the same size as the cells proper—which was surrounded by a high brick wall in every instance. The cells and floors and roofs were made of stone, and the corridors, which were only ten feet wide between the cells, and in the case of the single-story portion only fifteen feet high, were paved with stone. If you stood in the central room, or rotunda, and looked down the long stretches which departed from you in every direction, you had a sense of narrowness and confinement not compatible with their length. The iron doors, with their outer accompaniment of solid wooden ones, the latter used at times to shut the prisoner from all sight and sound, were grim and unpleasing to behold. The halls were light enough, being whitewashed frequently and set with the narrow skylights, which were closed with frosted glass in winter; but they were, as are all such matter-of-fact arrangements for incarceration, bare—wearisome to look upon. Life enough there was in all conscience, seeing that there were four hundred prisoners here at that time, and that nearly every cell was occupied; but it was a life of which no one individual was essentially aware as a spectacle. He was of it; but he was not. Some of the prisoners, after long service, were used as "trusties" or "runners," as they were locally called; but not many. There was a bakery, a machine-shop, a carpenter-shop, a store-room, a flour-mill, and a series of gardens, or truck patches; but the manipulation of these did not require the services of a large number.

The prison proper dated from 1822, and it had grown, wing by wing, until its present considerable size had been reached. Its population consisted of individuals of all degrees of intelligence and crime, from murderers to minor practitioners of larceny. It had what was known as the "Pennsylvania System" of regulation for its inmates, which was nothing more nor less than solitary confinement for all concerned—a life of absolute silence and separate labor in separate cells.

Barring his comparatively recent experience in the county jail, which after all was far from typical, Cowperwood had never been in a prison in his life. Once, when a boy, in one of his perambulations through several of the surrounding towns, he had passed a village "lock-up," as the town prisons were then called—a small, square, gray building with long iron-barred windows, and he had seen, at one of these rather depressing apertures on the second floor, a none too prepossessing drunkard or town ne'er-do-well who looked down on him with bleary eyes, unkempt hair, and a sodden, waxy, pallid face, and called—for it was summer and the jail window was open:

"Hey, sonny, get me a plug of tobacco, will you?"

Cowperwood, who had looked up, shocked and disturbed by the man's disheveled appearance, had called back, quite without stopping to think:

"Naw, I can't."

"Look out you don't get locked up yourself sometime, you little runt," the man had replied, savagely, only half recovered from his debauch of the day before.

He had not thought of this particular scene in years, but now suddenly it came back to him. Here he was on his way to be locked up in this dull, somber prison, and it was snowing, and he was being cut out of human affairs as much as it was possible for him to be cut out.

No friends were permitted to accompany him beyond the outer gate—not even Steger for the time being, though he might visit him later in the day. This was an inviolable rule. Zanders being known to the gate-keeper, and bearing his commitment paper, was admitted at once. The others turned solemnly away. They bade a gloomy if affectionate farewell to Cowperwood, who, on his part, attempted to give it all an air of inconsequence—as, in part and even here, it had for him.

"Well, good-by for the present," he said, shaking hands. "I'll be all right and I'll get out soon. Wait and see. Tell Lillian not to worry."

He stepped inside, and the gate clanked solemnly behind him. Zanders led the way through a dark, somber hall, wide and high-ceiled, to a farther gate, where a second gateman, trifling with a large key, unlocked a barred door at his bidding. Once inside the prison yard, Zanders turned to the left into a small office, presenting his prisoner before a small, chest-high desk, where stood a prison officer in uniform of blue. The latter, the receiving overseer of the prison—a thin, practical, executive-looking person with narrow gray eyes and light hair, took the paper which the sheriff's deputy handed him and read it. This was his authority for receiving Cowperwood. In his turn he handed Zanders a slip, showing that he had so received the prisoner; and then Zanders left, receiving gratefully the tip which Cowperwood pressed in his hand.

"Well, good-by, Mr. Cowperwood," he said, with a peculiar twist of his detective-like head. "I'm sorry. I hope you won't find it so bad here."

He wanted to impress the receiving overseer with his familiarity with this distinguished prisoner, and Cowperwood, true to his policy of make-believe, shook hands with him cordially.

"I'm much obliged to you for your courtesy, Mr. Zanders," he said, then turned to his new master with the air of a man who is determined to make a good impression. He was now in the hands of petty officials, he knew, who could modify or increase his comfort at will. He wanted to impress this man with his utter willingness to comply and obey—his sense of respect for his authority—without in any way demeaning himself. He was depressed but efficient, even here in the clutch of that eventual machine of the law, the State penitentiary, which he had been struggling so hard to evade.

The receiving overseer, Roger Kendall, though thin and clerical, was a rather capable man, as prison officials go—shrewd, not particularly well educated, not over-intelligent naturally, not over-industrious, but sufficiently energetic to hold his position. He knew something about convicts—considerable—for he had been dealing with them for nearly twenty-six years. His attitude toward them was cold, cynical, critical.

He did not permit any of them to come into personal contact with him, but he saw to it that underlings in his presence carried out the requirements of the law.

When Cowperwood entered, dressed in his very good clothing—a dark gray-blue twill suit of pure wool, a light, well-made gray overcoat, a black derby hat of the latest shape, his shoes new and of good leather, his tie of the best silk, heavy and conservatively colored, his hair and mustache showing the attention of an intelligent barber, and his hands well manicured—the receiving overseer saw at once that he was in the presence of some one of superior intelligence and force, such a man as the fortune of his trade rarely brought into his net.

Cowperwood stood in the middle of the room without apparently looking at any one or anything, though he saw all. "Convict number 3633," Kendall called to a clerk, handing him at the same time a yellow slip of paper on which was written Cowperwood's full name and his record number, counting from the beginning of the penitentiary itself.

The underling, a convict, took it and entered it in a book, reserving the slip at the same time for the penitentiary "runner" or "trusty," who would eventually take Cowperwood to the "manners" gallery.

"You will have to take off your clothes and take a bath," said Kendall to Cowperwood, eyeing him curiously. "I don't suppose you need one, but it's the rule."

"Thank you," replied Cowperwood, pleased that his personality was counting for something even here. "Whatever the rules are, I want to obey."

When he started to take off his coat, however, Kendall put up his hand delayingly and tapped a bell. There now issued from an adjoining room an assistant, a prison servitor, a weird-looking specimen of the genus "trusty." He was a small, dark, lopsided individual, one leg being slightly shorter, and therefore one shoulder lower, than the other. He was hollow-chested, squint-eyed, and rather shambling, but spry enough withal. He was dressed in a thin, poorly made, baggy suit of striped jeans, the prison stripes of the place, showing a soft roll-collar shirt underneath, and wearing a large, wide-striped cap, peculiarly offensive in its size and shape to Cowperwood. He could not help thinking how uncanny the man's squint eyes looked under its straight outstanding visor. The trusty had a silly, sycophantic manner of raising one hand in salute. He was a professional "second-story man," "up" for ten years, but by dint of good behavior he had attained to the honor of working about this office without the degrading hood customary for prisoners to wear over the cap. For this he was properly grateful. He now considered his superior with nervous dog-like eyes, and looked at Cowperwood with a certain cunning appreciation of his lot and a show of initial mistrust.

One prisoner is as good as another to the average convict; as a matter of fact, it is their only consolation in their degradation that all who come here are no better than they. The world may have misused them; but they misuse their confreres in their thoughts. The "holier than thou" attitude, intentional or otherwise, is quite the last and most deadly offense within prison walls. This particular "trusty" could no more understand Cowperwood than could a fly the motions of a fly-wheel; but with the cocky superiority of the underling of the world he did not hesitate to think that he could. A crook was a crook to him—Cowperwood no less than the shabbiest pickpocket. His one feeling was that he would like to demean him, to pull him down to his own level.

"You will have to take everything you have out of your pockets," Kendall now informed Cowperwood. Ordinarily he would have said, "Search the prisoner."

Cowperwood stepped forward and laid out a purse with twenty-five dollars in it, a pen-knife, a lead-pencil, a small note-book, and a little ivory elephant which Aileen had given him once, "for luck," and which he treasured solely because she gave it to him. Kendall looked at the latter curiously. "Now you can go on," he said to the "trusty," referring to the undressing and bathing process which was to follow.

"This way," said the latter, addressing Cowperwood, and preceding him into an adjoining room, where three closets held three old-fashioned, iron-bodied, wooden-top bath-tubs, with their attendant shelves for rough crash towels, yellow soap, and the like, and hooks for clothes.

"Get in there," said the trusty, whose name was Thomas Kuby, pointing to one of the tubs. Cowperwood realized that this was the beginning of petty official supervision; but he deemed it wise to appear friendly even here.

"I see," he said. "I will."

"That's right," replied the attendant, somewhat placated. "What did you bring?"

Cowperwood looked at him quizzically. He did not understand. The prison attendant realized that this man did not know the lingo of the place. "What did you bring?" he repeated. "How many years did you get?"

"Oh!" exclaimed Cowperwood, comprehendingly. "I understand. Four and three months." He decided to humor the man. It would probably be better so.

"What for?" inquired Kuby, familiarly.

Cowperwood's blood chilled slightly. "Larceny," he said.

"Yuh got off easy," commented Kuby. "I'm up for ten. A rube judge did that to me."

Kuby had never heard of Cowperwood's crime. He would not have understood its subtleties if he had. Cowperwood did not want to talk to this man; he did not know how. He wished he would go away; but that was not likely. He wanted to be put in his cell and let alone.

"That's too bad," he answered; and the convict realized clearly that this man was really not one of them, or he would not have said anything like that. Kuby went to the two hydrants opening into the bath-tub and turned them on. Cowperwood had been undressing the while, and now stood naked, but not ashamed, in front of this eighth-rate intelligence.

"Don't forget to wash your head, too," said Kuby, and went away.

Cowperwood stood there while the water ran, meditating on his fate. It was strange how life had dealt with him of late—so severely. Unlike most men in his position, he was not suffering from a consciousness of evil. He did not think he was evil. As he saw it, he was merely unfortunate. To think that he should be actually in this great, silent penitentiary, a convict, waiting here beside this cheap iron bathtub, not very sweet or hygienic to contemplate, with this crackbrained criminal to watch over him!

He stepped into the tub and washed himself briskly with the biting yellow soap, drying himself on one of the rough, only partially bleached towels. He looked for his underwear, but there was none. At this point the attendant looked in again. "Out here," he said, inconsiderately.

Cowperwood followed, naked. He was led through the receiving overseer's office into a room, where were scales, implements of measurement, a record-book, etc. The attendant who stood guard at the door now came over, and the clerk who sat in a corner automatically took down a record-blank. Kendall surveyed Cowperwood's decidedly graceful figure, already inclining to a slight thickening around the waist, and approved of it as superior to that of most who came here. His skin, as he particularly noted, was especially white.

"Step on the scale," said the attendant, brusquely.

Cowperwood did so, The former adjusted the weights and scanned the record carefully.

"Weight, one hundred and seventy-five," he called. "Now step over here."

He indicated a spot in the side wall where was fastened in a thin slat—which ran from the floor to about seven and one half feet above, perpendicularly—a small movable wooden indicator, which, when a man was standing under it, could be pressed down on his head. At the side of the slat were the total inches of height, laid off in halves, quarters, eighths, and so on, and to the right a length measurement for the arm. Cowperwood understood what was wanted and stepped under the indicator, standing quite straight.

"Feet level, back to the wall," urged the attendant. "So. Height, five feet nine and ten-sixteenths," he called. The clerk in the corner noted it. He now produced a tape-measure and began measuring Cowperwood's arms, legs, chest, waist, hips, etc. He called out the color of his eyes, his hair, his mustache, and, looking into his mouth, exclaimed, "Teeth, all sound."

After Cowperwood had once more given his address, age, profession, whether he knew any trade, etc.—which he did not—he was allowed to return to the bathroom, and put on the clothing which the prison provided for him—first the rough, prickly underwear, then the cheap soft roll-collar, white-cotton shirt, then the thick bluish-gray cotton socks of a quality such as he had never worn in his life, and over these a pair of indescribable rough-leather clogs, which felt to his feet as though they were made of wood or iron—oily and heavy. He then drew on the shapeless, baggy trousers with their telltale stripes, and over his arms and chest the loose-cut shapeless coat and waistcoat. He felt and knew of course that he looked very strange, wretched. And as he stepped out into the overseer's room again he experienced a peculiar sense of depression, a gone feeling which before this had not assailed him and which now he did his best to conceal. This, then, was what society did to the criminal, he thought to himself. It took him and tore away from his body and his life the habiliments of his proper state and left him these. He felt sad and grim, and, try as he would—he could not help showing it for a moment. It was always his business and his intention to conceal his real feelings, but now it was not quite possible. He felt degraded, impossible, in these clothes, and he knew that he looked it. Nevertheless, he did his best to pull himself together and look unconcerned, willing, obedient, considerate of those above him. After all, he said to himself, it was all a play of sorts, a dream even, if one chose to view it so, a miasma even, from which, in the course of time and with a little luck one might emerge safely enough. He hoped so. It could not last. He was only acting a strange, unfamiliar part on the stage, this stage of life that he knew so well.

Kendall did not waste any time looking at him, however. He merely said to his assistant, "See if you can find a cap for him," and the latter, going to a closet containing numbered shelves, took down a cap—a high-crowned, straight-visored, shabby, striped affair which Cowperwood was asked to try on. It fitted well enough, slipping down close over his ears, and he thought that now his indignities must be about complete. What could be added? There could be no more of these disconcerting accoutrements. But he was mistaken. "Now, Kuby, you take him to Mr. Chapin," said Kendall.

Kuby understood. He went back into the wash-room and produced what Cowperwood had heard of but never before seen—a blue-and-white-striped cotton bag about half the length of an ordinary pillow-case and half again as wide, which Kuby now unfolded and shook out as he came toward him. It was a custom. The use of this hood, dating from the earliest days of the prison, was intended to prevent a sense of location and direction and thereby obviate any attempt to escape. Thereafter during all his stay he was not supposed to walk with or talk to or see another prisoner—not even to converse with his superiors, unless addressed.

231

It was a grim theory, and yet one definitely enforced here, although as he was to learn later even this could be modified here.

"You'll have to put this on," Kuby said, and opened it in such a way that it could be put over Cowperwood's head.

Cowperwood understood. He had heard of it in some way, in times past. He was a little shocked—looked at it first with a touch of real surprise, but a moment after lifted his hands and helped pull it down.

"Never mind," cautioned the guard, "put your hands down. I'll get it over."

Cowperwood dropped his arms. When it was fully on, it came to about his chest, giving him little means of seeing anything. He felt very strange, very humiliated, very downcast. This simple thing of a blue-and-white striped bag over his head almost cost him his sense of self-possession. Why could not they have spared him this last indignity, he thought?

"This way," said his attendant, and he was led out to where he could not say.

"If you hold it out in front you can see to walk," said his guide; and Cowperwood pulled it out, thus being able to discern his feet and a portion of the floor below. He was thus conducted—seeing nothing in his transit—down a short walk, then through a long corridor, then through a room of uniformed guards, and finally up a narrow flight of iron steps, leading to the overseer's office on the second floor of one of the two-tier blocks. There, he heard the voice of Kuby saying: "Mr. Chapin, here's another prisoner for you from Mr. Kendall."

"I'll be there in a minute," came a peculiarly pleasant voice from the distance. Presently a big, heavy hand closed about his arm, and he was conducted still further.

"You hain't got far to go now," the voice said, "and then I'll take that bag off," and Cowperwood felt for some reason a sense of sympathy, perhaps—as though he would choke. The further steps were not many.

A cell door was reached and unlocked by the inserting of a great iron key. It was swung open, and the same big hand guided him through. A moment later the bag was pulled easily from his head, and he saw that he was in a narrow, whitewashed cell, rather dim, windowless, but lighted from the top by a small skylight of frosted glass three and one half feet long by four inches wide. For a night light there was a tin-bodied lamp swinging from a hook near the middle of one of the side walls. A rough iron cot, furnished with a straw mattress and two pairs of dark blue, probably unwashed blankets, stood in one corner. There was a hydrant and small sink in another. A small shelf occupied the wall opposite the bed. A plain wooden chair with a homely round back stood at the foot of the bed, and a fairly serviceable broom was standing in one corner. There was an iron stool or pot for excreta, giving, as he could see, into a large drain-pipe which ran along the inside wall, and which was obviously flushed by buckets of water being poured into it. Rats and other vermin infested this, and it gave off an unpleasant odor which filled the cell. The floor was of stone. Cowperwood's clear-seeing eyes took it all in at a glance. He noted the hard cell door, which was barred and cross-barred with great round rods of steel, and fastened with a thick, highly polished lock. He saw also that beyond this was a heavy wooden door, which could shut him in even more completely than the iron one. There was no chance for any clear, purifying sunlight here. Cleanliness depended entirely on whitewash, soap and water and sweeping, which in turn depended on the prisoners themselves.

He also took in Chapin, the homely, good-natured, cell overseer whom he now saw for the first time—a large, heavy, lumbering man, rather dusty and misshapen-looking, whose uniform did not fit him well, and whose manner of standing made him look as though he would much prefer to sit down. He was obviously bulky, but not strong, and his kindly face was covered with a short growth of grayish-brown whiskers. His hair was cut badly and stuck out in odd strings or wisps from underneath his big cap. Nevertheless, Cowperwood was not at all unfavorably impressed—quite the contrary—and he felt at once that this man might be more considerate of him than the others had been. He hoped so, anyhow. He did not know that he was in the presence of the overseer of the "manners squad," who would have him in charge for two weeks only, instructing him in the rules of the prison, and that he was only one of twenty-six, all told, who were in Chapin's care.

That worthy, by way of easy introduction, now went over to the bed and seated himself on it. He pointed to the hard wooden chair, which Cowperwood drew out and sat on.

"Well, now you're here, hain't yuh?" he asked, and answered himself quite genially, for he was an unlettered man, generously disposed, of long experience with criminals, and inclined to deal kindly with kindly temperament and a form of religious belief—Quakerism—had inclined him to be merciful, and yet his official duties, as Cowperwood later found out, seemed to have led him to the conclusion that most criminals were innately bad. Like Kendall, he regarded them as weaklings and ne'er-do-wells with evil streaks in them, and in the main he was not mistaken. Yet he could not help being what he was, a fatherly, kindly old man, having faith in those shibboleths of the weak and inexperienced mentally—human justice and human decency.

"Yes, I'm here, Mr. Chapin," Cowperwood replied, simply, remembering his name from the attendant, and flattering the keeper by the use of it.

To old Chapin the situation was more or less puzzling. This was the famous Frank A. Cowperwood whom he had read about, the noted banker and treasury-looter. He and his co-partner in crime, Stener, were destined to serve, as he had read, comparatively long terms here. Five hundred thousand dollars was a large sum of money in those days, much more than five million would have been forty years later. He was awed by the thought of what had become of it—how Cowperwood managed to do all the things the papers had said he had done. He had a little formula of questions which he usually went through with each new prisoner—asking him if he was sorry now for the crime he had committed, if he meant to do better with a new chance, if his father and mother were alive, etc.; and by the manner in which they answered these questions—simply, regretfully, defiantly, or otherwise—he judged whether they were being adequately punished or not. Yet he could not talk to Cowperwood as he now saw or as he would to the average second-story burglar, store-looter, pickpocket, and plain cheap thief and swindler. And yet he scarcely knew how else to talk.

"Well, now," he went on, "I don't suppose you ever thought you'd get to a place like this, did you, Mr. Cowperwood?"

"I never did," replied Frank, simply. "I wouldn't have believed it a few months ago, Mr. Chapin. I don't think I deserve to be here now, though of course there is no use of my telling you that."

He saw that old Chapin wanted to moralize a little, and he was only too glad to fall in with his mood. He would soon be alone with no one to talk to perhaps, and if a sympathetic understanding could be reached with this man now, so much the better. Any port in a storm; any straw to a drowning man.

"Well, no doubt all of us makes mistakes," continued Mr. Chapin, superiorly, with an amusing faith in his own value as a moral guide and reformer. "We can't just always tell how the plans we think so fine are coming out, can we? You're here now, an' I suppose you're sorry certain things didn't come out just as you thought; but if you had a chance I don't suppose you'd try to do just as you did before, now would yuh?"

"No, Mr. Chapin, I wouldn't, exactly," said Cowperwood, truly enough, "though I believed I was right in everything I did. I don't think legal justice has really been done me."

"Well, that's the way," continued Chapin, meditatively, scratching his grizzled head and looking genially about. "Sometimes, as I allers says to some of these here young fellers that comes in here, we don't know as much as we thinks we does. We forget that others are just as smart as we are, and that there are allers people that are watchin' us all the time. These here courts and jails and detectives—they're here all the time, and they get us. I gad"— Chapin's moral version of "by God"—"they do, if we don't behave."

"Yes," Cowperwood replied, "that's true enough, Mr. Chapin."

"Well," continued the old man after a time, after he had made a few more solemn, owl-like, and yet well-intentioned remarks, "now here's your bed, and there's your chair, and there's your wash-stand, and there's your water-closet. Now keep 'em all clean and use 'em right." (You would have thought he was making Cowperwood a present of a fortune.) "You're the one's got to make up your bed every mornin' and keep your floor swept and your toilet flushed and your cell clean. There hain't anybody here'll do that for yuh. You want to do all them things the first thing in the mornin' when you get up, and afterward you'll get sumpin' to eat, about six-thirty. You're supposed to get up at five-thirty."

"Yes, Mr. Chapin," Cowperwood said, politely. "You can depend on me to do all those things promptly."

"There hain't so much more," added Chapin. "You're supposed to wash yourself all over once a week an' I'll give you a clean towel for that. Next you gotta wash this floor up every Friday mornin'." Cowperwood winced at that. "You kin have hot water for that if you want it. I'll have one of the runners bring it to you. An' as for your friends and relations"—he got up and shook himself like a big Newfoundland dog. "You gotta wife, hain't you?"

"Yes," replied Cowperwood.

"Well, the rules here are that your wife or your friends kin come to see you once in three months, and your lawyer—you gotta lawyer hain't yuh?"

"Yes, sir," replied Cowperwood, amused.

"Well, he kin come every week or so if he likes—every day, I guess—there hain't no rules about lawyers. But you kin only write one letter once in three months yourself, an' if you want anything like tobaccer or the like o' that, from the store-room, you gotta sign an order for it, if you got any money with the warden, an' then I can git it for you."

The old man was really above taking small tips in the shape of money. He was a hold-over from a much more severe and honest regime, but subsequent presents or constant flattery were not amiss in making him kindly and generous. Cowperwood read him accurately.

"Very well, Mr. Chapin; I understand," he said, getting up as the old man did.

"Then when you have been here two weeks," added Chapin, rather ruminatively (he had forgot to state this to Cowperwood before), "the warden 'll come and git yuh and give yuh yer regular cell summers down-stairs. Yuh kin make up yer mind by that time what y'u'd like tuh do, what y'u'd like to work at. If you behave yourself proper, more'n like they'll give yuh a cell with a yard. Yuh never can tell."

He went out, locking the door with a solemn click; and Cowperwood stood there, a little more depressed than he had been, because of this latest intelligence. Only two weeks, and then he would be transferred from this kindly old man's care to another's, whom he did not know and with whom he might not fare so well.

"If ever you want me for anything—if ye're sick or sumpin' like that," Chapin now returned to say, after he had walked a few paces away, "we have a signal here of our own. Just hang your towel out through these here bars. I'll see it, and I'll stop and find out what yuh want, when I'm passin'."

Cowperwood, whose spirits had sunk, revived for the moment.

"Yes, sir," he replied; "thank you, Mr. Chapin."

The old man walked away, and Cowperwood heard his steps dying down the cement-paved hall. He stood and listened, his ears being greeted occasionally by a distant cough, a faint scraping of some one's feet, the hum or whir of a machine, or the iron scratch of a key in a lock. None of the noises was loud. Rather they were all faint and far away. He went over and looked at the bed, which was not very clean and without linen, and anything but wide or soft, and felt it curiously. So here was where he was to sleep from now on—he who so craved and appreciated luxury and refinement. If Aileen or some of his rich friends should see him here. Worse, he was sickened by the thought of possible vermin. How could he tell? How would he do? The one chair was abominable. The skylight was weak. He tried to think of himself as becoming accustomed to the situation, but he re-discovered the offal pot in one corner, and that discouraged him. It was possible that rats might come up here—it looked that way. No pictures, no books, no scene, no person, no space to walk— just the four bare walls and silence, which he would be shut into at night by the thick door. What a horrible fate!

He sat down and contemplated his situation. So here he was at last in the Eastern Penitentiary, and doomed, according to the judgment of the politicians (Butler among others), to remain here four long years and longer. Stener, it suddenly occurred to him, was probably being put through the same process he had just gone through. Poor old Stener! What a fool he had made of himself. But because of his foolishness he deserved all he was now getting. But the difference between himself and Stener was that they would let Stener out. It was possible that already they were easing his punishment in some way that he, Cowperwood, did not know. He put his hand to his chin, thinking—his business, his house, his friends, his family, Aileen. He felt for his watch, but remembered that they had taken that. There was no way of telling the time. Neither had he any notebook, pen, or pencil with which to amuse or interest himself. Besides he had had nothing to eat since morning. Still, that mattered little. What did matter was that he was shut up here away from the world, quite alone, quite lonely, without knowing what time it was, and that he could not attend to any of the things he ought to be attending to—his business affairs, his future. True, Steger would probably come to see him after a while. That would help a little. But even so—think of his position, his prospects up to the day of the fire and his state now. He sat looking at his shoes; his suit. God! He got up and walked to and fro, to and fro, but his own steps and movements sounded so loud. He walked to the cell door and looked out through the thick bars, but there was nothing to see—nothing save a portion of two cell doors opposite, something like his own. He came back and sat in his single chair, meditating, but, getting weary of that finally, stretched himself on the dirty prison bed to try it. It was not uncomfortable entirely. He got up after a while, however, and sat, then walked, then sat. What a narrow place to walk, he thought. This was horrible—something like a living tomb. And to think he should be here now, day after day and day after day, until—until what? Until the Governor pardoned him or his time was up, or his fortune eaten away—or—

So he cogitated while the hours slipped by. It was nearly five o'clock before Steger was able to return, and then only for a little while. He had been arranging for Cowperwood's appearance on the following Thursday, Friday, and Monday in his several court proceedings. When he was gone, however, and the night fell and Cowperwood had to trim his little, shabby oil-lamp and to drink the strong tea and eat the rough, poor bread made of bran and white flour, which was shoved to him through the small aperture in the door by the trencher trusty, who was accompanied by the overseer to see that it was done properly, he really felt very badly. And after that the center wooden door of his cell was presently closed and locked by a trusty who slammed it rudely and said no word. Nine o'clock would be sounded somewhere by a great bell, he understood, when his smoky oil-lamp would have to be put out promptly and he would have to undress and go to bed. There were punishments, no doubt, for infractions of these rules—reduced rations, the strait-jacket, perhaps stripes—he scarcely knew what. He felt disconsolate, grim, weary. He had put up such a long, unsatisfactory fight. After washing his heavy stone cup and tin plate at the hydrant, he took off the sickening uniform and shoes and even the drawers of the scratching underwear, and stretched himself wearily on the bed. The place was not any too warm, and he tried to make himself comfortable between the blankets—but it was of little use. His soul was cold.

"This will never do," he said to himself. "This will never do. I'm not sure whether I can stand much of this or not." Still he turned his face to the wall, and after several hours sleep eventually came.

235

Those who by any pleasing courtesy of fortune, accident of birth, inheritance, or the wisdom of parents or friends, have succeeded in avoiding making that anathema of the prosperous and comfortable, "a mess of their lives," will scarcely understand the mood of Cowperwood, sitting rather gloomily in his cell these first days, wondering what, in spite of his great ingenuity, was to become of him. The strongest have their hours of depression. There are times when life to those endowed with the greatest intelligence—perhaps mostly to those—takes on a somber hue. They see so many phases of its dreary subtleties. It is only when the soul of man has been built up into some strange self-confidence, some curious faith in its own powers, based, no doubt, on the actual presence of these same powers subtly involved in the body, that it fronts life unflinchingly. It would be too much to say that Cowperwood's mind was of the first order. It was subtle enough in all conscience— and involved, as is common with the executively great, with a strong sense of personal advancement. It was a powerful mind, turning, like a vast searchlight, a glittering ray into many a dark corner; but it was not sufficiently disinterested to search the ultimate dark. He realized, in a way, what the great astronomers, sociologists, philosophers, chemists, physicists, and physiologists were meditating; but he could not be sure in his own mind that, whatever it was, it was important for him. No doubt life held many strange secrets. Perhaps it was essential that somebody should investigate them. However that might be, the call of his own soul was in another direction. His business was to make money—to organize something which would make him much money, or, better yet, save the organization he had begun.

But this, as he now looked upon it, was almost impossible. It had been too disarranged and complicated by unfortunate circumstances. He might, as Steger pointed out to him, string out these bankruptcy proceedings for years, tiring out one creditor and another, but in the meantime the properties involved were being seriously damaged. Interest charges on his unsatisfied loans were making heavy inroads; court costs were mounting up; and, to cap it all, he had discovered with Steger that there were a number of creditors—those who had sold out to Butler, and incidentally to Mollenhauer—who would never accept anything except the full value of their claims. His one hope now was to save what he could by compromise a little later, and to build up some sort of profitable business through Stephen Wingate. The latter was coming in a day or two, as soon as Steger had made some working arrangement for him with Warden Michael Desmas who came the second day to have a look at the new prisoner.

Desmas was a large man physically—Irish by birth, a politician by training—who had been one thing and another in Philadelphia from a policeman in his early days and a corporal in the Civil War to a ward captain under Mollenhauer. He was a canny man, tall, raw-boned, singularly muscular-looking, who for all his fifty-seven years looked as though he could give a splendid account of himself in a physical contest. His hands were large and bony, his face more square than either round or long, and his forehead high. He had a vigorous growth of short-clipped, iron-gray hair, and a bristly iron-gray mustache, very short, keen, intelligent blue-gray eyes; a florid complexion; and even-edged, savage-looking teeth, which showed the least bit in a slightly wolfish way when he smiled. However, he was not as cruel a person as he looked to be; temperamental, to a certain extent hard, and on occasions savage, but with kindly hours also. His greatest weakness was that he was not quite mentally able to recognize that there were mental and social differences between prisoners, and that now and then one was apt to appear here who, with or without political influences, was eminently worthy of special consideration. What he could recognize was the differences pointed out to him by the politicians in special cases, such as that of Stener—not Cowperwood. However, seeing that the prison was a public institution apt to be visited at any time by lawyers, detectives, doctors, preachers, propagandists, and the public generally, and that certain rules and regulations had to be enforced (if for no other reason than to keep a moral and administrative control over his own help), it was necessary to maintain—and that even in the face of the politician—a certain amount of discipline, system, and order, and it was not possible to be too liberal with any one. There were, however, exceptional cases—men of wealth and refinement, victims of those occasional uprisings which so shocked the political leaders generally—who had to be looked after in a friendly way.

Desmas was quite aware, of course, of the history of Cowperwood and Stener. The politicians had already given him warning that Stener, because of his past services to the community, was to be treated with special consideration. Not so much was said about Cowperwood, although they did admit that his lot was rather hard. Perhaps he might do a little something for him but at his own risk.

"Butler is down on him," Strobik said to Desmas, on one occasion. "It's that girl of his that's at the bottom of it all. If you listened to Butler you'd feed him on bread and water, but he isn't a bad fellow. As a matter of fact, if George had had any sense Cowperwood wouldn't be where he is to-day. But the big fellows wouldn't let Stener alone. They wouldn't let him give Cowperwood any money."

Although Strobik had been one of those who, under pressure from Mollenhauer, had advised Stener not to let Cowperwood have any more money, yet here he was pointing out the folly of the victim's course. The thought of the inconsistency involved did not trouble him in the least.

Desmas decided, therefore, that if Cowperwood were persona non grata to the "Big Three," it might be necessary to be indifferent to him, or at least slow in extending him any special favors. For Stener a good chair, clean linen, special cutlery and dishes, the daily papers, privileges in the matter of mail, the visits of friends, and the like. For Cowperwood—well, he would have to look at Cowperwood and see what he thought. At the same time, Steger's intercessions were not without their effect on Desmas. So the morning after Cowperwood's entrance the warden received a letter from Terrence Relihan, the Harrisburg potentate, indicating that any kindness shown to Mr. Cowperwood would be duly appreciated by him. Upon the receipt of this letter Desmas went up and looked through Cowperwood's iron door. On the way he had a brief talk with Chapin, who told him what a nice man he thought Cowperwood was.

Desmas had never seen Cowperwood before, but in spite of the shabby uniform, the clog shoes, the cheap shirt, and the wretched cell, he was impressed. Instead of the weak, anaemic body and the shifty eyes of the average prisoner, he saw a man whose face and form blazed energy and power, and whose vigorous erectness no wretched clothes or conditions could demean. He lifted his head when Desmas appeared, glad that any form should have appeared at his door, and looked at him with large, clear, examining eyes—those eyes that in the past had inspired so much confidence and surety in all those who had known him. Desmas was stirred. Compared with Stener, whom he knew in the past and whom he had met on his entry, this man was a force. Say what you will, one vigorous man inherently respects another. And Desmas was vigorous physically. He eyed Cowperwood and Cowperwood eyed him. Instinctively Desmas liked him. He was like one tiger looking at another.

Instinctively Cowperwood knew that he was the warden. "This is Mr. Desmas, isn't it?" he asked, courteously and pleasantly.

"Yes, sir, I'm the man," replied Desmas interestedly. "These rooms are not as comfortable as they might be, are they?" The warden's even teeth showed in a friendly, yet wolfish, way.

"They certainly are not, Mr. Desmas," replied Cowperwood, standing very erect and soldier-like. "I didn't imagine I was coming to a hotel, however." He smiled.

"There isn't anything special I can do for you, is there, Mr. Cowperwood?" began Desmas curiously, for he was moved by a thought that at some time or other a man such as this might be of service to him. "I've been talking to your lawyer." Cowperwood was intensely gratified by the Mr. So that was the way the wind was blowing. Well, then, within reason, things might not prove so bad here. He would see. He would sound this man out.

"I don't want to be asking anything, Warden, which you cannot reasonably give," he now returned politely. "But there are a few things, of course, that I would change if I could. I wish I might have sheets for my bed, and I could afford better underwear if you would let me wear it. This that I have on annoys me a great deal."

"They're not the best wool, that's true enough," replied Desmas, solemnly. "They're made for the State out here in Pennsylvania somewhere. I suppose there's no objection to your wearing your own underwear if you want to. I'll see about that. And the sheets, too. We might let you use them if you have them. We'll have to go a little slow about this. There are a lot of people that take a special interest in showing the warden how to tend to his business."

"I can readily understand that, Warden," went on Cowperwood briskly, "and I'm certainly very much obliged to you. You may be sure that anything you do for me here will be appreciated, and not misused, and that I have friends on the outside who can reciprocate for me in the course of time." He talked slowly and emphatically, looking Desmas directly in the eye all of the time. Desmas was very much impressed.

"That's all right," he said, now that he had gone so far as to be friendly. "I can't promise much. Prison rules are prison rules. But there are some things that can be done, because it's the rule to do them for other men when they behave themselves. You can have a better chair than that, if you want it, and something to read too. If you're in business yet, I wouldn't want to do anything to stop that. We can't have people running in and out of here every fifteen minutes, and you can't turn a cell into a business office—that's not possible. It would break up the order of the place. Still, there's no reason why you shouldn't see some of your friends now and then. As for your mail—well, that will have to be opened in the ordinary way for the time being, anyhow. I'll have to see about that. I can't promise too much. You'll have to wait until you come out of this block and down-stairs. Some of the cells have a yard there; if there are any empty—" The warden cocked his eye wisely, and Cowperwood saw that his tot was not to be as bad as he had anticipated—though bad enough. The warden spoke to him about the different trades he might follow, and asked him to think about the one he would prefer. "You want to have something to keep your hands busy, whatever else you want. You'll find you'll need that. Everybody here wants to work after a time. I notice that."

Cowperwood understood and thanked Desmas profusely. The horror of idleness in silence and in a cell scarcely large enough to turn around in comfortably had already begun to creep over him, and the thought of being able to see Wingate and Steger frequently, and to have his mail reach him, after a time, untampered with, was a great relief. He was to have his own underwear, silk and wool—thank God!—and perhaps they would let him take off these shoes after a while. With these modifications and a trade, and perhaps the little yard which Desmas had referred to, his life would be, if not ideal, at least tolerable. The prison was still a prison, but it looked as though it might not be so much of a terror to him as obviously it must be to many.

During the two weeks in which Cowperwood was in the "manners squad," in care of Chapin, he learned nearly as much as he ever learned of the general nature of prison life; for this was not an ordinary penitentiary in the sense that the prison yard, the prison squad, the prison lock-step, the prison dining-room, and prison associated labor make the ordinary penitentiary. There was, for him and for most of those confined there, no general prison life whatsoever. The large majority were supposed to work silently in their cells at the particular tasks assigned them, and not to know anything of the remainder of the life which went on around them, the rule of this prison being solitary confinement, and few being permitted to work at the limited number of outside menial tasks provided. Indeed, as he sensed and as

238

old Chapin soon informed him, not more than seventy-five of the four hundred prisoners confined here were so employed, and not all of these regularly—cooking, gardening in season, milling, and general cleaning being the only avenues of escape from solitude. Even those who so worked were strictly forbidden to talk, and although they did not have to wear the objectionable hood when actually employed, they were supposed to wear it in going to and from their work. Cowperwood saw them occasionally tramping by his cell door, and it struck him as strange, uncanny, grim. He wished sincerely at times since old Chapin was so genial and talkative that he were to be under him permanently; but it was not to be.

His two weeks soon passed—drearily enough in all conscience but they passed, interlaced with his few commonplace tasks of bed-making, floor-sweeping, dressing, eating, undressing, rising at five-thirty, and retiring at nine, washing his several dishes after each meal, etc. He thought he would never get used to the food. Breakfast, as has been said, was at six-thirty, and consisted of coarse black bread made of bran and some white flour, and served with black coffee. Dinner was at eleven-thirty, and consisted of bean or vegetable soup, with some coarse meat in it, and the same bread. Supper was at six, of tea and bread, very strong tea and the same bread—no butter, no milk, no sugar. Cowperwood did not smoke, so the small allowance of tobacco which was permitted was without value to him. Steger called in every day for two or three weeks, and after the second day, Stephen Wingate, as his new business associate, was permitted to see him also—once every day, if he wished, Desmas stated, though the latter felt he was stretching a point in permitting this so soon. Both of these visits rarely occupied more than an hour, or an hour and a half, and after that the day was long. He was taken out on several days on a court order, between nine and five, to testify in the bankruptcy proceedings against him, which caused the time in the beginning to pass quickly.

It was curious, once he was in prison, safely shut from the world for a period of years apparently, how quickly all thought of assisting him departed from the minds of those who had been most friendly. He was done, so most of them thought. The only thing they could do now would be to use their influence to get him out some time; how soon, they could not guess. Beyond that there was nothing. He would really never be of any great importance to any one any more, or so they thought. It was very sad, very tragic, but he was gone—his place knew him not.

"A bright young man, that," observed President Davison of the Girard National, on reading of Cowperwood's sentence and incarceration. "Too bad! Too bad! He made a great mistake."

Only his parents, Aileen, and his wife—the latter with mingled feelings of resentment and sorrow—really missed him. Aileen, because of her great passion for him, was suffering most of all. Four years and three months; she thought. If he did not get out before then she would be nearing twenty-nine and he would be nearing forty. Would he want her then? Would she be so attractive? And would nearly five years change his point of view? He would have to wear a convict suit all that time, and be known as a convict forever after. It was hard to think about, but only made her more than ever determined to cling to him, whatever happened, and to help him all she could.

Indeed the day after his incarceration she drove out and looked at the grim, gray walls of the penitentiary. Knowing nothing absolutely of the vast and complicated processes of law and penal servitude, it seemed especially terrible to her. What might not they be doing to her Frank? Was he suffering much? Was he thinking of her as she was of him? Oh, the pity of it all! The pity! The pity of herself—her great love for him! She drove home, determined to see him; but as he had originally told her that visiting days were only once in three months, and that he would have to write her when the next one was, or when she could come, or when he could see her on the outside, she scarcely knew what to do. Secrecy was the thing.

The next day, however, she wrote him just the same, describing the drive she had taken on the stormy afternoon before—the terror of the thought that he was behind those grim gray walls—and declaring her determination to see him soon. And this letter, under the new arrangement, he received at once. He wrote her in reply, giving the letter to Wingate to mail. It ran:

My sweet girl:—I fancy you are a little downhearted to think I cannot be with you any more soon, but you mustn't be. I suppose you read all about the sentence in the paper. I came out here the same morning—nearly noon. If I had time, dearest, I'd write you a long letter describing the situation so as to ease your mind; but I haven't. It's against the rules, and I am really doing this secretly. I'm here, though, safe enough, and wish I were out, of course. Sweetest, you must be careful how you try to see me at first. You can't do me much service outside of cheering me up, and you may do yourself great harm. Besides, I think I have done you far more harm than I can ever make up to you and that you had best give me up, although I know you do not think so, and I would be sad, if you did. I am to be in the Court of Special Pleas, Sixth and Chestnut, on Friday at two o'clock; but you cannot see me there. I'll be out in charge of my counsel. You must be careful. Perhaps you'll think better, and not come here.

This last touch was one of pure gloom, the first Cowperwood had ever introduced into their relationship but conditions had changed him. Hitherto he had been in the position of the superior being, the one who was being sought—although Aileen was and had been well worth seeking—and he had thought that he might escape unscathed, and so grow in dignity and power until she might not possibly be worthy of him any longer. He had had that thought. But here, in stripes, it was a different matter. Aileen's position, reduced in value as it was by her long, ardent relationship with him, was now, nevertheless, superior to his— apparently so. For after all, was she not Edward Butler's daughter, and might she, after she had been away from him a while, wish to become a convict's bride. She ought not to want to, and she might not want to, for all he knew; she might change her mind. She ought not to wait for him. Her life was not yet ruined. The public did not know, so he thought—not generally anyhow—that she had been his mistress. She might marry. Why not, and so pass out of his life forever. And would not that be sad for him? And yet did he not owe it to her, to a sense of fair play in himself to ask her to give him up, or at least think over the wisdom of doing so?

He did her the justice to believe that she would not want to give him up; and in his position, however harmful it might be to her, it was an advantage, a connecting link with the finest period of his past life, to have her continue to love him. He could not, however, scribbling this note in his cell in Wingate's presence, and giving it to him to mail (Overseer Chapin was kindly keeping a respectful distance, though he was supposed to be present), refrain from adding, at the last moment, this little touch of doubt which, when she read it, struck Aileen to the heart. She read it as gloom on his part—as great depression. Perhaps, after all, the penitentiary and so soon, was really breaking his spirit, and he had held up so courageously so long. Because of this, now she was madly eager to get to him, to console him, even though it was difficult, perilous. She must, she said.

In regard to visits from the various members of his family—his mother and father, his brother, his wife, and his sister—Cowperwood made it plain to them on one of the days on which he was out attending a bankruptcy hearing, that even providing it could be arranged he did not think they should come oftener than once in three months, unless he wrote them or sent word by Steger. The truth was that he really did not care to see much of any of them at present. He was sick of the whole social scheme of things. In fact he wanted to be rid of the turmoil he had been in, seeing it had proved so useless. He had used nearly fifteen thousand dollars thus far in defending himself—court costs, family maintenance, Steger, etc.; but he did not mind that. He expected to make some little money working through Wingate. His family were not utterly without funds, sufficient to live on in a small way. He had advised them to remove into houses more in keeping with their reduced circumstances, which they had done—his mother and father and brothers and sister to a three-story brick house of about the caliber of the old Buttonwood Street house, and his wife to a smaller, less expensive two-story one on North Twenty-first Street, near the penitentiary, a portion of the money saved out of the thirty-five thousand dollars extracted from Stener under false pretenses aiding to sustain it. Of course all this was a terrible descent from the Girard Avenue mansion for the elder Cowperwood; for here was none of the furniture which characterized the other somewhat gorgeous domicile—merely store-bought, ready-made furniture, and neat but cheap hangings and fixtures generally. The assignees, to whom all Cowperwood's personal property belonged, and to whom Cowperwood, the elder, had surrendered all his holdings, would not permit anything of importance to be removed. It had all to be sold for the benefit of creditors. A few very small things, but only a few, had been kept, as everything had been inventoried some time before. One of the things which old Cowperwood wanted was his own desk which Frank had had designed for him; but as it was valued at five hundred dollars and could not be relinquished by the sheriff except on payment of that sum, or by auction, and as Henry Cowperwood had no such sum to spare, he had to let the desk go. There were many things they all wanted, and Anna Adelaide had literally purloined a few though she did not admit the fact to her parents until long afterward.

There came a day when the two houses in Girard Avenue were the scene of a sheriffs sale, during which the general public, without let or hindrance, was permitted to tramp through the rooms and examine the pictures, statuary, and objects of art generally, which were auctioned off to the highest bidder. Considerable fame had attached to Cowperwood's activities in this field, owing in the first place to the real merit of what he had brought together, and in the next place to the enthusiastic comment of such men as Wilton Ellsworth, Fletcher Norton, Gordon Strake—architects and art dealers whose judgment and taste were considered important in Philadelphia. All of the lovely things by which he had set great store—small bronzes, representative of the best period of the Italian Renaissance; bits of Venetian glass which he had collected with great care—a full curio case; statues by Powers, Hosmer, and Thorwaldsen—things which would be smiled at thirty years later, but which were of high value then; all of his pictures by representative American painters from Gilbert to Eastman Johnson, together with a few specimens of the current French and English schools, went for a song. Art judgment in Philadelphia at this time was not exceedingly high; and some of the pictures, for lack of appreciative understanding, were disposed of at much too low a figure. Strake, Norton, and Ellsworth were all present and bought liberally. Senator Simpson, Mollenhauer, and Strobik came to see what they could see. The small-fry politicians were there, en masse. But Simpson, calm judge of good art, secured practically the best of all that was offered. To him went the curio case of Venetian glass; one pair of tall blue-and-white Mohammedan cylindrical vases; fourteen examples of Chinese jade, including several artists' water-dishes and a pierced window-screen of the faintest tinge of green. To Mollenhauer went the furniture and decorations of the entry-hall and reception-room of Henry Cowperwood's house, and to Edward Strobik two of Cowperwood's bird's-eye maple bedroom suites for the most modest of prices. Adam Davis was present and secured the secretaire of buhl which the elder Cowperwood prized so highly. To Fletcher Norton went the four Greek vases—a kylix, a water-jar, and two amphorae—which he had sold to Cowperwood and which he valued highly. Various objects of art, including a Sevres dinner set, a Gobelin tapestry, Barye bronzes and pictures by Detaille, Fortuny, and George Inness, went to Walter Leigh, Arthur Rivers, Joseph Zimmerman, Judge Kitchen, Harper Steger, Terrence Relihan, Trenor Drake, Mr. and Mrs. Simeon Jones, W. C. Davison, Frewen Kasson, Fletcher Norton, and Judge Rafalsky.

Within four days after the sale began the two houses were bare of their contents. Even the objects in the house at 931 North Tenth Street had been withdrawn from storage where they had been placed at the time it was deemed advisable to close this institution, and placed on sale with the other objects in the two homes. It was at this time that the senior Cowperwoods first learned of something which seemed to indicate a mystery which had existed in connection with their son and his wife. No one of all the Cowperwoods was present during all this gloomy distribution; and Aileen, reading of the disposition of all the wares, and knowing their value to Cowperwood, to say nothing of their charm for her, was greatly depressed; yet she was not long despondent, for she was convinced that Cowperwood would some day regain his liberty and attain a position of even greater significance in the financial world. She could not have said why but she was sure of it.

CHAPTER LV

In the meanwhile Cowperwood had been transferred to a new overseer and a new cell in Block 3 on the ground door, which was like all the others in size, ten by sixteen, but to which was attached the small yard previously mentioned. Warden Desmas came up two days before he was transferred, and had another short conversation with him through his cell door.

"You'll be transferred on Monday," he said, in his reserved, slow way. "They'll give you a yard, though it won't be much good to you—we only allow a half-hour a day in it. I've told the overseer about your business arrangements. He'll treat you right in that matter. Just be careful not to take up too much time that way, and things will work out. I've decided to let you learn caning chairs. That'll be the best for you. It's easy, and it'll occupy your mind."

The warden and some allied politicians made a good thing out of this prison industry. It was really not hard labor—the tasks set were simple and not oppressive, but all of the products were promptly sold, and the profits pocketed. It was good, therefore, to see all the prisoners working, and it did them good. Cowperwood was glad of the chance to do something, for he really did not care so much for books, and his connection with Wingate and his old affairs were not sufficient to employ his mind in a satisfactory way. At the same time, he could not help thinking, if he seemed strange to himself, now, how much stranger he would seem then, behind these narrow bars working at so commonplace a task as caning chairs. Nevertheless, he now thanked Desmas for this, as well as for the sheets and the toilet articles which had just been brought in.

"That's all right," replied the latter, pleasantly and softly, by now much intrigued by Cowperwood. "I know that there are men and men here, the same as anywhere. If a man knows how to use these things and wants to be clean, I wouldn't be one to put anything in his way."

The new overseer with whom Cowperwood had to deal was a very different person from Elias Chapin. His name was Walter Bonhag, and he was not more than thirty-seven years of age—a big, flabby sort of person with a crafty mind, whose principal object in life was to see that this prison situation as he found it should furnish him a better income than his normal salary provided. A close study of Bonhag would have seemed to indicate that he was a stool-pigeon of Desmas, but this was really not true except in a limited way. Because Bonhag was shrewd and sycophantic, quick to see a point in his or anybody else's favor, Desmas instinctively realized that he was the kind of man who could be trusted to be lenient on order or suggestion. That is, if Desmas had the least interest in a prisoner he need scarcely say so much to Bonhag; he might merely suggest that this man was used to a different kind of life, or that, because of some past experience, it might go hard with him if he were handled roughly; and Bonhag would strain himself to be pleasant. The trouble was that to a shrewd man of any refinement his attentions were objectionable, being obviously offered for a purpose, and to a poor or ignorant man they were brutal and contemptuous. He had built up an extra income for himself inside the prison by selling the prisoners extra allowances of things which he secretly brought into the prison. It was strictly against the rules, in theory at least, to bring in anything which was not sold in the store-room—tobacco, writing paper, pens, ink, whisky, cigars, or delicacies of any kind. On the other hand, and excellently well for him, it was true that tobacco of an inferior grade was provided, as well as wretched pens, ink and paper, so that no self-respecting man, if he could help it, would endure them. Whisky was not allowed at all, and delicacies were abhorred as indicating rank favoritism; nevertheless, they were brought in. If a prisoner had the money and was willing to see that Bonhag secured something for his trouble, almost anything would be forthcoming. Also the privilege of being sent into the general yard as a "trusty," or being allowed to stay in the little private yard which some cells possessed, longer than the half-hour ordinarily permitted, was sold.

One of the things curiously enough at this time, which worked in Cowperwood's favor, was the fact that Bonhag was friendly with the overseer who had Stener in charge, and Stener, because of his political friends, was being liberally treated, and Bonhag knew of this. He was not a careful reader of newspapers, nor had he any intellectual grasp of important events; but he knew by now that both Stener and Cowperwood were, or had been, individuals of great importance in the community; also that Cowperwood had been the more important of the two. Better yet, as Bonhag now heard, Cowperwood still had money. Some prisoner, who was permitted to read the paper, told him so. And so, entirely aside from Warden Desmas's recommendation, which was given in a very quiet, noncommittal way, Bonhag was interested to see what he could do for Cowperwood for a price.

The day Cowperwood was installed in his new cell, Bonhag lolled up to the door, which was open, and said, in a semi-patronizing way, "Got all your things over yet?" It was his business to lock the door once Cowperwood was inside it.

"Yes, sir," replied Cowperwood, who had been shrewd enough to get the new overseer's name from Chapin; "this is Mr. Bonhag, I presume?"

"That's me," replied Bonhag, not a little flattered by the recognition, but still purely interested by the practical side of this encounter. He was anxious to study Cowperwood, to see what type of man he was.

"You'll find it a little different down here from up there," observed Bonhag. "It ain't so stuffy. These doors out in the yards make a difference."

"Oh, yes," said Cowperwood, observantly and shrewdly, "that is the yard Mr. Desmas spoke of."

At the mention of the magic name, if Bonhag had been a horse, his ears would have been seen to lift. For, of course, if Cowperwood was so friendly with Desmas that the latter had described to him the type of cell he was to have beforehand, it behooved Bonhag to be especially careful.

"Yes, that's it, but it ain't much," he observed. "They only allow a half-hour a day in it. Still it would be all right if a person could stay out there longer."

This was his first hint at graft, favoritism; and Cowperwood distinctly caught the sound of it in his voice.

"That's too bad," he said. "I don't suppose good conduct helps a person to get more." He waited to hear a reply, but instead Bonhag continued with: "I'd better teach you your new trade now. You've got to learn to cane chairs, so the warden says. If you want, we can begin right away." But without waiting for Cowperwood to acquiesce, he went off, returning after a time with three unvarnished frames of chairs and a bundle of cane strips or withes, which he deposited on the floor. Having so done—and with a flourish—he now continued: "Now I'll show you if you'll watch me," and he began showing Cowperwood how the strips were to be laced through the apertures on either side, cut, and fastened with little hickory pegs. This done, he brought a forcing awl, a small hammer, a box of pegs, and a pair of clippers.

243

After several brief demonstrations with different strips, as to how the geometric forms were designed, he allowed Cowperwood to take the matter in hand, watching over his shoulder. The financier, quick at anything, manual or mental, went at it in his customary energetic fashion, and in five minutes demonstrated to Bonhag that, barring skill and speed, which could only come with practice, he could do it as well as another. "You'll make out all right," said Bonhag. "You're supposed to do ten of those a day. We won't count the next few days, though, until you get your hand in. After that I'll come around and see how you're getting along. You understand about the towel on the door, don't you?" he inquired.

"Yes, Mr. Chapin explained that to me," replied Cowperwood. "I think I know what most of the rules are now. I'll try not to break any of them."

The days which followed brought a number of modifications of his prison lot, but not sufficient by any means to make it acceptable to him. Bonhag, during the first few days in which he trained Cowperwood in the art of caning chairs, managed to make it perfectly clear that there were a number of things he would be willing to do for him. One of the things that moved him to this, was that already he had been impressed by the fact that Stener's friends were coming to see him in larger numbers than Cowperwood's, sending him an occasional basket of fruit, which he gave to the overseers, and that his wife and children had been already permitted to visit him outside the regular visiting-day. This was a cause for jealousy on Bonhag's part. His fellow-overseer was lording it over him—telling him, as it were, of the high jinks in Block 4. Bonhag really wanted Cowperwood to spruce up and show what he could do, socially or otherwise.

And so now he began with: "I see you have your lawyer and your partner here every day. There ain't anybody else you'd like to have visit you, is there? Of course, it's against the rules to have your wife or sister or anybody like that, except on visiting days—" And here he paused and rolled a large and informing eye on Cowperwood—such an eye as was supposed to convey dark and mysterious things. "But all the rules ain't kept around here by a long shot."

Cowperwood was not the man to lose a chance of this kind. He smiled a little—enough to relieve himself, and to convey to Bonhag that he was gratified by the information, but vocally he observed: "I'll tell you how it is, Mr. Bonhag. I believe you understand my position better than most men would, and that I can talk to you. There are people who would like to come here, but I have been afraid to let them come. I did not know that it could be arranged. If it could be, I would be very grateful. You and I are practical men—I know that if any favors are extended some of those who help to bring them about must be looked after. If you can do anything to make it a little more comfortable for me here I will show you that I appreciate it. I haven't any money on my person, but I can always get it, and I will see that you are properly looked after."

Bonhag's short, thick ears tingled. This was the kind of talk he liked to hear. "I can fix anything like that, Mr. Cowperwood," he replied, servilely. "You leave it to me. If there's any one you want to see at any time, just let me know. Of course I have to be very careful, and so do you, but that's all right, too. If you want to stay out in that yard a little longer in the mornings or get out there afternoons or evenings, from now on, why, go ahead. It's all right. I'll just leave the door open. If the warden or anybody else should be around, I'll just scratch on your door with my key, and you come in and shut it. If there's anything you want from the outside I can get it for you—jelly or eggs or butter or any little thing like that. You might like to fix up your meals a little that way."

"I'm certainly most grateful, Mr. Bonhag," returned Cowperwood in his grandest manner, and with a desire to smile, but he kept a straight face.

"In regard to that other matter," went on Bonhag, referring to the matter of extra visitors, "I can fix that any time you want to. I know the men out at the gate. If you want anybody to come here, just write 'em a note and give it to me, and tell 'em to ask for me when they come. That'll get 'em in all right. When they get here you can talk to 'em in your cell. See!

Only when I tap they have to come out. You want to remember that. So just you let me know."

Cowperwood was exceedingly grateful. He said so in direct, choice language. It occurred to him at once that this was Aileen's opportunity, and that he could now notify her to come. If she veiled herself sufficiently she would probably be safe enough. He decided to write her, and when Wingate came he gave him a letter to mail.

Two days later, at three o'clock in the afternoon—the time appointed by him—Aileen came to see him. She was dressed in gray broadcloth with white-velvet trimmings and cut-steel buttons which glistened like silver, and wore, as additional ornaments, as well as a protection against the cold, a cap, stole, and muff of snow-white ermine. Over this rather striking costume she had slipped a long dark circular cloak, which she meant to lay off immediately upon her arrival. She had made a very careful toilet as to her shoes, gloves, hair, and the gold ornaments which she wore. Her face was concealed by a thick green veil, as Cowperwood had suggested; and she arrived at an hour when, as near as he had been able to prearrange, he would be alone. Wingate usually came at four, after business, and Steger in the morning, when he came at all. She was very nervous over this strange adventure, leaving the street-car in which she had chosen to travel some distance away and walking up a side street. The cold weather and the gray walls under a gray sky gave her a sense of defeat, but she had worked very hard to look nice in order to cheer her lover up. She knew how readily he responded to the influence of her beauty when properly displayed. Cowperwood, in view of her coming, had made his cell as acceptable as possible. It was clean, because he had swept it himself and made his own bed; and besides he had shaved and combed his hair, and otherwise put himself to rights. The caned chairs on which he was working had been put in the corner at the end of the bed. His few dishes were washed and hung up, and his clogs brushed with a brush which he now kept for the purpose. Never before, he thought to himself, with a peculiar feeling of artistic degradation, had Aileen seen him like this. She had always admired his good taste in clothes, and the way he carried himself in them; and now she was to see him in garments which no dignity of body could make presentable. Only a stoic sense of his own soul-dignity aided him here. After all, as he now thought, he was Frank A. Cowperwood, and that was something, whatever he wore. And Aileen knew it. Again, he might be free and rich some day, and he knew that she believed that. Best of all, his looks under these or any other circumstances, as he knew, would make no difference to Aileen. She would only love him the more. It was her ardent sympathy that he was afraid of. He was so glad that Bonhag had suggested that she might enter the cell, for it would be a grim procedure talking to her through a barred door.

When Aileen arrived she asked for Mr. Bonhag, and was permitted to go to the central rotunda, where he was sent for. When he came she murmured: "I wish to see Mr. Cowperwood, if you please"; and he exclaimed, "Oh, yes, just come with me." As he came across the rotunda floor from his corridor he was struck by the evident youth of Aileen, even though he could not see her face. This now was something in accordance with what he had expected of Cowperwood. A man who could steal five hundred thousand dollars and set a whole city by the ears must have wonderful adventures of all kinds, and Aileen looked like a true adventure. He led her to the little room where he kept his desk and detained visitors, and then bustled down to Cowperwood's cell, where the financier was working on one of his chairs and scratching on the door with his key, called: "There's a young lady here to see you. Do you want to let her come inside?"

"Thank you, yes," replied Cowperwood; and Bonhag hurried away, unintentionally forgetting, in his boorish incivility, to unlock the cell door, so that he had to open it in Aileen's presence. The long corridor, with its thick doors, mathematically spaced gratings and gray-stone pavement, caused Aileen to feel faint at heart. A prison, iron cells! And he was in one of them. It chilled her usually courageous spirit. What a terrible place for her Frank to be! What a horrible thing to have put him here! Judges, juries, courts, laws, jails seemed like so many foaming ogres ranged about the world, glaring down upon her and her love-affair. The clank of the key in the lock, and the heavy outward swinging of the door, completed her sense of the untoward. And then she saw Cowperwood.

Because of the price he was to receive, Bonhag, after admitting her, strolled discreetly away. Aileen looked at Cowperwood from behind her veil, afraid to speak until she was sure Bonhag had gone. And Cowperwood, who was retaining his self-possession by an effort, signaled her but with difficulty after a moment or two. "It's all right," he said. "He's gone away." She lifted her veil, removed her cloak, and took in, without seeming to, the stuffy, narrow thickness of the room, his wretched shoes, the cheap, misshapen suit, the iron door behind him leading out into the little yard attached to his cell. Against such a background, with his partially caned chairs visible at the end of the bed, he seemed unnatural, weird even. Her Frank! And in this condition. She trembled and it was useless for her to try to speak. She could only put her arms around him and stroke his head, murmuring: "My poor boy—my darling. Is this what they have done to you? Oh, my poor darling." She held his head while Cowperwood, anxious to retain his composure, winced and trembled, too. Her love was so full—so genuine. It was so soothing at the same time that it was unmanning, as now he could see, making of him a child again. And for the first time in his life, some inexplicable trick of chemistry—that chemistry of the body, of blind forces which so readily supersedes reason at times—he lost his self-control. The depth of Aileen's feelings, the cooing sound of her voice, the velvety tenderness of her hands, that beauty that had drawn him all the time—more radiant here perhaps within these hard walls, and in the face of his physical misery, than it had ever been before—completely unmanned him. He did not understand how it could; he tried to defy the moods, but he could not. When she held his head close and caressed it, of a sudden, in spite of himself, his breast felt thick and stuffy, and his throat hurt him. He felt, for him, an astonishingly strange feeling, a desire to cry, which he did his best to overcome; it shocked him so. There then combined and conspired to defeat him a strange, rich picture of the great world he had so recently lost, of the lovely, magnificent world which he hoped some day to regain. He felt more poignantly at this moment than ever he had before the degradation of the clog shoes, the cotton shirt, the striped suit, the reputation of a convict, permanent and not to be laid aside. He drew himself quickly away from her, turned his back, clinched his hands, drew his muscles taut; but it was too late. He was crying, and he could not stop.

"Oh, damn it!" he exclaimed, half angrily, half self-commiseratingly, in combined rage and shame. "Why should I cry? What the devil's the matter with me, anyhow?"

Aileen saw it. She fairly flung herself in front of him, seized his head with one hand, his shabby waist with the other, and held him tight in a grip that he could not have readily released.

"Oh, honey, honey, honey!" she exclaimed, pityingly feverishly. "I love you, I adore you. They could cut my body into bits if it would do you any good. To think that they should make you cry! Oh, my sweet, my sweet, my darling boy!"

She pulled his still shaking body tighter, and with her free hand caressed his head. She kissed his eyes, his hair, his cheeks. He pulled himself loose again after a moment, exclaiming, "What the devil's got into me?" but she drew him back.

"Never mind, honey darling, don't you be ashamed to cry. Cry here on my shoulder. Cry here with me. My baby—my honey pet!"

He quieted down after a few moments, cautioning her against Bonhag, and regaining his former composure, which he was so ashamed to have lost.

"You're a great girl, pet," he said, with a tender and yet apologetic smile. "You're all right—all that I need—a great help to me; but don't worry any longer about me, dear. I'm all right. It isn't as bad as you think. How are you?"

Aileen on her part was not to be soothed so easily. His many woes, including his wretched position here, outraged her sense of justice and decency. To think her fine, wonderful Frank should be compelled to come to this—to cry. She stroked his head, tenderly, while wild, deadly, unreasoning opposition to life and chance and untoward opposition surged in her brain. Her father—damn him! Her family—pooh! What did she care? Her Frank—her Frank. How little all else mattered where he was concerned. Never, never, never would she desert him—never—come what might. And now she clung to him in silence while she fought in her brain an awful battle with life and law and fate and circumstance. Law—nonsense! People—they were brutes, devils, enemies, hounds! She was delighted, eager, crazy to make a sacrifice of herself. She would go anywhere for or with her Frank now. She would do anything for him. Her family was nothing—life nothing, nothing, nothing. She would do anything he wished, nothing more, nothing less; anything she could do to save him, to make his life happier, but nothing for any one else.

CHAPTER LVI

The days passed. Once the understanding with Bonhag was reached, Cowperwood's wife, mother and sister were allowed to appear on occasions. His wife and the children were now settled in the little home for which he was paying, and his financial obligations to her were satisfied by Wingate, who paid her one hundred and twenty five dollars a month for him. He realized that he owed her more, but he was sailing rather close to the wind financially, these days. The final collapse of his old interests had come in March, when he had been legally declared a bankrupt, and all his properties forfeited to satisfy the claims against him. The city's claim of five hundred thousand dollars would have eaten up more than could have been realized at the time, had not a pro rata payment of thirty cents on the dollar been declared. Even then the city never received its due, for by some hocus-pocus it was declared to have forfeited its rights. Its claims had not been made at the proper time in the proper way. This left larger portions of real money for the others.

Fortunately by now Cowperwood had begun to see that by a little experimenting his business relations with Wingate were likely to prove profitable. The broker had made it clear that he intended to be perfectly straight with him. He had employed Cowperwood's two brothers, at very moderate salaries—one to take care of the books and look after the office, and the other to act on 'change with him, for their seats in that organization had never been sold. And also, by considerable effort, he had succeeded in securing Cowperwood, Sr., a place as a clerk in a bank. For the latter, since the day of his resignation from the Third National had been in a deep, sad quandary as to what further to do with his life. His son's disgrace! The horror of his trial and incarceration. Since the day of Frank's indictment and more so, since his sentence and commitment to the Eastern Penitentiary, he was as one who walked in a dream. That trial! That charge against Frank! His own son, a convict in stripes—and after he and Frank had walked so proudly in the front rank of the successful and respected here. Like so many others in his hour of distress, he had taken to reading the Bible, looking into its pages for something of that mind consolation that always, from youth up, although rather casually in these latter years, he had imagined was to be found there. The Psalms, Isaiah, the Book of Job, Ecclesiastes. And for the most part, because of the fraying nature of his present ills, not finding it.

But day after day secreting himself in his room—a little hall-bedroom office in his newest home, where to his wife, he pretended that he had some commercial matters wherewith he was still concerned—and once inside, the door locked, sitting and brooding on all that had befallen him—his losses; his good name. Or, after months of this, and because of the new position secured for him by Wingate—a bookkeeping job in one of the outlying banks—

slipping away early in the morning, and returning late at night, his mind a gloomy epitome of all that had been or yet might be.

To see him bustling off from his new but very much reduced home at half after seven in the morning in order to reach the small bank, which was some distance away and not accessible by street-car line, was one of those pathetic sights which the fortunes of trade so frequently offer. He carried his lunch in a small box because it was inconvenient to return home in the time allotted for this purpose, and because his new salary did not permit the extravagance of a purchased one. It was his one ambition now to eke out a respectable but unseen existence until he should die, which he hoped would not be long. He was a pathetic figure with his thin legs and body, his gray hair, and his snow-white side-whiskers. He was very lean and angular, and, when confronted by a difficult problem, a little uncertain or vague in his mind. An old habit which had grown on him in the years of his prosperity of putting his hand to his mouth and of opening his eyes in an assumption of surprise, which had no basis in fact, now grew upon him. He really degenerated, although he did not know it, into a mere automaton. Life strews its shores with such interesting and pathetic wrecks.

One of the things that caused Cowperwood no little thought at this time, and especially in view of his present extreme indifference to her, was how he would bring up this matter of his indifference to his wife and his desire to end their relationship. Yet apart from the brutality of the plain truth, he saw no way. As he could plainly see, she was now persisting in her pretense of devotion, uncolored, apparently, by any suspicion of what had happened. Yet since his trial and conviction, she had been hearing from one source and another that he was still intimate with Aileen, and it was only her thought of his concurrent woes, and the fact that he might possibly be spared to a successful financial life, that now deterred her from speaking. He was shut up in a cell, she said to herself, and she was really very sorry for him, but she did not love him as she once had. He was really too deserving of reproach for his general unseemly conduct, and no doubt this was what was intended, as well as being enforced, by the Governing Power of the world.

One can imagine how much such an attitude as this would appeal to Cowperwood, once he had detected it. By a dozen little signs, in spite of the fact that she brought him delicacies, and commiserated on his fate, he could see that she felt not only sad, but reproachful, and if there was one thing that Cowperwood objected to at all times it was the moral as well as the funereal air. Contrasted with the cheerful combative hopefulness and enthusiasm of Aileen, the wearied uncertainty of Mrs. Cowperwood was, to say the least, a little tame. Aileen, after her first burst of rage over his fate, which really did not develop any tears on her part, was apparently convinced that he would get out and be very successful again. She talked success and his future all the time because she believed in it. Instinctively she seemed to realize that prison walls could not make a prison for him. Indeed, on the first day she left she handed Bonhag ten dollars, and after thanking him in her attractive voice—without showing her face, however—for his obvious kindness to her, bespoke his further favor for Cowperwood—"a very great man," as she described him, which sealed that ambitious materialist's fate completely. There was nothing the overseer would not do for the young lady in the dark cloak. She might have stayed in Cowperwood's cell for a week if the visiting-hours of the penitentiary had not made it impossible.

The day that Cowperwood decided to discuss with his wife the weariness of his present married state and his desire to be free of it was some four months after he had entered the prison. By that time he had become inured to his convict life. The silence of his cell and the menial tasks he was compelled to perform, which had at first been so distressing, banal, maddening, in their pointless iteration, had now become merely commonplace—dull, but not painful. Furthermore he had learned many of the little resources of the solitary convict, such as that of using his lamp to warm up some delicacy which he had saved from a previous meal or from some basket which had been sent him by his wife or Aileen. He had partially gotten rid of the sickening odor of his cell by persuading Bonhag to bring him small packages of lime; which he used with great freedom. Also he succeeded in defeating some of the more venturesome rats with traps; and with Bonhag's permission, after his cell door had been properly locked at night, and sealed with the outer wooden door, he would take his chair, if it were not too cold, out into the little back yard of his cell and look at the sky, where, when the nights were clear, the stars were to be seen. He had never taken any interest in astronomy as a scientific study, but now the Pleiades, the belt of Orion, the Big Dipper and the North Star, to which one of its lines pointed, caught his attention, almost his fancy. He wondered why the stars of the belt of Orion came to assume the peculiar mathematical relation to each other which they held, as far as distance and arrangement were concerned, and whether that could possibly have any intellectual significance. The nebulous conglomeration of the suns in Pleiades suggested a soundless depth of space, and he thought of the earth floating like a little ball in immeasurable reaches of ether. His own life appeared very trivial in view of these things, and he found himself asking whether it was all really of any significance or importance. He shook these moods off with ease, however, for the man was possessed of a sense of grandeur, largely in relation to himself and his affairs; and his temperament was essentially material and vital. Something kept telling him that whatever his present state he must yet grow to be a significant personage, one whose fame would be heralded the world over—who must try, try, try. It was not given all men to see far or to do brilliantly; but to him it was given, and he must be what he was cut out to be. There was no more escaping the greatness that was inherent in him than there was for so many others the littleness that was in them.

Mrs. Cowperwood came in that afternoon quite solemnly, bearing several changes of linen, a pair of sheets, some potted meat and a pie. She was not exactly doleful, but Cowperwood thought that she was tending toward it, largely because of her brooding over his relationship to Aileen, which he knew that she knew. Something in her manner decided him to speak before she left; and after asking her how the children were, and listening to her inquiries in regard to the things that he needed, he said to her, sitting on his single chair while she sat on his bed:

"Lillian, there's something I've been wanting to talk with you about for some time. I should have done it before, but it's better late than never. I know that you know that there is something between Aileen Butler and me, and we might as well have it open and aboveboard. It's true I am very fond of her and she is very devoted to me, and if ever I get out of here I want to arrange it so that I can marry her. That means that you will have to give me a divorce, if you will; and I want to talk to you about that now. This can't be so very much of a surprise to you, because you must have seen this long while that our relationship hasn't been all that it might have been, and under the circumstances this can't prove such a very great hardship to you—I am sure." He paused, waiting, for Mrs. Cowperwood at first said nothing.

Her thought, when he first broached this, was that she ought to make some demonstration of astonishment or wrath: but when she looked into his steady, examining eyes, so free from the illusion of or interest in demonstrations of any kind, she realized how useless it would be. He was so utterly matter-of-fact in what seemed to her quite private and secret affairs—very shameless. She had never been able to understand quite how he could take the subtleties of life as he did, anyhow. Certain things which she always fancied should be hushed up he spoke of with the greatest nonchalance. Her ears tingled sometimes at his frankness in disposing of a social situation; but she thought this must be characteristic of notable men, and so there was nothing to be said about it. Certain men did as they pleased; society did not seem to be able to deal with them in any way. Perhaps God would, later— she was not sure. Anyhow, bad as he was, direct as he was, forceful as he was, he was far more interesting than most of the more conservative types in whom the social virtues of polite speech and modest thoughts were seemingly predominate.

"I know," she said, rather peacefully, although with a touch of anger and resentment in her voice. "I've known all about it all this time. I expected you would say something like this to me some day. It's a nice reward for all my devotion to you; but it's just like you, Frank. When you are set on something, nothing can stop you. It wasn't enough that you were getting along so nicely and had two children whom you ought to love, but you had to take up with this Butler creature until her name and yours are a by-word throughout the city. I know that she comes to this prison. I saw her out here one day as I was coming in, and I suppose every one else knows it by now. She has no sense of decency and she does not care—the wretched, vain thing—but I would have thought that you would be ashamed, Frank, to go on the way that you have, when you still have me and the children and your father and mother and when you are certain to have such a hard fight to get yourself on your feet, as it is. If she had any sense of decency she would not have anything to do with you—the shameless thing."

Cowperwood looked at his wife with unflinching eyes. He read in her remarks just what his observation had long since confirmed—that she was sympathetically out of touch with him. She was no longer so attractive physically, and intellectually she was not Aileen's equal. Also that contact with those women who had deigned to grace his home in his greatest hour of prosperity had proved to him conclusively she was lacking in certain social graces. Aileen was by no means so vastly better, still she was young and amenable and adaptable, and could still be improved. Opportunity as he now chose to think, might make Aileen, whereas for Lillian—or at least, as he now saw it—it could do nothing.

"I'll tell you how it is, Lillian," he said; "I'm not sure that you are going to get what I mean exactly, but you and I are not at all well suited to each other any more."

"You didn't seem to think that three or four years ago," interrupted his wife, bitterly.

"I married you when I was twenty-one," went on Cowperwood, quite brutally, not paying any attention to her interruption, "and I was really too young to know what I was doing. I was a mere boy. It doesn't make so much difference about that. I am not using that as an excuse. The point that I am trying to make is this—that right or wrong, important or not important, I have changed my mind since. I don't love you any more, and I don't feel that I want to keep up a relationship, however it may look to the public, that is not satisfactory to me. You have one point of view about life, and I have another. You think your point of view is the right one, and there are thousands of people who will agree with you; but I don't think so. We have never quarreled about these things, because I didn't think it was important to quarrel about them. I don't see under the circumstances that I am doing you any great injustice when I ask you to let me go. I don't intend to desert you or the children—you will get a good living-income from me as long as I have the money to give it to you—but I want my personal freedom when I come out of here, if ever I do, and I want you to let me have it. The money that you had and a great deal more, once I am out of here, you will get back when I am on my feet again. But not if you oppose me—only if you help me. I want, and intend to help you always—but in my way."

He smoothed the leg of his prison trousers in a thoughtful way, and plucked at the sleeve of his coat. Just now he looked very much like a highly intelligent workman as he sat here, rather than like the important personage that he was. Mrs. Cowperwood was very resentful.

"That's a nice way to talk to me, and a nice way to treat me!" she exclaimed dramatically, rising and walking the short space—some two steps—that lay between the wall and the bed. "I might have known that you were too young to know your own mind when you married me. Money, of course, that's all you think of and your own gratification. I don't believe you have any sense of justice in you. I don't believe you ever had. You only think of yourself, Frank. I never saw such a man as you. You have treated me like a dog all through this affair; and all the while you have been running with that little snip of an Irish thing, and telling her all about your affairs, I suppose. You let me go on believing that you cared for me up to the last moment, and then you suddenly step up and tell me that you want a divorce. I'll not do it. I'll not give you a divorce, and you needn't think it."

Cowperwood listened in silence. His position, in so far as this marital tangle was concerned, as he saw, was very advantageous. He was a convict, constrained by the exigencies of his position to be out of personal contact with his wife for a long period of time to come, which should naturally tend to school her to do without him. When he came out, it would be very easy for her to get a divorce from a convict, particularly if she could allege misconduct with another woman, which he would not deny. At the same time, he hoped to keep Aileen's name out of it. Mrs. Cowperwood, if she would, could give any false name if he made no contest. Besides, she was not a very strong person, intellectually speaking. He could bend her to his will. There was no need of saying much more now; the ice had been broken, the situation had been put before her, and time should do the rest.

"Don't be dramatic, Lillian," he commented, indifferently. "I'm not such a loss to you if you have enough to live on. I don't think I want to live in Philadelphia if ever I come out of here. My idea now is to go west, and I think I want to go alone. I sha'n't get married right away again even if you do give me a divorce. I don't care to take anybody along. It would be better for the children if you would stay here and divorce me. The public would think better of them and you."

"I'll not do it," declared Mrs. Cowperwood, emphatically. "I'll never do it, never; so there! You can say what you choose. You owe it to me to stick by me and the children after all I've done for you, and I'll not do it. You needn't ask me any more; I'll not do it."

"Very well," replied Cowperwood, quietly, getting up. "We needn't talk about it any more now. Your time is nearly up, anyhow." (Twenty minutes was supposed to be the regular allotment for visitors.) "Perhaps you'll change your mind sometime."

She gathered up her muff and the shawl-strap in which she had carried her gifts, and turned to go. It had been her custom to kiss Cowperwood in a make-believe way up to this time, but now she was too angry to make this pretense. And yet she was sorry, too—sorry for herself and, she thought, for him.

"Frank," she declared, dramatically, at the last moment, "I never saw such a man as you. I don't believe you have any heart. You're not worthy of a good wife. You're worthy of just such a woman as you're getting. The idea!" Suddenly tears came to her eyes, and she flounced scornfully and yet sorrowfully out.

Cowperwood stood there. At least there would be no more useless kissing between them, he congratulated himself. It was hard in a way, but purely from an emotional point of view. He was not doing her any essential injustice, he reasoned—not an economic one—which was the important thing. She was angry to-day, but she would get over it, and in time might come to see his point of view. Who could tell? At any rate he had made it plain to her what he intended to do and that was something as he saw it. He reminded one of nothing so much, as he stood there, as of a young chicken picking its way out of the shell of an old estate. Although he was in a cell of a penitentiary, with nearly four years more to serve, yet obviously he felt, within himself, that the whole world was still before him. He could go west if he could not reestablish himself in Philadelphia; but he must stay here long enough to win the approval of those who had known him formerly—to obtain, as it were, a letter of credit which he could carry to other parts.

"Hard words break no bones," he said to himself, as his wife went out. "A man's never done till he's done. I'll show some of these people yet." Of Bonhag, who came to close the cell door, he asked whether it was going to rain, it looked so dark in the hall.

"It's sure to before night," replied Bonhag, who was always wondering over Cowperwood's tangled affairs as he heard them retailed here and there.

CHAPTER LVII

The time that Cowperwood spent in the Eastern Penitentiary of Pennsylvania was exactly thirteen months from the day of his entry to his discharge. The influences which brought about this result were partly of his willing, and partly not. For one thing, some six months after his incarceration, Edward Malia Butler died, expired sitting in his chair in his private office at his home. The conduct of Aileen had been a great strain on him. From the time Cowperwood had been sentenced, and more particularly after the time he had cried on Aileen's shoulder in prison, she had turned on her father in an almost brutal way. Her attitude, unnatural for a child, was quite explicable as that of a tortured sweetheart. Cowperwood had told her that he thought Butler was using his influence to withhold a pardon for him, even though one were granted to Stener, whose life in prison he had been following with considerable interest; and this had enraged her beyond measure. She lost no chance of being practically insulting to her father, ignoring him on every occasion, refusing as often as possible to eat at the same table, and when she did, sitting next her mother in the place of Norah, with whom she managed to exchange. She refused to sing or play any more when he was present, and persistently ignored the large number of young political aspirants who came to the house, and whose presence in a way had been encouraged for her benefit. Old Butler realized, of course, what it was all about. He said nothing. He could not placate her.

Her mother and brothers did not understand it at all at first. (Mrs. Butler never understood.) But not long after Cowperwood's incarceration Callum and Owen became aware of what the trouble was. Once, when Owen was coming away from a reception at one of the houses where his growing financial importance made him welcome, he heard one of two men whom he knew casually, say to the other, as they stood at the door adjusting their coats, "You saw where this fellow Cowperwood got four years, didn't you?"

"Yes," replied the other. "A clever devil that—wasn't he? I knew that girl he was in with, too—you know who I mean. Miss Butler—wasn't that her name?"

Owen was not sure that he had heard right. He did not get the connection until the other guest, opening the door and stepping out, remarked: "Well, old Butler got even, apparently. They say he sent him up."

Owen's brow clouded. A hard, contentious look came into his eyes. He had much of his father's force. What in the devil were they talking about? What Miss Butler did they have in mind? Could this be Aileen or Norah, and how could Cowperwood come to be in with either of them? It could not possibly be Norah, he reflected; she was very much infatuated with a young man whom he knew, and was going to marry him. Aileen had been most friendly with the Cowperwoods, and had often spoken well of the financier. Could it be she? He could not believe it. He thought once of overtaking the two acquaintances and demanding to know what they meant, but when he came out on the step they were already some distance down the street and in the opposite direction from that in which he wished to go. He decided to ask his father about this.

On demand, old Butler confessed at once, but insisted that his son keep silent about it.

"I wish I'd have known," said Owen, grimly. "I'd have shot the dirty dog."

"Aisy, aisy," said Butler. "Yer own life's worth more than his, and ye'd only be draggin' the rest of yer family in the dirt with him. He's had somethin' to pay him for his dirty trick, and he'll have more. Just ye say nothin' to no one. Wait. He'll be wantin' to get out in a year or two. Say nothin' to her aither. Talkin' won't help there. She'll come to her sinses when he's been away long enough, I'm thinkin'." Owen had tried to be civil to his sister after that, but since he was a stickler for social perfection and advancement, and so eager to get up in the world himself, he could not understand how she could possibly have done any such thing. He resented bitterly the stumbling-block she had put in his path. Now, among other things, his enemies would have this to throw in his face if they wanted to—and they would want to, trust life for that.

Callum reached his knowledge of the matter in quite another manner, but at about the same time. He was a member of an athletic club which had an attractive building in the city, and a fine country club, where he went occasionally to enjoy the swimming-pool and the Turkish bath connected with it. One of his friends approached him there in the billiard-room one evening and said, "Say, Butler, you know I'm a good friend of yours, don't you?"

"Why, certainly, I know it," replied Callum. "What's the matter?"

"Well, you know," said the young individual, whose name was Richard Pethick, looking at Callum with a look of almost strained affection, "I wouldn't come to you with any story that I thought would hurt your feelings or that you oughtn't to know about, but I do think you ought to know about this." He pulled at a high white collar which was choking his neck.

"I know you wouldn't, Pethick," replied Callum; very much interested. "What is it? What's the point?"

"Well, I don't like to say anything," replied Pethick, "but that fellow Hibbs is saying things around here about your sister."

"What's that?" exclaimed Callum, straightening up in the most dynamic way and bethinking him of the approved social procedure in all such cases. He should be very angry. He should demand and exact proper satisfaction in some form or other—by blows very likely if his honor had been in any way impugned. "What is it he says about my sister? What right has he to mention her name here, anyhow? He doesn't know her."

Pethick affected to be greatly concerned lest he cause trouble between Callum and Hibbs. He protested that he did not want to, when, in reality, he was dying to tell. At last he came out with, "Why, he's circulated the yarn that your sister had something to do with this man Cowperwood, who was tried here recently, and that that's why he's just gone to prison."

"What's that?" exclaimed Callum, losing the make-believe of the unimportant, and taking on the serious mien of some one who feels desperately. "He says that, does he? Where is he? I want to see if he'll say that to me."

Some of the stern fighting ability of his father showed in his slender, rather refined young face.

"Now, Callum," insisted Pethick, realizing the genuine storm he had raised, and being a little fearful of the result, "do be careful what you say. You mustn't have a row in here. You know it's against the rules. Besides he may be drunk. It's just some foolish talk he's heard, I'm sure. Now, for goodness' sake, don't get so excited." Pethick, having evoked the storm, was not a little nervous as to its results in his own case. He, too, as well as Callum, himself as the tale-bearer, might now be involved.

But Callum by now was not so easily restrained. His face was quite pale, and he was moving toward the old English grill-room, where Hibbs happened to be, consuming a brandy-and-soda with a friend of about his own age. Callum entered and called him.

"Oh, Hibbs!" he said.

Hibbs, hearing his voice and seeing him in the door, arose and came over. He was an interesting youth of the collegiate type, educated at Princeton. He had heard the rumor concerning Aileen from various sources—other members of the club, for one—and had ventured to repeat it in Pethick's presence.

"What's that you were just saying about my sister?" asked Callum, grimly, looking Hibbs in the eye.

"Why—I—" hesitated Hibbs, who sensed trouble and was eager to avoid it. He was not exceptionally brave and looked it. His hair was straw-colored, his eyes blue, and his cheeks pink. "Why—nothing in particular. Who said I was talking about her?" He looked at Pethick, whom he knew to be the tale-bearer, and the latter exclaimed, excitedly:

"Now don't you try to deny it, Hibbs. You know I heard you?"

"Well, what did I say?" asked Hibbs, defiantly.

"Well, what did you say?" interrupted Callum, grimly, transferring the conversation to himself. "That's just what I want to know."

"Why," stammered Hibbs, nervously, "I don't think I've said anything that anybody else hasn't said. I just repeated that some one said that your sister had been very friendly with Mr. Cowperwood. I didn't say any more than I have heard other people say around here."

"Oh, you didn't, did you?" exclaimed Callum, withdrawing his hand from his pocket and slapping Hibbs in the face. He repeated the blow with his left hand, fiercely. "Perhaps that'll teach you to keep my sister's name out of your mouth, you pup!"

Hibbs's arms flew up. He was not without pugilistic training, and he struck back vigorously, striking Callum once in the chest and once in the neck. In an instant the two rooms of this suite were in an uproar. Tables and chairs were overturned by the energy of men attempting to get to the scene of action. The two combatants were quickly separated; sides were taken by the friends of each, excited explanations attempted and defied. Callum was examining the knuckles of his left hand, which were cut from the blow he had delivered. He maintained a gentlemanly calm. Hibbs, very much flustered and excited, insisted that he had been most unreasonably used. The idea of attacking him here. And, anyhow, as he maintained now, Pethick had been both eavesdropping and lying about him. Incidentally, the latter was protesting to others that he had done the only thing which an honorable friend could do. It was a nine days' wonder in the club, and was only kept out of the newspapers by the most strenuous efforts on the part of the friends of both parties. Callum was so outraged on discovering that there was some foundation for the rumor at the club in a general rumor which prevailed that he tendered his resignation, and never went there again.

"I wish to heaven you hadn't struck that fellow," counseled Owen, when the incident was related to him. "It will only make more talk. She ought to leave this place; but she won't. She's struck on that fellow yet, and we can't tell Norah and mother. We will never hear the last of this, you and I—believe me."

"Damn it, she ought to be made to go," exclaimed Callum.

"Well, she won't," replied Owen. "Father has tried making her, and she won't go. Just let things stand. He's in the penitentiary now, and that's probably the end of him. The public seem to think that father put him there, and that's something. Maybe we can persuade her to go after a while. I wish to God we had never had sight of that fellow. If ever he comes out, I've a good notion to kill him."

"Oh, I wouldn't do anything like that," replied Callum. "It's useless. It would only stir things up afresh. He's done for, anyhow."

They planned to urge Norah to marry as soon as possible. And as for their feelings toward Aileen, it was a very chilly atmosphere which Mrs. Butler contemplated from now on, much to her confusion, grief, and astonishment.

In this divided world it was that Butler eventually found himself, all at sea as to what to think or what to do. He had brooded so long now, for months, and as yet had found no solution. And finally, in a form of religious despair, sitting at his desk, in his business chair, he had collapsed—a weary and disconsolate man of seventy. A lesion of the left ventricle was the immediate physical cause, although brooding over Aileen was in part the mental one. His death could not have been laid to his grief over Aileen exactly, for he was a very large man—apoplectic and with sclerotic veins and arteries. For a great many years now he had taken very little exercise, and his digestion had been considerably impaired thereby. He was past seventy, and his time had been reached. They found him there the next morning, his hands folded in his lap, his head on his bosom, quite cold.

He was buried with honors out of St. Timothy's Church, the funeral attended by a large body of politicians and city officials, who discussed secretly among themselves whether his grief over his daughter had anything to do with his end. All his good deeds were

254

remembered, of course, and Mollenhauer and Simpson sent great floral emblems in remembrance. They were very sorry that he was gone, for they had been a cordial three. But gone he was, and that ended their interest in the matter. He left all of his property to his wife in one of the shortest wills ever recorded locally.

"I give and bequeath to my beloved wife, Norah, all my property of whatsoever kind to be disposed of as she may see fit."

There was no misconstruing this. A private paper drawn secretly for her sometime before by Butler, explained how the property should be disposed of by her at her death. It was Butler's real will masquerading as hers, and she would not have changed it for worlds; but he wanted her left in undisturbed possession of everything until she should die. Aileen's originally assigned portion had never been changed. According to her father's will, which no power under the sun could have made Mrs. Butler alter, she was left $250,000 to be paid at Mrs. Butler's death. Neither this fact nor any of the others contained in the paper were communicated by Mrs. Butler, who retained it to be left as her will. Aileen often wondered, but never sought to know, what had been left her. Nothing she fancied—but felt that she could not help this.

Butler's death led at once to a great change in the temper of the home. After the funeral the family settled down to a seemingly peaceful continuance of the old life; but it was a matter of seeming merely. The situation stood with Callum and Owen manifesting a certain degree of contempt for Aileen, which she, understanding, reciprocated. She was very haughty. Owen had plans of forcing her to leave after Butler's death, but he finally asked himself what was the use. Mrs. Butler, who did not want to leave the old home, was very fond of Aileen, so therein lay a reason for letting her remain. Besides, any move to force her out would have entailed an explanation to her mother, which was not deemed advisable. Owen himself was interested in Caroline Mollenhauer, whom he hoped some day to marry—as much for her prospective wealth as for any other reason, though he was quite fond of her. In the January following Butler's death, which occurred in August, Norah was married very quietly, and the following spring Callum embarked on a similar venture.

In the meanwhile, with Butler's death, the control of the political situation had shifted considerably. A certain Tom Collins, formerly one of Butler's henchmen, but latterly a power in the First, Second, Third, and Fourth Wards, where he had numerous saloons and control of other forms of vice, appeared as a claimant for political recognition. Mollenhauer and Simpson had to consult him, as he could make very uncertain the disposition of some hundred and fifteen thousand votes, a large number of which were fraudulent, but which fact did not modify their deadly character on occasion. Butler's sons disappeared as possible political factors, and were compelled to confine themselves to the street-railway and contracting business. The pardon of Cowperwood and Stener, which Butler would have opposed, because by keeping Stener in he kept Cowperwood in, became a much easier matter. The scandal of the treasury defalcation was gradually dying down; the newspapers had ceased to refer to it in any way. Through Steger and Wingate, a large petition signed by all important financiers and brokers had been sent to the Governor pointing out that Cowperwood's trial and conviction had been most unfair, and asking that he be pardoned. There was no need of any such effort, so far as Stener was concerned; whenever the time seemed ripe the politicians were quite ready to say to the Governor that he ought to let him go. It was only because Butler had opposed Cowperwood's release that they had hesitated. It was really not possible to let out the one and ignore the other; and this petition, coupled with Butler's death, cleared the way very nicely.

Nevertheless, nothing was done until the March following Butler's death, when both Stener and Cowperwood had been incarcerated thirteen months—a length of time which seemed quite sufficient to appease the anger of the public at large. In this period Stener had undergone a considerable change physically and mentally. In spite of the fact that a number of the minor aldermen, who had profited in various ways by his largess, called to see him

255

occasionally, and that he had been given, as it were, almost the liberty of the place, and that his family had not been allowed to suffer, nevertheless he realized that his political and social days were over. Somebody might now occasionally send him a basket of fruit and assure him that he would not be compelled to suffer much longer; but when he did get out, he knew that he had nothing to depend on save his experience as an insurance agent and real-estate dealer. That had been precarious enough in the days when he was trying to get some small political foothold. How would it be when he was known only as the man who had looted the treasury of five hundred thousand dollars and been sent to the penitentiary for five years? Who would lend him the money wherewith to get a little start, even so much as four or five thousand dollars? The people who were calling to pay their respects now and then, and to assure him that he had been badly treated? Never. All of them could honestly claim that they had not so much to spare. If he had good security to offer—yes; but if he had good security he would not need to go to them at all. The man who would have actually helped him if he had only known was Frank A. Cowperwood. Stener could have confessed his mistake, as Cowperwood saw it, and Cowperwood would have given him the money gladly, without any thought of return. But by his poor understanding of human nature, Stener considered that Cowperwood must be an enemy of his, and he would not have had either the courage or the business judgment to approach him.

During his incarceration Cowperwood had been slowly accumulating a little money through Wingate. He had paid Steger considerable sums from time to time, until that worthy finally decided that it would not be fair to take any more.

"If ever you get on your feet, Frank," he said, "you can remember me if you want to, but I don't think you'll want to. It's been nothing but lose, lose, lose for you through me. I'll undertake this matter of getting that appeal to the Governor without any charge on my part. Anything I can do for you from now on is free gratis for nothing."

"Oh, don't talk nonsense, Harper," replied Cowperwood. "I don't know of anybody that could have done better with my case. Certainly there isn't anybody that I would have trusted as much. I don't like lawyers you know."

"Yes—well," said Steger, "they've got nothing on financiers, so we'll call it even." And they shook hands.

So when it was finally decided to pardon Stener, which was in the early part of March, 1873—Cowperwood's pardon was necessarily but gingerly included. A delegation, consisting of Strobik, Harmon, and Winpenny, representing, as it was intended to appear, the unanimous wishes of the council and the city administration, and speaking for Mollenhauer and Simpson, who had given their consent, visited the Governor at Harrisburg and made the necessary formal representations which were intended to impress the public. At the same time, through the agency of Steger, Davison, and Walter Leigh, the appeal in behalf of Cowperwood was made. The Governor, who had had instructions beforehand from sources quite superior to this committee, was very solemn about the whole procedure. He would take the matter under advisement. He would look into the history of the crimes and the records of the two men. He could make no promises—he would see. But in ten days, after allowing the petitions to gather considerable dust in one of his pigeonholes and doing absolutely nothing toward investigating anything, he issued two separate pardons in writing. One, as a matter of courtesy, he gave into the hands of Messrs. Strobik, Harmon, and Winpenny, to bear personally to Mr. Stener, as they desired that he should. The other, on Steger's request, he gave to him. The two committees which had called to receive them then departed; and the afternoon of that same day saw Strobik, Harmon, and Winpenny arrive in one group, and Steger, Wingate, and Walter Leigh in another, at the prison gate, but at different hours.

256

CHAPTER LVIII

This matter of the pardon of Cowperwood, the exact time of it, was kept a secret from him, though the fact that he was to be pardoned soon, or that he had a very excellent chance of being, had not been denied—rather had been made much of from time to time. Wingate had kept him accurately informed as to the progress being made, as had Steger; but when it was actually ascertained, from the Governor's private secretary, that a certain day would see the pardon handed over to them, Steger, Wingate, and Walter Leigh had agreed between themselves that they would say nothing, taking Cowperwood by surprise. They even went so far—that is, Steger and Wingate did—as to indicate to Cowperwood that there was some hitch to the proceedings and that he might not now get out so soon. Cowperwood was somewhat depressed, but properly stoical; he assured himself that he could wait, and that he would be all right sometime. He was rather surprised therefore, one Friday afternoon, to see Wingate, Steger, and Leigh appear at his cell door, accompanied by Warden Desmas.

The warden was quite pleased to think that Cowperwood should finally be going out—he admired him so much—and decided to come along to the cell, to see how he would take his liberation. On the way Desmas commented on the fact that he had always been a model prisoner. "He kept a little garden out there in that yard of his," he confided to Walter Leigh. "He had violets and pansies and geraniums out there, and they did very well, too."

Leigh smiled. It was like Cowperwood to be industrious and tasteful, even in prison. Such a man could not be conquered. "A very remarkable man, that," he remarked to Desmas.

"Very," replied the warden. "You can tell that by looking at him."

The four looked in through the barred door where he was working, without being observed, having come up quite silently.

"Hard at it, Frank?" asked Steger.

Cowperwood glanced over his shoulder and got up. He had been thinking, as always these days, of what he would do when he did get out.

"What is this," he asked—"a political delegation?" He suspected something on the instant. All four smiled cheeringly, and Bonhag unlocked the door for the warden.

"Nothing very much, Frank," replied Stager, gleefully, "only you're a free man. You can gather up your traps and come right along, if you wish."

Cowperwood surveyed his friends with a level gaze. He had not expected this so soon after what had been told him. He was not one to be very much interested in the practical joke or the surprise, but this pleased him—the sudden realization that he was free. Still, he had anticipated it so long that the charm of it had been discounted to a certain extent. He had been unhappy here, and he had not. The shame and humiliation of it, to begin with, had been much. Latterly, as he had become inured to it all, the sense of narrowness and humiliation had worn off. Only the consciousness of incarceration and delay irked him. Barring his intense desire for certain things—success and vindication, principally—he found that he could live in his narrow cell and be fairly comfortable. He had long since become used to the limy smell (used to defeat a more sickening one), and to the numerous rats which he quite regularly trapped. He had learned to take an interest in chair-caning, having become so proficient that he could seat twenty in a day if he chose, and in working in the little garden in spring, summer, and fall. Every evening he had studied the sky from his narrow yard, which resulted curiously in the gift in later years of a great reflecting telescope to a famous university. He had not looked upon himself as an ordinary prisoner, by any means—had not felt himself to be sufficiently punished if a real crime had been involved. From Bonhag he had learned the history of many criminals here incarcerated, from murderers up and down, and many had been pointed out to him from time to time. He had been escorted into the general yard by Bonhag, had seen the general food of the place being prepared, had heard of Stener's modified life here, and so forth. It had finally struck him that it was not so bad, only that the delay to an individual like himself was wasteful. He could do so much now if he were out and did not have to fight court proceedings. Courts and jails! He shook his head when he thought of the waste involved in them.

"That's all right," he said, looking around him in an uncertain way. "I'm ready."

He stepped out into the hall, with scarcely a farewell glance, and to Bonhag, who was grieving greatly over the loss of so profitable a customer, he said: "I wish you would see that some of these things are sent over to my house, Walter. You're welcome to the chair, that clock, this mirror, those pictures—all of these things in fact, except my linen, razors, and so forth."

The last little act of beneficence soothed Bonhag's lacerated soul a little. They went out into the receiving overseer's office, where Cowperwood laid aside his prison suit and the soft shirt with a considerable sense of relief. The clog shoes had long since been replaced by a better pair of his own. He put on the derby hat and gray overcoat he had worn the year before, on entering, and expressed himself as ready. At the entrance of the prison he turned and looked back—one last glance—at the iron door leading into the garden.

"You don't regret leaving that, do you, Frank?" asked Steger, curiously.

"I do not," replied Cowperwood. "It wasn't that I was thinking of. It was just the appearance of it, that's all."

In another minute they were at the outer gate, where Cowperwood shook the warden finally by the hand. Then entering a carriage outside the large, impressive, Gothic entrance, the gates were locked behind them and they were driven away.

"Well, there's an end of that, Frank," observed Steger, gayly; "that will never bother you any more."

"Yes," replied Cowperwood. "It's worse to see it coming than going."

"It seems to me we ought to celebrate this occasion in some way," observed Walter Leigh. "It won't do just to take Frank home. Why don't we all go down to Green's? That's a good idea."

"I'd rather not, if you don't mind," replied Cowperwood, feelingly. "I'll get together with you all, later. Just now I'd like to go home and change these clothes."

He was thinking of Aileen and his children and his mother and father and of his whole future. Life was going to broaden out for him considerably from now on, he was sure of it. He had learned so much about taking care of himself in those thirteen months. He was going to see Aileen, and find how she felt about things in general, and then he was going to resume some such duties as he had had in his own concern, with Wingate & Co. He was going to secure a seat on 'change again, through his friends; and, to escape the effect of the prejudice of those who might not care to do business with an ex-convict, he was going to act as general outside man, and floor man on 'charge, for Wingate & Co. His practical control of that could not be publicly proved. Now for some important development in the market—some slump or something. He would show the world whether he was a failure or not.

They let him down in front of his wife's little cottage, and he entered briskly in the gathering gloom.

On September 18, 1873, at twelve-fifteen of a brilliant autumn day, in the city of Philadelphia, one of the most startling financial tragedies that the world has ever seen had its commencement. The banking house of Jay Cooke & Co., the foremost financial organization of America, doing business at Number 114 South Third Street in Philadelphia, and with branches in New York, Washington, and London, closed its doors. Those who know anything about the financial crises of the United States know well the significance of the panic which followed. It is spoken of in all histories as the panic of 1873, and the widespread ruin and disaster which followed was practically unprecedented in American history.

At this time Cowperwood, once more a broker—ostensibly a broker's agent—was doing business in South Third Street, and representing Wingate & Co. on 'change. During the six months which had elapsed since he had emerged from the Eastern Penitentiary he had been quietly resuming financial, if not social, relations with those who had known him before. Furthermore, Wingate & Co. were prospering, and had been for some time, a fact which redounded to his credit with those who knew. Ostensibly he lived with his wife in a small house on North Twenty-first Street. In reality he occupied a bachelor apartment on North Fifteenth Street, to which Aileen occasionally repaired. The difference between himself and his wife had now become a matter of common knowledge in the family, and, although there were some faint efforts made to smooth the matter over, no good resulted. The difficulties of the past two years had so inured his parents to expect the untoward and exceptional that, astonishing as this was, it did not shock them so much as it would have years before. They were too much frightened by life to quarrel with its weird developments. They could only hope and pray for the best.

The Butler family, on the other hand, what there was of it, had become indifferent to Aileen's conduct. She was ignored by her brothers and Norah, who now knew all; and her mother was so taken up with religious devotions and brooding contemplation of her loss that she was not as active in her observation of Aileen's life as she might have been. Besides, Cowperwood and his mistress were more circumspect in their conduct than they had ever been before. Their movements were more carefully guarded, though the result was the same. Cowperwood was thinking of the West—of reaching some slight local standing here in Philadelphia, and then, with perhaps one hundred thousand dollars in capital, removing to the boundless prairies of which he had heard so much—Chicago, Fargo, Duluth, Sioux City, places then heralded in Philadelphia and the East as coming centers of great life—and taking Aileen with him. Although the problem of marriage with her was insoluble unless Mrs. Cowperwood should formally agree to give him up—a possibility which was not manifest at this time, neither he nor Aileen were deterred by that thought. They were going to build a future together—or so they thought, marriage or no marriage. The only thing which Cowperwood could see to do was to take Aileen away with him, and to trust to time and absence to modify his wife's point of view.

This particular panic, which was destined to mark a notable change in Cowperwood's career, was one of those peculiar things which spring naturally out of the optimism of the American people and the irrepressible progress of the country. It was the result, to be accurate, of the prestige and ambition of Jay Cooke, whose early training and subsequent success had all been acquired in Philadelphia, and who had since become the foremost financial figure of his day. It would be useless to attempt to trace here the rise of this man to distinction; it need only be said that by suggestions which he made and methods which he devised the Union government, in its darkest hours, was able to raise the money wherewith to continue the struggle against the South. After the Civil War this man, who had built up a tremendous banking business in Philadelphia, with great branches in New York and Washington, was at a loss for some time for some significant thing to do, some constructive work which would be worthy of his genius. The war was over; the only thing which remained was the finances of peace, and the greatest things in American financial enterprise were those related to the construction of transcontinental railway lines. The Union Pacific, authorized in 1860, was already building; the Northern Pacific and the Southern Pacific were already dreams in various pioneer minds. The great thing was to connect the Atlantic and the Pacific by steel, to bind up the territorially perfected and newly solidified Union, or to enter upon some vast project of mining, of which gold and silver were the most important. Actually railway-building was the most significant of all, and railroad stocks were far and away the most valuable and important on every exchange in America. Here in Philadelphia, New York Central, Rock Island, Wabash, Central Pacific, St. Paul, Hannibal & St. Joseph, Union Pacific, and Ohio & Mississippi were freely traded in.

There were men who were getting rich and famous out of handling these things; and such towering figures as Cornelius Vanderbilt, Jay Gould, Daniel Drew, James Fish, and others in the East, and Fair, Crocker, W. R. Hearst, and Collis P. Huntington, in the West, were already raising their heads like vast mountains in connection with these enterprises. Among those who dreamed most ardently on this score was Jay Cooke, who without the wolfish cunning of a Gould or the practical knowledge of a Vanderbilt, was ambitious to thread the northern reaches of America with a band of steel which should be a permanent memorial to his name.

The project which fascinated him most was one that related to the development of the territory then lying almost unexplored between the extreme western shore of Lake Superior, where Duluth now stands, and that portion of the Pacific Ocean into which the Columbia River empties—the extreme northern one-third of the United States. Here, if a railroad were built, would spring up great cities and prosperous towns. There were, it was suspected, mines of various metals in the region of the Rockies which this railroad would traverse, and untold wealth to be reaped from the fertile corn and wheat lands. Products brought only so far east as Duluth could then be shipped to the Atlantic, via the Great Lakes and the Erie Canal, at a greatly reduced cost. It was a vision of empire, not unlike the Panama Canal project of the same period, and one that bade fair apparently to be as useful to humanity. It had aroused the interest and enthusiasm of Cooke. Because of the fact that the government had made a grant of vast areas of land on either side of the proposed track to the corporation that should seriously undertake it and complete it within a reasonable number of years, and because of the opportunity it gave him of remaining a distinguished public figure, he had eventually shouldered the project. It was open to many objections and criticisms; but the genius which had been sufficient to finance the Civil War was considered sufficient to finance the Northern Pacific Railroad. Cooke undertook it with the idea of being able to put the merits of the proposition before the people direct—not through the agency of any great financial corporation—and of selling to the butcher, the baker, and the candlestick-maker the stock or shares that he wished to dispose of.

It was a brilliant chance. His genius had worked out the sale of great government loans during the Civil War to the people direct in this fashion. Why not Northern Pacific certificates? For several years he conducted a pyrotechnic campaign, surveying the territory in question, organizing great railway-construction corps, building hundreds of miles of track under most trying conditions, and selling great blocks of his stock, on which interest of a certain percentage was guaranteed. If it had not been that he knew little of railroad-building, personally, and that the project was so vast that it could not well be encompassed by one man, even so great a man it might have proved successful, as under subsequent management it did. However, hard times, the war between France and Germany, which tied up European capital for the time being and made it indifferent to American projects, envy, calumny, a certain percentage of mismanagement, all conspired to wreck it. On September 18, 1873, at twelve-fifteen noon, Jay Cooke & Co. failed for approximately eight million dollars and the Northern Pacific for all that had been invested in it—some fifty million dollars more.

One can imagine what the result was—the most important financier and the most distinguished railway enterprise collapsing at one and the same time. "A financial thunderclap in a clear sky," said the Philadelphia Press. "No one could have been more surprised," said the Philadelphia Inquirer, "if snow had fallen amid the sunshine of a summer noon." The public, which by Cooke's previous tremendous success had been lulled into believing him invincible, could not understand it. It was beyond belief. Jay Cooke fail? Impossible, or anything connected with him. Nevertheless, he had failed; and the New York Stock Exchange, after witnessing a number of crashes immediately afterward, closed for eight days. The Lake Shore Railroad failed to pay a call-loan of one million seven hundred and fifty thousand dollars; and the Union Trust Company, allied to the Vanderbilt interests, closed its doors after withstanding a prolonged run. The National Trust Company of New York had eight hundred thousand dollars of government securities in its vaults, but not a dollar could be borrowed upon them; and it suspended. Suspicion was universal, rumor affected every one.

In Philadelphia, when the news reached the stock exchange, it came first in the form of a brief despatch addressed to the stock board from the New York Stock Exchange—"Rumor on street of failure of Jay Cooke & Co. Answer." It was not believed, and so not replied to. Nothing was thought of it. The world of brokers paid scarcely any attention to it. Cowperwood, who had followed the fortunes of Jay Cooke & Co. with considerable suspicion of its president's brilliant theory of vending his wares direct to the people—was perhaps the only one who had suspicions. He had once written a brilliant criticism to some inquirer, in which he had said that no enterprise of such magnitude as the Northern Pacific had ever before been entirely dependent upon one house, or rather upon one man, and that he did not like it. "I am not sure that the lands through which the road runs are so unparalleled in climate, soil, timber, minerals, etc., as Mr. Cooke and his friends would have us believe. Neither do I think that the road can at present, or for many years to come, earn the interest which its great issues of stock call for. There is great danger and risk there." So when the notice was posted, he looked at it, wondering what the effect would be if by any chance Jay Cooke & Co. should fail.

He was not long in wonder. A second despatch posted on 'change read: "New York, September 18th. Jay Cooke & Co. have suspended."

Cowperwood could not believe it. He was beside himself with the thought of a great opportunity. In company with every other broker, he hurried into Third Street and up to Number 114, where the famous old banking house was located, in order to be sure. Despite his natural dignity and reserve, he did not hesitate to run. If this were true, a great hour had struck. There would be wide-spread panic and disaster. There would be a terrific slump in prices of all stocks. He must be in the thick of it. Wingate must be on hand, and his two brothers. He must tell them how to sell and when and what to buy. His great hour had come!

CHAPTER LIX

The banking house of Jay Cooke & Co., in spite of its tremendous significance as a banking and promoting concern, was a most unpretentious affair, four stories and a half in height of gray stone and red brick. It had never been deemed a handsome or comfortable banking house. Cowperwood had been there often. Wharf-rats as long as the forearm of a man crept up the culverted channels of Dock Street to run through the apartments at will. Scores of clerks worked under gas-jets, where light and air were not any too abundant, keeping track of the firm's vast accounts. It was next door to the Girard National Bank, where Cowperwood's friend Davison still flourished, and where the principal financial business of the street converged. As Cowperwood ran he met his brother Edward, who was coming to the stock exchange with some word for him from Wingate.

"Run and get Wingate and Joe," he said. "There's something big on this afternoon. Jay Cooke has failed."

Edward waited for no other word, but hurried off as directed.

Cowperwood reached Cooke & Co. among the earliest. To his utter astonishment, the solid brown-oak doors, with which he was familiar, were shut, and a notice posted on them, which he quickly read, ran:

September 18, 1873.

To the Public—

We regret to be obliged to announce that, owing to
unexpected demands on us, our firm has been obliged to
suspend payment. In a few days we will be able to present a
statement to our creditors. Until which time we must ask
their patient consideration. We believe our assets to be
largely in excess of our liabilities.

Jay Cooke & Co.

A magnificent gleam of triumph sprang into Cowperwood's eye. In company with many others he turned and ran back toward the exchange, while a reporter, who had come for information knocked at the massive doors of the banking house, and was told by a porter, who peered out of a diamond-shaped aperture, that Jay Cooke had gone home for the day and was not to be seen.

"Now," thought Cowperwood, to whom this panic spelled opportunity, not ruin, "I'll get my innings. I'll go short of this—of everything."

Before, when the panic following the Chicago fire had occurred, he had been long—had been compelled to stay long of many things in order to protect himself. To-day he had nothing to speak of—perhaps a paltry seventy-five thousand dollars which he had managed to scrape together. Thank God! he had only the reputation of Wingate's old house to lose, if he lost, which was nothing. With it as a trading agency behind him—with it as an excuse for his presence, his right to buy and sell—he had everything to gain. Where many men were thinking of ruin, he was thinking of success. He would have Wingate and his two brothers under him to execute his orders exactly. He could pick up a fourth and a fifth man if necessary. He would give them orders to sell—everything—ten, fifteen, twenty, thirty points off, if necessary, in order to trap the unwary, depress the market, frighten the fearsome who would think he was too daring; and then he would buy, buy, buy, below these figures as much as possible, in order to cover his sales and reap a profit.

His instinct told him how widespread and enduring this panic would be. The Northern Pacific was a hundred-million-dollar venture. It involved the savings of hundreds of thousands of people—small bankers, tradesmen, preachers, lawyers, doctors, widows, institutions all over the land, and all resting on the faith and security of Jay Cooke. Once, not unlike the Chicago fire map, Cowperwood had seen a grand prospectus and map of the location of the Northern Pacific land-grant which Cooke had controlled, showing a vast stretch or belt of territory extending from Duluth—"The Zenith City of the Unsalted Seas," as Proctor Knott, speaking in the House of Representatives, had sarcastically called it— through the Rockies and the headwaters of the Missouri to the Pacific Ocean. He had seen how Cooke had ostensibly managed to get control of this government grant, containing millions upon millions of acres and extending fourteen hundred miles in length; but it was only a vision of empire. There might be silver and gold and copper mines there. The land was usable—would some day be usable. But what of it now? It would do to fire the imaginations of fools with—nothing more. It was inaccessible, and would remain so for years to come. No doubt thousands had subscribed to build this road; but, too, thousands would now fail if it had failed. Now the crash had come. The grief and the rage of the public would be intense. For days and days and weeks and months, normal confidence and courage would be gone. This was his hour. This was his great moment. Like a wolf prowling under glittering, bitter stars in the night, he was looking down into the humble folds of simple men and seeing what their ignorance and their unsophistication would cost them.

He hurried back to the exchange, the very same room in which only two years before he had fought his losing fight, and, finding that his partner and his brother had not yet come, began to sell everything in sight. Pandemonium had broken loose. Boys and men were fairly tearing in from all sections with orders from panic-struck brokers to sell, sell, sell, and later with orders to buy; the various trading-posts were reeling, swirling masses of brokers and their agents. Outside in the street in front of Jay Cooke & Co., Clark & Co., the Girard National Bank, and other institutions, immense crowds were beginning to form. They were hurrying here to learn the trouble, to withdraw their deposits, to protect their interests generally. A policeman arrested a boy for calling out the failure of Jay Cooke & Co., but nevertheless the news of the great disaster was spreading like wild-fire.

Among these panic-struck men Cowperwood was perfectly calm, deadly cold, the same Cowperwood who had pegged solemnly at his ten chairs each day in prison, who had baited his traps for rats, and worked in the little garden allotted him in utter silence and loneliness. Now he was vigorous and energetic. He had been just sufficiently about this exchange floor once more to have made his personality impressive and distinguished. He forced his way into the center of swirling crowds of men already shouting themselves hoarse, offering whatever was being offered in quantities which were astonishing, and at prices which allured the few who were anxious to make money out of the tumbling prices to buy. New York Central had been standing at 104 7/8 when the failure was announced; Rhode Island at 108 7/8; Western Union at 92 1/2; Wabash at 70 1/4; Panama at 117 3/8; Central Pacific at 99 5/8; St. Paul at 51; Hannibal & St. Joseph at 48; Northwestern at 63; Union Pacific at 26 3/4; Ohio and Mississippi at 38 3/4. Cowperwood's house had scarcely any of the stocks on hand. They were not carrying them for any customers, and yet he sold, sold, sold, to whoever would take, at prices which he felt sure would inspire them.

"Five thousand of New York Central at ninety-nine, ninety-eight, ninety-seven, ninety-six, ninety-five, ninety-four, ninety-three, ninety-two, ninety-one, ninety, eighty-nine," you might have heard him call; and when his sales were not sufficiently brisk he would turn to something else—Rock Island, Panama, Central Pacific, Western Union, Northwestern, Union Pacific. He saw his brother and Wingate hurrying in, and stopped in his work long enough to instruct them. "Sell everything you can," he cautioned them quietly, "at fifteen points off if you have to—no lower than that now—and buy all you can below it. Ed, you see if you cannot buy up some local street-railways at fifteen off. Joe, you stay near me and buy when I tell you."

The secretary of the board appeared on his little platform.

"E. W. Clark & Company," he announced, at one-thirty, "have just closed their doors."

"Tighe & Company," he called at one-forty-five, "announce that they are compelled to suspend."

"The First National Bank of Philadelphia," he called, at two o'clock, "begs to state that it cannot at present meet its obligations."

After each announcement, always, as in the past, when the gong had compelled silence, the crowd broke into an ominous "Aw, aw, aw."

"Tighe & Company," thought Cowperwood, for a single second, when he heard it. "There's an end of him." And then he returned to his task.

When the time for closing came, his coat torn, his collar twisted loose, his necktie ripped, his hat lost, he emerged sane, quiet, steady-mannered.

"Well, Ed," he inquired, meeting his brother, "how'd you make out?" The latter was equally torn, scratched, exhausted.

"Christ," he replied, tugging at his sleeves, "I never saw such a place as this. They almost tore my clothes off."

"Buy any local street-railways?"

"About five thousand shares."

"We'd better go down to Green's," Frank observed, referring to the lobby of the principal hotel. "We're not through yet. There'll be more trading there."

He led the way to find Wingate and his brother Joe, and together they were off, figuring up some of the larger phases of their purchases and sales as they went.

And, as he predicted, the excitement did not end with the coming of the night. The crowd lingered in front of Jay Cooke & Co.'s on Third Street and in front of other institutions, waiting apparently for some development which would be favorable to them. For the initiated the center of debate and agitation was Green's Hotel, where on the evening of the eighteenth the lobby and corridors were crowded with bankers, brokers, and speculators. The stock exchange had practically adjourned to that hotel en masse. What of the morrow? Who would be the next to fail? From whence would money be forthcoming? These were the topics from each mind and upon each tongue. From New York was coming momentarily more news of disaster. Over there banks and trust companies were falling like trees in a hurricane. Cowperwood in his perambulations, seeing what he could see and hearing what he could hear, reaching understandings which were against the rules of the exchange, but which were nevertheless in accord with what every other person was doing, saw about him men known to him as agents of Mollenhauer and Simpson, and congratulated himself that he would have something to collect from them before the week was over. He might not own a street-railway, but he would have the means to. He learned from hearsay, and information which had been received from New York and elsewhere, that things were as bad as they could be, and that there was no hope for those who expected a speedy return of normal conditions. No thought of retiring for the night entered until the last man was gone. It was then practically morning.

The next day was Friday, and suggested many ominous things. Would it be another Black Friday? Cowperwood was at his office before the street was fairly awake. He figured out his program for the day to a nicety, feeling strangely different from the way he had felt two years before when the conditions were not dissimilar. Yesterday, in spite of the sudden onslaught, he had made one hundred and fifty thousand dollars, and he expected to make as much, if not more, to-day. There was no telling what he could make, he thought, if he could only keep his small organization in perfect trim and get his assistants to follow his orders exactly. Ruin for others began early with the suspension of Fisk & Hatch, Jay Cooke's faithful lieutenants during the Civil War. They had calls upon them for one million five hundred thousand dollars in the first fifteen minutes after opening the doors, and at once closed them again, the failure being ascribed to Collis P. Huntington's Central Pacific Railroad and the Chesapeake & Ohio. There was a long-continued run on the Fidelity Trust Company. News of these facts, and of failures in New York posted on 'change, strengthened the cause Cowperwood was so much interested in; for he was selling as high as he could and buying as low as he could on a constantly sinking scale. By twelve o'clock he figured with his assistants that he had cleared one hundred thousand dollars; and by three o'clock he had two hundred thousand dollars more. That afternoon between three and seven he spent adjusting his trades, and between seven and one in the morning, without anything to eat, in gathering as much additional information as he could and laying his plans for the future. Saturday morning came, and he repeated his performance of the day before, following it up with adjustments on Sunday and heavy trading on Monday. By Monday afternoon at three o'clock he figured that, all losses and uncertainties to one side, he was once more a millionaire, and that now his future lay clear and straight before him.

As he sat at his desk late that afternoon in his office looking out into Third Street, where a hurrying of brokers, messengers, and anxious depositors still maintained, he had the feeling that so far as Philadelphia and the life here was concerned, his day and its day with him was over. He did not care anything about the brokerage business here any more or anywhere. Failures such as this, and disasters such as the Chicago fire, that had overtaken him two years before, had cured him of all love of the stock exchange and all feeling for Philadelphia. He had been very unhappy here in spite of all his previous happiness; and his experience as a convict had made, him, he could see quite plainly, unacceptable to the element with whom he had once hoped to associate. There was nothing else to do, now that he had reestablished himself as a Philadelphia business man and been pardoned for an offense which he hoped to make people believe he had never committed, but to leave Philadelphia to seek a new world.

"If I get out of this safely," he said to himself, "this is the end. I am going West, and going into some other line of business." He thought of street-railways, land speculation, some great manufacturing project of some kind, even mining, on a legitimate basis.

"I have had my lesson," he said to himself, finally getting up and preparing to leave. "I am as rich as I was, and only a little older. They caught me once, but they will not catch me again." He talked to Wingate about following up the campaign on the lines in which he had started, and he himself intended to follow it up with great energy; but all the while his mind was running with this one rich thought: "I am a millionaire. I am a free man. I am only thirty-six, and my future is all before me."

It was with this thought that he went to visit Aileen, and to plan for the future.

It was only three months later that a train, speeding through the mountains of Pennsylvania and over the plains of Ohio and Indiana, bore to Chicago and the West the young financial aspirant who, in spite of youth and wealth and a notable vigor of body, was a solemn, conservative speculator as to what his future might be. The West, as he had carefully calculated before leaving, held much. He had studied the receipts of the New York Clearing House recently and the disposition of bank-balances and the shipment of gold, and had seen that vast quantities of the latter metal were going to Chicago. He understood finance accurately. The meaning of gold shipments was clear. Where money was going trade was—a thriving, developing life. He wished to see clearly for himself what this world had to offer.

Two years later, following the meteoric appearance of a young speculator in Duluth, and after Chicago had seen the tentative opening of a grain and commission company labeled Frank A. Cowperwood & Co., which ostensibly dealt in the great wheat crops of the West, a quiet divorce was granted Mrs. Frank A. Cowperwood in Philadelphia, because apparently she wished it. Time had not seemingly dealt badly with her. Her financial affairs, once so bad, were now apparently all straightened out, and she occupied in West Philadelphia, near one of her sisters, a new and interesting home which was fitted with all the comforts of an excellent middle-class residence. She was now quite religious once more. The two children, Frank and Lillian, were in private schools, returning evenings to their mother. "Wash" Sims was once more the negro general factotum. Frequent visitors on Sundays were Mr. and Mrs. Henry Worthington Cowperwood, no longer distressed financially, but subdued and wearied, the wind completely gone from their once much-favored sails. Cowperwood, senior, had sufficient money wherewith to sustain himself, and that without slaving as a petty clerk, but his social joy in life was gone. He was old, disappointed, sad. He could feel that with his quondam honor and financial glory, he was the same—and he was not. His courage and his dreams were gone, and he awaited death.

Here, too, came Anna Adelaide Cowperwood on occasion, a clerk in the city water office, who speculated much as to the strange vicissitudes of life. She had great interest in her brother, who seemed destined by fate to play a conspicuous part in the world; but she could not understand him. Seeing that all those who were near to him in any way seemed to rise or fall with his prosperity, she did not understand how justice and morals were arranged in this world. There seemed to be certain general principles—or people assumed there were—but apparently there were exceptions. Assuredly her brother abided by no known rule, and yet seemed to be doing fairly well once more. What did this mean? Mrs. Cowperwood, his former wife, condemned his actions, and yet accepted of his prosperity as her due. What were the ethics of that?

Cowperwood's every action was known to Aileen Butler, his present whereabouts and prospects. Not long after his wife's divorce, and after many trips to and from this new world in which he was now living, these two left Philadelphia together one afternoon in the winter. Aileen explained to her mother, who was willing to go and live with Norah, that she had fallen in love with the former banker and wished to marry him. The old lady, gathering only a garbled version of it at first, consented.

Thus ended forever for Aileen this long-continued relationship with this older world. Chicago was before her—a much more distinguished career, Frank told her, than ever they could have had in Philadelphia.

"Isn't it nice to be finally going?" she commented.

"It is advantageous, anyhow," he said.

CONCERNING MYCTEROPERCA BONACI

There is a certain fish, the scientific name of which is Mycteroperca Bonaci, its common name Black Grouper, which is of considerable value as an afterthought in this connection, and which deserves to be better known. It is a healthy creature, growing quite regularly to a weight of two hundred and fifty pounds, and lives a comfortable, lengthy existence because of its very remarkable ability to adapt itself to conditions. That very subtle thing which we call the creative power, and which we endow with the spirit of the beatitudes, is supposed to build this mortal life in such fashion that only honesty and virtue shall prevail. Witness, then, the significant manner in which it has fashioned the black grouper. One might go far afield and gather less forceful indictments—the horrific spider spinning his trap for the unthinking fly; the lovely Drosera (Sundew) using its crimson calyx for a smothering-pit in which to seal and devour the victim of its beauty; the rainbow-colored jellyfish that spreads its prismed tentacles like streamers of great beauty, only to sting and torture all that falls within their radiant folds. Man himself is busy digging the pit and fashioning the snare, but he will not believe it. His feet are in the trap of circumstance; his eyes are on an illusion.

Mycteroperca moving in its dark world of green waters is as fine an illustration of the constructive genius of nature, which is not beatific, as any which the mind of man may discover. Its great superiority lies in an almost unbelievable power of simulation, which relates solely to the pigmentation of its skin. In electrical mechanics we pride ourselves on our ability to make over one brilliant scene into another in the twinkling of an eye, and flash before the gaze of an onlooker picture after picture, which appear and disappear as we look. The directive control of Mycteroperca over its appearance is much more significant. You cannot look at it long without feeling that you are witnessing something spectral and unnatural, so brilliant is its power to deceive. From being black it can become instantly white; from being an earth-colored brown it can fade into a delightful water-colored green. Its markings change as the clouds of the sky. One marvels at the variety and subtlety of its power.

Lying at the bottom of a bay, it can simulate the mud by which it is surrounded. Hidden in the folds of glorious leaves, it is of the same markings. Lurking in a flaw of light, it is like the light itself shining dimly in water. Its power to elude or strike unseen is of the greatest.

What would you say was the intention of the overruling, intelligent, constructive force which gives to Mycteroperca this ability? To fit it to be truthful? To permit it to present an unvarying appearance which all honest life-seeking fish may know? Or would you say that subtlety, chicanery, trickery, were here at work? An implement of illusion one might readily suspect it to be, a living lie, a creature whose business it is to appear what it is not, to simulate that with which it has nothing in common, to get its living by great subtlety, the power of its enemies to forefend against which is little. The indictment is fair.

Would you say, in the face of this, that a beatific, beneficent creative, overruling power never wills that which is either tricky or deceptive? Or would you say that this material seeming in which we dwell is itself an illusion? If not, whence then the Ten Commandments and the illusion of justice? Why were the Beatitudes dreamed of and how do they avail?

THE MAGIC CRYSTAL

If you had been a mystic or a soothsayer or a member of that mysterious world which divines by incantations, dreams, the mystic bowl, or the crystal sphere, you might have looked into their mysterious depths at this time and foreseen a world of happenings which concerned these two, who were now apparently so fortunately placed. In the fumes of the witches' pot, or the depths of the radiant crystal, might have been revealed cities, cities, cities; a world of mansions, carriages, jewels, beauty; a vast metropolis outraged by the power of one man; a great state seething with indignation over a force it could not control; vast halls of priceless pictures; a palace unrivaled for its magnificence; a whole world reading with wonder, at times, of a given name. And sorrow, sorrow, sorrow.

The three witches that hailed Macbeth upon the blasted heath might in turn have called to Cowperwood, "Hail to you, Frank Cowperwood, master of a great railway system! Hail to you, Frank Cowperwood, builder of a priceless mansion! Hail to you, Frank Cowperwood, patron of arts and possessor of endless riches! You shall be famed hereafter." But like the Weird Sisters, they would have lied, for in the glory was also the ashes of Dead Sea fruit— an understanding that could neither be inflamed by desire nor satisfied by luxury; a heart that was long since wearied by experience; a soul that was as bereft of illusion as a windless moon. And to Aileen, as to Macduff, they might have spoken a more pathetic promise, one that concerned hope and failure. To have and not to have! All the seeming, and yet the sorrow of not having! Brilliant society that shone in a mirage, yet locked its doors; love that eluded as a will-o'-the-wisp and died in the dark. "Hail to you, Frank Cowperwood, master and no master, prince of a world of dreams whose reality was disillusion!" So might the witches have called, the bowl have danced with figures, the fumes with vision, and it would have been true. What wise man might not read from such a beginning, such an end?

THE TITAN

CHAPTER I

THE NEW CITY

When Frank Algernon Cowperwood emerged from the Eastern District Penitentiary in Philadelphia he realized that the old life he had lived in that city since boyhood was ended. His youth was gone, and with it had been lost the great business prospects of his earlier manhood. He must begin again.

It would be useless to repeat how a second panic following upon a tremendous failure—that of Jay Cooke & Co.—had placed a second fortune in his hands. This restored wealth softened him in some degree. Fate seemed to have his personal welfare in charge. He was sick of the stock-exchange, anyhow, as a means of livelihood, and now decided that he would leave it once and for all. He would get in something else—street-railways, land deals, some of the boundless opportunities of the far West. Philadelphia was no longer pleasing to him. Though now free and rich, he was still a scandal to the pretenders, and the financial and social world was not prepared to accept him. He must go his way alone, unaided, or only secretly so, while his quondam friends watched his career from afar. So, thinking of this, he took the train one day, his charming mistress, now only twenty-six, coming to the station to see him off. He looked at her quite tenderly, for she was the quintessence of a certain type of feminine beauty.

"By-by, dearie," he smiled, as the train-bell signaled the approaching departure. "You and I will get out of this shortly. Don't grieve. I'll be back in two or three weeks, or I'll send for you. I'd take you now, only I don't know how that country is out there. We'll fix on some place, and then you watch me settle this fortune question. We'll not live under a cloud always. I'll get a divorce, and we'll marry, and things will come right with a bang. Money will do that."

He looked at her with his large, cool, penetrating eyes, and she clasped his cheeks between her hands.

"Oh, Frank," she exclaimed, "I'll miss you so! You're all I have."

"In two weeks," he smiled, as the train began to move, "I'll wire or be back. Be good, sweet."

She followed him with adoring eyes—a fool of love, a spoiled child, a family pet, amorous, eager, affectionate, the type so strong a man would naturally like—she tossed her pretty red gold head and waved him a kiss. Then she walked away with rich, sinuous, healthy strides— the type that men turn to look after.

"That's her—that's that Butler girl," observed one railroad clerk to another. "Gee! a man wouldn't want anything better than that, would he?"

It was the spontaneous tribute that passion and envy invariably pay to health and beauty. On that pivot swings the world.

Never in all his life until this trip had Cowperwood been farther west than Pittsburg. His amazing commercial adventures, brilliant as they were, had been almost exclusively confined to the dull, staid world of Philadelphia, with its sweet refinement in sections, its pretensions to American social supremacy, its cool arrogation of traditional leadership in commercial life, its history, conservative wealth, unctuous respectability, and all the tastes and avocations which these imply. He had, as he recalled, almost mastered that pretty world and made its sacred precincts his own when the crash came. Practically he had been admitted. Now he was an Ishmael, an ex-convict, albeit a millionaire. But wait! The race is to the swift, he said to himself over and over. Yes, and the battle is to the strong. He would test whether the world would trample him under foot or no.

Chicago, when it finally dawned on him, came with a rush on the second morning. He had spent two nights in the gaudy Pullman then provided—a car intended to make up for some of the inconveniences of its arrangements by an over-elaboration of plush and tortured glass—when the first lone outposts of the prairie metropolis began to appear. The side-tracks along the road-bed over which he was speeding became more and more numerous, the telegraph-poles more and more hung with arms and strung smoky-thick with wires. In the far distance, cityward, was, here and there, a lone working-man's cottage, the home of some adventurous soul who had planted his bare hut thus far out in order to reap the small but certain advantage which the growth of the city would bring.

The land was flat—as flat as a table—with a waning growth of brown grass left over from the previous year, and stirring faintly in the morning breeze. Underneath were signs of the new green—the New Year's flag of its disposition. For some reason a crystalline atmosphere enfolded the distant hazy outlines of the city, holding the latter like a fly in amber and giving it an artistic subtlety which touched him. Already a devotee of art, ambitious for connoisseurship, who had had his joy, training, and sorrow out of the collection he had made and lost in Philadelphia, he appreciated almost every suggestion of a delightful picture in nature.

The tracks, side by side, were becoming more and more numerous. Freight-cars were assembled here by thousands from all parts of the country—yellow, red, blue, green, white. (Chicago, he recalled, already had thirty railroads terminating here, as though it were the end of the world.) The little low one and two story houses, quite new as to wood, were frequently unpainted and already smoky—in places grimy. At grade-crossings, where ambling street-cars and wagons and muddy-wheeled buggies waited, he noted how flat the streets were, how unpaved, how sidewalks went up and down rhythmically—here a flight of steps, a veritable platform before a house, there a long stretch of boards laid flat on the mud of the prairie itself. What a city! Presently a branch of the filthy, arrogant, self-sufficient little Chicago River came into view, with its mass of sputtering tugs, its black, oily water, its tall, red, brown, and green grain-elevators, its immense black coal-pockets and yellowish-brown lumber-yards.

Here was life; he saw it at a flash. Here was a seething city in the making. There was something dynamic in the very air which appealed to his fancy. How different, for some reason, from Philadelphia! That was a stirring city, too. He had thought it wonderful at one time, quite a world; but this thing, while obviously infinitely worse, was better. It was more youthful, more hopeful. In a flare of morning sunlight pouring between two coal-pockets, and because the train had stopped to let a bridge swing and half a dozen great grain and lumber boats go by—a half-dozen in either direction—he saw a group of Irish stevedores idling on the bank of a lumber-yard whose wall skirted the water. Healthy men they were, in blue or red shirt-sleeves, stout straps about their waists, short pipes in their mouths, fine, hardy, nutty-brown specimens of humanity. Why were they so appealing, he asked himself. This raw, dirty town seemed naturally to compose itself into stirring artistic pictures. Why, it fairly sang! The world was young here. Life was doing something new. Perhaps he had better not go on to the Northwest at all; he would decide that question later.

In the mean time he had letters of introduction to distinguished Chicagoans, and these he would present. He wanted to talk to some bankers and grain and commission men. The stock-exchange of Chicago interested him, for the intricacies of that business he knew backward and forward, and some great grain transactions had been made here.

The train finally rolled past the shabby backs of houses into a long, shabbily covered series of platforms—sheds having only roofs—and amidst a clatter of trucks hauling trunks, and engines belching steam, and passengers hurrying to and fro he made his way out into Canal Street and hailed a waiting cab—one of a long line of vehicles that bespoke a metropolitan spirit. He had fixed on the Grand Pacific as the most important hotel—the one with the most social significance—and thither he asked to be driven. On the way he studied these streets as in the matter of art he would have studied a picture. The little yellow, blue, green, white, and brown street-cars which he saw trundling here and there, the tired, bony horses, jingling bells at their throats, touched him. They were flimsy affairs, these cars, merely highly varnished kindling-wood with bits of polished brass and glass stuck about them, but he realized what fortunes they portended if the city grew. Street-cars, he knew, were his natural vocation. Even more than stock-brokerage, even more than banking, even more than stock-organization he loved the thought of street-cars and the vast manipulative life it suggested.

CHAPTER II

A RECONNOITER

The city of Chicago, with whose development the personality of Frank Algernon Cowperwood was soon to be definitely linked! To whom may the laurels as laureate of this Florence of the West yet fall? This singing flame of a city, this all America, this poet in chaps and buckskin, this rude, raw Titan, this Burns of a city! By its shimmering lake it lay, a king of shreds and patches, a maundering yokel with an epic in its mouth, a tramp, a hobo among cities, with the grip of Caesar in its mind, the dramatic force of Euripides in its soul. A very bard of a city this, singing of high deeds and high hopes, its heavy brogans buried deep in the mire of circumstance. Take Athens, oh, Greece! Italy, do you keep Rome! This was the Babylon, the Troy, the Nineveh of a younger day. Here came the gaping West and the hopeful East to see. Here hungry men, raw from the shops and fields, idyls and romances in their minds, builded them an empire crying glory in the mud.

From New York, Vermont, New Hampshire, Maine had come a strange company, earnest, patient, determined, unschooled in even the primer of refinement, hungry for something the significance of which, when they had it, they could not even guess, anxious to be called great, determined so to be without ever knowing how. Here came the dreamy gentleman of the South, robbed of his patrimony; the hopeful student of Yale and Harvard and Princeton; the enfranchised miner of California and the Rockies, his bags of gold and silver in his hands. Here was already the bewildered foreigner, an alien speech confounding him—the Hun, the Pole, the Swede, the German, the Russian—seeking his homely colonies, fearing his neighbor of another race.

Here was the negro, the prostitute, the blackleg, the gambler, the romantic adventurer par excellence. A city with but a handful of the native-born; a city packed to the doors with all the riffraff of a thousand towns. Flaring were the lights of the bagnio; tinkling the banjos, zithers, mandolins of the so-called gin-mill; all the dreams and the brutality of the day seemed gathered to rejoice (and rejoice they did) in this new-found wonder of a metropolitan life in the West.

The first prominent Chicagoan whom Cowperwood sought out was the president of the Lake City National Bank, the largest financial organization in the city, with deposits of over fourteen million dollars. It was located in Dearborn Street, at Munroe, but a block or two from his hotel.

"Find out who that man is," ordered Mr. Judah Addison, the president of the bank, on seeing him enter the president's private waiting-room.

Mr. Addison's office was so arranged with glass windows that he could, by craning his neck, see all who entered his reception-room before they saw him, and he had been struck by Cowperwood's face and force. Long familiarity with the banking world and with great affairs generally had given a rich finish to the ease and force which the latter naturally possessed. He looked strangely replete for a man of thirty-six—suave, steady, incisive, with eyes as fine as those of a Newfoundland or a Collie and as innocent and winsome. They were wonderful eyes, soft and spring-like at times, glowing with a rich, human understanding which on the instant could harden and flash lightning. Deceptive eyes, unreadable, but alluring alike to men and to women in all walks and conditions of life.

The secretary addressed came back with Cowperwood's letter of introduction, and immediately Cowperwood followed.

Mr. Addison instinctively arose—a thing he did not always do. "I'm pleased to meet you, Mr. Cowperwood," he said, politely. "I saw you come in just now. You see how I keep my windows here, so as to spy out the country. Sit down. You wouldn't like an apple, would you?" He opened a left-hand drawer, producing several polished red winesaps, one of which he held out. "I always eat one about this time in the morning."

"Thank you, no," replied Cowperwood, pleasantly, estimating as he did so his host's temperament and mental caliber. "I never eat between meals, but I appreciate your kindness. I am just passing through Chicago, and I thought I would present this letter now rather than later. I thought you might tell me a little about the city from an investment point of view."

As Cowperwood talked, Addison, a short, heavy, rubicund man with grayish-brown sideburns extending to his ear-lobes and hard, bright, twinkling gray eyes—a proud, happy, self-sufficient man—munched his apple and contemplated Cowperwood. As is so often the case in life, he frequently liked or disliked people on sight, and he prided himself on his judgment of men. Almost foolishly, for one so conservative, he was taken with Cowperwood—a man immensely his superior—not because of the Drexel letter, which spoke of the latter's "undoubted financial genius" and the advantage it would be to Chicago to have him settle there, but because of the swimming wonder of his eyes. Cowperwood's personality, while maintaining an unbroken outward reserve, breathed a tremendous humanness which touched his fellow-banker. Both men were in their way walking enigmas, the Philadelphian far the subtler of the two. Addison was ostensibly a church-member, a model citizen; he represented a point of view to which Cowperwood would never have

271

stooped. Both men were ruthless after their fashion, avid of a physical life; but Addison was the weaker in that he was still afraid—very much afraid—of what life might do to him. The man before him had no sense of fear. Addison contributed judiciously to charity, subscribed outwardly to a dull social routine, pretended to love his wife, of whom he was weary, and took his human pleasure secretly. The man before him subscribed to nothing, refused to talk save to intimates, whom he controlled spiritually, and did as he pleased.

"Why, I'll tell you, Mr. Cowperwood," Addison replied. "We people out here in Chicago think so well of ourselves that sometimes we're afraid to say all we think for fear of appearing a little extravagant. We're like the youngest son in the family that knows he can lick all the others, but doesn't want to do it—not just yet. We're not as handsome as we might be—did you ever see a growing boy that was?—but we're absolutely sure that we're going to be. Our pants and shoes and coat and hat get too small for us every six months, and so we don't look very fashionable, but there are big, strong, hard muscles and bones underneath, Mr. Cowperwood, as you'll discover when you get to looking around. Then you won't mind the clothes so much."

Mr. Addison's round, frank eyes narrowed and hardened for a moment. A kind of metallic hardness came into his voice. Cowperwood could see that he was honestly enamoured of his adopted city. Chicago was his most beloved mistress. A moment later the flesh about his eyes crinkled, his mouth softened, and he smiled. "I'll be glad to tell you anything I can," he went on. "There are a lot of interesting things to tell."

Cowperwood beamed back on him encouragingly. He inquired after the condition of one industry and another, one trade or profession and another. This was somewhat different from the atmosphere which prevailed in Philadelphia—more breezy and generous. The tendency to expatiate and make much of local advantages was Western. He liked it, however, as one aspect of life, whether he chose to share in it or not. It was favorable to his own future. He had a prison record to live down; a wife and two children to get rid of—in the legal sense, at least (he had no desire to rid himself of financial obligation toward them). It would take some such loose, enthusiastic Western attitude to forgive in him the strength and freedom with which he ignored and refused to accept for himself current convention. "I satisfy myself" was his private law, but so to do he must assuage and control the prejudices of other men. He felt that this banker, while not putty in his hands, was inclined to a strong and useful friendship.

"My impressions of the city are entirely favorable, Mr. Addison," he said, after a time, though he inwardly admitted to himself that this was not entirely true; he was not sure whether he could bring himself ultimately to live in so excavated and scaffolded a world as this or not. "I only saw a portion of it coming in on the train. I like the snap of things. I believe Chicago has a future."

"You came over the Fort Wayne, I presume," replied Addison, loftily. "You saw the worst section. You must let me show you some of the best parts. By the way, where are you staying?"

"At the Grand Pacific."

"How long will you be here?"

"Not more than a day or two."

272

"Let me see," and Mr. Addison drew out his watch. "I suppose you wouldn't mind meeting a few of our leading men—and we have a little luncheon-room over at the Union League Club where we drop in now and then. If you'd care to do so, I'd like to have you come along with me at one. We're sure to find a few of them—some of our lawyers, business men, and judges."

"That will be fine," said the Philadelphian, simply. "You're more than generous. There are one or two other people I want to meet in between, and"—he arose and looked at his own watch—"I'll find the Union Club. Where is the office of Arneel & Co.?"

At the mention of the great beef-packer, who was one of the bank's heaviest depositors, Addison stirred slightly with approval. This young man, at least eight years his junior, looked to him like a future grand seigneur of finance.

At the Union Club, at this noontime luncheon, after talking with the portly, conservative, aggressive Arneel and the shrewd director of the stock-exchange, Cowperwood met a varied company of men ranging in age from thirty-five to sixty-five gathered about the board in a private dining-room of heavily carved black walnut, with pictures of elder citizens of Chicago on the walls and an attempt at artistry in stained glass in the windows. There were short and long men, lean and stout, dark and blond men, with eyes and jaws which varied from those of the tiger, lynx, and bear to those of the fox, the tolerant mastiff, and the surly bulldog. There were no weaklings in this selected company.

Mr. Arneel and Mr. Addison Cowperwood approved of highly as shrewd, concentrated men. Another who interested him was Anson Merrill, a small, polite, recherche soul, suggesting mansions and footmen and remote luxury generally, who was pointed out by Addison as the famous dry-goods prince of that name, quite the leading merchant, in the retail and wholesale sense, in Chicago.

Still another was a Mr. Rambaud, pioneer railroad man, to whom Addison, smiling jocosely, observed: "Mr. Cowperwood is on from Philadelphia, Mr. Rambaud, trying to find out whether he wants to lose any money out here. Can't you sell him some of that bad land you have up in the Northwest?"

Rambaud—a spare, pale, black-bearded man of much force and exactness, dressed, as Cowperwood observed, in much better taste than some of the others—looked at Cowperwood shrewdly but in a gentlemanly, retiring way, with a gracious, enigmatic smile. He caught a glance in return which he could not possibly forget. The eyes of Cowperwood said more than any words ever could. Instead of jesting faintly Mr. Rambaud decided to explain some things about the Northwest. Perhaps this Philadelphian might be interested.

To a man who has gone through a great life struggle in one metropolis and tested all the phases of human duplicity, decency, sympathy, and chicanery in the controlling group of men that one invariably finds in every American city at least, the temperament and significance of another group in another city is not so much, and yet it is. Long since Cowperwood had parted company with the idea that humanity at any angle or under any circumstances, climatic or otherwise, is in any way different. To him the most noteworthy characteristic of the human race was that it was strangely chemic, being anything or nothing, as the hour and the condition afforded. In his leisure moments—those free from practical calculation, which were not many—he often speculated as to what life really was. If he had not been a great financier and, above all, a marvelous organizer he might have become a highly individualistic philosopher—a calling which, if he had thought anything about it at all at this time, would have seemed rather trivial. His business as he saw it was with the material facts of life, or, rather, with those third and fourth degree theorems and syllogisms which control material things and so represent wealth. He was here to deal with the great general needs of the Middle West—to seize upon, if he might, certain well-springs of wealth and power and rise to recognized authority. In his morning talks he had learned of the extent and character of the stock-yards' enterprises, of the great railroad and ship interests, of the tremendous rising importance of real estate, grain speculation, the hotel business, the hardware business. He had learned of universal manufacturing companies— one that made cars, another elevators, another binders, another windmills, another engines. Apparently, any new industry seemed to do well in Chicago. In his talk with the one director of the Board of Trade to whom he had a letter he had learned that few, if any, local stocks were dealt in on 'change. Wheat, corn, and grains of all kinds were principally speculated in. The big stocks of the East were gambled in by way of leased wires on the New York Stock Exchange—not otherwise.

As he looked at these men, all pleasantly civil, all general in their remarks, each safely keeping his vast plans under his vest, Cowperwood wondered how he would fare in this community. There were such difficult things ahead of him to do. No one of these men, all of whom were in their commercial-social way agreeable, knew that he had only recently been in the penitentiary. How much difference would that make in their attitude? No one of them knew that, although he was married and had two children, he was planning to divorce his wife and marry the girl who had appropriated to herself the role which his wife had once played.

"Are you seriously contemplating looking into the Northwest?" asked Mr. Rambaud, interestedly, toward the close of the luncheon.

"That is my present plan after I finish here. I thought I'd take a short run up there."

"Let me put you in touch with an interesting party that is going as far as Fargo and Duluth. There is a private car leaving Thursday, most of them citizens of Chicago, but some Easterners. I would be glad to have you join us. I am going as far as Minneapolis."

Cowperwood thanked him and accepted. A long conversation followed about the Northwest, its timber, wheat, land sales, cattle, and possible manufacturing plants.

What Fargo, Minneapolis, and Duluth were to be civically and financially were the chief topics of conversation. Naturally, Mr. Rambaud, having under his direction vast railroad lines which penetrated this region, was confident of the future of it. Cowperwood gathered it all, almost by instinct. Gas, street-railways, land speculations, banks, wherever located, were his chief thoughts.

Finally he left the club to keep his other appointments, but something of his personality remained behind him. Mr. Addison and Mr. Rambaud, among others, were sincerely convinced that he was one of the most interesting men they had met in years. And he scarcely had said anything at all—just listened.

CHAPTER III

A CHICAGO EVENING

After his first visit to the bank over which Addison presided, and an informal dinner at the latter's home, Cowperwood had decided that he did not care to sail under any false colors so far as Addison was concerned. He was too influential and well connected. Besides, Cowperwood liked him too much. Seeing that the man's leaning toward him was strong, in reality a fascination, he made an early morning call a day or two after he had returned from Fargo, whither he had gone at Mr. Rambaud's suggestion, on his way back to Philadelphia, determined to volunteer a smooth presentation of his earlier misfortunes, and trust to Addison's interest to make him view the matter in a kindly light. He told him the whole story of how he had been convicted of technical embezzlement in Philadelphia and had served out his term in the Eastern Penitentiary. He also mentioned his divorce and his intention of marrying again.

Addison, who was the weaker man of the two and yet forceful in his own way, admired this courageous stand on Cowperwood's part. It was a braver thing than he himself could or would have achieved. It appealed to his sense of the dramatic. Here was a man who apparently had been dragged down to the very bottom of things, his face forced in the mire, and now he was coming up again strong, hopeful, urgent. The banker knew many highly respected men in Chicago whose early careers, as he was well aware, would not bear too close an inspection, but nothing was thought of that. Some of them were in society, some not, but all of them were powerful. Why should not Cowperwood be allowed to begin all over? He looked at him steadily, at his eyes, at his stocky body, at his smooth, handsome, mustached face. Then he held out his hand.

"Mr. Cowperwood," he said, finally, trying to shape his words appropriately, "I needn't say that I am pleased with this interesting confession. It appeals to me. I'm glad you have made it to me. You needn't say any more at any time. I decided the day I saw you walking into that vestibule that you were an exceptional man; now I know it. You needn't apologize to me. I haven't lived in this world fifty years and more without having my eye-teeth cut. You're welcome to the courtesies of this bank and of my house as long as you care to avail yourself of them. We'll cut our cloth as circumstances dictate in the future. I'd like to see you come to Chicago, solely because I like you personally. If you decide to settle here I'm sure I can be of service to you and you to me. Don't think anything more about it; I sha'n't ever say anything one way or another. You have your own battle to fight, and I wish you luck. You'll get all the aid from me I can honestly give you. Just forget that you told me, and when you get your matrimonial affairs straightened out bring your wife out to see us."

With these things completed Cowperwood took the train back to Philadelphia.

"Aileen," he said, when these two met again—she had come to the train to meet him—"I think the West is the answer for us. I went up to Fargo and looked around up there, but I don't believe we want to go that far. There's nothing but prairie-grass and Indians out in that country. How'd you like to live in a board shanty, Aileen," he asked, banteringly, "with nothing but fried rattlesnakes and prairie-dogs for breakfast? Do you think you could stand that?"

"Yes," she replied, gaily, hugging his arm, for they had entered a closed carriage; "I could stand it if you could. I'd go anywhere with you, Frank. I'd get me a nice Indian dress with leather and beads all over it and a feather hat like they wear, and—"

275

"There you go! Certainly! Pretty clothes first of all in a miner's shack. That's the way."

"You wouldn't love me long if I didn't put pretty clothes first," she replied, spiritedly. "Oh, I'm so glad to get you back!"

"The trouble is," he went on, "that that country up there isn't as promising as Chicago. I think we're destined to live in Chicago. I made an investment in Fargo, and we'll have to go up there from time to time, but we'll eventually locate in Chicago. I don't want to go out there alone again. It isn't pleasant for me." He squeezed her hand. "If we can't arrange this thing at once I'll just have to introduce you as my wife for the present."

"You haven't heard anything more from Mr. Steger?" she put in. She was thinking of Steger's efforts to get Mrs. Cowperwood to grant him a divorce.

"Not a word."

"Isn't it too bad?" she sighed.

"Well, don't grieve. Things might be worse."

He was thinking of his days in the penitentiary, and so was she. After commenting on the character of Chicago he decided with her that so soon as conditions permitted they would remove themselves to the Western city.

It would be pointless to do more than roughly sketch the period of three years during which the various changes which saw the complete elimination of Cowperwood from Philadelphia and his introduction into Chicago took place. For a time there were merely journeys to and fro, at first more especially to Chicago, then to Fargo, where his transported secretary, Walter Whelpley, was managing under his direction the construction of Fargo business blocks, a short street-car line, and a fair-ground. This interesting venture bore the title of the Fargo Construction and Transportation Company, of which Frank A. Cowperwood was president. His Philadelphia lawyer, Mr. Harper Steger, was for the time being general master of contracts.

For another short period he might have been found living at the Tremont in Chicago, avoiding for the time being, because of Aileen's company, anything more than a nodding contact with the important men he had first met, while he looked quietly into the matter of a Chicago brokerage arrangement—a partnership with some established broker who, without too much personal ambition, would bring him a knowledge of Chicago Stock Exchange affairs, personages, and Chicago ventures. On one occasion he took Aileen with him to Fargo, where with a haughty, bored insouciance she surveyed the state of the growing city.

"Oh, Frank!" she exclaimed, when she saw the plain, wooden, four-story hotel, the long, unpleasing business street, with its motley collection of frame and brick stores, the gaping stretches of houses, facing in most directions unpaved streets. Aileen in her tailored spick-and-spanness, her self-conscious vigor, vanity, and tendency to over-ornament, was a strange contrast to the rugged self-effacement and indifference to personal charm which characterized most of the men and women of this new metropolis. "You didn't seriously think of coming out here to live, did you?"

She was wondering where her chance for social exchange would come in—her opportunity to shine. Suppose her Frank were to be very rich; suppose he did make very much money—much more than he had ever had even in the past—what good would it do her here? In Philadelphia, before his failure, before she had been suspected of the secret liaison with him, he had been beginning (at least) to entertain in a very pretentious way. If she had been his wife then she might have stepped smartly into Philadelphia society. Out here, good gracious! She turned up her pretty nose in disgust. "What an awful place!" was her one comment at this most stirring of Western boom towns.

When it came to Chicago, however, and its swirling, increasing life, Aileen was much interested. Between attending to many financial matters Cowperwood saw to it that she was not left alone. He asked her to shop in the local stores and tell him about them; and this she did, driving around in an open carriage, attractively arrayed, a great brown hat emphasizing her pink-and-white complexion and red-gold hair. On different afternoons of their stay he took her to drive over the principal streets. When Aileen was permitted for the first time to see the spacious beauty and richness of Prairie Avenue, the North Shore Drive, Michigan Avenue, and the new mansions on Ashland Boulevard, set in their grassy spaces, the spirit, aspirations, hope, tang of the future Chicago began to work in her blood as it had in Cowperwood's. All of these rich homes were so very new. The great people of Chicago were all newly rich like themselves. She forgot that as yet she was not Cowperwood's wife; she felt herself truly to be so. The streets, set in most instances with a pleasing creamish-brown flagging, lined with young, newly planted trees, the lawns sown to smooth green grass, the windows of the houses trimmed with bright awnings and hung with intricate lace, blowing in a June breeze, the roadways a gray, gritty macadam—all these things touched her fancy. On one drive they skirted the lake on the North Shore, and Aileen, contemplating the chalky, bluish-green waters, the distant sails, the gulls, and then the new bright homes, reflected that in all certitude she would some day be the mistress of one of these splendid mansions. How haughtily she would carry herself; how she would dress! They would have a splendid house, much finer, no doubt, than Frank's old one in Philadelphia, with a great ball-room and dining-room where she could give dances and dinners, and where Frank and she would receive as the peers of these Chicago rich people.

"Do you suppose we will ever have a house as fine as one of these, Frank?" she asked him, longingly.

"I'll tell you what my plan is," he said. "If you like this Michigan Avenue section we'll buy a piece of property out here now and hold it. Just as soon as I make the right connections here and see what I am going to do we'll build a house—something really nice—don't worry. I want to get this divorce matter settled, and then we'll begin. Meanwhile, if we have to come here, we'd better live rather quietly. Don't you think so?"

It was now between five and six, that richest portion of a summer day. It had been very warm, but was now cooling, the shade of the western building-line shadowing the roadway, a moted, wine-like air filling the street. As far as the eye could see were carriages, the one great social diversion of Chicago, because there was otherwise so little opportunity for many to show that they had means. The social forces were not as yet clear or harmonious. Jingling harnesses of nickel, silver, and even plated gold were the sign manual of social hope, if not of achievement. Here sped homeward from the city—from office and manufactory—along this one exceptional southern highway, the Via Appia of the South Side, all the urgent aspirants to notable fortunes. Men of wealth who had met only casually in trade here nodded to each other. Smart daughters, society-bred sons, handsome wives came down-town in traps, Victorias, carriages, and vehicles of the latest design to drive

277

home their trade-weary fathers or brothers, relatives or friends. The air was gay with a social hope, a promise of youth and affection, and that fine flush of material life that recreates itself in delight. Lithe, handsome, well-bred animals, singly and in jingling pairs, paced each other down the long, wide, grass-lined street, its fine homes agleam with a rich, complaisant materiality.

"Oh!" exclaimed Aileen, all at once, seeing the vigorous, forceful men, the handsome matrons, and young women and boys, the nodding and the bowing, feeling a touch of the romance and wonder of it all. "I should like to live in Chicago. I believe it's nicer than Philadelphia."

Cowperwood, who had fallen so low there, despite his immense capacity, set his teeth in two even rows. His handsome mustache seemed at this moment to have an especially defiant curl. The pair he was driving was physically perfect, lean and nervous, with spoiled, petted faces. He could not endure poor horse-flesh. He drove as only a horse-lover can, his body bolt upright, his own energy and temperament animating his animals. Aileen sat beside him, very proud, consciously erect.

"Isn't she beautiful?" some of the women observed, as they passed, going north. "What a stunning young woman!" thought or said the men.

"Did you see her?" asked a young brother of his sister. "Never mind, Aileen," commented Cowperwood, with that iron determination that brooks no defeat. "We will be a part of this. Don't fret. You will have everything you want in Chicago, and more besides."

There was tingling over his fingers, into the reins, into the horses, a mysterious vibrating current that was his chemical product, the off-giving of his spirit battery that made his hired horses prance like children. They chafed and tossed their heads and snorted. Aileen was fairly bursting with hope and vanity and longing. Oh, to be Mrs. Frank Algernon Cowperwood here in Chicago, to have a splendid mansion, to have her cards of invitation practically commands which might not be ignored!

"Oh, dear!" she sighed to herself, mentally. "If only it were all true—now."

It is thus that life at its topmost toss irks and pains. Beyond is ever the unattainable, the lure of the infinite with its infinite ache.

"Oh, life! oh, youth! oh, hope! oh, years! Oh pain-winged fancy, beating forth with fears."

CHAPTER IV

PETER LAUGHLIN & CO.

The partnership which Cowperwood eventually made with an old-time Board of Trade operator, Peter Laughlin, was eminently to his satisfaction. Laughlin was a tall, gaunt speculator who had spent most of his living days in Chicago, having come there as a boy from western Missouri. He was a typical Chicago Board of Trade operator of the old school, having an Andrew Jacksonish countenance, and a Henry Clay—Davy Crockett— "Long John" Wentworth build of body.

Cowperwood from his youth up had had a curious interest in quaint characters, and he was interesting to them; they "took" to him. He could, if he chose to take the trouble, fit himself in with the odd psychology of almost any individual. In his early peregrinations in La Salle Street he inquired after clever traders on 'change, and then gave them one small commission after another in order to get acquainted. Thus he stumbled one morning on old Peter Laughlin, wheat and corn trader, who had an office in La Salle Street near Madison, and who did a modest business gambling for himself and others in grain and Eastern railway shares. Laughlin was a shrewd, canny American, originally, perhaps, of Scotch extraction, who had all the traditional American blemishes of uncouthness, tobacco-chewing, profanity, and other small vices. Cowperwood could tell from looking at him that he must have a fund of information concerning every current Chicagoan of importance, and this fact alone was certain to be of value. Then the old man was direct, plain-spoken, simple-appearing, and wholly unpretentious—qualities which Cowperwood deemed invaluable.

Once or twice in the last three years Laughlin had lost heavily on private "corners" that he had attempted to engineer, and the general feeling was that he was now becoming cautious, or, in other words, afraid. "Just the man," Cowperwood thought. So one morning he called upon Laughlin, intending to open a small account with him.

"Henry," he heard the old man say, as he entered Laughlin's fair-sized but rather dusty office, to a young, preternaturally solemn-looking clerk, a fit assistant for Peter Laughlin, "git me them there Pittsburg and Lake Erie sheers, will you?" Seeing Cowperwood waiting, he added, "What kin I do for ye?"

Cowperwood smiled. "So he calls them 'sheers,' does he?" he thought. "Good! I think I'll like him."

He introduced himself as coming from Philadelphia, and went on to say that he was interested in various Chicago ventures, inclined to invest in any good stock which would rise, and particularly desirous to buy into some corporation—public utility preferred—which would be certain to grow with the expansion of the city.

Old Laughlin, who was now all of sixty years of age, owned a seat on the Board, and was worth in the neighborhood of two hundred thousand dollars, looked at Cowperwood quizzically.

"Well, now, if you'd 'a' come along here ten or fifteen years ago you might 'a' got in on the ground floor of a lot of things," he observed. "There was these here gas companies, now, that them Otway and Apperson boys got in on, and then all these here street-railways. Why, I'm the feller that told Eddie Parkinson what a fine thing he could make out of it if he would go and organize that North State Street line. He promised me a bunch of sheers if he ever worked it out, but he never give 'em to me. I didn't expect him to, though," he added, wisely, and with a glint. "I'm too old a trader for that. He's out of it now, anyway. That Michaels-Kennelly crowd skinned him. Yep, if you'd 'a' been here ten or fifteen years ago you might 'a' got in on that. 'Tain't no use a-thinkin' about that, though, any more. Them sheers is sellin' fer clost onto a hundred and sixty."

Cowperwood smiled. "Well, Mr. Laughlin," he observed, "you must have been on 'change a long time here. You seem to know a good deal of what has gone on in the past."

"Yep, ever since 1852," replied the old man. He had a thick growth of upstanding hair looking not unlike a rooster's comb, a long and what threatened eventually to become a Punch-and-Judy chin, a slightly aquiline nose, high cheek-bones, and hollow, brown-skinned cheeks. His eyes were as clear and sharp as those of a lynx.

"To tell you the truth, Mr. Laughlin," went on Cowperwood, "what I'm really out here in Chicago for is to find a man with whom I can go into partnership in the brokerage business. Now I'm in the banking and brokerage business myself in the East. I have a firm in Philadelphia and a seat on both the New York and Philadelphia exchanges. I have some affairs in Fargo also. Any trade agency can tell you about me. You have a Board of Trade seat here, and no doubt you do some New York and Philadelphia exchange business. The new firm, if you would go in with me, could handle it all direct. I'm a rather strong outside man myself. I'm thinking of locating permanently in Chicago. What would you say now to going into business with me? Do you think we could get along in the same office space?"

Cowperwood had a way, when he wanted to be pleasant, of beating the fingers of his two hands together, finger for finger, tip for tip. He also smiled at the same time—or, rather, beamed—his eyes glowing with a warm, magnetic, seemingly affectionate light.

As it happened, old Peter Laughlin had arrived at that psychological moment when he was wishing that some such opportunity as this might appear and be available. He was a lonely man, never having been able to bring himself to trust his peculiar temperament in the hands of any woman. As a matter of fact, he had never understood women at all, his relations being confined to those sad immoralities of the cheapest character which only money— grudgingly given, at that—could buy. He lived in three small rooms in West Harrison Street, near Throup, where he cooked his own meals at times. His one companion was a small spaniel, simple and affectionate, a she dog, Jennie by name, with whom he slept. Jennie was a docile, loving companion, waiting for him patiently by day in his office until he was ready to go home at night. He talked to this spaniel quite as he would to a human being (even more intimately, perhaps), taking the dog's glances, tail-waggings, and general movements for answer. In the morning when he arose, which was often as early as half past four, or even four—he was a brief sleeper—he would begin by pulling on his trousers (he seldom bathed any more except at a down-town barber shop) and talking to Jennie.

"Git up, now, Jinnie," he would say. "It's time to git up. We've got to make our coffee now and git some breakfast. I can see yuh, lyin' there, pertendin' to be asleep. Come on, now! You've had sleep enough. You've been sleepin' as long as I have."

Jennie would be watching him out of the corner of one loving eye, her tail tap-tapping on the bed, her free ear going up and down.

When he was fully dressed, his face and hands washed, his old string tie pulled around into a loose and convenient knot, his hair brushed upward, Jennie would get up and jump demonstratively about, as much as to say, "You see how prompt I am."

"That's the way," old Laughlin would comment. "Allers last. Yuh never git up first, do yuh, Jinnie? Allers let yer old man do that, don't you?"

On bitter days, when the car-wheels squeaked and one's ears and fingers seemed to be in danger of freezing, old Laughlin, arrayed in a heavy, dusty greatcoat of ancient vintage and a square hat, would carry Jennie down-town in a greenish-black bag along with some of his beloved "sheers" which he was meditating on. Only then could he take Jennie in the cars.

On other days they would walk, for he liked exercise. He would get to his office as early as seven-thirty or eight, though business did not usually begin until after nine, and remain until four-thirty or five, reading the papers or calculating during the hours when there were no customers. Then he would take Jennie and go for a walk or to call on some business acquaintance. His home room, the newspapers, the floor of the exchange, his offices, and the streets were his only resources. He cared nothing for plays, books, pictures, music—and for women only in his one-angled, mentally impoverished way. His limitations were so marked that to a lover of character like Cowperwood he was fascinating—but Cowperwood only used character. He never idled over it long artistically.

As Cowperwood suspected, what old Laughlin did not know about Chicago financial conditions, deals, opportunities, and individuals was scarcely worth knowing. Being only a trader by instinct, neither an organizer nor an executive, he had never been able to make any great constructive use of his knowledge. His gains and his losses he took with reasonable equanimity, exclaiming over and over, when he lost: "Shucks! I hadn't orter have done that," and snapping his fingers. When he won heavily or was winning he munched tobacco with a seraphic smile and occasionally in the midst of trading would exclaim: "You fellers better come in. It's a-gonta rain some more." He was not easy to trap in any small gambling game, and only lost or won when there was a free, open struggle in the market, or when he was engineering some little scheme of his own.

The matter of this partnership was not arranged at once, although it did not take long. Old Peter Laughlin wanted to think it over, although he had immediately developed a personal fancy for Cowperwood. In a way he was the latter's victim and servant from the start. They met day after day to discuss various details and terms; finally, true to his instincts, old Peter demanded a full half interest.

"Now, you don't want that much, Laughlin," Cowperwood suggested, quite blandly. They were sitting in Laughlin's private office between four and five in the afternoon, and Laughlin was chewing tobacco with the sense of having a fine, interesting problem before him. "I have a seat on the New York Stock Exchange," he went on, "and that's worth forty thousand dollars. My seat on the Philadelphia exchange is worth more than yours here. They will naturally figure as the principal assets of the firm. It's to be in your name. I'll be liberal with you, though. Instead of a third, which would be fair, I'll make it forty-nine per cent., and we'll call the firm Peter Laughlin & Co. I like you, and I think you can be of a lot of use to me. I know you will make more money through me than you have alone. I could go in with a lot of these silk-stocking fellows around here, but I don't want to. You'd better decide right now, and let's get to work."

Old Laughlin was pleased beyond measure that young Cowperwood should want to go in with him. He had become aware of late that all of the young, smug newcomers on 'change considered him an old fogy. Here was a strong, brave young Easterner, twenty years his junior, evidently as shrewd as himself—more so, he feared—who actually proposed a business alliance. Besides, Cowperwood, in his young, healthy, aggressive way, was like a breath of spring.

"I ain't keerin' so much about the name," rejoined Laughlin. "You can fix it that-a-way if you want to. Givin' you fifty-one per cent. gives you charge of this here shebang. All right, though; I ain't a-kickin'. I guess I can manage allus to git what's a-comin' to me.

"It's a bargain, then," said Cowperwood. "We'll want new offices, Laughlin, don't you think? This one's a little dark."

"Fix it up any way you like, Mr. Cowperwood. It's all the same to me. I'll be glad to see how yer do it."

In a week the details were completed, and two weeks later the sign of Peter Laughlin & Co., grain and commission merchants, appeared over the door of a handsome suite of rooms on the ground floor of a corner at La Salle and Madison, in the heart of the Chicago financial district.

"Get onto old Laughlin, will you?" one broker observed to another, as they passed the new, pretentious commission-house with its splendid plate-glass windows, and observed the heavy, ornate bronze sign placed on either side of the door, which was located exactly on the corner. "What's struck him? I thought he was almost all through. Who's the Company?"

"I don't know. Some fellow from the East, I think."

"Well, he's certainly moving up. Look at the plate glass, will you?"

It was thus that Frank Algernon Cowperwood's Chicago financial career was definitely launched.

CHAPTER V

CONCERNING A WIFE AND FAMILY

If any one fancies for a moment that this commercial move on the part of Cowperwood was either hasty or ill-considered they but little appreciate the incisive, apprehensive psychology of the man. His thoughts as to life and control (tempered and hardened by thirteen months of reflection in the Eastern District Penitentiary) had given him a fixed policy. He could, should, and would rule alone. No man must ever again have the least claim on him save that of a suppliant. He wanted no more dangerous combinations such as he had had with Stener, the man through whom he had lost so much in Philadelphia, and others. By right of financial intellect and courage he was first, and would so prove it. Men must swing around him as planets around the sun.

Moreover, since his fall from grace in Philadelphia he had come to think that never again, perhaps, could he hope to become socially acceptable in the sense in which the so-called best society of a city interprets the phrase; and pondering over this at odd moments, he realized that his future allies in all probability would not be among the rich and socially important—the clannish, snobbish elements of society—but among the beginners and financially strong men who had come or were coming up from the bottom, and who had no social hopes whatsoever. There were many such. If through luck and effort he became sufficiently powerful financially he might then hope to dictate to society. Individualistic and even anarchistic in character, and without a shred of true democracy, yet temperamentally he was in sympathy with the mass more than he was with the class, and he understood the mass better. Perhaps this, in a way, will explain his desire to connect himself with a personality so naive and strange as Peter Laughlin. He had annexed him as a surgeon selects a special knife or instrument for an operation, and, shrewd as old Laughlin was, he was destined to be no more than a tool in Cowperwood's strong hands, a mere hustling messenger, content to take orders from this swiftest of moving brains. For the present Cowperwood was satisfied to do business under the firm name of Peter Laughlin & Co.— as a matter of fact, he preferred it; for he could thus keep himself sufficiently inconspicuous to avoid undue attention, and gradually work out one or two coups by which he hoped to firmly fix himself in the financial future of Chicago.

As the most essential preliminary to the social as well as the financial establishment of himself and Aileen in Chicago, Harper Steger, Cowperwood's lawyer, was doing his best all this while to ingratiate himself in the confidence of Mrs. Cowperwood, who had no faith in lawyers any more than she had in her recalcitrant husband. She was now a tall, severe, and rather plain woman, but still bearing the marks of the former passive charm that had once interested Cowperwood. Notable crows'-feet had come about the corners of her nose, mouth, and eyes. She had a remote, censorious, subdued, self-righteous, and even injured air.

The cat-like Steger, who had all the graceful contemplative air of a prowling Tom, was just the person to deal with her. A more suavely cunning and opportunistic soul never was. His motto might well have been, speak softly and step lightly.

"My dear Mrs. Cowperwood," he argued, seated in her modest West Philadelphia parlor one spring afternoon, "I need not tell you what a remarkable man your husband is, nor how useless it is to combat him. Admitting all his faults—and we can agree, if you please, that they are many"—Mrs. Cowperwood stirred with irritation—"still it is not worth while to attempt to hold him to a strict account. You know"—and Mr. Steger opened his thin, artistic hands in a deprecatory way—"what sort of a man Mr. Cowperwood is, and whether he can be coerced or not. He is not an ordinary man, Mrs. Cowperwood. No man could have gone through what he has and be where he is to day, and be an average man. If you take my advice you will let him go his way. Grant him a divorce. He is willing, even anxious to make a definite provision for you and your children. He will, I am sure, look liberally after their future. But he is becoming very irritable over your unwillingness to give him a legal separation, and unless you do I am very much afraid that the whole matter will be thrown into the courts. If, before it comes to that, I could effect an arrangement agreeable to you, I would be much pleased. As you know, I have been greatly grieved by the whole course of your recent affairs. I am intensely sorry that things are as they are."

Mr. Steger lifted his eyes in a very pained, deprecatory way. He regretted deeply the shifty currents of this troubled world.

Mrs. Cowperwood for perhaps the fifteenth or twentieth time heard him to the end in patience. Cowperwood would not return. Steger was as much her friend as any other lawyer would be. Besides, he was socially agreeable to her. Despite his Machiavellian profession, she half believed him. He went over, tactfully, a score of additional points. Finally, on the twenty-first visit, and with seemingly great distress, he told her that her husband had decided to break with her financially, to pay no more bills, and do nothing until his responsibility had been fixed by the courts, and that he, Steger, was about to retire from the case. Mrs. Cowperwood felt that she must yield; she named her ultimatum. If he would fix two hundred thousand dollars on her and the children (this was Cowperwood's own suggestion) and later on do something commercially for their only son, Frank, junior, she would let him go. She disliked to do it. She knew that it meant the triumph of Aileen Butler, such as it was. But, after all, that wretched creature had been properly disgraced in Philadelphia. It was not likely she could ever raise her head socially anywhere any more. She agreed to file a plea which Steger would draw up for her, and by that oily gentleman's machinations it was finally wormed through the local court in the most secret manner imaginable. The merest item in three of the Philadelphia papers some six weeks later reported that a divorce had been granted. When Mrs. Cowperwood read it she wondered greatly that so little attention had been attracted by it. She had feared a much more extended comment. She little knew the cat-like prowlings, legal and journalistic, of her husband's interesting counsel. When Cowperwood read it on one of his visits to Chicago he heaved a sigh of relief. At last it was really true. Now he could make Aileen his wife. He telegraphed her an enigmatic message of congratulation. When Aileen read it she thrilled from head to foot. Now, shortly, she would become the legal bride of Frank Algernon Cowperwood, the newly enfranchised Chicago financier, and then—

"Oh," she said, in her Philadelphia home, when she read it, "isn't that splendid! Now I'll be Mrs. Cowperwood. Oh, dear!"

Mrs. Frank Algernon Cowperwood number one, thinking over her husband's liaison, failure, imprisonment, pyrotechnic operations at the time of the Jay Cooke failure, and his present financial ascendancy, wondered at the mystery of life. There must be a God. The Bible said so. Her husband, evil though he was, could not be utterly bad, for he had made ample provision for her, and the children liked him. Certainly, at the time of the criminal prosecution he was no worse than some others who had gone free. Yet he had been convicted, and she was sorry for that and had always been. He was an able and ruthless man. She hardly knew what to think. The one person she really did blame was the wretched, vain, empty-headed, ungodly Aileen Butler, who had been his seductress and was probably now to be his wife. God would punish her, no doubt. He must. So she went to church on Sundays and tried to believe, come what might, that all was for the best.

CHAPTER VI

THE NEW QUEEN OF THE HOME

The day Cowperwood and Aileen were married—it was in an obscure village called Dalston, near Pittsburg, in western Pennsylvania, where they had stopped off to manage this matter—he had said to her: "I want to tell you, dear, that you and I are really beginning life all over. Now it depends on how well we play this game as to how well we succeed. If you will listen to me we won't try to do anything much socially in Chicago for the present. Of course we'll have to meet a few people. That can't be avoided. Mr. and Mrs. Addison are anxious to meet you, and I've delayed too long in that matter as it is. But what I mean is that I don't believe it's advisable to push this social exchange too far. People are sure to begin to make inquiries if we do. My plan is to wait a little while and then build a really fine house so that we won't need to rebuild. We're going to go to Europe next spring, if things go right, and we may get some ideas over there. I'm going to put in a good big gallery," he concluded. "While we're traveling we might as well see what we can find in the way of pictures and so on."

Aileen was thrilling with anticipation. "Oh, Frank," she said to him, quite ecstatically, "you're so wonderful! You do everything you want, don't you?"

"Not quite," he said, deprecatingly; "but it isn't for not wanting to. Chance has a little to say about some of these chings, Aileen."

She stood in front of him, as she often did, her plump, ringed hands on his shoulders, and looked into those steady, lucid pools—his eyes. Another man, less leonine, and with all his shifting thoughts, might have had to contend with the handicap of a shifty gaze; he fronted the queries and suspicions of the world with a seeming candor that was as disarming as that of a child. The truth was he believed in himself, and himself only, and thence sprang his courage to think as he pleased. Aileen wondered, but could get no answer.

"Oh, you big tiger!" she said. "You great, big lion! Boo!"

He pinched her cheek and smiled. "Poor Aileen!" he thought. She little knew the unsolvable mystery that he was even to himself—to himself most of all.

Immediately after their marriage Cowperwood and Aileen journeyed to Chicago direct, and took the best rooms that the Tremont provided, for the time being. A little later they heard of a comparatively small furnished house at Twenty-third and Michigan Avenue, which, with horses and carriages thrown in, was to be had for a season or two on lease. They contracted for it at once, installing a butler, servants, and the general service of a well-appointed home. Here, because he thought it was only courteous, and not because he thought it was essential or wise at this time to attempt a social onslaught, he invited the Addisons and one or two others whom he felt sure would come—Alexander Rambaud, president of the Chicago & Northwestern, and his wife, and Taylor Lord, an architect whom he had recently called into consultation and whom he found socially acceptable. Lord, like the Addisons, was in society, but only as a minor figure.

Trust Cowperwood to do the thing as it should be done. The place they had leased was a charming little gray-stone house, with a neat flight of granite, balustraded steps leading up to its wide-arched door, and a judicious use of stained glass to give its interior an artistically subdued atmosphere. Fortunately, it was furnished in good taste. Cowperwood turned over the matter of the dinner to a caterer and decorator. Aileen had nothing to do but dress, and wait, and look her best.

"I needn't tell you," he said, in the morning, on leaving, "that I want you to look nice to-night, pet. I want the Addisons and Mr. Rambaud to like you."

A hint was more than sufficient for Aileen, though really it was not needed. On arriving at Chicago she had sought and discovered a French maid. Although she had brought plenty of dresses from Philadelphia, she had been having additional winter costumes prepared by the best and most expensive mistress of the art in Chicago—Theresa Donovan. Only the day before she had welcomed home a golden-yellow silk under heavy green lace, which, with her reddish-gold hair and her white arms and neck, seemed to constitute an unusual harmony. Her boudoir on the night of the dinner presented a veritable riot of silks, satins, laces, lingerie, hair ornaments, perfumes, jewels—anything and everything which might contribute to the feminine art of being beautiful. Once in the throes of a toilet composition, Aileen invariably became restless and energetic, almost fidgety, and her maid, Fadette, was compelled to move quickly. Fresh from her bath, a smooth, ivory Venus, she worked quickly through silken lingerie, stockings and shoes, to her hair. Fadette had an idea to suggest for the hair. Would Madame let her try a new swirl she had seen? Madame would— yes. So there were movings of her mass of rich glinting tresses this way and that. Somehow it would not do. A braided effect was then tried, and instantly discarded; finally a double looping, without braids, low over the forehead, caught back with two dark-green bands, crossing like an X above the center of her forehead and fastened with a diamond sunburst, served admirably. In her filmy, lacy boudoir costume of pink silk Aileen stood up and surveyed herself in the full-length mirror.

"Yes," she said, turning her head this way and that.

Then came the dress from Donovan's, rustling and crisping. She slipped into it wonderingly, critically, while Fadette worked at the back, the arms, about her knees, doing one little essential thing after another.

"Oh, Madame!" she exclaimed. "Oh, charmant! Ze hair, it go weeth it perfect. It ees so full, so beyutiful here"—she pointed to the hips, where the lace formed a clinging basque. "Oh, tees varee, varee nize."

Aileen glowed, but with scarcely a smile. She was concerned. It wasn't so much her toilet, which must be everything that it should be—but this Mr. Addison, who was so rich and in society, and Mr. Rambaud, who was very powerful, Frank said, must like her. It was the necessity to put her best foot forward now that was really troubling her. She must interest these men mentally, perhaps, as well as physically, and with social graces, and that was not so easy. For all her money and comfort in Philadelphia she had never been in society in its best aspects, had never done social entertaining of any real importance. Frank was the most important man who had ever crossed her path. No doubt Mr. Rambaud had a severe, old-fashioned wife. How would she talk to her? And Mrs. Addison! She would know and see everything. Aileen almost talked out loud to herself in a consoling way as she dressed, so strenuous were her thoughts; but she went on, adding the last touches to her physical graces.

When she finally went down-stairs to see how the dining and reception rooms looked, and Fadette began putting away the welter of discarded garments—she was a radiant vision—a splendid greenish-gold figure, with gorgeous hair, smooth, soft, shapely ivory arms, a splendid neck and bust, and a swelling form. She felt beautiful, and yet she was a little nervous—truly. Frank himself would be critical. She went about looking into the dining-room, which, by the caterer's art, had been transformed into a kind of jewel-box glowing with flowers, silver, gold, tinted glass, and the snowy whiteness of linen. It reminded her of an opal flashing all its soft fires. She went into the general reception-room, where was a grand piano finished in pink and gold, upon which, with due thought to her one accomplishment—her playing—she had arranged the songs and instrumental pieces she did best. Aileen was really not a brilliant musician. For the first time in her life she felt matronly—as if now she were not a girl any more, but a woman grown, with some serious responsibilities, and yet she was not really suited to the role. As a matter of fact, her thoughts were always fixed on the artistic, social, and dramatic aspects of life, with unfortunately a kind of nebulosity of conception which permitted no condensation into anything definite or concrete. She could only be wildly and feverishly interested. Just then the door clicked to Frank's key—it was nearing six—and in he came, smiling, confident, a perfect atmosphere of assurance.

"Well!" he observed, surveying her in the soft glow of the reception-room lighted by wall candles judiciously arranged. "Who's the vision floating around here? I'm almost afraid to touch you. Much powder on those arms?"

He drew her into his arms, and she put up her mouth with a sense of relief. Obviously, he must think that she looked charming.

"I am chalky, I guess. You'll just have to stand it, though. You're going to dress, anyhow."

She put her smooth, plump arms about his neck, and he felt pleased. This was the kind of a woman to have—a beauty. Her neck was resplendent with a string of turquoise, her fingers too heavily jeweled, but still beautiful. She was faintly redolent of hyacinth or lavender. Her hair appealed to him, and, above all, the rich yellow silk of her dress, flashing fulgurously through the closely netted green.

"Charming, girlie. You've outdone yourself. I haven't seen this dress before. Where did you get it?"

"Here in Chicago."

He lifted her warm fingers, surveying her train, and turned her about.

"You don't need any advice. You ought to start a school."

"Am I all right?" she queried, smartly, but with a sense of self-distrust for the moment, and all because of him.

"You're perfect. Couldn't be nicer. Splendid!"

She took heart.

"I wish your friends would think so. You'd better hurry."

He went up-stairs, and she followed, looking first into the dining-room again. At least that was right. Surely Frank was a master.

At seven the plop of the feet of carriage-horses was heard, and a moment later Louis, the butler, was opening the door. Aileen went down, a little nervous, a little frigid, trying to think of many pleasant things, and wondering whether she would really succeed in being entertaining. Cowperwood accompanied her, a very different person in so far as mood and self-poise were concerned. To himself his own future was always secure, and that of Aileen's if he wished to make it so. The arduous, upward-ascending rungs of the social ladder that were troubling her had no such significance to him.

The dinner, as such simple things go, was a success from what might be called a managerial and pictorial point of view. Cowperwood, because of his varied tastes and interests, could discuss railroading with Mr. Rambaud in a very definite and illuminating way; could talk architecture with Mr. Lord as a student, for instance, of rare promise would talk with a master; and with a woman like Mrs. Addison or Mrs. Rambaud he could suggest or follow appropriate leads. Aileen, unfortunately, was not so much at home, for her natural state and mood were remote not so much from a serious as from an accurate conception of life. So many things, except in a very nebulous and suggestive way, were sealed books to Aileen— merely faint, distant tinklings. She knew nothing of literature except certain authors who to the truly cultured might seem banal. As for art, it was merely a jingle of names gathered from Cowperwood's private comments. Her one redeeming feature was that she was truly beautiful herself—a radiant, vibrating objet d'art. A man like Rambaud, remote, conservative, constructive, saw the place of a woman like Aileen in the life of a man like Cowperwood on the instant. She was such a woman as he would have prized himself in a certain capacity.

Sex interest in all strong men usually endures unto the end, governed sometimes by a stoic resignation. The experiment of such attraction can, as they well know, be made over and over, but to what end? For many it becomes too troublesome. Yet the presence of so glittering a spectacle as Aileen on this night touched Mr. Rambaud with an ancient ambition. He looked at her almost sadly. Once he was much younger. But alas, he had never attracted the flaming interest of any such woman. As he studied her now he wished that he might have enjoyed such good fortune.

In contrast with Aileen's orchid glow and tinted richness Mrs. Rambaud's simple gray silk, the collar of which came almost to her ears, was disturbing—almost reproving—but Mrs. Rambaud's ladylike courtesy and generosity made everything all right. She came out of intellectual New England—the Emerson-Thoreau-Channing Phillips school of philosophy—and was broadly tolerant. As a matter of fact, she liked Aileen and all the Orient richness she represented. "Such a sweet little house this is," she said, smilingly. "We've noticed it often. We're not so far removed from you but what we might be called neighbors."

Aileen's eyes spoke appreciation. Although she could not fully grasp Mrs. Rambaud, she understood her, in a way, and liked her. She was probably something like her own mother would have been if the latter had been highly educated. While they were moving into the reception-room Taylor Lord was announced. Cowperwood took his hand and brought him forward to the others.

"Mrs. Cowperwood," said Lord, admiringly—a tall, rugged, thoughtful person—"let me be one of many to welcome you to Chicago. After Philadelphia you will find some things to desire at first, but we all come to like it eventually."

"Oh, I'm sure I shall," smiled Aileen.

"I lived in Philadelphia years ago, but only for a little while," added Lord. "I left there to come here."

The observation gave Aileen the least pause, but she passed it over lightly. This sort of accidental reference she must learn to expect; there might be much worse bridges to cross.

"I find Chicago all right," she replied, briskly. "There's nothing the matter with it. It has more snap than Philadelphia ever had."

"I'm glad to hear you say that. I like it so much. Perhaps it's because I find such interesting things to do here."

He was admiring the splendor of her arms and hair. What need had beautiful woman to be intellectual, anyhow, he was saying to himself, sensing that Aileen might be deficient in ultimate refinement.

Once more an announcement from the butler, and now Mr. and Mrs. Addison entered. Addison was not at all concerned over coming here—liked the idea of it; his own position and that of his wife in Chicago was secure. "How are you, Cowperwood?" he beamed, laying one hand on the latter's shoulder. "This is fine of you to have us in to-night. Mrs. Cowperwood, I've been telling your husband for nearly a year now that he should bring you out here. Did he tell you?" (Addison had not as yet confided to his wife the true history of Cowperwood and Aileen.)

"Yes, indeed," replied Aileen, gaily, feeling that Addison was charmed by her beauty. "I've been wanting to come, too. It's his fault that I wasn't here sooner."

Addison, looking circumspectly at Aileen, said to himself that she was certainly a stunning-looking woman. So she was the cause of the first wife's suit. No wonder. What a splendid creature! He contrasted her with Mrs. Addison, and to his wife's disadvantage. She had never been as striking, as stand-upish as Aileen, though possibly she might have more sense. Jove! if he could find a woman like Aileen to-day. Life would take on a new luster. And yet he had women—very carefully, very subterraneously. But he had them.

"It's such a pleasure to meet you," Mrs. Addison, a corpulent, bejeweled lady, was saying to Aileen. "My husband and yours have become the best of friends, apparently. We must see more of each other."

She babbled on in a puffy social way, and Aileen felt as though she were getting along swiftly. The butler brought in a great tray of appetizers and cordials, and put them softly on a remote table. Dinner was served, and the talk flowed on; they discussed the growth of the city, a new church that Lord was building ten blocks farther out; Rambaud told about some humorous land swindles. It was quite gay. Meanwhile Aileen did her best to become interested in Mrs. Rambaud and Mrs. Addison. She liked the latter somewhat better, solely because it was a little easier to talk to her. Mrs. Rambaud Aileen knew to be the wiser and more charitable woman, but she frightened her a little; presently she had to fall back on Mr. Lord's help. He came to her rescue gallantly, talking of everything that came into his mind. All the men outside of Cowperwood were thinking how splendid Aileen was physically, how white were her arms, how rounded her neck and shoulders, how rich her hair.

CHAPTER VII

CHICAGO GAS

Old Peter Laughlin, rejuvenated by Cowperwood's electric ideas, was making money for the house. He brought many bits of interesting gossip from the floor, and such shrewd guesses as to what certain groups and individuals were up to, that Cowperwood was able to make some very brilliant deductions.

"By Gosh! Frank, I think I know exactly what them fellers are trying to do," Laughlin would frequently remark of a morning, after he had lain in his lonely Harrison Street bed meditating the major portion of the night. "That there Stock Yards gang" (and by gang he meant most of the great manipulators, like Arneel, Hand, Schryhart and others) "are after corn again. We want to git long o' that now, or I miss my guess. What do you think, huh?"

Cowperwood, schooled by now in many Western subtleties which he had not previously known, and daily becoming wiser, would as a rule give an instantaneous decision.

"You're right. Risk a hundred thousand bushels. I think New York Central is going to drop a point or two in a few days. We'd better go short a point."

Laughlin could never figure out quite how it was that Cowperwood always seemed to know and was ready to act quite as quickly in local matters as he was himself. He understood his wisdom concerning Eastern shares and things dealt in on the Eastern exchange, but these Chicago matters?

"Whut makes you think that?" he asked Cowperwood, one day, quite curiously.

"Why, Peter," Cowperwood replied, quite simply, "Anton Videra" (one of the directors of the Wheat and Corn Bank) "was in here yesterday while you were on 'change, and he was telling me." He described a situation which Videra had outlined.

Laughlin knew Videra as a strong, wealthy Pole who had come up in the last few years. It was strange how Cowperwood naturally got in with these wealthy men and won their confidence so quickly. Videra would never have become so confidential with him.

"Huh!" he exclaimed. "Well, if he says it it's more'n likely so."

So Laughlin bought, and Peter Laughlin & Co. won.

But this grain and commission business, while it was yielding a profit which would average about twenty thousand a year to each partner, was nothing more to Cowperwood than a source of information.

He wanted to "get in" on something that was sure to bring very great returns within a reasonable time and that would not leave him in any such desperate situation as he was at the time of the Chicago fire—spread out very thin, as he put it. He had interested in his ventures a small group of Chicago men who were watching him—Judah Addison, Alexander Rambaud, Millard Bailey, Anton Videra—men who, although not supreme figures by any means, had free capital. He knew that he could go to them with any truly sound proposition. The one thing that most attracted his attention was the Chicago gas situation, because there was a chance to step in almost unheralded in an as yet unoccupied territory; with franchises once secured—the reader can quite imagine how—he could present himself, like a Hamilcar Barca in the heart of Spain or a Hannibal at the gates of Rome, with a demand for surrender and a division of spoils.

There were at this time three gas companies operating in the three different divisions of the city—the three sections, or "sides," as they were called—South, West, and North, and of these the Chicago Gas, Light, and Coke Company, organized in 1848 to do business on the South Side, was the most flourishing and important. The People's Gas, Light, and Coke Company, doing business on the West Side, was a few years younger than the South Chicago company, and had been allowed to spring into existence through the foolish self-confidence of the organizer and directors of the South Side company, who had fancied that neither the West Side nor the North Side was going to develop very rapidly for a number of years to come, and had counted on the city council's allowing them to extend their mains at any time to these other portions of the city. A third company, the North Chicago Gas Illuminating Company, had been organized almost simultaneously with the West Side company by the same process through which the other companies had been brought into life—their avowed intention, like that of the West Side company, being to confine their activities to the sections from which the organizers presumably came.

Cowperwood's first project was to buy out and combine the three old city companies. With this in view he looked up the holders in all three corporations—their financial and social status. It was his idea that by offering them three for one, or even four for one, for every dollar represented by the market value of their stock he might buy in and capitalize the three companies as one. Then, by issuing sufficient stock to cover all his obligations, he would reap a rich harvest and at the same time leave himself in charge. He approached Judah Addison first as the most available man to help float a scheme of this kind. He did not want him as a partner so much as he wanted him as an investor.

"Well, I'll tell you how I feel about this," said Addison, finally. "You've hit on a great idea here. It's a wonder it hasn't occurred to some one else before. And you'll want to keep rather quiet about it, or some one else will rush in and do it. We have a lot of venturesome men out here. But I like you, and I'm with you. Now it wouldn't be advisable for me to go in on this personally—not openly, anyhow—but I'll promise to see that you get some of the money you want. I like your idea of a central holding company, or pool, with you in charge as trustee, and I'm perfectly willing that you should manage it, for I think you can do it. Anyhow, that leaves me out, apparently, except as an Investor. But you will have to get two or three others to help carry this guarantee with me. Have you any one in mind?"

"Oh yes," replied Cowperwood. "Certainly. I merely came to you first." He mentioned Rambaud, Videra, Bailey, and others.

"They're all right," said Addison, "if you can get them. But I'm not sure, even then, that you can induce these other fellows to sell out. They're not investors in the ordinary sense. They're people who look on this gas business as their private business. They started it. They like it. They built the gas-tanks and laid the mains. It won't be easy."

Cowperwood found, as Addison predicted, that it was not such an easy matter to induce the various stock-holders and directors in the old companies to come in on any such scheme of reorganization. A closer, more unresponsive set of men he was satisfied he had never met. His offer to buy outright at three or four for one they refused absolutely. The stock in each case was selling from one hundred and seventy to two hundred and ten, and intrinsically was worth more every year, as the city was growing larger and its need of gas greater. At the same time they were suspicious—one and all—of any combination scheme by an outsider. Who was he? Whom did he represent? He could make it clear that he had ample capital, but not who his backers were. The old officers and directors fancied that it was a scheme on the part of some of the officers and directors of one of the other companies to get control and oust them. Why should they sell? Why be tempted by greater profits from their stock when they were doing very well as it was? Because of his newness to Chicago and his lack of connection as yet with large affairs Cowperwood was eventually compelled to turn to another scheme—that of organizing new companies in the suburbs as an entering-wedge of attack upon the city proper. Suburbs such as Lake View and Hyde Park, having town or village councils of their own, were permitted to grant franchises to water, gas, and street-railway companies duly incorporated under the laws of the state. Cowperwood calculated that if he could form separate and seemingly distinct companies for each of the villages and towns, and one general company for the city later, he would be in a position to dictate terms to the older organizations. It was simply a question of obtaining his charters and franchises before his rivals had awakened to the situation.

The one difficulty was that he knew absolutely nothing of the business of gas—its practical manufacture and distribution—and had never been particularly interested in it. Street-railroading, his favorite form of municipal profit-seeking, and one upon which he had acquired an almost endless fund of specialized information, offered no present practical opportunity for him here in Chicago. He meditated on the situation, did some reading on the manufacture of gas, and then suddenly, as was his luck, found an implement ready to his hand.

It appeared that in the course of the life and growth of the South Side company there had once been a smaller organization founded by a man by the name of Sippens—Henry De Soto Sippens—who had entered and actually secured, by some hocus-pocus, a franchise to manufacture and sell gas in the down-town districts, but who had been annoyed by all sorts of legal processes until he had finally been driven out or persuaded to get out. He was now in the real-estate business in Lake View. Old Peter Laughlin knew him.

"He's a smart little cuss," Laughlin told Cowperwood. "I thort onct he'd make a go of it, but they ketched him where his hair was short, and he had to let go. There was an explosion in his tank over here near the river onct, an I think he thort them fellers blew him up. Anyhow, he got out. I ain't seen ner heard sight of him fer years."

Cowperwood sent old Peter to look up Mr. Sippens and find out what he was really doing, and whether he would be interested to get back in the gas business. Enter, then, a few days later into the office of Peter Laughlin & Co. Henry De Soto Sippens. He was a very little man, about fifty years of age; he wore a high, four-cornered, stiff felt hat, with a short brown business coat (which in summer became seersucker) and square-toed shoes; he looked for all the world like a country drug or book store owner, with perhaps the air of a country doctor or lawyer superadded. His cuffs protruded too far from his coat-sleeves, his necktie bulged too far out of his vest, and his high hat was set a little too far back on his forehead; otherwise he was acceptable, pleasant, and interesting. He had short side-burns— reddish brown—which stuck out quite defiantly, and his eyebrows were heavy.

"Mr. Sippens," said Cowperwood, blandly, "you were once in the gas manufacturing and distributing business here in Chicago, weren't you?"

"I think I know as much about the manufacture of gas as any one," replied Sippens, almost contentiously. "I worked at it for a number of years."

"Well, now, Mr. Sippens, I was thinking that it might be interesting to start a little gas company in one of these outlying villages that are growing so fast and see if we couldn't make some money out of it. I'm not a practical gas man myself, but I thought I might interest some one who was." He looked at Sippens in a friendly, estimating way. "I have heard of you as some one who has had considerable experience in this field here in Chicago. If I should get up a company of this kind, with considerable backing, do you think you might be willing to take the management of it?"

"Oh, I know all about this gas field," Mr. Sippens was about to say. "It can't be done." But he changed his mind before opening his lips. "If I were paid enough," he said, cautiously. "I suppose you know what you have to contend with?"

"Oh yes," Cowperwood replied, smiling. "What would you consider 'paid enough' to mean?"

"Oh, if I were given six thousand a year and a sufficient interest in the company—say, a half, or something like that—I might consider it," replied Sippens, determined, as he thought, to frighten Cowperwood off by his exorbitant demands. He was making almost six thousand dollars a year out of his present business.

"You wouldn't think that four thousand in several companies—say up to fifteen thousand dollars—and an interest of about a tenth in each would be better?"

Mr. Sippens meditated carefully on this. Plainly, the man before him was no trifling beginner. He looked at Cowperwood shrewdly and saw at once, without any additional explanation of any kind, that the latter was preparing a big fight of some sort. Ten years before Sippens had sensed the immense possibilities of the gas business. He had tried to "get in on it," but had been sued, waylaid, enjoined, financially blockaded, and finally blown up. He had always resented the treatment he had received, and he had bitterly regretted his inability to retaliate. He had thought his days of financial effort were over, but here was a man who was subtly suggesting a stirring fight, and who was calling him, like a hunter with horn, to the chase.

"Well, Mr. Cowperwood," he replied, with less defiance and more camaraderie, "if you could show me that you have a legitimate proposition in hand I am a practical gas man. I know all about mains, franchise contracts, and gas-machinery. I organized and installed the plant at Dayton, Ohio, and Rochester, New York. I would have been rich if I had got here a little earlier." The echo of regret was in his voice.

"Well, now, here's your chance, Mr. Sippens," urged Cowperwood, subtly. "Between you and me there's going to be a big new gas company in the field. We'll make these old fellows step up and see us quickly. Doesn't that interest you? There'll be plenty of money. It isn't that that's wanting—it's an organizer, a fighter, a practical gas man to build the plant, lay the mains, and so on." Cowperwood rose suddenly, straight and determined—a trick with him when he wanted to really impress any one. He seemed to radiate force, conquest, victory. "Do you want to come in?"

"Yes, I do, Mr. Cowperwood!" exclaimed Sippens, jumping to his feet, putting on his hat and shoving it far back on his head. He looked like a chest-swollen bantam rooster.

Cowperwood took his extended hand.

"Get your real-estate affairs in order. I'll want you to get me a franchise in Lake View shortly and build me a plant. I'll give you all the help you need. I'll arrange everything to your satisfaction within a week or so. We will want a good lawyer or two."

Sippens smiled ecstatically as he left the office. Oh, the wonder of this, and after ten years! Now he would show those crooks. Now he had a real fighter behind him—a man like himself. Now, by George, the fur would begin to fly! Who was this man, anyhow? What a wonder! He would look him up. He knew that from now on he would do almost anything Cowperwood wanted him to do.

CHAPTER VIII

NOW THIS IS FIGHTING

When Cowperwood, after failing in his overtures to the three city gas companies, confided to Addison his plan of organizing rival companies in the suburbs, the banker glared at him appreciatively. "You're a smart one!" he finally exclaimed. "You'll do! I back you to win!" He went on to advise Cowperwood that he would need the assistance of some of the strong men on the various village councils. "They're all as crooked as eels' teeth," he went on. "But there are one or two that are more crooked than others and safer—bell-wethers. Have you got your lawyer?"

"I haven't picked one yet, but I will. I'm looking around for the right man now.

"Well, of course, I needn't tell you how important that is. There is one man, old General Van Sickle, who has had considerable training in these matters. He's fairly reliable."

The entrance of Gen. Judson P. Van Sickle threw at the very outset a suggestive light on the whole situation. The old soldier, over fifty, had been a general of division during the Civil War, and had got his real start in life by filing false titles to property in southern Illinois, and then bringing suits to substantiate his fraudulent claims before friendly associates. He was now a prosperous go-between, requiring heavy retainers, and yet not over-prosperous. There was only one kind of business that came to the General—this kind; and one instinctively compared him to that decoy sheep at the stock-yards that had been trained to go forth into nervous, frightened flocks of its fellow-sheep, balking at being driven into the slaughtering-pens, and lead them peacefully into the shambles, knowing enough always to make his own way quietly to the rear during the onward progress and thus escape. A dusty old lawyer, this, with Heaven knows what welter of altered wills, broken promises, suborned juries, influenced judges, bribed councilmen and legislators, double-intentioned agreements and contracts, and a whole world of shifty legal calculations and false pretenses floating around in his brain. Among the politicians, judges, and lawyers generally, by reason of past useful services, he was supposed to have some powerful connections. He liked to be called into any case largely because it meant something to do and kept him from being bored. When compelled to keep an appointment in winter, he would slip on an old greatcoat of gray twill that he had worn until it was shabby, then, taking down a soft felt hat, twisted and pulled out of shape by use, he would pull it low over his dull gray eyes and amble forth. In summer his clothes looked as crinkled as though he had slept in them for weeks. He smoked. In cast of countenance he was not wholly unlike General Grant, with a short gray beard and mustache which always seemed more or less unkempt and hair that hung down over his forehead in a gray mass. The poor General! He was neither very happy nor very unhappy—a doubting Thomas without faith or hope in humanity and without any particular affection for anybody.

"I'll tell you how it is with these small councils, Mr. Cowperwood," observed Van Sickle, sagely, after the preliminaries of the first interview had been dispensed with.

"They're worse than the city council almost, and that's about as bad as it can be. You can't do anything without money where these little fellows are concerned. I don't like to be too hard on men, but these fellows—" He shook his head.

"I understand," commented Cowperwood. "They're not very pleasing, even after you make all allowances."

"Most of them," went on the General, "won't stay put when you think you have them. They sell out. They're just as apt as not to run to this North Side Gas Company and tell them all about the whole thing before you get well under way. Then you have to pay them more money, rival bills will be introduced, and all that." The old General pulled a long face. "Still, there are one or two of them that are all right," he added, "if you can once get them interested—Mr. Duniway and Mr. Gerecht."

"I'm not so much concerned with how it has to be done, General," suggested Cowperwood, amiably, "but I want to be sure that it will be done quickly and quietly. I don't want to be bothered with details. Can it be done without too much publicity, and about what do you think it is going to cost?"

"Well, that's pretty hard to say until I look into the matter," said the General, thoughtfully. "It might cost only four and it might cost all of forty thousand dollars—even more. I can't tell. I'd like to take a little time and look into it." The old gentleman was wondering how much Cowperwood was prepared to spend.

"Well, we won't bother about that now. I'm willing to be as liberal as necessary. I've sent for Mr. Sippens, the president of the Lake View Gas and Fuel Company, and he'll be here in a little while. You will want to work with him as closely as you can." The energetic Sippens came after a few moments, and he and Van Sickle, after being instructed to be mutually helpful and to keep Cowperwood's name out of all matters relating to this work, departed together. They were an odd pair—the dusty old General phlegmatic, disillusioned, useful, but not inclined to feel so; and the smart, chipper Sippens, determined to wreak a kind of poetic vengeance on his old-time enemy, the South Side Gas Company, via this seemingly remote Northside conspiracy. In ten minutes they were hand in glove, the General describing to Sippens the penurious and unscrupulous brand of Councilman Duniway's politics and the friendly but expensive character of Jacob Gerecht. Such is life.

In the organization of the Hyde Park company Cowperwood, because he never cared to put all his eggs in one basket, decided to secure a second lawyer and a second dummy president, although he proposed to keep De Soto Sippens as general practical adviser for all three or four companies. He was thinking this matter over when there appeared on the scene a very much younger man than the old General, one Kent Barrows McKibben, the only son of ex-Judge Marshall Scammon McKibben, of the State Supreme Court. Kent McKibben was thirty-three years old, tall, athletic, and, after a fashion, handsome. He was not at all vague intellectually—that is, in the matter of the conduct of his business—but dandified and at times remote. He had an office in one of the best blocks in Dearborn Street, which he reached in a reserved, speculative mood every morning at nine, unless something important called him down-town earlier. It so happened that he had drawn up the deeds and agreements for the real-estate company that sold Cowperwood his lots at Thirty-seventh Street and Michigan Avenue, and when they were ready he journeyed to the latter's office to ask if there were any additional details which Cowperwood might want to have taken into consideration. When he was ushered in, Cowperwood turned to him his keen, analytical eyes and saw at once a personality he liked. McKibben was just remote and artistic enough to suit him. He liked his clothes, his agnostic unreadableness, his social air. McKibben, on his part, caught the significance of the superior financial atmosphere at once. He noted Cowperwood's light-brown suit picked out with strands of red, his maroon tie, and small cameo cuff-links. His desk, glass-covered, looked clean and official. The woodwork of the rooms was all cherry, hand-rubbed and oiled, the pictures interesting steel-engravings of American life, appropriately framed. The typewriter—at that time just introduced—was in evidence, and the stock-ticker—also new—was ticking volubly the prices current. The secretary who waited on Cowperwood was a young Polish girl named Antoinette Nowak, reserved, seemingly astute, dark, and very attractive.

"What sort of business is it you handle, Mr. McKibben?" asked Cowperwood, quite casually, in the course of the conversation. And after listening to McKibben's explanation he added, idly: "You might come and see me some time next week. It is just possible that I may have something in your line."

In another man McKibben would have resented this remote suggestion of future aid. Now, instead, he was intensely pleased. The man before him gripped his imagination. His remote intellectuality relaxed. When he came again and Cowperwood indicated the nature of the work he might wish to have done McKibben rose to the bait like a fish to a fly.

"I wish you would let me undertake that, Mr. Cowperwood," he said, quite eagerly. "It's something I've never done, but I'm satisfied I can do it. I live out in Hyde Park and know most of the councilmen. I can bring considerable influence to bear for you."

Cowperwood smiled pleasantly.

So a second company, officered by dummies of McKibben's selection, was organized. De Soto Sippens, without old General Van Sickle's knowledge, was taken in as practical adviser. An application for a franchise was drawn up, and Kent Barrows McKibben began silent, polite work on the South Side, coming into the confidence, by degrees, of the various councilmen.

There was still a third lawyer, Burton Stimson, the youngest but assuredly not the least able of the three, a pale, dark-haired Romeoish youth with burning eyes, whom Cowperwood had encountered doing some little work for Laughlin, and who was engaged to work on the West Side with old Laughlin as ostensible organizer and the sprightly De Soto Sippens as practical adviser. Stimson was no mooning Romeo, however, but an eager, incisive soul, born very poor, eager to advance himself. Cowperwood detected that pliability of intellect which, while it might spell disaster to some, spelled success for him. He wanted the intellectual servants. He was willing to pay them handsomely, to keep them busy, to treat them with almost princely courtesy, but he must have the utmost loyalty. Stimson, while maintaining his calm and reserve, could have kissed the arch-episcopal hand. Such is the subtlety of contact.

Behold then at once on the North Side, the South Side, the West Side—dark goings to and fro and walkings up and down in the earth. In Lake View old General Van Sickle and De Soto Sippens, conferring with shrewd Councilman Duniway, druggist, and with Jacob Gerecht, ward boss and wholesale butcher, both of whom were agreeable but exacting, holding pleasant back-room and drug-store confabs with almost tabulated details of rewards and benefits. In Hyde Park, Mr. Kent Barrows McKibben, smug and well dressed, a Chesterfield among lawyers, and with him one J. J. Bergdoll, a noble hireling, long-haired and dusty, ostensibly president of the Hyde Park Gas and Fuel Company, conferring with Councilman Alfred B. Davis, manufacturer of willow and rattan ware, and Mr. Patrick Gilgan, saloon-keeper, arranging a prospective distribution of shares, offering certain cash consideration, lots, favors, and the like. Observe also in the village of Douglas and West Park on the West Side, just over the city line, the angular, humorous Peter Laughlin and Burton Stimson arranging a similar deal or deals.

The enemy, the city gas companies, being divided into three factions, were in no way prepared for what was now coming. When the news finally leaked out that applications for franchises had been made to the several corporate village bodies each old company

296

suspected the other of invasion, treachery, robbery. Pettifogging lawyers were sent, one by each company, to the village council in each particular territory involved, but no one of the companies had as yet the slightest idea who was back of it all or of the general plan of operations. Before any one of them could reasonably protest, before it could decide that it was willing to pay a very great deal to have the suburb adjacent to its particular territory left free, before it could organize a legal fight, councilmanic ordinances were introduced giving the applying company what it sought; and after a single reading in each case and one open hearing, as the law compelled, they were almost unanimously passed. There were loud cries of dismay from minor suburban papers which had almost been forgotten in the arrangement of rewards. The large city newspapers cared little at first, seeing these were outlying districts; they merely made the comment that the villages were beginning well, following in the steps of the city council in its distinguished career of crime.

Cowperwood smiled as he saw in the morning papers the announcement of the passage of each ordinance granting him a franchise. He listened with comfort thereafter on many a day to accounts by Laughlin, Sippens, McKibben, and Van Sickle of overtures made to buy them out, or to take over their franchises. He worked on plans with Sippens looking to the actual introduction of gas-plants. There were bond issues now to float, stock to be marketed, contracts for supplies to be awarded, actual reservoirs and tanks to be built, and pipes to be laid. A pumped-up public opposition had to be smoothed over. In all this De Soto Sippens proved a trump. With Van Sickle, McKibben, and Stimson as his advisers in different sections of the city he would present tabloid propositions to Cowperwood, to which the latter had merely to bow his head in assent or say no. Then De Soto would buy, build, and excavate. Cowperwood was so pleased that he was determined to keep De Soto with him permanently. De Soto was pleased to think that he was being given a chance to pay up old scores and to do large things; he was really grateful.

"We're not through with those sharpers," he declared to Cowperwood, triumphantly, one day. "They'll fight us with suits. They may join hands later. They blew up my gas-plant. They may blow up ours."

"Let them blow," said Cowperwood. "We can blow, too, and sue also. I like lawsuits. We'll tie them up so that they'll beg for quarter." His eyes twinkled cheerfully.

CHAPTER IX

IN SEARCH OF VICTORY

In the mean time the social affairs of Aileen had been prospering in a small way, for while it was plain that they were not to be taken up at once—that was not to be expected—it was also plain that they were not to be ignored entirely. One thing that helped in providing a nice harmonious working atmosphere was the obvious warm affection of Cowperwood for his wife. While many might consider Aileen a little brash or crude, still in the hands of so strong and capable a man as Cowperwood she might prove available. So thought Mrs. Addison, for instance, and Mrs. Rambaud. McKibben and Lord felt the same way. If Cowperwood loved her, as he seemed to do, he would probably "put her through" successfully. And he really did love her, after his fashion. He could never forget how splendid she had been to him in those old days when, knowing full well the circumstances of his home, his wife, his children, the probable opposition of her own family, she had

297

thrown over convention and sought his love. How freely she had given of hers! No petty, squeamish bickering and dickering here. He had been "her Frank" from the start, and he still felt keenly that longing in her to be with him, to be his, which had produced those first wonderful, almost terrible days. She might quarrel, fret, fuss, argue, suspect, and accuse him of flirtation with other women; but slight variations from the norm in his case did not trouble her—at least she argued that they wouldn't. She had never had any evidence. She was ready to forgive him anything, she said, and she was, too, if only he would love her.

"You devil," she used to say to him, playfully. "I know you. I can see you looking around. That's a nice stenographer you have in the office. I suppose it's her."

"Don't be silly, Aileen," he would reply. "Don't be coarse. You know I wouldn't take up with a stenographer. An office isn't the place for that sort of thing."

"Oh, isn't it? Don't silly me. I know you. Any old place is good enough for you."

He laughed, and so did she. She could not help it. She loved him so. There was no particular bitterness in her assaults. She loved him, and very often he would take her in his arms, kiss her tenderly, and coo: "Are you my fine big baby? Are you my red-headed doll? Do you really love me so much? Kiss me, then." Frankly, pagan passion in these two ran high. So long as they were not alienated by extraneous things he could never hope for more delicious human contact. There was no reaction either, to speak of, no gloomy disgust. She was physically acceptable to him. He could always talk to her in a genial, teasing way, even tender, for she did not offend his intellectuality with prudish or conventional notions. Loving and foolish as she was in some ways, she would stand blunt reproof or correction. She could suggest in a nebulous, blundering way things that would be good for them to do. Most of all at present their thoughts centered upon Chicago society, the new house, which by now had been contracted for, and what it would do to facilitate their introduction and standing. Never did a woman's life look more rosy, Aileen thought. It was almost too good to be true. Her Frank was so handsome, so loving, so generous. There was not a small idea about him. What if he did stray from her at times? He remained faithful to her spiritually, and she knew as yet of no single instance in which he had failed her. She little knew, as much as she knew, how blandly he could lie and protest in these matters. But he was fond of her just the same, and he really had not strayed to any extent.

By now also, Cowperwood had invested about one hundred thousand dollars in his gas-company speculations, and he was jubilant over his prospects; the franchises were good for twenty years. By that time he would be nearly sixty, and he would probably have bought, combined with, or sold out to the older companies at a great profit. The future of Chicago was all in his favor. He decided to invest as much as thirty thousand dollars in pictures, if he could find the right ones, and to have Aileen's portrait painted while she was still so beautiful. This matter of art was again beginning to interest him immensely. Addison had four or five good pictures—a Rousseau, a Greuze, a Wouverman, and one Lawrence— picked up Heaven knows where. A hotel-man by the name of Collard, a dry-goods and real-estate merchant, was said to have a very striking collection. Addison had told him of one Davis Trask, a hardware prince, who was now collecting. There were many homes, he knew where art was beginning to be assembled. He must begin, too.

Cowperwood, once the franchises had been secured, had installed Sippens in his own office, giving him charge for the time being. Small rented offices and clerks were maintained in the region where practical plant-building was going on. All sorts of suits to enjoin, annul, and restrain had been begun by the various old companies, but McKibben,

Stimson, and old General Van Sickle were fighting these with Trojan vigor and complacency. It was a pleasant scene. Still no one knew very much of Cowperwood's entrance into Chicago as yet. He was a very minor figure. His name had not even appeared in connection with this work. Other men were being celebrated daily, a little to his envy. When would he begin to shine? Soon, now, surely. So off they went in June, comfortable, rich, gay, in the best of health and spirits, intent upon enjoying to the full their first holiday abroad.

It was a wonderful trip. Addison was good enough to telegraph flowers to New York for Mrs. Cowperwood to be delivered on shipboard. McKibben sent books of travel. Cowperwood, uncertain whether anybody would send flowers, ordered them himself—two amazing baskets, which with Addison's made three—and these, with attached cards, awaited them in the lobby of the main deck. Several at the captain's table took pains to seek out the Cowperwoods. They were invited to join several card-parties and to attend informal concerts. It was a rough passage, however, and Aileen was sick. It was hard to make herself look just nice enough, and so she kept to her room. She was very haughty, distant to all but a few, and to these careful of her conversation. She felt herself coming to be a very important person.

Before leaving she had almost exhausted the resources of the Donovan establishment in Chicago. Lingerie, boudoir costumes, walking-costumes, riding-costumes, evening-costumes she possessed in plenty. She had a jewel-bag hidden away about her person containing all of thirty thousand dollars' worth of jewels. Her shoes, stockings, hats, and accessories in general were innumerable. Because of all this Cowperwood was rather proud of her. She had such a capacity for life. His first wife had been pale and rather anemic, while Aileen was fairly bursting with sheer physical vitality. She hummed and jested and primped and posed. There are some souls that just are, without previous revision or introspection. The earth with all its long past was a mere suggestion to Aileen, dimly visualized if at all. She may have heard that there were once dinosaurs and flying reptiles, but if so it made no deep impression on her. Somebody had said, or was saying, that we were descended from monkeys, which was quite absurd, though it might be true enough. On the sea the thrashing hills of green water suggested a kind of immensity and terror, but not the immensity of the poet's heart. The ship was safe, the captain at table in brass buttons and blue uniform, eager to be nice to her—told her so. Her faith really, was in the captain. And there with her, always, was Cowperwood, looking at this whole, moving spectacle of life with a suspicious, not apprehensive, but wary eye, and saying nothing about it.

In London letters given them by Addison brought several invitations to the opera, to dinner, to Goodwood for a weekend, and so on. Carriages, tallyhoes, cabs for riding were invoked. A week-end invitation to a houseboat on the Thames was secured. Their English hosts, looking on all this as a financial adventure, good financial wisdom, were courteous and civil, nothing more. Aileen was intensely curious. She noted servants, manners, forms. Immediately she began to think that America was not good enough, perhaps; it wanted so many things.

"Now, Aileen, you and I have to live in Chicago for years and years," commented Cowperwood. "Don't get wild. These people don't care for Americans, can't you see that? They wouldn't accept us if we were over here—not yet, anyhow. We're merely passing strangers, being courteously entertained." Cowperwood saw it all.

Aileen was being spoiled in a way, but there was no help. She dressed and dressed. The Englishmen used to look at her in Hyde Park, where she rode and drove; at Claridges' where they stayed; in Bond Street, where she shopped. The Englishwomen, the majority of them remote, ultra-conservative, simple in their tastes, lifted their eyes. Cowperwood sensed the situation, but said nothing. He loved Aileen, and she was satisfactory to him, at least for the present, anyhow, beautiful. If he could adjust her station in Chicago, that would be sufficient for a beginning. After three weeks of very active life, during which Aileen patronized the ancient and honorable glories of England, they went on to Paris.

Here she was quickened to a child-like enthusiasm. "You know," she said to Cowperwood, quite solemnly, the second morning, "the English don't know how to dress. I thought they did, but the smartest of them copy the French. Take those men we saw last night in the Cafe d'Anglais. There wasn't an Englishman I saw that compared with them."

"My dear, your tastes are exotic," replied Cowperwood, who was watching her with pleased interest while he adjusted his tie. "The French smart crowd are almost too smart, dandified. I think some of those young fellows had on corsets."

"What of it?" replied Aileen. "I like it. If you're going to be smart, why not be very smart?"

"I know that's your theory, my dear," he said, "but it can be overdone. There is such a thing as going too far. You have to compromise even if you don't look as well as you might. You can't be too very conspicuously different from your neighbors, even in the right direction."

"You know," she said, stopping and looking at him, "I believe you're going to get very conservative some day—like my brothers."

She came over and touched his tie and smoothed his hair.

"Well, one of us ought to be, for the good of the family," he commented, half smiling.

"I'm not so sure, though, that it will be you, either."

"It's a charming day. See how nice those white-marble statues look. Shall we go to the Cluny or Versailles or Fontainbleau? To-night we ought to see Bernhardt at the Francaise."

Aileen was so gay. It was so splendid to be traveling with her true husband at last.

It was on this trip that Cowperwood's taste for art and life and his determination to possess them revived to the fullest. He made the acquaintance in London, Paris, and Brussels of the important art dealers. His conception of great masters and the older schools of art shaped themselves. By one of the dealers in London, who at once recognized in him a possible future patron, he was invited with Aileen to view certain private collections, and here and there was an artist, such as Lord Leighton, Dante Gabriel Rossetti, or Whistler, to whom he was introduced casually, an interested stranger. These men only saw a strong, polite, remote, conservative man. He realized the emotional, egotistic, and artistic soul. He felt on the instant that there could be little in common between such men and himself in so far as personal contact was concerned, yet there was mutual ground on which they could meet. He could not be a slavish admirer of anything, only a princely patron. So he walked and saw, wondering how soon his dreams of grandeur were to be realized.

In London he bought a portrait by Raeburn; in Paris a plowing scene by Millet, a small Jan Steen, a battle piece by Meissonier, and a romantic courtyard scene by Isabey. Thus began the revival of his former interest in art; the nucleus of that future collection which was to mean so much to him in later years.

On their return, the building of the new Chicago mansion created the next interesting diversion in the lives of Aileen and Cowperwood. Because of some chateaux they saw in France that form, or rather a modification of it as suggested by Taylor Lord, was adopted. Mr. Lord figured that it would take all of a year, perhaps a year and a half, to deliver it in perfect order, but time was of no great importance in this connection. In the mean while they could strengthen their social connections and prepare for that interesting day when they should be of the Chicago elite.

There were, at this time, several elements in Chicago—those who, having grown suddenly rich from dull poverty, could not so easily forget the village church and the village social standards; those who, having inherited wealth, or migrated from the East where wealth was old, understood more of the savoir faire of the game; and those who, being newly born into wealth and seeing the drift toward a smarter American life, were beginning to wish they might shine in it—these last the very young people. The latter were just beginning to dream of dances at Kinsley's, a stated Kirmess, and summer diversions of the European kind, but they had not arrived as yet. The first class, although by far the dullest and most bovine, was still the most powerful because they were the richest, money as yet providing the highest standard. The functions which these people provided were stupid to the verge of distraction; really they were only the week-day receptions and Sunday-afternoon calls of Squeedunk and Hohokus raised to the Nth power. The purpose of the whole matter was to see and be seen. Novelty in either thought or action was decidedly eschewed. It was, as a matter of fact, customariness of thought and action and the quintessence of convention that was desired. The idea of introducing a "play actress," for instance, as was done occasionally in the East or in London—never; even a singer or an artist was eyed askance. One could easily go too far! But if a European prince should have strayed to Chicago (which he never did) or if an Eastern social magnate chanced to stay over a train or two, then the topmost circle of local wealth was prepared to strain itself to the breaking-point. Cowperwood had sensed all this on his arrival, but he fancied that if he became rich and powerful enough he and Aileen, with their fine house to help them, might well be the leaven which would lighten the whole lump. Unfortunately, Aileen was too obviously on the qui vive for those opportunities which might lead to social recognition and equality, if not supremacy. Like the savage, unorganized for protection and at the mercy of the horrific caprice of nature, she was almost tremulous at times with thoughts of possible failure. Almost at once she had recognized herself as unsuited temperamentally for association with certain types of society women. The wife of Anson Merrill, the great dry-goods prince, whom she saw in one of the down-town stores one day, impressed her as much too cold and remote. Mrs. Merrill was a woman of superior mood and education who found herself, in her own estimation, hard put to it for suitable companionship in Chicago. She was Eastern-bred-Boston—and familiar in an offhand way with the superior world of London, which she had visited several times. Chicago at its best was to her a sordid commercial mess. She preferred New York or Washington, but she had to live here. Thus she patronized nearly all of those with whom she condescended to associate, using an upward tilt of the head, a tired droop of the eyelids, and a fine upward arching of the brows to indicate how trite it all was.

It was a Mrs. Henry Huddlestone who had pointed out Mrs. Merrill to Aileen. Mrs. Huddlestone was the wife of a soap manufacturer living very close to the Cowperwoods' temporary home, and she and her husband were on the outer fringe of society. She had heard that the Cowperwoods were people of wealth, that they were friendly with the Addisons, and that they were going to build a two-hundred-thousand-dollar mansion. (The value of houses always grows in the telling.) That was enough. She had called, being three doors away, to leave her card; and Aileen, willing to curry favor here and there, had responded. Mrs. Huddlestone was a little woman, not very attractive in appearance, clever in a social way, and eminently practical.

"Speaking of Mrs. Merrill," commented Mrs. Huddlestone, on this particular day, "there she is—near the dress-goods counter. She always carries that lorgnette in just that way."

Aileen turned and examined critically a tall, dark, slender woman of the high world of the West, very remote, disdainful, superior.

"You don't know her?" questioned Aileen, curiously, surveying her at leisure.

"No," replied Mrs. Huddlestone, defensively. "They live on the North Side, and the different sets don't mingle so much."

As a matter of fact, it was just the glory of the principal families that they were above this arbitrary division of "sides," and could pick their associates from all three divisions.

"Oh!" observed Aileen, nonchalantly. She was secretly irritated to think that Mrs. Huddlestone should find it necessary to point out Mrs. Merrill to her as a superior person.

"You know, she darkens her eyebrows a little, I think," suggested Mrs. Huddlestone, studying her enviously. "Her husband, they say, isn't the most faithful person in the world. There's another woman, a Mrs. Gladdens, that lives very close to them that he's very much interested in."

"Oh!" said Aileen, cautiously. After her own Philadelphia experience she had decided to be on her guard and not indulge in too much gossip. Arrows of this particular kind could so readily fly in her direction.

"But her set is really much the smartest," complimented Aileen's companion.

Thereafter it was Aileen's ambition to associate with Mrs. Anson Merrill, to be fully and freely accepted by her. She did not know, although she might have feared, that that ambition was never to be realized.

But there were others who had called at the first Cowperwood home, or with whom the Cowperwoods managed to form an acquaintance. There were the Sunderland Sledds, Mr. Sledd being general traffic manager of one of the southwestern railways entering the city, and a gentleman of taste and culture and some wealth; his wife an ambitious nobody. There were the Walter Rysam Cottons, Cotton being a wholesale coffee-broker, but more especially a local social litterateur; his wife a graduate of Vassar. There were the Norrie Simmses, Simms being secretary and treasurer of the Douglas Trust and Savings Company, and a power in another group of financial people, a group entirely distinct from that represented by Addison and Rambaud.

Others included the Stanislau Hoecksemas, wealthy furriers; the Duane Kingslands, wholesale flour; the Webster Israelses, packers; the Bradford Candas, jewelers. All these people amounted to something socially. They all had substantial homes and substantial incomes, so that they were worthy of consideration. The difference between Aileen and most of the women involved a difference between naturalism and illusion. But this calls for some explanation.

To really know the state of the feminine mind at this time, one would have to go back to that period in the Middle Ages when the Church flourished and the industrious poet, half schooled in the facts of life, surrounded women with a mystical halo. Since that day the maiden and the matron as well has been schooled to believe that she is of a finer clay than man, that she was born to uplift him, and that her favors are priceless. This rose-tinted mist of romance, having nothing to do with personal morality, has brought about, nevertheless, a holier-than-thou attitude of women toward men, and even of women toward women. Now the Chicago atmosphere in which Aileen found herself was composed in part of this very illusion. The ladies to whom she had been introduced were of this high world of fancy. They conceived themselves to be perfect, even as they were represented in religious art and in fiction. Their husbands must be models, worthy of their high ideals, and other women must have no blemish of any kind. Aileen, urgent, elemental, would have laughed at all this if she could have understood. Not understanding, she felt diffident and uncertain of herself in certain presences.

Instance in this connection Mrs. Norrie Simms, who was a satellite of Mrs. Anson Merrill. To be invited to the Anson Merrills' for tea, dinner, luncheon, or to be driven down-town by Mrs. Merrill, was paradise to Mrs. Simms. She loved to recite the bon mots of her idol, to discourse upon her astonishing degree of culture, to narrate how people refused on occasion to believe that she was the wife of Anson Merrill, even though she herself declared it—those old chestnuts of the social world which must have had their origin in Egypt and Chaldea. Mrs. Simms herself was of a nondescript type, not a real personage, clever, good-looking, tasteful, a social climber. The two Simms children (little girls) had been taught all the social graces of the day—to pose, smirk, genuflect, and the like, to the immense delight of their elders. The nurse in charge was in uniform, the governess was a much put-upon person. Mrs. Simms had a high manner, eyes for those above her only, a serene contempt for the commonplace world in which she had to dwell.

During the first dinner at which she entertained the Cowperwoods Mrs. Simms attempted to dig into Aileen's Philadelphia history, asking if she knew the Arthur Leighs, the Trevor Drakes, Roberta Willing, or the Martyn Walkers. Mrs. Simms did not know them herself, but she had heard Mrs. Merrill speak of them, and that was enough of a handle whereby to swing them. Aileen, quick on the defense, ready to lie manfully on her own behalf, assured her that she had known them, as indeed she had—very casually—and before the rumor which connected her with Cowperwood had been voiced abroad. This pleased Mrs. Simms.

"I must tell Nellie," she said, referring thus familiarly to Mrs. Merrill.

Aileen feared that if this sort of thing continued it would soon be all over town that she had been a mistress before she had been a wife, that she had been the unmentioned corespondent in the divorce suit, and that Cowperwood had been in prison. Only his wealth and her beauty could save her; and would they?

One night they had been to dinner at the Duane Kingslands', and Mrs. Bradford Canda had asked her, in what seemed a very significant way, whether she had ever met her friend Mrs. Schuyler Evans, of Philadelphia. This frightened Aileen.

"Don't you suppose they must know, some of them, about us?" she asked Cowperwood, on the way home.

"I suppose so," he replied, thoughtfully. "I'm sure I don't know. I wouldn't worry about that if I were you. If you worry about it you'll suggest it to them. I haven't made any secret of my term in prison in Philadelphia, and I don't intend to. It wasn't a square deal, and they had no right to put me there."

"I know, dear," replied Aileen, "it might not make so much difference if they did know. I don't see why it should. We are not the only ones that have had marriage troubles, I'm sure.

"There's just one thing about this; either they accept us or they don't. If they don't, well and good; we can't help it. We'll go on and finish the house, and give them a chance to be decent. If they won't be, there are other cities. Money will arrange matters in New York— that I know. We can build a real place there, and go in on equal terms if we have money enough—and I will have money enough," he added, after a moment's pondering. "Never fear. I'll make millions here, whether they want me to or not, and after that—well, after that, we'll see what we'll see. Don't worry. I haven't seen many troubles in this world that money wouldn't cure."

His teeth had that even set that they always assumed when he was dangerously in earnest. He took Aileen's hand, however, and pressed it gently.

"Don't worry," he repeated. "Chicago isn't the only city, and we won't be the poorest people in America, either, in ten years. Just keep up your courage. It will all come out right. It's certain to."

Aileen looked out on the lamp-lit length of Michigan Avenue, down which they were rolling past many silent mansions. The tops of all the lamps were white, and gleamed through the shadows, receding to a thin point. It was dark, but fresh and pleasant. Oh, if only Frank's money could buy them position and friendship in this interesting world; if it only would! She did not quite realize how much on her own personality, or the lack of it, this struggle depended.

CHAPTER X

A TEST

The opening of the house in Michigan Avenue occurred late in November in the fall of eighteen seventy-eight. When Aileen and Cowperwood had been in Chicago about two years. Altogether, between people whom they had met at the races, at various dinners and teas, and at receptions of the Union and Calumet Clubs (to which Cowperwood, through Addison's backing, had been admitted) and those whom McKibben and Lord influenced, they were able to send invitations to about three hundred, of whom some two hundred and fifty responded. Up to this time, owing to Cowperwood's quiet manipulation of his affairs, there had been no comment on his past—no particular interest in it. He had money, affable ways, a magnetic personality. The business men of the city—those whom he met socially— were inclined to consider him fascinating and very clever. Aileen being beautiful and graceful for attention, was accepted at more or less her own value, though the kingly high world knew them not.

It is amazing what a showing the socially unplaced can make on occasion where tact and discrimination are used. There was a weekly social paper published in Chicago at this time, a rather able publication as such things go, which Cowperwood, with McKibben's assistance, had pressed into service. Not much can be done under any circumstances where the cause is not essentially strong; but where, as in this case, there is a semblance of respectability, considerable wealth, and great force and magnetism, all things are possible. Kent McKibben knew Horton Biggers, the editor, who was a rather desolate and disillusioned person of forty-five, gray, and depressed-looking—a sort of human sponge or barnacle who was only galvanized into seeming interest and cheerfulness by sheer necessity. Those were the days when the society editor was accepted as a member of society—de facto—and treated more as a guest than a reporter, though even then the tendency was toward elimination. Working for Cowperwood, and liking him, McKibben said to Biggers one evening:

"You know the Cowperwoods, don't you, Biggers?"

"No," replied the latter, who devoted himself barnacle-wise to the more exclusive circles. "Who are they?"

"Why, he's a banker over here in La Salle Street. They're from Philadelphia. Mrs. Cowperwood's a beautiful woman—young and all that. They're building a house out here on Michigan Avenue. You ought to know them. They're going to get in, I think. The Addisons like them. If you were to be nice to them now I think they'd appreciate it later. He's rather liberal, and a good fellow."

Biggers pricked up his ears. This social journalism was thin picking at best, and he had very few ways of turning an honest penny. The would be's and half-in's who expected nice things said of them had to subscribe, and rather liberally, to his paper. Not long after this brief talk Cowperwood received a subscription blank from the business office of the Saturday Review, and immediately sent a check for one hundred dollars to Mr. Horton Biggers direct. Subsequently certain not very significant personages noticed that when the Cowperwoods dined at their boards the function received comment by the Saturday Review, not otherwise. It looked as though the Cowperwoods must be favored; but who were they, anyhow?

The danger of publicity, and even moderate social success, is that scandal loves a shining mark. When you begin to stand out the least way in life, as separate from the mass, the cognoscenti wish to know who, what, and why. The enthusiasm of Aileen, combined with the genius of Cowperwood, was for making their opening entertainment a very exceptional affair, which, under the circumstances, and all things considered, was a dangerous thing to do. As yet Chicago was exceedingly slow socially. Its movements were, as has been said, more or less bovine and phlegmatic. To rush in with something utterly brilliant and pyrotechnic was to take notable chances. The more cautious members of Chicago society, even if they did not attend, would hear, and then would come ultimate comment and decision.

The function began with a reception at four, which lasted until six-thirty, and this was followed by a dance at nine, with music by a famous stringed orchestra of Chicago, a musical programme by artists of considerable importance, and a gorgeous supper from eleven until one in a Chinese fairyland of lights, at small tables filling three of the ground-floor rooms. As an added fillip to the occasion Cowperwood had hung, not only the important pictures which he had purchased abroad, but a new one—a particularly brilliant Gerome, then in the heyday of his exotic popularity—a picture of nude odalisques of the harem, idling beside the highly colored stone marquetry of an oriental bath. It was more or less "loose" art for Chicago, shocking to the uninitiated, though harmless enough to the illuminati; but it gave a touch of color to the art-gallery which the latter needed. There was also, newly arrived and newly hung, a portrait of Aileen by a Dutch artist, Jan van Beers, whom they had encountered the previous summer at Brussels. He had painted Aileen in nine sittings, a rather brilliant canvas, high in key, with a summery, out-of-door world behind her—a low stone-curbed pool, the red corner of a Dutch brick palace, a tulip-bed, and a blue sky with fleecy clouds. Aileen was seated on the curved arm of a stone bench, green grass at her feet, a pink-and-white parasol with a lacy edge held idly to one side; her rounded, vigorous figure clad in the latest mode of Paris, a white and blue striped-silk walking-suit, with a blue-and-white-banded straw hat, wide-brimmed, airy, shading her lusty, animal eyes. The artist had caught her spirit quite accurately, the dash, the assumption, the bravado based on the courage of inexperience, or lack of true subtlety. A refreshing thing in its way, a little showy, as everything that related to her was, and inclined to arouse jealousy in those not so liberally endowed by life, but fine as a character piece. In the warm glow of the guttered gas-jets she looked particularly brilliant here, pampered, idle, jaunty—the well-kept, stall-fed pet of the world. Many stopped to see, and many were the comments, private and otherwise.

This day began with a flurry of uncertainty and worried anticipation on the part of Aileen. At Cowperwood's suggestion she had employed a social secretary, a poor hack of a girl, who had sent out all the letters, tabulated the replies, run errands, and advised on one detail and another. Fadette, her French maid, was in the throes of preparing for two toilets which would have to be made this day, one by two o'clock at least, another between six and eight. Her "mon dieus" and "par bleus" could be heard continuously as she hunted for some article of dress or polished an ornament, buckle, or pin. The struggle of Aileen to be perfect was, as usual, severe. Her meditations, as to the most becoming gown to wear were trying. Her portrait was on the east wall in the art-gallery, a spur to emulation; she felt as though all society were about to judge her. Theresa Donovan, the local dressmaker, had given some advice; but Aileen decided on a heavy brown velvet constructed by Worth, of Paris—a thing of varying aspects, showing her neck and arms to perfection, and composing charmingly with her flesh and hair. She tried amethyst ear-rings and changed to topaz; she stockinged her legs in brown silk, and her feet were shod in brown slippers with red enamel buttons.

The trouble with Aileen was that she never did these things with that ease which is a sure sign of the socially efficient. She never quite so much dominated a situation as she permitted it to dominate her. Only the superior ease and graciousness of Cowperwood carried her through at times; but that always did. When he was near she felt quite the great lady, suited to any realm. When she was alone her courage, great as it was, often trembled in the balance. Her dangerous past was never quite out of her mind.

At four Kent McKibben, smug in his afternoon frock, his quick, receptive eyes approving only partially of all this show and effort, took his place in the general reception-room, talking to Taylor Lord, who had completed his last observation and was leaving to return later in the evening. If these two had been closer friends, quite intimate, they would have discussed the Cowperwoods' social prospects; but as it was, they confined themselves to dull conventionalities. At this moment Aileen came down-stairs for a moment, radiant. Kent McKibben thought he had never seen her look more beautiful. After all, contrasted with some of the stuffy creatures who moved about in society, shrewd, hard, bony, calculating, trading on their assured position, she was admirable. It was a pity she did not have more poise; she ought to be a little harder—not quite so genial. Still, with Cowperwood at her side, she might go far.

"Really, Mrs. Cowperwood," he said, "it is all most charming. I was just telling Mr. Lord here that I consider the house a triumph."

From McKibben, who was in society, and with Lord, another "in" standing by, this was like wine to Aileen. She beamed joyously.

Among the first arrivals were Mrs. Webster Israels, Mrs. Bradford Canda, and Mrs. Walter Rysam Cotton, who were to assist in receiving. These ladies did not know that they were taking their future reputations for sagacity and discrimination in their hands; they had been carried away by the show of luxury of Aileen, the growing financial repute of Cowperwood, and the artistic qualities of the new house. Mrs. Webster Israels's mouth was of such a peculiar shape that Aileen was always reminded of a fish; but she was not utterly homely, and to-day she looked brisk and attractive. Mrs. Bradford Canda, whose old rose and silver-gray dress made up in part for an amazing angularity, but who was charming withal, was the soul of interest, for she believed this to be a very significant affair. Mrs. Walter Rysam Cotton, a younger woman than either of the others, had the polish of Vassar life about her, and was "above" many things. Somehow she half suspected the Cowperwoods might not do, but they were making strides, and might possibly surpass all other aspirants. It behooved her to be pleasant.

Life passes from individuality and separateness at times to a sort of Monticelliesque mood of color, where individuality is nothing, the glittering totality all. The new house, with its charming French windows on the ground floor, its heavy bands of stone flowers and deep-sunk florated door, was soon crowded with a moving, colorful flow of people.

Many whom Aileen and Cowperwood did not know at all had been invited by McKibben and Lord; they came, and were now introduced. The adjacent side streets and the open space in front of the house were crowded with champing horses and smartly veneered carriages. All with whom the Cowperwoods had been the least intimate came early, and, finding the scene colorful and interesting, they remained for some time. The caterer, Kinsley, had supplied a small army of trained servants who were posted like soldiers, and carefully supervised by the Cowperwood butler. The new dining-room, rich with a Pompeian scheme of color, was aglow with a wealth of glass and an artistic arrangement of delicacies. The afternoon costumes of the women, ranging through autumnal grays, purples, browns, and greens, blended effectively with the brown-tinted walls of the entry-hall, the deep gray and gold of the general living-room, the old-Roman red of the dining-room, the white-and-gold of the music-room, and the neutral sepia of the art-gallery.

Aileen, backed by the courageous presence of Cowperwood, who, in the dining-room, the library, and the art-gallery, was holding a private levee of men, stood up in her vain beauty, a thing to see—almost to weep over, embodying the vanity of all seeming things, the mockery of having and yet not having. This parading throng that was more curious than interested, more jealous than sympathetic, more critical than kind, was coming almost solely to observe.

"Do you know, Mrs. Cowperwood," Mrs. Simms remarked, lightly, "your house reminds me of an art exhibit to-day. I hardly know why."

Aileen, who caught the implied slur, had no clever words wherewith to reply. She was not gifted in that way, but she flared with resentment.

"Do you think so?" she replied, caustically.

Mrs. Simms, not all dissatisfied with the effect she had produced, passed on with a gay air, attended by a young artist who followed amorously in her train.

Aileen saw from this and other things like it how little she was really "in." The exclusive set did not take either her or Cowperwood seriously as yet. She almost hated the comparatively dull Mrs. Israels, who had been standing beside her at the time, and who had heard the remark; and yet Mrs. Israels was much better than nothing. Mrs. Simms had condescended a mild "how'd do" to the latter.

It was in vain that the Addisons, Sledds, Kingslands, Hoecksemas, and others made their appearance; Aileen was not reassured. However, after dinner the younger set, influenced by McKibben, came to dance, and Aileen was at her best in spite of her doubts. She was gay, bold, attractive. Kent McKibben, a past master in the mazes and mysteries of the grand march, had the pleasure of leading her in that airy, fairy procession, followed by Cowperwood, who gave his arm to Mrs. Simms. Aileen, in white satin with a touch of silver here and there and necklet, bracelet, ear-rings, and hair-ornament of diamonds, glittered in almost an exotic way. She was positively radiant. McKibben, almost smitten, was most attentive.

"This is such a pleasure," he whispered, intimately. "You are very beautiful—a dream!"

"You would find me a very substantial one," returned Aileen. "Would that I might find," he laughed, gaily; and Aileen, gathering the hidden significance, showed her teeth teasingly. Mrs. Simms, engrossed by Cowperwood, could not hear as she would have liked.

After the march Aileen, surrounded by a half-dozen of gay, rudely thoughtless young bloods, escorted them all to see her portrait. The conservative commented on the flow of wine, the intensely nude Gerome at one end of the gallery, and the sparkling portrait of Aileen at the other, the enthusiasm of some of the young men for her company. Mrs. Rambaud, pleasant and kindly, remarked to her husband that Aileen was "very eager for life," she thought. Mrs. Addison, astonished at the material flare of the Cowperwoods, quite transcending in glitter if not in size and solidity anything she and Addison had ever achieved, remarked to her husband that "he must be making money very fast."

"The man's a born financier, Ella," Addison explained, sententiously. "He's a manipulator, and he's sure to make money. Whether they can get into society I don't know. He could if he were alone, that's sure. She's beautiful, but he needs another kind of woman, I'm afraid. She's almost too good-looking."

"That's what I think, too. I like her, but I'm afraid she's not going to play her cards right. It's too bad, too."

Just then Aileen came by, a smiling youth on either side, her own face glowing with a warmth of joy engendered by much flattery. The ball-room, which was composed of the music and drawing rooms thrown into one, was now the objective. It glittered before her with a moving throng; the air was full of the odor of flowers, and the sound of music and voices.

"Mrs. Cowperwood," observed Bradford Canda to Horton Biggers, the society editor, "is one of the prettiest women I have seen in a long time. She's almost too pretty."

"How do you think she's taking?" queried the cautious Biggers. "Charming, but she's hardly cold enough, I'm afraid; hardly clever enough. It takes a more serious type. She's a little too high-spirited. These old women would never want to get near her; she makes them look too old. She'd do better if she were not so young and so pretty."

"That's what I think exactly," said Biggers. As a matter of fact, he did not think so at all; he had no power of drawing any such accurate conclusions. But he believed it now, because Bradford Canda had said it.

CHAPTER XI

THE FRUITS OF DARING

Next morning, over the breakfast cups at the Norrie Simmses' and elsewhere, the import of the Cowperwoods' social efforts was discussed and the problem of their eventual acceptance or non-acceptance carefully weighed.

"The trouble with Mrs. Cowperwood," observed Mrs. Simms, "is that she is too gauche. The whole thing was much too showy. The idea of her portrait at one end of the gallery and that Gerome at the other! And then this item in the Press this morning! Why, you'd really think they were in society." Mrs. Simms was already a little angry at having let herself be used, as she now fancied she had been, by Taylor Lord and Kent McKibben, both friends of hers.

"What did you think of the crowd?" asked Norrie, buttering a roll.

"Why, it wasn't representative at all, of course. We were the most important people they had there, and I'm sorry now that we went. Who are the Israelses and the Hoecksemas, anyhow? That dreadful woman!" (She was referring to Mrs. Hoecksema.) "I never listened to duller remarks in my life."

"I was talking to Haguenin of the Press in the afternoon," observed Norrie. "He says that Cowperwood failed in Philadelphia before he came here, and that there were a lot of lawsuits. Did you ever hear that?"

"No. But she says she knows the Drakes and the Walkers there. I've been intending to ask Nellie about that. I have often wondered why he should leave Philadelphia if he was getting along so well. People don't usually do that."

Simms was envious already of the financial showing Cowperwood was making in Chicago. Besides, Cowperwood's manner bespoke supreme intelligence and courage, and that is always resented by all save the suppliants or the triumphant masters of other walks in life. Simms was really interested at last to know something more about Cowperwood, something definite.

Before this social situation had time to adjust itself one way or the other, however, a matter arose which in its way was far more vital, though Aileen might not have thought so. The feeling between the new and old gas companies was becoming strained; the stockholders of the older organization were getting uneasy. They were eager to find out who was back of these new gas companies which were threatening to poach on their exclusive preserves. Finally one of the lawyers who had been employed by the North Chicago Gas Illuminating Company to fight the machinations of De Soto Sippens and old General Van Sickle, finding that the Lake View Council had finally granted the franchise to the new company and that the Appellate Court was about to sustain it, hit upon the idea of charging conspiracy and wholesale bribery of councilmen. Considerable evidence had accumulated that Duniway, Jacob Gerecht, and others on the North Side had been influenced by cash, and to bring legal action would delay final approval of the franchises and give the old company time to think what else to do. This North Side company lawyer, a man by the name of Parsons, had been following up the movements of Sippens and old General Van Sickle, and had finally concluded that they were mere dummies and pawns, and that the real instigator in all this excitement was Cowperwood, or, if not he, then men whom he represented. Parsons visited Cowperwood's office one day in order to see him; getting no satisfaction, he proceeded to look up his record and connections. These various investigations and counter-schemings came to a head in a court proceeding filed in the United States Circuit Court late in November, charging Frank Algernon Cowperwood, Henry De Soto Sippens, Judson P. Van Sickle, and others with conspiracy; this again was followed almost immediately by suits begun by the West and South Side companies charging the same thing. In each case Cowperwood's name was mentioned as the secret power behind the new companies, conspiring to force the old companies to buy him out. His Philadelphia history was published, but only in part—a highly modified account he had furnished the newspapers some time before. Though conspiracy and bribery are ugly words, still lawyers' charges prove nothing. But a penitentiary record, for whatever reason served, coupled with previous failure, divorce, and scandal (though the newspapers made only the most guarded reference to all this), served to whet public interest and to fix Cowperwood and his wife in the public eye.

Cowperwood himself was solicited for an interview, but his answer was that he was merely a financial agent for the three new companies, not an investor; and that the charges, in so far as he was concerned, were untrue, mere legal fol-de-rol trumped up to make the situation as annoying as possible. He threatened to sue for libel. Nevertheless, although these suits eventually did come to nothing (for he had fixed it so that he could not be traced save as a financial agent in each case), yet the charges had been made, and he was now revealed as a shrewd, manipulative factor, with a record that was certainly spectacular.

"I see," said Anson Merrill to his wife, one morning at breakfast, "that this man Cowperwood is beginning to get his name in the papers." He had the Times on the table before him, and was looking at a headline which, after the old-fashioned pyramids then in vogue, read: "Conspiracy charged against various Chicago citizens. Frank Algernon Cowperwood, Judson P. Van Sickle, Henry De Soto Sippens, and others named in Circuit Court complaint." It went on to specify other facts. "I supposed he was just a broker."

"I don't know much about them," replied his wife, "except what Bella Simms tells me. What does it say?"

He handed her the paper.

"I have always thought they were merely climbers," continued Mrs. Merrill. "From what I hear she is impossible. I never saw her."

"He begins well for a Philadelphian," smiled Merrill. "I've seen him at the Calumet. He looks like a very shrewd man to me. He's going about his work in a brisk spirit, anyhow."

Similarly Mr. Norman Schryhart, a man who up to this time had taken no thought of Cowperwood, although he had noted his appearance about the halls of the Calumet and Union League Clubs, began to ask seriously who he was. Schryhart, a man of great physical and mental vigor, six feet tall, hale and stolid as an ox, a very different type of man from Anson Merrill, met Addison one day at the Calumet Club shortly after the newspaper talk began. Sinking into a great leather divan beside him, he observed:

"Who is this man Cowperwood whose name is in the papers these days, Addison? You know: all these people. Didn't you introduce him to me once?"

"I surely did," replied Addison, cheerfully, who, in spite of the attacks on Cowperwood, was rather pleased than otherwise. It was quite plain from the concurrent excitement that attended all this struggle, that Cowperwood must be managing things rather adroitly, and, best of all, he was keeping his backers' names from view. "He's a Philadelphian by birth. He came out here several years ago, and went into the grain and commission business. He's a banker now. A rather shrewd man, I should say. He has a lot of money."

"Is it true, as the papers say, that he failed for a million in Philadelphia in 1871?"

"In so far as I know, it is."

"Well, was he in the penitentiary down there?"

"I think so—yes. I believe it was for nothing really criminal, though. There appears to have been some political-financial mix-up, from all I can learn."

"And is he only forty, as the papers say?"

"About that, I should judge. Why?"

"Oh, this scheme of his looks rather pretentious to me—holding up the old gas companies here. Do you suppose he'll manage to do it?"

"I don't know that. All I know is what I have read in the papers," replied Addison, cautiously. As a matter of fact, he did not care to talk about this business at all. Cowperwood was busy at this very time, through an agent, attempting to effect a compromise and union of all interests concerned. It was not going very well.

"Humph!" commented Schryhart. He was wondering why men like himself, Merrill, Arneel, and others had not worked into this field long ago or bought out the old companies. He went away interested, and a day or two later—even the next morning—had formulated a scheme. Not unlike Cowperwood, he was a shrewd, hard, cold man. He believed in Chicago implicitly and in all that related to its future. This gas situation, now that Cowperwood had seen the point, was very clear to him. Even yet it might not be impossible for a third party to step in and by intricate manipulation secure the much coveted rewards. Perhaps Cowperwood himself could be taken over—who could tell?

311

Mr. Schryhart, being a very dominating type of person, did not believe in minor partnerships or investments. If he went into a thing of this kind it was his preference to rule. He decided to invite Cowperwood to visit the Schryhart office and talk matters over. Accordingly, he had his secretary pen a note, which in rather lofty phrases invited Cowperwood to call "on a matter of importance."

Now just at this time, it so chanced, Cowperwood was feeling rather secure as to his place in the Chicago financial world, although he was still smarting from the bitterness of the aspersions recently cast upon him from various quarters. Under such circumstances it was his temperament to evince a rugged contempt for humanity, rich and poor alike. He was well aware that Schryhart, although introduced, had never previously troubled to notice him.

"Mr. Cowperwood begs me to say," wrote Miss Antoinette Nowak, at his dictation, "that he finds himself very much pressed for time at present, but he would be glad to see Mr. Schryhart at his office at any time."

This irritated the dominating, self-sufficient Schryhart a little, but nevertheless he was satisfied that a conference could do no harm in this instance—was advisable, in fact. So one Wednesday afternoon he journeyed to the office of Cowperwood, and was most hospitably received.

"How do you do, Mr. Schryhart," observed Cowperwood, cordially, extending his hand. "I'm glad to see you again. I believe we met once before several years ago."

"I think so myself," replied Mr. Schryhart, who was broad-shouldered, square-headed, black-eyed, and with a short black mustache gracing a firm upper lip. He had hard, dark, piercing eyes. "I see by the papers, if they can be trusted," he said, coming direct to the point, "that you are interesting yourself in local gas. Is that true?"

"I'm afraid the papers cannot be generally relied on," replied Cowperwood, quite blandly. "Would you mind telling me what makes you interested to know whether I am or not?"

"Well, to tell the truth," replied Schryhart, staring at the financier, "I am interested in this local gas situation myself. It offers a rather profitable field for investment, and several members of the old companies have come to me recently to ask me to help them combine." (This was not true at all.) "I have been wondering what chance you thought you had of winning along the lines you are now taking."

Cowperwood smiled. "I hardly care to discuss that," he said, "unless I know much more of your motives and connections than I do at present. Do I understand that you have really been appealed to by stockholders of the old companies to come in and help adjust this matter?"

"Exactly," said Schryhart.

"And you think you can get them to combine? On what basis?"

"Oh, I should say it would be a simple matter to give each of them two or three shares of a new company for one in each of the old. We could then elect one set of officers, have one set of offices, stop all these suits, and leave everybody happy."

312

He said this in an easy, patronizing way, as though Cowperwood had not really thought it all out years before. It amazed the latter no little to see his own scheme patronizingly brought back to him, and that, too, by a very powerful man locally—one who thus far had chosen to overlook him utterly.

"On what basis," asked Cowperwood, cautiously, "would you expect these new companies to come in?"

"On the same basis as the others, if they are not too heavily capitalized. I haven't thought out all the details. Two or three for one, according to investment. Of course, the prejudices of these old companies have to be considered."

Cowperwood meditated. Should or should he not entertain this offer? Here was a chance to realize quickly by selling out to the old companies. Only Schryhart, not himself, would be taking the big end in this manipulative deal. Whereas if he waited—even if Schryhart managed to combine the three old companies into one—he might be able to force better terms. He was not sure. Finally he asked, "How much stock of the new company would be left in your hands—or in the hands of the organizing group—after each of the old and new companies had been provided for on this basis?"

"Oh, possibly thirty-five or forty per cent. of the whole," replied Schryhart, ingratiatingly. "The laborer is worthy of his hire."

"Quite so," replied Cowperwood, smiling, "but, seeing that I am the man who has been cutting the pole to knock this persimmon it seems to me that a pretty good share of that should come to me; don't you think so?"

"Just what do you mean?"

"Just what I have said. I personally have organized the new companies which have made this proposed combination possible. The plan you propose is nothing more than what I have been proposing for some time. The officers and directors of the old companies are angry at me merely because I am supposed to have invaded the fields that belong to them. Now, if on account of that they are willing to operate through you rather than through me, it seems to me that I should have a much larger share in the surplus. My personal interest in these new companies is not very large. I am really more of a fiscal agent than anything else." (This was not true, but Cowperwood preferred to have his guest think so.)

Schryhart smiled. "But, my dear sir," he explained, "you forget that I will be supplying nearly all the capital to do this."

"You forget," retorted Cowperwood, "that I am not a novice. I will guarantee to supply all the capital myself, and give you a good bonus for your services, if you want that. The plants and franchises of the old and new companies are worth something. You must remember that Chicago is growing."

"I know that," replied Schryhart, evasively, "but I also know that you have a long, expensive fight ahead of you. As things are now you cannot, of yourself, expect to bring these old companies to terms. They won't work with you, as I understand it. It will require an outsider like myself—some one of influence, or perhaps, I had better say, of old standing in

Chicago, some one who knows these people—to bring about this combination. Have you any one, do you think, who can do it better than I?"

"It is not at all impossible that I will find some one," replied Cowperwood, quite easily.

"I hardly think so; certainly not as things are now. The old companies are not disposed to work through you, and they are through me. Don't you think you had better accept my terms and allow me to go ahead and close this matter up?"

"Not at all on that basis," replied Cowperwood, quite simply. "We have invaded the enemies' country too far and done too much. Three for one or four for one—whatever terms are given the stockholders of the old companies—is the best I will do about the new shares, and I must have one-half of whatever is left for myself. At that I will have to divide with others." (This was not true either.)

"No," replied Schryhart, evasively and opposingly, shaking his square head. "It can't be done. The risks are too great. I might allow you one-fourth, possibly—I can't tell yet."

"One-half or nothing," said Cowperwood, definitely.

Schryhart got up. "That's the best you will do, is it?" he inquired.

"The very best."

"I'm afraid then," he said, "we can't come to terms. I'm sorry. You may find this a rather long and expensive fight."

"I have fully anticipated that," replied the financier.

CHAPTER XII

A NEW RETAINER

Cowperwood, who had rebuffed Schryhart so courteously but firmly, was to learn that he who takes the sword may well perish by the sword. His own watchful attorney, on guard at the state capitol, where certificates of incorporation were issued in the city and village councils, in the courts and so forth, was not long in learning that a counter-movement of significance was under way. Old General Van Sickle was the first to report that something was in the wind in connection with the North Side company. He came in late one afternoon, his dusty greatcoat thrown loosely about his shoulders, his small, soft hat low over his shaggy eyes, and in response to Cowperwood's "Evening, General, what can I do for you?" seated himself portentously.

"I think you'll have to prepare for real rough weather in the future, Captain," he remarked, addressing the financier with a courtesy title that he had fallen in the habit of using.

"What's the trouble now?" asked Cowperwood.

"No real trouble as yet, but there may be. Some one—I don't know who—is getting these three old companies together in one. There's a certificate of incorporation been applied for at Springfield for the United Gas and Fuel Company of Chicago, and there are some directors' meetings now going on at the Douglas Trust Company. I got this from Duniway, who seems to have friends somewhere that know."

Cowperwood put the ends of his fingers together in his customary way and began to tap them lightly and rhythmically.

"Let me see—the Douglas Trust Company. Mr. Simms is president of that. He isn't shrewd enough to organize a thing of that kind. Who are the incorporators?"

The General produced a list of four names, none of them officers or directors of the old companies.

"Dummies, every one," said Cowperwood, succinctly. "I think I know," he said, after a few moments' reflection, "who is behind it, General; but don't let that worry you. They can't harm us if they do unite. They're bound to sell out to us or buy us out eventually."

Still it irritated him to think that Schryhart had succeeded in persuading the old companies to combine on any basis; he had meant to have Addison go shortly, posing as an outside party, and propose this very thing. Schryhart, he was sure, had acted swiftly following their interview. He hurried to Addison's office in the Lake National.

"Have you heard the news?" exclaimed that individual, the moment Cowperwood appeared. "They're planning to combine. It's Schryhart. I was afraid of that. Simms of the Douglas Trust is going to act as the fiscal agent. I had the information not ten minutes ago."

"So did I," replied Cowperwood, calmly. "We should have acted a little sooner. Still, it isn't our fault exactly. Do you know the terms of agreement?"

"They're going to pool their stock on a basis of three to one, with about thirty per cent. of the holding company left for Schryhart to sell or keep, as he wants to. He guarantees the interest. We did that for him—drove the game right into his bag."

"Nevertheless," replied Cowperwood, "he still has us to deal with. I propose now that we go into the city council and ask for a blanket franchise. It can be had. If we should get it, it will bring them to their knees. We will really be in a better position than they are with these smaller companies as feeders. We can unite with ourselves."

"That will take considerable money, won't it?"

"Not so much. We may never need to lay a pipe or build a plant. They will offer to sell out, buy, or combine before that. We can fix the terms. Leave it to me. You don't happen to know by any chance this Mr. McKenty, who has so much say in local affairs here—John J. McKenty?"

Cowperwood was referring to a man who was at once gambler, rumored owner or controller of a series of houses of prostitution, rumored maker of mayors and aldermen, rumored financial backer of many saloons and contracting companies—in short, the patron saint of the political and social underworld of Chicago, and who was naturally to be reckoned with in matters which related to the city and state legislative programme.

315

"I don't," said Addison; "but I can get you a letter. Why?"

"Don't trouble to ask me that now. Get me as strong an introduction as you can."

"I'll have one for you to-day some time," replied Addison, efficiently. "I'll send it over to you."

Cowperwood went out while Addison speculated as to this newest move. Trust Cowperwood to dig a pit into which the enemy might fall. He marveled sometimes at the man's resourcefulness. He never quarreled with the directness and incisiveness of Cowperwood's action.

The man, McKenty, whom Cowperwood had in mind in this rather disturbing hour, was as interesting and forceful an individual as one would care to meet anywhere, a typical figure of Chicago and the West at the time. He was a pleasant, smiling, bland, affable person, not unlike Cowperwood in magnetism and subtlety, but different by a degree of animal coarseness (not visible on the surface) which Cowperwood would scarcely have understood, and in a kind of temperamental pull drawing to him that vast pathetic life of the underworld in which his soul found its solution. There is a kind of nature, not artistic, not spiritual, in no way emotional, nor yet unduly philosophical, that is nevertheless a sphered content of life; not crystalline, perhaps, and yet not utterly dark—an agate temperament, cloudy and strange. As a three-year-old child McKenty had been brought from Ireland by his emigrant parents during a period of famine. He had been raised on the far South Side in a shanty which stood near a maze of railroad-tracks, and as a naked baby he had crawled on its earthen floor. His father had been promoted to a section boss after working for years as a day-laborer on the adjoining railroad, and John, junior, one of eight other children, had been sent out early to do many things—to be an errand-boy in a store, a messenger-boy for a telegraph company, an emergency sweep about a saloon, and finally a bartender. This last was his true beginning, for he was discovered by a keen-minded politician and encouraged to run for the state legislature and to study law. Even as a stripling what things had he not learned—robbery, ballot-box stuffing, the sale of votes, the appointive power of leaders, graft, nepotism, vice exploitation—all the things that go to make up (or did) the American world of politics and financial and social strife. There is a strong assumption in the upper walks of life that there is nothing to be learned at the bottom. If you could have looked into the capacious but balanced temperament of John J. McKenty you would have seen a strange wisdom there and stranger memories—whole worlds of brutalities, tendernesses, errors, immoralities suffered, endured, even rejoiced in—the hardy, eager life of the animal that has nothing but its perceptions, instincts, appetites to guide it. Yet the man had the air and the poise of a gentleman.

To-day, at forty-eight, McKenty was an exceedingly important personage. His roomy house on the West Side, at Harrison Street and Ashland Avenue, was visited at sundry times by financiers, business men, office-holders, priests, saloon-keepers—in short, the whole range and gamut of active, subtle, political life. From McKenty they could obtain that counsel, wisdom, surety, solution which all of them on occasion were anxious to have, and which in one deft way and another—often by no more than gratitude and an acknowledgment of his leadership—they were willing to pay for. To police captains and officers whose places he occasionally saved, when they should justly have been discharged; to mothers whose erring boys or girls he took out of prison and sent home again; to keepers of bawdy houses whom he protected from a too harsh invasion of the grafting propensities of the local police; to politicians and saloon-keepers who were in danger of being destroyed by public upheavals of one kind and another, he seemed, in hours of stress, when his smooth, genial, almost artistic face beamed on them, like a heaven-sent son of light, a kind of Western god, all-powerful, all-merciful, perfect. On the other hand, there were ingrates, uncompromising or pharasaical religionists and reformers, plotting, scheming rivals, who found him deadly to contend with. There were many henchmen—runners from an almost imperial throne—to do his bidding. He was simple in dress and taste, married and (apparently) very happy, a professing though virtually non-practising Catholic, a suave, genial Buddha-like man, powerful and enigmatic.

When Cowperwood and McKenty first met, it was on a spring evening at the latter's home. The windows of the large house were pleasantly open, though screened, and the curtains were blowing faintly in a light air. Along with a sense of the new green life everywhere came a breath of stock-yards.

On the presentation of Addison's letter and of another, secured through Van Sickle from a well-known political judge, Cowperwood had been invited to call. On his arrival he was offered a drink, a cigar, introduced to Mrs. McKenty—who, lacking an organized social life of any kind, was always pleased to meet these celebrities of the upper world, if only for a moment—and shown eventually into the library. Mrs. McKenty, as he might have observed if he had had the eye for it, was plump and fifty, a sort of superannuated Aileen, but still showing traces of a former hardy beauty, and concealing pretty well the evidences that she had once been a prostitute. It so happened that on this particular evening McKenty was in a most genial frame of mind. There were no immediate political troubles bothering him just now. It was early in May. Outside the trees were budding, the sparrows and robins were voicing their several moods. A delicious haze was in the air, and some early mosquitoes were reconnoitering the screens which protected the windows and doors. Cowperwood, in spite of his various troubles, was in a complacent state of mind himself. He liked life—even its very difficult complications—perhaps its complications best of all. Nature was beautiful, tender at times, but difficulties, plans, plots, schemes to unravel and make smooth—these things were what made existence worth while.

"Well now, Mr. Cowperwood," McKenty began, when they finally entered the cool, pleasant library, "what can I do for you?"

"Well, Mr. McKenty," said Cowperwood, choosing his words and bringing the finest resources of his temperament into play, "it isn't so much, and yet it is. I want a franchise from the Chicago city council, and I want you to help me get it if you will. I know you may say to me why not go to the councilmen direct. I would do that, except that there are certain other elements—individuals—who might come to you. It won't offend you, I know, when I say that I have always understood that you are a sort of clearing-house for political troubles in Chicago."

Mr. McKenty smiled. "That's flattering," he replied, dryly.

"Now, I am rather new myself to Chicago," went on Cowperwood, softly. "I have been here only a year or two. I come from Philadelphia. I have been interested as a fiscal agent and an investor in several gas companies that have been organized in Lake View, Hyde Park, and elsewhere outside the city limits, as you may possibly have seen by the papers lately. I am not their owner, in the sense that I have provided all or even a good part of the money invested in them. I am not even their manager, except in a very general way. I might better be called their promoter and guardian; but I am that for other people and myself."

317

Mr. McKenty nodded.

"Now, Mr. McKenty, it was not very long after I started out to get franchises to do business in Lake View and Hyde Park before I found myself confronted by the interests which control the three old city gas companies. They were very much opposed to our entering the field in Cook County anywhere, as you may imagine, although we were not really crowding in on their field. Since then they have fought me with lawsuits, injunctions, and charges of bribery and conspiracy."

"I know," put in Mr. McKenty. "I have heard something of it."

"Quite so," replied Cowperwood. "Because of their opposition I made them an offer to combine these three companies and the three new ones into one, take out a new charter, and give the city a uniform gas service. They would not do that—largely because I was an outsider, I think. Since then another person, Mr. Schryhart"—McKenty nodded—"who has never had anything to do with the gas business here, has stepped in and offered to combine them. His plan is to do exactly what I wanted to do; only his further proposition is, once he has the three old companies united, to invade this new gas field of ours and hold us up, or force us to sell by obtaining rival franchises in these outlying places. There is talk of combining these suburbs with Chicago, as you know, which would allow these three down-town franchises to become mutually operative with our own. This makes it essential for us to do one of several things, as you may see—either to sell out on the best terms we can now, or to continue the fight at a rather heavy expense without making any attempt to strike back, or to get into the city council and ask for a franchise to do business in the down-town section—a general blanket franchise to sell gas in Chicago alongside of the old companies—with the sole intention of protecting ourselves, as one of my officers is fond of saying," added Cowperwood, humorously.

McKenty smiled again. "I see," he said. "Isn't that a rather large order, though, Mr. Cowperwood, seeking a new franchise? Do you suppose the general public would agree that the city needs an extra gas company? It's true the old companies haven't been any too generous. My own gas isn't of the best." He smiled vaguely, prepared to listen further.

"Now, Mr. McKenty, I know that you are a practical man," went on Cowperwood, ignoring this interruption, "and so am I. I am not coming to you with any vague story concerning my troubles and expecting you to be interested as a matter of sympathy. I realize that to go into the city council of Chicago with a legitimate proposition is one thing. To get it passed and approved by the city authorities is another. I need advice and assistance, and I am not begging it. If I could get a general franchise, such as I have described, it would be worth a very great deal of money to me. It would help me to close up and realize on these new companies which are entirely sound and needed. It would help me to prevent the old companies from eating me up. As a matter of fact, I must have such a franchise to protect my interests and give me a running fighting chance. Now, I know that none of us are in politics or finance for our health. If I could get such a franchise it would be worth from one-fourth to one-half of all I personally would make out of it, providing my plan of combining these new companies with the old ones should go through—say, from three to four hundred thousand dollars." (Here again Cowperwood was not quite frank, but safe.) "It is needless to say to you that I can command ample capital. This franchise would do that. Briefly, I want to know if you won't give me your political support in this matter and join in with me on the basis that I propose? I will make it perfectly clear to you beforehand who my associates are. I will put all the data and details on the table before you so that you can see for yourself how things are. If you should find at any time that I have misrepresented anything you are at full liberty, of course, to withdraw. As I said before," he concluded, "I am not a beggar. I am not coming here to conceal any facts or to hide anything which might deceive you as to the worth of all this to us. I want you to know the facts. I want you to give me your aid on such terms as you think are fair and equitable. Really the only trouble with me in this situation is that I am not a silk stocking. If I were this gas war would have been adjusted long ago. These gentlemen who are so willing to reorganize through Mr. Schryhart are largely opposed to me because I am—comparatively—a stranger in Chicago and not in their set. If I were"—he moved his hand slightly—"I don't suppose I would be here this evening asking for your favor, although that does not say that I am not glad to be here, or that I would not be glad to work with you in any way that I might. Circumstances simply have not thrown me across your path before."

As he talked his eye fixed McKenty steadily, almost innocently; and the latter, following him clearly, felt all the while that he was listening to a strange, able, dark, and very forceful man. There was no beating about the bush here, no squeamishness of spirit, and yet there was subtlety—the kind McKenty liked. While he was amused by Cowperwood's casual reference to the silk stockings who were keeping him out, it appealed to him. He caught the point of view as well as the intention of it. Cowperwood represented a new and rather pleasing type of financier to him. Evidently, he was traveling in able company if one could believe the men who had introduced him so warmly. McKenty, as Cowperwood was well aware, had personally no interest in the old companies and also—though this he did not say—no particular sympathy with them. They were just remote financial corporations to him, paying political tribute on demand, expecting political favors in return. Every few weeks now they were in council, asking for one gas-main franchise after another (special privileges in certain streets), asking for better (more profitable) light-contracts, asking for dock privileges in the river, a lower tax rate, and so forth and so on. McKenty did not pay much attention to these things personally. He had a subordinate in council, a very powerful henchman by the name of Patrick Dowling, a meaty, vigorous Irishman and a true watch-dog of graft for the machine, who worked with the mayor, the city treasurer, the city tax receiver—in fact, all the officers of the current administration—and saw that such minor matters were properly equalized. Mr. McKenty had only met two or three of the officers of the South Side Gas Company, and that quite casually. He did not like them very well. The truth was that the old companies were officered by men who considered politicians of the McKenty and Dowling stripe as very evil men; if they paid them and did other such wicked things it was because they were forced to do so.

"Well," McKenty replied, lingering his thin gold watch-chain in a thoughtful manner, "that's an interesting scheme you have. Of course the old companies wouldn't like your asking for a rival franchise, but once you had it they couldn't object very well, could they?" He smiled. Mr. McKenty spoke with no suggestion of a brogue. "From one point of view it might be looked upon as bad business, but not entirely. They would be sure to make a great cry, though they haven't been any too kind to the public themselves. But if you offered to combine with them I see no objection. It's certain to be as good for them in the long run as it is for you. This merely permits you to make a better bargain."

"Exactly," said Cowperwood.

"And you have the means, you tell me, to lay mains in every part of the city, and fight with them for business if they won't give in?"

"I have the means," said Cowperwood, "or if I haven't I can get them."

Mr. McKenty looked at Mr. Cowperwood very solemnly. There was a kind of mutual sympathy, understanding, and admiration between the two men, but it was still heavily veiled by self-interest. To Mr. McKenty Cowperwood was interesting because he was one of the few business men he had met who were not ponderous, pharasaical, even hypocritical when they were dealing with him.

"Well, I'll tell you what I'll do, Mr. Cowperwood," he said, finally. "I'll take it all under consideration. Let me think it over until Monday, anyhow. There is more of an excuse now for the introduction of a general gas ordinance than there would be a little later—I can see that. Why don't you draw up your proposed franchise and let me see it? Then we might find out what some of the other gentlemen of the city council think."

Cowperwood almost smiled at the word "gentlemen."

"I have already done that," he said. "Here it is."

McKenty took it, surprised and yet pleased at this evidence of business proficiency. He liked a strong manipulator of this kind—the more since he was not one himself, and most of those that he did know were thin-blooded and squeamish.

"Let me take this," he said. "I'll see you next Monday again if you wish. Come Monday."

Cowperwood got up. "I thought I'd come and talk to you direct, Mr. McKenty," he said, "and now I'm glad that I did. You will find, if you will take the trouble to look into this matter, that it is just as I represent it. There is a very great deal of money here in one way and another, though it will take some little time to work it out."

Mr. McKenty saw the point. "Yes," he said, sweetly, "to be sure."

They looked into each other's eyes as they shook hands.

"I'm not sure but you haven't hit upon a very good idea here," concluded McKenty, sympathetically. "A very good idea, indeed. Come and see me again next Monday, or about that time, and I'll let you know what I think. Come any time you have anything else you want of me. I'll always be glad to see you. It's a fine night, isn't it?" he added, looking out as they neared the door. "A nice moon that!" he added. A sickle moon was in the sky. "Good night."

CHAPTER XIII

THE DIE IS CAST

The significance of this visit was not long in manifesting itself. At the top, in large affairs, life goes off into almost inexplicable tangles of personalities. Mr. McKenty, now that the matter had been called to his attention, was interested to learn about this gas situation from all sides—whether it might not be more profitable to deal with the Schryhart end of the argument, and so on. But his eventual conclusion was that Cowperwood's plan, as he had outlined it, was the most feasible for political purposes, largely because the Schryhart faction, not being in a position where they needed to ask the city council for anything at present, were so obtuse as to forget to make overtures of any kind to the bucaneering forces at the City Hall.

When Cowperwood next came to McKenty's house the latter was in a receptive frame of mind. "Well," he said, after a few genial preliminary remarks, "I've been learning what's going on. Your proposition is fair enough. Organize your company, and arrange your plan conditionally. Then introduce your ordinance, and we'll see what can be done." They went into a long, intimate discussion as to how the forthcoming stock should be divided, how it was to be held in escrow by a favorite bank of Mr. McKenty's until the terms of the agreement under the eventual affiliation with the old companies or the new union company should be fulfilled, and details of that sort. It was rather a complicated arrangement, not as satisfactory to Cowperwood as it might have been, but satisfactory in that it permitted him to win. It required the undivided services of General Van Sickle, Henry De Soto Sippens, Kent Barrows McKibben, and Alderman Dowling for some little time. But finally all was in readiness for the coup.

On a certain Monday night, therefore, following the Thursday on which, according to the rules of the city council, an ordinance of this character would have to be introduced, the plan, after being publicly broached but this very little while, was quickly considered by the city council and passed. There had been really no time for public discussion. This was just the thing, of course, that Cowperwood and McKenty were trying to avoid. On the day following the particular Thursday on which the ordinance had been broached in council as certain to be brought up for passage, Schryhart, through his lawyers and the officers of the old individual gas companies, had run to the newspapers and denounced the whole thing as plain robbery; but what were they to do? There was so little time for agitation. True the newspapers, obedient to this larger financial influence, began to talk of "fair play to the old companies," and the uselessness of two large rival companies in the field when one would serve as well. Still the public, instructed or urged by the McKenty agents to the contrary, were not prepared to believe it. They had not been so well treated by the old companies as to make any outcry on their behalf.

Standing outside the city council door, on the Monday evening when the bill was finally passed, Mr. Samuel Blackman, president of the South Side Gas Company, a little, wispy man with shoe-brush whiskers, declared emphatically:

"This is a scoundrelly piece of business. If the mayor signs that he should be impeached. There is not a vote in there to-night that has not been purchased—not one. This is a fine element of brigandage to introduce into Chicago; why, people who have worked years and years to build up a business are not safe!"

"It's true, every word of it," complained Mr. Jordan Jules, president of the North Side company, a short, stout man with a head like an egg lying lengthwise, a mere fringe of hair, and hard, blue eyes. He was with Mr. Hudson Baker, tall and ambling, who was president of the West Chicago company. All of these had come to protest.

"It's that scoundrel from Philadelphia. He's the cause of all our troubles. It's high time the respectable business element of Chicago realized just what sort of a man they have to deal with in him. He ought to be driven out of here. Look at his Philadelphia record. They sent him to the penitentiary down there, and they ought to do it here."

321

Mr. Baker, very recently the guest of Schryhart, and his henchman, too, was also properly chagrined. "The man is a charlatan," he protested to Blackman. "He doesn't play fair. It is plain that he doesn't belong in respectable society."

Nevertheless, and in spite of this, the ordinance was passed. It was a bitter lesson for Mr. Norman Schryhart, Mr. Norrie Simms, and all those who had unfortunately become involved. A committee composed of all three of the old companies visited the mayor; but the latter, a tool of McKenty, giving his future into the hands of the enemy, signed it just the same. Cowperwood had his franchise, and, groan as they might, it was now necessary, in the language of a later day, "to step up and see the captain." Only Schryhart felt personally that his score with Cowperwood was not settled. He would meet him on some other ground later. The next time he would try to fight fire with fire. But for the present, shrewd man that he was, he was prepared to compromise.

Thereafter, dissembling his chagrin as best he could, he kept on the lookout for Cowperwood at both of the clubs of which he was a member; but Cowperwood had avoided them during this period of excitement, and Mahomet would have to go to the mountain. So one drowsy June afternoon Mr. Schryhart called at Cowperwood's office. He had on a bright, new, steel-gray suit and a straw hat. From his pocket, according to the fashion of the time, protruded a neat, blue-bordered silk handkerchief, and his feet were immaculate in new, shining Oxford ties.

"I'm sailing for Europe in a few days, Mr. Cowperwood," he remarked, genially, "and I thought I'd drop round to see if you and I could reach some agreement in regard to this gas situation. The officers of the old companies naturally feel that they do not care to have a rival in the field, and I'm sure that you are not interested in carrying on a useless rate war that won't leave anybody any profit. I recall that you were willing to compromise on a half-and-half basis with me before, and I was wondering whether you were still of that mind."

"Sit down, sit down, Mr. Schryhart," remarked Cowperwood, cheerfully, waving the new-comer to a chair. "I'm pleased to see you again. No, I'm no more anxious for a rate war than you are. As a matter of fact, I hope to avoid it; but, as you see, things have changed somewhat since I saw you. The gentlemen who have organized and invested their money in this new city gas company are perfectly willing—rather anxious, in fact—to go on and establish a legitimate business. They feel all the confidence in the world that they can do this, and I agree with them. A compromise might be effected between the old and the new companies, but not on the basis on which I was willing to settle some time ago. A new company has been organized since then, stock issued, and a great deal of money expended." (This was not true.) "That stock will have to figure in any new agreement. I think a general union of all the companies is desirable, but it will have to be on a basis of one, two, three, or four shares—whatever is decided—at par for all stock involved."

Mr. Schryhart pulled a long face. "Don't you think that's rather steep?" he said, solemnly.

"Not at all, not at all!" replied Cowperwood. "You know these new expenditures were not undertaken voluntarily." (The irony of this did not escape Mr. Schryhart, but he said nothing.)

"I admit all that, but don't you think, since your shares are worth practically nothing at present, that you ought to be satisfied if they were accepted at par?"

"I can't see why," replied Cowperwood. "Our future prospects are splendid. There must be an even adjustment here or nothing. What I want to know is how much treasury stock you would expect to have in the safe for the promotion of this new organization after all the old stockholders have been satisfied?"

"Well, as I thought before, from thirty to forty per cent. of the total issue," replied Schryhart, still hopeful of a profitable adjustment. "I should think it could be worked on that basis."

"And who gets that?"

"Why, the organizer," said Schryhart, evasively. "Yourself, perhaps, and myself."

"And how would you divide it? Half and half, as before?"

"I should think that would be fair."

"It isn't enough," returned Cowperwood, incisively. "Since I talked to you last I have been compelled to shoulder obligations and make agreements which I did not anticipate then. The best I can do now is to accept three-fourths."

Schryhart straightened up determinedly and offensively. This was outrageous, he thought, impossible! The effrontery of it!

"It can never be done, Mr. Cowperwood," he replied, forcefully. "You are trying to unload too much worthless stock on the company as it is. The old companies' stock is selling right now, as you know, for from one-fifty to two-ten. Your stock is worth nothing. If you are to be given two or three for one for that, and three-fourths of the remainder in the treasury, I for one want nothing to do with the deal. You would be in control of the company, and it will be water-logged, at that. Talk about getting something for nothing! The best I would suggest to the stockholders of the old companies would be half and half. And I may say to you frankly, although you may not believe it, that the old companies will not join in with you in any scheme that gives you control. They are too much incensed. Feeling is running too high. It will mean a long, expensive fight, and they will never compromise. Now, if you have anything really reasonable to offer I would be glad to hear it. Otherwise I am afraid these negotiations are not going to come to anything."

"Share and share alike, and three-fourths of the remainder," repeated Cowperwood, grimly. "I do not want to control. If they want to raise the money and buy me out on that basis I am willing to sell. I want a decent return for investments I have made, and I am going to have it. I cannot speak for the others behind me, but as long as they deal through me that is what they will expect."

Mr. Schryhart went angrily away. He was exceedingly wroth. This proposition as Cowperwood now outlined it was bucaneering at its best. He proposed for himself to withdraw from the old companies if necessary, to close out his holdings and let the old companies deal with Cowperwood as best they could. So long as he had anything to do with it, Cowperwood should never gain control of the gas situation. Better to take him at his suggestion, raise the money and buy him out, even at an exorbitant figure. Then the old gas companies could go along and do business in their old-fashioned way without being disturbed. This bucaneer! This upstart! What a shrewd, quick, forceful move he had made! It irritated Mr. Schryhart greatly.

The end of all this was a compromise in which Cowperwood accepted one-half of the surplus stock of the new general issue, and two for one of every share of stock for which his new companies had been organized, at the same time selling out to the old companies—clearing out completely. It was a most profitable deal, and he was enabled to provide handsomely not only for Mr. McKenty and Addison, but for all the others connected with him. It was a splendid coup, as McKenty and Addison assured him. Having now done so much, he began to turn his eyes elsewhere for other fields to conquer.

But this victory in one direction brought with it corresponding reverses in another: the social future of Cowperwood and Aileen was now in great jeopardy. Schryhart, who was a force socially, having met with defeat at the hands of Cowperwood, was now bitterly opposed to him. Norrie Simms naturally sided with his old associates. But the worst blow came through Mrs. Anson Merrill. Shortly after the housewarming, and when the gas argument and the conspiracy charges were rising to their heights, she had been to New York and had there chanced to encounter an old acquaintance of hers, Mrs. Martyn Walker, of Philadelphia, one of the circle which Cowperwood once upon a time had been vainly ambitious to enter. Mrs. Merrill, aware of the interest the Cowperwoods had aroused in Mrs. Simms and others, welcomed the opportunity to find out something definite.

"By the way, did you ever chance to hear of a Frank Algernon Cowperwood or his wife in Philadelphia?" she inquired of Mrs. Walker.

"Why, my dear Nellie," replied her friend, nonplussed that a woman so smart as Mrs. Merrill should even refer to them, "have those people established themselves in Chicago? His career in Philadelphia was, to say the least, spectacular. He was connected with a city treasurer there who stole five hundred thousand dollars, and they both went to the penitentiary. That wasn't the worst of it! He became intimate with some young girl—a Miss Butler, the sister of Owen Butler, by the way, who is now such a power down there, and—" She merely lifted her eyes. "While he was in the penitentiary her father died and the family broke up. I even heard it rumored that the old gentleman killed himself." (She was referring to Aileen's father, Edward Malia Butler.) "When he came out of the penitentiary Cowperwood disappeared, and I did hear some one say that he had gone West, and divorced his wife and married again. His first wife is still living in Philadelphia somewhere with his two children."

Mrs. Merrill was properly astonished, but she did not show it. "Quite an interesting story, isn't it?" she commented, distantly, thinking how easy it would be to adjust the Cowperwood situation, and how pleased she was that she had never shown any interest in them. "Did you ever see her—his new wife?"

"I think so, but I forget where. I believe she used to ride and drive a great deal in Philadelphia."

"Did she have red hair?"

"Oh yes. She was a very striking blonde."

"I fancy it must be the same person. They have been in the papers recently in Chicago. I wanted to be sure."

Mrs. Merrill was meditating some fine comments to be made in the future.

324

"I suppose now they're trying to get into Chicago society?" Mrs. Walker smiled condescendingly and contemptuously—as much at Chicago society as at the Cowperwoods.

"It's possible that they might attempt something like that in the East and succeed—I'm sure I don't know," replied Mrs. Merrill, caustically, resenting the slur, "but attempting and achieving are quite different things in Chicago."

The answer was sufficient. It ended the discussion. When next Mrs. Simms was rash enough to mention the Cowperwoods, or, rather, the peculiar publicity in connection with him, her future viewpoint was definitely fixed for her.

"If you take my advice," commented Mrs. Merrill, finally, "the less you have to do with these friends of yours the better. I know all about them. You might have seen that from the first. They can never be accepted."

Mrs. Merrill did not trouble to explain why, but Mrs. Simms through her husband soon learned the whole truth, and she was righteously indignant and even terrified. Who was to blame for this sort of thing, anyhow? she thought. Who had introduced them? The Addisons, of course. But the Addisons were socially unassailable, if not all-powerful, and so the best had to be made of that. But the Cowperwoods could be dropped from the lists of herself and her friends instantly, and that was now done. A sudden slump in their social significance began to manifest itself, though not so swiftly but what for the time being it was slightly deceptive.

The first evidence of change which Aileen observed was when the customary cards and invitations for receptions and the like, which had come to them quite freely of late, began to decline sharply in number, and when the guests to her own Wednesday afternoons, which rather prematurely she had ventured to establish, became a mere negligible handful. At first she could not understand this, not being willing to believe that, following so soon upon her apparent triumph as a hostess in her own home, there could be so marked a decline in her local importance. Of a possible seventy-five or fifty who might have called or left cards, within three weeks after the housewarming only twenty responded. A week later it had declined to ten, and within five weeks, all told, there was scarcely a caller. It is true that a very few of the unimportant—those who had looked to her for influence and the self-protecting Taylor Lord and Kent McKibben, who were commercially obligated to Cowperwood—were still faithful, but they were really worse than nothing. Aileen was beside herself with disappointment, opposition, chagrin, shame. There are many natures, rhinoceros-bided and iron-souled, who can endure almost any rebuff in the hope of eventual victory, who are almost too thick-skinned to suffer, but hers was not one of these. Already, in spite of her original daring in regard to the opinion of society and the rights of the former Mrs. Cowperwood, she was sensitive on the score of her future and what her past might mean to her. Really her original actions could be attributed to her youthful passion and the powerful sex magnetism of Cowperwood. Under more fortunate circumstances she would have married safely enough and without the scandal which followed. As it was now, her social future here needed to end satisfactorily in order to justify herself to herself, and, she thought, to him.

"You may put the sandwiches in the ice-box," she said to Louis, the butler, after one of the earliest of the "at home" failures, referring to the undue supply of pink-and-blue-ribboned titbits which, uneaten, honored some fine Sevres with their presence. "Send the flowers to the hospital. The servants may drink the claret cup and lemonade. Keep some of the cakes fresh for dinner."

The butler nodded his head. "Yes, Madame," he said. Then, by way of pouring oil on what appeared to him to be a troubled situation, he added: "Eet's a rough day. I suppose zat has somepsing to do weeth it."

Aileen was aflame in a moment. She was about to exclaim: "Mind your business!" but changed her mind. "Yes, I presume so," was her answer, as she ascended to her room. If a single poor "at home" was to be commented on by servants, things were coming to a pretty pass. She waited until the next week to see whether this was the weather or a real change in public sentiment. It was worse than the one before. The singers she had engaged had to be dismissed without performing the service for which they had come. Kent McKibben and Taylor Lord, very well aware of the rumors now flying about, called, but in a remote and troubled spirit. Aileen saw that, too. An affair of this kind, with only these two and Mrs. Webster Israels and Mrs. Henry Huddlestone calling, was a sad indication of something wrong. She had to plead illness and excuse herself. The third week, fearing a worse defeat than before, Aileen pretended to be ill. She would see how many cards were left. There were just three. That was the end. She realized that her "at homes" were a notable failure.

At the same time Cowperwood was not to be spared his share in the distrust and social opposition which was now rampant.

His first inkling of the true state of affairs came in connection with a dinner which, on the strength of an old invitation, they unfortunately attended at a time when Aileen was still uncertain. It had been originally arranged by the Sunderland Sledds, who were not so much socially, and who at the time it occurred were as yet unaware of the ugly gossip going about, or at least of society's new attitude toward the Cowperwoods. At this time it was understood by nearly all—the Simms, Candas, Cottons, and Kingslands—that a great mistake had been made, and that the Cowperwoods were by no means admissible.

To this particular dinner a number of people, whom the latter knew, had been invited. Uniformly all, when they learned or recalled that the Cowperwoods were expected, sent eleventh-hour regrets—"so sorry." Outside the Sledds there was only one other couple— the Stanislau Hoecksemas, for whom the Cowperwoods did not particularly care. It was a dull evening. Aileen complained of a headache, and they went home.

Very shortly afterward, at a reception given by their neighbors, the Haatstaedts, to which they had long since been invited, there was an evident shyness in regard to them, quite new in its aspect, although the hosts themselves were still friendly enough. Previous to this, when strangers of prominence had been present at an affair of this kind they were glad to be brought over to the Cowperwoods, who were always conspicuous because of Aileen's beauty. On this day, for no reason obvious to Aileen or Cowperwood (although both suspected), introductions were almost uniformly refused. There were a number who knew them, and who talked casually, but the general tendency on the part of all was to steer clear of them. Cowperwood sensed the difficulty at once. "I think we'd better leave early," he remarked to Aileen, after a little while. "This isn't very interesting."

They returned to their own home, and Cowperwood to avoid discussion went down-town. He did not care to say what he thought of this as yet.

It was previous to a reception given by the Union League that the first real blow was struck at him personally, and that in a roundabout way. Addison, talking to him at the Lake National Bank one morning, had said quite confidentially, and out of a clear sky:

"I want to tell you something, Cowperwood. You know by now something about Chicago society. You also know where I stand in regard to some things you told me about your past when I first met you. Well, there's a lot of talk going around about you now in regard to all that, and these two clubs to which you and I belong are filled with a lot of two-faced, double-breasted hypocrites who've been stirred up by this talk of conspiracy in the papers. There are four or five stockholders of the old companies who are members, and they are trying to drive you out. They've looked up that story you told me, and they're talking about filing charges with the house committees at both places. Now, nothing can come of it in either case—they've been talking to me; but when this next reception comes along you'll know what to do. They'll have to extend you an invitation; but they won't mean it." (Cowperwood understood.) "This whole thing is certain to blow over, in my judgment; it will if I have anything to do with it; but for the present—"

He stared at Cowperwood in a friendly way.

The latter smiled. "I expected something like this, Judah, to tell you the truth," he said, easily. "I've expected it all along. You needn't worry about me. I know all about this. I've seen which way the wind is blowing, and I know how to trim my sails."

Addison reached out and took his hand. "But don't resign, whatever you do," he said, cautiously. "That would be a confession of weakness, and they don't expect you to. I wouldn't want you to. Stand your ground. This whole thing will blow over. They're jealous, I think."

"I never intended to," replied Cowperwood. "There's no legitimate charge against me. I know it will all blow over if I'm given time enough." Nevertheless he was chagrined to think that he should be subjected to such a conversation as this with any one.

Similarly in other ways "society"—so called—was quite able to enforce its mandates and conclusions.

The one thing that Cowperwood most resented, when he learned of it much later, was a snub direct given to Aileen at the door of the Norrie Simmses'; she called there only to be told that Mrs. Simms was not at home, although the carriages of others were in the street. A few days afterward Aileen, much to his regret and astonishment—for he did not then know the cause—actually became ill.

If it had not been for Cowperwood's eventual financial triumph over all opposition—the complete routing of the enemy—in the struggle for control in the gas situation—the situation would have been hard, indeed. As it was, Aileen suffered bitterly; she felt that the slight was principally directed at her, and would remain in force. In the privacy of their own home they were compelled eventually to admit, the one to the other, that their house of cards, resplendent and forceful looking as it was, had fallen to the ground. Personal confidences between people so closely united are really the most trying of all. Human souls are constantly trying to find each other, and rarely succeeding.

"You know," he finally said to her once, when he came in rather unexpectedly and found her sick in bed, her eyes wet, and her maid dismissed for the day, "I understand what this is

327

all about. To tell you the truth, Aileen, I rather expected it. We have been going too fast, you and I. We have been pushing this matter too hard. Now, I don't like to see you taking it this way, dear. This battle isn't lost. Why, I thought you had more courage than this. Let me tell you something which you don't seem to remember. Money will solve all this sometime. I'm winning in this fight right now, and I'll win in others. They are coming to me. Why, dearie, you oughtn't to despair. You're too young. I never do. You'll win yet. We can adjust this matter right here in Chicago, and when we do we will pay up a lot of scores at the same time. We're rich, and we're going to be richer. That will settle it. Now put on a good face and look pleased; there are plenty of things to live for in this world besides society. Get up now and dress, and we'll go for a drive and dinner down-town. You have me yet. Isn't that something?"

"Oh yes," sighed Aileen, heavily; but she sank back again. She put her arms about his neck and cried, as much out of joy over the consolation he offered as over the loss she had endured. "It was as much for you as for me," she sighed.

"I know that," he soothed; "but don't worry about it now. You will come out all right. We both will. Come, get up." Nevertheless, he was sorry to see her yield so weakly. It did not please him. He resolved some day to have a grim adjustment with society on this score. Meanwhile Aileen was recovering her spirits. She was ashamed of her weakness when she saw how forcefully he faced it all.

"Oh, Frank," she exclaimed, finally, "you're always so wonderful. You're such a darling."

"Never mind," he said, cheerfully. "If we don't win this game here in Chicago, we will somewhere."

He was thinking of the brilliant manner in which he had adjusted his affairs with the old gas companies and Mr. Schryhart, and how thoroughly he would handle some other matters when the time came.

CHAPTER XIV

UNDERCURRENTS

It was during the year that followed their social repudiation, and the next and the next, that Cowperwood achieved a keen realization of what it would mean to spend the rest of his days in social isolation, or at least confined in his sources of entertainment to a circle or element which constantly reminded him of the fact that he was not identified with the best, or, at least, not the most significant, however dull that might be. When he had first attempted to introduce Aileen into society it was his idea that, however tame they might chance to find it to begin with, they themselves, once admitted, could make it into something very interesting and even brilliant. Since the time the Cowperwoods had been repudiated, however, they had found it necessary, if they wished any social diversion at all, to fall back upon such various minor elements as they could scrape an acquaintance with— passing actors and actresses, to whom occasionally they could give a dinner; artists and singers whom they could invite to the house upon gaining an introduction; and, of course, a number of the socially unimportant, such as the Haatstaedts, Hoecksemas, Videras, Baileys, and others still friendly and willing to come in a casual way. Cowperwood found it interesting from time to time to invite a business friend, a lover of pictures, or some young artist to the house to dinner or for the evening, and on these occasions Aileen was always present. The Addisons called or invited them occasionally. But it was a dull game, the more so since their complete defeat was thus all the more plainly indicated.

This defeat, as Cowperwood kept reflecting, was really not his fault at all. He had been getting along well enough personally. If Aileen had only been a somewhat different type of woman! Nevertheless, he was in no way prepared to desert or reproach her. She had clung to him through his stormy prison days. She had encouraged him when he needed encouragement. He would stand by her and see what could be done a little later; but this ostracism was a rather dreary thing to endure. Besides, personally, he appeared to be becoming more and more interesting to men and to women. The men friends he had made he retained—Addison, Bailey, Videra, McKibben, Rambaud, and others. There were women in society, a number of them, who regretted his disappearance if not that of Aileen. Occasionally the experiment would be tried of inviting him without his wife. At first he refused invariably; later he went alone occasionally to a dinner-party without her knowledge.

It was during this interregnum that Cowperwood for the first time clearly began to get the idea that there was a marked difference between him and Aileen intellectually and spiritually; and that while he might be in accord with her in many ways—emotionally, physically, idyllicly—there were, nevertheless, many things which he could do alone which she could not do—heights to which he could rise where she could not possibly follow. Chicago society might be a negligible quantity, but he was now to contrast her sharply with the best of what the Old World had to offer in the matter of femininity, for following their social expulsion in Chicago and his financial victory, he once more decided to go abroad. In Rome, at the Japanese and Brazilian embassies (where, because of his wealth, he gained introduction), and at the newly established Italian Court, he encountered at a distance charming social figures of considerable significance—Italian countesses, English ladies of high degree, talented American women of strong artistic and social proclivities. As a rule they were quick to recognize the charm of his manner, the incisiveness and grip of his mind, and to estimate at all its worth the high individuality of his soul; but he could also always see that Aileen was not so acceptable. She was too rich in her entourage, too showy. Her glowing health and beauty was a species of affront to the paler, more sublimated souls of many who were not in themselves unattractive.

"Isn't that the typical American for you," he heard a woman remark, at one of those large, very general court receptions to which so many are freely admitted, and to which Aileen had been determined to go. He was standing aside talking to an acquaintance he had made—an English-speaking Greek banker stopping at the Grand Hotel—while Aileen promenaded with the banker's wife. The speaker was an Englishwoman. "So gaudy, so self-conscious, and so naive!"

Cowperwood turned to look. It was Aileen, and the lady speaking was undoubtedly well bred, thoughtful, good-looking. He had to admit that much that she said was true, but how were you to gage a woman like Aileen, anyhow? She was not reprehensible in any way—just a full-blooded animal glowing with a love of life. She was attractive to him. It was too bad that people of obviously more conservative tendencies were so opposed to her. Why could they not see what he saw—a kind of childish enthusiasm for luxury and show which sprang, perhaps, from the fact that in her youth she had not enjoyed the social opportunities which she needed and longed for. He felt sorry for her. At the same time he was inclined to feel that perhaps now another type of woman would be better for him socially. If he had a harder type, one with keener artistic perceptions and a penchant for just the right social touch or note, how much better he would do! He came home bringing a Perugino, brilliant examples of Luini, Previtali, and Pinturrichio (this last a portrait of Caesar Borgia), which he picked up in Italy, to say nothing of two red African vases of great size that he found in Cairo, a tall gilt Louis Fifteenth standard of carved wood that he discovered in Rome, two ornate candelabra from Venice for his walls, and a pair of Italian torcheras from Naples to decorate the corners of his library. It was thus by degrees that his art collection was growing.

At the same time it should be said, in the matter of women and the sex question, his judgment and views had begun to change tremendously. When he had first met Aileen he had many keen intuitions regarding life and sex, and above all clear faith that he had a right to do as he pleased. Since he had been out of prison and once more on his upward way there had been many a stray glance cast in his direction; he had so often had it clearly forced upon him that he was fascinating to women. Although he had only so recently acquired Aileen legally, yet she was years old to him as a mistress, and the first engrossing—it had been almost all-engrossing—enthusiasm was over. He loved her not only for her beauty, but for her faithful enthusiasm; but the power of others to provoke in him a momentary interest, and passion even, was something which he did not pretend to understand, explain, or moralize about. So it was and so he was. He did not want to hurt Aileen's feelings by letting her know that his impulses thus wantonly strayed to others, but so it was.

Not long after he had returned from the European trip he stopped one afternoon in the one exclusive drygoods store in State Street to purchase a tie. As he was entering a woman crossed the aisle before him, from one counter to another—a type of woman which he was coming to admire, but only from a rather distant point of view, seeing them going here and there in the world. She was a dashing type, essentially smart and trig, with a neat figure, dark hair and eyes, an olive skin, small mouth, quaint nose—all in all quite a figure for Chicago at the time. She had, furthermore, a curious look of current wisdom in her eyes, an air of saucy insolence which aroused Cowperwood's sense of mastery, his desire to dominate. To the look of provocation and defiance which she flung him for the fraction of a second he returned a curiously leonine glare which went over her like a dash of cold water. It was not a hard look, however, merely urgent and full of meaning. She was the vagrom-minded wife of a prosperous lawyer who was absorbed in his business and in himself. She pretended indifference for a moment after the first glance, but paused a little way off as if to examine some laces. Cowperwood looked after her to catch a second fleeting, attracted look. He was on his way to several engagements which he did not wish to break, but he took out a note-book, wrote on a slip of paper the name of a hotel, and underneath: "Parlor, second floor, Tuesday, 1 P.M." Passing by where she stood, he put it into her gloved hand, which was hanging by her side. The fingers closed over it automatically. She had noted his action. On the day and hour suggested she was there, although he had given no name. That liaison, while delightful to him, was of no great duration. The lady was interesting, but too fanciful.

Similarly, at the Henry Huddlestones', one of their neighbors at the first Michigan Avenue house they occupied, he encountered one evening at a small dinner-party a girl of twenty-three who interested him greatly—for the moment. Her name was not very attractive—Ella F. Hubby, as he eventually learned—but she was not unpleasing. Her principal charm was a laughing, hoydenish countenance and roguish eyes. She was the daughter of a well-to-do commission merchant in South Water Street. That her interest should have been aroused by that of Cowperwood in her was natural enough. She was young, foolish, impressionable, easily struck by the glitter of a reputation, and Mrs. Huddlestone had spoken highly of Cowperwood and his wife and the great things he was doing or was going to do. When Ella saw him, and saw that he was still young-looking, with the love of beauty in his eyes and a force of presence which was not at all hard where she was concerned, she was charmed; and when Aileen was not looking her glance kept constantly wandering to his with a laughing signification of friendship and admiration. It was the most natural thing in the world for him to say to her, when they had adjourned to the drawing-room, that if she were in the neighborhood of his office some day she might care to look in on him. The look he gave her was one of keen understanding, and brought a look of its own kind, warm and flushing, in return. She came, and there began a rather short liaison. It was interesting but not brilliant. The girl did not have sufficient temperament to bind him beyond a period of rather idle investigation.

There was still, for a little while, another woman, whom he had known—a Mrs. Josephine Ledwell, a smart widow, who came primarily to gamble on the Board of Trade, but who began to see at once, on introduction, the charm of a flirtation with Cowperwood. She was a woman not unlike Aileen in type, a little older, not so good-looking, and of a harder, more subtle commercial type of mind. She rather interested Cowperwood because she was so trig, self-sufficient, and careful. She did her best to lure him on to a liaison with her, which finally resulted, her apartment on the North Side being the center of this relationship. It lasted perhaps six weeks. Through it all he was quite satisfied that he did not like her so very well. Any one who associated with him had Aileen's present attractiveness to contend with, as well as the original charm of his first wife. It was no easy matter.

It was during this period of social dullness, however, which somewhat resembled, though it did not exactly parallel his first years with his first wife, that Cowperwood finally met a woman who was destined to leave a marked impression on his life. He could not soon forget her. Her name was Rita Sohlberg. She was the wife of Harold Sohlberg, a Danish violinist who was then living in Chicago, a very young man; but she was not a Dane, and he was by no means a remarkable violinist, though he had unquestionably the musical temperament.

You have perhaps seen the would-be's, the nearly's, the pretenders in every field— interesting people all—devoted with a kind of mad enthusiasm to the thing they wish to do. They manifest in some ways all the externals or earmarks of their professional traditions, and yet are as sounding brass and tinkling cymbals. You would have had to know Harold Sohlberg only a little while to appreciate that he belonged to this order of artists. He had a wild, stormy, November eye, a wealth of loose, brownish-black hair combed upward from the temples, with one lock straggling Napoleonically down toward the eyes; cheeks that had almost a babyish tint to them; lips much too rich, red, and sensuous; a nose that was fine and large and full, but only faintly aquiline; and eyebrows and mustache that somehow seemed to flare quite like his errant and foolish soul. He had been sent away from Denmark (Copenhagen) because he had been a never-do-well up to twenty-five and because he was constantly falling in love with women who would not have anything to do with him. Here in Chicago as a teacher, with his small pension of forty dollars a month sent him by his mother, he had gained a few pupils, and by practising a kind of erratic economy, which kept him well dressed or hungry by turns, he had managed to make an interesting showing and pull himself through. He was only twenty-eight at the time he met Rita Greenough, of Wichita, Kansas, and at the time they met Cowperwood Harold was thirty-four and she twenty-seven.

She had been a student at the Chicago Fine Arts School, and at various student affairs had encountered Harold when he seemed to play divinely, and when life was all romance and art. Given the spring, the sunshine on the lake, white sails of ships, a few walks and talks on pensive afternoons when the city swam in a golden haze, and the thing was done. There was a sudden Saturday afternoon marriage, a runaway day to Milwaukee, a return to the studio now to be fitted out for two, and then kisses, kisses, kisses until love was satisfied or eased.

But life cannot exist on that diet alone, and so by degrees the difficulties had begun to manifest themselves. Fortunately, the latter were not allied with sharp financial want. Rita was not poor. Her father conducted a small but profitable grain elevator at Wichita, and, after her sudden marriage, decided to continue her allowance, though this whole idea of art and music in its upper reaches was to him a strange, far-off, uncertain thing. A thin, meticulous, genial person interested in small trade opportunities, and exactly suited to the rather sparse social life of Wichita, he found Harold as curious as a bomb, and preferred to handle him gingerly. Gradually, however, being a very human if simple person, he came to be very proud of it—boasted in Wichita of Rita and her artist husband, invited them home to astound the neighbors during the summer-time, and the fall brought his almost farmer-like wife on to see them and to enjoy trips, sight-seeing, studio teas. It was amusing, typically American, naive, almost impossible from many points of view.

Rita Sohlberg was of the semi-phlegmatic type, soft, full-blooded, with a body that was going to be fat at forty, but which at present was deliciously alluring. Having soft, silky, light-brown hair, the color of light dust, and moist gray-blue eyes, with a fair skin and even, white teeth, she was flatteringly self-conscious of her charms. She pretended in a gay, childlike way to be unconscious of the thrill she sent through many susceptible males, and yet she knew well enough all the while what she was doing and how she was doing it; it pleased her so to do. She was conscious of the wonder of her smooth, soft arms and neck, the fullness and seductiveness of her body, the grace and perfection of her clothing, or, at least, the individuality and taste which she made them indicate. She could take an old straw-hat form, a ribbon, a feather, or a rose, and with an innate artistry of feeling turn it into a bit of millinery which somehow was just the effective thing for her. She chose naive combinations of white and blues, pinks and white, browns and pale yellows, which somehow suggested her own soul, and topped them with great sashes of silky brown (or even red) ribbon tied about her waist, and large, soft-brimmed, face-haloing hats. She was a graceful dancer, could sing a little, could play feelingly—sometimes brilliantly—and could draw. Her art was a makeshift, however; she was no artist. The most significant thing about her was her moods and her thoughts, which were uncertain, casual, anarchic. Rita Sohlberg, from the conventional point of view, was a dangerous person, and yet from her own point of view at this time she was not so at all—just dreamy and sweet.

A part of the peculiarity of her state was that Sohlberg had begun to disappoint Rita—sorely. Truth to tell, he was suffering from that most terrible of all maladies, uncertainty of soul and inability to truly find himself. At times he was not sure whether he was cut out to be a great violinist or a great composer, or merely a great teacher, which last he was never willing really to admit. "I am an arteest," he was fond of saying. "Ho, how I suffer from my temperament!" And again: "These dogs! These cows! These pigs!" This of other people. The quality of his playing was exceedingly erratic, even though at times it attained to a kind of subtlety, tenderness, awareness, and charm which brought him some attention. As a rule, however, it reflected the chaotic state of his own brain. He would play violently, feverishly, with a wild passionateness of gesture which robbed him of all ability to control his own technic.

"Oh, Harold!" Rita used to exclaim at first, ecstatically. Later she was not so sure.

Life and character must really get somewhere to be admirable, and Harold, really and truly, did not seem to be getting anywhere. He taught, stormed, dreamed, wept; but he ate his three meals a day, Rita noticed, and he took an excited interest at times in other women. To be the be-all and end-all of some one man's life was the least that Rita could conceive or concede as the worth of her personality, and so, as the years went on and Harold began to be unfaithful, first in moods, transports, then in deeds, her mood became dangerous. She counted them up—a girl music pupil, then an art student, then the wife of a banker at whose house Harold played socially. There followed strange, sullen moods on the part of Rita, visits home, groveling repentances on the part of Harold, tears, violent, passionate reunions, and then the same thing over again. What would you?

Rita was not jealous of Harold any more; she had lost faith in his ability as a musician. But she was disappointed that her charms were not sufficient to blind him to all others. That was the fly in the ointment. It was an affront to her beauty, and she was still beautiful. She was unctuously full-bodied, not quite so tall as Aileen, not really as large, but rounder and plumper, softer and more seductive. Physically she was not well set up, so vigorous; but her eyes and mouth and the roving character of her mind held a strange lure. Mentally she was much more aware than Aileen, much more precise in her knowledge of art, music, literature, and current events; and in the field of romance she was much more vague and alluring. She knew many things about flowers, precious stones, insects, birds, characters in fiction, and poetic prose and verse generally.

At the time the Cowperwoods first met the Sohlbergs the latter still had their studio in the New Arts Building, and all was seemingly as serene as a May morning, only Harold was not getting along very well. He was drifting. The meeting was at a tea given by the Haatstaedts, with whom the Cowperwoods were still friendly, and Harold played. Aileen, who was there alone, seeing a chance to brighten her own life a little, invited the Sohlbergs, who seemed rather above the average, to her house to a musical evening. They came.

On this occasion Cowperwood took one look at Sohlberg and placed him exactly. "An erratic, emotional temperament," he thought. "Probably not able to place himself for want of consistency and application." But he liked him after a fashion. Sohlberg was interesting as an artistic type or figure—quite like a character in a Japanese print might be. He greeted him pleasantly.

"And Mrs. Sohlberg, I suppose," he remarked, feelingly, catching a quick suggestion of the rhythm and sufficiency and naive taste that went with her. She was in simple white and blue—small blue ribbons threaded above lacy flounces in the skin. Her arms and throat were deliciously soft and bare. Her eyes were quick, and yet soft and babyish—petted eyes.

"You know," she said to him, with a peculiar rounded formation of the mouth, which was a characteristic of her when she talked—a pretty, pouty mouth, "I thought we would never get heah at all. There was a fire"—she pronounced it fy-yah—"at Twelfth Street" (the Twelfth was Twalfth in her mouth) "and the engines were all about there. Oh, such sparks and smoke! And the flames coming out of the windows! The flames were a very dark red—almost orange and black. They're pretty when they're that way—don't you think so?"

Cowperwood was charmed. "Indeed, I do," he said, genially, using a kind of superior and yet sympathetic air which he could easily assume on occasion. He felt as though Mrs. Sohlberg might be a charming daughter to him—she was so cuddling and shy—and yet he could see that she was definite and individual. Her arms and face, he told himself, were lovely. Mrs. Sohlberg only saw before her a smart, cold, exact man—capable, very, she presumed—with brilliant, incisive eyes. How different from Harold, she thought, who would never be anything much—not even famous.

"I'm so glad you brought your violin," Aileen was saying to Harold, who was in another corner. "I've been looking forward to your coming to play for us."

"Very nize ov you, I'm sure," Sohlberg replied, with his sweety drawl. "Such a nize plaze you have here—all these loafly books, and jade, and glass."

He had an unctuous, yielding way which was charming, Aileen thought. He should have a strong, rich woman to take care of him. He was like a stormy, erratic boy.

After refreshments were served Sohlberg played. Cowperwood was interested by his standing figure—his eyes, his hair—but he was much more interested in Mrs. Sohlberg, to whom his look constantly strayed. He watched her hands on the keys, her fingers, the dimples at her elbows. What an adorable mouth, he thought, and what light, fluffy hair! But, more than that, there was a mood that invested it all—a bit of tinted color of the mind that reached him and made him sympathetic and even passionate toward her. She was the kind of woman he would like. She was somewhat like Aileen when she was six years younger (Aileen was now thirty-three, and Mrs. Sohlberg twenty-seven), only Aileen had always been more robust, more vigorous, less nebulous. Mrs. Sohlberg (he finally thought it out for himself) was like the rich tinted interior of a South Sea oyster-shell—warm, colorful, delicate. But there was something firm there, too. Nowhere in society had he seen any one like her. She was rapt, sensuous, beautiful. He kept his eyes on her until finally she became aware that he was gazing at her, and then she looked back at him in an arch, smiling way, fixing her mouth in a potent line. Cowperwood was captivated. Was she vulnerable? was his one thought. Did that faint smile mean anything more than mere social complaisance? Probably not, but could not a temperament so rich and full be awakened to feeling by his own? When she was through playing he took occasion to say: "Wouldn't you like to stroll into the gallery? Are you fond of pictures?" He gave her his arm.

"Now, you know," said Mrs. Sohlberg, quaintly—very captivatingly, he thought, because she was so pretty—"at one time I thought I was going to be a great artist. Isn't that funny! I sent my father one of my drawings inscribed 'to whom I owe it all.' You would have to see the drawing to see how funny that is."

She laughed softly.

Cowperwood responded with a refreshed interest in life. Her laugh was as grateful to him as a summer wind. "See," he said, gently, as they entered the room aglow with the soft light produced by guttered jets, "here is a Luini bought last winter." It was "The Mystic Marriage of St. Catharine." He paused while she surveyed the rapt expression of the attenuated saint. "And here," he went on, "is my greatest find so far." They were before the crafty countenance of Caesar Borgia painted by Pinturrichio.

"What a strange face!" commented Mrs. Sohlberg, naively. "I didn't know any one had ever painted him. He looks somewhat like an artist himself, doesn't he?" She had never read the involved and quite Satanic history of this man, and only knew the rumor of his crimes and machinations.

334

"He was, in his way," smiled Cowperwood, who had had an outline of his life, and that of his father, Pope Alexander VI., furnished him at the time of the purchase. Only so recently had his interest in Caesar Borgia begun. Mrs. Sohlberg scarcely gathered the sly humor of it.

"Oh yes, and here is Mrs. Cowperwood," she commented, turning to the painting by Van Beers. "It's high in key, isn't it?" she said, loftily, but with an innocent loftiness that appealed to him. He liked spirit and some presumption in a woman. "What brilliant colors! I like the idea of the garden and the clouds."

She stepped back, and Cowperwood, interested only in her, surveyed the line of her back and the profile of her face. Such co-ordinated perfection of line and color!

"Where every motion weaves and sings," he might have commented. Instead he said: "That was in Brussels. The clouds were an afterthought, and that vase on the wall, too."

"It's very good, I think," commented Mrs. Sohlberg, and moved away.

"How do you like this Israels?" he asked. It was the painting called "The Frugal Meal."

"I like it," she said, "and also your Bastien Le-Page," referring to "The Forge." "But I think your old masters are much more interesting. If you get many more you ought to put them together in a room. Don't you think so? I don't care for your Gerome very much." She had a cute drawl which he considered infinitely alluring.

"Why not?" asked Cowperwood.

"Oh, it's rather artificial; don't you think so? I like the color, but the women's bodies are too perfect, I should say. It's very pretty, though."

He had little faith in the ability of women aside from their value as objects of art; and yet now and then, as in this instance, they revealed a sweet insight which sharpened his own. Aileen, he reflected, would not be capable of making a remark such as this. She was not as beautiful now as this woman—not as alluringly simple, naive, delicious, nor yet as wise. Mrs. Sohlberg, he reflected shrewdly, had a kind of fool for a husband. Would she take an interest in him, Frank Cowperwood? Would a woman like this surrender on any basis outside of divorce and marriage? He wondered. On her part, Mrs. Sohlberg was thinking what a forceful man Cowperwood was, and how close he had stayed by her. She felt his interest, for she had often seen these symptoms in other men and knew what they meant. She knew the pull of her own beauty, and, while she heightened it as artfully as she dared, yet she kept aloof, too, feeling that she had never met any one as yet for whom it was worth while to be different. But Cowperwood—he needed someone more soulful than Aileen, she thought.

CHAPTER XV

A NEW AFFECTION

The growth of a relationship between Cowperwood and Rita Sohlberg was fostered quite accidentally by Aileen, who took a foolishly sentimental interest in Harold which yet was not based on anything of real meaning. She liked him because he was a superlatively gracious, flattering, emotional man where women—pretty women—were concerned. She had some idea she could send him pupils, and, anyhow, it was nice to call at the Sohlberg studio. Her social life was dull enough as it was. So she went, and Cowperwood, mindful of Mrs. Sohlberg, came also. Shrewd to the point of destruction, he encouraged Aileen in her interest in them. He suggested that she invite them to dinner, that they give a musical at which Sohlberg could play and be paid. There were boxes at the theaters, tickets for concerts sent, invitations to drive Sundays or other days.

The very chemistry of life seems to play into the hands of a situation of this kind. Once Cowperwood was thinking vividly, forcefully, of her, Rita began to think in like manner of him. Hourly he grew more attractive, a strange, gripping man. Beset by his mood, she was having the devil's own time with her conscience. Not that anything had been said as yet, but he was investing her, gradually beleaguering her, sealing up, apparently, one avenue after another of escape. One Thursday afternoon, when neither Aileen nor he could attend the Sohlberg tea, Mrs. Sohlberg received a magnificent bunch of Jacqueminot roses. "For your nooks and corners," said a card. She knew well enough from whom it came and what it was worth. There were all of fifty dollars worth of roses. It gave her breath of a world of money that she had never known. Daily she saw the name of his banking and brokerage firm advertised in the papers. Once she met him in Merrill's store at noon, and he invited her to lunch; but she felt obliged to decline. Always he looked at her with such straight, vigorous eyes. To think that her beauty had done or was doing this! Her mind, quite beyond herself, ran forward to an hour when perhaps this eager, magnetic man would take charge of her in a way never dreamed of by Harold. But she went on practising, shopping, calling, reading, brooding over Harold's inefficiency, and stopping oddly sometimes to think—the etherealized grip of Cowperwood upon her. Those strong hands of his—how fine they were—and those large, soft-hard, incisive eyes. The puritanism of Wichita (modified sometime since by the art life of Chicago, such as it was) was having a severe struggle with the manipulative subtlety of the ages—represented in this man.

"You know you are very elusive," he said to her one evening at the theater when he sat behind her during the entr'acte, and Harold and Aileen had gone to walk in the foyer. The hubbub of conversation drowned the sound of anything that might be said. Mrs. Sohlberg was particularly pleasing in a lacy evening gown.

"No," she replied, amusedly, flattered by his attention and acutely conscious of his physical nearness. By degrees she had been yielding herself to his mood, thrilling at his every word. "It seems to me I am very stable," she went on. "I'm certainly substantial enough."

She looked at her full, smooth arm lying on her lap.

Cowperwood, who was feeling all the drag of her substantiality, but in addition the wonder of her temperament, which was so much richer than Aileen's, was deeply moved. Those little blood moods that no words ever (or rarely) indicate were coming to him from her— faint zephyr-like emanations of emotions, moods, and fancies in her mind which allured him. She was like Aileen in animality, but better, still sweeter, more delicate, much richer spiritually. Or was he just tired of Aileen for the present, he asked himself at times. No, no, he told himself that could not be. Rita Sohlberg was by far the most pleasing woman he had ever known.

"Yes, but elusive, just the same," he went on, leaning toward her. "You remind me of something that I can find no word for—a bit of color or a perfume or tone—a flash of

336

something. I follow you in my thoughts all the time now. Your knowledge of art interests me. I like your playing—it is like you. You make me think of delightful things that have nothing to do with the ordinary run of my life. Do you understand?"

"It is very nice," she said, "if I do." She took a breath, softly, dramatically. "You make me think vain things, you know." (Her mouth was a delicious O.) "You paint a pretty picture." She was warm, flushed, suffused with a burst of her own temperament.

"You are like that," he went on, insistently. "You make me feel like that all the time. You know," he added, leaning over her chair, "I sometimes think you have never lived. There is so much that would complete your perfectness. I should like to send you abroad or take you—anyhow, you should go. You are very wonderful to me. Do you find me at all interesting to you?"

"Yes, but"—she paused—"you know I am afraid of all this and of you." Her mouth had that same delicious formation which had first attracted him. "I don't think we had better talk like this, do you? Harold is very jealous, or would be. What do you suppose Mrs. Cowperwood would think?"

"I know very well, but we needn't stop to consider that now, need we? It will do her no harm to let me talk to you. Life is between individuals, Rita. You and I have very much in common. Don't you see that? You are infinitely the most interesting woman I have ever known. You are bringing me something I have never known. Don't you see that? I want you to tell me something truly. Look at me. You are not happy as you are, are you? Not perfectly happy?"

"No." She smoothed her fan with her fingers.

"Are you happy at all?"

"I thought I was once. I'm not any more, I think."

"It is so plain why," he commented. "You are so much more wonderful than your place gives you scope for. You are an individual, not an acolyte to swing a censer for another. Mr. Sohlberg is very interesting, but you can't be happy that way. It surprises me you haven't seen it."

"Oh," she exclaimed, with a touch of weariness, "but perhaps I have."

He looked at her keenly, and she thrilled. "I don't think we'd better talk so here," she replied. "You'd better be—"

He laid his hand on the back of her chair, almost touching her shoulder.

"Rita," he said, using her given name again, "you wonderful woman!"

"Oh!" she breathed.

Cowperwood did not see Mrs. Sohlberg again for over a week—ten days exactly—when one afternoon Aileen came for him in a new kind of trap, having stopped first to pick up the Sohlbergs. Harold was up in front with her and she had left a place behind for Cowperwood with Rita. She did not in the vaguest way suspect how interested he was—his

337

manner was so deceptive. Aileen imagined that she was the superior woman of the two, the better-looking, the better-dressed, hence the more ensnaring. She could not guess what a lure this woman's temperament had for Cowperwood, who was so brisk, dynamic, seemingly unromantic, but who, just the same, in his nature concealed (under a very forceful exterior) a deep underlying element of romance and fire.

"This is charming," he said, sinking down beside Rita. "What a fine evening! And the nice straw hat with the roses, and the nice linen dress. My, my!" The roses were red; the dress white, with thin, green ribbon run through it here and there. She was keenly aware of the reason for his enthusiasm. He was so different from Harold, so healthy and out-of-doorish, so able. To-day Harold had been in tantrums over fate, life, his lack of success.

"Oh, I shouldn't complain so much if I were you," she had said to him, bitterly. "You might work harder and storm less."

This had produced a scene which she had escaped by going for a walk. Almost at the very moment when she had returned Aileen had appeared. It was a way out.

She had cheered up, and accepted, dressed. So had Sohlberg. Apparently smiling and happy, they had set out on the drive. Now, as Cowperwood spoke, she glanced about her contentedly. "I'm lovely," she thought, "and he loves me. How wonderful it would be if we dared." But she said aloud: "I'm not so very nice. It's just the day—don't you think so? It's a simple dress. I'm not very happy, though, to-night, either."

"What's the matter?" he asked, cheeringly, the rumble of the traffic destroying the carrying-power of their voices. He leaned toward her, very anxious to solve any difficulty which might confront her, perfectly willing to ensnare her by kindness. "Isn't there something I can do? We're going now for a long ride to the pavilion in Jackson Park, and then, after dinner, we'll come back by moonlight. Won't that be nice? You must be smiling now and like yourself—happy. You have no reason to be otherwise that I know of. I will do anything for you that you want done—that can be done. You can have anything you want that I can give you. What is it? You know how much I think of you. If you leave your affairs to me you would never have any troubles of any kind."

"Oh, it isn't anything you can do—not now, anyhow. My affairs! Oh yes. What are they? Very simple, all."

She had that delicious atmosphere of remoteness even from herself. He was enchanted.

"But you are not simple to me, Rita," he said, softly, "nor are your affairs. They concern me very much. You are so important to me. I have told you that. Don't you see how true it is? You are a strange complexity to me—wonderful. I'm mad over you. Ever since I saw you last I have been thinking, thinking. If you have troubles let me share them. You are so much to me—my only trouble. I can fix your life. Join it with mine. I need you, and you need me."

"Yes," she said, "I know." Then she paused. "It's nothing much," she went on—"just a quarrel."

"What over?"

"Over me, really." The mouth was delicious. "I can't swing the censer always, as you say." That thought of his had stuck. "It's all right now, though. Isn't the day lovely, be-yoot-i-ful!"

Cowperwood looked at her and shook his head. She was such a treasure—so inconsequential. Aileen, busy driving and talking, could not see or hear. She was interested in Sohlberg, and the southward crush of vehicles on Michigan Avenue was distracting her attention. As they drove swiftly past budding trees, kempt lawns, fresh-made flower-beds, open windows—the whole seductive world of spring—Cowperwood felt as though life had once more taken a fresh start. His magnetism, if it had been visible, would have enveloped him like a glittering aura. Mrs. Sohlberg felt that this was going to be a wonderful evening.

The dinner was at the Park—an open-air chicken a la Maryland affair, with waffles and champagne to help out. Aileen, flattered by Sohlberg's gaiety under her spell, was having a delightful time, jesting, toasting, laughing, walking on the grass. Sohlberg was making love to her in a foolish, inconsequential way, as many men were inclined to do; but she was putting him off gaily with "silly boy" and "hush." She was so sure of herself that she was free to tell Cowperwood afterward how emotional he was and how she had to laugh at him. Cowperwood, quite certain that she was faithful, took it all in good part. Sohlberg was such a dunce and such a happy convenience ready to his hand. "He's not a bad sort," he commented. "I rather like him, though I don't think he's so much of a violinist."

After dinner they drove along the lake-shore and out through an open bit of tree-blocked prairie land, the moon shining in a clear sky, filling the fields and topping the lake with a silvery effulgence. Mrs. Sohlberg was being inoculated with the virus Cowperwood, and it was taking deadly effect. The tendency of her own disposition, however lethargic it might seem, once it was stirred emotionally, was to act. She was essentially dynamic and passionate. Cowperwood was beginning to stand out in her mind as the force that he was. It would be wonderful to be loved by such a man. There would be an eager, vivid life between them. It frightened and drew her like a blazing lamp in the dark. To get control of herself she talked of art, people, of Paris, Italy, and he responded in like strain, but all the while he smoothed her hand, and once, under the shadow of some trees, he put his hand to her hair, turned her face, and put his mouth softly to her cheek. She flushed, trembled, turned pale, in the grip of this strange storm, but drew herself together. It was wonderful—heaven. Her old life was obviously going to pieces.

"Listen," he said, guardedly. "Will you meet me to-morrow at three just beyond the Rush Street bridge? I will pick you up promptly. You won't have to wait a moment."

She paused, meditating, dreaming, almost hypnotized by his strange world of fancy.

"Will you?" he asked, eagerly.

"Wait," she said, softly. "Let me think. Can I?"

She paused.

"Yes," she said, after a time, drawing in a deep breath. "Yes"—as if she had arranged something in her mind.

"My sweet," he whispered, pressing her arm, while he looked at her profile in the moonlight.

339

"But I'm doing a great deal," she replied, softly, a little breathless and a little pale.

CHAPTER XVI

A FATEFUL INTERLUDE

Cowperwood was enchanted. He kept the proposed tryst with eagerness and found her all that he had hoped. She was sweeter, more colorful, more elusive than anybody he had ever known. In their charming apartment on the North Side which he at once engaged, and where he sometimes spent mornings, evenings, afternoons, as opportunity afforded, he studied her with the most critical eye and found her almost flawless. She had that boundless value which youth and a certain insouciance of manner contribute. There was, delicious to relate, no melancholy in her nature, but a kind of innate sufficiency which neither looked forward to nor back upon troublesome ills. She loved beautiful things, but was not extravagant; and what interested him and commanded his respect was that no urgings of his toward prodigality, however subtly advanced, could affect her. She knew what she wanted, spent carefully, bought tastefully, arrayed herself in ways which appealed to him as the flowers did. His feeling for her became at times so great that he wished, one might almost have said, to destroy it—to appease the urge and allay the pull in himself, but it was useless. The charm of her endured. His transports would leave her refreshed apparently, prettier, more graceful than ever, it seemed to him, putting back her ruffled hair with her hand, mouthing at herself prettily in the glass, thinking of many remote delicious things at once.

"Do you remember that picture we saw in the art store the other day, Algernon?" she would drawl, calling him by his second name, which she had adopted for herself as being more suited to his moods when with her and more pleasing to her. Cowperwood had protested, but she held to it. "Do you remember that lovely blue of the old man's coat?" (It was an "Adoration of the Magi.") "Wasn't that be-yoot-i-ful?"

She drawled so sweetly and fixed her mouth in such an odd way that he was impelled to kiss her. "You clover blossom," he would say to her, coming over and taking her by the arms. "You sprig of cherry bloom. You Dresden china dream."

"Now, are you going to muss my hair, when I've just managed to fix it?"

The voice was the voice of careless, genial innocence—and the eyes.

"Yes, I am, minx."

"Yes, but you mustn't smother me, you know. Really, you know you almost hurt me with your mouth. Aren't you going to be nice to me?"

"Yes, sweet. But I want to hurt you, too."

"Well, then, if you must."

But for all his transports the lure was still there. She was like a butterfly, he thought, yellow and white or blue and gold, fluttering over a hedge of wild rose.

In these intimacies it was that he came quickly to understand how much she knew of social movements and tendencies, though she was just an individual of the outer fringe. She caught at once a clear understanding of his social point of view, his art ambition, his dreams of something better for himself in every way. She seemed to see clearly that he had not as yet realized himself, that Aileen was not just the woman for him, though she might be one. She talked of her own husband after a time in a tolerant way—his foibles, defects, weaknesses. She was not unsympathetic, he thought, just weary of a state that was not properly balanced either in love, ability, or insight. Cowperwood had suggested that she could take a larger studio for herself and Harold—do away with the petty economies that had hampered her and him—and explain it all on the grounds of a larger generosity on the part of her family. At first she objected; but Cowperwood was tactful and finally brought it about. He again suggested a little while later that she should persuade Harold to go to Europe. There would be the same ostensible reason—additional means from her relatives. Mrs. Sohlberg, thus urged, petted, made over, assured, came finally to accept his liberal rule—to bow to him; she became as contented as a cat. With caution she accepted of his largess, and made the cleverest use of it she could. For something over a year neither Sohlberg nor Aileen was aware of the intimacy which had sprung up. Sohlberg, easily bamboozled, went back to Denmark for a visit, then to study in Germany. Mrs. Sohlberg followed Cowperwood to Europe the following year. At Aix-les-Bains, Biarritz, Paris, even London, Aileen never knew that there was an additional figure in the background. Cowperwood was trained by Rita into a really finer point of view. He came to know better music, books, even the facts. She encouraged him in his idea of a representative collection of the old masters, and begged him to be cautious in his selection of moderns. He felt himself to be delightfully situated indeed.

The difficulty with this situation, as with all such where an individual ventures thus bucaneeringly on the sea of sex, is the possibility of those storms which result from misplaced confidence, and from our built-up system of ethics relating to property in women. To Cowperwood, however, who was a law unto himself, who knew no law except such as might be imposed upon him by his lack of ability to think, this possibility of entanglement, wrath, rage, pain, offered no particular obstacle. It was not at all certain that any such thing would follow. Where the average man might have found one such liaison difficult to manage, Cowperwood, as we have seen, had previously entered on several such affairs almost simultaneously; and now he had ventured on yet another; in the last instance with much greater feeling and enthusiasm. The previous affairs had been emotional makeshifts at best—more or less idle philanderings in which his deeper moods and feelings were not concerned. In the case of Mrs. Sohlberg all this was changed. For the present at least she was really all in all to him. But this temperamental characteristic of his relating to his love of women, his artistic if not emotional subjection to their beauty, and the mystery of their personalities led him into still a further affair, and this last was not so fortunate in its outcome.

Antoinette Nowak had come to him fresh from a West Side high school and a Chicago business college, and had been engaged as his private stenographer and secretary. This girl had blossomed forth into something exceptional, as American children of foreign parents are wont to do. You would have scarcely believed that she, with her fine, lithe body, her good taste in dress, her skill in stenography, bookkeeping, and business details, could be the daughter of a struggling Pole, who had first worked in the Southwest Chicago Steel Mills, and who had later kept a fifth-rate cigar, news, and stationery store in the Polish district, the merchandise of playing-cards and a back room for idling and casual gaming being the principal reasons for its existence. Antoinette, whose first name had not been Antoinette at all, but Minka (the Antoinette having been borrowed by her from an article in one of the

Chicago Sunday papers), was a fine dark, brooding girl, ambitious and hopeful, who ten days after she had accepted her new place was admiring Cowperwood and following his every daring movement with almost excited interest. To be the wife of such a man, she thought—to even command his interest, let alone his affection—must be wonderful. After the dull world she had known—it seemed dull compared to the upper, rarefied realms which she was beginning to glimpse through him—and after the average men in the real-estate office over the way where she had first worked, Cowperwood, in his good clothes, his remote mood, his easy, commanding manner, touched the most ambitious chords of her being. One day she saw Aileen sweep in from her carriage, wearing warm brown furs, smart polished boots, a street-suit of corded brown wool, and a fur toque sharpened and emphasized by a long dark-red feather which shot upward like a dagger or a quill pen. Antoinette hated her. She conceived herself to be better, or as good at least. Why was life divided so unfairly? What sort of a man was Cowperwood, anyhow? One night after she had written out a discreet but truthful history of himself which he had dictated to her, and which she had sent to the Chicago newspapers for him soon after the opening of his brokerage office in Chicago, she went home and dreamed of what he had told her, only altered, of course, as in dreams. She thought that Cowperwood stood beside her in his handsome private office in La Salle Street and asked her:

"Antoinette, what do you think of me?" Antoinette was nonplussed, but brave. In her dream she found herself intensely interested in him.

"Oh, I don't know what to think. I'm so sorry," was her answer. Then he laid his hand on hers, on her cheek, and she awoke. She began thinking, what a pity, what a shame that such a man should ever have been in prison. He was so handsome. He had been married twice. Perhaps his first wife was very homely or very mean-spirited. She thought of this, and the next day went to work meditatively. Cowperwood, engrossed in his own plans, was not thinking of her at present. He was thinking of the next moves in his interesting gas war. And Aileen, seeing her one day, merely considered her an underling. The woman in business was such a novelty that as yet she was declasse. Aileen really thought nothing of Antoinette at all.

Somewhat over a year after Cowperwood had become intimate with Mrs. Sohlberg his rather practical business relations with Antoinette Nowak took on a more intimate color. What shall we say of this—that he had already wearied of Mrs. Sohlberg? Not in the least. He was desperately fond of her. Or that he despised Aileen, whom he was thus grossly deceiving? Not at all. She was to him at times as attractive as ever—perhaps more so for the reason that her self-imagined rights were being thus roughly infringed upon. He was sorry for her, but inclined to justify himself on the ground that these other relations—with possibly the exception of Mrs. Sohlberg—were not enduring. If it had been possible to marry Mrs. Sohlberg he might have done so, and he did speculate at times as to whether anything would ever induce Aileen to leave him; but this was more or less idle speculation. He rather fancied they would live out their days together, seeing that he was able thus easily to deceive her. But as for a girl like Antoinette Nowak, she figured in that braided symphony of mere sex attraction which somehow makes up that geometric formula of beauty which rules the world. She was charming in a dark way, beautiful, with eyes that burned with an unsatisfied fire; and Cowperwood, although at first only in the least moved by her, became by degrees interested in her, wondering at the amazing, transforming power of the American atmosphere.

"Are your parents English, Antoinette?" he asked her, one morning, with that easy familiarity which he assumed to all underlings and minor intellects—an air that could not be resented in him, and which was usually accepted as a compliment.

Antoinette, clean and fresh in a white shirtwaist, a black walking-skirt, a ribbon of black velvet about her neck, and her long, black hair laid in a heavy braid low over her forehead and held close by a white celluloid comb, looked at him with pleased and grateful eyes. She had been used to such different types of men—the earnest, fiery, excitable, sometimes drunken and swearing men of her childhood, always striking, marching, praying in the Catholic churches; and then the men of the business world, crazy over money, and with no understanding of anything save some few facts about Chicago and its momentary possibilities. In Cowperwood's office, taking his letters and hearing him talk in his quick, genial way with old Laughlin, Sippens, and others, she had learned more of life than she had ever dreamed existed. He was like a vast open window out of which she was looking upon an almost illimitable landscape.

"No, sir," she replied, dropping her slim, firm, white hand, holding a black lead-pencil restfully on her notebook. She smiled quite innocently because she was pleased.

"I thought not," he said, "and yet you're American enough."

"I don't know how it is," she said, quite solemnly. "I have a brother who is quite as American as I am. We don't either of us look like our father or mother."

"What does your brother do?" he asked, indifferently.

"He's one of the weighers at Arneel & Co. He expects to be a manager sometime." She smiled.

Cowperwood looked at her speculatively, and after a momentary return glance she dropped her eyes. Slowly, in spite of herself, a telltale flush rose and mantled her brown cheeks. It always did when he looked at her.

"Take this letter to General Van Sickle," he began, on this occasion quite helpfully, and in a few minutes she had recovered. She could not be near Cowperwood for long at a time, however, without being stirred by a feeling which was not of her own willing. He fascinated and suffused her with a dull fire. She sometimes wondered whether a man so remarkable would ever be interested in a girl like her.

The end of this essential interest, of course, was the eventual assumption of Antoinette. One might go through all the dissolving details of days in which she sat taking dictation, receiving instructions, going about her office duties in a state of apparently chill, practical, commercial single-mindedness; but it would be to no purpose. As a matter of fact, without in any way affecting the preciseness and accuracy of her labor, her thoughts were always upon the man in the inner office—the strange master who was then seeing his men, and in between, so it seemed, a whole world of individuals, solemn and commercial, who came, presented their cards, talked at times almost interminably, and went away. It was the rare individual, however, she observed, who had the long conversation with Cowperwood, and that interested her the more. His instructions to her were always of the briefest, and he depended on her native intelligence to supply much that he scarcely more than suggested.

"You understand, do you?" was his customary phrase.

343

"Yes," she would reply.

She felt as though she were fifty times as significant here as she had ever been in her life before.

The office was clean, hard, bright, like Cowperwood himself. The morning sun, streaming in through an almost solid glass east front shaded by pale-green roller curtains, came to have an almost romantic atmosphere for her. Cowperwood's private office, as in Philadelphia, was a solid cherry-wood box in which he could shut himself completely— sight-proof, sound-proof. When the door was closed it was sacrosanct. He made it a rule, sensibly, to keep his door open as much as possible, even when he was dictating, sometimes not. It was in these half-hours of dictation—the door open, as a rule, for he did not care for too much privacy—that he and Miss Nowak came closest. After months and months, and because he had been busy with the other woman mentioned, of whom she knew nothing, she came to enter sometimes with a sense of suffocation, sometimes of maidenly shame. It would never have occurred to her to admit frankly that she wanted Cowperwood to make love to her. It would have frightened her to have thought of herself as yielding easily, and yet there was not a detail of his personality that was not now burned in her brain. His light, thick, always smoothly parted hair, his wide, clear, inscrutable eyes, his carefully manicured hands, so full and firm, his fresh clothing of delicate, intricate patterns—how these fascinated her! He seemed always remote except just at the moment of doing something, when, curiously enough, he seemed intensely intimate and near.

One day, after many exchanges of glances in which her own always fell sharply—in the midst of a letter—he arose and closed the half-open door. She did not think so much of that, as a rule—it had happened before—but now, to-day, because of a studied glance he had given her, neither tender nor smiling, she felt as though something unusual were about to happen. Her own body was going hot and cold by turns—her neck and hands. She had a fine figure, finer than she realized, with shapely limbs and torso. Her head had some of the sharpness of the old Greek coinage, and her hair was plaited as in ancient cut stone. Cowperwood noted it. He came back and, without taking his seat, bent over her and intimately took her hand.

"Antoinette," he said, lifting her gently.

She looked up, then arose—for he slowly drew her—breathless, the color gone, much of the capable practicality that was hers completely eliminated. She felt limp, inert. She pulled at her hand faintly, and then, lifting her eyes, was fixed by that hard, insatiable gaze of his. Her head swam—her eyes were filled with a telltale confusion.

"Antoinette!"

"Yes," she murmured.

"You love me, don't you?"

She tried to pull herself together, to inject some of her native rigidity of soul into her air— that rigidity which she always imagined would never desert her—but it was gone. There came instead to her a picture of the far Blue Island Avenue neighborhood from which she emanated—its low brown cottages, and then this smart, hard office and this strong man.

He came out of such a marvelous world, apparently. A strange foaming seemed to be in her blood. She was deliriously, deliciously numb and happy.

"Antoinette!"

"Oh, I don't know what I think," she gasped. "I— Oh yes, I do, I do."

"I like your name," he said, simply. "Antoinette." And then, pulling her to him, he slipped his arm about her waist.

She was frightened, numb, and then suddenly, not so much from shame as shock, tears rushed to her eyes. She turned and put her hand on the desk and hung her head and sobbed.

"Why, Antoinette," he asked, gently, bending over her, "are you so much unused to the world? I thought you said you loved me. Do you want me to forget all this and go on as before? I can, of course, if you can, you know."

He knew that she loved him, wanted him.

She heard him plainly enough, shaking.

"Do you?" he said, after a time, giving her moments in which to recover.

"Oh, let me cry!" she recovered herself sufficiently to say, quite wildly. "I don't know why I'm crying. It's just because I'm nervous, I suppose. Please don't mind me now."

"Antoinette," he repeated, "look at me! Will you stop?"

"Oh no, not now. My eyes are so bad."

"Antoinette! Come, look!" He put his hand under her chin. "See, I'm not so terrible."

"Oh," she said, when her eyes met his again, "I—" And then she folded her arms against his breast while he petted her hand and held her close.

"I'm not so bad, Antoinette. It's you as much as it is me. You do love me, then?"

"Yes, yes—oh yes!"

"And you don't mind?"

"No. It's all so strange." Her face was hidden.

"Kiss me, then."

She put up her lips and slipped her arms about him. He held her close.

He tried teasingly to make her say why she cried, thinking the while of what Aileen or Rita would think if they knew, but she would not at first—admitting later that it was a sense of evil. Curiously she also thought of Aileen, and how, on occasion, she had seen her sweep in and out. Now she was sharing with her (the dashing Mrs. Cowperwood, so vain and

345

superior) the wonder of his affection. Strange as it may seem, she looked on it now as rather an honor. She had risen in her own estimation—her sense of life and power. Now, more than ever before, she knew something of life because she knew something of love and passion. The future seemed tremulous with promise. She went back to her machine after a while, thinking of this. What would it all come to? she wondered, wildly. You could not have told by her eyes that she had been crying. Instead, a rich glow in her brown cheeks heightened her beauty. No disturbing sense of Aileen was involved with all this. Antoinette was of the newer order that was beginning to privately question ethics and morals. She had a right to her life, lead where it would. And to what it would bring her. The feel of Cowperwood's lips was still fresh on hers. What would the future reveal to her now? What?

CHAPTER XVII

AN OVERTURE TO CONFLICT

The result of this understanding was not so important to Cowperwood as it was to Antoinette. In a vagrant mood he had unlocked a spirit here which was fiery, passionate, but in his case hopelessly worshipful. However much she might be grieved by him, Antoinette, as he subsequently learned, would never sin against his personal welfare. Yet she was unwittingly the means of first opening the flood-gates of suspicion on Aileen, thereby establishing in the latter's mind the fact of Cowperwood's persistent unfaithfulness.

The incidents which led up to this were comparatively trivial—nothing more, indeed, at first than the sight of Miss Nowak and Cowperwood talking intimately in his office one afternoon when the others had gone and the fact that she appeared to be a little bit disturbed by Aileen's arrival. Later came the discovery—though of this Aileen could not be absolutely sure—of Cowperwood and Antoinette in a closed carriage one stormy November afternoon in State Street when he was supposed to be out of the city. She was coming out of Merrill's store at the time, and just happened to glance at the passing vehicle, which was running near the curb. Aileen, although uncertain, was greatly shocked. Could it be possible that he had not left town? She journeyed to his office on the pretext of taking old Laughlin's dog, Jennie, a pretty collar she had found; actually to find if Antoinette were away at the same time. Could it be possible, she kept asking herself, that Cowperwood had become interested in his own stenographer? The fact that the office assumed that he was out of town and that Antoinette was not there gave her pause. Laughlin quite innocently informed her that he thought Miss Nowak had gone to one of the libraries to make up certain reports. It left her in doubt.

What was Aileen to think? Her moods and aspirations were linked so closely with the love and success of Cowperwood that she could not, in spite of herself, but take fire at the least thought of losing him. He himself wondered sometimes, as he threaded the mesh-like paths of sex, what she would do once she discovered his variant conduct. Indeed, there had been little occasional squabbles, not sharp, but suggestive, when he was trifling about with Mrs. Kittridge, Mrs. Ledwell, and others. There were, as may be imagined, from time to time absences, brief and unimportant, which he explained easily, passional indifferences which were not explained so easily, and the like; but since his affections were not really involved in any of those instances, he had managed to smooth the matter over quite nicely.

"Why do you say that?" he would demand, when she suggested, apropos of a trip or a day when she had not been with him, that there might have been another. "You know there hasn't. If I am going in for that sort of thing you'll learn it fast enough. Even if I did, it wouldn't mean that I was unfaithful to you spiritually."

"Oh, wouldn't it?" exclaimed Aileen, resentfully, and with some disturbance of spirit. "Well, you can keep your spiritual faithfulness. I'm not going to be content with any sweet thoughts."

Cowperwood laughed even as she laughed, for he knew she was right and he felt sorry for her. At the same time her biting humor pleased him. He knew that she did not really suspect him of actual infidelity; he was obviously so fond of her. But she also knew that he was innately attractive to women, and that there were enough of the philandering type to want to lead him astray and make her life a burden. Also that he might prove a very willing victim.

Sex desire and its fruition being such an integral factor in the marriage and every other sex relation, the average woman is prone to study the periodic manifestations that go with it quite as one dependent on the weather—a sailor, or example—might study the barometer. In this Aileen was no exception. She was so beautiful herself, and had been so much to Cowperwood physically, that she had followed the corresponding evidences of feeling in him with the utmost interest, accepting the recurring ebullitions of his physical emotions as an evidence of her own enduring charm. As time went on, however—and that was long before Mrs. Sohlberg or any one else had appeared—the original flare of passion had undergone a form of subsidence, though not noticeable enough to be disturbing. Aileen thought and thought, but she did not investigate. Indeed, because of the precariousness of her own situation as a social failure she was afraid to do so.

With the arrival of Mrs. Sohlberg and then of Antoinette Nowak as factors in the potpourri, the situation became more difficult. Humanly fond of Aileen as Cowperwood was, and because of his lapses and her affection, desirous of being kind, yet for the time being he was alienated almost completely from her. He grew remote according as his clandestine affairs were drifting or blazing, without, however, losing his firm grip on his financial affairs, and Aileen noticed it. It worried her. She was so vain that she could scarcely believe that Cowperwood could long be indifferent, and for a while her sentimental interest in Sohlberg's future and unhappiness of soul beclouded her judgment; but she finally began to feel the drift of affairs. The pathos of all this is that it so quickly descends into the realm of the unsatisfactory, the banal, the pseudo intimate. Aileen noticed it at once. She tried protestations. "You don't kiss me the way you did once," and then a little later, "You haven't noticed me hardly for four whole days. What's the matter?"

"Oh, I don't know," replied Cowperwood, easily; "I guess I want you as much as ever. I don't see that I am any different." He took her in his arms and petted and caressed her; but Aileen was suspicious, nervous.

The psychology of the human animal, when confronted by these tangles, these ripping tides of the heart, has little to do with so-called reason or logic. It is amazing how in the face of passion and the affections and the changing face of life all plans and theories by which we guide ourselves fall to the ground. Here was Aileen talking bravely at the time she invaded Mrs. Lillian Cowperwood's domain of the necessity of "her Frank" finding a woman suitable to his needs, tastes, abilities, but now that the possibility of another woman equally or possibly better suited to him was looming in the offing—although she had no idea who it might be—she could not reason in the same way. Her ox, God wot, was the one that was being gored. What if he should find some one whom he could want more than he did her? Dear heaven, how terrible that would be! What would she do? she asked herself, thoughtfully. She lapsed into the blues one afternoon—almost cried—she could scarcely say why. Another time she thought of all the terrible things she would do, how difficult she would make it for any other woman who invaded her preserves. However, she was not sure. Would she declare war if she discovered another? She knew she would eventually; and yet she knew, too, that if she did, and Cowperwood were set in his passion, thoroughly alienated, it would do no good. It would be terrible, but what could she do to win him back? That was the issue. Once warned, however, by her suspicious questioning, Cowperwood was more mechanically attentive than ever. He did his best to conceal his altered mood—his enthusiasms for Mrs. Sohlberg, his interest in Antoinette Nowak—and this helped somewhat.

But finally there was a detectable change. Aileen noticed it first after they had been back from Europe nearly a year. At this time she was still interested in Sohlberg, but in a harmlessly flirtatious way. She thought he might be interesting physically, but would he be as delightful as Cowperwood? Never! When she felt that Cowperwood himself might be changing she pulled herself up at once, and when Antoinette appeared—the carriage incident—Sohlberg lost his, at best, unstable charm. She began to meditate on what a terrible thing it would be to lose Cowperwood, seeing that she had failed to establish herself socially. Perhaps that had something to do with his defection. No doubt it had. Yet she could not believe, after all his protestations of affection in Philadelphia, after all her devotion to him in those dark days of his degradation and punishment, that he would really turn on her. No, he might stray momentarily, but if she protested enough, made a scene, perhaps, he would not feel so free to injure her—he would remember and be loving and devoted again. After seeing him, or imagining she had seen him, in the carriage, she thought at first that she would question him, but later decided that she would wait and watch more closely. Perhaps he was beginning to run around with other women. There was safety in numbers—that she knew. Her heart, her pride, was hurt, but not broken.

CHAPTER XVIII

THE CLASH

The peculiar personality of Rita Sohlberg was such that by her very action she ordinarily allayed suspicion, or rather distracted it. Although a novice, she had a strange ease, courage, or balance of soul which kept her whole and self-possessed under the most trying of circumstances. She might have been overtaken in the most compromising of positions, but her manner would always have indicated ease, a sense of innocence, nothing unusual, for she had no sense of moral degradation in this matter—no troublesome emotion as to what was to flow from a relationship of this kind, no worry as to her own soul, sin, social opinion, or the like. She was really interested in art and life—a pagan, in fact. Some people are thus hardily equipped. It is the most notable attribute of the hardier type of personalities—not necessarily the most brilliant or successful. You might have said that her soul was naively unconscious of the agony of others in loss. She would have taken any loss to herself with an amazing equableness—some qualms, of course, but not many—because her vanity and sense of charm would have made her look forward to something better or as good.

348

She had called on Aileen quite regularly in the past, with or without Harold, and had frequently driven with the Cowperwoods or joined them at the theater or elsewhere. She had decided, after becoming intimate with Cowperwood, to study art again, which was a charming blind, for it called for attendance at afternoon or evening classes which she frequently skipped. Besides, since Harold had more money he was becoming gayer, more reckless and enthusiastic over women, and Cowperwood deliberately advised her to encourage him in some liaison which, in case exposure should subsequently come to them, would effectually tie his hands.

"Let him get in some affair," Cowperwood told Rita. "We'll put detectives on his trail and get evidence. He won't have a word to say."

"We don't really need to do that," she protested sweetly, naively. "He's been in enough scrapes as it is. He's given me some of the letters—" (she pronounced it "lettahs")—"written him."

"But we'll need actual witnesses if we ever need anything at all. Just tell me when he's in love again, and I'll do the rest."

"You know I think," she drawled, amusingly, "that he is now. I saw him on the street the other day with one of his students—rather a pretty girl, too."

Cowperwood was pleased. Under the circumstances he would almost have been willing—not quite—for Aileen to succumb to Sohlberg in order to entrap her and make his situation secure. Yet he really did not wish it in the last analysis—would have been grieved temporarily if she had deserted him. However, in the case of Sohlberg, detectives were employed, the new affair with the flighty pupil was unearthed and sworn to by witnesses, and this, combined with the "lettahs" held by Rita, constituted ample material wherewith to "hush up" the musician if ever he became unduly obstreperous. So Cowperwood and Rita's state was quite comfortable.

But Aileen, meditating over Antoinette Nowak, was beside herself with curiosity, doubt, worry. She did not want to injure Cowperwood in any way after his bitter Philadelphia experience, and yet when she thought of his deserting her in this way she fell into a great rage. Her vanity, as much as her love, was hurt. What could she do to justify or set at rest her suspicions? Watch him personally? She was too dignified and vain to lurk about street-corners or offices or hotels. Never! Start a quarrel without additional evidence—that would be silly. He was too shrewd to give her further evidence once she spoke. He would merely deny it. She brooded irritably, recalling after a time, and with an aching heart, that her father had put detectives on her track once ten years before, and had actually discovered her relations with Cowperwood and their rendezvous. Bitter as that memory was—torturing—yet now the same means seemed not too abhorrent to employ under the circumstances. No harm had come to Cowperwood in the former instance, she reasoned to herself—no especial harm—from that discovery (this was not true), and none would come to him now. (This also was not true.) But one must forgive a fiery, passionate soul, wounded to the quick, some errors of judgment. Her thought was that she would first be sure just what it was her beloved was doing, and then decide what course to take. But she knew that she was treading on dangerous ground, and mentally she recoiled from the consequences which might follow. He might leave her if she fought him too bitterly. He might treat her as he had treated his first wife, Lillian.

She studied her liege lord curiously these days, wondering if it were true that he had deserted her already, as he had deserted his first wife thirteen years before, wondering if he could really take up with a girl as common as Antoinette Nowak—wondering, wondering, wondering—half afraid and yet courageous. What could be done with him? If only he still loved her all would be well yet—but oh!

The detective agency to which she finally applied, after weeks of soul-racking suspense, was one of those disturbingly human implements which many are not opposed to using on occasion, when it is the only means of solving a troublous problem of wounded feelings or jeopardized interests. Aileen, being obviously rich, was forthwith shamefully overcharged; but the services agreed upon were well performed. To her amazement, chagrin, and distress, after a few weeks of observation Cowperwood was reported to have affairs not only with Antoinette Nowak, whom she did suspect, but also with Mrs. Sohlberg. And these two affairs at one and the same time. For the moment it left Aileen actually stunned and breathless.

The significance of Rita Sohlberg to her in this hour was greater than that of any woman before or after. Of all living things, women dread women most of all, and of all women the clever and beautiful. Rita Sohlberg had been growing on Aileen as a personage, for she had obviously been prospering during this past year, and her beauty had been amazingly enhanced thereby. Once Aileen had encountered Rita in a light trap on the Avenue, very handsome and very new, and she had commented on it to Cowperwood, whose reply had been: "Her father must be making some money. Sohlberg could never earn it for her."

Aileen sympathized with Harold because of his temperament, but she knew that what Cowperwood said was true.

Another time, at a box-party at the theater, she had noted the rich elaborateness of Mrs. Sohlberg's dainty frock, the endless pleatings of pale silk, the startling charm of the needlework and the ribbons—countless, rosetted, small—that meant hard work on the part of some one.

"How lovely this is," she had commented.

"Yes," Rita had replied, airily; "I thought, don't you know, my dressmaker would never get done working on it."

It had cost, all told, two hundred and twenty dollars, and Cowperwood had gladly paid the bill.

Aileen went home at the time thinking of Rita's taste and of how well she had harmonized her materials to her personality. She was truly charming.

Now, however, when it appeared that the same charm that had appealed to her had appealed to Cowperwood, she conceived an angry, animal opposition to it all. Rita Sohlberg! Ha! A lot of satisfaction she'd get knowing as she would soon, that Cowperwood was sharing his affection for her with Antoinette Nowak—a mere stenographer. And a lot of satisfaction Antoinette would get—the cheap upstart—when she learned, as she would, that Cowperwood loved her so lightly that he would take an apartment for Rita Sohlberg and let a cheap hotel or an assignation-house do for her.

But in spite of this savage exultation her thoughts kept coming back to herself, to her own predicament, to torture and destroy her. Cowperwood, the liar! Cowperwood, the pretender! Cowperwood, the sneak! At one moment she conceived a kind of horror of the man because of all his protestations to her; at the next a rage—bitter, swelling; at the next a pathetic realization of her own altered position. Say what one will, to take the love of a man like Cowperwood away from a woman like Aileen was to leave her high and dry on land, as a fish out of its native element, to take all the wind out of her sails—almost to kill her. Whatever position she had once thought to hold through him, was now jeopardized. Whatever joy or glory she had had in being Mrs. Frank Algernon Cowperwood, it was now tarnished. She sat in her room, this same day after the detectives had given their report, a tired look in her eyes, the first set lines her pretty mouth had ever known showing about it, her past and her future whirling painfully and nebulously in her brain. Suddenly she got up, and, seeing Cowperwood's picture on her dresser, his still impressive eyes contemplating her, she seized it and threw it on the floor, stamping on his handsome face with her pretty foot, and raging at him in her heart. The dog! The brute! Her brain was full of the thought of Rita's white arms about him, of his lips to hers. The spectacle of Rita's fluffy gowns, her enticing costumes, was in her eyes. Rita should not have him; she should not have anything connected with him, nor, for that matter, Antoinette Nowak, either—the wretched upstart, the hireling. To think he should stoop to an office stenographer! Once on that thought, she decided that he should not be allowed to have a woman as an assistant any more. He owed it to her to love her after all she had done for him, the coward, and to let other women alone. Her brain whirled with strange thoughts. She was really not sane in her present state. She was so wrought up by her prospective loss that she could only think of rash, impossible, destructive things to do. She dressed swiftly, feverishly, and, calling a closed carriage from the coach-house, ordered herself to be driven to the New Arts Building. She would show this rosy cat of a woman, this smiling piece of impertinence, this she-devil, whether she would lure Cowperwood away. She meditated as she rode. She would not sit back and be robbed as Mrs. Cowperwood had been by her. Never! He could not treat her that way. She would die first! She would kill Rita Sohlberg and Antoinette Nowak and Cowperwood and herself first. She would prefer to die that way rather than lose his love. Oh yes, a thousand times! Fortunately, Rita Sohlberg was not at the New Arts Building, or Sohlberg, either. They had gone to a reception. Nor was she at the apartment on the North Side, where, under the name of Jacobs, as Aileen had been informed by the detectives, she and Cowperwood kept occasional tryst. Aileen hesitated for a moment, feeling it useless to wait, then she ordered the coachman to drive to her husband's office. It was now nearly five o'clock. Antoinette and Cowperwood had both gone, but she did not know it. She changed her mind, however, before she reached the office—for it was Rita Sohlberg she wished to reach first—and ordered her coachman to drive back to the Sohlberg studio. But still they had not returned. In a kind of aimless rage she went home, wondering how she should reach Rita Sohlberg first and alone. Then, to her savage delight, the game walked into her bag. The Sohlbergs, returning home at six o'clock from some reception farther out Michigan Avenue, had stopped, at the wish of Harold, merely to pass the time of day with Mrs. Cowperwood. Rita was exquisite in a pale-blue and lavender concoction, with silver braid worked in here and there. Her gloves and shoes were pungent bits of romance, her hat a dream of graceful lines. At the sight of her, Aileen, who was still in the hall and had opened the door herself, fairly burned to seize her by the throat and strike her; but she restrained herself sufficiently to say, "Come in." She still had sense enough and self-possession enough to conceal her wrath and to close the door. Beside his wife Harold was standing, offensively smug and inefficient in the fashionable frock-coat and silk hat of the time, a restraining influence as yet. He was bowing and smiling:

"Oh." This sound was neither an "oh" nor an "ah," but a kind of Danish inflected "awe," which was usually not unpleasing to hear. "How are you, once more, Meeses Cowperwood? It eez sudge a pleasure to see you again—awe."

"Won't you two just go in the reception-room a moment," said Aileen, almost hoarsely. "I'll be right in. I want to get something." Then, as an afterthought, she called very sweetly: "Oh, Mrs. Sohlberg, won't you come up to my room for a moment? I have something I want to show you."

Rita responded promptly. She always felt it incumbent upon her to be very nice to Aileen.

"We have only a moment to stay," she replied, archly and sweetly, and coming out in the hall, "but I'll come up."

Aileen stayed to see her go first, then followed up-stairs swiftly, surely, entered after Rita, and closed the door. With a courage and rage born of a purely animal despair, she turned and locked it; then she wheeled swiftly, her eyes lit with a savage fire, her cheeks pale, but later aflame, her hands, her fingers working in a strange, unconscious way.

"So," she said, looking at Rita, and coming toward her quickly and angrily, "you'll steal my husband, will you? You'll live in a secret apartment, will you? You'll come here smiling and lying to me, will you? You beast! You cat! You prostitute! I'll show you now! You tow-headed beast! I know you now for what you are! I'll teach you once for all! Take that, and that, and that!"

Suiting action to word, Aileen had descended upon her whirlwind, animal fashion, striking, scratching, choking, tearing her visitor's hat from her head, ripping the laces from her neck, beating her in the face, and clutching violently at her hair and throat to choke and mar her beauty if she could. For the moment she was really crazy with rage.

By the suddenness of this onslaught Rita Sohlberg was taken back completely. It all came so swiftly, so terribly, she scarcely realized what was happening before the storm was upon her. There was no time for arguments, pleas, anything. Terrified, shamed, nonplussed, she went down quite limply under this almost lightning attack. When Aileen began to strike her she attempted in vain to defend herself, uttering at the same time piercing screams which could be heard throughout the house. She screamed shrilly, strangely, like a wild dying animal. On the instant all her fine, civilized poise had deserted her. From the sweetness and delicacy of the reception atmosphere—the polite cooings, posturings, and mouthings so charming to contemplate, so alluring in her—she had dropped on the instant to that native animal condition that shows itself in fear. Her eyes had a look of hunted horror, her lips and cheeks were pale and drawn. She retreated in a staggering, ungraceful way; she writhed and squirmed, screaming in the strong clutch of the irate and vigorous Aileen.

Cowperwood entered the hall below just before the screams began. He had followed the Sohlbergs almost immediately from his office, and, chancing to glance in the reception-room, he had observed Sohlberg smiling, radiant, an intangible air of self-ingratiating, social, and artistic sycophancy about him, his long black frock-coat buttoned smoothly around his body, his silk hat still in his hands.

"Awe, how do you do, Meezter Cowperwood," he was beginning to say, his curly head shaking in a friendly manner, "I'm soa glad to see you again" when—but who can imitate a scream of terror? We have no words, no symbols even, for those essential sounds of fright and agony. They filled the hall, the library, the reception-room, the distant kitchen even, and basement with a kind of vibrant terror.

Cowperwood, always the man of action as opposed to nervous cogitation, braced up on the instant like taut wire. What, for heaven's sake, could that be? What a terrible cry! Sohlberg the artist, responding like a chameleon to the various emotional complexions of life, began to breathe stertorously, to blanch, to lose control of himself.

"My God!" he exclaimed, throwing up his hands, "that's Rita! She's up-stairs in your wife's room! Something must have happened. Oh—" On the instant he was quite beside himself, terrified, shaking, almost useless. Cowperwood, on the contrary, without a moment's hesitation had thrown his coat to the floor, dashed up the stairs, followed by Sohlberg. What could it be? Where was Aileen? As he bounded upward a clear sense of something untoward came over him; it was sickening, terrifying. Scream! Scream! Scream! came the sounds. "Oh, my God! don't kill me! Help! Help!" SCREAM—this last a long, terrified, ear-piercing wail.

Sohlberg was about to drop from heart failure, he was so frightened. His face was an ashen gray. Cowperwood seized the door-knob vigorously and, finding the door locked, shook, rattled, and banged at it.

"Aileen!" he called, sharply. "Aileen! What's the matter in there? Open this door, Aileen!"

"Oh, my God! Oh, help! help! Oh, mercy—o-o-o-o-oh!" It was the moaning voice of Rita.

"I'll show you, you she-devil!" he heard Aileen calling. "I'll teach you, you beast! You cat, you prostitute! There! there! there!"

"Aileen!" he called, hoarsely. "Aileen!" Then, getting no response, and the screams continuing, he turned angrily.

"Stand back!" he exclaimed to Sohlberg, who was moaning helplessly. "Get me a chair, get me a table—anything." The butler ran to obey, but before he could return Cowperwood had found an implement. "Here!" he said, seizing a long, thin, heavily carved and heavily wrought oak chair which stood at the head of the stairs on the landing. He whirled it vigorously over his head. Smash! The sound rose louder than the screams inside.

Smash! The chair creaked and almost broke, but the door did not give.

Smash! The chair broke and the door flew open. He had knocked the lock loose and had leaped in to where Aileen, kneeling over Rita on the floor, was choking and beating her into insensibility. Like an animal he was upon her.

"Aileen," he shouted, fiercely, in a hoarse, ugly, guttural voice, "you fool! You idiot—let go! What the devil's the matter with you? What are you trying to do? Have you lost your mind?—you crazy idiot!"

He seized her strong hands and ripped them apart. He fairly dragged her back, half twisting and half throwing her over his knee, loosing her clutching hold. She was so insanely furious that she still struggled and cried, saying: "Let me at her! Let me at her! I'll teach her! Don't you try to hold me, you dog! I'll show you, too, you brute—oh—"

"Pick up that woman," called Cowperwood, firmly, to Sohlberg and the butler, who had entered. "Get her out of here quick! My wife has gone crazy. Get her out of here, I tell you! This woman doesn't know what she's doing. Take her out and get a doctor. What sort of a hell's melee is this, anyway?"

"Oh," moaned Rita, who was torn and fainting, almost unconscious from sheer terror.

"I'll kill her!" screamed Aileen. "I'll murder her! I'll murder you too, you dog! Oh"—she began striking at him—"I'll teach you how to run around with other women, you dog, you brute!"

Cowperwood merely gripped her hands and shook her vigorously, forcefully.

"What the devil has got into you, anyway, you fool?" he said to her, bitterly, as they carried Rita out. "What are you trying to do, anyway—murder her? Do you want the police to come in here? Stop your screaming and behave yourself, or I'll shove a handkerchief in your mouth! Stop, I tell you! Stop! Do you hear me? This is enough, you fool!" He clapped his hand over her mouth, pressing it tight and forcing her back against him. He shook her brutally, angrily. He was very strong. "Now will you stop," he insisted, "or do you want me to choke you quiet? I will, if you don't. You're out of your mind. Stop, I tell you! So this is the way you carry on when things don't go to suit you?" She was sobbing, struggling, moaning, half screaming, quite beside herself.

"Oh, you crazy fool!" he said, swinging her round, and with an effort getting out a handkerchief, which he forced over her face and in her mouth. "There," he said, relievedly, "now will you shut up?" holding her tight in an iron grip, he let her struggle and turn, quite ready to put an end to her breathing if necessary.

Now that he had conquered her, he continued to hold her tightly, stooping beside her on one knee, listening and meditating. Hers was surely a terrible passion. From some points of view he could not blame her. Great was her provocation, great her love. He knew her disposition well enough to have anticipated something of this sort. Yet the wretchedness, shame, scandal of the terrible affair upset his customary equilibrium. To think any one should give way to such a storm as this! To think that Aileen should do it! To think that Rita should have been so mistreated! It was not at all unlikely that she was seriously injured, marred for life—possibly even killed. The horror of that! The ensuing storm of public rage! A trial! His whole career gone up in one terrific explosion of woe, anger, death! Great God!

He called the butler to him by a nod of his head, when the latter, who had gone out with Rita, hurried back.

"How is she?" he asked, desperately. "Seriously hurt?"

"No, sir; I think not. I believe she's just fainted. She'll be all right in a little while, sir. Can I be of any service, sir?"

Ordinarily Cowperwood would have smiled at such a scene. Now he was cold, sober.

"Not now," he replied, with a sigh of relief, still holding Aileen firmly. "Go out and close the door. Call a doctor. Wait in the hall. When he comes, call me."

354

Aileen, conscious of things being done for Rita, of sympathy being extended to her, tried to get up, to scream again; but she couldn't; her lord and master held her in an ugly hold. When the door was closed he said again: "Now, Aileen, will you hush? Will you let me get up and talk to you, or must we stay here all night? Do you want me to drop you forever after to-night? I understand all about this, but I am in control now, and I am going to stay so. You will come to your senses and be reasonable, or I will leave you to-morrow as sure as I am here." His voice rang convincingly. "Now, shall we talk sensibly, or will you go on making a fool of yourself—disgracing me, disgracing the house, making yourself and myself the laughing-stock of the servants, the neighborhood, the city? This is a fine showing you've made to-day. Good God! A fine showing, indeed! A brawl in this house, a fight! I thought you had better sense—more self-respect—really I did. You have seriously jeopardized my chances here in Chicago. You have seriously injured and possibly killed a woman. You could even be hanged for that. Do you hear me?"

"Oh, let them hang me," groaned Aileen. "I want to die."

He took away his hand from her mouth, loosened his grip upon her arms, and let her get to her feet. She was still torrential, impetuous, ready to upbraid him, but once standing she was confronted by him, cold, commanding, fixing her with a fishy eye. He wore a look now she had never seen on his face before—a hard, wintry, dynamic flare, which no one but his commercial enemies, and only those occasionally, had seen.

"Now stop!" he exclaimed. "Not one more word! Not one! Do you hear me?"

She wavered, quailed, gave way. All the fury of her tempestuous soul fell, as the sea falls under a lapse of wind. She had had it in heart, on her lips, to cry again, "You dog! you brute!" and a hundred other terrible, useless things, but somehow, under the pressure of his gaze, the hardness of his heart, the words on her lips died away. She looked at him uncertainly for a moment, then, turning, she threw herself on the bed near by, clutched her cheeks and mouth and eyes, and, rocking back and forth in an agony of woe, she began to sob:

"Oh, my God! my God! My heart! My life! I want to die! I want to die!"

Standing there watching her, there suddenly came to Cowperwood a keen sense of her soul hurt, her heart hurt, and he was moved.

"Aileen," he said, after a moment or two, coming over and touching her quite gently, "Aileen! Don't cry so. I haven't left you yet. Your life isn't utterly ruined. Don't cry. This is bad business, but perhaps it is not without remedy. Come now, pull yourself together, Aileen!"

For answer she merely rocked and moaned, uncontrolled and uncontrollable.

Being anxious about conditions elsewhere, he turned and stepped out into the hall. He must make some show for the benefit of the doctor and the servants; he must look after Rita, and offer some sort of passing explanation to Sohlberg.

"Here," he called to a passing servant, "shut that door and watch it. If Mrs. Cowperwood comes out call me instantly."

CHAPTER XIX

"HELL HATH NO FURY—"

Rita was not dead by any means—only seriously bruised, scratched, and choked. Her scalp was cut in one place. Aileen had repeatedly beaten her head on the floor, and this might have resulted seriously if Cowperwood had not entered as quickly as he had. Sohlberg for the moment—for some little time, in fact—was under the impression that Aileen had truly lost her mind, had suddenly gone crazy, and that those shameless charges he had heard her making were the emanations of a disordered brain. Nevertheless the things she had said haunted him. He was in a bad state himself—almost a subject for the doctor. His lips were bluish, his cheeks blanched. Rita had been carried into an adjoining bedroom and laid upon a bed; cold water, ointments, a bottle of arnica had been procured; and when Cowperwood appeared she was conscious and somewhat better. But she was still very weak and smarting from her wounds, both mental and physical. When the doctor arrived he had been told that a lady, a guest, had fallen down-stairs; when Cowperwood came in the physician was dressing her wounds.

As soon as he had gone Cowperwood said to the maid in attendance, "Go get me some hot water." As the latter disappeared he bent over and kissed Rita's bruised lips, putting his finger to his own in warning sign.

"Rita," he asked, softly, "are you fully conscious?"

She nodded weakly.

"Listen, then," he said, bending over and speaking slowly. "Listen carefully. Pay strict attention to what I'm saying. You must understand every word, and do as I tell you. You are not seriously injured. You will be all right. This will blow over. I have sent for another doctor to call on you at your studio. Your husband has gone for some fresh clothes. He will come back in a little while. My carriage will take you home when you are a little stronger. You mustn't worry. Everything will be all right, but you must deny everything, do you hear? Everything! In so far as you know, Mrs. Cowperwood is insane. I will talk to your husband to-morrow. I will send you a trained nurse. Meantime you must be careful of what you say and how you say it. Be perfectly calm. Don't worry. You are perfectly safe here, and you will be there. Mrs. Cowperwood will not trouble you any more. I will see to that. I am so sorry; but I love you. I am near you all the while. You must not let this make any difference. You will not see her any more."

Still he knew that it would make a difference.

Reassured as to Rita's condition, he went back to Aileen's room to plead with her again—to soothe her if he could. He found her up and dressing, a new thought and determination in her mind. Since she had thrown herself on the bed sobbing and groaning, her mood had gradually changed; she began to reason that if she could not dominate him, could not make him properly sorry, she had better leave. It was evident, she thought, that he did not love her any more, seeing that his anxiety to protect Rita had been so great; his brutality in restraining her so marked; and yet she did not want to believe that this was so. He had been so wonderful to her in times past. She had not given up all hope of winning a victory over him, and these other women—she loved him too much—but only a separation would do it. That might bring him to his senses. She would get up, dress, and go down-town to a hotel. He should not see her any more unless he followed her. She was satisfied that she had broken up the liaison with Rita Sohlberg, anyway for the present, and as for Antoinette Nowak, she would attend to her later. Her brain and her heart ached. She was so full of woe and rage, alternating, that she could not cry any more now. She stood before her mirror trying with trembling fingers to do over her toilet and adjust a street-costume. Cowperwood was disturbed, nonplussed at this unexpected sight.

"Aileen," he said, finally, coming up behind her, "can't you and I talk this thing over peacefully now? You don't want to do anything that you'll be sorry for. I don't want you to. I'm sorry. You don't really believe that I've ceased to love you, do you? I haven't, you know. This thing isn't as bad as it looks. I should think you would have a little more sympathy with me after all we have been through together. You haven't any real evidence of wrong-doing on which to base any such outburst as this."

"Oh, haven't I?" she exclaimed, turning from the mirror, where, sorrowfully and bitterly, she was smoothing her red-gold hair. Her cheeks were flushed, her eyes red. Just now she seemed as remarkable to him as she had seemed that first day, years ago, when in a red cape he had seen her, a girl of sixteen, running up the steps of her father's house in Philadelphia. She was so wonderful then. It mellowed his mood toward her.

"That's all you know about it, you liar!" she declared. "It's little you know what I know. I haven't had detectives on your trail for weeks for nothing. You sneak! You'd like to smooth around now and find out what I know. Well, I know enough, let me tell you that. You won't fool me any longer with your Rita Sohlbergs and your Antoinette Nowaks and your apartments and your houses of assignation. I know what you are, you brute! And after all your protestations of love for me! Ugh!"

She turned fiercely to her task while Cowperwood stared at her, touched by her passion, moved by her force. It was fine to see what a dramatic animal she was—really worthy of him in many ways.

"Aileen," he said, softly, hoping still to ingratiate himself by degrees, "please don't be so bitter toward me. Haven't you any understanding of how life works—any sympathy with it? I thought you were more generous, more tender. I'm not so bad."

He eyed her thoughtfully, tenderly, hoping to move her through her love for him.

"Sympathy! Sympathy!" She turned on him blazing. "A lot you know about sympathy! I suppose I didn't give you any sympathy when you were in the penitentiary in Philadelphia, did I? A lot of good it did me—didn't it? Sympathy! Bah! To have you come out here to Chicago and take up with a lot of prostitutes—cheap stenographers and wives of musicians! You have given me a lot of sympathy, haven't you?—with that woman lying in the next room to prove it!"

She smoothed her lithe waist and shook her shoulders preparatory to putting on a hat and adjusting her wrap. She proposed to go just as she was, and send Fadette back for all her belongings.

"Aileen," he pleaded, determined to have his way, "I think you're very foolish. Really I do. There is no occasion for all this—none in the world. Here you are talking at the top of your voice, scandalizing the whole neighborhood, fighting, leaving the house. It's abominable. I don't want you to do it. You love me yet, don't you? You know you do. I know you don't

357

mean all you say. You can't. You really don't believe that I have ceased to love you, do you, Aileen?"

"Love!" fired Aileen. "A lot you know about love! A lot you have ever loved anybody, you brute! I know how you love. I thought you loved me once. Humph! I see how you loved me—just as you've loved fifty other women, as you love that snippy little Rita Sohlberg in the next room—the cat!—the dirty little beast!—the way you love Antoinette Nowak—a cheap stenographer! Bah! You don't know what the word means." And yet her voice trailed off into a kind of sob and her eyes filled with tears, hot, angry, aching. Cowperwood saw them and came over, hoping in some way to take advantage of them. He was truly sorry now—anxious to make her feel tender toward him once more.

"Aileen," he pleaded, "please don't be so bitter. You shouldn't be so hard on me. I'm not so bad. Aren't you going to be reasonable?" He put out a smoothing hand, but she jumped away.

"Don't you touch me, you brute!" she exclaimed, angrily. "Don't you lay a hand on me. I don't want you to come near me. I'll not live with you. I'll not stay in the same house with you and your mistresses. Go and live with your dear, darling Rita on the North Side if you want to. I don't care. I suppose you've been in the next room comforting her—the beast! I wish I had killed her—Oh, God!" She tore at her throat in a violent rage, trying to adjust a button.

Cowperwood was literally astonished. Never had he seen such an outburst as this. He had not believed Aileen to be capable of it. He could not help admiring her. Nevertheless he resented the brutality of her assault on Rita and on his own promiscuous tendency, and this feeling vented itself in one last unfortunate remark.

"I wouldn't be so hard on mistresses if I were you, Aileen," he ventured, pleadingly. "I should have thought your own experience would have—"

He paused, for he saw on the instant that he was making a grave mistake. This reference to her past as a mistress was crucial. On the instant she straightened up, and her eyes filled with a great pain. "So that's the way you talk to me, is it?" she asked. "I knew it! I knew it! I knew it would come!"

She turned to a tall chest of drawers as high as her breasts, laden with silverware, jewel-boxes, brushes and combs, and, putting her arms down, she laid her head upon them and began to cry. This was the last straw. He was throwing up her lawless girlhood love to her as an offense.

"Oh!" she sobbed, and shook in a hopeless, wretched paroxysm. Cowperwood came over quickly. He was distressed, pained. "I didn't mean that, Aileen," he explained. "I didn't mean it in that way—not at all. You rather drew that out of me; but I didn't mean it as a reproach. You were my mistress, but good Lord, I never loved you any the less for that—rather more. You know I did. I want you to believe that; it's true. These other matters haven't been so important to me—they really haven't—"

He looked at her helplessly as she moved away to avoid him; he was distressed, nonplussed, immensely sorry. As he walked to the center of the room again she suddenly suffered a great revulsion of feeling, but only in the direction of more wrath. This was too much.

"So this is the way you talk to me," she exclaimed, "after all I have done for you! You say that to me after I waited for you and cried over you when you were in prison for nearly two years? Your mistress! That's my reward, is it? Oh!"

Suddenly she observed her jewel-case, and, resenting all the gifts he had given her in Philadelphia, in Paris, in Rome, here in Chicago, she suddenly threw open the lid and, grabbing the contents by handfuls, began to toss them toward him—to actually throw them in his face. Out they came, handfuls of gauds that he had given her in real affection: a jade necklace and bracelet of pale apple-green set in spun gold, with clasps of white ivory; a necklace of pearls, assorted as to size and matched in color, that shone with a tinted, pearly flame in the evening light; a handful of rings and brooches, diamonds, rubies, opals, amethysts; a dog-collar of emeralds, and a diamond hair-ornament. She flung them at him excitedly, strewing the floor, striking him on the neck, the face, the hands. "Take that! and that! and that! There they are! I don't want anything more of yours. I don't want anything more to do with you. I don't want anything that belongs to you. Thank God, I have money enough of my own to live on! I hate you—I despise you—I never want to see you any more. Oh—" And, trying to think of something more, but failing, she dashed swiftly down the hall and down the stairs, while he stood for just one moment overwhelmed. Then he hurried after.

"Aileen!" he called. "Aileen, come back here! Don't go, Aileen!" But she only hurried faster; she opened and closed the door, and actually ran out in the dark, her eyes wet, her heart bursting. So this was the end of that youthful dream that had begun so beautifully. She was no better than the others—just one of his mistresses. To have her past thrown up to her as a defense for the others! To be told that she was no better than they! This was the last straw. She choked and sobbed as she walked, vowing never to return, never to see him any more. But as she did so Cowperwood came running after, determined for once, as lawless as he was, that this should not be the end of it all. She had loved him, he reflected. She had laid every gift of passion and affection on the altar of her love. It wasn't fair, really. She must be made to stay. He caught up at last, reaching her under the dark of the November trees.

"Aileen," he said, laying hold of her and putting his arms around her waist. "Aileen, dearest, this is plain madness. It is insanity. You're not in your right mind. Don't go! Don't leave me! I love you! Don't you know I do? Can't you really see that? Don't run away like this, and don't cry. I do love you, and you know it. I always shall. Come back now. Kiss me. I'll do better. Really I will. Give me another chance. Wait and see. Come now—won't you? That's my girl, my Aileen. Do come. Please!"

She pulled on, but he held her, smoothing her arms, her neck, her face.

"Aileen!" he entreated.

She tugged so that he was finally compelled to work her about into his arms; then, sobbing, she stood there agonized but happy once more, in a way.

"But I don't want to," she protested. "You don't love me any more. Let me go."

But he kept hold of her, urging, and finally she said, her head upon his shoulder as of old, "Don't make me come back to-night. I don't want to. I can't. Let me go down-town. I'll come back later, maybe."

"Then I'll go with you," he said, endearingly. "It isn't right. There are a lot of things I should be doing to stop this scandal, but I'll go."

And together they sought a street-car.

CHAPTER XX

"MAN AND SUPERMAN"

It is a sad commentary on all save the most chemic unions—those dark red flowers of romance that bloom most often only for a tragic end—that they cannot endure the storms of disaster that are wont to overtake them. A woman like Rita Sohlberg, with a seemingly urgent feeling for Cowperwood, was yet not so charmed by him but that this shock to her pride was a marked sedative. The crushing weight of such an exposure as this, the Homeric laughter inherent, if not indicated in the faulty planning, the failure to take into account beforehand all the possibilities which might lead to such a disaster, was too much for her to endure. She was stung almost to desperation, maddened, at the thought of the gay, idle way in which she had walked into Mrs. Cowperwood's clutches and been made into a spectacle and a laughing-stock by her. What a brute she was—what a demon! Her own physical weakness under the circumstances was no grief to her—rather a salve to her superior disposition; but just the same she had been badly beaten, her beauty turned into a ragamuffin show, and that was enough. This evening, in the Lake Shore Sanitarium, where she had been taken, she had but one thought—to get away when it should all be over and rest her wearied brain. She did not want to see Sohlberg any more; she did not want to see Cowperwood any more. Already Harold, suspicious and determined to get at the truth, was beginning to question her as to the strangeness of Aileen's attack—her probable reason. When Cowperwood was announced, Sohlberg's manner modified somewhat, for whatever his suspicions were, he was not prepared to quarrel with this singular man as yet.

"I am so sorry about this unfortunate business," said Cowperwood, coming in with brisk assurance. "I never knew my wife to become so strangely unbalanced before. It was most fortunate that I arrived when I did. I certainly owe you both every amend that can be made. I sincerely hope, Mrs. Sohlberg, that you are not seriously injured. If there is anything I can possibly do—anything either of you can suggest"—he looked around solicitously at Sohlberg—"I shall only be too glad to do it. How would it do for you to take Mrs. Sohlberg away for a little while for a rest? I shall so gladly pay all expenses in connection with her recovery."

Sohlberg, brooding and heavy, remained unresponsive, smoldering; Rita, cheered by Cowperwood's presence, but not wholly relieved by any means, was questioning and disturbed. She was afraid there was to be a terrific scene between them. She declared she was better and would be all right—that she did not need to go away, but that she preferred to be alone.

"It's very strange," said Sohlberg, sullenly, after a little while. "I daunt onderstand it! I daunt onderstand it at all. Why should she do soach a thing? Why should she say soach things? Here we have been the best of friends opp to now. Then suddenly she attacks my wife and sais all these strange things."

"But I have assured you, my dear Mr. Sohlberg, that my wife was not in her right mind. She has been subject to spells of this kind in the past, though never to anything so violent as this to-night. Already she has recovered her normal state, and she does not remember. But, perhaps, if we are going to discuss things now we had better go out in the hall. Your wife will need all the rest she can get."

Once outside, Cowperwood continued with brilliant assurance: "Now, my dear Sohlberg, what is it I can say? What is it you wish me to do? My wife has made a lot of groundless charges, to say nothing of injuring your wife most seriously and shamefully. I cannot tell you, as I have said, how sorry I am. I assure you Mrs. Cowperwood is suffering from a gross illusion. There is absolutely nothing to do, nothing to say, so far as I can see, but to let the whole matter drop. Don't you agree with me?"

Harold was twisting mentally in the coils of a trying situation. His own position, as he knew, was not formidable. Rita had reproached him over and over for infidelity. He began to swell and bluster at once.

"That is all very well for you to say, Mr. Cowperwood," he commented, defiantly, "but how about me? Where do I come in? I daunt know what to theenk yet. It ees very strange. Supposing what your wife sais was true? Supposing my wife has been going around weeth some one? That ees what I want to find out. Eef she has! Eef eet is what I theenk it ees I shall—I shall—I daunt know what I shall do. I am a very violent man."

Cowperwood almost smiled, concerned as he was over avoiding publicity; he had no fear of Sohlberg physically.

"See here," he exclaimed, suddenly, looking sharply at the musician and deciding to take the bull by the horns, "you are in quite as delicate a situation as I am, if you only stop to think. This affair, if it gets out, will involve not only me and Mrs. Cowperwood, but yourself and your wife, and if I am not mistaken, I think your own affairs are not in any too good shape. You cannot blacken your wife without blackening yourself—that is inevitable. None of us is exactly perfect. For myself I shall be compelled to prove insanity, and I can do this easily. If there is anything in your past which is not precisely what it should be it could not long be kept a secret. If you are willing to let the matter drop I will make handsome provision for you both; if, instead, you choose to make trouble, to force this matter into the daylight, I shall leave no stone unturned to protect myself, to put as good a face on this matter as I can."

"What!" exclaimed Sohlberg. "You threaten me? You try to frighten me after your wife charges that you have been running around weeth my wife? You talk about my past! I like that. Haw! We shall see about dis! What is it you knaw about me?"

"Well, Mr. Sohlberg," rejoined Cowperwood, calmly, "I know, for instance, that for a long while your wife has not loved you, that you have been living on her as any pensioner might, that you have been running around with as many as six or seven women in as many years or less. For months I have been acting as your wife's financial adviser, and in that time, with the aid of detectives, I have learned of Anna Stelmak, Jessie Laska, Bertha Reese, Georgia Du Coin—do I need to say any more? As a matter of fact, I have a number of your letters in my possession."

"Saw that ees it!" exclaimed Sohlberg, while Cowperwood eyed him fixedly. "You have been running around weeth my wife? Eet ees true, then. A fine situation! And you come here now weeth these threats, these lies to booldoze me. Haw! We weel see about them. We weel see what I can do. Wait teel I can consult a lawyer first. Then we weel see!"

Cowperwood surveyed him coldly, angrily. "What an ass!" he thought.

"See here," he said, urging Sohlberg, for privacy's sake, to come down into the lower hall, and then into the street before the sanitarium, where two gas-lamps were fluttering fitfully in the dark and wind, "I see very plainly that you are bent on making trouble. It is not enough that I have assured you that there is nothing in this—that I have given you my word. You insist on going further. Very well, then. Supposing for argument's sake that Mrs. Cowperwood was not insane; that every word she said was true; that I had been misconducting myself with your wife? What of it? What will you do?"

He looked at Sohlberg smoothly, ironically, while the latter flared up.

"Haw!" he shouted, melodramatically. "Why, I would keel you, that's what I would do. I would keel her. I weel make a terrible scene. Just let me knaw that this is so, and then see!"

"Exactly," replied Cowperwood, grimly. "I thought so. I believe you. For that reason I have come prepared to serve you in just the way you wish." He reached in his coat and took out two small revolvers, which he had taken from a drawer at home for this very purpose. They gleamed in the dark. "Do you see these?" he continued. "I am going to save you the trouble of further investigation, Mr. Sohlberg. Every word that Mrs. Cowperwood said to-night— and I am saying this with a full understanding of what this means to you and to me—is true. She is no more insane than I am. Your wife has been living in an apartment with me on the North Side for months, though you cannot prove that. She does not love you, but me. Now if you want to kill me here is a gun." He extended his hand. "Take your choice. If I am to die you might as well die with me."

He said it so coolly, so firmly, that Sohlberg, who was an innate coward, and who had no more desire to die than any other healthy animal, paled. The look of cold steel was too much. The hand that pressed them on him was hard and firm. He took hold of one, but his fingers trembled. The steely, metallic voice in his ear was undermining the little courage that he had. Cowperwood by now had taken on the proportions of a dangerous man—the lineaments of a demon. He turned away mortally terrified.

"My God!" he exclaimed, shaking like a leaf. "You want to keel me, do you? I weel not have anything to do with you! I weel not talk to you! I weel see my lawyer. I weel talk to my wife first."

"Oh, no you won't," replied Cowperwood, intercepting him as he turned to go and seizing him firmly by the arm. "I am not going to have you do anything of the sort. I am not going to kill you if you are not going to kill me; but I am going to make you listen to reason for once. Now here is what else I have to say, and then I am through. I am not unfriendly to you. I want to do you a good turn, little as I care for you. To begin with, there is nothing in those charges my wife made, not a thing. I merely said what I did just now to see if you were in earnest. You do not love your wife any more. She doesn't love you. You are no good to her. Now, I have a very friendly proposition to make to you. If you want to leave Chicago and stay away three years or more, I will see that you are paid five thousand dollars every year on January first—on the nail—five thousand dollars! Do you hear? Or you can stay here in Chicago and hold your tongue and I will make it three thousand—monthly or yearly, just as you please. But—and this is what I want you to remember—if you don't get

362

out of town or hold your tongue, if you make one single rash move against me, I will kill you, and I will kill you on sight. Now, I want you to go away from here and behave yourself. Leave your wife alone. Come and see me in a day or two—the money is ready for you any time." He paused while Sohlberg stared—his eyes round and glassy. This was the most astonishing experience of his life. This man was either devil or prince, or both. "Good God!" he thought. "He will do that, too. He will really kill me." Then the astounding alternative—five thousand dollars a year—came to his mind. Well, why not? His silence gave consent.

"If I were you I wouldn't go up-stairs again to-night," continued Cowperwood, sternly. "Don't disturb her. She needs rest. Go on down-town and come and see me to-morrow— or if you want to go back I will go with you. I want to say to Mrs. Sohlberg what I have said to you. But remember what I've told you."

"Nau, thank you," replied Sohlberg, feebly. "I will go down-town. Good night." And he hurried away.

"I'm sorry," said Cowperwood to himself, defensively. "It is too bad, but it was the only way."

CHAPTER XXI

A MATTER OF TUNNELS

The question of Sohlberg adjusted thus simply, if brutally, Cowperwood turned his attention to Mrs. Sohlberg. But there was nothing much to be done. He explained that he had now completely subdued Aileen and Sohlberg, that the latter would make no more trouble, that he was going to pension him, that Aileen would remain permanently quiescent. He expressed the greatest solicitude for her, but Rita was now sickened of this tangle. She had loved him, as she thought, but through the rage of Aileen she saw him in a different light, and she wanted to get away. His money, plentiful as it was, did not mean as much to her as it might have meant to some women; it simply spelled luxuries, without which she could exist if she must. His charm for her had, perhaps, consisted mostly in the atmosphere of flawless security, which seemed to surround him—a glittering bubble of romance. That, by one fell attack, was now burst. He was seen to be quite as other men, subject to the same storms, the same danger of shipwreck. Only he was a better sailor than most. She recuperated gradually; left for home; left for Europe; details too long to be narrated. Sohlberg, after much meditating and fuming, finally accepted the offer of Cowperwood and returned to Denmark. Aileen, after a few days of quarreling, in which he agreed to dispense with Antoinette Nowak, returned home.

Cowperwood was in no wise pleased by this rough denouement. Aileen had not raised her own attractions in his estimation, and yet, strange to relate, he was not unsympathetic with her. He had no desire to desert her as yet, though for some time he had been growing in the feeling that Rita would have been a much better type of wife for him. But what he could not have, he could not have. He turned his attention with renewed force to his business; but it was with many a backward glance at those radiant hours when, with Rita in his presence or enfolded by his arms, he had seen life from a new and poetic angle. She was so charming, so naive—but what could he do?

For several years thereafter Cowperwood was busy following the Chicago street-railway situation with increasing interest. He knew it was useless to brood over Rita Sohlberg—she would not return—and yet he could not help it; but he could work hard, and that was something. His natural aptitude and affection for street-railway work had long since been demonstrated, and it was now making him restless. One might have said of him quite truly that the tinkle of car-bells and the plop of plodding horses' feet was in his blood. He surveyed these extending lines, with their jingling cars, as he went about the city, with an almost hungry eye. Chicago was growing fast, and these little horse-cars on certain streets were crowded night and morning—fairly bulging with people at the rush-hours. If he could only secure an octopus-grip on one or all of them; if he could combine and control them all! What a fortune! That, if nothing else, might salve him for some of his woes—a tremendous fortune—nothing less. He forever busied himself with various aspects of the scene quite as a poet might have concerned himself with rocks and rills. To own these street-railways! To own these street-railways! So rang the song of his mind.

Like the gas situation, the Chicago street-railway situation was divided into three parts— three companies representing and corresponding with the three different sides or divisions of the city. The Chicago City Railway Company, occupying the South Side and extending as far south as Thirty-ninth Street, had been organized in 1859, and represented in itself a mine of wealth. Already it controlled some seventy miles of track, and was annually being added to on Indiana Avenue, on Wabash Avenue, on State Street, and on Archer Avenue. It owned over one hundred and fifty cars of the old-fashioned, straw-strewn, no-stove type, and over one thousand horses; it employed one hundred and seventy conductors, one hundred and sixty drivers, a hundred stablemen, and blacksmiths, harness-makers, and repairers in interesting numbers. Its snow-plows were busy on the street in winter, its sprinkling-cars in summer. Cowperwood calculated its shares, bonds, rolling-stock, and other physical properties as totaling in the vicinity of over two million dollars. The trouble with this company was that its outstanding stock was principally controlled by Norman Schryhart, who was now decidedly inimical to Cowperwood, or anything he might wish to do, and by Anson Merrill, who had never manifested any signs of friendship. He did not see how he was to get control of this property. Its shares were selling around two hundred and fifty dollars.

The North Chicago City Railway was a corporation which had been organized at the same time as the South Side company, but by a different group of men. Its management was old, indifferent, and incompetent, its equipment about the same. The Chicago West Division Railway had originally been owned by the Chicago City or South Side Railway, but was now a separate corporation. It was not yet so profitable as the other divisions of the city, but all sections of the city were growing. The horse-bell was heard everywhere tinkling gaily.

Standing on the outside of this scene, contemplating its promise, Cowperwood much more than any one else connected financially with the future of these railways at this time was impressed with their enormous possibilities—their enormous future if Chicago continued to grow, and was concerned with the various factors which might further or impede their progress.

Not long before he had discovered that one of the chief handicaps to street-railway development, on the North and West Sides, lay in the congestion of traffic at the bridges spanning the Chicago River. Between the street ends that abutted on it and connected the two sides of the city ran this amazing stream—dirty, odorous, picturesque, compact of a heavy, delightful, constantly crowding and moving boat traffic, which kept the various bridges momentarily turning, and tied up the street traffic on either side of the river until it seemed at times as though the tangle of teams and boats would never any more be straightened out. It was lovely, human, natural, Dickensesque—a fit subject for a Daumier, a Turner, or a Whistler. The idlest of bridge-tenders judged for himself when the boats and when the teams should be made to wait, and how long, while in addition to the regular pedestrians a group of idlers stood at gaze fascinated by the crowd of masts, the crush of wagons, and the picturesque tugs in the foreground below. Cowperwood, as he sat in his light runabout, annoyed by a delay, or dashed swiftly forward to get over before a bridge turned, had long since noted that the street-car service in the North and West Sides was badly hampered. The unbroken South Side, unthreaded by a river, had no such problem, and was growing rapidly.

Because of this he was naturally interested to observe one day, in the course of his peregrinations, that there existed in two places under the Chicago River—in the first place at La Salle Street, running north and south, and in the second at Washington Street, running east and west—two now soggy and rat-infested tunnels which were never used by anybody—dark, dank, dripping affairs only vaguely lighted with oil-lamp, and oozing with water. Upon investigation he learned that they had been built years before to accommodate this same tide of wagon traffic, which now congested at the bridges, and which even then had been rapidly rising. Being forced to pay a toll in time to which a slight toll in cash, exacted for the privilege of using a tunnel, had seemed to the investors and public infinitely to be preferred, this traffic had been offered this opportunity of avoiding the delay. However, like many another handsome commercial scheme on paper or bubbling in the human brain, the plan did not work exactly. These tunnels might have proved profitable if they had been properly built with long, low-per-cent. grades, wide roadways, and a sufficiency of light and air; but, as a matter of fact, they had not been judiciously adapted to public convenience. Norman Schryhart's father had been an investor in these tunnels, and Anson Merrill. When they had proved unprofitable, after a long period of pointless manipulation—cost, one million dollars—they had been sold to the city for exactly that sum each, it being poetically deemed that a growing city could better afford to lose so disturbing an amount than any of its humble, ambitious, and respectable citizens. That was a little affair by which members of council had profited years before; but that also is another story.

After discovering these tunnels Cowperwood walked through them several times—for though they were now boarded up, there was still an uninterrupted footpath—and wondered why they could not be utilized. It seemed to him that if the street-car traffic were heavy enough, profitable enough, and these tunnels, for a reasonable sum, could be made into a lower grade, one of the problems which now hampered the growth of the North and West Sides would be obviated. But how? He did not own the tunnels. He did not own the street-railways. The cost of leasing and rebuilding the tunnels would be enormous. Helpers and horses and extra drivers on any grade, however slight, would have to be used, and that meant an extra expense. With street-car horses as the only means of traction, and with the long, expensive grades, he was not so sure that this venture would be a profitable one.

However, in the fall of 1880, or a little earlier (when he was still very much entangled with the preliminary sex affairs that led eventually to Rita Sohlberg), he became aware of a new system of traction relating to street-cars which, together with the arrival of the arc-light, the telephone, and other inventions, seemed destined to change the character of city life entirely.

Recently in San Francisco, where the presence of hills made the movement of crowded street-railway cars exceedingly difficult, a new type of traction had been introduced—that of the cable, which was nothing more than a traveling rope of wire running over guttered wheels in a conduit, and driven by immense engines, conveniently located in adjacent stations or "power-houses." The cars carried a readily manipulated "grip-lever," or steel hand, which reached down through a slot into a conduit and "gripped" the moving cable. This invention solved the problem of hauling heavily laden street-cars up and down steep grades. About the same time he also heard, in a roundabout way, that the Chicago City Railway, of which Schryhart and Merrill were the principal owners, was about to introduce this mode of traction on its lines—to cable State Street, and attach the cars of other lines running farther out into unprofitable districts as "trailers." At once the solution of the North and West Side problems flashed upon him—cables.

Outside of the bridge crush and the tunnels above mentioned, there was one other special condition which had been for some time past attracting Cowperwood's attention. This was the waning energy of the North Chicago City Railway Company—the lack of foresight on the part of its directors which prevented them from perceiving the proper solution of their difficulties. The road was in a rather unsatisfactory state financially—really open to a coup of some sort. In the beginning it had been considered unprofitable, so thinly populated was the territory they served, and so short the distance from the business heart. Later, however, as the territory filled up, they did better; only then the long waits at the bridges occurred. The management, feeling that the lines were likely to be poorly patronized, had put down poor, little, light-weight rails, and run slimpsy cars which were as cold as ice in winter and as hot as stove-ovens in summer. No attempt had been made to extend the down-town terminus of the several lines into the business center—they stopped just over the river which bordered it at the north. (On the South Side Mr. Schryhart had done much better for his patrons. He had already installed a loop for his cable about Merrill's store.) As on the West Side, straw was strewn in the bottom of all the cars in winter to keep the feet of the passengers warm, and but few open cars were used in summer. The directors were averse to introducing them because of the expense. So they had gone on and on, adding lines only where they were sure they would make a good profit from the start, putting down the same style of cheap rail that had been used in the beginning, and employing the same antique type of car which rattled and trembled as it ran, until the patrons were enraged to the point of anarchy. Only recently, because of various suits and complaints inaugurated, the company had been greatly annoyed, but they scarcely knew what to do, how to meet the onslaught. Though there was here and there a man of sense—such as Terrence Mulgannon, the general superintendent; Edwin Kaffrath, a director; William Johnson, the constructing engineer of the company—yet such other men as Onias C. Skinner, the president, and Walter Parker, the vice-president, were reactionaries of an elderly character, conservative, meditative, stingy, and, worst of all, fearful or without courage for great adventure. It is a sad commentary that age almost invariably takes away the incentive to new achievement and makes "Let well enough alone" the most appealing motto.

Mindful of this, Cowperwood, with a now splendid scheme in his mind, one day invited John J. McKenty over to his house to dinner on a social pretext. When the latter, accompanied by his wife, had arrived, and Aileen had smiled on them both sweetly, and was doing her best to be nice to Mrs. McKenty, Cowperwood remarked:

"McKenty, do you know anything about these two tunnels that the city owns under the river at Washington and La Salle streets?"

"I know that the city took them over when it didn't need them, and that they're no good for anything. That was before my time, though," explained McKenty, cautiously. "I think the city paid a million for them. Why?"

"Oh, nothing much," replied Cowperwood, evading the matter for the present. "I was wondering whether they were in such condition that they couldn't be used for anything. I see occasional references in the papers to their uselessness."

"They're in pretty bad shape, I'm afraid," replied McKenty. "I haven't been through either of them in years and years. The idea was originally to let the wagons go through them and break up the crowding at the bridges. But it didn't work. They made the grade too steep and the tolls too high, and so the drivers preferred to wait for the bridges. They were pretty hard on horses. I can testify to that myself. I've driven a wagon-load through them more than once. The city should never have taken them over at all by rights. It was a deal. I don't know who all was in it. Carmody was mayor then, and Aldrich was in charge of public works."

He relapsed into silence, and Cowperwood allowed the matter of the tunnels to rest until after dinner when they had adjourned to the library. There he placed a friendly hand on McKenty's arm, an act of familiarity which the politician rather liked.

"You felt pretty well satisfied with the way that gas business came out last year, didn't you?" he inquired.

"I did," replied McKenty, warmly. "Never more so. I told you that at the time." The Irishman liked Cowperwood, and was grateful for the swift manner in which he had been made richer by the sum of several hundred thousand dollars.

"Well, now, McKenty," continued Cowperwood, abruptly, and with a seeming lack of connection, "has it ever occurred to you that things are shaping up for a big change in the street-railway situation here? I can see it coming. There's going to be a new motor power introduced on the South Side within a year or two. You've heard of it?"

"I read something of it," replied McKenty, surprised and a little questioning. He took a cigar and prepared to listen. Cowperwood, never smoking, drew up a chair.

"Well, I'll tell you what that means," he explained. "It means that eventually every mile of street-railway track in this city—to say nothing of all the additional miles that will be built before this change takes place—will have to be done over on an entirely new basis. I mean this cable-conduit system. These old companies that are hobbling along now with an old equipment will have to make the change. They'll have to spend millions and millions before they can bring their equipment up to date. If you've paid any attention to the matter you must have seen what a condition these North and West Side lines are in."

"It's pretty bad; I know that," commented McKenty.

"Just so," replied Cowperwood, emphatically. "Well, now, if I know anything about these old managements from studying them, they're going to have a hard time bringing themselves to do this. Two to three million are two to three million, and it isn't going to be an easy matter for them to raise the money—not as easy, perhaps, as it would be for some of the rest of us, supposing we wanted to go into the street-railway business."

"Yes, supposing," replied McKenty, jovially. "But how are you to get in it? There's no stock for sale that I know of."

"Just the same," said Cowperwood, "we can if we want to, and I'll show you how. But at present there's just one thing in particular I'd like you to do for me. I want to know if there is any way that we can get control of either of those two old tunnels that I was talking to you about a little while ago. I'd like both if I might. Do you suppose that is possible?"

"Why, yes," replied McKenty, wondering; "but what have they got to do with it? They're not worth anything. Some of the boys were talking about filling them in some time ago— blowing them up. The police think crooks hide in them."

"Just the same, don't let any one touch them—don't lease them or anything," replied Cowperwood, forcefully. "I'll tell you frankly what I want to do. I want to get control, just as soon as possible, of all the street-railway lines I can on the North and West Sides—new or old franchises. Then you'll see where the tunnels come in."

He paused to see whether McKenty caught the point of all he meant, but the latter failed.

"You don't want much, do you?" he said, cheerfully. "But I don't see how you can use the tunnels. However, that's no reason why I shouldn't take care of them for you, if you think that's important."

"It's this way," said Cowperwood, thoughtfully. "I'll make you a preferred partner in all the ventures that I control if you do as I suggest. The street-railways, as they stand now, will have to be taken up lock, stock, and barrel, and thrown into the scrap heap within eight or nine years at the latest. You see what the South Side company is beginning to do now. When it comes to the West and North Side companies they won't find it so easy. They aren't earning as much as the South Side, and besides they have those bridges to cross. That means a severe inconvenience to a cable line. In the first place, the bridges will have to be rebuilt to stand the extra weight and strain. Now the question arises at once—at whose expense? The city's?"

"That depends on who's asking for it," replied Mr. McKenty, amiably.

"Quite so," assented Cowperwood. "In the next place, this river traffic is becoming impossible from the point of view of a decent street-car service. There are waits now of from eight to fifteen minutes while these tows and vessels get through. Chicago has five hundred thousand population to-day. How much will it have in 1890? In 1900? How will it be when it has eight hundred thousand or a million?"

"You're quite right," interpolated McKenty. "It will be pretty bad."

"Exactly. But what is worse, the cable lines will carry trailers, or single cars, from feeder lines. There won't be single cars waiting at these draws—there will be trains, crowded trains. It won't be advisable to delay a cable-train from eight to fifteen minutes while boats are making their way through a draw. The public won't stand for that very long, will it, do you think?"

"Not without making a row, probably," replied McKenty.

"Well, that means what, then?" asked Cowperwood. "Is the traffic going to get any lighter? Is the river going to dry up?"

Mr. McKenty stared. Suddenly his face lighted. "Oh, I see," he said, shrewdly. "It's those tunnels you're thinking about. Are they in any shape to be used?"

"They can be made over cheaper than new ones can be built."

"True for you," replied McKenty, "and if they're in any sort of repair they'd be just what you'd want." He was emphatic, almost triumphant. "They belong to the city. They cost pretty near a million apiece, those things."

"I know it," said Cowperwood. "Now, do you see what I'm driving at?"

"Do I see!" smiled McKenty. "That's a real idea you have, Cowperwood. I take off my hat to you. Say what you want."

"Well, then, in the first place," replied Cowperwood, genially, "it is agreed that the city won't part with those two tunnels under any circumstances until we can see what can be done about this other matter?"

"It will not."

"In the next place, it is understood, is it, that you won't make it any easier than you can possibly help for the North and West Side companies to get ordinances extending their lines, or anything else, from now on? I shall want to introduce some franchises for feeders and outlying lines myself."

"Bring in your ordinances," replied McKenty, "and I'll do whatever you say. I've worked with you before. I know that you keep your word."

"Thanks," said Cowperwood, warmly. "I know the value of keeping it. In the mean while I'll go ahead and see what can be done about the other matter. I don't know just how many men I will need to let in on this, or just what form the organization will take. But you may depend upon it that your interests will be properly taken care of, and that whatever is done will be done with your full knowledge and consent."

"All very good," answered McKenty, thinking of the new field of activity before them. A combination between himself and Cowperwood in a matter like this must prove very beneficial to both. And he was satisfied, because of their previous relations, that his own interests would not be neglected.

"Shall we go and see if we can find the ladies?" asked Cowperwood, jauntily, laying hold of the politician's arm.

"To be sure," assented McKenty, gaily. "It's a fine house you have here—beautiful. And your wife is as pretty a woman as I ever saw, if you'll pardon the familiarity."

"I have always thought she was rather attractive myself," replied Cowperwood, innocently.

CHAPTER XXII

STREET-RAILWAYS AT LAST

Among the directors of the North Chicago City company there was one man, Edwin L. Kaffrath, who was young and of a forward-looking temperament. His father, a former heavy stockholder of this company, had recently died and left all his holdings and practically his directorship to his only son. Young Kaffrath was by no means a practical street-railway man, though he fancied he could do very well at it if given a chance. He was the holder of nearly eight hundred of the five thousand shares of stock; but the rest of it was so divided that he could only exercise a minor influence. Nevertheless, from the day of his entrance into the company—which was months before Cowperwood began seriously to think over the situation—he had been strong for improvements—extensions, more franchises, better cars, better horses, stoves in the cars in winter, and the like, all of which suggestions sounded to his fellow-directors like mere manifestations of the reckless impetuosity of youth, and were almost uniformly opposed.

"What's the matter with them cars?" asked Albert Thorsen, one of the elder directors, at one of the meetings at which Kaffrath was present and offering his usual protest. "I don't see anything the matter with 'em. I ride in em."

Thorsen was a heavy, dusty, tobacco-bestrewn individual of sixty-six, who was a little dull but genial. He was in the paint business, and always wore a very light steel-gray suit much crinkled in the seat and arms.

"Perhaps that's what's the matter with them, Albert," chirped up Solon Kaempfaert, one of his cronies on the board.

The sally drew a laugh.

"Oh, I don't know. I see the rest of you on board often enough."

"Why, I tell you what's the matter with them," replied Kaffrath. "They're dirty, and they're flimsy, and the windows rattle so you can't hear yourself think. The track is no good, and the filthy straw we keep in them in winter is enough to make a person sick. We don't keep the track in good repair. I don't wonder people complain. I'd complain myself."

"Oh, I don't think things are as bad as all that," put in Onias C. Skinner, the president, who had a face which with its very short side-whiskers was as bland as a Chinese god. He was sixty-eight years of age. "They're not the best cars in the world, but they're good cars. They need painting and varnishing pretty badly, some of them, but outside of that there's many a good year's wear in them yet. I'd be very glad if we could put in new rolling-stock, but the item of expense will be considerable. It's these extensions that we have to keep building and the long hauls for five cents which eat up the profits." The so-called "long hauls" were only two or three miles at the outside, but they seemed long to Mr. Skinner.

"Well, look at the South Side," persisted Kaffrath. "I don't know what you people are thinking of. Here's a cable system introduced in Philadelphia. There's another in San Francisco. Some one has invented a car, as I understand it, that's going to run by electricity, and here we are running cars—barns, I call them—with straw in them. Good Lord, I should think it was about time that some of us took a tumble to ourselves!"

370

"Oh, I don't know," commented Mr. Skinner. "It seems to me we have done pretty well by the North Side. We have done a good deal."

Directors Solon Kaempfaert, Albert Thorsen, Isaac White, Anthony Ewer, Arnold C. Benjamin, and Otto Matjes, being solemn gentlemen all, merely sat and stared.

The vigorous Kaffrath was not to be so easily repressed, however. He repeated his complaints on other occasions. The fact that there was also considerable complaint in the newspapers from time to time in regard to this same North Side service pleased him in a way. Perhaps this would be the proverbial fire under the terrapin which would cause it to move along.

By this time, owing to Cowperwood's understanding with McKenty, all possibility of the North Side company's securing additional franchises for unoccupied streets, or even the use of the La Salle Street tunnel, had ended. Kaffrath did not know this. Neither did the directors or officers of the company, but it was true. In addition, McKenty, through the aldermen, who were at his beck and call on the North Side, was beginning to stir up additional murmurs and complaints in order to discredit the present management. There was a great to-do in council over a motion on the part of somebody to compel the North Side company to throw out its old cars and lay better and heavier tracks. Curiously, this did not apply so much to the West and South Sides, which were in the same condition. The rank and file of the city, ignorant of the tricks which were constantly being employed in politics to effect one end or another, were greatly cheered by this so-called "public uprising." They little knew the pawns they were in the game, or how little sincerity constituted the primal impulse.

Quite by accident, apparently, one day Addison, thinking of the different men in the North Side company who might be of service to Cowperwood, and having finally picked young Kaffrath as the ideal agent, introduced himself to the latter at the Union League.

"That's a pretty heavy load of expense that's staring you North and West Side street-railway people in the face," he took occasion to observe.

"How's that?" asked Kaffrath, curiously, anxious to hear anything which concerned the development of the business.

"Well, unless I'm greatly mistaken, you, all of you, are going to be put to the expense of doing over your lines completely in a very little while—so I hear—introducing this new motor or cable system that they are getting on the South Side." Addison wanted to convey the impression that the city council or public sentiment or something was going to force the North Chicago company to indulge in this great and expensive series of improvements.

Kaffrath pricked up his ears. What was the city Council going to do? He wanted to know all about it. They discussed the whole situation—the nature of the cable-conduits, the cost of the power-houses, the need of new rails, and the necessity of heavier bridges, or some other means of getting over or under the river. Addison took very good care to point out that the Chicago City or South Side Railway was in a much more fortunate position than either of the other two by reason of its freedom from the river-crossing problem. Then he again commiserated the North Side company on its rather difficult position. "Your company will have a very great deal to do, I fancy," he reiterated.

371

Kaffrath was duly impressed and appropriately depressed, for his eight hundred shares would be depressed in value by the necessity of heavy expenditures for tunnels and other improvements. Nevertheless, there was some consolation in the thought that such betterment, as Addison now described, would in the long run make the lines more profitable. But in the mean time there might be rough sailing. The old directors ought to act soon now, he thought. With the South Side company being done over, they would have to follow suit. But would they? How could he get them to see that, even though it were necessary to mortgage the lines for years to come, it would pay in the long run? He was sick of old, conservative, cautious methods.

After the lapse of a few weeks Addison, still acting for Cowperwood, had a second and private conference with Kaffrath. He said, after exacting a promise of secrecy for the present, that since their previous conversation he had become aware of new developments. In the interval he had been visited by several men of long connection with street-railways in other localities. They had been visiting various cities, looking for a convenient outlet for their capital, and had finally picked on Chicago. They had looked over the various lines here, and had decided that the North Chicago City Railway was as good a field as any. He then elaborated with exceeding care the idea which Cowperwood had outlined to him. Kaffrath, dubious at first, was finally won over. He had too long chafed under the dusty, poky attitude of the old regime. He did not know who these new men were, but this scheme was in line with his own ideas. It would require, as Addison pointed out, the expenditure of several millions of dollars, and he did not see how the money could be raised without outside assistance, unless the lines were heavily mortgaged. If these new men were willing to pay a high rate for fifty-one per cent. of this stock for ninety-nine years and would guarantee a satisfactory rate of interest on all the stock as it stood, besides inaugurating a forward policy, why not let them? It would be just as good as mortgaging the soul out of the old property, and the management was of no value, anyhow. Kaffrath could not see how fortunes were to be made for these new investors out of subsidiary construction and equipment companies, in which Cowperwood would be interested, how by issuing watered stock on the old and new lines the latter need scarcely lay down a dollar once he had the necessary opening capital (the "talking capital," as he was fond of calling it) guaranteed. Cowperwood and Addison had by now agreed, if this went through, to organize the Chicago Trust Company with millions back of it to manipulate all their deals. Kaffrath only saw a better return on his stock, possibly a chance to get in on the "ground plan," as a new phrase expressed it, of the new company.

"That's what I've been telling these fellows for the past three years," he finally exclaimed to Addison, flattered by the latter's personal attention and awed by his great influence; "but they never have been willing to listen to me. The way this North Side system has been managed is a crime. Why, a child could do better than we have done. They've saved on track and rolling-stock, and lost on population. People are what we want up there, and there is only one way that I know of to get them, and that is to give them decent car service. I'll tell you frankly we've never done it."

Not long after this Cowperwood had a short talk with Kaffrath, in which he promised the latter not only six hundred dollars a share for all the stock he possessed or would part with on lease, but a bonus of new company stock for his influence. Kaffrath returned to the North Side jubilant for himself and for his company. He decided after due thought that a roundabout way would best serve Cowperwood's ends, a line of subtle suggestion from some seemingly disinterested party. Consequently he caused William Johnson, the directing engineer, to approach Albert Thorsen, one of the most vulnerable of the directors, declaring he had heard privately that Isaac White, Arnold C. Benjamin, and Otto Matjes, three other directors and the heaviest owners, had been offered a very remarkable price for their stock, and that they were going to sell, leaving the others out in the cold.

Thorsen was beside himself with grief. "When did you hear that?" he asked.

Johnson told him, but for the time being kept the source of his information secret. Thorsen at once hurried to his friend, Solon Kaempfaert, who in turn went to Kaffrath for information.

"I have heard something to that effect," was Kaffrath's only comment, "but really I do not know."

Thereupon Thorsen and Kaempfaert imagined that Kaffrath was in the conspiracy to sell out and leave them with no particularly valuable pickings. It was very sad.

Meanwhile, Cowperwood, on the advice of Kaffrath, was approaching Isaac White, Arnold C. Benjamin, and Otto Matjes direct—talking with them as if they were the only three he desired to deal with. A little later Thorsen and Kaempfaert were visited in the same spirit, and agreed in secret fear to sell out, or rather lease at the very advantageous terms Cowperwood offered, providing he could get the others to do likewise. This gave the latter a strong backing of sentiment on the board. Finally Isaac White stated at one of the meetings that he had been approached with an interesting proposition, which he then and there outlined. He was not sure what to think, he said, but the board might like to consider it. At once Thorsen and Kaempfaert were convinced that all Johnson had suggested was true. It was decided to have Cowperwood come and explain to the full board just what his plan was, and this he did in a long, bland, smiling talk. It was made plain that the road would have to be put in shape in the near future, and that this proposed plan relieved all of them of work, worry, and care. Moreover, they were guaranteed more interest at once than they had expected to earn in the next twenty or thirty years. Thereupon it was agreed that Cowperwood and his plan should be given a trial. Seeing that if he did not succeed in paying the proposed interest promptly the property once more became theirs, so they thought, and that he assumed all obligations—taxes, water rents, old claims, a few pensions—it appeared in the light of a rather idyllic scheme.

"Well, boys, I think this is a pretty good day's work myself," observed Anthony Ewer, laying a friendly hand on the shoulder of Mr. Albert Thorsen. "I'm sure we can all unite in wishing Mr. Cowperwood luck with his adventure." Mr. Ewer's seven hundred and fifteen shares, worth seventy-one thousand five hundred dollars, having risen to a valuation of four hundred and twenty-nine thousand dollars, he was naturally jubilant.

"You're right," replied Thorsen, who was parting with four hundred and eighty shares out of a total of seven hundred and ninety, and seeing them all bounce in value from two hundred to six hundred dollars. "He's an interesting man. I hope he succeeds."

Cowperwood, waking the next morning in Aileen's room—he had been out late the night before with McKenty, Addison, Videra, and others—turned and, patting her neck where she was dozing, said: "Well, pet, yesterday afternoon I wound up that North Chicago Street Railway deal. I'm president of the new North Side company just as soon as I get my board of directors organized. We're going to be of some real consequence in this village, after all, in a year or two."

He was hoping that this fact, among other things, would end in mollifying Aileen toward him. She had been so gloomy, remote, weary these many days—ever since the terrific assault on Rita.

"Yes?" she replied, with a half-hearted smile, rubbing her waking eyes. She was clad in a foamy nightgown of white and pink. "That's nice, isn't it?"

Cowperwood brought himself up on one elbow and looked at her, smoothing her round, bare arms, which he always admired. The luminous richness of her hair had never lost its charm completely.

"That means that I can do the same thing with the Chicago West Division Company in a year or so," he went on. "But there's going to be a lot of talk about this, I'm afraid, and I don't want that just now. It will work out all right. I can see Schryhart and Merrill and some of these other people taking notice pretty soon. They've missed out on two of the biggest things Chicago ever had—gas and railways."

"Oh yes, Frank, I'm glad for you," commented Aileen, rather drearily, who, in spite of her sorrow over his defection, was still glad that he was going on and forward. "You'll always do all right."

"I wish you wouldn't feel so badly, Aileen," he said, with a kind of affectional protest. "Aren't you going to try and be happy with me? This is as much for you as for me. You will be able to pay up old scores even better than I will."

He smiled winningly.

"Yes," she replied, reproachfully but tenderly at that, a little sorrowfully, "a lot of good money does me. It was your love I wanted."

"But you have that," he insisted. "I've told you that over and over. I never ceased to care for you really. You know I didn't."

"Yes, I know," she replied, even as he gathered her close in his arms. "I know how you care." But that did not prevent her from responding to him warmly, for back of all her fuming protest was heartache, the wish to have his love intact, to restore that pristine affection which she had once assumed would endure forever.

CHAPTER XXIII

THE POWER OF THE PRESS

The morning papers, in spite of the efforts of Cowperwood and his friends to keep this transfer secret, shortly thereafter were full of rumors of a change in "North Chicago." Frank Algernon Cowperwood, hitherto unmentioned in connection with Chicago street-railways, was pointed to as the probable successor to Onias C. Skinner, and Edwin L. Kaffrath, one of the old directors, as future vice-president. The men back of the deal were referred to as "in all likelihood Eastern capitalists." Cowperwood, as he sat in Aileen's room examining the various morning papers, saw that before the day was over he would be sought out for an expression of opinion and further details. He proposed to ask the newspaper men to wait a few days until he could talk to the publishers of the papers themselves—win their confidence—and then announce a general policy; it would be something that would please the city, and the residents of the North Side in particular. At the same time he did not care to promise anything which he could not easily and profitably perform. He wanted fame and reputation, but he wanted money even more; he intended to get both.

To one who had been working thus long in the minor realms of finance, as Cowperwood considered that he had so far been doing, this sudden upward step into the more conspicuous regions of high finance and control was an all-inspiring thing. So long had he been stirring about in a lesser region, paving the way by hours and hours of private thought and conference and scheming, that now when he actually had achieved his end he could scarcely believe for the time being that it was true. Chicago was such a splendid city. It was growing so fast. Its opportunities were so wonderful. These men who had thus foolishly parted with an indefinite lease of their holdings had not really considered what they were doing. This matter of Chicago street-railways, once he had them well in hand, could be made to yield such splendid profits! He could incorporate and overcapitalize. Many subsidiary lines, which McKenty would secure for him for a song, would be worth millions in the future, and they should be his entirely; he would not be indebted to the directors of the old North Chicago company for any interest on those. By degrees, year by year, as the city grew, the lines which were still controlled by this old company, but were practically his, would become a mere item, a central core, in the so very much larger system of new lines which he would build up about it. Then the West Side, and even the South Side sections— but why dream? He might readily become the sole master of street-railway traffic in Chicago! He might readily become the most princely financial figure in the city—and one of the few great financial magnates of the nation.

In any public enterprise of any kind, as he knew, where the suffrages of the people or the privileges in their possessions are desired, the newspapers must always be considered. As Cowperwood even now was casting hungry eyes in the direction of the two tunnels—one to be held in view of an eventual assumption of the Chicago West Division Company, the other to be given to the North Chicago Street Railway, which he had now organized, it was necessary to make friends with the various publishers. How to go about it?

Recently, because of the influx of a heavy native and foreign-born population (thousands and thousands of men of all sorts and conditions looking for the work which the growth of the city seemed to promise), and because of the dissemination of stirring ideas through radical individuals of foreign groups concerning anarchism, socialism, communism, and the like, the civic idea in Chicago had become most acute. This very May, in which Cowperwood had been going about attempting to adjust matters in his favor, there had been a tremendous national flare-up, when in a great public place on the West Side known as the Haymarket, at one of a number of labor meetings, dubbed anarchistic because of the principles of some of the speakers, a bomb had been hurled by some excited fanatic, which had exploded and maimed or killed a number of policemen, injuring slightly several others. This had brought to the fore, once and for all, as by a flash of lightning, the whole problem of mass against class, and had given it such an airing as in view of the cheerful, optimistic, almost inconsequential American mind had not previously been possible. It changed, quite as an eruption might, the whole face of the commercial landscape. Man thought thereafter somewhat more accurately of national and civic things. What was anarchism? What socialism? What rights had the rank and file, anyhow, in economic and governmental development? Such were interesting questions, and following the bomb—which acted as a great stone cast in the water—these ripple-rings of thought were still widening and emanating until they took in such supposedly remote and impregnable quarters as editorial offices, banks and financial institutions generally, and the haunts of political dignitaries and their jobs.

In the face of this, however, Cowperwood was not disturbed. He did not believe in either the strength of the masses or their ultimate rights, though he sympathized with the condition of individuals, and did believe that men like himself were sent into the world to better perfect its mechanism and habitable order. Often now, in these preliminary days, he looked at the large companies of men with their horses gathered in and about the several carbarns of the company, and wondered at their state. So many of them were so dull. They were rather like animals, patient, inartistic, hopeless. He thought of their shabby homes, their long hours, their poor pay, and then concluded that if anything at all could be done for them it would be pay them decent living wages, which he proposed to do—nothing more. They could not be expected to understand his dreams or his visions, or to share in the magnificence and social dominance which he craved. He finally decided that it would be as well for him to personally visit the various newspaper publishers and talk the situation over with them. Addison, when consulted as to this project, was somewhat dubious. He had small faith in the newspapers.

He had seen them play petty politics, follow up enmities and personal grudges, and even sell out, in certain cases, for pathetically small rewards.

"I tell you how it is, Frank," remarked Addison, on one occasion. "You will have to do all this business on cotton heels, practically. You know that old gas crowd are still down on you, in spite of the fact that you are one of their largest stockholders. Schryhart isn't at all friendly, and he practically owns the Chronicle. Ricketts will just about say what he wants him to say. Hyssop, of the Mail and the Transcript, is an independent man, but he's a Presbyterian and a cold, self-righteous moralist. Braxton's paper, the Globe, practically belongs to Merrill, but Braxton's a nice fellow, at that. Old General MacDonald, of the Inquirer, is old General MacDonald. It's all according to how he feels when he gets up in the morning. If he should chance to like your looks he might support you forever and forever until you crossed his conscience in some way. He's a fine old walrus. I like him. Neither Schryhart nor Merrill nor any one else can get anything out of him unless he wants to give it. He may not live so many years, however, and I don't trust that son of his. Haguenin, of the Press, is all right and friendly to you, as I understand. Other things being equal, I think he'd naturally support you in anything he thought was fair and reasonable. Well, there you have them. Get them all on your side if you can. Don't ask for the LaSalle Street tunnel right away. Let it come as an afterthought—a great public need. The main thing will be to avoid having the other companies stirring up a real fight against you. Depend on it, Schryhart will be thinking pretty hard about this whole business from now on. As for Merrill—well, if you can show him where he can get something out of it for his store, I guess he'll be for you."

It is one of the splendid yet sinister fascinations of life that there is no tracing to their ultimate sources all the winds of influence that play upon a given barque—all the breaths of chance that fill or desert our bellied or our sagging sails. We plan and plan, but who by taking thought can add a cubit to his stature? Who can overcome or even assist the Providence that shapes our ends, rough hew them as we may. Cowperwood was now entering upon a great public career, and the various editors and public personalities of the city were watching him with interest. Augustus M. Haguenin, a free agent with his organ, the Press, and yet not free, either, because he was harnessed to the necessity of making his paper pay, was most interested. Lacking the commanding magnetism of a man like MacDonald, he was nevertheless an honest man, well-intentioned, thoughtful, careful. Haguenin, ever since the outcome of Cowperwood's gas transaction, had been intensely interested in the latter's career. It seemed to him that Cowperwood was probably destined to become a significant figure. Raw, glittering force, however, compounded of the cruel Machiavellianism of nature, if it be but Machiavellian, seems to exercise a profound attraction for the conventionally rooted. Your cautious citizen of average means, looking out through the eye of his dull world of seeming fact, is often the first to forgive or condone the grim butcheries of theory by which the strong rise. Haguenin, observing Cowperwood, conceived of him as a man perhaps as much sinned against as sinning, a man who would be faithful to friends, one who could be relied upon in hours of great stress. As it happened, the Haguenins were neighbors of the Cowperwoods, and since those days when the latter had attempted unsuccessfully to enter Chicago society this family had been as acceptable as any of those who had remained friendly.

And so, when Cowperwood arrived one day at the office of the Press in a blowing snow-storm—it was just before the Christmas holidays—Haguenin was glad to see him. "It's certainly real winter weather we're having now, isn't it?" he observed, cheerfully. "How goes the North Chicago Street Railway business?" For months he, with the other publishers, had been aware that the whole North Side was to be made over by fine cable-tracks, power-houses, and handsome cars; and there already was talk that some better arrangement was to be made to bring the passengers into the down-town section.

"Mr. Haguenin," said Cowperwood, smilingly—he was arrayed in a heavy fur coat, with a collar of beaver and driving-gauntlets of dogskin—"we have reached the place in this street-railway problem on the North Side where we are going to require the assistance of the newspapers, or at least their friendly support. At present our principal difficulty is that all our lines, when they come down-town, stop at Lake Street—just this side of the bridges. That means a long walk for everybody to all the streets south of it, and, as you probably know, there has been considerable complaint. Besides that, this river traffic is becoming more and more what I may say it has been for years—an intolerable nuisance. We have all suffered from it. No effort has ever been made to regulate it, and because it is so heavy I doubt whether it ever can be systematized in any satisfactory way. The best thing in the long run would be to tunnel under the river; but that is such an expensive proposition that, as things are now, we are in no position to undertake it. The traffic on the North Side does not warrant it. It really does not warrant the reconstruction of the three bridges which we now use at State, Dearborn, and Clark; yet, if we introduce the cable system, which we now propose, these bridges will have to be done over. It seems to me, seeing that this is an enterprise in which the public is as much interested almost as we are, that it would only be fair if the city should help pay for this reconstruction work. All the land adjacent to these lines, and the property served by them, will be greatly enhanced in value. The city's taxing power will rise tremendously. I have talked to several financiers here in Chicago, and they agree with me; but, as is usual in all such cases, I find that some of the politicians are against me. Since I have taken charge of the North Chicago company the attitude of one or two papers has not been any too friendly." (In the Chronicle, controlled by Schryhart, there had already been a number of references to the probability that now, since Cowperwood and his friends were in charge, the sky-rocketing tactics of the old Lake View, Hyde Park, and other gas organizations would be repeated. Braxton's Globe, owned by Merrill, being semi-neutral, had merely suggested that it hoped that no such methods would be repeated here.) "Perhaps you may know," Cowperwood continued, "that we have a very sweeping programme of improvement in mind, if we can obtain proper public consideration and assistance."

At this point he reached down in one of his pockets and drew forth astutely drafted maps and blue-prints, especially prepared for this occasion. They showed main cable lines on North Clark, La Salle, and Wells streets. These lines coming down-town converged at Illinois and La Salle streets on the North Side—and though Cowperwood made no reference to it at the moment, they were indicated on the map in red as running over or under the river at La Salle Street, where was no bridge, and emerging therefrom, following a loop along La Salle to Munroe, to Dearborn, to Randolph, and thence into the tunnel again. Cowperwood allowed Haguenin to gather the very interesting traffic significance of it all before he proceeded.

"On the map, Mr. Haguenin, I have indicated a plan which, if we can gain the consent of the city, will obviate any quarrel as to the great expense of reconstructing the bridges, and will make use of a piece of property which is absolutely without value to the city at present, but which can be made into something of vast convenience to the public. I am referring, as you see"—he laid an indicative finger on the map in Mr. Haguenin's hands—"to the old La Salle Street tunnel, which is now boarded up and absolutely of no use to any one. It was built apparently under a misapprehension as to the grade the average loaded wagon could negotiate. When it was found to be unprofitable it was sold to the city and locked up. If you have ever been through it you know what condition it is in. My engineers tell me the walls are leaking, and that there is great danger of a cave-in unless it is very speedily repaired. I am also told that it will require about four hundred thousand dollars to put it in suitable condition for use. My theory is that if the North Chicago Street Railway is willing to go to this expense for the sake of solving this bridge-crush problem, and giving the residents of the North Side a sensible and uninterrupted service into the business heart, the city ought to be willing to make us a present of this tunnel for the time being, or at least a long lease at a purely nominal rental."

Cowperwood paused to see what Haguenin would say.

The latter was looking at the map gravely, wondering whether it was fair for Cowperwood to make this demand, wondering whether the city should grant it to him without compensation, wondering whether the bridge-traffic problem was as serious as he pointed out, wondering, indeed, whether this whole move was not a clever ruse to obtain something for nothing.

"And what is this?" he asked, laying a finger on the aforementioned loop.

"That," replied Cowperwood, "is the only method we have been able to figure out of serving the down-town business section and the North Side, and of solving this bridge problem. If we obtain the tunnel, as I hope we shall, all the cars of these North Side lines will emerge here"—he pointed to La Salle and Randolph—"and swing around—that is, they will if the city council give us the right of way. I think, of course, there can be no reasonable objection to that. There is no reason why the citizens of the North Side shouldn't have as comfortable an access to the business heart as those of the West or South Side."

"None in the world," Mr. Haguenin was compelled to admit. "Are you satisfied, however, that the council and the city should sanction the gift of a loop of this kind without some form of compensation?"

"I see no reason why they shouldn't," replied Cowperwood, in a somewhat injured tone. "There has never been any question of compensation where other improvements have been suggested for the city in the past. The South Side company has been allowed to turn in a loop around State and Wabash. The Chicago City Passenger Railway has a loop in Adams and Washington streets."

"Quite so," said Mr. Haguenin, vaguely. "That is true. But this tunnel, now—do you think that should fall in the same category of public beneficences?"

At the same time he could not help thinking, as he looked at the proposed loop indicated on the map, that the new cable line, with its string of trailers, would give down-town Chicago a truly metropolitan air and would provide a splendid outlet for the North Side. The streets in question were magnificent commercial thoroughfares, crowded even at this date with structures five, six, seven, and even eight stories high, and brimming with heavy streams of eager life—young, fresh, optimistic. Because of the narrow area into which the commercial life of the city tended to congest itself, this property and these streets were immensely valuable—among the most valuable in the whole city. Also he observed that if this loop did come here its cars, on their return trip along Dearborn Street, would pass by his very door—the office of the Press—thereby enhancing the value of that property of which he was the owner.

"I certainly do, Mr. Haguenin," returned Cowperwood, emphatically, in answer to his query. "Personally, I should think Chicago would be glad to pay a bonus to get its street-railway service straightened out, especially where a corporation comes forward with a liberal, conservative programme such as this. It means millions in growth of property values on the North Side. It means millions to the business heart to have this loop system laid down just as I suggest."

He put his finger firmly on the map which he had brought, and Haguenin agreed with him that the plan was undoubtedly a sound business proposition. "Personally, I should be the last to complain," he added, "for the line passes my door. At the same time this tunnel, as I understand it, cost in the neighborhood of eight hundred thousand or a million dollars. It is a delicate problem. I should like to know what the other editors think of it, and how the city council itself would feel toward it."

Cowperwood nodded. "Certainly, certainly," he said. "With pleasure. I would not come here at all if I did not feel that I had a perfectly legitimate proposition—one that the press of the city should unite in supporting. Where a corporation such as ours is facing large expenditures, which have to be financed by outside capital, it is only natural that we should wish to allay useless, groundless opposition in advance. I hope we may command your support."

"I hope you may," smiled Mr. Haguenin. They parted the best of friends.

The other publishers, guardians of the city's privileges, were not quite so genial as Haguenin in their approval of Cowperwood's proposition. The use of a tunnel and several of the most important down-town streets might readily be essential to the development of Cowperwood's North Side schemes, but the gift of them was a different matter. Already, as a matter of fact, the various publishers and editors had been consulted by Schryhart, Merrill, and others with a view to discovering how they felt as to this new venture, and whether Cowperwood would be cheerfully indorsed or not. Schryhart, smarting from the wounds he had received in the gas war, viewed this new activity on Cowperwood's part with a suspicious and envious eye. To him much more than to the others it spelled a new and dangerous foe in the street-railway field, although all the leading citizens of Chicago were interested.

"I suppose now," he said one evening to the Hon. Walter Melville Hyssop, editor and publisher of the Transcript and the Evening Mail, whom he met at the Union League, "that this fellow Cowperwood will attempt some disturbing coup in connection with street-railway affairs. He is just the sort. I think, from an editorial point of view, his political connections will bear watching." Already there were rumors abroad that McKenty might have something to do with the new company.

Hyssop, a medium-sized, ornate, conservative person, was not so sure. "We shall find out soon enough, no doubt, what propositions Mr. Cowperwood has in hand," he remarked. "He is very energetic and capable, as I understand it."

Hyssop and Schryhart, as well as the latter and Merrill, had been social friends for years and years.

After his call on Mr. Haguenin, Cowperwood's naturally selective and self-protective judgment led him next to the office of the Inquirer, old General MacDonald's paper, where he found that because of rhuematism and the severe, inclement weather of Chicago, the old General had sailed only a few days before for Italy. His son, an aggressive, mercantile type of youth of thirty-two, and a managing editor by the name of Du Bois were acting in his stead. In the son, Truman Leslie MacDonald, an intense, calm, and penetrating young man, Cowperwood encountered some one who, like himself, saw life only from the point of view of sharp, self-centered, personal advantage. What was he, Truman Leslie MacDonald, to derive from any given situation, and how was he to make the Inquirer an even greater property than it had been under his father before him? He did not propose to be overwhelmed by the old General's rather flowery reputation. At the same time he meant to become imposingly rich. An active member of a young and very smart set which had been growing up on the North Side, he rode, drove, was instrumental in organizing a new and exclusive country club, and despised the rank and file as unsuited to the fine atmosphere to which he aspired. Mr. Clifford Du Bois, the managing editor, was a cool reprobate of forty, masquerading as a gentleman, and using the Inquirer in subtle ways for furthering his personal ends, and that under the old General's very nose. He was osseous, sandy-haired, blue-eyed, with a keen, formidable nose and a solid chin. Clifford Du Bois was always careful never to let his left hand know what his right hand did.

It was this sapient pair that received Cowperwood in the old General's absence, first in Mr. Du Bois's room and then in that of Mr. MacDonald. The latter had already heard much of Cowperwood's doings. Men who had been connected with the old gas war—Jordan Jules, for instance, president of the old North Chicago Gas Company, and Hudson Baker, president of the old West Chicago Gas Company—had denounced him long before as a bucaneer who had pirated them out of very comfortable sinecures. Here he was now invading the North Chicago street-railway field and coming with startling schemes for the reorganization of the down-town business heart. Why shouldn't the city have something in return; or, better yet, those who helped to formulate the public opinion, so influential in the success of Cowperwood's plans? Truman Leslie MacDonald, as has been said, did not see life from his father's point of view at all. He had in mind a sharp bargain, which he could drive with Cowperwood during the old gentleman's absence. The General need never know.

"I understand your point of view, Mr. Cowperwood," he commented, loftily, "but where does the city come in? I see very clearly how important this is to the people of the North Side, and even to the merchants and real-estate owners in the down-town section; but that simply means that it is ten times as important to you. Undoubtedly, it will help the city, but the city is growing, anyhow, and that will help you. I've said all along that these public franchises were worth more than they used to be worth. Nobody seems to see it very clearly as yet, but it's true just the same. That tunnel is worth more now than the day it was built. Even if the city can't use it, somebody can."

He was meaning to indicate a rival car line.

Cowperwood bristled internally.

"That's all very well," he said, preserving his surface composure, "but why make fish of one and flesh of another? The South Side company has a loop for which it never paid a dollar. So has the Chicago City Passenger Railway. The North Side company is planning more extensive improvements than were ever undertaken by any single company before. I hardly think it is fair to raise the question of compensation and a franchise tax at this time, and in connection with this one company only."

"Um—well, that may be true of the other companies. The South Side company had those streets long ago. They merely connected them up. But this tunnel, now—that's a different matter, isn't it? The city bought and paid for that, didn't it?"

"Quite true—to help out men who saw that they couldn't make another dollar out of it," said Cowperwood, acidly. "But it's of no use to the city. It will cave in pretty soon if it isn't repaired. Why, the consent of property-owners alone, along the line of this loop, is going to aggregate a considerable sum. It seems to me instead of hampering a great work of this kind the public ought to do everything in its power to assist it. It means giving a new metropolitan flavor to this down-town section. It is time Chicago was getting out of its swaddling clothes."

Mr. MacDonald, the younger, shook his head. He saw clearly enough the significance of the points made, but he was jealous of Cowperwood and of his success. This loop franchise and tunnel gift meant millions for some one. Why shouldn't there be something in it for him? He called in Mr. Du Bois and went over the proposition with him. Quite without effort the latter sensed the drift of the situation.

"It's an excellent proposition," he said. "I don't see but that the city should have something, though. Public sentiment is rather against gifts to corporations just at present."

Cowperwood caught the drift of what was in young MacDonald's mind.

"Well, what would you suggest as a fair rate of compensation to the city?" he asked, cautiously, wondering whether this aggressive youth would go so far as to commit himself in any way.

"Oh, well, as to that," MacDonald replied, with a deprecatory wave of his hand, "I couldn't say. It ought to bear a reasonable relationship to the value of the utility as it now stands. I should want to think that over. I shouldn't want to see the city demand anything unreasonable. Certainly, though, there is a privilege here that is worth something."

Cowperwood flared inwardly. His greatest weakness, if he had one, was that he could but ill brook opposition of any kind. This young upstart, with his thin, cool face and sharp, hard eyes! He would have liked to tell him and his paper to go to the devil. He went away, hoping that he could influence the Inquirer in some other way upon the old General's return.

As he was sitting next morning in his office in North Clark Street he was aroused by the still novel-sounding bell of the telephone—one of the earliest in use—on the wall back of him. After a parley with his secretary, he was informed that a gentleman connected with the Inquirer wished to speak with him.

"This is the Inquirer," said a voice which Cowperwood, his ear to the receiver, thought he recognized as that of young Truman MacDonald, the General's son. "You wanted to know," continued the voice, "what would be considered adequate compensation so far as that tunnel matter is concerned. Can you hear me?"

"Yes," replied Cowperwood.

"Well, I should not care to influence your judgment one way or the other; but if my opinion were asked I should say about fifty thousand dollars' worth of North Chicago Street Railway stock would be satisfactory."

The voice was young, clear, steely.

"To whom would you suggest that it might be paid?" Cowperwood asked, softly, quite genially.

"That, also, I would suggest, might be left to your very sound judgment."

The voice ceased. The receiver was hung up.

"Well, I'll be damned!" Cowperwood said, looking at the floor reflectively. A smile spread over his face. "I'm not going to be held up like that. I don't need to be. It isn't worth it. Not at present, anyhow." His teeth set.

He was underestimating Mr. Truman Leslie MacDonald, principally because he did not like him. He thought his father might return and oust him. It was one of the most vital mistakes he ever made in his life.

CHAPTER XXIV

THE COMING OF STEPHANIE PLATOW

During this period of what might have been called financial and commercial progress, the affairs of Aileen and Cowperwood had been to a certain extent smoothed over. Each summer now, partly to take Aileen's mind off herself and partly to satisfy his own desire to see the world and collect objects of art, in which he was becoming more and more interested, it was Cowperwood's custom to make with his wife a short trip abroad or to foreign American lands, visiting in these two years Russia, Scandinavia, Argentine, Chili, and Mexico. Their plan was to leave in May or June with the outward rush of traffic, and return in September or early October. His idea was to soothe Aileen as much as possible, to fill her mind with pleasing anticipations as to her eventual social triumph somewhere—in New York or London, if not Chicago—to make her feel that in spite of his physical desertion he was still spiritually loyal.

By now also Cowperwood was so shrewd that he had the ability to simulate an affection and practise a gallantry which he did not feel, or, rather, that was not backed by real passion. He was the soul of attention; he would buy her flowers, jewels, knickknacks, and ornaments; he would see that her comfort was looked after to the last detail; and yet, at the very same moment, perhaps, he would be looking cautiously about to see what life might offer in the way of illicit entertainment. Aileen knew this, although she could not prove it to be true. At the same time she had an affection and an admiration for the man which gripped her in spite of herself.

You have, perhaps, pictured to yourself the mood of some general who has perhaps suffered a great defeat; the employee who after years of faithful service finds himself discharged. What shall life say to the loving when their love is no longer of any value, when all that has been placed upon the altar of affection has been found to be a vain sacrifice? Philosophy? Give that to dolls to play with. Religion? Seek first the metaphysical-minded. Aileen was no longer the lithe, forceful, dynamic girl of 1865, when Cowperwood first met her. She was still beautiful, it is true, a fair, full-blown, matronly creature not more than thirty-five, looking perhaps thirty, feeling, alas, that she was a girl and still as attractive as ever. It is a grim thing to a woman, however fortunately placed, to realize that age is creeping on, and that love, that singing will-o'-the-wisp, is fading into the ultimate dark. Aileen, within the hour of her greatest triumph, had seen love die. It was useless to tell herself, as she did sometimes, that it might come back, revive. Her ultimately realistic temperament told her this could never be. Though she had routed Rita Sohlberg, she was fully aware that Cowperwood's original constancy was gone. She was no longer happy. Love was dead. That sweet illusion, with its pearly pink for heart and borders, that laughing cherub that lures with Cupid's mouth and misty eye, that young tendril of the vine of life that whispers of eternal spring-time, that calls and calls where aching, wearied feet by legion follow, was no longer in existence.

In vain the tears, the storms, the self-tortures; in vain the looks in the mirror, the studied examination of plump, sweet features still fresh and inviting. One day, at the sight of tired circles under her eyes, she ripped from her neck a lovely ruche that she was adjusting and, throwing herself on her bed, cried as though her heart would break. Why primp? Why ornament? Her Frank did not love her. What to her now was a handsome residence in Michigan Avenue, the refinements of a French boudoir, or clothing that ran the gamut of the dressmaker's art, hats that were like orchids blooming in serried rows? In vain, in vain! Like the raven that perched above the lintel of the door, sad memory was here, grave in her widow weeds, crying "never more." Aileen knew that the sweet illusion which had bound Cowperwood to her for a time had gone and would never come again. He was here. His step was in the room mornings and evenings; at night for long prosaic, uninterrupted periods she could hear him breathing by her side, his hand on her body. There were other nights when he was not there—when he was "out of the city"—and she resigned herself to accept his excuses at their face value. Why quarrel? she asked herself. What could she do? She was waiting, waiting, but for what?

And Cowperwood, noting the strange, unalterable changes which time works in us all, the inward lap of the marks of age, the fluted recession of that splendor and radiance which is youth, sighed at times perhaps, but turned his face to that dawn which is forever breaking where youth is. Not for him that poetic loyalty which substitutes for the perfection of young love its memories, or takes for the glitter of passion and desire that once was the happy thoughts of companionship—the crystal memories that like early dews congealed remain beaded recollections to comfort or torture for the end of former joys. On the contrary, after the vanishing of Rita Sohlberg, with all that she meant in the way of a delicate insouciance which Aileen had never known, his temperament ached, for he must have something like that. Truth to say, he must always have youth, the illusion of beauty, vanity in womanhood, the novelty of a new, untested temperament, quite as he must have pictures, old porcelain, music, a mansion, illuminated missals, power, the applause of the great, unthinking world.

As has been said, this promiscuous attitude on Cowperwood's part was the natural flowering out of a temperament that was chronically promiscuous, intellectually uncertain, and philosophically anarchistic. From one point of view it might have been said of him that he was seeking the realization of an ideal, yet to one's amazement our very ideals change at times and leave us floundering in the dark. What is an ideal, anyhow? A wraith, a mist, a perfume in the wind, a dream of fair water. The soul-yearning of a girl like Antoinette Nowak was a little too strained for him. It was too ardent, too clinging, and he had gradually extricated himself, not without difficulty, from that particular entanglement. Since then he had been intimate with other women for brief periods, but to no great satisfaction—Dorothy Ormsby, Jessie Belle Hinsdale, Toma Lewis, Hilda Jewell; but they shall be names merely. One was an actress, one a stenographer, one the daughter of one of his stock patrons, one a church-worker, a solicitor for charity coming to him to seek help for an orphan's home. It was a pathetic mess at times, but so are all defiant variations from the accustomed drift of things. In the hardy language of Napoleon, one cannot make an omelette without cracking a number of eggs.

The coming of Stephanie Platow, Russian Jewess on one side of her family, Southwestern American on the other, was an event in Cowperwood's life. She was tall, graceful, brilliant, young, with much of the optimism of Rita Sohlberg, and yet endowed with a strange fatalism which, once he knew her better, touched and moved him. He met her on shipboard on the way to Goteborg. Her father, Isadore Platow, was a wealthy furrier of Chicago. He was a large, meaty, oily type of man—a kind of ambling, gelatinous formula of the male, with the usual sound commercial instincts of the Jew, but with an errant philosophy which led him to believe first one thing and then another so long as neither interfered definitely with his business. He was an admirer of Henry George and of so altruistic a programme as that of Robert Owen, and, also, in his way, a social snob. And yet he had married Susetta Osborn, a Texas girl who was once his bookkeeper. Mrs. Platow was lithe, amiable, subtle, with an eye always to the main social chance—in other words, a climber. She was shrewd enough to realize that a knowledge of books and art and current events was essential, and so she "went in" for these things.

It is curious how the temperaments of parents blend and revivify in their children. As Stephanie grew up she had repeated in her very differing body some of her father's and mother's characteristics—an interesting variability of soul. She was tall, dark, sallow, lithe, with a strange moodiness of heart and a recessive, fulgurous gleam in her chestnut-brown, almost brownish-black eyes. She had a full, sensuous, Cupid's mouth, a dreamy and even languishing expression, a graceful neck, and a heavy, dark, and yet pleasingly modeled face. From both her father and mother she had inherited a penchant for art, literature, philosophy, and music. Already at eighteen she was dreaming of painting, singing, writing poetry, writing books, acting—anything and everything. Serene in her own judgment of what was worth while, she was like to lay stress on any silly mood or fad, thinking it exquisite—the last word. Finally, she was a rank voluptuary, dreaming dreams of passionate union with first one and then another type of artist, poet, musician—the whole gamut of the artistic and emotional world.

Cowperwood first saw her on board the Centurion one June morning, as the ship lay at dock in New York. He and Aileen were en route for Norway, she and her father and mother for Denmark and Switzerland. She was hanging over the starboard rail looking at a flock of wide-winged gulls which were besieging the port of the cook's galley. She was musing soulfully—conscious (fully) that she was musing soulfully. He paid very little attention to her, except to note that she was tall, rhythmic, and that a dark-gray plaid dress, and an immense veil of gray silk wound about her shoulders and waist and over one arm, after the manner of a Hindu shawl, appeared to become her much. Her face seemed very sallow, and her eyes ringed as if indicating dyspepsia. Her black hair under a chic hat did not escape his critical eye. Later she and her father appeared at the captain's table, to which the Cowperwoods had also been invited.

Cowperwood and Aileen did not know how to take this girl, though she interested them both. They little suspected the chameleon character of her soul. She was an artist, and as formless and unstable as water. It was a mere passing gloom that possessed her. Cowperwood liked the semi-Jewish cast of her face, a certain fullness of the neck, her dark, sleepy eyes. But she was much too young and nebulous, he thought, and he let her pass. On this trip, which endured for ten days, he saw much of her, in different moods, walking with a young Jew in whom she seemed greatly interested, playing at shuffleboard, reading solemnly in a corner out of the reach of the wind or spray, and usually looking naive, preternaturally innocent, remote, dreamy. At other times she seemed possessed of a wild animation, her eyes alight, her expression vigorous, an intense glow in her soul. Once he saw her bent over a small wood block, cutting a book-plate with a thin steel graving tool.

Because of Stephanie's youth and seeming unimportance, her lack of what might be called compelling rosy charm, Aileen had become reasonably friendly with the girl. Far subtler, even at her years, than Aileen, Stephanie gathered a very good impression of the former, of her mental girth, and how to take her. She made friends with her, made a book-plate for her, made a sketch of her. She confided to Aileen that in her own mind she was destined for the stage, if her parents would permit; and Aileen invited her to see her husband's pictures on their return. She little knew how much of a part Stephanie would play in Cowperwood's life.

The Cowperwoods, having been put down at Goteborg, saw no more of the Platows until late October. Then Aileen, being lonely, called to see Stephanie, and occasionally thereafter Stephanie came over to the South Side to see the Cowperwoods. She liked to roam about their house, to dream meditatively in some nook of the rich interior, with a book for company. She liked Cowperwood's pictures, his jades, his missals, his ancient radiant glass. From talking with Aileen she realized that the latter had no real love for these things, that her expressions of interest and pleasure were pure make-believe, based on their value as possessions. For Stephanie herself certain of the illuminated books and bits of glass had a heavy, sensuous appeal, which only the truly artistic can understand. They unlocked dark dream moods and pageants for her. She responded to them, lingered over them, experienced strange moods from them as from the orchestrated richness of music.

And in doing so she thought of Cowperwood often. Did he really like these things, or was he just buying them to be buying them? She had heard much of the pseudo artistic—the

385

people who made a show of art. She recalled Cowperwood as he walked the deck of the Centurion. She remembered his large, comprehensive, embracing blue-gray eyes that seemed to blaze with intelligence. He seemed to her quite obviously a more forceful and significant man than her father, and yet she could not have said why. He always seemed so trigly dressed, so well put together. There was a friendly warmth about all that he said or did, though he said or did little. She felt that his eyes were mocking, that back in his soul there was some kind of humor over something which she did not understand quite.

After Stephanie had been back in Chicago six months, during which time she saw very little of Cowperwood, who was busy with his street-railway programme, she was swept into the net of another interest which carried her away from him and Aileen for the time being. On the West Side, among a circle of her mother's friends, had been organized an Amateur Dramatic League, with no less object than to elevate the stage. That world-old problem never fails to interest the new and the inexperienced. It all began in the home of one of the new rich of the West Side—the Timberlakes. They, in their large house on Ashland Avenue, had a stage, and Georgia Timberlake, a romantic-minded girl of twenty with flaxen hair, imagined she could act. Mrs. Timberlake, a fat, indulgent mother, rather agreed with her. The whole idea, after a few discursive performances of Milton's "The Masque of Comus," "Pyramus and Thisbe," and an improved Harlequin and Columbine, written by one of the members, was transferred to the realm of the studios, then quartered in the New Arts Building. An artist by the name of Lane Cross, a portrait-painter, who was much less of an artist than he was a stage director, and not much of either, but who made his living by hornswaggling society into the belief that he could paint, was induced to take charge of these stage performances.

By degrees the "Garrick Players," as they chose to call themselves, developed no little skill and craftsmanship in presenting one form and another of classic and semi-classic play. "Romeo and Juliet," with few properties of any kind, "The Learned Ladies" of Moliere, Sheridan's "The Rivals," and the "Elektra" of Sophocles were all given. Considerable ability of one kind and another was developed, the group including two actresses of subsequent repute on the American stage, one of whom was Stephanie Platow. There were some ten girls and women among the active members, and almost as many men—a variety of characters much too extended to discuss here. There was a dramatic critic by the name of Gardner Knowles, a young man, very smug and handsome, who was connected with the Chicago Press. Whipping his neatly trousered legs with his bright little cane, he used to appear at the rooms of the players at the Tuesday, Thursday, and Saturday teas which they inaugurated, and discuss the merits of the venture. Thus the Garrick Players were gradually introduced into the newspapers. Lane Cross, the smooth-faced, pasty-souled artist who had charge, was a rake at heart, a subtle seducer of women, who, however, escaped detection by a smooth, conventional bearing. He was interested in such girls as Georgia Timberlake, Irma Ottley, a rosy, aggressive maiden who essayed comic roles, and Stephanie Platow. These, with another girl, Ethel Tuckerman, very emotional and romantic, who could dance charmingly and sing, made up a group of friends which became very close. Presently intimacies sprang up, only in this realm, instead of ending in marriage, they merely resulted in sex liberty. Thus Ethel Tuckerman became the mistress of Lane Cross; an illicit attachment grew up between Irma Ottley and a young society idler by the name of Bliss Bridge; and Gardner Knowles, ardently admiring Stephanie Platow literally seized upon her one afternoon in her own home, when he went ostensibly to interview her, and overpersuaded her. She was only reasonably fond of him, not in love; but, being generous, nebulous, passionate, emotional, inexperienced, voiceless, and vainly curious, without any sense of the meums and teums that govern society in such matters, she allowed this rather brutal thing to happen. She was not a coward—was too nebulous and yet forceful to be such. Her parents never knew. And once so launched, another world—that of sex satisfaction—began to dawn on her.

Were these young people evil? Let the social philosopher answer. One thing is certain: They did not establish homes and raise children. On the contrary, they led a gay, butterfly existence for nearly two years; then came a gift in the lute. Quarrels developed over parts, respective degrees of ability, and leadership. Ethel Tuckerman fell out with Lane Cross, because she discovered him making love to Irma Ottley. Irma and Bliss Bridge released each other, the latter transferring his affections to Georgia Timberlake. Stephanie Platow, by far the most individual of them all, developed a strange inconsequence as to her deeds. It was when she was drawing near the age of twenty that the affair with Gardner Knowles began. After a time Lane Cross, with his somewhat earnest attempt at artistic interpretation and his superiority in the matter of years—he was forty, and young Knowles only twenty-four—seemed more interesting to Stephanie, and he was quick to respond. There followed an idle, passionate union with this man, which seemed important, but was not so at all. And then it was that Stephanie began dimly to perceive that it was on and on that the blessings lie, that somewhere there might be some man much more remarkable than either of these; but this was only a dream. She thought of Cowperwood at times; but he seemed to her to be too wrapped up in grim tremendous things, far apart from this romantic world of amateur dramatics in which she was involved.

CHAPTER XXV

AIRS FROM THE ORIENT

Cowperwood gained his first real impression of Stephanie at the Garrick Players, where he went with Aileen once to witness a performance of "Elektra." He liked Stephanie particularly in this part, and thought her beautiful. One evening not long afterward he noticed her in his own home looking at his jades, particularly a row of bracelets and ear-rings. He liked the rhythmic outline of her body, which reminded him of a letter S in motion. Quite suddenly it came over him that she was a remarkable girl—very—destined, perhaps, to some significant future. At the same time Stephanie was thinking of him.

"Do you find them interesting?" he asked, stopping beside her.

"I think they're wonderful. Those dark-greens, and that pale, fatty white! I can see how beautiful they would be in a Chinese setting. I have always wished we could find a Chinese or Japanese play to produce sometime."

"Yes, with your black hair those ear-rings would look well," said Cowperwood.

He had never deigned to comment on a feature of hers before. She turned her dark, brown-black eyes on him—velvety eyes with a kind of black glow in them—and now he noticed how truly fine they were, and how nice were her hands—brown almost as a Malay's.

He said nothing more; but the next day an unlabeled box was delivered to Stephanie at her home containing a pair of jade ear-rings, a bracelet, and a brooch with Chinese characters intagliated. Stephanie was beside herself with delight. She gathered them up in her hands and kissed them, fastening the ear-rings in her ears and adjusting the bracelet and ring.

Despite her experience with her friends and relatives, her stage associates, and her paramours, she was still a little unschooled in the world. Her heart was essentially poetic and innocent. No one had ever given her much of anything—not even her parents. Her allowance thus far in life had been a pitiful six dollars a week outside of her clothing. As she surveyed these pretty things in the privacy of her room she wondered oddly whether Cowperwood was growing to like her. Would such a strong, hard business man be interested in her? She had heard her father say he was becoming very rich. Was she a great actress, as some said she was, and would strong, able types of men like Cowperwood take to her—eventually? She had heard of Rachel, of Nell Gwynne, of the divine Sarah and her loves. She took the precious gifts and locked them in a black-iron box which was sacred to her trinkets and her secrets.

The mere acceptance of these things in silence was sufficient indication to Cowperwood that she was of a friendly turn of mind. He waited patiently until one day a letter came to his office—not his house—addressed, "Frank Algernon Cowperwood, Personal." It was written in a small, neat, careful hand, almost printed.

I don't know how to thank you for your wonderful present. I didn't mean you should give them to me, and I know you sent them. I shall keep them with pleasure and wear them with delight. It was so nice of you to do this.

STEPHANIE PLATOW.

Cowperwood studied the handwriting, the paper, the phraseology. For a girl of only a little over twenty this was wise and reserved and tactful. She might have written to him at his residence. He gave her the benefit of a week's time, and then found her in his own home one Sunday afternoon. Aileen had gone calling, and Stephanie was pretending to await her return.

"It's nice to see you there in that window," he said. "You fit your background perfectly."

"Do I?" The black-brown eyes burned soulfully. The panneling back of her was of dark oak, burnished by the rays of an afternoon winter sun.

Stephanie Platow had dressed for this opportunity. Her full, rich, short black hair was caught by a childish band of blood-red ribbon, holding it low over her temples and ears. Her lithe body, so harmonious in its graven roundness, was clad in an apple-green bodice, and a black skirt with gussets of red about the hem; her smooth arms, from the elbows down, were bare. On one wrist was the jade bracelet he had given her. Her stockings were apple-green silk, and, despite the chill of the day, her feet were shod in enticingly low slippers with brass buckles.

Cowperwood retired to the hall to hang up his overcoat and came back smiling.

"Isn't Mrs. Cowperwood about?"

"The butler says she's out calling, but I thought I'd wait a little while, anyhow. She may come back."

She turned up a dark, smiling face to him, with languishing, inscrutable eyes, and he recognized the artist at last, full and clear.

"I see you like my bracelet, don't you?"

"It's beautiful," she replied, looking down and surveying it dreamily. "I don't always wear it. I carry it in my muff. I've just put it on for a little while. I carry them all with me always. I love them so. I like to feel them."

She opened a small chamois bag beside her—lying with her handkerchief and a sketch-book which she always carried—and took out the ear-rings and brooch.

Cowperwood glowed with a strange feeling of approval and enthusiasm at this manifestation of real interest. He liked jade himself very much, but more than that the feeling that prompted this expression in another. Roughly speaking, it might have been said of him that youth and hope in women—particularly youth when combined with beauty and ambition in a girl—touched him. He responded keenly to her impulse to do or be something in this world, whatever it might be, and he looked on the smart, egoistic vanity of so many with a kindly, tolerant, almost parental eye. Poor little organisms growing on the tree of life—they would burn out and fade soon enough. He did not know the ballad of the roses of yesteryear, but if he had it would have appealed to him. He did not care to rifle them, willy-nilly; but should their temperaments or tastes incline them in his direction, they would not suffer vastly in their lives because of him. The fact was, the man was essentially generous where women were concerned.

"How nice of you!" he commented, smiling. "I like that." And then, seeing a note-book and pencil beside her, he asked, "What are you doing?"

"Just sketching."

"Let me see?"

"It's nothing much," she replied, deprecatingly. "I don't draw very well."

"Gifted girl!" he replied, picking it up. "Paints, draws, carves on wood, plays, sings, acts."

"All rather badly," she sighed, turning her head languidly and looking away. In her sketch-book she had put all of her best drawings; there were sketches of nude women, dancers, torsos, bits of running figures, sad, heavy, sensuous heads and necks of sleeping girls, chins up, eyelids down, studies of her brothers and sister, and of her father and mother.

"Delightful!" exclaimed Cowperwood, keenly alive to a new treasure. Good heavens, where had been his eyes all this while? Here was a jewel lying at his doorstep—innocent, untarnished—a real jewel. These drawings suggested a fire of perception, smoldering and somber, which thrilled him.

"These are beautiful to me, Stephanie," he said, simply, a strange, uncertain feeling of real affection creeping over him. The man's greatest love was for art. It was hypnotic to him. "Did you ever study art?" he asked.

"No."

"And you never studied acting?"

"No."

She shook her head in a slow, sad, enticing way. The black hair concealing her ears moved him strangely.

"I know the art of your stage work is real, and you have a natural art which I just seem to see. What has been the matter with me, anyhow?"

"Oh no," she sighed. "It seems to me that I merely play at everything. I could cry sometimes when I think how I go on."

"At twenty?"

"That is old enough," she smiled, archly.

"Stephanie," he asked, cautiously, "how old are you, exactly?"

"I will be twenty-one in April," she answered.

"Have your parents been very strict with you?"

She shook her head dreamily. "No; what makes you ask? They haven't paid very much attention to me. They've always liked Lucille and Gilbert and Ormond best." Her voice had a plaintive, neglected ring. It was the voice she used in her best scenes on the stage.

"Don't they realize that you are very talented?"

"I think perhaps my mother feels that I may have some ability. My father doesn't, I'm sure. Why?"

She lifted those languorous, plaintive eyes.

"Why, Stephanie, if you want to know, I think you're wonderful. I thought so the other night when you were looking at those jades. It all came over me. You are an artist, truly, and I have been so busy I have scarcely seen it. Tell me one thing."

"Yes."

She drew in a soft breath, filling her chest and expanding her bosom, while she looked at him from under her black hair. Her hands were crossed idly in her lap. Then she looked demurely down.

"Look, Stephanie! Look up! I want to ask you something. You have known something of me for over a year. Do you like me?"

"I think you're very wonderful," she murmured.

"Is that all?"

"Isn't that much?" she smiled, shooting a dull, black-opal look in his direction.

"You wore my bracelet to-day. Were you very glad to get it?"

"Oh yes," she sighed, with aspirated breath, pretending a kind of suffocation.

"How beautiful you really are!" he said, rising and looking down at her.

She shook her head.

"No."

"Yes!"

"No."

"Come, Stephanie! Stand by me and look at me. You are so tall and slender and graceful. You are like something out of Asia."

She sighed, turning in a sinuous way, as he slipped his arm her. "I don't think we should, should we?" she asked, naively, after a moment, pulling away from him.

"Stephanie!"

"I think I'd better go, now, please."

CHAPTER XXVI

LOVE AND WAR

It was during the earlier phases of his connection with Chicago street-railways that Cowperwood, ardently interesting himself in Stephanie Platow, developed as serious a sex affair as any that had yet held him. At once, after a few secret interviews with her, he adopted his favorite ruse in such matters and established bachelor quarters in the downtown section as a convenient meeting-ground. Several conversations with Stephanie were not quite as illuminating as they might have been, for, wonderful as she was—a kind of artistic godsend in this dull Western atmosphere—she was also enigmatic and elusive, very. He learned speedily, in talking with her on several days when they met for lunch, of her dramatic ambitions, and of the seeming spiritual and artistic support she required from some one who would have faith in her and inspire her by his or her confidence. He learned all about the Garrick Players, her home intimacies and friends, the growing quarrels in the dramatic organization. He asked her, as they sat in a favorite and inconspicuous resort of his finding, during one of those moments when blood and not intellect was ruling between them, whether she had ever—

"Once," she naively admitted.

It was a great shock to Cowperwood. He had fancied her refreshingly innocent. But she explained it was all so accidental, so unintentional on her part, very. She described it all so gravely, soulfully, pathetically, with such a brooding, contemplative backward searching of the mind, that he was astonished and in a way touched. What a pity! It was Gardner Knowles who had done this, she admitted. But he was not very much to blame, either. It just happened. She had tried to protest, but— Wasn't she angry? Yes, but then she was sorry to do anything to hurt Gardner Knowles. He was such a charming boy, and he had such a lovely mother and sister, and the like.

Cowperwood was astonished. He had reached that point in life where the absence of primal innocence in a woman was not very significant; but in Stephanie, seeing that she was so utterly charming, it was almost too bad. He thought what fools the Platows must be to tolerate this art atmosphere for Stephanie without keeping a sharp watch over it. Nevertheless, he was inclined to believe from observation thus far that Stephanie might be hard to watch. She was ingrainedly irresponsible, apparently—so artistically nebulous, so non-self-protective. To go on and be friends with this scamp! And yet she protested that never after that had there been the least thing between them. Cowperwood could scarcely believe it. She must be lying, and yet he liked her so. The very romantic, inconsequential way in which she narrated all this staggered, amused, and even fascinated him.

"But, Stephanie," he argued, curiously, "there must been some aftermath to all this. What happened? What did you do?"

"Nothing." She shook her head.

He had to smile.

"But oh, don't let's talk about it!" she pleaded. "I don't want to. It hurts me. There was nothing more."

She sighed, and Cowperwood meditated. The evil was now done, and the best that he could do, if he cared for her at all—and he did—was to overlook it. He surveyed her oddly, wonderingly. What a charming soul she was, anyhow! How naive—how brooding! She had art—lots of it. Did he want to give her up?

As he might have known, it was dangerous to trifle with a type of this kind, particularly once awakened to the significance of promiscuity, and unless mastered by some absorbing passion. Stephanie had had too much flattery and affection heaped upon her in the past two years to be easily absorbed. Nevertheless, for the time being, anyhow, she was fascinated by the significance of Cowperwood. It was wonderful to have so fine, so powerful a man care for her. She conceived of him as a very great artist in his realm rather than as a business man, and he grasped this fact after a very little while and appreciated it. To his delight, she was even more beautiful physically than he had anticipated—a smoldering, passionate girl who met him with a fire which, though somber, quite rivaled his own. She was different, too, in her languorous acceptance of all that he bestowed from any one he had ever known. She was as tactful as Rita Sohlberg—more so—but so preternaturally silent at times.

"Stephanie," he would exclaim, "do talk. What are you thinking of? You dream like an African native."

She merely sat and smiled in a dark way or sketched or modeled him. She was constantly penciling something, until moved by the fever of her blood, when she would sit and look at him or brood silently, eyes down. Then, when he would reach for her with seeking hands, she would sigh, "Oh yes, oh yes!"

Those were delightful days with Stephanie.

In the matter of young MacDonald's request for fifty thousand dollars in securities, as well as the attitude of the other editors—Hyssop, Braxton, Ricketts, and so on—who had proved subtly critical, Cowperwood conferred with Addison and McKenty.

"A likely lad, that," commented McKenty, succinctly, when he heard it. "He'll do better than his father in one way, anyhow. He'll probably make more money."

McKenty had seen old General MacDonald just once in his life, and liked him.

"I should like to know what the General would think of that if he knew," commented Addison, who admired the old editor greatly. "I'm afraid he wouldn't sleep very well."

"There is just one thing," observed Cowperwood, thoughtfully. "This young man will certainly come into control of the Inquirer sometime. He looks to me like some one who would not readily forget an injury." He smiled sardonically. So did McKenty and Addison.

"Be that as it may," suggested the latter, "he isn't editor yet." McKenty, who never revealed his true views to any one but Cowperwood, waited until he had the latter alone to observe:

What can they do? Your request is a reasonable one. Why shouldn't the city give you the tunnel? It's no good to anyone as it is. And the loop is no more than the other roads have now. I'm thinking it's the Chicago City Railway and that silk-stocking crowd on State Street or that gas crowd that's talking against you. I've heard them before. Give them what they want, and it's a fine moral cause. Give it to anyone else, and there's something wrong with it. It's little attention I pay to them. We have the council, let it pass the ordinances. It can't be proved that they don't do it willingly. The mayor is a sensible man. He'll sign them. Let young MacDonald talk if he wants to. If he says too much you can talk to his father. As for Hyssop, he's an old grandmother anyhow. I've never known him to be for a public improvement yet that was really good for Chicago unless Schryhart or Merrill or Arneel or someone else of that crowd wanted it. I know them of old. My advice is to go ahead and never mind them. To hell with them! Things will be sweet enough, once you are as powerful as they are. They'll get nothing in the future without paying for it. It's little enough they've ever done to further anything that I wanted.

Cowperwood, however, remained cool and thoughtful. Should he pay young MacDonald? he asked himself. Addison knew of no influence that he could bring to bear. Finally, after much thought, he decided to proceed as he had planned. Consequently, the reporters around the City Hall and the council-chamber, who were in touch with Alderman Thomas Dowling, McKenty's leader on the floor of council, and those who called occasionally— quite regularly, in fact—at the offices of the North Chicago Street Railway Company, Cowperwood's comfortable new offices in the North Side, were now given to understand that two ordinances—one granting the free use of the La Salle Street tunnel for an unlimited period (practically a gift of it), and another granting a right of way in La Salle, Munroe, Dearborn, and Randolph streets for the proposed loop—would be introduced in council very shortly. Cowperwood granted a very flowery interview, in which he explained quite enthusiastically all that the North Chicago company was doing and proposed to do, and made clear what a splendid development it would assure to the North Side and to the business center.

At once Schryhart, Merrill, and some individuals connected with the Chicago West Division Company, began to complain in the newspaper offices and at the clubs to Ricketts, Braxton, young MacDonald, and the other editors. Envy of the pyrotechnic progress of the man was as much a factor in this as anything else. It did not make the slightest difference, as Cowperwood had sarcastically pointed out, that every other corporation of any significance in Chicago had asked and received without money and without price. Somehow his career in connection with Chicago gas, his venturesome, if unsuccessful effort to enter Chicago society, his self-acknowledged Philadelphia record, rendered the sensitive cohorts of the ultra-conservative exceedingly fearful. In Schryhart's Chronicle appeared a news column which was headed, "Plain Grab of City Tunnel Proposed." It was a very truculent statement, and irritated Cowperwood greatly. The Press (Mr. Haguenin's paper), on the other hand, was most cordial to the idea of the loop, while appearing to be a little uncertain as to whether the tunnel should be granted without compensation or not. Editor Hyssop felt called upon to insist that something more than merely nominal compensation should be made for the tunnel, and that "riders" should be inserted in the loop ordinance making it incumbent upon the North Chicago company to keep those thoroughfares in full repair and well lighted. The Inquirer, under Mr. MacDonald, junior, and Mr. Du Bois, was in rumbling opposition. No free tunnels, it cried; no free ordinances for privileges in the down-town heart. It had nothing to say about Cowperwood personally. The Globe, Mr. Braxton's paper, was certain that no free rights to the tunnel should be given, and that a much better route for the loop could be found—one larger and more serviceable to the public, one that might be made to include State Street or Wabash Avenue, or both, where Mr. Merrill's store was located. So it went, and one could see quite clearly to what extent the interests of the public figured in the majority of these particular viewpoints.

Cowperwood, individual, reliant, utterly indifferent to opposition of any kind, was somewhat angered by the manner in which his overtures had been received, but still felt that the best way out of his troubles was to follow McKenty's advice and get power first. Once he had his cable-conduit down, his new cars running, the tunnel rebuilt, brilliantly lighted, and the bridge crush disposed of, the public would see what a vast change for the better had been made and would support him. Finally all things were in readiness and the ordinance jammed through. McKenty, being a little dubious of the outcome, had a rocking-chair brought into the council-chamber itself during the hours when the ordinances were up for consideration. In this he sat, presumably as a curious spectator, actually as a master dictating the course of liquidation in hand. Neither Cowperwood nor any one else knew of McKenty's action until too late to interfere with it. Addison and Videra, when they read about it as sneeringly set forth in the news columns of the papers, lifted and then wrinkled their eyebrows.

"That looks like pretty rough work to me," commented Addison. "I thought McKenty had more tact. That's his early Irish training."

Alexander Rambaud, who was an admirer and follower of Cowperwood's, wondered whether the papers were lying, whether it really could be true that Cowperwood had a serious political compact with McKenty which would allow him to walk rough-shod over public opinion. Rambaud considered Cowperwood's proposition so sane and reasonable that he could not understand why there should be serious opposition, or why Cowperwood and McKenty should have to resort to such methods.

However, the streets requisite for the loop were granted. The tunnel was leased for nine hundred and ninety-nine years at the nominal sum of five thousand dollars per year. It was understood that the old bridges over State, Dearborn, and Clark streets should be put in repair or removed; but there was "a joker" inserted elsewhere which nullified this. Instantly there were stormy outbursts in the Chronicle, Inquirer, and Globe; but Cowperwood, when he read them, merely smiled. "Let them grumble," he said to himself. "I put a very reasonable proposition before them. Why should they complain? I'm doing more now than the Chicago City Railway. It's jealousy, that's all. If Schryhart or Merrill had asked for it, there would have been no complaint."

McKenty called at the offices of the Chicago Trust Company to congratulate Cowperwood. "The boys did as I thought they would," he said. "I had to be there, though, for I heard some one say that about ten of them intended to ditch us at the last moment."

"Good work, good work!" replied Cowperwood, cheerfully. "This row will all blow over. It would be the same whenever we asked. The air will clear up. We'll give them such a fine service that they'll forget all about this, and be glad they gave us the tunnel."

Just the same, the morning after the enabling ordinances had passed, there was much derogatory comment in influential quarters. Mr. Norman Schryhart, who, through his publisher, had been fulminating defensively against Cowperwood, stared solemnly at Mr. Ricketts when they met.

"Well," said the magnate, who imagined he foresaw a threatened attack on his Chicago City Street Railway preserves, "I see our friend Mr. Cowperwood has managed to get his own way with the council. I am morally certain he uses money to get what he is after as freely as a fireman uses water. He's as slippery as an eel. I should be glad if we could establish that there is a community of interest between him and these politicians around City Hall, or between him and Mr. McKenty. I believe he has set out to dominate this city politically as well as financially, and he'll need constant watching. If public opinion can be aroused against him he may be dislodged in the course of time. Chicago may get too uncomfortable for him. I know Mr. McKenty personally, but he is not the kind of man I care to do business with."

Mr. Schryhart's method of negotiating at City Hall was through certain reputable but somewhat slow-going lawyers who were in the employ of the South Side company. They had never been able to reach Mr. McKenty at all. Ricketts echoed a hearty approval. "You're very right," he said, with owlish smugness, adjusting a waistcoat button that had come loose, and smoothing his cuffs. "He's a prince of politicians. We'll have to look sharp if we ever trap him" Mr. Ricketts would have been glad to sell out to Mr. Cowperwood, if he had not been so heavily obligated to Mr. Schryhart. He had no especial affection for Cowperwood, but he recognized in him a coming man.

Young MacDonald, talking to Clifford Du Bois in the office of the Inquirer, and reflecting how little his private telephone message had availed him, was in a waspish, ironic frame of mind.

"Well," he said, "it seems our friend Cowperwood hasn't taken our advice. He may make his mark, but the Inquirer isn't through with him by a long shot. He'll be wanting other things from the city in the future."

Clifford Du Bois regarded his acid young superior with a curious eye. He knew nothing of MacDonald's private telephone message to Cowperwood; but he knew how he himself would have dealt with the crafty financier had he been in MacDonald's position.

"Yes, Cowperwood is shrewd," was his comment. "Pritchard, our political man, says the ways of the City Hall are greased straight up to the mayor and McKenty, and that Cowperwood can have anything he wants at any time. Tom Dowling eats out of his hand,

and you know what that means. Old General Van Sickle is working for him in some way. Did you ever see that old buzzard flying around if there wasn't something dead in the woods?"

"He's a slick one," remarked MacDonald. "But as for Cowperwood, he can't get away with this sort of thing very long. He's going too fast. He wants too much."

Mr. Du Bois smiled quite secretly. It amused him to see how Cowperwood had brushed MacDonald and his objections aside—dispensed for the time being with the services of the Inquirer. Du Bois confidently believed that if the old General had been at home he would have supported the financier.

Within eight months after seizing the La Salle Street tunnel and gobbling four of the principal down-town streets for his loop, Cowperwood turned his eyes toward the completion of the second part of the programme—that of taking over the Washington Street tunnel and the Chicago West Division Company, which was still drifting along under its old horse-car regime. It was the story of the North Side company all over again. Stockholders of a certain type—the average—are extremely nervous, sensitive, fearsome. They are like that peculiar bivalve, the clam, which at the slightest sense of untoward pressure withdraws into its shell and ceases all activity. The city tax department began by instituting proceedings against the West Division company, compelling them to disgorge various unpaid street-car taxes which had hitherto been conveniently neglected. The city highway department was constantly jumping on them for neglect of street repairs. The city water department, by some hocus-pocus, made it its business to discover that they had been stealing water. On the other hand were the smiling representatives of Cowperwood, Kaifrath, Addison, Videra, and others, approaching one director or stockholder after another with glistening accounts of what a splendid day would set in for the Chicago West Division Company if only it would lease fifty-one per cent. of its holdings—fifty-one per cent. of twelve hundred and fifty shares, par value two hundred dollars—for the fascinating sum of six hundred dollars per share, and thirty per cent. interest on all stock not assumed.

Who could resist? Starve and beat a dog on the one hand; wheedle, pet, and hold meat in front of it on the other, and it can soon be brought to perform. Cowperwood knew this. His emissaries for good and evil were tireless. In the end—and it was not long in coming— the directors and chief stockholders of the Chicago West Division Company succumbed; and then, ho! the sudden leasing by the Chicago West Division Company of all its property—to the North Chicago Street Railway Company, lessee in turn of the Chicago City Passenger Railway, a line which Cowperwood had organized to take over the Washington Street tunnel. How had he accomplished it? The question was on the tip of every financial tongue. Who were the men or the organization providing the enormous sums necessary to pay six hundred dollars per share for six hundred and fifty shares of the twelve hundred and fifty belonging to the old West Division company, and thirty per cent. per year on all the remainder? Where was the money coming from to cable all these lines? It was simple enough if they had only thought. Cowperwood was merely capitalizing the future.

Before the newspapers or the public could suitably protest, crowds of men were at work day and night in the business heart of the city, their flaring torches and resounding hammers making a fitful bedlamic world of that region; they were laying the first great cable loop and repairing the La Salle Street tunnel. It was the same on the North and West Sides, where concrete conduits were being laid, new grip and trailer cars built, new car-barns erected, and large, shining power-houses put up. The city, so long used to the old bridge delays, the straw-strewn, stoveless horse-cars on their jumping rails, was agog to see how fine this new service would be. The La Salle Street tunnel was soon aglow with white plaster and electric lights. The long streets and avenues of the North Side were threaded with concrete-lined conduits and heavy street-rails. The powerhouses were completed and the system was started, even while the contracts for the changes on the West Side were being let.

Schryhart and his associates were amazed at this swiftness of action, this dizzy phantasmagoria of financial operations. It looked very much to the conservative traction interests of Chicago as if this young giant out of the East had it in mind to eat up the whole city. The Chicago Trust Company, which he, Addison, McKenty, and others had organized to manipulate the principal phases of the local bond issues, and of which he was rumored to be in control, was in a flourishing condition. Apparently he could now write his check for millions, and yet he was not beholden, so far as the older and more conservative multimillionaires of Chicago were concerned, to any one of them. The worst of it was that this Cowperwood—an upstart, a jail-bird, a stranger whom they had done their best to suppress financially and ostracize socially, had now become an attractive, even a sparkling figure in the eyes of the Chicago public. His views and opinions on almost any topic were freely quoted; the newspapers, even the most antagonistic, did not dare to neglect him. Their owners were now fully alive to the fact that a new financial rival had appeared who was worthy of their steel.

CHAPTER XXVII

A FINANCIER BEWITCHED

It was interesting to note how, able though he was, and bound up with this vast street-railway enterprise which was beginning to affect several thousand men, his mind could find intense relief and satisfaction in the presence and actions of Stephanie Platow. It is not too much to say that in her, perhaps, he found revivified the spirit and personality of Rita Sohlberg. Rita, however, had not contemplated disloyalty—it had never occurred to her to be faithless to Cowperwood so long as he was fond of her any more than for a long time it had been possible for her, even after all his philanderings, to be faithless to Sohlberg. Stephanie, on the other hand, had the strange feeling that affection was not necessarily identified with physical loyalty, and that she could be fond of Cowperwood and still deceive him—a fact which was based on her lack as yet of a true enthusiasm for him. She loved him and she didn't. Her attitude was not necessarily identified with her heavy, lizardish animality, though that had something to do with it; but rather with a vague, kindly generosity which permitted her to feel that it was hard to break with Gardner Knowles and Lane Cross after they had been so nice to her. Gardner Knowles had sung her praises here, there, and everywhere, and was attempting to spread her fame among the legitimate theatrical enterprises which came to the city in order that she might be taken up and made into a significant figure. Lane Cross was wildly fond of her in an inadequate way which made it hard to break with him, and yet certain that she would eventually. There was still another man—a young playwright and poet by the name of Forbes Gurney—tall, fair, passionate—who had newly arrived on the scene and was courting her, or, rather, being courted by her at odd moments, for her time was her own. In her artistically errant way she had refused to go to school like her sister, and was idling about, developing, as she phrased it, her artistic possibilities.

Cowperwood, as was natural, heard much of her stage life. At first he took all this palaver with a grain of salt, the babbling of an ardent nature interested in the flighty romance of the studio world. By degrees, however, he became curious as to the freedom of her actions, the ease with which she drifted from place to place—Lane Cross's studio; Bliss Bridge's bachelor rooms, where he appeared always to be receiving his theatrical friends of the Garrick Players; Mr. Gardner Knowles's home on the near North Side, where he was frequently entertaining a party after the theater. It seemed to Cowperwood, to say the least, that Stephanie was leading a rather free and inconsequential existence, and yet it reflected her exactly—the color of her soul. But he began to doubt and wonder.

"Where were you, Stephanie, yesterday?" he would ask, when they met for lunch, or in the evenings early, or when she called at his new offices on the North Side, as she sometimes did to walk or drive with him.

"Oh, yesterday morning I was at Lane Cross's studio trying on some of his Indian shawls and veils. He has such a lot of those things—some of the loveliest oranges and blues. You just ought to see me in them. I wish you might."

"Alone?"

"For a while. I thought Ethel Tuckerman and Bliss Bridge would be there, but they didn't come until later. Lane Cross is such a dear. He's sort of silly at times, but I like him. His portraits are so bizarre."

She went off into a description of his pretentious but insignificant art.

Cowperwood marveled, not at Lane Cross's art nor his shawls, but at this world in which Stephanie moved. He could not quite make her out. He had never been able to make her explain satisfactorily that first single relationship with Gardner Knowles, which she declared had ended so abruptly. Since then he had doubted, as was his nature; but this girl was so sweet, childish, irreconcilable with herself, like a wandering breath of air, or a pale-colored flower, that he scarcely knew what to think. The artistically inclined are not prone to quarrel with an enticing sheaf of flowers. She was heavenly to him, coming in, as she did at times when he was alone, with bland eyes and yielding herself in a kind of summery ecstasy. She had always something artistic to tell of storms, winds, dust, clouds, smoke forms, the outline of buildings, the lake, the stage. She would cuddle in his arms and quote long sections from "Romeo and Juliet," "Paolo and Francesca," "The Ring and the Book," Keats's "Eve of St. Agnes." He hated to quarrel with her, because she was like a wild rose or some art form in nature. Her sketch-book was always full of new things. Her muff, or the light silk shawl she wore in summer, sometimes concealed a modeled figure of some kind which she would produce with a look like that of a doubting child, and if he wanted it, if he liked it, he could have it. Cowperwood meditated deeply. He scarcely knew what to think.

The constant atmosphere of suspicion and doubt in which he was compelled to remain, came by degrees to distress and anger him. While she was with him she was clinging enough, but when she was away she was ardently cheerful and happy. Unlike the station he had occupied in so many previous affairs, he found himself, after the first little while, asking her whether she loved him instead of submitting to the same question from her.

He thought that with his means, his position, his future possibilities he had the power to bind almost any woman once drawn to his personality; but Stephanie was too young and too poetic to be greatly impaired by wealth and fame, and she was not yet sufficiently gripped by the lure of him. She loved him in her strange way; but she was interested also by the latest arrival, Forbes Gurney. This tall, melancholy youth, with brown eyes and pale-brown hair, was very poor. He hailed from southern Minnesota, and what between a penchant for journalism, verse-writing, and some dramatic work, was somewhat undecided as to his future. His present occupation was that of an instalment collector for a furniture company, which set him free, as a rule, at three o'clock in the afternoon. He was trying, in a mooning way, to identify himself with the Chicago newspaper world, and was a discovery of Gardner Knowles.

Stephanie had seen him about the rooms of the Garrick Players. She had looked at his longish face with its aureole of soft, crinkly hair, his fine wide mouth, deep-set eyes, and good nose, and had been touched by an atmosphere of wistfulness, or, let us say, life-hunger. Gardner Knowles brought a poem of his once, which he had borrowed from him, and read it to the company, Stephanie, Ethel Tuckerman, Lane Cross, and Irma Ottley assembled.

"Listen to this," Knowles had suddenly exclaimed, taking it out of his pocket.

It concerned a garden of the moon with the fragrance of pale blossoms, a mystic pool, some ancient figures of joy, a quavered Lucidian tune.

"With eerie flute and rhythmic thrum Of muted strings and beaten drum."

Stephanie Platow had sat silent, caught by a quality that was akin to her own. She asked to see it, and read it in silence.

"I think it's charming," she said.

Thereafter she hovered in the vicinity of Forbes Gurney. Why, she could scarcely say. It was not coquetry. She just drew near, talked to him of stage work and her plays and her ambitions. She sketched him as she had Cowperwood and others, and one day Cowperwood found three studies of Forbes Gurney in her note-book idyllicly done, a note of romantic feeling about them.

"Who is this?" he asked.

"Oh, he's a young poet who comes up to the Players—Forbes Gurney. He's so charming; he's so pale and dreamy."

Cowperwood contemplated the sketches curiously. His eyes clouded.

"Another one of Stephanie's adherents," he commented, teasingly. "It's a long procession I've joined. Gardner Knowles, Lane Cross, Bliss Bridge, Forbes Gurney."

Stephanie merely pouted moodily.

"How you talk! Bliss Bridge, Gardner Knowles! I admit I like them all, but that's all I do do. They're just sweet and dear. You'd like Lane Cross yourself; he's such a foolish old Polly. As for Forbes Gurney, he just drifts up there once in a while as one of the crowd. I scarcely know him."

"Exactly," said Cowperwood, dolefully; "but you sketch him." For some reason Cowperwood did not believe this. Back in his brain he did not believe Stephanie at all, he did not trust her. Yet he was intensely fond of her—the more so, perhaps, because of this.

"Tell me truly, Stephanie," he said to her one day, urgently, and yet very diplomatically. "I don't care at all, so far as your past is concerned. You and I are close enough to reach a perfect understanding. But you didn't tell me the whole truth about you and Knowles, did you? Tell me truly now. I sha'n't mind. I can understand well enough how it could have happened. It doesn't make the least bit of difference to me, really."

Stephanie was off her guard for once, in no truly fencing mood. She was troubled at times about her various relations, anxious to put herself straight with Cowperwood or with any one whom she truly liked. Compared to Cowperwood and his affairs, Cross and Knowles were trivial, and yet Knowles was interesting to her. Compared to Cowperwood, Forbes Gurney was a stripling beggar, and yet Gurney had what Cowperwood did not have—a sad, poetic lure. He awakened her sympathies. He was such a lonely boy. Cowperwood was so strong, brilliant, magnetic.

Perhaps it was with some idea of clearing up her moral status generally that she finally said: "Well, I didn't tell you the exact truth about it, either. I was a little ashamed to."

At the close of her confession, which involved only Knowles, and was incomplete at that, Cowperwood burned with a kind of angry resentment. Why trifle with a lying prostitute? That she was an inconsequential free lover at twenty-one was quite plain. And yet there was something so strangely large about the girl, so magnetic, and she was so beautiful after her kind, that he could not think of giving her up. She reminded him of himself.

"Well, Stephanie," he said, trampling under foot an impulse to insult or rebuke and dismiss her, "you are strange. Why didn't you tell me this before? I have asked and asked. Do you really mean to say that you care for me at all?"

"How can you ask that?" she demanded, reproachfully, feeling that she had been rather foolish in confessing. Perhaps she would lose him now, and she did not want to do that. Because his eyes blazed with a jealous hardness she burst into tears. "Oh, I wish I had never told you! There is nothing to tell, anyhow. I never wanted to."

Cowperwood was nonplussed. He knew human nature pretty well, and woman nature; his common sense told him that this girl was not to be trusted, and yet he was drawn to her. Perhaps she was not lying, and these tears were real.

"And you positively assure me that this was all—that there wasn't any one else before, and no one since?"

Stephanie dried her eyes. They were in his private rooms in Randolph Street, the bachelor rooms he had fitted for himself as a changing place for various affairs.

"I don't believe you care for me at all," she observed, dolefully, reproachfully. "I don't believe you understand me. I don't think you believe me. When I tell you how things are you don't understand. I don't lie. I can't. If you are so doubting now, perhaps you had better not see me any more. I want to be frank with you, but if you won't let me—"

She paused heavily, gloomily, very sorrowfully, and Cowperwood surveyed her with a kind of yearning. What an unreasoning pull she had for him! He did not believe her, and yet he could not let her go.

"Oh, I don't know what to think," he commented, morosely. "I certainly don't want to quarrel with you, Stephanie, for telling me the truth. Please don't deceive me. You are a remarkable girl. I can do so much for you if you will let me. You ought to see that."

"But I'm not deceiving you," she repeated, wearily. "I should think you could see."

"I believe you," he went on, trying to deceive himself against his better judgment. "But you lead such a free, unconventional life."

"Ah," thought Stephanie, "perhaps I talk too much."

"I am very fond of you. You appeal to me so much. I love you, really. Don't deceive me. Don't run with all these silly simpletons. They are really not worthy of you. I shall be able to get a divorce one of these days, and then I would be glad to marry you."

"But I'm not running with them in the sense that you think. They're not anything to me beyond mere entertainment. Oh, I like them, of course. Lane Cross is a dear in his way, and so is Gardner Knowles. They have all been nice to me."

Cowperwood's gorge rose at her calling Lane Cross dear. It incensed him, and yet he held his peace.

"Do give me your word that there will never be anything between you and any of these men so long as you are friendly with me?" he almost pleaded—a strange role for him. "I don't care to share you with any one else. I won't. I don't mind what you have done in the past, but I don't want you to be unfaithful in the future."

"What a question! Of course I won't. But if you don't believe me—oh, dear—"

Stephanie sighed painfully, and Cowperwood's face clouded with angry though well-concealed suspicion and jealousy.

"Well, I'll tell you, Stephanie, I believe you now. I'm going to take your word. But if you do deceive me, and I should find it out, I will quit you the same day. I do not care to share you with any one else. What I can't understand, if you care for me, is how you can take so much interest in all these affairs? It certainly isn't devotion to your art that's impelling you, is it?"

"Oh, are you going to go on quarreling with me?" asked Stephanie, naively. "Won't you believe me when I say that I love you? Perhaps—" But here her histrionic ability came to her aid, and she sobbed violently.

Cowperwood took her in his arms. "Never mind," he soothed. "I do believe you. I do think you care for me. Only I wish you weren't such a butterfly temperament, Stephanie."

So this particular lesion for the time being was healed.

CHAPTER XXVIII

THE EXPOSURE OF STEPHANIE

At the same time the thought of readjusting her relations so that they would avoid disloyalty to Cowperwood was never further from Stephanie's mind. Let no one quarrel with Stephanie Platow. She was an unstable chemical compound, artistic to her finger-tips, not understood or properly guarded by her family. Her interest in Cowperwood, his force and ability, was intense. So was her interest in Forbes Gurney—the atmosphere of poetry that enveloped him. She studied him curiously on the various occasions when they met, and, finding him bashful and recessive, set out to lure him. She felt that he was lonely and depressed and poor, and her womanly capacity for sympathy naturally bade her be tender.

Her end was easily achieved. One night, when they were all out in Bliss Bridge's single-sticker—a fast-sailing saucer—Stephanie and Forbes Gurney sat forward of the mast looking at the silver moon track which was directly ahead. The rest were in the cockpit "cutting up"—laughing and singing. It was very plain to all that Stephanie was becoming interested in Forbes Gurney; and since he was charming and she wilful, nothing was done to interfere with them, except to throw an occasional jest their way. Gurney, new to love and romance, scarcely knew how to take his good fortune, how to begin. He told Stephanie of his home life in the wheat-fields of the Northwest, how his family had moved from Ohio when he was three, and how difficult were the labors he had always undergone. He had stopped in his plowing many a day to stand under a tree and write a poem—such as it was—or to watch the birds or to wish he could go to college or to Chicago. She looked at him with dreamy eyes, her dark skin turned a copper bronze in the moonlight, her black hair irradiated with a strange, luminous grayish blue. Forbes Gurney, alive to beauty in all its forms, ventured finally to touch her hand—she of Knowles, Cross, and Cowperwood—and she thrilled from head to toe. This boy was so sweet. His curly brown hair gave him a kind of Greek innocence and aspect. She did not move, but waited, hoping he would do more.

"I wish I might talk to you as I feel," he finally said, hoarsely, a catch in his throat.

She laid one hand on his.

"You dear!" she said.

He realized now that he might. A great ecstasy fell upon him. He smoothed her hand, then slipped his arm about her waist, then ventured to kiss the dark cheek turned dreamily from him. Artfully her head sunk to his shoulder, and he murmured wild nothings—how divine she was, how artistic, how wonderful! With her view of things, it could only end one way. She manoeuvered him into calling on her at her home, into studying her books and plays on the top-floor sitting-room, into hearing her sing. Once fully in his arms, the rest was easy by suggestion. He learned she was no longer innocent, and then— In the mean time Cowperwood mingled his speculations concerning large power-houses, immense reciprocating engines, the problem of a wage scale for his now two thousand employees, some of whom were threatening to strike, the problem of securing, bonding, and equipping the La Salle Street tunnel and a down-town loop in La Salle, Munroe, Dearborn, and Randolph streets, with mental inquiries and pictures as to what possibly Stephanie Platow might be doing. He could only make appointments with her from time to time. He did not fail to note that, after he began to make use of information she let drop as to her whereabouts from day to day and her free companionship, he heard less of Gardner Knowles, Lane Cross, and Forbes Gurney, and more of Georgia Timberlake and Ethel

Tuckerman. Why this sudden reticence? On one occasion she did say of Forbes Gurney "that he was having such a hard time, and that his clothes weren't as nice as they should be, poor dear!" Stephanie herself, owing to gifts made to her by Cowperwood, was resplendent these days. She took just enough to complete her wardrobe according to her taste.

"Why not send him to me?" Cowperwood asked. "I might find something to do for him." He would have been perfectly willing to put him in some position where he could keep track of his time. However, Mr. Gurney never sought him for a position, and Stephanie ceased to speak of his poverty. A gift of two hundred dollars, which Cowperwood made her in June, was followed by an accidental meeting with her and Gurney in Washington Street. Mr. Gurney, pale and pleasant, was very well dressed indeed. He wore a pin which Cowperwood knew had once belonged to Stephanie. She was in no way confused. Finally Stephanie let it out that Lane Cross, who had gone to New Hampshire for the summer, had left his studio in her charge. Cowperwood decided to have this studio watched.

There was in Cowperwood's employ at this time a young newspaper man, an ambitious spark aged twenty-six, by the name of Francis Kennedy. He had written a very intelligent article for the Sunday Inquirer, describing Cowperwood and his plans, and pointing out what a remarkable man he was. This pleased Cowperwood. When Kennedy called one day, announcing smartly that he was anxious to get out of reportorial work, and inquiring whether he couldn't find something to do in the street-railway world, Cowperwood saw in him a possibly useful tool.

"I'll try you out as secretary for a while," he said, pleasantly. "There are a few special things I want done. If you succeed in those, I may find something else for you later."

Kennedy had been working for him only a little while when he said to him one day: "Francis, did you ever hear of a young man by the name of Forbes Gurney in the newspaper world?"

They were in Cowperwood's private office.

"No, sir," replied Francis, briskly.

"You have heard of an organization called the Garrick Players, haven't you?"

"Yes, sir."

"Well, Francis, do you suppose you could undertake a little piece of detective work for me, and handle it intelligently and quietly?"

"I think so," said Francis, who was the pink of perfection this morning in a brown suit, garnet tie, and sard sleeve-links. His shoes were immaculately polished, and his young, healthy face glistened.

"I'll tell you what I want you to do. There is a young actress, or amateur actress, by the name of Stephanie Platow, who frequents the studio of an artist named Cross in the New Arts Building. She may even occupy it in his absence—I don't know. I want you to find out for me what the relations of Mr. Gurney and this woman are. I have certain business reasons for wanting to know."

Young Kennedy was all attention.

"You couldn't tell me where I could find out anything about this Mr. Gurney to begin with, could you?" he asked.

"I think he is a friend of a critic here by the name of Gardner Knowles. You might ask him. I need not say that you must never mention me.

"Oh, I understand that thoroughly, Mr. Cowperwood." Young Kennedy departed, meditating. How was he to do this? With true journalistic skill he first sought other newspaper men, from whom he learned—a bit from one and a scrap from another—of the character of the Garrick Players, and of the women who belonged to it. He pretended to be writing a one-act play, which he hoped to have produced.

He then visited Lane Cross's studio, posing as a newspaper interviewer. Mr. Cross was out of town, so the elevator man said. His studio was closed.

Mr. Kennedy meditated on this fact for a moment.

"Does any one use his studio during the summer months?" he asked.

"I believe there is a young woman who comes here—yes."

"You don't happen to know who it is?"

"Yes, I do. Her name is Platow. What do you want to know for?"

"Looky here," exclaimed Kennedy, surveying the rather shabby attendant with a cordial and persuasive eye, "do you want to make some money—five or ten dollars, and without any trouble to you?"

The elevator man, whose wages were exactly eight dollars a week, pricked up his ears.

"I want to know who comes here with this Miss Platow, when they come—all about it. I'll make it fifteen dollars if I find out what I want, and I'll give you five right now."

The elevator factotum had just sixty-five cents in his pocket at the time. He looked at Kennedy with some uncertainty and much desire.

"Well, what can I do?" he repeated. "I'm not here after six. The janitor runs this elevator from six to twelve."

"There isn't a room vacant anywhere near this one, is there?" Kennedy asked, speculatively.

The factotum thought. "Yes, there is. One just across the hall."

"What time does she come here as a rule?"

"I don't know anything about nights. In the day she sometimes comes mornings, sometimes in the afternoon."

"Anybody with her?"

404

"Sometimes a man, sometimes a girl or two. I haven't really paid much attention to her, to tell you the truth."

Kennedy walked away whistling.

From this day on Mr. Kennedy became a watcher over this very unconventional atmosphere. He was in and out, principally observing the comings and goings of Mr. Gurney. He found what he naturally suspected, that Mr. Gurney and Stephanie spent hours here at peculiar times—after a company of friends had jollified, for instance, and all had left, including Gurney, when the latter would quietly return, with Stephanie sometimes, if she had left with the others, alone if she had remained behind. The visits were of varying duration, and Kennedy, to be absolutely accurate, kept days, dates, the duration of the hours, which he left noted in a sealed envelope for Cowperwood in the morning. Cowperwood was enraged, but so great was his interest in Stephanie that he was not prepared to act. He wanted to see to what extent her duplicity would go.

The novelty of this atmosphere and its effect on him was astonishing. Although his mind was vigorously employed during the day, nevertheless his thoughts kept returning constantly. Where was she? What was she doing? The bland way in which she could lie reminded him of himself. To think that she should prefer any one else to him, especially at this time when he was shining as a great constructive factor in the city, was too much. It smacked of age, his ultimate displacement by youth. It cut and hurt.

One morning, after a peculiarly exasperating night of thought concerning her, he said to young Kennedy: "I have a suggestion for you. I wish you would get this elevator man you are working with down there to get you a duplicate key to this studio, and see if there is a bolt on the inside. Let me know when you do. Bring me the key. The next time she is there of an evening with Mr. Gurney step out and telephone me."

The climax came one night several weeks after this discouraging investigation began. There was a heavy yellow moon in the sky, and a warm, sweet summer wind was blowing. Stephanie had called on Cowperwood at his office about four to say that instead of staying down-town with him, as they had casually planned, she was going to her home on the West Side to attend a garden-party of some kind at Georgia Timberlake's. Cowperwood looked at her with—for him—a morbid eye. He was all cheer, geniality, pleasant badinage; but he was thinking all the while what a shameless enigma she was, how well she played her part, what a fool she must take him to be. He gave her youth, her passion, her attractiveness, her natural promiscuity of soul due credit; but he could not forgive her for not loving him perfectly, as had so many others. She had on a summery black-and-white frock and a fetching brown Leghorn hat, which, with a rich-red poppy ornamenting a flare over her left ear and a peculiar ruching of white-and-black silk about the crown, made her seem strangely young, debonair, a study in Hebraic and American origins.

"Going to have a nice time, are you?" he asked, genially, politically, eying her in his enigmatic and inscrutable way. "Going to shine among that charming company you keep! I suppose all the standbys will be there—Bliss Bridge, Mr. Knowles, Mr. Cross—dancing attendance on you?"

He failed to mention Mr. Gurney.

Stephanie nodded cheerfully. She seemed in an innocent outing mood.

Cowperwood smiled, thinking how one of these days—very shortly, perhaps—he was certain to take a signal revenge. He would catch her in a lie, in a compromising position somewhere—in this studio, perhaps—and dismiss her with contempt. In an elder day, if they had lived in Turkey, he would have had her strangled, sewn in a sack, and thrown into the Bosporus. As it was, he could only dismiss her. He smiled and smiled, smoothing her hand. "Have a good time," he called, as she left. Later, at his own home—it was nearly midnight—Mr. Kennedy called him up.

"Mr. Cowperwood?"

"Yes."

"You know the studio in the New Arts Building?"

"Yes."

"It is occupied now."

Cowperwood called a servant to bring him his runabout. He had had a down-town locksmith make a round keystem with a bored clutch at the end of it—a hollow which would fit over the end of such a key as he had to the studio and turn it easily from the outside. He felt in his pocket for it, jumped in his runabout, and hurried away. When he reached the New Arts Building he found Kennedy in the hall and dismissed him. "Thanks," he observed, brusquely. "I will take care of this."

He hurried up the stairs, avoiding the elevator, to the vacant room opposite, and thence reconnoitered the studio door. It was as Kennedy had reported. Stephanie was there, and with Gurney. The pale poet had been brought there to furnish her an evening of delight. Because of the stillness of the building at this hour he could hear their muffled voices speaking alternately, and once Stephanie singing the refrain of a song. He was angry and yet grateful that she had, in her genial way, taken the trouble to call and assure him that she was going to a summer lawn-party and dance. He smiled grimly, sarcastically, as he thought of her surprise. Softly he extracted the clutch-key and inserted it, covering the end of the key on the inside and turning it. It gave solidly without sound. He next tried the knob and turned it, feeling the door spring slightly as he did so. Then inaudibly, because of a gurgled laugh with which he was thoroughly familiar, he opened it and stepped in.

At his rough, firm cough they sprang up—Gurney to a hiding position behind a curtain, Stephanie to one of concealment behind draperies on the couch. She could not speak, and could scarcely believe that her eyes did not deceive her. Gurney, masculine and defiant, but by no means well composed, demanded: "Who are you? What do you want here?" Cowperwood replied very simply and smilingly: "Not very much. Perhaps Miss Platow there will tell you." He nodded in her direction.

Stephanie, fixed by his cold, examining eye, shrank nervously, ignoring Gurney entirely. The latter perceived on the instant that he had a previous liaison to deal with—an angry and outraged lover—and he was not prepared to act either wisely or well.

"Mr. Gurney," said Cowperwood, complacently, after staring at Stephanie grimly and scorching her with his scorn, "I have no concern with you, and do not propose to do anything to disturb you or Miss Platow after a very few moments. I am not here without reason. This young woman has been steadily deceiving me. She has lied to me frequently,
406

and pretended an innocence which I did not believe. To-night she told me she was to be at a lawn-party on the West Side. She has been my mistress for months. I have given her money, jewelry, whatever she wanted. Those jade ear-rings, by the way, are one of my gifts." He nodded cheerfully in Stephanie's direction. "I have come here simply to prove to her that she cannot lie to me any more. Heretofore, every time I have accused her of things like this she has cried and lied. I do not know how much you know of her, or how fond you are of her. I merely wish her, not you, to know"—and he turned and stared at Stephanie—"that the day of her lying to me is over."

During this very peculiar harangue Stephanie, who, nervous, fearful, fixed, and yet beautiful, remained curled up in the corner of the suggestive oriental divan, had been gazing at Cowperwood in a way which plainly attested, trifle as she might with others, that she was nevertheless fond of him—intensely so. His strong, solid figure, confronting her so ruthlessly, gripped her imagination, of which she had a world. She had managed to conceal her body in part, but her brown arms and shoulders, her bosom, trim knees, and feet were exposed in part. Her black hair and naive face were now heavy, distressed, sad. She was frightened really, for Cowperwood at bottom had always overawed her—a strange, terrible, fascinating man. Now she sat and looked, seeking still to lure him by the pathetic cast of her face and soul, while Cowperwood, scornful of her, and almost openly contemptuous of her lover, and his possible opposition, merely stood smiling before them. It came over her very swiftly now just what it was she was losing—a grim, wonderful man. Beside him Gurney, the pale poet, was rather thin—a mere breath of romance. She wanted to say something, to make a plea; but it was so plain Cowperwood would have none of it, and, besides, here was Gurney. Her throat clogged, her eyes filled, even here, and a mystical bog-fire state of emotion succeeded the primary one of opposition. Cowperwood knew the look well. It gave him the only sense of triumph he had.

"Stephanie," he remarked, "I have just one word to say to you now. We will not meet any more, of course. You are a good actress. Stick to your profession. You may shine in it if you do not merge it too completely with your loves. As for being a free lover, it isn't incompatible with what you are, perhaps, but it isn't socially advisable for you. Good night."

He turned and walked quickly out.

"Oh, Frank," called Stephanie, in a strange, magnetized, despairing way, even in the face of her astonished lover. Gurney stared with his mouth open.

Cowperwood paid no heed. Out he went through the dark hall and down the stairs. For once the lure of a beautiful, enigmatic, immoral, and promiscuous woman—poison flower though she was—was haunting him. "D— her!" he exclaimed. "D— the little beast, anyhow! The ——! The ——!" He used terms so hard, so vile, so sad, all because he knew for once what it was to love and lose—to want ardently in his way and not to have—now or ever after. He was determined that his path and that of Stephanie Platow should never be allowed to cross again.

CHAPTER XXIX

A FAMILY QUARREL

It chanced that shortly before this liaison was broken off, some troubling information was quite innocently conveyed to Aileen by Stephanie Platow's own mother. One day Mrs. Platow, in calling on Mrs. Cowperwood, commented on the fact that Stephanie was gradually improving in her art, that the Garrick Players had experienced a great deal of trouble, and that Stephanie was shortly to appear in a new role—something Chinese.

"That was such a charming set of jade you gave her," she volunteered, genially. "I only saw it the other day for the first time. She never told me about it before. She prizes it so very highly, that I feel as though I ought to thank you myself."

Aileen opened her eyes. "Jade!" she observed, curiously. "Why, I don't remember." Recalling Cowperwood's proclivities on the instant, she was suspicious, distraught. Her face showed her perplexity.

"Why, yes," replied Mrs. Platow, Aileen's show of surprise troubling her. "The ear-rings and necklet, you know. She said you gave them to her."

"To be sure," answered Aileen, catching herself as by a hair. "I do recall it now. But it was Frank who really gave them. I hope she likes them."

She smiled sweetly.

"She thinks they're beautiful, and they do become her," continued Mrs. Platow, pleasantly, understanding it all, as she fancied. The truth was that Stephanie, having forgotten, had left her make-up box open one day at home, and her mother, rummaging in her room for something, had discovered them and genially confronted her with them, for she knew the value of jade. Nonplussed for the moment, Stephanie had lost her mental, though not her outward, composure and referred them back casually to an evening at the Cowperwood home when Aileen had been present and the gauds had been genially forced upon her.

Unfortunately for Aileen, the matter was not to be allowed to rest just so, for going one afternoon to a reception given by Rhees Crier, a young sculptor of social proclivities, who had been introduced to her by Taylor Lord, she was given a taste of what it means to be a neglected wife from a public point of view. As she entered on this occasion she happened to overhear two women talking in a corner behind a screen erected to conceal wraps. "Oh, here comes Mrs. Cowperwood," said one. "She's the street-railway magnate's wife. Last winter and spring he was running with that Platow girl—of the Garrick Players, you know."

The other nodded, studying Aileen's splendiferous green—velvet gown with envy.

"I wonder if she's faithful to him?" she queried, while Aileen strained to hear. "She looks daring enough."

Aileen managed to catch a glimpse of her observers later, when they were not looking, and her face showed her mingled resentment and feeling; but it did no good. The wretched gossipers had wounded her in the keenest way. She was hurt, angry, nonplussed. To think that Cowperwood by his variability should expose her to such gossip as this!

One day not so long after her conversation with Mrs. Platow, Aileen happened to be standing outside the door of her own boudoir, the landing of which commanded the lower hall, and there overheard two of her servants discussing the Cowperwood menage in particular and Chicago life in general. One was a tall, angular girl of perhaps twenty-seven or eight, a chambermaid, the other a short, stout woman of forty who held the position of assistant housekeeper. They were pretending to dust, though gossip conducted in a whisper was the matter for which they were foregathered. The tall girl had recently been employed in the family of Aymar Cochrane, the former president of the Chicago West Division Railway, and now a director of the new West Chicago Street Railway Company.

"And I was that surprised," Aileen heard this girl saying, "to think I should be coming here. I cud scarcely believe me ears when they told me. Why, Miss Florence was runnin' out to meet him two and three times in the week. The wonder to me was that her mother never guessed."

"Och," replied the other, "he's the very divil and all when it comes to the wimmin." (Aileen did not see the upward lift of the hand that accompanied this). "There was a little girl that used to come here. Her father lives up the street here. Haguenin is his name. He owns that morning paper, the Press, and has a fine house up the street here a little way. Well, I haven't seen her very often of late, but more than once I saw him kissing her in this very room. Sure his wife knows all about it. Depend on it. She had an awful fight with some woman here onct, so I hear, some woman that he was runnin' with and bringin' here to the house. I hear it's somethin' terrible the way she beat her up—screamin' and carryin' on. Oh, they're the divil, these men, when it comes to the wimmin."

A slight rustling sound from somewhere sent the two gossipers on their several ways, but Aileen had heard enough to understand. What was she to do? How was she to learn more of these new women, of whom she had never heard at all? She at once suspected Florence Cochrane, for she knew that this servant had worked in the Cochrane family. And then Cecily Haguenin, the daughter of the editor with whom they were on the friendliest terms! Cowperwood kissing her! Was there no end to his liaisons—his infidelity?

She returned, fretting and grieving, to her room, where she meditated and meditated, wondering whether she should leave him, wondering whether she should reproach him openly, wondering whether she should employ more detectives. What good would it do? She had employed detectives once. Had it prevented the Stephanie Platow incident? Not at all. Would it prevent other liaisons in the future? Very likely not. Obviously her home life with Cowperwood was coming to a complete and disastrous end. Things could not go on in this way. She had done wrong, possibly, in taking him away from Mrs. Cowperwood number one, though she could scarcely believe that, for Mrs. Lillian Cowperwood was so unsuited to him—but this repayment! If she had been at all superstitious or religious, and had known her Bible, which she didn't, she might have quoted to herself that very fatalistic statement of the New Testament, "With what measure ye mete it shall be measured unto you again."

The truth was that Cowperwood's continued propensity to rove at liberty among the fair sex could not in the long run fail of some results of an unsatisfactory character. Coincident with the disappearance of Stephanie Platow, he launched upon a variety of episodes, the charming daughter of so worthy a man as Editor Haguenin, his sincerest and most sympathetic journalistic supporter; and the daughter of Aymar Cochrane, falling victims, among others, to what many would have called his wiles. As a matter of fact, in most cases he was as much sinned against as sinning, since the provocation was as much offered as given.

The manner in which he came to get in with Cecily Haguenin was simple enough. Being an old friend of the family, and a frequent visitor at her father's house, he found this particular daughter of desire an easy victim. She was a vigorous blonde creature of twenty at this time, very full and plump, with large, violet eyes, and with considerable alertness of mind—a sort of doll girl with whom Cowperwood found it pleasant to amuse himself. A playful gamboling relationship had existed between them when she was a mere child attending school, and had continued through her college years whenever she happened to be at home on a vacation. In these very latest days when Cowperwood on occasion sat in the Haguenin library consulting with the journalist-publisher concerning certain moves which he wished to have put right before the public he saw considerably more of Cecily. One night, when her father had gone out to look up the previous action of the city council in connection with some matter of franchises, a series of more or less sympathetic and understanding glances suddenly culminated in Cecily's playfully waving a new novel, which she happened to have in her hand, in Cowperwood's face; and he, in reply, laid hold caressingly of her arms.

"You can't stop me so easily," she observed, banteringly.

"Oh yes, I can," he replied.

A slight struggle ensued, in which he, with her semiwilful connivance, managed to manoeuver her into his arms, her head backward against his shoulder.

"Well," she said, looking up at him with a semi-nervous, semi-provocative glance, "now what? You'll just have to let me go."

"Not very soon, though."

"Oh yes, you will. My father will be here in a moment."

"Well, not until then, anyhow. You're getting to be the sweetest girl."

She did not resist, but remained gazing half nervously, half dreamily at him, whereupon he smoothed her cheek, and then kissed her. Her father's returning step put an end to this; but from this point on ascent or descent to a perfect understanding was easily made.

In the matter of Florence Cochrane, the daughter of Aymar Cochrane, the president of the Chicago West Division Company—a second affair of the period—the approach was only slightly different, the result the same. This girl, to furnish only a brief impression, was a blonde of a different type from Cecily—delicate, picturesque, dreamy. She was mildly intellectual at this time, engaged in reading Marlowe and Jonson; and Cowperwood, busy in the matter of the West Chicago Street Railway, and conferring with her father, was conceived by her as a great personage of the Elizabethan order. In a tentative way she was in revolt against an apple-pie order of existence which was being forced upon her. Cowperwood recognized the mood, trifled with her spiritedly, looked into her eyes, and found the response he wanted. Neither old Aymar Cochrane nor his impeccably respectable wife ever discovered.

Subsequently Aileen, reflecting upon these latest developments, was from one point of view actually pleased or eased. There is always safety in numbers, and she felt that if Cowperwood were going to go on like this it would not be possible for him in the long run to take a definite interest in any one; and so, all things considered, and other things being equal, he would probably just as leave remain married to her as not.

But what a comment, she could not help reflecting, on her own charms! What an end to an ideal union that had seemed destined to last all their days! She, Aileen Butler, who in her youth had deemed herself the peer of any girl in charm, force, beauty, to be shoved aside thus early in her life—she was only forty—by the younger generation. And such silly snips as they were—Stephanie Platow! and Cecily Haguenin! and Florence Cochrane, in all likelihood another pasty-faced beginner! And here she was—vigorous, resplendent, smooth of face and body, her forehead, chin, neck, eyes without a wrinkle, her hair a rich golden reddish glow, her step springing, her weight no more than one hundred and fifty pounds for her very normal height, with all the advantages of a complete toilet cabinet, jewels, clothing, taste, and skill in material selection—being elbowed out by these upstarts. It was almost unbelievable. It was so unfair. Life was so cruel, Cowperwood so temperamentally unbalanced. Dear God! to think that this should be true! Why should he not love her? She studied her beauty in the mirror from time to time, and raged and raged. Why was her body not sufficient for him? Why should he deem any one more beautiful? Why should he not be true to his reiterated protestations that he cared for her? Other men were true to other women. Her father had been faithful to her mother. At the thought of her own father and his opinion of her conduct she winced, but it did not change her point of view as to her present rights. See her hair! See her eyes! See her smooth, resplendent arms! Why should Cowperwood not love her? Why, indeed?

One night, shortly afterward, she was sitting in her boudoir reading, waiting for him to come home, when the telephone-bell sounded and he informed her that he was compelled to remain at the office late. Afterward he said he might be obliged to run on to Pittsburg for thirty-six hours or thereabouts; but he would surely be back on the third day, counting the present as one. Aileen was chagrined. Her voice showed it. They had been scheduled to go to dinner with the Hoecksemas, and afterward to the theater. Cowperwood suggested that she should go alone, but Aileen declined rather sharply; she hung up the receiver without even the pretense of a good-by. And then at ten o'clock he telephoned again, saying that he had changed his mind, and that if she were interested to go anywhere—a later supper, or the like—she should dress, otherwise he would come home expecting to remain.

Aileen immediately concluded that some scheme he had had to amuse himself had fallen through. Having spoiled her evening, he was coming home to make as much hay as possible out of this bit of sunshine. This infuriated her. The whole business of uncertainty in the matter of his affections was telling on her nerves. A storm was in order, and it had come. He came bustling in a little later, slipped his arms around her as she came forward and kissed her on the mouth. He smoothed her arms in a make-believe and yet tender way, and patted her shoulders. Seeing her frown, he inquired, "What's troubling Babykins?"

"Oh, nothing more than usual," replied Aileen, irritably. "Let's not talk about that. Have you had your dinner?"

"Yes, we had it brought in." He was referring to McKenty, Addison, and himself, and the statement was true. Being in an honest position for once, he felt called upon to justify himself a little. "It couldn't be avoided to-night. I'm sorry that this business takes up so much of my time, but I'll get out of it some day soon. Things are bound to ease up."

Aileen withdrew from his embrace and went to her dressing-table. A glance showed her that her hair was slightly awry, and she smoothed it into place. She looked at her chin, and then went back to her book—rather sulkily, he thought.

"Now, Aileen, what's the trouble?" he inquired. "Aren't you glad to have me up here? I know you have had a pretty rough road of it of late, but aren't you willing to let bygones be bygones and trust to the future a little?"

"The future! The future! Don't talk to me about the future. It's little enough it holds in store for me," she replied.

Cowperwood saw that she was verging on an emotional storm, but he trusted to his powers of persuasion, and her basic affection for him, to soothe and quell her.

"I wish you wouldn't act this way, pet," he went on. "You know I have always cared for you. You know I always shall. I'll admit that there are a lot of little things which interfere with my being at home as much as I would like at present; but that doesn't alter the fact that my feeling is the same. I should think you could see that."

"Feeling! Feeling!" taunted Aileen, suddenly. "Yes, I know how much feeling you have. You have feeling enough to give other women sets of jade and jewels, and to run around with every silly little snip you meet. You needn't come home here at ten o'clock, when you can't go anywhere else, and talk about feeling for me. I know how much feeling you have. Pshaw!"

She flung herself irritably back in her chair and opened her book. Cowperwood gazed at her solemnly, for this thrust in regard to Stephanie was a revelation. This woman business could grow peculiarly exasperating at times.

"What do you mean, anyhow?" he observed, cautiously and with much seeming candor. "I haven't given any jade or jewels to any one, nor have I been running around with any 'little snips,' as you call them. I don't know what you are talking about, Aileen."

"Oh, Frank," commented Aileen, wearily and incredulously, "you lie so! Why do you stand there and lie? I'm so tired of it; I'm so sick of it all. How should the servants know of so many things to talk of here if they weren't true? I didn't invite Mrs. Platow to come and ask me why you had given her daughter a set of jade. I know why you lie; you want to hush me up and keep quiet. You're afraid I'll go to Mr. Haguenin or Mr. Cochrane or Mr. Platow, or to all three. Well, you can rest your soul on that score. I won't. I'm sick of you and your lies. Stephanie Platow—the thin stick! Cecily Haguenin—the little piece of gum! And Florence Cochrane—she looks like a dead fish!" (Aileen had a genius for characterization at times.) "If it just weren't for the way I acted toward my family in Philadelphia, and the talk it would create, and the injury it would do you financially, I'd act to-morrow. I'd leave you—that's what I'd do. And to think that I should ever have believed that you really loved me, or could care for any woman permanently. Bosh! But I don't care. Go on! Only I'll tell you one thing. You needn't think I'm going to go on enduring all this as I have in the past. I'm not. You're not going to deceive me always. I'm not going to stand it. I'm not so old yet. There are plenty of men who will be glad to pay me attention if you won't. I told you once that I wouldn't be faithful to you if you weren't to me, and I won't be. I'll show you. I'll go with other men. I will! I will! I swear it."

"Aileen," he asked, softly, pleadingly, realizing the futility of additional lies under such circumstances, "won't you forgive me this time? Bear with me for the present. I scarcely understand myself at times. I am not like other men. You and I have run together a long time now. Why not wait awhile? Give me a chance! See if I do not change. I may."

"Oh yes, wait! Change. You may change. Haven't I waited? Haven't I walked the floor night after night! when you haven't been here? Bear with you—yes, yes! Who's to bear with me when my heart is breaking? Oh, God!" she suddenly added, with passionate vigor, "I'm miserable! I'm miserable! My heart aches! It aches!"

She clutched her breast and swung from the room, moving with that vigorous stride that had once appealed to him so, and still did. Alas, alas! it touched him now, but only as a part of a very shifty and cruel world. He hurried out of the room after her, and (as at the time of the Rita Sohlberg incident) slipped his arm about her waist; but she pulled away irritably. "No, no!" she exclaimed. "Let me alone. I'm tired of that."

"You're really not fair to me, Aileen," with a great show of feeling and sincerity. "You're letting one affair that came between us blind your whole point of view. I give you my word I haven't been unfaithful to you with Stephanie Platow or any other woman. I may have flirted with them a little, but that is really nothing. Why not be sensible? I'm not as black as you paint me. I'm moving in big matters that are as much for your concern and future as for mine. Be sensible, be liberal."

There was much argument—the usual charges and countercharges—but, finally, because of her weariness of heart, his petting, the unsolvability of it all, she permitted him for the time being to persuade her that there were still some crumbs of affection left. She was soul-sick, heartsick. Even he, as he attempted to soothe her, realized clearly that to establish the reality of his love in her belief he would have to make some much greater effort to entertain and comfort her, and that this, in his present mood, and with his leaning toward promiscuity, was practically impossible. For the time being a peace might be patched up, but in view of what she expected of him—her passion and selfish individuality—it could not be. He would have to go on, and she would have to leave him, if needs be; but he could not cease or go back. He was too passionate, too radiant, too individual and complex to belong to any one single individual alone.

CHAPTER XXX

OBSTACLES

The impediments that can arise to baffle a great and swelling career are strange and various. In some instances all the cross-waves of life must be cut by the strong swimmer. With other personalities there is a chance, or force, that happily allies itself with them; or they quite unconsciously ally themselves with it, and find that there is a tide that bears them on. Divine will? Not necessarily. There is no understanding of it. Guardian spirits? There are many who so believe, to their utter undoing. (Witness Macbeth). An unconscious drift in the direction of right, virtue, duty? These are banners of mortal manufacture. Nothing is proved; all is permitted.

413

Not long after Cowperwood's accession to control on the West Side, for instance, a contest took place between his corporation and a citizen by the name of Redmond Purdy—real-estate investor, property-trader, and money-lender—which set Chicago by the ears. The La Salle and Washington Street tunnels were now in active service, but because of the great north and south area of the West Side, necessitating the cabling of Van Buren Street and Blue Island Avenue, there was need of a third tunnel somewhere south of Washington Street, preferably at Van Buren Street, because the business heart was thus more directly reached. Cowperwood was willing and anxious to build this tunnel, though he was puzzled how to secure from the city a right of way under Van Buren Street, where a bridge loaded with heavy traffic now swung. There were all sorts of complications. In the first place, the consent of the War Department at Washington had to be secured in order to tunnel under the river at all. Secondly, the excavation, if directly under the bridge, might prove an intolerable nuisance, necessitating the closing or removal of the bridge. Owing to the critical, not to say hostile, attitude of the newspapers which, since the La Salle and Washington tunnel grants, were following his every move with a searchlight, Cowperwood decided not to petition the city for privileges in this case, but instead to buy the property rights of sufficient land just north of the bridge, where the digging of the tunnel could proceed without interference.

The piece of land most suitable for this purpose, a lot 150 x 150, lying a little way from the river-bank, and occupied by a seven-story loft-building, was owned by the previously mentioned Redmond Purdy, a long, thin, angular, dirty person, who wore celluloid collars and cuffs and spoke with a nasal intonation.

Cowperwood had the customary overtures made by seemingly disinterested parties endeavoring to secure the land at a fair price. But Purdy, who was as stingy as a miser and as incisive as a rat-trap, had caught wind of the proposed tunnel scheme. He was all alive for a fine profit. "No, no, no," he declared, over and over, when approached by the representatives of Mr. Sylvester Toomey, Cowperwood's ubiquitous land-agent. "I don't want to sell. Go away."

Mr. Sylvester Toomey was finally at his wit's end, and complained to Cowperwood, who at once sent for those noble beacons of dark and stormy waters, General Van Sickle and the Hon. Kent Barrows McKibben. The General was now becoming a little dolty, and Cowperwood was thinking of pensioning him; but McKibben was in his prime—smug, handsome, deadly, smooth. After talking it over with Mr. Toomey they returned to Cowperwood's office with a promising scheme. The Hon. Nahum Dickensheets, one of the judges of the State Court of Appeals, and a man long since attached, by methods which need not here be described, to Cowperwood's star, had been persuaded to bring his extensive technical knowledge to bear on the emergency. At his suggestion the work of digging the tunnel was at once begun—first at the east or Franklin Street end; then, after eight months' digging, at the west or Canal Street end. A shaft was actually sunk some thirty feet back of Mr. Purdy's building—between it and the river—while that gentleman watched with a quizzical gleam in his eye this defiant procedure. He was sure that when it came to the necessity of annexing his property the North and West Chicago Street Railways would be obliged to pay through the nose.

"Well, I'll be cussed," he frequently observed to himself, for he could not see how his exaction of a pound of flesh was to be evaded, and yet he felt strangely restless at times. Finally, when it became absolutely necessary for Cowperwood to secure without further delay this coveted strip, he sent for its occupant, who called in pleasant anticipation of a profitable conversation; this should be worth a small fortune to him.

"Mr. Purdy," observed Cowperwood, glibly, "you have a piece of land on the other side of the river that I need. Why don't you sell it to me? Can't we fix this up now in some amicable way?"

He smiled while Purdy cast shrewd, wolfish glances about the place, wondering how much he could really hope to exact. The building, with all its interior equipment, land, and all, was worth in the neighborhood of two hundred thousand dollars.

"Why should I sell? The building is a good building. It's as useful to me as it would be to you. I'm making money out of it."

"Quite true," replied Cowperwood, "but I am willing to pay you a fair price for it. A public utility is involved. This tunnel will be a good thing for the West Side and any other land you may own over there. With what I will pay you you can buy more land in that neighborhood or elsewhere, and make a good thing out of it. We need to put this tunnel just where it is, or I wouldn't trouble to argue with you.

"That's just it," replied Purdy, fixedly. "You've gone ahead and dug your tunnel without consulting me, and now you expect me to get out of the way. Well, I don't see that I'm called on to get out of there just to please you."

"But I'll pay you a fair price."

"How much will you pay me?"

"How much do you want?"

Mr. Purdy scratched a fox-like ear. "One million dollars."

"One million dollars!" exclaimed Cowperwood. "Don't you think that's a little steep, Mr. Purdy?"

"No," replied Purdy, sagely. "It's not any more than it's worth."

Cowperwood sighed.

"I'm sorry," he replied, meditatively, "but this is really too much. Wouldn't you take three hundred thousand dollars in cash now and consider this thing closed?"

"One million," replied Purdy, looking sternly at the ceiling. "Very well, Mr. Purdy," replied Cowperwood. "I'm very sorry. It's plain to me that we can't do business as I had hoped. I'm willing to pay you a reasonable sum; but what you ask is far too much—preposterous! Don't you think you'd better reconsider? We might move the tunnel even yet."

"One million dollars," said Purdy.

"It can't be done, Mr. Purdy. It isn't worth it. Why won't you be fair? Call it three hundred and twenty-five thousand dollars cash, and my check to-night."

"I wouldn't take five or six hundred thousand dollars if you were to offer it to me, Mr. Cowperwood, to-night or any other time. I know my rights."

"Very well, then," replied Cowperwood, "that's all I can say. If you won't sell, you won't sell. Perhaps you'll change your mind later."

Mr. Purdy went out, and Cowperwood called in his lawyers and his engineers. One Saturday afternoon, a week or two later, when the building in question had been vacated for the day, a company of three hundred laborers, with wagons, picks, shovels, and dynamite sticks, arrived. By sundown of the next day (which, being Sunday, was a legal holiday, with no courts open or sitting to issue injunctions) this comely structure, the private property of Mr. Redmond Purdy, was completely razed and a large excavation substituted in its stead. The gentleman of the celluloid cuffs and collars, when informed about nine o'clock of this same Sunday morning that his building had been almost completely removed, was naturally greatly perturbed. A portion of the wall was still standing when he arrived, hot and excited, and the police were appealed to.

But, strange to say, this was of little avail, for they were shown a writ of injunction issued by the court of highest jurisdiction, presided over by the Hon. Nahum Dickensheets, which restrained all and sundry from interfering. (Subsequently on demand of another court this remarkable document was discovered to have disappeared; the contention was that it had never really existed or been produced at all.)

The demolition and digging proceeded. Then began a scurrying of lawyers to the door of one friendly judge after another. There were apoplectic cheeks, blazing eyes, and gasps for breath while the enormity of the offense was being noised abroad. Law is law, however. Procedure is procedure, and no writ of injunction was either issuable or returnable on a legal holiday, when no courts were sitting. Nevertheless, by three o'clock in the afternoon an obliging magistrate was found who consented to issue an injunction staying this terrible crime. By this time, however, the building was gone, the excavation complete. It remained merely for the West Chicago Street Railway Company to secure an injunction vacating the first injunction, praying that its rights, privileges, liberties, etc., be not interfered with, and so creating a contest which naturally threw the matter into the State Court of Appeals, where it could safely lie. For several years there were numberless injunctions, writs of errors, doubts, motions to reconsider, threats to carry the matter from the state to the federal courts on a matter of constitutional privilege, and the like. The affair was finally settled out of court, for Mr. Purdy by this time was a more sensible man. In the mean time, however, the newspapers had been given full details of the transaction, and a storm of words against Cowperwood ensued.

But more disturbing than the Redmond Purdy incident was the rivalry of a new Chicago street-railway company. It appeared first as an idea in the brain of one James Furnivale Woolsen, a determined young Westerner from California, and developed by degrees into consents and petitions from fully two-thirds of the residents of various streets in the extreme southwest section of the city where it was proposed the new line should be located. This same James Furnivale Woolsen, being an ambitious person, was not to be so easily put down. Besides the consent and petitions, which Cowperwood could not easily get away from him, he had a new form of traction then being tried out in several minor cities—a form of electric propulsion by means of an overhead wire and a traveling pole, which was said to be very economical, and to give a service better than cables and cheaper even than horses.

Cowperwood had heard all about this new electric system some time before, and had been studying it for several years with the greatest interest, since it promised to revolutionize the whole business of street-railroading. However, having but so recently completed his excellent cable system, he did not see that it was advisable to throw it away. The trolley was as yet too much of a novelty; certainly it was not advisable to have it introduced into Chicago until he was ready to introduce it himself—first on his outlying feeder lines, he thought, then perhaps generally.

But before he could take suitable action against Woolsen, that engaging young upstart, who was possessed of a high-power imagination and a gift of gab, had allied himself with such interested investors as Truman Leslie MacDonald, who saw here a heaven-sent opportunity of mulcting Cowperwood, and Jordan Jules, once the president of the North Chicago Gas Company, who had lost money through Cowperwood in the gas war. Two better instruments for goading a man whom they considered an enemy could not well be imagined—Truman Leslie with his dark, waspish, mistrustful, jealous eyes, and his slim, vital body; and Jordan Jules, short, rotund, sandy, a sickly crop of thin, oily, light hair growing down over his coat-collar, his forehead and crown glisteningly bald, his eyes a seeking, searching, revengeful blue. They in turn brought in Samuel Blackman, once president of the South Side Gas Company; Sunderland Sledd, of local railroad management and stock-investment fame; and Norrie Simms, president of the Douglas Trust Company, who, however, was little more than a fiscal agent. The general feeling was that Cowperwood's defensive tactics—which consisted in having the city council refuse to act—could be easily met.

"Well, I think we can soon fix that," exclaimed young MacDonald, one morning at a meeting. "We ought to be able to smoke them out. A little publicity will do it."

He appealed to his father, the editor of the Inquirer, but the latter refused to act for the time being, seeing that his son was interested. MacDonald, enraged at the do-nothing attitude of the council, invaded that body and demanded of Alderman Dowling, still leader, why this matter of the Chicago general ordinances was still lying unconsidered. Mr. Dowling, a large, mushy, placid man with blue eyes, an iron frame, and a beefy smile, vouchsafed the information that, although he was chairman of the committee on streets and alleys, he knew nothing about it. "I haven't been payin' much attention to things lately," he replied.

Mr. MacDonald went to see the remaining members of this same committee. They were non-committal. They would have to look into the matter. Somebody claimed that there was a flaw in the petitions.

Evidently there was crooked work here somewhere. Cowperwood was to blame, no doubt. MacDonald conferred with Blackman and Jordan Jules, and it was determined that the council should be harried into doing its duty. This was a legitimate enterprise. A new and better system of traction was being kept out of the city. Schryhart, since he was offered an interest, and since there was considerable chance of his being able to dominate the new enterprise, agreed that the ordinances ought to be acted upon. In consequence there was a renewed hubbub in the newspapers.

It was pointed out through Schryhart's Chronicle, through Hyssop's and Merrill's papers, and through the Inquirer that such a situation was intolerable. If the dominant party, at the behest of so sinister an influence as Cowperwood, was to tie up all outside traction legislation, there could be but one thing left—an appeal to the voters of the city to turn the rascals out. No party could survive such a record of political trickery and financial jugglery. McKenty, Dowling, Cowperwood, and others were characterized as unreasonable

417

obstructionists and debasing influences. But Cowperwood merely smiled. These were the caterwaulings of the enemy. Later, when young MacDonald threatened to bring legal action to compel the council to do its duty, Cowperwood and his associates were not so cheerful. A mandamus proceeding, however futile, would give the newspapers great opportunity for chatter; moreover, a city election was drawing near. However, McKenty and Cowperwood were by no means helpless. They had offices, jobs, funds, a well-organized party system, the saloons, the dives, and those dark chambers where at late hours ballot-boxes are incontinently stuffed.

Did Cowperwood share personally in all this? Not at all. Or McKenty? No. In good tweed and fine linen they frequently conferred in the offices of the Chicago Trust Company, the president's office of the North Chicago Street Railway System, and Mr. Cowperwood's library. No dark scenes were ever enacted there. But just the same, when the time came, the Schryhart-Simms-MacDonald editorial combination did not win. Mr. McKenty's party had the votes. A number of the most flagrantly debauched aldermen, it is true, were defeated; but what is an alderman here and there? The newly elected ones, even in the face of pre-election promises and vows, could be easily suborned or convinced. So the anti-Cowperwood element was just where it was before; but the feeling against him was much stronger, and considerable sentiment generated in the public at large that there was something wrong with the Cowperwood method of street-railway control.

CHAPTER XXXI

UNTOWARD DISCLOSURES

Coincident with these public disturbances and of subsequent hearing upon them was the discovery by Editor Haguenin of Cowperwood's relationship with Cecily. It came about not through Aileen, who was no longer willing to fight Cowperwood in this matter, but through Haguenin's lady society editor, who, hearing rumors in the social world, springing from heaven knows where, and being beholden to Haguenin for many favors, had carried the matter to him in a very direct way. Haguenin, a man of insufficient worldliness in spite of his journalistic profession, scarcely believed it. Cowperwood was so suave, so commercial. He had heard many things concerning him—his past—but Cowperwood's present state in Chicago was such, it seemed to him, as to preclude petty affairs of this kind. Still, the name of his daughter being involved, he took the matter up with Cecily, who under pressure confessed. She made the usual plea that she was of age, and that she wished to live her own life—logic which she had gathered largely from Cowperwood's attitude. Haguenin did nothing about it at first, thinking to send Cecily off to an aunt in Nebraska; but, finding her intractable, and fearing some counter-advice or reprisal on the part of Cowperwood, who, by the way, had indorsed paper to the extent of one hundred thousand dollars for him, he decided to discuss matters first. It meant a cessation of relations and some inconvenient financial readjustments; but it had to be. He was just on the point of calling on Cowperwood when the latter, unaware as yet of the latest development in regard to Cecily, and having some variation of his council programme to discuss with Haguenin, asked him over the 'phone to lunch. Haguenin was much surprised, but in a way relieved. "I am busy," he said, very heavily, "but cannot you come to the office some time to-day? There is something I would like to see you about."

Cowperwood, imagining that there was some editorial or local political development on foot which might be of interest to him, made an appointment for shortly after four. He drove to the publisher's office in the Press Building, and was greeted by a grave and almost despondent man.

"Mr. Cowperwood," began Haguenin, when the financier entered, smart and trig, his usual air of genial sufficiency written all over him, "I have known you now for something like fourteen years, and during this time I have shown you nothing but courtesy and good will. It is true that quite recently you have done me various financial favors, but that was more due, I thought, to the sincere friendship you bore me than to anything else. Quite accidentally I have learned of the relationship that exists between you and my daughter. I have recently spoken to her, and she admitted all that I need to know. Common decency, it seems to me, might have suggested to you that you leave my child out of the list of women you have degraded. Since it has not, I merely wish to say to you"—and Mr. Haguenin's face was very tense and white—"that the relationship between you and me is ended. The one hundred thousand dollars you have indorsed for me will be arranged for otherwise as soon as possible, and I hope you will return to me the stock of this paper that you hold as collateral. Another type of man, Mr. Cowperwood, might attempt to make you suffer in another way. I presume that you have no children of your own, or that if you have you lack the parental instinct; otherwise you could not have injured me in this fashion. I believe that you will live to see that this policy does not pay in Chicago or anywhere else."

Haguenin turned slowly on his heel toward his desk. Cowperwood, who had listened very patiently and very fixedly, without a tremor of an eyelash, merely said: "There seems to be no common intellectual ground, Mr. Haguenin, upon which you and I can meet in this matter. You cannot understand my point of view. I could not possibly adopt yours. However, as you wish it, the stock will be returned to you upon receipt of my indorsements. I cannot say more than that."

He turned and walked unconcernedly out, thinking that it was too bad to lose the support of so respectable a man, but also that he could do without it. It was silly the way parents insisted on their daughters being something that they did not wish to be.

Haguenin stood by his desk after Cowperwood had gone, wondering where he should get one hundred thousand dollars quickly, and also what he should do to make his daughter see the error of her ways. It was an astonishing blow he had received, he thought, in the house of a friend. It occurred to him that Walter Melville Hyssop, who was succeeding mightily with his two papers, might come to his rescue, and that later he could repay him when the Press was more prosperous. He went out to his house in a quandary concerning life and chance; while Cowperwood went to the Chicago Trust Company to confer with Videra, and later out to his own home to consider how he should equalize this loss. The state and fate of Cecily Haguenin was not of so much importance as many other things on his mind at this time.

Far more serious were his cogitations with regard to a liaison he had recently ventured to establish with Mrs. Hosmer Hand, wife of an eminent investor and financier. Hand was a solid, phlegmatic, heavy-thinking person who had some years before lost his first wife, to whom he had been eminently faithful. After that, for a period of years he had been a lonely speculator, attending to his vast affairs; but finally because of his enormous wealth, his rather presentable appearance and social rank, he had been entrapped by much social attention on the part of a Mrs. Jessie Drew Barrett into marrying her daughter Caroline, a dashing skip of a girl who was clever, incisive, calculating, and intensely gay. Since she was socially ambitious, and without much heart, the thought of Hand's millions, and how advantageous would be her situation in case he should die, had enabled her to overlook quite easily his heavy, unyouthful appearance and to see him in the light of a lover. There was criticism, of course. Hand was considered a victim, and Caroline and her mother designing minxes and cats; but since the wealthy financier was truly ensnared it behooved friends and future satellites to be courteous, and so they were. The wedding was very well attended. Mrs. Hand began to give house-parties, teas, musicales, and receptions on a lavish scale.

Cowperwood never met either her or her husband until he was well launched on his street-car programme. Needing two hundred and fifty thousand dollars in a hurry, and finding the Chicago Trust Company, the Lake City Bank, and other institutions heavily loaded with his securities, he turned in a moment of inspirational thought to Hand. Cowperwood was always a great borrower. His paper was out in large quantities. He introduced himself frequently to powerful men in this way, taking long or short loans at high or low rates of interest, as the case might be, and sometimes finding some one whom he could work with or use. In the case of Hand, though the latter was ostensibly of the enemies' camp—the Schryhart-Union-Gas-Douglas-Trust-Company crowd—nevertheless Cowperwood had no hesitation in going to him. He wished to overcome or forestall any unfavorable impression. Though Hand, a solemn man of shrewd but honest nature, had heard a number of unfavorable rumors, he was inclined to be fair and think the best. Perhaps Cowperwood was merely the victim of envious rivals.

When the latter first called on him at his office in the Rookery Building, he was most cordial. "Come in, Mr. Cowperwood," he said. "I have heard a great deal about you from one person and another—mostly from the newspapers. What can I do for you?"

Cowperwood exhibited five hundred thousand dollars' worth of West Chicago Street Railway stock. "I want to know if I can get two hundred and fifty thousand dollars on those by to-morrow morning."

Hand, a placid man, looked at the securities peacefully. "What's the matter with your own bank?" He was referring to the Chicago Trust Company. "Can't it take care of them for you?"

"Loaded up with other things just now," smiled Cowperwood, ingratiatingly.

"Well, if I can believe all the papers say, you're going to wreck these roads or Chicago or yourself; but I don't live by the papers. How long would you want it for?"

"Six months, perhaps. A year, if you choose."

Hand turned over the securities, eying their gold seals. "Five hundred thousand dollars' worth of six per cent. West Chicago preferred," he commented. "Are you earning six per cent.?"

"We're earning eight right now. You'll live to see the day when these shares will sell at two hundred dollars and pay twelve per cent. at that."

"And you've quadrupled the issue of the old company? Well, Chicago's growing. Leave them here until to-morrow or bring them back. Send over or call me, and I'll tell you."

They talked for a little while on street-railway and corporation matters. Hand wanted to know something concerning West Chicago land—a region adjoining Ravenswood. Cowperwood gave him his best advice.

The next day he 'phoned, and the stocks, so Hand informed him, were available. He would send a check over. So thus a tentative friendship began, and it lasted until the relationship between Cowperwood and Mrs. Hand was consummated and discovered.

In Caroline Barrett, as she occasionally preferred to sign herself, Cowperwood encountered a woman who was as restless and fickle as himself, but not so shrewd. Socially ambitious, she was anything but socially conventional, and she did not care for Hand. Once married, she had planned to repay herself in part by a very gay existence. The affair between her and Cowperwood had begun at a dinner at the magnificent residence of Hand on the North Shore Drive overlooking the lake. Cowperwood had gone to talk over with her husband various Chicago matters. Mrs. Hand was excited by his risque reputation. A little woman in stature, with intensely white teeth, red lips which she did not hesitate to rouge on occasion, brown hair, and small brown eyes which had a gay, searching, defiant twinkle in them, she did her best to be interesting, clever, witty, and she was.

"I know Frank Cowperwood by reputation, anyhow," she exclaimed, holding out a small, white, jeweled hand, the nails of which at their juncture with the flesh were tinged with henna, and the palms of which were slightly rouged. Her eyes blazed, and her teeth gleamed. "One can scarcely read of anything else in the Chicago papers."

Cowperwood returned his most winning beam. "I'm delighted to meet you, Mrs. Hand. I have read of you, too. But I hope you don't believe all the papers say about me."

"And if I did it wouldn't hurt you in my estimation. To do is to be talked about in these days."

Cowperwood, because of his desire to employ the services of Hand, was at his best. He kept the conversation within conventional lines; but all the while he was exchanging secret, unobserved smiles with Mrs. Hand, whom he realized at once had married Hand for his money, and was bent, under a somewhat jealous espionage, to have a good time anyhow. There is a kind of eagerness that goes with those who are watched and wish to escape that gives them a gay, electric awareness and sparkle in the presence of an opportunity for release. Mrs. Hand had this. Cowperwood, a past master in this matter of femininity, studied her hands, her hair, her eyes, her smile. After some contemplation he decided, other things being equal, that Mrs. Hand would do, and that he could be interested if she were very much interested in him. Her telling eyes and smiles, the heightened color of her cheeks indicated after a time that she was.

Meeting him on the street one day not long after they had first met, she told him that she was going for a visit to friends at Oconomowoc, in Wisconsin.

"I don't suppose you ever get up that far north in summer, do you?" she asked, with an air, and smiled.

"I never have," he replied; "but there's no telling what I might do if I were bantered. I suppose you ride and canoe?"

"Oh yes; and play tennis and golf, too."

"But where would a mere idler like me stay?"

"Oh, there are several good hotels. There's never any trouble about that. I suppose you ride yourself?"

"After a fashion," replied Cowperwood, who was an expert.

Witness then the casual encounter on horseback, early one Sunday morning in the painted hills of Wisconsin, of Frank Algernon Cowperwood and Caroline Hand. A jaunty, racing canter, side by side; idle talk concerning people, scenery, conveniences; his usual direct suggestions and love-making, and then, subsequently—

The day of reckoning, if such it might be called, came later.

Caroline Hand was, perhaps, unduly reckless. She admired Cowperwood greatly without really loving him. He found her interesting, principally because she was young, debonair, sufficient—a new type. They met in Chicago after a time instead of in Wisconsin, then in Detroit (where she had friends), then in Rockford, where a sister had gone to live. It was easy for him with his time and means. Finally, Duane Kingsland, wholesale flour merchant, religious, moral, conventional, who knew Cowperwood and his repute, encountered Mrs. Hand and Cowperwood first near Oconomowoc one summer's day, and later in Randolph Street, near Cowperwood's bachelor rooms. Being the man that he was and knowing old Hand well, he thought it was his duty to ask the latter if his wife knew Cowperwood intimately. There was an explosion in the Hand home. Mrs. Hand, when confronted by her husband, denied, of course, that there was anything wrong between her and Cowperwood. Her elderly husband, from a certain telltale excitement and resentment in her manner, did not believe this. He thought once of confronting Cowperwood; but, being heavy and practical, he finally decided to sever all business relationships with him and fight him in other ways. Mrs. Hand was watched very closely, and a suborned maid discovered an old note she had written to Cowperwood. An attempt to persuade her to leave for Europe—as old Butler had once attempted to send Aileen years before—raised a storm of protest, but she went. Hand, from being neutral if not friendly, became quite the most dangerous and forceful of all Cowperwood's Chicago enemies. He was a powerful man. His wrath was boundless. He looked upon Cowperwood now as a dark and dangerous man—one of whom Chicago would be well rid.

CHAPTER XXXII

A SUPPER PARTY

Since the days in which Aileen had been left more or less lonely by Cowperwood, however, no two individuals had been more faithful in their attentions than Taylor Lord and Kent McKibben. Both were fond of her in a general way, finding her interesting physically and temperamentally; but, being beholden to the magnate for many favors, they were exceedingly circumspect in their attitude toward her, particularly during those early years in which they knew that Cowperwood was intensely devoted to her. Later they were not so careful.

It was during this latter period that Aileen came gradually, through the agency of these two men, to share in a form of mid-world life that was not utterly dull. In every large city there is a kind of social half world, where artists and the more adventurous of the socially unconventional and restless meet for an exchange of things which cannot be counted mere social form and civility. It is the age-old world of Bohemia. Hither resort those "accidentals" of fancy that make the stage, the drawing-room, and all the schools of artistic endeavor interesting or peculiar. In a number of studios in Chicago such as those of Lane Cross and Rhees Crier, such little circles were to be found. Rhees Crier, for instance, a purely parlor artist, with all the airs, conventions, and social adaptability of the tribe, had quite a following. Here and to several other places by turns Taylor Lord and Kent McKibben conducted Aileen, both asking and obtaining permission to be civil to her when Cowperwood was away.

Among the friends of these two at this time was a certain Polk Lynde, an interesting society figure, whose father owned an immense reaper works, and whose time was spent in idling, racing, gambling, socializing—anything, in short, that it came into his head to do. He was tall, dark, athletic, straight, muscular, with a small dark mustache, dark, black-brown eyes, kinky black hair, and a fine, almost military carriage—which he clothed always to the best advantage. A clever philanderer, it was quite his pride that he did not boast of his conquests. One look at him, however, by the initiated, and the story was told. Aileen first saw him on a visit to the studio of Rhees Grier. Being introduced to him very casually on this occasion, she was nevertheless clearly conscious that she was encountering a fascinating man, and that he was fixing her with a warm, avid eye. For the moment she recoiled from him as being a little too brazen in his stare, and yet she admired the general appearance of him. He was of that smart world that she admired so much, and from which now apparently she was hopelessly debarred. That trig, bold air of his realized for her at last the type of man, outside of Cowperwood, whom she would prefer within limits to admire her. If she were going to be "bad," as she would have phrased it to herself, she would be "bad" with a man such as he. He would be winsome and coaxing, but at the same time strong, direct, deliciously brutal, like her Frank. He had, too, what Cowperwood could not have, a certain social air or swagger which came with idleness, much loafing, a sense of social superiority and security—a devil-may-care insouciance which recks little of other people's will or whims.

When she next saw him, which was several weeks later at an affair of the Courtney Tabors, friends of Lord's, he exclaimed:

"Oh yes. By George! You're the Mrs. Cowperwood I met several weeks ago at Rhees Grier's studio. I've not forgotten you. I've seen you in my eye all over Chicago. Taylor Lord introduced me to you. Say, but you're a beautiful woman!"

He leaned ingratiatingly, whimsically, admiringly near.

Aileen realized that for so early in the afternoon, and considering the crowd, he was curiously enthusiastic. The truth was that because of some rounds he had made elsewhere he was verging toward too much liquor. His eye was alight, his color coppery, his air swagger, devil-may-care, bacchanal. This made her a little cautious; but she rather liked his brown, hard face, handsome mouth, and crisp Jovian curls. His compliment was not utterly improper; but she nevertheless attempted coyly to avoid him.

"Come, Polk, here's an old friend of yours over here—Sadie Boutwell—she wants to meet you again," some one observed, catching him by the arm.

"No, you don't," he exclaimed, genially, and yet at the same time a little resentfully—the kind of disjointed resentment a man who has had the least bit too much is apt to feel on being interrupted. "I'm not going to walk all over Chicago thinking of a woman I've seen somewhere only to be carried away the first time I do meet her. I'm going to talk to her first."

Aileen laughed. "It's charming of you, but we can meet again, perhaps. Besides, there's some one here"—Lord was tactfully directing her attention to another woman. Rhees Grier and McKibben, who were present also, came to her assistance. In the hubbub that ensued Aileen was temporarily extricated and Lynde tactfully steered out of her way. But they had met again, and it was not to be the last time. Subsequent to this second meeting, Lynde thought the matter over quite calmly, and decided that he must make a definite effort to become more intimate with Aileen. Though she was not as young as some others, she suited his present mood exactly. She was rich physically—voluptuous and sentient. She was not of his world precisely, but what of it? She was the wife of an eminent financier, who had been in society once, and she herself had a dramatic record. He was sure of that. He could win her if he wanted to. It would be easy, knowing her as he did, and knowing what he did about her.

So not long after, Lynde ventured to invite her, with Lord, McKibben, Mr. and Mrs. Rhees Grier, and a young girl friend of Mrs. Grier who was rather attractive, a Miss Chrystobel Lanman, to a theater and supper party. The programme was to hear a reigning farce at Hooley's, then to sup at the Richelieu, and finally to visit a certain exclusive gambling-parlor which then flourished on the South Side—the resort of actors, society gamblers, and the like—where roulette, trente-et-quarante, baccarat, and the honest game of poker, to say nothing of various other games of chance, could be played amid exceedingly recherche surroundings.

The party was gay, especially after the adjournment to the Richelieu, where special dishes of chicken, lobster, and a bucket of champagne were served. Later at the Alcott Club, as the gambling resort was known, Aileen, according to Lynde, was to be taught to play baccarat, poker, and any other game that she wished. "You follow my advice, Mrs. Cowperwood," he observed, cheerfully, at dinner—being host, he had put her between himself and McKibben—"and I'll show you how to get your money back anyhow. That's more than some others can do," he added, spiritedly, recalling by a look a recent occasion when he and McKibben, being out with friends, the latter had advised liberally and had seen his advice go wrong.

"Have you been gambling, Kent?" asked Aileen, archly, turning to her long-time social mentor and friend.

"No, I can honestly say I haven't," replied McKibben, with a bland smile. "I may have thought I was gambling, but I admit I don't know how. Now Polk, here, wins all the time, don't you, Polk? Just follow him."

A wry smile spread over Lynde's face at this, for it was on record in certain circles that he had lost as much as ten and even fifteen thousand in an evening. He also had a record of winning twenty-five thousand once at baccarat at an all-night and all-day sitting, and then losing it.

Lynde all through the evening had been casting hard, meaning glances into Aileen's eyes. She could not avoid this, and she did not feel that she wanted to. He was so charming. He was talking to her half the time at the theater, without apparently addressing or even seeing her. Aileen knew well enough what was in his mind. At times, quite as in those days when she had first met Cowperwood, she felt an unwilled titillation in her blood. Her eyes brightened. It was just possible that she could come to love a man like this, although it would be hard. It would serve Cowperwood right for neglecting her. Yet even now the shadow of Cowperwood was over her, but also the desire for love and a full sex life.

In the gambling-rooms was gathered an interested and fairly smart throng—actors, actresses, clubmen, one or two very emancipated women of the high local social world, and a number of more or less gentlemanly young gamblers. Both Lord and McKibben began suggesting column numbers for first plays to their proteges, while Lynde leaned caressingly over Aileen's powdered shoulders. "Let me put this on quatre premier for you," he suggested, throwing down a twenty-dollar gold piece.

"Oh, but let it be my money," complained Aileen. "I want to play with my money. I won't feel that it's mine if I don't."

"Very well, but you can't just now. You can't play with bills." She was extracting a crisp roll from her purse. "I'll have to exchange them later for you for gold. You can pay me then. He's going to call now, anyhow. There you are. He's done it. Wait a moment. You may win." And he paused to study the little ball as it circled round and round above the receiving pockets.

"Let me see. How much do I get if I win quatre premier?" She was trying to recall her experiences abroad.

"Ten for one," replied Lynde; "but you didn't get it. Let's try it once more for luck. It comes up every so often—once in ten or twelve. I've made it often on a first play. How long has it been since the last quatre premier?" he asked of a neighbor whom he recognized.

"Seven, I think, Polk. Six or seven. How's tricks?"

"Oh, so so." He turned again to Aileen. "It ought to come up now soon. I always make it a rule to double my plays each time. It gets you back all you've lost, some time or other." He put down two twenties.

"Goodness," she exclaimed, "that will be two hundred! I had forgotten that."

Just then the call came for all placements to cease, and Aileen directed her attention to the ball. It circled and circled in its dizzy way and then suddenly dropped.

"Lost again," commented Lynde. "Well, now we'll make it eighty," and he threw down four twenties. "Just for luck we'll put something on thirty-six, and thirteen, and nine." With an easy air he laid one hundred dollars in gold on each number.

Aileen liked his manner. This was like Frank. Lynde had the cool spirit of a plunger. His father, recognizing his temperament, had set over a large fixed sum to be paid to him annually. She recognized, as in Cowperwood, the spirit of adventure, only working out in another way. Lynde was perhaps destined to come to some startlingly reckless end, but

425

what of it? He was a gentleman. His position in life was secure. That had always been Aileen's sad, secret thought. Hers had not been and might never be now.

"Oh, I'm getting foozled already," she exclaimed, gaily reverting to a girlhood habit of clapping her hands. "How much will I win if I win?" The gesture attracted attention even as the ball fell.

"By George, you have it!" exclaimed Lynde, who was watching the croupier. "Eight hundred, two hundred, two hundred"—he was counting to himself—"but we lose thirteen. Very good, that makes us nearly one thousand ahead, counting out what we put down. Rather nice for a beginning, don't you think? Now, if you'll take my advice you'll not play quatre premier any more for a while. Suppose you double a thirteen—you lost on that— and play Bates's formula. I'll show you what that is."

Already, because he was known to be a plunger, Lynde was gathering a few spectators behind him, and Aileen, fascinated, and not knowing these mysteries of chance, was content to watch him. At one stage of the playing Lynde leaned over and, seeing her smile, whispered:

"What adorable hair and eyes you have! You glow like a great rose. You have a radiance that is wonderful."

"Oh, Mr. Lynde! How you talk! Does gambling always affect you this way?"

"No, you do. Always, apparently!" And he stared hard into her upturned eyes. Still playing ostensibly for Aileen's benefit, he now doubled the cash deposit on his system, laying down a thousand in gold. Aileen urged him to play for himself and let her watch. "I'll just put a little money on these odd numbers here and there, and you play any system you want. How will that do?"

"No, not at all," he replied, feelingly. "You're my luck. I play with you. You keep the gold for me. I'll make you a fine present if I win. The losses are mine."

"Just as you like. I don't know really enough about it to play. But I surely get the nice present if you win?"

"You do, win or lose," he murmured. "And now you put the money on the numbers I call. Twenty on seven. Eighty on thirteen. Eighty on thirty. Twenty on nine. Fifty on twenty-four." He was following a system of his own, and in obedience Aileen's white, plump arm reached here and there while the spectators paused, realizing that heavier playing was being done by this pair than by any one else. Lynde was plunging for effect. He lost a thousand and fifty dollars at one clip.

"Oh, all that good money!" exclaimed Aileen, mock-pathetically, as the croupier raked it in.

"Never mind, we'll get it back," exclaimed Lynde, throwing two one-thousand-dollar bills to the cashier. "Give me gold for those."

The man gave him a double handful, which he put down between Aileen's white arms.

"One hundred on two. One hundred on four. One hundred on six. One hundred on eight."

The pieces were five-dollar gold pieces, and Aileen quickly built up the little yellow stacks and shoved them in place. Again the other players stopped and began to watch the odd pair. Aileen's red-gold head, and pink cheeks, and swimming eyes, her body swathed in silks and rich laces; and Lynde, erect, his shirt bosom snowy white, his face dark, almost coppery, his eyes and hair black—they were indeed a strikingly assorted pair.

"What's this? What's this?" asked Grier, coming up. "Who's plunging? You, Mrs. Cowperwood?"

"Not plunging," replied Lynde, indifferently. "We're merely working out a formula—Mrs. Cowperwood and I. We're doing it together."

Aileen smiled. She was in her element at last. She was beginning to shine. She was attracting attention.

"One hundred on twelve. One hundred on eighteen. One hundred on twenty-six."

"Good heavens, what are you up to, Lynde?" exclaimed Lord, leaving Mrs. Rhees and coming over. She followed. Strangers also were gathering. The business of the place was at its topmost toss—it being two o'clock in the morning—and the rooms were full.

"How interesting!" observed Miss Lanman, at the other end of the table, pausing in her playing and staring. McKibben, who was beside her, also paused. "They're plunging. Do look at all the money! Goodness, isn't she daring-looking—and he?" Aileen's shining arm was moving deftly, showily about.

"Look at the bills he's breaking!" Lynde was taking out a thick layer of fresh, yellow bills which he was exchanging for gold. "They make a striking pair, don't they?"

The board was now practically covered with Lynde's gold in quaint little stacks. He had followed a system called Mazarin, which should give him five for one, and possibly break the bank. Quite a crowd swarmed about the table, their faces glowing in the artificial light. The exclamation "plunging!" "plunging!" was to be heard whispered here and there. Lynde was delightfully cool and straight. His lithe body was quite erect, his eyes reflective, his teeth set over an unlighted cigarette. Aileen was excited as a child, delighted to be once more the center of comment. Lord looked at her with sympathetic eyes. He liked her. Well, let her be amused. It was good for her now and then; but Lynde was a fool to make a show of himself and risk so much money.

"Table closed!" called the croupier, and instantly the little ball began to spin. All eyes followed it. Round and round it went—Aileen as keen an observer as any. Her face was flushed, her eyes bright.

"If we lose this," said Lynde, "we will make one more bet double, and then if we don't win that we'll quit." He was already out nearly three thousand dollars.

"Oh yes, indeed! Only I think we ought to quit now. Here goes two thousand if we don't win. Don't you think that's quite enough? I haven't brought you much luck, have I?"

"You are luck," he whispered. "All the luck I want. One more. Stand by me for one more try, will you? If we win I'll quit."

The little ball clicked even as she nodded, and the croupier, paying out on a few small stacks here and there, raked all the rest solemnly into the receiving orifice, while murmurs of sympathetic dissatisfaction went up here and there.

"How much did they have on the board?" asked Miss Lanman of McKibben, in surprise. "It must have been a great deal, wasn't it?"

"Oh, two thousand dollars, perhaps. That isn't so high here, though. People do plunge for as much as eight or ten thousand. It all depends." McKibben was in a belittling, depreciating mood.

"Oh yes, but not often, surely."

"For the love of heavens, Polk!" exclaimed Rhees Grier, coming up and plucking at his sleeve; "if you want to give your money away give it to me. I can gather it in just as well as that croupier, and I'll go get a truck and haul it home, where it will do some good. It's perfectly terrible the way you are carrying on."

Lynde took his loss with equanimity. "Now to double it," he observed, "and get all our losses back, or go downstairs and have a rarebit and some champagne. What form of a present would please you best?—but never mind. I know a souvenir for this occasion."

He smiled and bought more gold. Aileen stacked it up showily, if a little repentantly. She did not quite approve of this—his plunging—and yet she did; she could not help sympathizing with the plunging spirit. In a few moments it was on the board—the same combination, the same stacks, only doubled—four thousand all told. The croupier called, the ball rolled and fell. Barring three hundred dollars returned, the bank took it all.

"Well, now for a rarebit," exclaimed Lynde, easily, turning to Lord, who stood behind him smiling. "You haven't a match, have you? We've had a run of bad luck, that's sure."

Lynde was secretly the least bit disgruntled, for if he had won he had intended to take a portion of the winnings and put it in a necklace or some other gewgaw for Aileen. Now he must pay for it. Yet there was some satisfaction in having made an impression as a calm and indifferent, though heavy loser. He gave Aileen his arm.

"Well, my lady," he observed, "we didn't win; but we had a little fun out of it, I hope? That combination, if it had come out, would have set us up handsomely. Better luck next time, eh?"

He smiled genially.

"Yes, but I was to have been your luck, and I wasn't," replied Aileen.

"You are all the luck I want, if you're willing to be. Come to the Richelieu to-morrow with me for lunch—will you?"

"Let me see," replied Aileen, who, observing his ready and somewhat iron fervor, was doubtful. "I can't do that," she said, finally, "I have another engagement."

"How about Tuesday, then?"

Aileen, realizing of a sudden that she was making much of a situation that ought to be handled with a light hand, answered readily: "Very well—Tuesday! Only call me up before. I may have to change my mind or the time." And she smiled good-naturedly.

After this Lynde had no opportunity to talk to Aileen privately; but in saying good night he ventured to press her arm suggestively. She suffered a peculiar nervous thrill from this, but decided curiously that she had brought it upon herself by her eagerness for life and revenge, and must make up her mind. Did she or did she not wish to go on with this? This was the question uppermost, and she felt that she must decide. However, as in most such cases, circumstances were to help decide for her, and, unquestionably, a portion of this truth was in her mind as she was shown gallantly to her door by Taylor Lord.

CHAPTER XXXIII

MR. LYNDE TO THE RESCUE

The interested appearance of a man like Polk Lynde at this stage of Aileen's affairs was a bit of fortuitous or gratuitous humor on the part of fate, which is involved with that subconscious chemistry of things of which as yet we know nothing. Here was Aileen brooding over her fate, meditating over her wrongs, as it were; and here was Polk Lynde, an interesting, forceful Lothario of the city, who was perhaps as well suited to her moods and her tastes at this time as any male outside of Cowperwood could be.

In many respects Lynde was a charming man. He was comparatively young—not more than Aileen's own age—schooled, if not educated, at one of the best American colleges, of excellent taste in the matter of clothes, friends, and the details of living with which he chose to surround himself, but at heart a rake. He loved, and had from his youth up, to gamble. He was in one phase of the word a HARD and yet by no means a self-destructive drinker, for he had an iron constitution and could consume spirituous waters with the minimum of ill effect. He had what Gibbon was wont to call "the most amiable of our vices," a passion for women, and he cared no more for the cool, patient, almost penitent methods by which his father had built up the immense reaper business, of which he was supposedly the heir, than he cared for the mysteries or sacred rights of the Chaldees. He realized that the business itself was a splendid thing. He liked on occasion to think of it with all its extent of ground-space, plain red-brick buildings, tall stacks and yelling whistles; but he liked in no way to have anything to do with the rather commonplace routine of its manipulation.

The principal difficulty with Aileen under these circumstances, of course, was her intense vanity and self-consciousness. Never was there a vainer or more sex-troubled woman. Why, she asked herself, should she sit here in loneliness day after day, brooding about Cowperwood, eating her heart out, while he was flitting about gathering the sweets of life elsewhere? Why should she not offer her continued charms as a solace and a delight to other men who would appreciate them? Would not such a policy have all the essentials of justice in it? Yet even now, so precious had Cowperwood been to her hitherto, and so wonderful, that she was scarcely able to think of serious disloyalty. He was so charming when he was nice—so splendid. When Lynde sought to hold her to the proposed luncheon engagement she at first declined. And there, under slightly differing conditions, the matter might easily have stood. But it so happened that just at this time Aileen was being almost daily harassed by additional evidence and reminders of Cowperwood's infidelity.

For instance, going one day to call on the Haguenins—for she was perfectly willing to keep up the pretense of amity in so long as they had not found out the truth—she was informed that Mrs. Haguenin was "not at home." Shortly thereafter the Press, which had always been favorable to Cowperwood, and which Aileen regularly read because of its friendly comment, suddenly veered and began to attack him. There were solemn suggestions at first that his policy and intentions might not be in accord with the best interests of the city. A little later Haguenin printed editorials which referred to Cowperwood as "the wrecker," "the Philadelphia adventurer," "a conscienceless promoter," and the like. Aileen guessed instantly what the trouble was, but she was too disturbed as to her own position to make any comment. She could not resolve the threats and menaces of Cowperwood's envious world any more than she could see her way through her own grim difficulties.

One day, in scanning the columns of that faithful chronicle of Chicago social doings, the Chicago Saturday Review, she came across an item which served as a final blow. "For some time in high social circles," the paragraph ran, "speculation has been rife as to the amours and liaisons of a certain individual of great wealth and pseudo social prominence, who once made a serious attempt to enter Chicago society. It is not necessary to name the man, for all who are acquainted with recent events in Chicago will know who is meant. The latest rumor to affect his already nefarious reputation relates to two women—one the daughter, and the other the wife, of men of repute and standing in the community. In these latest instances it is more than likely that he has arrayed influences of the greatest importance socially and financially against himself, for the husband in the one case and the father in the other are men of weight and authority. The suggestion has more than once been made that Chicago should and eventually would not tolerate his bucaneering methods in finance and social matters; but thus far no definite action has been taken to cast him out. The crowning wonder of all is that the wife, who was brought here from the East, and who—so rumor has it—made a rather scandalous sacrifice of her own reputation and another woman's heart and home in order to obtain the privilege of living with him, should continue so to do."

Aileen understood perfectly what was meant. "The father" of the so-called "one" was probably Haguenin or Cochrane, more than likely Haguenin. "The husband of the other"—but who was the husband of the other? She had not heard of any scandal with the wife of anybody. It could not be the case of Rita Sohlberg and her husband—that was too far back. It must be some new affair of which she had not the least inkling, and so she sat and reflected. Now, she told herself, if she received another invitation from Lynde she would accept it.

It was only a few days later that Aileen and Lynde met in the gold-room of the Richelieu. Strange to relate, for one determined to be indifferent she had spent much time in making a fetching toilet. It being February and chill with glittering snow on the ground, she had chosen a dark-green broadcloth gown, quite new, with lapis-lazuli buttons that worked a "Y" pattern across her bosom, a seal turban with an emerald plume which complemented a sealskin jacket with immense wrought silver buttons, and bronze shoes. To perfect it all, Aileen had fastened lapis-lazuli ear-rings of a small flower-form in her ears, and wore a plain, heavy gold bracelet. Lynde came up with a look of keen approval written on his handsome brown face. "Will you let me tell you how nice you look?" he said, sinking into the chair opposite. "You show beautiful taste in choosing the right colors. Your ear-rings go so well with your hair."

Although Aileen feared because of his desperateness, she was caught by his sleek force—that air of iron strength under a parlor mask. His long, brown, artistic hands, hard and muscular, indicated an idle force that might be used in many ways. They harmonized with his teeth and chin.

"So you came, didn't you?" he went on, looking at her steadily, while she fronted his gaze boldly for a moment, only to look evasively down.

He still studied her carefully, looking at her chin and mouth and piquant nose. In her colorful cheeks and strong arms and shoulders, indicated by her well-tailored suit, he recognized the human vigor he most craved in a woman. By way of diversion he ordered an old-fashioned whisky cocktail, urging her to join him. Finding her obdurate, he drew from his pocket a little box.

"We agreed when we played the other night on a memento, didn't we?" he said. "A sort of souvenir? Guess?"

Aileen looked at it a little nonplussed, recognizing the contents of the box to be jewelry. "Oh, you shouldn't have done that," she protested. "The understanding was that we were to win. You lost, and that ended the bargain. I should have shared the losses. I haven't forgiven you for that yet, you know."

"How ungallant that would make me!" he said, smilingly, as he trifled with the long, thin, lacquered case. "You wouldn't want to make me ungallant, would you? Be a good fellow—a good sport, as they say. Guess, and it's yours."

Aileen pursed her lips at this ardent entreaty.

"Oh, I don't mind guessing," she commented, superiorly, "though I sha'n't take it. It might be a pin, it might be a set of ear-rings, it might be a bracelet—"

He made no comment, but opened it, revealing a necklace of gold wrought into the form of a grape-vine of the most curious workmanship, with a cluster of leaves artistically carved and arranged as a breastpiece, the center of them formed by a black opal, which shone with an enticing luster. Lynde knew well enough that Aileen was familiar with many jewels, and that only one of ornate construction and value would appeal to her sense of what was becoming to her. He watched her face closely while she studied the details of the necklace.

"Isn't it exquisite!" she commented. "What a lovely opal—what an odd design." She went over the separate leaves. "You shouldn't be so foolish. I couldn't take it. I have too many things as it is, and besides—" She was thinking of what she would say if Cowperwood chanced to ask her where she got it. He was so intuitive.

"And besides?" he queried.

"Nothing," she replied, "except that I mustn't take it, really." "Won't you take it as a souvenir even if—our agreement, you know."

"Even if what?" she queried.

"Even if nothing else comes of it. A memento, then—truly—you know."

He laid hold of her fingers with his cool, vigorous ones. A year before, even six months, Aileen would have released her hand smilingly. Now she hesitated. Why should she be so squeamish with other men when Cowperwood was so unkind to her?

"Tell me something," Lynde asked, noting the doubt and holding her fingers gently but firmly, "do you care for me at all?"

"I like you, yes. I can't say that it is anything more than that."

She flushed, though, in spite of herself.

He merely gazed at her with his hard, burning eyes. The materiality that accompanies romance in so many temperaments awakened in her, and quite put Cowperwood out of her mind for the moment. It was an astonishing and revolutionary experience for her. She quite burned in reply, and Lynde smiled sweetly, encouragingly.

"Why won't you be friends with me, my sweetheart? I know you're not happy—I can see that. Neither am I. I have a wreckless, wretched disposition that gets me into all sorts of hell. I need some one to care for me. Why won't you? You're just my sort. I feel it. Do you love him so much"—he was referring to Cowperwood—"that you can't love any one else?"

"Oh, him!" retorted Aileen, irritably, almost disloyally. "He doesn't care for me any more. He wouldn't mind. It isn't him."

"Well, then, what is it? Why won't you? Am I not interesting enough? Don't you like me? Don't you feel that I'm really suited to you?" His hand sought hers softly.

Aileen accepted the caress.

"Oh, it isn't that," she replied, feelingly, running back in her mind over her long career with Cowperwood, his former love, his keen protestations. She had expected to make so much out of her life with him, and here she was sitting in a public restaurant flirting with and extracting sympathy from a comparative stranger. It cut her to the quick for the moment and sealed her lips. Hot, unbidden tears welled to her eyes.

Lynde saw them. He was really very sorry for her, though her beauty made him wish to take advantage of her distress. "Why should you cry, dearest?" he asked, softly, looking at her flushed cheeks and colorful eyes. "You have beauty; you are young; you're lovely. He's not the only man in the world. Why should you be faithful when he isn't faithful to you? This Hand affair is all over town. When you meet some one that really would care for you, why shouldn't you? If he doesn't want you, there are others."

At the mention of the Hand affair Aileen straightened up. "The Hand affair?" she asked, curiously. "What is that?"

"Don't you know?" he replied, a little surprised. "I thought you did, or I certainly wouldn't have mentioned it."

"Oh, I know about what it is," replied Aileen, wisely, and with a touch of sardonic humor. "There have been so many or the same kind. I suppose it must be the case the Chicago Review was referring to—the wife of the prominent financier. Has he been trifling with Mrs. Hand?"

"Something like that," replied Lynde. "I'm sorry that I spoke, though? really I am. I didn't mean to be carrying tales."

"Soldiers in a common fight, eh?" taunted Aileen, gaily.

"Oh, not that, exactly. Please don't be mean. I'm not so bad. It's just a principle with me. We all have our little foibles."

"Yes, I know," replied Aileen; but her mind was running on Mrs. Hand. So she was the latest. "Well, I admire his taste, anyway, in this case," she said, archly. "There have been so many, though. She is just one more."

Lynde smiled. He himself admired Cowperwood's taste. Then he dropped the subject.

"But let's forget that," he said. "Please don't worry about him any more. You can't change that. Pull yourself together." He squeezed her fingers. "Will you?" he asked, lifting his eyebrows in inquiry.

"Will I what?" replied Aileen, meditatively.

"Oh, you know. The necklace for one thing. Me, too." His eyes coaxed and laughed and pleaded.

Aileen smiled. "You're a bad boy," she said, evasively. This revelation in regard to Mrs. Hand had made her singularly retaliatory in spirit. "Let me think. Don't ask me to take the necklace to-day. I couldn't. I couldn't wear it, anyhow. Let me see you another time." She moved her plump hand in an uncertain way, and he smoothed her wrist.

"I wonder if you wouldn't like to go around to the studio of a friend of mine here in the tower?" he asked, quite nonchalantly. "He has such a charming collection of landscapes. You're interested in pictures, I know. Your husband has some of the finest."

Instantly Aileen understood what was meant—quite by instinct. The alleged studio must be private bachelor quarters.

"Not this afternoon," she replied, quite wrought up and disturbed. "Not to-day. Another time. And I must be going now. But I will see you."

"And this?" he asked, picking up the necklace.

"You keep it until I do come," she replied. "I may take it then."

She relaxed a little, pleased that she was getting safely away; but her mood was anything but antagonistic, and her spirits were as shredded as wind-whipped clouds. It was time she wanted—a little time—that was all.

CHAPTER XXXIV

ENTER HOSMER HAND

It is needless to say that the solemn rage of Hand, to say nothing of the pathetic anger of Haguenin, coupled with the wrath of Redmond Purdy, who related to all his sad story, and of young MacDonald and his associates of the Chicago General Company, constituted an atmosphere highly charged with possibilities and potent for dramatic results. The most serious element in this at present was Hosmer Hand, who, being exceedingly wealthy and a director in a number of the principal mercantile and financial institutions of the city, was in a position to do Cowperwood some real financial harm. Hand had been extremely fond of his young wife. Being a man of but few experiences with women, it astonished and enraged him that a man like Cowperwood should dare to venture on his preserves in this reckless way, should take his dignity so lightly. He burned now with a hot, slow fire of revenge.

Those who know anything concerning the financial world and its great adventures know how precious is that reputation for probity, solidarity, and conservatism on which so many of the successful enterprises of the world are based. If men are not absolutely honest themselves they at least wish for and have faith in the honesty of others. No set of men know more about each other, garner more carefully all the straws of rumor which may affect the financial and social well being of an individual one way or another, keep a tighter mouth concerning their own affairs and a sharper eye on that of their neighbors. Cowperwood's credit had hitherto been good because it was known that he had a "soft thing" in the Chicago street-railway field, that he paid his interest charges promptly, that he had organized the group of men who now, under him, controlled the Chicago Trust Company and the North and West Chicago Street Railways, and that the Lake City Bank, of which Addison was still president, considered his collateral sound. Nevertheless, even previous to this time there had been a protesting element in the shape of Schryhart, Simms, and others of considerable import in the Douglas Trust, who had lost no chance to say to one and all that Cowperwood was an interloper, and that his course was marked by political and social trickery and chicanery, if not by financial dishonesty. As a matter of fact, Schryhart, who had once been a director of the Lake City National along with Hand, Arneel, and others, had resigned and withdrawn all his deposits sometime before because he found, as he declared, that Addison was favoring Cowperwood and the Chicago Trust Company with loans, when there was no need of so doing—when it was not essentially advantageous for the bank so to do. Both Arneel and Hand, having at this time no personal quarrel with Cowperwood on any score, had considered this protest as biased. Addison had maintained that the loans were neither unduly large nor out of proportion to the general loans of the bank. The collateral offered was excellent. "I don't want to quarrel with Schryhart," Addison had protested at the time; "but I am afraid his charge is unfair. He is trying to vent a private grudge through the Lake National. That is not the way nor this the place to do it."

Both Hand and Arneel, sober men both, agreed with this—admiring Addison—and so the case stood. Schryhart, however, frequently intimated to them both that Cowperwood was merely building up the Chicago Trust Company at the expense of the Lake City National, in order to make the former strong enough to do without any aid, at which time Addison would resign and the Lake City would be allowed to shift for itself. Hand had never acted on this suggestion but he had thought.

It was not until the incidents relating to Cowperwood and Mrs. Hand had come to light that things financial and otherwise began to darken up. Hand, being greatly hurt in his pride, contemplated only severe reprisal. Meeting Schryhart at a directors' meeting one day not long after his difficulty had come upon him, he remarked:

"I thought a few years ago, Norman, when you talked to me about this man Cowperwood that you were merely jealous—a dissatisfied business rival. Recently a few things have come to my notice which cause me to think differently. It is very plain to me now that the man is thoroughly bad—from the crown of his head to the soles of his feet. It's a pity the city has to endure him."

"So you're just beginning to find that out, are you, Hosmer?" answered Schryhart. "Well, I'll not say I told you so. Perhaps you'll agree with me now that the responsible people of Chicago ought to do something about it."

Hand, a very heavy, taciturn man, merely looked at him. "I'll be ready enough to do," he said, "when I see how and what's to be done."

A little later Schryhart, meeting Duane Kingsland, learned the true source of Hand's feeling against Cowperwood, and was not slow in transferring this titbit to Merrill, Simms, and others. Merrill, who, though Cowperwood had refused to extend his La Salle Street tunnel loop about State Street and his store, had hitherto always liked him after a fashion— remotely admired his courage and daring—was now appropriately shocked.

"Why, Anson," observed Schryhart, "the man is no good. He has the heart of a hyena and the friendliness of a scorpion. You heard how he treated Hand, didn't you?"

"No," replied Merrill, "I didn't."

"Well, it's this way, so I hear." And Schryhart leaned over and confidentially communicated considerable information into Mr. Merrill's left ear.

The latter raised his eyebrows. "Indeed!" he said.

"And the way he came to meet her," added Schryhart, contemptuously, "was this. He went to Hand originally to borrow two hundred and fifty thousand dollars on West Chicago Street Railway. Angry? The word is no name for it."

"You don't say so," commented Merrill, dryly, though privately interested and fascinated, for Mrs. Hand had always seemed very attractive to him. "I don't wonder."

He recalled that his own wife had recently insisted on inviting Cowperwood once.

Similarly Hand, meeting Arneel not so long afterward, confided to him that Cowperwood was trying to repudiate a sacred agreement. Arneel was grieved and surprised. It was enough for him to know that Hand had been seriously injured. Between the two of them they now decided to indicate to Addison, as president of the Lake City Bank, that all relations with Cowperwood and the Chicago Trust Company must cease. The result of this was, not long after, that Addison, very suave and gracious, agreed to give Cowperwood due warning that all his loans would have to be taken care of and then resigned—to become, seven months later, president of the Chicago Trust Company. This desertion created a great stir at the time, astonishing the very men who had suspected that it might come to pass. The papers were full of it.

"Well, let him go," observed Arneel to Hand, sourly, on the day that Addison notified the board of directors of the Lake City of his contemplated resignation. "If he wants to sever his connection with a bank like this to go with a man like that, it's his own lookout. He may live to regret it."

It so happened that by now another election was pending Chicago, and Hand, along with Schryhart and Arneel—who joined their forces because of his friendship for Hand—decided to try to fight Cowperwood through this means.

Hosmer Hand, feeling that he had the burden of a great duty upon him, was not slow in acting. He was always, when aroused, a determined and able fighter. Needing an able lieutenant in the impending political conflict, he finally bethought himself of a man who had recently come to figure somewhat conspicuously in Chicago politics—one Patrick Gilgan, the same Patrick Gilgan of Cowperwood's old Hyde Park gas-war days. Mr. Gilgan was now a comparatively well-to-do man. Owing to a genial capacity for mixing with people, a close mouth, and absolutely no understanding of, and consequently no conscience in matters of large public import (in so far as they related to the so-called rights of the mass), he was a fit individual to succeed politically. His saloon was the finest in all Wentworth Avenue. It fairly glittered with the newly introduced incandescent lamp reflected in a perfect world of beveled and faceted mirrors. His ward, or district, was full of low, rain-beaten cottages crowded together along half-made streets; but Patrick Gilgan was now a state senator, slated for Congress at the next Congressional election, and a possible successor of the Hon. John J. McKenty as dictator of the city, if only the Republican party should come into power. (Hyde Park, before it had been annexed to the city, had always been Republican, and since then, although the larger city was normally Democratic, Gilgan could not conveniently change.) Hearing from the political discussion which preceded the election that Gilgan was by far the most powerful politician on the South Side, Hand sent for him. Personally, Hand had far less sympathy with the polite moralistic efforts of men like Haguenin, Hyssop, and others, who were content to preach morality and strive to win by the efforts of the unco good, than he had with the cold political logic of a man like Cowperwood himself. If Cowperwood could work through McKenty to such a powerful end, he, Hand, could find some one else who could be made as powerful as McKenty.

"Mr. Gilgan," said Hand, when the Irishman came in, medium tall, beefy, with shrewd, twinkling gray eyes and hairy hands, "you don't know me—"

"I know of you well enough," smiled the Irishman, with a soft brogue. "You don't need an introduction to talk to me."

"Very good," replied Hand, extending his hand. "I know of you, too. Then we can talk. It's the political situation here in Chicago I'd like to discuss with you. I'm not a politician myself, but I take some interest in what's going on. I want to know what you think will be the probable outcome of the present situation here in the city."

Gilgan, having no reason for laying his private political convictions bare to any one whose motive he did not know, merely replied: "Oh, I think the Republicans may have a pretty good show. They have all but one or two of the papers with them, I see. I don't know much outside of what I read and hear people talk."

Mr. Hand knew that Gilgan was sparring, and was glad to find his man canny and calculating.

436

"I haven't asked you to come here just to be talking over politics in general, as you may imagine, Mr. Gilgan. I want to put a particular problem before you. Do you happen to know either Mr. McKenty or Mr. Cowperwood?"

"I never met either of them to talk to," replied Gilgan. "I know Mr. McKenty by sight, and I've seen Mr. Cowperwood once." He said no more.

"Well," said Mr. Hand, "suppose a group of influential men here in Chicago were to get together and guarantee sufficient funds for a city-wide campaign; now, if you had the complete support of the newspapers and the Republican organization in the bargain, could you organize the opposition here so that the Democratic party could be beaten this fall? I'm not talking about the mayor merely and the principal city officers, but the council, too—the aldermen. I want to fix things so that the McKenty-Cowperwood crowd couldn't get an alderman or a city official to sell out, once they are elected. I want the Democratic party beaten so thoroughly that there won't be any question in anybody's mind as to the fact that it has been done. There will be plenty of money forthcoming if you can prove to me, or, rather, to the group of men I am thinking of, that the thing can be done."

Mr. Gilgan blinked his eyes solemnly. He rubbed his knees, put his thumbs in the armholes of his vest, took out a cigar, lit it, and gazed poetically at the ceiling. He was thinking very, very hard. Mr. Cowperwood and Mr. McKenty, as he knew, were very powerful men. He had always managed to down the McKenty opposition in his ward, and several others adjacent to it, and in the Eighteenth Senatorial District, which he represented. But to be called upon to defeat him in Chicago, that was different. Still, the thought of a large amount of cash to be distributed through him, and the chance of wresting the city leadership from McKenty by the aid of the so-called moral forces of the city, was very inspiring. Mr. Gilgan was a good politician. He loved to scheme and plot and make deals—as much for the fun of it as anything else. Just now he drew a solemn face, which, however, concealed a very light heart.

"I have heard," went on Hand, "that you have built up a strong organization in your ward and district."

"I've managed to hold me own," suggested Gilgan, archly. "But this winning all over Chicago," he went on, after a moment, "now, that's a pretty large order. There are thirty-one wards in Chicago this election, and all but eight of them are nominally Democratic. I know most of the men that are in them now, and some of them are pretty shrewd men, too. This man Dowling in council is nobody's fool, let me tell you that. Then there's Duvanicki and Ungerich and Tiernan and Kerrigan—all good men." He mentioned four of the most powerful and crooked aldermen in the city. "You see, Mr. Hand, the way things are now the Democrats have the offices, and the small jobs to give out. That gives them plenty of political workers to begin with. Then they have the privilege of collecting money from those in office to help elect themselves. That's another great privilege." He smiled. "Then this man Cowperwood employs all of ten thousand men at present, and any ward boss that's favorable to him can send a man out of work to him and he'll find a place for him. That's a gre-a-eat help in building up a party following. Then there's the money a man like Cowperwood and others can contribute at election time. Say what you will, Mr. Hand, but it's the two, and five, and ten dollar bills paid out at the last moment over the saloon bars and at the polling-places that do the work. Give me enough money"—and at this noble thought Mr. Gilgan straightened up and slapped one fist lightly in the other, adjusting at the same time his half-burned cigar so that it should not burn his hand—"and I can carry every ward in Chicago, bar none. If I have money enough," he repeated, emphasizing the last two words. He put his cigar back in his mouth, blinked his eyes defiantly, and leaned back in his chair.

"Very good," commented Hand, simply; "but how much money?"

"Ah, that's another question," replied Gilgan, straightening up once more. "Some wards require more than others. Counting out the eight that are normally Republican as safe, you would have to carry eighteen others to have a majority in council. I don't see how anything under ten to fifteen thousand dollars to a ward would be safe to go on. I should say three hundred thousand dollars would be safer, and that wouldn't be any too much by any means."

Mr. Gilgan restored his cigar and puffed heavily the while he leaned back and lifted his eyes once more.

"And how would that money be distributed exactly?" inquired Mr. Hand.

"Oh, well, it's never wise to look into such matters too closely," commented Mr. Gilgan, comfortably. "There's such a thing as cutting your cloth too close in politics. There are ward captains, leaders, block captains, workers. They all have to have money to do with—to work up sentiment—and you can't be too inquiring as to just how they do it. It's spent in saloons, and buying coal for mother, and getting Johnnie a new suit here and there. Then there are torch-light processions and club-rooms and jobs to look after. Sure, there's plenty of places for it. Some men may have to be brought into these wards to live—kept in boarding-houses for a week or ten days." He waved a hand deprecatingly.

Mr. Hand, who had never busied himself with the minutiae of politics, opened his eyes slightly. This colonizing idea was a little liberal, he thought.

"Who distributes this money?" he asked, finally.

"Nominally, the Republican County Committee, if it's in charge; actually, the man or men who are leading the fight. In the case of the Democratic party it's John J. McKenty, and don't you forget it. In my district it's me, and no one else."

Mr. Hand, slow, solid, almost obtuse at times, meditated under lowering brows. He had always been associated with a more or less silk-stocking crew who were unused to the rough usage of back-room saloon politics, yet every one suspected vaguely, of course, at times that ballot-boxes were stuffed and ward lodging-houses colonized. Every one (at least every one of any worldly intelligence) knew that political capital was collected from office-seekers, office-holders, beneficiaries of all sorts and conditions under the reigning city administration. Mr. Hand had himself contributed to the Republican party for favors received or about to be. As a man who had been compelled to handle large affairs in a large way he was not inclined to quarrel with this. Three hundred thousand dollars was a large sum, and he was not inclined to subscribe it alone, but fancied that at his recommendation and with his advice it could be raised. Was Gilgan the man to fight Cowperwood? He looked him over and decided—other things being equal—that he was. And forthwith the bargain was struck. Gilgan, as a Republican central committeeman—chairman, possibly—was to visit every ward, connect up with every available Republican force, pick strong, suitable anti-Cowperwood candidates, and try to elect them, while he, Hand, organized the money element and collected the necessary cash. Gilgan was to be given money personally. He was to have the undivided if secret support of all the high Republican elements in the city. His business was to win at almost any cost. And as a reward he was to have the Republican support for Congress, or, failing that, the practical Republican leadership in city and county.

"Anyhow," said Hand, after Mr. Gilgan finally took his departure, "things won't be so easy for Mr. Cowperwood in the future as they were in the past. And when it comes to getting his franchises renewed, if I'm alive, we'll see whether he will or not."

The heavy financier actually growled a low growl as he spoke out loud to himself. He felt a boundless rancor toward the man who had, as he supposed, alienated the affections of his smart young wife.

CHAPTER XXXV

A POLITICAL AGREEMENT

In the first and second wards of Chicago at this time—wards including the business heart, South Clark Street, the water-front, the river-levee, and the like—were two men, Michael (alias Smiling Mike) Tiernan and Patrick (alias Emerald Pat) Kerrigan, who, for picturequeness of character and sordidness of atmosphere, could not be equaled elsewhere in the city, if in the nation at large. "Smiling" Mike Tiernan, proud possessor of four of the largest and filthiest saloons of this area, was a man of large and genial mold—perhaps six feet one inch in height, broad-shouldered in proportion, with a bovine head, bullet-shaped from one angle, and big, healthy, hairy hands and large feet. He had done many things from digging in a ditch to occupying a seat in the city council from this his beloved ward, which he sold out regularly for one purpose and another; but his chief present joy consisted in sitting behind a solid mahogany railing at a rosewood desk in the back portion of his largest Clark Street hostelry—"The Silver Moon." Here he counted up the returns from his various properties—salons, gambling resorts, and houses of prostitution—which he manipulated with the connivance or blinking courtesy of the present administration, and listened to the pleas and demands of his henchmen and tenants.

The character of Mr. Kerrigan, Mr. Tiernan's only rival in this rather difficult and sordid region, was somewhat different. He was a small man, quite dapper, with a lean, hollow, and somewhat haggard face, but by no means sickly body, a large, strident mustache, a wealth of coal-black hair parted slickly on one side, and a shrewd, genial brown-black eye—constituting altogether a rather pleasing and ornate figure whom it was not at all unsatisfactory to meet. His ears were large and stood out bat-wise from his head; and his eyes gleamed with a smart, evasive light. He was cleverer financially than Tiernan, richer, and no more than thirty-five, whereas Mr. Tiernan was forty-five years of age. Like Mr. Tiernan in the first ward, Mr. Kerrigan was a power in the second, and controlled a most useful and dangerous floating vote. His saloons harbored the largest floating element that was to be found in the city—longshoremen, railroad hands, stevedores, tramps, thugs, thieves, pimps, rounders, detectives, and the like. He was very vain, considered himself handsome, a "killer" with the ladies. Married, and with two children and a sedate young wife, he still had his mistress, who changed from year to year, and his intermediate girls. His clothes were altogether noteworthy, but it was his pride to eschew jewelry, except for one enormous emerald, value fourteen thousand dollars, which he wore in his necktie on occasions, and the wonder of which, pervading all Dearborn Street and the city council, had won him the soubriquet of "Emerald Pat." At first he rejoiced heartily in this title, as he did in a gold and diamond medal awarded him by a Chicago brewery for selling the largest number of barrels of beer of any saloon in Chicago. More recently, the newspapers having begun to pay humorous attention to both himself and Mr. Tiernan, because of their prosperity and individuality, he resented it.

The relation of these two men to the present political situation was peculiar, and, as it turned out, was to constitute the weak spot in the Cowperwood-McKenty campaign. Tiernan and Kerrigan, to begin with, being neighbors and friends, worked together in politics and business, on occasions pooling their issues and doing each other favors. The enterprises in which they were engaged being low and shabby, they needed counsel and consolation. Infinitely beneath a man like McKenty in understanding and a politic grasp of life, they were, nevertheless, as they prospered, somewhat jealous of him and his high estate. They saw with speculative and somewhat jealous eyes how, after his union with Cowperwood, he grew and how he managed to work his will in many ways—by extracting tolls from the police department, and heavy annual campaign contributions from manufacturers favored by the city gas and water departments. McKenty—a born manipulator in this respect—knew where political funds were to be had in an hour of emergency, and he did not hesitate to demand them. Tiernan and Kerrigan had always been fairly treated by him as politics go; but they had never as yet been included in his inner council of plotters. When he was down-town on one errand or another, he stopped in at their places to shake hands with them, to inquire after business, to ask if there was any favor he could do them; but never did he stoop to ask a favor of them or personally to promise any form of reward. That was the business of Dowling and others through whom he worked.

Naturally men of strong, restive, animal disposition, finding no complete outlet for all their growing capacity, Tiernan and Kerrigan were both curious to see in what way they could add to their honors and emoluments. Their wards, more than any in the city, were increasing in what might be called a vote-piling capacity, the honest, legitimate vote not being so large, but the opportunities afforded for colonizing, repeating, and ballot-box stuffing being immense. In a doubtful mayoralty campaign the first and second wards alone, coupled with a portion of the third adjoining them, would register sufficient illegitimate votes (after voting-hours, if necessary) to completely change the complexion of the city as to the general officers nominated. Large amounts of money were sent to Tiernan and Kerrigan around election time by the Democratic County Committee to be disposed of as they saw fit. They merely sent in a rough estimate of how much they would need, and always received a little more than they asked for. They never made nor were asked to make accounting afterward. Tiernan would receive as high as fifteen and eighteen, Kerrigan sometimes as much as twenty to twenty-five thousand dollars, his being the pivotal ward under such circumstances.

McKenty had recently begun to recognize that these two men would soon have to be given fuller consideration, for they were becoming more or less influential. But how? Their personalities, let alone the reputation of their wards and the methods they employed, were not such as to command public confidence. In the mean time, owing to the tremendous growth of the city, the growth of their own private business, and the amount of ballot-box stuffing, repeating, and the like which was required of them, they were growing more and more restless. Why should not they be slated for higher offices? they now frequently asked themselves. Tiernan would have been delighted to have been nominated for sheriff or city treasurer. He considered himself eminently qualified. Kerrigan at the last city convention had privately urged on Dowling the wisdom of nominating him for the position of

440

commissioner of highways and sewers, which office he was anxious to obtain because of its reported commercial perquisites; but this year, of all times, owing to the need of nominating an unblemished ticket to defeat the sharp Republican opposition, such a nomination was not possible. It would have drawn the fire of all the respectable elements in the city. As a result both Tiernan and Kerrigan, thinking over their services, past and future, felt very much disgruntled. They were really not large enough mentally to understand how dangerous—outside of certain fields of activity—they were to the party.

After his conference with Hand, Gilgan, going about the city with the promise of ready cash on his lips, was able to arouse considerable enthusiasm for the Republican cause. In the wards and sections where the so-called "better element" prevailed it seemed probable, because of the heavy moral teaching of the newspapers, that the respectable vote would array itself almost solidly this time against Cowperwood. In the poorer wards it would not be so easy. True, it was possible, by a sufficient outlay of cash, to find certain hardy bucaneers who could be induced to knife their own brothers, but the result was not certain. Having heard through one person and another of the disgruntled mood of both Kerrigan and Tiernan, and recognizing himself, even if he was a Republican, to be a man much more of their own stripe than either McKenty or Dowling, Gilgan decided to visit that lusty pair and see what could be done by way of alienating them from the present center of power.

After due reflection he first sought out "Emerald Pat" Kerrigan, whom he knew personally but with whom he was by no means intimate politically, at his "Emporium Bar" in Dearborn Street. This particular saloon, a feature of political Chicago at this time, was a large affair containing among other marvelous saloon fixtures a circular bar of cherry wood twelve feet in diameter, which glowed as a small mountain with the customary plain and colored glasses, bottles, labels, and mirrors. The floor was a composition of small, shaded red-and-green marbles; the ceiling a daub of pinky, fleshy nudes floating among diaphanous clouds; the walls were alternate panels of cerise and brown set in rosewood. Mr. Kerrigan, when other duties were not pressing, was usually to be found standing chatting with several friends and surveying the wonders of his bar trade, which was very large. On the day of Mr. Gilgan's call he was resplendent in a dark-brown suit with a fine red stripe in it, Cordovan leather shoes, a wine-colored tie ornamented with the emerald of so much renown, and a straw hat of flaring proportions and novel weave. About his waist, in lieu of a waistcoat, was fastened one of the eccentricities of the day, a manufactured silk sash. He formed an interesting contrast with Mr. Gilgan, who now came up very moist, pink, and warm, in a fine, light tweed of creamy, showy texture, straw hat, and yellow shoes.

"How are you, Kerrigan?" he observed, genially, there being no political enmity between them. "How's the first, and how's trade? I see you haven't lost the emerald yet?"

"No. No danger of that. Oh, trade's all right. And so's the first. How's Mr. Gilgan?" Kerrigan extended his hand cordially.

"I have a word to say to you. Have you any time to spare?"

For answer Mr. Kerrigan led the way into the back room. Already he had heard rumors of a strong Republican opposition at the coming election.

Mr. Gilgan sat down. "It's about things this fall I've come to see you, of course," he began, smilingly. "You and I are supposed to be on opposite sides of the fence, and we are as a rule, but I am wondering whether we need be this time or not?"

Mr. Kerrigan, shrewd though seemingly simple, fixed him with an amiable eye. "What's your scheme?" he said. "I'm always open to a good idea."

"Well, it's just this," began Mr. Gilgan, feeling his way. "You have a fine big ward here that you carry in your vest pocket, and so has Tiernan, as we all know; and we all know, too, that if it wasn't for what you and him can do there wouldn't always be a Democratic mayor elected. Now, I have an idea, from looking into the thing, that neither you nor Tiernan have got as much out of it so far as you might have."

Mr. Kerrigan was too cautious to comment as to that, though Mr. Gilgan paused for a moment.

"Now, I have a plan, as I say, and you can take it or leave it, just as you want, and no hard feelings one way or the other. I think the Republicans are going to win this fall—McKenty or no McKenty—first, second, and third wards with us or not, as they choose. The doings of the big fellow"—he was referring to McKenty—"with the other fellow in North Clark Street"—Mr. Gilgan preferred to be a little enigmatic at times—"are very much in the wind just now. You see how the papers stand. I happen to know where there's any quantity of money coming into the game from big financial quarters who have no use for this railroad man. It's a solid La Salle and Dearborn Street line-up, so far as I can see. Why, I don't know. But so it is. Maybe you know better than I do. Anyhow, that's the way it stands now. Add to that the fact that there are eight naturally Republican wards as it is, and ten more where there is always a fighting chance, and you begin to see what I'm driving at. Count out these last ten, though, and bet only on the eight that are sure to stand. That leaves twenty-three wards that we Republicans always conceded to you people; but if we manage to carry thirteen of them along with the eight I'm talking about, we'll have a majority in council, and"—flick! he snapped his fingers—"out you go—you, McKenty, Cowperwood, and all the rest. No more franchises, no more street-paving contracts, no more gas deals. Nothing—for two years, anyhow, and maybe longer. If we win we'll take the jobs and the fat deals." He paused and surveyed Kerrigan cheerfully but defiantly.

"Now, I've just been all over the city," he continued, "in every ward and precinct, so I know something of what I am talking about. I have the men and the cash to put up a fight all along the line this time. This fall we win—me and the big fellows over there in La Salle Street, and all the Republicans or Democrats or Prohibitionists, or whoever else comes in with us—do you get me? We're going to put up the biggest political fight Chicago has ever seen. I'm not naming any names just yet, but when the time comes you'll see. Now, what I want to ask of you is this, and I'll not mince me words nor beat around the bush. Will you and Tiernan come in with me and Edstrom to take over the city and run it during the next two years? If you will, we can win hands down. It will be a case of share and share alike on everything—police, gas, water, highways, street-railways, everything—or we'll divide beforehand and put it down in black and white. I know that you and Tiernan work together, or I wouldn't talk about this. Edstrom has the Swedes where he wants them, and he'll poll twenty thousand of them this fall. There's Ungerich with his Germans; one of us might make a deal with him afterward, give him most any office he wants. If we win this time we can hold the city for six or eight years anyhow, most likely, and after that—well, there's no use lookin' too far in the future—Anyhow we'd have a majority of the council and carry the mayor along with it."

"If—" commented Mr. Kerrigan, dryly.

"If," replied Mr. Gilgan, sententiously. "You're very right. There's a big 'if' in there, I'll admit. But if these two wards—yours and Tiernan's—could by any chance be carried for the Republicans they'd be equal to any four or five of the others."

"Very true," replied Mr. Kerrigan, "if they could be carried for the Republicans. But they can't be. What do you want me to do, anyhow? Lose me seat in council and be run out of the Democratic party? What's your game? You don't take me for a plain damn fool, do you?"

"Sorry the man that ever took 'Emerald Pat' for that," answered Gilgan, with honeyed compliment. "I never would. But no one is askin' ye to lose your seat in council and be run out of the Democratic party. What's to hinder you from electin' yourself and droppin' the rest of the ticket?" He had almost said "knifing."

Mr. Kerrigan smiled. In spite of all his previous dissatisfaction with the Chicago situation he had not thought of Mr. Gilgan's talk as leading to this. It was an interesting idea. He had "knifed" people before—here and there a particular candidate whom it was desirable to undo. If the Democratic party was in any danger of losing this fall, and if Gilgan was honest in his desire to divide and control, it might not be such a bad thing. Neither Cowperwood, McKenty, nor Dowling had ever favored him in any particular way. If they lost through him, and he could still keep himself in power, they would have to make terms with him. There was no chance of their running him out. Why shouldn't he knife the ticket? It was worth thinking over, to say the least.

"That's all very fine," he observed, dryly, after his meditations had run their course; "but how do I know that you wouldn't turn around and 'welch' on the agreement afterward?" (Mr. Gilgan stirred irritably at the suggestion.) "Dave Morrissey came to me four years ago to help him out, and a lot of satisfaction I got afterward." Kerrigan was referring to a man whom he had helped make county clerk, and who had turned on him when he asked for return favors and his support for the office of commissioner of highways. Morrissey had become a prominent politician.

"That's very easy to say," replied Gilgan, irritably, "but it's not true of me. Ask any man in my district. Ask the men who know me. I'll put my part of the bargain in black and white if you'll put yours. If I don't make good, show me up afterward. I'll take you to the people that are backing me. I'll show you the money. I've got the goods this time. What do you stand to lose, anyhow? They can't run you out for cutting the ticket. They can't prove it. We'll bring police in here to make it look like a fair vote. I'll put up as much money as they will to carry this district, and more."

Mr. Kerrigan suddenly saw a grand coup here. He could "draw down" from the Democrats, as he would have expressed it, twenty to twenty-five thousand dollars to do the dirty work here. Gilgan would furnish him as much and more—the situation being so critical. Perhaps fifteen or eighteen thousand would be necessary to poll the number of votes required either way. At the last hour, before stuffing the boxes, he would learn how the city was going. If it looked favorable for the Republicans it would be easy to complete the victory and complain that his lieutenants had been suborned. If it looked certain for the Democrats he could throw Gilgan and pocket his funds. In either case he would be "in" twenty-five to thirty thousand dollars, and he would still be councilman.

"All very fine," replied Mr. Kerrigan, pretending a dullness which he did not feel; "but it's damned ticklish business at best. I don't know that I want anything to do with it even if we

443

could win. It's true the City Hall crowd have never played into my hands very much; but this is a Democratic district, and I'm a Democrat. If it ever got out that I had thrown the party it would be pretty near all day with me.

"I'm a man of my word," declared Mr. Gilgan, emphatically, getting up. "I never threw a man or a bet in my life. Look at me record in the eighteenth. Did you ever hear any one say that I had?"

"No, I never did," returned Kerrigan, mildly. "But it's a pretty large thing you're proposing, Mr. Gilgan. I wouldn't want to say what I thought about it offhand. This ward is supposed to be Democratic. It couldn't be swung over into the Republican column without a good bit of fuss being made about it. You'd better see Mr. Tiernan first and hear what he has to say. Afterward I might be willing to talk about it further. Not now, though—not now."

Mr. Gilgan went away quite jauntily and cheerfully. He was not at all downcast.

CHAPTER XXXVI

AN ELECTION DRAWS NEAR

Subsequently Mr. Kerrigan called on Mr. Tiernan casually. Mr. Tiernan returned the call. A little later Messrs. Tiernan, Kerrigan, and Gilgan, in a parlor-room in a small hotel in Milwaukee (in order not to be seen together), conferred. Finally Messrs. Tiernan, Edstrom, Kerrigan, and Gilgan met and mapped out a programme of division far too intricate to be indicated here. Needless to say, it involved the division of chief clerks, pro rata, of police graft, of gambling and bawdy-house perquisites, of returns from gas, street-railway, and other organizations. It was sealed with many solemn promises. If it could be made effective this quadrumvirate was to endure for years. Judges, small magistrates, officers large and small, the shrievalty, the water office, the tax office, all were to come within its purview. It was a fine, handsome political dream, and as such worthy of every courtesy and consideration but it was only a political dream in its ultimate aspects, and as such impressed the participants themselves at times.

The campaign was now in full blast. The summer and fall (September and October) went by to the tune of Democratic and Republican marching club bands, to the sound of lusty political voices orating in parks, at street-corners, in wooden "wigwams," halls, tents, and parlors—wherever a meager handful of listeners could be drummed up and made by any device to keep still. The newspapers honked and bellowed, as is the way with those profit-appointed advocates and guardians of "right" and "justice." Cowperwood and McKenty were denounced from nearly every street-corner in Chicago. Wagons and sign-boards on wheels were hauled about labeled "Break the partnership between the street-railway corporations and the city council." "Do you want more streets stolen?" "Do you want Cowperwood to own Chicago?" Cowperwood himself, coming down-town of a morning or driving home of an evening, saw these things. He saw the huge signs, listened to speeches denouncing himself, and smiled. By now he was quite aware as to whence this powerful uprising had sprung. Hand was back of it, he knew—for so McKenty and Addison had quickly discovered—and with Hand was Schryhart, Arneel, Merrill, the Douglas Trust Company, the various editors, young Truman Leslie MacDonald, the old gas crowd, the Chicago General Company—all. He even suspected that certain aldermen might possibly be suborned to desert him, though all professed loyalty. McKenty, Addison, Videra, and himself were planning the details of their defenses as carefully and effectively as possible. Cowperwood was fully alive to the fact that if he lost this election—the first to be vigorously contested—it might involve a serious chain of events; but he did not propose to be unduly disturbed, since he could always fight in the courts by money, and by preferment in the council, and with the mayor and the city attorney. "There is more than one way to kill a cat," was one of his pet expressions, and it expressed his logic and courage exactly. Yet he did not wish to lose.

One of the amusing features of the campaign was that the McKenty orators had been instructed to shout as loudly for reforms as the Republicans, only instead of assailing Cowperwood and McKenty they were to point out that Schryhart's Chicago City Railway was far more rapacious, and that this was a scheme to give it a blanket franchise of all streets not yet covered by either the Cowperwood or the Schryhart-Hand-Arneel lines. It was a pretty argument. The Democrats could point with pride to a uniformly liberal interpretation of some trying Sunday laws, whereby under Republican and reform administrations it had been occasionally difficult for the honest working-man to get his glass or pail of beer on Sunday. On the other hand it was possible for the Republican orators to show how "the low dives and gin-mills" were everywhere being operated in favor of McKenty, and that under the highly respectable administration of the Republican candidate for mayor this partnership between the city government and vice and crime would be nullified.

"If I am elected," declared the Honorable Chaffee Thayer Sluss, the Republican candidate, "neither Frank Cowperwood nor John McKenty will dare to show his face in the City Hall unless he comes with clean hands and an honest purpose.

"Hooray!" yelled the crowd.

"I know that ass," commented Addison, when he read this in the Transcript. "He used to be a clerk in the Douglas Trust Company. He's made a little money recently in the paper business. He's a mere tool for the Arneel-Schryhart interests. He hasn't the courage of a two-inch fish-worm."

When McKenty read it he simply observed: "There are other ways of going to City Hall than by going yourself." He was depending upon a councilmanic majority at least.

However, in the midst of this uproar the goings to and fro of Gilgan, Edstrom, Kerrigan, and Tiernan were nor fully grasped. A more urbanely shifty pair than these latter were never seen. While fraternizing secretly with both Gilgan and Edstrom, laying out their political programme most neatly, they were at the same time conferring with Dowling, Duvanicki, even McKenty himself. Seeing that the outcome was, for some reason—he could scarcely see why—looking very uncertain, McKenty one day asked the two of them to come to see him. On getting the letter Mr. Tiernan strolled over to Mr. Kerrigan's place to see whether he also had received a message.

"Sure, sure! I did!" replied Mr. Kerrigan, gaily. "Here it is now in me outside coat pocket. 'Dear Mr. Kerrigan,'" he read, "'won't you do me the favor to come over to-morrow evening at seven and dine with me? Mr. Ungerich, Mr. Duvanicki, and several others will very likely drop in afterward. I have asked Mr. Tiernan to come at the same time. Sincerely, John J. McKenty.' That's the way he does it," added Mr. Kerrigan; "just like that."

He kissed the letter mockingly and put it back into his pocket.

"Sure I got one, jist the same way. The very same langwidge, nearly," commented Mr. Tiernan, sweetly. "He's beginning to wake up, eh? What! The little old first and second are beginning to look purty big just now, eh? What!"

"Tush!" observed Mr. Kerrigan to Mr. Tiernan, with a marked sardonic emphasis, "that combination won't last forever. They've been getting too big for their pants, I'm thinking. Well, it's a long road, eh? It's pretty near time, what?"

"You're right," responded Mr. Tiernan, feelingly. "It is a long road. These are the two big wards of the city, and everybody knows it. If we turn on them at the last moment where will they be, eh?"

He put a fat finger alongside of his heavy reddish nose and looked at Mr. Kerrigan out of squinted eyes.

"You're damned right," replied the little politician, cheerfully.

They went to the dinner separately, so as not to appear to have conferred before, and greeted each other on arriving as though they had not seen each other for days.

"How's business, Mike?"

"Oh, fair, Pat. How's things with you?"

"So so."

"Things lookin' all right in your ward for November?"

Mr. Tiernan wrinkled a fat forehead. "Can't tell yet." All this was for the benefit of Mr. McKenty, who did not suspect rank party disloyalty.

Nothing much came of this conference, except that they sat about discussing in a general way wards, pluralities, what Zeigler was likely to do with the twelfth, whether Pinski could make it in the sixth, Schlumbohm in the twentieth, and so on. New Republican contestants in old, safe Democratic wards were making things look dubious.

"And how about the first, Kerrigan?" inquired Ungerich, a thin, reflective German-American of shrewd presence. Ungerich was one who had hitherto wormed himself higher in McKenty's favor than either Kerrigan or Tiernan.

"Oh, the first's all right," replied Kerrigan, archly. "Of course you never can tell. This fellow Scully may do something, but I don't think it will be much. If we have the same police protection—"

Ungerich was gratified. He was having a struggle in his own ward, where a rival by the name of Glover appeared to be pouring out money like water. He would require considerably more money than usual to win. It was the same with Duvanicki.

McKenty finally parted with his lieutenants—more feelingly with Kerrigan and Tiernan than he had ever done before. He did not wholly trust these two, and he could not exactly admire them and their methods, which were the roughest of all, but they were useful.

"I'm glad to learn," he said, at parting, "that things are looking all right with you, Pat, and you, Mike," nodding to each in turn. "We're going to need the most we can get out of everybody. I depend on you two to make a fine showing—the best of any. The rest of us will not forget it when the plums are being handed around afterward."

"Oh, you can depend on me to do the best I can always," commented Mr. Kerrigan, sympathetically. "It's a tough year, but we haven't failed yet."

"And me, Chief! That goes for me," observed Mr. Tiernan, raucously. "I guess I can do as well as I have."

"Good for you, Mike!" soothed McKenty, laying a gentle hand on his shoulder. "And you, too, Kerrigan. Yours are the key wards, and we understand that. I've always been sorry that the leaders couldn't agree on you two for something better than councilmen; but next time there won't be any doubt of it, if I have any influence then." He went in and closed the door. Outside a cool October wind was whipping dead leaves and weed stalks along the pavements. Neither Tiernan nor Kerrigan spoke, though they had come away together, until they were two hundred feet down the avenue toward Van Buren.

"Some talk, that, eh?" commented Mr. Tiernan, eying Mr. Kerrigan in the flare of a passing gas-lamp.

"Sure. That's the stuff they always hand out when they're up against it. Pretty kind words, eh?"

"And after ten years of about the roughest work that's done, eh? It's about time, what? Say, it's a wonder he didn't think of that last June when the convention was in session.

"Tush! Mikey," smiled Mr. Kerrigan, grimly. "You're a bad little boy. You want your pie too soon. Wait another two or four or six years, like Paddy Kerrigan and the others."

"Yes, I will—not," growled Mr. Tiernan. "Wait'll the sixth."

"No more, will I," replied Mr. Kerrigan. "Say, we know a trick that beats that next-year business to a pulp. What?"

"You're dead right," commented Mr. Tiernan.

And so they went peacefully home.

CHAPTER XXXVII

AILEEN'S REVENGE

The interesting Polk Lynde, rising one morning, decided that his affair with Aileen, sympathetic as it was, must culminate in the one fashion satisfactory to him here and now—this day, if possible, or the next. Since the luncheon some considerable time had elapsed, and although he had tried to seek her out in various ways, Aileen, owing to a certain feeling that she must think and not jeopardize her future, had evaded him. She realized well enough that she was at the turning of the balance, now that opportunity was knocking so loudly at her door, and she was exceedingly coy and distrait. In spite of herself the old grip of Cowperwood was over her—the conviction that he was such a tremendous figure in the world—and this made her strangely disturbed, nebulous, and meditative. Another type of woman, having troubled as much as she had done, would have made short work of it, particularly since the details in regard to Mrs. Hand had been added. Not so Aileen. She could not quite forget the early vows and promises exchanged between them, nor conquer the often-fractured illusions that he might still behave himself.

On the other hand, Polk Lynde, marauder, social adventurer, a bucaneer of the affections, was not so easily to be put aside, delayed, and gainsaid. Not unlike Cowperwood, he was a man of real force, and his methods, in so far as women were concerned, were even more daring. Long trifling with the sex had taught him that they were coy, uncertain, foolishly inconsistent in their moods, even with regard to what they most desired. If one contemplated victory, it had frequently to be taken with an iron hand.

From this attitude on his part had sprung his rather dark fame. Aileen felt it on the day that she took lunch with him. His solemn, dark eyes were treacherously sweet. She felt as if she might be paving the way for some situation in which she would find herself helpless before his sudden mood—and yet she had come.

But Lynde, meditating Aileen's delay, had this day decided that he should get a definite decision, and that it should be favorable. He called her up at ten in the morning and chafed her concerning her indecision and changeable moods. He wanted to know whether she would not come and see the paintings at his friend's studio—whether she could not make up her mind to come to a barn-dance which some bachelor friends of his had arranged. When she pleaded being out of sorts he urged her to pull herself together. "You're making things very difficult for your admirers," he suggested, sweetly.

Aileen fancied she had postponed the struggle diplomatically for some little time without ending it, when at two o'clock in the afternoon her door-bell was rung and the name of Lynde brought up. "He said he was sure you were in," commented the footman, on whom had been pressed a dollar, "and would you see him for just a moment? He would not keep you more than a moment."

Aileen, taken off her guard by this effrontery, uncertain as to whether there might not be something of some slight import concerning which he wished to speak to her, quarreling with herself because of her indecision, really fascinated by Lynde as a rival for her affections, and remembering his jesting, coaxing voice of the morning, decided to go down. She was lonely, and, clad in a lavender housegown with an ermine collar and sleeve cuffs, was reading a book.

"Show him into the music-room," she said to the lackey. When she entered she was breathing with some slight difficulty, for so Lynde affected her. She knew she had displayed fear by not going to him before, and previous cowardice plainly manifested does not add to one's power of resistance.

"Oh!" she exclaimed, with an assumption of bravado which she did not feel. "I didn't expect to see you so soon after your telephone message. You have never been in our house before, have you? Won't you put up your coat and hat and come into the gallery? It's brighter there, and you might be interested in some of the pictures."

Lynde, who was seeking for any pretext whereby he might prolong his stay and overcome her nervous mood, accepted, pretending, however, that he was merely passing and with a moment to spare.

"Thought I'd get just one glimpse of you again. Couldn't resist the temptation to look in. Stunning room, isn't it? Spacious—and there you are! Who did that? Oh, I see—Van Beers. And a jolly fine piece of work it is, too, charming."

He surveyed her and then turned back to the picture where, ten years younger, buoyant, hopeful, carrying her blue-and-white striped parasol, she sat on a stone bench against the Dutch background of sky and clouds. Charmed by the picture she presented in both cases, he was genially complimentary. To-day she was stouter, ruddier—the fiber of her had hardened, as it does with so many as the years come on; but she was still in full bloom—a little late in the summer, but in full bloom.

"Oh yes; and this Rembrandt—I'm surprised! I did not know your husband's collection was so representative. Israels, I see, and Gerome, and Meissonier! Gad! It is a representative collection, isn't it?"

"Some of the things are excellent," she commented, with an air, aping Cowperwood and others, "but a number will be weeded out eventually—that Paul Potter and this Goy—as better examples come into the market."

She had heard Cowperwood say as much, over and over.

Finding that conversation was possible between them in this easy, impersonal way, Aileen became quite natural and interested, pleased and entertained by his discreet and charming presence. Evidently he did not intend to pay much more than a passing social call. On the other hand, Lynde was studying her, wondering what effect his light, distant air was having. As he finished a very casual survey of the gallery he remarked:

"I have always wondered about this house. I knew Lord did it, of course, and I always heard it was well done. That is the dining-room, I suppose?"

Aileen, who had always been inordinately vain of the house in spite of the fact that it had proved of small use socially, was delighted to show him the remainder of the rooms. Lynde, who was used, of course, to houses of all degrees of material splendor—that of his own family being one of the best—pretended an interest he did not feel. He commented as he went on the taste of the decorations and wood-carving, the charm of the arrangement that permitted neat brief vistas, and the like.

"Just wait a moment," said Aileen, as they neared the door of her own boudoir. "I've forgotten whether mine is in order. I want you to see that."

She opened it and stepped in.

"Yes, you may come," she called.

449

He followed. "Oh yes, indeed. Very charming. Very graceful—those little lacy dancing figures—aren't they? A delightful color scheme. It harmonizes with you exactly. It is quite like you."

He paused, looking at the spacious rug, which was of warm blues and creams, and at the gilt ormolu bed. "Well done," he said, and then, suddenly changing his mood and dropping his talk of decoration (Aileen was to his right, and he was between her and the door), he added: "Tell me now why won't you come to the barn-dance to-night? It would be charming. You will enjoy it."

Aileen saw the sudden change in his mood. She recognized that by showing him the rooms she had led herself into an easily made disturbing position. His dark engaging eyes told their own story.

"Oh, I don't feel in the mood to. I haven't for a number of things for some time. I—"

She began to move unconcernedly about him toward the door, but he detained her with his hand. "Don't go just yet," he said. "Let me talk to you. You always evade me in such a nervous way. Don't you like me at all?"

"Oh yes, I like you; but can't we talk just as well down in the music-room as here? Can't I tell you why I evade you down there just as well as I can here?" She smiled a winning and now fearless smile.

Lynde showed his even white teeth in two gleaming rows. His eyes filled with a gay maliciousness. "Surely, surely," he replied; "but you're so nice in your own room here. I hate to leave it."

"Just the same," replied Aileen, still gay, but now slightly disturbed also, "I think we might as well. You will find me just as entertaining downstairs."

She moved, but his strength, quite as Cowperwood's, was much too great for her. He was a strong man.

"Really, you know," she said, "you mustn't act this way here. Some one might come in. What cause have I given you to make you think you could do like this with me?"

"What cause?" he asked, bending over her and smoothing her plump arms with his brown hands. "Oh, no definite cause, perhaps. You are a cause in yourself. I told you how sweet I thought you were, the night we were at the Alcott. Didn't you understand then? I thought you did."

"Oh, I understood that you liked me, and all that, perhaps. Any one might do that. But as for anything like—well—taking such liberties with me—I never dreamed of it. But listen. I think I hear some one coming." Aileen, making a sudden vigorous effort to free herself and failing, added: "Please let me go, Mr. Lynde. It isn't very gallant of you, I must say, restraining a woman against her will. If I had given you any real cause—I shall be angry in a moment."

Again the even smiling teeth and dark, wrinkling, malicious eyes.

"Really! How you go on! You would think I was a perfect stranger. Don't you remember what you said to me at lunch? You didn't keep your promise. You practically gave me to understand that you would come. Why didn't you? Are you afraid of me, or don't you like me, or both? I think you're delicious, splendid, and I want to know."

He shifted his position, putting one arm about her waist, pulling her close to him, looking into her eyes. With the other he held her free arm. Suddenly he covered her mouth with his and then kissed her cheeks. "You care for me, don't you? What did you mean by saying you might come, if you didn't?"

He held her quite firm, while Aileen struggled. It was a new sensation this—that of the other man, and this was Polk Lynde, the first individual outside of Cowperwood to whom she had ever felt drawn. But now, here, in her own room—and it was within the range of possibilities that Cowperwood might return or the servants enter.

"Oh, but think what you are doing," she protested, not really disturbed as yet as to the outcome of the contest with him, and feeling as though he were merely trying to make her be sweet to him without intending anything more at present—"here in my own room! Really, you're not the man I thought you were at all, if you don't instantly let me go. Mr. Lynde! Mr. Lynde!" (He had bent over and was kissing her). "Oh, you shouldn't do this! Really! I—I said I might come, but that was far from doing it. And to have you come here and take advantage of me in this way! I think you're horrid. If I ever had any interest in you, it is quite dead now, I can assure you. Unless you let me go at once, I give you my word I will never see you any more. I won't! Really, I won't! I mean it! Oh, please let me go! I'll scream, I tell you! I'll never see you again after this day! Oh—" It was an intense but useless struggle.

Coming home one evening about a week later, Cowperwood found Aileen humming cheerfully, and yet also in a seemingly deep and reflective mood. She was just completing an evening toilet, and looked young and colorful—quite her avid, seeking self of earlier days.

"Well," he asked, cheerfully, "how have things gone to-day?" Aileen, feeling somehow, as one will on occasions, that if she had done wrong she was justified and that sometime because of this she might even win Cowperwood back, felt somewhat kindlier toward him. "Oh, very well," she replied. "I stopped in at the Hoecksemas' this afternoon for a little while. They're going to Mexico in November. She has the darlingest new basket-carriage— if she only looked like anything when she rode in it. Etta is getting ready to enter Bryn Mawr. She is all fussed up about leaving her dog and cat. Then I went down to one of Lane Cross's receptions, and over to Merrill's"—she was referring to the great store—"and home. I saw Taylor Lord and Polk Lynde together in Wabash Avenue."

"Polk Lynde?" commented Cowperwood. "Is he interesting?"

"Yes, he is," replied Aileen. "I never met a man with such perfect manners. He's so fascinating. He's just like a boy, and yet, Heaven knows, he seems to have had enough worldly experience."

"So I've heard," commented Cowperwood. "Wasn't he the one that was mixed up in that Carmen Torriba case here a few years ago?" Cowperwood was referring to the matter of a Spanish dancer traveling in America with whom Lynde had been apparently desperately in love.

451

"Oh yes," replied Aileen, maliciously; "but that oughtn't to make any difference to you. He's charming, anyhow. I like him."

"I didn't say it did, did I? You don't object to my mentioning a mere incident?"

"Oh, I know about the incident," replied Aileen, jestingly. "I know you."

"What do you mean by that?" he asked, studying her face.

"Oh, I know you," she replied, sweetly and yet defensively. "You think I'll stay here and be content while you run about with other women—play the sweet and loving wife? Well, I won't. I know why you say this about Lynde. It's to keep me from being interested in him, possibly. Well, I will be if I want to. I told you I would be, and I will. You can do what you please about that. You don't want me, so why should you be disturbed as to whether other men are interested in me or not?"

The truth was that Cowperwood was not clearly thinking of any probable relation between Lynde and Aileen any more than he was in connection with her and any other man, and yet in a remote way he was sensing some one. It was this that Aileen felt in him, and that brought forth her seemingly uncalled-for comment. Cowperwood, under the circumstances, attempted to be as suave as possible, having caught the implication clearly.

"Aileen," he cooed, "how you talk! Why do you say that? You know I care for you. I can't prevent anything you want to do, and I'm sure you know I don't want to. It's you that I want to see satisfied. You know that I care."

"Yes, I know how you care," replied Aileen, her mood changing for the moment. "Don't start that old stuff, please. I'm sick of it. I know how you're running around. I know about Mrs. Hand. Even the newspapers make that plain. You've been home just one evening in the last eight days, long enough for me to get more than a glimpse of you. Don't talk to me. Don't try to bill and coo. I've always known. Don't think I don't know who your latest flame is. But don't begin to whine, and don't quarrel with me if I go about and get interested in other men, as I certainly will. It will be all your fault if I do, and you know it. Don't begin and complain. It won't do you any good. I'm not going to sit here and be made a fool of. I've told you that over and over. You don't believe it, but I'm not. I told you that I'd find some one one of these days, and I will. As a matter of fact, I have already."

At this remark Cowperwood surveyed her coolly, critically, and yet not unsympathetically; but she swung out of the room with a defiant air before anything could be said, and went down to the music-room, from whence a few moments later there rolled up to him from the hall below the strains of the second Hungarian Rhapsodie, feelingly and for once movingly played. Into it Aileen put some of her own wild woe and misery. Cowperwood hated the thought for the moment that some one as smug as Lynde—so good-looking, so suave a society rake—should interest Aileen; but if it must be, it must be. He could have no honest reason for complaint. At the same time a breath of real sorrow for the days that had gone swept over him. He remembered her in Philadelphia in her red cape as a school-girl—in his father's house—out horseback-riding, driving. What a splendid, loving girl she had been—such a sweet fool of love. Could she really have decided not to worry about him any more? Could it be possible that she might find some one else who would be interested in her, and in whom she would take a keen interest? It was an odd thought for him.

452

He watched her as she came into the dining-room later, arrayed in green silk of the shade of copper patina, her hair done in a high coil—and in spite of himself he could not help admiring her. She looked very young in her soul, and yet moody—loving (for some one), eager, and defiant. He reflected for a moment what terrible things passion and love are—how they make fools of us all. "All of us are in the grip of a great creative impulse," he said to himself. He talked of other things for a while—the approaching election, a poster-wagon he had seen bearing the question, "Shall Cowperwood own the city?" "Pretty cheap politics, I call that," he commented. And then he told of stopping in a so-called Republican wigwam at State and Sixteenth streets—a great, cheaply erected, unpainted wooden shack with seats, and of hearing himself bitterly denounced by the reigning orator. "I was tempted once to ask that donkey a few questions," he added, "but I decided I wouldn't."

Aileen had to smile. In spite of all his faults he was such a wonderful man—to set a city thus by the ears. "Yet, what care I how fair he be, if he be not fair to me."

"Did you meet any one else besides Lynde you liked?" he finally asked, archly, seeking to gather further data without stirring up too much feeling.

Aileen, who had been studying him, feeling sure the subject would come up again, replied: "No, I haven't; but I don't need to. One is enough."

"What do you mean by that?" he asked, gently.

"Oh, just what I say. One will do."

"You mean you are in love with Lynde?"

"I mean—oh!" She stopped and surveyed him defiantly. "What difference does it make to you what I mean? Yes, I am. But what do you care? Why do you sit there and question me? It doesn't make any difference to you what I do. You don't want me. Why should you sit there and try to find out, or watch? It hasn't been any consideration for you that has restrained me so far. Suppose I am in love? What difference would it make to you?"

"Oh, I care. You know I care. Why do you say that?"

"Yes, you care," she flared. "I know how you care. Well, I'll just tell you one thing"—rage at his indifference was driving her on—"I am in love with Lynde, and what's more, I'm his mistress. And I'll continue to be. But what do you care? Pshaw!"

Her eyes blazed hotly, her color rose high and strong. She breathed heavily.

At this announcement, made in the heat of spite and rage generated by long indifference, Cowperwood sat up for a moment, and his eyes hardened with quite that implacable glare with which he sometimes confronted an enemy. He felt at once there were many things he could do to make her life miserable, and to take revenge on Lynde, but he decided after a moment he would not. It was not weakness, but a sense of superior power that was moving him. Why should he be jealous? Had he not been unkind enough? In a moment his mood changed to one of sorrow for Aileen, for himself, for life, indeed—its tangles of desire and necessity. He could not blame Aileen. Lynde was surely attractive. He had no desire to part with her or to quarrel with him—merely to temporarily cease all intimate relations with her and allow her mood to clear itself up. Perhaps she would want to leave him of her own accord. Perhaps, if he ever found the right woman, this might prove good grounds for his leaving her. The right woman—where was she? He had never found her yet.

"Aileen," he said, quite softly, "I wish you wouldn't feel so bitterly about this. Why should you? When did you do this? Will you tell me that?"

"No, I'll not tell you that," she replied, bitterly. "It's none of your affair, and I'll not tell you. Why should you ask? You don't care."

"But I do care, I tell you," he returned, irritably, almost roughly. "When did you? You can tell me that, at least." His eyes had a hard, cold look for the moment, dying away, though, into kindly inquiry.

"Oh, not long ago. About a week," Aileen answered, as though she were compelled.

"How long have you known him?" he asked, curiously.

"Oh, four or five months, now. I met him last winter."

"And did you do this deliberately—because you were in love with him, or because you wanted to hurt me?"

He could not believe from past scenes between them that she had ceased to love him.

Aileen stirred irritably. "I like that," she flared. "I did it because I wanted to, and not because of any love for you—I can tell you that. I like your nerve sitting here presuming to question me after the way you have neglected me." She pushed back her plate, and made as if to get up.

"Wait a minute, Aileen," he said, simply, putting down his knife and fork and looking across the handsome table where Sevres, silver, fruit, and dainty dishes were spread, and where under silk-shaded lights they sat opposite each other. "I wish you wouldn't talk that way to me. You know that I am not a petty, fourth-rate fool. You know that, whatever you do, I am not going to quarrel with you. I know what the trouble is with you. I know why you are acting this way, and how you will feel afterward if you go on. It isn't anything I will do—" He paused, caught by a wave of feeling.

"Oh, isn't it?" she blazed, trying to overcome the emotion that was rising in herself. The calmness of him stirred up memories of the past. "Well, you keep your sympathy for yourself. I don't need it. I will get along. I wish you wouldn't talk to me."

She shoved her plate away with such force that she upset a glass in which was champagne, the wine making a frayed, yellowish splotch on the white linen, and, rising, hurried toward the door. She was choking with anger, pain, shame, regret.

"Aileen! Aileen!" he called, hurrying after her, regardless of the butler, who, hearing the sound of stirring chairs, had entered. These family woes were an old story to him. "It's love you want—not revenge. I know—I can tell. You want to be loved by some one completely. I'm sorry. You mustn't be too hard on me. I sha'n't be on you." He seized her by the arm and detained her as they entered the next room. By this time Aileen was too ablaze with emotion to talk sensibly or understand what he was doing.

454

"Let me go!" she exclaimed, angrily, hot tears in her eyes. "Let me go! I tell you I don't love you any more. I tell you I hate you!" She flung herself loose and stood erect before him. "I don't want you to talk to me! I don't want you to speak to me! You're the cause of all my troubles. You're the cause of whatever I do, when I do it, and don't you dare to deny it! You'll see! You'll see! I'll show you what I'll do!"

She twisted and turned, but he held her firmly until, in his strong grasp, as usual, she collapsed and began to cry. "Oh, I cry," she declared, even in her tears, "but it will be just the same. It's too late! too late!"

CHAPTER XXXVIII .

AN HOUR OF DEFEAT

The stoic Cowperwood, listening to the blare and excitement that went with the fall campaign, was much more pained to learn of Aileen's desertion than to know that he had arrayed a whole social element against himself in Chicago. He could not forget the wonder of those first days when Aileen was young, and love and hope had been the substance of her being. The thought ran through all his efforts and cogitations like a distantly orchestrated undertone. In the main, in spite of his activity, he was an introspective man, and art, drama, and the pathos of broken ideals were not beyond him. He harbored in no way any grudge against Aileen—only a kind of sorrow over the inevitable consequences of his own ungovernable disposition, the will to freedom within himself. Change! Change! the inevitable passing of things! Who parts with a perfect thing, even if no more than an unreasoning love, without a touch of self-pity?

But there followed swiftly the sixth of November, with its election, noisy and irrational, and the latter resulted in a resounding defeat. Out of the thirty-two Democratic aldermen nominated only ten were elected, giving the opposition a full two-thirds majority in council, Messrs. Tiernan and Kerrigan, of course, being safely in their places. With them came a Republican mayor and all his Republican associates on the ticket, who were now supposed to carry out the theories of the respectable and the virtuous. Cowperwood knew what it meant and prepared at once to make overtures to the enemy. From McKenty and others he learned by degrees the full story of Tiernan's and Kerrigan's treachery, but he did not store it up bitterly against them. Such was life. They must be looked after more carefully in future, or caught in some trap and utterly undone. According to their own accounts, they had barely managed to scrape through.

"Look at meself! I only won by three hundred votes," archly declared Mr. Kerrigan, on divers and sundry occasions. "By God, I almost lost me own ward!"

Mr. Tiernan was equally emphatic. "The police was no good to me," he declared, firmly. "They let the other fellows beat up me men. I only polled six thousand when I should have had nine."

But no one believed them.

While McKenty meditated as to how in two years he should be able to undo this temporary victory, and Cowperwood was deciding that conciliation was the best policy for him,

Schryhart, Hand, and Arneel, joining hands with young MacDonald, were wondering how they could make sure that this party victory would cripple Cowperwood and permanently prevent him from returning to power. It was a long, intricate fight that followed, but it involved (before Cowperwood could possibly reach the new aldermen) a proposed reintroduction and passage of the much-opposed General Electric franchise, the granting of rights and privileges in outlying districts to various minor companies, and last and worst—a thing which had not previously dawned on Cowperwood as in any way probable—the projection of an ordinance granting to a certain South Side corporation the privilege of erecting and operating an elevated road. This was as severe a blow as any that had yet been dealt Cowperwood, for it introduced a new factor and complication into the Chicago street-railway situation which had hitherto, for all its troubles, been comparatively simple.

In order to make this plain it should be said that some eighteen or twenty years before in New York there had been devised and erected a series of elevated roads calculated to relieve the congestion of traffic on the lower portion of that long and narrow island, and they had proved an immense success. Cowperwood had been interested in them, along with everything else which pertained to public street traffic, from the very beginning. In his various trips to New York he had made a careful physical inspection of them. He knew all about their incorporation, backers, the expense connected with them, their returns, and so forth. Personally, in so far as New York was concerned, he considered them an ideal solution of traffic on that crowded island. Here in Chicago, where the population was as yet comparatively small—verging now toward a million, and widely scattered over a great area—he did not feel that they would be profitable—certainly not for some years to come. What traffic they gained would be taken from the surface lines, and if he built them he would be merely doubling his expenses to halve his profits. From time to time he had contemplated the possibility of their being built by other men—providing they could secure a franchise, which previous to the late election had not seemed probable—and in this connection he had once said to Addison: "Let them sink their money, and about the time the population is sufficient to support the lines they will have been driven into the hands of receivers. That will simply chase the game into my bag, and I can buy them for a mere song." With this conclusion Addison had agreed. But since this conversation circumstances made the construction of these elevated roads far less problematic.

In the first place, public interest in the idea of elevated roads was increasing. They were a novelty, a factor in the life of New York; and at this time rivalry with the great cosmopolitan heart was very keen in the mind of the average Chicago citizen. Public sentiment in this direction, however naive or unworthy, was nevertheless sufficient to make any elevated road in Chicago popular for the time being. In the second place, it so happened that because of this swelling tide of municipal enthusiasm, this renaissance of the West, Chicago had finally been chosen, at a date shortly preceding the present campaign, as the favored city for an enormous international fair—quite the largest ever given in America. Men such as Hand, Schryhart, Merrill, and Arneel, to say nothing of the various newspaper publishers and editors, had been enthusiastic supporters of the project, and in this Cowperwood had been one with them. No sooner, however, had the award actually been granted than Cowperwood's enemies made it their first concern to utilize the situation against him.

To begin with, the site of the fair, by aid of the new anti-Cowperwood council, was located on the South Side, at the terminus of the Schryhart line, thus making the whole city pay tribute to that corporation. Simultaneously the thought suddenly dawned upon the Schryhart faction that it would be an excellent stroke of business if the New York elevated-road idea were now introduced into the city—not so much with the purpose of making money immediately, but in order to bring the hated magnate to an understanding that he had a formidable rival which might invade the territory that he now monopolized, curtailing his and thus making it advisable for him to close out his holdings and depart. Bland and interesting were the conferences held by Mr. Schryhart with Mr. Hand, and by Mr. Hand with Mr. Arneel on this subject. Their plan as first outlined was to build an elevated road on the South Side—south of the proposed fair-grounds—and once that was popular—having previously secured franchises which would cover the entire field, West, South, and North— to construct the others at their leisure, and so to bid Mr. Cowperwood a sweet and smiling adieu.

Cowperwood, awaiting the assembling of the new city council one month after election, did not propose to wait in peace and quiet until the enemy should strike at him unprepared. Calling those familiar agents, his corporation attorneys, around him, he was shortly informed of the new elevated-road idea, and it gave him a real shock. Obviously Hand and Schryhart were now in deadly earnest. At once he dictated a letter to Mr. Gilgan asking him to call at his office. At the same time he hurriedly adjured his advisers to use due diligence in discovering what influences could be brought to bear on the new mayor, the honorable Chaffee Thayer Sluss, to cause him to veto the ordinances in case they came before him— to effect in him, indeed, a total change of heart.

The Hon. Chaffee Thayer Sluss, whose attitude in this instance was to prove crucial, was a tall, shapely, somewhat grandiloquent person who took himself and his social and commercial opportunities and doings in the most serious and, as it were, elevated light. You know, perhaps, the type of man or woman who, raised in an atmosphere of comparative comfort and some small social pretension, and being short of those gray convolutions in the human brain-pan which permit an individual to see life in all its fortuitousness and uncertainty, proceed because of an absence of necessity and the consequent lack of human experience to take themselves and all that they do in the most reverential and Providence-protected spirit. The Hon. Chaffee Thayer Sluss reasoned that, because of the splendid ancestry on which he prided himself, he was an essentially honest man. His father had amassed a small fortune in the wholesale harness business. The wife whom at the age of twenty-eight he had married—a pretty but inconsequential type of woman—was the daughter of a pickle manufacturer, whose wares were in some demand and whose children had been considered good "catches" in the neighborhood from which the Hon. Chaffee Sluss emanated. There had been a highly conservative wedding feast, and a honeymoon trip to the Garden of the Gods and the Grand Canon. Then the sleek Chaffee, much in the grace of both families because of his smug determination to rise in the world, had returned to his business, which was that of a paper-broker, and had begun with the greatest care to amass a competence on his own account.

The Honorable Chaffee, be it admitted, had no particular faults, unless those of smugness and a certain over-carefulness as to his own prospects and opportunities can be counted as such. But he had one weakness, which, in view of his young wife's stern and somewhat Puritanic ideas and the religious propensities of his father and father-in-law, was exceedingly disturbing to him. He had an eye for the beauty of women in general, and particularly for plump, blonde women with corn-colored hair. Now and then, in spite of the fact that he had an ideal wife and two lovely children, he would cast a meditative and speculative eye after those alluring forms that cross the path of all men and that seem to beckon slyly by implication if not by actual, open suggestion.

However, it was not until several years after Mr. Sluss had married, and when he might have been considered settled in the ways of righteousness, that he actually essayed to any extent the role of a gay Lothario. An experience or two with the less vigorous and vicious girls of the streets, a tentative love affair with a girl in his office who was not new to the practices she encouraged, and he was fairly launched. He lent himself at first to the great folly of pretending to love truly; but this was taken by one and another intelligent young woman with a grain of salt. The entertainment and preferment he could provide were accepted as sufficient reward. One girl, however, actually seduced, had to be compensated by five thousand dollars—and that after such terrors and heartaches (his wife, her family, and his own looming up horribly in the background) as should have cured him forever of a penchant for stenographers and employees generally. Thereafter for a long time he confined himself strictly to such acquaintances as he could make through agents, brokers, and manufacturers who did business with him, and who occasionally invited him to one form of bacchanalian feast or another.

As time went on he became wiser, if, alas, a little more eager. By association with merchants and some superior politicians whom he chanced to encounter, and because the ward in which he lived happened to be a pivotal one, he began to speak publicly on occasion and to gather dimly the import of that logic which sees life as a pagan wild, and religion and convention as the forms man puts on or off to suit his fancy, mood, and whims during the onward drift of the ages. Not for Chaffee Thayer Sluss to grasp the true meaning of it all. His brain was not big enough. Men led dual lives, it was true; but say what you would, and in the face of his own erring conduct, this was very bad. On Sunday, when he went to church with his wife, he felt that religion was essential and purifying. In his own business he found himself frequently confronted by various little flaws of logic relating to undue profits, misrepresentations, and the like; but say what you would, nevertheless and notwithstanding, God was God, morality was superior, the church was important. It was wrong to yield to one's impulses, as he found it so fascinating to do. One should be better than his neighbor, or pretend to be.

What is to be done with such a rag-bag, moralistic ass as this? In spite of all his philanderings, and the resultant qualms due to his fear of being found out, he prospered in business and rose to some eminence in his own community. As he had grown more lax he had become somewhat more genial and tolerant, more generally acceptable. He was a good Republican, a follower in the wake of Norrie Simms and young Truman Leslie MacDonald. His father-in-law was both rich and moderately influential. Having lent himself to some campaign speaking, and to party work in general, he proved quite an adept. Because of all these things—his ability, such as it was, his pliability, and his thoroughly respectable savor—he had been slated as candidate for mayor on the Republican ticket, which had subsequently been elected.

Cowperwood was well aware, from remarks made in the previous campaign, of the derogatory attitude of Mayor Sluss. Already he had discussed it in a conversation with the Hon. Joel Avery (ex-state senator), who was in his employ at the time. Avery had recently been in all sorts of corporation work, and knew the ins and outs of the courts—lawyers, judges, politicians—as he knew his revised statutes. He was a very little man—not more than five feet one inch tall—with a wide forehead, saffron hair and brows, brown, cat-like eyes and a mushy underlip that occasionally covered the upper one as he thought. After years and years Mr. Avery had learned to smile, but it was in a strange, exotic way. Mostly he gazed steadily, folded his lower lip over his upper one, and expressed his almost unchangeable conclusions in slow Addisonian phrases. In the present crisis it was Mr. Avery who had a suggestion to make.

"One thing that I think could be done," he said to Cowperwood one day in a very confidential conference, "would be to have a look into the—the—shall I say the heart affairs—of the Hon. Chaffee Thayer Sluss." Mr. Avery's cat-like eyes gleamed sardonically. "Unless I am greatly mistaken, judging the man by his personal presence merely, he is the sort of person who probably has had, or if not might readily be induced to have, some compromising affair with a woman which would require considerable sacrifice on his part to smooth over. We are all human and vulnerable"—up went Mr. Avery's lower lip covering the upper one, and then down again—"and it does not behoove any of us to be too severely ethical and self-righteous. Mr. Sluss is a well-meaning man, but a trifle sentimental, as I take it."

As Mr. Avery paused Cowperwood merely contemplated him, amused no less by his personal appearance than by his suggestion.

"Not a bad idea," he said, "though I don't like to mix heart affairs with politics."

"Yes," said Mr. Avery, soulfully, "there may be something in it. I don't know. You never can tell."

The upshot of this was that the task of obtaining an account of Mr. Sluss's habits, tastes, and proclivities was assigned to that now rather dignified legal personage, Mr. Burton Stimson, who in turn assigned it to an assistant, a Mr. Marchbanks. It was an amazing situation in some respects, but those who know anything concerning the intricacies of politics, finance, and corporate control, as they were practised in those palmy days, would never marvel at the wells of subtlety, sinks of misery, and morasses of disaster which they represented.

From another quarter, the Hon. Patrick Gilgan was not slow in responding to Cowperwood's message. Whatever his political connections and proclivities, he did not care to neglect so powerful a man.

"And what can I be doing for you to-day, Mr. Cowperwood?" he inquired, when he arrived looking nice and fresh, very spick and span after his victory.

"Listen, Mr. Gilgan," said Cowperwood, simply, eying the Republican county chairman very fixedly and twiddling his thumbs with fingers interlocked, "are you going to let the city council jam through the General Electric and that South Side 'L' road ordinance without giving me a chance to say a word or do anything about it?"

Mr. Gilgan, so Cowperwood knew, was only one of a new quadrumvirate setting out to rule the city, but he pretended to believe that he was the last word—an all power and authority—after the fashion of McKenty. "Me good man," replied Gilgan, archly, "you flatter me. I haven't the city council in me vest pocket. I've been county chairman, it's true, and helped to elect some of these men, but I don't own 'em. Why shouldn't they pass the General Electric ordinance? It's an honest ordinance, as far as I know. All the newspapers have been for it. As for this 'L' road ordinance, I haven't anything to do with it. It isn't anything I know much about. Young MacDonald and Mr. Schryhart are looking after that."

As a matter of fact, all that Mr. Gilgan was saying was decidedly true. A henchman of young MacDonald's who was beginning to learn to play politics—an alderman by the name of Klemm—had been scheduled as a kind of field-marshal, and it was MacDonald—not Gilgan, Tiernan, Kerrigan, or Edstrom—who was to round up the recalcitrant aldermen, telling them their duty. Gilgan's quadrumvirate had not as yet got their machine in good working order, though they were doing their best to bring this about. "I helped to elect every one of these men, it's true; but that doesn't mean I'm running 'em by any means," concluded Gilgan. "Not yet, anyhow."

At the "not yet" Cowperwood smiled.

"Just the same, Mr. Gilgan," he went on, smoothly, "you're the nominal head and front of this whole movement in opposition to me at present, and you're the one I have to look to. You have this present Republican situation almost entirely in your own fingers, and you can do about as you like if you're so minded. If you choose you can persuade the members of council to take considerable more time than they otherwise would in passing these ordinances—of that I'm sure. I don't know whether you know or not, Mr. Gilgan, though I suppose you do, that this whole fight against me is a strike campaign intended to drive me out of Chicago. Now you're a man of sense and judgment and considerable business experience, and I want to ask you if you think that is fair. I came here some sixteen or seventeen years ago and went into the gas business. It was an open field, the field I undertook to develop—outlying towns on the North, South, and West sides. Yet the moment I started the old-line companies began to fight me, though I wasn't invading their territory at all at the time."

"I remember it well enough," replied Gilgan. "I was one of the men that helped you to get your Hyde Park franchise. You'd never have got it if it hadn't been for me. That fellow McKibben," added Gilgan, with a grin, "a likely chap, him. He always walked as if he had on rubber shoes. He's with you yet, I suppose?"

"Yes, he's around here somewhere," replied Cowperwood, loftily. "But to go back to this other matter, most of the men that are behind this General Electric ordinance and this 'L' road franchise were in the gas business—Blackman, Jules, Baker, Schryhart, and others— and they are angry because I came into their field, and angrier still because they had eventually to buy me out. They're angry because I reorganized these old-fashioned street-railway companies here and put them on their feet. Merrill is angry because I didn't run a loop around his store, and the others are angry because I ever got a loop at all. They're all angry because I managed to step in and do the things that they should have done long before. I came here—and that's the whole story in a nutshell. I've had to have the city council with me to be able to do anything at all, and because I managed to make it friendly and keep it so they've turned on me in that section and gone into politics. I know well enough, Mr. Gilgan," concluded Cowperwood, "who has been behind you in this fight. I've known all along where the money has been coming from. You've won, and you've won handsomely, and I for one don't begrudge you your victory in the least; but what I want to know now is, are you going to help them carry this fight on against me in this way, or are you not? Are you going to give me a fighting chance? There's going to be another election in two years. Politics isn't a bed of roses that stays made just because you make it once. These fellows that you have got in with are a crowd of silk stockings. They haven't any sympathy with you or any one like you. They're willing to be friendly with you now—just long enough to get something out of you and club me to death. But after that how long do you think they will have any use for you—how long?"

"Not very long, maybe," replied Gilgan, simply and contemplatively, "but the world is the world, and we have to take it as we find it."

"Quite so," replied Cowperwood, undismayed; "but Chicago is Chicago, and I will be here as long as they will. Fighting me in this fashion—building elevated roads to cut into my profits and giving franchises to rival companies—isn't going to get me out or seriously injure me, either. I'm here to stay, and the political situation as it is to-day isn't going to remain the same forever and ever. Now, you are an ambitious man; I can see that. You're not in politics for your health—that I know. Tell me exactly what it is you want and whether I can't get it for you as quick if not quicker than these other fellows? What is it I can do for you that will make you see that my side is just as good as theirs and better? I am playing a legitimate game in Chicago. I've been building up an excellent street-car service. I don't want to be annoyed every fifteen minutes by a rival company coming into the field. Now, what can I do to straighten this out? Isn't there some way that you and I can come together without fighting at every step? Can't you suggest some programme we can both follow that will make things easier?"

Cowperwood paused, and Gilgan thought for a long time. It was true, as Cowperwood said, that he was not in politics for his health. The situation, as at present conditioned, was not inherently favorable for the brilliant programme he had originally mapped out for himself. Tiernan, Kerrigan, and Edstrom were friendly as yet; but they were already making extravagant demands; and the reformers—those who had been led by the newspapers to believe that Cowperwood was a scoundrel and all his works vile—were demanding that a strictly moral programme be adhered to in all the doings of council, and that no jobs, contracts, or deals of any kind be entered into without the full knowledge of the newspapers and of the public. Gilgan, even after the first post-election conference with his colleagues, had begun to feel that he was between the devil and the deep sea, but he was feeling his way, and not inclined to be in too much of a hurry.

"It's rather a flat proposition you're makin' me," he said softly, after a time, "askin' me to throw down me friends the moment I've won a victory for 'em. It's not the way I've been used to playin' politics. There may be a lot of truth in what you say. Still, a man can't be jumpin' around like a cat in a bag. He has to be faithful to somebody sometime." Mr. Gilgan paused, considerably nonplussed by his own position.

"Well," replied Cowperwood, sympathetically, "think it over. It's difficult business, this business of politics. I'm in it, for one, only because I have to be. If you see any way you can help me, or I can help you, let me know. In the mean time don't take in bad part what I've just said. I'm in the position of a man with his back to the wall. I'm fighting for my life. Naturally, I'm going to fight. But you and I needn't be the worse friends for that. We may become the best of friends yet."

"It's well I know that," said Gilgan, "and it's the best of friends I'd like to be with you. But even if I could take care of the aldermen, which I couldn't alone as yet, there's the mayor. I don't know him at all except to say how-do-ye-do now and then; but he's very much opposed to you, as I understand it. He'll be running around most likely and talking in the papers. A man like that can do a good deal."

"I may be able to arrange for that," replied Cowperwood. "Perhaps Mr. Sluss can be reached. It may be that he isn't as opposed to me as he thinks he is. You never can tell."

CHAPTER XXXIX

THE NEW ADMINISTRATION

Oliver Marchbanks, the youthful fox to whom Stimson had assigned the task of trapping Mr. Sluss in some legally unsanctioned act, had by scurrying about finally pieced together enough of a story to make it exceedingly unpleasant for the Honorable Chaffee in case he were to become the too willing tool of Cowperwood's enemies. The principal agent in this affair was a certain Claudia Carlstadt—adventuress, detective by disposition, and a sort of smiling prostitute and hireling, who was at the same time a highly presentable and experienced individual. Needless to say, Cowperwood knew nothing of these minor proceedings, though a genial nod from him in the beginning had set in motion the whole machinery of trespass in this respect.

Claudia Carlstadt—the instrument of the Honorable Chaffee's undoing—was blonde, slender, notably fresh as yet, being only twenty-six, and as ruthless and unconsciously cruel as only the avaricious and unthinking type—unthinking in the larger philosophic meaning of the word—can be. To grasp the reason for her being, one would have had to see the spiritless South Halstead Street world from which she had sprung—one of those neighborhoods of old, cracked, and battered houses where slatterns trudge to and fro with beer-cans and shutters swing on broken hinges. In her youth Claudia had been made to "rush the growler," to sell newspapers at the corner of Halstead and Harrison streets, and to buy cocaine at the nearest drug store. Her little dresses and underclothing had always been of the poorest and shabbiest material—torn and dirty, her ragged stockings frequently showed the white flesh of her thin little legs, and her shoes were worn and cracked, letting the water and snow seep through in winter. Her companions were wretched little street boys of her own neighborhood, from whom she learned to swear and to understand and indulge in vile practices, though, as is often the case with children, she was not utterly depraved thereby, at that. At eleven, when her mother died, she ran away from the wretched children's home to which she had been committed, and by putting up a piteous tale she was harbored on the West Side by an Irish family whose two daughters were clerks in a large retail store. Through these Claudia became a cash-girl. Thereafter followed an individual career as strange and checkered as anything that had gone before. Sufficient to say that Claudia's native intelligence was considerable. At the age of twenty she had managed—through her connections with the son of a shoe manufacturer and with a rich jeweler—to amass a little cash and an extended wardrobe. It was then that a handsome young Western Congressman, newly elected, invited her to Washington to take a position in a government bureau. This necessitated a knowledge of stenography and typewriting, which she soon acquired. Later she was introduced by a Western Senator into that form of secret service which has no connection with legitimate government, but which is profitable. She was used to extract secrets by flattery and cajolery where ordinary bribery would not avail. A matter of tracing the secret financial connections of an Illinois Congressman finally brought her back to Chicago, and here young Stimson encountered her. From him she learned of the political and financial conspiracy against Cowperwood, and was in an odd manner fascinated. From her Congressmen friends she already knew something of Sluss. Stimson indicated that it would be worth two or three thousand dollars and expenses if the mayor were successfully compromised. Thus Claudia Carlstadt was gently navigated into Mr. Sluss's glowing life.

The matter was not so difficult of accomplishment. Through the Hon. Joel Avery, Marchbanks secured a letter from a political friend of Mr. Sluss in behalf of a young widow—temporarily embarrassed, a competent stenographer, and the like—who wished a place under the new administration. Thus equipped, Claudia presented herself at the mayor's office armed for the fray, as it were, in a fetching black silk of a strangely heavy grain, her throat and fingers ornamented with simple pearls, her yellow hair arranged about her temples in exquisite curls. Mr. Sluss was very busy, but made an appointment. The next time she appeared a yellow and red velvet rose had been added to her corsage. She was a shapely, full-bosomed young woman who had acquired the art of walking, sitting, standing, and bending after the most approved theories of the Washington cocotte. Mr. Sluss was interested at once, but circumspect and careful. He was now mayor of a great city, the cynosure of all eyes. It seemed to him he remembered having already met Mrs. Brandon, as the lady styled herself, and she reminded him where. It had been two years before in the grill of the Richelieu. He immediately recalled details of the interesting occasion.

"Ah, yes, and since then, as I understand it, you married and your husband died. Most unfortunate."

Mr. Sluss had a large international manner suited, as he thought, to a man in so exalted a position.

Mrs. Brandon nodded resignedly. Her eyebrows and lashes were carefully darkened so as to sweeten the lines of her face, and a dimple had been made in one cheek by the aid of an orange stick. She was the picture of delicate femininity appealingly distressful, and yet to all appearance commercially competent.

"At the time I met you you were connected with the government service in Washington, I believe."

"Yes, I had a small place in the Treasury Department, but this new administration put me out."

She lifted her eyes and leaned forward, thus bringing her torso into a ravishing position. She had the air of one who has done many things besides work in the Treasury Department. No least detail, as she observed, was lost on Mr. Sluss. He noted her shoes, which were button patent leather with cloth tops; her gloves, which were glace black kid with white stitching at the back and fastened by dark-gamet buttons; the coral necklace worn on this occasion, and her yellow and red velvet rose. Evidently a trig and hopeful widow, even if so recently bereaved.

"Let me see," mused Mr. Sluss, "where are you living? Just let me make a note of your address. This is a very nice letter from Mr. Barry. Suppose you give me a few days to think what I can do? This is Tuesday. Come in again on Friday. I'll see if anything suggests itself."

He strolled with her to the official door, and noted that her step was light and springy. At parting she turned a very melting gaze upon him, and at once he decided that if he could he would find her something. She was the most fascinating applicant that had yet appeared.

The end of Chaffee Thayer Sluss was not far distant after this. Mrs. Brandon returned, as requested, her costume enlivened this time by a red-silk petticoat which contrived to show its ingratiating flounces beneath the glistening black broadcloth of her skirt.

"Say, did you get on to that?" observed one of the doormen, a hold-over from the previous regime, to another of the same vintage. "Some style to the new administration, hey? We're not so slow, do you think?"

He pulled his coat together and fumbled at his collar to give himself an air of smartness, and gazed gaily at his partner, both of them over sixty and dusty specimens, at that.

The other poked him in the stomach. "Hold your horses there, Bill. Not so fast. We ain't got a real start yet. Give us another six months, and then watch out."

Mr. Sluss was pleased to see Mrs. Brandon. He had spoken to John Bastienelli, the new commissioner of taxes, whose offices were directly over the way on the same hall, and the latter, seeing that he might want favors of the mayor later on, had volubly agreed to take care of the lady.

"I am very glad to be able to give you this letter to Mr. Bastienelli," commented Mr. Sluss, as he rang for a stenographer, "not only for the sake of my old friend Mr. Barry, but for your own as well. Do you know Mr. Barry very well?" he asked, curiously.

"Only slightly," admitted Mrs. Brandon, feeling that Mr. Sluss would be glad to know she was not very intimate with those who were recommending her. "I was sent to him by a Mr. Amerman." (She named an entirely fictitious personage.)

Mr. Sluss was relieved. As he handed her the note she once more surveyed him with those grateful, persuasive, appealing eyes. They made him almost dizzy, and set up a chemical perturbation in his blood which quite dispelled his good resolutions in regard to the strange woman and his need of being circumspect.

"You say you are living on the North Side?" he inquired, smiling weakly, almost foolishly.

"Yes, I have taken such a nice little apartment over-looking Lincoln Park. I didn't know whether I was going to be able to keep it up, but now that I have this position— You've been so very kind to me, Mr. Sluss," she concluded, with the same I-need-to-be-cared-for air. "I hope you won't forget me entirely. If I could be of any personal service to you at any time—"

Mr. Sluss was rather beside himself at the thought that this charming baggage of femininity, having come so close for the minute, was now passing on and might disappear entirely. By a great effort of daring, as they walked toward the door, he managed to say: "I shall have to look into that little place of yours sometime and see how you are getting along. I live up that way myself."

"Oh, do!" she exclaimed, warmly. "It would be so kind. I am practically alone in the world. Perhaps you play cards. I know how to make a most wonderful punch. I should like you to see how cozily I am settled."

At this Mr. Sluss, now completely in tow of his principal weakness, capitulated. "I will," he said, "I surely will. And that sooner than you expect, perhaps. You must let me know how you are getting along."

He took her hand. She held his quite warmly. "Now I'll hold you to your promise," she gurgled, in a throaty, coaxing way. A few days later he encountered her at lunch-time in his hall, where she had been literally lying in wait for him in order to repeat her invitation. Then he came.

The hold-over employees who worked about the City Hall in connection with the mayor's office were hereafter instructed to note as witnesses the times of arrival and departure of Mrs. Brandon and Mr. Sluss. A note that he wrote to Mrs. Brandon was carefully treasured, and sufficient evidence as to their presence at hotels and restaurants was garnered to make out a damaging case. The whole affair took about four months; then Mrs. Brandon suddenly received an offer to return to Washington, and decided to depart. The letters that followed her were a part of the data that was finally assembled in Mr. Stimson's office to be used against Mr. Sluss in case he became too obstreperous in his opposition to Cowperwood.

In the mean time the organization which Mr. Gilgan had planned with Mr. Tiernan, Mr. Kerrigan, and Mr. Edstrom was encountering what might be called rough sledding. It was discovered that, owing to the temperaments of some of the new aldermen, and to the self-righteous attitude of their political sponsors, no franchises of any kind were to be passed unless they had the moral approval of such men as Hand, Sluss, and the other reformers; above all, no money of any kind was to be paid to anybody for anything.

"Whaddye think of those damn four-flushers and come-ons, anyhow?" inquired Mr. Kerrigan of Mr. Tiernan, shortly subsequent to a conference with Gilgan, from which Tiernan had been unavoidably absent. "They've got an ordinance drawn up covering the whole city in an elevated-road scheme, and there ain't anything in it for anybody. Say, whaddye think they think we are, anyhow? Hey?"

Mr. Tiernan himself, after his own conference with Edstrom, had been busy getting the lay of the land, as he termed it; and his investigations led him to believe that a certain alderman by the name of Klemm, a clever and very respectable German-American from the North Side, was to be the leader of the Republicans in council, and that he and some ten or twelve others were determined, because of moral principles alone, that only honest measures should be passed. It was staggering.

At this news Mr. Kerrigan, who had been calculating on a number of thousands of dollars for his vote on various occasions, stared incredulously. "Well, I'll be damned!" he commented. "They've got a nerve! What?"

"I've been talking to this fellow Klemm of the twentieth," said Mr. Tiernan, sardonically. "Say, he's a real one! I met him over at the Tremont talkin' to Hvranek. He shakes hands like a dead fish. Whaddye think he had the nerve to say to me. 'This isn't the Mr. Tiernan of the second?' he says.

"'I'm the same,' says I.

"'Well, you don't look as savage as I thought you did,' says he. Haw-haw! I felt like sayin', 'If you don't go way I'll give you a slight tap on the wrist.' I'd like just one pass at a stiff like that up a dark alley." (Mr. Tiernan almost groaned in anguish.) "And then he begins to say he doesn't see how there can be any reasonable objection to allowin' various new companies to enter the street-car field. 'It's sufficiently clear,' he says, 'that the public is against monopolies in any form.'" (Mr. Tiernan was mocking Mr. Klemm's voice and language.) "My eye!" he concluded, sententiously. "Wait till he tries to throw that dope into Gumble and Pinski and Schlumbohm—haw, haw, haw!"

Mr. Kerrigan, at the thought of these hearty aldermen accustomed to all the perquisites of graft and rake-off, leaned back and gave vent to a burst of deep-chested laughter. "I'll tell you what it is, Mike," he said, archly, hitching up his tight, very artistic, and almost English trousers, "we're up against a bunch of pikers in this Gilgan crowd, and they've gotta be taught a lesson. He knows it as well as anybody else. None o' that Christian con game goes

465

around where I am. I believe this man Cowperwood's right when he says them fellows are a bunch of soreheads and jealous. If Cowperwood's willing to put down good hard money to keep 'em out of his game, let them do as much to stay in it. This ain't no charity grab-bag. We ought to be able to round up enough of these new fellows to make Schryhart and MacDonald come down good and plenty for what they want. From what Gilgan said all along, I thought he was dealing with live ones. They paid to win the election. Now let 'em pay to pull off a swell franchise if they want it, eh?"

"You're damn right," echoed Tiernan. "I'm with you to a T."

It was not long after this conversation that Mr. Truman Leslie MacDonald, acting through Alderman Klemm, proceeded to make a count of noses, and found to his astonishment that he was not as strong as he had thought he was. Political loyalty is such a fickle thing. A number of aldermen with curious names—Horback, Fogarty, McGrane, Sumulsky— showed signs of being tampered with. He hurried at once to Messrs. Hand, Schryhart, and Arneel with this disconcerting information. They had been congratulating themselves that the recent victory, if it resulted in nothing else, would at least produce a blanket 'L' road franchise, and that this would be sufficient to bring Cowperwood to his knees.

Upon receiving MacDonald's message Hand sent at once for Gilgan. When he inquired as to how soon a vote on the General Electric franchise—which had been introduced by Mr. Klemm—could reasonably be expected, Gilgan declared himself much grieved to admit that in one direction or other considerable opposition seemed to have developed to the measure.

"What's that?" said Hand, a little savagely. "Didn't we make a plain bargain in regard to this? You had all the money you asked for, didn't you? You said you could give me twenty-six aldermen who would vote as we agreed. You're not going to go back on your bargain, are you?"

"Bargain! bargain!" retorted Gilgan, irritated because of the spirit of the assault. "I agreed to elect twenty-six Republican aldermen, and that I did. I don't own 'em body and soul. I didn't name 'em in every case. I made deals with the men in the different wards that had the best chance, and that the people wanted. I'm not responsible for any crooked work that's going on behind my back, am I? I'm not responsible for men's not being straight if they're not?"

Mr. Gilgan's face was an aggrieved question-mark.

"But you had the picking of these men," insisted Mr. Hand, aggressively. "Every one of them had your personal indorsement. You made the deals with them. You don't mean to say they're going back on their sacred agreement to fight Cowperwood tooth and nail? There can't be any misunderstanding on their part as to what they were elected to do. The newspapers have been full of the fact that nothing favorable to Cowperwood was to be put through."

"That's all true enough," replied Mr. Gilgan; "but I can't be held responsible for the private honesty of everybody. Sure I selected these men. Sure I did! But I selected them with the help of the rest of the Republicans and some of the Democrats. I had to make the best terms I could—to pick the men that could win. As far as I can find out most of 'em are satisfied not to do anything for Cowperwood. It's passing these ordinances in favor of other people that's stirring up the trouble."

Mr. Hand's broad forehead wrinkled, and his blue eyes surveyed Mr. Gilgan with suspicion. "Who are these men, anyhow?" he inquired. "I'd like to get a list of them."

Mr. Gilgan, safe in his own subtlety, was ready with a toll of the supposed recalcitrants. They must fight their own battles. Mr. Hand wrote down the names, determining meanwhile to bring pressure to bear. He decided also to watch Mr. Gilgan. If there should prove to be a hitch in the programme the newspapers should be informed and commanded to thunder appropriately. Such aldermen as proved unfaithful to the great trust imposed on them should be smoked out, followed back to the wards which had elected them, and exposed to the people who were behind them. Their names should be pilloried in the public press. The customary hints as to Cowperwood's deviltry and trickery should be redoubled.

But in the mean time Messrs. Stimson, Avery, McKibben, Van Sickle, and others were on Cowperwood's behalf acting separately upon various unattached aldermen—those not temperamentally and chronically allied with the reform idea—and making them understand that if they could find it possible to refrain from supporting anti-Cowperwood measures for the next two years, a bonus in the shape of an annual salary of two thousand dollars or a gift in some other form—perhaps a troublesome note indorsed or a mortgage taken care of—would be forthcoming, together with a guarantee that the general public should never know. In no case was such an offer made direct. Friends or neighbors, or suave unidentified strangers, brought mysterious messages. By this method some eleven aldermen—quite apart from the ten regular Democrats who, because of McKenty and his influence, could be counted upon—had been already suborned. Although Schryhart, Hand, and Arneel did not know it, their plans—even as they planned—were being thus undermined, and, try as they would, the coveted ordinance for a blanket franchise persistently eluded them. They had to content themselves for the time being with a franchise for a single 'L' road line on the South Side in Schryhart's own territory, and with a franchise to the General Electric covering only one unimportant line, which it would be easy for Cowperwood, if he continued in power, to take over at some later time.

CHAPTER XL

A TRIP TO LOUISVILLE

The most serious difficulty confronting Cowperwood from now on was really not so much political as financial. In building up and financing his Chicago street-railway enterprises he had, in those days when Addison was president of the Lake City National, used that bank as his chief source of supply. Afterward, when Addison had been forced to retire from the Lake City to assume charge of the Chicago Trust Company, Cowperwood had succeeded in having the latter designated as a central reserve and in inducing a number of rural banks to keep their special deposits in its vaults. However, since the war on him and his interests had begun to strengthen through the efforts of Hand and Arneel—men most influential in the control of the other central-reserve banks of Chicago, and in close touch with the money barons of New York—there were signs not wanting that some of the country banks depositing with the Chicago Trust Company had been induced to withdraw because of pressure from outside inimical forces, and that more were to follow. It was some time before Cowperwood fully realized to what an extent this financial opposition might be directed against himself. In its very beginning it necessitated speedy hurryings to New York,

467

Philadelphia, Cincinnati, Baltimore, Boston—even London at times—on the chance that there would be loose and ready cash in someone's possession. It was on one of these peregrinations that he encountered a curious personality which led to various complications in his life, sentimental and otherwise, which he had not hitherto contemplated.

In various sections of the country Cowperwood had met many men of wealth, some grave, some gay, with whom he did business, and among these in Louisville, Kentucky, he encountered a certain Col. Nathaniel Gillis, very wealthy, a horseman, inventor, roue, from whom he occasionally extracted loans. The Colonel was an interesting figure in Kentucky society; and, taking a great liking to Cowperwood, he found pleasure, during the brief periods in which they were together, in piloting him about. On one occasion in Louisville he observed: "To-night, Frank, with your permission, I am going to introduce you to one of the most interesting women I know. She isn't good, but she's entertaining. She has had a troubled history. She is the ex-wife of two of my best friends, both dead, and the ex-mistress of another. I like her because I knew her father and mother, and because she was a clever little girl and still is a nice woman, even if she is getting along. She keeps a sort of house of convenience here in Louisville for a few of her old friends. You haven't anything particular to do to-night, have you? Suppose we go around there?"

Cowperwood, who was always genially sportive when among strong men—a sort of bounding collie—and who liked to humor those who could be of use to him, agreed.

"It sounds interesting to me. Certainly I'll go. Tell me more about her. Is she good-looking?"

"Rather. But better yet, she is connected with a number of women who are." The Colonel, who had a small, gray goatee and sportive dark eyes, winked the latter solemnly.

Cowperwood arose.

"Take me there," he said.

It was a rainy night. The business on which he was seeing the Colonel required another day to complete. There was little or nothing to do. On the way the Colonel retailed more of the life history of Nannie Hedden, as he familiarly called her, and explained that, although this was her maiden name, she had subsequently become first Mrs. John Alexander Fleming, then, after a divorce, Mrs. Ira George Carter, and now, alas! was known among the exclusive set of fast livers, to which he belonged, as plain Hattie Starr, the keeper of a more or less secret house of ill repute. Cowperwood did not take so much interest in all this until he saw her, and then only because of two children the Colonel told him about, one a girl by her first marriage, Berenice Fleming, who was away in a New York boarding-school, the other a boy, Rolfe Carter, who was in a military school for boys somewhere in the West.

"That daughter of hers," observed the Colonel, "is a chip of the old block, unless I miss my guess. I only saw her two or three times a few years ago when I was down East at her mother's summer home; but she struck me as having great charm even for a girl of ten. She's a lady born, if ever there was one. How her mother is to keep her straight, living as she does, is more than I know. How she keeps her in that school is a mystery. There's apt to be a scandal here at any time. I'm very sure the girl doesn't know anything about her mother's business. She never lets her come out here."

468

"Berenice Fleming," Cowperwood thought to himself. "What a pleasing name, and what a peculiar handicap in life."

"How old is the daughter now?" he inquired.

"Oh, she must be about fifteen—not more than that."

When they reached the house, which was located in a rather somber, treeless street, Cowperwood was surprised to find the interior spacious and tastefully furnished. Presently Mrs. Carter, as she was generally known in society, or Hattie Starr, as she was known to a less satisfying world, appeared. Cowperwood realized at once that he was in the presence of a woman who, whatever her present occupation, was not without marked evidences of refinement. She was exceedingly intelligent, if not highly intellectual, trig, vivacious, anything but commonplace. A certain spirited undulation in her walk, a seeming gay, frank indifference to her position in life, an obvious accustomedness to polite surroundings took his fancy. Her hair was built up in a loose Frenchy way, after the fashion of the empire, and her cheeks were slightly mottled with red veins. Her color was too high, and yet it was not utterly unbecoming. She had friendly gray-blue eyes, which went well with her light-brown hair; along with a pink flowered house-gown, which became her fulling figure, she wore pearls.

"The widow of two husbands," thought Cowperwood; "the mother of two children!" With the Colonel's easy introduction began a light conversation. Mrs. Carter gracefully persisted that she had known of Cowperwood for some time. His strenuous street-railway operations were more or less familiar to her.

"It would be nice," she suggested, "since Mr. Cowperwood is here, if we invited Grace Deming to call."

The latter was a favorite of the Colonel's.

"I would be very glad if I could talk to Mrs. Carter," gallantly volunteered Cowperwood—he scarcely knew why. He was curious to learn more of her history. On subsequent occasions, and in more extended conversation with the Colonel, it was retailed to him in full.

Nannie Hedden, or Mrs. John Alexander Fleming, or Mrs. Ira George Carter, or Hattie Starr, was by birth a descendant of a long line of Virginia and Kentucky Heddens and Colters, related in a definite or vague way to half the aristocracy of four or five of the surrounding states. Now, although still a woman of brilliant parts, she was the keeper of a select house of assignation in this meager city of perhaps two hundred thousand population. How had it happened? How could it possibly have come about? She had been in her day a reigning beauty. She had been born to money and had married money. Her first husband, John Alexander Fleming, who had inherited wealth, tastes, privileges, and vices from a long line of slave-holding, tobacco-growing Flemings, was a charming man of the Kentucky-Virginia society type. He had been trained in the law with a view to entering the diplomatic service, but, being an idler by nature, had never done so. Instead, horse-raising, horse-racing, philandering, dancing, hunting, and the like, had taken up his time. When their wedding took place the Kentucky-Virginia society world considered it a great match. There was wealth on both sides. Then came much more of that idle social whirl which had produced the marriage. Even philanderings of a very vital character were not barred, though deception, in some degree at least, would be necessary. As a natural result there followed

469

the appearance in the mountains of North Carolina during a charming autumn outing of a gay young spark by the name of Tucker Tanner, and the bestowal on him by the beautiful Nannie Fleming—as she was then called—of her temporary affections. Kind friends were quick to report what Fleming himself did not see, and Fleming, roue that he was, encountering young Mr. Tanner on a high mountain road one evening, said to him, "You get out of this party by night, or I will let daylight through you in the morning." Tucker Tanner, realizing that however senseless and unfair the exaggerated chivalry of the South might be, the end would be bullets just the same, departed. Mrs. Fleming, disturbed but unrepentant, considered herself greatly abused. There was much scandal. Then came quarrels, drinking on both sides, finally a divorce. Mr. Tucker Tanner did not appear to claim his damaged love, but the aforementioned Ira George Carter, a penniless never-do-well of the same generation and social standing, offered himself and was accepted. By the first marriage there had been one child, a girl. By the second there was another child, a boy. Ira George Carter, before the children were old enough to impress Mrs. Carter with the importance of their needs or her own affection for them, had squandered, in one ridiculous venture after another, the bulk of the property willed to her by her father, Major Wickham Hedden. Ultimately, after drunkenness and dissipation on the husband's side, and finally his death, came the approach of poverty. Mrs. Carter was not practical, and still passionate and inclined to dissipation. However, the aimless, fatuous going to pieces of Ira George Carter, the looming pathos of the future of the children, and a growing sense of affection and responsibility had finally sobered her. The lure of love and life had not entirely disappeared, but her chance of sipping at those crystal founts had grown sadly slender. A woman of thirty-eight and still possessing some beauty, she was not content to eat the husks provided for the unworthy. Her gorge rose at the thought of that neglected state into which the pariahs of society fall and on which the inexperienced so cheerfully comment. Neglected by her own set, shunned by the respectable, her fortune quite gone, she was nevertheless determined that she would not be a back-street seamstress or a pensioner upon the bounty of quondam friends. By insensible degrees came first unhallowed relationships through friendship and passing passion, then a curious intermediate state between the high world of fashion and the half world of harlotry, until, finally, in Louisville, she had become, not openly, but actually, the mistress of a house of ill repute. Men who knew how these things were done, and who were consulting their own convenience far more than her welfare, suggested the advisability of it. Three or four friends like Colonel Gillis wished rooms— convenient place in which to loaf, gamble, and bring their women. Hattie Starr was her name now, and as such she had even become known in a vague way to the police—but only vaguely—as a woman whose home was suspiciously gay on occasions.

Cowperwood, with his appetite for the wonders of life, his appreciation of the dramas which produce either failure or success, could not help being interested in this spoiled woman who was sailing so vaguely the seas of chance. Colonel Gillis once said that with some strong man to back her, Nannie Fleming could be put back into society. She had a pleasant appeal—she and her two children, of whom she never spoke. After a few visits to her home Cowperwood spent hours talking with Mrs. Carter whenever he was in Louisville. On one occasion, as they were entering her boudoir, she picked up a photograph of her daughter from the dresser and dropped it into a drawer. Cowperwood had never seen this picture before. It was that of a girl of fifteen or sixteen, of whom he obtained but the most fleeting glance. Yet, with that instinct for the essential and vital which invariably possessed him, he gained a keen impression of it. It was of a delicately haggard child with a marvelously agreeable smile, a fine, high-poised head upon a thin neck, and an air of bored superiority. Combined with this was a touch of weariness about the eyelids which drooped in a lofty way. Cowperwood was fascinated. Because of the daughter he professed an interest in the mother, which he really did not feel.

A little later Cowperwood was moved to definite action by the discovery in a photographer's window in Louisville of a second picture of Berenice—a rather large affair which Mrs. Carter had had enlarged from a print sent her by her daughter some time before. Berenice was standing rather indifferently posed at the corner of a colonial mantel, a soft straw outing-hat held negligently in one hand, one hip sunk lower than the other, a faint, elusive smile playing dimly around her mouth. The smile was really not a smile, but only the wraith of one, and the eyes were wide, disingenuous, mock-simple. The picture because of its simplicity, appealed to him. He did not know that Mrs. Carter had never sanctioned its display. "A personage," was Cowperwood's comment to himself, and he walked into the photographer's office to see what could be done about its removal and the destruction of the plates. A half-hundred dollars, he found, would arrange it all—plates, prints, everything. Since by this ruse he secured a picture for himself, he promptly had it framed and hung in his Chicago rooms, where sometimes of an afternoon when he was hurrying to change his clothes he stopped to look at it. With each succeeding examination his admiration and curiosity grew. Here was perhaps, he thought, the true society woman, the high-born lady, the realization of that ideal which Mrs. Merrill and many another grande dame had suggested.

It was not so long after this again that, chancing to be in Louisville, he discovered Mrs. Carter in a very troubled social condition. Her affairs had received a severe setback. A certain Major Hagenback, a citizen of considerable prominence, had died in her home under peculiar circumstances. He was a man of wealth, married, and nominally living with his wife in Lexington. As a matter of fact, he spent very little time there, and at the time of his death of heart failure was leading a pleasurable existence with a Miss Trent, an actress, whom he had introduced to Mrs. Carter as his friend. The police, through a talkative deputy coroner, were made aware of all the facts. Pictures of Miss Trent, Mrs. Carter, Major Hagenback, his wife, and many curious details concerning Mrs. Carter's home were about to appear in the papers when Colonel Gillis and others who were powerful socially and politically interfered; the affair was hushed up, but Mrs. Carter was in distress. This was more than she had bargained for.

Her quondam friends were frightened away for the nonce. She herself had lost courage. When Cowperwood saw her she had been in the very human act of crying, and her eyes were red.

"Well, well," he commented, on seeing her—she was in moody gray in the bargain—"you don't mean to tell me you're worrying about anything, are you?"

"Oh, Mr. Cowperwood," she explained, pathetically, "I have had so much trouble since I saw you. You heard of Major Hagenback's death, didn't you?" Cowperwood, who had heard something of the story from Colonel Gillis, nodded. "Well, I have just been notified by the police that I will have to move, and the landlord has given me notice, too. If it just weren't for my two children—"

She dabbed at her eyes pathetically.

Cowperwood meditated interestedly.

"Haven't you any place you can go?" he asked.

"I have a summer place in Pennsylvania," she confessed; "but I can't go there very well in February. Besides, it's my living I'm worrying about. I have only this to depend on."

She waved her hand inclusively toward the various rooms. "Don't you own that place in Pennsylvania?" he inquired.

"Yes, but it isn't worth much, and I couldn't sell it. I've been trying to do that anyhow for some time, because Berenice is getting tired of it."

"And haven't you any money laid away?"

"It's taken all I have to run this place and keep the children in school. I've been trying to give Berenice and Rolfe a chance to do something for themselves."

At the repetition of Berenice's name Cowperwood consulted his own interest or mood in the matter. A little assistance for her would not bother him much. Besides, it would probably eventually bring about a meeting with the daughter.

"Why don't you clear out of this?" he observed, finally. "It's no business to be in, anyhow, if you have any regard for your children. They can't survive anything like this. You want to put your daughter back in society, don't you?"

"Oh yes," almost pleaded Mrs. Carter.

"Precisely," commented Cowperwood, who, when he was thinking, almost invariably dropped into a short, cold, curt, business manner. Yet he was humanely inclined in this instance.

"Well, then, why not live in your Pennsylvania place for the present, or, if not that, go to New York? You can't stay here. Ship or sell these things." He waved a hand toward the rooms.

"I would only too gladly," replied Mrs. Carter, "if I knew what to do."

"Take my advice and go to New York for the present. You will get rid of your expenses here, and I will help you with the rest—for the present, anyhow. You can get a start again. It is too bad about these children of yours. I will take care of the boy as soon as he is old enough. As for Berenice"—he used her name softly—"if she can stay in her school until she is nineteen or twenty the chances are that she will make social connections which will save her nicely. The thing for you to do is to avoid meeting any of this old crowd out here in the future if you can. It might be advisable to take her abroad for a time after she leaves school."

"Yes, if I just could," sighed Mrs. Carter, rather lamely.

"Well, do what I suggest now, and we will see," observed Cowperwood. "It would be a pity if your two children were to have their lives ruined by such an accident as this."

Mrs. Carter, realizing that here, in the shape of Cowperwood, if he chose to be generous, was the open way out of a lowering dungeon of misery, was inclined to give vent to a bit of grateful emotion, but, finding him subtly remote, restrained herself. His manner, while warmly generous at times, was also easily distant, except when he wished it to be otherwise.

472

Just now he was thinking of the high soul of Berenice Fleming and of its possible value to him.

CHAPTER XLI

THE DAUGHTER OF MRS. FLEMING

Berenice Fleming, at the time Cowperwood first encountered her mother, was an inmate of the Misses Brewster's School for Girls, then on Riverside Drive, New York, and one of the most exclusive establishments of its kind in America. The social prestige and connections of the Heddens, Flemings, and Carters were sufficient to gain her this introduction, though the social fortunes of her mother were already at this time on the down grade. A tall girl, delicately haggard, as he had imagined her, with reddish-bronze hair of a tinge but distantly allied to that of Aileen's, she was unlike any woman Cowperwood had ever known. Even at seventeen she stood up and out with an inexplicable superiority which brought her the feverish and exotic attention of lesser personalities whose emotional animality found an outlet in swinging a censer at her shrine.

A strange maiden, decidedly! Even at this age, when she was, as one might suppose, a mere slip of a girl, she was deeply conscious of herself, her sex, her significance, her possible social import. Armed with a fair skin, a few freckles, an almost too high color at times, strange, deep, night-blue, cat-like eyes, a long nose, a rather pleasant mouth, perfect teeth, and a really good chin, she moved always with a feline grace that was careless, superior, sinuous, and yet the acme of harmony and a rhythmic flow of lines. One of her mess-hall tricks, when unobserved by her instructors, was to walk with six plates and a water-pitcher all gracefully poised on the top of her head after the fashion of the Asiatic and the African, her hips moving, her shoulders, neck, and head still. Girls begged weeks on end to have her repeat this "stunt," as they called it. Another was to put her arms behind her and with a rush imitate the Winged Victory, a copy of which graced the library hall.

"You know," one little rosy-cheeked satellite used to urge on her, adoringly, "she must have been like you. Her head must have been like yours. You are lovely when you do it."

For answer Berenice's deep, almost black-blue eyes turned on her admirer with solemn unflattered consideration. She awed always by the something that she did not say.

The school, for all the noble dames who presided over it—solemn, inexperienced owl-like conventionalists who insisted on the last tittle and jot of order and procedure—was a joke to Berenice. She recognized the value of its social import, but even at fifteen and sixteen she was superior to it. She was superior to her superiors and to the specimens of maidenhood—supposed to be perfect socially—who gathered about to hear her talk, to hear her sing, declaim, or imitate. She was deeply, dramatically, urgently conscious of the value of her personality in itself, not as connected with any inherited social standing, but of its innate worth, and of the artistry and wonder of her body. One of her chief delights was to walk alone in her room—sometimes at night, the lamp out, the moon perhaps faintly illuminating her chamber—and to pose and survey her body, and dance in some naive, graceful, airy Greek way a dance that was singularly free from sex consciousness—and yet was it? She was conscious of her body—of every inch of it—under the ivory-white clothes which she frequently wore. Once she wrote in a secret diary which she maintained—

473

another art impulse or an affectation, as you will: "My skin is so wonderful. It tingles so with rich life. I love it and my strong muscles underneath. I love my hands and my hair and my eyes. My hands are long and thin and delicate; my eyes are a dark, deep blue; my hair is a brown, rusty red, thick and sleepy. My long, firm, untired limbs can dance all night. Oh, I love life! I love life!"

You would not have called Berenice Fleming sensuous—though she was—because she was self-controlled. Her eyes lied to you. They lied to all the world. They looked you through and through with a calm savoir faire, a mocking defiance, which said with a faint curl of the lips, barely suggested to help them out, "You cannot read me, you cannot read me." She put her head to one side, smiled, lied (by implication), assumed that there was nothing. And there was nothing, as yet. Yet there was something, too—her inmost convictions, and these she took good care to conceal. The world—how little it should ever, ever know! How little it ever could know truly!

The first time Cowperwood encountered this Circe daughter of so unfortunate a mother was on the occasion of a trip to New York, the second spring following his introduction to Mrs. Carter in Louisville. Berenice was taking some part in the closing exercises of the Brewster School, and Mrs. Carter, with Cowperwood for an escort, decided to go East. Cowperwood having located himself at the Netherlands, and Mrs. Carter at the much humbler Grenoble, they journeyed together to visit this paragon whose picture he had had hanging in his rooms in Chicago for months past. When they were introduced into the somewhat somber reception parlor of the Brewster School, Berenice came slipping in after a few moments, a noiseless figure of a girl, tall and slim, and deliciously sinuous. Cowperwood saw at first glance that she fulfilled all the promise of her picture, and was delighted. She had, he thought, a strange, shrewd, intelligent smile, which, however, was girlish and friendly. Without so much as a glance in his direction she came forward, extending her arms and hands in an inimitable histrionic manner, and exclaimed, with a practised and yet natural inflection: "Mother, dear! So here you are really! You know, I've been thinking of you all morning. I wasn't sure whether you would come to-day, you change about so. I think I even dreamed of you last night."

Her skirts, still worn just below the shoe-tops, had the richness of scraping silk then fashionable. She was also guilty of using a faint perfume of some kind.

Cowperwood could see that Mrs. Carter, despite a certain nervousness due to the girl's superior individuality and his presence, was very proud of her. Berenice, he also saw quickly, was measuring him out of the tail of her eye—a single sweeping glance which she vouchsafed from beneath her long lashes sufficing; but she gathered quite accurately the totality of Cowperwood's age, force, grace, wealth, and worldly ability. Without hesitation she classed him as a man of power in some field, possibly finance, one of the numerous able men whom her mother seemed to know. She always wondered about her mother. His large gray eyes, that searched her with lightning accuracy, appealed to her as pleasant, able eyes. She knew on the instant, young as she was, that he liked women, and that probably he would think her charming; but as for giving him additional attention it was outside her code. She preferred to be interested in her dear mother exclusively.

"Berenice," observed Mrs. Carter, airily, "let me introduce Mr. Cowperwood."

Berenice turned, and for the fraction of a second leveled a frank and yet condescending glance from wells of what Cowperwood considered to be indigo blue.

474

"Your mother has spoken of you from time to time," he said, pleasantly.

She withdrew a cool, thin hand as limp and soft as wax, and turned to her mother again without comment, and yet without the least embarrassment. Cowperwood seemed in no way important to her.

"What would you say, dear," pursued Mrs. Carter, after a brief exchange of commonplaces, "if I were to spend next winter in New York?"

"It would be charming if I could live at home. I'm sick of this silly boarding-school."

"Why, Berenice! I thought you liked it."

"I hate it, but only because it's so dull. The girls here are so silly."

Mrs. Carter lifted her eyebrows as much as to say to her escort, "Now what do you think?" Cowperwood stood solemnly by. It was not for him to make a suggestion at present. He could see that for some reason—probably because of her disordered life—Mrs. Carter was playing a game of manners with her daughter; she maintained always a lofty, romantic air. With Berenice it was natural—the expression of a vain, self-conscious, superior disposition.

"A rather charming garden here," he observed, lifting a curtain and looking out into a blooming plot.

"Yes, the flowers are nice," commented Berenice.

"Wait; I'll get some for you. It's against the rules, but they can't do more than send me away, and that's what I want."

"Berenice! Come back here!"

It was Mrs. Carter calling.

The daughter was gone in a fling of graceful lines and flounces. "Now what do you make of her?" asked Mrs. Carter, turning to her friend.

"Youth, individuality, energy—a hundred things. I see nothing wrong with her."

"If I could only see to it that she had her opportunities unspoiled."

Already Berenice was returning, a subject for an artist in almost studied lines. Her arms were full of sweet-peas and roses which she had ruthlessly gathered.

"You wilful girl!" scolded her mother, indulgently. "I shall have to go and explain to your superiors. Whatever shall I do with her, Mr. Cowperwood?"

"Load her with daisy chains and transport her to Cytherea," commented Cowperwood, who had once visited this romantic isle, and therefore knew its significance.

Berenice paused. "What a pretty speech that is!" she exclaimed. "I have a notion to give you a special flower for that. I will, too." She presented him with a rose.

For a girl who had slipped in shy and still, Cowperwood commented, her mood had certainly changed. Still, this was the privilege of the born actress, to change. And as he viewed Berenice Fleming now he felt her to be such—a born actress, lissome, subtle, wise, indifferent, superior, taking the world as she found it and expecting it to obey—to sit up like a pet dog and be told to beg. What a charming character! What a pity it should not be allowed to bloom undisturbed in its make-believe garden! What a pity, indeed!

CHAPTER XLII

F. A. COWPERWOOD, GUARDIAN

It was some time after this first encounter before Cowperwood saw Berenice again, and then only for a few days in that region of the Pocono Mountains where Mrs. Carter had her summer home. It was an idyllic spot on a mountainside, some three miles from Stroudsburg, among a peculiar juxtaposition of hills which, from the comfortable recesses of a front veranda, had the appearance, as Mrs. Carter was fond of explaining, of elephants and camels parading in the distance. The humps of the hills—some of them as high as eighteen hundred feet—rose stately and green. Below, quite visible for a mile or more, moved the dusty, white road descending to Stroudsburg. Out of her Louisville earnings Mrs. Carter had managed to employ, for the several summer seasons she had been here, a gardener, who kept the sloping front lawn in seasonable flowers. There was a trig two-wheeled trap with a smart horse and harness, and both Rolfe and Berenice were possessed of the latest novelty of the day—low-wheeled bicycles, which had just then superseded the old, high-wheel variety. For Berenice, also, was a music-rack full of classic music and song collections, a piano, a shelf of favorite books, painting-materials, various athletic implements, and several types of Greek dancing-tunics which she had designed herself, including sandals and fillet for her hair. She was an idle, reflective, erotic person dreaming strange dreams of a near and yet far-off social supremacy, at other times busying herself with such social opportunities as came to her. A more safely calculating and yet wilful girl than Berenice Fleming would have been hard to find. By some trick of mental adjustment she had gained a clear prevision of how necessary it was to select the right socially, and to conceal her true motives and feelings; and yet she was by no means a snob, mentally, nor utterly calculating. Certain things in her own and in her mother's life troubled her—quarrels in her early days, from her seventh to her eleventh year, between her mother and her stepfather, Mr. Carter; the latter's drunkenness verging upon delirium tremens at times; movings from one place to another—all sorts of sordid and depressing happenings. Berenice had been an impressionable child. Some things had gripped her memory mightily—once, for instance, when she had seen her stepfather, in the presence of her governess, kick a table over, and, seizing the toppling lamp with demoniac skill, hurl it through a window. She, herself, had been tossed by him in one of these tantrums, when, in answer to the cries of terror of those about her, he had shouted: "Let her fall! It won't hurt the little devil to break a few bones." This was her keenest memory of her stepfather, and it rather softened her judgment of her mother, made her sympathetic with her when she was inclined to be critical. Of her own father she only knew that he had divorced her mother— why, she could not say. She liked her mother on many counts, though she could not feel that she actually loved her—Mrs. Carter was too fatuous at times, and at other times too restrained. This house at Pocono, or Forest Edge, as Mrs. Carter had named it, was conducted after a peculiar fashion. From June to October only it was open, Mrs. Carter, in the past, having returned to Louisville at that time, while Berenice and Rolfe went back to their respective schools. Rolfe was a cheerful, pleasant-mannered youth, well bred, genial, and courteous, but not very brilliant intellectually. Cowperwood's judgment of him the first time he saw him was that under ordinary circumstances he would make a good confidential clerk, possibly in a bank. Berenice, on the other hand, the child of the first husband, was a creature of an exotic mind and an opalescent heart. After his first contact with her in the reception-room of the Brewster School Cowperwood was deeply conscious of the import of this budding character. He was by now so familiar with types and kinds of women that an exceptional type—quite like an exceptional horse to a judge of horse-flesh—stood out in his mind with singular vividness. Quite as in some great racing-stable an ambitious horseman might imagine that he detected in some likely filly the signs and lineaments of the future winner of a Derby, so in Berenice Fleming, in the quiet precincts of the Brewster School, Cowperwood previsioned the central figure of a Newport lawn fete or a London drawing-room. Why? She had the air, the grace, the lineage, the blood—that was why; and on that score she appealed to him intensely, quite as no other woman before had ever done.

It was on the lawn of Forest Edge that Cowperwood now saw Berenice. The latter had had the gardener set up a tall pole, to which was attached a tennis-ball by a cord, and she and Rolfe were hard at work on a game of tether-ball. Cowperwood, after a telegram to Mrs. Carter, had been met at the station in Pocono by her and rapidly driven out to the house. The green hills pleased him, the up-winding, yellow road, the silver-gray cottage with the brown-shingle roof in the distance. It was three in the afternoon, and bright for a sinking sun.

"There they are now," observed Mrs. Carter, cheerful and smiling, as they came out from under a low ledge that skirted the road a little way from the cottage. Berenice, executing a tripping, running step to one side, was striking the tethered ball with her racquet. "They are hard at it, as usual. Two such romps!"

She surveyed them with pleased motherly interest, which Cowperwood considered did her much credit. He was thinking that it would be too bad if her hopes for her children should not be realized. Yet possibly they might not be. Life was very grim. How strange, he thought, was this type of woman—at once a sympathetic, affectionate mother and a panderer to the vices of men. How strange that she should have these children at all. Berenice had on a white skirt, white tennis-shoes, a pale-cream silk waist or blouse, which fitted her very loosely. Because of exercise her color was high—quite pink—and her dusty, reddish hair was blowy. Though they turned into the hedge gate and drove to the west entrance, which was at one side of the house, there was no cessation of the game, not even a glance from Berenice, so busy was she.

He was merely her mother's friend to her. Cowperwood noted, with singular vividness of feeling, that the lines of her movements—the fleeting, momentary positions she assumed— were full of a wondrous natural charm. He wanted to say so to Mrs. Carter, but restrained himself.

"It's a brisk game," he commented, with a pleased glance. "You play, do you?"

"Oh, I did. I don't much any more. Sometimes I try a set with Rolfe or Bevy; but they both beat me so badly."

"Bevy? Who is Bevy?"

"Oh, that's short of Berenice. It's what Rolfe called her when he was a baby."

"Bevy! I think that rather nice."

"I always like it, too. Somehow it seems to suit her, and yet I don't know why."

Before dinner Berenice made her appearance, freshened by a bath and clad in a light summer dress that appeared to Cowperwood to be all flounces, and the more graceful in its lines for the problematic absence of a corset. Her face and hands, however—a face thin, long, and sweetly hollow, and hands that were slim and sinewy—gripped and held his fancy. He was reminded in the least degree of Stephanie; but this girl's chin was firmer and more delicately, though more aggressively, rounded. Her eyes, too, were shrewder and less evasive, though subtle enough.

"So I meet you again," he observed, with a somewhat aloof air, as she came out on the porch and sank listlessly into a wicker chair. "The last time I met you you were hard at work in New York."
"Breaking the rules. No, I forget; that was my easiest work. Oh, Rolfe," she called over her shoulder, indifferently, "I see your pocket-knife out on the grass."

Cowperwood, properly suppressed, waited a brief space. "Who won that exciting game?"

"I did, of course. I always win at tether-ball."

"Oh, do you?" commented Cowperwood.

"I mean with brother, of course. He plays so poorly." She turned to the west—the house faced south—and studied the road which came up from Stroudsburg. "I do believe that's Harry Kemp," she added, quite to herself. "If so, he'll have my mail, if there is any."

She got up again and disappeared into the house, coming out a few moments later to saunter down to the gate, which was over a hundred feet away. To Cowperwood she seemed to float, so hale and graceful was she. A smart youth in blue serge coat, white trousers, and white shoes drove by in a high-seated trap.

"Two letters for you," he called, in a high, almost falsetto voice. "I thought you would have eight or nine. Blessed hot, isn't it?" He had a smart though somewhat effeminate manner, and Cowperwood at once wrote him down as an ass. Berenice took the mail with an engaging smile. She sauntered past him reading, without so much as a glance. Presently he heard her voice within.

"Mother, the Haggertys have invited me for the last week in August. I have half a mind to cut Tuxedo and go. I like Bess Haggerty."

"Well, you'll have to decide that, dearest. Are they going to be at Tarrytown or Loon Lake?"

"Loon Lake, of course," came Berenice's voice.

What a world of social doings she was involved in, thought Cowperwood. She had begun well. The Haggertys were rich coal-mine operators in Pennsylvania. Harris Haggerty, to whose family she was probably referring, was worth at least six or eight million. The social world they moved in was high.

They drove after dinner to The Saddler, at Saddler's Run, where a dance and "moonlight promenade" was to be given. On the way over, owing to the remoteness of Berenice, Cowperwood for the first time in his life felt himself to be getting old. In spite of the vigor of his mind and body, he realized constantly that he was over fifty-two, while she was only seventeen. Why should this lure of youth continue to possess him? She wore a white concoction of lace and silk which showed a pair of smooth young shoulders and a slender, queenly, inimitably modeled neck. He could tell by the sleek lines of her arms how strong she was.

"It is perhaps too late," he said to himself, in comment. "I am getting old."

The freshness of the hills in the pale night was sad.

Saddler's, when they reached there after ten, was crowded with the youth and beauty of the vicinity. Mrs. Carter, who was prepossessing in a ball costume of silver and old rose, expected that Cowperwood would dance with her. And he did, but all the time his eyes were on Berenice, who was caught up by one youth and another of dapper mien during the progress of the evening and carried rhythmically by in the mazes of the waltz or schottische. There was a new dance in vogue that involved a gay, running step—kicking first one foot and then the other forward, turning and running backward and kicking again, and then swinging with a smart air, back to back, with one's partner. Berenice, in her lithe, rhythmic way, seemed to him the soul of spirited and gracious ease—unconscious of everybody and everything save the spirit of the dance itself as a medium of sweet emotion, of some far-off, dreamlike spirit of gaiety. He wondered. He was deeply impressed.

"Berenice," observed Mrs. Carter, when in an intermission she came forward to where Cowperwood and she were sitting in the moonlight discussing New York and Kentucky social life, "haven't you saved one dance for Mr. Cowperwood?"

Cowperwood, with a momentary feeling of resentment, protested that he did not care to dance any more. Mrs. Carter, he observed to himself, was a fool.

"I believe," said her daughter, with a languid air, "that I am full up. I could break one engagement, though, somewhere."

"Not for me, though, please," pleaded Cowperwood. "I don't care to dance any more, thank you."

He almost hated her at the moment for a chilly cat. And yet he did not.

"Why, Bevy, how you talk! I think you are acting very badly this evening."

"Please, please," pleaded Cowperwood, quite sharply. "Not any more. I don't care to dance any more."

Bevy looked at him oddly for a moment—a single thoughtful glance.

"But I have a dance, though," she pleaded, softly. "I was just teasing. Won't you dance it with me?

"I can't refuse, of course," replied Cowperwood, coldly.

"It's the next one," she replied.

They danced, but he scarcely softened to her at first, so angry was he. Somehow, because of all that had gone before, he felt stiff and ungainly. She had managed to break in upon his natural savoir faire—this chit of a girl. But as they went on through a second half the spirit of her dancing soul caught him, and he felt more at ease, quite rhythmic. She drew close and swept him into a strange unison with herself.

"You dance beautifully," he said.

"I love it," she replied. She was already of an agreeable height for him.

It was soon over. "I wish you would take me where the ices are," she said to Cowperwood.

He led her, half amused, half disturbed at her attitude toward him.

"You are having a pleasant time teasing me, aren't you?" he asked.

"I am only tired," she replied. "The evening bores me. Really it does. I wish we were all home."

"We can go when you say, no doubt."

As they reached the ices, and she took one from his hand, she surveyed him with those cool, dull blue eyes of hers—eyes that had the flat quality of unglazed Dutch tiles.

"I wish you would forgive me," she said. "I was rude. I couldn't help it. I am all out of sorts with myself."

"I hadn't felt you were rude," he observed, lying grandly, his mood toward her changing entirely.

"Oh yes I was, and I hope you will forgive me. I sincerely wish you would."

"I do with all my heart—the little that there is to forgive."

He waited to take her back, and yielded her to a youth who was waiting. He watched her trip away in a dance, and eventually led her mother to the trap. Berenice was not with them on the home drive; some one else was bringing her. Cowperwood wondered when she would come, and where was her room, and whether she was really sorry, and— As he fell asleep Berenice Fleming and her slate-blue eyes were filling his mind completely.

CHAPTER XLIII

THE PLANET MARS

The banking hostility to Cowperwood, which in its beginning had made necessary his trip to Kentucky and elsewhere, finally reached a climax. It followed an attempt on his part to

480

furnish funds for the building of elevated roads. The hour for this new form of transit convenience had struck. The public demanded it. Cowperwood saw one elevated road, the South Side Alley Line, being built, and another, the West Side Metropolitan Line, being proposed, largely, as he knew, in order to create sentiment for the idea, and so to make his opposition to a general franchise difficult. He was well aware that if he did not choose to build them others would. It mattered little that electricity had arrived finally as a perfected traction factor, and that all his lines would soon have to be done over to meet that condition, or that it was costing him thousands and thousands to stay the threatening aspect of things politically. In addition he must now plunge into this new realm, gaining franchises by the roughest and subtlest forms of political bribery. The most serious aspect of this was not political, but rather financial. Elevated roads in Chicago, owing to the sparseness of the population over large areas, were a serious thing to contemplate. The mere cost of iron, right of way, rolling-stock, and power-plants was immense. Being chronically opposed to investing his private funds where stocks could just as well be unloaded on the public, and the management and control retained by him, Cowperwood, for the time being, was puzzled as to where he should get credit for the millions to be laid down in structural steel, engineering fees, labor, and equipment before ever a dollar could be taken out in passenger fares. Owing to the advent of the World's Fair, the South Side 'L'—to which, in order to have peace and quiet, he had finally conceded a franchise—was doing reasonably well. Yet it was not making any such return on the investment as the New York roads. The new lines which he was preparing would traverse even less populous sections of the city, and would in all likelihood yield even a smaller return. Money had to be forthcoming—something between twelve and fifteen million dollars—and this on the stocks and bonds of a purely paper corporation which might not yield paying dividends for years to come. Addison, finding that the Chicago Trust Company was already heavily loaded, called upon various minor but prosperous local banks to take over the new securities (each in part, of course). He was astonished and chagrined to find that one and all uniformly refused.

"I'll tell you how it is, Judah," one bank president confided to him, in great secrecy. "We owe Timothy Arneel at least three hundred thousand dollars that we only have to pay three per cent. for. It's a call-loan. Besides, the Lake National is our main standby when it comes to quick trades, and he's in on that. I understand from one or two friends that he's at outs with Cowperwood, and we can't afford to offend him. I'd like to, but no more for me—not at present, anyhow."

"Why, Simmons," replied Addison, "these fellows are simply cutting off their noses to spite their faces. These stock and bond issues are perfectly good investments, and no one knows it better than you do. All this hue and cry in the newspapers against Cowperwood doesn't amount to anything. He's perfectly solvent. Chicago is growing. His lines are becoming more valuable every year."

"I know that," replied Simmons. "But what about this talk of a rival elevated system? Won't that injure his lines for the time being, anyhow, if it comes into the field?"

"If I know anything about Cowperwood," replied Addison, simply, "there isn't going to be any rival elevated road. It's true they got the city council to give them a franchise for one line on the South Side; but that's out of his territory, anyhow, and that other one to the Chicago General Company doesn't amount to anything. It will be years and years before it can be made to pay a dollar, and when the time comes he will probably take it over if he wants it. Another election will be held in two years, and then the city administration may not be so unfavorable. As it is, they haven't been able to hurt him through the council as much as they thought they would."

"Yes; but he lost the election."

"True; but it doesn't follow he's going to lose the next one, or every one."

"Just the same," replied Simmons, very secretively, "I understand there's a concerted effort on to drive him out. Schryhart, Hand, Merrill, Arneel—they're the most powerful men we have. I understand Hand says that he'll never get his franchises renewed except on terms that'll make his lines unprofitable. There's going to be an awful smash here one of these days if that's true." Mr. Simmons looked very wise and solemn.

"Never believe it," replied Addison, contemptuously. "Hand isn't Chicago, neither is Schryhart, nor Arneel. Cowperwood is a brainy man. He isn't going to be put under so easily. Did you ever hear what was the real bottom cause of all this disturbance?"

"Yes, I've heard," replied Simmons.

"Do you believe it?"

"Oh, I don't know. Yes, I suppose I do. Still, I don't know that that need have anything to do with it. Money envy is enough to make any man fight. This man Hand is very powerful."

Not long after this Cowperwood, strolling into the president's office of the Chicago Trust Company, inquired: "Well, Judah, how about those Northwestern 'L' bonds?"

"It's just as I thought, Frank," replied Addison, softly. "We'll have to go outside of Chicago for that money. Hand, Arneel, and the rest of that crowd have decided to combine against us. That's plain. Something has started them off in full cry. I suppose my resignation may have had something to do with it. Anyhow, every one of the banks in which they have any hand has uniformly refused to come in. To make sure that I was right I even called up the little old Third National of Lake View and the Drovers and Traders on Forty-seventh Street. That's Charlie Wallin's bank. When I was over in the Lake National he used to hang around the back door asking for anything I could give him that was sound. Now he says his orders are from his directors not to share in anything we have to offer. It's the same story everywhere—they daren't. I asked Wallin if he knew why the directors were down on the Chicago Trust or on you, and at first he said he didn't. Then he said he'd stop in and lunch with me some day. They're the silliest lot of old ostriches I ever heard of. As if refusing to let us have money on any loan here was going to prevent us from getting it! They can take their little old one-horse banks and play blockhouses with them if they want to. I can go to New York and in thirty-six hours raise twenty million dollars if we need it."

Addison was a little warm. It was a new experience for him. Cowperwood merely curled his mustaches and smiled sardonically.

"Well, never mind," he said. "Will you go down to New York, or shall I?"

It was decided, after some talk, that Addison should go. When he reached New York he found, to his surprise, that the local opposition to Cowperwood had, for some mysterious reason, begun to take root in the East.

"I'll tell you how it is," observed Joseph Haeckelheimer, to whom Addison applied—a short, smug, pussy person who was the head of Haeckelheimer, Gotloeb & Co., international bankers. "We hear odd things concerning Mr. Cowperwood out in Chicago. Some people say he is sound—some not. He has some very good franchises covering a large portion of the city, but they are only twenty-year franchises, and they will all run out by 1903 at the latest. As I understand it, he has managed to stir up all the local elements— some very powerful ones, too—and he is certain to have a hard time to get his franchises renewed. I don't live in Chicago, of course. I don't know much about it, but our Western correspondent tells me this is so. Mr. Cowperwood is a very able man, as I understand it, but if all these influential men are opposed to him they can make him a great deal of trouble. The public is very easily aroused."

"You do a very able man a great injustice, Mr. Haeckelheimer," Addison retorted. "Almost any one who starts out to do things successfully and intelligently is sure to stir up a great deal of feeling. The particular men you mention seem to feel that they have a sort of proprietor's interest in Chicago. They really think they own it. As a matter of fact, the city made them; they didn't make the city."

Mr. Haeckelheimer lifted his eyebrows. He laid two fine white hands, plump and stubby, over the lower buttons of his protuberant waistcoat. "Public favor is a great factor in all these enterprises," he almost sighed. "As you know, part of a man's resources lies in his ability to avoid stirring up opposition. It may be that Mr. Cowperwood is strong enough to overcome all that. I don't know. I've never met him. I'm just telling you what I hear."

This offish attitude on the part of Mr. Haeckelheimer was indicative of a new trend. The man was enormously wealthy. The firm of Haeckelheimer, Gotloeb & Co. represented a controlling interest in some of the principal railways and banks in America. Their favor was not to be held in light esteem.

It was plain that these rumors against Cowperwood in New York, unless offset promptly by favorable events in Chicago, might mean—in the large banking quarters, anyhow—the refusal of all subsequent Cowperwood issues. It might even close the doors of minor banks and make private investors nervous.

Addison's report of all this annoyed Cowperwood no little. It made him angry. He saw in it the work of Schryhart, Hand, and others who were trying their best to discredit him. "Let them talk," he declared, crossly. "I have the street-railways. They're not going to rout me out of here. I can sell stocks and bonds to the public direct if need be! There are plenty of private people who are glad to invest in these properties."

At this psychological moment enter, as by the hand of Fate, the planet Mars and the University. This latter, from having been for years a humble Baptist college of the cheapest character, had suddenly, through the beneficence of a great Standard Oil multimillionaire, flared upward into a great university, and was causing a stir throughout the length and breadth of the educational world.

It was already a most noteworthy spectacle, one of the sights of the city. Millions were being poured into it; new and beautiful buildings were almost monthly erected. A brilliant, dynamic man had been called from the East as president. There were still many things needed—dormitories, laboratories of one kind and another, a great library; and, last but not least, a giant telescope—one that would sweep the heavens with a hitherto unparalleled receptive eye, and wring from it secrets not previously decipherable by the eye and the mind of man.

Cowperwood had always been interested in the heavens and in the giant mathematical and physical methods of interpreting them. It so happened that the war-like planet, with its sinister aspect, was just at this time to be seen hanging in the west, a fiery red; and the easily aroused public mind was being stirred to its shallow depth by reflections and speculations regarding the famous canals of the luminary. The mere thought of the possibility of a larger telescope than any now in existence, which might throw additional light on this evasive mystery, was exciting not only Chicago, but the whole world. Late one afternoon Cowperwood, looking over some open fields which faced his new power-house in West Madison Street, observed the planet hanging low and lucent in the evening sky, a warm, radiant bit of orange in a sea of silver. He paused and surveyed it. Was it true that there were canals on it, and people? Life was surely strange.

One day not long after this Alexander Rambaud called him up on the 'phone and remarked, jocosely:

"I say, Cowperwood, I've played a rather shabby trick on you just now. Doctor Hooper, of the University, was in here a few minutes ago asking me to be one of ten to guarantee the cost of a telescope lens that he thinks he needs to run that one-horse school of his out there. I told him I thought you might possibly be interested. His idea is to find some one who will guarantee forty thousand dollars, or eight or ten men who will guarantee four or five thousand each. I thought of you, because I've heard you discuss astronomy from time to time."

"Let him come," replied Cowperwood, who was never willing to be behind others in generosity, particularly where his efforts were likely to be appreciated in significant quarters.

Shortly afterward appeared the doctor himself—short, rotund, rubicund, displaying behind a pair of clear, thick, gold-rimmed glasses, round, dancing, incisive eyes. Imaginative grip, buoyant, self-delusive self-respect were written all over him. The two men eyed each other—one with that broad-gage examination which sees even universities as futile in the endless shift of things; the other with that faith in the balance for right which makes even great personal forces, such as financial magnates, serve an idealistic end.

"It's not a very long story I have to tell you, Mr. Cowperwood," said the doctor. "Our astronomical work is handicapped just now by the simple fact that we have no lens at all, no telescope worthy of the name. I should like to see the University do original work in this field, and do it in a great way. The only way to do it, in my judgment, is to do it better than any one else can. Don't you agree with me?" He showed a row of shining white teeth.

Cowperwood smiled urbanely.

"Will a forty-thousand-dollar lens be a better lens than any other lens?" he inquired.

"Made by Appleman Brothers, of Dorchester, it will," replied the college president. "The whole story is here, Mr. Cowperwood. These men are practical lens-makers. A great lens, in the first place, is a matter of finding a suitable crystal. Large and flawless crystals are not common, as you may possibly know. Such a crystal has recently been found, and is now owned by Mr. Appleman. It takes about four or five years to grind and polish it. Most of the polishing, as you may or may not know, is done by the hand—smoothing it with the thumb and forefinger. The time, judgment, and skill of an optical expert is required. To-day, unfortunately, that is not cheap. The laborer is worthy of his hire, however, I suppose"—he waved a soft, full, white hand—"and forty thousand is little enough. It would be a great honor if the University could have the largest, most serviceable, and most perfect lens in the world. It would reflect great credit, I take it, on the men who would make this possible."

Cowperwood liked the man's artistically educational air; obviously here was a personage of ability, brains, emotion, and scientific enthusiasm. It was splendid to him to see any strong man in earnest, for himself or others.

"And forty thousand will do this?" he asked.

"Yes, sir. Forty thousand will guarantee us the lens, anyhow."

"And how about land, buildings, a telescope frame? Have you all those things prepared for it?"

"Not as yet, but, since it takes four years at least to grind the lens, there will be time enough, when the lens is nearing completion, to look after the accessories. We have picked our site, however—Lake Geneva—and we would not refuse either land or accessories if we knew where to get them."

Again the even, shining teeth, the keen eyes boring through the glasses.

Cowperwood saw a great opportunity. He asked what would be the cost of the entire project. Dr. Hooper presumed that three hundred thousand would do it all handsomely— lens, telescope, land, machinery, building—a great monument.

"And how much have you guaranteed on the cost of your lens?" "Sixteen thousand dollars, so far."

"To be paid when?"

"In instalments—ten thousand a year for four years. Just enough to keep the lens-maker busy for the present."

Cowperwood reflected. Ten thousand a year for four years would be a mere salary item, and at the end of that time he felt sure that he could supply the remainder of the money quite easily. He would be so much richer; his plans would be so much more mature. On such a repute (the ability to give a three-hundred-thousand-dollar telescope out of hand to be known as the Cowperwood telescope) he could undoubtedly raise money in London, New York, and elsewhere for his Chicago enterprise. The whole world would know him in a day. He paused, his enigmatic eyes revealing nothing of the splendid vision that danced before them. At last! At last!

"How would it do, Mr. Hooper," he said, sweetly, "if, instead of ten men giving you four thousand each, as you plan, one man were to give you forty thousand in annual instalments of ten thousand each? Could that be arranged as well?"

"My dear Mr. Cowperwood," exclaimed the doctor, glowing, his eyes alight, "do I understand that you personally might wish to give the money for this lens?"

"I might, yes. But I should have to exact one pledge, Mr. Hooper, if I did any such thing."

"And what would that be?"

"The privilege of giving the land and the building—the whole telescope, in fact. I presume no word of this will be given out unless the matter is favorably acted upon?" he added, cautiously and diplomatically.

The new president of the university arose and eyed him with a peculiarly approbative and grateful gaze. He was a busy, overworked man. His task was large. Any burden taken from his shoulders in this fashion was a great relief.

"My answer to that, Mr. Cowperwood, if I had the authority, would be to agree now in the name of the University, and thank you. For form's sake, I must submit the matter to the trustees of the University, but I have no doubt as to the outcome. I anticipate nothing but grateful approbation. Let me thank you again."

They shook hands warmly, and the solid collegian bustled forth. Cowperwood sank quietly in his chair. He pressed his fingers together, and for a moment or two permitted himself to dream. Then he called a stenographer and began a bit of dictation. He did not care to think even to himself how universally advantageous all this might yet prove to be.

The result was that in the course of a few weeks the proffer was formally accepted by the trustees of the University, and a report of the matter, with Cowperwood's formal consent, was given out for publication. The fortuitous combination of circumstances already described gave the matter a unique news value. Giant reflectors and refractors had been given and were in use in other parts of the world, but none so large or so important as this. The gift was sufficient to set Cowperwood forth in the light of a public benefactor and patron of science. Not only in Chicago, but in London, Paris, and New York, wherever, indeed, in the great capitals scientific and intellectual men were gathered, this significant gift of an apparently fabulously rich American became the subject of excited discussion. Banking men, among others, took sharp note of the donor, and when Cowperwood's emissaries came around later with a suggestion that the fifty-year franchises about to be voted him for elevated roads should be made a basis of bond and mortgage loans, they were courteously received. A man who could give three-hundred-thousand-dollar telescopes in the hour of his greatest difficulties must be in a rather satisfactory financial condition. He must have great wealth in reserve. After some preliminaries, during which Cowperwood paid a flying visit to Threadneedle Street in London, and to Wall Street in New York, an arrangement was made with an English-American banking company by which the majority of the bonds for his proposed roads were taken over by them for sale in Europe and elsewhere, and he was given ample means wherewith to proceed. Instantly the stocks of his surface lines bounded in price, and those who had been scheming to bring about Cowperwood's downfall gnashed impotent teeth. Even Haeckelheimer & Co. were interested.

Anson Merrill, who had only a few weeks before given a large field for athletic purposes to the University, pulled a wry face over this sudden eclipse of his glory. Hosmer Hand, who had given a chemical laboratory, and Schryhart, who had presented a dormitory, were depressed to think that a benefaction less costly than theirs should create, because of the distinction of the idea, so much more notable comment. It was merely another example of the brilliant fortune which seemed to pursue the man, the star that set all their plans at defiance.

CHAPTER XLIV

A FRANCHISE OBTAINED

The money requisite for the construction of elevated roads having been thus pyrotechnically obtained, the acquisition of franchises remained no easy matter. It involved, among other problems, the taming of Chaffee Thayer Sluss, who, quite unconscious of the evidence stored up against him, had begun to fulminate the moment it was suggested in various secret political quarters that a new ordinance was about to be introduced, and that Cowperwood was to be the beneficiary. "Don't you let them do that, Mr. Sluss," observed Mr. Hand, who for purposes of conference had courteously but firmly bidden his hireling, the mayor, to lunch. "Don't you let them pass that if you can help it." (As chairman or president of the city council Mr. Sluss held considerable manipulative power over the machinery of procedure.) "Raise such a row that they won't try to pass it over your head. Your political future really depends on it—your standing with the people of Chicago. The newspapers and the respectable financial and social elements will fully support you in this. Otherwise they will wholly desert you. Things have come to a handsome pass when men sworn and elected to perform given services turn on their backers and betray them in this way!"

Mr. Hand was very wroth.

Mr. Sluss, immaculate in black broadcloth and white linen, was very sure that he would fulfil to the letter all of Mr. Hand's suggestions. The proposed ordinance should be denounced by him; its legislative progress heartily opposed in council.

"They shall get no quarter from me!" he declared, emphatically. "I know what the scheme is. They know that I know it."

He looked at Mr. Hand quite as one advocate of righteousness should look at another, and the rich promoter went away satisfied that the reins of government were in safe hands. Immediately afterward Mr. Sluss gave out an interview in which he served warning on all aldermen and councilmen that no such ordinance as the one in question would ever be signed by him as mayor.

At half past ten on the same morning on which the interview appeared—the hour at which Mr. Sluss usually reached his office—his private telephone bell rang, and an assistant inquired if he would be willing to speak with Mr. Frank A. Cowperwood. Mr. Sluss, somehow anticipating fresh laurels of victory, gratified by the front-page display given his announcement in the morning papers, and swelling internally with civic pride, announced, solemnly: "Yes; connect me."

"Mr. Sluss," began Cowperwood, at the other end, "this is Frank A. Cowperwood."

"Yes. What can I do for you, Mr. Cowperwood?"

"I see by the morning papers that you state that you will have nothing to do with any proposed ordinance which looks to giving me a franchise for any elevated road on the North or West Side?"

"That is quite true," replied Mr. Sluss, loftily. "I will not."

"Don't you think it is rather premature, Mr. Sluss, to denounce something which has only a rumored existence?" (Cowperwood, smiling sweetly to himself, was quite like a cat playing with an unsuspicious mouse.) "I should like very much to talk this whole matter over with you personally before you take an irrevocable attitude. It is just possible that after you have heard my side you may not be so completely opposed to me. From time to time I have sent to you several of my personal friends, but apparently you do not care to receive them."

"Quite true," replied Mr. Sluss, loftily; "but you must remember that I am a very busy man, Mr. Cowperwood, and, besides, I do not see how I can serve any of your purposes. You are working for a set of conditions to which I am morally and temperamentally opposed. I am working for another. I do not see that we have any common ground on which to meet. In fact, I do not see how I can be of any service to you whatsoever."

"Just a moment, please, Mr. Mayor," replied Cowperwood, still very sweetly, and fearing that Sluss might choose to hang up the receiver, so superior was his tone. "There may be some common ground of which you do not know. Wouldn't you like to come to lunch at my residence or receive me at yours? Or let me come to your office and talk this matter over. I believe you will find it the part of wisdom as well as of courtesy to do this."

"I cannot possibly lunch with you to-day," replied Sluss, "and I cannot see you, either. There are a number of things pressing for my attention. I must say also that I cannot hold any back-room conferences with you or your emissaries. If you come you must submit to the presence of others."

"Very well, Mr. Sluss," replied Cowperwood, cheerfully. "I will not come to your office. But unless you come to mine before five o'clock this afternoon you will face by noon to-morrow a suit for breach of promise, and your letters to Mrs. Brandon will be given to the public. I wish to remind you that an election is coming on, and that Chicago favors a mayor who is privately moral as well as publicly so. Good morning."

Mr. Cowperwood hung up his telephone receiver with a click, and Mr. Sluss sensibly and visibly stiffened and paled. Mrs. Brandon! The charming, lovable, discreet Mrs. Brandon who had so ungenerously left him! Why should she be thinking of suing him for breach of promise, and how did his letter to her come to be in Cowperwood's hands? Good heavens—those mushy letters! His wife! His children! His church and the owlish pastor thereof! Chicago! And its conventional, moral, religious atmosphere! Come to think of it, Mrs. Brandon had scarcely if ever written him a note of any kind. He did not even know her history.

At the thought of Mrs. Sluss—her hard, cold, blue eyes—Mr. Sluss arose, tall and distrait, and ran his hand through his hair. He walked to the window, snapping his thumb and middle finger and looking eagerly at the floor. He thought of the telephone switchboard just outside his private office, and wondered whether his secretary, a handsome young Presbyterian girl, had been listening, as usual. Oh, this sad, sad world! If the North Side ever learned of this—Hand, the newspapers, young MacDonald—would they protect him? They would not. Would they run him for mayor again? Never! Could the public be induced to vote for him with all the churches fulminating against private immorality, hypocrites, and whited sepulchers? Oh, Lord! Oh, Lord! And he was so very, very much respected and looked up to—that was the worst of it all. This terrible demon Cowperwood had descended on him, and he had thought himself so secure. He had not even been civil to Cowperwood. What if the latter chose to avenge the discourtesy?

Mr. Sluss went back to his chair, but he could not sit in it. He went for his coat, took it down, hung it up again, took it down, announced over the 'phone that he could not see any one for several hours, and went out by a private door. Wearily he walked along North Clark Street, looking at the hurly-burly of traffic, looking at the dirty, crowded river, looking at the sky and smoke and gray buildings, and wondering what he should do. The world was so hard at times; it was so cruel. His wife, his family, his political career. He could not conscientiously sign any ordinances for Mr. Cowperwood—that would be immoral, dishonest, a scandal to the city. Mr. Cowperwood was a notorious traitor to the public welfare. At the same time he could not very well refuse, for here was Mrs. Brandon, the charming and unscrupulous creature, playing into the hands of Cowperwood. If he could only meet her, beg of her, plead; but where was she? He had not seen her for months and months. Could he go to Hand and confess all? But Hand was a hard, cold, moral man also. Oh, Lord! Oh, Lord! He wondered and thought, and sighed and pondered—all without avail.

Pity the poor earthling caught in the toils of the moral law. In another country, perhaps, in another day, another age, such a situation would have been capable of a solution, one not utterly destructive to Mr. Sluss, and not entirely favorable to a man like Cowperwood. But here in the United States, here in Chicago, the ethical verities would all, as he knew, be lined up against him. What Lake View would think, what his pastor would think, what Hand and all his moral associates would think—ah, these were the terrible, the incontrovertible consequences of his lapse from virtue.

At four o'clock, after Mr. Sluss had wandered for hours in the snow and cold, belaboring himself for a fool and a knave, and while Cowperwood was sitting at his desk signing papers, contemplating a glowing fire, and wondering whether the mayor would deem it advisable to put in an appearance, his office door opened and one of his trim stenographers entered announcing Mr. Chaffee Thayer Sluss. Enter Mayor Sluss, sad, heavy, subdued, shrunken, a very different gentleman from the one who had talked so cavalierly over the wires some five and a half hours before. Gray weather, severe cold, and much contemplation of seemingly irreconcilable facts had reduced his spirits greatly. He was a little pale and a little restless. Mental distress has a reducing, congealing effect, and Mayor Sluss seemed somewhat less than his usual self in height, weight, and thickness. Cowperwood had seen him more than once on various political platforms, but he had never met him. When the troubled mayor entered he arose courteously and waved him to a chair.

"Sit down, Mr. Sluss," he said, genially. "It's a disagreeable day out, isn't it? I suppose you have come in regard to the matter we were discussing this morning?"

Nor was this cordiality wholly assumed. One of the primal instincts of Cowperwood's nature—for all his chicane and subtlety—was to take no rough advantage of a beaten enemy. In the hour of victory he was always courteous, bland, gentle, and even sympathetic; he was so to-day, and quite honestly, too.

Mayor Sluss put down the high sugar-loaf hat he wore and said, grandiosely, as was his manner even in the direst extremity: "Well, you see, I am here, Mr. Cowperwood. What is it you wish me to do, exactly?"

"Nothing unreasonable, I assure you, Mr. Sluss," replied Cowperwood. "Your manner to me this morning was a little brusque, and, as I have always wanted to have a sensible private talk with you, I took this way of getting it. I should like you to dismiss from your mind at once the thought that I am going to take an unfair advantage of you in any way. I have no present intention of publishing your correspondence with Mrs. Brandon." (As he said this he took from his drawer a bundle of letters which Mayor Sluss recognized at once as the enthusiastic missives which he had sometime before penned to the fair Claudia. Mr. Sluss groaned as he beheld this incriminating evidence.) "I am not trying," continued Cowperwood, "to wreck your career, nor to make you do anything which you do not feel that you can conscientiously undertake. The letters that I have here, let me say, have come to me quite by accident. I did not seek them. But, since I do have them, I thought I might as well mention them as a basis for a possible talk and compromise between us."

Cowperwood did not smile. He merely looked thoughtfully at Sluss; then, by way of testifying to the truthfulness of what he had been saying, thumped the letters up and down, just to show that they were real.

"Yes," said Mr. Sluss, heavily, "I see."

He studied the bundle—a small, solid affair—while Cowperwood looked discreetly elsewhere. He contemplated his own shoes, the floor. He rubbed his hands and then his knees.

Cowperwood saw how completely he had collapsed. It was ridiculous, pitiable.

"Come, Mr. Sluss," said Cowperwood, amiably, "cheer up. Things are not nearly as desperate as you think. I give you my word right now that nothing which you yourself, on mature thought, could say was unfair will be done. You are the mayor of Chicago. I am a citizen. I merely wish fair play from you. I merely ask you to give me your word of honor that from now on you will take no part in this fight which is one of pure spite against me. If you cannot conscientiously aid me in what I consider to be a perfectly legitimate demand for additional franchises, you will, at least, not go out of your way to publicly attack me. I will put these letters in my safe, and there they will stay until the next campaign is over, when I will take them out and destroy them. I have no personal feeling against you—none in the world. I do not ask you to sign any ordinance which the council may pass giving me elevated-road rights. What I do wish you to do at this time is to refrain from stirring up public sentiment against me, especially if the council should see fit to pass an ordinance over your veto. Is that satisfactory?"

"But my friends? The public? The Republican party? Don't you see it is expected of me that I should wage some form of campaign against you?" queried Sluss, nervously.

"No, I don't," replied Cowperwood, succinctly, "and, anyhow, there are ways and ways of waging a public campaign. Go through the motions, if you wish, but don't put too much heart in it. And, anyhow, see some one of my lawyers from time to time when they call on you. Judge Dickensheets is an able and fair man. So is General Van Sickle. Why not confer with them occasionally?—not publicly, of course, but in some less conspicuous way. You will find both of them most helpful."

Cowperwood smiled encouragingly, quite beneficently, and Chaffee Thayer Sluss, his political hopes gone glimmering, sat and mused for a few moments in a sad and helpless quandary.

"Very well," he said, at last, rubbing his hands feverishly. "It is what I might have expected. I should have known. There is no other way, but—" Hardly able to repress the hot tears now burning beneath his eyelids, the Hon. Mr. Sluss picked up his hat and left the room. Needless to add that his preachings against Cowperwood were permanently silenced.

CHAPTER XLV

CHANGING HORIZONS

The effect of all this was to arouse in Cowperwood the keenest feelings of superiority he had ever yet enjoyed. Hitherto he had fancied that his enemies might worst him, but at last his path seemed clear. He was now worth, all in all, the round sum of twenty million dollars. His art-collection had become the most important in the West—perhaps in the nation, public collections excluded. He began to envision himself as a national figure, possibly even an international one. And yet he was coming to feel that, no matter how complete his financial victory might ultimately be, the chances were that he and Aileen would never be socially accepted here in Chicago. He had done too many boisterous things—alienated too many people. He was as determined as ever to retain a firm grip on the Chicago street-railway situation. But he was disturbed for a second time in his life by the thought that, owing to the complexities of his own temperament, he had married unhappily and would find the situation difficult of adjustment. Aileen, whatever might be said of her deficiencies, was by no means as tractable or acquiescent as his first wife. And, besides, he felt that he owed her a better turn. By no means did he actually dislike her as yet; though she was no longer soothing, stimulating, or suggestive to him as she had formerly been. Her woes, because of him, were too many; her attitude toward him too censorious. He was perfectly willing to sympathize with her, to regret his own change of feeling, but what would you? He could not control his own temperament any more than Aileen could control hers.

The worst of this situation was that it was now becoming complicated on Cowperwood's part with the most disturbing thoughts concerning Berenice Fleming. Ever since the days when he had first met her mother he had been coming more and more to feel for the young girl a soul-stirring passion—and that without a single look exchanged or a single word spoken. There is a static something which is beauty, and this may be clothed in the habiliments of a ragged philosopher or in the silks and satins of pampered coquetry. It was a suggestion of this beauty which is above sex and above age and above wealth that shone in the blowing hair and night-blue eyes of Berenice Fleming. His visit to the Carter family at Pocono had been a disappointment to him, because of the apparent hopelessness of arousing Berenice's interest, and since that time, and during their casual encounters, she had remained politely indifferent. Nevertheless, he remained true to his persistence in the pursuit of any game he had fixed upon.

Mrs. Carter, whose relations with Cowperwood had in the past been not wholly platonic, nevertheless attributed much of his interest in her to her children and their vital chance. Berenice and Rolfe themselves knew nothing concerning the nature of their mother's arrangements with Cowperwood. True to his promise of protectorship and assistance, he had established her in a New York apartment adjacent to her daughter's school, and where he fancied that he himself might spend many happy hours were Berenice but near. Proximity to Berenice! The desire to arouse her interest and command her favor! Cowperwood would scarcely have cared to admit to himself how great a part this played in a thought which had recently been creeping into his mind. It was that of erecting a splendid house in New York.

By degrees this idea of building a New York house had grown upon him. His Chicago mansion was a costly sepulcher in which Aileen sat brooding over the woes which had befallen her. Moreover, aside from the social defeat which it represented, it was becoming merely as a structure, but poorly typical of the splendor and ability of his imaginations. This second dwelling, if he ever achieved it, should be resplendent, a monument to himself. In his speculative wanderings abroad he had seen many such great palaces, designed with the utmost care, which had housed the taste and culture of generations of men. His art-collection, in which he took an immense pride, had been growing, until it was the basis if not the completed substance for a very splendid memorial. Already in it were gathered paintings of all the important schools; to say nothing of collections of jade, illumined missals, porcelains, rugs, draperies, mirror frames, and a beginning at rare originals of sculpture. The beauty of these strange things, the patient laborings of inspired souls of various times and places, moved him, on occasion, to a gentle awe. Of all individuals he respected, indeed revered, the sincere artist. Existence was a mystery, but these souls who set themselves to quiet tasks of beauty had caught something of which he was dimly conscious. Life had touched them with a vision, their hearts and souls were attuned to sweet harmonies of which the common world knew nothing. Sometimes, when he was weary after a strenuous day, he would enter—late in the night—his now silent gallery, and turning on the lights so that the whole sweet room stood revealed, he would seat himself before some treasure, reflecting on the nature, the mood, the time, and the man that had produced it. Sometimes it would be one of Rembrandt's melancholy heads—the sad "Portrait of a Rabbi"—or the sweet introspection of a Rousseau stream. A solemn Dutch housewife, rendered with the bold fidelity and resonant enameled surfaces of a Hals or the cold elegance of an Ingres, commanded his utmost enthusiasm. So he would sit and wonder at the vision and skill of the original dreamer, exclaiming at times: "A marvel! A marvel!"

At the same time, so far as Aileen was concerned things were obviously shaping up for additional changes. She was in that peculiar state which has befallen many a woman—trying to substitute a lesser ideal for a greater, and finding that the effort is useless or nearly so. In regard to her affair with Lynde, aside from the temporary relief and diversion it had afforded her, she was beginning to feel that she had made a serious mistake. Lynde was delightful, after his fashion. He could amuse her with a different type of experience from any that Cowperwood had to relate. Once they were intimate he had, with an easy, genial air, confessed to all sorts of liaisons in Europe and America. He was utterly pagan—a faun—and at the same time he was truly of the smart world. His open contempt of all but one or two of the people in Chicago whom Aileen had secretly admired and wished to associate with, and his easy references to figures of importance in the East and in Paris and London, raised him amazingly in her estimation; it made her feel, sad to relate, that she had by no means lowered herself in succumbing so readily to his forceful charms.

Nevertheless, because he was what he was—genial, complimentary, affectionate, but a playboy, merely, and a soldier of fortune, with no desire to make over her life for her on any new basis—she was now grieving over the futility of this romance which had got her nowhere, and which, in all probability, had alienated Cowperwood for good. He was still outwardly genial and friendly, but their relationship was now colored by a sense of mistake and uncertainty which existed on both sides, but which, in Aileen's case, amounted to a subtle species of soul-torture. Hitherto she had been the aggrieved one, the one whose loyalty had never been in question, and whose persistent affection and faith had been greatly sinned against. Now all this was changed. The manner in which he had sinned against her was plain enough, but the way in which, out of pique, she had forsaken him was in the other balance. Say what one will, the loyalty of woman, whether a condition in nature or an evolved accident of sociology, persists as a dominating thought in at least a section of the race; and women themselves, be it said, are the ones who most loudly and openly subscribe to it. Cowperwood himself was fully aware that Aileen had deserted him, not because she loved him less or Lynde more, but because she was hurt—and deeply so. Aileen knew that he knew this. From one point of view it enraged her and made her defiant; from another it grieved her to think she had uselessly sinned against his faith in her. Now he had ample excuse to do anything he chose. Her best claim on him—her wounds— she had thrown away as one throws away a weapon. Her pride would not let her talk to him about this, and at the same time she could not endure the easy, tolerant manner with which he took it. His smiles, his forgiveness, his sometimes pleasant jesting were all a horrible offense.

To complete her mental quandary, she was already beginning to quarrel with Lynde over this matter of her unbreakable regard for Cowperwood. With the sufficiency of a man of the world Lynde intended that she should succumb to him completely and forget her wonderful husband. When with him she was apparently charmed and interested, yielding herself freely, but this was more out of pique at Cowperwood's neglect than from any genuine passion for Lynde. In spite of her pretensions of anger, her sneers, and criticisms whenever Cowperwood's name came up, she was, nevertheless, hopelessly fond of him and identified with him spiritually, and it was not long before Lynde began to suspect this. Such a discovery is a sad one for any master of women to make. It jolted his pride severely.

"You care for him still, don't you?" he asked, with a wry smile, upon one occasion. They were sitting at dinner in a private room at Kinsley's, and Aileen, whose color was high, and who was becomingly garbed in metallic-green silk, was looking especially handsome. Lynde had been proposing that she should make special arrangements to depart with him for a three-months' stay in Europe, but she would have nothing to do with the project. She did not dare. Such a move would make Cowperwood feel that she was alienating herself forever; it would give him an excellent excuse to leave her.

"Oh, it isn't that," she had declared, in reply to Lynde's query. "I just don't want to go. I can't. I'm not prepared. It's nothing but a notion of yours, anyhow. You're tired of Chicago because it's getting near spring. You go and I'll be here when you come back, or I may decide to come over later." She smiled.

Lynde pulled a dark face.

"Hell!" he said. "I know how it is with you. You still stick to him, even when he treats you like a dog. You pretend not to love him when as a matter of fact you're mad about him. I've seen it all along. You don't really care anything about me. You can't. You're too crazy about him."

"Oh, shut up!" replied Aileen, irritated greatly for the moment by this onslaught. "You talk like a fool. I'm not anything of the sort. I admire him. How could any one help it?" (At this time, of course, Cowperwood's name was filling the city.) "He's a very wonderful man. He was never brutal to me. He's a full-sized man—I'll say that for him."

By now Aileen had become sufficiently familiar with Lynde to criticize him in her own mind, and even outwardly by innuendo, for being a loafer and idler who had never created in any way the money he was so freely spending. She had little power to psychologize concerning social conditions, but the stalwart constructive persistence of Cowperwood along commercial lines coupled with the current American contempt of leisure reflected somewhat unfavorably upon Lynde, she thought.

Lynde's face clouded still more at this outburst. "You go to the devil," he retorted. "I don't get you at all. Sometimes you talk as though you were fond of me. At other times you're all wrapped up in him. Now you either care for me or you don't. Which is it? If you're so crazy about him that you can't leave home for a month or so you certainly can't care much about me."

Aileen, however, because of her long experience with Cowperwood, was more than a match for Lynde. At the same time she was afraid to let go of him for fear that she should have no one to care for her. She liked him. He was a happy resource in her misery, at least for the moment. Yet the knowledge that Cowperwood looked upon this affair as a heavy blemish on her pristine solidarity cooled her. At the thought of him and of her whole tarnished and troubled career she was very unhappy.

"Hell!" Lynde had repeated, irritably, "stay if you want to. I'll not be trying to over-persuade you—depend on that."

They quarreled still further over this matter, and, though they eventually made up, both sensed the drift toward an ultimately unsatisfactory conclusion.

It was one morning not long after this that Cowperwood, feeling in a genial mood over his affairs, came into Aileen's room, as he still did on occasions, to finish dressing and pass the time of day.

"Well," he observed, gaily, as he stood before the mirror adjusting his collar and tie, "how are you and Lynde getting along these days—nicely?"

"Oh, you go to the devil!" replied Aileen, flaring up and struggling with her divided feelings, which pained her constantly. "If it hadn't been for you there wouldn't be any chance for your smarty 'how-am-I-getting-alongs.' I am getting along all right—fine—regardless of anything you may think. He's as good a man as you are any day, and better. I like him. At least he's fond of me, and that's more than you are. Why should you care what I do? You don't, so why talk about it? I want you to let me alone."

"Aileen, Aileen, how you carry on! Don't flare up so. I meant nothing by it. I'm sorry as much for myself as for you. I've told you I'm not jealous. You think I'm critical. I'm not anything of the kind. I know how you feel. That's all very good."

"Oh yes, yes," she replied. "Well, you can keep your feelings to yourself. Go to the devil! Go to the devil, I tell you!" Her eyes blazed.

He stood now, fully dressed, in the center of the rug before her, and Aileen looked at him, keen, valiant, handsome—her old Frank. Once again she regretted her nominal faithlessness, and raged at him in her heart for his indifference. "You dog," she was about to add, "you have no heart!" but she changed her mind. Her throat tightened and her eyes filled. She wanted to run to him and say: "Oh, Frank, don't you understand how it all is, how it all came about? Won't you love me again—can't you?" But she restrained herself. It seemed to her that he might understand—that he would, in fact—but that he would never again be faithful, anyhow. And she would so gladly have discarded Lynde and any and all men if he would only have said the word, would only have really and sincerely wished her to do so.

It was one day not long after their morning quarrel in her bedroom that Cowperwood broached the matter of living in New York to Aileen, pointing out that thereby his art-collection, which was growing constantly, might be more suitably housed, and that it would give her a second opportunity to enter social life.

"So that you can get rid of me out here," commented Aileen, little knowing of Berenice Fleming.

"Not at all," replied Cowperwood, sweetly. "You see how things are. There's no chance of our getting into Chicago society. There's too much financial opposition against me here. If we had a big house in New York, such as I would build, it would be an introduction in itself. After all, these Chicagoans aren't even a snapper on the real society whip. It's the Easterners who set the pace, and the New-Yorkers most of all. If you want to say the word, I can sell this place and we can live down there, part of the time, anyhow. I could spend as much of my time with you there as I have been doing here—perhaps more."

Because of her soul of vanity Aileen's mind ran forward in spite of herself to the wider opportunities which his words suggested. This house had become a nightmare to her—a place of neglect and bad memories. Here she had fought with Rita Sohlberg; here she had seen society come for a very little while only to disappear; here she had waited this long time for the renewal of Cowperwood's love, which was now obviously never to be restored in its original glamour. As he spoke she looked at him quizzically, almost sadly in her great doubt. At the same time she could not help reflecting that in New York where money counted for so much, and with Cowperwood's great and growing wealth and prestige behind her, she might hope to find herself socially at last. "Nothing venture, nothing have" had always been her motto, nailed to her mast, though her equipment for the life she now craved had never been more than the veriest make-believe—painted wood and tinsel. Vain, radiant, hopeful Aileen! Yet how was she to know?

"Very well," she observed, finally. "Do as you like. I can live down there as well as I can here, I presume—alone."

Cowperwood knew the nature of her longings. He knew what was running in her mind, and how futile were her dreams. Life had taught him how fortuitous must be the circumstances which could enable a woman of Aileen's handicaps and defects to enter that cold upper world. Yet for all the courage of him, for the very life of him, he could not tell her. He could not forget that once, behind the grim bars in the penitentiary for the Eastern District of Pennsylvania, he had cried on her shoulder. He could not be an ingrate and wound her with his inmost thoughts any more than he could deceive himself. A New York mansion and the dreams of social supremacy which she might there entertain would soothe her ruffled vanity and assuage her disappointed heart; and at the same time he would be nearer Berenice Fleming. Say what one will of these ferret windings of the human mind, they are, nevertheless, true and characteristic of the average human being, and Cowperwood was no exception. He saw it all, he calculated on it—he calculated on the simple humanity of Aileen.

CHAPTER XLVI

DEPTHS AND HEIGHTS

The complications which had followed his various sentimental affairs left Cowperwood in a quandary at times as to whether there could be any peace or satisfaction outside of monogamy, after all. Although Mrs. Hand had gone to Europe at the crisis of her affairs, she had returned to seek him out. Cecily Haguenin found many opportunities of writing him letters and assuring him of her undying affection. Florence Cochrane persisted in seeing or attempting to see him even after his interest in her began to wane. For another thing Aileen, owing to the complication and general degeneracy of her affairs, had recently begun to drink. Owing to the failure of her affair with Lynde—for in spite of her yielding she had never had any real heart interest in it—and to the cavalier attitude with which Cowperwood took her disloyalty, she had reached that state of speculative doldrums where the human animal turns upon itself in bitter self-analysis; the end with the more sensitive or the less durable is dissipation or even death. Woe to him who places his faith in illusion—the only reality—and woe to him who does not. In one way lies disillusion with its pain, in the other way regret.

After Lynde's departure for Europe, whither she had refused to follow him, Aileen took up with a secondary personage by the name of Watson Skeet, a sculptor. Unlike most artists, he was the solitary heir of the president of an immense furniture-manufacturing company in which he refused to take any interest. He had studied abroad, but had returned to Chicago with a view to propagating art in the West. A large, blond, soft-fleshed man, he had a kind of archaic naturalness and simplicity which appealed to Aileen. They had met at the Rhees Griers'. Feeling herself neglected after Lynde's departure, and dreading loneliness above all things, Aileen became intimate with Skeet, but to no intense mental satisfaction. That driving standard within—that obsessing ideal which requires that all things be measured by it—was still dominant. Who has not experienced the chilling memory of the better thing? How it creeps over the spirit of one's current dreams! Like the specter at the banquet it stands, its substanceless eyes viewing with a sad philosophy the makeshift feast. The what-might-have-been of her life with Cowperwood walked side by side with her wherever she went. Once occasionally indulging in cigarettes, she now smoked almost constantly. Once barely sipping at wines, cocktails, brandy-and-soda, she now took to the latter, or, rather, to a new whisky-and-soda combination known as "highball" with a kind of vehemence which had little to do with a taste for the thing itself. True, drinking is, after all, a state of mind, and not an appetite. She had found on a number of occasions when she had been quarreling with Lynde or was mentally depressed that in partaking of these drinks a sort of warm, speculative indifference seized upon her. She was no longer so sad. She might cry, but it was in a soft, rainy, relieving way. Her sorrows were as strange, enticing figures in dreams. They moved about and around her, not as things actually identical with her, but as ills which she could view at a distance. Sometimes both she and they (for she saw herself also as in a kind of mirage or inverted vision) seemed beings of another state, troubled, but not bitterly painful. The old nepenthe of the bottle had seized upon her. After a few accidental lapses, in which she found it acted as a solace or sedative, the highball visioned itself to her as a resource. Why should she not drink if it relieved her, as it actually did, of physical and mental pain? There were apparently no bad after-effects. The whisky involved was diluted to an almost watery state. It was her custom now when at home alone to go to the butler's pantry where the liquors were stored and prepare a drink for herself, or to order a tray with a siphon and bottle placed in her room. Cowperwood, noticing the persistence of its presence there and the fact that she drank heavily at table, commented upon it.

"You're not taking too much of that, are you, Aileen?" he questioned one evening, watching her drink down a tumbler of whisky and water as she sat contemplating a pattern of needlework with which the table was ornamented.

"Certainly I'm not," she replied, irritably, a little flushed and thick of tongue. "Why do you ask?" She herself had been wondering whether in the course of time it might not have a depreciating effect on her complexion. This was the only thing that still concerned her—her beauty.

"Well, I see you have that bottle in your room all the time. I was wondering if you might not be forgetting how much you are using it."

Because she was so sensitive he was trying to be tactful.

"Well," she answered, crossly, "what if I am? It wouldn't make any particular difference if I did. I might as well drink as do some other things that are done."

It was a kind of satisfaction to her to bait him in this way. His inquiry, being a proof of continued interest on his part, was of some value. At least he was not entirely indifferent to her.

"I wish you wouldn't talk that way, Aileen," he replied. "I have no objection to your drinking some. I don't suppose it makes any difference to you now whether I object or not. But you are too good-looking, too well set up physically, to begin that. You don't need it, and it's such a short road to hell. Your state isn't so bad. Good heavens! many another woman has been in your position. I'm not going to leave you unless you want to leave me. I've told you that over and over. I'm just sorry people change—we all do. I suppose I've changed some, but that's no reason for your letting yourself go to pieces. I wish you wouldn't be desperate about this business. It may come out better than you think in the long run."

He was merely talking to console her.

"Oh! oh! oh!" Aileen suddenly began to rock and cry in a foolish drunken way, as though her heart would break, and Cowperwood got up. He was horrified after a fashion.

"Oh, don't come near me!" Aileen suddenly exclaimed, sobering in an equally strange way. "I know why you come. I know how much you care about me or my looks. Don't you worry whether I drink or not. I'll drink if I please, or do anything else if I choose. If it helps me over my difficulties, that's my business, not yours," and in defiance she prepared another glass and drank it.

Cowperwood shook his head, looking at her steadily and sorrowfully. "It's too bad, Aileen," he said. "I don't know what to do about you exactly. You oughtn't to go on this way. Whisky won't get you anywhere. It will simply ruin your looks and make you miserable in the bargain."

"Oh, to hell with my looks!" she snapped. "A lot of good they've done me." And, feeling contentious and sad, she got up and left the table. Cowperwood followed her after a time, only to see her dabbing at her eyes and nose with powder. A half-filled glass of whisky and water was on the dressing-table beside her. It gave him a strange feeling of responsibility and helplessness.

Mingled with his anxiety as to Aileen were thoughts of the alternate rise and fall of his hopes in connection with Berenice. She was such a superior girl, developing so definitely as an individual. To his satisfaction she had, on a few recent occasions when he had seen her, unbent sufficiently to talk to him in a friendly and even intimate way, for she was by no means hoity-toity, but a thinking, reasoning being of the profoundest intellectual, or, rather, the highest artistic tendencies. She was so care-free, living in a high and solitary world, at times apparently enwrapt in thoughts serene, at other times sharing vividly in the current interests of the social world of which she was a part, and which she dignified as much as it dignified her.

One Sunday morning at Pocono, in late June weather, when he had come East to rest for a few days, and all was still and airy on the high ground which the Carter cottage occupied, Berenice came out on the veranda where Cowperwood was sitting, reading a fiscal report of one of his companies and meditating on his affairs. By now they had become somewhat more sympatica than formerly, and Berenice had an easy, genial way in his presence. She liked him, rather. With an indescribable smile which wrinkled her nose and eyes, and played about the corners of her mouth, she said: "Now I am going to catch a bird."

"A what?" asked Cowperwood, looking up and pretending he had not heard, though he had. He was all eyes for any movement of hers. She was dressed in a flouncy morning gown eminently suitable for the world in which she was moving.

"A bird," she replied, with an airy toss of her head. "This is June-time, and the sparrows are teaching their young to fly."

Cowperwood, previously engrossed in financial speculations, was translated, as by the wave of a fairy wand, into another realm where birds and fledglings and grass and the light winds of heaven were more important than brick and stone and stocks and bonds. He got up and followed her flowing steps across the grass to where, near a clump of alder bushes, she had seen a mother sparrow enticing a fledgling to take wing. From her room upstairs, she had been watching this bit of outdoor sociology. It suddenly came to Cowperwood, with great force, how comparatively unimportant in the great drift of life were his own affairs when about him was operative all this splendid will to existence, as sensed by her. He saw her stretch out her hands downward, and run in an airy, graceful way, stooping here and there, while before her fluttered a baby sparrow, until suddenly she dived quickly and then, turning, her face agleam, cried: "See, I have him! He wants to fight, too! Oh, you little dear!"

She was holding "him," as she chose to characterize it, in the hollow of her hand, the head between her thumb and forefinger, with the forefinger of her free hand petting it the while she laughed and kissed it. It was not so much bird-love as the artistry of life and of herself that was moving her. Hearing the parent bird chirping distractedly from a nearby limb, she turned and called: "Don't make such a row! I sha'n't keep him long."

Cowperwood laughed—trig in the morning sun. "You can scarcely blame her," he commented.

"Oh, she knows well enough I wouldn't hurt him," Berenice replied, spiritedly, as though it were literally true.

"Does she, indeed?" inquired Cowperwood. "Why do you say that?"

"Because it's true. Don't you think they know when their children are really in danger?"

"But why should they?" persisted Cowperwood, charmed and interested by the involute character of her logic. She was quite deceptive to him. He could not be sure what she thought.

She merely fixed him a moment with her cool, slate-blue eyes. "Do you think the senses of the world are only five?" she asked, in the most charming and non-reproachful way. "Indeed, they know well enough. She knows." She turned and waved a graceful hand in the direction of the tree, where peace now reigned. The chirping had ceased. "She knows I am not a cat."

Again that enticing, mocking smile that wrinkled her nose, her eye-corners, her mouth. The word "cat" had a sharp, sweet sound in her mouth. It seemed to be bitten off closely with force and airy spirit. Cowperwood surveyed her as he would have surveyed the ablest person he knew. Here was a woman, he saw, who could and would command the utmost reaches of his soul in every direction. If he interested her at all, he would need them all. The eyes of her were at once so elusive, so direct, so friendly, so cool and keen. "You will have to be interesting, indeed, to interest me," they seemed to say; and yet they were by no means averse, apparently, to a hearty camaraderie. That nose-wrinkling smile said as much. Here was by no means a Stephanie Platow, nor yet a Rita Sohlberg. He could not assume her as he had Ella Hubby, or Florence Cochrane, or Cecily Haguenin. Here was an iron individuality with a soul for romance and art and philosophy and life. He could not take her as he had those others. And yet Berenice was really beginning to think more than a little about Cowperwood. He must be an extraordinary man; her mother said so, and the newspapers were always mentioning his name and noting his movements.

A little later, at Southampton, whither she and her mother had gone, they met again. Together with a young man by the name of Greanelle, Cowperwood and Berenice had gone into the sea to bathe. It was a wonderful afternoon.

To the east and south and west spread the sea, a crinkling floor of blue, and to their left, as they faced it, was a lovely outward-curving shore of tawny sand. Studying Berenice in blue-silk bathing costume and shoes, Cowperwood had been stung by the wonder of passing life—how youth comes in, ever fresh and fresh, and age goes out. Here he was, long crowded years of conflict and experience behind him, and yet this twenty-year-old girl, with her incisive mind and keen tastes, was apparently as wise in matters of general import as himself. He could find no flaw in her armor in those matters which they could discuss. Her knowledge and comments were so ripe and sane, despite a tendency to pose a little, which was quite within her rights. Because Greanelle had bored her a little she had shunted him off and was amusing herself talking to Cowperwood, who fascinated her by his compact individuality.

"Do you know," she confided to him, on this occasion, "I get so very tired of young men sometimes. They can be so inane. I do declare, they are nothing more than shoes and ties and socks and canes strung together in some unimaginable way. Vaughn Greanelle is for all the world like a perambulating manikin to-day. He is just an English suit with a cane attached walking about."

"Well, bless my soul," commented Cowperwood, "what an indictment!"

"It's true," she replied. "He knows nothing at all except polo, and the latest swimming-stroke, and where everybody is, and who is going to marry who. Isn't it dull?"

She tossed her head back and breathed as though to exhale the fumes of the dull and the inane from her inmost being.

"Did you tell him that?" inquired Cowperwood, curiously.

"Certainly I did."

"I don't wonder he looks so solemn," he said, turning and looking back at Greanelle and Mrs. Carter; they were sitting side by side in sand-chairs, the former beating the sand with his toes. "You're a curious girl, Berenice," he went on, familiarly. "You are so direct and vital at times."

"Not any more than you are, from all I can hear," she replied, fixing him with those steady eyes. "Anyhow, why should I be bored? He is so dull. He follows me around out here all the time, and I don't want him."

She tossed her head and began to run up the beach to where bathers were fewer and fewer, looking back at Cowperwood as if to say, "Why don't you follow?" He developed a burst of enthusiasm and ran quite briskly, overtaking her near some shallows where, because of a sandbar offshore, the waters were thin and bright.

"Oh, look!" exclaimed Berenice, when he came up. "See, the fish! O-oh!"

She dashed in to where a few feet offshore a small school of minnows as large as sardines were playing, silvery in the sun. She ran as she had for the bird, doing her best to frighten them into a neighboring pocket or pool farther up on the shore. Cowperwood, as gay as a boy of ten, joined in the chase. He raced after them briskly, losing one school, but pocketing another a little farther on and calling to her to come.

"Oh!" exclaimed Berenice at one point. "Here they are now. Come quick! Drive them in here!"

Her hair was blowy, her face a keen pink, her eyes an electric blue by contrast. She was bending low over the water—Cowperwood also—their hands outstretched, the fish, some five in all, nervously dancing before them in their efforts to escape. All at once, having forced them into a corner, they dived; Berenice actually caught one. Cowperwood missed by a fraction, but drove the fish she did catch into her hands.

"Oh," she exclaimed, jumping up, "how wonderful! It's alive. I caught it."

She danced up and down, and Cowperwood, standing before her, was sobered by her charm. He felt an impulse to speak to her of his affection, to tell her how delicious she was to him.

"You," he said, pausing over the word and giving it special emphasis—"you are the only thing here that is wonderful to me."

She looked at him a moment, the live fish in her extended hands, her eyes keying to the situation. For the least fraction of a moment she was uncertain, as he could see, how to take

500

this. Many men had been approximative before. It was common to have compliments paid to her. But this was different. She said nothing, but fixed him with a look which said quite plainly, "You had better not say anything more just now, I think." Then, seeing that he understood, that his manner softened, and that he was troubled, she crinkled her nose gaily and added: "It's like fairyland. I feel as though I had caught it out of another world." Cowperwood understood. The direct approach was not for use in her case; and yet there was something, a camaraderie, a sympathy which he felt and which she felt. A girls' school, conventions, the need of socially placing herself, her conservative friends, and their viewpoint—all were working here. If he were only single now, she told herself, she would be willing to listen to him in a very different spirit, for he was charming. But this way— And he, for his part, concluded that here was one woman whom he would gladly marry if she would have him.

CHAPTER XLVII

AMERICAN MATCH

Following Cowperwood's coup in securing cash by means of his seeming gift of three hundred thousand dollars for a telescope his enemies rested for a time, but only because of a lack of ideas wherewith to destroy him. Public sentiment—created by the newspapers— was still against him. Yet his franchises had still from eight to ten years to run, and meanwhile he might make himself unassailably powerful. For the present he was busy, surrounded by his engineers and managers and legal advisers, constructing his several elevated lines at a whirlwind rate. At the same time, through Videra, Kaffrath, and Addison, he was effecting a scheme of loaning money on call to the local Chicago banks—the very banks which were most opposed to him—so that in a crisis he could retaliate. By manipulating the vast quantity of stocks and bonds of which he was now the master he was making money hand over fist, his one rule being that six per cent. was enough to pay any holder who had merely purchased his stock as an outsider. It was most profitable to himself. When his stocks earned more than that he issued new ones, selling them on 'change and pocketing the difference. Out of the cash-drawers of his various companies he took immense sums, temporary loans, as it were, which later he had charged by his humble servitors to "construction," "equipment," or "operation." He was like a canny wolf prowling in a forest of trees of his own creation.

The weak note in this whole project of elevated lines was that for some time it was destined to be unprofitable. Its very competition tended to weaken the value of his surface-line companies. His holdings in these as well as in elevated-road shares were immense. If anything happened to cause them to fall in price immense numbers of these same stocks held by others would be thrown on the market, thus still further depreciating their value and compelling him to come into the market and buy. With the most painstaking care he began at once to pile up a reserve in government bonds for emergency purposes, which he decided should be not less than eight or nine million dollars, for he feared financial storms as well as financial reprisal, and where so much was at stake he did not propose to be caught napping.

At the time that Cowperwood first entered on elevated-road construction there was no evidence that any severe depression in the American money-market was imminent. But it was not long before a new difficulty began to appear. It was now the day of the trust in all its watery magnificence. Coal, iron, steel, oil, machinery, and a score of other commercial necessities had already been "trustified," and others, such as leather, shoes, cordage, and the like, were, almost hourly, being brought under the control of shrewd and ruthless men. Already in Chicago Schryhart, Hand, Arneel, Merrill, and a score of others were seeing their way to amazing profits by underwriting these ventures which required ready cash, and to which lesser magnates, content with a portion of the leavings of Dives's table, were glad to bring to their attention. On the other hand, in the nation at large there was growing up a feeling that at the top there were a set of giants—Titans—who, without heart or soul, and without any understanding of or sympathy with the condition of the rank and file, were setting forth to enchain and enslave them. The vast mass, writhing in ignorance and poverty, finally turned with pathetic fury to the cure-all of a political leader in the West. This latter prophet, seeing gold becoming scarcer and scarcer and the cash and credits of the land falling into the hands of a few who were manipulating them for their own benefit, had decided that what was needed was a greater volume of currency, so that credits would be easier and money cheaper to come by in the matter of interest. Silver, of which there was a superabundance in the mines, was to be coined at the ratio of sixteen dollars of silver for every one of gold in circulation, and the parity of the two metals maintained by fiat of government. Never again should the few be able to make a weapon of the people's medium of exchange in order to bring about their undoing. There was to be ample money, far beyond the control of central banks and the men in power over them. It was a splendid dream worthy of a charitable heart, but because of it a disturbing war for political control of the government was shortly threatened and soon began. The money element, sensing the danger of change involved in the theories of the new political leader, began to fight him and the element in the Democratic party which he represented. The rank and file of both parties—the more or less hungry and thirsty who lie ever at the bottom on both sides—hailed him as a heaven-sent deliverer, a new Moses come to lead them out of the wilderness of poverty and distress. Woe to the political leader who preaches a new doctrine of deliverance, and who, out of tenderness of heart, offers a panacea for human ills. His truly shall be a crown of thorns.

Cowperwood, no less than other men of wealth, was opposed to what he deemed a crack-brained idea—that of maintaining a parity between gold and silver by law. Confiscation was his word for it—the confiscation of the wealth of the few for the benefit of the many. Most of all was he opposed to it because he feared that this unrest, which was obviously growing, foreshadowed a class war in which investors would run to cover and money be locked in strong-boxes. At once he began to shorten sail, to invest only in the soundest securities, and to convert all his weaker ones into cash.

To meet current emergencies, however, he was compelled to borrow heavily here and there, and in doing so he was quick to note that those banks representing his enemies in Chicago and elsewhere were willing to accept his various stocks as collateral, providing he would accept loans subject to call. He did so gladly, at the same time suspecting Hand, Schryhart, Arneel, and Merrill of some scheme to wreck him, providing they could get him where the calling of his loans suddenly and in concert would financially embarrass him. "I think I know what that crew are up to," he once observed to Addison, at this period. "Well, they will have to rise very early in the morning if they catch me napping."

The thing that he suspected was really true. Schryhart, Hand, and Arneel, watching him through their agents and brokers, had soon discovered—in the very earliest phases of the silver agitation and before the real storm broke—that he was borrowing in New York, in London, in certain quarters of Chicago, and elsewhere. "It looks to me," said Schryhart, one day, to his friend Arneel, "as if our friend has gotten in a little too deep. He has overreached himself. These elevated-road schemes of his have eaten up too much capital. There is another election coming on next fall, and he knows we are going to fight tooth and nail. He needs money to electrify his surface lines. If we could trace out exactly where he stands, and where he has borrowed, we might know what to do."

"Unless I am greatly mistaken," replied Arneel, "he is in a tight place or is rapidly getting there. This silver agitation is beginning to weaken stocks and tighten money. I suggest that our banks here loan him all the money he wants on call. When the time comes, if he isn't ready, we can shut him up tighter than a drum. If we can pick up any other loans he's made anywhere else, well and good."

Mr. Arneel said this without a shadow of bitterness or humor. In some tight hour, perhaps, now fast approaching, Mr. Cowperwood would be promised salvation—"saved" on condition that he should leave Chicago forever. There were those who would take over his property in the interest of the city and upright government and administer it accordingly.

Unfortunately, at this very time Messrs. Hand, Schryhart, and Arneel were themselves concerned in a little venture to which the threatened silver agitation could bode nothing but ill. This concerned so simple a thing as matches, a commodity which at this time, along with many others, had been trustified and was yielding a fine profit. "American Match" was a stock which was already listed on every exchange and which was selling steadily around one hundred and twenty.

The geniuses who had first planned a combination of all match concerns and a monopoly of the trade in America were two men, Messrs. Hull and Stackpole—bankers and brokers, primarily. Mr. Phineas Hull was a small, ferret-like, calculating man with a sparse growth of dusty-brown hair and an eyelid, the right one, which was partially paralyzed and drooped heavily, giving him a characterful and yet at times a sinister expression.

His partner, Mr. Benoni Stackpole, had been once a stage-driver in Arkansas, and later a horse-trader. He was a man of great force and calculation—large, oleaginous, politic, and courageous. Without the ultimate brain capacity of such men as Arneel, Hand, and Merrill, he was, nevertheless, resourceful and able. He had started somewhat late in the race for wealth, but now, with all his strength, he was endeavoring to bring to fruition this plan which, with the aid of Hull, he had formulated. Inspired by the thought of great wealth, they had first secured control of the stock of one match company, and had then put themselves in a position to bargain with the owners of others. The patents and processes controlled by one company and another had been combined, and the field had been broadened as much as possible.

But to do all this a great deal of money had been required, much more than was in possession of either Hull or Stackpole. Both of them being Western men, they looked first to Western capital. Hand, Schryhart, Arneel, and Merrill were in turn appealed to, and great blocks of the new stock were sold to them at inside figures. By the means thus afforded the combination proceeded apace. Patents for exclusive processes were taken over from all sides, and the idea of invading Europe and eventually controlling the market of the world had its inception. At the same time it occurred to each and all of their lordly patrons that it would be a splendid thing if the stock they had purchased at forty-five, and which was now selling in open market at one hundred and twenty, should go to three hundred, where, if these monopolistic dreams were true, it properly belonged. A little more of this stock—the destiny of which at this time seemed sure and splendid—would not be amiss. And so there began a quiet campaign on the part of each capitalist to gather enough of it to realize a true fortune on the rise.

A game of this kind is never played with the remainder of the financial community entirely unaware of what is on foot. In the inner circles of brokerage life rumors were soon abroad that a tremendous boom was in store for American Match. Cowperwood heard of it through Addison, always at the center of financial rumor, and the two of them bought heavily, though not so heavily but that they could clear out at any time with at least a slight margin in their favor. During a period of eight months the stock slowly moved upward, finally crossing the two-hundred mark and reaching two-twenty, at which figure both Addison and Cowperwood sold, realizing nearly a million between them on their investment.

In the mean time the foreshadowed political storm was brewing. At first a cloud no larger than a man's hand, it matured swiftly in the late months of 1895, and by the spring of 1896 it had become portentous and was ready to burst. With the climacteric nomination of the "Apostle of Free Silver" for President of the United States, which followed in July, a chill settled down over the conservative and financial elements of the country. What Cowperwood had wisely proceeded to do months before, others less far-seeing, from Maine to California and from the Gulf to Canada, began to do now. Bank-deposits were in part withdrawn; feeble or uncertain securities were thrown upon the market. All at once Schryhart, Arneel, Hand, and Merrill realized that they were in more or less of a trap in regard to their large holdings in American Match. Having gathered vast quantities of this stock, which had been issued in blocks of millions, it was now necessary to sustain the market or sell at a loss. Since money was needed by many holders, and this stock was selling at two-twenty, telegraphic orders began to pour in from all parts of the country to sell on the Chicago Exchange, where the deal was being engineered and where the market obviously existed. All of the instigators of the deal conferred, and decided to sustain the market. Messrs. Hull and Stackpole, being the nominal heads of the trust, were delegated to buy, they in turn calling on the principal investors to take their share, pro rata. Hand, Schryhart, Arneel, and Merrill, weighted with this inpouring flood of stock, which they had to take at two-twenty, hurried to their favorite banks, hypothecating vast quantities at one-fifty and over, and using the money so obtained to take care of the additional shares which they were compelled to buy.

At last, however, their favorite banks were full to overflowing and at the danger-point. They could take no more.

"No, no, no!" Hand declared to Phineas Hull over the 'phone. "I can't risk another dollar in this venture, and I won't! It's a perfect proposition. I realize all its merits just as well as you do. But enough is enough. I tell you a financial slump is coming. That's the reason all this stock is coming out now. I am willing to protect my interests in this thing up to a certain point. As I told you, I agree not to throw a single share on the market of all that I now have. But more than that I cannot do. The other gentlemen in this agreement will have to protect themselves as best they can. I have other things to look out for that are just as important to me, and more so, than American Match."

It was the same with Mr. Schryhart, who, stroking a crisp, black mustache, was wondering whether he had not better throw over what holdings he had and clear out; however, he feared the rage of Hand and Arneel for breaking the market and thus bringing on a local panic. It was risky business. Arneel and Merrill finally agreed to hold firm to what they had;

but, as they told Mr. Hull, nothing could induce them to "protect" another share, come what might.

In this crisis naturally Messrs. Hull and Stackpole—estimable gentlemen both—were greatly depressed. By no means so wealthy as their lofty patrons, their private fortunes were in much greater jeopardy. They were eager to make any port in so black a storm. Witness, then, the arrival of Benoni Stackpole at the office of Frank Algernon Cowperwood. He was at the end of his tether, and Cowperwood was the only really rich man in the city not yet involved in this speculation. In the beginning he had heard both Hand and Schryhart say that they did not care to become involved if Cowperwood was in any way, shape, or manner to be included, but that had been over a year ago, and Schryhart and Hand were now, as it were, leaving both him and his partner to their fates. They could have no objection to his dealing with Cowperwood in this crisis if he could make sure that the magnate would not sell him out. Mr. Stackpole was six feet one in his socks and weighed two hundred and thirty pounds. Clad in a brown linen suit and straw hat (for it was late July), he carried a palm-leaf fan as well as his troublesome stocks in a small yellow leather bag. He was wet with perspiration and in a gloomy state of mind. Failure was staring him in the face—giant failure. If American Match fell below two hundred he would have to close his doors as banker and broker and, in view of what he was carrying, he and Hull would fail for approximately twenty million dollars. Messrs. Hand, Schryhart, Arneel, and Merrill would lose in the neighborhood of six or eight millions between them. The local banks would suffer in proportion, though not nearly so severely, for, loaning at one-fifty, they would only sacrifice the difference between that and the lowest point to which the stock might fall.

Cowperwood eyed the new-comer, when he entered, with an equivocal eye, for he knew well now what was coming. Only a few days before he had predicted an eventual smash to Addison.

"Mr. Cowperwood," began Stackpole, "in this bag I have fifteen thousand shares of American Match, par value one million five hundred thousand dollars, market value three million three hundred thousand at this moment, and worth every cent of three hundred dollars a share and more. I don't know how closely you have been following the developments of American Match. We own all the patents on labor-saving machines and, what's more, we're just about to close contracts with Italy and France to lease our machines and processes to them for pretty nearly one million dollars a year each. We're dickering with Austria and England, and of course we'll take up other countries later. The American Match Company will yet make matches for the whole world, whether I'm connected with it or not. This silver agitation has caught us right in mid-ocean, and we're having a little trouble weathering the storm. I'm a perfectly frank man when it comes to close business relations of this kind, and I'm going to tell you just how things stand. If we can scull over this rough place that has come up on account of the silver agitation our stock will go to three hundred before the first of the year. Now, if you want to take it you can have it outright at one hundred and fifty dollars—that is, providing you'll agree not to throw any of it back on the market before next December; or, if you won't promise that" (he paused to see if by any chance he could read Cowperwood's inscrutable face) "I want you to loan me one hundred and fifty dollars a share on these for thirty days at least at ten or fifteen, or whatever rate you care to fix."

Cowperwood interlocked his fingers and twiddled his thumbs as he contemplated this latest evidence of earthly difficulty and uncertainty. Time and chance certainly happened to all men, and here was one opportunity of paying out those who had been nagging him. To take this stock at one-fifty on loan and peddle it out swiftly and fully at two-twenty or less would bring American Match crumbling about their ears. When it was selling at one-fifty or less he could buy it back, pocket his profit, complete his deal with Mr. Stackpole, pocket his interest, and smile like the well-fed cat in the fable. It was as simple as twiddling his thumbs, which he was now doing.

"Who has been backing this stock here in Chicago besides yourself and Mr. Hull?" he asked, pleasantly. "I think that I already know, but I should like to be certain if you have no objection."

"None in the least, none in the least," replied Mr. Stackpole, accommodatingly. "Mr. Hand, Mr. Schryhart, Mr. Arneel, and Mr. Merrill."

"That is what I thought," commented Cowperwood, easily. "They can't take this up for you? Is that it? Saturated?"

"Saturated," agreed Mr. Stackpole, dully. "But there's one thing I'd have to stipulate in accepting a loan on these. Not a share must be thrown on the market, or, at least, not before I have failed to respond to your call. I have understood that there is a little feeling between you and Mr. Hand and the other gentlemen I have mentioned. But, as I say—and I'm talking perfectly frankly now—I'm in a corner, and it's any port in a storm. If you want to help me I'll make the best terms I can, and I won't forget the favor."

He opened the bag and began to take out the securities—long greenish-yellow bundles, tightly gripped in the center by thick elastic bands. They were in bundles of one thousand shares each. Since Stackpole half proffered them to him, Cowperwood took them in one hand and lightly weighed them up and down.

"I'm sorry, Mr. Stackpole," he said, sympathetically, after a moment of apparent reflection, "but I cannot possibly help you in this matter. I'm too involved in other things myself, and I do not often indulge in stock-peculations of any kind. I have no particular malice toward any one of the gentlemen you mention. I do not trouble to dislike all who dislike me. I might, of course, if I chose, take these stocks and pay them out and throw them on the market to-morrow, but I have no desire to do anything of the sort. I only wish I could help you, and if I thought I could carry them safely for three or four months I would. As it is—" He lifted his eyebrows sympathetically. "Have you tried all the bankers in town?"

"Practically every one."

"And they can't help you?"

"They are carrying all they can stand now."

"Too bad. I'm sorry, very. By the way, do you happen, by any chance, to know Mr. Millard Bailey or Mr. Edwin Kaffrath?"

"No, I don't," replied Stackpole, hopefully.

"Well, now, there are two men who are much richer than is generally supposed. They often have very large sums at their disposal. You might look them up on a chance. Then there's my friend Videra. I don't know how he is fixed at present. You can always find him at the Twelfth Ward Bank. He might be inclined to take a good portion of that—I don't know.

He's much better off than most people seem to think. I wonder you haven't been directed to some one of these men before." (As a matter of fact, no one of the individuals in question would have been interested to take a dollar of this loan except on Cowperwood's order, but Stackpole had no reason for knowing this. They were not prominently identified with the magnate.)

"Thank you very much. I will," observed Stackpole, restoring his undesired stocks to his bag.

Cowperwood, with an admirable show of courtesy, called a stenographer, and pretended to secure for his guest the home addresses of these gentlemen. He then bade Mr. Stackpole an encouraging farewell. The distrait promoter at once decided to try not only Bailey and Kaffrath, but Videra; but even as he drove toward the office of the first-mentioned Cowperwood was personally busy reaching him by telephone.

"I say, Bailey," he called, when he had secured the wealthy lumberman on the wire, "Benoni Stackpole, of Hull & Stackpole, was here to see me just now."

"Yes."

"He has with him fifteen thousand shares of American Match—par value one hundred, market value to-day two-twenty."

"Yes."

"He is trying to hypothecate the lot or any part of it at one-fifty."

"Yes."

"You know what the trouble with American Match is, don't you?"

"No. I only know it's being driven up to where it is now by a bull campaign."

"Well, listen to me. It's going to break. American Match is going to bust."

"Yes."

"But I want you to loan this man five hundred thousand dollars at one-twenty or less and then recommend that he go to Edwin Kaffrath or Anton Videra for the balance."

"But, Frank, I haven't any five hundred thousand to spare. You say American Match is going to bust."

"I know you haven't, but draw the check on the Chicago Trust, and Addison will honor it. Send the stock to me and forget all about it. I will do the rest. But under no circumstances mention my name, and don't appear too eager. Not more than one-twenty at the outside, do you hear? and less if you can get it. You recognize my voice, do you?"

"Perfectly."

"Drive over afterward if you have time and let me know what happens."

507

"Very good," commented Mr. Bailey, in a businesslike way.

Cowperwood next called for Mr. Kaffrath. Conversing to similar effect with that individual and with Videra, before three-quarters of an hour Cowperwood had arranged completely for Mr. Stackpole's tour. He was to have his total loan at one-twenty or less. Checks were to be forthcoming at once. Different banks were to be drawn on—banks other than the Chicago Trust Company. Cowperwood would see, in some roundabout way, that these checks were promptly honored, whether the cash was there or not. In each case the hypothecated stocks were to be sent to him. Then, having seen to the perfecting of this little programme, and that the banks to be drawn upon in this connection understood perfectly that the checks in question were guaranteed by him or others, he sat down to await the arrival of his henchmen and the turning of the stock into his private safe.

CHAPTER XLVIII

PANIC

On August 4, 1896, the city of Chicago, and for that matter the entire financial world, was startled and amazed by the collapse of American Match, one of the strongest of market securities, and the coincident failure of Messrs. Hull and Stackpole, its ostensible promoters, for twenty millions. As early as eleven o'clock of the preceding day the banking and brokerage world of Chicago, trading in this stock, was fully aware that something untoward was on foot in connection with it. Owing to the high price at which the stock was "protected," and the need of money to liquidate, blocks of this stock from all parts of the country were being rushed to the market with the hope of realizing before the ultimate break. About the stock-exchange, which frowned like a gray fortress at the foot of La Salle Street, all was excitement—as though a giant anthill had been ruthlessly disturbed. Clerks and messengers hurried to and fro in confused and apparently aimless directions. Brokers whose supply of American Match had been apparently exhausted on the previous day now appeared on 'change bright and early, and at the clang of the gong began to offer the stock in sizable lots of from two hundred to five hundred shares. The agents of Hull & Stackpole were in the market, of course, in the front rank of the scrambling, yelling throng, taking up whatever stock appeared at the price they were hoping to maintain. The two promoters were in touch by 'phone and wire not only with those various important personages whom they had induced to enter upon this bull campaign, but with their various clerks and agents on 'change. Naturally, under the circumstances both were in a gloomy frame of mind. This game was no longer moving in those large, easy sweeps which characterize the more favorable aspects of high finance. Sad to relate, as in all the troubled flumes of life where vast currents are compressed in narrow, tortuous spaces, these two men were now concerned chiefly with the momentary care of small but none the less heartbreaking burdens. Where to find fifty thousand to take care of this or that burden of stock which was momentarily falling upon them? They were as two men called upon, with their limited hands and strength, to seal up the ever-increasing crevices of a dike beyond which raged a mountainous and destructive sea.

At eleven o'clock Mr. Phineas Hull rose from the chair which sat before his solid mahogany desk, and confronted his partner.

"I'll tell you, Ben," he said, "I'm afraid we can't make this. We've hypothecated so much of this stock around town that we can't possibly tell who's doing what. I know as well as I'm standing on this floor that some one, I can't say which one, is selling us out. You don't suppose it could be Cowperwood or any of those people he sent to us, do you?"

Stackpole, worn by his experiences of the past few weeks, was inclined to be irritable.

"How should I know, Phineas?" he inquired, scowling in troubled thought. "I don't think so. I didn't notice any signs that they were interested in stock-gambling. Anyhow, we had to have the money in some form. Any one of the whole crowd is apt to get frightened now at any moment and throw the whole thing over. We're in a tight place, that's plain."

For the fortieth time he plucked at a too-tight collar and pulled up his shirt-sleeves, for it was stifling, and he was coatless and waistcoatless. Just then Mr. Hull's telephone bell rang—the one connecting with the firm's private office on 'change, and the latter jumped to seize the receiver.

"Yes?" he inquired, irritably.

"Two thousand shares of American offered at two-twenty! Shall I take them?"

The man who was 'phoning was in sight of another man who stood at the railing of the brokers' gallery overlooking "the pit," or central room of the stock-exchange, and who instantly transferred any sign he might receive to the man on the floor. So Mr. Hull's "yea" or "nay" would be almost instantly transmuted into a cash transaction on 'change.

"What do you think of that?" asked Hull of Stackpole, putting his hand over the receiver's mouth, his right eyelid drooping heavier than ever. "Two thousand more to take up! Where d'you suppose they are coming from? Tch!"

"Well, the bottom's out, that's all," replied Stackpole, heavily and gutturally. "We can't do what we can't do. I say this, though: support it at two-twenty until three o'clock. Then we'll figure up where we stand and what we owe. And meanwhile I'll see what I can do. If the banks won't help us and Arneel and that crowd want to get from under, we'll fail, that's all; but not before I've had one more try, by Jericho! They may not help us, but—"

Actually Mr. Stackpole did not see what was to be done unless Messrs. Hand, Schryhart, Merrill, and Arneel were willing to risk much more money, but it grieved and angered him to think he and Hull should be thus left to sink without a sigh. He had tried Kaffrath, Videra, and Bailey, but they were adamant. Thus cogitating, Stackpole put on his wide-brimmed straw hat and went out. It was nearly ninety-six in the shade. The granite and asphalt pavements of the down-town district reflected a dry, Turkish-bath-room heat. There was no air to speak of. The sky was a burning, milky blue, with the sun gleaming feverishly upon the upper walls of the tall buildings.

Mr. Hand, in his seventh-story suite of offices in the Rookery Building, was suffering from the heat, but much more from mental perturbation. Though not a stingy or penurious man, it was still true that of all earthly things he suffered most from a financial loss. How often had he seen chance or miscalculation sweep apparently strong and valiant men into the limbo of the useless and forgotten! Since the alienation of his wife's affections by Cowperwood, he had scarcely any interest in the world outside his large financial holdings, which included profitable investments in a half-hundred companies. But they must pay, pay,

509

pay heavily in interest—all of them—and the thought that one of them might become a failure or a drain on his resources was enough to give him an almost physical sensation of dissatisfaction and unrest, a sort of spiritual and mental nausea which would cling to him for days and days or until he had surmounted the difficulty. Mr. Hand had no least corner in his heart for failure.

As a matter of fact, the situation in regard to American Match had reached such proportions as to be almost numbing. Aside from the fifteen thousand shares which Messrs. Hull and Stackpole had originally set aside for themselves, Hand, Arneel, Schryhart, and Merrill had purchased five thousand shares each at forty, but had since been compelled to sustain the market to the extent of over five thousand shares more each, at prices ranging from one-twenty to two-twenty, the largest blocks of shares having been bought at the latter figure. Actually Hand was caught for nearly one million five hundred thousand dollars, and his soul was as gray as a bat's wing. At fifty-seven years of age men who are used only to the most successful financial calculations and the credit that goes with unerring judgment dread to be made a mark by chance or fate. It opens the way for comment on their possibly failing vitality or judgment. And so Mr. Hand sat on this hot August afternoon, ensconced in a large carved mahogany chair in the inner recesses of his inner offices, and brooded. Only this morning, in the face of a falling market, he would have sold out openly had he not been deterred by telephone messages from Arneel and Schryhart suggesting the advisability of a pool conference before any action was taken. Come what might on the morrow, he was determined to quit unless he saw some clear way out—to be shut of the whole thing unless the ingenuity of Stackpole and Hull should discover a way of sustaining the market without his aid. While he was meditating on how this was to be done Mr. Stackpole appeared, pale, gloomy, wet with perspiration.

"Well, Mr. Hand," he exclaimed, wearily, "I've done all I can. Hull and I have kept the market fairly stable so far. You saw what happened between ten and eleven this morning. The jig's up. We've borrowed our last dollar and hypothecated our last share. My personal fortune has gone into the balance, and so has Hull's. Some one of the outside stockholders, or all of them, are cutting the ground from under us. Fourteen thousand shares since ten o'clock this morning! That tells the story. It can't be done just now—not unless you gentlemen are prepared to go much further than you have yet gone. If we could organize a pool to take care of fifteen thousand more shares—"

Mr. Stackpole paused, for Mr. Hand was holding up a fat, pink digit.

"No more of that," he was saying, solemnly. "It can't be done. I, for one, won't sink another dollar in this proposition at this time. I'd rather throw what I have on the market and take what I can get. I am sure the others feel the same way."

Mr. Hand, to play safe, had hypothecated nearly all his shares with various banks in order to release his money for other purposes, and he knew he would not dare to throw over all his holdings, just as he knew he would have to make good at the figure at which they had been margined. But it was a fine threat to make.

Mr. Stackpole stared ox-like at Mr. Hand.

"Very well," he said, "I might as well go back, then, and post a notice on our front door. We bought fourteen thousand shares and held the market where it is, but we haven't a dollar to pay for them with. Unless the banks or some one will take them over for us we're gone—we're bankrupt."

Mr. Hand, who knew that if Mr. Stackpole carried out this decision it meant the loss of his one million five hundred thousand, halted mentally. "Have you been to all the banks?" he asked. "What does Lawrence, of the Prairie National, have to say?"

"It's the same with all of them," replied Stackpole, now quite desperate, "as it is with you. They have all they can carry—every one. It's this damned silver agitation—that's it, and nothing else. There's nothing the matter with this stock. It will right itself in a few months. It's sure to."

"Will it?" commented Mr. Hand, sourly. "That depends on what happens next November." (He was referring to the coming national election.)

"Yes, I know," sighed Mr. Stackpole, seeing that it was a condition, and not a theory, that confronted him. Then, suddenly clenching his right hand, he exclaimed, "Damn that upstart!" (He was thinking of the "Apostle of Free Silver.") "He's the cause of all this. Well, if there's nothing to be done I might as well be going. There's all those shares we bought to-day which we ought to be able to hypothecate with somebody. It would be something if we could get even a hundred and twenty on them."

"Very true," replied Hand. "I wish it could be done. I, personally, cannot sink any more money. But why don't you go and see Schryhart and Arneel? I've been talking to them, and they seem to be in a position similar to my own; but if they are willing to confer, I am. I don't see what's to be done, but it may be that all of us together might arrange some way of heading off the slaughter of the stock to-morrow. I don't know. If only we don't have to suffer too great a decline."

Mr. Hand was thinking that Messrs. Hull and Stackpole might be forced to part with all their remaining holdings at fifty cents on the dollar or less. Then if it could possibly be taken and carried by the united banks for them (Schryhart, himself, Arneel) and sold at a profit later, he and his associates might recoup some of their losses. The local banks at the behest of the big quadrumvirate might be coerced into straining their resources still further. But how was this to be done? How, indeed?

It was Schryhart who, in pumping and digging at Stackpole when he finally arrived there, managed to extract from him the truth in regard to his visit to Cowperwood. As a matter of fact, Schryhart himself had been guilty this very day of having thrown two thousand shares of American Match on the market unknown to his confreres. Naturally, he was eager to learn whether Stackpole or any one else had the least suspicion that he was involved. As a consequence he questioned Stackpole closely, and the latter, being anxious as to the outcome of his own interests, was not unwilling to make a clean breast. He had the justification in his own mind that the quadrumvirate had been ready to desert him anyhow.

"Why did you go to him?" exclaimed Schryhart, professing to be greatly astonished and annoyed, as, indeed, in one sense he was. "I thought we had a distinct understanding in the beginning that under no circumstances was he to be included in any portion of this. You might as well go to the devil himself for assistance as go there." At the same time he was thinking "How fortunate!" Here was not only a loophole for himself in connection with his own subtle side-plays, but also, if the quadrumvirate desired, an excuse for deserting the troublesome fortunes of Hull & Stackpole.

511

"Well, the truth is," replied Stackpole, somewhat sheepishly and yet defiantly, "last Thursday I had fifteen thousand shares on which I had to raise money. Neither you nor any of the others wanted any more. The banks wouldn't take them. I called up Rambaud on a chance, and he suggested Cowperwood."

As has been related, Stackpole had really gone to Cowperwood direct, but a lie under the circumstances seemed rather essential.

"Rambaud!" sneered Schryhart. "Cowperwood's man—he and all the others. You couldn't have gone to a worse crowd if you had tried. So that's where this stock is coming from, beyond a doubt. That fellow or his friends are selling us out. You might have known he'd do it. He hates us. So you're through, are you?—not another single trick to turn?"

"Not one," replied Stackpole, solemnly.

"Well, that's too bad. You have acted most unwisely in going to Cowperwood; but we shall have to see what can be done."

Schryhart's idea, like that of Hand, was to cause Hull & Stackpole to relinquish all their holdings for nothing to the banks in order that, under pressure, the latter might carry the stocks he and the others had hypothecated with them until such a time as the company might be organized at a profit. At the same time he was intensely resentful against Cowperwood for having by any fluke of circumstance reaped so large a profit as he must have done. Plainly, the present crisis had something to do with him. Schryhart was quick to call up Hand and Arneel, after Stackpole had gone, suggesting a conference, and together, an hour later, at Arneel's office, they foregathered along with Merrill to discuss this new and very interesting development. As a matter of fact, during the course of the afternoon all of these gentlemen had been growing more and more uneasy. Not that between them they were not eminently capable of taking care of their own losses, but the sympathetic effect of such a failure as this (twenty million dollars), to say nothing of its reaction upon the honor of themselves and the city as a financial center, was a most unsatisfactory if not disastrous thing to contemplate, and now this matter of Cowperwood's having gained handsomely by it all was added to their misery. Both Hand and Arneel growled in opposition when they heard, and Merrill meditated, as he usually did, on the wonder of Cowperwood's subtlety. He could not help liking him.

There is a sort of municipal pride latent in the bosoms of most members of a really thriving community which often comes to the surface under the most trying circumstances. These four men were by no means an exception to this rule. Messrs. Schryhart, Hand, Arneel, and Merrill were concerned as to the good name of Chicago and their united standing in the eyes of Eastern financiers. It was a sad blow to them to think that the one great enterprise they had recently engineered—a foil to some of the immense affairs which had recently had their genesis in New York and elsewhere—should have come to so untimely an end. Chicago finance really should not be put to shame in this fashion if it could be avoided. So that when Mr. Schryhart arrived, quite warm and disturbed, and related in detail what he had just learned, his friends listened to him with eager and wary ears.

It was now between five and six o'clock in the afternoon and still blazing outside, though the walls of the buildings on the opposite side of the street were a cool gray, picked out with pools of black shadow. A newsboy's strident voice was heard here and there calling an extra, mingled with the sound of homing feet and street-cars—Cowperwood's street-cars.

"I'll tell you what it is," said Schryhart, finally. "It seems to me we have stood just about enough of this man's beggarly interference. I'll admit that neither Hull nor Stackpole had any right to go to him. They laid themselves and us open to just such a trick as has been worked in this case." Mr. Schryhart was righteously incisive, cold, immaculate, waspish. "At the same time," he continued, "any other moneyed man of equal standing with ourselves would have had the courtesy to confer with us and give us, or at least our banks, an opportunity for taking over these securities. He would have come to our aid for Chicago's sake. He had no occasion for throwing these stocks on the market, considering the state of things. He knows very well what the effect of their failure will be. The whole city is involved, but it's little he cares. Mr. Stackpole tells me that he had an express understanding with him, or, rather, with the men who it is plain have been representing him, that not a single share of this stock was to be thrown on the market. As it is, I venture to say not a single share of it is to be found anywhere in any of their safes. I can sympathize to a certain extent with poor Stackpole. His position, of course, was very trying. But there is no excuse—none in the world—for such a stroke of trickery on Cowperwood's part. It's just as we've known all along—the man is nothing but a wrecker. We certainly ought to find some method of ending his career here if possible."

Mr. Schryhart kicked out his well-rounded legs, adjusted his soft-roll collar, and smoothed his short, crisp, wiry, now blackish-gray mustache. His black eyes flashed an undying hate.

At this point Mr. Arneel, with a cogency of reasoning which did not at the moment appear on the surface, inquired: "Do any of you happen to know anything in particular about the state of Mr. Cowperwood's finances at present? Of course we know of the Lake Street 'L' and the Northwestern. I hear he's building a house in New York, and I presume that's drawing on him somewhat. I know he has four hundred thousand dollars in loans from the Chicago Central; but what else has he?"

"Well, there's the two hundred thousand he owes the Prairie National," piped up Schrybart, promptly. "From time to time I've heard of several other sums that escape my mind just now."

Mr. Merrill, a diplomatic mouse of a man—gray, Parisian, dandified—was twisting in his large chair, surveying the others with shrewd though somewhat propitiatory eyes. In spite of his old grudge against Cowperwood because of the latter's refusal to favor him in the matter of running street-car lines past his store, he had always been interested in the man as a spectacle. He really disliked the thought of plotting to injure Cowperwood. Just the same, he felt it incumbent to play his part in such a council as this. "My financial agent, Mr. Hill, loaned him several hundred thousand not long ago," he volunteered, a little doubtfully. "I presume he has many other outstanding obligations."

Mr. Hand stirred irritably.

"Well, he's owing the Third National and the Lake City as much if not more," he commented. "I know where there are five hundred thousand dollars of his loans that haven't been mentioned here. Colonel Ballinger has two hundred thousand. He must owe Anthony Ewer all of that. He owes the Drovers and Traders all of one hundred and fifty thousand."

On the basis of these suggestions Arneel made a mental calculation, and found that Cowperwood was indebted apparently to the tune of about three million dollars on call, if not more.

"I haven't all the facts," he said, at last, slowly and distinctly. "If we could talk with some of the presidents of our banks to-night, we should probably find that there are other items of which we do not know. I do not like to be severe on any one, but our own situation is serious. Unless something is done to-night Hull & Stackpole will certainly fail in the morning. We are, of course, obligated to the various banks for our loans, and we are in honor bound to do all we can for them. The good name of Chicago and its rank as a banking center is to a certain extent involved. As I have already told Mr. Stackpole and Mr. Hull, I personally have gone as far as I can in this matter. I suppose it is the same with each of you. The only other resources we have under the circumstances are the banks, and they, as I understand it, are pretty much involved with stock on hypothecation. I know at least that this is true of the Lake City and the Douglas Trust."

"It's true of nearly all of them," said Hand. Both Schryhart and Merrill nodded assent.

"We are not obligated to Mr. Cowperwood for anything so far as I know," continued Mr. Arneel, after a slight but somewhat portentous pause. "As Mr. Schryhart has suggested here to-day, he seems to have a tendency to interfere and disturb on every occasion. Apparently he stands obligated to the various banks in the sums we have mentioned. Why shouldn't his loans be called? It would help strengthen the local banks, and possibly permit them to aid in meeting this situation for us. While he might be in a position to retaliate, I doubt it."

Mr. Arneel had no personal opposition to Cowperwood—none, at least, of a deep-seated character. At the same time Hand, Merrill, and Schryhart were his friends. In him, they felt, centered the financial leadership of the city. The rise of Cowperwood, his Napoleonic airs, threatened this. As Mr. Arneel talked he never raised his eyes from the desk where he was sitting. He merely drummed solemnly on the surface with his fingers. The others contemplated him a little tensely, catching quite clearly the drift of his proposal.

"An excellent idea—excellent!" exclaimed Schryhart. "I will join in any programme that looks to the elimination of this man. The present situation may be just what is needed to accomplish this. Anyhow, it may help to solve our difficulty. If so, it will certainly be a case of good coming out of evil."

"I see no reason why these loans should not be called," Hand commented. "I'm willing to meet the situation on that basis."

"And I have no particular objection," said Merrill. "I think, however, it would be only fair to give as much notice as possible of any decision we may reach," he added.

"Why not send for the various bankers now," suggested Schryhart, "and find out exactly where he stands, and how much it will take to carry Hull & Stackpole? Then we can inform Mr. Cowperwood of what we propose to do."

To this proposition Mr. Hand nodded an assent, at the same time consulting a large, heavily engraved gold watch of the most ponderous and inartistic design. "I think," he said, "that we have found the solution to this situation at last. I suggest that we get Candish and Kramer, of the stock-exchange" (he was referring to the president and secretary, respectively, of that organization), "and Simmons, of the Douglas Trust. We should soon be able to tell what we can do."

The library of Mr. Arneel's home was fixed upon as the most suitable rendezvous. Telephones were forthwith set ringing and messengers and telegrams despatched in order that the subsidiary financial luminaries and the watch-dogs of the various local treasuries might come and, as it were, put their seal on this secret decision, which it was obviously presumed no minor official or luminary would have the temerity to gainsay.

CHAPTER XLIX

MOUNT OLYMPUS

By eight o'clock, at which hour the conference was set, the principal financial personages of Chicago were truly in a great turmoil. Messrs. Hand, Schryhart, Merrill, and Arneel were personally interested! What would you? As early as seven-thirty there was a pattering of horses' hoofs and a jingle of harness, as splendid open carriages were drawn up in front of various exclusive mansions and a bank president, or a director at least, issued forth at the call of one of the big quadrumvirate to journey to the home of Mr. Arneel. Such interesting figures as Samuel Blackman, once president of the old Chicago Gas Company, and now a director of the Prairie National; Hudson Baker, once president of the West Chicago Gas Company, and now a director of the Chicago Central National; Ormonde Ricketts, publisher of the Chronicle and director of the Third National; Norrie Simms, president of the Douglas Trust Company; Walter Rysam Cotton, once an active wholesale coffee-broker, but now a director principally of various institutions, were all en route. It was a procession of solemn, superior, thoughtful gentlemen, and all desirous of giving the right appearance and of making the correct impression. For, be it known, of all men none are so proud or vainglorious over the minor trappings of materialism as those who have but newly achieved them. It is so essential apparently to fulfil in manner and air, if not in fact, the principle of "presence" which befits the role of conservator of society and leader of wealth. Every one of those named and many more—to the number of thirty—rode thus loftily forth in the hot, dry evening air and were soon at the door of the large and comfortable home of Mr. Timothy Arneel.

That important personage was not as yet present to receive his guests, and neither were Messrs. Schryhart, Hand, nor Merrill. It would not be fitting for such eminent potentates to receive their underlings in person on such an occasion. At the hour appointed these four were still in their respective offices, perfecting separately the details of the plan upon which they had agreed and which, with a show of informality and of momentary inspiration, they would later present. For the time being their guests had to make the best of their absence. Drinks and liquors were served, but these were of small comfort. A rack provided for straw hats was for some reason not used, every one preferring to retain his own head-gear. Against the background of wood panneling and the chairs covered with summer linen the company presented a galleryesque variety and interest. Messrs. Hull and Stackpole, the corpses or victims over which this serious gathering were about to sit in state, were not actually present within the room, though they were within call in another part of the house, where, if necessary, they could be reached and their advice or explanations heard. This presumably brilliant assemblage of the financial weight and intelligence of the city appeared as solemn as owls under the pressure of a rumored impending financial crisis. Before Arneel's appearance there was a perfect buzz of minor financial gossip, such as:

"You don't say?"

"Is it as serious as that?"

"I knew things were pretty shaky, but I was by no means certain how shaky."

"Fortunately, we are not carrying much of that stock." (This from one of the few really happy bankers.)

"This is a rather serious occasion, isn't it?"

"You don't tell me!"

"Dear, dear!"

Never a word in criticism from any source of either Hand or Schryhart or Arneel or Merrill, though the fact that they were back of the pool was well known. Somehow they were looked upon as benefactors who were calling this conference with a view of saving others from disaster rather than for the purpose of assisting themselves. Such phrases as, "Oh, Mr. Hand! Marvelous man! Marvelous!" or, "Mr. Schryhart—very able—very able indeed!" or, "You may depend on it these men are not going to allow anything serious to overtake the affairs of the city at this time," were heard on every hand. The fact that immense quantities of cash or paper were involved in behalf of one or other of these four was secretly admitted by one banker to another. No rumor that Cowperwood or his friends had been profiting or were in any way involved had come to any one present—not as yet.

At eight-thirty exactly Mr. Arneel first ambled in quite informally, Hand, Schryhart, and Merrill appearing separately very shortly after. Rubbing their hands and mopping their faces with their handkerchiefs, they looked about them, making an attempt to appear as nonchalant and cheerful as possible under such trying circumstances. There were many old acquaintances and friends to greet, inquiries to be made as to the health of wives and children. Mr. Arneel, clad in yellowish linen, with a white silk shirt of lavender stripe, and carrying a palm-leaf fan, seemed quite refreshed; his fine expanse of neck and bosom looked most paternal, and even Abrahamesque. His round, glistening pate exuded beads of moisture. Mr. Schryhart, on the contrary, for all the heat, appeared quite hard and solid, as though he might be carved out of some dark wood. Mr. Hand, much of Mr. Arneel's type, but more solid and apparently more vigorous, had donned for the occasion a blue serge coat with trousers of an almost gaudy, bright stripe. His ruddy, archaic face was at once encouraging and serious, as though he were saying, "My dear children, this is very trying, but we will do the best we can." Mr. Merrill was as cool and ornate and lazy as it was possible for a great merchant to be. To one person and another he extended a cool, soft hand, nodding and smiling half the time in silence. To Mr. Arneel as the foremost citizen and the one of largest wealth fell the duty (by all agreed as most appropriate) of assuming the chair—which in this case was an especially large one at the head of the table.

There was a slight stir as he finally, at the suggestion of Schryhart, went forward and sat down. The other great men found seats.

"Well, gentlemen," began Mr. Arneel, dryly (he had a low, husky voice), "I'll be as brief as I can. This is a very unusual occasion which brings us together. I suppose you all know how it is with Mr. Hull and Mr. Stackpole. American Match is likely to come down with a crash in the morning if something very radical isn't done to-night. It is at the suggestion of a number of men and banks that this meeting is called."

Mr. Arneel had an informal, tete-a-tete way of speaking as if he were sitting on a chaise-longue with one other person.

"The failure," he went on, firmly, "if it comes, as I hope it won't, will make a lot of trouble for a number of banks and private individuals which we would like to avoid, I am sure. The principal creditors of American Match are our local banks and some private individuals who have loaned money on the stock. I have a list of them here, along with the amounts for which they are responsible. It is in the neighborhood of ten millions of dollars."

Mr. Arneel, with the unconscious arrogance of wealth and power, did not trouble to explain how he got the list, neither did he show the slightest perturbation. He merely fished down in one pocket in a heavy way and produced it, spreading it out on the table before him. The company wondered whose names and what amounts were down, and whether it was his intention to read it.

"Now," resumed Mr. Arneel, seriously, "I want to say here that Mr. Stackpole, Mr. Merrill, Mr. Hand, and myself have been to a certain extent investors in this stock, and up to this afternoon we felt it to be our duty, not so much to ourselves as to the various banks which have accepted this stock as collateral and to the city at large, to sustain it as much as possible. We believed in Mr. Hull and Mr. Stackpole. We might have gone still further if there had been any hope that a number of others could carry the stock without seriously injuring themselves; but in view of recent developments we know that this can't be done. For some time Mr. Hull and Mr. Stackpole and the various bank officers have had reason to think that some one has been cutting the ground from under them, and now they know it. It is because of this, and because only concerted action on the part of banks and individuals can save the financial credit of the city at this time, that this meeting is called. Stocks are going to continue to be thrown on the market. It is possible that Hull & Stackpole may have to liquidate in some way. One thing is certain: unless a large sum of money is gathered to meet the claim against them in the morning, they will fail. The trouble is due indirectly, of course, to this silver agitation; but it is due a great deal more, we believe, to a piece of local sharp dealing which has just come to light, and which has really been the cause of putting the financial community in the tight place where it stands to-night. I might as well speak plainly as to this matter. It is the work of one man—Mr. Cowperwood. American Match might have pulled through and the city been have spared the danger which now confronts it if Mr. Hull and Mr. Stackpole had not made the mistake of going to this man."

Mr. Arneel paused, and Mr. Norrie Simms, more excitable than most by temperament, chose to exclaim, bitterly: "The wrecker!" A stir of interest passed over the others accompanied by murmurs of disapproval.

"The moment he got the stock in his hands as collateral," continued Mr. Arneel, solemnly, "and in the face of an agreement not to throw a share on the market, he has been unloading steadily. That is what has been happening yesterday and to-day. Over fifteen thousand shares of this stock, which cannot very well be traced to outside sources, have been thrown on the market, and we have every reason to believe that all of it comes from the same place. The result is that American Match, and Mr. Hull and Mr. Stackpole, are on the verge of collapse."

"The scoundrel!" repeated Mr. Norrie Simms, bitterly, almost rising to his feet. The Douglas Trust Company was heavily interested in American Match.

517

"What an outrage!" commented Mr. Lawrence, of the Prairie National, which stood to lose at least three hundred thousand dollars in shrinkage of values on hypothecated stock alone. To this bank that Cowperwood owed at least three hundred thousand dollars on call.

"Depend on it to find his devil's hoof in it somewhere," observed Jordan Jules, who had never been able to make any satisfactory progress in his fight on Cowperwood in connection with the city council and the development of the Chicago General Company. The Chicago Central, of which he was now a director, was one of the banks from which Cowperwood had judiciously borrowed.

"It's a pity he should be allowed to go on bedeviling the town in this fashion," observed Mr. Sunderland Sledd to his neighbor, Mr. Duane Kingsland, who was a director in a bank controlled by Mr. Hand.

The latter, as well as Schryhart, observed with satisfaction the effect of Mr. Arneel's words on the company.

Mr. Arneel now again fished in his pocket laboriously, and drew forth a second slip of paper which he spread out before him. "This is a time when frankness must prevail," he went on, solemnly, "if anything is to be done, and I am in hopes that we can do something. I have here a memorandum of some of the loans which the local banks have made to Mr. Cowperwood and which are still standing on their books. I want to know if there are any further loans of which any of you happen to know and which you are willing to mention at this time."

He looked solemnly around.

Immediately several loans were mentioned by Mr. Cotton and Mr. Osgood which had not been heard of previously. The company was now very well aware, in a general way, of what was coming.

"Well, gentlemen," continued Mr. Arneel, "I have, previous to this meeting, consulted with a number of our leading men. They agree with me that, since so many banks are in need of funds to carry this situation, and since there is no particular obligation on anybody's part to look after the interests of Mr. Cowperwood, it might be just as well if these loans of his, which are outstanding, were called and the money used to aid the banks and the men who have been behind Mr. Hull and Mr. Stackpole. I have no personal feeling against Mr. Cowperwood—that is, he has never done me any direct injury—but naturally I cannot approve of the course he has seen fit to take in this case. Now, if there isn't money available from some source to enable you gentlemen to turn around, there will be a number of other failures. Runs may be started on a half-dozen banks. Time is the essence of a situation like this, and we haven't any time."

Mr. Arneel paused and looked around. A slight buzz of conversation sprang up, mostly bitter and destructive criticism of Cowperwood.

"It would be only just if he could be made to pay for this," commented Mr. Blackman to Mr. Sledd. "He has been allowed to play fast and loose long enough. It is time some one called a halt on him."

"Well, it looks to me as though it would be done tonight," Mr. Sledd returned.

Meanwhile Mr. Schryhart was again rising to his feet. "I think," he was saying, "if there is no objection on any one's part, Mr. Arneel, as chairman, might call for a formal expression of opinion from the different gentlemen present which will be on record as the sense of this meeting."

At this point Mr. Kingsland, a tall, whiskered gentleman, arose to inquire exactly how it came that Cowperwood had secured these stocks, and whether those present were absolutely sure that the stock has been coming from him or from his friends. "I would not like to think we were doing any man an injustice," he concluded.

In reply to this Mr. Schryhart called in Mr. Stackpole to corroborate him. Some of the stocks had been positively identified. Stackpole related the full story, which somehow seemed to electrify the company, so intense was the feeling against Cowperwood.

"It is amazing that men should be permitted to do things like this and still hold up their heads in the business world," said one, Mr. Vasto, president of the Third National, to his neighbor.

"I should think there would be no difficulty in securing united action in a case of this kind," said Mr. Lawrence, president of the Prairie National, who was very much beholden to Hand for past and present favors.

"Here is a case," put in Schryhart, who was merely waiting for an opportunity to explain further, "in which an unexpected political situation develops an unexpected crisis, and this man uses it for his personal aggrandizement and to the detriment of every other person. The welfare of the city is nothing to him. The stability of the very banks he borrows from is nothing. He is a pariah, and if this opportunity to show him what we think of him and his methods is not used we will be doing less than our duty to the city and to one another."

"Gentlemen," said Mr. Arneel, finally, after Cowperwood's different loans had been carefully tabulated, "don't you think it would be wise to send for Mr. Cowperwood and state to him directly the decision we have reached and the reasons for it? I presume all of us would agree that he should be notified."

"I think he should be notified," said Mr. Merrill, who saw behind this smooth talk the iron club that was being brandished.

Both Hand and Schryhart looked at each other and Arneel while they politely waited for some one else to make a suggestion. When no one ventured, Hand, who was hoping this would prove a ripping blow to Cowperwood, remarked, viciously:

"He might as well be told—if we can reach him. It's sufficient notice, in my judgment. He might as well understand that this is the united action of the leading financial forces of the city."

"Quite so," added Mr. Schryhart. "It is time he understood, I think, what the moneyed men of this community think of him and his crooked ways."

A murmur of approval ran around the room.

"Very well," said Mr. Arneel. "Anson, you know him better than some of the rest of us. Perhaps you had better see if you can get him on the telephone and ask him to call. Tell him that we are here in executive session."

"I think he might take it more seriously if you spoke to him, Timothy," replied Merrill.

Arneel, being always a man of action, arose and left the room, seeking a telephone which was located in a small workroom or office den on the same floor, where he could talk without fear of being overheard.

Sitting in his library on this particular evening, and studying the details of half a dozen art-catalogues which had accumulated during the week, Cowperwood was decidedly conscious of the probable collapse of American Match on the morrow. Through his brokers and agents he was well aware that a conference was on at this hour at the house of Arneel. More than once during the day he had seen bankers and brokers who were anxious about possible shrinkage in connection with various hypothecated securities, and to-night his valet had called him to the 'phone half a dozen times to talk with Addison, with Kaffrath, with a broker by the name of Prosser who had succeeded Laughlin in active control of his private speculations, and also, be it said, with several of the banks whose presidents were at this particular conference. If Cowperwood was hated, mistrusted, or feared by the overlords of these institutions, such was by no means the case with the underlings, some of whom, through being merely civil, were hopeful of securing material benefits from him at some future time. With a feeling of amused satisfaction he was meditating upon how heavily and neatly he had countered on his enemies. Whereas they were speculating as to how to offset their heavy losses on the morrow, he was congratulating himself on corresponding gains. When all his deals should be closed up he would clear within the neighborhood of a million dollars. He did not feel that he had worked Messrs. Hull and Stackpole any great injustice. They were at their wit's end. If he had not seized this opportunity to undercut them Schryhart or Arneel would have done so, anyhow.

Mingled with thoughts of a forthcoming financial triumph were others of Berenice Fleming. There are such things as figments of the brain, even in the heads of colossi. He thought of Berenice early and late; he even dreamed of her. He laughed at himself at times for thus being taken in the toils of a mere girl—the strands of her ruddy hair—but working in Chicago these days he was always conscious of her, of what she was doing, of where she was going in the East, of how happy he would be if they were only together, happily mated.

It had so happened, unfortunately, that in the course of this summer's stay at Narragansett Berenice, among other diversions, had assumed a certain interest in one Lieutenant Lawrence Braxmar, U.S.N., whom she found loitering there, and who was then connected with the naval station at Portsmouth, New Hampshire. Cowperwood, coming East at this time for a few days' stay in order to catch another glimpse of his ideal, had been keenly disturbed by the sight of Braxmar and by what his presence might signify. Up to this time he had not given much thought to younger men in connection with her. Engrossed in her personality, he could think of nothing as being able to stand long between him and the fulfilment of his dreams. Berenice must be his. That radiant spirit, enwrapt in so fair an outward seeming, must come to see and rejoice in him. Yet she was so young and airy in her mood that he sometimes wondered. How was he to draw near? What say exactly? What do? Berenice was in no way hypnotized by either his wealth or fame. She was accustomed (she little knew to what extent by his courtesy) to a world more resplendent in its social security than his own. Surveying Braxmar keenly upon their first meeting, Cowperwood had liked his face and intelligence, had judged him to be able, but had wondered instantly how he could get rid of him. Viewing Berenice and the Lieutenant as they strolled off together along a summery seaside veranda, he had been for once lonely, and had sighed. These uncertain phases of affection could become very trying at times. He wished he were young again, single.

To-night, therefore, this thought was haunting him like a gloomy undertone, when at half past eleven the telephone rang once more, and he heard a low, even voice which said:

"Mr. Cowperwood? This is Mr. Arneel."

"Yes."

"A number of the principal financial men of the city are gathered here at my house this evening. The question of ways and means of preventing a panic to-morrow is up for discussion. As you probably know, Hull & Stackpole are in trouble. Unless something is done for them tonight they will certainly fail to-morrow for twenty million dollars. It isn't so much their failure that we are considering as it is the effect on stocks in general, and on the banks. As I understand it, a number of your loans are involved. The gentlemen here have suggested that I call you up and ask you to come here, if you will, to help us decide what ought to be done. Something very drastic will have to be decided on before morning."

During this speech Cowperwood's brain had been reciprocating like a well-oiled machine.

"My loans?" he inquired, suavely. "What have they to do with the situation? I don't owe Hull & Stackpole anything."

"Very true. But a number of the banks are carrying securities for you. The idea is that a number of these will have to be called—the majority of them—unless some other way can be devised to-night. We thought you might possibly wish to come and talk it over, and that you might be able to suggest some other way out."

"I see," replied Cowperwood, caustically. "The idea is to sacrifice me in order to save Hull & Stackpole. Is that it?"

His eyes, quite as though Arneel were before him, emitted malicious sparks.

"Well, not precisely that," replied Arneel, conservatively; "but something will have to be done. Don't you think you had better come over?"

"Very good. I'll come," was the cheerful reply. "It isn't anything that can be discussed over the 'phone, anyhow."

He hung up the receiver and called for his runabout. On the way over he thanked the prevision which had caused him, in anticipation of some such attack as this, to set aside in the safety vaults of the Chicago Trust Company several millions in low-interest-bearing government bonds. Now, if worst came to worst, these could be drawn on and hypothecated. These men should see at last how powerful he was and how secure.

As he entered the home of Arneel he was a picturesque and truly representative figure of his day. In a light summer suit of cream and gray twill, with a straw hat ornamented by a blue-and-white band, and wearing yellow quarter-shoes of the softest leather, he appeared a very model of trig, well-groomed self-sufficiency. As he was ushered into the room he gazed about him in a brave, leonine way.

"A fine night for a conference, gentlemen," he said, walking toward a chair indicated by Mr. Arneel. "I must say I never saw so many straw hats at a funeral before. I understand that my obsequies are contemplated. What can I do?"

He beamed in a genial, sufficient way, which in any one else would have brought a smile to the faces of the company. In him it was an implication of basic power which secretly enraged and envenomed nearly all those present. They merely stirred in a nervous and wholly antagonistic way. A number of those who knew him personally nodded—Merrill, Lawrence, Simms; but there was no friendly light in their eyes.

"Well, gentlemen?" he inquired, after a moment or two of ominous silence, observing Hand's averted face and Schryhart's eyes, which were lifted ceilingward.

"Mr. Cowperwood," began Mr. Arneel, quietly, in no way disturbed by Cowperwood's jaunty air, "as I told you over the 'phone, this meeting is called to avert, if possible, what is likely to be a very serious panic in the morning. Hull & Stackpole are on the verge of failure. The outstanding loans are considerable—in the neighborhood of seven or eight million here in Chicago. On the other hand, there are assets in the shape of American Match stocks and other properties sufficient to carry them for a while longer if the banks can only continue their loans. As you know, we are all facing a falling market, and the banks are short of ready money. Something has to be done. We have canvassed the situation here to-night as thoroughly as possible, and the general conclusion is that your loans are among the most available assets which can be reached quickly. Mr. Schryhart, Mr. Merrill, Mr. Hand, and myself have done all we can thus far to avert a calamity, but we find that some one with whom Hull & Stackpole have been hypothecating stocks has been feeding them out in order to break the market. We shall know how to avoid that in the future" (and he looked hard at Cowperwood), "but the thing at present is immediate cash, and your loans are the largest and the most available. Do you think you can find the means to pay them back in the morning?"

Arneel blinked his keen, blue eyes solemnly, while the rest, like a pack of genial but hungry wolves, sat and surveyed this apparently whole but now condemned scapegoat and victim. Cowperwood, who was keenly alive to the spirit of the company, looked blandly and fearlessly around. On his knee he held his blue—banded straw hat neatly balanced on one edge. His full mustache curled upward in a jaunty, arrogant way.

"I can meet my loans," he replied, easily. "But I would not advise you or any of the gentlemen present to call them." His voice, for all its lightness, had an ominous ring.

"Why not?" inquired Hand, grimly and heavily, turning squarely about and facing him. "It doesn't appear that you have extended any particular courtesy to Hull or Stackpole." His face was red and scowling.

"Because," replied Cowperwood, smiling, and ignoring the reference to his trick, "I know why this meeting was called. I know that these gentlemen here, who are not saying a word, are mere catspaws and rubber stamps for you and Mr. Schryhart and Mr. Arneel and Mr. Merrill. I know how you four gentlemen have been gambling in this stock, and what your probable losses are, and that it is to save yourselves from further loss that you have decided to make me the scapegoat. I want to tell you here"—and he got up, so that in his full stature he loomed over the room—"you can't do it. You can't make me your catspaw to pull your chestnuts out of the fire, and no rubber-stamp conference can make any such attempt successful. If you want to know what to do, I'll tell you—close the Chicago Stock Exchange to-morrow morning and keep it closed. Then let Hull & Stackpole fail, or if not you four put up the money to carry them. If you can't, let your banks do it. If you open the day by calling a single one of my loans before I am ready to pay it, I'll gut every bank from here to the river. You'll have panic, all the panic you want. Good evening, gentlemen."

He drew out his watch, glanced at it, and quickly walked to the door, putting on his hat as he went. As he bustled jauntily down the wide interior staircase, preceded by a footman to open the door, a murmur of dissatisfaction arose in the room he had just left.

"The wrecker!" re-exclaimed Norrie Simms, angrily, astounded at this demonstration of defiance.

"The scoundrel!" declared Mr. Blackman. "Where does he get the wealth to talk like that?"

"Gentlemen," said Mr. Arneel, stung to the quick by this amazing effrontery, and yet made cautious by the blazing wrath of Cowperwood, "it is useless to debate this question in anger. Mr. Cowperwood evidently refers to loans which can be controlled in his favor, and of which I for one know nothing. I do not see what can be done until we do know. Perhaps some of you can tell us what they are."

But no one could, and after due calculation advice was borrowed of caution. The loans of Frank Algernon Cowperwood were not called.

CHAPTER L

A NEW YORK MANSION

The failure of American Match the next morning was one of those events that stirred the city and the nation and lingered in the minds of men for years. At the last moment it was decided that in lieu of calling Cowperwood's loans Hull & Stackpole had best be sacrificed, the stock-exchange closed, and all trading ended. This protected stocks from at least a quotable decline and left the banks free for several days (ten all told) in which to repair their disrupted finances and buttress themselves against the eventual facts. Naturally, the minor speculators throughout the city—those who had expected to make a fortune out of this crash—raged and complained, but, being faced by an adamantine exchange directorate, a subservient press, and the alliance between the big bankers and the heavy quadrumvirate, there was nothing to be done. The respective bank presidents talked solemnly of "a mere temporary flurry," Hand, Schryhart, Merrill, and Arneel went still further into their pockets to protect their interests, and Cowperwood, triumphant, was roundly denounced by the smaller fry as a "bucaneer," a "pirate," a "wolf"—indeed, any opprobrious term that came into their minds. The larger men faced squarely the fact that here was an enemy worthy of their steel. Would he master them? Was he already the dominant money power in Chicago? Could he thus flaunt their helplessness and his superiority in their eyes and before their underlings and go unwhipped?

"I must give in!" Hosmer Hand had declared to Arneel and Schryhart, at the close of the Arneel house conference and as they stood in consultation after the others had departed. "We seem to be beaten to-night, but I, for one, am not through yet. He has won to-night, but he won't win always. This is a fight to a finish between me and him. The rest of you can stay in or drop out, just as you wish."

"Hear, hear!" exclaimed Schryhart, laying a fervently sympathetic hand on his shoulder. "Every dollar that I have is at your service, Hosmer. This fellow can't win eventually. I'm with you to the end."

Arneel, walking with Merrill and the others to the door, was silent and dour. He had been cavalierly affronted by a man who, but a few short years before, he would have considered a mere underling. Here was Cowperwood bearding the lion in his den, dictating terms to the principal financial figures of the city, standing up trig and resolute, smiling in their faces and telling them in so many words to go to the devil. Mr. Arneel glowered under lowering brows, but what could he do? "We must see," he said to the others, "what time will bring. Just now there is nothing much to do. This crisis has been too sudden. You say you are not through with him, Hosmer, and neither am I. But we must wait. We shall have to break him politically in this city, and I am confident that in the end we can do it." The others were grateful for his courage even though to-morrow he and they must part with millions to protect themselves and the banks. For the first time Merrill concluded that he would have to fight Cowperwood openly from now on, though even yet he admired his courage. "But he is too defiant, too cavalier! A very lion of a man," he said to himself. "A man with the heart of a Numidian lion."

It was true.

From this day on for a little while, and because there was no immediate political contest in sight, there was comparative peace in Chicago, although it more resembled an armed camp operating under the terms of some agreed neutrality than it did anything else. Schryhart, Hand, Arneel, and Merrill were quietly watchful. Cowperwood's chief concern was lest his enemies might succeed in their project of worsting him politically in one or all three of the succeeding elections which were due to occur every two years between now and 1903, at which time his franchises would have to be renewed. As in the past they had made it necessary for him to work against them through bribery and perjury, so in ensuing struggles they might render it more and more difficult for him or his agents to suborn the men elected to office. The subservient and venal councilmen whom he now controlled might be replaced by men who, if no more honest, would be more loyal to the enemy, thus blocking the extension of his franchises. Yet upon a renewal period of at least twenty and preferably fifty years depended the fulfilment of all the colossal things he had begun—his art-collection, his new mansion, his growing prestige as a financier, his rehabilitation socially, and the celebration of his triumph by a union, morganatic or otherwise, with some one who would be worthy to share his throne.

It is curious how that first and most potent tendency of the human mind, ambition, becomes finally dominating. Here was Cowperwood at fifty-seven, rich beyond the wildest dream of the average man, celebrated in a local and in some respects in a national way, who was nevertheless feeling that by no means had his true aims been achieved. He was not yet all-powerful as were divers Eastern magnates, or even these four or five magnificently moneyed men here in Chicago who, by plodding thought and labor in many dreary fields such as Cowperwood himself frequently scorned, had reaped tremendous and uncontended profits. How was it, he asked himself, that his path had almost constantly been strewn with stormy opposition and threatened calamity? Was it due to his private immorality? Other men were immoral; the mass, despite religious dogma and fol-de-rol theory imposed from the top, was generally so. Was it not rather due to his inability to control without dominating personally—without standing out fully and clearly in the sight of all men? Sometimes he thought so. The humdrum conventional world could not brook his daring, his insouciance, his constant desire to call a spade a spade. His genial sufficiency was a taunt and a mockery to many. The hard implication of his eye was dreaded by the weaker as fire is feared by a burnt child. Dissembling enough, he was not sufficiently oily and make-believe.

Well, come what might, he did not need to be or mean to be so, and there the game must lie; but he had not by any means attained the height of his ambition. He was not yet looked upon as a money prince. He could not rank as yet with the magnates of the East—the serried Sequoias of Wall Street. Until he could stand with these men, until he could have a magnificent mansion, acknowledged as such by all, until he could have a world-famous gallery, Berenice, millions—what did it avail?

The character of Cowperwood's New York house, which proved one of the central achievements of his later years, was one of those flowerings—out of disposition which eventuate in the case of men quite as in that of plants. After the passing of the years neither a modified Gothic (such as his Philadelphia house had been), nor a conventionalized Norman-French, after the style of his Michigan Avenue home, seemed suitable to him. Only the Italian palaces of medieval or Renaissance origin which he had seen abroad now appealed to him as examples of what a stately residence should be. He was really seeking something which should not only reflect his private tastes as to a home, but should have the more enduring qualities of a palace or even a museum, which might stand as a monument to his memory. After much searching Cowperwood had found an architect in New York who suited him entirely—one Raymond Pyne, rake, raconteur, man-about-town—who was still first and foremost an artist, with an eye for the exceptional and the perfect. These two spent days and days together meditating on the details of this home museum. An immense gallery was to occupy the west wing of the house and be devoted to pictures; a second gallery should occupy the south wing and be given over to sculpture and large whorls of art; and these two wings were to swing as an L around the house proper, the latter standing in the angle between them. The whole structure was to be of a rich brownstone, heavily carved. For its interior decoration the richest woods, silks, tapestries, glass, and marbles were canvassed. The main rooms were to surround a great central court with a colonnade of pink-veined alabaster, and in the center there would be an electrically lighted fountain of alabaster and silver. Occupying the east wall a series of hanging baskets of orchids, or of other fresh flowers, were to give a splendid glow of color, a morning-sun effect, to this richly artificial realm. One chamber—a lounge on the second floor—was to be entirely lined with thin-cut transparent marble of a peach-blow hue, the lighting coming only through these walls and from without. Here in a perpetual atmosphere of sunrise were to be racks for exotic birds, a trellis of vines, stone benches, a central pool of glistening water, and an echo of music. Pyne assured him that after his death this room would make an excellent chamber in which to exhibit porcelains, jades, ivories, and other small objects of value.

Cowperwood was now actually transferring his possessions to New York, and had persuaded Aileen to accompany him. Fine compound of tact and chicane that he was, he had the effrontery to assure her that they could here create a happier social life. His present plan was to pretend a marital contentment which had no basis solely in order to make this transition period as undisturbed as possible. Subsequently he might get a divorce, or he might make an arrangement whereby his life would be rendered happy outside the social pale.

Of all this Berenice Fleming knew nothing at all. At the same time the building of this splendid mansion eventually awakened her to an understanding of the spirit of art that occupied the center of Cowperwood's iron personality and caused her to take a real interest in him. Before this she had looked on him as a kind of Western interloper coming East and taking advantage of her mother's good nature to scrape a little social courtesy. Now, however, all that Mrs. Carter had been telling her of his personality and achievements was becoming crystallized into a glittering chain of facts. This house, the papers were fond of repeating, would be a jewel of rare workmanship. Obviously the Cowperwoods were going to try to enter society. "What a pity it is," Mrs. Carter once said to Berenice, "that he couldn't have gotten a divorce from his wife before he began all this. I am so afraid they will never be received. He would be if he only had the right woman; but she—" Mrs. Carter, who had once seen Aileen in Chicago, shook her head doubtfully. "She is not the type," was her comment. "She has neither the air nor the understanding."

"If he is so unhappy with her," observed Berenice, thoughtfully, "why doesn't he leave her? She can be happy without him. It is so silly—this cat-and-dog existence. Still I suppose she values the position he gives her," she added, "since she isn't so interesting herself."

"I suppose," said Mrs. Carter, "that he married her twenty years ago, when he was a very different man from what he is to-day. She is not exactly coarse, but not clever enough. She cannot do what he would like to see done. I hate to see mismatings of this kind, and yet they are so common. I do hope, Bevy, that when you marry it will be some one with whom you can get along, though I do believe I would rather see you unhappy than poor."

This was delivered as an early breakfast peroration in Central Park South, with the morning sun glittering on one of the nearest park lakes. Bevy, in spring-green and old-gold, was studying the social notes in one of the morning papers.

"I think I should prefer to be unhappy with wealth than to be without it," she said, idly, without looking up.

Her mother surveyed her admiringly, conscious of her imperious mood. What was to become of her? Would she marry well? Would she marry in time? Thus far no breath of the wretched days in Louisville had affected Berenice. Most of those with whom Mrs. Carter had found herself compelled to deal would be kind enough to keep her secret. But there were others. How near she had been to drifting on the rocks when Cowperwood had appeared!

"After all," observed Berenice, thoughtfully, "Mr. Cowperwood isn't a mere money-grabber, is he? So many of these Western moneyed men are so dull."

"My dear," exclaimed Mrs. Carter, who by now had become a confirmed satellite of her secret protector, "you don't understand him at all. He is a very astonishing man, I tell you. The world is certain to hear a lot more of Frank Cowperwood before he dies. You can say what you please, but some one has to make the money in the first place. It's little enough that good breeding does for you in poverty. I know, because I've seen plenty of our friends come down."

In the new house, on a scaffold one day, a famous sculptor and his assistants were at work on a Greek frieze which represented dancing nymphs linked together by looped wreaths. Berenice and her mother happened to be passing. They stopped to look, and Cowperwood joined them. He waved his hand at the figures of the frieze, and said to Berenice, with his old, gay air, "If they had copied you they would have done better."

"How charming of you!" she replied, with her cool, strange, blue eyes fixed on him. "They are beautiful." In spite of her earlier prejudices she knew now that he and she had one god in common—Art; and that his mind was fixed on things beautiful as on a shrine.

He merely looked at her.

"This house can be little more than a museum to me," he remarked, simply, when her mother was out of hearing; "but I shall build it as perfectly as I can. Perhaps others may enjoy it if I do not."

She looked at him musingly, understandingly, and he smiled. She realized, of course, that he was trying to convey to her that he was lonely.

CHAPTER LI

THE REVIVAL OF HATTIE STARR

Engrossed in the pleasures and entertainments which Cowperwood's money was providing, Berenice had until recently given very little thought to her future. Cowperwood had been most liberal. "She is young," he once said to Mrs. Carter, with an air of disinterested liberality, when they were talking about Berenice and her future. "She is an exquisite. Let her have her day. If she marries well she can pay you back, or me. But give her all she needs now." And he signed checks with the air of a gardener who is growing a wondrous orchid.

The truth was that Mrs. Carter had become so fond of Berenice as an object of beauty, a prospective grande dame, that she would have sold her soul to see her well placed; and as the money to provide the dresses, setting, equipage had to come from somewhere, she had placed her spirit in subjection to Cowperwood and pretended not to see the compromising position in which she was placing all that was near and dear to her.

"Oh, you're so good," she more than once said to him a mist of gratitude commingled with joy in her eyes. "I would never have believed it of any one. But Bevy—"

"An esthete is an esthete," Cowperwood replied. "They are rare enough. I like to see a spirit as fine as hers move untroubled. She will make her way."

Seeing Lieutenant Braxmar in the foreground of Berenice's affairs, Mrs. Carter was foolish enough to harp on the matter in a friendly, ingratiating way. Braxmar was really interesting after his fashion. He was young, tall, muscular, and handsome, a graceful dancer; but, better yet, he represented in his moods lineage, social position, a number of the things which engaged Berenice most. He was intelligent, serious, with a kind of social grace which was gay, courteous, wistful. Berenice met him first at a local dance, where a new step was being practised—"dancing in the barn," as it was called—and so airily did he tread it with her in his handsome uniform that she was half smitten for the moment.

"You dance delightfully," she said. "Is this a part of your life on the ocean wave?"

"Deep-sea-going dancing," he replied, with a heavenly smile. "All battles are accompanied by balls, don't you know?"

"Oh, what a wretched jest!" she replied. "It's unbelievably bad."

"Not for me. I can make much worse ones."

"Not for me," she replied, "I can't stand them." And they went prancing on. Afterward he came and sat by her; they walked in the moonlight, he told her of naval life, his Southern home and connections.

Mrs. Carter, seeing him with Berenice, and having been introduced, observed the next morning, "I like your Lieutenant, Bevy. I know some of his relatives well. They come from the Carolinas. He's sure to come into money. The whole family is wealthy. Do you think he might be interested in you?"

"Oh, possibly—yes, I presume so," replied Berenice, airily, for she did not take too kindly to this evidence of parental interest. She preferred to see life drift on in some nebulous way at present, and this was bringing matters too close to home. "Still, he has so much machinery on his mind I doubt whether he could take any serious interest in a woman. He is almost more of a battle-ship than he is a man."

She made a mouth, and Mrs. Carter commented gaily: "You rogue! All the men take an interest in you. You don't think you could care for him, then, at all?"

"Why, mother, what a question! Why do you ask? Is it so essential that I should?"

"Oh, not that exactly," replied Mrs. Carter, sweetly, bracing herself for a word which she felt incumbent upon her; "but think of his position. He comes of such a good family, and he must be heir to a considerable fortune in his own right. Oh, Bevy, I don't want to hurry or spoil your life in any way, but do keep in mind the future. With your tastes and instincts money is so essential, and unless you marry it I don't know where you are to get it. Your father was so thoughtless, and Rolfe's was even worse."

She sighed.

Berenice, for almost the first time in her life, took solemn heed of this thought. She pondered whether she could endure Braxmar as a life partner, follow him around the world, perhaps retransferring her abode to the South; but she could not make up her mind. This suggestion on the part of her mother rather poisoned the cup for her. To tell the truth, in this hour of doubt her thoughts turned vaguely to Cowperwood as one who represented in his avid way more of the things she truly desired. She remembered his wealth, his plaint that his new house could be only a museum, the manner in which he approached her with looks and voiceless suggestions. But he was old and married—out of the question, therefore—and Braxmar was young and charming. To think her mother should have been so tactless as to suggest the necessity for consideration in his case! It almost spoiled him for her. And was their financial state, then, as uncertain as her mother indicated?

In this crisis some of her previous social experiences became significant. For instance, only a few weeks previous to her meeting with Braxmar she had been visiting at the country estate of the Corscaden Batjers, at Redding Hills, Long Island, and had been sitting with her hostess in the morning room of Hillcrest, which commanded a lovely though distant view of Long Island Sound.

Mrs. Fredericka Batjer was a chestnut blonde, fair, cool, quiescent—a type out of Dutch art. Clad in a morning gown of gray and silver, her hair piled in a Psyche knot, she had in her lap on this occasion a Java basket filled with some attempt at Norwegian needlework.

"Bevy," she said, "you remember Kilmer Duelma, don't you? Wasn't he at the Haggertys' last summer when you were there?"

Berenice, who was seated at a small Chippendale writing-desk penning letters, glanced up, her mind visioning for the moment the youth in question. Kilmer Duelma—tall, stocky, swaggering, his clothes the loose, nonchalant perfection of the season, his walk ambling, studied, lackadaisical, aimless, his color high, his cheeks full, his eyes a little vacuous, his mind acquiescing in a sort of genial, inconsequential way to every query and thought that was put to him. The younger of the two sons of Auguste Duelma, banker, promoter, multimillionaire, he would come into a fortune estimated roughly at between six and eight millions. At the Haggertys' the year before he had hung about her in an aimless fashion.

Mrs. Batjer studied Berenice curiously for a moment, then returned to her needlework. "I've asked him down over this week-end," she suggested.

"Yes?" queried Berenice, sweetly. "Are there others?"

"Of course," assented Mrs. Batjer, remotely. "Kilmer doesn't interest you, I presume."

Berenice smiled enigmatically.

"You remember Clarissa Faulkner, don't you, Bevy?" pursued Mrs. Batjer. "She married Romulus Garrison."

"Perfectly. Where is she now?"

"They have leased the Chateau Brieul at Ars for the winter. Romulus is a fool, but Clarissa is so clever. You know she writes that she is holding a veritable court there this season. Half the smart set of Paris and London are dropping in. It is so charming for her to be able to do those things now. Poor dear! At one time I was quite troubled over her."

Without giving any outward sign Berenice did not fail to gather the full import of the analogy. It was all true. One must begin early to take thought of one's life. She suffered a disturbing sense of duty. Kilmer Duelma arrived at noon Friday with six types of bags, a special valet, and a preposterous enthusiasm for polo and hunting (diseases lately acquired from a hunting set in the Berkshires). A cleverly contrived compliment supposed to have emanated from Miss Fleming and conveyed to him with tact by Mrs. Batjer brought him ambling into Berenice's presence suggesting a Sunday drive to Saddle Rock.

"Haw! haw! You know, I'm delighted to see you again. Haw! haw! It's been an age since I've seen the Haggertys. We missed you after you left. Haw! haw! I did, you know. Since I saw you I have taken up polo—three ponies with me all the time now—haw! haw!—a regular stable nearly."

Berenice strove valiantly to retain a serene interest. Duty was in her mind, the Chateau Brieul, the winter court of Clarissa Garrison, some first premonitions of the flight of time. Yet the drive was a bore, conversation a burden, the struggle to respond titanic, impossible. When Monday came she fled, leaving three days between that and a week-end at Morristown. Mrs. Batjer—who read straws most capably—sighed. Her own Corscaden was not much beyond his money, but life must be lived and the ambitious must inherit wealth or gather it wisely. Some impossible scheming silly would soon collect Duelma, and then— She considered Berenice a little difficult.

Berenice could not help piecing together the memory of this incident with her mother's recent appeal in behalf of Lieutenant Braxmar. A great, cloying, disturbing, disintegrating factor in her life was revealed by the dawning discovery that she and her mother were without much money, that aside from her lineage she was in a certain sense an interloper in society. There were never rumors of great wealth in connection with her—no flattering whispers or public notices regarding her station as an heiress. All the smug minor manikins of the social world were on the qui vive for some cotton-headed doll of a girl with an endless bank-account. By nature sybaritic, an intense lover of art fabrics, of stately functions, of power and success in every form, she had been dreaming all this while of a great soul-freedom and art-freedom under some such circumstances as the greatest individual wealth of the day, and only that, could provide. Simultaneously she had vaguely cherished the idea that if she ever found some one who was truly fond of her, and whom she could love or even admire intensely—some one who needed her in a deep, sincere way—she would give herself freely and gladly. Yet who could it be? She had been charmed by Braxmar, but her keen, analytic intelligence required some one harder, more vivid, more ruthless, some one who would appeal to her as an immense force. Yet she must be conservative, she must play what cards she had to win.

During his summer visit at Narragansett Cowperwood had not been long disturbed by the presence of Braxmar, for, having received special orders, the latter was compelled to hurry away to Hampton Roads. But the following November, forsaking temporarily his difficult affairs in Chicago for New York and the Carter apartment in Central Park South, Cowperwood again encountered the Lieutenant, who arrived one evening brilliantly arrayed in full official regalia in order to escort Berenice to a ball. A high military cap surmounting his handsome face, his epaulets gleaming in gold, the lapels of his cape thrown back to reveal a handsome red silken lining, his sword clanking by his side, he seemed a veritable singing flame of youth. Cowperwood, caught in the drift of circumstance—age, unsuitableness, the flaring counter-attractions of romance and vigor—fairly writhed in pain.

Berenice was so beautiful in a storm of diaphanous clinging garments. He stared at them from an adjacent room, where he pretended to be reading, and sighed. Alas, how was his cunning and foresight—even his—to overcome the drift of life itself? How was he to make himself appealing to youth? Braxmar had the years, the color, the bearing. Berenice seemed to-night, as she prepared to leave, to be fairly seething with youth, hope, gaiety. He arose after a few moments and, giving business as an excuse, hurried away. But it was only to sit in his own rooms in a neighboring hotel and meditate. The logic of the ordinary man under such circumstances, compounded of the age-old notions of chivalry, self-sacrifice, duty to higher impulses, and the like, would have been to step aside in favor of youth, to give convention its day, and retire in favor of morality and virtue. Cowperwood saw things in no such moralistic or altruistic light. "I satisfy myself," had ever been his motto, and under that, however much he might sympathize with Berenice in love or with love itself, he was not content to withdraw until he was sure that the end of hope for him had really come. There had been moments between him and Berenice—little approximations toward intimacy—which had led him to believe that by no means was she seriously opposed to him. At the same time this business of the Lieutenant, so Mrs. Carter confided to him a little later, was not to be regarded lightly. While Berenice might not care so much, obviously Braxmar did.

"Ever since he has been away he has been storming her with letters," she remarked to Cowperwood, one afternoon. "I don't think he is the kind that can be made to take no for an answer.

"A very successful kind," commented Cowperwood, dryly. Mrs. Carter was eager for advice in the matter. Braxmar was a man of parts. She knew his connections. He would inherit at least six hundred thousand dollars at his father's death, if not more. What about her Louisville record? Supposing that should come out later? Would it not be wise for Berenice to marry, and have the danger over with?

"It is a problem, isn't it?" observed Cowperwood, calmly. "Are you sure she's in love?"

"Oh, I wouldn't say that, but such things so easily turn into love. I have never believed that Berenice could be swept off her feet by any one—she is so thoughtful—but she knows she has her own way to make in the world, and Mr. Braxmar is certainly eligible. I know his cousins, the Clifford Porters, very well."

Cowperwood knitted his brows. He was sick to his soul with this worry over Berenice. He felt that he must have her, even at the cost of inflicting upon her a serious social injury. Better that she should surmount it with him than escape it with another. It so happened, however, that the final grim necessity of acting on any such idea was spared him.

Imagine a dining-room in one of the principal hotels of New York, the hour midnight, after an evening at the opera, to which Cowperwood, as host, had invited Berenice, Lieutenant Braxmar, and Mrs. Carter. He was now playing the role of disinterested host and avuncular mentor.

His attitude toward Berenice, meditating, as he was, a course which should be destructive to Braxmar, was gentle, courteous, serenely thoughtful. Like a true Mephistopheles he was waiting, surveying Mrs. Carter and Berenice, who were seated in front chairs clad in such exotic draperies as opera-goers affect—Mrs. Carter in pale-lemon silk and diamonds; Berenice in purple and old-rose, with a jeweled comb in her hair. The Lieutenant in his dazzling uniform smiled and talked blandly, complimented the singers, whispered pleasant nothings to Berenice, descanted at odd moments to Cowperwood on naval personages who happened to be present. Coming out of the opera and driving through blowy, windy streets to the Waldorf, they took the table reserved for them, and Cowperwood, after consulting with regard to the dishes and ordering the wine, went back reminiscently to the music, which had been "La Boheme." The death of Mimi and the grief of Rodolph, as voiced by the splendid melodies of Puccini, interested him.

"That makeshift studio world may have no connection with the genuine professional artist, but it's very representative of life," he remarked.

"I don't know, I'm sure," said Braxmar, seriously.

"All I know of Bohemia is what I have read in books—Trilby, for instance, and—" He could think of no other, and stopped. "I suppose it is that way in Paris."

He looked at Berenice for confirmation and to win a smile. Owing to her mobile and sympathetic disposition, she had during the opera been swept from period to period by surges of beauty too gay or pathetic for words, but clearly comprehended of the spirit. Once when she had been lost in dreamy contemplation, her hands folded on her knees, her eyes fixed on the stage, both Braxmar and Cowperwood had studied her parted lips and fine profile with common impulses of emotion and enthusiasm. Realizing after the mood was gone that they had been watching her, Berenice had continued the pose for a moment, then had waked as from a dream with a sigh. This incident now came back to her as well as her feeling in regard to the opera generally.

"It is very beautiful," she said; "I do not know what to say. People are like that, of course. It is so much better than just dull comfort. Life is really finest when it's tragic, anyhow."

She looked at Cowperwood, who was studying her; then at Braxmar, who saw himself for the moment on the captain's bridge of a battle-ship commanding in time of action. To Cowperwood came back many of his principal moments of difficulty. Surely his life had been sufficiently dramatic to satisfy her.

"I don't think I care so much for it," interposed Mrs. Carter. "One gets tired of sad happenings. We have enough drama in real life."

Cowperwood and Braxmar smiled faintly. Berenice looked contemplatively away. The crush of diners, the clink of china and glass, the bustling to and fro of waiters, and the strumming of the orchestra diverted her somewhat, as did the nods and smiles of some entering guests who recognized Braxmar and herself, but not Cowperwood.

Suddenly from a neighboring door, opening from the men's cafe and grill, there appeared the semi-intoxicated figure of an ostensibly swagger society man, his clothing somewhat awry, an opera-coat hanging loosely from one shoulder, a crush-opera-hat dangling in one hand, his eyes a little bloodshot, his under lip protruding slightly and defiantly, and his whole visage proclaiming that devil-may-care, superior, and malicious aspect which the drunken rake does not so much assume as achieve. He looked sullenly, uncertainly about; then, perceiving Cowperwood and his party, made his way thither in the half-determined, half-inconsequential fashion of one not quite sound after his cups. When he was directly opposite Cowperwood's table—the cynosure of a number of eyes—he suddenly paused as if in recognition, and, coming over, laid a genial and yet condescending hand on Mrs. Carter's bare shoulder.

"Why, hello, Hattie!" he called, leeringly and jeeringly. "What are you doing down here in New York? You haven't given up your business in Louisville, have you, eh, old sport? Say, lemme tell you something. I haven't had a single decent girl since you left—not one. If you open a house down here, let me know, will you?"

He bent over her smirkingly and patronizingly the while he made as if to rummage in his white waistcoat pocket for a card. At the same moment Cowperwood and Braxmar, realizing quite clearly the import of his words, were on their feet. While Mrs. Carter was pulling and struggling back from the stranger, Braxmar's hand (he being the nearest) was on him, and the head waiter and two assistants had appeared.

"What is the trouble here? What has he done?" they demanded.

Meanwhile the intruder, leering contentiously at them all, was exclaiming in very audible tones: "Take your hands off. Who are you? What the devil have you got to do with this? Don't you think I know what I'm about? She knows me—don't you, Hattie? That's Hattie Starr, of Louisville—ask her! She kept one of the swellest ever run in Louisville. What do you people want to be so upset about? I know what I'm doing. She knows me."

He not only protested, but contested, and with some vehemence. Cowperwood, Braxmar, and the waiters forming a cordon, he was shoved and hustled out into the lobby and the outer entranceway, and an officer was called.

"This man should be arrested," Cowperwood protested, vigorously, when the latter appeared. "He has grossly insulted lady guests of mine. He is drunk and disorderly, and I wish to make that charge. Here is my card. Will you let me know where to come?" He handed it over, while Braxmar, scrutinizing the stranger with military care, added: "I should like to thrash you within an inch of your life. If you weren't drunk I would. If you are a gentleman and have a card I want you to give it to me. I want to talk to you later." He leaned over and presented a cold, hard face to that of Mr. Beales Chadsey, of Louisville, Kentucky.

"Tha's all right, Captain," leered Chadsey, mockingly. "I got a card. No harm done. Here you are. You c'n see me any time you want—Hotel Buckingham, Fifth Avenue and Fiftieth Street. I got a right to speak to anybody I please, where I please, when I please. See?"

He fumbled and protested while the officer stood by read to take him in charge. Not finding a card, he added: "Tha's all right. Write it down. Beales Chadsey, Hotel Buckingham, or Louisville, Kentucky. See me any time you want to. Tha's Hattie Starr. She knows me. I couldn't make a mistake about her—not once in a million. Many's the night I spent in her house."

Braxmar was quite ready to lunge at him had not the officer intervened.

Back in the dining-room Berenice and her mother were sitting, the latter quite flustered, pale, distrait, horribly taken aback—by far too much distressed for any convincing measure of deception.

"Why, the very idea!" she was saying. "That dreadful man! How terrible! I never saw him before in my life."

Berenice, disturbed and nonplussed, was thinking of the familiar and lecherous leer with which the stranger had addressed her mother—the horror, the shame of it. Could even a drunken man, if utterly mistaken, be so defiant, so persistent, so willing to explain? What shameful things had she been hearing?

"Come, mother," she said, gently, and with dignity; "never mind, it is all right. We can go home at once. You will feel better when you are out of here."

She called a waiter and asked him to say to the gentlemen that they had gone to the women's dressing-room. She pushed an intervening chair out of the way and gave her mother her arm.

533

"To think I should be so insulted," Mrs. Carter mumbled on, "here in a great hotel, in the presence of Lieutenant Braxmar and Mr. Cowperwood! This is too dreadful. Well, I never."

She half whimpered as she walked; and Berenice, surveying the room with dignity, a lofty superiority in her face, led solemnly forth, a strange, lacerating pain about her heart. What was at the bottom of these shameful statements? Why should this drunken roisterer have selected her mother, of all other women in the dining-room, for the object of these outrageous remarks? Why should her mother be stricken, so utterly collapsed, if there were not some truth in what he had said? It was very strange, very sad, very grim, very horrible. What would that gossiping, scandal-loving world of which she knew so much say to a scene like this? For the first time in her life the import and horror of social ostracism flashed upon her.

The following morning, owing to a visit paid to the Jefferson Market Police Court by Lieutenant Braxmar, where he proposed, if satisfaction were not immediately guaranteed, to empty cold lead into Mr. Beales Chadsey's stomach, the following letter on Buckingham stationery was written and sent to Mrs. Ira George Carter—36 Central Park South:

DEAR MADAM:

Last evening, owing to a drunken debauch, for which I have no satisfactory or suitable explanation to make, I was the unfortunate occasion of an outrage upon your feelings and those of your daughter and friends, for which I wish most humbly to apologize. I cannot tell you how sincerely I regret whatever I said or did, which I cannot now clearly recall. My mental attitude when drinking is both contentious and malicious, and while in this mood and state I was the author of statements which I know to be wholly unfounded. In my drunken stupor I mistook you for a certain notorious woman of Louisville—why, I have not the slightest idea. For this wholly shameful and outrageous conduct I sincerely ask your pardon—beg your forgiveness. I do not know what amends I can make, but anything you may wish to suggest I shall gladly do. In the mean while I hope you will accept this letter in the spirit in which it is written and as a slight attempt at recompense which I know can never fully be made.

Very sincerely,
BEALES CHADSEY.

At the same time Lieutenant Braxmar was fully aware before this letter was written or sent that the charges implied against Mrs. Carter were only too well founded. Beales Chadsey had said drunk what twenty men in all sobriety and even the police at Louisville would corroborate. Chadsey had insisted on making this clear to Braxmar before writing the letter.

CHAPTER LII

BEHIND THE ARRAS

Berenice, perusing the apology from Beales Chadsey, which her mother—very much fagged and weary—handed her the next morning, thought that it read like the overnight gallantry of some one who was seeking to make amends without changing his point of view. Mrs.

Carter was too obviously self-conscious. She protested too much. Berenice knew that she could find out for herself if she chose, but would she choose? The thought sickened her, and yet who was she to judge too severely?

Cowperwood came in bright and early to put as good a face on the matter as he could. He explained how he and Braxmar had gone to the police station to make a charge; how Chadsey, sobered by arrest, had abandoned his bravado and humbly apologized. When viewing the letter handed him by Mrs. Carter he exclaimed:

"Oh yes. He was very glad to promise to write that if we would let him off. Braxmar seemed to think it was necessary that he should. I wanted the judge to impose a fine and let it go at that. He was drunk, and that's all there was to it."

He assumed a very unknowing air when in the presence of Berenice and her mother, but when alone with the latter his manner changed completely.

"Brazen it out," he commanded. "It doesn't amount to anything. Braxmar doesn't believe that this man really knows anything. This letter is enough to convince Berenice. Put a good face on it; more depends on your manner than on anything else. You're much too upset. That won't do at all; you'll tell the whole story that way."

At the same time he privately regarded this incident as a fine windfall of chance—in all likelihood the one thing which would serve to scare the Lieutenant away. Outwardly, however, he demanded effrontery, assumption; and Mrs. Carter was somewhat cheered, but when she was alone she cried. Berenice, coming upon her accidentally and finding her eyes wet, exclaimed:

"Oh, mother, please don't be foolish. How can you act this way? We had better go up in the country and rest a little while if you are so unstrung."

Mrs. Carter protested that it was merely nervous reaction, but to Berenice it seemed that where there was so much smoke there must be some fire.

Her manner in the aftermath toward Braxmar was gracious, but remote. He called the next day to say how sorry he was, and to ask her to a new diversion. She was sweet, but distant. In so far as she was concerned it was plain that the Beales Chadsey incident was closed, but she did not accept his invitation.

"Mother and I are planning to go to the country for a few days," she observed, genially. "I can't say just when we shall return, but if you are still here we shall meet, no doubt. You must be sure and come to see us." She turned to an east court-window, where the morning sun was gleaming on some flowers in a window-box, and began to pinch off a dead leaf here and there.

Braxmar, full of the tradition of American romance, captivated by her vibrant charm, her poise and superiority under the circumstances, her obvious readiness to dismiss him, was overcome, as the human mind frequently is, by a riddle of the spirit, a chemical reaction as mysterious to its victim as to one who is its witness. Stepping forward with a motion that was at once gallant, reverent, eager, unconscious, he exclaimed:

"Berenice! Miss Fleming! Please don't send me away like this. Don't leave me. It isn't anything I have done, is it? I am mad about you. I can't bear to think that anything that has happened could make any difference between you and me. I haven't had the courage to tell you before, but I want to tell you now. I have been in love with you from the very first night I saw you. You are such a wonderful girl! I don't feel that I deserve you, but I love you. I love you with all the honor and force in me. I admire and respect you. Whatever may or may not be true, it is all one and the same to me. Be my wife, will you? Marry me, please! Oh, I'm not fit to be the lacer of your shoes, but I have position and I'll make a name for myself, I hope. Oh, Berenice!" He extended his arms in a dramatic fashion, not outward, but downward, stiff and straight, and declared: "I don't know what I shall do without you. Is there no hope for me at all?"

An artist in all the graces of sex—histrionic, plastic, many-faceted—Berenice debated for the fraction of a minute what she should do and say. She did not love the Lieutenant as he loved her by any means, and somehow this discovery concerning her mother shamed her pride, suggesting an obligation to save herself in one form or another, which she resented bitterly. She was sorry for his tactless proposal at this time, although she knew well enough the innocence and virtue of the emotion from which it sprung.

"Really, Mr. Braxmar," she replied, turning on him with solemn eyes, "you mustn't ask me to decide that now. I know how you feel. I'm afraid, though, that I may have been a little misleading in my manner. I didn't mean to be. I'm quite sure you'd better forget your interest in me for the present anyhow. I could only make up my mind in one way if you should insist. I should have to ask you to forget me entirely. I wonder if you can see how I feel—how it hurts me to say this?"

She paused, perfectly poised, yet quite moved really, as charming a figure as one would have wished to see—part Greek, part Oriental—contemplative, calculating.

In that moment, for the first time, Braxmar realized that he was talking to some one whom he could not comprehend really. She was strangely self-contained, enigmatic, more beautiful perhaps because more remote than he had ever seen her before. In a strange flash this young American saw the isles of Greece, Cytherea, the lost Atlantis, Cyprus, and its Paphian shrine. His eyes burned with a strange, comprehending luster; his color, at first high, went pale.

"I can't believe you don't care for me at all, Miss Berenice," he went on, quite strainedly. "I felt you did care about me. But here," he added, all at once, with a real, if summoned, military force, "I won't bother you. You do understand me. You know how I feel. I won't change. Can't we be friends, anyhow?"

He held out his hand, and she took it, feeling now that she was putting an end to what might have been an idyllic romance.

"Of course we can," she said. "I hope I shall see you again soon."

After he was gone she walked into the adjoining room and sat down in a wicker chair, putting her elbows on her knees and resting her chin in her hands. What a denouement to a thing so innocent, so charming! And now he was gone. She would not see him any more, would not want to see him—not much, anyhow. Life had sad, even ugly facts. Oh yes, yes, and she was beginning to perceive them clearly.

Some two days later, when Berenice had brooded and brooded until she could endure it no longer, she finally went to Mrs. Carter and said: "Mother, why don't you tell me all about this Louisville matter so that I may really know? I can see something is worrying you. Can't you trust me? I am no longer a child by any means, and I am your daughter. It may help me to straighten things out, to know what to do."

Mrs. Carter, who had always played a game of lofty though loving motherhood, was greatly taken aback by this courageous attitude. She flushed and chilled a little; then decided to lie.

"I tell you there was nothing at all," she declared, nervously and pettishly. "It is all an awful mistake. I wish that dreadful man could be punished severely for what he said to me. To be outraged and insulted this way before my own child!"

"Mother," questioned Berenice, fixing her with those cool, blue eyes, "why don't you tell me all about Louisville? You and I shouldn't have things between us. Maybe I can help you."

All at once Mrs. Carter, realizing that her daughter was no longer a child nor a mere social butterfly, but a woman superior, cool, sympathetic, with intuitions much deeper than her own, sank into a heavily flowered wing-chair behind her, and, seeking a small pocket-handkerchief with one hand, placed the other over her eyes and began to cry.

"I was so driven, Bevy, I didn't know which way to turn. Colonel Gillis suggested it. I wanted to keep you and Rolfe in school and give you a chance. It isn't true—anything that horrible man said. It wasn't anything like what he suggested. Colonel Gillis and several others wanted me to rent them bachelor quarters, and that's the way it all came about. It wasn't my fault; I couldn't help myself, Bevy."

"And what about Mr. Cowperwood?" inquired Berenice curiously. She had begun of late to think a great deal about Cowperwood. He was so cool, deep, dynamic, in a way resourceful, like herself.

"There's nothing about him," replied Mrs. Carter, looking up defensively. Of all her men friends she best liked Cowperwood. He had never advised her to evil ways or used her house as a convenience to himself alone. "He never did anything but help me out. He advised me to give up my house in Louisville and come East and devote myself to looking after you and Rolfe. He offered to help me until you two should be able to help yourselves, and so I came. Oh, if I had only not been so foolish—so afraid of life! But your father and Mr. Carter just ran through everything."

She heaved a deep, heartfelt sigh.

"Then we really haven't anything at all, have we, mother—property or anything else?"

Mrs. Carter shook her head, meaning no.

"And the money we have been spending is Mr. Cowperwood's?"

"Yes."

Berenice paused and looked out the window over the wide stretch of park which it commanded. Framed in it like a picture were a small lake, a hill of trees, with a Japanese pagoda effect in the foreground. Over the hill were the yellow towering walls of a great hotel in Central Park West. In the street below could be heard the jingle of street-cars. On a road in the park could be seen a moving line of pleasure vehicles—society taking an airing in the chill November afternoon.

"Poverty, ostracism," she thought. And should she marry rich? Of course, if she could. And whom should she marry? The Lieutenant? Never. He was really not masterful enough mentally, and he had witnessed her discomfiture. And who, then? Oh, the long line of sillies, light-weights, rakes, ne'er-do-wells, who, combined with sober, prosperous, conventional, muddle-headed oofs, constituted society. Here and there, at far jumps, was a real man, but would he be interested in her if he knew the whole truth about her?

"Have you broken with Mr. Braxmar?" asked her mother, curiously, nervously, hopefully, hopelessly.

"I haven't seen him since," replied Berenice, lying conservatively. "I don't know whether I shall or not. I want to think." She arose. "But don't you mind, mother. Only I wish we had some other way of living besides being dependent on Mr. Cowperwood."

She walked into her boudoir, and before her mirror began to dress for a dinner to which she had been invited. So it was Cowperwood's money that had been sustaining them all during the last few years; and she had been so liberal with his means—so proud, vain, boastful, superior. And he had only fixed her with those inquiring, examining eyes. Why? But she did not need to ask herself why. She knew now. What a game he had been playing, and what a silly she had been not to see it. Did her mother in any way suspect? She doubted it. This queer, paradoxical, impossible world! The eyes of Cowperwood burned at her as she thought.

CHAPTER LIII

A DECLARATION OF LOVE

For the first time in her life Berenice now pondered seriously what she could do. She thought of marriage, but decided that instead of sending for Braxmar or taking up some sickening chase of an individual even less satisfactory it might be advisable to announce in a simple social way to her friends that her mother had lost her money, and that she herself was now compelled to take up some form of employment—the teaching of dancing, perhaps, or the practice of it professionally. She suggested this calmly to her mother one day. Mrs. Carter, who had been long a parasite really, without any constructive monetary notions of real import, was terrified. To think that she and "Bevy," her wonderful daughter, and by reaction her son, should come to anything so humdrum and prosaic as ordinary struggling life, and after all her dreams. She sighed and cried in secret, writing Cowperwood a cautious explanation and asking him to see her privately in New York when he returned.

"Don't you think we had best go on a little while longer?" she suggested to Berenice. "It just wrings my heart to think that you, with your qualifications, should have to stoop to giving dancing-lessons. We had better do almost anything for a while yet. You can make a suitable marriage, and then everything will be all right for you. It doesn't matter about me. I can live. But you—" Mrs. Carter's strained eyes indicated the misery she felt. Berenice was moved by this affection for her, which she knew to be genuine; but what a fool her mother had been, what a weak reed, indeed, she was to lean upon! Cowperwood, when he conferred with

Mrs. Carter, insisted that Berenice was quixotic, nervously awry, to wish to modify her state, to eschew society and invalidate her wondrous charm by any sort of professional life. By prearrangement with Mrs. Carter he hurried to Pocono at a time when he knew that Berenice was there alone. Ever since the Beales Chadsey incident she had been evading him.

When he arrived, as he did about one in the afternoon of a crisp January day, there was snow on the ground, and the surrounding landscape was bathed in a crystalline light that gave back to the eye endless facets of luster—jewel beams that cut space with a flash. The automobile had been introduced by now, and he rode in a touring-car of eighty horse-power that gave back from its dark-brown, varnished surface a lacquered light. In a great fur coat and cap of round, black lamb's-wool he arrived at the door.

"Well, Bevy," he exclaimed, pretending not to know of Mrs. Carter's absence, "how are you? How's your mother? Is she in?"

Berenice fixed him with her cool, steady-gazing eyes, as frank and incisive as they were daring, and smiled him an equivocal welcome. She wore a blue denim painter's apron, and a palette of many colors glistened under her thumb. She was painting and thinking—thinking being her special occupation these days, and her thoughts had been of Braxmar, Cowperwood, Kilmer Duelma, a half-dozen others, as well as of the stage, dancing, painting. Her life was in a melting-pot, as it were, before her; again it was like a disarranged puzzle, the pieces of which might be fitted together into some interesting picture if she could but endure.

"Do come in," she said. "It's cold, isn't it? Well, there's a nice fire here for you. No, mother isn't here. She went down to New York. I should think you might have found her at the apartment. Are you in New York for long?"

She was gay, cheerful, genial, but remote. Cowperwood felt the protective gap that lay between him and her. It had always been there. He felt that, even though she might understand and like him, yet there was something—convention, ambition, or some deficiency on his part—that was keeping her from him, keeping her eternally distant.

He looked about the room, at the picture she was attempting (a snow-scape, of a view down a slope), at the view itself which he contemplated from the window, at some dancing sketches she had recently executed and hung on the wall for the time being—lovely, short tunic motives. He looked at her in her interesting and becoming painter's apron. "Well, Berenice," he said, "always the artist first. It is your world. You will never escape it. These things are beautiful." He waved an ungloved hand in the direction of a choric line. "It wasn't your mother I came to see, anyhow. It is you. I had such a curious letter from her. She tells me you want to give up society and take to teaching or something of that sort. I came because I wanted to talk to you about that. Don't you think you are acting rather hastily?"

He spoke now as though there were some reason entirely disassociated from himself that was impelling him to this interest in her.

Berenice, brush in hand, standing by her picture, gave him a look that was cool, curious, defiant, equivocal.

"No, I don't think so," she replied, quietly. "You know how things have been, so I may speak quite frankly. I know that mother's intentions were always of the best."

Her mouth moved with the faintest touch of sadness. "Her heart, I am afraid, is better than her head. As for your motives, I am satisfied to believe that they have been of the best also. I know that they have been, in fact—it would be ungenerous of me to suggest anything else." (Cowperwood's fixed eyes, it seemed to her, had moved somewhere in their deepest depths.) "Yet I don't feel we can go on as we have been doing. We have no money of our own. Why shouldn't I do something? What else can I really do?"

She paused, and Cowperwood gazed at her, quite still. In her informal, bunchy painter's apron, and with her blue eyes looking out at him from beneath her loose red hair, it seemed to him she was the most perfect thing he had ever known. Such a keen, fixed, enthroned mind. She was so capable, so splendid, and, like his own, her eyes were unafraid. Her spiritual equipoise was undisturbed.

"Berenice," he said, quietly, "let me tell you something. You did me the honor just now to speak of my motives ingiving your mother money as of the best. They were—from my own point of view—the best I have ever known. I will not say what I thought they were in the beginning. I know what they were now. I am going to speak quite frankly with you, if you will let me, as long as we are here together. I don't know whether you know this or not, but when I first met your mother I only knew by chance that she had a daughter, and it was of no particular interest to me then. I went to her house as the guest of a financial friend of mine who admired her greatly. From the first I myself admired her, because I found her to be a lady to the manner born—she was interesting. One day I happened to see a photograph of you in her home, and before I could mention it she put it away. Perhaps you recall the one. It is in profile—taken when you were about sixteen."

"Yes, I remember," replied Berenice, simply—as quietly as though she were hearing a confession.

"Well, that picture interested me intensely. I inquired about you, and learned all I could. After that I saw another picture of you, enlarged, in a Louisville photographer's window. I bought it. It is in my office now—my private office—in Chicago. You are standing by a mantelpiece."

"I remember," replied Berenice, moved, but uncertain.

"Let me tell you a little something about my life, will you? It won't take long. I was born in Philadelphia. My family had always belonged there. I have been in the banking and street-railway business all my life. My first wife was a Presbyterian girl, religious, conventional. She was older than I by six or seven years. I was happy for a while—five or six years. We had two children—both still living. Then I met my present wife. She was younger than myself—at least ten years, and very good-looking. She was in some respects more intelligent than my first wife—at least less conventional, more generous, I thought. I fell in love with her, and when I eventually left Philadelphia I got a divorce and married her. I was greatly in love with her at the time. I thought she was an ideal mate for me, and I still think she has many qualities which make her attractive. But my own ideals in regard to women have all the time been slowly changing. I have come to see, through various experiments, that she is not the ideal woman for me at all. She does not understand me. I don't pretend to understand myself, but it has occurred to me that there might be a woman somewhere who would understand me better than I understand myself, who would see the things that I don't see about myself, and would like me, anyhow. I might as well tell you that I have been a lover of women always. There is just one ideal thing in this world to me, and that is the woman that I would like to have."

"I should think it would make it rather difficult for any one woman to discover just which woman you would like to have?" smiled Berenice, whimsically. Cowperwood was unabashed.

"It would, I presume, unless she should chance to be the very one woman I am talking about," he replied, impressively.

"I should think she would have her work cut out for her under any circumstances," added Berenice, lightly, but with a touch of sympathy in her voice.

"I am making a confession," replied Cowperwood, seriously and a little heavily. "I am not apologizing for myself. The women I have known would make ideal wives for some men, but not for me. Life has taught me that much. It has changed me."

"And do you think the process has stopped by any means?" she replied, quaintly, with that air of superior banter which puzzled, fascinated, defied him.

"No, I will not say that. My ideal has become fixed, though, apparently. I have had it for a number of years now. It spoils other matters for me. There is such a thing as an ideal. We do have a pole-star in physics."

As he said this Cowperwood realized that for him he was making a very remarkable confession. He had come here primarily to magnetize her and control her judgment. As a matter of fact, it was almost the other way about. She was almost dominating him. Lithe, slender, resourceful, histrionic, she was standing before him making him explain himself, only he did not see her so much in that light as in the way of a large, kindly, mothering intelligence which could see, feel, and understand. She would know how it was, he felt sure. He could make himself understood if he tried. Whatever he was or had been, she would not take a petty view. She could not. Her answers thus far guaranteed as much.

"Yes," she replied, "we do have a pole-star, but you do not seem able to find it. Do you expect to find your ideal in any living woman?"

"I have found it," he answered, wondering at the ingenuity and complexity of her mind— and of his own, for that matter—of all mind indeed. Deep below deep it lay, staggering him at times by its fathomless reaches. "I hope you will take seriously what I am going to say, for it will explain so much. When I began to be interested in your picture I was so because it coincided with the ideal I had in mind—the thing that you think changes swiftly. That was nearly seven years ago. Since then it has never changed. When I saw you at your school on Riverside Drive I was fully convinced. Although I have said nothing, I have remained so. Perhaps you think I had no right to any such feelings. Most people would agree with you. I had them and do have them just the same, and it explains my relation to your mother. When she came to me once in Louisville and told me of her difficulties I was glad to help her for your sake. That has been my reason ever since, although she does not know that. In some respects, Berenice, your mother is a little dull. All this while I have been in love with you—intensely so. As you stand there now you seem to me amazingly beautiful—the ideal I have been telling you about. Don't be disturbed; I sha'n't press any attentions on you." (Berenice had moved very slightly. She was concerned as much for him as for herself. His power was so wide, his power so great. She could not help taking him seriously when he was so serious.) "I have done whatever I have done in connection with you and your mother because I have been in love with you and because I wanted you to become the splendid thing I thought you ought to become. You have not known it, but you are the cause of my building the house on Fifth Avenue—the principal reason. I wanted to build something worthy of you. A dream? Certainly. Everything we do seems to have something of that quality. Its beauty, if there is any, is due to you. I made it beautiful thinking of you."

He paused, and Berenice gave no sign. Her first impulse had been to object, but her vanity, her love of art, her love of power—all were touched. At the same time she was curious now as to whether he had merely expected to take her as his mistress or to wait until he could honor her as his wife.

"I suppose you are wondering whether I ever expected to marry you or not," he went on, getting the thought out of her mind. "I am no different from many men in that respect, Berenice. I will be frank. I wanted you in any way that I could get you. I was living in the hope all along that you would fall in love with me—as I had with you. I hated Braxmar here, not long ago, when he appeared on the scene, but I could never have thought of interfering. I was quite prepared to give you up. I have envied every man I have ever seen with you—young and old. I have even envied your mother for being so close to you when I could not be. At the same time I have wanted you to have everything that would help you in any way. I did not want to interfere with you in case you found some one whom you could truly love if I knew that you could not love me. There is the whole story outside of anything you may know. But it is not because of this that I came to-day. Not to tell you this."

He paused, as if expecting her to say something, though she made no comment beyond a questioning "Yes?"

"The thing that I have come to say is that I want you to go on as you were before. Whatever you may think of me or of what I have just told you, I want you to believe that I am sincere and disinterested in what I am telling you now. My dream in connection with you is not quite over. Chance might make me eligible if you should happen to care. But I want you to go on and be happy, regardless of me. I have dreamed, but I dare say it has been a mistake. Hold your head high—you have a right to. Be a lady. Marry any one you really love. I will see that you have a suitable marriage portion. I love you, Berenice, but I will make it a fatherly affection from now on. When I die I will put you in my will. But go on now in the spirit you were going before. I really can't be happy unless I think you are going to be."

He paused, still looking at her, believing for the time being what he said. If he should die she would find herself in his will. If she were to go on and socialize and seek she might find some one to love, but also she might think of him more kindly before she did so. What would be the cost of her as a ward compared to his satisfaction and delight in having her at least friendly and sympathetic and being in her good graces and confidence?

Berenice, who had always been more or less interested in him, temperamentally biased, indeed, in his direction because of his efficiency, simplicity, directness, and force, was especially touched in this instance by his utter frankness and generosity. She might question his temperamental control over his own sincerity in the future, but she could scarcely question that at present he was sincere. Moreover, his long period of secret love and admiration, the thought of so powerful a man dreaming of her in this fashion, was so

542

flattering. It soothed her troubled vanity and shame in what had gone before. His straightforward confession had a kind of nobility which was electric, moving. She looked at him as he stood there, a little gray about the temples—the most appealing ornament of some men to some women—and for the life of her she could not help being moved by a kind of tenderness, sympathy, mothering affection. Obviously he did need the woman his attitude seemed to show that he needed, some woman of culture, spirit, taste, amorousness; or, at least, he was entitled to dream of her. As he stood before her he seemed a kind of superman, and yet also a bad boy—handsome, powerful, hopeful, not so very much older than herself now, impelled by some blazing internal force which harried him on and on. How much did he really care for her? How much could he? How much could he care for any one? Yet see all he had done to interest her. What did that mean? To say all this? To do all this? Outside was his car brown and radiant in the snow. He was the great Frank Algernon Cowperwood, of Chicago, and he was pleading with her, a mere chit of a girl, to be kind to him, not to put him out of her life entirely. It touched her intellect, her pride, her fancy.

Aloud she said: "I like you better now. I really believe in you. I never did, quite, before. Not that I think I ought to let you spend your money on me or mother—I don't. But I admire you. You make me. I understand how it is, I think. I know what your ambitions are. I have always felt that I did, in part. But you mustn't talk to me any more now. I want to think. I want to think over what you have said. I don't know whether I can bring myself to it or not." (She noticed that his eyes seemed to move somehow in their deepest depths again.) "But we won't talk about it any more at present."

"But, Berenice," he added, with a real plea in his voice, "I wonder if you do understand. I have been so lonely—I am—"

"Yes, I do," she replied, holding out her hand. "We are going to be friends, whatever happens, from now on, because I really like you. You mustn't ask me to decide about the other, though, to-day. I can't do it. I don't want to. I don't care to."

"Not when I would so gladly give you everything—when I need it so little?"

"Not until I think it out for myself. I don't think so, though. No," she replied, with an air. "There, Mr. Guardian Father," she laughed, pushing his hand away.

Cowperwood's heart bounded. He would have given millions to take her close in his arms. As it was he smiled appealingly.

"Don't you want to jump in and come to New York with me? If your mother isn't at the apartment you could stop at the Netherland."

"No, not to-day. I expect to be in soon. I will let you know, or mother will."

He bustled out and into the machine after a moment of parley, waving to her over the purpling snow of the evening as his machine tore eastward, planning to make New York by dinner-time. If he could just keep her in this friendly, sympathetic attitude. If he only could!

CHAPTER LIV

WANTED—FIFTY-YEAR FRANCHISES

Whatever his momentary satisfaction in her friendly acceptance of his confession, the uncertain attitude of Berenice left Cowperwood about where he was before. By a strange stroke of fate Braxmar, his young rival, had been eliminated, and Berenice had been made to see him, Cowperwood, in his true colors of love and of service for her. Yet plainly she did not accept them at his own valuation. More than ever was he conscious of the fact that he had fallen in tow of an amazing individual, one who saw life from a distinct and peculiar point of view and who was not to be bent to his will. That fact more than anything else— for her grace and beauty merely emblazoned it—caused him to fall into a hopeless infatuation.

He said to himself over and over, "Well, I can live without her if I must," but at this stage the mere thought was an actual stab in his vitals. What, after all, was life, wealth, fame, if you couldn't have the woman you wanted—love, that indefinable, unnamable coddling of the spirit which the strongest almost more than the weakest crave? At last he saw clearly, as within a chalice-like nimbus, that the ultimate end of fame, power, vigor was beauty, and that beauty was a compound of the taste, the emotion, the innate culture, passion, and dreams of a woman like Berenice Fleming. That was it: that was it. And beyond was nothing save crumbling age, darkness, silence.

In the mean time, owing to the preliminary activity and tact of his agents and advisers, the Sunday newspapers were vying with one another in describing the wonders of his new house in New York—its cost, the value of its ground, the wealthy citizens with whom the Cowperwoods would now be neighbors. There were double-column pictures of Aileen and Cowperwood, with articles indicating them as prospective entertainers on a grand scale who would unquestionably be received because of their tremendous wealth. As a matter of fact, this was purely newspaper gossip and speculation. While the general columns made news and capital of his wealth, special society columns, which dealt with the ultra-fashionable, ignored him entirely. Already the machination of certain Chicago social figures in distributing information as to his past was discernible in the attitude of those clubs, organizations, and even churches, membership in which constitutes a form of social passport to better and higher earthly, if not spiritual, realms. His emissaries were active enough, but soon found that their end was not to be gained in a day. Many were waiting locally, anxious enough to get in, and with social equipments which the Cowperwoods could scarcely boast. After being blackballed by one or two exclusive clubs, seeing his application for a pew at St. Thomas's quietly pigeon-holed for the present, and his invitations declined by several multimillionaires whom he met in the course of commercial transactions, he began to feel that his splendid home, aside from its final purpose as an art-museum, could be of little value.

At the same time Cowperwood's financial genius was constantly being rewarded by many new phases of materiality chiefly by an offensive and defensive alliance he was now able to engineer between himself and the house of Haeckelheimer, Gotloeb & Co. Seeing the iron manner in which he had managed to wrest victory out of defeat after the first seriously contested election, these gentlemen had experienced a change of heart and announced that they would now gladly help finance any new enterprise which Cowperwood might undertake. Among many other financiers, they had heard of his triumph in connection with the failure of American Match.

"Dot must be a right cleffer man, dot Cowperwood," Mr. Gotloeb told several of his partners, rubbing his hands and smiling. "I shouldt like to meet him."

And so Cowperwood was manoeuvered into the giant banking office, where Mr. Gotloeb extended a genial hand.

"I hear much of Chicawkgo," he explained, in his semi-German, semi-Hebraic dialect, "but almozd more uff you. Are you goink to swallow up all de street-railwaiss unt elefated roats out dere?"

Cowperwood smiled his most ingenuous smile.

"Why? Would you like me to leave a few for you?"

"Not dot exzagly, but I might not mint sharink in some uff dem wit you."

"You can join with me at any time, Mr. Gotloeb, as you must know. The door is always very, very wide open for you."

"I musd look into dot some more. It loogs very promising to me. I am gladt to meet you."

The great external element in Cowperwood's financial success—and one which he himself had foreseen from the very beginning—was the fact that Chicago was developing constantly. What had been when he arrived a soggy, messy plain strewn with shanties, ragged sidewalks, a higgledy-piggledy business heart, was now truly an astounding metropolis which had passed the million mark in population and which stretched proud and strong over the greater part of Cook County. Where once had been a meager, makeshift financial section, with here and there only a splendid business building or hotel or a public office of some kind, there were now canon-like streets lined with fifteen and even eighteen story office buildings, from the upper stories of which, as from watch-towers, might be surveyed the vast expanding regions of simple home life below. Farther out were districts of mansions, parks, pleasure resorts, great worlds of train-yards and manufacturing areas. In the commercial heart of this world Frank Algernon Cowperwood had truly become a figure of giant significance. How wonderful it is that men grow until, like colossi, they bestride the world, or, like banyan-trees, they drop roots from every branch and are themselves a forest—a forest of intricate commercial life, of which a thousand material aspects are the evidence. His street-railway properties were like a net—the parasite Gold Thread—linked together as they were, and draining two of the three important "sides" of the city.

In 1886, when he had first secured a foothold, they had been capitalized at between six and seven millions (every device for issuing a dollar on real property having been exhausted). To-day, under his management, they were capitalized at between sixty and seventy millions. The majority of the stock issued and sold was subject to a financial device whereby twenty per cent. controlled eighty per cent., Cowperwood holding that twenty per cent. and borrowing money on it as hypothecated collateral. In the case of the West Side corporation, a corporate issue of over thirty millions had been made, and these stocks, owing to the tremendous carrying power of the roads and the swelling traffic night and morning of poor sheep who paid their hard-earned nickels, had a market value which gave the road an assured physical value of about three times the sum for which it could have been built. The North Chicago company, which in 1886 had a physical value of little more than a million, could not now be duplicated for less than seven millions, and was capitalized at nearly fifteen millions. The road was valued at over one hundred thousand dollars more per mile than the sum for which it could actually have been replaced. Pity the poor groveling hack at the bottom who has not the brain-power either to understand or to control that which his very presence and necessities create.

These tremendous holdings, paying from ten to twelve per cent. on every hundred-dollar share, were in the control, if not in the actual ownership, of Cowperwood. Millions in loans that did not appear on the books of the companies he had converted into actual cash, wherewith he had bought houses, lands, equipages, paintings, government bonds of the purest gold value, thereby assuring himself to that extent of a fortune vaulted and locked, absolutely secure. After much toiling and moiling on the part of his overworked legal department he had secured a consolidation, under the title of the Consolidated Traction Company of Illinois, of all outlying lines, each having separate franchises and capitalized separately, yet operated by an amazing hocus-pocus of contracts and agreements in single, harmonious union with all his other properties. The North and West Chicago companies he now proposed to unite into a third company to be called the Union Traction Company. By taking up the ten and twelve per cent. issues of the old North and West companies and giving two for one of the new six-per-cent one-hundred-dollar-share Union Traction stocks in their stead, he could satisfy the current stockholders, who were apparently made somewhat better off thereby, and still create and leave for himself a handsome margin of nearly eighty million dollars. With a renewal of his franchises for twenty, fifty, or one hundred years he would have fastened on the city of Chicago the burden of yielding interest on this somewhat fictitious value and would leave himself personally worth in the neighborhood of one hundred millions.

This matter of extending his franchises was a most difficult and intricate business, however. It involved overcoming or outwitting a recent and very treacherous increase of local sentiment against him. This had been occasioned by various details which related to his elevated roads. To the two lines already built he now added a third property, the Union Loop. This he prepared to connect not only with his own, but with other outside elevated properties, chief among which was Mr. Schryhart's South Side "L." He would then farm out to his enemies the privilege of running trains on this new line. However unwillingly, they would be forced to avail themselves of the proffered opportunity, because within the region covered by the new loop was the true congestion—here every one desired to come either once or twice during the day or night. By this means Cowperwood would secure to his property a paying interest from the start.

This scheme aroused a really unprecedented antagonism in the breasts of Cowperwood's enemies. By the Arneel-Hand-Schryhart contingent it was looked upon as nothing short of diabolical. The newspapers, directed by such men as Haguenin, Hyssop, Ormonde Ricketts, and Truman Leslie MacDonald (whose father was now dead, and whose thoughts as editor of the Inquirer were almost solely directed toward driving Cowperwood out of Chicago), began to shout, as a last resort, in the interests of democracy. Seats for everybody (on Cowperwood's lines), no more straps in the rush hours, three-cent fares for workingmen, morning and evening, free transfers from all of Cowperwood's lines north to west and west to north, twenty per cent. of the gross income of his lines to be paid to the city. The masses should be made cognizant of their individual rights and privileges. Such a course, while decidedly inimical to Cowperwood's interests at the present time, and as such strongly favored by the majority of his opponents, had nevertheless its disturbing elements to an ultra-conservative like Hosmer Hand.

"I don't know about this, Norman," he remarked to Schryhart, on one occasion. "I don't know about this. It's one thing to stir up the public, but it's another to make them forget.

This is a restless, socialistic country, and Chicago is the very hotbed and center of it. Still, if it will serve to trip him up I suppose it will do for the present. The newspapers can probably smooth it all over later. But I don't know."

Mr. Hand was of that order of mind that sees socialism as a horrible importation of monarchy-ridden Europe. Why couldn't the people be satisfied to allow the strong, intelligent, God-fearing men of the community to arrange things for them? Wasn't that what democracy meant? Certainly it was—he himself was one of the strong. He could not help distrusting all this radical palaver. Still, anything to hurt Cowperwood—anything.

Cowperwood was not slow to realize that public sentiment was now in danger of being thoroughly crystallized against him by newspaper agitation. Although his franchises would not expire—the large majority of them—before January 1, 1903, yet if things went on at this rate it would be doubtful soon whether ever again he would be able to win another election by methods legitimate or illegitimate. Hungry aldermen and councilmen might be venal and greedy enough to do anything he should ask, provided he was willing to pay enough, but even the thickest-hided, the most voracious and corrupt politician could scarcely withstand the searching glare of publicity and the infuriated rage of a possibly aroused public opinion. By degrees this last, owing to the untiring efforts of the newspapers, was being whipped into a wild foam. To come into council at this time and ask for a twenty-year extension of franchises not destined to expire for seven years was too much. It could not be done. Even suborned councilmen would be unwilling to undertake it just now. There are some things which even politically are impossible.

To make matters worse, the twenty-year-franchise limit was really not at all sufficient for his present needs. In order to bring about the consolidation of his North and West surface lines, which he was now proposing and on the strength of which he wished to issue at least two hundred million dollars' worth of one-hundred-dollar-six-per-cent. shares in place of the seventy million dollars current of ten and twelve per cents., it was necessary for him to secure a much more respectable term of years than the brief one now permitted by the state legislature, even providing that this latter could be obtained.

"Peeble are not ferry much indrested in tees short-time frangizes," observed Mr. Gotloeb once, when Cowperwood was talking the matter over with him. He wanted Haeckelheimer & Co. to underwrite the whole issue. "Dey are so insigure. Now if you couldt get, say, a frangize for fifty or one hunnert years or something like dot your stocks wouldt go off like hot cakes. I know where I couldt dispose of fifty million dollars off dem in Cermany alone."

He was most unctuous and pleading.

Cowperwood understood this quite as well as Gotloeb, if not better. He was not at all satisfied with the thought of obtaining a beggarly twenty-year extension for his giant schemes when cities like Philadelphia, Boston, New York, and Pittsburg were apparently glad to grant their corporations franchises which would not expire for ninety-nine years at the earliest, and in most cases were given in perpetuity. This was the kind of franchise favored by the great moneyed houses of New York and Europe, and which Gotloeb, and even Addison, locally, were demanding.

"It is certainly important that we get these franchises renewed for fifty years," Addison used to say to him, and it was seriously and disagreeably true.

The various lights of Cowperwood's legal department, constantly on the search for new legislative devices, were not slow to grasp the import of the situation. It was not long before the resourceful Mr. Joel Avery appeared with a suggestion.

"Did you notice what the state legislature of New York is doing in connection with the various local transit problems down there?" asked this honorable gentleman of Cowperwood, one morning, ambling in when announced and seating himself in the great presence. A half-burned cigar was between his fingers, and a little round felt hat looked peculiarly rakish above his sinister, intellectual, constructive face and eyes.

"No, I didn't," replied Cowperwood, who had actually noted and pondered upon the item in question, but who did not care to say so. "I saw something about it, but I didn't pay much attention to it. What of it?"

"Well, it plans to authorize a body of four or five men—one branch in New York, one in Buffalo, I presume—to grant all new franchises and extend old ones with the consent of the various local communities involved. They are to fix the rate of compensation to be paid to the state or the city, and the rates of fare. They can regulate transfers, stock issues, and all that sort of thing. I was thinking if at any time we find this business of renewing the franchises too uncertain here we might go into the state legislature and see what can be done about introducing a public-service commission of that kind into this state. We are not the only corporation that would welcome it. Of course, it would be better if there were a general or special demand for it outside of ourselves. It ought not to originate with us."

He stared at Cowperwood heavily, the latter returning a reflective gaze.

"I'll think it over," he said. "There may be something in that."

Henceforth the thought of instituting such a commission never left Cowperwood's mind. It contained the germ of a solution—the possibility of extending his franchises for fifty or even a hundred years.

This plan, as Cowperwood was subsequently to discover, was a thing more or less expressly forbidden by the state constitution of Illinois. The latter provided that no special or exclusive privilege, immunity, or franchise whatsoever should be granted to any corporation, association, or individual. Yet, "What is a little matter like the constitution between friends, anyhow?" some one had already asked. There are fads in legislation as well as dusty pigeonholes in which phases of older law are tucked away and forgotten. Many earlier ideals of the constitution-makers had long since been conveniently obscured or nullified by decisions, appeals to the federal government, appeals to the state government, communal contracts, and the like—fine cobwebby figments, all, but sufficient, just the same, to render inoperative the original intention. Besides, Cowperwood had but small respect for either the intelligence or the self-protective capacity of such men as constituted the rural voting element of the state. From his lawyers and from others he had heard innumerable droll stories of life in the state legislature, and the state counties and towns—on the bench, at the rural huskings where the state elections were won, in country hotels, on country roads and farms. "One day as I was getting on the train at Petunkey," old General Van Sickle, or Judge Dickensheets, or ex-Judge Avery would begin—and then would follow some amazing narration of rural immorality or dullness, or political or social misconception. Of the total population of the state at this time over half were in the city itself, and these he had managed to keep in control. For the remaining million, divided between twelve small cities and an agricultural population, he had small respect. What did this handful of yokels amount to, anyhow?—dull, frivoling, barn-dancing boors.

The great state of Illinois—a territory as large as England proper and as fertile as Egypt, bordered by a great lake and a vast river, and with a population of over two million free-born Americans—would scarcely seem a fit subject for corporate manipulation and control. Yet a more trade-ridden commonwealth might not have been found anywhere at this time within the entire length and breadth of the universe. Cowperwood personally, though contemptuous of the bucolic mass when regarded as individuals, had always been impressed by this great community of his election. Here had come Marquette and Joliet, La Salle and Hennepin, dreaming a way to the Pacific. Here Lincoln and Douglas, antagonist and protagonist of slavery argument, had contested; here had arisen "Joe" Smith, propagator of that strange American dogma of the Latter-Day Saints. What a state, Cowperwood sometimes thought; what a figment of the brain, and yet how wonderful! He had crossed it often on his way to St. Louis, to Memphis, to Denver, and had been touched by its very simplicity—the small, new wooden towns, so redolent of American tradition, prejudice, force, and illusion. The white-steepled church, the lawn-faced, tree-shaded village streets, the long stretches of flat, open country where corn grew in serried rows or where in winter the snow bedded lightly—it all reminded him a little of his own father and mother, who had been in many respects suited to such a world as this. Yet none the less did he hesitate to press on the measure which was to adjust his own future, to make profitable his issue of two hundred million dollars' worth of Union Traction, to secure him a fixed place in the financial oligarchy of America and of the world.

The state legislature at this time was ruled over by a small group of wire-pulling, pettifogging, corporation-controlled individuals who came up from the respective towns, counties, and cities of the state, but who bore the same relation to the communities which they represented and to their superiors and equals in and out of the legislative halls at Springfield that men do to such allies anywhere in any given field. Why do we call them pettifogging and dismiss them? Perhaps they were pettifogging, but certainly no more so than any other shrewd rat or animal that burrows its way onward—and shall we say upward? The deepest controlling principle which animated these individuals was the oldest and first, that of self-preservation. Picture, for example, a common occurrence—that of Senator John H. Southack, conversing with, perhaps, Senator George Mason Wade, of Gallatin County, behind a legislative door in one of the senate conference chambers toward the close of a session—Senator Southack, blinking, buttonholing his well-dressed colleague and drawing very near; Senator Wade, curious, confidential, expectant (a genial, solid, experienced, slightly paunchy but well-built Senator Wade—and handsome, too).

"You know, George, I told you there would be something eventually in the Quincy water-front improvement if it ever worked out. Well, here it is. Ed Truesdale was in town yesterday." (This with a knowing eye, as much as to say, "Mum's the word.") "Here's five hundred; count it."

A quick flashing out of some green and yellow bills from a vest pocket, a light thumbing and counting on the part of Senator Wade. A flare of comprehension, approval, gratitude, admiration, as though to signify, "This is something like." "Thanks, John. I had pretty near forgot all about it. Nice people, eh? If you see Ed again give him my regards. When that Bellville contest comes up let me know."

Mr. Wade, being a good speaker, was frequently in request to stir up the populace to a sense of pro or con in connection with some legislative crisis impending, and it was to some such future opportunity that he now pleasantly referred. O life, O politics, O necessity, O hunger, O burning human appetite and desire on every hand!

Mr. Southack was an unobtrusive, pleasant, quiet man of the type that would usually be patronized as rural and pettifogging by men high in commercial affairs. He was none the less well fitted to his task, a capable and diligent beneficiary and agent. He was well dressed, middle-aged,—only forty-five—cool, courageous, genial, with eyes that were material, but not cold or hard, and a light, springy, energetic step and manner. A holder of some C. W. & I. R.R. shares, a director of one of his local county banks, a silent partner in the Effingham Herald, he was a personage in his district, one much revered by local swains. Yet a more game and rascally type was not to be found in all rural legislation.

It was old General Van Sickle who sought out Southack, having remembered him from his earlier legislative days. It was Avery who conducted the negotiations. Primarily, in all state scheming at Springfield, Senator Southack was supposed to represent the C. W. I., one of the great trunk-lines traversing the state, and incidentally connecting Chicago with the South, West, and East. This road, having a large local mileage and being anxious to extend its franchises in Chicago and elsewhere, was deep in state politics. By a curious coincidence it was mainly financed by Haeckelheimer, Gotloeb & Co., of New York, though Cowperwood's connection with that concern was not as yet known. Going to Southack, who was the Republican whip in the senate, Avery proposed that he, in conjunction with Judge Dickensheets and one Gilson Bickel, counsel for the C. W. I., should now undertake to secure sufficient support in the state senate and house for a scheme introducing the New York idea of a public-service commission into the governing machinery of the state of Illinois. This measure, be it noted, was to be supplemented by one very interesting and important little proviso to the effect that all franchise-holding corporations should hereby, for a period of fifty years from the date of the enactment of the bill into law, be assured of all their rights, privileges, and immunities—including franchises, of course. This was justified on the ground that any such radical change as that involved in the introduction of a public-service commission might disturb the peace and well-being of corporations with franchises which still had years to run.

Senator Southack saw nothing very wrong with this idea, though he naturally perceived what it was all about and whom it was truly designed to protect.

"Yes," he said, succinctly, "I see the lay of that land, but what do I get out of it?"

"Fifty thousand dollars for yourself if it's successful, ten thousand if it isn't—provided you make an honest effort; two thousand dollars apiece for any of the boys who see fit to help you if we win. Is that perfectly satisfactory?"

"Perfectly," replied Senator Southack.

CHAPTER LV

COWPERWOOD AND THE GOVERNOR

A Public-service-commission law might, ipso facto, have been quietly passed at this session, if the arbitrary franchise-extending proviso had not been introduced, and this on the thin excuse that so novel a change in the working scheme of the state government might bring about hardship to some. This redounded too obviously to the benefit of one particular corporation. The newspaper men—as thick as flies about the halls of the state capitol at Springfield, and essentially watchful and loyal to their papers—were quick to sense the true state of affairs. Never were there such hawks as newspapermen. These wretches (employed by sniveling, mud-snouting newspapers of the opposition) were not only in the councils of politicians, in the pay of rival corporations, in the confidence of the governor, in the secrets of the senators and local representatives, but were here and there in one another's confidence. A piece of news—a rumor, a dream, a fancy—whispered by Senator Smith to Senator Jones, or by Representative Smith to Representative Jones, and confided by him in turn to Charlie White, of the Globe, or Eddie Burns, of the Democrat, would in turn be communicated to Robert Hazlitt, of the Press, or Harry Emonds, of the Transcript.

All at once a disturbing announcement in one or other of the papers, no one knowing whence it came. Neither Senator Smith nor Senator Jones had told any one. No word of the confidence imposed in Charlie White or Eddie Burns had ever been breathed. But there you were—the thing was in the papers, the storm of inquiry, opinion, opposition was on. No one knew, no one was to blame, but it was on, and the battle had henceforth to be fought in the open.

Consider also the governor who presided at this time in the executive chamber at Springfield. He was a strange, tall, dark, osseous man who, owing to the brooding, melancholy character of his own disposition, had a checkered and a somewhat sad career behind him. Born in Sweden, he had been brought to America as a child, and allowed or compelled to fight his own way upward under all the grinding aspects of poverty. Owing to an energetic and indomitable temperament, he had through years of law practice and public labors of various kinds built up for himself a following among Chicago Swedes which amounted to adoration. He had been city tax-collector, city surveyor, district attorney, and for six or eight years a state circuit judge. In all these capacities he had manifested a tendency to do the right as he saw it and play fair—qualities which endeared him to the idealistic. Honest, and with a hopeless brooding sympathy for the miseries of the poor, he had as circuit judge, and also as district attorney, rendered various decisions which had made him very unpopular with the rich and powerful—decisions in damage cases, fraud cases, railroad claim cases, where the city or the state was seeking to oust various powerful railway corporations from possession of property—yards, water-frontages, and the like, to which they had no just claim. At the same time the populace, reading the news items of his doings and hearing him speak on various and sundry occasions, conceived a great fancy for him. He was primarily soft-hearted, sweet-minded, fiery, a brilliant orator, a dynamic presence. In addition he was woman-hungry—a phase which homely, sex-starved intellectuals the world over will understand, to the shame of a lying age, that because of quixotic dogma belies its greatest desire, its greatest sorrow, its greatest joy. All these factors turned an ultra-conservative element in the community against him, and he was considered dangerous. At the same time he had by careful economy and investment built up a fair sized fortune. Recently, however, owing to the craze for sky-scrapers, he had placed much of his holdings in a somewhat poorly constructed and therefore unprofitable office building. Because of this error financial wreck was threatening him. Even now he was knocking at the doors of large bonding companies for assistance.

This man, in company with the antagonistic financial element and the newspapers, constituted, as regards Cowperwood's public-service-commission scheme, a triumvirate of difficulties not easy to overcome. The newspapers, in due time, catching wind of the true purport of the plan, ran screaming to their readers with the horrible intelligence. In the offices of Schryhart, Arneel, Hand, and Merrill, as well as in other centers of finance, there was considerable puzzling over the situation, and then a shrewd, intelligent deduction was made.

"Do you see what he's up to, Hosmer?" inquired Schryhart of Hand. "He sees that we have him scotched here in Chicago. As things stand now he can't go into the city council and ask for a franchise for more than twenty years under the state law, and he can't do that for three or four years yet, anyhow. His franchises don't expire soon enough. He knows that by the time they do expire we will have public sentiment aroused to such a point that no council, however crooked it may be, will dare to give him what he asks unless he is willing to make a heavy return to the city. If he does that it will end his scheme of selling any two hundred million dollars of Union Traction at six per cent. The market won't back him up. He can't pay twenty per cent. to the city and give universal transfers and pay six per cent. on two hundred million dollars, and everybody knows it. He has a fine scheme of making a cool hundred million out of this. Well, he can't do it. We must get the newspapers to hammer this legislative scheme of his to death. When he comes into the local council he must pay twenty or thirty per cent. of the gross receipts of his roads to the city. He must give free transfers from every one of his lines to every other one. Then we have him. I dislike to see socialistic ideas fostered, but it can't be helped. We have to do it. If we ever get him out of here we can hush up the newspapers, and the public will forget about it; at least we can hope so."

In the mean time the governor had heard the whisper of "boodle"—a word of the day expressive of a corrupt legislative fund. Not at all a small-minded man, nor involved in the financial campaign being waged against Cowperwood, nor inclined to be influenced mentally or emotionally by superheated charges against the latter, he nevertheless speculated deeply. In a vague way he sensed the dreams of Cowperwood. The charge of seducing women so frequently made against the street-railway magnate, so shocking to the yoked conventionalists, did not disturb him at all. Back of the onward sweep of the generations he himself sensed the mystic Aphrodite and her magic. He realized that Cowperwood had traveled fast—that he was pressing to the utmost a great advantage in the face of great obstacles. At the same time he knew that the present street-car service of Chicago was by no means bad. Would he be proving unfaithful to the trust imposed on him by the great electorate of Illinois if he were to advantage Cowperwood's cause? Must he not rather in the sight of all men smoke out the animating causes here—greed, over-weening ambition, colossal self-interest as opposed to the selflessness of a Christian ideal and of a democratic theory of government?

Life rises to a high plane of the dramatic, and hence of the artistic, whenever and wherever in the conflict regarding material possession there enters a conception of the ideal. It was this that lit forever the beacon fires of Troy, that thundered eternally in the horses' hoofs at Arbela and in the guns at Waterloo. Ideals were here at stake—the dreams of one man as opposed perhaps to the ultimate dreams of a city or state or nation—the grovelings and wallowings of a democracy slowly, blindly trying to stagger to its feet. In this conflict— taking place in an inland cottage-dotted state where men were clowns and churls, dancing fiddlers at country fairs—were opposed, as the governor saw it, the ideals of one man and the ideals of men.

Governor Swanson decided after mature deliberation to veto the bill. Cowperwood, debonair as ever, faithful as ever to his logic and his conception of individuality, was determined that no stone should be left unturned that would permit him to triumph, that would carry him finally to the gorgeous throne of his own construction. Having first

552

engineered the matter through the legislature by a tortuous process, fired upon at every step by the press, he next sent various individuals—state legislators, representatives of the C. W. & I., members of outside corporations to see the governor, but Swanson was adamant. He did not see how he could conscientiously sanction the bill. Finally, one day, as he was seated in his Chicago business office—a fateful chamber located in the troublesome building which was subsequently to wreck his fortune and which was the raison d'etre of a present period of care and depression—enter the smug, comfortable presence of Judge Nahum Dickensheets, at present senior counsel of the North Chicago Street Railway. He was a very mountain of a man physically—smooth-faced, agreeably clothed, hard and yet ingratiating of eye, a thinker, a reasoner. Swanson knew much of him by reputation and otherwise, although personally they were no more than speaking acquaintances.

"How are you, Governor? I'm glad to see you again. I heard you were back in Chicago. I see by the morning papers that you have that Southack public-service bill up before you. I thought I would come over and have a few words with you about it if you have no objection. I've been trying to get down to Springfield for the last three weeks to have a little chat with you before you reached a conclusion one way or the other. Do you mind if I inquire whether you have decided to veto it?"

The ex-judge, faintly perfumed, clean and agreeable, carried in his hand a large-sized black hand-satchel which he put down beside him on the floor.

"Yes, Judge," replied Swanson, "I've practically decided to veto it. I can see no practical reason for supporting it. As I look at it now, it's specious and special, not particularly called for or necessary at this time."

The governor talked with a slight Swedish accent, intellectual, individual.

A long, placid, philosophic discussion of all the pros and cons of the situation followed. The governor was tired, distrait, but ready to listen in a tolerant way to more argument along a line with which he was already fully familiar. He knew, of course, that Dickensheets was counsel for the North Chicago Street Railway Company.

"I'm very glad to have heard what you have to say, Judge," finally commented the governor. I don't want you to think I haven't given this matter serious thought—I have. I know most of the things that have been done down at Springfield. Mr. Cowperwood is an able man; I don't charge any more against him than I do against twenty other agencies that are operating down there at this very moment. I know what his difficulties are. I can hardly be accused of sympathizing with his enemies, for they certainly do not sympathize with me. I am not even listening to the newspapers. This is a matter of faith in democracy—a difference in ideals between myself and many other men. I haven't vetoed the bill yet. I don't say that something may not arise to make me sign it. My present intention, unless I hear something much more favorable in its behalf than I have already heard, is to veto it.

"Governor," said Dickensheets, rising, "let me thank you for your courtesy. I would be the last person in the world to wish to influence you outside the line of your private convictions and your personal sense of fair play. At the same time I have tried to make plain to you how essential it is, how only fair and right, that this local street-railway-franchise business should be removed out of the realm of sentiment, emotion, public passion, envy, buncombe, and all the other influences that are at work to frustrate and make difficult the work of Mr. Cowperwood. All envy, I tell you. His enemies are willing to sacrifice every principle of justice and fair play to see him eliminated. That sums it up."

"That may all be true," replied Swanson. "Just the same, there is another principle involved here which you do not seem to see or do not care to consider—the right of the people under the state constitution to a consideration, a revaluation, of their contracts at the time and in the manner agreed upon under the original franchise. What you propose is sumptuary legislation; it makes null and void an agreement between the people and the street-railway companies at a time when the people have a right to expect a full and free consideration of this matter aside from state legislative influence and control. To persuade the state legislature, by influence or by any other means, to step in at this time and interfere is unfair. The propositions involved in those bills should be referred to the people at the next election for approval or not, just as they see fit. That is the way this matter should be arranged. It will not do to come into the legislature and influence or buy votes, and then expect me to write my signature under the whole matter as satisfactory."

Swanson was not heated or antipathetic. He was cool, firm, well-intentioned.

Dickensheets passed his hand over a wide, high temple. He seemed to be meditating something—some hitherto untried statement or course of action.

"Well, Governor," he repeated, "I want to thank you, anyhow. You have been exceedingly kind. By the way, I see you have a large, roomy safe here." He had picked up the bag he was carrying. "I wonder if I might leave this here for a day or two in your care? It contains some papers that I do not wish to carry into the country with me. Would you mind locking it up in your safe and letting me have it when I send for it?"

"With pleasure," replied the governor.

He took it, placed it in lower storage space, and closed and locked the door. The two men parted with a genial hand-shake. The governor returned to his meditations, the judge hurried to catch a car.

About eleven o'clock the next morning Swanson was still working in his office, worrying greatly over some method whereby he could raise one hundred thousand dollars to defray interest charges, repairs, and other payments, on a structure that was by no means meeting expenses and was hence a drain. At this juncture his office door opened, and his very youthful office-boy presented him the card of F. A. Cowperwood. The governor had never seen him before. Cowperwood entered brisk, fresh, forceful. He was as crisp as a new dollar bill—as clean, sharp, firmly limned.

"Governor Swanson, I believe?"

"Yes, sir."

The two were scrutinizing each other defensively.

"I am Mr. Cowperwood. I come to have a very few words with you. I will take very little of your time. I do not wish to go over any of the arguments that have been gone over before. I am satisfied that you know all about them."

"Yes, I had a talk with Judge Dickensheets yesterday."

"Just so, Governor. Knowing all that you do, permit me to put one more matter before you. I know that you are, comparatively, a poor man—that every dollar you have is at present practically tied in this building. I know of two places where you have applied for a loan of one hundred thousand dollars and have been refused because you haven't sufficient security to offer outside of this building, which is mortgaged up to its limit as it stands. The men, as you must know, who are fighting you are fighting me. I am a scoundrel because I am selfish and ambitious—a materialist. You are not a scoundrel, but a dangerous person because you are an idealist. Whether you veto this bill or not, you will never again be elected Governor of Illinois if the people who are fighting me succeed, as they will succeed, in fighting you."

Swanson's dark eyes burned illuminatively. He nodded his head in assent.

"Governor, I have come here this morning to bribe you, if I can. I do not agree with your ideals; in the last analysis I do not believe that they will work. I am sure I do not believe in most of the things that you believe in. Life is different at bottom perhaps from what either you or I may think. Just the same, as compared with other men, I sympathize with you. I will loan you that one hundred thousand dollars and two or three or four hundred thousand dollars more besides if you wish. You need never pay me a dollar—or you can if you wish. Suit yourself. In that black bag which Judge Dickensheets brought here yesterday, and which is in your safe, is three hundred thousand dollars in cash. He did not have the courage to mention it. Sign the bill and let me beat the men who are trying to beat me. I will support you in the future with any amount of money or influence that I can bring to bear in any political contest you may choose to enter, state or national."

Cowperwood's eyes glowed like a large, genial collie's. There was a suggestion of sympathetic appeal in them, rich and deep, and, even more than that, a philosophic perception of ineffable things. Swanson arose. "You really don't mean to say that you are trying to bribe me openly, do you?" he inquired. In spite of a conventional impulse to burst forth in moralistic denunciation, solemnly phrased, he was compelled for the moment to see the other man's viewpoint. They were working in different directions, going different ways, to what ultimate end?

"Mr. Cowperwood," continued the governor, his face a physiognomy out of Goya, his eye alight with a kind of understanding sympathy, "I suppose I ought to resent this, but I can't. I see your point of view. I'm sorry, but I can't help you nor myself. My political belief, my ideals, compel me to veto this bill; when I forsake these I am done politically with myself. I may not be elected governor again, but that does not matter, either. I could use your money, but I won't. I shall have to bid you good morning."

He moved toward the safe, slowly, opened it, took out the bag and brought it over.

"You must take that with you," he added.

The two men looked at each other a moment curiously, sadly—the one with a burden of financial, political, and moral worry on his spirit, the other with an unconquerable determination not to be worsted even in defeat.

"Governor," concluded Cowperwood, in the most genial, contented, undisturbed voice, "you will live to see another legislature pass and another governor sign some such bill. It will not be done this session, apparently, but it will be done. I am not through, because my case is right and fair. Just the same, after you have vetoed the bill, come and see me, and I will loan you that one hundred thousand if you want it."

Cowperwood went out. Swanson vetoed the bill. It is on record that subsequently he borrowed one hundred thousand dollars from Cowperwood to stay him from ruin.

CHAPTER LVI

THE ORDEAL OF BERENICE

At the news that Swanson had refused to sign the bill and that the legislature lacked sufficient courage to pass it over his veto both Schryhart and Hand literally rubbed their hands in comfortable satisfaction.

"Well, Hosmer," said Schryhart the next day, when they met at their favorite club—the Union League—"it looks as though we were making some little progress, after all, doesn't it? Our friend didn't succeed in turning that little trick, did he?"

He beamed almost ecstatically upon his solid companion.

"Not this time. I wonder what move he will decide to make next."

"I don't see very well what it can be. He knows now that he can't get his franchises without a compromise that will eat into his profits, and if that happens he can't sell his Union Traction stock. This legislative scheme of his must have cost him all of three hundred thousand dollars, and what has he to show for it? The new legislature, unless I'm greatly mistaken, will be afraid to touch anything in connection with him. It's hardly likely that any of the Springfield politicians will want to draw the fire of the newspapers again."

Schryhart felt very powerful, imposing—sleek, indeed—now that his theory of newspaper publicity as a cure was apparently beginning to work. Hand, more saturnine, more responsive to the uncertainty of things mundane—the shifty undercurrents that are perpetually sapping and mining below—was agreeable, but not sure. Perhaps so.

In regard to his Eastern life during this interlude, Cowperwood had been becoming more and more keenly alive to the futility of the attempt to effect a social rescue for Aileen. "What was the use?" he often asked himself, as he contemplated her movements, thoughts, plans, as contrasted with the natural efficiency, taste, grace, and subtlety of a woman like Berenice. He felt that the latter could, if she would, smooth over in an adroit way all the silly social antagonisms which were now afflicting him. It was a woman's game, he frequently told himself, and would never be adjusted till he had the woman.

Simultaneously Aileen, looking at the situation from her own point of view and nonplussed by the ineffectiveness of mere wealth when not combined with a certain social something which she did not appear to have, was, nevertheless, unwilling to surrender her dream. What was it, she asked herself over and over, that made this great difference between women and women? The question contained its own answer, but she did not know that. She was still good-looking—very—and an adept in self-ornamentation, after her manner and taste. So great had been the newspaper palaver regarding the arrival of a new multimillionaire from the West and the palace he was erecting that even tradesmen, clerks, and hall-boys knew of her. Almost invariably, when called upon to state her name in such quarters, she was greeted by a slight start of recognition, a swift glance of examination, whispers, even open comment. That was something. Yet how much more, and how different were those rarefied reaches of social supremacy to which popular repute bears scarcely any relationship at all. How different, indeed? From what Cowperwood had said in Chicago she had fancied that when they took up their formal abode in New York he would make an attempt to straighten out his life somewhat, to modify the number of his indifferent amours and to present an illusion of solidarity and unity. Yet, now that they had actually arrived, she noticed that he was more concerned with his heightened political and financial complications in Illinois and with his art-collection than he was with what might happen to be going on in the new home or what could be made to happen there. As in the days of old, she was constantly puzzled by his persistent evenings out and his sudden appearances and disappearances. Yet, determine as she might, rage secretly or openly as she would, she could not cure herself of the infection of Cowperwood, the lure that surrounded and substantiated a mind and spirit far greater than any other she had ever known. Neither honor, virtue, consistent charity, nor sympathy was there, but only a gay, foamy, unterrified sufficiency and a creative, constructive sense of beauty that, like sunlit spray, glowing with all the irradiative glories of the morning, danced and fled, spun driftwise over a heavy sea of circumstance. Life, however dark and somber, could never apparently cloud his soul. Brooding and idling in the wonder palace of his construction, Aileen could see what he was like. The silver fountain in the court of orchids, the peach-like glow of the pink marble chamber, with its birds and flowers, the serried brilliance of his amazing art-collections were all like him, were really the color of his soul. To think that after all she was not the one to bind him to subjection, to hold him by golden yet steely threads of fancy to the hem of her garment! To think that he should no longer walk, a slave of his desire, behind the chariot of her spiritual and physical superiority. Yet she could not give up.

By this time Cowperwood had managed through infinite tact and a stoic disregard of his own aches and pains to re-establish at least a temporary working arrangement with the Carter household. To Mrs. Carter he was still a Heaven-sent son of light. Actually in a mournful way she pleaded for Cowperwood, vouching for his disinterestedness and long-standing generosity. Berenice, on the other hand, was swept between her craving for a great state for herself—luxury, power—and her desire to conform to the current ethics and morals of life. Cowperwood was married, and because of his attitude of affection for her his money was tainted. She had long speculated on his relation to Aileen, the basis of their differences, had often wondered why neither she nor her mother had ever been introduced. What type of woman was the second Mrs. Cowperwood? Beyond generalities Cowperwood had never mentioned her. Berenice actually thought to seek her out in some inconspicuous way, but, as it chanced, one night her curiosity was rewarded without effort. She was at the opera with friends, and her escort nudged her arm.

"Have you noticed Box 9—the lady in white satin with the green lace shawl?"

"Yes." Berenice raised her glasses.

"Mrs. Frank Algernon Cowperwood, the wife of the Chicago millionaire. They have just built that house at 68th Street. He has part lease of number 9, I believe."

Berenice almost started, but retained her composure, giving merely an indifferent glance. A little while after, she adjusted her glasses carefully and studied Mrs. Cowperwood. She noted curiously that Aileen's hair was somewhat the color of her own—more carroty red. She studied her eyes, which were slightly ringed, her smooth cheeks and full mouth, thickened somewhat by drinking and dissipation. Aileen was good-looking, she thought—

handsome in a material way, though so much older than herself. Was it merely age that was alienating Cowperwood, or was it some deep-seated intellectual difference? Obviously Mrs. Cowperwood was well over forty—a fact which did not give Berenice any sense of satisfaction or of advantage. She really did not care enough. It did occur to her, however, that this woman whom she was observing had probably given the best years of her life to Cowperwood—the brilliant years of her girlhood. And now he was tired of her! There were small carefully powdered lines at the tails of Aileen's eyes and at the corners of her mouth. At the same time she seemed preternaturally gay, kittenish, spoiled. With her were two men—one a well-known actor, sinisterly handsome, a man with a brutal, unclean reputation, the other a young social pretender—both unknown to Berenice. Her knowledge was to come from her escort, a loquacious youth, more or less versed, as it happened, in the gay life of the city.

"I hear that she is creating quite a stir in Bohemia," he observed. "If she expects to enter society it's a poor way to begin, don't you think?"

"Do you know that she expects to?"

"All the usual signs are out—a box here, a house on Fifth Avenue."

This study of Aileen puzzled and disturbed Berenice a little. Nevertheless, she felt immensely superior. Her soul seemed to soar over the plain Aileen inhabited. The type of the latter's escorts suggested error—a lack of social discrimination. Because of the high position he had succeeded in achieving Cowperwood was entitled, no doubt, to be dissatisfied. His wife had not kept pace with him, or, rather, had not eluded him in his onward flight—had not run swiftly before, like a winged victory. Berenice reflected that if she were dealing with such a man he should never know her truly—he should be made to wonder and to doubt. Lines of care and disappointment should never mar her face. She would scheme and dream and conceal and evade. He should dance attendance, whoever he was.

Nevertheless, here she herself was, at twenty-two, unmarried, her background insecure, the very ground on which she walked treacherous. Braxmar knew, and Beales Chadsey, and Cowperwood. At least three or four of her acquaintances must have been at the Waldorf on that fatal night. How long would it be before others became aware? She tried eluding her mother, Cowperwood, and the situation generally by freely accepting more extended invitations and by trying to see whether there was not some opening for her in the field of art. She thought of painting and essayed several canvases which she took to dealers. The work was subtle, remote, fanciful—a snow scene with purple edges; a thinking satyr, iron-like in his heaviness, brooding over a cloudy valley; a lurking devil peering at a praying Marguerite; a Dutch interior inspired by Mrs. Batjer, and various dancing figures. Phlegmatic dealers of somber mien admitted some promise, but pointed out the difficulty of sales. Beginners were numerous. Art was long. If she went on, of course.... Let them see other things. She turned her thoughts to dancing.

This art in its interpretative sense was just being introduced into America, a certain Althea Baker having created a good deal of stir in society by this means. With the idea of duplicating or surpassing the success of this woman Berenice conceived a dance series of her own. One was to be "The Terror"—a nymph dancing in the spring woods, but eventually pursued and terrorized by a faun; another, "The Peacock," a fantasy illustrative of proud self-adulation; another, "The Vestal," a study from Roman choric worship. After spending considerable time at Pocono evolving costumes, poses, and the like, Berenice finally hinted at the plan to Mrs. Batjer, declaring that she would enjoy the artistic outlet it would afford, and indicating at the same time that it might provide the necessary solution of a problem of ways and means.

"Why, Bevy, how you talk!" commented Mrs. Batjer. "And with your possibilities. Why don't you marry first, and do your dancing afterward? You might compel a certain amount of attention that way."

"Because of hubby? How droll! Whom would you suggest that I marry at once?"

"Oh, when it comes to that—" replied Mrs. Batjer, with a slight reproachful lift in her voice, and thinking of Kilmer Duelma. "But surely your need isn't so pressing. If you were to take up professional dancing I might have to cut you afterward—particularly if any one else did."

She smiled the sweetest, most sensible smile. Mrs. Batjer accompanied her suggestions nearly always with a slight sniff and cough. Berenice could see that the mere fact of this conversation made a slight difference. In Mrs. Batjer's world poverty was a dangerous topic. The mere odor of it suggested a kind of horror—perhaps the equivalent of error or sin. Others, Berenice now suspected, would take affright even more swiftly.

Subsequent to this, however, she made one slight investigation of those realms that govern professional theatrical engagements. It was a most disturbing experience. The mere color and odor of the stuffy offices, the gauche, material attendants, the impossible aspirants and participants in this make-believe world! The crudeness! The effrontery! The materiality! The sensuality! It came to her as a sickening breath and for the moment frightened her. What would become of refinement there? What of delicacy? How could one rise and sustain an individual dignity and control in such a world as this?

Cowperwood was now suggesting as a binding link that he should buy a home for them in Park Avenue, where such social functions as would be of advantage to Berenice and in some measure to himself as an occasional guest might be indulged in. Mrs. Carter, a fool of comfort, was pleased to welcome this idea. It promised to give her absolute financial security for the future.

"I know how it is with you, Frank," she declared. "I know you need some place that you can call a home. The whole difficulty will be with Bevy. Ever since that miserable puppy made those charges against me I haven't been able to talk to her at all. She doesn't seem to want to do anything I suggest. You have much more influence with her than I have. If you explain, it may be all right."

Instantly Cowperwood saw an opportunity. Intensely pleased with this confession of weakness on the part of the mother, he went to Berenice, but by his usual method of indirect direction.

"You know, Bevy," he said, one afternoon when he found her alone, "I have been wondering if it wouldn't be better if I bought a large house for you and your mother here in New York, where you and she could do entertaining on a large scale. Since I can't spend my money on myself, I might as well spend it on some one who would make an interesting use of it. You might include me as an uncle or father's cousin or something of that sort," he added, lightly.

Berenice, who saw quite clearly the trap he was setting for her, was nonplussed. At the same time she could not help seeing that a house, if it were beautifully furnished, would be an interesting asset. People in society loved fixed, notable dwellings; she had observed that. What functions could not be held if only her mother's past were not charged against her! That was the great difficulty. It was almost an Arabian situation, heightened by the glitter of gold. And Cowperwood was always so diplomatic. He came forward with such a bland, engaging smile. His hands were so shapely and seeking.

"A house such as you speak of would enlarge the debt beyond payment, I presume," she remarked, sardonically and with a sad, almost contemptuous gesture. Cowperwood realized how her piercing intellect was following his shifty trail, and winced. She must see that her fate was in his hands, but oh! if she would only surrender, how swiftly every dollar of his vast fortune should be piled humbly at her feet. She should have her heart's desire, if money would buy it. She could say to him go, and he would go; come, and he would come.

"Berenice," he said, getting up, "I know what you think. You fancy I am trying to further my own interests in this way, but I'm not. I wouldn't compromise you ultimately for all the wealth of India. I have told you where I stand. Every dollar that I have is yours to do with as you choose on any basis that you may care to name. I have no future outside of you, none except art. I do not expect you to marry me. Take all that I have. Wipe society under your feet. Don't think that I will ever charge it up as a debt. I won't. I want you to hold your own. Just answer me one question; I won't ever ask another."

"Yes?"

"If I were single now, and you were not in love or married, would you consider me at all?"

His eyes pleaded as never had they pleaded before.

She started, looked concerned, severe, then relaxed as suddenly. "Let me see," she said, with a slight brightening of the eyes and a toss of her head. "That is a second cousin to a proposal, isn't it? You have no right to make it. You aren't single, and aren't likely to be. Why should I try to read the future?"

She walked indifferently out of the room, and Cowperwood stayed a moment to think. Obviously he had triumphed in a way. She had not taken great offense. She must like him and would marry him if only...

Only Aileen.

And now he wished more definitely and forcefully than ever that he were really and truly free. He felt that if ever he wished to attain Berenice he must persuade Aileen to divorce him.

CHAPTER LVII

AILEEN'S LAST CARD

It was not until some little time after they were established in the new house that Aileen first came upon any evidence of the existence of Berenice Fleming. In a general way she assumed that there were women—possibly some of whom she had known—Stephanie, Mrs. Hand, Florence Cochrane, or later arrivals—yet so long as they were not obtruded on her she permitted herself the semi-comforting thought that things were not as bad as they might be. So long, indeed, as Cowperwood was genuinely promiscuous, so long as he trotted here and there, not snared by any particular siren, she could not despair, for, after all, she had ensnared him and held him deliciously—without variation, she believed, for all of ten years—a feat which no other woman had achieved before or after. Rita Sohlberg might have succeeded—the beast! How she hated the thought of Rita! By this time, however, Cowperwood was getting on in years. The day must come when he would be less keen for variability, or, at least, would think it no longer worth while to change. If only he did not find some one woman, some Circe, who would bind and enslave him in these Later years as she had herself done in his earlier ones all might yet be well. At the same time she lived in daily terror of a discovery which was soon to follow.

She had gone out one day to pay a call on some one to whom Rhees Grier, the Chicago sculptor, had given her an introduction. Crossing Central Park in one of the new French machines which Cowperwood had purchased for her indulgence, her glance wandered down a branch road to where another automobile similar to her own was stalled. It was early in the afternoon, at which time Cowperwood was presumably engaged in Wall Street. Yet there he was, and with him two women, neither of whom, in the speed of passing, could Aileen quite make out. She had her car halted and driven to within seeing-distance behind a clump of bushes. A chauffeur whom she did not know was tinkering at a handsome machine, while on the grass near by stood Cowperwood and a tall, slender girl with red hair somewhat like Aileen's own. Her expression was aloof, poetic, rhapsodical. Aileen could not analyze it, but it fixed her attention completely. In the tonneau sat an elderly lady, whom Aileen at once assumed to be the girl's mother. Who were they? What was Cowperwood doing here in the Park at this hour? Where were they going? With a horrible retch of envy she noted upon Cowperwood's face a smile the like and import of which she well knew. How often she had seen it years and years before! Having escaped detection, she ordered her chauffeur to follow the car, which soon started, at a safe distance. She saw Cowperwood and the two ladies put down at one of the great hotels, and followed them into the dining-room, where, from behind a screen, after the most careful manoeuvering, she had an opportunity of studying them at her leisure. She drank in every detail of Berenice's face—the delicately pointed chin, the clear, fixed blue eyes, the straight, sensitive nose and tawny hair. Calling the head waiter, she inquired the names of the two women, and in return for a liberal tip was informed at once. "Mrs. Ira Carter, I believe, and her daughter, Miss Fleming, Miss Berenice Fleming. Mrs. Carter was Mrs. Fleming once." Aileen followed them out eventually, and in her own car pursued them to their door, into which Cowperwood also disappeared. The next day, by telephoning the apartment to make inquiry, she learned that they actually lived there. After a few days of brooding she employed a detective, and learned that Cowperwood was a constant visitor at the Carters', that the machine in which they rode was his maintained at a separate garage, and that they were of society truly. Aileen would never have followed the clue so vigorously had it not been for the look she had seen Cowperwood fix on the girl in the Park and in the restaurant—an air of soul-hunger which could not be gainsaid.

Let no one ridicule the terrors of unrequited love. Its tentacles are cancerous, its grip is of icy death. Sitting in her boudoir immediately after these events, driving, walking, shopping, calling on the few with whom she had managed to scrape an acquaintance, Aileen thought morning, noon, and night of this new woman. The pale, delicate face haunted her. What were those eyes, so remote in their gaze, surveying? Love? Cowperwood? Yes! Yes! Gone in a flash, and permanently, as it seemed to Aileen, was the value of this house, her dream of a new social entrance. And she had already suffered so much; endured so much. Cowperwood being absent for a fortnight, she moped in her room, sighed, raged, and then began to drink. Finally she sent for an actor who had once paid attention to her in Chicago, and whom she had later met here in the circle of the theaters. She was not so much burning with lust as determined in her drunken gloom that she would have revenge. For days there followed an orgy, in which wine, bestiality, mutual recrimination, hatred, and despair were involved. Sobering eventually, she wondered what Cowperwood would think of her now if he knew this? Could he ever love her any more? Could he even tolerate her? But what did he care? It served him right, the dog! She would show him, she would wreck his dream, she would make her own life a scandal, and his too! She would shame him before all the world. He should never have a divorce! He should never be able to marry a girl like that and leave her alone—never, never, never! When Cowperwood returned she snarled at him without vouchsafing an explanation.

He suspected at once that she had been spying upon his manoeuvers. Moreover, he did not fail to notice her heavy eyes, superheated cheeks, and sickly breath. Obviously she had abandoned her dream of a social victory of some kind, and was entering on a career of what—debauchery? Since coming to New York she had failed utterly, he thought, to make any single intelligent move toward her social rehabilitation. The banal realms of art and the stage, with which in his absence or neglect she had trifled with here, as she had done in Chicago, were worse than useless; they were destructive. He must have a long talk with her one of these days, must confess frankly to his passion for Berenice, and appeal to her sympathy and good sense. What scenes would follow! Yet she might succumb, at that. Despair, pride, disgust might move her. Besides, he could now bestow upon her a very large fortune. She could go to Europe or remain here and live in luxury. He would always remain friendly with her—helpful, advisory—if she would permit it.

The conversation which eventually followed on this topic was of such stuff as dreams are made of. It sounded hollow and unnatural within the walls where it took place. Consider the great house in upper Fifth Avenue, its magnificent chambers aglow, of a stormy Sunday night. Cowperwood was lingering in the city at this time, busy with a group of Eastern financiers who were influencing his contest in the state legislature of Illinois. Aileen was momentarily consoled by the thought that for him perhaps love might, after all, be a thing apart—a thing no longer vital and soul-controlling. To-night he was sitting in the court of orchids, reading a book—the diary of Cellini, which some one had recommended to him—stopping to think now and then of things in Chicago or Springfield, or to make a note. Outside the rain was splashing in torrents on the electric-lighted asphalt of Fifth Avenue—the Park opposite a Corot-like shadow. Aileen was in the music-room strumming indifferently. She was thinking of times past—Lynde, from whom she had not heard in half a year; Watson Skeet, the sculptor, who was also out of her ken at present. When Cowperwood was in the city and in the house she was accustomed from habit to remain indoors or near. So great is the influence of past customs of devotion that they linger long past the hour when the act ceases to become valid.

"What an awful night!" she observed once, strolling to a window to peer out from behind a brocaded valance.

"It is bad, isn't it?" replied Cowperwood, as she returned. "Hadn't you thought of going anywhere this evening?"

"No—oh no," replied Aileen, indifferently. She rose restlessly from the piano, and strolled on into the great picture-gallery. Stopping before one of Raphael Sanzio's Holy Families, only recently hung, she paused to contemplate the serene face—medieval, Madonnaesque, Italian.

The lady seemed fragile, colorless, spineless—without life. Were there such women? Why did artists paint them? Yet the little Christ was sweet. Art bored Aileen unless others were enthusiastic. She craved only the fanfare of the living—not painted resemblances. She returned to the music-room, to the court of orchids, and was just about to go up-stairs to prepare herself a drink and read a novel when Cowperwood observed:

"You're bored, aren't you?"

"Oh no; I'm used to lonely evenings," she replied, quietly and without any attempt at sarcasm.

Relentless as he was in hewing life to his theory—hammering substance to the form of his thought—yet he was tender, too, in the manner of a rainbow dancing over an abyss. For the moment he wanted to say, "Poor girlie, you do have a hard time, don't you, with me?" but he reflected instantly how such a remark would be received. He meditated, holding his book in his hand above his knee, looking at the purling water that flowed and flowed in sprinkling showers over the sportive marble figures of mermaids, a Triton, and nymphs astride of fishes.

"You're really not happy in this state, any more, are you?" he inquired. "Would you feel any more comfortable if I stayed away entirely?"

His mind had turned of a sudden to the one problem that was fretting him and to the opportunities of this hour.

"You would," she replied, for her boredom merely concealed her unhappiness in no longer being able to command in the least his interest or his sentiment.

"Why do you say that in just that way?" he asked.

"Because I know you would. I know why you ask. You know well enough that it isn't anything I want to do that is concerned. It's what you want to do. You'd like to turn me off like an old horse now that you are tired of me, and so you ask whether I would feel any more comfortable. What a liar you are, Frank! How really shifty you are! I don't wonder you're a multimillionaire. If you could live long enough you would eat up the whole world. Don't you think for one moment that I don't know of Berenice Fleming here in New York, and how you're dancing attendance on her—because I do. I know how you have been hanging about her for months and months—ever since we have been here, and for long before. You think she's wonderful now because she's young and in society. I've seen you in the Waldorf and in the Park hanging on her every word, looking at her with adoring eyes. What a fool you are, to be so big a man! Every little snip, if she has pink cheeks and a doll's face, can wind you right around her finger. Rita Sohlberg did it; Stephanie Platow did it; Florence Cochrane did it; Cecily Haguenin—and Heaven knows how many more that I never heard of. I suppose Mrs. Hand still lives with you in Chicago—the cheap strumpet! Now it's Berenice Fleming and her frump of a mother. From all I can learn you haven't been able to get her yet—because her mother's too shrewd, perhaps—but you probably will in the end. It isn't you so much as your money that they're after. Pah! Well, I'm unhappy enough, but it isn't anything you can remedy any more. Whatever you could do to make me unhappy you have done, and now you talk of my being happier away from you. Clever boy, you! I know you the way I know my ten fingers. You don't deceive me at any time in any way any more. I can't do anything about it. I can't stop you from making a fool of yourself with every woman you meet, and having people talk from one end of the country to the other. Why, for a woman to be seen with you is enough to fix her reputation forever. Right now all Broadway knows you're running after Berenice Fleming. Her name will soon be as sweet as those of the others you've had. She might as well give herself to you. If she ever had a decent reputation it's gone by now, you can depend upon that."

These remarks irritated Cowperwood greatly—enraged him—particularly her references to Berenice. What were you to do with such a woman? he thought. Her tongue was becoming unbearable; her speech in its persistence and force was that of a termagant. Surely, surely, he had made a great mistake in marrying her. At the same time the control of her was largely in his own hands even yet.

"Aileen," he said, coolly, at the end of her speech, "you talk too much. You rave. You're growing vulgar, I believe. Now let me tell you something." And he fixed her with a hard, quieting eye. "I have no apologies to make. Think what you please. I know why you say what you do. But here is the point. I want you to get it straight and clear. It may make some difference eventually if you're any kind of a woman at all. I don't care for you any more. If you want to put it another way—I'm tired of you. I have been for a long while. That's why I've run with other women. If I hadn't been tired of you I wouldn't have done it. What's more, I'm in love with somebody else—Berenice Fleming, and I expect to stay in love. I wish I were free so I could rearrange my life on a different basis and find a little comfort before I die. You don't really care for me any more. You can't. I'll admit I have treated you badly; but if I had really loved you I wouldn't have done it, would I? It isn't my fault that love died in me, is it? It isn't your fault. I'm not blaming you. Love isn't a bunch of coals that can be blown by an artificial bellows into a flame at any time. It's out, and that's an end of it. Since I don't love you and can't, why should you want me to stay near you? Why shouldn't you let me go and give me a divorce? You'll be just as happy or unhappy away from me as with me. Why not? I want to be free again. I'm miserable here, and have been for a long time. I'll make any arrangement that seems fair and right to you. I'll give you this house—these pictures, though I really don't see what you'd want with them." (Cowperwood had no intention of giving up the gallery if he could help it.) "I'll settle on you for life any income you desire, or I'll give you a fixed sum outright. I want to be free, and I want you to let me be. Now why won't you be sensible and let me do this?"

During this harangue Cowperwood had first sat and then stood. At the statement that his love was really dead—the first time he had ever baldly and squarely announced it—Aileen had paled a little and put her hand to her forehead over her eyes. It was then he had arisen. He was cold, determined, a little revengeful for the moment. She realized now that he meant this—that in his heart was no least feeling for all that had gone before—no sweet memories, no binding thoughts of happy hours, days, weeks, years, that were so glittering and wonderful to her in retrospect. Great Heavens, it was really true! His love was dead; he had said it! But for the nonce she could not believe it; she would not. It really couldn't be true.

"Frank," she began, coming toward him, the while he moved away to evade her. Her eyes were wide, her hands trembling, her lips moving in an emotional, wavy, rhythmic way. "You really don't mean that, do you? Love isn't wholly dead, is it? All the love you used to feel for me? Oh, Frank, I have raged, I have hated, I have said terrible, ugly things, but it has been because I have been in love with you! All the time I have. You know that. I have felt so bad—O God, how bad I have felt! Frank, you don't know it—but my pillow has been wet many and many a night. I have cried and cried. I have got up and walked the floor. I have drunk whisky—plain, raw whisky—because something hurt me and I wanted to kill the pain. I have gone with other men, one after another—you know that—but, oh! Frank, Frank, you know that I didn't want to, that I didn't mean to! I have always despised the thought of them afterward. It was only because I was lonely and because you wouldn't pay any attention to me or be nice to me. Oh, how I have longed and longed for just one loving hour with you—one night, one day! There are women who could suffer in silence, but I can't. My mind won't let me alone, Frank—my thoughts won't. I can't help thinking how I used to run to you in Philadelphia, when you would meet me on your way home, or when I used to come to you in Ninth Street or on Eleventh. Oh, Frank, I probably did wrong to your first wife. I see it now—how she must have suffered! But I was just a silly girl then, and I didn't know. Don't you remember how I used to come to you in Ninth Street and how I saw you day after day in the penitentiary in Philadelphia? You said then you would love me always and that you would never forget. Can't you love me any more—just a little? Is it really true that your love is dead? Am I so old, so changed? Oh, Frank, please don't say that—please don't—please, please please! I beg of you!"

She tried to reach him and put a hand on his arm, but he stepped aside. To him, as he looked at her now, she was the antithesis of anything he could brook, let alone desire artistically or physically. The charm was gone, the spell broken. It was another type, another point of view he required, but, above all and principally, youth, youth—the spirit, for instance, that was in Berenice Fleming. He was sorry—in his way. He felt sympathy, but it was like the tinkling of a far-off sheep-bell—the moaning of a whistling buoy heard over the thrash of night-black waves on a stormy sea.

"You don't understand how it is, Aileen," he said. "I can't help myself. My love is dead. It is gone. I can't recall it. I can't feel it. I wish I could, but I can't; you must understand that. Some things are possible and some are not."

He looked at her, but with no relenting. Aileen, for her part, saw in his eyes nothing, as she believed, save cold philosophic logic—the man of business, the thinker, the bargainer, the plotter. At the thought of the adamantine character of his soul, which could thus definitely close its gates on her for ever and ever, she became wild, angry, feverish—not quite sane.

"Oh, don't say that!" she pleaded, foolishly. "Please don't. Please don't say that. It might come back a little if—if—you would only believe in it. Don't you see how I feel? Don't you see how it is?"

She dropped to her knees and clasped him about the waist. "Oh, Frank! Oh, Frank! Oh, Frank!" she began to call, crying. "I can't stand it! I can't! I can't! I can't! I shall die."

"Don't give way like that, Aileen," he pleaded. "It doesn't do any good. I can't lie to myself. I don't want to lie to you. Life is too short. Facts are facts. If I could say and believe that I loved you I would say so now, but I can't. I don't love you. Why should I say that I do?"

In the content of Aileen's nature was a portion that was purely histrionic, a portion that was childish—petted and spoiled—a portion that was sheer unreason, and a portion that was splendid emotion—deep, dark, involved. At this statement of Cowperwood's which seemed to throw her back on herself for ever and ever to be alone, she first pleaded willingness to compromise—to share. She had not fought Stephanie Platow, she had not fought Florence

Cochrane, nor Cecily Haguenin, nor Mrs. Hand, nor, indeed, anybody after Rita, and she would fight no more. She had not spied on him in connection with Berenice—she had accidentally met them. True, she had gone with other men, but? Berenice was beautiful, she admitted it, but so was she in her way still—a little, still. Couldn't he find a place for her yet in his life? Wasn't there room for both?

At this expression of humiliation and defeat Cowperwood was sad, sick, almost nauseated. How could one argue? How make her understand?

"I wish it were possible, Aileen," he concluded, finally and heavily, "but it isn't."

All at once she arose, her eyes red but dry.

"You don't love me, then, at all, do you? Not a bit?"

"No, Aileen, I don't. I don't mean by that that I dislike you. I don't mean to say that you aren't interesting in your way as a woman and that I don't sympathize with you. I do. But I don't love you any more. I can't. The thing I used to feel I can't feel any more."

She paused for a moment, uncertain how to take this, the while she whitened, grew more tense, more spiritual than she had been in many a day. Now she felt desperate, angry, sick, but like the scorpion that ringed by fire can turn only on itself. What a hell life was, she told herself. How it slipped away and left one aging, horribly alone! Love was nothing, faith nothing—nothing, nothing!

A fine light of conviction, intensity, intention lit her eye for the moment. "Very well, then," she said, coolly, tensely. "I know what I'll do. I'll not live this way. I'll not live beyond to-night. I want to die, anyhow, and I will."

It was by no means a cry, this last, but a calm statement. It should prove her love. To Cowperwood it seemed unreal, bravado, a momentary rage intended to frighten him. She turned and walked up the grand staircase, which was near—a splendid piece of marble and bronze fifteen feet wide, with marble nereids for newel-posts, and dancing figures worked into the stone. She went into her room quite calmly and took up a steel paper-cutter of dagger design—a knife with a handle of bronze and a point of great sharpness. Coming out and going along the balcony over the court of orchids, where Cowperwood still was seated, she entered the sunrise room with its pool of water, its birds, its benches, its vines. Locking the door, she sat down and then, suddenly baring an arm, jabbed a vein—ripped it for inches—and sat there to bleed. Now she would see whether she could die, whether he would let her.

Uncertain, astonished, not able to believe that she could be so rash, not believing that her feeling could be so great, Cowperwood still remained where she had left him wondering. He had not been so greatly moved—the tantrums of women were common—and yet— Could she really be contemplating death? How could she? How ridiculous! Life was so strange, so mad. But this was Aileen who had just made this threat, and she had gone up the stairs to carry it out, perhaps. Impossible! How could it be? Yet back of all his doubts there was a kind of sickening feeling, a dread. He recalled how she had assaulted Rita Sohlberg.

He hurried up the steps now and into her room. She was not there. He went quickly along the balcony, looking here and there, until he came to the sunrise room. She must be there, for the door was shut. He tried it—it was locked.

"Aileen," he called. "Aileen! Are you in there?" No answer. He listened. Still no answer. "Aileen!" he repeated. "Are you in there? What damned nonsense is this, anyhow?"

"George!" he thought to himself, stepping back; "she might do it, too—perhaps she has." He could not hear anything save the odd chattering of a toucan aroused by the light she had switched on. Perspiration stood out on his brow. He shook the knob, pushed a bell for a servant, called for keys which had been made for every door, called for a chisel and hammer.

"Aileen," he said, "if you don't open the door this instant I will see that it is opened. It can be opened quick enough."

Still no sound.

"Damn it!" he exclaimed, becoming wretched, horrified. A servant brought the keys. The right one would not enter. A second was on the other side. "There is a bigger hammer somewhere," Cowperwood said. "Get it! Get me a chair!" Meantime, with terrific energy, using a large chisel, he forced the door.

There on one of the stone benches of the lovely room sat Aileen, the level pool of water before her, the sunrise glow over every thing, tropic birds in their branches, and she, her hair disheveled, her face pale, one arm—her left—hanging down, ripped and bleeding, trickling a thick stream of rich, red blood. On the floor was a pool of blood, fierce, scarlet, like some rich cloth, already turning darker in places.

Cowperwood paused—amazed. He hurried forward, seized her arm, made a bandage of a torn handkerchief above the wound, sent for a surgeon, saying the while: "How could you, Aileen? How impossible! To try to take your life! This isn't love. It isn't even madness. It's foolish acting."

"Don't you really care?" she asked.

"How can you ask? How could you really do this?"

He was angry, hurt, glad that she was alive, shamed—many things.

"Don't you really care?" she repeated, wearily.

"Aileen, this is nonsense. I will not talk to you about it now. Have you cut yourself anywhere else?" he asked, feeling about her bosom and sides.

"Then why not let me die?" she replied, in the same manner. "I will some day. I want to."

"Well, you may, some day," he replied, "but not to-night. I scarcely think you want to now. This is too much, Aileen—really impossible."

He drew himself up and looked at her—cool, unbelieving, the light of control, even of victory, in his eyes. As he had suspected, it was not truly real. She would not have killed herself. She had expected him to come—to make the old effort. Very good. He would see her safely in bed and in a nurse's hands, and would then avoid her as much as possible in the future. If her intention was genuine she would carry it out in his absence, but he did not believe she would.

CHAPTER LVIII

A MARAUDER UPON THE COMMONWEALTH

The spring and summer months of 1897 and the late fall of 1898 witnessed the final closing battle between Frank Algernon Cowperwood and the forces inimical to him in so far as the city of Chicago, the state of Illinois, and indeed the United States of America, were concerned. When in 1896 a new governor and a new group of state representatives were installed Cowperwood decided that it would be advisable to continue the struggle at once. By the time this new legislature should convene for its labors a year would have passed since Governor Swanson had vetoed the original public-service-commission bill. By that time public sentiment as aroused by the newspapers would have had time to cool. Already through various favorable financial interests—particularly Haeckelheimer, Gotloeb & Co. and all the subsurface forces they represented—he had attempted to influence the incoming governor, and had in part succeeded.

The new governor in this instance—one Corporal A. E. Archer—or ex-Congressman Archer, as he was sometimes called—was, unlike Swanson, a curious mixture of the commonplace and the ideal—one of those shiftily loyal and loyally shifty who make their upward way by devious, if not too reprehensible methods. He was a little man, stocky, brown-haired, brown-eyed, vigorous, witty, with the ordinary politician's estimate of public morality—namely, that there is no such thing. A drummer-boy at fourteen in the War of the Rebellion, a private at sixteen and eighteen, he had subsequently been breveted for conspicuous military service. At this later time he was head of the Grand Army of the Republic, and conspicuous in various stirring eleemosynary efforts on behalf of the old soldiers, their widows and orphans. A fine American, flag-waving, tobacco-chewing, foul-swearing little man was this—and one with noteworthy political ambitions. Other Grand Army men had been conspicuous in the lists for Presidential nominations. Why not he? An excellent orator in a high falsetto way, and popular because of good-fellowship, presence, force, he was by nature materially and commercially minded—therefore without basic appeal to the higher ranks of intelligence. In seeking the nomination for governorship he had made the usual overtures and had in turn been sounded by Haeckelheimer, Gotloeb, and various other corporate interests who were in league with Cowperwood as to his attitude in regard to a proposed public-service commission. At first he had refused to commit himself. Later, finding that the C. W. & I. and the Chicago & Pacific (very powerful railroads both) were interested, and that other candidates were running him a tight chase in the gubernatorial contest, he succumbed in a measure, declaring privately that in case the legislature proved to be strongly in favor of the idea and the newspapers not too crushingly opposed he might be willing to stand as its advocate. Other candidates expressed similar views, but Corporal Archer proved to have the greater following, and was eventually nominated and comfortably elected.

Shortly after the new legislature had convened, it so chanced that a certain A. S. Rotherhite, publisher of the South Chicago Journal, was one day accidentally sitting as a visitor in the seat of a state representative by the name of Clarence Mulligan. While so occupied Rotherhite was familiarly slapped on the back by a certain Senator Ladrigo, of Menard, and was invited to come out into the rotunda, where, posing as Representative Mulligan, he was introduced by Senator Ladrigo to a stranger by the name of Gerard. The latter, with but few preliminary remarks, began as follows:

"Mr. Mulligan, I want to fix it with you in regard to this Southack bill which is soon to come up in the house. We have seventy votes, but we want ninety. The fact that the bill has gone to a second reading in the senate shows our strength. I am authorized to come to terms with you this morning if you would like. Your vote is worth two thousand dollars to you the moment the bill is signed."

Mr. Rotherhite, who happened to be a newly recruited member of the Opposition press, proved very canny in this situation.

"Excuse me," he stammered, "I did not understand your name?"

"Gerard. G-er-ard. Henry A. Gerard," replied this other.

"Thank you. I will think it over," was the response of the presumed Representative Mulligan.

Strange to state, at this very instant the authentic Mulligan actually appeared—heralded aloud by several of his colleagues who happened to be lingering near by in the lobby. Whereupon the anomalous Mr. Gerard and the crafty Senator Ladrigo discreetly withdrew. Needless to say that Mr. Rotherhite hurried at once to the forces of righteousness. The press should spread this little story broadcast. It was a very meaty incident; and it brought the whole matter once more into the fatal, poisonous field of press discussion.

At once the Chicago papers flew to arms. The cry was raised that the same old sinister Cowperwoodian forces were at work. The members of the senate and the house were solemnly warned. The sterling attitude of ex-Governor Swanson was held up as an example to the present Governor Archer. "The whole idea," observed an editorial in Truman Leslie MacDonald's Inquirer, "smacks of chicane, political subtlety, and political jugglery. Well do the citizens of Chicago and the people of Illinois know who and what particular organization would prove the true beneficiaries. We do not want a public-service commission at the behest of a private street-railway corporation. Are the tentacles of Frank A. Cowperwood to envelop this legislature as they did the last?"

This broadside, coming in conjunction with various hostile rumblings in other papers, aroused Cowperwood to emphatic language.

"They can all go to the devil," he said to Addison, one day at lunch. "I have a right to an extension of my franchises for fifty years, and I am going to get it. Look at New York and Philadelphia. Why, the Eastern houses laugh. They don't understand such a situation. It's all the inside work of this Hand-Schryhart crowd. I know what they're doing and who's pulling the strings. The newspapers yap-yap every time they give an order. Hyssop waltzes every time Arneel moves. Little MacDonald is a stool-pigeon for Hand. It's got down so low now that it's anything to beat Cowperwood. Well, they won't beat me. I'll find a way out. The legislature will pass a bill allowing for a fifty-year franchise, and the governor will sign it. I'll see to that personally. I have at least eighteen thousand stockholders who want a decent run for their money, and I propose to give it to them. Aren't other men getting rich? Aren't other corporations earning ten and twelve per cent? Why shouldn't I? Is Chicago any the worse? Don't I employ twenty thousand men and pay them well? All this palaver about the rights of the people and the duty to the public—rats! Does Mr. Hand acknowledge any duty to the public where his special interests are concerned? Or Mr. Schryhart? Or Mr. Arneel? The newspapers be damned! I know my rights. An honest legislature will give me a decent franchise to save me from the local political sharks."

By this time, however, the newspapers had become as subtle and powerful as the politicians themselves. Under the great dome of the capitol at Springfield, in the halls and conference chambers of the senate and house, in the hotels, and in the rural districts wherever any least information was to be gathered, were their representatives—to see, to listen, to pry. Out of this contest they were gaining prestige and cash. By them were the reform aldermen persuaded to call mass-meetings in their respective districts. Property-owners were urged to organize; a committee of one hundred prominent citizens led by Hand and Schryhart was formed. It was not long before the halls, chambers, and committee-rooms of the capitol at Springfield and the corridors of the one principal hotel were being tramped over almost daily by rampant delegations of ministers, reform aldermen, and civil committeemen, who arrived speechifying, threatening, and haranguing, and departed, only to make room for another relay.

"Say, what do you think of these delegations, Senator?" inquired a certain Representative Greenough of Senator George Christian, of Grundy, one morning, the while a group of Chicago clergymen accompanied by the mayor and several distinguished private citizens passed through the rotunda on their way to the committee on railroads, where the house bill was privily being discussed. "Don't you think they speak well for our civic pride and moral upbringing?" He raised his eyes and crossed his fingers over his waistcoat in the most sanctimonious and reverential attitude.

"Yes, dear Pastor," replied the irreverent Christian, without the shadow of a smile. He was a little sallow, wiry man with eyes like a ferret, a small mustache and goatee ornamenting his face. "But do not forget that the Lord has called us also to this work."

"Even so," acquiesced Greenough. "We must not weary in well doing. The harvest is truly plenteous and the laborers are few."

"Tut, tut, Pastor. Don't overdo it. You might make me larf," replied Christian; and the twain parted with knowing and yet weary smiles.

Yet how little did the accommodating attitude of these gentlemen avail in silencing the newspapers. The damnable newspapers! They were here, there, and everywhere reporting each least fragment of rumor, conversation, or imaginary programme. Never did the citizens of Chicago receive so keen a drilling in statecraft—its subtleties and ramifications. The president of the senate and the speaker of the house were singled out and warned separately as to their duty. A page a day devoted to legislative proceeding in this quarter was practically the custom of the situation. Cowperwood was here personally on the scene, brazen, defiant, logical, the courage of his convictions in his eyes, the power of his magnetism fairly enslaving men. Throwing off the mask of disinterestedness—if any might be said to have covered him—he now frankly came out in the open and, journeying to Springfield, took quarters at the principal hotel. Like a general in time of battle, he marshaled his forces about him. In the warm, moonlit atmosphere of June nights when the streets of Springfield were quiet, the great plain of Illinois bathed for hundreds of miles from north to south in a sweet effulgence and the rurals slumbering in their simple homes, he sat conferring with his lawyers and legislative agents.

Pity in such a crisis the poor country-jake legislator torn between his desire for a justifiable and expedient gain and his fear lest he should be assailed as a betrayer of the people's interests. To some of these small-town legislators, who had never seen as much as two thousand dollars in cash in all their days, the problem was soul-racking. Men gathered in private rooms and hotel parlors to discuss it. They stood in their rooms at night and thought about it alone. The sight of big business compelling its desires the while the people went begging was destructive. Many a romantic, illusioned, idealistic young country editor, lawyer, or statesman was here made over into a minor cynic or bribe-taker. Men were robbed of every vestige of faith or even of charity; they came to feel, perforce, that there was nothing outside the capacity for taking and keeping. The surface might appear commonplace—ordinary men of the state of Illinois going here and there—simple farmers and small-town senators and representatives conferring and meditating and wondering what they could do—yet a jungle-like complexity was present, a dark, rank growth of horrific but avid life—life at the full, life knife in hand, life blazing with courage and dripping at the jaws with hunger.

However, because of the terrific uproar the more cautious legislators were by degrees becoming fearful. Friends in their home towns, at the instigation of the papers, were beginning to write them. Political enemies were taking heart. It meant too much of a sacrifice on the part of everybody. In spite of the fact that the bait was apparently within easy reach, many became evasive and disturbed. When a certain Representative Sparks, cocked and primed, with the bill in his pocket, arose upon the floor of the house, asking leave to have it spread upon the minutes, there was an instant explosion. The privilege of the floor was requested by a hundred. Another representative, Disback, being in charge of the opposition to Cowperwood, had made a count of noses and was satisfied in spite of all subtlety on the part of the enemy that he had at least one hundred and two votes, the necessary two-thirds wherewith to crush any measure which might originate on the floor. Nevertheless, his followers, because of caution, voted it to a second and a third reading. All sorts of amendments were made—one for a three-cent fare during the rush-hours, another for a 20 per cent. tax on gross receipts. In amended form the measure was sent to the senate, where the changes were stricken out and the bill once more returned to the house. Here, to Cowperwood's chagrin, signs were made manifest that it could not be passed. "It can't be done, Frank," said Judge Dickensheets. "It's too grilling a game. Their home papers are after them. They can't live."

Consequently a second measure was devised—more soothing and lulling to the newspapers, but far less satisfactory to Cowperwood. It conferred upon the Chicago City Council, by a trick of revising the old Horse and Dummy Act of 1865, the right to grant a franchise for fifty instead of for twenty years. This meant that Cowperwood would have to return to Chicago and fight out his battle there. It was a severe blow, yet better than nothing. Providing that he could win one more franchise battle within the walls of the city council in Chicago, it would give him all that he desired. But could he? Had he not come here to the legislature especially to evade such a risk? His motives were enduring such a blistering exposure. Yet perhaps, after all, if the price were large enough the Chicago councilmen would have more real courage than these country legislators—would dare more. They would have to.

So, after Heaven knows what desperate whisperings, conferences, arguments, and heartening of members, there was originated a second measure which—after the defeat of the first bill, 104 to 49—was introduced, by way of a very complicated path, through the judiciary committee. It was passed; and Governor Archer, after heavy hours of contemplation and self-examination, signed it. A little man mentally, he failed to estimate an aroused popular fury at its true import to him. At his elbow was Cowperwood in the clear light of day, snapping his fingers in the face of his enemies, showing by the hard, cheerful glint in his eye that he was still master of the situation, giving all assurance that he would yet live to whip the Chicago papers into submission. Besides, in the event of the passage of the bill, Cowperwood had promised to make Archer independently rich—a cash reward of five hundred thousand dollars.

CHAPTER LIX

CAPITAL AND PUBLIC RIGHTS

Between the passage on June 5, 1897, of the Mears bill—so christened after the doughty representative who had received a small fortune for introducing it—and its presentation to the Chicago City Council in December of the same year, what broodings, plottings, politickings, and editorializings on the part of all and sundry! In spite of the intense feeling of opposition to Cowperwood there was at the same time in local public life one stratum of commercial and phlegmatic substance that could not view him in an altogether unfavorable light. They were in business themselves. His lines passed their doors and served them. They could not see wherein his street-railway service differed so much from that which others might give. Here was the type of materialist who in Cowperwood's defiance saw a justification of his own material point of view and was not afraid to say so. But as against these there were the preachers—poor wind-blown sticks of unreason who saw only what the current palaver seemed to indicate. Again there were the anarchists, socialists, single-taxers, and public-ownership advocates. There were the very poor who saw in Cowperwood's wealth and in the fabulous stories of his New York home and of his art-collection a heartless exploitation of their needs. At this time the feeling was spreading broadcast in America that great political and economic changes were at hand—that the tyranny of iron masters at the top was to give way to a richer, freer, happier life for the rank and file. A national eight-hour-day law was being advocated, and the public ownership of public franchises. And here now was a great street-railway corporation, serving a population of a million and a half, occupying streets which the people themselves created by their presence, taking toll from all these humble citizens to the amount of sixteen or eighteen millions of dollars in the year and giving in return, so the papers said, poor service, shabby cars, no seats at rush-hours, no universal transfers (as a matter of fact, there were in operation three hundred and sixty-two separate transfer points) and no adequate tax on the immense sums earned. The workingman who read this by gas or lamp light in the kitchen or parlor of his shabby flat or cottage, and who read also in other sections of his paper of the free, reckless, glorious lives of the rich, felt himself to be defrauded of a portion of his rightful inheritance. It was all a question of compelling Frank A. Cowperwood to do his duty by Chicago. He must not again be allowed to bribe the aldermen; he must not be allowed to have a fifty-year franchise, the privilege of granting which he had already bought from the state legislature by the degradation of honest men. He must be made to succumb, to yield to the forces of law and order. It was claimed—and with a justice of which those who made the charge were by no means fully aware—that the Mears bill had been put through the house and senate by the use of cold cash, proffered even to the governor himself. No legal proof of this was obtainable, but Cowperwood was assumed to be a briber on a giant scale. By the newspaper cartoons he was represented as a pirate commander ordering his men to scuttle another vessel—the ship of Public Rights. He was pictured as a thief, a black mask over his eyes, and as a seducer, throttling Chicago, the fair maiden, while he stole her purse. The fame of this battle was by now becoming world-wide. In Montreal, in Cape Town, in Buenos Ayres and Melbourne, in London and Paris, men were reading of this singular struggle. At last, and truly, he was a national and international figure. His original dream, however, modified by circumstances, had literally been fulfilled.

Meanwhile be it admitted that the local elements in finance which had brought about this terrific onslaught on Cowperwood were not a little disturbed as to the eventual character of the child of their own creation. Here at last was a public opinion definitely inimical to Cowperwood; but here also were they themselves, tremendous profit-holders, with a desire for just such favors as Cowperwood himself had exacted, deliberately setting out to kill the goose that could lay the golden egg. Men such as Haeckelheimer, Gotloeb, Fishel, tremendous capitalists in the East and foremost in the directorates of huge transcontinental lines, international banking-houses, and the like, were amazed that the newspapers and the anti-Cowperwood element should have gone so far in Chicago. Had they no respect for capital? Did they not know that long-time franchises were practically the basis of all modern capitalistic prosperity? Such theories as were now being advocated here would spread to other cities unless checked. America might readily become anti-capitalistic—socialistic. Public ownership might appear as a workable theory—and then what?

"Those men out there are very foolish," observed Mr. Haeckelheimer at one time to Mr. Fishel, of Fishel, Stone & Symons. "I can't see that Mr. Cowperwood is different from any other organizer of his day. He seems to me perfectly sound and able. All his companies pay. There are no better investments than the North and West Chicago railways. It would be advisable, in my judgment, that all the lines out there should be consolidated and be put in his charge. He would make money for the stockholders. He seems to know how to run street-railways."

"You know," replied Mr. Fishel, as smug and white as Mr. Haeckelheimer, and in thorough sympathy with his point of view, "I have been thinking of something like that myself. All this quarreling should be hushed up. It's very bad for business—very. Once they get that public-ownership nonsense started, it will be hard to stop. There has been too much of it already."

Mr. Fishel was stout and round like Mr. Haeckelheimer, but much smaller. He was little more than a walking mathematical formula. In his cranium were financial theorems and syllogisms of the second, third, and fourth power only.

And now behold a new trend of affairs. Mr. Timothy Arneel, attacked by pneumonia, dies and leaves his holdings in Chicago City to his eldest son, Edward Arneel. Mr. Fishel and Mr. Haeckelheimer, through agents and then direct, approach Mr. Merrill in behalf of Cowperwood. There is much talk of profits—how much more profitable has been the Cowperwood regime over street-railway lines than that of Mr. Schryhart. Mr. Fishel is interested in allaying socialistic excitement. So, by this time, is Mr. Merrill. Directly hereafter Mr. Haeckelheimer approaches Mr. Edward Arneel, who is not nearly so forceful as his father, though he would like to be so. He, strange to relate, has come rather to admire Cowperwood and sees no advantage in a policy that can only tend to municipalize local lines. Mr. Merrill, for Mr. Fishel, approaches Mr. Hand. "Never! never! never!" says Hand. Mr. Haeckelheimer approaches Mr. Hand. "Never! never! never! To the devil with Mr. Cowperwood!" But as a final emissary for Mr. Haeckelheimer and Mr. Fishel there now appears Mr. Morgan Frankhauser, the partner of Mr. Hand in a seven-million-dollar traction scheme in Minneapolis and St. Paul. Why will Mr. Hand be so persistent? Why pursue a scheme of revenge which only stirs up the masses and makes municipal ownership a valid political idea, thus disturbing capital elsewhere? Why not trade his Chicago holdings to him, Frankhauser, for Pittsburg traction stock—share and share alike—and then fight Cowperwood all he pleases on the outside?

Mr. Hand, puzzled, astounded, scratching his round head, slaps a heavy hand on his desk. "Never!" he exclaims. "Never, by God—as long as I am alive and in Chicago!" And then he yields. Life does shifty things, he is forced to reflect in a most puzzled way. Never would he have believed it! "Schryhart," he declared to Frankhauser, "will never come in. He will die first. Poor old Timothy—if he were alive—he wouldn't either."

"Leave Mr. Schryhart out of it, for Heaven's sake," pleaded Mr. Frankhauser, a genial American German. "Haven't I troubles enough?"

Mr. Schryhart is enraged. Never! never! never! He will sell out first—but he is in a minority, and Mr. Frankhauser, for Mr. Fishel or Mr. Haeckelheimer, will gladly take his holdings.

Now behold in the autumn of 1897 all rival Chicago street-railway lines brought to Mr. Cowperwood on a platter, as it were—a golden platter.

"Ve haff it fixed," confidentially declared Mr. Gotloeb to Mr. Cowperwood, over an excellent dinner in the sacred precincts of the Metropolitan Club in New York. Time, 8.30 P.M. Wine—sparkling burgundy. "A telegram come shusst to-day from Frankhauser. A nice man dot. You shouldt meet him sometime. Hant—he sells out his stock to Frankhauser. Merrill unt Edward Arneel vork vit us. Ve hantle efferyt'ing for dem. Mr. Fishel vill haff his friends pick up all de local shares he can, unt mit dees tree ve control de board. Schryhart iss out. He sess he vill resign. Very goot. I don't subbose dot vill make you veep any. It all hintges now on vether you can get dot fifty-year-franchise ordinance troo de city council or not. Haeckelheimer sess he prefers you to all utters to run t'ings. He vill leef everytink positifely in your hands. Frankhauser sess de same. Vot Haeckelheimer sess he doess. Now dere you are. It's up to you. I vish you much choy. It is no small chop you haff, beating de newspapers, unt you still haff Hant unt Schryhart against you. Mr. Haeckelheimer askt me to pay his complimends to you unt to say vill you dine vit him next veek, or may he dine vit you—vicheffer iss most conveniend. So."

In the mayor's chair of Chicago at this time sat a man named Walden H. Lucas. Aged thirty-eight, he was politically ambitious. He had the elements of popularity—the knack or luck of fixing public attention. A fine, upstanding, healthy young buck he was, subtle, vigorous, a cool, direct, practical thinker and speaker, an eager enigmatic dreamer of great political honors to come, anxious to play his cards just right, to make friends, to be the pride of the righteous, and yet the not too uncompromising foe of the wicked. In short, a youthful, hopeful Western Machiavelli, and one who could, if he chose, serve the cause of the anti-Cowperwood struggle exceedingly well indeed.

Cowperwood, disturbed, visits the mayor in his office.

"Mr. Lucas, what is it you personally want? What can I do for you? Is it future political preferment you are after?"

"Mr. Cowperwood, there isn't anything you can do for me. You do not understand me, and I do not understand you. You cannot understand me because I am an honest man."

"Ye gods!" replied Cowperwood. "This is certainly a case of self-esteem and great knowledge. Good afternoon."

Shortly thereafter the mayor was approached by one Mr. Carker, who was the shrewd, cold, and yet magnetic leader of Democracy in the state of New York. Said Carker:

"You see, Mr. Lucas, the great money houses of the East are interested in this local contest here in Chicago. For example, Haeckelheimer, Gotloeb & Co. would like to see a consolidation of all the lines on a basis that will make them an attractive investment for buyers generally and will at the same time be fair and right to the city. A twenty-year contract is much too short a term in their eyes. Fifty is the least they could comfortably contemplate, and they would prefer a hundred. It is little enough for so great an outlay. The policy now being pursued here can lead only to the public ownership of public utilities, and that is something which the national Democratic party at large can certainly not afford to advocate at present. It would antagonize the money element from coast to coast. Any man whose political record was definitely identified with such a movement would have no possible chance at even a state nomination, let alone a national one. He could never be elected. I make myself clear, do I not?"

"You do."

"A man can just as easily be taken from the mayor's office in Chicago as from the governor's office at Springfield," pursued Mr. Carker. "Mr. Haeckelheimer and Mr. Fishel have personally asked me to call on you. If you want to be mayor of Chicago again for two years or governor next year, until the time for picking a candidate for the Presidency arrives, suit yourself. In the mean time you will be unwise, in my judgment, to saddle yourself with this public-ownership idea. The newspapers in fighting Mr. Cowperwood have raised an issue which never should have been raised."

After Mr. Carker's departure, arrived Mr. Edward Arneel, of local renown, and then Mr. Jacob Bethal, the Democratic leader in San Francisco, both offering suggestions which if followed might result in mutual support. There were in addition delegations of powerful Republicans from Minneapolis and from Philadelphia. Even the president of the Lake City Bank and the president of the Prairie National—once anti-Cowperwood—arrived to say what had already been said. So it went. Mr. Lucas was greatly nonplussed. A political career was surely a difficult thing to effect. Would it pay to harry Mr. Cowperwood as he had set out to do? Would a steadfast policy advocating the cause of the people get him anywhere? Would they be grateful? Would they remember? Suppose the current policy of the newspapers should be modified, as Mr. Carker had suggested that it might be. What a mess and tangle politics really were!

"Well, Bessie," he inquired of his handsome, healthy, semi-blonde wife, one evening, "what would you do if you were I?"

She was gray-eyed, gay, practical, vain, substantially connected in so far as family went, and proud of her husband's position and future. He had formed the habit of talking over his various difficulties with her.

"Well, I'll tell you, Wally," she replied. "You've got to stick to something. It looks to me as though the winning side was with the people this time. I don't see how the newspapers can change now after all they've done. You don't have to advocate public ownership or anything unfair to the money element, but just the same I'd stick to my point that the fifty-year franchise is too much. You ought to make them pay the city something and get their franchise without bribery. They can't do less than that. I'd stick to the course you've begun on. You can't get along without the people, Wally. You just must have them. If you lose their good will the politicians can't help you much, nor anybody else."

Plainly there were times when the people had to be considered. They just had to be!

CHAPTER LX

THE NET

The storm which burst in connection with Cowperwood's machinations at Springfield early in 1897, and continued without abating until the following fall, attracted such general attention that it was largely reported in the Eastern papers. F. A. Cowperwood versus the state of Illinois—thus one New York daily phrased the situation. The magnetizing power of fame is great. Who can resist utterly the luster that surrounds the individualities of some men, causing them to glow with a separate and special effulgence? Even in the case of Berenice this was not without its value. In a Chicago paper which she found lying one day on a desk which Cowperwood had occupied was an extended editorial which interested her greatly. After reciting his various misdeeds, particularly in connection with the present state legislature, it went on to say: "He has an innate, chronic, unconquerable contempt for the rank and file. Men are but slaves and thralls to draw for him the chariot of his greatness. Never in all his history has he seen fit to go to the people direct for anything. In Philadelphia, when he wanted public-franchise control, he sought privily and by chicane to arrange his affairs with a venal city treasurer. In Chicago he has uniformly sought to buy and convert to his own use the splendid privileges of the city, which should really redound to the benefit of all. Frank Algernon Cowperwood does not believe in the people; he does not trust them. To him they constitute no more than a field upon which corn is to be sown, and from which it is to be reaped. They present but a mass of bent backs, their knees and faces in the mire, over which as over a floor he strides to superiority. His private and inmost faith is in himself alone. Upon the majority he shuts the gates of his glory in order that the sight of their misery and their needs may not disturb nor alloy his selfish bliss. Frank Algernon Cowperwood does not believe in the people."

This editorial battle-cry, flung aloft during the latter days of the contest at Springfield and taken up by the Chicago papers generally and by those elsewhere, interested Berenice greatly. As she thought of him—waging his terrific contests, hurrying to and fro between New York and Chicago, building his splendid mansion, collecting his pictures, quarreling with Aileen—he came by degrees to take on the outlines of a superman, a half-god or demi-gorgon. How could the ordinary rules of life or the accustomed paths of men be expected to control him? They could not and did not. And here he was pursuing her, seeking her out with his eyes, grateful for a smile, waiting as much as he dared on her every wish and whim.

Say what one will, the wish buried deep in every woman's heart is that her lover should be a hero. Some, out of the veriest stick or stone, fashion the idol before which they kneel, others demand the hard reality of greatness; but in either case the illusion of paragon-worship is maintained.

Berenice, by no means ready to look upon Cowperwood as an accepted lover, was nevertheless gratified that his erring devotion was the tribute of one able apparently to command thought from the whole world. Moreover, because the New York papers had taken fire from his great struggle in the Middle West and were charging him with bribery, perjury, and intent to thwart the will of the people, Cowperwood now came forward with an attempt to explain his exact position to Berenice and to justify himself in her eyes. During visits to the Carter house or in entr'actes at the opera or the theater, he recounted to her bit by bit his entire history. He described the characters of Hand, Schryhart, Arneel, and the motives of jealousy and revenge which had led to their attack upon him in Chicago. "No human being could get anything through the Chicago City Council without paying for it," he declared. "It's simply a question of who's putting up the money." He told how Truman Leslie MacDonald had once tried to "shake him down" for fifty thousand dollars, and how the newspapers had since found it possible to make money, to increase their circulation, by attacking him. He frankly admitted the fact of his social ostracism, attributing it partially to Aileen's deficiencies and partially to his own attitude of Promethean defiance, which had never yet brooked defeat.

"And I will defeat them now," he said, solemnly, to Berenice one day over a luncheon-table at the Plaza when the room was nearly empty. His gray eyes were a study in colossal enigmatic spirit. "The governor hasn't signed my fifty-year franchise bill" (this was before the closing events at Springfield), "but he will sign it. Then I have one more fight ahead of me. I'm going to combine all the traffic lines out there under one general system. I am the logical person to provide it. Later on, if public ownership ever arrives, the city can buy it."

"And then—" asked Berenice sweetly, flattered by his confidences.

"Oh, I don't know. I suppose I'll live abroad. You don't seem to be very much interested in me. I'll finish my picture collection—"

"But supposing you should lose?"

"I don't contemplate losing," he remarked, coolly. "Whatever happens, I'll have enough to live on. I'm a little tired of contest."

He smiled, but Berenice saw that the thought of defeat was a gray one. With victory was his heart, and only there. Owing to the national publicity being given to Cowperwood's affairs at this time the effect upon Berenice of these conversations with him was considerable. At the same time another and somewhat sinister influence was working in his favor. By slow degrees she and her mother were coming to learn that the ultra-conservatives of society were no longer willing to accept them. Berenice had become at last too individual a figure to be overlooked. At an important luncheon given by the Harris Haggertys, some five months after the Beales Chadsey affair, she had been pointed out to Mrs. Haggerty by a visiting guest from Cincinnati as some one with whom rumor was concerning itself. Mrs. Haggerty wrote to friends in Louisville for information, and received it. Shortly after, at the coming-out party of a certain Geraldine Borga, Berenice, who had been her sister's schoolmate, was curiously omitted. She took sharp note of that. Subsequently the Haggertys failed to include her, as they had always done before, in their generous summer invitations. This was true also of the Lanman Zeiglers and the Lucas Demmigs. No direct affront was offered; she was simply no longer invited. Also one morning she read in the Tribune that Mrs. Corscaden Batjer had sailed for Italy. No word of this had been sent to Berenice. Yet Mrs. Batjer was supposedly one of her best friends. A hint to some is of more avail than an open statement to others. Berenice knew quite well in which direction the tide was setting.

True, there were a number—the ultra-smart of the smart world—who protested. Mrs. Patrick Gilbennin, for instance: "No! You don't tell me? What a shame! Well, I like Bevy and shall always like her. She's clever, and she can come here just as long as she chooses. It isn't her fault. She's a lady at heart and always will be. Life is so cruel." Mrs. Augustus Tabreez: "Is that really true? I can't believe it. Just the same, she's too charming to be dropped. I for one propose to ignore these rumors just as long as I dare. She can come here if she can't go anywhere else." Mrs. Pennington Drury: "That of Bevy Fleming! Who says so? I don't believe it. I like her anyhow. The idea of the Haggertys cutting her—dull fools! Well, she can be my guest, the dear thing, as long as she pleases. As though her mother's career really affected her!"

Nevertheless, in the world of the dull rich—those who hold their own by might of possession, conformity, owl-eyed sobriety, and ignorance—Bevy Fleming had become persona non grata. How did she take all this? With that air of superior consciousness which knows that no shift of outer material ill-fortune can detract one jot from an inward mental superiority. The truly individual know themselves from the beginning and rarely, if ever, doubt. Life may play fast and loose about them, running like a racing, destructive tide in and out, but they themselves are like a rock, still, serene, unmoved. Bevy Fleming felt herself to be so immensely superior to anything of which she was a part that she could afford to hold her head high even now Just the same, in order to remedy the situation she now looked about her with an eye single to a possible satisfactory marriage. Braxmar had gone for good. He was somewhere in the East—in China, she heard—his infatuation for her apparently dead. Kilmer Duelma was gone also—snapped up—an acquisition on the part of one of those families who did not now receive her. However, in the drawing-rooms where she still appeared—and what were they but marriage markets?—one or two affairs did spring up— tentative approachments on the part of scions of wealth. They were destined to prove abortive. One of these youths, Pedro Ricer Marcado, a Brazilian, educated at Oxford, promised much for sincerity and feeling until he learned that Berenice was poor in her own right—and what else? Some one had whispered something in his ear. Again there was a certain William Drake Bowdoin, the son of a famous old family, who lived on the north side of Washington Square. After a ball, a morning musicale, and one other affair at which they met Bowdoin took Berenice to see his mother and sister, who were charmed. "Oh, you serene divinity!" he said to her, ecstatically, one day. "Won't you marry me?" Bevy looked at him and wondered. "Let us wait just a little longer, my dear," she counseled. "I want you to be sure that you really love me. Shortly thereafter, meeting an old classmate at a club, Bowdoin was greeted as follows:

"Look here, Bowdoin. You're a friend of mine. I see you with that Miss Fleming. Now, I don't know how far things have gone, and I don't want to intrude, but are you sure you are aware of all the aspects of the case?"

"What do you mean?" demanded Bowdoin. "I want you to speak out."

"Oh, pardon, old man. No offense, really. You know me. I couldn't. College—and all that. Just this, though, before you go any further. Inquire about. You may hear things. If they're true you ought to know. If not, the talking ought to stop. If I'm wrong call on me for amends. I hear talk, I tell you. Best intentions in the world, old man. I do assure you."

More inquiries. The tongues of jealousy and envy. Mr. Bowdoin was sure to inherit three million dollars. Then a very necessary trip to somewhere, and Berenice stared at herself in the glass. What was it? What were people saying, if anything? This was strange. Well, she was young and beautiful. There were others. Still, she might have come to love Bowdoin. He was so airy, artistic in an unconscious way. Really, she had thought better of him.

The effect of all this was not wholly depressing. Enigmatic, disdainful, with a touch of melancholy and a world of gaiety and courage, Berenice heard at times behind joy the hollow echo of unreality. Here was a ticklish business, this living. For want of light and air the finest flowers might die. Her mother's error was not so inexplicable now. By it had she not, after all, preserved herself and her family to a certain phase of social superiority? Beauty was of such substance as dreams are made of, and as fleeting. Not one's self alone— one's inmost worth, the splendor of one's dreams—but other things—name, wealth, the presence or absence of rumor, and of accident—were important. Berenice's lip curled. But life could be lived. One could lie to the world. Youth is optimistic, and Berenice, in spite of her splendid mind, was so young. She saw life as a game, a good chance, that could be played in many ways. Cowperwood's theory of things began to appeal to her. One must create one's own career, carve it out, or remain horribly dull or bored, dragged along at the chariot wheels of others. If society was so finicky, if men were so dull—well, there was one thing she could do. She must have life, life—and money would help some to that end.

Besides, Cowperwood by degrees was becoming attractive to her; he really was. He was so much better than most of the others, so very powerful. She was preternaturally gay, as one who says, "Victory shall be mine anyhow."

CHAPTER LXI

THE CATACLYSM

And now at last Chicago is really facing the thing which it has most feared. A giant monopoly is really reaching out to enfold it with an octopus-like grip. And Cowperwood is its eyes, its tentacles, its force! Embedded in the giant strength and good will of Haeckelheimer, Gotloeb & Co., he is like a monument based on a rock of great strength. A fifty-year franchise, to be delivered to him by a majority of forty-eight out of a total of sixty-eight aldermen (in case the ordinance has to be passed over the mayor's veto), is all that now stands between him and the realization of his dreams. What a triumph for his iron policy of courage in the face of all obstacles! What a tribute to his ability not to flinch in the face of storm and stress! Other men might have abandoned the game long before, but not he. What a splendid windfall of chance that the money element should of its own accord take fright at the Chicago idea of the municipalization of public privilege and should hand him this giant South Side system as a reward for his stern opposition to fol-de-rol theories.

Through the influence of these powerful advocates he was invited to speak before various local commercial bodies—the Board of Real Estate Dealers, the Property Owners' Association, the Merchants' League, the Bankers' Union, and so forth, where he had an opportunity to present his case and justify his cause. But the effect of his suave speechifyings in these quarters was largely neutralized by newspaper denunciation. "Can any good come out of Nazareth?" was the regular inquiry. That section of the press formerly beholden to Hand and Schryhart stood out as bitterly as ever; and most of the other newspapers, being under no obligation to Eastern capital, felt it the part of wisdom to support the rank and file. The most searching and elaborate mathematical examinations were conducted with a view to showing the fabulous profits of the streetcar trust in future years. The fine hand of Eastern banking-houses was detected and their sinister motives noised abroad. "Millions for everybody in the trust, but not one cent for Chicago," was the Inquirer's way of putting it. Certain altruists of the community were by now so aroused that in the destruction of Cowperwood they saw their duty to God, to humanity, and to democracy straight and clear. The heavens had once more opened, and they saw a great light. On the other hand the politicians—those in office outside the mayor—constituted a petty band of guerrillas or free-booters who, like hungry swine shut in a pen, were ready to fall upon any and all propositions brought to their attention with but one end in view: that they might eat, and eat heartily. In times of great opportunity and contest for privilege life always sinks to its lowest depths of materialism and rises at the same time to its highest reaches of the ideal. When the waves of the sea are most towering its hollows are most awesome.

Finally the summer passed, the council assembled, and with the first breath of autumn chill the very air of the city was touched by a premonition of contest. Cowperwood, disappointed by the outcome of his various ingratiatory efforts, decided to fall back on his old reliable method of bribery. He fixed on his price—twenty thousand dollars for each favorable vote, to begin with. Later, if necessary, he would raise it to twenty-five thousand, or even thirty thousand, making the total cost in the neighborhood of a million and a half. Yet it was a small price indeed when the ultimate return was considered. He planned to have his ordinance introduced by an alderman named Ballenberg, a trusted lieutenant, and handed thereafter to the clerk, who would read it, whereupon another henchman would rise to move that it be referred to the joint committee on streets and alleys, consisting of thirty-four members drawn from all the standing committees. By this committee it would be considered for one week in the general council-chamber, where public hearings would be held. By keeping up a bold front Cowperwood thought the necessary iron could be put into his followers to enable them to go through with the scorching ordeal which was sure to follow. Already aldermen were being besieged at their homes and in the precincts of the ward clubs and meeting-places. Their mail was being packed with importuning or threatening letters. Their very children were being derided, their neighbors urged to chastise them. Ministers wrote them in appealing or denunciatory vein. They were spied upon and abused daily in the public prints. The mayor, shrewd son of battle that he was, realizing that he had a whip of terror in his hands, excited by the long contest waged, and by the smell of battle, was not backward in urging the most drastic remedies.

"Wait till the thing comes up," he said to his friends, in a great central music-hall conference in which thousands participated, and when the matter of ways and means to defeat the venal aldermen was being discussed. "We have Mr. Cowperwood in a corner, I think. He cannot do anything for two weeks, once his ordinance is in, and by that time we shall be able to organize a vigilance committee, ward meetings, marching clubs, and the like. We ought to organize a great central mass-meeting for the Sunday night before the Monday when the bill comes up for final hearing. We want overflow meetings in every ward at the same time. I tell you, gentlemen, that, while I believe there are enough honest voters in the city council to prevent the Cowperwood crowd from passing this bill over my veto, yet I don't think the matter ought to be allowed to go that far. You never can tell what these rascals will do once they see an actual cash bid of twenty or thirty thousand dollars before them. Most of them, even if they were lucky, would never make the half of that in a lifetime. They don't expect to be returned to the Chicago City Council. Once is enough. There are too many others behind them waiting to get their noses in the trough. Go into your respective wards and districts and organize meetings. Call your particular alderman before you. Don't let him evade you or quibble or stand on his rights as a private citizen or a public officer. Threaten—don't cajole. Soft or kind words won't go with that type of man.

Threaten, and when you have managed to extract a promise be on hand with ropes to see that he keeps his word. I don't like to advise arbitrary methods, but what else is to be done? The enemy is armed and ready for action right now. They're just waiting for a peaceful moment. Don't let them find it. Be ready. Fight. I'm your mayor, and ready to do all I can, but I stand alone with a mere pitiful veto right. You help me and I'll help you. You fight for me and I'll fight for you."

Witness hereafter the discomfiting situation of Mr. Simon Pinski at 9 P.M. on the second evening following the introduction of the ordinance, in the ward house of the Fourteenth Ward Democratic Club. Rotund, flaccid, red-faced, his costume a long black frock-coat and silk hat, Mr. Pinski was being heckled by his neighbors and business associates. He had been called here by threats to answer for his prospective high crimes and misdemeanors. By now it was pretty well understood that nearly all the present aldermen were criminal and venal, and in consequence party enmities were practically wiped out. There were no longer for the time being Democrats and Republicans, but only pro or anti Cowperwoods— principally anti. Mr. Pinski, unfortunately, had been singled out by the Transcript, the Inquirer, and the Chronicle as one of those open to advance questioning by his constituents. Of mixed Jewish and American extraction, he had been born and raised in the Fourteenth and spoke with a decidedly American accent. He was neither small nor large— sandy-haired, shifty-eyed, cunning, and on most occasions amiable. Just now he was decidedly nervous, wrathy, and perplexed, for he had been brought here against his will. His slightly oleaginous eye—not unlike that of a small pig—had been fixed definitely and finally on the munificent sum of thirty thousand dollars, no less, and this local agitation threatened to deprive him of his almost unalienable right to the same. His ordeal took place in a large, low-ceiled room illuminated by five very plain, thin, two-armed gas-jets suspended from the ceiling and adorned by posters of prizefights, raffles, games, and the "Simon Pinski Pleasure Association" plastered here and there freely against dirty, long-unwhitewashed walls. He stood on the low raised platform at the back of the room, surrounded by a score or more of his ward henchmen, all more or less reliable, all black-frocked, or at least in their Sunday clothes; all scowling, nervous, defensive, red-faced, and fearing trouble. Mr. Pinski has come armed. This talk of the mayor's concerning guns, ropes, drums, marching clubs, and the like has been given very wide publicity, and the public seems rather eager for a Chicago holiday in which the slaughter of an alderman or so might furnish the leading and most acceptable feature.

"Hey, Pinski!" yells some one out of a small sea of new and decidedly unfriendly faces. (This is no meeting of Pinski followers, but a conglomerate outpouring of all those elements of a distrait populace bent on enforcing for once the principles of aldermanic decency. There are even women here—local church-members, and one or two advanced civic reformers and W. C. T. U. bar-room smashers. Mr. Pinski has been summoned to their presence by the threat that if he didn't come the noble company would seek him out later at his own house.)

"Hey, Pinski! You old boodler! How much do you expect to get out of this traction business?" (This from a voice somewhere in the rear.)

Mr. Pinski (turning to one side as if pinched in the neck). "The man that says I am a boodler is a liar! I never took a dishonest dollar in my life, and everybody in the Fourteenth Ward knows it."

The Five Hundred People Assembled. "Ha! ha! ha! Pinski never took a dollar! Ho! ho! ho! Whoop-ee!"

Mr. Pinski (very red-faced, rising). "It is so. Why should I talk to a lot of loafers that come here because the papers tell them to call me names? I have been an alderman for six years now. Everybody knows me."

A Voice. "You call us loafers. You crook!"

Another Voice (referring to his statement of being known). "You bet they do!"

Another Voice (this from a small, bony plumber in workclothes). "Hey, you old grafter! Which way do you expect to vote? For or against this franchise? Which way?"

Still Another Voice (an insurance clerk). "Yes, which way?"

Mr. Pinski (rising once more, for in his nervousness he is constantly rising or starting to rise, and then sitting down again). "I have a right to my own mind, ain't I? I got a right to think. What for am I an alderman, then? The constitution..."

An Anti-Pinski Republican (a young law clerk). "To hell with the constitution! No fine words now, Pinski. Which way do you expect to vote? For or against? Yes or no?"

A Voice (that of a bricklayer, anti-Pinski). "He daresn't say. He's got some of that bastard's money in his jeans now, I'll bet."

A Voice from Behind (one of Pinski's henchmen—a heavy, pugilistic Irishman). "Don't let them frighten you, Sim. Stand your ground. They can't hurt you. We're here."

Pinski (getting up once more). "This is an outrage, I say. Ain't I gon' to be allowed to say what I think? There are two sides to every question. Now, I think whatever the newspapers say that Cowperwood—"

A Journeyman Carpenter (a reader of the Inquirer). "You're bribed, you thief! You're beating about the bush. You want to sell out."

The Bony Plumber. "Yes, you crook! You want to get away with thirty thousand dollars, that's what you want, you boodler!"

Mr. Pinski (defiantly, egged on by voices from behind). "I want to be fair—that's what. I want to keep my own mind. The constitution gives everybody the right of free speech— even me. I insist that the street-car companies have some rights; at the same time the people have rights too."

A Voice. "What are those rights?"

Another Voice. "He don't know. He wouldn't know the people's rights from a sawmill."

Another Voice. "Or a load of hay."

Pinski (continuing very defiantly now, since he has not yet been slain). "I say the people have their rights. The companies ought to be made to pay a fair tax. But this twenty-year-franchise idea is too little, I think. The Mears bill now gives them fifty years, and I think all told—"

The Five Hundred (in chorus). "Ho, you robber! You thief! You boodler! Hang him! Ho! ho! ho! Get a rope!"

Pinski (retreating within a defensive circle as various citizens approach him, their eyes blazing, their teeth showing, their fists clenched). "My friends, wait! Ain't I goin' to be allowed to finish?"

A Voice. "We'll finish you, you stiff!"

A Citizen (advancing; a bearded Pole). "How will you vote, hey? Tell us that! How? Hey?"

A Second Citizen (a Jew). "You're a no-good, you robber. I know you for ten years now already. You cheated me when you were in the grocery business."

A Third Citizen (a Swede. In a sing-song voice). "Answer me this, Mr. Pinski. If a majority of the citizens of the Fourteenth Ward don't want you to vote for it, will you still vote for it?"

Pinski (hesitating).

The Five Hundred. "Ho! look at the scoundrel! He's afraid to say. He don't know whether he'll do what the people of this ward want him to do. Kill him! Brain him!"

A Voice from Behind. "Aw, stand up, Pinski. Don't be afraid." Pinski (terrorized as the five hundred make a rush for the stage). "If the people don't want me to do it, of course I won't do it. Why should I? Ain't I their representative?"

A Voice. "Yes, when you think you're going to get the wadding kicked out of you."

Another Voice. "You wouldn't be honest with your mother, you bastard. You couldn't be!"

Pinski. "If one-half the voters should ask me not to do it I wouldn't do it."

A Voice. "Well, we'll get the voters to ask you, all right. We'll get nine-tenths of them to sign before to-morrow night."

An Irish-American (aged twenty-six; a gas collector; coming close to Pinski). "If you don't vote right we'll hang you, and I'll be there to help pull the rope myself."

One of Pinski's Lieutenants. "Say, who is that freshie? We want to lay for him. One good kick in the right place will just about finish him."

The Gas Collector. "Not from you, you carrot-faced terrier. Come outside and see." (Business of friends interfering).

The meeting becomes disorderly. Pinski is escorted out by friends—completely surrounded—amid shrieks and hisses, cat-calls, cries of "Boodler!" "Thief!" "Robber!"

There were many such little dramatic incidents after the ordinance had been introduced.

Henceforth on the streets, in the wards and outlying sections, and even, on occasion, in the business heart, behold the marching clubs—those sinister, ephemeral organizations which on demand of the mayor had cropped out into existence—great companies of the unheralded, the dull, the undistinguished—clerks, working-men, small business men, and minor scions of religion or morality; all tramping to and fro of an evening, after working-hours, assembling in cheap halls and party club-houses, and drilling themselves to what end? That they might march to the city hall on the fateful Monday night when the street-railway ordinances should be up for passage and demand of unregenerate lawmakers that they do their duty. Cowperwood, coming down to his office one morning on his own elevated lines, was the observer of a button or badge worn upon the coat lapel of stolid, inconsequential citizens who sat reading their papers, unconscious of that presence which epitomized the terror and the power they all feared. One of these badges had for its device a gallows with a free noose suspended; another was blazoned with the query: "Are we going to be robbed?" On sign-boards, fences, and dead walls huge posters, four by six feet in dimension, were displayed.

WALDEN H. LUCAS

against the

BOODLERS
===========================
Every citizen of Chicago should
come down to the City Hall

TO-NIGHT
MONDAY, DEC. 12
===========================
and every Monday night
thereafter while the Street-car
Franchises are under consideration,
and see that the interests
of the city are protected against

BOODLEISM
=========
Citizens, Arouse and Defeat the Boodlers!
In the papers were flaring head-lines; in the clubs, halls, and churches fiery speeches could nightly be heard. Men were drunk now with a kind of fury of contest. They would not succumb to this Titan who was bent on undoing them. They would not be devoured by this gorgon of the East. He should be made to pay an honest return to the city or get out. No fifty-year franchise should be granted him. The Mears law must be repealed, and he must come into the city council humble and with clean hands. No alderman who received as much as a dollar for his vote should in this instance be safe with his life.

Needless to say that in the face of such a campaign of intimidation only great courage could win. The aldermen were only human. In the council committee-chamber Cowperwood went freely among them, explaining as he best could the justice of his course and making it plain that, although willing to buy his rights, he looked on them as no more than his due. The rule of the council was barter, and he accepted it. His unshaken and unconquerable defiance heartened his followers greatly, and the thought of thirty thousand dollars was as a buttress against many terrors. At the same time many an alderman speculated solemnly as to what he would do afterward and where he would go once he had sold out.

At last the Monday night arrived which was to bring the final test of strength. Picture the large, ponderous structure of black granite—erected at the expense of millions and suggesting somewhat the somnolent architecture of ancient Egypt—which served as the city hall and county court-house combined. On this evening the four streets surrounding it were packed with thousands of people. To this throng Cowperwood has become an astounding figure: his wealth fabulous, his heart iron, his intentions sinister—the acme of cruel, plotting deviltry. Only this day, the Chronicle, calculating well the hour and the occasion, has completely covered one of its pages with an intimate, though exaggerated, description of Cowperwood's house in New York: his court of orchids, his sunrise room, the baths of pink and blue alabaster, the finishings of marble and intaglio. Here Cowperwood was represented as seated in a swinging divan, his various books, art treasures, and comforts piled about him. The idea was vaguely suggested that in his sybaritic hours odalesques danced before him and unnamable indulgences and excesses were perpetrated.

At this same hour in the council-chamber itself were assembling as hungry and bold a company of gray wolves as was ever gathered under one roof. The room was large, ornamented to the south by tall windows, its ceiling supporting a heavy, intricate chandelier, its sixty-six aldermanic desks arranged in half-circles, one behind the other; its woodwork of black oak carved and highly polished; its walls a dark blue-gray decorated with arabesques in gold—thus giving to all proceedings an air of dignity and stateliness. Above the speaker's head was an immense portrait in oil of a former mayor—poorly done, dusty, and yet impressive. The size and character of the place gave on ordinary occasions a sort of resonance to the voices of the speakers. To-night through the closed windows could be heard the sound of distant drums and marching feet. In the hall outside the council door were packed at least a thousand men with ropes, sticks, a fife-and-drum corps which occasionally struck up "Hail! Columbia, Happy Land," "My Country, 'Tis of Thee," and "Dixie." Alderman Schlumbohm, heckled to within an inch of his life, followed to the council door by three hundred of his fellow-citizens, was there left with the admonition that they would be waiting for him when he should make his exit. He was at last seriously impressed.

"What is this?" he asked of his neighbor and nearest associate, Alderman Gavegan, when he gained the safety of his seat. "A free country?"

"Search me!" replied his compatriot, wearily. "I never seen such a band as I have to deal with out in the Twentieth. Why, my God! a man can't call his name his own any more out here. It's got so now the newspapers tell everybody what to do."

Alderman Pinski and Alderman Hoherkorn, conferring together in one corner, were both very dour. "I'll tell you what, Joe," said Pinski to his confrere; "it's this fellow Lucas that has got the people so stirred up. I didn't go home last night because I didn't want those fellows to follow me down there. Me and my wife stayed down-town. But one of the boys was over here at Jake's a little while ago, and he says there must 'a' been five hundred people around my house at six o'clock, already. Whad ye think o' that?"

"Same here. I don't take much stock in this lynching idea. Still, you can't tell. I don't know whether the police could help us much or not. It's a damned outrage. Cowperwood has a fair proposition. What's the matter with them, anyhow?"

Renewed sounds of "Marching Through Georgia" from without.

Enter at this time Aldermen Ziner, Knudson, Revere, Rogers, Tiernan, and Kerrigan. Of all the aldermen perhaps Messrs. Tiernan and Kerrigan were as cool as any. Still the spectacle of streets blocked with people who carried torches and wore badges showing slip-nooses attached to a gallows was rather serious.

"I'll tell you, Pat," said "Smiling Mike," as they eventually made the door through throngs of jeering citizens; "it does look a little rough. Whad ye think?"

"To hell with them!" replied Kerrigan, angry, waspish, determined. "They don't run me or my ward. I'll vote as I damn please."

"Same here," replied Tiernan, with a great show of courage. "That goes for me. But it's putty warm, anyhow, eh?"

"Yes, it's warm, all right," replied Kerrigan, suspicious lest his companion in arms might be weakening, "but that'll never make a quitter out of me."

"Nor me, either," replied the Smiling One.

Enter now the mayor, accompanied by a fife-and-drum corps rendering "Hail to the Chief." He ascends the rostrum. Outside in the halls the huzzas of the populace. In the gallery overhead a picked audience. As the various aldermen look up they contemplate a sea of unfriendly faces. "Get on to the mayor's guests," commented one alderman to another, cynically.

A little sparring for time while minor matters are considered, and the gallery is given opportunity for comment on the various communal lights, identifying for itself first one local celebrity and then another. "There's Johnnie Dowling, that big blond fellow with the round head; there's Pinski—look at the little rat; there's Kerrigan. Get on to the emerald. Eh, Pat, how's the jewelry? You won't get any chance to do any grafting to-night, Pat. You won't pass no ordinance to-night."

Alderman Winkler (pro-Cowperwood). "If the chair pleases, I think something ought to be done to restore order in the gallery and keep these proceedings from being disturbed. It seems to me an outrage, that, on an occasion of this kind, when the interests of the people require the most careful attention—"

A Voice. "The interests of the people!"

Another Voice. "Sit down. You're bought!"

Alderman Winkler. "If the chair pleases—"

The Mayor. "I shall have to ask the audience in the gallery to keep quiet in order that the business in hand may be considered." (Applause, and the gallery lapses into silence.)

Alderman Guigler (to Alderman Sumulsky). "Well trained, eh?"

Alderman Ballenberg (pro-Cowperwood, getting up—large, brown, florid, smooth-faced). "Before calling up an ordinance which bears my name I should like to ask permission of the council to make a statement. When I introduced this ordinance last week I said—"

A Voice. "We know what you said."

Alderman Ballenberg. "I said that I did so by request. I want to explain that it was at the request of a number of gentlemen who have since appeared before the committee of this council that now has this ordinance—"

A Voice. "That's all right, Ballenberg. We know by whose request you introduced it. You've said your little say."

Alderman Ballenberg. "If the chair pleases—"

A Voice. "Sit down, Ballenberg. Give some other boodler a chance."

The Mayor. "Will the gallery please stop interrupting."

Alderman Horanek (jumping to his feet). "This is an outrage. The gallery is packed with people come here to intimidate us. Here is a great public corporation that has served this city for years, and served it well, and when it comes to this body with a sensible proposition we ain't even allowed to consider it. The mayor packs the gallery with his friends, and the papers stir up people to come down here by thousands and try to frighten us. I for one—"

A Voice. "What's the matter, Billy? Haven't you got your money yet?"

Alderman Hvranek (Polish-American, intelligent, even artistic looking, shaking his fist at the gallery). "You dare not come down here and say that, you coward!"

A Chorus of Fifty Voices. "Rats!" (also) "Billy, you ought to have wings."

Alderman Tiernan (rising). "I say now, Mr. Mayor, don't you think we've had enough of this?"

A Voice. "Well, look who's here. If it ain't Smiling Mike."

Another Voice. "How much do you expect to get, Mike?"

Alderman Tiernan (turning to gallery). "I want to say I can lick any man that wants to come down here and talk to me to my face. I'm not afraid of no ropes and no guns. These corporations have done everything for the city—"

A Voice. "Aw!"

Alderman Tiernan. "If it wasn't for the street-car companies we wouldn't have any city."

Ten Voices. "Aw!"

Alderman Tiernan (bravely). "My mind ain't the mind of some people."

A Voice. "I should say not."

Alderman Tiernan. "I'm talking for compensation for the privileges we expect to give."

A Voice. "You're talking for your pocket-book."

Alderman Tiernan. "I don't give a damn for these cheap skates and cowards in the gallery. I say treat these corporations right. They have helped make the city."

A Chorus of Fifty Voices. "Aw! You want to treat yourself right, that's what you want. You vote right to-night or you'll be sorry."

By now the various aldermen outside of the most hardened characters were more or less terrified by the grilling contest. It could do no good to battle with this gallery or the crowd outside. Above them sat the mayor, before them reporters, ticking in shorthand every phrase and word. "I don't see what we can do," said Alderman Pinski to Alderman Hvranek, his neighbor. "It looks to me as if we might just as well not try."

At this point arose Alderman Gilleran, small, pale, intelligent, anti-Cowperwood. By prearrangement he had been scheduled to bring the second, and as it proved, the final test of strength to the issue. "If the chair pleases," he said, "I move that the vote by which the Ballenberg fifty-year ordinance was referred to the joint committee of streets and alleys be reconsidered, and that instead it be referred to the committee on city hall."

This was a committee that hitherto had always been considered by members of council as of the least importance. Its principal duties consisted in devising new names for streets and regulating the hours of city-hall servants. There were no perquisites, no graft. In a spirit of ribald defiance at the organization of the present session all the mayor's friends—the reformers—those who could not be trusted—had been relegated to this committee. Now it was proposed to take this ordinance out of the hands of friends and send it here, from whence unquestionably it would never reappear. The great test had come.

Alderman Hoberkorn (mouthpiece for his gang because the most skilful in a parliamentary sense). "The vote cannot be reconsidered." He begins a long explanation amid hisses.

A Voice. "How much have you got?"

A Second Voice. "You've been a boodler all your life."

Alderman Hoberkorn (turning to the gallery, a light of defiance in his eye). "You come here to intimidate us, but you can't do it. You're too contemptible to notice."

A Voice. "You hear the drums, don't you?"

A Second Voice. "Vote wrong, Hoberkorn, and see. We know you."

Alderman Tiernan (to himself). "Say, that's pretty rough, ain't it?"

The Mayor. "Motion overruled. The point is not well taken."

Alderman Guigler (rising a little puzzled). "Do we vote now on the Gilleran resolution?"

A Voice. "You bet you do, and you vote right."

The Mayor. "Yes. The clerk will call the roll."

The Clerk (reading the names, beginning with the A's). "Altvast?" (pro-Cowperwood).

Alderman Altvast. "Yea." Fear had conquered him.

Alderman Tiernan (to Alderman Kerrigan). "Well, there's one baby down."

Alderman Kerrigan. "Yep."

"Ballenberg?" (Pro-Cowperwood; the man who had introduced the ordinance.)

"Yea."

Alderman Tiernan. "Say, has Ballenberg weakened?"

Alderman Kerrigan. "It looks that way."

"Canna?"

"Yea."

"Fogarty?"

"Yea."

Alderman Tiernan (nervously). "There goes Fogarty."

"Hvranek?"

"Yea."

Alderman Tiernan. "And Hvranek!"

Alderman Kerrigan (referring to the courage of his colleagues). "It's coming out of their hair."

In exactly eighty seconds the roll-call was in and Cowperwood had lost—41 to 25. It was plain that the ordinance could never be revived.

CHAPTER LXII

THE RECOMPENSE

You have seen, perhaps, a man whose heart was weighted by a great woe. You have seen the eye darken, the soul fag, and the spirit congeal under the breath of an icy disaster. At ten-thirty of this particular evening Cowperwood, sitting alone in the library of his Michigan Avenue house, was brought face to face with the fact that he had lost. He had built so much on the cast of this single die. It was useless to say to himself that he could go into the council a week later with a modified ordinance or could wait until the storm had died out. He refused himself these consolations. Already he had battled so long and so vigorously, by every resource and subtlety which his mind had been able to devise. All week long on divers occasions he had stood in the council-chamber where the committee had been conducting its hearings. Small comfort to know that by suits, injunctions, appeals, and writs to intervene he could tie up this transit situation and leave it for years and years the prey of lawyers, the despair of the city, a hopeless muddle which would not be unraveled until he and his enemies should long be dead. This contest had been so long in the brewing, he had gone about it with such care years before. And now the enemy had been heartened by a great victory. His aldermen, powerful, hungry, fighting men all—like those picked soldiers of the ancient Roman emperors—ruthless, conscienceless, as desperate as himself, had in their last redoubt of personal privilege fallen, weakened, yielded. How could he hearten them to another struggle—how face the blazing wrath of a mighty populace that had once learned how to win? Others might enter here—Haeckelheimer, Fishel, any one of a half-dozen Eastern giants—and smooth out the ruffled surface of the angry sea that he had blown to fury. But as for him, he was tired, sick of Chicago, sick of this interminable contest. Only recently he had promised himself that if he were to turn this great trick he would never again attempt anything so desperate or requiring so much effort. He would not need to. The size of his fortune made it of little worth. Besides, in spite of his tremendous vigor, he was getting on.

Since he had alienated Aileen he was quite alone, out of touch with any one identified with the earlier years of his life. His all-desired Berenice still evaded him. True, she had shown lately a kind of warming sympathy; but what was it? Gracious tolerance, perhaps—a sense of obligation? Certainly little more, he felt. He looked into the future, deciding heavily that he must fight on, whatever happened, and then—

While he sat thus drearily pondering, answering a telephone call now and then, the door-bell rang and the servant brought a card which he said had been presented by a young woman who declared that it would bring immediate recognition. Glancing at it, Cowperwood jumped to his feet and hurried down-stairs into the one presence he most craved.

There are compromises of the spirit too elusive and subtle to be traced in all their involute windings. From that earliest day when Berenice Fleming had first set eyes on Cowperwood she had been moved by a sense of power, an amazing and fascinating individuality. Since then by degrees he had familiarized her with a thought of individual freedom of action and a disregard of current social standards which were destructive to an earlier conventional view of things. Following him through this Chicago fight, she had been caught by the wonder of his dreams; he was on the way toward being one of the world's greatest money giants. During his recent trips East she had sometimes felt that she was able to read in the cast of his face the intensity of this great ambition, which had for its ultimate aim—herself. So he had once assured her. Always with her he had been so handsome, so pleading, so patient.

So here she was in Chicago to-night, the guest of friends at the Richelieu, and standing in Cowperwood's presence.

"Why, Berenice!" he said, extending a cordial hand.

"When did you arrive in town? Whatever brings you here?" He had once tried to make her promise that if ever her feeling toward him changed she would let him know of it in some way. And here she was to-night—on what errand? He noted her costume of brown silk and velvet—how well it seemed to suggest her cat-like grace!

"You bring me here," she replied, with an indefinable something in her voice which was at once a challenge and a confession. "I thought from what I had just been reading that you might really need me now."

"You mean—?" he inquired, looking at her with vivid eyes. There he paused.

"That I have made up my mind. Besides, I ought to pay some time."

"Berenice!" he exclaimed, reproachfully.

"No, I don't mean that, either," she replied. "I am sorry now. I think I understand you better. Besides," she added, with a sudden gaiety that had a touch of self-consolation in it, "I want to."

"Berenice! Truly?"

"Can't you tell?" she queried.

"Well, then," he smiled, holding out his hands; and, to his amazement, she came forward.

"I can't explain myself to myself quite," she added, in a hurried low, eager tone, "but I couldn't stay away any longer. I had the feeling that you might be going to lose here for the present. But I want you to go somewhere else if you have to—London or Paris. The world won't understand us quite—but I do."

"Berenice!" He smothered her cheek and hair.

"Not so close, please. And there aren't to be any other ladies, unless you want me to change my mind."

"Not another one, as I hope to keep you. You will share everything I have..."

For answer—

How strange are realities as opposed to illusion!

IN RETROSPECT

The world is dosed with too much religion. Life is to be learned from life, and the professional moralist is at best but a manufacturer of shoddy wares. At the ultimate remove, God or the life force, if anything, is an equation, and at its nearest expression for man—the contract social—it is that also. Its method of expression appears to be that of generating the individual, in all his glittering variety and scope, and through him progressing to the mass with its problems. In the end a balance is invariably struck wherein the mass subdues the individual or the individual the mass—for the time being. For, behold, the sea is ever dancing or raging.

In the mean time there have sprung up social words and phrases expressing a need of balance—of equation. These are right, justice, truth, morality, an honest mind, a pure heart—all words meaning: a balance must be struck. The strong must not be too strong; the weak not too weak. But without variation how could the balance be maintained? Nirvana! Nirvana! The ultimate, still, equation.

Rushing like a great comet to the zenith, his path a blazing trail, Cowperwood did for the hour illuminate the terrors and wonders of individuality. But for him also the eternal equation—the pathos of the discovery that even giants are but pygmies, and that an ultimate balance must be struck. Of the strange, tortured, terrified reflection of those who, caught in his wake, were swept from the normal and the commonplace, what shall we say? Legislators by the hundred, who were hounded from politics into their graves; a half-hundred aldermen of various councils who were driven grumbling or whining into the limbo of the dull, the useless, the commonplace. A splendid governor dreaming of an ideal on the one hand, succumbing to material necessity on the other, traducing the spirit that aided him the while he tortured himself with his own doubts. A second governor, more amenable, was to be greeted by the hisses of the populace, to retire brooding and discomfited, and finally to take his own life. Schryhart and Hand, venomous men both, unable to discover whether they had really triumphed, were to die eventually, puzzled. A mayor whose greatest hour was in thwarting one who contemned him, lived to say: "It is a great mystery. He was a strange man." A great city struggled for a score of years to untangle that which was all but beyond the power of solution—a true Gordian knot.

And this giant himself, rushing on to new struggles and new difficulties in an older land, forever suffering the goad of a restless heart—for him was no ultimate peace, no real understanding, but only hunger and thirst and wonder. Wealth, wealth, wealth! A new grasp of a new great problem and its eventual solution. Anew the old urgent thirst for life, and only its partial quenchment. In Dresden a palace for one woman, in Rome a second for another. In London a third for his beloved Berenice, the lure of beauty ever in his eye. The lives of two women wrecked, a score of victims despoiled; Berenice herself weary, yet brilliant, turning to others for recompense for her lost youth. And he resigned, and yet not—loving, understanding, doubting, caught at last by the drug of a personality which he could not gainsay.

What shall we say of life in the last analysis—"Peace, be still"? Or shall we battle sternly for that equation which we know will be maintained whether we battle or no, in order that the strong become not too strong or the weak not too weak? Or perchance shall we say (sick of dullness): "Enough of this. I will have strong meat or die!" And die? Or live?

Each according to his temperament—that something which he has not made and cannot always subdue, and which may not always be subdued by others for him. Who plans the steps that lead lives on to splendid glories, or twist them into gnarled sacrifices, or make of them dark, disdainful, contentious tragedies? The soul within? And whence comes it? Of God?

What thought engendered the spirit of Circe, or gave to a Helen the lust of tragedy? What lit the walls of Troy? Or prepared the woes of an Andromache? By what demon counsel was the fate of Hamlet prepared? And why did the weird sisters plan ruin to the murderous Scot?

Double, double toil and trouble,
Fire burn and cauldron bubble.

In a mulch of darkness are bedded the roots of endless sorrows—and of endless joys. Canst thou fix thine eye on the morning? Be glad. And if in the ultimate it blind thee, be glad also! Thou hast lived.

Note from the Editor

Odin's Library Classics strives to bring you unedited and unabridged works of classical literature. As such, this is the complete and unabridged version of the original English text unless noted. In some instances, obvious typographical errors have been corrected. This is done to preserve the original text as much as possible. The English language has evolved since the writing and some of the words appear in their original form, or at least the most commonly used form at the time. This is done to protect the original intent of the author. If at any time you are unsure of the meaning of a word, please do your research on the etymology of that word. It is important to preserve the history of the English language.

Taylor Anderson

62948932R00328

Made in the USA
Columbia, SC
06 July 2019